Heavy Metal Movies

GUITAR BARBARIANS, MUTANT BIMBOS & CULT ZOMBIES AMOK IN THE 666 MOST EAR- AND EYE-RIPPING BIG-SCREAM FILMS EVER!

MIKE "McBEARDO" McPADDEN

Bazillion Points

HEAVY METAL MOVIES
Guitar Barbarians, Mutant Bimbos & Cult Zombies Amok
in the 666 Most Ear- and Eye-Ripping Big-Scream Films Ever!
by Mike "McBeardo" McPadden

Copyright © 2014

First printing, published in 2014 by

Bazillion Points
61 Greenpoint Ave. #504
Brooklyn, New York 11222
United States
www.bazillionpoints.com
www.heavymetalmovies.com

Produced for Bazillion Points by Ian Christe
Cover painting by Andrei Bouzikov
Cover layout and design by Bazillion Points
Copyedited by Polly Watson

Photographs © Vaticanus, Chris Roo. All rights reserved.
McBeardo mural by Scott R. Miller

A bazillion thank-yous to Magnus Henriksson, Dianna Dilworth, Vivienne Christe,
Rachel McPadden, David Szulkin, Richard Christy, Alice Cooper, Andrei Bouzikov,
Thor, John Fasano, Jeff Krulik, Robin Bougie, Carole Ann Christe

ISBN 978-1-935950-06-6

Printed in the United States

TO DANNY PEARY

YOUR *CULT MOVIES* BOOKS TAUGHT ME TO EXPERIENCE FILM
AND MUSIC—AND, THEREFORE, LIFE ITSELF—THROUGH THE
EYES AND EARS (AND HEART AND BRAIN) OF A WRITER

The Key to the Curse of the Oath of Heavy Metal Movies:

- Occult Rock 'n Roll Horror
- Headbanger Stories
- Metal Soundtracks
- Concert Performances
- Raw Documentaries
- Metal Musicians Acting
- Namesakes & Lyrical References
- Iconic Metal Film Characters
- Swords & Sorcery! Devils! Witchcraft! Demonic Possession! Post- Apocalypse! Sci-Fi! Slashers! Cannibals! Zombies! Vampires! Goth Chicks! Psycho 'Nam Vets! Metal Reality! Laser Vision! Nuns! Violent Apes! Medical Deviants! World Metal! Urban Warfare! Torture!!!

Table of Contents

Mighty Monsters, Delinquent Double Features, and Sticky Seats: My Life in Heavy Metal Movies

Liberty Theatre, 1980, 42nd Street, New York City. Photo by Vaticanus

ONE SUMMER NIGHT IN 1933 in the bayside amusement hamlet of Keansburg, New Jersey, *King Kong*, the movie and the giant ape star himself, delightfully terrified my grandmother and set in motion a spectacular chain of events. Twenty-year-old Frances Jean Mackey had just come from a screening up the block at the Casino Theater, built in 1914 and active under a series of different names until late 1982. Accompanying Granny, as I would much later know her, was a gentleman caller of whom I know not much except I respect his ideas as far as what makes a proper date movie.

That night long ago, Granny and her Raritan Bay beau sat on the front porch of her humble home, reliving *King Kong*'s unprecedented thrills and wonders. Suddenly— BOOOM!!!—right before their eyes, the back half of the house across the street exploded, the victim of a badly repaired boiler. Nobody, I have been repeatedly assured, was injured when the spirit of Kong mashed his mighty foot down on that beach-town bungalow. On the contrary, the sidewalks buckled and my fate was sealed in a sudden furious moment of volcanic visual mayhem, deafening sound, chaos, horror, amazement, and hilarity. My granny experienced a perfect event that rippled through the generations until I was born in its echo. I came into this world craving the larger-than-life film experience that erupts off the screen and storms into consciousness and remakes your very being from the inside out. The Heavy Metal Movie!

I first felt that great madness in 1972 at the age of four, as the lights went down for a showing of Walt Disney's bonkers *Pinocchio* at the very same theater where my grandmother had experienced *King Kong* four decades earlier. I felt the curse, for sure, growing up in Brooklyn's lordly Flatbush and watching excitedly as WOR-TV (the legendary Channel 9) reran its hardworking *King Kong* print, seemingly several times every single week throughout the first half of the '70s. From kindergarten onward, I tore out newspaper ads for movies; mostly kids' stuff at first, but also anything with a horror and exploitation bent. The titles and the images grew more lurid the nearer I lurched toward puberty. I assembled the clippings into scrapbooks that I revered like talismanic runes— which they were (and still are!)

The giant monkeys, the madmen, the cannibals, the motorcycles—they exploded in smudged black print across the listings each week. To make sense of the mayhem, I turned to seemingly biblical film tomes like the annual *TV Movies* compendium edited by super-nerd Leonard Maltin. This brick-size paperback, as thick as a phone book, listed thousands of capsule reviews of seemingly every movie ever made. The book utilized a scale of one to four stars plus "BOMB!" for movies that Lenny really hated. I pored over every page and circled each "BOMB!", then combed the TV listings and tried to catch every one of them. I kept this up for years, and I was never disappointed. Not once.

As my movie mania advanced and I grew a little older, I discovered the same thunderous transcendence provided by movies through music, first through AM radio rock, and then FM radio hard rock. The Ramones and *The Uncle Floyd Show* introduced punk rock. Suddenly heavy metal appeared all around, courtesy of everything and nothing, and never left. I devoted myself to heavy metal wholeheartedly and headbangingly, arriving via my gateway to the heavy stuff, Kiss.

I discovered heavy metal and movies to be two byways of a single continuum. Each stream led to uncharted, unpredictable, unlimited oceans of experience and expression and elation. The combined powers proved to be packed with almost lethal transformative potential. In 1978, my thoughts were not nearly so fancily splayed out while I watched *Kiss Meets the Phantom of the Park*—but, believe me, all that bombastic shit was exactly what I was feeling.

♆

Soon, the Heavy Metal Movie gods smiled most glitteringly upon me. Decamped, as I was every summer from birth, at my grandparents' house in Keansburg and perusing the newspaper's film section with no other concern in the world, I noticed an ad for *The Rocky Horror Picture Show* that was emblazoned with the rating PG. This information was incorrect, of course—the glam horror movie is rated R. But for my purposes, the error was oh so right. I was fascinated with *Rocky Horror* based on New York media reports of the movie somehow involving rock and roll, monsters, and naked women in the audience. After memorizing the songs by taping them off *Dr. Demento*, I had finagled the soundtrack cassette for my tenth birthday. Grabbing the misprinted ad, I set upon Moms McBeardo in a frenzy, barking: "Look! Ma! Look! *Rocky Horror* is rated PG! It's PG! SEE! That means I can see it! Right?! RIGHT?! PG! PG! PEEEE-JEEEE!"

Fooled and exhausted, Moms relented. "Yes. Fine. You can go. Ask one of your aunts or uncles to take you." My hippie aunt Carol lived in Greenwich Village and my super-cool uncle Freddy was crashing with us in Keansburg, so I suggested that he and I go visit his sister and take in the movie at its home base, Manhattan's Eighth Street Playhouse. During the 1970s, ten-year-old kids really could pull off master capers like this.

My plan was flawless. The movie blew my mind and the teenage girl who played Janet in the live *Rocky Horror* shadow cast nearly blew every other one of my circuits by sitting on my lap momentarily and then flashing her boobs up onstage, the first pair I wasn't related to on which I ever laid eyes. "Don't dream it," *Rocky Horror* famously advises. "Be it!" Point taken! Hard and deep.

By time I saw *Pinocchio* back at that ramshackle boardwalk movie house in Keansburg, New Jersey, the venue was called the Colonial. When I turned eleven, I took in my first parent-sanctioned R-rated movie there, *Alien*. Over the course of the next two summers—1980 and 1981—the Colonial transformed into an unholy Heavy Metal Movie temple where my buddy Mickey Cosgrove and I slunk past the reddened ganja-zonked eyes of the local teens who manned the ticket counter and basked in atrocities: *Dawn of the Dead, Maniac, Mother's Day, Phantasm*, the first two *Friday the 13th* movies, *Don't Go in the House*, and *Prom Night*. I kept my eyes clamped shut during most of the reissue screening of *The Texas Chain Saw Massacre*.

During this period, I stumbled upon a couple books by brothers Harry and Michael Medved: *The Fifty Worst Films of All Time* (1978) and *The Golden Turkey Awards* (1980). These were detail-laden textbooks exploding with information about the men and the madness behind all those fantastic "BOMB!" extravaganzas. I can still recite long passages from those books.

Then came 1982, the Year Everything Broke. In April '82, the Easter Bunny enriched my basket with a copy of *Cult Movies: The Classics, the Sleepers, the Weird and the Wonderful* by Danny Peary. This and its two follow-up volumes became the crucial texts of my human existence. That same spring, the *New York Daily News* ran an article on the *Gore Gazette*, a xeroxed screed-sheet that came screaming twice a month out of New Jersey. In its pages, mad publisher the Right Reverend Rick Sullivan reviewed every exploitation film that blew through the tristate area in the manner of a jocular misanthrope. I subscribed and, unknowingly, opened the door on the rest of my life.

Come September 1982, I started attending Xavier High School on Sixteenth Street and Sixth Avenue in Manhattan, a long subway ride from home in Flatbush. The Village loomed just minutes away, awash in an cinema-lover dream venues like the aforementioned Eighth Street Playhouse, which boasted a new double feature every day and midnight movies seven nights a week. St. Mark's Cinema was pure punk, with more double features, more midnight movies, and real popcorn. The Waverly was totally new wave, and home to *Eraserhead* and *Forbidden Zone*. The Thalia was heavy on the black-and-white classics. The Bleecker Street Cinema aimed for the glands, playing *Toxic Avenger* on weekends for more than a year. Many others threw motion pictures up on the walls; only the Quad among them is still breathing.

More foreboding and infinitely more fulfilling was the golden heavy metal wasteland festering two subway stops north of my high school: Times Square at its unreal psycho-orgasmic peak of pimps, prostitutes, peep shows, and porn palaces. Forty-Second Street in its mega-squalor was dirtily awash with a dozen or so rough-and-tumble, open-all-night, triple-feature discount exploitation grindhouse theaters. These life-or-death casinos showcased the best and worst (and newest and oldest) from the chum buckets of cinematic sleaze, horror, hooker, splatter, kung fu, slasher, zombie, cannibal, rape-revenge, women in prison, sci-fi, cheerleader, teen sex, and nut-crushing action nuggets to float up from the bottommost gutters of the international motion picture trade. The slow-burning anthem "The Zoo" by Germany's beloved metal masters Scorpions perfectly nails this time, place, and overall feel. Listen to that precisely harmonized sleaze. How could I resist? How could *anybody*?

The first picture I saw on Forty-Second Street, or the Deuce, was the gorily tormented teen monster quickie *The Beast Within*. I was killing time while I accompanied my older cousin Martin to pick up his sister Mary at Grand Central Station, after her train was delayed. Martin and I ducked into the Lyric Theatre, and caught the flick for $1.99 each. (I think it might have been even cheaper). Martin subsequently got on with his life. In many ways, I never left that moment.

Meanwhile, back at home in Flatbush, I was a quick B9 bus ride's distance from storied Kings County metal mecca L'Amour: The Rock Capitol of Brooklyn. As a frequent patron there, I can tell you exactly how it should be properly pronounced, "La-MAWZ," inexplicably plural, with the second syllable rhyming (fittingly) with "jaws."

Now that I was trusted to make my way via public transportation between Brooklyn and Manhattan every day without adult supervision (another aspect of life that would be impossible now), my immediate daily destination after last period was Forty-Second Street. At first, I'd just walk around and attempt to mentally tattoo the area's overwhelming porn propaganda into the pit of my psyche (I think it worked). Soon enough, I ponied up for a ticket to a double feature of the high school horndog romp *Goin' All the Way* and the babes-behind-bars bruiser *The Concrete Jungle*. The audience, as legends do tell, was absolutely apeshit, but no one bothered me. I watched the show and then went home, and I lied to Moms about hanging out with nonexistent friends. Only it wasn't exactly a lie. I had just rammed open an entire new universe of . . . friends. And there were so many more to come.

The New Amsterdam, the grandest of Forty-Second Street's fallen movie palaces, closed in 1982, so I got never inside that one. But the others became my cathedrals. Aside from the Lyric, there were the Selwyn, the Harris, the Anco, the Empire, the Liberty, the Rialto, the Times Square, and the nastily hardscrabble Cine 42 Twin, which, unlike the others, wasn't a time-trashed jewel of classic architecture, but a warehouse for post-human reprobates strewn about deadly hard plastic seats that really seemed to fit the particularly insane fare that ran there.

On Columbus Day weekend in 1982, Keansburg's little fleapit auditorium (then called the Midway), where King Kong rattled my ancestor's genes, was shuttered forever. I caught the last movie ever screened there: *The Road Warrior*, on the bottom of a double bill with *Night Shift*, a warmhearted comedy about a prostitution ring run out of a morgue. The shotguns and hot pants made a mighty send-off for one era, and a fittingly spectacular heralding in of another.

Christmas 1982 delivered me the final socially ruinous yet divinely transmogrifying Heavy Metal Movie haymaker: *The Psychotronic Encyclopedia of Film* by Michael Weldon, which featured write-ups of about two thousand movies that Weldon himself had seen on Forty-Second Street. And Santa's death blow was a VCR. Now there was no movie I could not see and, maybe even better still, there was no movie I could write about myself. Destiny beckoned.

Happyland, a zine I published under the pen(is) name Selwyn Harris from 1991 to 2002, trafficked largely in hard movie and heavy music coverage, and I parlayed that early on into a weird professional journey that has included editing *Hustler* magazine, raving about metal bands for the metal-hating *New York Press,* slaving at Troma Films for two long weeks, writing porno screenplays, serving as head writer for eleven years (and counting) at celebrity nudity Internet powerhouse Mr. Skin, and playing guitar for bacchanalian shock rock platoon Gays in the Military, whose albums were filed at Chicago's legendary Metal Haven Records —appropriately—under "Noise."

Heavy Metal Movies is the summation of forty-five years of movie-devouring, music-hoovering passion, and maniacal attention to detail alchemized by three and a half years of brute labor into a reading experience that I hope will rock you, ravage you, light up your inner screen, and stomp your very being like the heel of King Kong slamming down on that beach house across the street from my grandmother in 1933. The airplanes didn't kill Kong after all; they only liberated the savage beauty of Heavy Metal Movies and helped give birth to this beast!

Enjoy what is positively the most horrifying book ever written...

Clockwise from top left: *Alice meets Jason; the Alice behind the mask for* Friday the 13th Part VI *(1986); Alice Cooper pulls the juice on Dave Mustaine of Megadeth at the SBK Records release party for Wes Craven's* Shocker *in 1989*

An Audience with the Godfather of Heavy Metal Movies
Alice Cooper

Since the twilight of the 1960s, Alice Cooper has pummeled spellbound audiences with scary music about spiders, dead babies, and disturbing ephemera of every sick stripe. His access-all-areas status in the heavy metal arena is indisputable. For nearly as long, he has reigned unrelentingly over the realm of Heavy Metal Movies. Beginning with a *Diary of a Mad Housewife* (1970), he progressed through numerous parts large and small in all kinds of productions. Alice hit a big-screen high note in *Wayne's World* (1992) that he sustained through myriad movie appearances and soundtrack contributions all the way up to a monstrous performance of "The Ballad of Dwight Frye" in *Dark Shadows* (2012).

Beyond the concert films and documentaries, and the 1975 *Welcome to My Nightmare* TV special that took on a second life as a midnight movie, the master showman of the macabre has also plunged into the kind of B-movie undertakings that Heavy Metal Movie devotees like Alice himself love best: offerings such as the gore-sopped *Monster Dog* (1986), John Carpenter's *Prince of Darkness* (1987), and the flamboyantly unhinged Mae West fantasia *Sextette* (1978).

Welcome to the Heavy Metal Movies nightmare, with a few introductory words from our maestro. The following vignettes are Alice's first recounting of his movie roles and adventures. No hypnosis was needed. As you might imagine, talking to Alice is just . . . *killer*.

Welcome to My Nightmare (1975)

Back when we were planning *Welcome to My Nightmare*, we wanted an iconic character to be the voice—the conscience of this nightmare. We thought about Christopher Lee, and this guy and that guy, and of course someone suggested Vincent Price. I said, "Well, what are the chances of getting Vincent Price?"

Our producer, Bob Ezrin, called him, and Price said, "I'll be there." I couldn't believe it. We couldn't do better than that. Bela Lugosi or Boris Karloff would have been the only two that might have been comparable. We had Vincent Price, with that great voice!

When he came to read that whole section in the nightmare about the spider museum, he said: "Hey, can I rewrite some of this?"

I told him, "You're Vincent Price—you can do anything you want to do! We're just happy to have you here."

He had so much fun doing the role. He recorded his part on video with us, and then he performed it onstage with us. We actually played the first two shows of *Welcome to My Nightmare* in Lake Tahoe. Vincent Price did his part before the audience, which was like—you just can't get that. Nobody gets anything that good. So what a prize it was having Vincent in our movie.

Sextette (1978)

Everybody wanted to be in *Sextette* at the time. Mae West was probably not going to be around much longer, and she was still Mae West, you know? All the people who signed on for it were my friends. Keith Moon was in it, and Ringo Starr was in it. Timothy Dalton, Dom DeLuise, and all these people who were all very hot at the time were also involved. Then there was George Raft—I thought, "Oh man, how cool is that? George Raft!" I'm a fan of the old gangster movies.

The producers wanted me to play an Italian waiter. I loved it, because I didn't have to play me. I thought that would be great, not to mention I would get to do a song with Mae West. I mean, how many people get to sing with Mae West?

My costume was a waiter's tuxedo. I brought in her food, and then I sat down at a piano and started playing. Mae sat down next to me, and we did a song together. At the end of the song, the moment that the director yelled, "Cut," Mae literally leaned over and said, "Why don't you come on back to my trailer?"

At first I thought she was kidding. I realized quickly that she wasn't kidding at all. So I said, "Well, first of all, you're eighty-six years old, and I'm not sure if you're a woman!"

Mae said, "Oh, I'm *all* woman!"

I told her, "I'm very married, okay? I'm very married!" She said, "Oh well, you know, that's never stopped most of the guys!'

So I found out from Keith Moon and Ringo that she came on to everybody. Every single male in the cast, she tried to get back to her trailer. It was great to have an eighty-six-year-old woman coming on to you, and then kind of thinking about that for a second. Well, that's something to talk about!

Sgt Pepper's Lonely Hearts Club Band (1978)

In 1978 the Bee Gees were the hottest band in the world, and I really liked them. As much as disco was our enemy, *Saturday Night Fever* was one of the greatest albums ever made. I mean it was the *Sgt. Pepper* of disco. Even a heavy metal guy could listen to that and say, "You know, this is an exception. As much as I hate disco, this is an exception."

On paper, this movie sounded like a great idea—now it's considered one of the great turkeys of all time. Somehow I looked at it, and Aerosmith was in it, and Steve Martin was in it, and the Bee Gees, who were well respected. Then Peter Frampton was a friend of mine. Everybody involved in this movie was friends with each other. Halfway through the production, though, the producers realized that most of the actors couldn't deliver dialogue. For that reason, they added George Burns doing the narration, which actually kind of helped.

In the end, there was just no way that *Sgt. Pepper* was going to work without the Beatles. No matter who else was involved, you couldn't make this movie without the Beatles—it was almost heresy. *Sgt. Pepper's Lonely Hearts Club Band* was the Beatles' best album, and then here we were doing the movie without the Beatles, so it was doomed from the beginning.

This Is Spinal Tap (1984)

I loved *Spinal Tap*. It's one of the most quoted movies ever. I think every musician who has ever gone on the road watched *Spinal Tap* and said: "Hey, that happened to us!"

I saw so many things happen in that movie that happened to us: getting lost backstage; going to an autograph signing where the guy forgot to publicize it, so nobody's there when you show up; the girlfriend of the lead player deciding she knew more than the manager—oh my gosh, have I seen that! Every band that ever watched this movie totally got it, so the comedy worked on a bunch of different levels.

Monster Dog (1986)

Monster Dog is exactly the kind of movie I rent. It's exactly crappy enough and stupid enough for me to really like it. If I were to have rented this movie, I would have been very happy. It was fun. There was so much blood in this movie that the film crew was wearing raincoats. You know I loved that.

I took the role when I first got out of the institution to get sober. I told my manager, Shep Gordon, that I needed to do something where I would have to work every day sober. When I'm on tour, I really work two hours a night, and that's about it. I thought a movie would be much better. So I took this movie where I played the lead. I actually had to learn a lot of dialogue. I had to get up at six in the morning, do makeup, know my lines, and work all day. I had to make sure I could work sober. And that's why I took *Monster Dog*. They also told me it would only be released in the Philippines!

Jason Lives: Friday the 13th Part VI (1986)

Freddy's Dead: The Final Nightmare (1991)

We were all fans of the slasher movies. When they asked me to do some music for *Friday the 13th Part VI*, I had an idea for "Man Behind the Mask." I thought that was a great title, along with "Hard Rock Summer." I wasn't really in the movie, but I did get to play Freddy Krueger's father later on, in *Freddy's Dead: The Final Nightmare* (*Nightmare on Elm Street 6*). That was great for me, because I got to play someone other than Alice Cooper. I played Freddie's father as this dysfunctional drunk Southern bastard of a father. It was fun to work as a character.

Prince of Darkness (1987)

I actually just showed up to watch John Carpenter shoot the movie. He called me and said he would be shooting in downtown L.A. John had just come to one of our shows, and he had worked with my manager, Shep, on two or three different movies. I said I would love to go down and watch John Carpenter shooting in this old mission downtown. He wanted to show me this thing they were doing with mercury; they had a special-effects mirror that looked like glass but was liquid mercury.

While I was watching him and the crew at work, I noticed all these "street zombie" kind of people in the scene. John said, "Hey Alice, you know what would be great? If you put on this stocking cap and were just like standing in the middle of all these zombies." That sounded okay to me. The idea was that the camera would just pan across the scene, and it would be funny if someone watching the movie thought for half a minute, "Hey, wait! That was Alice Cooper!"

After we shot that scene, John said, "You know, you're the scariest guy out there, so why don't you be sort of the leader of these guys?" That sounded okay to me, so they took two or three more shots with me set up as the head street zombie.

Then John said, "You know that thing onstage that you do with the microphone, where you put it through a guy's chest? Well, we could put a bicycle through this guy's chest!" The next thing I know, I'm the main villain in this movie, and I'd never even seen the script! I was just accidentally there, sort of having fun, but John Carpenter is always thinking, always moving. He just kept building the part. Years later, I picked up the DVD, and I was on the cover!

I never said a word in *Prince of Darkness*. I never played any music. I just got to do all the stuff that was fun. That was the easiest acting job I've ever had.

The Decline of Western Civilization Part II: The Metal Years (1988)

The bass player in W.A.S.P., Chris Holmes, he sort of stole the movie—uh, in a pathetic way. I kind of felt so sorry for his mother in the whole thing. I'm sure that's not going to be the movie they play at Thanksgiving when all the family's there, you know.

Wayne's World (1992)

We all knew the bit on *Saturday Night Live*, we all laughed at Wayne because we knew guys who were just like that! In fact, Garth looked exactly like our lead guitar player, Glenn Buxton. In fact, I think he might have been based on Glenn. He was exactly like Glenn.

Mike Myers called up and said, "We need someone of your status, because we need someone for the 'we're not worthy' thing—someone from the classic mythical rock gods."

I said, "Okay, great! I'll do it!" I got there, and Mike said, "Alice, I know that you act, so can you do a few lines for us?" I said sure, so he handed me five pages of dialogue. You know, all this stuff about socialist governors.

I kind of hesitated and said, "Uh, when are we shooting this?"

He said, "In about twenty minutes," so that's how we did it. We did the whole bit about this rock band sounding like somebody on *Jeopardy,* and we knew every answer to everything. Mike Myers and Dana Carvey stood off camera, doing everything they could to make me laugh. So I found a spot between them, at the back of the room, and I just focused on looking past them toward that spot. Every take was different, because I was making half of it up.

Isn't it funny? That little movie didn't cost anything to make, yet it actually made more money than *Batman*? As a result, I've been stuck with that "we're not worthy!" thing ever since.

The Devil's Rejects (2005)

Dark Shadows (2012)

Rob Zombie has ended up being sort of my little brother, you know. We toured together, and there's not a reference that he can make that I don't know. Likewise, there's not a quote I can throw at him that he doesn't know, especially when it comes to horror movies or TV or trivia or anything like that. We're both on the same page—and he gets the fact that horror and comedy are very, very close.

If Rob Zombie's movies had come out in the 1970s, they would have been XXX-rated. *Devil's Rejects* really had that edge of those movies you weren't supposed to see in the 1960s. Now it's hard to capture that, because audiences have seen so much. I don't think that people get the sense of humor. When you're doing violence so over the top that it becomes funny, and you start laughing—that's where I think he's best.

The first time I ever experienced that was in *Evil Dead*. I was sitting and thinking, "Wow! Could there be any more blood in this movie?" Just at that point, he hits a pipe and gets soaked in blood and I just burst out laughing. After that point I felt like I was watching one of the funniest movies I had ever seen. It was disturbing at first, and then it got really funny.

Rob Zombie has a great, great sense of humor when it comes to his movies.

Rob's wife is such a lovely girl—she is such a doll, and she plays the most horrific characters. The stuff that comes out of her mouth . . .

Maybe *Lords of Salem* could be the ultimate Heavy Metal Movie. My daughter auditioned for it, as a witch. Then she found out that she would have to take her top off and run through the city, and she had a problem with that.

I can see exactly where Rob's going. He's like Tim Burton, who always kind of takes a left-handed look at everything. I'm always interested in seeing what he's going to do next. Rob likes to look at these movies in a different sense. When I did *Dark Shadows*, with Tim Burton, I honestly didn't know what to expect, but I knew it was going to be tilted to the left and way off-kilter. That's exactly how it ended up being, and that's exactly how I like things to be.

Thank you to the intrepid Katherine Turman!

Clockwise from top left: 2020 Texas Gladiators *(1982); French poster for* 2019: After the Fall of New York *(1983);* 1990: The Bronx Warriors *(1982) VHS;* 976-Evil *(1988) VHS;* 2001 *(1968)*

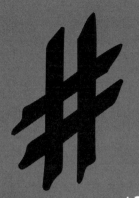

3 Inches of Blood: Warriors of the Great White North

(2014)

(Dir. Tom MacLeod; w/Cam Pipes, Shane Clark, Justin Hagberg, Ash Pearson)

✖ Metal Reality ✖ Bon Scott's Grave

My worst day as a musician really would have been the best day of my life when I was working construction," declares guitarist Shane Clark at the start of the film about his band 3 Inches of Blood. This thoroughly agreeable good-time documentary then demonstrates the appeal of hitting the road with 3 Inches of Blood—even with all the low-budget travel challenges, and, as discussed in hilarious detail, putrid body odor.

Headbanging highlights of the Canadian quartet's trek through their homeland include Clark displaying a mini Crown Royal bottle filled with dirt from the grave of fallen AC/DC front-man Bon Scott; Justin Hagberg showing off a collection of pages marked "666" that he has ripped out of every hotel-room Bible; Arnold Schwarzenegger imitations; and the code word "Windows!" which means somebody in the van is about to fart. Industrial metal gods Frontline Assembly (with whom Hagberg has collabo-

rated) visit the band in Ottawa, and we meet 3 Inches' colorful tour manager Mathias "Staddy" Stadlbauer—a German who somehow sounds like a Scot. Notes Clark: "He doesn't mind being the asshole."

Every single show seems to be followed by a Viking bacchanal of cold beer, hot metal babes, and beard-quaking belly laughs. *3 Inches of Blood: Warriors of the Great White North* truly makes us feel as though we've been invited to the rolling party of a band that remembers the fundamental metal concept of enjoying success to the hilt.

200 Motels (1971)

(Dirs. Tony Palmer, Frank Zappa; w/Frank Zappa, Ringo Starr, Mark Volman, Howard Kaylan)

✖ Nunsploitation ✖ Concert Footage

Before earning metal sainthood for battling the censor-witches of the PMRC and being name-checked by Deep Purple in "Smoke on the Water," musical visionary Frank Zappa led many rock fans to heavy metal. In the other direction, he also opened countless headbanging minds to the far reaches of rock, jazz, classical, doo-wop, and any other art form that could involve brilliant noise and brilliantly dumb dirty jokes.

200 Motels is Zappa's first crack at motion picture madness, embodying the forgotten cultural mo-ment when acid rock tumbled into the black pits of rising heavy metal. Surrealistic sketches and psychedelic set pieces about the insanity of touring are interspersed with performances of the Mothers of Invention jamming with the London Philharmonic. Ringo Starr plays Zappa during the talking parts. A psychedelic cartoon interlude admiringly tweaks Black Sabbath and Grand Funk Railroad. Keith Moon, madman drummer of the Who, pops in and out as "The Hot Nun."

Zappa himself plays lots of guitar, demonstrating what a six-string maestro he was, every lick on par with those of his future protégé Steve Vai.

300 (2007)

(DIR. ZACK SNYDER; W/GERARD BUTLER, LENA HEADEY, KELLY CRAIG, DOMINIC WEST)
✠ SWORDS & SORCERY ✠ BATTLE ELEPHANTS

Spartans, ready your breakfast and eat hearty, for tonight...we dine in HELL!" Adapted from a graphic novel by Frank Miller (*The Dark Knight Returns*), and inspired by the Battle of Thermopylae circa 480 b.c., *300* pits Sparta's King Leonidas (Gerard Butler) against Persia's Xerxes (Rodrigo Santoro), a "god-king" of gender-flexibility and exotic quadruped transportation. His battle rhinos rule. The action kicks off when Xerxes sends a messenger to Sparta, demanding that the independent nation bow to Persian control. Leonidas replies by whomping a boot to the messenger's chest and sending the fellow tumbling down Sparta's precariously open-access "Pit of Death." The Persian military numbers one million troops, while Spartan forces top out at 300. Hence the title. Each side's army strips down and oils up, marching into battle like a-million-and-300 Manowar album covers brought to loincdothed, spear-chucking, earth-scorching life.

300 then brings the gift of carnage—shiny, gory, and spectacular, end-to-end, pure molten power metal cascading off the screen, like a Frank Frazetta–designed Xbox 360 game based on Iced Earth lyrics that plays *you*. No wonder bands named Sparta, Spartan Warrior, Leonidas, and Xerxes have sprouted up all over the place. This

looks like no other previous movie, and sounds like an all-out apocalypse in Dolby 6.66. *300* ripples, sweats, bleeds, pierces your brain, and then detonates your nervous system as you are propelled upward, arms pumping overhead, involuntarily grunting in a prehuman tongue: "Holy flaming fuck!"

976-EVIL (1988)

(DIR. ROBERT ENGLUND; W/STEPHEN GEOFFREYS)
✠ SATAN ✠ YOUTH GONE WILD ✠ TELEPHONES

Freddy Krueger directs Evil Ed from *Fright Night* (he was also Wendell Tvedt in *Fraternity Vacation*) in a gimmicky, effects-heavy fright flick about Satan possessing callers by means of a "horror-scope" telephone line. The ring-dings include our bedraggled teen nerd hero, who soon turns into a purple-faced demon hell-bent on wasting his bully tormentors.

Upon release, *976-Evil* was a relative disappointment. A quarter century later, the VHS special is an automatic blast back to an extremely specific, knuckleheaded headbanger past. Aside from Robert Englund (yes, Freddy) behind the camera and Stephen Geoffreys (the aforementioned Ed/Wendell) in the lead, *976-Evil* traffics in rubber monsters, sticky gore, Satanic Panic, Spencer Gifts–ish punk chicks, and, in its every moment, the look and feel of an MTV hair metal video.

Besides all that, the central plot device is a pay-per-minute call-in number for a dubious entertainment service hustled hard via late-night TV ads. Circa 1988, these semi-scams were everywhere, offering prerecorded messages from teen idols, scandal queens, pro wrestlers, rappers, Howard Stern, and no dearth of metal bands, including Kiss (of course) and Warrant. There were also 900-number Heavy Metal Movie spin-offs such as the Freddy Krueger line, where he'd tell you a scary story, and a Bill and Ted touch-tone time-travel game that touted the Wyld Stallyns van as a grand prize. I'd love to meet the winner.

976-Evil generated a useless 1992 sequel, and the Deftones recorded the 2010 tribute "976-Evil."

1984 (1984)

(DIR. MICHAEL RADFORD; W/JOHN HURT, SUZANNA HAMILTON, RICHARD BURTON, BOB FLAG)

✠ POST-APOCALYPSE ✠ BIG BROTHER

Heavy metal is music's loudest cry against oppression. *1984* by George Orwell performed the same function for literature. Director Michael Radford's stark, well-made, and very British movie adaptation potently realizes the soul-poisoning dread of omnipresent state authority as viewed through the struggles of dissatisfied citizen Winston Smith (John Hurt) and Julia (Suzanna Hamilton), the woman with whom he dares to fall in love.

"War is peace," spouts Big Brother (Bob Flag), the face of a government that offers "protection" through constant, inescapable surveillance. "Freedom is slavery. Ignorance is strength." Bullshit then, bullshit now. The rebellion of *1984* is heavy metal. That's the truth. And in a metal context, Suzanna Hamilton's lushly overgrown lap brush during her full-frontal nude scene looks as though she's using her thighs to apply a headlock on Buzz Osborne of the Melvins and Claudio Sanchez of Coheed and Cambria.

1990: THE BRONX WARRIORS (1982)

(DIR. ENZO G. CASTELLARI; W/MARK GREGORY, STEFANIA GIROLAMI, FRED WILLIAMSON, VIC MORROW)

✠ POST-APOCALYPSE ✠ '80s ITALIAN EXPLOITATION

At the turn of the final decade of the twentieth century, the basic scenario of *Escape from New York* is replayed in the Big Apple's northernmost borough, whose only occupants are homicidal hooligans clad in Dumpster discards from *The Warriors*. Only a bare-chested, hippie-haired brutalist in the mold of *Conan the Barbarian* could survive, and then only by being handy with motorized vehicles and handmade oversize weaponry; just like in *The Road Warrior*!

That cavalcade of movie names explains all any-one needs to know about *1990: Bronx Warriors*. Small surprise that the movie was made in 1982, and more specifically by the Italian exploitation outfit behind *Zombie* (1979), *Zombie Holocaust* (1980), *The Beyond* (1981), and *New York Ripper* (1982). In the early '80s, the country of Caligula went plumb *pazzo* for Hollywood's dystopian action outbursts, especially the Big Four named above. Even Italy's most hard-charging metal export of the moment was named Bulldozer, as in the *Road Warrior* kill machine.

Debuting in the lead as skinny-jeaned street gang leader Trash is Mark Gregory, all of seventeen years old, whom director Enzo G. Castellari reportedly discovered at either a shoe store or a gym. Perfectly adequate in the role of teenager in a leather vest, Gregory seems just tough enough to defend runaway debutante Ann (Stefania Girolami) and throttle the asses of rival roller-skating street gang the Zombies. One piece of semi-official trivia floated after the fact hilariously reports that Gregory "beat off 2,000 other hopefuls for the role." Now that's a man's man.

In 1983, the sequel *Bronx Warriors 2*, aka *Escape From the Bronx*, brawled its way into theaters.

2001: A SPACE ODYSSEY (1968)

(DIR. STANLEY KUBRICK; W/KEIR DULLEA, GARY LOCKWOOD, DOUGLAS RAIN)

✠ VIOLENT APES ✠ MONOLITH ✠ EVIL COMPUTER

Stanley Kubrick's *2001: A Space Odyssey* stands, monolith-like indeed, as one of the definitive heavy metal statements—all the way from the Dawn of Man to Jupiter and Beyond the Infinite. The film profoundly influenced contemporary British solid-rock mind-blowers Earth who, after catching sight of another movie, changed their name to Black Sabbath.

The on-screen events of *2001* are almost as familiar as its five-note musical refrain ("Also Sprach Zarathustra" by Richard Strauss). In the beginning, a black monolith appears to a society of simians, emits a drone, and seems to change them from peaceful to violent. After beating another animal to death, one of the apes throws a bone into the sky and we cut to a spaceship floating gracefully among others through the heavens. The year is 2001, and the same black monolith appears on the moon. Astronaut Dave Bowman (Keir Dullea) takes off to investigate. The monolith vanishes and turns up again on Jupiter. Bowman and Dr. Frank Poole (Gary Lockwood) set off to find it on a ship controlled by HAL 9000, an all-seeing computer with a mind, and a very distinct voice, of its own. In time, HAL goes "insane" and kills Poole. Bowman is forced to shut HAL down as the computer pleads for its life. Bowman then flies directly into the monolith, experiences the ultimate psychedelic sound and light show, and turns up in a fancy room as a very old man. He is transformed into the Starchild, an infant floating in the vastness of space whose face radiates pure hope.

There are as many theories as to what *2001* is "about" as there are those who've seen the movie. My own, quickly: The monolith is God, or a divine spirit or higher power. The monolith appears when man is ready, and empowers him to surge forward via intelligence and technology. Immediately, though, consequences occur: the apes learn to use tools and build shelter, but they also learn greed and war. In the space age, man is entirely reliant on ever fancier tools and ever more intricate shelters. The monolith materializes far away, so that man must travel to reach it and, in the process, grow. When HAL, the ultimate tool and the ultimate shelter, not only fails man but works to destroy him, Bowman reaches within and conjures his humanity. In doing so, he directly confronts the divine. Bowman then hurls himself headlong into this higher power, undergoes an entire transformation, and emerges reborn, the embodiment of limitless possibilities.

As for Black Sabbath, the band also formed in 1968, landing smack in a mud pit of hairy, unwashed grunters. Sabbath also pulsated and overwhelmed and emitted its hypnotic drone to serve as the propulsive force driving the primitives upright and onward through a gateway to previously inconceivable creativity and creations, as well as being the very gateway itself. Whether that makes any sense to you or not, your head just got banged!

2019: AFTER THE FALL OF NEW YORK (1983)

(DIR. SERGIO MARTINO; W/MICHAEL SOPKIW, ANNA KANAKIS, GEORGE EASTMAN)

✶ POST-APOCALYPSE ✶ '80S ITALIAN EXPLOITATION
✶ EVIL APEMEN

Italians must like it when bad stuff happens to New York City. That's the only logical deduction one can make after mopping up the heaps of Gotham-based slasher movies and post-nuke adventures made by friendly Roman countrymen in the 1980s. One shell-shocked survivor in *2019* calls the city "the Baked Apple." Done and done.

This go-around, Parsifal (Michael Sopkiw) is our requisite leather-headbanded motorcycle hero. The bad guys, who dropped the big one in 1999, are the Eurax. They dress like Darth Vader, ride horses, and fuck shit up with flamethrowers. Rats are food, eyes exist for gouging out, and entertainment comes in the form of circus-like "car fights." Rape and torture serve as the main forms of currency. All the women are hot punk chicks, but none of them can reproduce.

Word bubbles up into this radioactive spew-stew that a single fertile female has been discovered. Just as surely as the main dwarf character is called "Shorty," this sole beacon of hope for human breeding is named—what else?—"Mary." She needs safe transport to Alaska, where she'll presumably be kept extremely busy repopulating the planet. Parsifal is up to the challenge.

Then *After the Fall of New York* ups the ante by ripping off *Planet of the Apes* in the most enjoyably literal way—by introducing a tribe of apemen with no explanation as to how and why they got to the big city. Out of nowhere, just: "Hey, hey! Some monkeys!"

2020 Texas Gladiators (1982)

(Dir. Joe D'Amato; w/Al Cliver, Harrison Muller, Jr., Hal Yamanouchi)

✵ Post-Apocalypse Texas ✵ Italy ✵ Nun Rape
✵ Priest Crucifixion

The Lone Star State backdrop immediately sets *2020 Texas Gladiators* apart from its Italian-born, post-apocalypse peers of 1982. The film opens a world of extreme entertainment even blacker than Black Sabbath: The villains meld Nazi aesthetics with *Star Wars* stormtrooper stuff; director Joe D'Amato mines *The Deer Hunter* for P.O.W. Russian-roulette action; the Texas setting allows for dips into spaghetti western and Native American iconography; and the vehicles of the final battle look like the kind of mutant multi-wheelers Sid from *Toy Story* would knock together out of old Tonka trucks and Malibu Barbie convertibles.

The film's first five minutes conjure a black-metal milieu unequaled in cinema. A gaggle of nuns and a kindly priest go about their solemn business in a quiet convent. Mad marauders storm the place and turn it into Unholy Rape Central Station—slashing, stripping, stabbing, burning, and gouging new holes in virgin flesh for penile plunging purposes. The nuns scream, cry, and bleed. The priest who rushes to help is graphically crucified. The youngest sister, seeing no lesser agony, slashes her own throat with a piece of jagged debris, making sure to cut all the way down between her visibly bare breasts.

After this relentless body-fluid basting runs for a while, the scene's *real* kick in the nuts is revealed: The good guys have assembled their bulging muscles above the melee, readying to descend upon the raiders at any moment. That means the movie's heroes just stood by and witnessed all these lovely Texas nuns get sodomized into armadillo soup, and nice Father Longhorn having to accept nails through his appendages, wailing, and they could have stopped it, but they chose to wait —so that we, the audience, could see it all happen. Thank you!

Our debt of gratitude is due the heroic Nisus (Al Cliver), who sports long locks and mounts numerous motorcycles in defense of a small band of survivors, as is required of any Italian post-apocalypse-movie hero. The leading lady is tiny-titted, badonka-butted Stefania Sandrelli, one of the great beauties of heinous European exploitation flicks. Bringing up the rear, so to speak, is a sexy, chubby machine-gun chick dressed in an S&M outfit that completely exposes her naked boobs every time she's on camera.

You may have been told to not mess with Texas, but by all means, let *2020 Texas Gladiators* mess with you. I did, and look at me now!

THE ABOMINABLE DR. PHIBES ✠ ABSENT ✠ ABSURD ✠ AC/DC: LET THERE BE ROCK ✠ ACE VENTURA: PET DETECTIVE ✠ ACTRESS APOCALYPSE ✠ THE ADVENTURES OF UNCLE COLT AND CLETUS: HEDGE-HOGGIN' ✠ AFTER PARTY MASSACRE ✠ AIRHEADS ✠ ALICE COOPER: THE NIGHTMARE ✠ ALICE COOPER: WELCOME TO MY NIGHTMARE ✠ ALICE SWEET ALICE ✠ ALIEN ✠ ALL THE COLORS OF THE DARK ✠ ALUCARDA ✠ AMEBIX RISEN: A HISTORY OF AMEBIX ✠ AMERICA 3000 ✠ AMERICAN MOVIE ✠ AN AMERICAN WEREWOLF IN LONDON ✠ AMITYVILLE 2: THE POSSESSION ✠ ANGEL AT MIDNIGHT ✠ ANGEL HEART ✠ ANIMAL INSTINCTS III: THE SEDUCTRESS ✠ AN-THOR-OLOGY (1976-1985) ✠ ANTICHRIST ✠ THE ANTICHRIST ✠ ANTHROPOPHAGUS: THE GRIM REAPER ✠ ANVIL!: THE STORY OF ANVIL ✠ APOCALYPSE NOW ✠ AQUA TEEN HUNGER FORCE COLON MOVIE FILM FOR THEATERS ✠ ARENA: HEAVY METAL ✠ ARISE: THE SRI LANKAN METAL MUSIC DOCUMENTARY ✠ ARMY OF DARKNESS ✠ AS THE PALACES BURN ✠ THE ASPHYX ✠ ASSORTED ATROCITIES: THE EXODUS DOCUMENTARY ✠ AT MIDNIGHT I'LL TAKE YOUR SOUL ✠ ATOR THE FIGHTING EAGLE ✠ AUGUST UNDERGROUND ✠ AURAL AMPHETAMINE: METALLICA AND THE DAWN OF THRASH ✠ AUTOPSY

The Abominable Dr. Phibes (1971)

(Dir. Robert Fuest; w/Vincent Price, Joseph Cotten, Virginia North, Peter Jeffrey)
✠ Vincent Price ✠ Goth Babe ✠ Biblical Plagues ✠ Ancient Egypt

As horror movies evolved from the unprec-edented intensity of *Night of the Living Dead* (1968) into the dead-hearted, documentary-style shocks of *Last House on the Left* (1972) and *The Texas Chain Saw Massacre* (1974), old-school master Vincent Price reclaimed his fright film crown one final time with his campy tour de force *The Abominable Dr. Phibes*.

Anton Phibes (Price) is a world-renowned British organ-player with doctorates in music and theology. As the movie begins, in 1925, it is believed that Phibes was killed four years earlier in a car accident that resulted in the death of wife Victoria during surgery. Alas, the mad maestro is hardly dead. He is alive and unwell—a scarred, mouthless monster who rigs up a perfect face mask and sound system that, when hooked to a gramophone, enable him to "speak." Phibes lives in a mansion full of music-playing automatons, where he's tended to and accompanied by black-clad and mute (a miracle when it comes to goth chicks!) Vulnavia (Virginia North). All he does is plot his revenge, until the time comes to put his wicked plans into action.

The diabolical doctor blames Victoria's death on incompetent medical practices, so, one by one, he inflicts the ten Old Testament plagues that befell Egypt upon the attending doctors and one nurse. Bees, locusts, rats, blood, a head-crushing mechanical frog mask, and on and on—check your scripture. Dr. Phibes's weapons of choice are each eloquently employed while Vulnavia looks on adoringly. Scotland Yard's Inspector Trout (Peter Jeffrey) is on the case, but fails to catch the fiend.

Dr. Phibes is funny, scary, vicious, and classy. In other words, the film is the perfect embodiment of its star, Vincent Price—as unholy a Heavy Metal Movie god as has ever reigned in blood and hailstones. NWOBHM greats Angel Witch summed it up with their song "Dr. Phibes."

ΛBSENT (2010)
(DIR. JUSTIN HUNT; W/JAMES HETFIELD, JOHNNY TAPIA, JOHN ELDREDGE)
✶ JAMES HETFIELD

Heavy metal fan Justin Hunt gets heavy, and deep, with his documentary *Absent*, starting with this proclamation: "The father is the first person in the world who chooses you...or doesn't." Many a young headbanger has been molded, at least in part, by the soul-deep wounds left by a dad who ditches his familial responsibilities. Hunt sits with a series of adults to ponder their own childhood betrayals, including *Wild at Heart* novelist John Eldredge, boxer Johnny Tapia (a shattered soul who was led to believe his father was murdered), and, most surprisingly, Metallica's James Hetfield.

Metallica's ferocious frontman reveals himself, even more so than in *Some Kind of Monster* (2004), to be just another battle-fatigued human trying hard, again and again, to do better.

Hetfield remarkably drops his notorious guard here, opening up to the point of near tears and even sharing family pictures. He musically addressed his Christian Science upbringing in the furious song "The God That Failed," but this

sit-down provides a more nuanced picture—and one that is even more heartfelt when it comes to his inability to heal emotional hurts by sheer faith. By the end, *Absent* drains and devastates, all for a higher purpose.

ΛBSURD (1981), AKA
MONSTER HUNTER; HORRIBLE;
ROSSO SANGUE
(DIR. JOE D'AMATO; W/GEORGE EASTMAN, EDMUND PERDOM)
✶ ITALIAN HORROR ✶ BANNED VIDEO NASTY

While fleeing a furious priest (Edmund Perdom), bearded burly-man Mikos Stenopolis (George Eastman) climbs a spiked fence, slips, and gorily disembowels himself all over the place. With his guts spilling out, Mikos amazes doctors at a hospital with his ability to spontaneously heal. He then also brutally murders all those doctors. And nurses. And anyone and everyone else who gets in his path. So goes the appropriately absurd opening of *Absurd*, splatter legend Joe D'Amato's pseudo-sequel to his legendary fetus-eating atrocity parade from earlier in 1981, *The Grim Reaper*, aka *Anthropophagus*.

Mikos leaves a trail of bloodshed in his wake until arriving at a house with a babysitter and two kids. A family friend gets pickaxed in the skull; the babysitter has her face forced into a lit oven; and, ultimately, our villain gets stabbed in the eye with a drawing compass by an infirm little girl, who goes on to decapitate him.

Absurd, an extreme black metal band from Germany, took its name directly as a tribute to this film upon forming in 1992. The teenage group's love of violent movies was apparent in their songs, and spilled into real life in 1993 when members overpowered a fifteen-year-old associate and strangled him to death with an electrical cord. While in prison, leader Hendrik Möbus released a tape with a cover featuring the grave of their murder victim. And in case anyone didn't get it, the liner notes explain: "The cover shows the grave of Sandro B. murdered by horde ABSURD on 29.04.93 AB." This earned Möbus further jail time for mocking his victim. Truly Absurd. Less damaged bands named Absurd hailed from Belgium, France, Poland, Russia, Sweden, and Switzerland.

AC/DC: Let There Be Rock (1980)

(DIRS. ERIC DIONYSIUS, ERIC MISTLER; W/BON SCOTT, ANGUS YOUNG, MALCOLM YOUNG, PHIL RUDD)
✠ CONCERT FOOTAGE

Let there be light. During my first week of work on this book, *AC/DC: Let There Be Rock*, after decades as a semi-lost classic, emerged in a special edition Blu-ray package. I like to imagine Bon Scott, from the beyond, somehow puked that convergence into being.

Anything seems possible seeing AC/DC's original singer alive onstage, and this is the defining document of the end of the Bon Scott era. He rides on the vital apex of his frontman prowess during a Paris show in December 1979, just prior to his alcoholically exiting this mortal coil, at thirty-three, in February 1980. Watch him, wonder what might have been, and weep. Then watch him again, in just plain wonder.

Let There Be Rock also provides permanent proof positive that AC/DC's pipsqueak guitarist Angus Young really did wail and rail nonstop onstage, as though the electrical current for which his band is named was coursing through his body in places where the rest of us have mere blood.

The concert consists of thirteen songs, many from *Highway to Hell*, bookended by stalwarts "Live Wire" and closing with "Let There Be Rock." Every performance is great. Between numbers, the band chats and clowns around. These bits were likely designed for pee and popcorn breaks, but they stand as invaluable treasures. These are goofy glimpses of the men who were members of what would become of one of history's most successful rock bands. At this point, they had no clue that they were about

to lose their vividly live wire Bon Scott and yet somehow reemerge from that tragedy as giants.

The legend persists that some theaters screening *Let There Be Rock* ran the movie's sound through stacks of Marshall amplifiers. No proof of this exists, and eyewitnesses who caught the flick on its first run do not recall any stacks. But if is not true, it certainly should be. Let there always be *Let There Be Rock*.

Ace Ventura—Pet Detective (1994)

(DIR. TOM SHADYAC; W/JIM CARREY, COURTENEY COX, SEAN YOUNG, TONE LOC, CANNIBAL CORPSE)
✠ KILLER CAMEOS

For a wiseacre generation that came of age in the '90s, *Ace Ventura: Pet Detective* served as the gateway to three of life's most profound pleasures: slapstick comedy; talking out of your butt, literally; and death metal.

During his lunatic quest to recover the Miami Dolphins' kidnapped bottlenose mascot, Jim Carrey as our pointy-haired hero stumbles into a metal show. After joking with a reveler whose face is entirely covered by hair ("I think Uncle Fester is looking for you!"), Ace leaps on stage and jams along with Cannibal Corpse. Driven into a frenzy by the blast beats, Ace tears off his shirt, headbangs, roars into a microphone in classic Cookie Monster style, spazzes out to the song "Hammer Smashed Face," and announces, "I gotta go, guys! I got a date with your mothers!" *Ace Ventura: Pet Detective* made Jim Carrey a superstar and, for a few months in 1994, turned Cannibal Corpse into the house band at kiddie movie matinees in multiplexes everywhere.

Cannibal Corpse appearing in *Ace Ventura* is certainly surprising. That they got the gig at the insistence of Jim Carrey himself is even more of a brain-banger. Upon seeing a rock band scene in the original *Ace Ventura* script, Carrey insisted that the job go to Cannibal Corpse. The rubber-faced funnyman was an avowed death metal nut

Clockwise from top left: Welcome to My Nightmare *(1975)*; AC/DC Let There Be Rock *(1980) VHS; the poster is better than the movie—* Alien Contamination *(1980); alternate* Alice, Sweet Alice *(1976) moniker* Holy Terror; An American Werewolf in London *(1981) lobby card; Bruce Campbell as Ash in* Army of Darkness *(1993), aka* Evil Dead 3.

His taste for Florida death metal mellowed over time, however—twenty years later he tapped far more cerebral Cynic/Death guitarist Paul Masvidal to collaborate on a children's record.

In the documentary *Cannibal Corpse: Centuries of Torment* (2008), the band members talk at length about flying from Buffalo to Miami to shoot the scene and how they felt when Carrey seemed even more excited to meet them than they were to meet him. Carrey provided similar big-screen exposure to satanic noise punks the Dwarves in *Me, Myself, and Irene* (2000), where he sings along in a car to the band's song "Motherfucker."

Actress Apocalypse

(2005)

(Dir. Richard R. Anasky; w/Garo Nigoghossian, Greg G. Freeman, Jay Ingle, Dahlia Legault)
✠ Slasher ✠ Doom Metal

Frustrated by the difficulties facing his unreleased acid opus *I Am Vengeance* (2006), writer-director Richard R. Anasky shot *Actress Apocalypse*, a mock documentary about the shooting of an independent horror movie that goes nakedly and messily off course.

The Lincoln brothers, square David (Garo Nigoghossian) and wildman Vance (Greg G. Freeman), attempt to shoot a slasher film. Vance loses his mind due to filmmaking pressures, he sets up a succession of starlet auditions that begin with nudity and add up to the title of the movie. *Actress Apocalypse* is trippy and ingenious, making terrific use of adroit editing, impressive gore, and the greatest visual effect of all: female nudity.

Albums by pioneering British doom band Witchfinder General feature on-screen repeatedly in *Actress Apocalypse*. Director Anasky is a worshipfully devoted fan and wanted the group's influence to be seen all over the movie. Fuzzed-out Swedish stoner rock outfit Space Probe Taurus provides the rocket ride soundtrack.

The Adventures of Uncle Colt and Cletus — Hedge-Hoggin' (2013)

(Dir. Nathan Cox; w/Jeremy Spencer, Bobby Watson, Ron Jeremy, Verne Troyer)
✠ Killer Cameos ✠ Headbanger Buddies

Bill and Ted, Wayne and Garth, and Terry and Dean of *Fubar*: the notion of two hesher buds looking to bang heads and score babes en route to delusional rock stardom is a grand Heavy Metal Movie archetype. *The Adventures of Uncle Colt and Cletus: Hedge-Hoggin'* introduces another long-locked numbskull duo, with the twist being that one is a real-life rock star. Jeremy Spencer, drummer of platinum-selling Five Finger Death Punch, plays Colt. His actual drum tech Bobby Watson costars as Cletus. Spencer and Watson created the slapstick yokel characters to amuse themselves on tour.

During the nine-minute movie, Colt and Cletus do yard work for Ron Jeremy and unleash Verne Troyer as a genie. When Troyer, the former Mini-Me, is displeased by a limp handshake, he yips: "Shake like a man, bitch!" Uncle Colt and Cletus then magically become MTV-type pop sensations with bikini-clad groupies, but before long they end up losing it all. Multiple follow-ups are promised to come gushing through the pipeline.

After Party Massacre (2011)

(Dirs. Kristoff Bates, Kyle Severn; w/Scarlett Von Sinn, Kyle Severn)
✠ Slasher ✠ Rape and Revenge ✠ Soundtrack
(16 Volt, Asphyx, Denial Fiend, Master)

The bloodily bile-spattered brainchild of online culture maven Kristoff Bates (proprietor of the sites Horror Merch and Spooky Girls) and musician Kyle Severn (member of Incantation and Acheron), *After Party Massacre* supplies a properly outlandish volume of death metal slasher righteousness. Whatever plot peeks through is centered on sexy alt-nude model Scarlett Von Sinn as (yes) Scarlett. She attends a death metal show, where she is uncomfortably manhandled, and she retaliates (and then some) by torturing, murdering, and/or mutilating anyone she encounters—including some of her hot friends. Amidst seas of Spooky Girl nudity and lesbianism, a wire hanger is jammed into peehole, a dildo is hammered into a skull, limbs are removed by a power saw, and vats of gore pour down over Scarlett's targets. Overwhelmingly, the visual effects rock; the nudity 100 percent entirely rocks.

After Party Massacre also boasts more than twenty bands on its soundtrack. The music is laid end-to-end, underscoring every single moment of activity. Incantation and Soulless also deliver ripping live performances. Opeth fans be warned: numerous jokes here come at the expense of you.

Airheads (1994)

(Dir. Michael Lehmann; w/Brendan Fraser, Adam Sandler, Steve Buscemi, Harold Ramis)

✠ Sunset Strip ✠ Killer Cameos

The year 1994 was a great time for anybody who liked watching metalheads suffer. Lollapalooza ruled. L.A.'s once-towering all-metal KNAC-FM flipped to a foreign-tongue format. *Headbangers Ball* limped toward the first in its series of executions by MTV. Not long after Kurt Cobain gave himself the ultimate makeover from the neck up, Metallica took to pondering how much of his audience they might acquire if they abbreviated their hairdos.

Into this toxic terrain, *Airheads* arrived, born ready for VHS video rental. Brendan Fraser is atypically zesty in *Airheads*, not long after his likable caveman turn in the near-metal laffer *Encino Man* (1992). He plays the frontman of a power trio, backed by Adam Sandler and Steve Buscemi—who is especially good in Adam Sandler movies. This band, the Lone Rangers, fills a water gun with hot sauce and takes over a radio station. They receive sympathy from a DJ (Joe Mantegna), grief from a broadcast exec (Michael McKean), and butt-kissing from a Columbia Records bigwig (Harold Ramis). Sunset Strip hordes, outside the station, lap it all up.

White Zombie plays the Whisky A Go Go, showcasing Sean Yseult's mesmerizing hair-spins. Beavis and Butt-head make a surprise vocal cameo. Lemmy mouths a scripted line, as does *The Howard Stern Show*'s Stuttering John Melendez, who also scored a pleasant toe-tapper on the soundtrack—"I'm Gonna Talk My Way Out of This"—which lives up to the Lone Rangers' description of their sound as "power slop."

Alice Cooper: The Nightmare (1975)

(Dir. Jorn Winther; w/Alice Cooper, Vincent Price, Sheryl Cooper, Steve Hunter, Dick Wagner)

✠ Vincent Price ✠ Haunted House

Alice Cooper: The Nightmare aired April 25, 1975, on ABC. The prime-time special is an hour-long, shot-on-video phantasmagoria with Alice in the role of Steven, an innocent youth trapped inside a nightmare. Vincent Price emerges as the Spirit of the Nightmare, and Alice's real-life lady, Sheryl Cooper, plays Cold Ethyl.

Alice Cooper: The Nightmare, the TV show, is often confused with *Alice Cooper: Welcome to My Nightmare*, the concert film. They are two separate entities, although they often both get referred to as simply *Welcome to My Nightmare*.

Looking like it was shot inside a haunted house designed by Sid and Marty Kroft, replete with ghouls and puppets and a Bat Woman (Robin Blythe), *The Nightmare* is a ghoulish delight. The music covers the entire *Welcome to My Nightmare* album, plus the early song "The Ballad of Dwight Frye." The action, art direction, and general aura are a warm-up for Alice's classic guest host shot on *The Muppet Show*.

The Nightmare was scripted by Alan Rudolph, who worked extensively on *The Brady Bunch* and served as assistant director to Robert Altman on *The Long Goodbye* (1973) and *Nashville* (1975). He went on to direct the rock and roll comedy *Roadie* (1980). Just prior to this, Rudolph directed *Barn of the Naked Dead* (1974), about a maniac who kidnaps women and forces them to learn circus tricks—a perfect precursor to Alice's *Nightmare*.

Alice Cooper: Welcome to My Nightmare (1975)

(Dir. David Winters; w/Alice Cooper, Dick Wagner, Steve Hunter, Jozef Chirowski, Whitey Glan)

✠ Mutants ✠ Giant Cyclops ✠ Rock Concert

Not to be confused with the ABC-TV special *Alice Cooper: The Nightmare*, this better-known offering is a feature-length theatrical concert film that bombed upon release, but lived on through the late '70s as a regular midnight movie.

The film documents Alice on tour promoting the album of the same name, his first without the original Alice Cooper Group, with footage mostly shot at London's Wembley Arena in September 1975. Glam vixen Suzi Quatro, aka Leather Tuscadero from *Happy Days*, was the opening act. In addition to entirety of the *Welcome to My Nightmare* album, the band plays "I'm Eighteen," "School's Out," and "Department of Youth."

The *Nightmare* stage opus takes place in the bedroom of young naïf Steven, played by Alice. The setting transforms into a graveyard into which an array of monsters and mutants drop by or pop up. Among these are dancing skeletons, flashy demons, a behemoth spider with the voice of Vincent Price, and, most fan-friggin'-tastically, a nine-foot-tall Cyclops. The sheer scope of the production makes it seem like this show could have only played in soccer stadiums.

Thanks to master choreographer David Winters, the action onstage is positively stupefying. One amazing effect has Alice jumping into a movie being projected on a giant screen behind the band, running wild among some phantoms, and then tumbling back out. Apparently, the production cost $600,000—more than a Broadway musical of that era—and all that spending shows.

As a movie, though, *Nightmare* is point-and-shoot concert footage, which is more than fine when the subject is Alice Cooper at the peak of his powers as the Greatest Showman on Earth... or any other planet. Rhino's *Welcome to My Nightmare* DVD includes a great commentary track by Cooper. Director David Winters went on to make the skateboard movie *Thrashin'* in 1986.

Alice Sweet Alice (1976), aka Communion; Holy Terror

(Dir. Albert Sole; w/Linda Miller, Paula Sheppard, Lillian Roth, Brooke Shields)

✠ Slasher ✠ Evil Masks

Described by *Psychotronic Encyclopedia of Film* author Michael Weldon as "violently anti-Catholic," *Alice, Sweet Alice* is a tantrum that oozes forward from an old, deep, and very clearly Church-of-Rome-inflicted wound, drawing you into a hellishly thrilling and intriguing mystery.

Alice (Paula Sheppard) is an angry twelve-year-old in the highly Italian, entirely Catholic town of Paterson, NJ, in 1962. She dons a unnerving clear mask to scare church housekeeper Mrs. Tredoni (Mildred Clinton) and her goody two-shoes nine-year-old sister, Karen (Brooke Shields). Karen's First Communion arrives. Before she can receive the sacrament, the girl is strangled and set ablaze by someone in a yellow raincoat and a mask like the one Alice wore.

Alice's world is dominated by despicable grown-ups: her miserably divorced mother; a morbidly obese child-molesting landlord; some nasty kids her own age who hate her; and the dictatorial misery of pre≠Vatican II East Coast ethnic Catholicism. An obviously intelligent and creative child, she takes refuge in a basement lair with her mask, a hideous three-faced baby doll, and strange rituals she performs involving a candle. In another time and place, Alice could have turned onto Black Sabbath, Coven, and other burgeoning heavy metal routes to occult exploration. Instead she goes someplace darker.

Alice, Sweet Alice evolves into a devious maze involving multiple murders in and near the local parish. The crisis leads to a logical but terrifying solution, compounded by a multitiered shock ending that may well prompt lapsed Catholics to involuntarily make the sign of the cross.

Alice, Sweet Alice opened in theaters three times. First as *Communion*, in 1976, then under its most familiar title, and finally as *Holy Terror*, in 1981. The last campaign cashed in on Brooke Shields's star power at the time, being careful to hide the fact that she is only nine in the movie, too young even by *Blue Lagoon* standards (not to mention that she gets offed in the first ten minutes). Paula Sheppard, like Brooke, makes her movie debut here. She went on to one other film role, as Adrian, the heroin-pushing bisexual, in the new wave midnight movie *Liquid Sky* (1982).

ALIEN (1979)

(DIR. RIDLEY SCOTT; W/SIGOURNEY WEAVER, JOHN HURT, TOM SKERRIT, YAPHET KOTTO, HARRY DEAN STANTON, IAN HOLM)

✠ H. R. GIGER ✠ SCIENCE FICTION ✠ SPLATTER

An out-of-nowhere box-office smash turned genre-buster, *Alien* exerted enormous impact on sci-fi and horror in the years to come. None of the imitators picked up on what really made Ridley Scott's slow-building masterpiece unique: the story is really a gritty, Method-acted '70s blue-collar drama set in a haunted house—but the house happens to be a spaceship. And a womb.

Alien rip-offs focused on two of the most talked-about visuals: The infant creature bursting out of John Hurt's chest, and the full-grown alien itself, a raging, acid-bleeding eight-foot-tall exoskeletal insect that somehow also looks like a giant penis covered in fanged vaginas. Any living person will be struck dumb by each of these sights, the first for its sudden, visceral shock, and the latter for its masterfully intricate, horrifyingly sexual originality courtesy of Swiss surrealist H. R. Giger.

Alien matches silvery prog-rock visuals with the hammer-blow terror of sleek metal. The film remains the shining high point of a golden age of heady, adult science-fiction cinema that spanned from *2001: A Space Odyssey* (1968) to Ridley Scott's *Blade Runner* (1982). We've seen so many films and other entertainments copping *Alien*'s surface elements, but nothing truly like it since.

H. R. Giger's heavy metal connections are profuse—witness his hugely influential, often-tattooed "bio-mechanical" imagery. Most familiar is his painting "Satan I," depicting the horned one aiming a crucifix slingshot right at you, that graces the cover of Celtic Frost's *To Mega Therion*. Giger artwork also features on albums from Danzig, Atrocity, Necronomicon, Sacrosanct, and Triptykon—not to mention punk giants the Dead Kennedys and prog masters Magma and Emerson, Lake and Palmer. The landmark Carcass album *Heartwork* features a photo of a Giger sculpture. Singer Jonathan Davis of nü-metal troupe Korn uses a custom microphone stand designed by Giger, so that, unlike in space, everyone can hear him scream.

ALL THE COLORS OF THE DARK (1972)

(DIR. SERGIO MARTINO; W/EDWIGE FENECH, GEORGE HILTON, MARINA MALFATTI)

✠ SATAN ✠ BLACK MASS ✠ GIALLO

Beginning with its eerie, evocative title, *All the Colors of the Dark* puts a fresh spin on two horror genres: rip-offs of *Rosemary's Baby* (1968) and Italian *giallo* crime thrillers. Gorgeous Edwige Fenech stars as Jane, a woman whose pregnancy ends in a car crash. She is subsequently inundated with striking, surreal nightmares involving a blue-eyed knife-wielder, an old lady in a baby bonnet, and the slaughter of a screaming nude nubile. Neighbor Mary (Marina Malfatti) reasonably suggests to Jane that participating in a satanic mass ritual will put end such mental torment. Unfortunately, after Jane drinks fox blood from a golden goblet and participates in an occult orgy, her torments only intensify—and so do the jolts and brain-popping visuals of this well-crafted acid rock devil shocker.

Jus Oborn, high unholy magician of Electric Wizard, has raved about the "really hallucinatory vibe" of *All the Colors of the Dark*. The little-known bands Blue Holocaust and Chains have written songs titled "All the Colors of the Dark."

ALUCARDA (1978), AKA SISTERS OF SATAN

(DIR. JUAN LOPEZ MOCTEZUMA; W/TINA ROMERO, SUSANA KAMINI, CLAUDIO BROOK, DAVID SILVA)

✠ SATAN ✠ DEMONIC POSSESSION ✠ NUNS

Mexican horror director Juan Lopez Moctezuma (*Mansion of Madness*; *Mary, Mary, Bloody Mary*) hits his peak in *Alucarda*, a surreal blend of Catholic spookery, blood-drenched teenage lesbianism, and proto-retro torture porn. Who could ask for anything more? The title is simply "Dracula" spelled backwards, with an *a* at the end because the story is about a chick.

Alucarda (Tina Romero) and Justine (Susana Kamini) are orphan girls being raised in a convent. After a run-in with Gypsies and a stray coffin in the woods, Alucarda conjures Satan in their bedroom. From then on, they're converts to his unholy cause. The girls proclaim their new love of the Dark Lord in Bible study class. As evidenced by the Spanish Inquisition, the Catholic Church has ways of quieting such talk. But then so, too, does Satan when it comes time to respond.

Moctezuma produced the original midnight movie, *El Topo* (1970), and maintained a close friendship with its mad genius creator, Alejandro Jodorowsky (*Santa Sangre*). After being a hot ticket among bootleg video traders in the 1990s, *Alucarda* attained wider cult status on DVD, thanks to Mondo Macabro's killer 2003 special-edition release. Moctezuma's set design, costuming, and commitment to outrage remain astounding throughout *Alucarda*. His female stars rise to the movie's high standards. They may even be the most prolific screamers in any horror film I've ever seen. I bow to them, while wearing earplugs.

AMEBIX RISEN: A HISTORY OF AMEBIX (2008)

(DIR. ROY WALLACE; W/ROB "THE BARON" MILLER, STIG, MARTIN, JELLO BIAFRA, SCOTT KELLY)

✠ CRUST PUNK ✠ ALEISTER CROWLEY

In the course of just two official albums, fascinating genre-busters Amebix forever altered the extreme music landscape. Bedecked in sunglasses and black leather amidst multicolor-mohawked UK punks in the late '70s, the squat-dwelling bikers in Amebix commingled occult sorcery with antiauthority street-riot philosophy to conjure the heaviness of Black Sabbath, the rocket thrust of Motörhead, the rebelliousness of Crass, and the apocalyptic firestorms of Killing Joke, along with their own uniquely energetic and inventive take on raising the roof.

Amebix Risen is a straightforward documentary on the band, consisting of talking-head interviews, performance footage, and rudimentary graphics, all of which serve the subject well. Core Amebix members Rob "The Baron" Miller and Stig prove particularly compelling and well-spoken on screen, chronicling their rise and fall with good humor and a shockingly clear perspective.

Rob Miller reveals his post-Amebix career as a professional sword maker with amusement over how people are not surprised by it. He recounts reading: "Rob Miller went on from being a singer in the band Amebix to making swords on the Isle of Skye—of course he did!"

Singularly named drummer Martin discusses at length his psychic involvement with the ghost of

Aleister Crowley, and how he introduced occultism into the overall Amebix mix. Scott Kelly and Steve Von Till of Neurosis wax lovingly on the band, too, citing how Amebix managed to convey anarchic spirit and pagan spirituality while never spouting specifically political or religious lyrics. "Everybody else was getting caught up in details," Scott says. "They were way past that."

Rob Miller talks about Amebix's sonic drift from punk to metal on their 1985 full-length debut, *Arise*: "I was always interested in heavy metal as a musical form, but I thought the lyrics were shit. I loved Black Sabbath—the way the music made you feel something, other than just the words. I liked Crass, and the words would make you feel something, but the music didn't have much resonance. That's why I thought—we can make good music and good lyrics, to get a bit of force together, to push a point home with intensity." Hence, the English take on the punk-metal crossover was born.

AMERICA 3000 (1986)
(DIR. DAVID ENGELBACH; W/CHUCK WAGNER, LAURENE LANDON, STEVE MALOVIC)
✠ POST-APOCALYPSE ✠ AMAZONS ✠ MUTANTS
✠ CANNON FILMS

America 3000 begins by sharing this information: "Nine hundred years after the Great Nuke. The world man created, he destroyed. Out of the darkness and ignorance of the radioactive rubble emerged a new order. And the world was woggos." As you could never guess, "woggos" is future-speak for "totally cuckoo." Battle-savvy Amazons, complete with Sunset Strip–ready giant hair and animal-print bikinis, rule the desert landscape. Men, who are ape-dumb and defenseless, work as slaves or, if they're lucky, "seeders." Mutants wander about. Then Corbus (Chuck Wagner), a resident of "Camp Reagan," falls into a bunker stocked with laser guns, grenades, and a ghetto blaster equipped with hard rock cassettes. The revolution is on.

The post-nuke setting and Cannon Films pedi-gree earn *America 3000* its Heavy Metal Movies stripes, but the real metal beast here is a Wookie-like mutant named "Aargh the Awful." The on-screen function of this head-to-toe hirsute, stoner-metal monstrosity is to whoop and wail along with the rock jams pouring out of the unearthed boom box. After Corbus and an Amazon leader (Laurene Landon) swap some sweat and lots of mega-jiggy plastic lingo, *America 3000* wraps up with a charging-cavalry action climax. Divert your eyes if you're sensitive to the old movie stunt trick of "horse-tripping."

AMERICAN MOVIE (1999)
(DIR. CHRIS SMITH; W/MARC BORCHARDT, MIKE SCHANK, TOM SCHIMMELS, BILL BORCHARDT)
✠ METAL REALITY ✠ HORROR ✠ OBSESSION

The narrative American movie at the heart of the documentary *American Movie* is titled *Coven*, a short supernatural horror film written and directed by gangly Milwaukee auteur Mark Borchardt. He hopes that the success of *Coven* will finance his full-length coming-of-age drama, *Northwestern*. Aiding and abetting Mark at every turn is his hefty, sweetly dim, mightily mustachioed metalhead best friend Mike Schank.

Replete with a long, floppy mane of dark hair, a cheesy goatee, active alcoholism, multiple children out of wedlock, a volatile temper, an inability to finish seemingly any task, and a hilarious insistence on mispronouncing "Coven" with a long *o*, so it rhymes with "cloven," Borchardt embodies the Midwestern hesher stereotype—including a lopsided, often inexplicable, likability.

Tom Schimmels, the spookily aristocratic local thespian who plays the lead in *Coven*, is like Wisconsin's answer to Brazilian horror host Coffin Joe—and that's when he's not even on the set. He is some find. Uncle Bill Borchardt, Mark's chief financier, has a single line in *Coven* that he repeats maniacally, to the point that, even in the midst of this upbeat, life-affirming documentary, it packs a real chill: "It's all right, it's okay, there's something to live for...Jesus told me so!"

Clockwise from top left: *Golan-Globus gets mega jiggy plastic with* America 3000 *(1986);* Alucarda *(1978) displays a cross properly in a special edition;* American Movie *(1999) stars Mark Borchardt and Mike Schank relaxing*

American Movie mines the most admirable and relatable traits of its central figure, and unironically salutes his ambition. Ultimately, when Mark completes *Coven*, we see pieces of it, along with its premiere audience's genuinely delighted reaction. Borchardt does possess talent on par with his ambition, no matter how much he muddles both. What a great surprise ending.

The heart of *American Movie*, though, is the tirelessly supportive Mike Schank. Trading in booze and hallucinogen addictions for a very healthy electric guitar enthusiasm and a potentially not-so-swell fondness for scratch-off game cards, this soft-spoken, gentlest of headbangers—who, frankly, seems to have never quite fully returned from his previous psychedelic drug excursions—is one of the most huggable personalities in American movies. Long may he shred.

The special-edition DVD of *American Movie* comes with the complete *Coven*—which is great—plus a bonus scene titled, "I Wish I Were a Member of AC/DC," which depicts Mark and Mike stranded by the side of a road on a freezing, rainy afternoon. Poor Mike laments: "I wish I were a member of AC/DC." When asked why, he says: "Because then I wouldn't be here. I'd be in one of my mansions."

An American Werewolf in London

(1981)

(Dir. John Landis; w/David Naughton, Jenny Agutter, Griffin Dunne)

✠ Werewolves ✠ England

A pair of college-age backpackers look wet and worried on the poster for *An American Werewolf in London*. They're eyeing something in the distance while a full moon beams through the cloudy night sky above. "From the director of *Animal House*," reads the tagline, "a different kind of animal." Earlier in 1981, Joe Dante's *The Howling* most excellently resurrected lycanthropic cinema. That film's approach was summed up by the image of long claws crazily tearing through a curtain to reveal screaming female facial features on the other side. *American Werewolf* is both subtler and more startling; the movie fulfills its promise with a perfect blend of gothic chills, lilting comedy, visceral shocks, and eyeball-blasting terror visuals.

American friends David (David Naughton) and Jack (Griffin Dunne) are traveling the English moors on a foggy evening. They stop at the Slaughtered Lamb, a foreboding country pub straight out of a classic Hammer gothic horror film. Locals warn of a werewolf on the loose. The boys don't listen. Jack is killed as a result and David suffers a worse fate: he is only bitten.

Recovering in London, David takes up with sexy nurse Alex (Jenny Agutter), but is plagued by horrific visions. Jack's ghost visits him in progressively grotesque states of decay; a jiggling piece of skin on his neck is a real gut-churner. David sees himself nude in the woods, stalking and eating a live deer. In the last, most jolting nightmare, David is at home in America with his family when Nazi werewolves suddenly kick the door in and slaughter them all with machine guns. (Slayer adapted this gruesome image for its Slatanic Wehrmacht fan club).

Soon, the full moon rises again and David transforms into a werewolf. The masterful onscreen metamorphosis, so familiar now, broke new ground in the realm of special effects. David runs the streets, feeds, and awakens nude the next day in the wolf cage at the London Zoo. That night, David ducks into a porno theater. Jack and David's victims from the previous night confront him, saying he should kill himself before he changes again. It's too late. Dave wolfs out and embarks on a wild massacre through Piccadilly Circus. A stalking sequence in the London Underground, shot from the point of the view of the werewolf, perfectly captures the feel of Iron Maiden's "Killers," released earlier that year: "You walk through the subway, his eyes burn a hole in your back." When police bullets cut David down, he shockingly reverts to human form.

Makeup master Rick Baker, whose work on *American Werewolf* earned him the first-ever Academy Award for Outstanding Achievement in Makeup, exposed audiences to what they could only previously imagine. He spoke of childhood frustration with movies where a guy sees a full moon, ducks behind a rock, and steps out a full-fledged wolfman. "Show me what's happening behind that rock!" Baker recalls thinking.

The *American Werewolf* soundtrack consists almost solely of songs that comment on the action, including "Moondance" by Van Morrison and "Bad Moon Rising" by Creedence Clearwater Revival. Religion quashed other components of the proposed *American Werewolf* song list. Cat Stevens forbade the use of his "Moonshadow" as he was in full Koran-waving "Yusuf Islam" mode. Bob Dylan, a born-again Christian at the point of filming, similarly passed on allowing his cover of "Blue Moon," citing the movie's R rating.

The film's violence, frank sexuality, and humor mirrored exactly the changes happening in rock music; heavy metal leapt forward to tear away all veneers and expose the loudest, scariest, most perilous, and most electrifying components lying dormant in rock music. The new era was opened wide like a gaping wound, and heavy metal came gushing forth. Once the beast was loose, we could never go back. *American Werewolf* heralded a new breed of no-blinking, explicit terror. The American werewolf's death in London gave birth to the age of heavy metal horror in Hollywood.

Amityville 2: The Possession (1982)

(Dir. Damiano Damiani; w/Jack Magner, Diane Franklin, Burt Young, James Olson)

✴ Haunted House ✴ Exorcism

The best-selling 1977 book *The Amityville Horror* tells the supposedly true story of a haunted house on New York's Long Island, replete with an invisible pig, rooms swarming with flies, and disembodied voices that moan: "For God's sake, *get out!*" This well-told urban legend blew up to be a monstrous pop-culture phenomenon, spawning no fewer than ten films. At least one element was undeniably true; several years prior to the events described in the book, teenager Ronald DeFeo really did murder six members of his family on the premises. Besides, the half-moon windows in the attic make the house seem to have evil jack-o'-lantern eyes.

The useless 1979 *Amityville Horror* movie made sufficient dough to warrant a follow-up, produced by Dino De Laurentiis (*King Kong*), which tastefully commingles the real-life DeFeo tragedy with exorcism exploitation and sexy incest. Jack Magner plays Sonny Montelli, a troubled Italian-American teen who, upon moving into 112 Ocean Avenue, increases the disobedience quotient. He seduces his topless sister (Diane Franklin) and hears demonic voices through his headphones that say, "Kill 'em!" Sonny undergoes full possession from there and he does, for sure, kill 'em all. An exorcism saves the day, as well as Sonny's soul—but no amount of Latin chants and holy water could stop the sequels.

Director Damiano Damiani (*A Bullet for the General*, *The Devil is a Woman*, *How to Kill a Judge*), came to Amityville with dozens of sleazy Italian crime thrillers under his belt. Not surprisingly, his rather extreme entry in the *Amityville Horror* annals stands out, and is praised as a favorite by Phil Anselmo of Pantera. I would further endorse *Amityville 3D* (1983) as an *objet d'schlock*, while *Amityville Dollhouse* (1996) deserves a cheerful mention just for its title. Though the original *Amityville Horror* story is pooh-poohed today when remembered at all, as a horror brand name the legend remains unstoppable. To further scare you away from Long Island, it's worth mentioning that "say you love Satan" killer Ricky Kasso was institutionalized in Amityville prior to committing a drug-addled 1984 murder.

The *Amityville* movies inspired the song "High Hopes: The Amityville Murders" by Wind Wraith, and others by Hellbilly, Nominon, and Sodomizer, and Carpatia Castle; plus bands named Amityville hailing from Germany and the U.S. New York act Amityville Dollhouse is named after the straight-to-video eighth movie in this series.

ANGEL AT MIDNIGHT (1977)

(DIR. PETER LAKE; W/PUNKY MEADOWS, MICKIE JONES, GREGG GIUFFRIA, FRANK DIMINO)

✣ SUNSET STRIP ✣ GLAM ✣ CONCERT FOOTAGE

Gene Simmons brought Washington, D.C.'s, semi-prog, hard-edged glam-rockers Angel to Casablanca Records—the home of Kiss throughout the 1970s. Yet no matter how many times Casablanca pitched Angel to the public, the overwhelming response was "Go to hell." That is a shame, because Angel was a genuine curiosity. Draped with flowing flaxen locks and pristine white robes, the band posited itself as the yin to Kiss's yang, complete with equally elaborate stage shows. Instead of blood and fire, however, Angel projected the giant face of the Archangel Gabriel descending from on high to summon the band members forth from a giant plastic re-creation of their *White Hot* album cover.

Casablanca had enough faith in Angel to invest $150,000 in this 35mm film. As executive Larry Harris writes in his thoroughly readable memoir *And Party Every Day: The Inside Story of Casablanca Records*: "Given the recent release of *The Song Remains the Same* [and] the wildly popular midnight screenings of *The Rocky Horror Picture Show*..., an Angel movie wasn't that hard a sell. Cleveland, one of the band's biggest strongholds, was chosen as the location of the live segments. Attendees were strongly encouraged to wear white, so that in the film it would look like they were in Heaven with the band."

Shooting went well and editing was under way when Casablanca began to panic over Angel's lack of album sales. Then the group fired bassist Mickie Jones before his proper "beauty footage" was shot. Alas, *Angel at Midnight* never took public flight, although enough footage was completed for Casablanca to ponder a LaserDisc release at one point. For now, *Angel at Midnight*

is languishing, somewhere, yearning to spread its gorgeous, feathery wings. Casablanca again tried to sell the band via the movies by making them a centerpiece of the teen-angels-on-the-road-to-ruin movie *Foxes* (1980), starring Jodie Foster and Cherie Currie, but most of Angel's footage ended up on the cutting room floor.

At least Frank Zappa noticed. He was so amused/appalled by the archly effeminate Angel that he wrote "Punky's Whips," one of the most savage take-downs in rock, directly satirizing frontman Punky Meadows. The lyrics ooze about Zappa drummer Terry Bozzio hopelessly falling in love with poofy Punky, rhyming "bite his neck" with "more fluid than Jeff Beck."

ANGEL HEART (1987)

(DIR. ALAN PARKER; W/MICKEY ROURKE, ROBERT DE NIRO, LISA BONET, CHARLOTTE RAMPLING)

✣ VOODOO ✣ SATAN ✣ CHICKEN BLOOD

In 1955 New York City, hard-boiled private dick Harry Angel (Mickey Rourke) is summoned by a thorny man of wealth and taste identifying himself as Lou Cyphre (Robert De Niro), who hires him to track down a lost crooner named Johnny Favorite. Ace investigator though he is, Harry doesn't put together that his goateed, raven-maned, wizard-fingered, never-before-seen client's moniker adds up to "Lucifer." Instead, he hightails it way down yonder to New Orleans for some voodoo sex and violence.

In keeping with the "Get it? GET IT!?!" nomenclature of *Angel Heart*'s opening, erstwhile Cosby kid Lisa Bonet also plays topless hoodoo hottie Epiphany Proudfoot. She bones Harry Angel in a barn where black magic chicken blood rains down on them in buckets from on high.

Subtle, *Angel Heart* ain't. It also never comes close to the fake movie critic quote on its TV commercials hyping *Angel Heart* as "*Chinatown* meets *The Exorcist*." For metalheads in 1987, though—particularly metalheads equipped with smokable enhancers—*Angel Heart*'s stylish imagery and ham-hoofed satanic shenanigans provided plenty of late-night viewing pleasure, occasionally at midnight screenings and more often while gathered with cohorts for home video viewing and boot-stomping.

Angel Heart courted controversy, earning an X rating before release, due to the graphic Rourke-Bonet get-down. Several seconds were scraped to secure an R rating. Lisa Bonet was bounced from *The Cosby Show* due to *Angel Heart*. No longer pristine enough to continue playing teen daughter Denise Huxtable, she was banished to her own sitcom, *A Different World*. After that, she actually did punish herself by marrying Lenny Kravitz. Metal bands including Dark Age, Insanity, and Manimal wrote songs about this movie.

Animal Instincts III: The Seductress (1996)

(Dir. Gregory Hyppolyte [Gregory Dark]; w/Wendy Schumacher, James Matthew, Marcus Grahm)

✴ Sunset Strip ✴ Hair Metal ✴ Selwyn Harris

You don't need to have seen *Animal Instincts* (1992) or *Animal Instincts II* (1994) to follow what happens in *Animal Instincts III: The Seductress*. I didn't—and I wrote the goddamn movie! If you tuned into Showtime after 1 a.m. during the tail end of the 1990s, odds are you caught at least one unhappy gander at this erotic thriller. *Animal Instincts III* (*AI3* for short) was a soft-core effort by director Gregory Dark (*New Wave Hookers*, credited here as Gregory Hyppolyte), following our decidedly metal XXX collaboration *Devil in Miss Jones 5: The Inferno* (1995).

After crafting the first two *Animal Instinct* movies, Greg wanted to work a couple of his personal passions—knife throwing and hip-hop—into the third installment. I asked if we could throw in some heavy metal and rock and roll groupies. Greg replied, "Why the fuck wouldn't you?"

The result was this plot: Joanna Coles (Wendy Schumacher), the World's Greatest Exhibitionist, falls in love with Alex Savage (James Matthew), a big-shot record producer and a champion knife thrower. Alex also happens to be blind. But wait!

He isn't really blind. He's just faking, because, as we find out, Alex is actually the World's Greatest Voyeur. The knife skill, he explains, is just a Zen thing, like the deaf, dumb, and blind kid who had that reputation for pinball.

In the course of Joanna and Alex's courtship, they come across various and sundry musician types, a sexy groupie played by porn star Jen Teal, and couple of Hollywood strippers wearing maid costumes. Joanna fucks all comers right in front of Alex's face, and he pretends he can't see anything happen. But, oh, is he ever taking it all in! Among the secretly seduced rock stars is heavy metal guitar whiz and operatic vocalist Trick Willy (John Bates). Trouble storms upon the arrival of gangsta rapper Stone Chill (Marcus Grahm). Over the course of a dinner party, Stone, believing Alex can't see, terrorizes Joanna, has his bodyguard nail her on the fully set table, and kills his manager. Alex ends the one-man crime wave by winging a knife into Stone's heart. Everybody ends up happy and/or dead.

I want to state outright, here and now, that I was certifiably insane when I wrote *Animal Instincts III*. The film is a psychographic snapshot of a deranged mind in a condition of severe tumult. And all that would be extremely metal if the movie weren't just so mortifyingly *terrible*, mainly due to the screenplay. But, hey, headbangers, I gave you Trick Willy!

At one point, Joanna reads aloud from a newspaper about how Stone Chill beat a previous record producer hideously close to death. Upset, she repeatedly talks about all the horrible stuff that befell the producer named "Mr. Albini." Fortunately, no Steve Albinis were actually harmed during the production of the film, leaving him healthy enough to record Burning Witch and High on Fire records in coming years.

The name Trick Willy was an homage to my friend Peter Landau and his genuinely great NYC bluesy scum-punk band Da Willys. In the mid-1980s, Peter Landau served as the original drummer in White Zombie. After playing on the group's first record, Pete informed Rob Zombie that he was quitting, as he was hitching his drumsticks to yet another Lower East Side supernova in hot ascent toward stardom, GG Allin. We all know how that turned out.

AN-THOR-OLOGY (1976-1985) (2005)

(DIRS. FRANK MEYER, PAUL HARB; W/JON MIKL THOR)

✠ Thor ✠ Music Videos ✠ Concert Footage
✠ Midway Mayhem

An-Thor-Ology (1976–1985) serves up muscle-bound Canadian metal titan Jon Mikl Thor unchained, uncensored, and unfettered by any level of professional production. First, strangest, and best is a 1976 *Merv Griffin Show* clip from the Aladdin resort in Las Vegas. Thor is introduced as a member of the hotel's "Red, Hot, and Blue" revue. He takes the stage, short-haired and long-mustachioed, to strip out of a superhero costume in proto-Chippendales fashion while singing the most lackluster version of Sweet's "Action" ever emitted by a human being. Then he blows into a hot-water bottle until it explodes.

A 1979 Canadian TV report, played twice, describes Thor as "The King of Muscle Rock...sort of a male Dolly Parton" and dubiously claims that "he's been offered Conan and Tarzan movies...and a Broadway show." Dearest to me is Thor on *The Uncle Floyd Show* in 1982, during the beloved New Jersey garage-punk kiddie program's brief tenure as an NBC overnight series. Again, Thor puffs a water bottle into combustive oblivion. A few years later, Thor visits U68, a New York–area UHF music video channel (and the only music video platform anywhere for bands like Voivod and Razor). Glaring, flexing, and flashing his steel-bending teeth, Thor pumps up the U68 *Power Hour*, snarling: "This is Thor, reminding all you headbangers to tune in every night to U68 at eleven for some bone-crushing metal. Get your rocks off!"

After thirty-three minutes of these disconnected jewels, the title "Thorumentary" floats on screen, and Jon Mikl starts narrating, or rather boasting

about his bodybuilding titles and revealing how as a boy he got other kids to throw bricks at his head to prove he was invincible. He confesses that he once starred in "a blue musical" titled *What Do You Say to a Naked Waiter?* "There was nudity," Thor states. "Yes, I was naked. But it was classy. Hey! It was the swingin' '70s." Shortly thereafter, during a live cover of the Troggs' "Wild Thing" Thor voraciously sucks the tongues of entranced female audience members.

Beyond that, *An-Thor-Ology* is mostly dawn-of-the-VCR camcorder live footage; our boy in some TV commercial bit parts; a couple of run-of-the-mill music videos. Thor peaks while playing "Thunder on the Tundra" on a bargain-budget UK comedy show called *Channel 72*. While messing with all of this, do not lose track of time and forget to watch Thor's *Rock-'N'-Roll Nightmare*.

ANTICHRIST (2009)

(DIR. LARS VON TRIER; W/CHARLOTTE GAINSBOURG, WILLEM DAFOE)

✠ Chaos ✠ Witchcraft ✠ Antichrist

The Scandinavian kingdom of Denmark, which whelped unto heavy metal Mercyful Fate and Lars Ulrich, also gifted cinema with an invigorating and debate-inspiring fellow traveler named Lars von Trier. The first firebrand of global art cinema since his whore-for-God saga *Breaking the Waves* (1996), von Trier finally went for broke with *Antichrist*, dividing critics, converting new fans to his extreme experiences, and creating the most respectable indie cinema release since the '70s that could lay claim to *Cannibal Holocaust*'s tagline: "the one that goes ALL the way!"

As married characters He and She (Willem Dafoe and Charlotte Gainsbourg) have rhapsodic sex, their baby son toddles from his crib and tumbles right out a window. We watch him fall to his death in slow motion, set to soothing classical music. Willem Dafoe's character, He, is a psychiatrist composing a thesis on "Gynocide," a grindcore band name if ever there was one. When She goes into complete mental collapse after the baby's funeral, He then whisks her to a cabin in lush woodland area called Eden. Hell follows with them.

She spins out into unreachable salvos of madness. He comes across a talking fox who plainly states, "Chaos reigns!" A crow and a deer also prove unnaturally communicative. Hail falls hard. Eden's former resident is revealed to have been a weather-changing witch. By the end, She provides He (and herself) with the ultimate lesson in gynocide, although we can't imagine what the hundreds of blur-faced women ascending up a hill toward the cabin might have in store.

Antichrist is a benchmark midnight-movie grossout/freak-out on a par with the works of Alejandro Jodorowsky (*El Topo*, *The Holy Mountain*), but reduced from epic scale to agonizing intimacy. Often, metal music is praised as "ear-bleeding." *Antichrist* warrants similar descriptive lauding, but draws plasma from organs well south of one's ears, both metaphorically and on-screen.

Antichrist's biblical references and pagan-conjuring nature setting create an air of heady spirituality that packs a soul-quaking wallop when the interpersonal Armageddon comes down. When He and She make love under a tree, hundreds of hands emerge from the roots. The *Antichrist* poster uses this scary, trippy image.

But this abstract description is unsatisfying, so here's the deal with the big, bloody climax: She pulverizes He's testicles with a wooden block, then jacks him off until he comes blood. While He is passed out, She drills a hole into his leg and bolts a hefty grindstone through it so He can't escape. After He makes it to a foxhole, She beats him with a shovel and partly buries him alive. She takes a pair of scissors, cuts off her clitoris, and masturbates to screaming orgasm as blood spews from the wound. All of this is well-lit and in close-up. The sex acts are actually performed in hardcore pornographic detail. To the extreme!

THE ANTICHRIST (1974), AKA THE TEMPTER

(DIR. ALBERTO DE MARTINO; W/CARLA GRAVINA, MEL FERRER, ARTHUR KENNEDY)

✵ SEX WITH SATAN ✵ EXORCISM ✵ INQUISITION

The Antichrist is one of many grotesquely delightful Italian *Exorcist* rip-offs from the mid-1970s. Retitled *The Tempter*, the film enjoyed a second life in theaters in 1978. After that, it filled out drive-in and grindhouse double and triple bills for nearly a decade, even getting a sizable release in Portugal in 1986. The movie still stood out as weird enough to warrant C-level circulation.

After crippled Ippolita Oderisi (Carla Gravina) visits a spooky shrine to the Virgin Mary and undergoes hypnosis, she experiences flashbacks to her previous life as a witch who was burned at the stake. Ippolita transports herself to that realm, where she nakedly submits to a ritual in an eye-popping, all-gray hell, building to a frenzy as she copulates with a goat-horned Satan. Newly able to walk in the present day, she then goes on a sex rampage that includes snapping one conquest's neck and seducing her brother. She also pukes green and wills the furniture to fly around the room.

The Antichrist's standout segment is not just Ippolina making sex with Old Scratch, but the gnarly rites she performs to make it happen: she laps up blood, eats a toad's head, and then lustfully licks the ass of a goat. Such gross rites sounds like the sort of nonsense Ricky Kasso–type burnouts would try in the vicinity of a barnyard while whacked out of their minds on PCP and Venom records. If we are to believe *The Antichrist*, it works!

Anthropophagus: The Grim Reaper

(1981), aka The Grim Reaper; Anthropophagus: The Beast; The Zombie's Rage

(Dir. Joe D'Amato; w/George Eastman, Tisa Farrow, Saverio Vallone, Serena Grandi)

✻ Cannibalism ✻ '80s Italian Horror
✻ Banned Video Nasty

A group of tourists sails to an uninhabited Greek island. A diary indicates that murder most barf-bag-conducive befell whoever landed there before them. A prior traveler, Nikos Karamanlis (George Eastman), was the source of the slaughter. He arrived on the island some time ago with a wife and child who died and ultimately became his sole food source. Nikos is still around now—lurking as a scabby-skinned, zombie-like madman—and hungrier than ever.

Anthropophagus: The Grim Reaper (as the film is now definitively known) opened in the United States as *The Grim Reaper* and marked the straightforward horror debut of Italian sleaze specialist Joe D'Amato (*Emanuelle in America*). In unedited form, the only form that counts, *Anthropophagus* stakes a strong claim among the other European regurgitation exercises of era.

One transgression truly elevates the film to grindcore gross-out greatness. In graphic close-up, Nikos overpowers the hugely pregnant Maggie (Serena Grandi), tears open her belly, yanks out the living contents, and devours the mewling fetus in front of her and the rest of us. Happy Mother's Day—Joe D'Amato style!

Anthropophagy is the Greek root term for the eating of human flesh, but the fetus eaten by Nikos is actually a skinned rabbit. The film was cowritten by director D'Amato and star Eastman. They reteamed later in 1981 to serve the same functions on the pseudo-sequel, and fellow banned UK video nasty, *Absurd*.

Anvil! The Story of Anvil (2008)

(Dir. Sacha Gervasi; w/Steve "Lips" Kudlow, Robb Reiner, Ivan Hurd)

✻ Metal History ✻ Concert Footage
✻ Vibrator Guitar Solo

Anvil! The Story of Anvil is a heartfelt, soulful, touchingly funny, and finally inspiring chronicle of one the great '80s metal bands that could have, would have, and should have, but didn't. The movie makes that point immediately, opening at Japan's 1984 Super Rock festival. Hot off the albums *Metal on Metal* and *Forged in Fire*, Anvil, led by best friends Steve "Lips" Kudlow (singer/guitarist) and Robb Reiner (drummer), plays to a stadium of roaring fans alongside Scorpions, Bon Jovi, and Whitesnake.

We know what became of those other groups. Now we see what's up with Anvil. Today in their native Canada, Lips drives a truck for a school catering company, and Robb works construction. For fun, they play a local bar, always to the delight of the crowd and the odd old-time admirer who happens by. Incongruously, the former greatness of Anvil is praised on-camera in interviews with metal giants on the order of Lars Ulrich, Slash, Lemmy, Tom Araya, and Scott Ian.

Lips gets a shaky offer for a European tour from a fan named Tiziana Arrigoni. Robb is not immediately enthusiastic, but these lifelong partners promised to ride the rock train to the very end so, along with guitarist Ivan Hurd and bassist Glenn Five, off they go, tumbling headlong into one calamity after another. Five weeks later, after making exactly no money, they return home. One catch: Ivan Hurd takes up romantically with Tiziana. Anvil, hilariously inappropriately, plays their wedding. Glenn Five becomes homeless.

Lips and Robb begin work on the band's thirteenth album, *This Is Thirteen*. To finance the recording, Robb attempts to sell sunglasses by phone. It doesn't work. And so it goes. We fall in love with these guys as they remain steadfastly committed to the spark that launched them as teenagers. We also see that, despite the real-life slapstick all around them, Lips and Robb are not easy rock and roll clowns. Each is sharp and witty, with Reiner being particularly well spoken. He paints, too!

Anvil ends on a fantastic up note, with the band returning to where the movie began: Japan. The final scene is a pure surprise and an even purer outburst of inspiration. Metal on metal forever.

Following the critical acclaim and popular success of *Anvil!: The Story of Anvil*, the reinvigorated band scored opening tour gigs for AC/DC and Saxon, followed by their headlining tours of Europe and festival slots alongside Alice Cooper. The movie proved to be an endless blessing for the band. Noted Lips: "One of my heroes is Ian Anderson from Jethro Tull, and he came up to me in Heathrow Airport and told me the movie had completely inspired him to keep playing music. He just kept thanking me for all of the inspiration my band gave him. I mean, this is Ian Anderson from Jethro Tull—how cool is that?"

Many critics incorrectly pegged *Anvil!: The Story of Anvil* as a modern-day mockumentary made in tribute to Spinal Tap. There are many uncanny similarities: Anvil plays a disastrous tour; the band members visit Stonehenge; scuzzy record execs shaft them (one of whom spews the Artie Fufkin–worthy line, "You've been around a long time, and that has currency!"); and they launch a comeback in Japan. In addition, Anvil drummer Robb Reiner's name was mistaken as homage to *This Is Spinal Tap* director Rob Reiner. Sometimes, metal is just stranger than life.

𝕬POCALYPSE 𝕹OW (1979)
(DIR. FRANCIS FORD COPPOLA; W/MARTIN SHEEN, MARLON BRANDO, ROBERT DUVALL)
✣ VIETNAM WAR ✣ LITERAL NAPALM DEATH
✣ ANIMAL SACRIFICE ✣ WAGNER

The images that leap immediately to mind when *Apocalypse Now* comes up are all those helicopters. Iron and steel birds of prey descend from the sky to the Götterdämmerung strains of Richard Wagner's "Ride of the Valkyries," whereupon they scorch a seaside Vietnamese village with a rain of napalm death. Once the hostiles have been leveled, attack leader Lt. Col. Bill Kilgore (Robert Duvall) surveys the utter destruction his team has wrought and declares: "I love the smell of napalm in the morning!" Then he goes surfing. Horns all the way up.

Adapted by screenwriter John Milius (director of *Conan the Barbarian*) from the 1899 Joseph Conrad novel *Heart of Darkness*, and originally titled *The Psychedelic Soldier*, *Apocalypse Now* documents the Vietnam War journey of Captain Benjamin Willard (Martin Sheen) on an assignment to "terminate with extreme prejudice" the rogue Colonel Kurtz (Marlon Brando). Kurtz has installed himself as a demigod in the Cambodian jungle, surrounded by worshippers and leading his own army. Willard joins a beat-to-shit crew on a beat-down boat, named *Erebus* after the son of the Greek god of total darkness, and together they experience an overwhelming complement of every bizarre high and unimaginable horror that quasi-legal combat in Southeast Asia can offer.

The heaviest of war films about the heaviest of American wars, the genuinely epic *Apocalypse Now* opens on a bombastic note and only metallicizes further until imploding into a crescendo of darker-than-death doom that resonates, indeed, apocalyptic. The very first scene is a masterwork of tension and release. Willard boozes in a hotel room to the slow build proto-goth of the Doors' "The End". He freaks out, spastically launches into martial arts moves, and trashes the place while Jim Morrison wails about Oedipus and mass murder and a mythic travail to hell.

That opening gambit is bookended with a reprise of "The End" that underscores *Apocalypse Now*'s final bloody payoff. Willard, who suffers through agonies after arriving at Kurtz's compound, seizes a moment to complete his mission. Morrison moans and the music escalates as Willard's machete execution of Kurtz is intercut with a (very real) ritual decapitation of a water buffalo.

Kurtz's jungle lair of face-painted natives, bamboo cages, heads on pikes, and makeshift torture devices was imitated by nearly every Italian cannibal horror movie of the subsequent decade—as was the actual footage of locals slaying a live animal. Echoing in the final moments are Kurtz's dying words: "The horror...the horror..."

The film is in league with Apocalypse Now bands and albums by Discharge, Goregod, Undergang, and Total Fucking Destruction, not to mention songs by Cro-Mags, Fortress, Goregod, M.A.C.E., Mephisto, Torment, and Trance.

Aqua Teen Hunger Force Colon Movie Film for Theaters

(2007)

(DIRS. MATT MAIELLARO, DAVE WILLIS; W/DANA SNYDER, CAREY MEANS, DAVE WILLIS, NEIL PEART)
✣ ANIMATION ✣ CAMEOS

Kicking off with a poster painted in the tradition of Frank Frazetta fantasy art, the big-screen adaptation of Adult Swim's late-night stoner favorite opens with a parody of 1950s drive-in movie intermission cartoons, depicting a cute parade of snacks singing pleasantly about moviegoing etiquette. The sweets are promptly overpowered by Mastodon—in the form of a wailing gumdrop, pretzel, candy box, and cheesy nachos sampler—blasting through an updated set of rules and consequences: "Do not crinkle your food wrappers loudly! Be considerate to others or I will bite your torso and give you a disease!"

Aqua Teen Hunger Force Colon Movie Film for Theaters proper then starts off with Frylock, Master Shake, and Meatwad caroming through time and space on their typically absurd, non sequitur–driven adventures. Whereas Glenn Danzig voiced himself on the *Aqua Teen* TV show, for the movie, we get Neil Peart of Rush, who mans his drum kit aboard a spaceship piloted by a talking

slice of watermelon named Walter Melon. The soundtrack boasts still more Mastodon, along with Andrew W.K., Early Man, Unearth, and Brass Castle.

Arena: Heavy Metal

(1989)

(DIR. HELEN GALLAGHER; W/OZZY OSBOURNE, TONY IOMMI, JIMMY PAGE, AXL ROSE)
✣ CONCERT FOOTAGE

After fifteen long years on air, the BBC series *Arena* finally set its heady gaze upon contemporary hard rock. *Arena: Heavy Metal* is a kaleidoscopic hour loosely centered on England's 1989 Monsters of Rock festival at Donington. Seemingly devoid of structure, the documentary opens with footage of misery-torn Birmingham, leading into Ozzy Osbourne yukking it up with Tony Iommi at a diner, and some-odd minutes later concluding with Napalm Death onstage roaring through "Scum."

Between the Brummie highlights are plenty of metal superstars turned talking heads, and performance clips including uniformly excellent live footage of Sabbath, Deep Purple, Iron Maiden, Motörhead, Metallica, Slayer, Megadeth, and Japanese thrashers Outrage. The real juice comes from the interviews, though. Tom Araya talks Satan, illustrated here by B-roll footage from 1968's *The Devil Rides Out.* Jim Marshall takes us through a history of his namesake amplifiers. Bill Steer and Shane Embury groove on George Romero's *Day of the Dead.*

Three of the Q&As are truly extraordinary. Jimmy Page, perched on a stool with an acoustic guitar and loose as a Crowleyan goose, picks and strums through "Kashmir" and "Over the Hills and Far Away." Bruce Dickinson, ever the affable ham, demonstrates his fencing skills, then leads a tour of classic metal wardrobe items, including the aforementioned Mr. Page's glittery trousers and Gene Simmons's dragon boots. He wraps up with a tribute to Blackie Lawless's exploding chainsaw codpiece.

Finally, witness W. Axl Rose at a noxious height of rock-god assholery. Axl disses Kiss, and then lays into Iron Maiden. "Have you got anything in common with Iron Maiden?" an interviewer asks. "I hope not," Axl replies. "[Iron Maiden] doesn't have anything to do with rock and roll as far as I'm concerned. We're a rock and roll band. What they do is what they do, I don't know what it is, and I hope to never be like that. I hope it's not catching." Unfortunately for him, he never did catch Iron Maiden's magic.

Arena: Heavy Metal's final moments belong to ten-year-old guitar prodigy and Steve Vai protégé Thomas McRocklin, wailing for awestruck headbangers at a pub. This parting shot is intended signal that the kids are all right, except that McRocklin, after an early-'90s stint in the kid band Bad4Good, dropped off the metalsphere and has been MIA for decades.

The BBC reran *Arena: Heavy Metal* in 2009 as part of a multi-night *Heavy Metal Heaven* series hosted by Elvira, alongside heavy viewing including *Get Thrashed* (2006), *Hysteria: The Def Leppard Story* (2001), and *Metallica Live at Hammersmith Odeon* (2008).

Arise: The Sri Lankan Metal Music Documentary

(2010)

(Dirs. Naveen Marasinghe, Dinesh Guneratne; w/ Cannibis, Fallen Grace, Merlock)
✵ World Metal ✵ Metal Reality

Few headbangers outside of Southeast Asia were hip to the Sri Lankan metal scene before this movie. Shot on the fly throughout 2008 and 2009 by young fans with borrowed video cameras, *Arise* opens up the world of heavy metal in Sri Lanka by focusing on four bands practicing distinct forms of the music. Cannibis drips stoner sludge. Fallen Grace plays melodic death metal. Funeral in Heaven rages black metal. Mer-

lock blows minds with progressive thrash.

Home recording and tape trading planted heavy metal seeds all over the globe. The musicians of *Arise* represent the flowering of that never-ending stream of rich metal bounty. Cheap cameras and the Internet have now made the documentary form the next powerful stage of metal's grassroots revolution. Stomping like their homeland's elephants, and soaring like spiritual holy men, these Sri Lankan headbangers redefine the concept of "unleashed in the East."

Army of Darkness (1993)

(Dir. Sam Raimi; w/Bruce Campbell, Embeth Davidtz, Marcus Gilbert, Richard Grove)
✵ Swords & Sorcery ✵ Necronomicon ✵ Demonic Possession

Beginning exactly where *Evil Dead 2* (1987) left off, the film starts with Ash (Bruce Campbell) being time-warped back to AD 1300, where he is caught in a conflict between Lord Arthur (Marcus Gilbert) and Duke Henry (Richard Grove). Hence the movie's original title: *The Medieval Dead*. Good thing his right arm is still a chainsaw, and he brought along a shotgun—which he famously calls his "boomstick."

Ash wins over the locals by kicking a Deadite's keister, something that comes naturally after he's spent two movies doing just that. When he lands in yet another haunted forest, he contends with miniature versions of himself that form into his evil double. He soon sets out to find the Necronomicon, the book of spells that can send him back home.

The search eventually entails Ash leading royal forces against a battalion of the living dead led by his doppelgänger. Victory ensures his return to the 1990s, where he is just another S-Mart employee who can really effectively eliminate anybody possessed by demons. And when someone fitting that description wanders into the store, he does just that!

The words Ash must speak to do the time warp again are "Klaatu barada nikto," a quote from

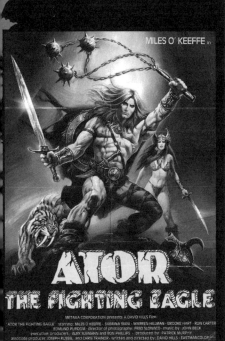

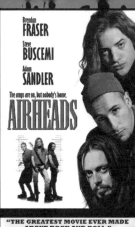

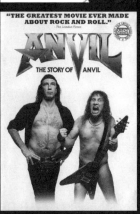

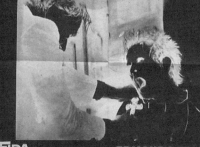

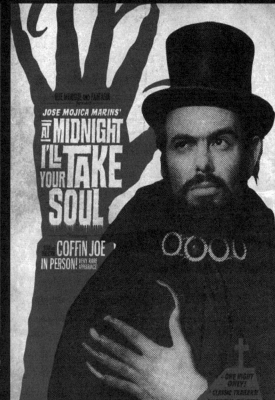

Clockwise from top left: Ator the Fighting Eagle *(1982)*; Airheads *(1994)*; Anvil! *(2008)*; no-budget thrash; Coffin Joe *U.S. event poster*; The Antichrist *(1978)* as it spooked Italian theaters

the alien in the 1951 sci-fi classic *The Day the Earth Stood Still*. (In 1973, a Canadian prog band named Klaatu inspired rumors that they were the Beatles recording in disguise. They were not.)

After the convulsively brutal *The Evil Dead* (1981) and the more comedic second installment, the entirely self-aware *Army of Darkness* revs right into straight-up slapstick. Countless horror-comedies have followed this model. Campbell's Ash became one of the great icons of fantasy cinema because, frankly, this was the *Evil Dead* movie kids could watch. Even more so than in *Darkman* (1990), with *Army of Darkness* director Sam Raimi announced himself as the talent to whom the previously unfilmable *Spider-Man* could be entrusted. Good for him.

As the Palaces Burn (2014)

(Dir. Don Argott; w/Randy Blythe, Mark Morton, Willie Adler, John Campbell, Chris Adler)

✠ Metal Reality ✠ Justice ✠ World Metal

As he stepped off an airplane in the Czech Republic on June 27, 2012, Lamb of God vocalist Randy Blythe was seized by police and arrested on charges of intentional infliction of bodily harm resulting in death. Czech authorities had been waiting to apprehend Blythe following the 2010 death of Daniel Nosek, a nineteen-year-old fan who died hours after repeatedly stage-diving during a heated Lamb of God show in Prague. Caught completely by surprise, Blythe was taken from the airport directly to a Czech prison. After five confusing weeks behind bars, Blythe was granted bail. The singer returned to the U.S. but bravely vowed to return to Prague to stand trial and face his charges as a matter of honor.

These events and Blythe's subsequent return to court became the unexpected core of director Don Argott's powerful documentary about modern Virginia metal band Lamb of God. His film-in-progress, initially a look at the band's widely varied audience, turned into an unforgettably powerful true-crime chronicle that masterfully shapes horrible happenstance into a stranger-than-fiction narrative. This is the second time Argott has caught metal lightning in bottle, having luckily captured similarly pivotal events in cosmically troubled Pentagram frontman Bobby Liebling's life in the 2011 movie *Last Days Here*.

In fact, *As the Palaces Burn* flies nearly halfway through before the Czech intrigue arises. Blythe and the rest of the Lamb of God boys make great on-camera subjects, whether talking or fist-fighting backstage. The film compellingly tracks a newly sober Blythe approaching life sans liquid assistance. We meet two remarkable die-hard Lamb of God lovers: a guy who headbangs while driving a taxi in Colombia, and a female death metal vocalist in India. Their lives tell the power of metal, specifically as channeled through Lamb of God. They will make believers out of anybody.

The second half of *As the Palaces Burn* focuses on Blythe's trial overseas, and how the other members of Lamb of God scramble to help him back home. They display almost parental and at least brotherly concern for the teen who lost his life, and his family. Leading up to the verdict, sufficient twists and turns emerge in court that make the movie suspenseful even if you're aware of the verdict. Come the final scene, there is no way to avoid being moved, shaken, saddened, uplifted, and inspired. Lamb of God is an extraordinary collection of humans first and musicians second, and they are extraordinarily well served by Argott's best effort to date.

The Asphyx (1973), AKA The Horror of Death; Spirit of the Dead

(Dir. Peter Newbrook; w/Robert Powell, Jane Lapotaire)

✠ Supernatural Horror

After making the kinky, metal-plated shocker *Crucible of Terror*—about a mad sculptor who slays London nubiles for his bronze statues—intensely British director Peter Newbrook went retro and supernatural in *The Asphyx*. At the turn of the twentieth century, ghost-hunting London photographer Sir Hugo Cunningham (Robert Stephens) captures an "asphyx," a floating phantom that yanks the spirit from the body of a dying being. If an asphyx is seized, though, whoever was about to die becomes impossible to kill. Cunningham becomes hell-bent on achieving immortality for himself and his loved ones. Nothing goes as planned. Corpses result.

The Asphyx is a high-class, lushly mounted, and vividly photographed production, and exudes enough heaviness that the veteran Dutch doom-drenched death metal group Asphyx were inspired to take their name from the film.

ASSORTED ATROCITIES: THE EXODUS DOCUMENTARY (2010)

(DIR. CRAIG CEFOLA; W/ROB DUKES, GARY HOLT, LEE ALTUS, TOM HUNTING, PAUL BOSTAPH)

✠ THRASH METAL ✠ CONCERT FOOTAGE

Assorted Atrocities: The Exodus Documentary takes an invigorating look at the Bay Area thrash legends at work and play around the twenty-fifth anniversary of the band's 1984 masterwork, *Bonded by Blood*. Beginning in 2005 as a rejiggered Exodus lineup comes together to record the album *Shovel Headed Kill Machine*, *Assorted Atrocities* covers the next five years onward as the group tours Australia, Japan, Europe, and the ever metal-inflamed South America.

The movie also depicts making of two Exodus music videos ("Riot Act" and "Now Thy Death Day Come"), and shows the band supplying voices to the cartoon *Metalocalypse*. Life on the road never gets easy, but for veterans such as the survivors in Exodus, exporting metal to the masses worldwide is its own reward. Racking up frequent flyer miles sure beats the fuck out of working for a living. Stories about Exodus's late, legendary front-beast Paul Baloff abound in *Assorted Atrocities*, and they never, ever disappoint. The *Assorted Atrocities* DVD includes Exodus performing the *Bonded by Blood* album in its entirety at the 2008 Wacken Open Air festival.

AT MIDNIGHT I'LL TAKE YOUR SOUL (1964), AKA À MEIA-NOITE LEVAREI SUA ALMA

(DIR. JOSÉ MOJICA MARINS; W/JOSÉ MOJICA MARINS, MAGDA MEI, VALÉRIA VASQUEZ, NIVALDO LIMA)

✠ COFFIN JOE ✠ ZOMBIES ✠ SPIDERS

The character who became nothing short of "The Boogeyman of Brazil," Zé do Caixão—"Coffin Joe"—debuted in *At Midnight I'll Take Your Soul*. This black-clad gravedigger wears a top hat and a flowing black cape, and sports jarringly long and curvy fingernails. To see him once is to carry Coffin Joe in your unsafe soul forever. Referenced by White Zombie in the song "I, Zombie," José Mojica Marins plays Coffin Joe, as only he can, with simmering morbid intensity. Marins also wrote and directed *At Midnight*. In the movie, our antihero's hatred of religion is surpassed only by his obsession with finding "one perfect woman" to carry his unholy seed.

Joe's mission involves him killing his infertile wife with a spider, bludgeoning and drowning a rival in a bathtub, using his talon-like nails to gouge a doctor's eyes out, and raping young Terazhina (Magda Mei), who hangs herself with a pledge to return from hell to drag him down there with her. The action climaxes with ghosts, maggotty faces in a mausoleum, and Joe getting his hellfire comeuppance, just as nighttime church bells strike twelve.

At Midnight I'll Take Your Soul is great gothic spookery from the early 1960s, spiked with some genuinely nasty flourishes. Marins made horror history with his film and his memorable character. Coffin Joe transformed Brazil into a fertile wellspring for the dark arts, from the nation's vibrant fright film culture to a Sepultura-led heavy metal explosion in the '80s. Righteously united in the 1990s, Coffin Joe in fact cut his famous fingernails at a Sepultura concert and presented them to the band as a bizarre sort of blessing. He has introduced the band often since, and appears on their *Live in São Paulo* DVD (2005).

Coffin Joe returned in numerous other films, as well as TV shows, documentaries, and comic books. Many cite the second Coffin Joe movie, *This Night I'll Possess Your Corpse* (1967), as his best. Oddly, in *The Strange World of Coffin Joe* (1968), Coffin Joe himself only appears on the poster for the movie, not in the film itself. He does appear, if only as a prolonged LSD vision, in *Awakening of the Beast* (1970).

The Bloody Exorcism of Coffin Joe (1974) is a meta-commentary on the CJ phenomenon, with Marins appearing as both himself and his ghastly creation. They actually get into a fistfight. I remain partial to the outrageous and surreal *Hallucinations of a Deranged Mind* (1978). It consists of lurid, nonsensical sequences of sexy horror and bright red gore that were censored or otherwise discarded from previous Coffin Joe productions. These scenes are presented as nightmares plaguing a psychiatrist who lives in terror that Coffin Joe is trying to steal his wife.

The Embodiment of Evil (2008) is the final installment in what Marins calls "The Coffin Joe Trilogy." It completes the story set in motion by the very first two films about CJ's quest for "one perfect woman" with whom he can procreate. Although he is impaled through the heart with a crucifix, the movie ends with every female at Coffin Joe's funeral pregnant with his children.

Outside of the movies, Coffin Joe has been a beloved TV horror host in Brazil for decades. Liz Marins, real-life daughter of Jose Mojica Marins, has followed in her father's spooky footsteps. Brazil knows her as "Liz Vamp" and she's the sexy, fang-mouthed face of "Vampires Day," when citizens are encouraged to donate blood to hospitals and blood banks. Necrophagia has feted him in song with "Zé do Caixão."

ATOR THE FIGHTING EAGLE (1982), AKA ATOR L'INVINCIBILE

(DIR. JOE D'AMATO; W/MILES O'KEEFE, SABRINA SIANI, EDMUND PURDOM, DAKAR, RITZA BROWN)
✣ **SWORDS & SORCERY**

Mega-muscled Miles O'Keefe, the titular swinger in Bo Derek's 1981 *Tarzan the Ape Man*, returns in the title role of *Ator the Fighting Eagle*. He lives in a setting familiar to swords and sorcery fans, and he is the grown-up survivor of a massacre perpetrated on his childhood village by the High Priest of the Spider Cult (Dakar). All Ator wants to do is marry his sister Sunya (Ritza Brown). The High Priest poops their nuptial plans by kidnapping Sunya and forcing Ator to battle a giant eight-legged attack arachnid. Also, there are witches.

Italian B-movie machine Joe D'Amato, arguably the fastest celluloid slinger in schlockdom, rushed out *Ator* as a quickie rip-off of *Conan the Barbarian* (1982). D'Amato is credited with making no fewer than six films in 1982, the same year he directed *Ator*. Among them is *Emperor Caligula: The Untold Story*, one of D'Amato's multiple cash-ins on the *Penthouse* magazine blockbuster *Caligula* (1979).

As has happened more than once with D'Amato movies, *Ator* achieved its own cult, independent of *Conan*, running endlessly on HBO in the mid-'80s. *Ator* is heavily metal in its milieu and will be as happy a relic of '80s adolescent nostalgia as an arcade token or a silk Judas Priest tour jacket. As a reward for completing its quest and earning back the production budget, *Ator* spawned three sequels: *The Blade Master* (1984), *Iron Warrior* (1987), and *Quest for the Mighty Sword* (1990).

August Underground

(2001)

(Dir. Fred Vogel; w/Fred Vogel, Allen Peters, AnnMarie Reveruzzi, Erika Risovich)

✠ Serial Killers ✠ Snuff ✠ Censorship

August Underground shoves the "video diary of a homicidal maniac" framework of such aboveground art house hits as *Henry: Portrait of a Serial Killer* (1985) and *Man Bites Dog* (1992) to a heinous new low (or high)—then pushes the threshold for sick and sadistic explicit degradation past the nauseating point into anger and, ultimately, sadness. Presented without plot or overarching commentary as a "found" VHS tape, *August Underground* consists of camcorder footage of Peter (director Fred Vogel) and an unnamed cameraman (cowriter Allen Peters) wandering from one atrocity to another.

How bad could it be? A naked girl tied to a chair, covered in blood, urine, and feces, has her nipple cut off and is forced to eat her dead boyfriend's toe. A hitchhiker is orally raped and beaten to death. A store clerk is stabbed. Twin brother tattoo artists are murdered and dismembered. Peter sodomizes a prostitute while smashing her skull to liquid nothingness with a hammer. Between such episodes, these two creeps mellow out in high creep style by visiting a cemetery and—bringing to mind the Big Black song "Cables"—a slaughterhouse. The entire seventy minutes is exhausting and soul-sullying. Take that as a recommendation, if you're so inclined.

August Underground's initial death blow brought mixed reactions from horror fans. Roger Watkins, director of his own tape-traded, quasi-legal cult outrage *Last House on Dead End Street* (1977), once declared *August Underground* "the *Citizen Kane* of horror movies." Not long after that, he died.

Among the most immediate and outspoken proponents was singer Killjoy of Necrophagia, who went on to cowrite and codirect the sequel, the upsetting *August Underground's Mordum* (2003), in which the word *fuck* is spoken more than five hundred times in seventy-seven minutes. Killjoy's death metal side project with members of Autopsy and Brutal Truth, the Ravenous, also recorded an homage, "August Underground."

En route to the Rue Morgue Festival of Fear horror convention in Toronto in 2005, Fred Vogel was arrested by Canadian authorities for attempting to transport "obscene materials" over their border. Vogel spent about ten hours behind bars, and the charges were later dismissed.

His vicious vision returned via a second, even more repellent, sequel, *August Underground's Penance* (2007). Vogel had at this point long been an instructor with supreme splatter effects artist Tom Savini in the macabre master's Special Makeup Effects program. The visuals in *Penance* appear more hideously realistic than ever, with a burbling, fluid-secreting organ achieving a singular new level of gag-inducing grossness. Merle Allin, GG's musician brother, cameos by playing guitar onstage at a rock club. He fits right in perfectly with everything else here.

Aural Amphetamine: Metallica and the Dawn of Thrash (2008)

(Dir. Rob Johnstone; w/Metallica, Malcolm Dome, Lonn Friend)

✠ Thrash Metal ✠ NWOBHM ✠ Metal History

The UK documentary *Aural Amphetamine: Metallica and the Dawn of Thrash* views metal's early-'80s Bay Area revolution by way of Ol' Blighty, putting an interesting spin on an otherwise very familiar story. A Cockney-accented narrator guides us through a lengthy history of the New Wave of British Heavy Metal, with just a quick detour into punk before hopping back to the States to chronicle the making of Metallica's *Kill 'Em All*. From that point, *Aural Amphetamine* focuses on Metallica and the band's rise through 1988's *...And Justice for All*. Photomontages and archive videos fill the screen effectively. Metal journalists Malcolm Dome, Lonn Friend, and Joel McIver do what they do at such times.

Although *Aural Amphetamine* contains no original Metallica interviews, the rock doc scores satisfying sit-downs with Diamond Head guitarist Brian Tatler, Megadeth's Chris Poland, D.R.I. bassist Harald Oimoen, and NWOBHM band Elixir, among others. Though better viewed in its original context in the *20th Century Box* documentary, the black-and-white footage of early London headbangers carrying paper guitars into the Bandwagon rock club is beguiling as ever.

AUTOPSY (1975), AKA TENSION
(DIR. ARMANDO CRISPINO; W/MIMSY FARMER, BARRY PRIMUS, RAY LOVELOCK, ANGELA GOODWIN)
✠ HORROR ✠ GIALLO ✠ ITALY

Autopsy puts a weird spin on the Italian horror-mystery *giallo* genre by introducing *sunspots* as a lethal threat to the population of Rome. A sexy pathologist (Mimsy Farmer) and a semi-lunatic priest (Barry Primus) join forces to prove that a wave of gory suicides has actually been a wave of gory murders. Aside from shock shots of nude bodies on slabs, *Autopsy* achieves metal intensity by way of wild, hallucinatory visions that Mimsy repeatedly suffers in which the bashed, burned, and broken bodies in her morgue arise, attack, and run wild. Two of them even fuck!

Autopsy makes a good movie out of these very bad trips. Akin to *Snuff* generating publicity by indicating it contained real murder footage, *Autopsy*'s American release benefited from whispers that its on-camera corpse dissections were the real deal. Take even a brief look: they are not.

The landmark movie is celebrated by the mighty band Autopsy and songs titled "Autopsy" by the Accüsed, Becoming the Archetype, Dark Autopsy, Dismember, E-X-E, Eternal Hate, Rampage, Sixgun Symphony, Trencher, and, of course, Ultra Vomit.

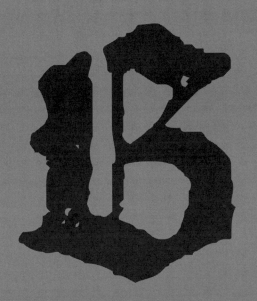

BABA YAGA ✠ BACK TO THE FUTURE ✠ BAD CHANNELS ✠ BAD NEWS TOUR ✠ BAD RONALD ✠ BARBARIAN QUEEN ✠ THE BARBARIANS ✠ BASKET CASE ✠ BATTLE ROYALE ✠ BEACH BALLS ✠ THE BEASTMASTER ✠ BEAVIS AND BUTT-HEAD DO AMERICA ✠ BEGOTTEN ✠ BENEATH THE PLANET OF THE APES ✠ BERSERKER ✠ BEST WORST MOVIE ✠ BEWARE OF MR. BAKER ✠ THE BEYOND ✠ BEYOND THE DOOR ✠ BILL & TED'S EXCELLENT ADVENTURE ✠ BILL & TED'S BOGUS JOURNEY ✠ BILLY JACK ✠ BIOHAZARD ✠ THE BIRD WITH THE CRYSTAL PLUMAGE ✠ BLACK AND BLUE ✠ BLACK BLOODED BRIDES OF SATAN ✠ BLACK CHRISTMAS ✠ BLACK CIRCLE BOYS ✠ BLACK DEATH ✠ BLACK METAL: A DOCUMENTARY ✠ BLACK METAL SATANICA ✠ BLACK ROSES ✠ BLACK SABBATH ✠ BLACK SABBATH: THE LAST SUPPER ✠ BLACK SUNDAY ✠ THE BLADE MASTER ✠ BLADE RUNNER ✠ THE BLAIR WITCH PROJECT ✠ BLÖDAREN ✠ BLOOD BATH AND BEYOND ✠ BLOOD CULT ✠ BLOOD FEAST ✠ BLOOD INTO WINE ✠ BLOOD ON SATAN'S CLAW ✠ BLOOD TRACKS ✠ BLOODSTONE: SUBSPECIES II ✠ BLOODSUCKING FREAKS ✠ BLUE VENGEANCE ✠ BOOK OF SHADOWS: BLAIR WITCH 2 ✠ BORDELLO OF BLOOD ✠ BORN IN THE BASEMENT ✠ BRAINSCAN ✠ BRIDE OF CHUCKY ✠ BUMMER ✠ THE BUNNY GAME ✠ BURIAL GROUND: THE NIGHTS OF TERROR ✠ THE BURNING ✠ THE BURNING MOON ✠ THE BUTTERFLY BALL

BABA YAGA (1973), AKA DEVIL WITCH; KISS ME, KILL ME

(DIR. CORRADO FARINA; W/CARROLL BAKER, ISABELLE DE FUNES, ELY GALLEANI, GEORGE EASTMAN)

✠ WITCHCRAFT ✠ SLAVIC FOLKLORE ✠ VOODOO

Adapted from a pornographic comic by master Italian eroticist Guido Crepax, *Baba Yaga* is a groovily erotic Italian scare flick that follows sexy hippie photographer Valentina (De Funès) as she falls under the spell of the titular witch (Baker). Voodoo, S&M, a kinky doll that comes to life, and Nazi underwear nightmares add up to a memorably psychedelic '70s Euro skin fright flick.

Bands named Baba Yaga have been spotted in the UK and U.S., and prog weirdoes Mekong Delta penned the song "The Hut of Baba Yaga."

BACK TO THE FUTURE (1985)

(DIR. ROBERT ZEMECKIS; W/MICHAEL J. FOX, LEA THOMPSON, CHRISTOPHER LLOYD, CRISPIN GLOVER)

✠ TIME TRAVEL ✠ GUITAR SOLOS

Marty McFly (Michael J. Fox) time-travels by DeLorean from 1985 to 1955, where he almost boffs his teenage mom. In order to motivate nebbish George McFly (Crispin Glover) into ultimately becoming his father, Marty slips Walkman earphones on George's sleeping head and blares a cassette marked "Van Halen." The dad-to-be bolts upright and listens hard. Huey Lewis, as a music teacher, tells Marty his electric guitar audition for the high school talent show is "just too loud." Somebody melt that dingleberry's brain with Van Halen!

Bad Channels (1992)

(Dir. Ted Nicolaou; w/Martha Quinn, Paul Hipp, Blue Öyster Cult)

✡ Blue Öyster Cult

Whatever scant budget existed for *Bad Channels* must have been lavished on fees for MTV VJ Martha Quinn and Blue Öyster Cult. Even at the time, it was tough not to wonder what Ms. Quinn, Eric Bloom, Buck Dharma, and company must have thought of *Bad Channels*. Exactly ten years earlier, Martha had been the breakout star of MTV's first wave of world conquest, and BÖC were selling out stadiums alongside Black Sabbath (see also: *Black and Blue*).

This is what they had come to: Quinn joins wacky morning disc jockey Dangerous Dan O'Dare (Paul Hipp) to combat puppet-headed aliens who shrink hot earth women and put them in bottles. Once captured, the ladies dream of appearing in Blue Öyster Cult music videos. In 1992, this is definitely odd.

BÖC is always welcome and, boy, does this film offer a big dose; aside from the three videos, they contribute more than twenty compositions to the soundtrack. Neither can anyone entirely dismiss a movie that serves as the connecting chapter between *Dollman* (1991), *Demonic Toys* (1992), and *Dollman vs. Demonic Toys* (1993).

Bad News Tour (1983)

(Dir. Sandy Johnson; w/Adrian Edmonson, Rik Mayall, Nigel Planer, Peter Richardson)

✡ Ozzy Osbourne ✡ Lemmy ✡ Castle Donington ✡ The Young Ones

Unlike the lead characters in *This Is Spinal Tap*, the fictitious heavy rockers of *Bad News Tour* actually hail from Ye Olde Metal England. Americans best know funnymen Adrian Edmonson (playing singer Vim Fuego), Nigel Planer (guitarist Den Dennis), and Rik Mayall (bassist Colin Grigson) as the brilliant leads on the vintage MTV sitcom import *The Young Ones*. The comedy partners had previously launched Bad News on the BBC Channel Four TV series, *The Comic Strip Presents...*, and this VHS release combines two *Comic Strip* episodes as a single feature.

The first portion, "Bad News Tour," from 1985, follows the dim-bulb headbangers on a tour of England's dinky Grantham area, accompanied by an amazingly inept documentary crew. The longer-running sequel, "More Bad News," from 1987, sees the band reuniting to play the 1986 Monsters of Rock Festival at Castle Donington. The band actually did play! The audience may not have been in on the joke, but they obligingly bombard Bad News with bottles, many clearly filled with human discharge, as is the custom in Britain. After a noble battle, Bad News retreats.

Bad News Tour is a riot, but unfortunately was overshadowed by *This Is Spinal Tap*—to the chagrin of die-hard metalheads and comedy devotees alike. The first episode is a fascinating frontline look at the remnants of the New Wave of British Heavy Metal, and the second portrays the lagging UK rock world being eclipsed by Bay Area thrash and L.A. glam. Most importantly, it's hilarious. Ozzy Osbourne and Lemmy cameo.

Bad News also issued a self-titled album in 1987, produced by Brian May of Queen, and a 1988 follow-up, *Bootleg*. The band toured throughout the second half of the '80s, where they were occasionally joined by May and, once, by Jeff Beck. The Bad News music video for their cover of Queen's "Bohemian Rhapsody" nearly surpasses Spinal Tap for onstage laugh riots, and predates comic use of the song in *Wayne's World* by years.

Bad Ronald (1974)

(Dir. Buzz Kulik; w/Scott Jacoby, Pippa Scott, Kim Hunter, Dabney Coleman)

✡ Horror

The Ronald of *Bad Ronald* isn't a bad kid, really. He's just a jittery high school nerd who, after accidentally killing a younger girl for taunting him, becomes a fugitive in his own home. As played by Scott Jacoby (who resembles the youthful Howard Stern), Ronald is a creep for sure, and he only grows creepier while living in a tiny hidden room in his house. Meanwhile, his mother tells everyone he ran away.

The ploy works until Mom dies. Ronald, who occupied his time creating the elaborate fantasy world Atranta, has to contend with the family that moves into the house. Staying put proves especially challenging, as the new residents include three sexy blonde teenage girls. Eventually, Ronald comes to believe the youngest is the Princess of Atranta. As the Prince, he must rescue her from the Devil that threatens their happiness. No part of this plan works out for him.

Made for ABC and rerun frequently as an afternoon movie on local stations, *Bad Ronald* touched a deep nerve with the generation of kids that came of age in the '70s. Part of the power lies with director Buzz Kulik's eerie and unnerving atmosphere, but *Bad Ronald* also realizes the fantasy kids have of living in the walls of somebody else's house—spying, stalking, hiding, eavesdropping, and, of course, making copious lewd use of peepholes.

Ronald himself is a classic lost soul in desperate need of heavy metal. His whole story would be different if the movie started with him shaking off a hot chick's rejection by stopping into a record store and stumbling across "Burn" by Deep Purple or "Secret Treaties" by Blue Öyster Cult or "Phenomenon" by UFO or the self-titled debuts from Kiss and Rush. From there, Ronald could and would have started composing concept albums about Atranta. And then the girls would want to kidnap him.

Barbarian Queen (1985)
(Dir. Héctor Olivera; w/Lana Clarkson, Katt Shea, Dawn Dunlap, Frank Zagarino)
✱ Swords & Sorcery

In a better world, blonde stunner Lana Clarkson would be hailed for her dominant, dynamic star turn in the title role of sexed-up sword-and-sorcery B-movie *Barbarian Queen*. Alas, in our bullet-riddled reality, she's remembered for

being shot to death (in the mouth) by crackpot record producer Phil Spector in February 2003.

Reports on Clarkson's murder typically mention *Barbarian Queen* as an afterthought, and that's surely because the reporters have never bothered to watch it. Make sure you do.

A mid-cycle highlight of schlock mogul Roger Corman's prolific Conan rip-off period (which also gave us *Sorceress* and the *Deathstalker* movies), *Barbarian Queen* opens, as was the style of the day, with a virgin getting gang-raped. The victim is Taramis (Dawn Dunlap), the sister of royal figure Amethea (Clarkson). Her wedding party to virtuous King Argan (Frank Zagarino) is further pooped upon by marauders leveling their village, then rounding up what few survivors remain to serve as hookers or gladiators. Amethea makes it out alive and embarks on a vengeance quest with fellow female freedom fighters Tiniara (Susana Traverso) and Estrild (Katt Shea—future director of *Stripped to Kill* and *Poison Ivy*).

Blood-raining battles, black sorcery, and naked concubines all contribute mightily to *Barbarian Queen*'s hyper-metal quotient, but Clarkson's performance is worthy of full horns raised. Her nudity is powerful, too—most effective when she kicks a mad torture-sadist into his own acid bath.

The Barbarians (1987)
(Dir. Ruggero Deodato; w/David Paul, Peter Paul, Richard Lynch, Michael Berryman, Eva Larue)
✱ Swords & Sorcery ✱ Barbarians

As the "Barbarian Brothers," professional bodybuilding twins David and Peter Paul enjoyed a fourth-tier '80s Hollywood career perfectly in sync with the bubblegum cheese of the high hair-metal era. After donning memorably matching overalls in the underrated Mr. T comedy *D.C. Cab* (1983), the Brothers flexed their way up rung-by-rung through the showbiz gutter and were rewarded with a late-in-the-fray Italian-made *Conan* rip-off, *The Barbarians*.

Here, identical musclemen portray, yes, identical musclemen who have been raised by circus folk in a medieval world of cheap special effects. Baddie Kadar (Richard Lynch in Bo Derek braids) kidnaps their queen, then captures the brothers and unloads them on wicked fight trainer Michael Berryman (*The Hills Have Eyes*), a demented lowlife known as "The Dirtmaster." The brawls occasionally turn shockingly gory en route to a big showdown. Naturally, the Barbarian Brothers win, and nobody, not even the Italian producers, ever thought about a sequel.

The Barbarian Brothers parlayed their massiveness into a subsequent direct-to-video movie career that included 1989's *Think Big* ("All they had was strength, determination, and a lucky chicken bone. Brains aren't everything!"); 1992's *Double Trouble* ("Twin brothers: one's a good cop, the other's bad news!"); and 1994's *Twin Sitters* ("You're never home alone when you're a twin!"). They also appeared, with legs severed, as "The Hun Brothers" in the director's cut of Oliver Stone's *Natural Born Killers* (1994).

BASKET CASE (1982)

(DIR. FRANK HENENLOTTER; W/KEVIN VAN HENTENRYCK, TERRI SUSAN SMITH, BEVERLY BONNER)
✣ GRINDHOUSE HORROR ✣ BANNED VIDEO NASTY

Labeled by fragile flower Rex Reed as "the sickest movie I've ever seen," *Basket Case* was writer-director Frank Henenlotter's attempt to contribute to the storied array of outrages he watched in grindhouses along New York City's fabled Forty-Second Street of the 1970s and early '80s. Inexplicably, *Basket Case* bombed on that theater strip nicknamed "The Deuce," but caught on big and bloody as a midnight movie down at Greenwich Village's Waverly Theater, prior to becoming a rite-of-home-video-passage for head-banging horror fans over the next two decades.

Wide-eyed youth Duane (Kevin Van Hentenryck) strolls up Forty-Second Street carrying a locked wicker basket. He takes in the neon peep show signs and glowing porn theater marquees, is propositioned by hookers and pushers, and, with seeming naïveté, checks into a Times

Square flophouse hotel. Inside the basket is Belial, his twin brother, who is about the size of a large pumpkin. Belial looks like a fanged face squished on the front of a big pile of putty. The brothers were born conjoined, until surgeons separated them and cast Belial in the trash to die. Duane saved him. Now, together, they're hunting down the doctors who did them wrong. The scheme goes gorily well until Duane takes up romantically with medical receptionist Sharon (Terri Susan Smith). Belial boils over with jealousy. He rapes Sharon to death, and sets off a tragic conclusion for the siblings (particularly tragic is what happens to Duane's testes).

Basket Case rocks like fuck, and is embraced as a classic especially for its rough edges and inventive solutions to realizing its makers' dreams with limited resources. Belial is a wondrous, nauseating creation, played most of the time by a puppet controlled by Van Hentenryck. *Basket Case*'s most deliriously engaging scene is a stop-motion animated segment wherein Belial freaks out and trashes his hotel room.

Reports of offended audience members storming out of horror movie screenings are plentiful. *Basket Case*'s lethal rape scene so repulsed the movie's crew that several of them walked off the set during filming. Director Henenlotter went from *Basket Case* to a sporadic but consistently admirable career with titles including *Basket Case*'s two sequels, plus *Brain Damage* (1988), *Frankenhooker* (1990), and the documentary *Herschell Gordon Lewis: The Godfather of Gore* (2010).

BATTLE ROYALE (2000)

(DIR. KINJI FUKASAKU; W/TATSUYA FUJIWARA, AKI MAEDA, TARO YAMAMOTO, MASANOBU ANDO)
✣ SCHOOL SHOOTINGS ✣ YOUTH GONE WILD

To assure obedience among emerging generations, an oppressively routine government selects one entire high school class and deposits its members on an island with a mighty passel of weaponry and the instructions to kill one another until only one student is left standing. Should a student hesitate to kill, an electronic collar will blow his or her head off. The island is wired for broadcast, and the entire nation watches.

Director Kinji Fukasaku crafts a thrilling, nail-biting action movie while simultaneously communicating the Orwellian horror of the premise. Old men in charge, clinging to power, prove capable of limitless atrocities. What begins with warning labels slapped on music and horror movies forcibly withdrawn from circulation can lead, quickly and easily, to totalitarianism. Heavy metal has always threatened that agenda, making it at once a target and a weapon. *Battle Royale* embodies such a concept: it demonstrates a metal wail for freedom, while righteously allowing us to enjoy the on-screen carnage. Everybody wins.

Battle Royale was a blockbuster in Japan, ranking in the top ten highest grossing films of all time there. A U.S. remake was planned, despite skittishness over the subject matter after the 1999 Columbine school shootings, but the 2007 Virginia Tech shootings put the project on the far back burner. *Battle Royale* didn't properly play theaters in the U.S. until 2011, and finally received an official DVD release in 2012.

Fans latched on to the movie through bootleg videos and region-free DVD releases. Many believe that *Hunger Games* creator Suzanne Collins must count among those viewers, but she denies having ever seen *Battle Royale* or read the book.

BEACH BALLS (1988)
(DIR: JOE RITTER; PHILIP PALEY, HEIDI HELMER)
✠ SUNSET STRIP ✠ BACKMASKING

*B*each Balls introduces us to teen beach bum Charlie (Philip Paley), who pines for spunky surf babe Wendy (Heidi Helmer). The catch: Heidi only digs dudes in bands. The solution: Charlie trades his long board for a six-string and shreds for broke. Potential wipeouts arise by way of Charlie's parents, who are Jesus nuts hell-bent on decoding backward-masked calls to satanism on hard rock LPs. Furthermore, Wendy seems particularly fixated on a glam metal group called

Severed Heads in a Bag, portrayed by real-life Sunset Strip fixture D.R. Starr.

Fate intercedes when Charlie's mom and dad leave town on a record-burning tour the very same weekend that Severed Heads needs a location to play a showcase for some music biz honchos. Guess where the big metal concert will be? Charlie's house! The best-laid plans of horny teens often go zanily astray en route to getting laid, of course, and *Beach Balls* climaxes with a slapstick free-for-all in which Charlie's house is trashed by lifeguards battling metal dudes, bikini twins invade on roller-skates, and a blowup sex doll bounces across every inch of the screen. Happily for Charlie, Wendy is burned by a sexist Severed Head and turns to him for comfort, ensuring that *Beach Balls* doesn't end with our hero suffering blue balls.

Philip Paley, who plays Charlie, was Cha-Ka the monkey boy on the classic '70s prehistoric TV adventure series *Land of the Lost*. He grew up to be the lead in *Beach Balls*. And he has acted in nothing since. Watch for Sunset Strip metal entrepreneur Bill Gazzarri, who you'll never forget leading the "Odin! Odin!" chant in *Decline of Western Civilization Part II*, introducing Severed Heads in a Bag on stage at his famous club.

THE BEASTMASTER (1982)
(DIR: DON COSCARELLI; W/MARC SINGER, TANYA ROBERTS, RIP TORN, JOHN AMOS)
✠ SWORDS & SORCERY

*B*eastmaster is a *Conan* cash-in aimed at kids; and the movie sufficiently entertains across the board, through color and action and fun use of animal actors, ultimately becoming a knuckle-headed classic in its own right. The Beastmaster himself is Dar (Marc Singer), a blonde barbarian in a loincloth (very proto-He-Man), who is sucked out of his mother's uterus by a witch and implanted in the womb of a cow. This switcheroo results in Dar developing telepathic communion with all creatures great and small, essentially making him the Aquaman of dry land. As an adult, Dar can see through the eyes of his pet hawk Sharak, and draws his strength from a black tiger, Ruh, and his cunning from Kodo and Podo, a pair of ferrets. He teams with slave girl Kiri (Tanya Roberts) and leather-bound muscle-warrior Seth (John Amos, head of the Evans clan on TV's *Good Times*) to battle evil warlock Maax (Rip Torn). Further assistance comes from flying bat-people who wrap their wings around bad guys and mulch them into slop.

Director Don Coscarelli (*Phantasm*) whips up a mirthful adventure that only improves with age. The campy parts grow campier, and the metal parts always loom more monolithic. *Beastmaster*'s PG rating seems especially remarkable now given Tanya Roberts's multiple displays of her own breast-masters. Somehow, she topped her toplessness here in the semi-metal *Sheena* (1984), where she bares all—and that was also rated PG! In the 1980s kids had no choice but to choose metal! *Beastmaster*'s omnipresence on TV throughout the '80s and '90s pointed countless young minds in the direction of classic-style pulp fantasy and post-*Conan* saber-slaying. TBS aired the movie to the point that its call letters were said to stand for "The *Beastmaster* Station." Similarly, HBO got tagged: "Hey, *Beastmaster*'s On!"

Although the film was a modest success upon its first release, *Beastmaster*'s cult sufficiently swelled over the ensuing decade to warrant a theatrically released sequel nine years later. *Beastmaster 2: Through the Portal of Time* (1991) sends Dar to modern-day Los Angeles in pursuit of his wicked half-brother Arklon (Wings Hauser, looking a bit like Sam Kinison). It is terrible, and not just because there's no nudity. The cable movie *Beastmaster III: The Eye of Braxus* followed in 1996. The TV series *BeastMaster* launched in 1999 and ran in syndication for three seasons.

Ruh, the Beastmaster's "black tiger," is an actual tiger dyed black. Look around the corners of his mouth for orange smears. Sadly, Ruh died two years after shooting the movie, allegedly as a result of toxic poisoning from the color treatments. This review is dedicated to Ruh's memory.

Beavis and Butt-Head Do America (1996)

(Dir. Mike Judge; w/Mike Judge, Bruce Willis, Demi Moore, David Letterman)

✠ Animation ✠ Headbanger Buddies
✠ Soundtrack (AC/DC, Ozzy Osbourne)

From their AC/DC and Metallica shirts, their spontaneous celebratory chants of "Breakin' the Law" by Judas Priest, their role in turning White Zombie from a Lower East Side noise cult into stadium-packing international superstars (by goofily worshiping the "Thunderkiss '65" video), heavy metal in the '90s had no better ambassadors than MTV's animated couch-bound headbangers, Beavis and Butt-head. The TV show creator Mike Judge's comedy was brilliant; then the musical taste of the two nachos-for-brains stars created a metal oasis during the Lollapalooza decade. Alone in the alt-pop wilderness, the maniacally giggling voices of Beavis and Butt-head cried out against college rock and lovingly reminisced about when Ozzy Osbourne bit the head off a cow and "milk squirted out."

Beavis and Butt-head Do America translates the pair to the big screen, expanding their world from school-work-sofa-repeat to a cross-country misadventure from Las Vegas to Washington, D.C., after their precious TV is stolen. Our heroes are mistaken for assassins, and they unwittingly transport a biological weapon from state to state. Cars pile up behind them, and national security is raised to Defcon 4. Along the way, Beavis trips on peyote. Butt-head attempts to romance First Daughter Chelsea Clinton.

Real-life *Beavis* superfan David Letterman vocal cameos as a homeless Mötley Crüe roadie who is likely Butt-head's father. All confusion is cleared up by the end, and Chelsea's dad, President Bill Clinton, makes the boys honorary ATF agents. Beavis, who was forbidden for years to speak the word on TV due to a tragic copycat arson, erupts with glee when he finds out that that the last letter stands for "FIRE! FIRE! FIRE!" Free at last.

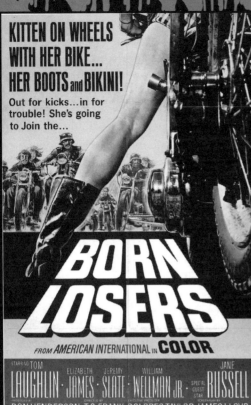

KITTEN ON WHEELS
WITH HER BIKE...
HER BOOTS and BIKINI!

Out for kicks...in for
trouble! She's going
to Join the...

BORN LOSERS

FROM AMERICAN INTERNATIONAL IN **COLOR**

STARRING TOM **LAUGHLIN** · Elizabeth **JAMES** · Jeremy **SLATE** · William **WELLMAN JR.** · SPEC'AL GUEST STAR Jane **RUSSELL**

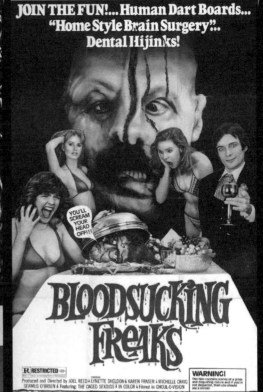

JOIN THE FUN!...Human Dart Boards...
"Home Style Brain Surgery"...
Dental Hijinks!

YOU'LL SCREAM YOUR HEAD OFF!!!

BLOODSUCKING FREAKS

R RESTRICTED

Produced and Directed by JOEL REED · LYNETTE SHELDON & KAREN FRASER & MICHELLE CRAIG
SEAMUS O'BRIEN · Featuring THE CAGED SEXDIDS · IN COLOR · Filmed in GHOUL-O-VISION

WARNING!
This film contains scenes of a gross and disgusting nature and if you're not disposed, then you should see a shrink!

THE EVIL SPIRIT MUST CHOOSE EVIL...

THE BLACK MASS...THE SPELLS...THE INCANTATIONS...
THE CURSES...THE CEREMONIAL SEX...

JOE SOLOMON presents

SIMON· KING of the WITCHES

THE TENANT IN ROOM 7 IS VERY SMALL,
VERY TWISTED, AND VERY MAD

BASKET CASE

an IEVINS / HENENLOTTER production starring KEVIN VanHENTENRYCK · TERRI SUSAN SMITH
BEVERLY BONNER Director of Photography BRUCE TORBET Music GUS RUSSO
Executive Producers ARNIE BRUCK TOM KAYE Production Executive RAY SUNDLIN
Produced by EDGAR IEVINS Written and Directed by FRANK HENENLOTTER

DISTRIBUTED BY
RFI **RUGGED FILMS INC.**

Clockwise from top left: *early Billy Jack trouble in* Born Losers *(1967);*
join the fun with Bloodsucking Freaks *(1976);* Times Square turmoil in
Basket Case *(1982);* Simon, King of the Witches *(1971)* chooses evil

BEGOTTEN (1990)

(DIR. E. ELIAS MERHIGE; W/BRIAN SALZBERG, DONNA DEMPSEY, STEPHEN CHARLES BARRY)

✠ BLASPHEMY

The creation myth of the Bible gets a shit-rape-suicide makeover in *Begotten*, E. Elias Merhige's black-and-white psych-doom trip downward that, momentarily, looked poised to be an *Eraserhead* for the '90s. That *Begotten* ended up just being the weirdest midnight movie of its moment is more than okay, as it chronicles, unflinchingly, God (Brian Salzberg) slicing out his own guts with a straight razor, followed by Mother Earth (Donna Dempsey) committing divine necrophilia upon the disemboweled Almighty's post-mortem-potent erection.

Moms subsequently gives birth to the adult-size Son of Earth/Flesh on Bone (Stephen Charles Barry). Her offspring's life amidst the roving cannibals and gang rapists of the movie's ravaged landscape is one huge pain-heap of anti-happiness. All this tumbles toward a sudden conclusion after seventy-eight cornea-melting, impressively committed minutes.

Writer-director Merhige was a star pupil in the film department at SUNY Purchase. His most notorious student production ends with a close-up of his own defecating anus. Aside from Hollywood efforts *Shadow of the Vampire* (2000) and *Suspect Zero* (2004), Merge has helmed music videos for Danzig and Marilyn Manson.

BENEATH the PLANET of the APES (1970)

(DIR. TED POST; W/JAMES FRANCISCUS, KIM HUNTER, MAURICE EVANS, LINDA HARRISON, CHARLTON HESTON)

✠ TALKING APES ✠ APOCALYPSE ✠ NUCLEAR BOMB

Beneath *the Planet of the Apes* is a world-class, only-in-the-'70s sci-fi noggin-scratcher that, while not on par with its classic predecessor, may actually contain more individual heavy metal surface elements. Shortly after Taylor (Charlton Heston) freaks out beneath the beached Statue of Liberty—one of cinema's all-time defining moments of doom—the ground splits open and swallows him whole while mute hottie Nova (Linda Harrison) watches. U.S. astronaut Brent (James Franciscus) then lands on the planet to look for Taylor. He runs into Nova, plus Cornelius (David Watson), Zira (Kim Hunter), and Dr. Zaius (Maurice Evans) from the first film.

With gorilla General Ursus (James Gregory) out to kill them, Brent and Nova escape to a caved-in New York City subway station and, eventually, the remains of St. Patrick's Cathedral. There, telepathic mutants worship the "Divine Bomb," a nuclear weapon left over from humanity's reign that is singularly capable of destroying the entire planet. Taylor turns up, General Ursus invades... and let us just deem the ending "explosive."

Beneath the Planet of the Apes is cheap, weird, and lovable. Then came the further sequels, all cheap, mostly weird, and some lovable. *Escape From the Planet of the Apes* (1972), depicting Cornelius and Zira blasting off into the past and landing in modern America, is great. *Conquest of the Planet of the Apes* (1972) is a riot in a very real sense, chronicling the initial uprising of primates against their human captors. *Battle for the Planet of the Apes* (1973), rated G in reaction to parents expressing grief over *Conquest's* intensity and violence, is a bust—and that's despite Paul Williams (*Phantom of the Paradise*) as an orangutan and an awesome crying statue at the end.

BERSERKER (1987)

(DIR. JEFFERSON RICHARD; W/MIKE RILEY, JOSEPH ALAN JOHNSON, VALERIE SHELDON)

✠ VIKINGS ✠ SLASHER

Along with *Scalps* (1983), which features a homicidal Native American antagonist, *Berserker* is the most noteworthy entry in the already highly metal '80s slasher cycle to focus on a specifically metal archetype: a kill-crazy Viking. Apologies to Scandinavians, but the creators here have recast your ancestors as cannibals.

Half a dozen dumb "teens," played by actors in their mid-twenties, venture predictably into the woods and fall prey to the fangs and claws of the title slayer, a thousand-year-young Norse warrior bedecked in bearskin, complete with a bear's head for a hat. He wreaks a lot of havoc. Somehow one chick, post-coitus, gets messed up by an actual bear, or so it seems.

Actually, yes, she does. *Berserker*, bizarrely, is all about how the Viking uses the bear to carry out his camper killing via Asgardian telekinesis or some such power. The Viking has a great time, until the bear turns on him in a final climax filled with Norse-god black magic that, in terms of unintentional hilarity, warrants one helmet horn and half a hairy paw up.

This *Berserker* is not to be confused with *Berserker: Hell's Warrior* (2004), a low-budget action flick spin on Eric the Red starring reliable direct-to-video stalwarts Craig Sheffer and Patrick Bergin. Nor is this the unmade *Berserker* written by Mel Gibson in 2012, who also planned to star and direct. That one may well have been the gore-sopped Viking carnage opera cinema has been waiting for, but we all know how Mel's future plans turned out now, don't we, Sugartits?

The movie is in league with the band the Berzerker, and "Berserker" songs by Aurora Borealis, Belmez, Guillotine, Thor, Viking, and more.

Best Worst Movie

(2009)

(Dir. Michael Stephenson; w/Michael Stephenson, George Hardy)

✠ Goblins ✠ Obsession

The documentary *Best Worst Movie* tells the story of *Troll 2*, a 1990 B-flick boondoogle turned cult phenomenon. *Troll 2* is often described as "perfectly terrible" and, for some time, it ruled as the single lowest-rated movie on the IMDB.

For a generation of burgeoning horror nuts and headbangers, *Troll 2* was a perennial sleepover video and a ubiquitous after-school presence on cable TV. Fan sites sprang up, screenings were mounted, and in 2007, devotees from all over the world descended on the town where the movie was filmed for a multi-day *Troll 2* festival. The audience-driven aspect of *Troll 2* almost sounds like the origins of a niche metal festival, not a movie about flesh-eating goblins.

Director Michael Stephenson starred in *Troll 2* as a kid and he reunites the entire cast to take the movie on the road and meet up with all these cockeyed admirers. The standout presence of *Best Worst Movie* is George Hardy, a well-liked dentist who costarred as the dad in *Troll 2* and delivered the film's most celebrated line: "You can't piss on hospitality!" Hardy forgot about his acting turn for years until patients took to looking askance at him and asking, incredulously, about *Troll 2*.

Best Worst Movie starts off with Hardy and Stephenson hitting the road to roaring crowds and gushing declarations. By the end, *Troll 2*'s public party moment has passed, and they're sitting alone at a horror expo, accepting the inevitable return to real life. Fame is fleeting. Only the uniquely insane ineptitude of *Troll 2* is forever.

Or, as dentist George Hardy observes as he scans the black-clad, heavily made-up, metal-bent denizens of a horror convention: "There's a lot of gingivitis in this room."

Beware of Mr. Baker

(2012)

(Dir. Jay Bulger; w/Ginger Baker, Eric Clapton, Jack Bruce, John Lydon)

✠ Proto-Metal ✠ Concert Footage

Cream pioneered the hard rock, heavy blues sound that Black Sabbath would alchemize into metal. *Beware of Mr. Baker*, a documentary on the band's louder-than-life drum legend Ginger Baker, takes its title from a sign hung on the gate of the musician's South African estate. Clarifying the warning in no uncertain terms, the movie opens with the infamously volatile Baker unloading on director Jay Bulger,

"I'm gonna fucking put you in a hospital!" and promptly smashing the filmmaker square in the nose with a silver-handled walking stick.

Entrenched at his ranch, Baker allows Bulger to film him under the false pretense that it's for a *Rolling Stone* magazine profile. He retracts his approval and prevents Bulger from filming him sometimes, as so violently demonstrated. Baker's bandmates in Cream, Eric Clapton and Jack Bruce are amused and alarmed as they describe dealing with the demonic drummer. One hilarious segment intercuts Baker contradicting everything the other two say. Rock legends, one by one, testify to Baker's unparalleled power behind the kit and how dangerous he is elsewhere. Sabbath drummer Bill Ward pays tribute, as do drummers Neil Peart (Rush), Charlie Watts (Rolling Stones), Chad Smith (Red Hot Chili Peppers), Marky Ramone (Ramones), and Carmine Appice (Ozzy Osbourne, Cactus, King Kobra).

Cream's 2005 reunion shows at the Royal Albert Hall are a highlight of the movie, although it's no surprise that Baker, in the most obscene and enraged manner possible, insists that no such thing will ever happen again. *Beware of Mr. Baker* deftly slams home an intimate portrait of a percussive genius and combustive madman. You'll appreciate seeing it within safe distance of Ginger's walking stick. Pure satanic abandon reigns behind Baker's wild eyes, both in the new material and archival footage, with the wild red mane and beard from which his nickname "Ginger" arise flailing like bursts of hellfire.

The Beyond (1987), aka 7 Doors of Death

(Dir. Lucio Fulci; w/Catriona MacColl, David Warbeck, Cinzia Monreale, Veronica Lazar)

✠ Italian Horror ✠ Hell ✠ Demons ✠ Zombies ✠ Black Magic

Dreamy and inviting in its fluidity, yet ruthless in its violence and grotesquery, *The Beyond* is Lucio Fulci's surrealistic tone poem about a gothic New Orleans hotel that houses one of Earth's seven doors to hell. Decades after we witness a warlock chemically melted down to his bones there, New York painter Liza (Catriona MacColl) acquires the hotel to renovate it. Naturally, she opens the damned door in the basement by mistake, and all hell comes pouring through.

Perhaps even more than any other major '80s Italian splatter opera, *The Beyond* is entirely experienced as nightmare imagery and consciousness-shattering sounds courtesy of maestro Fabio Frizzi's (*Zombie, City of the Living Dead*) chilling score. Indelible sights include a creamy-eyed blind girl with a ferocious guide dog standing in the middle of a highway, tarantulas eating eyeballs and lips, internal organs suddenly being rendered external; sauntering Louisiana zombies; and an apocalyptic, cosmos-spanning wrap-up that is truly beyond even the beyond.

Quentin Tarantino revived *The Beyond* as a midnight movie in 1998 through his Rolling Thunder Pictures, in association with Grindhouse Releasing. Grindhouse became major players in the extreme horror DVD world, counting among its honchos David Szulkin, aka Dave Depraved of the mighty doom metal band Blood Farmers.

Beyond the Door (1974), aka The Devil Within Her; Diabolica

(Dir. Ovidio G. Assonitis; w/Juliet Mills, Richard Johnson, Gabriele Lavia)

✠ Satan ✠ Demonic Possession ✠ Satan Spawn

Ripping off both *Rosemary's Baby* (1968) and *The Exorcist* (1973) at once, *Beyond the Door* introduces a very pregnant San Francisco housewife, Jessica, who quickly becomes very demonically possessed. It's the kid's fault, in this case, as the son of Satan swells inside Jessica's belly.

At first, abnormality manifests pretty hilariously with Jessica eating a banana peel off the sidewalk, demolishing her husband's fancy fish tank, and uncomfortably planting a wet kiss on her other young son's mouth. In due time, though,

Jessica levitates, curses in baritone, rotates her head 360 degrees, and power-pukes repeatedly in multiple colors. Her creep ex-boyfriend Dimitri (Richard Johnson) shows up and says he can help, but he's in cahoots with the underworld. Nobody ends up happy. Except Satan. Hail Satan.

Beyond the Door packed theaters, many patrons no doubt drawn in by the gimmick of "Possessound," a specialized knock-off of Universal Studio's booming bass "Sensurround" developed for the disaster epic *Earthquake* (1974). Warner Bros. noticed how well *Beyond the Door* was doing and filed a lawsuit, claiming it infringed on their *Exorcist* property. The court decided Warners couldn't claim ownership of gross-out devil scenes, and drive-ins were free to continue filling their bills with possession flicks for years.

Beyond the Door II, which opened in the U.S. in 1979, is totally unrelated and actually just a retitling of Mario Bava's (*Black Sabbath*) swan song film, *Shock* (1977). The Serbian film *Beyond the Door III* (1989) is related in title only.

Bill & Ted's Excellent Adventure

(1989)

(Dir. Stephen Herek; w/Keanu Reeves, Alex Winter, George Carlin, Jane Wiedlin)
✸ Air Guitar ✸ Soundtrack (Warrant, Extreme, Bang Tango, Tora Tora, Shark Island)

Wyld Stallyns rule. That's the first thing we learn in *Bill & Ted's Excellent Adventure*, as Rufus (George Carlin) readies a time-traveling phone booth in the utopian society of San Dimas, CA, during the year 2688. His mission is to assure the musical success of mighty metal squadron Wyld Stallyns, led by a pair of heroes known as the Two Great Ones—Bill S. Preston, Esq. (Alex Winter) and Ted "Theodore" Logan (Keanu Reeves). The ideal future world is centered on both Wyld Stallyns' music and its two core philosophies: "Be excellent to each other" and "Party on, dudes!"

Landing in 1988 San Dimas, Rufus discovers that Bill and Ted are goofball high school metalheads of an affably air-brained order. So that they may complete a history project, and therefore be able to form Wyld Stallyns, Rufus enables Bill and Ted to travel through time and interact with actual historical figures. Complications arise when they accidentally bring Napoleon back to modern California. (Ted's kid brother's big line has always cracked me up: "Napoleon is a dick!")

After romancing fifteenth-century royals Princess Elizabeth (Kimberley Kates) and Princess Joanna (Diane Franklin), our heroes round up Billy the Kid (Dan Shor), Sigmund Freud (Rod Loomis), Beethoven (Clifford David), Genghis Khan (Al Leong), Joan of Arc (Jane Wiedlin), Abraham Lincoln (Robert V. Barron), and "Socrates" (Tony Steedman). For their final school presentation, Bill and Ted roll out each of these figures in the style of a major stadium rock show, earning a good grade and ensuring the formation and transformative triumph of Wyld Stallyns.

Like *Wayne's World* a few years hence, the high-energy, funny-from-end-to-end *Bill & Ted* spotlights the overwhelmingly benign aspects of metal fandom typically eclipsed by lurid reports of occult rituals and teen suicide. For example, Bill and Ted salute one another and others they deem "most excellent" with a signature air-guitar shred. This celebration of knuckleheaded youthful good times elevates dreams of riding hard-rock lightning into something comically cosmic.

This movie proved such an appealing hit, it spawned a cartoon series, *Bill & Ted's Excellent Adventures*, featuring the voices of Reeves, Winter, and Carlin. The show ran for two seasons and spun off its own line of rock band toys. Even more impressive, Bill & Ted's Excellent Cere*al* hit supermarket shelves in 1990.

Director Stephen Herek previously made the supremely likable Gremlins rip-off *Critters* (1986), and went on to direct the pseudo–Judas Priest flick *Rock Star* (2001).

For curly-maned Diane Franklin, who plays Princess Joanna, *Bill & Ted* capped a remarkable run of '80s cult movies. She debuted as the ice-hearted Karen in *The Last American Virgin* (1982), had incestuous sex with her brother in *Amityville II: The Possession* (1982), played French exchange student Monique Junot in *Better Off Dead* (1984), starred as the biblical Eve in *Second Time Lucky* (1984), and teamed with her heavy metal boyfriend to battle a satellite-dish frog monster in *TerrorVision* (1986).

In planning Wyld Stallyns, Bill and Ted insist they will need "Edward Van Halen" on guitar. After the premiere, Eddie said that if they ever really got the band together, he'd be happy to join. Be excellent to each other. Party on, dudes.

Bill & Ted's Bogus Journey (1991)

(Dir. Peter Hewitt; w/Keanu Reeves, Alex Winter, George Carlin, William Sadler, Pam Grier)

✣ Grim Reaper ✣ Satan ✣ Soundtrack (Steve Vai, Primus, Kiss, Megadeth, Faith No More, King's X, Slaughter, Winger)

The second time around, Bill and Ted must defend their destiny of fronting metal combo Wyld Stallyns in order to create a future utopia in San Dimas, CA. This quest, *Bill & Ted's Bogus Journey*, involves them traveling to hell; hence the original title of the film, *Bill & Ted Go to Hell*. The drama begins as twenty-seventh-century evildoer Chuck De Nomolos (Joss Ackland) sends robotic lookalikes of Bill (Alex Winter) and Ted (Keanu Reeves) back to 1991 in order to sabotage Wyld Stallyns' attempt to win the Fourth Annual San Dimas Battle of the Bands. The first thing the robots do is throw Bill and Ted off a cliff, killing them. All is not lost, however, as Death (William Sadler), in full Grim Reaper resplendence, proposes a game with their souls at stake. Bill and Ted try to squirm out of it, but Satan scares them into rising to the occasion. The game parodies the excruciating fatalism of Ingmar Bergman's *The Seventh Seal* (1957). There, Death plays a soul-gambling round of chess with a medieval knight. Here, our heroes defeat the Reaper at Battleship, Clue, Coleco Football, and Twister. Sadler, as Death, steals *Journey*. His winces, frowns, and pitiful headshakes at little defeats and defiled dignity are a scream.

After the boys storm heaven, this bogus journey spans time, space, and metaphysics, affably and amusingly. Upon the actual "Stairway to Heaven," Ted pleads his case for salvation by quoting extensively from Poison's "Every Rose Has Its Thorn." An alien shape-shifter and good Bill and Ted robots save the day, resulting in an even funnier film than the first, already a Heavy Metal Movie classic. Much like Kiss battling their duplicate robots in *Kiss Meets the Phantom of the Park* (1978), Bill and Ted going at it with mechanical lookalikes works fabulously as comedy.

What I grew up calling a "wedgie," Bill and Ted call a "Melvin"—as did the Melvins, when selecting a band name. An underpants-hiking-up by any other name is still hilarious when administered to the Grim Reaper. Also, you will see Pam Grier unzip a costume of herself and have George Carlin emerge. The band portraying Wyld Stallyns is Primus. They wail through "Tommy the Cat." Guest shredder Steve Vai provides the band's guitar solos.

The return of Bill & Ted was again a commercial success. Fox aired the live-action TV series *Bill & Ted's Excellent Adventures* during summer 1992. Twenty years later, in 2012, Alex Winter and Keanu Reeves announced the imminent arrival of a third *Bill & Ted* excursion. Excellent!

Billy Jack (1971)

(Dir. Tom Laughlin; w/Tom Laughlin, Delores Taylor, Clark Howat, Howard Hesseman)

✣ Hippies vs. Rednecks ✣ Native American Spirituality ✣ Fistfights

A tour de force by writer-director-star Tom Laughlin, *Billy Jack* is the searing saga of a half-Indian Green Beret turned hapkido-kicking pacifist. He is a frontline revolutionary in defense of wild horses, Native Americans, hippie

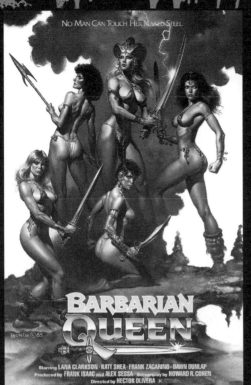

Clockwise from top left: Barbarian Queen *(1985); Oedipus plus zombies in* Burial Ground *(1981); the* Barbarians *invade 1987, peak year of VHS; Swedish Sensationsfilm* Blood Tracks *(1985)*

kids, and Howard Hesseman. And you. And me, probably. Hopefully. That *Billy Jack*—along with its righteous one-man-smashing-the-system cinematic soul brother *Walking Tall* (1973)—seems to have fallen through the cultural cracks in recent years is just wrong. Maybe even evil!

Consider that *Billy Jack* was the number one box office hit of 1971, predating Bruce Lee at the movies and the Wounded Knee occupation in South Dakota in the news, firing up the public about martial arts and the American Indian movement. The three-hour head-trip sequel, *The Trial of Billy Jack* (1974), earned back ten times its budget within a month of being released.

The action opens in the scenic New Mexico desert, as a posse of calculating rednecks rounds up free-roaming mustangs to slaughter for dog food. "One Tin Soldier" by Coven accompanies the sweeping helicopter camera. Coven's 1969 debut album *Witchcraft Destroys Minds and Reaps Souls* features the band members waving devil horns and a performing a song called "Black Sabbath." They were the first satanic rock band to top the Billboard Pop Singles chart.

Our hero appears on horseback, clad in denim, topped by his signature black hat and pointing a shotgun at the would-be Alpo accomplices, who desperately identify themselves as lawmen. Billy Jack, informing them that they are on Indian land where *he* is the law, points out that "when policemen break the law, there is no law. Just the fight for survival." Pure metal.

From there, the story is narrated by Jean (Delores Taylor, the real-life Mrs. Laughlin), who runs the nearby Freedom School for "throwaway kids"— Mexicans, blacks, Indians, longhairs, gender-questioning yoga practitioners, and the acid-fried improv comedy troupe the Committee (featuring *WKRP*'s Dr. Johnny Fever, Howard Hesseman). Be sure that metal burnouts would have comprised no small segment of that student body.

Jean is aided in her good work by upstanding Sheriff Cole (Clark Howat) and the kindly village doctor (Victor Izay). All the other locals—suburban squares and hell-raising shit-kickers—detest the Freedom School. Led by corrupt town boss Posner (Bert Freed) and his sniveling rapist son Bernard, the neighbors aim to send the place to a most Unhappy Hunting Ground.

Billy Jack quintessentially metal moments include his informing Old Man Posner, "I'm gonna take this right foot and whop you on the left side of your face and there's not a damn thing you can do about it," and then doing exactly that. Billy's speech to Bernard in an ice cream shop after the spoiled creep humiliates a group of young Indians is an all-time great slow burn. "When I think about the savagery of this idiotic moment of yours," he seethes, "I just go berserk!" An unparalleled hapkido rampage follows.

There's no doubt that the main character sweats nails. During Billy Jack's psychedelic spirit ritual, he communes with his "brother"—a rattlesnake. If he's not on a horse, he's driving an old army jeep or a motorcycle. The only more metal means of transport would be tank or levitation. Offscreen, Laughlin even took a metal approach to marketing *Billy Jack*. Disappointed by Warner Brothers' initial release, he bought back the rights and drove across the country renting theaters and dealing direct. This practice, called "four-walling," forever changed film distribution. He booked his own tour and got in the van, and drew crowds by pitching *Billy Jack* to a youth generation that had just soured on flower power, buying ads near campuses and saturating TV with commercials during after-school hours.

The sequel, *The Trial of Billy Jack* (1974), may actually be more purely metal. No doubt Laughlin was angrier. Studios, an old Hollywood insider once told me, killed the 1977 release of *Billy Jack Goes to Washington* and pulled the plug, mid-filming, on a 1986 installment in which our hero, disguised as a priest, takes on the New York mob. For the next three decades, Laughlin lingered in exile, but he never backed down until his death in December 2013.

BIOHAZARD (1985)

(DIR. FRED OLEN RAY; W/ALDO RAY, ANGELIQUE PETTYJOHN, WILLIAM FAIR, DAVID O'HARA)

✳ ALIENS

In *Biohazard*, tireless one-man B-movie grinder Fred Olen Ray (*Scalps, Hollywood Chainsaw Hookers*) directs Hollywood tough guy legend Aldo Ray (*Shock 'Em Dead*) and veteran *Star Trek* vixen Angelique Pettyjohn through a goofy swirl of sci-fi horror, extrasensory claptrap, and naked knockers. Angelique plays a busty psychic employed by the U.S. military to travel to other dimensions. Occasionally, she returns with tagalongs, including, for the purposes of some semblance of plot, a toddler-size "Bio Monster," played by the director's five-year-old son, Christopher Ray. At one point, the Bio Monster tears apart an *E.T. the Extra-Terrestrial* poster. Struggling to pass a one-hour running time, *Biohazard* ends with a ten-minute blooper reel.

Angelique Pettyjohn is a permanent knockout after her turn as Shahna on the 1968 *Star Trek* episode "The Gamesters of Triskelion." *Star Trek* is a metal endeavor of course (especially the first series) and so, too, are numerous other cult titles from Angelique's filmography, including *Repo Man* (1984) and the *Lost Empire* (1985), along with her numerous hardcore-porn films, the heaviest of which involves a nude lesbian Ilsa homage in the XXX-rated *Stalag 69* (1982).

THE BIRD WITH THE CRYSTAL PLUMAGE (1970)

(DIR. DARIO ARGENTO; W/TONY MUSANTE, SUZY KENDALL, ENRICO SALERNO, EVA RENZI)

✳ GIALLO ✳ DARIO ARGENTO

While in Rome, American writer Sam Dalmas (Tony Musante) witnesses a figure in black attempting to murder Monica (Eva Renzi), the wife of an art gallery owner. Monica survives, but the would-be killer—in fact, a mad slasher terrorizing the city—soon turns his attention to Sam and his model girlfriend Julia (Suzy Kendall).

The title fowl of Italian terror maestro Dario Argento's *The Bird With the Crystal Plumage* proves to be an essential clue in tracking down the villain. The twist ending, which is chock-full of sadomasochistic knife play, and the gleaming black leather gloves (worn by first-time director Argento himself), became two of the director's trademarks. Ennio Morricone's spine-tingling, stop-and-start score is nail-biting on its own. As Heavy Metal Movies go, this is the violent virtuoso variety, not hairy brute box office.

BLACK AND BLUE (1981)

(DIR. JAY DUBIN; BLACK SABBATH, BLUE ÖYSTER CULT)

✳ CONCERT FOOTAGE

Like a many metal fan of 1980s vintage, I received my first in-depth exposure to Black Sabbath via the Ronnie James Dio–fronted albums *Heaven and Hell* and *Mob Rules*. Also, I grew up in Flatbush, Brooklyn, where hooked-cross graffiti in honor of Blue Öyster Cult was as plentiful as the band's "secret" gigs under the pseudonym Soft White Underbelly at places like Zappa's and the Brooklyn Zoo. As a result, those two metal megaliths coheadlining 1980 tour stop at Nassau Coliseum on Long Island rocked the very foundations of my neighborhood, both as a live concert and the movie version—*Black and Blue*—that played local theaters the following spring.

A few decades later, *Black and Blue* still shakes the soul. The film presents alternating songs by Blue Öyster Cult and Black Sabbath, kicking off with "The Marshall Plan" and "War Pigs", and ending with BÖC covering Steppenwolf's "Born to Be Wild" and Sabbath tearing up "Die Young".

Each band is at a particular peak of its dark powers, electrifying the world's most famous rock concert hall and commanding its assembled throngs of denim-and-leather disciples with abilities that plainly seem beyond any godly realm. *Scary* might seem a strong word, but the horned salute fits. Also, *Black and Blue* has never been released on DVD, so it maintains a mystique in this instant-access era.

Black Blooded Brides of Satan (2009)

(Dir. Sami Haavisto; w/Anne Rajala, Sami Haavisto, Tomi Kerminen, Jukka Lapi)

✠ Black Mass ✠ Human Sacrifice ✠ Rape and Revenge ✠ Soundtrack (black metal)

A bilingual black metal horror film in Finnish and Swedish, *Black Blooded Brides of Satan* takes a pedestrian plot regarding a teen girl falling in with a rough crowd, and brutalizes it up impressively with rape, snuff videos, human sacrifice, and naked female corpses littering Helsinki. Anne Rajala, as wayward black metal maiden Linda, makes a strong heroine, and her delicious-looking bare derriere makes a strong exploitation DVD cover. This is the highest-profile project to date for Blood Ceremony Films, the studio that describes itself as "the harbinger of Finnish horror since 2001."

Black Christmas (1974), aka Silent Night, Evil Night

(Dir. Bob Clark; w/Olivia Hussey, Keir Dullea, Margot Kidder, John Saxon)

✠ Slasher ✠ Holiday Hell

Sorority girls making plans for their holiday break are disturbed by a series of obscene phone calls, and then they start turning up dead. The killer taunts them by telephone, and here come the screams when they discover their tormentor is calling from inside the house!

An early and eerie slasher film that shakes the most sacred holiday to its core, *Black Christmas* is an innovative horror movie that so many others ripped off to the point of turning its scares into clichés. The movie is searingly terrifying, and, especially given the juxtaposition of Yuletide cheer with heinous serial slaughter, more than worthy of the Venom song that bears its name.

NBC planned to air *Black Christmas* under the title *Stranger in the House* but ultimately deemed it "too scary" for network broadcast. NBC was right! Director Bob Clark went on to make *Porky's* (1982) and eventually wimped out or warmed up and directed a very different type of holiday movie, *A Christmas Story* (1983).

Black Circle Boys (1997)

(Dir. Matthew Carnahan; w/Scott Bairstow, Eric Mabius, Tara Subkoff, Donnie Wahlberg)

✠ Satan ✠ Soundtrack (Rorschach Test)

Kyle (Scott Bairstow), a metal-loving high school swim champ, moves to a new town and falls in with a clique of drug-puffing, beer-huffing, occult-studying goth teens. The group of friends is putting together a band. Kyle's a drummer. Everything works out great—until it all goes wrong. Leader Shane (Eric Mabius) entices Kyle into a black-lipsticked life of demon-summoning, mescaline-amped crime sprees that we see in frequent montages. We all meet Greggo (Don "Donnie Don" Wahlberg), his deep-into-the-dark-arts, attempting-to-be-androgynous mentor. Upon meeting Kyle, Greggo lovingly massages his own chest and asks, "You wanna fuck me?"

The fun goes too far. Kyle wants out. Shane's not quick to let him go. The ensuing showdown for a shirtless teen jock's soul sets a template for homoerotic boy horror that director David De Cocteau would perfect and exploit charmingly a few years hence in *The Brotherhood* (2001) and its manifold sequels and rip-offs.

Even the most downtrodden metal outcast will feel superior to these characters. Rather than invoke Satan proper, the Black Circle Boys exclusively call him "The Father." In biology class, Kyle chomps the head off a harmless frog. The Ozzy precedent demands something at least as dangerous as a rabid bat. Even the music is sterile industrial dance, not red-blooded metal. But given the lack of proper portrayals of metal life in the 1990s, this might have been close enough.

BLACK DEATH (2010)

(DIR. CHRISTOPHER SMITH; W/SEAN BEAN, EDDIE REDMAYNE, CARICE VAN HOUTEN)

✤ WITCH BURNING ✤ PLAGUE

An excellent, low-budget surprise bolstered by beautiful cinematography and perfect casting, *Black Death* provokes throughout its haunting course across plague-wracked 1300s England. The time and place bleeds multiple genres of heavy metal, and the execution by director Christopher Smith varies from gothic operatic to pagan folk to doom and doom again. Pursuing a woman he loves, boyish monk Osmund (Eddie Redmayne) departs with a party of pagan punishers for England's marshlands. As Ulric, the God squad's head heathen-buster-in-charge, Sean Bean finds a top-notch reason to keep his hair long after *Lord of the Rings* and *Game of Thrones*. Carice van Houten is appropriately spellbinding as Langiva, leader of a village populated by literal anti-Christ-types.

Black Death's plot offers a medieval thumbscrew-twist on *The Wicker Man* (1973), flipping the script just when you think you know where your sympathies lie. Everybody hurts by the end, and they all put their hurt on someone else. Given the setting, these punishments are often worse than permanent. En route to the final confrontation, Ulric is revealed as a witch burner with unexpected mercy, only to fall helplessly to witches who burn with unexpected mercilessness.

BLACK METAL: A DOCUMENTARY (2007)

(DIR. BILL ZEBUB; W/ABBATH DOOM OCCULTA, CRONOS, MORTIIS, FENRIZ, TOM WARRIOR, KING DIAMOND)

✤ BLACK METAL ✤ NAZIS

Bill Zebub, purveyor of the legendary underground metal publication *The Grimoire of Exalted Deeds* and maker of impressively offensive shot-on-video B-movies, turns documentarian. Given the subject, the rough-and-raw results fit. This educational effort includes interviews with and songs by King Diamond, Mortiis, and members of Arkhon Infaustus, Celtic Frost, Darkthrone, Enslaved, Gloomy Grim, Gorgoroth, and Immortal.

Black Metal parades these subjects before the camera without narration or comment, allowing numerous key purveyors of evil metal to sound off on their art, philosophies, and general happiness with being anti-happy. All agree that there is no one black metal sound, let alone look. Points of debate include whether or not it's okay to don corpse paint, or play keyboards, or worship Satan, or torch churches. A lively discussion arises.

The topic of neo-Nazi National Socialist Black Metal (NSBM) is bandied about, with some musicians arguing that since they despise all God-centered religion, why stop at Christianity and not just as vehemently include Muslims and Jews? Though the NSBM era has faded since this film was made, presenting ideas from the back pages of fanzines spoken aloud sets *Black Metal: A Documentary* apart from numerous efforts by filmmakers less familiar with black metal.

When it comes to church arson, Mortiis seems to embody many in the Norwegian metal scene when he essentially echoes Chris Rock's take on the O. J. Simpson murders: "I can't condone it... but I understand!" For others, everything still boils down to show business. Backstage at an Immortal show, frontman Abbath Doom Occulta breaks into a huge grin when asked about the inspiration for his corpse paint, beaming: "Arthur Brown! Alice Cooper! Kiss! I love the old shit!"

BLACK METAL SATANICA (2008)

(DIR. MATS LUNDBERG; W/WATAIN, VREID, SHINING, SVARTAHRID, RIMSFROST, ONDSKAPT, MORDICHRIST)

✤ SCANDINAVIAN BLACK METAL ✤ BLOODLETTING

The deep-breathing narrator intones during the opening moments of this film, "Scandinavia is one of the richest parts of the world,

Clockwise from top left: *Satanic rock is real in* Black Roses *(1988); Karloff loses his head for* Black Sabbath *(1963); Beavis and Butthead reach the promised land (1996); shit gets heavy in* Begotten *(1990); Bill and Ted and George Carlin*

with almost no unemployment, and a low crime rate. Everything is clean and nice." Quickly, we free-fall hell-deep into the blazing extreme metal underground. The story line runs through requisite highlights of black metal history: The Christian church usurping paganism at swordpoint hundreds of years ago; then Venom begetting Bathory; corpse-painted arsonists igniting thousand-year-old houses of worship; and Varg Vikernes knifing Euronymous out of the scene.

The movie, produced by L.A.-based goth powerhouse Cleopatra Records, then leaps into contemporary issues gripping black metal. At odds here are Norse pagans and various sects of Satanists. Each camp is united by love of their own interpretation of black metal, and by their hatred of Jesus—except for a curious few working to introduce the curious concept of "Christian black metal."

Even casual observers of the genre might be ready to yawn and move on before the appearance of Niklas "Kvarforth" Olsson of the "suicidal black metal" group Shining. Clear-eyed and plainspoken, Olsson explains his agenda for deliberately encouraging listeners to mutilate and kill themselves. His soul-deep glee in describing "pure white bone" sticking out of a blood-spewing, self-inflicted gash elicits a real chill.

As with seemingly every black metal documentary to date, the music gets short shrift. With a subject dominated by grave robbery, corpse defilement, and various related transgressions, perhaps that's understandable. But the music is ultimately the only thing many of these disparate extremists have in common.

BLACK ROSES (1988)
(DIR. JOHN FASANO; W/SAL VIVIANO, JOHN MARTIN, CARMINE APPICE, JULIE ADAMS, VINCENT PASTORE)
✷ SATANIC PANIC ✷ DEMONIC POSSESSION
✷ SOUNDTRACK (KING KOBRA, LIZZY BORDEN)

Writer-director-lunatic John Fasano's evenmore-metal follow-up to *Rock N Roll Nightmare* (1987) begins when a wild hard rock combo interrupts the boredom of small-town Mill Basin. They roar down Main Street in a fleet of Lamborghini Countachs. An ordinary hair metal threat would have arrived via Trans Ams with eagles on the hoods, so this intercontinental touch signals a far greater peril. Once they climb out of their high horses, Black Roses come off as an FM-friendly group with an ear for a crunchy hook. They catch on big-time with the local youth, but distress the local anti-rock forces of repression. When concerned parents crash a Black Roses gig to see just how dire this menace may be, however, the group charms them with "(Paradise) We're on Our Way," a harmless AOR power ballad. Seeing no problem, the mom-andpop contingent splits the scene so the kids can enjoy themselves.

From there, *Black Roses* unleashes total hell itself upon all comers via diabolical heavy metal. "It's a rock invasion!" screams lead singer Damian (Sal Viviano). Damian is the very picture of bewitching charisma in a foot-high steroid-Fabio wig. He wails further about carrying a sword to tear down the Lord and, in order to "roam the world alone," he instructs the teens to "destroy your happy home." The kids hear and obey the message, and soon Mill Basin's adults begin turning up slaughtered, often in impressively creative fashion.

Vincent Pastore—"Big Pussy" from *The Sopranos*—debuts as a dad with zero patience for his son's metal makeover. "Only two types of men wear earrings: pirates and faggots," he says. "I don't see no ship in the driveway!" Big Papa aims to silence his son's Black Roses listening parties by tinkering with the home stereo system. A saber-toothed demonic hand puppet with a taste for Italian emerges from the speaker and gorily dashes that plan. Across town, another youngster, zombified and loving it, simply pumps six shotgun rounds into his old man's stomach.

Only Mr. Moorhouse (John Martin), the very John Stossel–like "cool teacher" at the high school, connects the rash of deaths to the coming of Black Roses. The students help him draw his conclusion by chanting in unison at their desks.

"Da-mi-an! Da-mi-an! Da-mi-an!" Moorhouse thwarts a topless seduction effort by star student Julie (Karen Planden), so she turns into a flesh-famished rubber gorgon. Quick-thinking Moorhouse fends off Monster Julie by grabbing a tennis racket and firing a succession of fuzzy balls into her ungodly maw.

As the madness escalates, more boobs escape bras. More latex abominations emerge to feed and fight. More hairdos stand ever higher. Black Roses is somehow dispatched back to the undying flames from whence they came—yet now Mill Basin's misfortune is the world's peril! The band emerges six months later, playing a sold-out show at Madison Square Garden in New York City. The last we see of Damian, the diabolical singer is smiling and hissing the word "Evil!"

Black Roses is cheap and silly in the best possible ways, but also remarkably professional and continually engaging. Even blind metalheads could marvel at the majesty of Black Roses, thanks to the raised-print, relief-map-style vacuum-formed plastic VHS box shell. Pawing that bumpy copy of *Black Roses* in the video store must be a unifying Heavy Metal Movies cultural moment.

The music performed by Black Roses comes largely courtesy of King Kobra, a peroxide-blonde glam combo led by raven-haired Brooklyn-born drummer Carmine Appice, real-life legend of Vanilla Fudge, Cactus, Ted Nugent, and Ozzy Osbourne fame. His character's name is "Vinny Apache," a nod to younger brother Vinny Appice, who handled the sticks for Black Sabbath and Dio. Appice the elder also cowrote "Da Ya Think I'm Sexy?" with Rod Stewart.

The semi-official Black Roses theme song, "Me Against the World"—as performed by the band in full plastic-faced hell-spawn form—is by Lizzy Borden. Aside from their *Black Roses* soundtrack work, Lizzy Borden also appears in *The Decline of Western Civilization Part II: The Metal Years*.

Like TV's *The Twilight Zone*, where the most paranoid character is always proved to be correct, *Black Roses* takes an interesting stand against censorship and seemingly irrational fears about heavy metal. Mill Basin's grown-up population is portrayed as prudish and overprotective regarding Black Roses. Yet Black Roses really are Satan's messengers and heavy metal is their mind-warping medium. Though the film shows very little respect for metal fans, it's fun to see the worst nightmares come true instead of patiently explaining the virtues of heavy metal yet again!

BLACK SABBATH (1963), AKA THE THREE FACES OF FEAR
(DIR. MARIO BAVA; W/BORIS KARLOFF, JACQUELINE PIERREUX, MICHELE MERCIER, LIDIA ALFONSI)
✷ WITCHCRAFT ✷ VAMPIRES

Fright great Boris Karloff drolly introduces a trio of terror tales from Italian maestro Mario Bava. The European cut of the movie, titled *The Three Faces of Fear*, features more gore and a lesbian subplot missing from the American International Pictures cut, as well as a different order of the stories. But the AIP version actually inspired the birth of heavy metal.

The first story, "The Drop of Water," chronicles the hard lesson learned by a greedy nurse (Jacqueline Pierreux), not to steal rings from the fingers of dead witches. The story is tense, spooky, and legitimately hair-raising. Bava's use of color, lighting, and the witch's mobile, horribly smiling corpse make this mini-movie an absolute classic.

The second segment, "The Telephone," is a snooze. Sexy Rosy (Michele Mercier) is crank-called by her dead boyfriend. Mary (Lidia Alfonsi) comes over to calm her down. A guy we think is the dead boyfriend shows up and strangles Mary, and Rosy knifes him—only to immediately get another phone call from the dead boyfriend. You will see that coming. In the European cut, Mary and Rosy also shared a bed, which probably made the segment much more interesting.

The final piece, "The Wurdalak," is a darkly comic number with Karloff as a Russian patriarch who turns his rural family into vampires, one by one. For the record, this is the only time the man who created the world's definitive Frankenstein monster ever portrayed a vampire.

Here is the story often told: In 1969, hippie blues-rock band Earth played in Birmingham, UK. Across the street, a crowd lined up outside a movie theater showing *Black Sabbath*. Bassist Geezer Butler noticed "it was strange that people spend so much money to see scary movies."

When Butler shortly thereafter had a nightmare about a "figure in black" at the foot of his bed, he and Ozzy wrote lyrics set by Iommi to "the devil's tritone" and they called the piece—as you already know—"Black Sabbath." And then—as you also already know—that's what they called their band. And now Boris Karloff's bloodthirsty spawn number in the millions.

Black Sabbath: The Last Supper (1999)

(Dirs. Jeb Brian, Monica Hardiman; w/Ozzy Osbourne, Tony Iommi, Geezer Butler, Bill Ward)

✻ Black Sabbath ✻ Bill Ward

Those fearing that Ozzy Osbourne's naked taint might never be immortalized on film can rest easy. About forty-five minutes into the 1999 reunion tour documentary *Black Sabbath: The Last Supper*, Ozzy drops trou on stage, aims his exposed perineum at the camera, and offers an up-close view what's going on down there, along with the stretched and bobbling bits above and below that—specifically, his taint.

The rest of the movie is an eye-opener too. *The Last Supper*, in fact, proves that not only were all four Founding Fathers of Heavy Metal aboveground come the turn of the century, but they were vital and godlike and, in short, The Real Black Sabbath. Still.

The film's sole caveat is that several times, in the midst of song performances we never thought we'd witness these four horsemen gallop through again, the directors intercut interview footage. That is just—please sing the next three

words to the opening riff of "Black Sabbath"—dumb-DUMB-duhhhhhmb!

Otherwise, the interviews are sheer joy: we witness, time and again, loving and good-natured band squabbles immediately locking into a three-against-one dynamic. In this case, the drummer is usually on the poky end of that stick. But drummer Bill Ward repeatedly steals the show. Particularly moving is his confession that while enjoying long-term sobriety after years of barely surviving the living death of addiction, he had to search his soul to see if he could still, in good conscience, parade the likes of "Sweet Leaf" and "Snowblind" out to a new generation. He concluded that those songs, like the vices they celebrate, are part of his story. But the most important chapter is the one on display, in which Ward is alive and strong and awesomely shirtless as he pounds down the doors to Hades.

Black Sunday (1960), aka The Mask of Satan

(Dir. Mario Bava; w/Barbara Steele, John Richardson, Arturo Dominici, Ivo Garrani)

✻ Witchcraft ✻ Vampires

Italian horror maestro Mario Bava unveiled his craft with the grand gothic rhapsody *Black Sunday*. All hell followed. In 1630 Moldavia, Princess Asa Vajda (Barbara Steele), a malicious witch, and her henchman Javuto (Arturo Dominici) stare down an angry mob in a foggy forest. The pair are to be burned at the stake, with the executioner first hammering devil masks with long spikes inside them into the faces of the condemned. Just before the mallet hits, Asa vows revenge. Two hundred years later, Asa is revived when blood accidentally drips on her remains. She psychically summons Javuto, and the pair arise, now as vampires, to hunt her ancestors.

Black Sunday is an extended exercise in lush horror and elegant suspense with lurid carnality, unexpected shocks, and a nightmare-black soul. *Black Sunday* was markedly more violent than other fright films of its time. Three minutes were cut for the U.S. run. In England, the movie was banned outright until 1968. Mario Bava thus established Italy as the new blood-spring for cinematic terror. He became a new kind of thriller maker, the type of which had yet to be named. A few years hence, Bava followed up *Black Sunday* with *Black Sabbath* (1963), and doom wiped the floor with helter skelter.

Blessed with the most bewitching eyes ever photographed, Barbara Steele became an international star after *Black Sunday*, specializing in European gothic horror films and stylish American exploitation fare. Her follow-up spookers include *The Pit and the Pendulum* (1961), *The Horrible Dr. Hitchcock* (1962), *Castle of Blood* (1964), *Nightmare Castle* (1965), and *Curse of the Crimson Altar* (1968), as well as Fellini's *8 1/2* (1963). Among her drive-in films are *Caged Heat* (1974); *Shivers*, aka *They Came From Within* (1975); *Piranha* (1978); and *Silent Scream* (1980).

THE BLADE MASTER
(1984), AKA ATOR L'INVINCIBILE 2; THE CAVE DWELLERS
(DIR. JOE D'AMATO; W/MILES O'KEEFE, LISA FOSTER, CHEN WONG, DAVID BRANDON)
✵ SWORDS & SORCERY ✵ NUCLEAR CARNAGE

Just as 1982 begat *Ator the Fighting Eagle* to cash in on *Conan the Barbarian*, 1984 delivered *Ator*'s sequel, *The Blade Master*, just in time to ride the leather loincloth of *Conan the Destroyer*. Director Joe D'Amato reteamed with star Miles O'Keefe for a fresh adventure wherein Ator, his Asian sidekick Thong (Chen Wong), and miniskirt chick Mila (Lisa Foster) fight to save their magical world from a "geometric nucleus" weapon wielded by evil warlord Zor (David Brandon). The journey pits our crew against cannibal cavemen and a giant snake before it climaxes with the greatest "What the fucking FUCK?!" incident in all of cheeseball cinema: Ator constructs a working hang glider that he uses to fly over Zor's castle and drop bombs on the soldiers below. At the end, Ator safely dis-

poses of the "geometric nucleus" and we enjoy stock footage of atomic bomb tests. What a blast.

In 1991, *The Blade Master* was spoofed on the television program *Mystery Science Theater 3000*. Far from being insulted, Miles O'Keefe felt so tickled by Blade Master's *MST3K* treatment that he called the production office, complimented all involved, and requested a copy of the episode.

BLADE RUNNER (1982)
(DIR. RIDLEY SCOTT; W/HARRISON FORD, RUTGER HAUER, DARYL HANNAH, SEAN YOUNG)
✵ POST-APOCALYPSE ✵ SEX ROBOTS

Blade Runner bombed upon its release in summer 1982, smack between the mega-metal hits *Conan the Barbarian* and *The Road Warrior*. Adapted from the brain-bending Philip K. Dick novel *Do Androids Dream of Electric Sheep?*, *Blade Runner* may have put audiences off with its complex look or hard-to-decipher title. Regardless, punks and new wave film fans first adopted *Blade Runner* as their own; and the film's dystopian setting, technological terror, hatred of authority, questions on the nature of existence, and sheer robot brutality spoke directly to cold, powerful 1980s heavy metal.

One of *Blade Runner*'s primary visual influences was the French magazine *Metal Hurlant*, the American version of which is known as *Heavy Metal*. Of particular impact was the comic "The Long Tomorrow" by mega-metal artist Moebius. Iron Maiden ran with the theme on *Somewhere in Time* in 1986, White Zombie and countless others wrote songs cribbed from the *Blade Runner* story line, and Fear Factory made an entire career at the sizzling juicy intersection of machine and flesh, getting into the heads of replicants. Initially one of the great cult films of all time, *Blade Runner* has since come to be revered as one of cinema's defining science-fiction masterworks. The picture brings together seemingly disparate audiences who see themselves in its mysteries and draw inspiration from what it reveals.

After a catastrophic environmental disaster,

2019 Los Angeles is a rain-drenched cesspool of hustlers, crooks, and the dregs of society. The wealthy have colonized the moon, and that's where they are. The rich also enjoy androids known as "replicants" that look and act indistinguishable from people—their sales tagline, in fact, is: "More human than human." Replicants are used for warfare and slave labor, and as sexual playthings.

Sometimes, replicants rebel. Agents known as "blade runners" then hunt the androids down and terminate them. Ex–blade runner Rick Deckard (Harrison Ford) is forced out of retirement and goes in search of renegade androids Roy Batty (Rutger Hauer), Zhora (Joanna Cassidy), and Pris (Daryl Hannah), who have made it back from space to kill their creators.

Deckard's pursuit of the replicants through the neon hell of post-scorched L.A. is an awe-inspiring journey. The art direction and visual effects are history-making achievements—but also notable is the resilient humanity and commitment to connection that pulsates at *Blade Runner*'s core. Among its other pioneering accomplishments, *Blade Runner: The Director's Cut*, released theatrically in 1992, kicked off a movement enabling successful directors such as Ridley Scott to rework their commercial masterpieces.

The movie's surface elements are incandescently metal. As Rutger Hauer laments in his departing speech: "All those moments lost in time, like tears in the rain." Heavy!

The Blair Witch Project (1999)

(DIRS. DANIEL MYRICK, EDUARDO SÁNCHEZ; W/ HEATHER DONAHUE, JOSHUA LEONARD)

✵ WITCHCRAFT

If you've seen *The Blair Witch Project*—and chances are that you have seen the most famous witch movie of all time—you realize the connection to metal is tenuous, as the film consists of nothing but of shaky footage of '90s slackers traipsing through the woods and hurling F-bombs. Well, in honor of Acid Witch, Angel Witch, Witchcraft, and a hundred other awesome bands named after witches, here's a nod to the cool-looking bunches of sticks left behind by the never-seen witch, and a tip of the hat to the parting image of the bad-boy-in-the-corner being punished to certain death. That final bang of the camera rings true as a heavy doom metal riff, to be sure. For all of one second.

As with other online crazes, *The Blair Witch Project* seemed fun at the time, but there wasn't much to it, and the film has now aged about as well as any relationship with an Internet girl- or boyfriend kindled in an AOL chat room in 1999.

Blödaren (1983), aka The Bleeder

(DIR. HANS HATWIG; W/"DR. ÅKE" ERIKSSON, SUSSI AX, EVA DANIELSSON, MIA HANSSON)

✵ SLASHER ✵ SWEDEN ✵ FAKE BAND (ROCK CATS)

Sweden's first slasher film, *The Bleeder* tells the tale of a scraggly murder junkie who wags his tongue vociferously in Gene Simmons/Miley Cyrus fashion and who weeps blood constantly because his mommy was mean to him.

The existence of this freak is bad news for the Rock Cats, an all-female lite-metal combo touring the backwoods of Sweden, playing outdoor shows in the woods to all-boy audiences. Somewhere outside of Bifors, they suffer a breakdown of their extremely European-looking tour vehicle (picture a knockoff Barbie camper crossed with a quaalude). Clad in neon leopard prints, shoulder pads, hoop earrings, and (I *skit* you not) spandex jingle-bell pants, they saunter into town and cross deadly paths with the Bleeder.

After a surreal moment with a human skull in a baby carriage, *Blödaren* quickly (but, oh, so slowly) becomes a stalk-and-strangle demo reel as the Bleeder picks off a succession of Rock Cats with his bare mitts. Nice Swedish countryside. Dull murders. At least all the Rock Cats' fans grew up to start death metal bands.

Director Hans Hatwig created *Poster* magazine, a rock glossy geared to fans of Kiss and AC/DC. He used this media stranglehold to nurture the absurd misconception that the Bleeder was, in fact, an unmasked Gene Simmons. In those days, nobody knew any better. In fact, the Bleeder was portrayed by Sweden's own multi-talented prog drummer "Dr. Åke" Eriksson, who also cowrote the script.

BLOOD BATH aND BEYOND (2006)

(DIR. DON DRAKULICH; W/DAVE BROCKIE, DON DRAKULICH)

✠ SCARY PUPPETS ✠ CONCERT FOOTAGE

Blood Bath and Beyond gathers Gwar performances, music videos, lost footage, and other visual odds-and-sods for an entertaining but hardly complete retrospective of the planet-destroying career of theatrical metal's most explosively over-the-top artists and technicians. Gwar frontman Oderus Urungus (Dave Brockie) and monster-pompadour-sporting manager Sleazy P. Martini (Don Drakulich) attend an awards show and look back on the body of destruction built by everyone's favorite heavy metal collective from outer space. We see many clips from the many stages of the bands three decades of mayhem.

A proper Gwar documentary is beyond overdue. Humanity requires a fun but serious cinematic account of the history of this remarkable ensemble and its unique place in rock. *Blood Bath and Beyond* is more like Cheech and Chong's VHS release *Get Out of My Room* (1985): too little, too lackadaisical, and too loose. A squib too far. As Gwar's video productions lost steam in the 2000s, Oderus Urungus took on new media life as an occasional contributor to Fox News. As much as that sounds like a detail from one of their berserk stage shows, it is actually true.

BLOOD CULT (1985)

(DIR. CHRISTOPHER LEWIS; W/JULI ANDELMAN, CHARLES ELLIS, JAMES VANCE)

✠ SLASHER ✠ SATAN ✠ BLACK MASS ✠ HUMAN SACRIFICE ✠ DUNGEONS & DRAGONS

Blood Cult turned cheapness into an effective ballyhoo gimmick. The movie was shot on camcorders in 1985, and the big sales pitch was the chance to view the first extreme gore movie "made for the home video market!" At the time, seeing occult dismemberment in a format akin to afternoon soap operas actually did seem pretty cool. Now that we modern B-horror fanatics see almost nothing but, one is tempted to sneer, "Thanks a lot, *Blood Cult*!"

An unknown slasher stalks an Oklahoma campus, slaughtering coeds and leaving gold trinkets in place of stolen body parts. Charles Ellis portrays the gruff cop on the killer's trail, and his main hunch is that the crimes might be connected to Dungeons & Dragons. In fact, it's all the work of a satanic cult, but all we care about is seeing the bad guy beat one screamer senseless with her roommate's decapitated head.

Misleading ad copy notwithstanding, many other shot-on-video horror movies beat *Blood Cult* out of the box, including *Blood Beat* (1983), *Sledgehammer* (1983), and *Twisted Illusions* (1985). Most remarkable is *Boardinghouse* (1982), which was transferred to film for a 1985 theatrical release. This fantastically insane film's resulting washed-out blurriness was promoted as "Horrorvision."

BLOOD FEAST (1963)

(DIR. HERSCHELL GORDON LEWIS; W/MAL ARNOLD, CONNIE MASON, WILLIAM KERWIN, LYN BOLTON)

✠ GORE ✠ CANNIBALISM ✠ EGYPT

Let us now, as fans of gory horror films—as I assume we all probably are—take a moment to pay sanguine respect to *Blood Feast*, the pioneering outrage by director Herschell Gordon Lewis and producer David F. Friedman.

In this film, the first gore movie, Fuad Ramses (Mal Arnold), an Egyptian caterer servicing well-to-do housewives of Miami, murders nubile young women and cooks their bodies in the dishes he feeds to his customers. It's part of a ritual he hopes will bring the ancient goddess Ishtar to life. Ramses commits graphic killings before our eyes and the blood-red carnage is captured in unflinching, close-up detail: a bathing woman is stabbed in the eye and dismembered with a machete; a teen girl's scalp is sliced open and her brain is pulled out of her skull; and a drunken sailor's motel room conquest has her tongue ripped from her mouth. One survivor merely has her face flayed off.

After attending a local lecture on Egyptian blood rites and perusing the book *Ancient Weird Religious Rites*, which is ubiquitous in this movie, Detective Pete Thornton (William Kerwin) tries to connect the death spree to the intensely eyebrowed caterer. Thornton's lackadaisical ineptitude as a cop is topped only by the acting anti-ability of his sexual target, *Playboy* centerfold Connie Mason, who is also unknowingly the final female sacrifice impotent Ramses needs to finish his Ishtar project.

Blood Feast ends, hilariously, with Ramses lurching across a landfill, the cripple somehow outrunning the Miami Beach police force. He jumps into a garbage truck to escape the cops, only to be crushed in the compactor. "A fitting end," lawman Thornton says, "for the garbage that he was!"

For all the campy ridiculousness of *Blood Feast*, Lewis's masterpiece barrels recklessly through the limits of cinema violence and still rates as effective extreme horror. That breakthrough changed art and culture overall, setting the stage, musically, for hard rock expanding its reach to such far-flung genres as death metal twenty years later. Just as there had to be a Screaming Lord Sutch and a Crazy World of Arthur Brown before there could be an Alice Cooper and a King Diamond, *Blood Feast* made possible every subsequent fright-film boundary pusher, high-

and lowbrow alike, from *Night of the Living Dead* (1968) to *The Texas Chain Saw Massacre* (1974) to *Cannibal Holocaust* (1982) to *Martyrs* (2008) to *Antichrist* (2009).

Blood Feast's moronic timpani theme and lunatic organ score were composed and performed by director Lewis himself. Had he waited a few decades, he might have asked for music from the B-level New Jersey thrash metal band Blood Feast, or any of the countless "Blood Feast" songs by bands including Ghoul, Krampus, Six Feet Under, and Misfits.

BLOOD INTO WINE (2010)

(DIRS. RYAN PAGE, CHRISTOPHER POMERENKE; W/ MAYNARD JAMES KEENAN, ERIC GLOMSKI, MILLA JOVOVICH, PATTON OSWALT, TIM HEIDECKER)

✣ METAL REALITY ✣ OBSESSION

As a documentary concept, "rock star opens winery" seems like the basis for a gross commercial puff piece. When the side-jobbing musician is Maynard James Keenan of Tool, A Perfect Circle, and Puscifer, and he is joined by comedy mutants Tim and Eric, *Blood Into Wine* all of a sudden turns intriguing.

The finished movie makes good on a cockeyed promise. Turns out Keenan is a third-generation *vino* maker, hailing from grape-crushing stock in northern Italy. Eric Glomski, his partner in an Arizona vineyard, makes his artful and scientific approach to winemaking look engaging for the camera. Comedian Patton Oswalt busts balls about the inherent douchebaggery of wine culture, and actress Milla Jovovich pretties things up. Many bands have created much worse documents of the recordings of their latest CDs; as is par for the course, Keenan tries something different and proves there is blood running in his wine-sopped heart.

BLOOD ON SATAN'S CLAW (1971), AKA SATAN'S SKIN

(DIR. PIERS HAGGARD; W/PATRICK HYMARK, BARRY ANDREWS, LINDA HAYDEN)

✴ DEMON WORSHIP ✴ WITCHCRAFT

In always-so-less-than-jolly seventeenth-century England, farmer Ralph Gower (Barry Andrews) unearths a mutant skull covered in patches of ugly fur. The eye still peering out from one of its sockets appears to Ralph to be evidence of some kind of monster. The town judge (Patrick Hymark) laughs off such a notion. And then the strangeness starts.

Area youths begin playing strange and violent games, culminating in human sacrifice to resurrect an evil god called Behemoth. Ralph dug up his skull, and now his claw is stirring up trouble in an attic. Other locals sprout hairy body parts, which they deem "Satan's Skin." These appendages need to be hacked off, quite bloodily, in order to physically reassemble Behemoth, bit by bit. In addition to this delectably diabolical setup, *Blood on Satan's Claw* supplies demon rape in an attic, a witch's coven taking over a church, and full-frontal devil-dance nudity from a demonic teenage temptress named Angel (Linda Hayden).

A too-abrupt, even laughable ending after all that is the only factor keeping *Blood on Satan's Claw* from the uppermost echelons of British horror. And British horror is what gave the world heavy metal to begin with, you know. Finnish doom band Reverend Bizarre paid homage with their song "Blood on Satan's Claw..

In the 2010 BBC documentary *A History of Horror*, Mark Gatiss of UK comedy troupe the League of Gentlemen grouped *Blood on Satan's Claw* in with *Witchfinder General* (1968) and *The Wicker Man* (1973) as prime examples of the short-lived "folk horror" film subgenre. All three films were released by Tigon Productions, and each branded the flesh of heavy metal with hot irons.

BLOOD TRACKS (1985), AKA HEAVY METAL; SHOCKING HEAVY METAL

(DIR. MATS HELGE; W/JEFF HARDING, MICHAEL FITZPATRICK, NAOMI KANEDA, BRAD POWELL)

✴ MUTANTS ✴ HAIR METAL ✴ SWEDISH SENSATIONSFILM

Eighty quick minutes long and made in Sweden, *Blood Tracks* opens in 1945 with a wife murdering her drunken lout husband and hightailing it with her kids to parts unknown. The action then jumps ahead forty years to a mountainside music video shoot for the band Solid Gold (played by the real band Easy Action), who rock so hard they bring on an avalanche!

The band and the groupies spend the rest of the film trapped in a cabin, alternately fucking, futzing with walkie-talkies, and getting all kinds of fucked up by the family from the beginning of the movie who are now inbred snow cannibals living nearby in an abandoned factory.

Unlike so many other wrongheaded gore flicks of its day, the poodle-headed *Blood Tracks* actually gets better as it goes along. Easy Action would get their forty-eight-inch-platform bootlaces tied together by even the most flamboyant cast members of *Decline and Fall of Western Civilization II*. So what starts out dopey and amiably embarrassing steadily swells into genuine lunacy and mirthful mortification. At one point, a nubile groupie is trapped in a Volvo, and during her rescue her clothes are torn apart.

Blood Tracks should be watched looking up at the screen so the movie's copious idiotic glam metal joys can pummel down like all those boobs and snowdrifts do to our cabin-bound heroes. Nutbar auteur Mats Helge previously directed the off-the-wall martial arts romp *The Ninja Mission* (1984). For the U.S. release of *Blood Tracks*, he's credited as "Mike Jackson." His further escapades are chronicled in the Daniel Ekeroth book *Swedish Sensationsfilms*, and the documentary *The Director Who Disappeared* (2013).

Stretching their range in the collective role of Solid Gold, Stockholm-based Easy Action in reality began as a hard-edged metal band in 1981 before heading in a more glam direction with some success in Scandinavia. Guitarist and leader Kee Marcello departed Easy Action in 1986 and joined Europe just in time for *The Final Countdown*. Singer Zinny Zan moved to America and became the frontman of Shotgun Messiah.

BLOODSTONE: SUBSPECIES II (1993)

(DIR. TED NICOLAOU; W/ANDERS HOVE, DENICE DUFF, KEVIN SPIRTAS, PAMELA GORDON)

✠ VAMPIRES ✠ CONCERT FOOTAGE ✠ ROMANIA

From the late 1980s through pretty deep into the 1990s, filmmaker Charles Band's Full Moon Studios maintained a high standard in low-budget horror. The outfit pumped out a long parade of entertaining B-movies such as *Trancers, Demonic Toys,* and the popular *Puppet Master* movies. (Three cheers for *Puppet Master 4,* where we meet Decapitron!) The *Subspecies* franchise saw the studio team with *Fangoria* magazine to create something barely more polished, shot on location in Romania with visual effects that go beyond marionettes with knife hands.

Vampire Radu Vladislas (Anders Hove) is the *Subspecies* antihero: a full-blown, slobbering, white-faced demon-ghoul who dwells in a spooky castle. He lords over extremely cool stop-motion-animated creatures—the creepy-crawly subspecies of the title. Radu has been doing standard bloodsucking for centuries, but in the anything-goes early 1990s, his existence is rocked by Michelle Morgan, a traveling college student. He goes batshit trying to make her his unholy bride, and their doomed, one-sided romance drives the entire multipart *Subspecies* saga. Adding to the delirium, Michelle is portrayed by different actresses in different installments.

The original *Subspecies* (1991) boasts *Phantasm*'s Tall Man, Angus Scrimm, as Radu's father, but *Subspecies II* wins the Heavy Metal Movies prize, thanks to 13 Ghosts. This highly competent thrash band tears up the stage at the club Vex. Graffiti over the entrance declares "Metal Rules" and "No Future," uncovering the punk-metal crossover in vampire-inundated Eastern Europe. Michelle (Denice Duff) navigates Vex's dance floor, populated by exactly the type of headbangers you'd expect to see in a low-budget vampire movie shot in Romania. Meanwhile, the metal quotient goes through the roof as 13 Ghosts performs two admirably slow-style Slayer-like numbers, the burning "Beneath the Gravestone" (which also appears in the previously praised *Puppet Master 4*) and "Death of Innocence," an all-out neck-snapper. The 13 Ghosts band, apparently consisting of guys from the in-house FX department, plays a doomy, captivating thrash metal. Too bad they never released any material or even a soundtrack for this film.

Bloodlust: Subspecies III (1994) is next in the series, followed by *Vampire Journals* (1997), a spin-off film about a supporting vampire named Ash. *Subspecies IV: Bloodstorm* finally put a stake in the whole bloody affair. Despite multiple unrelated films titled *13 Ghosts*, the 13 Ghosts band in *Bloodstone* never rose again.

BLOODSUCKING FREAKS (1976), AKA THE INCREDIBLE TORTURE SHOW

(DIR. JOEL M. REED; W/SEAMUS O'BRIEN, LUIS DE JESUS, VIJU KREM)

✠ TORTURE ✠ SNUFF ✠ BANNED VIDEO NASTY

You won't believe the eye. Nine minutes into *Bloodsucking Freaks*, the torture porn that begat all torture porn, the nastiest of all video nasties, the death metal freak show from the decade prior to the freak-birth of death metal—a giddy dwarf on a theater stage hacksaws through the wrist of a screaming nude blonde. He removes her hand, kisses it, and holds it aloft in triumph. The well-dressed audience applauds.

"Now the eye, Ralphus!" instructs the saturnine

emcee. The devious dwarf reaches into the weeping victim's ocular cavity, plucks out her meaty, dripping peeper, and pops it into his mouth. Then he chews it up and swallows it—right on camera. Again, the hoity-toity audience applauds.

And so a challenge line is drawn in *Bloodsucking Freaks*, and over its filthy course the movie itself repeatedly crosses that border, brandishing chains, chainsaws, whips, thumbscrews, starvation, brainwashing, brain-siphoning, and an unholy host of other atrocious demonstrations of man's inhumanity to man; or, more specifically, man's inhumanity to naked woman. The gates of grossness were afterward forever open wide.

Bloodsucking Freaks is sick, and very funny, but unlike the best-known products of the studio it helped launch, Troma, this movie is no joke. Our hero, Sardu (Seamus O'Brien), is an elegant, highly histrionic older gentleman in warlock garb who runs the Theater of the Macabre in Manhattan's SoHo district, at the time a burgeoning enclave of artists and "cutting-edge" performers. Ralphus (Luis De Jesus) is Sardu's midget assistant and constant companion.

To secure performers for their nightly extravaganzas, Sardu runs a white-slavery ring. Virginal young women are delivered in crates, kept nude and unfed in a basement cage, and then requisitioned as needed for grotesque sexual tortures, both onstage and off. Sardu and Ralphus also use these bedraggled slaves as furniture and, in one rib-tickler of a scene, as a dartboard. While quaffing steins of beer, they toss darts at a target painted on one girl's anus. Then they play backgammon using severed fingers.

Among the theater's human resource suppliers is The Doctor (Ernie Pysher), a mad dentist who yanks out a woman's teeth with pliers and then drills a hole into her head, into which he inserts a straw and sucks out the goop inside. Between such sensory-overloading set pieces, *Bloodsucking Freaks'* plot hinges on Sardu kidnapping snooty theater critic Creasy Silo (Allan Dellay) and famous ballerina Natasha D'Natalie (Viju Krem). The dancer's boyfriend, NFL superstar

Tom Maverick (Niles McMaster), and the NYPD's Sergeant John Tucci (Dan Fauci) pursue her into the pits of Sardu's diabolical dominion.

The real meat, of course, is the human meat being pulled, prodded, spiked, flayed, and flambéed every which way in the set pieces that separate the story sequences. Especially uproarious is the exposé of Sardu as a mincing masochist. *Bloodsucking Freaks* violates every taboo short of committing actual murder on camera, in a spirit of jubilant celebration. It wants you to smile as you wince and salute with devil horns as you retch.

Aside from Joel M. Reed's well-paced, consistently effective film (if you ever see his lesser-known works, you'll understand this one was a fluke), the performances elevate *Bloodsucking Freaks* further still from mere geek show to something unforgettable. Dellay, Fauci, and McMaster (who appeared on the ABC soap *Edge of Night*) are great, as is Krem, a real-life fashion model who convincingly pulls off her deadly pas de deux.

Seamus O'Brien gives one of the loftiest high camp performances in the annals of wrongheaded entertainment. It's impossible not to believe that this lanky, crystal-eyed, effete weirdo really exists somewhere; that once the cameras shut off, somehow this ghoul just took off his sorcerer robe and went home. O'Brien starred in the long-running Off-Broadway institution *The Fantasticks* throughout the filming of *Bloodsucking Freaks*. His only other movie credit is *The Happy Hooker* (1975). After Sardu, whatever body of berserk work might have lain ahead of him got snuffed out in 1977 during a knife fight with a burglar in O'Brien's New York apartment.

The overwhelmingly iconic character in *Bloodsucking Freaks*, though, is homicidal half-pint Ralphus. Luis De Jesus danced as a space alien in funk group Parliament Funkadelic's lavish concert productions and later donned an Ewok costume for *Return of the Jedi*. Luis's most celebrated non-Ralphus film role, however, is as the title character opposite porn star Vanessa Del Rio in the 1971 hard-core loop *The Anal Dwarf*.

Bloodsucking Freaks premiered in 1976 as *The Incredible Torture Show*. After making no particular waves, Troma retitled it *Bloodsucking Freaks* and put it back on the grindhouse/drive-in circuit. Technically speaking, *Bloodsucking Freaks* is the first movie produced and distributed by Troma Films, and is unquestionably their best movie.

Soon, *Bloodsucking Freaks* caught on as a VHS sensation worldwide. Teenagers everywhere submitted to the litmus test of whether they could stand the onscreen sickness instead of cringing and turning away. The watchdog group Women Against Pornography protested the showing of *Bloodsucking Freaks* in Times Square, just as they would the mighty *Maniac* in 1980. The group of course, was tipped off well in advance by Troma's publicity department. Pickets sell tickets.

The specific imagery—bondage, kidnapping, physical torment, sexual degradation, body eating—brings to life the stuff of countless death metal albums, even tumbling into the antic arena of gore-grind. Also as with death and grind, the engine of *Bloodsucking Freaks* is its joy in its own ceaseless bombastic transgression.

As with metal in general, as well, the movie raises questions of cyclical outrage. Why so much brouhaha over *Saw* and *Hostel* and Rob Zombie movies when, multiple decades earlier, *Bloodsucking Freaks* displayed way worse scenes, in greater numbers, at a higher level of intensity? Any movie where evil dwarf Ralphus gets head from an actual decapitated noggin should only end, as this one does, by showing a naked nubile biting with relish into a hot-dog bun containing a freshly torn-off human penis.

BLUE VENGEANCE (1989)

(DIRS. J. CHRISTIAN INGVORDSEN, DANNY KUCHUCK; W/J. CHRISTIAN INGVORDSEN, JOHN WEINER, JAKE LAMOTTA, THE LUNACHICKS)
✙ SLASHER ✙ REVENGE

As was expected of many teens, Mark Trax (John Weiner) hears some heavy metal and goes kill crazy. In capturing the young fiend,

known by his *nom de blood* Mirrorman, NYPD detective Mickey McCardle (J. Christian Ingvordsen) loses his partner to crossfire. Ten years later, Mirrorman escapes. Somebody starts gorily offing various New York rock scene figures, including members of the band that inspired Mirrorman to go mad in the first place. McCardle is the only one who recognizes the pattern, and he'll stop at nothing to get his man.

Blue Vengeance is a late-'80s/early-'90s standard not-quite-ready-for-cable VHS revenge thriller. The metal spin helps, but what will actually stick in your head are Mirrorman's fantasies of being a medieval knight battling rubber-suit monsters. He believes them to be enemies of heavy metal. Obviously, that's insane! NYC scum-rock she-legends the Lunachicks literally bust things up on stage at CBGB, and watch for a cameo by Jake LaMotta, the real-life boxer on whom *Raging Bull* (1980) was based.

BOOK OF SHADOWS: BLAIR WITCH 2 (2000)

(DIR. JOE BERLINGER; W/KIM DIRECTOR, JEFFREY DONOVAN, ERICA LEERHSEN, TRISTINE SKYLER)
✙ WITCHCRAFT ✙ GOTH CHICKS ✙ BACKWARD MASKING ✙ SOUNDTRACK (TONY IOMMI)

The widely panned sequel to the previous year's *The Blair Witch Project* is actually an okay neo-dead-teenager movie that makes good use of a solid metal soundtrack. *Book of Shadows* even attempts a meta-commentary on the original phenomenon, tracking a gaggle of *Blair Witch* fans traveling to the movie's location. The premise is intriguing: what if events that you clearly remember exist on video as something violently different?

Alas, not a lot is made of these big ideas, just some murder and spookery and a pair of goth chicks who embody contemporary teen-witch archetypes: lithe Erica Leerhsen as a tree-humping, free-love Wiccan and voluptuous, corpse-skinned, raven-maned Kim Director as a cynical, chain-smoking death-rock betty in big black boots. Her character name, "Kim Diamond," is a tribute to King Diamond of Mercyful Fate.

Director Joe Berlinger also co-helmed the *Paradise Lost* documentaries about the West Memphis Three, heavy metal victims of an unjust legal system. Here he indulged in a different form of gravitas, staging an omnisexual drug-and-booze orgy in the woods to Queens of the Stone Age's mighty "Feel Good Hit of the Summer." The gimmick for the *Book of Shadows* home video release was "The Secret of Esrever." At certain points in the movie, viewers were encouraged to rewird a scene to see semi-subliminal messages; pretty "bmud" either way.

Bordello of Blood

(1996)

(Dir. Gilbert Adler; w/Dennis Miller, Erika Eleniak, Angie Everhart, Corey Feldman)

✠ Vampire Hookers ✠ Soundtrack (Cinderella, Scorpions, Sweet, Thin Lizzy, Anthrax)

The second big-screen venture for HBO's *Tales From the Crypt* series introduces Dennis Miller as a wisecracking private eye. When a busty blonde (Erika Eleniak) hires him to hunt down her missing degenerate brother (Corey Feldman), the trail leads to a funeral home run by vampires that acts as a front for undead prostitutes—yes, a bordello of blood! Corey Feldman, one of the vampire-slaying Frog brothers in *The Lost Boys* (1987), plays a vampire, hunted here by a priest portrayed by Chris Sarandon, the vampire from *Fright Night* (1985).

As with the TV series, everything here is slick and self-aware, and the stench of Spielbergian fake edginess abounds. Miller is funny, though, and the very of-the-moment idea to load Super Soaker water rifles with holy water is clever. Miller's climactic siege of the unholy whorehouse, set to Sweet's "Ballroom Blitz," is where the movie comes closest to scoring.

The cackling corpse Crypt Keeper puppet, who does the pun-filled intros and outros, has never charmed me, though Lord knows I've tried to love him. On the other hand, Anthrax's "Bordello of Blood" theme song is hard charging and flecked with cool absorption of grunge revamping of dirty-bluesy '70s heaviness.

Born in the Basement

(2007)

(Dir. Lori DeAngelis-Kundrat; w/Rat Skates, Chris Antonucci, Ralph Iovino)

✠ Thrash Metal ✠ Metal Reality ✠ Obsession

Energetic and affable, drummer Rat Skates tells his story, from slamming skins for New York City punks the Lubricunts to ultimately masterminding New Jersey thrash machine Overkill. Skates spins one great yarn after another, each of which is visualized on-screen by effectively edited archival footage and scenes incorporating actual remnants of his storied hard rock past.

All along, we see Rat designing Overkill's logo, rubber-stamping every record, and plastering posters up and down the East Coast. But the absolute highlight is Skates covering dozens of milk crates with cardboard painted to look like dungeon bricks. Like that, Skates not only builds Overkill's gothic stage set, but he constructs a huge riser for his drum—complete with a working gate underneath so that vocalist Bobby Blitz could make a dramatic entrance in concert.

Born in the Basement fills in cracks left by official accounts. For example: the Lubricunts stuff. With video from *The Uncle Floyd Show* and newspaper clippings demonstrating the wildly all-encompassing music scene circa 1980, Skates shows us first-wave New York punk played by dirty-faced, dirty-minded dirtbags who went heavy metal once they got their technical chops up. In the way that many describe the New Wave of British Heavy Metal as "metal played with punk attitude," Skates points to the Dead Boys as his early idols, noting how singer Stiv Bators and guitarist Cheetah Chrome, in particular, were "punks who played hard rock like metal guys."

Typically, the telling of thrash metal's story begins in California, with Metallica, Slayer, and Exodus, but here we see how Overkill evolved from Garden State punk gumption to world-class technical virtuosity, and from horror theatrics to "street" aesthetics. The rule of Skates came to a complete stop when he departed Overkill in 1987 due to general burnout. The version of the band's early years on display here is his and his alone—and an entertaining and informative ride.

BRAINSCAN (1994)

(DIR. JOHN FLYNN; W/EDWARD FURLONG, FRANK LANGELLA, T. RYDER SMITH, AMY HARGREAVES)

✡ HORROR ✡ SOUNDTRACK (WHITE ZOMBIE, PRIMUS, BUTTHOLE SURFERS, MUDHONEY)

Edward Furlong caromed from *Terminator 2* (1991) to Aerosmith's monumental "Livin' on the Edge" music video to *Brainscan*, a misguided attempt to create a new horror antihero in the vein of Freddy and Jason. The supernatural slayer of the hour, Trickster, comes with a '90s tie-in soundtrack stacked high with Lollapalooza stars, but a name saddled with memories of '80s New Jersey hair-glam band Trixter.

Furlong plays a kid with Aerosmith posters on his wall who monkeys with the wrong technology. Since this film is set in 1995, the "wrong technology" means novelties such as virtual reality, CD-ROM discs, and anything that can be labeled "interactive." Like Clint Howard hacking his way to hell in *Evilspeak*, Furlong downloads Trickster to real life, and subpar horror movie crap happens. The movie sets up a sequel that never made it to any reality, virtual or otherwise. Contributing to *Brainscan*'s limpness is a killer sporting a ludicrous flaming red Mohawk-mullet, a pirate shirt, a velvet jacket, and leather pants, with exquisitely buffed cocaine-scoop fingernails from the mousse-metal era. Who could fear that?

BRIDE OF CHUCKY (1998)

(DIR. RONNY YU; W/BRAD DOURIF, JENNIFER TILLY, KATHERINE HEIGL, ALEXIS ARQUETTE, JOHN RITTER)

✡ EVIL DOLL ✡ BLACK MAGIC ✡ SOUNDTRACK (COAL CHAMBER, BRUCE DICKINSON, JUDAS PRIEST, MOTÖRHEAD, SLAYER, STATIC-X, WHITE ZOMBIE)

Chucky, the killer doll from *Child's Play* (1988) and its two sequels, goes officially, fantastically metal in *Bride of Chucky*. He's burnt, banged-up, scarred all over, and, thanks to botched voodoo involving an androgynous goth (Alexis Arquette), partnered with sexy rubber love toy Tiffany. Brad Dourif again voices Chucky, the serial murderer trapped in a toddler-size plastic toy body. Jennifer Tilly camps it up, first in voluptuous human form, then as lethally living plaything Tiffany.

The very gory *Bride of Chucky* is fleet-footed, ferociously funny, and exciting way beyond what anyone could rightly expect from a long-delayed fourth series installment. Solid horror jolts abound, and one sequence guarantees wincing, moaning, and, ultimately, nauseated laughter; Chucky and Tiffany's lengthy sexual encounter involves horrendously passionate French kissing with very human, very saliva-soaked tongues.

Hong Kong director Ronny Yu delivers the goods in grand fashion, as he would again in *Freddy vs. Jason* (2003). Add in a state-of-the-late-'90s nu metal party soundtrack, and *Bride of Chucky* is forever worth celebrating. After *Bride of Chucky*, Universal Studios officially anointed Chucky one of the classic "Universal Monsters," joining the ranks of Boris Karloff's Frankenstein, Bela Lugosi's Dracula, and Lon Chaney Jr.'s Wolfman.

Bummer (1973),
aka The Sadist
(Dir. William Allen Castleman; w/Dennis Burkley, Connie Strickland, Carol Speed)
✠ Proto-Metal ✠ Sunset Strip ✠ Groupies

The original tagline for rock and roll murder freak-out *Bummer* was "You don't have to rape a groupie—you just have to ask!" For the final poster (a painting of a dazed Paul McCartney lookalike embracing a topless blonde nubile), the word *rape* was softened to *assault*, but this schlock flick's nasty edge was hardly dulled.

The Group, as the rock band at the center of the story is called, attracts three female followers called the Groupies. Flaxen-haired Barbara (Connie Strickland), redhead Dolly (Diane Lee Hart), and African-American Janyce (Carol Speed) spread their affections among the members of a garage-psych combo that sounds like the Strawberry Alarm Clock with a broken spring. Nobody breaks off a piece for obese, sweaty, antisocial bass player Butts (Dennis Burkley). It's all fun and head games until Butts blows a mental gasket and goes shotgun and forced-sex bonkers.

Duke (Kipp Whitman), the singer, looks a bit like Rob Tyner of the MC5, and Butts is a dead-on lard-ass harbinger of the today's elite population of out-of-shape stoner dudes with beards. The setting—drug-numbed early-1970s Sunset Strip—is worth the trip just for the neon lights. *Bummer* director William Allen Castleman came by the job naturally. He wrote and performed the scores of numerous exploitation films including *She Freak* (1967), *The Big Bird Cage* (1972), and *The Swinging Cheerleaders* (1974).

The Bunny Game (2010)
(Dir. Adam Rehmeier; w/Rodleen Getsic, Norwood Fisher, Gregg Gilmore, Paul Ill, Jeff F. Renfro)
✠ Torture ✠ Soundtrack (Harassor)

The *Bunny Game* opens with a close-up of a woman's face. There's a plastic bag drawn tight over her head and she's gasping and flailing and on fire with a will to not die. The rest of this stark, black-and-white horror-drama is an attempt to make you feel like she does in that moment. Sometimes, it really works.

Bunny (Rodleen Getsic) is a druggie streetwalker who picks up trucker Hog (Jeff F. Renfro)—very much the wrong kind of trick. Like *Scrapbook* (2000), *The Bunny Game* goes on to unflinchingly chronicle the ensuing abuse, so it's up to the actors to keep us compelled. The entire film is improvised. Renfro, for sure, is completely unpleasant. Getsic commits to the point of actually getting beaten bloody, burned with a blowtorch, and branded with hot metal on camera.

Unlike in *Scrapbook*, though, the arch artiness of the black-and-white photography and, worse, the occasionally epileptic editing mean that at no point will you have to remind yourself, "It's only a movie.... It's only a movie...." That's certainly counterproductive in a movie where what's special about the effects is that they're not effects, but real documented explosions of violence. Death metal band Harassor provides appropriately atonal and hurtful songs to the soundtrack.

Rodleen Getsic, in interviews, says she used to be a prostitute and endured numerous abductions. She also says she went right from filming *The Bunny Game* to a spa and spiritual retreat to recover. The film itself in 2011 went right to Los Angeles's first-ever Heavy Metal Film Festival.

Burial Ground: The Nights of Terror

(1981), aka Nights of Terror; Flesheater; Zombi 3

(Dir. Andrea Bianchi; w/Peter Bark, Mariangela Giordano, Karin Well, Gianluigi Chirizzi)

✠ Italian Horror ✠ Zombies

The most rabidly insane among the many, many zombie chunk-blowers to rise up from Italy in the gore-sopped wake of George Romero's *Dawn of the Dead* (1978) and Lucio Fulci's *Zombie* (1979), this film is soaked in ungodly and unsavory sexuality, courtesy of the director of venereal Euro-sleaze gems such as *What the Peeper Saw* (1972), *Strip Nude for Your Killer* (1975), and *Malabimba, the Malicious Whore* (1979). The zombies in this landmark transgression descend inexplicably from the ancient Etruscan people of Tuscany. The plot is minimal—a reckless professor invites three couples and a kid to a castle—and is meant to deliver as much graphic flesh flaying and wound chewing as can be packed into the film cans. Truly the most bat-guano berserk undead Italo-splatter epic of all, this movie delivers some delightful abominations not contained in any other celluloid outrage.

Unforgettably freaky, wig-wearing, twenty-five-year-old small person Peter Bark is cast in the role of Michael, a twelve-year-old perv obsessed with sucking on the hot tits of his sexy mom (Mariangela Giordano). Best of all, after he goes zombie, young Michael gets to enjoy more than just an Oedipal mouthful. Bark ranks among the greatest of cinema's "one and done" thespians. His single credited movie performance is as Michael in *Burial Ground: The Nights of Terror.* In the aftermath of *Burial Ground*'s rediscovery and cult embracement in the 2000s, sleuths spotted and made a record of Bark in several unacknowledged roles in Italian obscurities. Among them: Whistling Guy in *Liquirizia* (1979) and Boy Scout in Train in *Vai Alla Grande* (1983).

Mariangela Giordano, who plays Michael's reluctant (at first) breast-feeder mom, was a veteran vixen of Italian cinema who later in her career nakedly embraced her country's fantastically lurid grindhouse output. Aside from *Burial Ground*, Mariangela starred nude in the aforementioned *Malabimba, the Malicious Whore*, and in *Patrick Still Lives* (1980), *Eroticón* (1981), and *Satan's Baby Doll* (1982). At age fifty-nine, Mariangela made a nude comeback in *Killer Barbys* (1996), a vehicle for Spain's eponymous garage-punk band, directed by gore legend Jess Franco.

Drunkenly paced; loaded with kill scenes that will make you moan and cheer out loud, and even genuinely spooky, *Burial Ground* is a pioneering death metal movie that embodies the early days of Venom, Slayer, Possessed, and Death. Everything a headbanger could hope for in a zombie film rises up and attacks.

Burial Ground: Nights of Terror blipped briefly on U.S. screens, doing a quick drive-in and fleapit theater run in 1986. One lucky critic who caught it was Rick Sullivan, publisher of the revered horror zine *Gore Gazette*, which named *Burial Ground* the "G.G. Movie of the Year."

The Burning (1981)

(Dir. Tony Maylam; w/Brian Matthews, Leah Ayers, Lou David, Jason Alexander, Holly Hunter)

✠ Slasher ✠ Tom Savini ✠ Soundtrack (Yes/ Black Sabbath keyboard man Rick Wakeman)

The Burning was the first film to specifically invoke the summer camp legend of Cropsy—the caretaker who's the victim of a prank gone wrong who then haunts the woods forever to exact revenge on future campers. I first heard of Cropsy in 1978, as a nine-year-old cub scout at Camp Alpine in the Catskills. The tale that kept me up that night was that some past scouts pulled a stunt that burned down Cropsy's cabin. The prank killed his wife and baby, and left him physically scarred and permanently pissed off.

The Burning's version of the tale opens sans wife and baby, with a bachelor Cropsy screaming in flames. The action jumps five years ahead in time, with Cropsy getting out of the hospital and, like any burn victim, immediately hitting glorious old Forty-Second Street for some double-sawbuck companionship. Once the first professional orgasm deliverer he encounters gets a load of Cropsy's melted Madball complexion, though, she freaks. He cools the situation by gutting her with scissors. Immediately, Cropsy dreams bigger: he picks up some industrial-size garden shears and heads back to the camp.

The imperiled campers are the typical mixed bag of jokers, jocks, hotties, and virgins, with young Jason Alexander (*Seinfeld*) standing out with a full head of luxurious locks. Holly Hunter and Fisher Stevens, who loses his fingers and how, also debuted in *The Burning*. Essentially a litany of active ingredients, *The Burning* is one of the purest *Friday the 13th* cash-ins of the early '80s.

Behind the scenes, *The Burning* was written by future movie moguls Harvey and Bob Weinstein, and was the inaugural release of the Miramax Films empire. Tom Savini passed up *Friday the 13th Part 2* to create *The Burning*'s blood and guts. In some territories, it was probably passed off as a sequel—and plenty prefer it to *Friday the 13th*; but similar to what could be said of the proliferation of Bruce Dickinson knockoffs during the same era, there is only one Jason Voorhees.

The Burning Moon

(1997)

(Dir. Olaf Ittenbach; w/Beate Neumeyer, Bernd Muggenthaler, Ellen Fischer)

✠ German Gore ✠ Hell ✠ Serial Killer

"No matter what you have heard," boasts the official DVD cover of director Olaf Ittenbach's long-bootlegged barf bag horror legend, "You have never seen anything like *The Burning Moon*." If we have learned anything from the likes of *Nekromantik* and *Violent Shit*—it's to trust the "Holy *scheiße*!" hype when it comes to extreme splatter outrages from Germany.

Shot on video in 1992, *The Burning Moon* pukes out mad, manic energy from its first moment, spinning a pair of sick and sadistic sagas that are perversely set up as bedtime stories read by a belligerent junkie (played by Ittenbach) to his kid sister. The first tale regards a rape-and-decapitation-happy serial murderer running roughshod over a suburban hamlet. The second is a relatively elaborate fantasia of a priest who, like the initial anti-hero, is in no way averse to fatal sexual assault and creative mutilation. The difference is that when the creepozoid man of the cloth pins his crimes on a local dimwit, mob justice is meted out; then, direct from Hell, supernatural torture vengeance befalls the vigilantes. *The Burning Moon* is all about the brilliantly executed gore effects, amphetamine editing rhythms, and intermittent forays of inexplicable lunacy.

Necrophagia pays proper homage via its 2001 track, "Burning Moon Sickness."

The Butterfly Ball

(1977)

(Dir. Tony Klinger; w/Roger Glover, Twiggy, Vincent Price, Ian Gillan, Ronnie James Dio)

✠ Concert Footage ✠ Proto-Metal

The Butterfly Ball documents a live rock opera at the Royal Albert Hall, adapted from a solo album of the same name by Deep Purple's Roger Glover. Based on a children's book about woodland animals, the LP features vocal performances by Ronnie James Dio and David Coverdale. Vincent Price narrates, Ian Gillan sings, and adults in animal costumes cavort about relaying the insanely psychedelic story.

The Ronnie James Dio–voiced single "Love Is All" was a semi-hit, and produced an animated video used in kids' TV shows worldwide. Dio had to miss the live performance, though, so his role on-screen is sung by Deep Purple frontman Ian Gillan, who takes the stage to ecstatic cheers. Dio did get to sing his *Butterfly Ball* number at the Royal Albert Hall in 1999, as part of a guest appearance with Deep Purple.

THE CABINET OF DR. CALIGARI ✦ CALIGULA ✦ THE CALL OF CTHULU ✦ CANNIBAL APOCALYPSE ✦ CANNIBAL CORPSE: CENTURIES OF TORMENT ✦ CANNIBAL FEROX ✦ CANNIBAL HOLOCAUST ✦ CAPTAIN CLEGG ✦ CARRIE ✦ CELTIC FROST: A DYING GOD ✦ CHAOS ✦ UN CHIEN ANDALOU ✦ CHILDREN OF THE CORN ✦ CHILDREN OF THE DAMNED ✦ CHIMAIRA: THE DEHUMANIZING PROCESS ✦ CHOPPING MALL ✦ CHRISTIANE F. ✦ C.H.U.D. ✦ CITY OF THE LIVING DEAD ✦ CLASH OF THE TITANS ✦ CLASS OF 1984 ✦ CLASSIC ALBUMS: MOTÖRHEAD—ACE OF SPADES ✦ CLIFF 'EM ALL: THE $19.98 HOME VIDEO ✦ A CLOCKWORK ORANGE ✦ CLUB SATAN: THE WITCHES' SABBATH ✦ COMBAT SHOCK ✦ CONAN THE BARBARIAN ✦ CONAN THE DESTROYER ✦ CONFLICT OF INTEREST ✦ CONQUEST ✦ THE COUNTESS ✦ COUNTESS DRACULA ✦ THE COVENANT ✦ CRADLE OF FEAR ✦ THE CRAFT ✦ CREAM: STRANGE BREW ✦ CREEPSHOW ✦ CREMASTER 2 ✦ THE CRIMSON GHOST ✦ CROMWELL ✦ CROSSROADS ✦ THE CROW ✦ THE CROW: CITY OF ANGELS ✦ CROWLEY ✦ CYCLONE

THE CABINET OF DR. CALIGARI (1920)

(DIR. ROBERT WIENE; W/WERNER KRAUSS, CONRAD VEIDT, LIL DAGOVER, FRIEDRICH FEHER)

✦ MEDICAL DEVIANT ✦ MIND CONTROL

With its abstract architecture, whirling cutout sets, and demonically herky-jerky physicality, director Robert Weine's *The Cabinet of Dr. Caligari* is a masterpiece of German expressionism and silent filmmaking, and remains one of the most influential horror tales ever mounted. The medico Dr. Caligari (Werner Krauss) runs a carnival act wherein hypnotized sleepwalker Cesare (Conrad Veidt) does his bidding and prophesizes the future. Trouble bubbles when an audience member asks how long he will live. Cesare says the guy will be dead by dawn. Come sunrise, Cesare is proven correct.

The dead dude's pal Francis (Friedrich Feher) investigates Caligari and discovers a fiendish plot. This leads to Cesare kidnapping Francis's fiancée, Jane (Lil Dagover). A chase ensues and a serial murder conspiracy is revealed, building to one of the first—and still most surprising—twist endings in cinema.

Dr. Caligari's eye-popping costumes, set design, and art direction remain one of a kind. Rob Zombie's "Living Dead Girl" video does an expert job of paying tribute by re-creating the movie's motifs, which only adds to the mind-blowing fact that this film was created and became a worldwide hit the better part of a century earlier, all the way back in 1920.

Another tribute, *Dr. Caligari* (1989), is a neon-scorched variation on this classic by avant-garde filmmaker Steven Sayadian (, AKA Rinse Dream). After brilliantly blending hard-core porn with new wave pop art in *Nightdreams* (1981) and *Café Flesh* (1982), he had potential to become the next visionary in crackpot art films after David Lynch. Alas, it was not to be.

CALIGULA (1979)

(DIRS. TINTO BRASS, BOB GUCCIONE; W/MALCOLM McDOWELL, HELEN MIRREN, PETER O'TOOLE)
✴ ROMAN DECADENCE ✴ CENSORSHIP

For all of heavy metal's fixation on medieval Europe, the historic era that next most embodies the excess of hedonist heavy metal is Rome under the rule of the caesars. The maddest, most metal emperor of them all must have been Gaius Julius Caesar Augustus Germanicus, better known by his nickname, "Little Boots," or Caligula. Taking the bait, metal bands have written dozens of songs in tribute to Caligula, and names from the film have resurfaced as band names in Argentina, Belgium, Paraguay, Sweden, Australia, Chile, the U.S., and Japan.

New York City in the 1970s skirted the high-end hedonism and down-and-dirty decadence of Caligula's reign. One of the perverse princes of gauche Gotham was *Penthouse* magazine publisher Bob Guccione. How fitting that Gooch pushed *Penthouse* into movie production by way of his pernicious predecessor, Little Boots. *Caligula* is Bible-size in scope and scale and *Satanic Bible*–intense in its elaborate indulgence and hard-core realization of every gory impulse of its creators.

Malcolm McDowell devours the lead role. Helen Mirren exudes eternal lust as his wife Caesonia. Teresa Ann Savoy is Drusilla, Caligua's sister who has sex with him and with Caesonia. Filling out the main cast are giant British thespians (Peter O'Toole, John Gielgud) and some *Penthouse* Pets who happily engage in full-penetration lesbianism, including Lori Wagner and Anneka Di Lorenzo. Surrounding all that acting is an avalanche of elaborate, meticulously rendered grotesqueries that takes any previously held concept of on-screen obscenity, buries it up to

the neck, and then tosses rotten tomatoes at its screaming face just before it gets decapitated by a street-cleaning device affixed with giant, spinning razor blades.

The damage *Caligula* does to viewers is nothing compared to the inhuman treatment of the on-screen personalities. An offender of the god Bacchus has a knot tied in his penis, then is subjected to having gallons of wine poured down his throat. Once his stomach is the size of a medicine ball, it is punctured with a sword, and out explodes the recycled wine! Another disfavored sod has his dick cut off and tossed to dogs; those hungry curs happily chew it up on camera.

In a famously foul sequence, Caligula is offended to learn that a young betrothed couple is a pair of virgins. On their wedding night, he forcibly deflowers the bride and then giddily fists the groom. The brutal streak is contagious. Caligula's toddler son offends all of humanity by being related to Caligula. An angry citizen scoops the little guy up, swings him by the legs, and smashes his tiny Roman head apart all over a stone staircase.

The plot is otherwise unnaturally preoccupied with gnarly incest; a whorehouse of physically deformed prostitutes, including one with either one eye or three eyes; and the relatively subtle hilarity of Caligula declaring war on the god Neptune. As part of that lost cause, he orders his soldiers to attack by tossing spears into the sea, and then parades around Rome holding shells and starfish aloft as spoils of victory.

As a film, this is a long, bloody, incomprehensible mess, but as a jaw-dropping spectacle *Caligula* shreds and slays and with toga-torching amazing stamina. *Psychotronic Encyclopedia of Film* author Michael J. Weldon swears that even the most psychotically jaded grindhouse audiences of New York's Forty-Second Street jumped up from their seats and screamed at *Caligula* during its first run there.

World-renowned novelist and intellectual Gore Vidal wrote the first version of Caligula's screenplay. When he saw which way the red tide was turning, he actually fought to remove his name from the finished film. He only partially won that fight—the final credit reads: "Based on an original screenplay by Gore Vidal."

Director Tinto Brass also fought to remove his name from Caligula. Guccione had hired the upstart Italian filmmaker after failing to persuade top-ticket directors John Huston and Lina Wertmüller to take the job. Brass had previously made the (kick-ass) Nazi whorehouse epic *Salon Kitty* (1976), proving his ability to engagingly blend sexual overkill with historic atrocities. Brass clashed with Guccione repeatedly and finally split when the *Penthouse* publisher shot and inserted his own hard-core porn footage.

On the other hand, Helen Mirren has remained very close to Brass since making Caligula. On her warm, hilarious DVD commentary, she says she loves the film, reasoning: "It bought me my first house!"

Countless edits of this epic exist, as in the U.S. alone it was rolled out in X-rated, R-rated, and unrated versions, all commercially successful. Critics hated *Caligula* with apocalyptic gall. No doubt their wrath helped pack all those theaters. Guccione even had the gumption to charge a premium of $7.50 for tickets to the original, extremely limited release, at a time when the average ticket price in New York was $3.00. The movie also faced censorship nearly everywhere on earth, and remains banned in some countries. Once *Caligula* became an early home video blockbuster, all that banning was really hopeless.

The Call of Cthulhu (2005)

(Dir. Andrew Leman; w/Matt Foyer, John Bolen)

✠ H. P. Lovecraft

H. P. Lovecraft is one of literature's most prolific heavy metal wellsprings, inspiring songs by Metallica, Morbid Angel, Electric Wizard, Mortician, and, of course, Necronomicon and Re-Animator. Lovecraft's story "The Call of Cthulhu" had long been thought "unfilmable," but director Andrew Leman and the his fellow Lovecraft devotees cracked the code by going silent. The result is feverish and, quite literally, nightmare-like. The plot centers on college professor George Angell (Ralph Lucas) delving into his granduncle's collection of occult paperwork. There he learns of the Cult of Cthulhu, whose worshippers make human sacrifice to an evil, octopus-like god from outer space who causes violent delirium and terrifying hallucinations in those who get too close.

The H. P. Lovecraft Historical Society credibly adapts the horror master's revolutionary work into what a movie would have looked like if released alongside the story's 1928 publication. *The Call of Cthulhu* is silent and shot in black-and-white, with art direction and performances in the vein of *The Cabinet of Dr. Caligari* (1920) and *Nosferatu* (1922). The total budget was $50,000. The creators are to be saluted: Tentacles up!

Cannibal Apocalypse (1980), aka Apocalypse Domani; Invasion of the Flesh Hunters

(Dir. Antonio Margheriti; w/John Saxon, Elizabeth Turner, John Morghen)

✠ Cannibals ✠ Zombies ✠ Psycho 'Nam Vet
✠ Banned Video Nasty

Circa 1980, psycho Vietnam vet movies abounded, as did zombie films and cannibal flicks. Here, in one gross swoop, are all three of these supremely metal genres in one burbling gutbucket of righteous hideousness. *Cannibal Apocalypse* opens with a 'Nam flashback. Captain Norman Hopper (John Saxon) feverishly recalls stumbling on two GIs feasting on the body of a local villager.

The action picks up years later in Atlanta, where Hopper's life as a TV reporter is upended by a call from one of those flesh-eating soldiers, the hilariously named Charles Bukowski (John Morghen, aka Giovanni Radice). Hopper passes on meeting Charlie for a drink, and soon we discover Charlie has retained his taste for human skin. He violently bites the neck of girl in a theater, then battles bikers and slaughters bystanders. Before long, the troubled ex-soldier barricades himself in a strip mall.

Meanwhile, Hopper is not very feeling well, either. A doctor informs him that the bite he got in Vietnam has given him a zombie virus. *Cannibal Apocalypse* quickly escalates into urban warfare inflamed with body eating, in which, memorably, a tongue and a naked female breast are consumed. Geysers of gore erupt as the virus engulfs Atlanta while the trained killers do their stuff. Italian filmmakers sure didn't fuck around back in the day.

John Saxon, who also played the bad guy in *Enter the Dragon* (1973) and the police chief Dad in *Nightmare on Elm Street* (1984), has since taken pains to distance himself from *Cannibal Apocalypse*. He claims he didn't know how horrifically explicit the violence would be, and says he's never watched the finished film. He should.

Cannibal Corpse: Centuries of Torment (2008)

(Dirs. Nic Izzi, Denise Korycki, David Stuart; w/Cannibal Corpse, Vincent Locke, Jim Carrey)

✠ Death Metal

Seven hours and twenty minutes is a lot of documentary time to be dedicated to any one subject, let alone one band, but the sheer uniqueness of these death metal demons and, by 2008, their decades-spanning breadth of work make *Cannibal Corpse: Centuries of Torment* yet another landmark achievement for these Buffalo, New York–born hate bombardiers.

Centuries of Torment is spread out over three DVDs. The first is a straight, three-hour history, beginning in the frozen nothingness along the New York–Canada border in 1988. When we first meet these young fans of Slayer, Kreator, and the embryonic death metal rumblings of Autopsy and Death, Bob Rusay is Cannibal Corpse's hotshot guitarist, while Chris Barnes mans the microphone. Rusay, fired in '93 and now a golf instructor, has little to say. Barnes, whose gravel-puking ogre vocals defined the Cannibal Corpse sound front and center, contributes a lot, even acknowledging the talent of his 1995 replacement, George "Corpsegrinder" Fisher.

Centuries of Torment treats us to a brutally revealing level of access and detail. The production and reception of the band's early-'90s classics *Eaten Back to Life*, *Butchered at Birth*, and *Tomb of the Mutilated* are catalogued, along with international controversies. Both Australia and Germany enacted government-enforced bans on the sale of Cannibal Corpse music. Their stature as death metal elder statesmen also plays a part. In 2003, CC officially earned the title "the biggest-selling death metal band of the SoundScan era."

Gory details include some time with Vincent Locke, the painter responsible for Cannibal Corpse's often literally eye-popping album covers and associated imagery, as well as the inside skinny on Jim Carrey securing the band a cameo in *Ace Ventura: Pet Detective*. The second disc features Cannibal Corpse concert footage. Disc three is bonus footage, with the band addressing ephemera from fan tattoos to the awesomeness of the animated series *Metalocalypse*.

Cannibal Ferox (1981), aka Make Them Die Slowly

(Dir. Umberto Lenzi; w/Giovanni Lombardo Radice, Lorraine De Selle, Danilo Mattei, Zora Kerova)

✠ Splatter Horror ✠ Cannibals

The gnawing dilemma is whether to list this film by the preferred Italian title, *Cannibal Ferox*, or the name under which I first saw this gut-ripper during its uninterrupted two-year run at the Liberty grindhouse on Forty-Second Street, *Make Them Die Slowly*. I defer to convention with *Cannibal Ferox*, but this vicious, immoral, repulsive sensory overload of wrongness would still burst barf bags under any name.

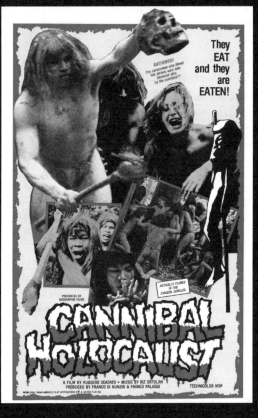

Clockwise from top left: *killer sales in* Chopping Mall *(1986); raising the reaper for* Children of the Corn *(1984);* City of the Living Dead *(1980), aka* The Gates of Hell; *H.P. Lovecraft revival* The Call of Cthulhu *(2005);* Cannibal Holocaust *(1980) spawned posters for every country where it was banned*

After some introductory violence in Manhattan regarding a missing drug dealer, *Cannibal Ferox* skulks down to Paraguay, where noted anthropologist Gloria Davis (Lorraine De Selle) is joined by her brother Rudy (Danilo Mattei) and their pal Pat (Zora Kerova) on a journey into the jungle to disprove the "myth" of human-eating primitive peoples. This mission will fail, of course.

En route to a friendly village, the trio comes across bedraggled Americans Mike (Giovanni Lombardo Radice) and Joe (Walter Lucchini), who claim that cannibals tortured, castrated, and chowed down on their guide. The truth soon comes to light when drugged-up Mike murders a local girl. When the natives see the girl's body, they go from restless to vengeful to hungry, and it's really too bloody bad for any non-locals within chewing distance.

The tribe immediately feasts on Joe's not-quite-dead body, graphically savoring his intestines and organ meats. Mike is then tied to a tree where, up close and in repugnantly believable detail, a native slices off his penis and eats it. Other tribesman cauterize the wound to keep Mike alive and dickless, graphically forcing upon viewers the worst thing anyone can possibly imagine (until *A Serbian Film* ([2010] came along, anyway).

Remarkably, the cock chomping isn't even the movie's most iconic abomination. That honor goes to poor Pat having hooks thrust through her naked breasts, by which she is then hoisted up and hung in midair. In many parts of the world, that image adorned the *Cannibal Ferox* promotional poster. The parade of other *Cannibal Ferox* affronts includes Rudy being reduced to piranha chow, Mike having the top of his head chopped off with a machete to enable a full-on brain feast, and totally unnecessary displays of actual animal killing. To keep up the generally unwell feeling, the filmmakers intersplice unrelated footage of a pig and a sea turtle slaughtered for food, a leopard munching on a monkey, and a giant snake snarfing down some kind of cute rodent that someone kindly tethered to a tree as bait.

When all is said and digested, a rescue party whisks Gloria back to New York. Once there, the atrocity-hardened scholar says that crocodiles have eaten her companions, and she writes the book that she had intended to all along, *Cannibalism: End of a Myth*. What a phony!

Cannibal Ferox is preceded by an on-screen announcement: "The following feature is one of the most violent films ever made. There are at least two dozen scenes of barbaric torture and sadistic cruelty graphically shown. If the presentation of disgusting and repulsive subject matter upsets you, please do not view this film." Robert Kerman (, AKA veteran '70s and '80s porn star R. Bolla) plays a cop. He's wearing the exact same suit and tie he had on when he starred as the lead in the previous year's milestone chunk-blower, *Cannibal Holocaust* (1980).

The litany of tributes in metal includes the songs titled "Cannibal Ferox" and "Make Them Die Slowly" by White Zombie, 7000 Dying Rats, Burial Ground, Cardiac Arrest, Gore Obsessed, and One Man Army and the Undead Quartet. White Zombie named an album *Make Them Die Slowly*, and Rob Zombie has also mentioned seeing the film during that infamous two-year stretch at the Liberty on Forty-Second Street. I saw it there, too; who doesn't remember where they were?

Cannibal Holocaust (1980)

(Dir. Ruggero Deodato; w/Robert Kerman)

✠ Splatter ✠ Cannibals

Cannibal Holocaust is the gore-sopped king of the unholy mountain in 1980s post–*Dawn of the Dead* flesh-eating barf bag cinema. I feel slightly greater affection for the film that has become its companion—Umberto Lenzi's *Cannibal Ferox* (1981), aka *Make Them Die Slowly*—but *Cannibal Holocaust* got there first. The title alone has yet to be surpassed in simple, savage evocation of gross atrocities. *Cannibal Holocaust* also effectively invented the "found footage" horror genre, which would grow to greater effect in the age of the Internet by way of *The Blair Witch Project* (1999) and countless Asian films.

A documentary film crew descends into the Amazon rain forest to chronicle indigenous cannibal tribes. They never really leave, except as semi-digested chunks inside the natives' stools. New York anthropologist Harold Monroe (Robert Kerman) later embarks on a search for this missing team. He befriends the locals and finds the films the documentarians left behind.

Returning to Manhattan, Monroe expresses his outrage at a TV network that wishes to air footage of the tribes at work, at war, and preparing live animals as meals. Monroe forces the network execs to watch every bit of film he found, including that which exposes heinous crimes committed by the filmmakers: arson, gang rape, impaling a young girl on a pole that runs up through her vagina and out her mouth. They also view the equally barbaric revenge perpetrated on the outsiders: more rape, torture, mutilation, beheading, and lots of human-meat consumption.

Horrified, the TV bigwigs order the films destroyed, which is just a hilarious reaction. They have this unimaginably fascinating, never-before-possible evidence of a profound culture clash, and their attitude suddenly becomes: "It's too gross. Burn it." Monroe, his mind likely blown permanently, wanders out into the New York City streets wondering who the real cannibals are.

Cannibal Holocaust really is a layered, thought-provoking film, due largely to the way-ahead-of-its-time "found footage" innovation. Kerman also makes for a convincingly noble hero, in contrast to the just as credible thugs who abuse the natives. Deodato's direction is powerful, bolstered by his use of actual Amazon Basin residents, truly delivering a wrenching "you are there" immediacy—and culpability.

Plus, to use the parlance of gross-out horror geeks who watched *Cannibal Holocaust* until the VHS tapes disintegrated, it's a chunk-blower nonpareil. The actual on-camera animal kill-

ings will keep it forever controversial. Even in the extremes of the heavy world, the sensibility is split between Ozzy Osbourne chomping live doves and bats and Watain dunking themselves in cow's blood before a show on the one hand, versus a large contingent of vegan or vegetarian musicians, including Ozzy's Black Sabbath bandmate Geezer Butler, plus members of Napalm Death, Carcass, Kreator, Cattle Decapitation, and Dillinger Escape Plan.

In *Cannibal Holocaust*, we witness six animal slaughters, the most gruesome of which are the shell removal of a large sea turtle and a spider monkey getting its face sliced off for brain-sucking purposes. A tarantula, a snake, a pig, and a raccoon-like coatimundi also bite it. It's upsetting and nauseating, but those of us watching are implicated in those deaths—especially while chomping hot dogs and pork nachos at the same time that the humans on-screen consume the turtle and the monkey.

After the film's release, the director was actually charged with murder. As rumors swirled about *Cannibal Holocaust* containing human snuff footage, the French magazine *Photo* reported that Deodato had four actors, including the girl with the pole running through her, killed in order to film their deaths. Complicating the matter, the movie's stars had agreed to stay out of the media for a year in order to increase the movie's inherent mystery. The ploy worked too well. Italian authorities arrested Deodato and held him until he was able to produce the still-living performers. The "impaled" girl explained to a judge exactly how they pulled off the effect. The court settled for banning *Cannibal Holocaust* from Italy, and convicting Deodato on charges of obscenity and "violence." He got a suspended sentence.

Star Robert Kerman performed in more than one hundred adult films between 1975 and 1998. Under the name "R. Bolla" or "Richard Bolla," he appears in X-rated classics such as *Sex Wish* (1976), *Punk Rock* (1977), and *The Devil in Miss Jones Part II* (1982). Kerman's non-porn credits, including *Cannibal Holocaust*, make for a weird list: *The Goodbye Girl* (1977), *The Concorde: Airport '79* (1979), *Eaten Alive!* (1980), *Night of the Creeps* (1986), and *Spider-Man* (2002).

Cannibal Holocaust broke box office records in Japan. In the land of Loudness, Sabbat, Sigh, Boris, and Merzbow, this was the second highest-earning film of 1983, behind only *E.T. the Extra-Terrestrial*. South America took notice, too. When asked in 1991 what a Sepultura movie might be like, various members of the mighty band answered in unison: "*Cannibal Holocaust*!" Ex-Sepultura frontman Max Cavalera has recorded a "Cannibal Holocaust" with his band Soulfly, and so have the bands Necrophagia, Grotesque, Virus, and a lot of others.

Captain Clegg (1962), aka Night Creatures

(Dir. Peter Graham Scott; w/Peter Cushing, Oliver Reed, Yvonne Roman, Patrick Allen)

✠ Hammer Horror ✠ Pirates

Hammer Films reached out past monster movies here and into the gothic skullduggery of smuggling and "land pirates" on the English moors. In 1792, Captain Collier (Patrick Allen) is dispatched to investigate violations of an embargo against French wines that seems to be centered in the village of Dymchurch. When a snitch turns up dead, locals tell the captain it was "marsh phantoms," hooded skeleton ghost riders who run riot every so often. Most mysterious of all is Dymchurch clergyman Parson Blyss (Peter Cushing). A huge, brutish ex-pirate whose tongue was cut out recognizes Blyss as Captain Clegg, a scourge of the seas. Rampages result.

Captain Clegg is based on *Dr. Syn*, a series of early twentieth-century novels by Russell Thorndike. *Dr. Syn* also provided the basis for a very spooky Disney TV movie, *The Scarecrow of Romney Marsh* (1963), starring Patrick McGoohan. English doom lords Cathedral gave the movie their seal of approval with "Captain Clegg," a tribute to the night-riding man.

Carrie (1976)

(Dir. Brian De Palma; w/Sissy Spacek, Piper Laurie, Amy Irving, Betty Buckley, John Travolta)

✠ Religious Fanatics ✠ Animal Sacrifice ✠ School Massacre

Carrie is the ultimate doomed-youth anthem. This dazzling, thrilling, funny, and heartbreaking horror classic is a realization of the fears and fantasies of every adolescent outsider afflicted with inner anguish so furious that he or she wishes a single mind-bomb could just burn the entire shittiness of existence to cinders.

Sissy Spacek as Carrie, Piper Laurie as her Bible-psycho mother, and the rest of the cast deliver performances of stunning clarity. No viewer in America can resist identifying with poor, picked-on Carrie White. And though this trembling, confused young girl in her slip is a far cry from a leather titan, the heavy metal tone and imagery never stop. Brian De Palma's adaptation of Stephen King's novel illustrates the infernal travails of puberty with the sufferings of Christian martyrs, over-the-top sexual hysteria, and of course the pig slaughter and blood ritual of Carrie's prom night humiliation.

Though school shootings were the last thing on the creators' minds in 1976, Carrie's climactic massacre of her teachers and classmates is a harrowing foreshadowing of Columbine and too many similar fatal outbursts. Even in the context of nightmarish revenge, the final note of terror indicates that hell itself is not as terrible as a teenage untouchable's need for human contact.

Stephen King says he based Carrie on one girl with whom he attended high school, and another who was his student when he taught English. Both were social pariahs from crazily religious families, and each one died in her twenties.

CARRIE WHITE BURNS IN HELL! is scrawled on our heroine's grave at the end. It's true. And there she's our prom queen for eternity.

CELTIC FROST: A DYING GOD (2008)

(DIR. ADRIAN WINKLER; W/TOM GABRIEL FISCHER, MARTIN AIN, H. R. GIGER)

✠ DEATH METAL ✠ DOOM ✠ SWITZERLAND

The one-hour documentary *Celtic Frost: A Dying God* was originally broadcast in Swiss Standard German on Switzerland's national TV in November 2008. The time is well spent with Frost's key members, Tom Gabriel Fischer (AKA Tom Warrior) and Martin Ain, around the era of the band's remarkable 2006 comeback album, *Monotheist*. Despite the mass-media pedigree, *A Dying God* speaks most effectively to fans who are already familiar with the band, moving quickly and fairly presumptuously through Frost's origins in Hellhammer, the disaster of 1988's *Cold Lake* album, specific frictions between Fischer and Ain, and other such intricacies. For devotees, *A Dying God* is as deep an immersion into the procreation of the wicked as ever experienced.

A Dying God features frequent highlights from vintage TV footage. Appearing on a 1985 teen music show, Tom explains to clean-cut kids about the role of satanism in metal, explaining, "I do not perform black masses! I do not sacrifice young girls!" The band performs "Into the Crypts of Rays." In a 1986 clip, Tom aligns Celtic Frost with death metal, a term he helped coin years earlier. A 1987 interview features Martin declaring the band's new direction to be classical music. Then comes a hyper-glam music video for 1988's "Cherry Orchards" single, a teased-hair horror beyond anything in *The Decline of Western Civilization Part II*.

Undying devotion is palpable between Fischer and Ain—as is loads of unresolved tension. Playful 1986 footage shows the two joking about Tom seducing and stealing Martin's first-ever girlfriend. They laugh and act lighthearted, but the documentary implies that rift in fact prevented Martin from playing on Frost's landmark '86 LP, *To Mega Therion*. A quarter-century later, the wound has not entirely healed. "Tom is like a brother to me," says the present-day Ain, "but a brother doesn't always have to be a friend."

There are triumphs. At an event in Switzerland, artist H. R. Giger (*Alien*) poses with the band, demonstrating a bond formed in 1985 when he bestowed his *Satan I* for use on the cover of *To Mega Therion*. There is lightness. After a Tokyo show befouled by technical problems, the band's spirits are elevated by a jam with Gallhammer, a local all-girl band inspired by the pre-Celtic Frost band Hellhammer.

Then comes finality. A climactic band meeting on whether to add three shows in Mexico is calm but tempers smolder. Fischer wants to soldier on and not be "pussies." Drummer Franco Sesa wants out, saying: "I don't need any one of you around me more than one month. If this is my dream, it's a fucking nightmare." Soon after, the film concludes, and so did the band. A postscript notes simply that Fischer and Ain have decided to "bury Celtic Frost."

CHAOS (2005)

(DIR. DAVID DEFALCO; W/KEVIN GAGE, MAYA BAROVICH, CHANTAL DEGROAT, SAGE STALLONE)

✠ EXTREME GORE ✠ RAPE AND REVENGE

Early reports mistakenly hyped the pernicious *Chaos* as as an unofficial remake of *Last House on the Left* (1972). The movie retains the plot of Wes Craven's grindhouse shocker and, by extension, Swedish director Ingmar Bergman's *The Virgin Spring* (*Jungfrukällan* [1960]).

Two suburban teenage innocents, blonde Angelica (Maya Barovich) and African-American Emily (Chantal Degroat), fall prey to a scumbag cabal lorded over by psycho-sadist Chaos (Kevin Gage). The gang includes violent Frankie (Stephen Wozniak), sexually berserk Daisy (Kelly K. C. Quann), and morose junkie Swan (Sage Stallone). The degree of carnal horrors to which Chaos and company subject the girls (and viewers at home) far, far surpasses the crimes depicted in *Last House on the Left*. For example,

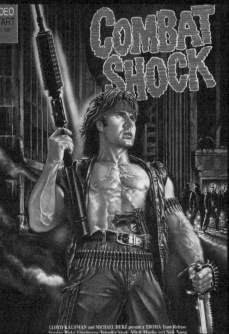

Clockwise from top: *Arnold Schwarzenegger as* Conan the Destroyer *(1984); England's burning in* Cromwell *(1970); "psycho shocker...extraordinaire" German promotion for* Carrie *(1976); Lucio Fulci pulls a gory sword out for* Conquest *(1983); Staten Island's sickest:* Combat Shock *(1985)*

Chaos carves off Angelica's nipple and forces her to eat it. As in the original, the killers mess up by seeking refuge at the home of Emily's parents, who exact hard-core revenge.

Chaos definitely departs from Last House in its conclusion, with a twist you don't want to see coming. I found it chilling. Others term it depressing. Either way, it's a downer. Chaos is like a cover song that outpaces its inspiration in numerous areas, occasionally matches it in gut effect, and delivers a commendable update despite its essential unoriginality.

Sage Stallone, who plays Swan, was the son of Sylvester. He died in 2012, and is missed sorely. He was a horror fan to the end, and he put his Hollywood muscle to work restoring and distributing fright classics as the co-founder and cornerstone of Grindhouse Releasing.

Chaos creator David DeFalco also directed and starred in the VHS anti-masterpiece Heavy Metal Massacre (1989). When Chaos opened in Chicago, the ever-enterprising DeFalco got into a publicity-generating (and hugely entertaining) pissing contest with movie critic Roger Ebert. Although famously supportive of the original Last House film, Ebert gave Chaos no stars, and seemed to be weeping when he wrote his condemning review. DeFalco replied with an ad in Ebert's newspaper, the Chicago Sun-Times, calling out the critic for not wanting to see "evil portrayed as it really is."

Ebert then penned a column, titled "Evil in Film: To What End?" in which he replied: "Your real purpose in making Chaos, I suspect, was not to educate, but to create a scandal that would draw an audience." He was right, of course. When Chaos ran for an entire summer at the Village Art Theater in Chicago, the box office displayed giant blowups of DeFalco and Ebert's public communiqués, peddling untold numbers of tickets to easily scandalized viewers and me.

Un Chien Andalou (1929)

(Dirs. Luis Buñuel, Salvador Dali; w/Simone Mareuil, Luis Buñuel, Salvador Dali)

✳ Gore ✳ Surrealism

Avant-garde filmmaker Luis Buñuel and surrealist painter Salvador Dalí redirected the course of cinema with their sixteen-minute silent collaboration Un Chien Andalou. They did it in proto-headbanger fashion: with shock, awe, bare boobs, dead animals, and scorn for Christianity.

Un Chien Andalou (An Andalusian Dog) opens with a man (Buñuel) sharpening a straight razor. Clouds cut across the moon. A woman (Simone Mareuil) sits wide-eyed, staring into the camera. The man comes behind her, spreads her eyelids apart with his fingers and, in extreme close-up, drags the razor across her eyeball. Slime spills out. Though horrifying to watch now, imagine seeing that, unprepared, in 1929!

The movie, written by Buñuel and Dalí, progresses as a series of bizarre actions and images strewn together with the logic-free nature of a dream, spiked by flashes of a nightmare. Among the alternately upsetting, arousing, and thoroughly scandalous visuals are those of ants emerging endlessly from a hole in a man's palm, horny hands groping a woman's breasts as her clothes disappear, a cross-dressing nun, pianos containing rotting donkey carcasses, and freaked-out priests (one of whom is Dalí) tethered to the Ten Commandments.

By consciously expanding the parameters of art by way of the harsh, the frightening, and the grotesque, Un Chien Andalou set in motion the cultural changes that, musically, resulted in experimental jazz and then rock and roll and then, ultimately, heavy metal. More or less directly, every other film contained in this book owes something to Un Chien Andalou.

After much public speculation, Buñuel revealed that the sliced eye belonged to a butchered calf, and that he over-lit the animal's hide to make it resemble human skin. However, both of Un

Chien Andalou's lead actors committed suicide. In 1932, Pierre Batcheff, the guy with the ant hands, overdosed on pills. In 1954, Simone Mareuil offed herself in a surrealist manner that must have humbled even the filmmakers. She stepped into a public square in France, dumped gasoline all over her body, and lit herself up.

Children of the Corn (1984)

(Dir. Fritz Kiersch; w/John Franklin, Courtney Gains, Linda Hamilton, Peter Horton)

✠ Youth Gone Wild ✠ Cults ✠ Stephen King

Children of the Corn is one of the most fondly remembered horror films of the 1980s. Certainly this Stephen King adaptation ranks high and hard among the most metal, due to how easy it is to identify with the empowered cult of diabolic teens and small children taking over a remote country town. Even though the *Corn* is a little unsalted and unpopped, two explosive elements blow the lid right off the movie.

The plot involves out-of-towners who turn off a paved road and run into big hillbilly trouble. The unkempt and unfriendly children they encounter are unnerving, as there has never been a less welcoming presence than the unseen, human-hungry corn-demon to whom the youngsters make sacrifices: He Who Walks Behind the Rows. Then come Isaac (John Franklin) and Malachi (Courtney Gains), two towering, underage villains played by awesomely freakazoic actors.

Thanks to these two icons, *Children of the Corn* remains an object of profound horror-metal affection. Isaac is a pint-size Elmer Gantry–*cum*–Jim Jones bedecked in Amish wear. John Franklin, who seems born to play the part, looks like a third-grader and a retirement-home grouch all at once, and he mesmerizes his flock and viewers at home when he preaches prophecies regarding the righteousness of spilling "outlander" blood. Malachi is Isaac's tall, gangly, bucktoothed enforcer with long red hair and a threatening way with a scythe. He's played by newcomer Courtney Gains, later familiar from *Colors* (1988). In *Hardbodies* (1984), he displayed a "multilingual" ability to flip people off in forty-eight languages. Truly, this is one gruesome twosome. Isaac brings the heavy; Malachi is all metal.

"Outlander! Outlander! We have your woman!" shouts Malachi, one of the great quotations of Heavy Metal Movies. In the original Stephen King story, Isaac was named William Renfrew and Malachi was called Craig Boardman. Evil farmer hats off to screenwriter George Goldsmith for those two massive upgrades.

Director Fritz Kiersch went on to make *Tuff Turf* (1985) and *Gor* (1987). John Franklin costarred under a full-body wig as Cousin Itt in the big-screen *Addams Family* (1991) and its 1993 sequel.

Children of the Corn spawned a numbing eight sequels of varying loose relation to the original, plus a 2009 Syfy channel remake; not bad for a short story first published in *Penthouse* in 1977. Even after seeing all of them, all I remember is an old lady in a wheelchair being launched through a plate-glass window in *Children of the Corn III: Urban Harvest* (1995), and I can vouch that Isaac did indeed return as promised in *Children of the Corn 666: Isaac's Return* (1996). A PG-13 remake seems inevitable.

Children of the Damned (1963)

(Dir. Anton M. Leader; w/Ian Hendry, Alan Badel, Barbara Ferris, Alfred Burke)

✠ Creepy Children

Village of the Damned (1960) is one of science-fiction cinema's most fundamentally English fright efforts, about a freak mass impregnation of all fertile women, and the Aryan, glowing-eyed, psychic-terror moppets that result. The sequel, *Children of the Damned*, takes a sympathetic view of the creepy-peepered kids and even points out parallels with Christ in their virgin births and ability to raise the dead. In the end, they all get blown up, so maybe they are even martyrs.

Never one to shy away from a definitely British oddity, Iron Maiden penned the song "Children of the Damned" for their breakthrough *Number of the Beast* album. The lyrics to the Iron Maiden song actually seem to describe the climax of *Village of the Damned*, a writing technique known as metallic license. Anything that makes things heavier is perfectly okay.

CHIMAIRA: THE DEHUMANIZING PROCESS (2004)

(DIRS. TODD BELL, NICK KLECZEWSKI; W/MARK HUNTER, EMIL WERSTLER, MATT DEVRIES)
✳ CONCERT FOOTAGE

Cleveland groove-metal stompers Chimaira practice relentlessly, play ruthlessly, and talk loud in the "video album" *Chimaira: The Dehumanizing Process*. Between exceptionally well-presented songs, band members recount their history, ruminate on their various processes, and sound off about their horror over being lumped in among nü-metal rap-rockers around the turn of the century. After each gripe, Chimaira launches into a wall-of-hurt sound-storm in order to clarify the distance between them and, say, Linkin Park. Point taken, and taken hard. Disproving any connection to nü-metal is the band name itself; a chimera is a multiheaded beast from Greek mythology. The creature appears fearsome in Dungeons & Dragons rules, which specify that a chimera can gore with its goat head, tear with its lion fangs, and bite or breathe fire with its dragon head.

CHOPPING MALL (1986), AKA KILLBOTS

(DIR. JIM WYNORSKI; W/PAUL BARTEL, MARY WORONOV)
✳ KILLER ROBOTS ✳ CANNIBALISM

Technology runs amok alongside huge hair, tight spandex, and loud rock in a mid-1980s shopping mall. Headbangers, preppies, burn-outs, and squares convene in peace in a consumer paradise, until the establishment's tank-turreted, semi-anthropomorphic robot security guards are turned murder-crazy by a stray lightning bolt.

A group of teens spends the night in a shopping center, not knowing that the mechanized rent-a-cops all around them are out for blood. Engaging cat-and-mouse pursuits rule the wee hours, with death-beams making for mostly clean fatalities. Nothing happens to merit *Chopping Mall*'s VHS box cover image of a paper bag stuffed with gory body scraps. Devotees of '80s slasher films have nonetheless always warmed to *Chopping Mall* for its unique spin on dispatching adolescents (one of which results in a geyser-like exploding head).

Also known by the inherently more metal title *Killbots*, *Chopping Mall* essentially imbues cutesy "No. 5" from the same summer's *Short Circuit* with the corrupted brain of the trigger-happy, chicken-legged automaton in the following year's *RoboCop*. Paul Bartel and Mary Woronov wittily bring back their cannibal chef characters from *Eating Raoul* (1982), and Dick Miller reprises the homicide-happy sculptor role he plays in *A Bucket of Blood* (1959). This movie kicks the crap out of *Phantom of the Mall: Eric's Revenge* (1989).

CHRISTIANE F. (1981)

(DIR. ULI EDEL; W/NATJA BRUNCKHORST, THOMAS HAUSTEIN, DAVID BOWIE)
✳ GRIM REALITY ✳ BERLIN ✳ JUNKIES

An oddball art house hit powered by traditional mondo puke-o shock tactics, *Christiane F.* is adapted from a book based on interviews with real-life underage Berlin heroin addict and prostitute Vera Christiane Felscherinow. The movie re-creates its subject's downward sputter between the ages of thirteen and fifteen with documentary-style filmmaking, nonprofessional actors, and guerilla intensity.

The German kids of *Christiane F.* suck dicks and shoot junk and puke and die—or, worse, they don't die—amidst the thrashing hellscape that would (very) soon birth the likes of Destruction,

Kreator, Sodom. Those bands sound like what *Christiane F.* feels like, even if it is Bowie who cameos and provides the actual soundtrack. This is the total alienation of Cold War Europe. As the Narcotically Thin White Duke (whose concert footage sticks out like a sore track mark) would proclaim a few years hence in a death-march MTV campaign: "Too much is never enough!"

C.H.U.D. (1984)

(Dir. Douglas Cheek; w/John Heard, Daniel Stern, Christopher Curry, Kim Greist)

✣ Cannibalistic Humanoids ✣ Underground Dwellers

For as few people as have actually seen the movie *C.H.U.D.*, seemingly everyone knows that the acronym stands for "Cannibalistic Humanoid Underground Dwellers." Strangely, everyone knows these are human-size, glowing-eyed mutants created by toxic waste, living in the sewers of New York City and feasting on anybody who gets too close to an open grate. Three decades after the film debuted, C.H.U.D.s remain affectionate joke fodder. Although they're really stupid-looking and the movie itself is largely dullsville, their nickname may be the most fun word to say in the history of any language.

Not every beloved heavy metal album is a classic. Many might not even be good. Some are terrible, but the love we feel is genuine, and the same goes for some Heavy Metal Movies. Especially *C.H.U.D.* That explains why I have a C.H.U.D. emerging from a sewer tattooed on my left wrist.

While C.H.U.D. metal bands surfaced in Australia and France, *C.H.U.D.* has been parodied endlessly in pop culture, notably in four episodes of *The Simpsons*, as well as on *Robot Chicken*, *Aqua Teen Hunger Force*, *Workaholics*, *The Tom Green Show*, and in the video game *Tony Hawk's Underground*. *C.H.U.D. II: Bud the Chud* (1989) is the only sequel to date. The movie misses the mark by attempting straight-up horror comedy; the original is so affectionately rib tickling because it is played straight.

City of the Living Dead (1980), aka The Gates of Hell; Twilight of the Dead

(Dir. Lucio Fulci; w/Christopher George, Catriona MacColl, Carlo De Mejo, Fabrizio Jovine)

✣ Italian Horror ✣ Banned Video Nasty ✣ Hell ✣ Zombies ✣ Dunwich

As so many spaghetti splatter movies do, *City of the Living Dead* starts in New York City, where the ghost of a hanged priest (Fabrizio Jovine) scares a psychic (Catriona MacColl) to death, then brings her back to life with a mission. His suicide apparently opened the gates of hell, which must now be closed. The psychic works with a crack journalist (Christopher George) to lock up the gates on a tight deadline before All Saints Day. After that, the dead will rise en masse to munch on the living.

All the proper elements are set up perfectly for '80s Italian power-gore, complete with a field trip to H. P. Lovecraft territory, a spooky town called Dunwich. Hot off *Zombie* (1979), director Lucio Fulci goes more rambunctiously off the rails in *City*. With weirdness that is almost poetry, Fulci bombards us with bleeding walls, teleporting undead, cinema's greatest electric-drill-to-the-brain encounter, and a girl literally doing what many in the original audience must have felt was inevitable: puking her actual guts out.

Don't get the wrong idea. *City* more than a pastiche of hurl-baiting stunts. Sergio Salvati's cinematography, Gino de Rossi's exquisitely grotesque special effects, and the unnerving score by Fabio Frizzi enhance Fulci's vision with haunting force. Many hail *The Beyond* (1981) as Fulci's masterpiece. Watch that film back-to-back with *City of the Living Dead* before deciding. Keep your artisan *Heavy Metal Movies* barf bag handy.

City of the Living Dead lent more than its share of scary images to heavy metal. The movie poster's one-eyed, green, goblin-like zombie head looming over a skyscraper skyline seems to have carved a special place in metal consciousness, appearing and reappearing in Xeroxed flyer art and bootleg T-shirts. When there is a photo of an underground band posing in its poster-adorned practice space, between the Slayer and Motörhead artwork, look for *The Gates of Hell*.

Clash of the Titans

(1981)

(Dir. Desmond Davis; w/Harry Hamlin, Laurence Olivier, Ursula Andress, Claire Bloom)

✠ Greek Myths ✠ Norse Myths ✠ Witches

The original heavy metal generation was introduced to Classics 101 by way of *Clash of the Titans*, the final cavalcade of marvels concocted by special effects wizard Ray Harryhausen (*Jason and the Argonauts*). The story borrows liberally from many Greek and Norse myths and whips up plenty of new stuff. Harry Hamlin makes a heroic Perseus sent forth to battle gods, Gorgons, and all nemeses in between. Laurence Olivier strikes a charming, befuddled note as Zeus.

As always, the true stars are Harryhausen's stop-motion animated visuals. Chief among his amazing creations are snake-headed Medusa, whose blood drops turn into giant scorpions; the giant, multiarmed sea monster the Kraken; the winged horse Pegasus; two-headed attack dog Dioskilos; and Bubo, a robotic owl that Harryhausen swears he devised before ever seeing *Star Wars'* R2-D2.

In 1984, Harryhausen pursued a sequel to be called *Force of the Trojans*. It never materialized, perhaps because some young studio executives couldn't stop snickering at the condom-tastic title. If only to underscore the wonderful originality of Harryhausen's techniques, Hollywood mustered a 2010 CGI remake and a 2012 CGI sequel to the remake, both utterly useless.

Class of 1984 (1982), aka Guerilla High

(Dir. Mark L. Lester; w/Perry King, Timothy Van Patten, Michael J. Fox, Roddy McDowall)

✠ Youth Gone Wild ✠ Revenge

Class of 1984 kicks, slashes, screams, pukes, and bleeds punk rock, but a very Plasmatics-style metalhead version of punk rock. There's the hyper-punk gang at the center of the story, a serrated-edged foursome adorned with Mohawk haircuts, angular makeup, neon dye jobs, torn-up fashions, spikes, boots, and all the other outrageous and once-futuristic accoutrements. Our antiheroes go out slam dancing to a live performance by Canuck punk faves Teenage Head. Additional soundtrack nuggets come from L.A. hardcore terrorists Fear. Alice Cooper, punk godfather and metal's man in mascara, delivers the theme song "I Am the Future."

Head thug Stegman (Timothy Van Patten, of the famed Van Patten clan) loves pushing dope, pulping skulls, and knife-raping the pregnant wife of Mr. Norris (Perry King)—the teacher who only wanted to help him! Terrible, right? But Stegman is also a piano prodigy! Effortlessly, this black-leather-jacketed monster improvises a classical-style concerto. His moody chops would hold up well next to Glenn Tipton's playing on *Sad Wings of Destiny*, if not for Stegman's dedication to a gang instead of Judas Priest.

Unlike Penelope Spheeris's punk *verité* exploitation picture *Suburbia*, *Class of 1984* shuns overt artiness and launches a pure all-out attack. A drive-in or a grindhouse movie like this will always out-metal anything with a veneer of respectability. This movie's sole motivation is to make your blood boil and then pay off with spectacular revenge. We witness one sick, sadistic misdeed by Stegman's crew after another as they terrorize teachers and students alike while Mr. Norris, with his every fiber, tries to keep cool.

Michael J. Fox gets shanked in the school cafeteria. Biology teacher Roddy McDowall's lab animals are sacrificed. After the incident with Mrs. Norris, though, our inflamed educator explodes into a homicidal rampage that utilizes highly specific high school bricolage including the woodshop buzz saw and the auditorium catwalk with its noose-like ropes as he delivers the punks to a painful and permanent detention from life.

Barnyard, the punk gang's jumbo-size enforcer, is played by Keith Knight. His other best-known role is as hot-dog-eating champion Larry "Fink" Finkelstein in *Meatballs* (1979). *Class of 1984* also generated two little-known sci-fi sequels: *Class of 1999* (1990), about cyborg teachers brought in to discipline unruly students; and *Class of 1999 II: The Substitute* (1994), where one rogue robot teacher slips back onto a high school faculty and commences lethal lesson-giving.

Class of 1984, like the *Texas Chain Saw Massacre* (1974) and so many other exploitation greats, opens with a claim to be based on true events. I'd like to see the newspaper report about the real-life Stegman's swinging corpse messing up the high school orchestra recital. *Newsweek*'s 1982 review praised the film for its precision and suspense, but recoiled from its graphic imagery and relentless tone, finally asking, "Who wants to get mugged by a movie?" Metalheads, that's who. We were—and are—the future!

Classic Albums: Motörhead—Ace of Spades (2005)

(Dir. Tim Kirkby; w/Lemmy Kilmister, Fast Eddie Clarke, Phil Taylor, Slash, Lars Ulrich)

✠ Warts ✠ Metal History ✠ Concert Footage

The kick-ass British documentary series *Classic Albums* consists of one-hour breakdowns of landmark rock recordings, explored and explained by original group members along with the engineers and producers who created the disc at hand. The *Classic Albums* canon contains no lack of heavy metal platters, but no single installment stands out like the one devoted to Motörhead's 1980 masterwork, *Ace of Spades.*

For this strange pseudo-reunion, bassist and frontman Lemmy Kilmister is joined in person by the *Ace of Spades* master tapes and classic drummer Phil "Philthy Animal" Taylor. Together, they reminisce and needle one another while isolating various instruments and pieces of music. A montage of Marlboro Reds and unfiltered Camels being ignited and dragged on is quite literally breathtaking.

Ex-Motörhead guitarist Fast Eddie Clarke is present, but, alas, not at the same time as his ex-mates. Clarke does his interviews solo. Later, when Lemmy and Philthy jam next to one another, Eddie plays along from a remote location. At one point, shoddy green-screen technology assembles an awkward "illusion" of the three band members playing "We Are the Road Crew" together, though Clarke seems to be suspended in some sort of Hawkwind-style interstellar vacuum. (Aimee Mann flying around the studio in Rush's "Time Stand Still" video is more convincing.)

Lemmy and Phil having a go, side by side, is British comedy platinum. Their exchanges run from ash-dry wit (Lemmy: "It's called the dead man's hand because it was in Wild Bill Hickock's hand when he died." Phil: "Yeah, before that it was just a hand, aces and eights, wasn't it?"); to several degrees past cheeky (Lemmy: "I'm getting a tattoo on my dick of a dick, only bigger"; Phil: "Good idea. I'm getting a third buttock tattooed right here on my buttock").

Among choice bits of history dislodged are some details on *Ace of Spades*' famous cover photo, which suggests a gritty spaghetti western. Instead of Mexico, the shot was taken in a British quarry. Fast Eddie was primarily interested in paying tribute to Clint Eastwood. Phil wanted to be Marlon Brando in *One-Eyed Jacks* (1961). Lemmy is done up as James Garner's '60s TV cowboy Brett Maverick—or so Phil claims.

Ultimately, *Ace of Spades* is the star, but Phil Taylor, a reality comic in the making, comes dangerously close to stealing the show. He introduces himself by showing a (real) hole in the sole of his shoe to match the prominent gapes within his (plastic) hillbilly choppers. He also slams the skins like a teenager, saves a booger to eat later, recounts how he broke his neck in a "who can lift the other guy highest" contest with a "big Irish kid," and claims Fast Eddie gets his guitar wah effects by keeping a live hamster underneath his pedal. Still every bit the cartoon dervish we see in the archive footage, Taylor bounces around the screen relentlessly one-upping Lemmy. When the singer says he wants to go to a strip club, Phil chimes in: "You going there to take your clothes off in front of all those men, *again*?"

Other metal-focused *Classic Albums* features include editions on *Paranoid* by Black Sabbath, *Disraeli Gears* by Cream, *Machine Head* by Deep Purple, *Hysteria* by Def Leppard, *Number of the Beast* by Iron Maiden, *Electric Ladyland* by Jimi Hendrix, *British Steel* by Judas Priest, *Metallica* by Metallica, *2112* and *Moving Pictures* by Rush, and *Apostrophe (')/Overnite Sensation* by Frank Zappa. Each documentary is excellently informative and entertaining.

Cliff 'Em All: The $19.98 Home Video (1987)

(Dirs. Doug Freel, Jean Pellerin; w/Cliff Burton, James Hetfield, Lars Ulrich, Kirk Hammett)

✠ Cliff Burton ✠ Metal History ✠ Bass Solo

On September 27, 1986, on Swedish highway in the early-morning hours, Metallica's tour bus flipped over and removed twenty-four-year-old Clifford Lee Burton from the living. Compounding the horror of life lost was the magnitude of talented bass master Burton's unfulfilled expectations. Not to diminish the agonizing and untimely loss of John Lennon or Dimebag Darrell, but those giants each left behind mythic bodies of work. Burton died prior to his prime, just as the Metallica starship was ascending.

Metallica paid visual homage to their bassist via the warts-and-all *Cliff 'Em All* camcorder assemblage, an immediate fan favorite. The directors cleverly culled candid clips from friends and trawled the underground for bootleg concert footage to portray Cliff as he was, onstage and off, rocking and reveling, blowing away hometown headbangers and international festival crowds alike. James Hetfield sums up *Cliff 'Em All* in the video's liner notes: "A compilation of bootleg footage shot by sneaky Metallifux, stuff shot for TV that was never used, but we've held onto, home footage, personal fotos and us drunk." All of this is terrifically accurate.

"But most important," Hetfield continues, "it's really a look back at the 3-1/2 years that Cliff was with us and includes his best bass solos and the home footage and pix that we feel best capture his unique personality and style."

Watching Burton in action at tiny Bay Area club the Stone, alongside former Metallica axeman Dave Mustaine, or having his name chanted at the massive Roskilde Festival is marvelous. His skill and smile shine during exquisite solos that smolder with his Bach-obsessed classical training. Keeping it real, *Cliff 'Em All*'s final image is a shot of Burton carefully holding a flower in one hand and, with the other, shooting an unwavering, defiant middle finger straight upward.

A Clockwork Orange (1971)

(Dir. Stanley Kubrick; w/Malcolm McDowell, Patrick Magee, Adrienne Corri, Miriam Karlin)

✠ Dystopia ✠ Youth Uprising ✠ Mind Control

One of the cornerstones of heavy metal cinema, visionary filmmaker Stanley Kubrick's follow-up to his monolithically metal *2001: A Space Odyssey*, *A Clockwork Orange* elevates Anthony Burgess's 1962 future-cool novel of teen gang violence to a pornographic pop-art visual universe of beautiful repugnance.

Alex (Malcolm McDowell) and his gang of "droogs" get high on drinkable drug "milk plus" and storm England's public alleys and private homes. One beating-and-rape spree culminates in Alex murdering a woman with a penis statue. The droogs betray him when the cops arrive, and Alex goes to jail. Ten years into his prison sentence, Alex submits to the "Ludovico Technique," aversion therapy that will make him sick when confronted with violence. It will also viscerally put Alex off his other two great passions, classical music and sex with young girls.

Released back into society, Alex is rejected by his parents and throttled by his ex-droogs, who are now cops. He falls into the hands of Mr. Alexander (Patrick Magee), a famous writer he crippled. (Alex also raped Mrs. Alexander.) Liberal Mr. Alexander intends to use Alex to expose the cruelty of the Ludovico Technique, until he realizes that Alex was his attacker. He then goes for revenge, via Beethoven's Ninth Symphony.

Kubrick and his astonishing cast—particularly, of course, McDowell in star-making terrorist mode—hold up a mirror to government-backed censor groups such as the metal-hunting PMRC and the nation of scolds that longs for the state to save it from its own children. *Clockwork* further lays bare the destructive loop of a society whose upper echelons are bent on indulging pornographic decadence and high-end hedonism while forbidding such pleasures to the untouchable classes and, when necessary, controlling them through totalitarian torture and mind control.

Numerous visual high points from *Clockwork* have later appeared in heavy metal album artwork and music videos: the nude woman furniture of the Korova milk bar; the black bowler hats, white thermals, false eyelashes, and phallic-nosed costumes; Alex having high-speed sex with two teen girls to the "William Tell Overture"; Alex's mechanically peeled-apart eyelids as he undergoes Ludovico treatment; Alex envisioning himself as a Roman centurion whipping Christ en route to crucifixion; and many more.

The connection between classical music and heavy metal takes an interesting turn in *Clockwork*, as the former is depicted as underlying violent antisocial behavior that typically gets pinned on the latter. The use of Beethoven's soaring Ninth Symphony especially hammers home the irony, such beautiful music tied to such ugliness.

Slipknot percussionist Chris Fehn's stage mask is a tribute to the long-nosed mask worn by Alex. Sepultura's 2009 release *A-Lex* is a concept-album adaptation of *A Clockwork Orange*. Its title is also a pun: in Latin, *a lex* means "without law." Other examples are numerous; two standouts are Death Angel's 1987 debut album *The Ultra-Violence*, and Megadeth's adoption of the term *droogies* to describe followers of the band.

Club Satan: The Witches' Sabbath (2007)

(Dir. Shane Bugbee; Cassandra Cruz, Dakota, Heather Gables, Scott Lyons)

✠ Black Metal ✠ Satan ✠ Black Mass ✠ Soundtrack (Acheron, Society 1)

Multimedia provocateur Shane Bugbee (Mike Hunt Publishing) detours from underground publishing and into hard-core porn with *Club Satan: The Witches' Sabbath*. Bugbee directs a coven of porn lovelies through a psychedelic occult sex freak-out that includes an actual Black Mass, fisting, pissing nuns, crucifixes as orifice stuffers, Satan getting his salad tossed, and Christ taking a money shot in the kisser (upside-down, of course). There's no questioning that the various penetrations and expulsions are legit, but lest anyone question the devil worship's authenticity, the movie's box cover assures, "Church of Satan officials oversaw each and every aspect of the making of *Club Satan: The Witches' Sabbath*."

Tripped-out rectal blasphemies and pentagram-staining gang bangs are tied together with a slaying all-metal soundtrack—Swedish black metal titans Dark Funeral bust out "King Antichrist" and "The New Society." *Club Satan* boils over, stickily, with the very definition of the term *goddamned*. The movie debuted on April 30, 2007, Walpurgis Night, for those keeping track, playing simultaneously in bars, galleries, screening rooms, and a Detroit fetish boutique.

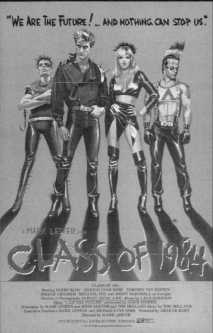

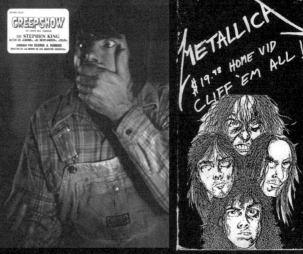

Clockwise from top: The Crimson Ghost (1946); *Metallica's*
Cliff 'Em All *(1987); Dali and Buñuel's shock horror* Un Chien
Andalusian *(1929); Stephen King in* Creepshow *(1982); the unruly*
Class of 1984 *(1982)*

Combat Shock (1985),
aka American Nightmares
(Dir. Buddy Giovinazzo; w/Rick Giovinazzo, Veronica Stork, Mitch Maglio)
✤ Psycho 'Nam Vet ✤ Staten Island

Writer-director Buddy Giovinazzo made one of cinema's most searing deadbeat-on-a-bum-trip downers with *American Nightmare*. When schlock house Troma Films picked up the movie for a grindhouse release (during a weird period when they also put out the arty *Story of a Junky*) the studio gave it the better, more fitting title of *Combat Shock*. However genuinely relatable the story of lead loser Frankie Dunlan (Rick Giovinazzo, the director's brother) may have been among Vietnam vets returning to an America enflamed by social and financial shit storms, *Combat Shock* is uniquely inseparable from its setting, the most disconnected and landfill-spotted New York City borough, Staten Island.

Frankie's Staten Island is a cold, concrete slab of weeds, broken glass, and burned-out buildings that serve as shooting galleries. The streets buckle with gang violence and ten-year-old prostitutes. At home, Frankie's dumpy, sour wife Cathy (Veronica Stork) tends to their deformed monster-baby and shrieks at our hero to get a job. But nobody's got a job for Frankie.

Escape comes in the form of Frankie's frequent, splat-tastically gory jungle-fighting flashbacks. And heroin. The latter has caused Frankie to run up a bill with scumbag crime lord Paco (Mitch Maglio); the former makes him need dope more than ever. For Frankie, as for his equally damaged Vietnam-era colleagues Travis Bickle (*Taxi Driver*), John Eastland (*The Exterminator*), and Major Charles Rane (*Rolling Thunder*), the pushed-too-far point ultimately arrives, triggering his subsequent hyper-violent revenge. Unlike those classic Ministers of Retribution, though, Frankie acts not to correct the wrongs of others but simply to blow the perpetrators away. The dealers and the leg-breakers go down in a

barrage of bloodletting. So do Mrs. Dunlan and Junior. Then Frankie turns the gun on himself.

Combat Shock is a declaration of the one-of-a-kind talent of creator Buddy Giovinazzo, and should have propelled him at least into a proper B-movie career. That never happened, but he has produced four novels and worked as a film instructor at New York's School of the Visual Arts and NYU. *Combat Shock* remains not only a cult favorite, but also the sole case of Troma consistently doing right by one of its acquisitions; witness the expansive double-disc Blu-ray edition.

The wasted look, feel, and locale of *Combat Shock* certainly explain how Staten Island became a heavy metal hotbed in the 1980s, home to historic Metallica and Venom shows in early 1983, and birthplace of hairy bands including Cities and Savage Thrust. The film is actually partially inspired by the song "Frankie Teardrop," a ten-minute odyssey of bleakness by the metallic electro-noise duo Suicide. One of the standouts from the mid-'70s CBGB period that begat the Ramones et al, Suicide is psycho-intense frontman Alan Vega wailing over the hissing and chugging of Martin Rev's dispassionate and repetitive synths. From Suicide comes industrial (Ministry, Godflesh), power electronics (Whitehouse, Grey Wolves), noise (Wolf Eyes, Bloodyminded), drone (Sunn o))), Jesu) and myriad more subgenres hell-bent on annihilation of the senses.

Conan the Barbarian
(1982)
(Dir. John Milius; w/Arnold Schwarzenegger, Sandahl Bergman, James Earl Jones)
✤ Barbarians ✤ Swords & Sorcery

Featuring the ultimate metal pulp icon and power fantasy personified, portrayed here by the ultimate metal '80s movie icon, Arnold Schwarzenegger, *Conan* is a pivotal landmark in heavy metal movie history. Steel, sweat, spell casting, snake worship, meat, muscle, massacres, cannibalism, camel punching, war paint, witch sex, and overall flawless awesomeness are the active ingredients of *Conan the Barbarian*. All of those things, and der Arnold, who transforms here from bodybuilding curiosity to biggest movie star in the world.

We first meet young Conan the Cimmerian in the Hyborian Age, when his happy childhood is cut short by merciless marauders who sack his village, slaughter his parents, and march him into slavery. He spends his formative years pushing the blades of a giant mill for the benefit of evil overlord Thulsa Doom (James Earl Jones), head of a flesh-eating cult that prays to snakes. For years, Conan stomps, endlessly building physical strength and a rage for revenge.

Adult Conan (Arnold Schwarzenegger) escapes the daily grind by engaging in bare-knuckle fighting for his cruel masters, eventually punching, strangling, and snapping spines to freedom. Then time comes to really slay some ass. After Conan stirs up a supernatural storm by sticking his flesh saber into a witch (Cassandra Gava), he hooks up with crafty Mongol thief Subotai (pro surfer Gerry Lopez) and falls for valiant swordswoman Valeria (badass Broadway dancer Sandahl Bergman). Together, they take a job from King Osric (Max von Sydow) to rescue his daughter (Valerie Quennessen), who has fallen in with Thulsa Doom's mesmerized devotees. Along the way, Conan turns to Crom, the god of steel, for guidance and inspiration.

"Crom is strong!" Conan explains. "If I die, I have to go before him, and he will ask me, 'What is the riddle of steel?' If I don't know it, he will cast me out of Valhalla and laugh at me!" That's a heavy trip.

The bloodletting, brutality, and, oh yes, barbarism that erupt from their mission, culminating with the painted-up trio invading one of Thulsa Doom's cannibal orgies, is as perfect an embodiment of classic heavy metal visuals as has ever been conveyed by motion pictures. Conan's charging, spellbinding neoclassical score comes courtesy of composer Basil Poledouris. Even without electric guitars, his orchestra thunders pure metal, breaching a chasm to musically

inspire Celtic Frost, Morbid Angel, and many others grappling with their own riddles of steel.

Thulsa Doom demonstrates to the always-quick-to-decapitate Conan that power can be even greater when wielded lightly. At the base of his mountain chamber, Doom turns to a robe-clad female worshipper on the rocks above them. He smiles at her, gestures with his hand, and calmly says, "Come to me, my child." The girl happily leaps to her death at their feet. "That is strength, boy," Doom says. "That is power: the strength and power of flesh. What is steel compared to the hand that wields it?"

During his saga, Conan is crucified. He stays alive by killing vultures with his teeth, until his friends can rescue him. When he's asked what is best in life, Conan lays out the ultimate power trip: "To crush your enemies, to see them driven before you and to hear the lamentation of the women." These words to live by are made infinitely more metal by Arnold's pronunciation.

Originally, Conan the Barbarian was created in a series of stories and novels by fantasy author Robert E. Howard in the 1930s. They sold well and built a growing following for decades, spawning a Marvel Comics spin-off in 1970 that exploded in popularity. Conan's emergence and domination as a comic book hero directly paralleled the rise of heavy metal. Like that of *Lord of the Rings*, the reach of *Conan the Barbarian* into heavy metal music is vast, profound, and ongoing. Bands like Conan and Virgin Steele dressed like Conan, and Manilla Road and hundreds of others wrote songs about his exploits.

Although Italian painter Renato Casaro created the *Conan* movie poster, the influence of Brooklyn-born über-metal visual artist Frank Frazetta is all over the film. Frazetta contributed covers to numerous Conan novels, as well as countless fantasy images that motivated the psyche of early heavy metal. In one of the most famous cases of false advertising in the form of a record cover, his mighty painting *The Death Dealer* was used by party-hearty Southern rock band Molly Hatchet on the cover of their self-titled debut.

Director John Milius previously scripted *Magnum Force* (1973) and *Apocalypse Now* (1979), and went on to direct *Red Dawn* (1985). In the documentary *Frazetta: Painting With Fire* (2003), Milius points out several scenes in the movie that pay direct homage to the master: the princess chained to a pillar; Thulsa Doom transforming into a giant snake; and the final battle in the blood-drenched orgy chamber.

The mysticism surrounding Crom and "the riddle of steel" has proven nearly as beguiling to metalheads as Tolkien's spiritual system laid out in *Lord of the Rings*. When Conan breaks his father's sword in battle, he find the answer to the riddle: whether one worships steel, flesh, or anything else (heavy metal music, say), strength and power come directly from the passion of one's dedication and belief.

Conan the Destroyer

(1984)

(Dir. Richard Fleischer; w/Olivia d'Abo, Arnold Schwarzenegger, Grace Jones, Wilt Chamberlain)
✠ **Barbarians**

Witness one of the great bungles in Heavy Metal Movies. The charms of this sequel to the landmark *Conan the Barbarian* (1982) are inexorably intertwined with what sank the movie upon release. Lethally, this *Conan* is cute. After original director John Milius proved unavailable (while working on *Red Dawn*), producer Dino De Laurentiis toned down the solemnity and ultraviolence in order to turn the Conan franchise into an international family franchise. The result pleased no one. Still, we've only got so many *Conan* movies. While not in a league with *Barbarian*, you can't really hate *Destroyer*.

Arnold is his usual perfect self, and the stunt casting of Grace Jones and Wilt Chamberlain as sidekicks works well. Tracey Walter, a shar-pei-faced comic character actor best known as Miller in *Repo Man* (1984), is amusing as a two-bit thief. Olivia d'Abo, the big sister on *The Wonder Years*, debuts as a suitably luminous teen princess in

need of rescue by sorcery and broadsword.

Nonetheless, there's not much destructive about *Conan the Destroyer*. In terms of the metal of the day, this movie is all Ratt, Night Ranger, and Van Halen's *1984*, when it could have been Metallica and Slayer. Good times in any case, but sadly not a great Conan movie. At least *Conan the Destroyer*, the painting by Frank Frazetta for which the film is named, sold for $1.5 million. Also, the mook in the suit playing the monstrous Dagoth is pro wrestling super-legend Andre the Giant.

Conflict of Interest

(1993)

(Dir. Gary Davis; w/Judd Nelson, Christopher McDonald, Joey Katz, Alyssa Milano)
✠ **Motorcycles**

Brat pack nostril-flare kingpin Judd Nelson fell into a solid B-movie spree after his big-screen roles dried up, doing particularly impressive serial-killer work in William Lustig's *Relentless* (1989). Judd may be no Eric Roberts, but his late-night cable action thrillers like *Conflict of Interest* are dependable. As villain Gideon, Nelson runs the Wreck, which is described as "the deffest metal club in town," decorated with real motorcycle chandeliers.

Gideon has a good racket going in San Pedro, Metal City, with his elaborate pirate shirts, fake-boobed booty dancers, and underground illegal activities. Then along comes crazed cop Mickey Flannery (mustachioed Christopher McDonald), and we have a direct-to-VHS showdown set to a blazingly generic faux-metal soundtrack.

Director Gary Davis is a legendary stunt performer. He has abused his body a thousand different ways in more than eighty movies, including *Race With the Devil* (1975), *Return From Witch Mountain* (1978), *Knightriders* (1981), *Megaforce* (1982), *They Live* (1988), *Terminator 2* (1991), *The Devil's Advocate* (1997), and *Thor* (2011). The stunts here come off better than the movie's budget should allow, thanks to snazzy work by Davis.

CONQUEST (1983)

(DIR. LUCIO FULCI; W/JORGE RIVERO, SABRINA SIANI, CONRADO SAN MARTIN, ANDREA OCHIPINTI)

✤ **SWORDS & SORCERY** ✤ **WOLFMEN**

My favorite of all the myriad early-'80s *Conan* rip-offs, *Conquest* is a crazily imaginative swirl of sword-and-sorcery tropes rendered unique by its stylized sights and sounds, its one-of-a-kind topless villainess, and the go-for-barbaric-broke direction of Italian splatter specialist Lucio Fulci (1979's *Zombie*). The entire film is rendered in a gauzy fog, quite the opposite of Fulci's typical lurid red gore and gristle.

At issue in this post-*Conan* action fantasy is ownership of a magic bow, once wielded by the god Kronos and said to be able to make arrows from beams of sunlight. The action commences with Ocron (Sabrina Siani), a permanently bare-breasted, decidedly evil sorceress whose entire head is encased in a golden mask. She leads an army of dog-faced wolfmen. For kicks, she snorts drugs and trips out over visions of being murdered by the magic wonder weapon.

Mace (Jorge Rivero) is our Schwarzenegger stand-in. His best friend is a hawk, the better to toss in some co-opted *Beastmaster* moments. He teams with Ilias (Andrea Occhipinti), an archer, to take out Ocron. The two good guys and one bad lady's various exploits comprise the remainder of *Conquest*, in weird and exciting fashion.

In the annals of heavy metal movie goddess figures, evil or otherwise, we can't quite worship Sabrina Sinai's Ocron hard enough. Her golden head, lithely naked torso, and spiritual communion with snakes are pure metal lyricism made supple flesh. Twenty years old when the film was made, Siani began acting in Italy as a teenager. Her big break was portraying the commandingly credible title figure in *White Cannibal Queen* (1980), and she costarred in Joe D'Amato's famous *Conan* cash-in *Ator the Fighting Eagle* (1982). She then went on to D'Amato's laudably insane *2020: Texas Gladiators* (1984).

THE COUNTESS (2009)

(DIR. JULIE DELPY; W/JULIE DELPY, WILLIAM HURT)

✤ **COUNTESS BATHORY**

The closest we will get to a *Masterpiece Theater* take on the true story of Elizabeth Bathory, *The Countess* is a labor of love (and bloodlust) for esteemed French actress Julie Delpy. She stars as the notorious seventeenth-century noblewoman who bathed in the blood of female virgins, and she also wrote and directed this good-looking, nicely paced retelling of available facts.

Elizabeth Bathory as a topic is tailor-made for both high art and exploitation cinema. We've gotten the former in the unstoppable form of *Immoral Tales* (1974), and the latter numerous times over, ranging from *Countess Dracula* (1971) to *Hostel: Part II* (2007). Julie Delpy's *The Countess* provides a bloody good middle ground.

The countess socks it to a dandified Catholic cleric who challenges the equality of women: "I am a woman. I love beautiful dresses and shiny jewelry. Just like you, Bishop." After a private trial, Bathory is convicted of her crimes and sentenced to be walled up in her bedroom. The sense of doom Delpy communicates in the movie's final scenes as the layers of bricks rise really brings down the house.

COUNTESS DRACULA (1971)

(DIR. PETER SASDY; W/INGRID PITT, NIGEL GREEN, ANDREA LAWRENCE, SUSAN BRODRICK)

✤ **COUNTESS BATHORY** ✤ **HAMMER HORROR**

Hammer Films took a bold, salacious step away from their typical top-notch vampire and Frankenstein fare with the tawdry, R-rated *Countess Dracula*, based on the Eastern European legend of Countess Elizabeth Bathory. Polish-born scream queen Ingrid Pitt stars as an ignoble Hungarian noblewoman who discovers that bathing in the blood of female virgins keeps her young. The countess is soon dispatching henchmen to round up and drain dry the local teen girl population so she can plop in and out of plasma baths with glee. Such antics can't go on forever and, of course, given the angry nature of villagers with fluid-depleted daughters, they don't.

Countess Dracula combines Hammer's trademark gothic atmospherics (fog, castles, tombstones) with the new freedom of the early '70s (nude peasant babes galore). It's not really scary, but Ingrid's really, really naked. She later reprised the role of the Countess Bathory on English black metal band Cradle of Filth's 1998 concept album, *Cruelty and the Beast*.

The Covenant (2006)

(Dir. Renny Harlin; w/Taylor Kitsch, Laura Ramsey, Steven Strait, Toby Hemingway)

✠ Black Magic ✠ Witch Trials ✠ Soundtrack (White Zombie, Killing Joke)

In the dwindling days of VHS, teenagers futzing around with occult hellfire became a genre unto itself in by way of dude-objectifying B-movie franchises such as *Black Circle Boys* (1997) and *The Brotherhood* (2001). Like a "mockbuster" in reverse, *The Covenant* amps that formula up for the big screen, scrubs the homoeroticism down to a PG-13, and rips off *X-Men* and *Harry Potter*.

Four prep school muscleheads, one played by Taylor Kitsch (*John Carter*), are warlocks descended from survivors of a seventeenth-century Salem witch purge. Each bohunk boasts various magic powers and they use them to do wicked cool stuff like lead local cops on a chase and then pull up behind the patrol car, pointing and laughing. When a fifth frat-boy sorcerer shows up looking to consume all their mystic abilities, the battle of the stupid CGI effects is on.

Pulsating throughout *The Covenant* is a serviceable techno-metal score by movie composer duo tomandandy, and canned industrial metal by White Zombie and Frontline Assembly.

Cradle of Fear (2001)

(Dir. Alex Chandon; w/Dani Filth, Emily Booth, David McEwen, Eileen Daly, Edmund Dehn)

✠ Satan ✠ British Horror ✠ Goth Chicks ✠ Soundtrack (Cradle of Filth)

Like infamous metal compilations such as *Metal for Muthas* and *Metal Fatigue*, the British horror anthology is a grand Heavy Metal Movie tradition. What Hammer Films was to classic monsters and gothic bloodletting, Amicus Productions was to anthologies. Among the best of Amicus's releases are *Dr. Terror's House of Horrors* (1965), *Torture Garden* (1967), *Tales From the Crypt* (1972), *The Vault of Horror* (1973), and the rock-and-roll-centric *The Monster Club* (1980).

Given how much he resembles a scary puppet, Dani Filth is ideally cast as "The Man," a Crypt Keeper–like host in the fright anthology *Cradle of Fear*. The Man doesn't wisecrack, but he does slit throats with his shadow and crush skulls like tomatoes. He's a demon in cahoots with Satan-worshipping child rapist and serial murderer Kemper (David McEwen), who begins the film in prison. The mission of The Man is to knock off the jury members who put Kemper behind bars. We see each of their stories.

First up, Emily Booth (credited as Emily Bouffante) is a goth chick who is banged by a hell-spawn and so must give herself a gore-geyser of an abortion. Next, a pair of lesbian cat burglars (Rebecca Eden and Emma Rice) attempt to beat an old man to death; but in the beloved fashion of old E.C. horror comics, he simply will not stay dead. Third is a kinky amputee who will do anything to obtain a new leg. The leg, however, has an agenda of its own. Finally, an Internet pervert happens upon a room where one can direct a snuff video remotely. Karma turns out to be a bitch—with a hammer. Cradle of Filth band members cameo throughout each segment.

Cradle of Fear looks cheap and shoddy but keeps your attention. Notably, distinct elements of each story are impressive affronts to good taste. Essentially, this is a Cradle of Filth horror movie and delivers exactly what fans and foes alike would expect, to both its credit and detriment.

The Craft (1996)

(Dir. Andrew Fleming; w/Robin Tunney, Fairuza Balk, Neve Campbell, Rachel True)

✡ Witchcraft

The Craft was sold as the dark sister of *Clueless* (1995), and as a spelunk into the rites of teen girl drama and trauma that would provide a sinister parallel to the latter film's ebullient pop pleasures. For preteen female heavy metal fans in particular, *The Craft* acted as a gateway into the deeper revels and heady perils of occult exploration and increasingly extreme music.

Robin Tunney plays an edgy telepath who falls in with a high school coven; Fairuza Balk, Neve Campbell, and Rachel True. They solve their typical adolescent issues by casting spells that reap unforeseen consequences—e.g., zapping romantic feelings into the high school hunk turns him into an obsessed stalker. A few of the special effects pack an iron punch, particularly the disturbing scenes involving bugs, thousands of snakes, and a nastily beached whale.

The Craft was a sleeper hit that swelled into a bona fide cult among budding death-betties. It even inspired a mini-genre of ongoing direct-to-video rip-offs, including *Little Witches* (1996), *I've Been Waiting for You* (1998), and *5ive Girls* (2006). The young coven's chant is catchy and, given the proper harmonic deepening, would make a good doom record sample: "Now is the time. This is the hour. Ours is the magic. Ours is the power. Now is the time. This is the hour. Ours is the magic. Ours is the power."

Cream: Strange Brew (1991)

(Dir. Paul Justman; w/Eric Clapton, Jack Bruce, Ginger Baker)

✡ Proto-Metal ✡ Concert Footage

A succint hour-long overview of proto-metal's most towering power trio, *Cream: Strange Brew* combines good interviews with all three members and hit-or-miss performance footage. VH1's *Behind the Music* series perfected this formula a few years later. Among the highlights, Jimi Hendrix tips his headband to Cream with a wailing cover of "Sunshine of Your Love."

Creepshow (1982)

(Dir. George Romero; w/E. G. Marshall, Adrienne Barbeau, Hal Holbrook, Leslie Nielsen, Ted Danson, Stephen King)

✡ Stephen King ✡ Tom Savini ✡ Zombies

Creepshow brought together writer Stephen King and director George Romero, two defining horror brand names of the early 1980s, to revel in the retro ghoulishness of their own childhoods. The film combines 1950s E.C. Comics frights with 1970s Amicus Productions horror story anthology films, updated for the callous and high-splatter 1980s. Vividly gruesome for its day, at least on a mainstream level, the movie immediately snared a cult following among heavy metal fans (and inspired a Skid Row song).

A cool opening cartoon unfolds into an okay framing story regarding a belligerent dad confiscating a young kid's fright comic. From there, we get quite the mixed bag of horror shorts.

The first story, "Father's Day," ends memorably with a severed head being served with icing and candles. "The Lonesome Death of Jordy Verrill," starring Stephen King himself as a farmer being consumed by alien plant life, is just depressing.

Better is "Something to Tide You Over," with Leslie Nielsen slowly drowning his wife (Gaylen Ross) and her side piece (Ted Danson) by burying them up to their necks in sand as the waves roll in over their heads. Unfortunately, he couldn't quite get them to stay buried. "The Crate" is ponderous monster-in-a-box stuff, leading to the movie's high point, "They're Creeping Up on You!"

Alone in his high-tech penthouse, millionaire E. G. Marshall is a raving nut billionaire germophobe in the mad mold of Howard Hughes. He steadily and understandably descends into lunacy as thousands upon thousands of cockroaches overrun his spotless home fortress. Romero shoots the glisteningly antiseptic sets to maximize the gross-out impact of the bugs and builds wittily to the flesh-crawling inevitable.

Though *Creepshow* is too long and too slow, the movie is a glowing nostalgic benchmark for the first VCR generation of headbanging horror fanatics. In fact, the syndicated late-night horror anthology television series *Tales From the Darkside* (1984–88) began as a *Creepshow* spin-off, produced by George Romero and featuring occasional contributions from Stephen King. *Tales From the Darkside: The Movie* (1990) is that show's perfectly respectable big-screen adaptation. Makeup artist Tom Savini says he considers that film to be "the real *Creepshow 3*."

Lighter, loopier, and more memorable than its much-ballyhooed 1982 predecessor, *Creepshow 2* (1987) cuts the number of King stories from five to three. George Romero produces, handing directorial reins to frequent collaborator Michael Gornick. The results, less geared to a preteen crowd, are a lot of fun, with copious gore and ghoulishness. Makeup maestro Tom Savini appears as the monster-faced "Creepshow Creep."

Creepshow 2 ends with a quote from *Colliers* magazine published in 1949, defending comic books against the witch hunt of the era but surely with contemporary anti–heavy metal moves by the PMRC in mind: "Juvenile delinquency is the product of pent-up frustrations, stored-up resentments, and bottled-up fears. But the comics are a handy, obvious, uncomplicated scapegoat. If the

adults who crusade against them would only get as steamed up over such basic causes of delinquency as parental ignorance, indifference, and cruelty, they might discover that comic books are no more a menace than *Treasure Island* or *Jack the Giant Killer*."

CREMASTER 2 (1999)
(DIR. MATTHEW BARNEY; W/MATTHEW BARNEY, DAVE LOMBARDO, STEVE TUCKER, NORMAN MAILER)
✠ DEATH METAL ✠ BEES

The husband of Björk, who herself had commissioned a Carcass remix years earlier, Matthew Barney scored high-art pay dirt with his nonsensical *Cremaster* film series. *Cremaster 2*, the fourth entry in this lushly photographed nonsense cycle, warrants special attention thanks to appearances by Slayer and Morbid Angel personnel (with a nod to hard-boiled literary icon Norman Mailer costarring as Harry Houdini).

In this film, Slayer's Dave Lombardo barrels through a drum solo in a recording studio, accompanied by buzzing sounds. Then a guy covered with bees roars into a telephone, his voice provided by longtime Morbid Angel singer Steve Tucker. Matthew Barney gets paid insane amounts of money for this sort of *mishegoss*, and his metal fetish resulted in some bizarre society scenes, such as Mortician main man and heavy metal movie proponent extraordinaire Will Rahmer rubbing shoulders with the chin-tucked grand society dames of New York.

THE CRIMSON GHOST
(1946), AKA CYCLOTRODE X
(DIRS. FRED C. BANNON, WILLIAM WITNEY; W/CHARLES QUIGLEY, LINDA STIRLING, CLAYTON MOORE)
✠ MISFITS SKULL ✠ IRON MAIDEN VIDEO

The Crimson Ghost is a supervillain in the twelve-part movie serial that bears his name. He wears a hood, a cape, and the coolest skull mask ever devised for motion pictures; no disrespect intended to *Halloween III: Season of the*

Witch. The Ghost aims to steal the Cyclotrode X, a device that can nullify atomic bombs and shut down any electrical device.

While exciting and visually creative, *The Crimson Ghost* is now remembered primarily for the title character's bone-faced mask. In the late 1970s, the Misfits appropriated the image as their logo and mascot. Metallica bassist Cliff Burton famously had the Crimson Ghost skull image tattooed on his upper arm. That toothy skull expanded the visual iconography of hard rock, as well, and has become an all-purpose cultural icon appropriated by anyone and everyone, including hip-hop shoe designers.

Following are the twelve chapters of the Crimson Ghost saga, reproduced here for any up-and-comer looking for a dozen solid song titles: 1. "Atomic Peril"; 2. "Thunderbolt"; 3. "The Fatal Sacrifice"; 4. "The Laughing Skull"; 5. "Flaming Death"; 6. "Mystery of the Mountain"; 7. "Electrocution"; 8. "The Slave Collar"; 9. "Blazing Fury"; 10. "The Trap That Failed"; 11. "Double Murder"; 12. "The Invisible Trail."

CROMWELL (1970)

(DIR. KEN HUGHES; W/RICHARD HARRIS, ALEC GUINNESS, ROBERT MORLEY, DOROTHY TUTIN)
✣ RELIGIOUS FANATICS ✣ MEDIEVAL WARFARE

Oliver Cromwell, Lord Protector of England during the early seventeenth century, hated Catholics. Like Nuclear Assault, he wanted to see the pope on the end of a rope. He was a violently pious Anglican and anti-papist who created the New Model Army to wage a coup d'état against the British throne, and then waged God-on-his-side genocidal invasions of Ireland and Scotland. This movie focuses on the strongman's rise to power. Richard Harris fills out the frightfully metal suit of armor with the most righteous war helmet in UK history. Alec Guinness is a great foil as King Charles I.

Full of epic battles, florid costumes, and fiery fanaticism, *Cromwell* brings to life a very old wave of British heaviness. Charles Gray plays

the Earl of Essex, a breather role for him between embodying an ersatz Aleister Crowley in *The Devil Rides Out* (1968) and narrating as the Criminologist in *The Rocky Horror Picture Show* (1975). Though British history admittedly has to overcome a PBS stodginess to breathe fire on-screen, *Cromwell* deserves the good dusting. Among the metal bands that have dared to trade in this subject matter are Finland's impossibly heavy Reverend Bizarre and bands named Cromwell from Finland, Italy, and Spain.

CROSSROADS (1986)

(DIR. WALTER HILL; W/RALPH MACCHIO, STEVE VAI, JOE SENECA, JAMI GERTZ)
✣ SATAN ✣ GUITARS

Like a blues-metal movie version of the 1979 Charlie Daniels Band romp "The Devil Went Down to Georgia," *Crossroads* pits the karate kid himself (Ralph Macchio) as a Julliard guitar student thwarting the number one shredder in hell (the mighty Steve Vai) in a battle of the jams to win back the soul of blues legend Willie Brown (Joe Seneca). Ry Cooder delivers a nice musical score, supplementing lots of Robert Johnson songs, all of which seem quaint when Steve Vai summons fire and brimstone during his big solo.

In addition to teaching Daniel-san how to credibly wail on an axe, Zappa and David Lee Roth collaborator Vai exudes a diabolical screen presence. He should play the devil's music in more movies. This *Crossroads* has no connection to the 2002 Britney Spears vehicle of the same name, although that does raise the question of whether she might be another Deep South musician who signed her soul away to Old Scratch.

The Crow (1994)

(Dir. Alex Proyas; w/Brandon Lee, Sofia Shinas, Michael Wincott, Bai Ling, Ernie Hudson)

✠ Goth ✠ Curse ✠ Soundtrack (Helmet, Pantera, Rollins Band)

Melancholy enveloped *The Crow* long before the movie made it to theaters. Brandon Lee, the movie's twenty-eight-year-old star and the son of the gone-too-soon martial arts legend Bruce Lee, was killed on the set when a gun thought to contain blanks fired a live bullet. The sudden loss of rising talent Lee was a tragedy on every level, and made a morbid backstory for a semi-futuristic rock-and-roll spectacle about a murdered goth singer who returns on Devil's Night as a dark angel of vengeance.

Lee plays Eric Draven, frontman for Detroit gloom band Hangman's Joke. He's murdered while attempting to rescue his girlfriend from rapist thugs. A year later, a crow taps on Eric's tombstone and the rocker rises from the grave. He has gained the power to heal spontaneously and, after donning a black leather body suit and applying sad ghost makeup, Draven hunts down the drug lord who caused his death. All kinds of brutes get royally wasted along the way.

Director Alex Proyas mounts *The Crow* as a fluid series of moody, ultra-stylized set pieces flash-flooded with brain-bashing action and maniacal gunplay. Lee seems to have been born to be an off-kilter A-list movie star. His actual death is inevitably draped over every frame of the film, but he carries the entire mammoth production flawlessly during the pulse-pounding punch-ups and he can be quite moving when *The Crow* frequently slows down to languish in gloom.

The Crow was adapted from a late-'80s cult comic book series by James O'Barr. The Detroit-based writer and artist created the comic to help cope with the death of his fiancée, who was killed by a drunk driver. Yes, everything about *The Crow* is soaked in bummer. O'Barr himself is a musician, performing with avant-garde metal band Trust Obey. They were briefly signed to Trent Reznor's Nothing Records. Orgiastic industrial metal act My Life With the Thrill Kill Kult appears on stage in a rock club.

The soundtrack offers an excellent sampling of mid-'90s alt-metal. The covers are great. Pantera plays Poison Idea's "The Badge"; Nine Inch Nails performs Joy Division's "Dead Souls"; Rollins Band does Suicide's "Ghost Rider." Stone Temple Pilots scored a huge, lasting hit with "Big Empty." Outliving its star, *The Crow* then spawned three movie sequels and a TV series, which lasted two seasons in syndication, called *The Crow: Stairway to Heaven*.

The Crow: City of Angels (1996)

(Dir. Tim Pope; w/Vincent Perez, Mia Kirshner, Richard Brooks, Iggy Pop)

✠ Soundtrack (Deftones, Korn, Iggy Pop, White Zombie)

For *The Crow: City of Angels*, Swiss actor Vincent Perez dons the fancy corpse paint first worn by Brandon Lee in *The Crow* (1994). Perez plays Ashe Corven, yet another murdered innocent resurrected by a mythic crow to wreak vengeful havoc on a pack of gangsters. *City of Angels* delivers satisfying violence and two standout sequences. First, Ashe slaughters a thug in a porno peep show and decimates the place, sending jizz mops, filthy tokens, and cracked video screens blaring smut everywhere. Then head baddie Judah Earl (Richard Brooks) crucifies the crow with knives and sucks its blood as a Day of the Dead sacrifice.

Beyond those epic dustups, the movie never really takes flight, but it prepped the Crow cult for two more movie follow-ups, *The Crow: Salvation* (2000) and *The Crow: Wicked Prayer* (2005), plus the syndicated TV series, *The Crow: Stairway to Heaven*. Iggy Pop is great here as a throat-stomping villain named Curve. He should make more movies. On the other end of the spectrum, Jon Bon Jovi allegedly auditioned to play Ashe.

CROWLEY (2008),

AKA CHEMICAL WEDDING

(DIR. JULIAN DOYLE; W/SIMON CALLOW, KAL WEBER, LUCY CUDDEN, JUD CHARLTON)

✸ ALEISTER CROWLEY ✸ SOUNDTRACK (IRON MAIDEN, BRUCE DICKINSON)

Ozzy Osbourne may sing about "Mr. Crowley," but Iron Maiden frontman Bruce Dickinson wrote the screenplay to an entire movie about the famed occult-obsessed Victorian hedonist. Dickinson also cameos as Crowley's landlord. *Crowley* casts esteemed British thespian Simon Callow as Professor Oliver Haddo, a stuttering bumbler of a Cambridge instructor who undergoes quite the personality change once the spirit of Crowley possesses him. (That name, Oliver Haddo, is taken from W. Somerset Maugham's novel *The Magician*, inspired by Crowley.)

Let loose on campus, the famously do-what-thou-wilt Crowley pisses on his students, jizzes onto a photocopier, fucks and kills hookers, fucks and kills homeless people, gets drunk, gets high, and whoops it up nonstop while seeking a "scarlet bride" for a "chemical wedding." Relishing the role, Callow devours the screen as "The Great Beast 666," aka "The Wickedest Man in the World." But even as Callow lets his penis fly freely in the wind, he can't counter the movie's inherent clunkiness and crippling chintziness. Given Crowley's storied place in British history and heavy metal, his first film of note should do more to bewitch and beguile generations of dark-streaked spiritual seekers. Two horns thrown high to Dickinson for writing the film and getting it made, in any case. .

CYCLONE (1987)

(DIR. FRED OLEN RAY; W/HEATHER THOMAS, JEFFREY COMBS, MARTIN LANDAU, DUKEY FLYSWATTER)

✸ BIKERS ✸ DEVIL METAL

Heather Thomas, the bodacious bikini blonde from TV's *The Fall Guy* who was not Heather Locklear, stars in schlockmeister Fred Olen Ray's likable motorcycle cheapie. She plays the girlfriend of the inventor of a $5 million wonder-bike. When the whiz kid is knocked off by corporate thugs who want his secrets, Heather protects the Cyclone, blowing baddies to firecracker bits with built-in rocket launchers and laser cannons.

The premise already smells of classic early-'80s heavy metal fodder by bands like Razor and Rogue Male, and proper musical input is delivered here by the band Haunted Garage. Though they look like Oingo Boingo, the combo wails through a great number about the perils of Satan in song, titled "Devil Metal." Haunted Garage was the demented and awful "headbanger" project of B-movie actor and screenwriter Michael Sonye, who, adorned in white fur cape and rib-cage shirt, assumed the very metal stage name Dukey Flyswatter for this role. Sonye also played Mengele in *Surf Nazis Must Die*, and he wrote *Blood Diner*. Somehow the band continued on to provide music for *Nightmare Sisters* (1988) and *The Dead Hate the Living* (2000).

DAGON ✠ DAHMER ✠ DAHMER VS. GACY ✠ DAMIEN: OMEN II ✠ THE DARK ✠ THE DARK CRYSTAL ✠ DARKNESS ✠ DARKON ✠ THE DARWIN AWARDS ✠ DAUGHTERS OF DARKNESS ✠ DAWN OF THE DAY OF THE NIGHT OF THE PENGUINS ✠ DAWN OF THE DEAD (1978) ✠ DAWN OF THE DEAD (2004) ✠ DAWN: PORTRAIT OF A TEENAGE RUNAWAY ✠ THE DAY OF THE BEAST ✠ DAZED AND CONFUSED ✠ DEAD ALIVE ✠ DEAD GIRLS ✠ DEAD MEADOW: THREE KINGS ✠ THE DEAD POOL ✠ DEAD SNOW ✠ DEADBEAT AT DAWN ✠ DEADLY BLESSING ✠ DEATH METAL: A DOCUMENTARY ✠ DEATH METAL ANGOLA ✠ DEATH METAL: ARE WE WATCHING YOU DIE? ✠ DEATH METAL ZOMBIES ✠ DEATH RACE 2000 ✠ DEATH RIDERS ✠ DEATH WISH II ✠ DEATH WISH 3 ✠ DEATHDREAM ✠ DEATHSPORT ✠ DEATHSTALKER ✠ THE DECLINE OF WESTERN CIVILIZATION PART II: THE METAL YEARS ✠ DEEP RED ✠ DEEP THROAT ✠ THE DEMON LOVER ✠ DEMONOID: MESSENGER OF DEATH ✠ DEMONS ✠ DESPERATE TEENAGE LOVEDOLLS ✠ DETROIT METAL CITY ✠ DETROIT ROCK CITY ✠ THE DEVIL IN MISS JONES ✠ THE DEVIL RIDES OUT ✠ DEVIL'S ANGELS ✠ THE DEVIL'S RAIN ✠ THE DEVIL'S REJECTS ✠ THE DEVILS ✠ DIARY OF A MADMAN ✠ DISASTERPIECES ✠ DOGTOWN AND Z-BOYS ✠ DOMINATOR ✠ DON'T GO IN THE HOUSE ✠ DON'T LOOK NOW ✠ THE DOOM GENERATION ✠ THE DOORS ✠ DOWN: DIARY OF A MAD BAND–EUROPE IN THE YEAR OF VI ✠ DR. ALIEN ✠ DR. BUTCHER, M.D. (MEDICAL DEVIATE) ✠ DRACULA ✠ DRACULA 2000 ✠ DRACULA'S DAUGHTER ✠ DRAGONSLAYER ✠ DREAM DECEIVERS: THE STORY BEHIND JAMES VANCE VS. JUDAS PRIEST ✠ DREAMANIAC ✠ DREDD ✠ DRIVE ANGRY ✠ DRIVER 23 ✠ DROP DEAD ROCK ✠ DUCK! THE CARBINE HIGH MASSACRE ✠ DUNE ✠ DUNE WARRIORS ✠ THE DUNGEONMASTER ✠ DUNGEONS & DRAGONS ✠ DUNKELHEIT: THE TALE OF VARG VIKERNES ✠ THE DUNWICH HORROR

DAGON (2001)

(DIR. STUART GORDON; W/EZRA GODDEN, FRANCISCO RABAL, RACQUEL MEROÑO, MACARENA GOMEZ)

✠ H. P. LOVECRAFT ✠ WATER ✠ EVIL FISH

Dagon is an ancient Mesopotamian god of fertility who figures mightily in multiple pre-Judeo-Christian religions. He is so closely associated with fishing that, over centuries of worship throughout the Middle East, Dagon's image evolved into a part-man, part-fish manifestation. (Just don't call him a mermaid.) Numerous literary heavy hitters have incorporated Dagon into their work, including John Milton, George Eliot, Saul Bellow, and, most importantly, headbanger icon H. P. Lovecraft.

The movie *Dagon* adapts the water-god-intensive Lovecraft novella *The Shadow Over Innsmouth* into a witty, agreeably disgusting horror romp that hits like a tidal wave and jolts like an electric eel. Director Stuart Gordon delivers his greatest, most assured work since he first spectacularly took on Lovecraft in the all-time splatter classic, *Re-Animator* (1985). *Dagon* is another worthy entry in the short list of heavy horror greats.

After a storm at sea smashes their pleasure vessel against a rocky shore and traps their friends in the lower cabin, vacationers Paul (Ezra Godden) and Barbara (Raquel Meroño) row a lifeboat into the Spanish fishing village of Imbocca to seek help. Instead, they find spooky terra-cotta terrain populated by fish-loopy locals who practice an unfamiliar, sea-rooted religion. These beach-town beasts also collect human skins and prove not to be wholly human themselves. The array of awesomely rendered aqua-mutants on parade includes Uxia (Macarena Gómez), a scary-sexy dream figure made partly scaly flesh, cinema's premier death-mermaid to date. Paul's many shocking discoveries are all part of the frightful fun of *Dagon*, as the plot packs a succession of tricky twists.

Dagon, released just as horror and heavy metal were finding footing again in 2001, has only garnered a small cult following. Dagon, the deity, has inspired extremely loud devotees to form bands in France, Mexico, and the U.S., both as Dagon and with variation names such as Altar of Dagon, Daegonism, Dagon Storm, and Temple of Dagon. In addition, the number of metal anthems honoring Dagon numbers well into three digits. Stuart Gordon's film does all of that ferociously fishy passion proud.

ᗝAHMER (2002)
(DIR. DAVID JACOBSON; W/JEREMY RENNER, BRUCE DAVISON, ARTEL GREAT)
✠ CANNIBALISM ✠ SERIAL KILLERS

Dahmer stood out amidst a glut of camcorder-budget serial killer biopics cluttering Blockbuster Video shelves in the early 2000s, including *Ed Gein* (2000), *Nightstalker* (2002), *Ted Bundy* (2002), and *Gacy* (2003). This straightforward, detail-heavy docudrama on Jeffrey Dah-

mer is distinguished by subtle construction and execution from writer-director David Jacobson, and a stellar performance by Jeremy Renner as the notorious Milwaukee cannibal. A scene of Dahmer trying to keep his father from discovering a severed head stashed in his bedroom is unexpectedly suspenseful, and it unexpectedly generates sympathy for a guy who really did stash severed heads in his bedroom.

A whole bunch of sick, mostly tongue-in-cheek heavy metal songs have been written about man-eater Dahmer by bands including Nightstick, Blood Duster, Amoebic Dysentery, Soulfly, Fuck I'm Dead, and Church of Misery; a band from Cuba even named itself Jeffrey Dahmer. All pale next to Chicago-area death-thrashers Macabre, who recount the life and jailhouse toilet stall murder of Jeffrey Dahmer in loving, lurid detail on their 2000 release, the twenty-six-song concept album *Dahmer*.

ᗝAHMER ᗪS. ᏀACY (2010)
(DIR. FORD AUSTIN; W/FORD AUSTIN, RANDAL MALONE, PETER ZHMUTSKI, HARLAND WILLIAMS)
✠ SERIAL KILLERS

The U.S. government is attempting to create the ultimate killer by mashing up the DNA of Milwaukee cannibal Jeffrey Dahmer (Ford Austin) with Chicago's kid-killing clown John Wayne Gacy (Randal Malone). Clones of the notorious murderers escape and go on simultaneous slaying rampages before a redneck warrior named Ringo (Austin, again) who talks to God (Harland Williams) can hunt them down. Steven Adler of Guns N' Roses, or maybe a clone of him, makes a cameo as "Stevie."

ᗝAMIEN: ᗝMEN ᏠᏠ (1978)
(DIR. DON TAYLOR; W/WILLIAM HOLDEN, LEE GRANT, JONATHAN SCOTT-TAYLOR, LEW AYRES)
✠ ANTICHRIST

Damien: *Omen II* flashes forward seven years from the chilling conclusion of *The Omen* (1976). Up-and-coming Antichrist Damien

Thorn (Jonathan Scott-Taylor), now twelve, attends a military academy outside of Chicago. His uncle Richard (William Holden), overseer of the Thorn Industries business empire, has raised him in stern fashion. Bad stuff happens to those who cross Damien. Eventually, Damien discovers the famous 666 birthmark on his scalp and decides he is down with heralding Armageddon for the glory of Satan, his true father. The movie ends with Damien inheriting the Thorn fortune and all the global power that comes with it. He is the Antichrist as a yawn-inducing CEO terrorist.

Omen II is largely a hell-forsaken botch job save for two terror sequences. First, a pesky reporter (Elizabeth Sheperd) is attacked by a raven that flies into her car and pecks out her eyes. Upon fleeing, she steps directly into the path of an oncoming truck. The surprise tractor-trailer splatter has been repeated in many subsequent films, as in 1998's *Bride of Chucky* and 2005's *The Devil's Rejects*, but *Omen II* got in the first jolt.

The truly blood-chilling set piece takes place at a pickup hockey match in the frozen Wisconsin wilderness. An industrial do-gooder (Lew Ayres) who poses a threat to Damien falls through the ice and is carried away by the current. The panicked players scramble to break through the surface, but he just floats helplessly up against the transparent ceiling of death, wide-eyed and desperate, until he drowns. Breathtaking!

THE DARK (1979)
(DIR. JOHN "BUD" CARLOS; W/WILLIAM DEVANE, CATHY LEE CROSBY, RICHARD JAECKAL, CASEY KASEM)
✳ SCIENCE FICTION ✳ HORROR ✳ LASER-SHOOTING EYEBALLS

The Mangler, a seven-foot-tall hulk from another planet (seven-foot-tall actor John Bloom), stalks Los Angeles leaving headless corpses in his wake that instantly explain how he got his nickname. He also strikes, as the film's title indicates, in *The Dark*. Among the victims is the daughter of novelist Roy Warner (William Devane). Warner teams with TV reporter Zoe

Owens (Cathy Lee Crosby) to crack the case. They do—but only after lots more body parts pile up, and The Mangler reveals a talent for blasting lasers out of his eyes. Up until that point, *The Dark* radiated righteousness just by way of the Mangler's huge size, horrific menace, and penchant for really ugly mangling. One he starts squinting death-rays, *The Dark* goes interstellar heavy.

The Dark was first conceived as a slasher movie about a guy kept in an attic all his life until breaking free and going decapitation-happy. Then it was to be a zombie movie, and the Mangler was designed as such. After *Alien* stormed the box office in 1979, though, the villain was changed to extraterrestrial, and the eye-beam effects were added at the last minute. Somewhere along this odyssey of revisions, director John "Bud" Carlos (*Kingdom of the Spiders*) replaced Tobe Hooper (*The Texas Chain Saw Massacre*).

The Mangler's first victim is Kathy Richards, who survived in real life to one day give birth to Paris Hilton. She's also the sister of preteen heartthrob Kim Richards (*Tuff Turf*, Disney's *Witch Mountain* movies). Legendary American Top 40 DJ Casey Kasem, the man who introduced Ratt and Quiet Riot to families on long drives in station wagons, plays an LAPD pathologist. Aside from voicing slacker-*cum*-stoner-rock-icon Shaggy on *Scooby-Doo*, Casey enjoyed a live acting career that teems with metal-friendly credits: *The Glory Stompers* (1967), *2000 Years Later* (1969), *Wild Wheels* (1969), *The Cycle Savages* (1969), *The Incredible Two-Headed Transplant* (1971), and *The Doomsday Machine* (1972).

THE DARK CRYSTAL (1982)
(DIRS. JIM HENSON, FRANK OZ; W/JIM HENSON, FRANK OZ, KATHRYN MULLEN, DAVE GOETZ)
✳ SWORDS & SORCERY ✳ SCARY PUPPETS

Muppet-meisters Jim Henson and Frank Oz apply their visionary character designing powers to a heavier-than-Kermit realm. *The Dark*

Crystal chronicles the quest of "gelflings" Jen and Kira, along with their dog-thing, Fizzgig, to upend an age of misery on their planet, Thra, by swiping the titular crystal from the buzzard-faced Skeksis, who presently rule, and thereby restore the power of the wise and kindly Mystics, who used to be cool. This realm is very reminiscent of Tolkien, *Star Wars*, pulp fantasy novels, and '70s custom vans, but Henson's brilliance elevates every frame above and beyond anything that could be deemed a rip-off. Like its 1982 brethren *Blade Runner* and *The Thing*, *The Dark Crystal* was not a critical or commercial hit upon its release, but it has since endured as a beloved cult film.

The Dark Crystal is not Jim Henson at his most metallic, though. For the first season of *Saturday Night Live*, Henson created a new batch of Muppets "who can stay up late" as part of a recurring sketch, "The Land of Gorch." The swampy Gorch creatures engaged in goofy bits that involved huffing bog gas and sacrificing chickens to a rock god who flushed like a toilet.

DARKNESS (1993)
(DIR. LEIF JONKER; W/GARY MILLER, RANDALL AVIKS, MICHAEL GISICK, CENA DONHAM)
✠ VAMPIRES ✠ SOUNDTRACK (APOSTASY, SCEPTER)

Writer-director Leif Jonker, a talented and ambitious Wichita headbanger and horror nut, literally sold his own blood to finance the $5,000 vampire opus *Darkness*. Jonker was just nineteen, and the movie preserves its creator's youthful exuberance—which some might deem insanity. In fact, almost everyone in *Darkness* is a teenager, parading around in Iron Maiden, Dio, and other metal shirts, grounding the proceedings in enjoyably nutty, anything-goes energy.

A posse of young rockers returns to their small town after a metal concert to discover it raided by a demonic bloodsucker named Liven (Randall Aviks). It's then up to the kids, led by convenience store massacre survivor Tobe (Gary Miller), to shut down Liven and his newly vampiric army of the undead. War ensues, and to merely state that blood flows would be to describe Niagara Falls as a dripping tap. The fantastically splatterific gross-out gore effects, which baste the screen frequently and ferociously, come across as the joyful works of boys going berserk.

Darkness remains a shining beacon of what's possible with drive, ability, imagination, and deep, dark heavy metal soul. Randall Aviks, who stars as the head vampire, told Jonker he finally wrapped his head around the production by saying, "I get it—it's a garage band movie!"

In 1996, when *Darkness: Vampire Version* was coming out on two-disc DVD from Barrel, Jonker was sent an interview from a relatively known journalist who began with the question: "I absolutely hate when filmmakers put heavy metal music in their movies. Why did you decide to put it in *Darkness*?"

"First off," says Jonker, "it obviously was an assholish and unprofessional question, but it also showed that this guy had such a stick up his butt. There was no middle ground I was interested in finding with him, and I shut him down right then and said, 'Thanks but no thanks' for the interview. You either have at least some spark of love in your heart for the majesty of metal, or you're dead to me."

Asked to pick the most metal movie of all time, Jonker names *Demons*, but adds: "I haven't made the most metal movie yet. That film would be *Raw Steel*, about the late 1980s and the heyday of MTV and an alternate timeline in the history of the world where heavy metal demons attempt to take over the planet."

DARKON (2006)
(DIRS. LUKE MEYER, ANDREW NEEL; W/SKIP LIPMAN, KENYON WELLS, DANIEL MCARTHUR)
✠ METAL REALITY ✠ SWORDS & SORCERY
✠ DUNGEONS & DRAGONS

The title of this documentary refers to the make-believe medieval domain in a real game in Maryland of live-action role-playing—LARP, for short. LARPing, for the unfamiliar, is a dress-up-and-act-out extension of quintessentially heavy metal story-telling games such as Dungeons & Dragons, the specific universe of which seems to provide Darkon's essential blueprint. So you know the types you'll meet here.

More than two hundred strong, Darkon's LARPers converge each Sunday on soccer fields and public parks all over suburban Baltimore. They dress in full Middle Ages battle gear and combat each other with foam rubber swords and cardboard shields. They also wield spells, potions, curses, and other ephemera that they concoct and trade among one another during the week. Among this lot are royals, wizards, elves, necromancers, alchemists, and all the usual suspects in this type of realm, each embodied with great passion by grown men with day jobs that seem to correspond unnervingly to the status of each player in the game. Here the fabric of fantasy and reality goes a little haywire.

Single dad Skip Lipman narrates. His Darkon persona is Bannor of Laconia. His main opponent is Keldar of Mordom, who exists elsewhere as Kenyon Wells. Through these team captains, we meet other LARPers. To the high credit of filmmakers Meyer and Neel, the movie never condescends to them. A brouhaha at a Denny's over a broken treaty packs real dramatic punch. By the end, Darkon takes on the narrative of a solid, compelling sports movie. You'll root for your favorites to win, and appreciate that at no point is anyone painted as merely a loser.

THE DARWIN AWARDS (2006)

(DIR. FINN TAYLOR; W/WYNONA RYDER, JOSEPH FIENNES, JUDAH FRIEDLANDER, LUKAS HAAS)
✣ CONCERT FOOTAGE ✣ SOUNDTRACK (METALLICA, JUDAS PRIEST) ✣ DANISH DRUMMER

In the mid-2000s, Hollywood scrambled to somehow convert zillions of Internet eyeballs into ass-filled theater seats. Among those dot-com bombs (The Onion Movie [2008], anyone?), The Darwin Awards (2006) is an ill-advised curiosity made infinitely more quizzical by the participation of Metallica. The Darwin Awards took off online as a gathering place for true stories of ridiculous fatalities caused by the victims' own stupidity. Here, Winona Ryder and Joseph Fiennes play insurance investigators running down the facts of a series of popular stories from the Darwin Awards website, among them "Misadventure at a Metallica Concert."

Judah Friedlander and Lukas Haas portray stoned, drunken heshers attempting to crash an outdoor stadium show by backing their pickup truck next to a fence and hopping inside. As the band plays below them, however, Judah falls down a hill and gets squashed, while Lukas gets to go backstage. There, all four members of Metallica appear in the flesh, rattling off dumb dialogue about sex, drugs, and rock and roll. Lars Ulrich chews a toothpick throughout.

During the concert segment, Metallica performs "No Leaf Clover" and "Sad but True." The soundtrack also prominently features "Hell Bent for Leather" by Judas Priest. Metallica is typically reluctant to allow their music to be used in movies and TV shows, which adds an extra "What the...?" element to band members actually appearing in, of all things, The Darwin Awards. "Misadventure at a Metallica Concert" has since been discredited as an urban legend, so no actual dirtbags were harmed in being made fun of by this motion picture.

DAUGHTERS OF DARKNESS (1971)

(DIR. HARRY KÜMEL; W/DELPHINE SEYRIG, DANIELLE OUIMET, ANDREA RAU, JOHN KARLEN)
✣ COUNTESS BATHORY ✣ LESBIAN VAMPIRES

The most understated take on the legend of Countess Elizabeth Bathory, Daughters of Darkness is très chic European art-trash/trash-art that's archly gothic and beautifully shot, but frustratingly restrained when it comes to flesh, blood, and lesbian sex by the bathtub-full. Delphine Seyrig stars as the undying blood countess;

visiting a grand hotel in contemporary Belgium, she takes a shine to newlyweds Valerie (Danielle Ouimet) and Stefan (John Karlen). Sexy Andrea Rau plays the countess's handmaiden who ends up sporting fangs for eternity.

A cult item throughout the '70s and a ubiquitous big-box VHS rental in the early '80s, *Daughters of Darkness* warrants mentioning for its stately take on metal movie majesty, but you can see better, gorier bisexual bloodsucking elsewhere. Art houses and revival theaters often paired *Daughters of Darkness* with Jose Ramon Larraz's much sexier and overall superior *Vampyres* (1974), aka *Daughters of Dracula*.

DAWN OF THE DAY OF THE NIGHT OF THE PENGUINS (1997)

(DIRS. DAVE BROCKIE, HUNTER JACKSON; W/GWAR)
✳ BODY FLUIDS ✳ EVIL PUPPETS

Gwar, the space alien heavy metal warrior collective stranded in Antarctica, returns to skirmish with longtime nemesis Techno Destructo in *Dawn of the Day of the Night of the Penguins*. Yes, the mayhem involves penguins, crack, a killer vagina, mass slaughter, and blood, diarrhea, jizz, and puke raining down on the audience.

Dawn consists of Gwar performing a plot-intensive show from their 1997 *Carnival of Chaos* tour in Washington, D.C. The costumes, puppets, and amazingly rendered special effects never fail to make one's eyes pop, but the intricacy of the band's ongoing story line—continued here from previous tours and home videos—is also enough to get your brain spraying fluid in every direction. The concert on display features the farewell performance of Peter Lee as Gwar character Flattus Maximus. He was shot in the stomach during a carjacking a few years prior and never fully recovered.

DAWN OF THE DEAD (1978)

(DIR. GEORGE ROMERO; W/KEN FOREE, DAVID EMGE, SCOTT H. REINIGER, GAYLEN ROSS)
✳ ZOMBIES ✳ BIKERS ✳ POST-APOCALYPSE
✳ SOUNDTRACK (GOBLIN)

With *Dawn of the Dead*, writer-director George Romero and special effects gore-god Tom Savini aimed to make the *Moby-Dick* of horror cinema and, bite by bite, skull blast by skull blast, Goblin riff by Goblin riff, they pulled off the genre's broadest, deepest, grossest, and most powerful leap forward to date. Much has been made of *Dawn* and its 1968 predecessor, *Night of the Living Dead*, containing "social commentary," all of which is nonsense, but there's no denying that the film embodies an extreme, lunging moment in art and culture and the overall human zeitgeist. The times, they were a-detonatin'.

In 1979 terms, think of *Dawn*'s unprecedented explicit exploding-head scene as fright film's equivalent of Eddie Van Halen's volcanic guitar solo "Eruption." Both were dumbfounding visions of the great beyond, now made possible.

As for the content of the movie, *Dawn* tracks a band of zombie attack survivors camped out in Pennsylvania's luxurious Monroeville Mall as they wage war against an endless onslaught of flesh-starved zombies. Romero delivers suspense. Savini delivers eye-pops. Each master makes *Dawn* scary where it should be and funny in ways you don't see coming. The action sequences excite ferociously, and an undercurrent of dread pulsates throughout, lending cataclysmic gravitas to every frame. Even stuff like a biker gang battling ghouls on motorcycles, and a shot of a disembodied arm in a drug store blood-pressure-machine cuff are genuinely unsettling.

Now, regarding the postgame analysis of *Dawn* as some sort of satire of consumerism or political commentary or metaphor for class warfare; palaver like that arises from lofty academic and media gatekeeper types wanting in on the fun being had by the "bad kids." The same overthink-

Clockwise from top: Death Riders *(1976)
do it; Kyle MacLachlan's mighty fine* Dune
(1984); Deathstalker *(1983)*; Detroit Metal
City *(2008)*; The Dark *(1979)*; *David
Markey's* Desperate Teenage Lovedolls
(1984). Center: *Heaven help the copy editor
of* The Devil's Rain *(1975) poster*

ers worked their tragic magic on punk, and the result was U2. In recent years, the highbrows have finally noticed and tried to dignify metal, though so far they have failed. Same goes for the campaign to assimilate splatter horror into the canon of acceptable outrageousness, thankfully.

Romero, to his artistic discredit but with understandable career-extending canniness, dove into such blather gigantic-black-square-eyeglasses first. He'll tell you or the *New York Times* or NPR or anybody about the Chomskyite underpinnings of his bone-munchers. Here's my take on the deal: *Dawn of the Dead* is the result of some fantastically creative guys thinking it would be really cool to show what it was like to battle walking, cannibalistic corpses in a fortress with every modern convenience available—i.e., a suburban shopping mall—and then figuring out how best to execute that vision. From their mighty effort and achievement has come all ensuing horror filmdom, paralleling the way the late-'70s rock revolution quickly begat black metal, death metal, and hardcore, and has steadily seeped into all heavy music since then. And in both cases, the key ingredient is instinct—and guts.

Italian horror maestro Dario Argento is the executive producer of *Dawn of the Dead*. He flew Romero to Rome to write the script and turned him on to the heavy sounds of Goblin, the prog rock group that scored Argento classics including *Deep Red* (1975) and *Suspiria* (1977). Along with Argento, the band composed and performs *Dawn*'s mind-melting soundtrack.

Dawn of the Dead boasted the most terrifying TV commercial of all time. On a shot of what looks like a blank wall, a word crawl scrawls upward while voice-over great Adolph Caesar intones about how George Romero terrified the world with *Night of the Living Dead* and now he's back. Then—AIEEEEE!–the wall slides open, revealing that it was in fact an elevator door, and a throng of zombies charges the screen.

The ad campaign worked. *Dawn of the Dead* stormed through Europe and Japan for a few months before devastating America in spring-time 1979. With no hope of avoiding an X rating, *Dawn* hit theaters with the weird warning: "There is no explicit sex in this picture. However, there are scenes of violence that may be considered shocking. No one under 17 will be admitted." It remained a first-run attraction for more than a year before going into perpetual theatrical revival and, on a budget of $650,000, grossing $55 million worldwide. In Italy, executive producer Argento presented his own edit of the film, titled *Zombi*.

Romero had grand plans to follow *Dawn* with a cosmic-scaled zombie gottadammerung in *Day of the Dead* (1985). When financing fell short, he shot what he could, and the scrappy, snarling movie that resulted is a minor masterpiece.

DAWN OF THE DEAD (2004)

(DIR. ZACK SNYDER; W/SARAH POLLEY, VING RHAMES, MEKHI PHIFER, TY BURRELL)

✠ ZOMBIES ✠ POST-APOCALYPSE ✠ SOUNDTRACK (DISTURBED)

This wholly unnecessary, but, shock of shocks, highly enjoyable, *Dawn of the Dead* remake (by director Zack Snyder, from a script by James Gunn) works as a way-better-than-average mid-2000s action movie dropped into a zombie setting. A scary opening sequence features an attack by an undead neighbor kid. That's followed by sharply edited credits during which we witness society collapse as the dead rise to the sounds of "The Man Comes Around" by Johnny Cash. Make no mistake, the new *Dawn* is trite and beyond predictable. Yet somehow, Snyder and company make it work.

In amongst the fun factors, the improvised anti-zombie tank is especially pulverizing. Easy-listening parodists Richard Cheese and Lounge Against the Machine perform their ersatz Muzak take on Disturbed's 1999 anthem "Down With the Sickness" while the survivors settle into their adopted shopping mall turned fortress. The original song plays under a closing sequence that leads to a surprisingly downbeat payoff.

Dawn: Portrait of a Teenage Runaway (1976)

(Dir. Randal Kleiser; w/Eve Plumb, Leigh McCloskey, Bo Hopkins, Georg Sanford Brown)

✡ Soundtrack (Runaways)

Along with sweaty hard rock and proto-metal, tawdry network-TV teen sex movies rank as the greatest cultural contributions of the 1970s. None is tawdrier or teen-sexier than *Dawn: Portrait of a Teenage Runaway*. Eve Plumb—yes, Jan Brady herself—stars as fifteen-year-old Dawn, an ambitious blonde who hightails it out of small-town dullsville for the thrills and pills of scummy Hollywood Boulevard. In short order, Dawn turns tricks for cracker pimp Swan (Bo Hopkins), and begins a romance with fellow rent-a-teen Alexander (Leigh McCloskey). Aside from the warped reality of a Brady girl peddling herself to every Tom, Dick, and George Glass in front of the Pussycat Theater, the movie includes a montage set to "Cherry Bomb" by the Runaways.

Joan Jett's power chords stomp, Lita Ford's lead axe electrifies, and Cherie Currie wails over our plucky heroine exploring the adult book stores, back alleys, shit-bum bars, and other opportune blow job–dispensation outposts in and around scummy Hollywood. Like millions of other horndogs, I was lured to *Dawn: Portrait of a Teenage Runaway* by the boilerplate-porno plot, hoping against hope that, somehow, this would be the time that NBC showed nudity. Though my puerile prayers were in vain, I did take immediate notice of "Cherry Bomb." I was eight years old and I wanted more and ultimately headed out for the sights accompanied by the sounds of the Runaways. I wasn't alone; how else do you explain the interview subjects in *The Decline of Western Civilization Part II*?

Despite all the puberty-unbound obsessions of '70s TV films, hard rock and heavy metal remained under deep cover in movies-of-the-week. *The Day My Kid Went Punk* didn't even air until 1987! *Kiss Meets the Phantom of the Park* (1978) was one awesome exception. In *Cotton Candy* (1978), directed by Ron Howard, a charming garage band battles their foils, Rapid Fire, but even those bad guys can only manage a hilariously terrible cover of "I Shot the Sheriff." Closer to metal is *Sooner or Later* (1979). Jessie (Denise Miller) is a mousy thirteen-year-old smitten with budding rock bohunk Michael Skye (Rex Smith). He's seventeen, and she convinces him she's of appropriate age for making out. It happens. The jailbait angle gets a nod, but Smith is essentially a goody-goody Andy Gibb stand-in. Wrong Australian—they should have gone for Bon Scott!

The Day of the Beast (1995), aka El Dia de la Bestia

(Dir. Lex de la Iglesia; w/Lex Angulo, Santiago Segura, Armando De Razza)

✡ Antichrist ✡ Satan

Catholic priest Father Angel (Álex Angulo) believes the Antichrist will be born somewhere in Madrid on December 25. Teaming with heavy metal record store clerk Shorty Dee (Santiago Segura), Angel kidnaps a TV clairvoyant and sets out to find evil by doing evil. Specifically, that means sinning like mad (robbing a beggar, coldcocking a mime), committing crippling and deadly violence, and embarking on a psychedelic trip that conjures Satan himself (Higinio Barbero) in order to murder the newborn Antichrist just before dawn on Christmas morning.

Day of the Beast is a frenetic fright farce that melds nasty visuals with joyful blasphemy and manages to be dark-hearted but not mean-spirited. Spanish filmmaker Álex de la Iglesia announces his cinematic voice with a frantic, heavy metal roar. From the movie's epileptic pacing to its outrageous physical barbarity, the director's love of comic books is clear. And with horror-comedy soaring into vogue by the mid-'90s, this *Beast* had its day, right on time, everywhere.

Segura's Shorty Dee is one of metal's most towering representations in film. Rotund, pierced, tattooed, bearded, greasy-maned, and clad in a devil T-shirt beneath a sleeveless leather vest that's in turn beneath a patch-adorned sleeveless denim vest, Segura looks the part perfectly and he plays it with *mucho gusto*. Father Angel stops into Shorty's record shop after spotting a demon-horned, red-eyed baby doll in the display window. Surrounded by skulls, Cannibal Corpse T-shirts, and Venom albums, Angel hands over a list of requests: "Iron Maiden, Napalm Dez, Hace De Ce." The last is the priest's best guess at the spelling of AC/DC. When Satan ultimately appears, he is a full-blown, twelve-foot-tall, fang-faced, horn-headed antelope-man. You'll be inclined to bow before him.

Dazed and Confused

(1993)

(Dir. Richard Linklater; w/Jason London, Matthew McConaughey, Milla Jovovich)

✵ Stoners ✵ Soundtrack (Alice Cooper, Black Sabbath, Black Oak Arkansas, Deep Purple, Kiss, the Runaways, Sweet, ZZ Top)

Dazed and Confused is writer-director Richard Linklater's highly amusing stoner rock kaleidoscope. The film is set on May 28, 1976, the last day of the semester at Lee High School outside Austin, Texas. *Seniors* on their way out of school paddle the asses of freshmen on their way in. Football hero Randall "Pink" Floyd (Jason London) struggles over whether to sign a pledge to not do drugs all summer. That night, the teens blare heavy tunes while they cruise in cars, play mailbox baseball, and surge in and out of a hamburger stand and the Emporium, a rock club. An after-hours keg party in a field sparks conflicts until the central characters crash out on the school's football field. The whole time, everybody's getting stoned. Everywhere.

The fluidity of action in *Dazed and Confused* is beguiling. Fantastically nostalgic costume choices and set decorations wash in and out of funny scenes performed by a cast of up-and-comers that percolates, lava-lamp-like, with talent and enthusiasm.

Pink celebrates his decision not to sign the pledge by buying tickets to see Aerosmith. A pilfered statue of the Spirit of '76 turns up with the faces of its three figures wearing Kiss makeup. The scene of the freshmen being paddled to "No More Mister Nice Guy" by Alice Cooper is among the film's most famous, second only to Matthew McConaughey's star-making moment as oily David Wooderson ("That's what I love about these high school girls, man: I get older, they stay the same age!").

Connecting the flow is a powerful and inspirational assemblage of FM-radio hard rock hits that will rank alongside the best of your own vintage mixtapes. With a handful of exceptions (most involving Cameron Crowe), Led Zeppelin refuses to allow their music in movies. Linklater petitioned the group to let him include "Rock and Roll." Jimmy Page and John Paul Jones were cool with it. Robert Plant nixed the idea. Even without them, the *Dazed and Confused* soundtrack proved so popular that a sequel album, *Even More Dazed and Confused*, was issued in 1994.

Overenthusiastic reviewers congratulated *Dazed and Confused* for being "plotless," which is ludicrous as a point of praise, and in this case patently not true. Personally, I was also irritated that lead character's surname was "Floyd," which seemed like a lazy screenwriting decision so that his nickname could be "Pink." Lo and behold, in 2004, three of Richard Linklater's high school classmates filed suit against the filmmaker for appropriating their names for his script. The litigants were a Mr. Wooderson, a Mr. Slater, and a Mr. Floyd. The lawsuit was dismissed, which means there must be a lot of Floyds out there!

Dead Alive (1992),

aka Braindead

(Dir. Peter Jackson; w/Timothy Balme, Diana Peñalver, Elizabeth Moody, Ian Watkin)

✵ Zombies ✵ Extreme Gore

Peter Jackson bellied up to the *Fangoria*-friendly extreme-gore filmmaking game with two powerful hands of over-the-top, beyond-the-barf-bag gambits: the humans-as-alien-fast-food farce *Bad Taste* (1987); and his masterpiece of oozing puppet perversion, *Meet the Feebles* (1989). For *Dead Alive*, the nutty New Zealander loaded everything possible into the pot and let it all spew in blood red, bone white, intestine gray, and organ purple.

In 1957, the buttoned-up life of Lionel (Timothy Balme) gets blown asunder when his domineering mother, Vera (Elizabeth Moody), is infected by a Sumatran monkey-rat with some kind of zombifying ailment. With cheeky humor and genuinely unprecedented violence, Vera turns the entire local population into zombies, including naughty baby Selwyn (Daniel Sabic); Lionel desperately struggles to maintain an illusion of control.

Dead Alive's climax is an operatic outpouring of bloodshed and flesh-shredding in which Lionel thrusts an upended lawnmower into dozens upon dozens of oncoming zombies. Even then, their limbs, spines, and other body parts keep attacking until they are completely reduced to crimson mush. Vera, in the midst of the melee, becomes the size of King Kong, swoops up Lionel, and forces him back inside her womb—the hard way—where he stays until his sweetheart Paquita (Diana Peñalver) can manually bring about Lionel's slimy "rebirth." The lawnmower scene called for blood to be pumped out at a rate of five gallons per second. And it goes on for many, many seconds.

From the skin-stripping leg scene on down, *Dead Alive* is absolutely the most fun movie you can watch at a midnight screening or during a horror festival in a theater packed with sugared-up madpeople. The public viewings of this movie become as much a ritualistic bonding experience as the most transcendent heavy metal concerts. In short, Sumatran rat-monkeys rule.

A scene in which Lionel takes baby Selwyn to the park was shot after the rest of the film, to make use of money Jackson had saved by remaining under budget. The man-versus-infant donnybrook is a slapstick marvel, with a desperate Lionel violently trying to subdue the pint-size zombie while baby Selwyn fights back with one barbaric blow after another before horrified onlookers.

DEAD GIRLS (1990)

(DIRS. DENNIS DEVINE, STEVE JARVIS; W/DIANA KARANIKAS, ILENE B. SINGER, ANGELA EADS)
✸ SLASHER ✸ FAKE BAND (DEAD GIRLS)

The Dead Girls of *Dead Girls* are a fast-rising female musical quintet specializing in the realm of "death rock." Sexy psychic Bertha Beirut (Diana Karanikas) sings lead. The other Dead Girls include Lucy Lethal, Cynthia Slayed, Nancy Napalm, and a dude drummer, Randy Rot. After declaring, "Life's a dog! A total bummer!" Bertha's sister Brooke joins her friends in a gothy, candlelit ritual leading to an all-out suicide pact, except Brooke survives. She then spends some time in a coma, with Black Sabbath and Iron Maiden posters hanging above her head.

Picking up on uncool juju, the Dead Girls cart Brooke, their manager, and a nurse off to a cabin in the woods for some head-clearing time. A slasher in a giallo-style skull mask, a fedora, and a black overcoat poops that plan. One by one, the killer picks off the assembled victims, each time leaving a note containing Dead Girls lyrics that pertain to the specific crime at hand. To make it easy, Dead Girls songs boast titles such as "Drown Your Sorrows" and "Nail Gun Murder."

For a two-buck VHS flick, *Dead Girls* does try to explore the cause-and-effect relationship between heavy metal music and real world violence. But *Dead Girls* at heart is simply a cheap thrills heavy metal horror movie. Though the film doesn't really contain any actual heavy metal, the action does provide plenty of girls. Some are naked. All are screaming. Codirector Dennis Devine went on to shoot the heavier metal horror flick *Sawblade* (2010).

Dead Meadow: Three Kings (2010)

(DIRS. SIMON CHAN, JOE RUBALCABA; W/JASON SIMON, STEVE KILLE, STEPHEN MCCARTY, DAVE KOENIG)

✠ CONCERT FOOTAGE ✠ TRIP SEQUENCE

Dead Meadow: Three Kings is a concert film capturing the way-out eponymous stoner rock power trio (whose name sounds like "death metal" under the right conditions) tearing it up in L.A. on the last night of their tour for the 2008 album *Old Growth*. In homage to Led Zep's *The Song Remains the Same* (1977), *Three Kings* intersperses onstage performance action with loopy, fairly elaborate, and totally tripped-out fantasy sequences. Each Dead Meadow member wanders the desert in a robe. A cartoon sun gets stoned. Goddess figures in see-through tunics arise. And there's smoke and murder and floating obelisks. If you dig hallucinogenic '70s midnight movie weirdness alternately set to "freak-out" and "mellow-out" modes, then you will dig the mythical bits. I dug it all the way to the dark side of *Dune*.

Dead Meadow: Three Kings premiered in 2010 at the Hollywood Forever cemetery, projected through tombstones onto a white wall. Dig that.

The Dead Pool (1988)

(DIR. BUDDY VAN HORN; W/CLINT EASTWOOD, PATRICIA CLARKSON, LIAM NEESON, JIM CARREY)

✠ FAKE BAND (JIM CARREY IN GUNS N' ROSES)

For Clint Eastwood's most famous recurring cop character, Dirty Harry, the fifth movie was not the charm. But this film does showcase the lone big-screen acting efforts of the original lineup of Guns N' Roses, even Axl. *The Dead Pool* is also weirdly set largely in the world of '80s splatter movies. Liam Neeson plays a horror director whose obsessed fan is offing San Francisco celebrities to rig the odds of a "death pool" betting circle. Dirty Harry is on his "to kill" list.

Real-life Cannibal Corpse advocate Jim Carrey makes a memorable impact early on as Johnny Squares, a doomed rocker who lip-synchs "Welcome to the Jungle" on the set of a production titled *Hotel Satan*. At his funeral, we see Guns N' Roses assembled, prominently, to mourn. Later on, Slash fires a harpoon gun on the set of *Hotel Satan*. Dirty Harry will find use for that weapon at the movie's climax but not, unfortunately, while wearing Slash's top hat.

Dead Snow (2009)

(DIR. TOMMY WIRKOLA; W/CHARLOTTE FROGNER, STIG FRODE HENRIKSEN)

✠ ZOMBIES ✠ NAZIS ✠ NORWAY

Dead Snow is a product of the cutesy clone mentality of the Internet age, in which we are inundated with cat videos, bacon (or whatever has replaced bacon in the last few seconds), and, infuriatingly, zombies as kitsch objects. Here, Nazi soldiers frozen since the World War II occupation of Norway are thawed out and attack college students on a ski trip. At no point is there a moment of danger, or suspense, or anything resembling horror aside from an attempt to up the "wink-wink" aspects of splatter comedies past. Emanating from *Evil Dead 2*'s ersatz horror boilerplate and incorporating the latest affordable technology, *Dead Snow* is a popularized extreme-gore exercise for the twenty-first century: an easily summarized gimmick pumped up with CGI slapstick.

The Nazi touch got the movie noticed and the fact that it's in Norwegian got it booked at art theaters. False metal must contain some elements of metal to even be false. Nazis, like it or not, are metal. Zombies started out as metal, but they've recently evolved into cultural accessories for costumed pub crawls. How about a bar tour for people who get their giggles dressing up as Nazis? *That* would present a challenge! *Dead Snow* is the right movie for these false-metal flesh-eater times, and Norway looks nice.

Deadbeat at Dawn (1988)

(Dir. Jim VanBebber; w/Jim VanBebber, Paul Harper, Megan Murphy, Ric Walker, Marc Pitman)

✠ Motorcycles ✠ Psycho 'Nam Vet ✠ Witches

In decidedly non-scenic Dayton, Ohio, Goose (Jim VanBebber) leads the Ravens street gang. Danny (Paul Harper) heads up rival outfit the Spiders. Kristy (Megan Murphy) is Goose's groovy, witchcraft-practicing old lady; at least she is until a pair of golf-club-wielding Spiders graphically beat her into a heap of puree. Goose concocts a smashingly killer double-cross plan to get even. After respectfully disposing of Kristy's remains in a trash compactor and crashing with his junkie 'Nam vet dad, Goose unites the Ravens and the Spiders for an armored car heist. Then he hunts down his enemies and dispatches them, one by one, with savage gross-out grace.

Deadbeat at Dawn is a microbudget grindhouse wonder that stunned viewers with bare-knuckled impact that has only grown more impressive. VanBebber wrote, directed, produced, edited, and performed all the death-defying stunts. In the lead role, he's terrifying when necessary and magnetic throughout. With *Deadbeat*, VanBebber meticulously crafted and explosively released an underground headbanger cinema classic and became a unique, howling voice in the most brutal echelons of truly independent filmmaking.

Deadbeat at Dawn took four years just to film. As revealed in the documentary *Diary of a Deadbeat*, that intense level of persistence is a VanBebber hallmark. He followed up with the Ricky Kasso–inspired *My Sweet Satan* (1994), and music videos for Necrophagia and Skinny Puppy. He also labored for more than a decade on *The Manson Family* (2003), watching his cast age from thrill-seeking nubile teens to thirtysomething Midwesterners with families. French doom band Horrors of the Black Museum and Missouri sludge act the Lion's Daughter have honored him with songs called "Deadbeat After Dawn."

Deadly Blessing (1981)

(Dir. Wes Craven; w/Ernest Borgnine, Maren Jensen, Sharon Stone, Michael Berryman)

✠ Cult Sect

The Hittites are a rural religious sect wherein men sport Amish-style facial hair and everybody pays heed to spiritual leader Isaiah Schmidt. As Ernest Borgnine portrays Isaiah, Hittite-ism immediately has appeal. City girl Martha (Maren Jensen) marries in to the Hittites, but in short order her husband is killed by a tractor. Outsider pals Lana (Sharon Stone) and Vicky (Susan Buckner) drop by to comfort her.

All seems serene until the Hittites start blathering about an incubus in their midst. Then the dead hubby's corpse turns up hanging from a rafter; a snake surfaces in a Martha's bath; a spider pops out of Sharon Stone's mouth; a surprise scare makes a cameo (something borrowed from "Z-Man/Superwoman" in *Beyond the Valley of the Dolls*); and the feared incubus puts in an appearance, leading to a tense chase scene in a barn

Deadly Blessing was hated upon its release. This lesser Wes Craven movie is off-kilter enough, opening with cornball narration and introducing an endless series of female characters, to be fondly revisited. The film did inspire the band Deadly Blessing and a great song by splatter rock kings the Accüsed. Michael Berryman from *The Hills Have Eyes* (1977) plays a threatening farmhand. Prior to Freddy Krueger, the bald, bug-eyed Berryman was Craven's most familiar visual signature.

Death Metal: A Documentary (2004)

(Dir. Bill Zebub; w/Amon Amarth, Brutal Truth, Cannibal Corpse, Immolation, Malignancy, Mortician, Type O Negative, Suffocation, Venom)

✠ Death Metal ✠ Metal Reality

New Jersey's multimedia metal maven Bill Zebub hits various backstage areas with camera in not-always-steady hand to chat with death metal players. Music videos and concert footage are sprinkled throughout. Unlike many black metal documentaries, including those by Zebub himself, the focus remains on the music itself.

The opening credits juxtapose bizarre, lushly detailed illustrations (showing Ernie from Sesame Street being crucified, Satan carving Baby Jesus like a turkey) with sexy cover shots of Zebub's magazine *The Grimoire of Exalted Deeds*, snippets of death metal, and odd audio drops.

At its best, *Death Metal: A Documentary* creates the feeling of a casual sit-down with these musicians, and that's a pretty good feeling. When Dan Lilker of Brutal Truth appears, the words beneath him identify him as being a member of "Brutal Ruth." How much more down-to-earth can the treatment of metal gods be?

Death Metal Angola

(2013)

(Dir: Jeremy Xido; w/Sonia Ferreira, Wilker Flores)
✴ World Metal ✴ Soundtrack (Before Crush, Black Soul, Dor Fantasma, Neblina) ✴

Detroit-born documentary maker (and actor and professional dancer) Jeremy Xido hopped half a world away to create *Death Metal Angola*, a rousing testament to the power of extreme hard rock to energize, uplift, and inspire in even potentially life-or-death circumstances. This movie's setting is the Angolan city Huambo as it slowly emerges from a quarter century of civil war—and most of the film takes place in an orphanage.

DMA's heroine is Sonia Ferreira, the saintly operator of the Okutiuka orphanage. She is a lifelong fan of thrash, black metal, and death metal who serves as a beloved matriarch to the local rock community. Aided by her boyfriend Wilker Flores, Sonia organizes a daylong music festival featuring local acts Before Crush, Black Soul, Dor Fantasma, Neblina, and Nothing to Lose. Much time is spent with the couple, as well as with the kids who drift in and out of the orphanage, as

the impeccably shot movie surges forward to a suspenseful countdown to showtime.

The final concert portion of *Death Metal Angola* is a hard and heavy jolt from an area of the world unfamiliar to most who will view this documentary, but it strikes in all the best and (to headbangers) all the best-known places where metal makes its mark most deeply felt. The connection between the performers and the crowd, bonded by metal unleashed with painful passion, is palpably spiritual, alive with hope, and undeniably real.

As Sonia herself beautifully puts it: "Rock was one of the ways that helped me to fight for my freedom." *Death Metal Angola* stands as proof that ugly music can be entirely liberating and life-affirming, absolutely anywhere on this insane planet.

Death Metal: Are We Watching You Die? (2010)

(Dir: Bill Zebub; w/Amon Amarth, Cradle of Filth, Deranged, Immolation, Marduk, Mayhem, Krisiun)
✴ Death Metal ✴ Metal Reality

Director Bill Zebub dips into outtakes from *Black Metal: A Documentary* (2007), and adds new shot-on-the-fly talks with various figures for a satisfying look at death metal. To explain the amount of non–death metal artists here, Zebub dons a plastic Viking helmet and says: "In the original era of death metal, black metal gaylords who tried to wage war against death metal were the enemy, but it's not the case anymore."

Operatic beauty Liv Kristine exudes feminine allure so out of place with everything else on display it's chuckle-inducing. A lengthy, good-naturedly ball-busting tour bus sit-down with George "Corpsegrinder" Fisher of Cannibal Corpse actually feels like you're hanging out with him. Bill Zebub brings up Cookie Monster to Corpsegrinder. "Cookie Monster is the coolest

Muppet," says the Cannibal Corpse vocalist. "I had a Cookie Monster puppet when I was a kid. But if Cookie Monster is a death metal singer, he's a tame version. He doesn't go all out. He's only using half his voice." Exactly—the comic shorthand used by the mainstream to explain heavy metal always falls short of the built-in absurdity of the real thing.

Death Metal Zombies

(1995), aka Dead Rock Zombies

(Dir. Todd Jason Cook; w/Todd Jason Cook, Lisa Cook, Bill DeWild, Thomas Banta)

✚ Death Metal ✚ Zombies ✚ Soundtrack (Amorphis, Brutality, Count Raven, Deceased, Pungent Stench) ✚ Fake Band (Living Corpse)

From Houston it came and to hell it will take you! *Death Metal Zombies*, a labor of no money and puked-up buckets of headbanging love from writer-director-star Todd Jason Cook, directly and disgustingly confronts the perils of false death metal. The falseness in question is embodied by the band Living Corpse, which is not death metal at all. However, one listen to their track "Zombified" turns hero Brad (Cook) and his headbanging pals into the walking dead. Brad's lady Angel (Lisa Cook, the auteur's real-life wife) confronts Living Corpse frontman Shengar (Thomas Banta), who is "leader of the dead world."

As far as I can tell, watching all eighty-three minutes of *Death Metal Zombies* in one sitting is biologically impossible. The action, if you want to call it that, is set mostly in the director's house, shot on what must have been the oldest camcorder on earth in 1995, with no lighting adjustments. Two bits display a modicum of nicely wrongheaded wit: a killer in a Nixon mask, and a guy sitting on an upturned knife and demonstrating what would happen if you used the toilet on the cover of Metallica's *Metal Up Your Ass.*

The sheer artlessness of *Death Metal Zombies* does weave an inspiring spell in smaller doses. Some local Texas metal honeys also offer some wonderfully welcome nudity to the cause. How-ever piss-poor the actual movie aspect of *Death Metal Zombie* may be, the soundtrack is a rip-snorting cross section of Relapse Records' 1995 roster at its most ferocious.

Death Race 2000 (1975)

(Dir. Paul Bartel; w/David Carradine, Sylvester Stallone, Mary Woronov, Roberta Collins)

✚ Dystopian Science Fiction ✚ Death Machines

In a financially ruined, totalitarian America of the near future, the state entertains its citizenry by sponsoring an annual televised Transcontinental Death Race. Drivers have three days to speed from coast to coast, racking up points based on how many pedestrians they can kill along the way. Frankenstein (David Carradine) is the all-time Death Race champion. He's a dashing figure in head-to-toe black leather, including a full face mask and long, flowing cape. His competitors include throwback gangster Machine Gun Joe Viterbo (Sylvester Stallone), cowgirl Calamity Jane Kelly (Mary Woronov), and Nazi maiden Matilda the Hun (Roberta Collins).

A rebel faction sabotages the race, and we learn that Frankenstein is a double agent. His aim is to win the contest, and, when being congratulated by the president, to assassinate him with an explosive in his prosthetic right hand. This will be the Death Race to end all Death Races.

Director Paul Bartel (*Eating Raoul*) conjures wondrous sci-fi visuals and avalanches of energy on a miniscule budget, and he stages the race brilliantly. This landmark film is a manic masterwork of black comedy, slapstick, social satire, and straight-up exploitation excitement. *Death Race 2000* is among the most metal enterprises in spirit and ideas and high-octane execution in any medium. Bartel's vision, while savagely hilarious, also provides a vortex view of a future that seems to have largely become our terribly less entertaining present. We wage our own individual social media death races day in and day out, where we watch and then report on reality TV and Internet snuff videos. Free thrills for everybody, everywhere, all the time, keep us all distracted from noticing the powers behind this nonstop destruction disguised as stimulation.

An early interloper in pinball and air hockey hangouts, humped by headband-wearing teens in fringed leather boots and pot leaf necklaces, the 1976 video game *Death Race* was inspired by the movie. Players control on-screen cars with steering wheels while stick-figure pedestrians run about. The goal is to hit those little people. When you nail one, it screams and becomes a tombstone. Eventually, the tombstones become their own obstacle course.

For years, Tom Cruise was attached to a straightforward *Death Race 2000* remake. That eventually turned into director Paul W. S. Anderson's unnecessary *Death Race* (2008) with Jason Statham.

DEATH RIDERS (1976)

(DIR. JIM WILSON; LARRY MANN, RUSS SMITH, DANNY REED, CLAIRE REED)

✠ METAL REALITY ✠ YOUTH GONE WILD ✠ ANIMAL SACRIFICE

The Black Sabbath song title "Killing Yourself To Live" takes on a thunderously profound meaning for the daredevils who comprise the Danville, Illinois–based Death Riders Motorcycle Thrill Show. Along with flaming heaps of twisted metal, these literal headbangers are the stars of *Death Riders,* a demolition derby documentary made expressly for the 1970s drive-in circuit. You have to wonder how many outdoor theaters turned into impromptu bumper-car rallies every time the movie played.

Death Riders opens with a dedication to all the Thrill Show veterans who can smash motor vehicles into one another no more, getting extremely specific by listing each fatally fallen comrade along with the stunt that did him in. We then meet the current crop of performers, including narrator Larry Mann, who informs us that the Death Riders "aren't like the stuntmen you see on TV or movies. We do all our own stunts with no tricky gimmicks, no rehearsals, and no safety precautions." And why? "That's the way we like it." Evel Knievel be damned!

Mann also points out something that explains why heavy metal could only be violently born in the 1970s, and not during our current hyper-protective age: most of the Death Riders are actual teenage volunteers, wild boys who are happily redefining the concept of a headbanging youth. Danny Reed is one such high-school-age hell-raiser. Much the way you might have blasted Slayer or Slipknot for thrills, Danny flips a car through the air in front of his mom, Claire, to get her to pass out. Floyd Reed, Danny's dad and the Death Riders' owner/operator, hoots in approval.

Beyond the explosive derby action, which includes a few painful mishaps, the proto-*Jackass* antics of these reckless teens running wild include swallowing goldfish, feeding a hamburger made of dog food to their nerdy announcer, riding bulls, getting their vans a-rockin' with stunt groupies, and enduring razzes from one of the few adults on hand, Squeeks the Clown. In case the raving antics of grave-mocking stunt nuts isn't '70s enough, the film also covers a visit to a nudist colony.

DEATH WISH II (1982)

(DIR. MICHAEL WINNER; W/CHARLES BRONSON, JILL IRELAND, VINCENT GARDENIA)

✠ VIGILANTE JUSTICE ✠ SOUNDTRACK (JIMMY PAGE) ✠ CANNON FILMS

Bronson's back, and he's carrying Cannon Films, the most metal exploitation studio of the '80s, with him. Eight years after *Death Wish* (1974), New York's beloved mugger hunter Paul Kersey (Charles Bronson) has absconded to Los Angeles and kicked his hoodlum-sniping habit. That is, of course, until life again kicks him where it hurts the most—right in his family. Enter a multiracial new wave/punk rock/roller disco street gang (the ranks of which include Laurence Fishburne), cut from the template used in the ensuing decade's most gonad-pummeling urban revenge movies and street-fighting videogames. These flamboyant degenerates break into Kersey's apartment and perpetrate atrocities against his daughter that out-heinous her similar attack eight years earlier, and back then she got a spray-paint douche! The housekeeper gets it even worse.

From that home invasion on, *Death Wish II* announces itself as a lower, more feral beast than its classy predecessor. Bronson plays the revenge scenes accordingly. Seeing a cross on the necklace of one of his targets, our unholy avenger asks: "Do you believe in Jesus?"

"Y-yeah! Yeah!" the skell stutters.

Kersey cocks his pistol and deadpans, "You're gonna meet him!" Blammo.

The *Death Wish* movies' shift in tone and budget parallels the changes in metal from the '70s to the '80s. The grand, classical, Hollywood-made original belonged to the era of long, flowing hair and polished costumes. The sequel is pure gritty indie metal mayhem. The same way Metallica's debut launched New Jersey's Megaforce Records, *Death Wish II*'s surprise blockbuster grosses launched Cannon Films. The grindhouse empire of Israeli moguls Menaham Golan and Yoram Globus went on to bring us more Bronson, a lot more Chuck Norris, and like-fisted classics on the order of *Cobra*, *Bloodsport*, *Masters of the Universe*, and the *Breakin'* movies.

Prior to *Death Wish II*, Led Zeppelin maestro Jimmy Page's only film work had been on occultist Kenneth Anger's *Lucifer Rising* (1972). Their collaboration ended with Anger putting a demonic curse on the guitarist. Director Michael Winner, apparently more agreeable than Anger, was Page's neighbor and simply asked him to do the music. Page, inactive since the 1980 breakup of Led Zeppelin, even worked for free, conjuring the bluesy, surprisingly synth-heavy themes that underscore *Death Wish II*'s crazy action.

ᗪEATH ᗯISH 3 (1985)
(DIR. MICHAEL WINNER; W/CHARLES BRONSON, MARTIN BALSAM, DEBORAH RAFFIN, ED LAUTER)
✤ VIGILANTE ✤ SOUNDTRACK (JIMMY PAGE)

The only thing weirder than there being a *Death Wish II* soundtrack by Jimmy Page on Swan Song Records is that there were enough tracks left over to fill up the *Death Wish 3* soundtrack by Jimmy Page on Swan Song Records. The third time was the harm in the continuing adventures of mild-mannered architect turned superhuman vigilante Paul Kersey (Charles Bronson). *Death Wish 3* is not just the most violent film in the series, it's the least plausible, the least concerned with inconveniences such as the physics of rocket launchers in Bronx alleyways, and, without question, the most giddily deranged. Taken on those terms, *Death Wish 3* is also the most enjoyable of the bunch.

The movie opens with Kersey fleeing the L.A. setting of the 1982 sequel and returning to the New York of the original. Life there isn't just cheap, it wears a new wave/punk rock/roller disco street hood costume, and the only way to stop it from gang-raping its way to some sort of new hyper-predator species is to pump it full of multiple holes. Kersey holes up in a tenement surrounded by urban chaos and multicolor Mohawks that would make Mad Max blush. Within five minutes, he's out killing gutter scum. Curiously, the overwhelmed local police chief (Ed Lauter) offers our hero a deal: exterminate all the human vermin you want, just keep the five-o in the loop. Kersey takes him up on the first part.

From there, *Death Wish 3* lunges toward the format of *Night of the Living Dead*, only way zanier, with Kersey and a handful of shut-in elderly ethnics mowing down and blowing away the entire street criminal element of New York City, which, circa 1985, really was a job fit only for Bronson. Martin Balsam is a riot as old Jewish neighbor Bennet. With endless chutzpah, he busts out bazookas and other anti-artillery firepower he smuggled back from World War II. Lanky, demon-eyed Gavan O'Herlihy makes an indelible creep out of head baddie Manny Fraker, a nightmare sadist out of a Carnivore or Sodom song, replete with denim, leather, and an otherworldly ugliness. Kersey blows Fraker up real good; don't complain to me that that's any kind of spoiler.

DEATHDREAM (1974),
AKA DEAD OF NIGHT
(DIR. BOB CLARK; W/RICHARD BACKUS, JOHN MARLEY, LYNN CARLIN, ANYA ORMSBY)

✷ ZOMBIE ✷ VIETNAM CONFLICT

Deathdream updates the 1902 gothic horror story *The Monkey's Paw* by W. W. Jacobs for the Vietnam era. The movie is spooky and sad, and plays like out a supernatural doom metal opus at half speed, compounding its effectiveness. After being told that her son Andy (Richard Backus) has been killed in combat, Christine Brooks (Lynn Carlin) simply refuses to accept the news. Later that night, Andy shows up at home, clearly not quite right.

Blood-draining murders accompany Andy's return and he takes to hanging out after dark at the local cemetery. Everything leads back to a grave that Andy had been digging for himself. Once he runs out of fresh blood to inject, he turns into a skeleton, free at last to be dead.

Bob Clark directed *Deathdream* the same year that he made the groundbreaking campus slasher film *Black Christmas* (1974), and this is the first film to feature makeup effects by master of the art Tom Savini.

DEATHSPORT (1978), AKA
DEATH RACE 2050
(DIRS. ALLAN ARKUSH, NICHOLAS NICIPHOR; W/DAVID CARRADINE, CLAUDIA JENNINGS, RICHARD LYNCH)

✷ POST-APOCALYPSE ✷ DEATH MACHINES

Set one thousand years in the future, some time after the Neutron Wars, *Deathsport* is producer Roger Corman's follow-up to the masterpiece *Death Race 2000* (1975). For the most part, it fizzles, no mean feat for a scorched-earth sci-fi adventure centering on motor combat between gladiators on "destructocycles." The movie stars David Carradine as the hero, Claudia Jennings (*Gator Bait*) as the female lead, and real-life burn victim Richard Lynch (*Invasion U.S.A.*) as the baddie. The score is surreal, patched together on dark, droning synthesizers. Codirector Allan Arkush is the revered mastermind behind *Rock 'n' Roll High School* (1979) and *Get Crazy* (1983). *Deathsport* is a distracted mess that is way less than the sum of these parts, but individually, these parts are still worth a look.

Not long after filming *Deathsport*, Claudia Jennings died in a car accident. The radiant, naturally redheaded Minnesota native was *Playboy*'s 1970 Playmate of the Year, and she had transformed, throughout the ensuing decade, into an emerging queen of cult cinema. Her movie career highlights include *Unholy Rollers* (1972), *Truck Stop Women* (1974), *Gator Bait* (1974), *The Man Who Fell to Earth* (1975), and *The Great Texas Dynamite Chase* (1977). Each is worth seeking out, as is Jennings's swan song, *Fast Company* (1979), a drag racing drama written and directed by David Cronenberg.

DEATHSTALKER (1983)
(DIR. JAMES SBARDELLATI; W/RICK HILL, BARBI BENTON, LANA CLARKSON, RICHARD BROOKER)

✷ SWORDS & SORCERY

In the title role of *Deathstalker*, square-jawed Rick Hill fills the screen with muscular clunk and an affable lack of grace befitting the mad fun thrust upon him here. However, nobody has more thrust upon her in *Deathstalker* than Barbi Benton. Hugh Hefner's high-profile head house bunny of the swinging '60s plays Princess Codille, kidnapped slave of tyrant wizard Munkar (Bernard Erhard) and rape target extraordinaire. Faring better (although, cripes, not in real life, where she was shot in the face by Phil Spector) is fellow Playboy vet Lana Clarkson as Kaira. She's a fierce warrior in her own right with an even fiercer costume that consists of a cape, a thong, and nothing else. The action centers on saving the princess and toppling Munkar during a tournament of mercenary gladiators.

On its own movie terms, *Deathstalker* is a skull-flattening *Conan*-knockoff classic. The plot is standard sword-and-sorcery stuff, but the delights of *Deathstalker* are in the delirious details. The movie's makeup team runs wild with what appears to be several dozen dollars' worth of latex. The screen buckles under the sight of rubber-mugged trolls and a pig-faced beast-man who goes cannibal at a feast by chowing down on an actual pig face. Then Munkar magically sex-changes his number-two stooge into Barbi Benton. Dwarves and acrobats frolic. Deathstalker's pal Oghris (Richard Brooker) wears a midriff-baring shirt that offers the most hilarious variation on male modeling this side of Manowar.

Tribute must be paid, as well, to the importance of the *Deathstalker* poster to the film's enduring popularity. The lushly painted scene of our workout-happy hero raising his saber against a hog-snouted, hottie-squeezing ogre is one of artist Boris Vallejo's most familiar images. Even without Vallejo's canon of cover art—which includes Ozzy's *Ultimate Sin*, *Take No Prisoners* by Molly Hatchet, and *No Place for Disgrace* by Flotsam and Jetsam—the *Deathstalker* poster stands as one of the most archetypical metal images of the 1980s.

Also produced in Argentina by Roger Corman, *Deathstalker II* (1987) allowed writer-director Jim Wynorski to send up *Conan* rip-offs by creating his own decent *Conan* rip-off. *Deathstalker II* boasts splatter, black magic, monstrous beasties, nude maidens, a likable hero and a terrifically hissable villain. And then Wynorski just goes berserk. Despite the laugh lines, *Deathstalker II* is the real deal, from its Boris Vallejo oil-painting poster to its all-girl army of Amazon avengers to its final bloodbath and concubine orgy.

THE DECLINE OF WESTERN CIVILIZATION PART II: THE METAL YEARS (1988)

(DIR. PENELOPE SPHEERIS; W/ALICE COOPER, OZZY OSBOURNE, GENE SIMMONS, PAUL STANLEY, STEVEN TYLER, LEMMY KILMISTER, DAVE MUSTAINE, POISON, CHRIS HOLMES, RIKI RACHTMAN, BILL GAZZARRI)
✠ HAIR METAL ✠ SUNSET STRIP ✠ METAL REALITY

The Decline II is a masterpiece without qualification, and this documentary of life on the glitzy metal skids of the Sunset Strip during the fin de 1980s has only gotten better with time, distance, and a return to manageable hairstyles. Like *Heavy Metal Parking Lot* (1986) gone Hollywood, director Penelope Spheeris's follow-up to her 1981 portrait of punk rock life in L.A. surges beyond a mere snapshot of one subculture into one of the greatest examples of documentary film. Spheeris's interview skills, barbed editing, and out-of-nowhere sound effects act as the director's pithy but never condescending commentary, guiding us through L.A.'s Sunset Strip between August 1987 and February 1988.

Unlike its punk-focused predecessor, *Part II* has one high-heeled boot planted securely in mainstream culture. Part one's arty, hardcore outcasts seceded from society to forge their own parallel playing field. These hair-hoppers are hell-bent on remaking the world in their glitter-dripping image, scrambling to the climb the Top 40/MTV/*Tiger Beat* heap as fast as they can. As demonstrated by Megadeth, Faster Pussycat, Lizzy Borden, London, Odin, and Seduce, this wave of bands make an unabashed case for success.

Decline II enjoys participation from biggest-of-big-league hard rock icons (Ozzy, Kiss, Alice Cooper, Aerosmith), and it's notable that almost none of the A-league actually moved to L.A. until they were already successful. Poison chimes in at the crest of their breakthrough to pop superstar-

Clockwise from top left: *Jim Carrey's in the jungle, baby, in* The Dead Pool; *Satanic scares in* Damien: Omen II; Deathsport; *Lizzy Borden prepares to give 'em the axe in* Decline II; *Africa rages in* Death Metal Angola

dom, and even the relatively more gritty acts like Megadeth, W.A.S.P., and Lemmy have already packed stadiums and racked up gold records. Ozzy Osbourne charms while he makes breakfast. Toxic Twins Steven Tyler and Joe Perry are warm and amusing in their first bout with sobriety. Lemmy (described by Spheeris as "a brat" during filming) expounds on the dynamics of his adopted city with his mountaintop guru turn. After hearing from the metal gods, we know exactly what caliber and what specifics of success the kids we meet want and expect.

Alice Cooper, next to upended female mannequin legs onstage, says: "Heavy metal saved rock 'n' roll for the '80s". He is followed immediately by Paul Stanley, in bed with a quartet of live, not-quite-nude lingerie models. "Heavy metal is the rock 'n' roll of the '80s," he states. Both Steven Tyler of Aerosmith and Chris Holmes of W.A.S.P., with ample hand gestures, compare playing heavy metal favorably to masturbation. Even Poison are unexpectedly hilarious. Amidst an avalanche of talk about penis size, singer Brett Michaels shouts out, "Sixteen inches . . . between all four of us! That's four apiece!"

Darlyne Pettinicchio, an executive at the anti-metal parents' organization Back in Control, demonstrates a run-through of heavy metal body armor—chains, collars, arm-bands, all of it heavily spiked and awesome. She points out how the "devil horns" hand salutes contains an image of three sixes between the curled and outstretched fingers. (I can only ever find two). Made the same year as *Decline II*, *America's Best Kept Secret* (1988), a hard-hitting one-hour exposé of our troubled nation's raging satanic underground, features Pettinicchio as a probation officer.

Bill Gazzarri is *Decline*'s other "grown-up" of note, the self-anointed "Godfather of Rock 'n' Roll." Decked out in the fashion of a Depression-era Chicago gangster, the owner of Sunset Strip stronghold Gazzarri's was best known for shepherding numerous Hollywood acts from their practice spaces to the world stage, most notably the Doors in the '60s and Van Halen in the '70s.

The '80s incarnation of Gazzarri, still brandishing the cigar and white fedora, and looking a hard decade older than his sixty-three years here, specializes in poodle metal punctuated by fantastically tacky "Miss Gazzarri's Dancer" near-strip contests that nod back to the Sunset Strip's go-go heyday in the 1960s, and to vaudeville before that. Along with a bikini-clad Miss Gazzarri's, who notes that winning the title can help her focus on her "actressing," crusty old Bill hilariously introduces the band Odin leading a chant of "OH-din! OH-din!" Not mentioned in the movie is that Gazzarri's was one of L.A.'s most notorious "pay to play" establishments, charging bands to perform. Do you think the Miss Gazzarri's Dancers competitors escaped scot-free?

Chris Holmes, of W.A.S.P., provides one of the saddest and scariest interludes in the annals of documentary filmmaking as he floats in a pool, his mother, Sandy, seated nearby, and babbles about not caring whether he lives or dies while literally dousing himself with vodka.

Spheeris presents her young subjects in rapid-fire interviews. They rattle off their band names: Sex, Vixen, Tuff, Dirty Blonde, Wet Cherri, Untimely Death, Jaded Lady. We meet a poofy-coifed mom and her even poofier-coifed toddler, two fleshy groupies who declare, "Men in makeup are where it's at!" and a succession of power-rocking hopefuls, the standout of which is the leader of combo Wet Cherri. "I can't picture not making it," he says. "If you came and heard us, you'd think the same thing, too."

In live action, we see Van Halen disciples Faster Pussycat at the peak of their near-popularity, and a few songs each from also-rans Lizzy Borden, London, Seduce, and, most memorably, Odin, butt-rockers who live up to the notion literally as the lead singer performs hapkido kicks across the stage in assless pants.

"What do you have to say to kids who want to make it as a rock star," Spheeris asks, off-camera, to Dave Mustaine of Megadeth. Frowning right into the lens, he snarls, "Don't!"

Presented (admirably without explicit explanation) as an antidote to the mousse-and-mascara madness running rampant for the previous hour, Mustaine and the other members of Megadeth come off thoughtful and funny. The band rips through "In My Darkest Hour" first in a studio and then before a mosh-ablaze throng of true believers at a rock club. The Dead Kennedys sticker on Dave Ellefson's bass harkens back to the punks of the first *Decline,* as does, in its personal nature and blunt-impact delivery, the music.

As Megadeth plays, the manic slam-dancing of the thrashers onstage and off builds to a spine-snapping crescendo so that when "Darkest Hour" finally simmers to a close and the credit "A Film by Penelope Spheeris" fades in onscreen, the effect is that of total exhilaration, designed to launch leather-jacketed headbangers bounding out of theater seats and raising a ruckus through the mall. Spheeris knew which of her subjects would have lasting power, and she chose wisely.

DEEP RED (1975), AKA PROFONDO ROSSO; THE HATCHET MURDERS

(DIR. DARIO ARGENTO; W/DAVID HEMMINGS, DARIA NICOLODI, GABRIELE LAVIA, MACHA MERIL)

✠ GIALLO ✠ SLASHER ✠ SOUNDTRACK (GOBLIN)

After directing *The Bird With the Crystal Plumage* (1970), *The Cat O' Nine Tails* (1971), and *Four Flies on Grey Velvet* (1975), Dario Argento established himself as one of horror's most ferociously promising talents. *Deep Red* is the fulfillment of that promise, and the effective starting point of one of the most metal cinematic categories: Italian extreme splatter horror.

David Hemmings plays Marcus Daly, a piano teacher who witnesses the murder of psychic Helga (Macha Meril). He teams with reporter Gianni Brezzi (Daria Nicolodi) to investigate and unleashes a barrage of surreal, discombobulating, and terrifying sights and sounds that would define Argento's signature style. The supernatural mingles seamlessly with the masked killer motifs of the Italian giallo fright film genre in *Deep Red*, while also calling to mind Michelangelo Antonioni's mod mystery *Blow-Up* (1967). Colors lunge off the screen in attack mode. Gore spews and spatters. At the movie's often-cited peak of terror, an evil doll the size of a human dwarf cackles and swings a knife—never to leave your brain for the rest of your existence.

As usual with Argento, *Deep Red* should not be followed too closely. His first true masterpiece is, fittingly, his first true exercise in incomprehensible insanity. The visuals fit perfectly with the jabbing, scalding, frightening score by prog-rock ear-benders Goblin, just as they would on future Argento-Goblin collaborations, particularly *Suspiria* and *Phenomena*. Larger than death and full of frames that would later become metal album covers, *Deep Red* is the first fully metal movement in Argento's horrific cinematic symphony.

After seeing *Deep Red,* the Master of Suspense himself, Alfred Hitchcock, allegedly said: "This young Italian guy is starting to worry me!" *Deep Red* showcases Argento's most iconic visual trademark: the killer's black-gloved hands. Shown in close-up performing the most violent of violations, these symbols of death and power belonged to the director himself.

DEEP THROAT (1972)

(DIR. GERARD DAMIANO; W/LINDA LOVELACE, HARRY REEMS, CAROL CONNORS, DOLLY SHARP)

✠ PORN CHIC

The porno feature toward which all earlier sex films led and from which all subsequent porno has proceeded, *Deep Throat* shook the world, groin first, in the 1970s. More than a movie, *Deep Throat* was a milestone, ushering in an era of "porn chic" and unprecedented permissiveness that oozed into every crack of the culture.

The movie itself is a giggle-worthy trifle about a woman (Linda Lovelace) who discovers her clitoris is in her throat, and so develops a technique to achieve orgasm via tonsils-to-the-testicles fellatio. Celebrities and suburban couples lined up to experience *Deep Throat* at theaters that were previously the sole domain of raincoated reprobates. Lovelace became one of the most famous women on earth. And the movie's lurid title entered the lexicon in serious ways; "Deep Throat" became the covert code name of the Watergate informant who took down President Nixon.

Aside from the bottomless blow job gimmick, *Deep Throat* boasts an array of "deviant" sex acts in hard-core close-up, images that the general public had never previously seen. In obliterating cinematic taboos, *Deep Throat* paved the way for hard rock to explore its outer extremes. Heavy metal, as always, led the forward assault, and the new freedom to be freaky affected everyone from Frank Zappa to later bands like the Mentors. Cover artwork began to feature nudity and overt sexuality, quickly going too far, as with the naked jailbait under broken glass depicted by Scorpions on the *Virgin Killer* jacket.

Deep Throat is also the name of a short-lived German metal band. If any doubt existed as to the inspiration for their moniker, the title of their only album, 1982's *The Devil in Miss Jones*, is taken from the second-most famous porno movie of all time. The cover shows the group standing in front of an adult theater with *Deep Throat* on its marquee.

The Demon Lover

(1977), AKA The Devil Master

(DIRS. DONALD G. JACKSON, JERRY YOUNKINS; W/ JERRY YOUNKINS, VAL MAYERIK, GUNNAR HANSEN)
✤ DEMON ✤ SATANIC ORGY

The Demon Lover is a legendary no-budget occult hair-raiser, shot quickly and messily in the vicinity of Detroit. Burly, bearded, long-haired warlock Laval Blessing (codirector Jerry Younkins) and his pal Damian (Val Mayerik) stage a bacchanal at their party castle in rural Michigan with their usual naked nubile coven. When the gathering turns sour and the girls

split, Laval conjures a demon (David J. Howard) to exact bloody and painful-looking revenge.

Ex-cult members die horrendously, a cop investigates, Gunnar Hansen (the original Leatherface) plays a psychic, Laval spends some time at a karate gym, and—after the slam-bang climax featuring Ted Nugent's actual guns and ammo (thanks to a personal connection to the filmmakers)—the demon wins. Character names in *Demon Lover*, overwhelmingly, are tributes to Heavy Metal Movie icons, including: (Forrest J.) Ackerman, (Frank) Frazetta, (Alan) Ormsby, Sam (Peckinpah), and (George) Romero.

Cast member Val Mayerik is the cocreator of comic book character Howard the Duck. Codirector Donald G. Jackson went on to a prolific exploitation career. He even made a handful of heavy metal favorites, including *Roller Blade* (1986) and *Hell Comes to Frogtown* (1988).

The documentary *Demon Lover Diary* (1980), about the making of this film, is a trip in and of itself. Shot as it happened, *DLD* showcases genuinely frightening meltdowns and freak-outs as production continually wobbles toward collapse. Given the nature of the film-within-a-film and the combustible personalities all around it, *DLD* plays like an earlier version of *American Movie* (1999). *DLD* ends with the documentary makers running for their lives away from Ted Nugent's compound to the sound of gunfire. The last line of the movie is classic: "They're firing at us!"

Demonoid: Messenger of Death (1981), AKA

Macabra; La Mano del Diablo

(DIR. ALFREDO ZACARÍAS; W/SAMANTHA EGGAR, STUART WHITMAN, ROY JENSON, LEW SAUNDERS, HAJI)
✤ SATAN ✤ KILLER ✤ DISEMBODIED HAND

The fun and likable Mexploitation mess *Demonoid* opens with a bare-breasted lovely in a cave, getting her left hand chopped off. The plot then follows the disembodied appendage, which is from hell, after all, as it crawls about possessing other people's left hands willy-nilly. Russ Meyer mammazon Haji cameos as a gangster's gazongariffic gal pal.

Demonoid exerts a special hold due largely to a gripping promotional campaign. The movie poster is brain smoking; a perfect early-'80s fantasy painting that depicts a roaring, sword-raising, long-tailed, black-skinned Satan, with mesmerized chain-mail-clad bikini chicks at his feet, astride a giant crawling hand. In the background a massive screaming female face looms with one terrified eye popped wide open. Toward the bottom, little adobe villages burn. The tagline screams: "Up from the depths of hell comes the ultimate horror!" In bold print at the bottom, bright yellow letters blare: "Warning: Certain scenes could be too shocking for those of you who are not true believers in the devil!"

Better still for young Catholics in the crowd, the movie employed a unique marketing gimmick: "Become a Disciple of the Devil!" At participating theaters, *Demonoid* patrons could get their names written in calligraphy on a certificate that declared them a "Disciple of the Devil." Years later, Rick Sullivan, publisher of the beloved horror movie zine *Gore Gazette*, showed me his *Demonoid* certificate. I wish I had stolen it.

Demonoid was made in 1979, but only made it to theaters north of the border in 1981 to cash in on the high-profile Hollywood release *The Hand*, an early Oliver Stone effort with Michael Caine on the run from his own free-wheeling fist. Other metal-caliber monster-mitt movies include *The Children* (1980), in which toxic gas turns a town's kiddie population into killers who can only be cured by having their hands severed with a sword; *Evil Dead 2* (1987), with its prized bird-flipping hand on the loose; *Body Parts* (1991), about a murderer's spirit returning to take back his transplanted limbs; and *Idle Hands* (1999), a surprisingly clever and nasty teen horror comedy wherein a jerky high school principal is jerked off by villainous disembodied digits.

DEMONS (1985)

(DIR. LAMBERTO BAVA; W/URBANO BARBERINI, NATASHA HOVEY, KARL ZINNY, FIORE ARGENTO)
✷ ITALIAN HORROR ✷ DEMONS ✷ SOUNDTRACK (ACCEPT, MÖTLEY CRÜE, PRETTY MAIDS, SAXON)

Produced and written by Dario Argento and directed by Lamberto Bava (son of Mario Bava), *Demons* is Italy's hallucinogenic meta-commentary on its own berserk splatter movies of the '80s. The film takes place in a theater showing a berserk splatter movie from Italy. An unnamed fright film is playing at the Metropol, which is packed with patrons who accepted a screening invite from a freaky dude (Michael Soavi) wearing a Terminator-skull mask. The movie-within-a-movie features a silver monster mask that transforms its wearer into a demon. The same mask is on display in the Metropol lobby. In fact, on her way inside, a hooker cut herself on the mask. Before long, the prostitute's wound spews goo, and she grotesquely mutates into a demon a lot like the one up on screen.

From there, *Demons* is an electrically kinetic orgy of body-breaking and gore-spraying, as one patron after another gets bitten and infected, flailing wildly in some truly awesome monster makeup. The exits, in the meantime, have been bricked up to prevent escape. Amidst gushers of blood, bile, entrails, green puke, and other wet foulnesses, youthful George (Urbano Barberini) and Cheryl (Natasha Hovey) make their way to the fateful lobby display, which also includes a motorcycle and a samurai sword.

The couple mounts the bike and speeds around the theater, hacking and slashing demons as they go, in a sustained assault of homicidal heavy metal joy while "Fast as a Shark" by Accept blares on the soundtrack. A group of punk rockers breaks into the theater, only to get demon-bit and go running around spreading the plague to the general populace. George and Cheryl nastily dispatch the original ticket giver and then take to the demon overrun streets while "Everybody Up" by Saxon closes out the action.

A heavily armed family in a Jeep rescues our heroes. As Cheryl tragically transforms into a demon during the closing credits, a ten-year-old kid in the front seat blasts her with a shotgun. Twice. Right in the gut.

Demons makes effective use of the metal songs on its soundtrack. "Night Danger" by Pretty Maids turns out to be really good rioting music. The big surprise is the bizarre, even scary "Walking on the Edge" by Rick Springfield. It's a five-minute opus, the first one of which consists of swirling synths and a deep devil voice moaning about war and "the Beast" before launching into hard rock bombast. Posters lining the Metropol lobby include those for *AC/DC: Let There Be Rock* (1980), *Four Flies on Grey Velvet* (1971), *No Nukes* (1980), and *Nosferatu* (1979). The video game Silent Hill features a re-creation of the Metropol theater adorned with posters for *Demons*.

DESPERATE TEENAGE LOVEDOLLS (1984)
(DIR. DAVID MARKEY; W/JENNIFER SCHWARTZ, HILARY RUBENS, JANET HOUSDEN, STEVE MCDONALD)
✣ GLAM ROCK ✣ SUNSET STRIP ✣ YOUTH REVOLT

How strong is the connection between heavy metal and bubblegum pop? Early embodiments of a solid nexus turned up in the 1970s via Kiss, Thor, Slade, and Sweet, as well as Suzi Quatro and the Runaways. Right in the crosshairs is the Osmonds' "Crazy Horses" single from 1972, a romp so monstrous that dirtbag NWOBHM band Tank's cover a decade later is actually more subdued than the original! Lawnmower Deth didn't reach the power of the original, either. Pop and power reached the ultimate collision point of Motörhead and the Monkees in Hawthorne, California, longhairs Redd Kross.

Led by brothers Jeff and Steve McDonald, Redd Kross arose from the same early-'80s L.A. punk storm that begat Black Flag, the Germs, and Fear. They covered Blue Cheer and sang about Ronnie James Dio, and their every note elicits the same delirious rush as the greatest overflowing bowl of sugar cereal ever downed during the greatest Saturday morning cartoon marathon. Redd Kross never translated their electrifying live shows into the global eternal pop rock stardom they deserved, but the McDonalds did star in and score *Desperate Teenage Lovedolls*, director David Markey's madcap underground masterpiece.

Essentially a parody of the real-life Runaways story, *Desperate Teenage Lovedolls* chronicles the triumphs and tragedies of an all-girl rock group, comprised of frontwoman Kitty Carryall (Jennifer Schwartz), guitar goddess Bunny Tremolo (Hilary Rubens), and skin-slammer Patch Kelly (Janet Housden and, in performance, an amusingly "disguised" Jeff McDonald). After busking and surviving gang violence on the mean shores of Venice Beach, the Lovedolls fall under the spell of ruthless rock impresario Johnny Tremaine (Steve McDonald). Their rocket ride to the top of the pop charts is only slightly less spectacular than their cataclysmic downfall. What a trip.

Desperate Teenage Lovedolls is a guerilla maelstrom of catfights, LSD flip-outs, *Bewitched* and *Brady Bunch* music cues, references to *Valley of the Dolls* and *Switchblade Sisters*, a quick cameo by young, hatless Saul Hudson (aka Slash of Guns N' Roses), and even murder! Best of all, the action goes down to the tune of great Redd Kross originals (with the Lovedolls on vocals where needed) and their amazingly illegal covers of "Strutter," "Purple Haze," and, most uproariously, "Stairway to Heaven." The subject matter is *River's Edge* all the way, but the attitude is punk rock sitcom overload; dig the epic sound bite: "Thanks for killing my mom!"

DETROIT METAL CITY (2008)
(DIR. TOSHIO LEE; W/KEN'ICHI MATSUYAMA)
✣ CONCERT FOOTAGE ✣ CORPSE PAINT

Soft-spoken farm boy Soichi Negishi (Ken'ichi Matsuyama) longs for Swedish-style pop stardom. Not in Sweden, though. In Tokyo. When his JapABBA dreams die hard, he splashes on corpse paint and supervillain gear as "demon emperor" Johannes Krauser II, lead shrieker and guitarist for death metal extremists DMC—which is short for *Detroit Metal City*.

Japan's headbangers immediately worship both Krauser and his maniacal bandmates. Unfortunately, Soichi hates the music, hates the audience, and hates himself for selling out, so much so that the inner torment he channels to portray Krauser begins to explode out at inopportune times—like when he's reunited with old crush Yuri (Rosa Kato). The catch is that the angrier Soichi gets, the more powerful—and popular—Krauser becomes, leading to an ultimate blowout after supreme metal god Jack II Dark (Gene Simmons) announces his retirement.

With a plot so impossible in terms of its own reality and ours, *Detroit Metal City* is a zesty, energizing roar of weirdness. The movie is based on a best-selling manga comic that was also adapted into a pretty cool anime series. Matsuyama is terrific in the dual-lead role, hilariously juggling his personas as they duke it out for his soul, and convincingly rocking in front of DMC. His pop music is funny and sweet, too.

DETROIT ROCK CITY

(1999)

(DIR. ADAM RIFKIN; W/EDWARD FURLONG, GIUSEPPE ANDREWS, SHANNON TWEED, KISS)

✠ ROCK CONCERT ✠ SOUNDTRACK (KISS, BLACK SABBATH, AC/DC, VAN HALEN, BLUE ÖYSTER CULT)

In 1978, a teenage garage band scores Kiss tickets, but one dude's mom burns them. The dudes spend the rest of the rest of the movie trying to crash the concert. What should have been a Kiss-centric jam-kicker on par with *Dazed and Confused* (1993) and *The Stoned Age* (1994)—or even *That '70s Show*—fizzles instead of pops. The "party-hearty" atmosphere never takes flight, and moments of dumb fun rarely transcend from dumbness to funny.

When Kiss finally takes the stage, there's no

mistaking that it's the lumpen lugs of *Psycho Circus* and definitely not the demonic foursome of *Destroyer*. However much I slag *Detroit Rock City*, though, my four-year-old nephew, Simon Landau, watched the film with me and after seeing the rock show at the end came to the greatest realizations of his young life. He turned to me, wide-eyed and wonder-struck, and breathlessly said: "Wait a minute! Uncle Mike! KISS IS REAL?!" He's been a Kiss Army member ever since. Those guys will *always* find a way!

THE DEVIL IN MISS JONES (1973)

(DIR. GERARD DAMIANO; W/GEORGINA SPELVIN, HARRY REEMS, MARC "10 ½ INCH" STEVENS)

✠ SATAN ✠ SEXUAL DAMNATION ✠ PORN CHIC

The Devil in Miss Jones is heavy, man. Heavy like hellfire. Heavy like metal. Yet despite the movie's entirely downbeat air—it opens with a spinster slitting her wrists in a bathtub and going to hell—coupled with the homeliness of thirty-six-year-old Georgina Spelvin as Miss Jones, *Devil* was a massive box office success and cultural phenomenon. After Miss Jones gorily offs herself, we learn she's a virgin who denied herself the earthly pleasures of the flesh. The Devil, depicted here as a professorial gentleman, sends her careening through a full palate of sexual sensations.

Straight intercourse leads to lesbianism leads to double penetration by a pair of dudes (one of whom is loin legend Marc "10 1/2 Inch" Stevens) leads to essentially fellating an entire live snake. And it goes on for eternity. What makes this situation hellish is that Miss Jones will never, ever be able to climax. She is condemned to remain forever sexualized—and thereby, inflamed with a will to live—but trapped in a netherworld on the brink of an orgasm that will never arrive. She's as doomed as doom comes (or doesn't come).

A year after inventing "porn chic" with the jocular crotch comedy *Deep Throat* (1972), Queens, New York, hairdresser-turned-sudden-blockbuster-filmmaker Gerard Damiano got all kinds of existentially serious with *The Devil in Miss Jones*. It's a series of arty meditations connected by hard-core sex, shot through with an haunting hopelessness makes *DMJ* a milestone of doom metal cinema. The initial release played in standard (i.e., non-porn) theaters, and ranked as the seventh highest grossing attraction of 1973 (between *Live and Let Die* and *Paper Moon*). It garnered rave reviews like one in *Variety* that invoked Jean-Paul Sartre and proclaimed, "With *The Devil in Miss Jones*, the hard-core porno feature approaches an art form, one that critics may have a tough time ignoring in the future."

Sequels to the film, some quite remarkable, continue to be produced today. Avant-garde smut maker Gregory Dark (under his "Dark Brothers" guise) assumed the *Devil in Miss Jones* mantle in 1986, unleashing the über–new wave *Devil in Miss Jones Part III* and *Devil in Miss Jones Part IV* in rapid succession to huge acclaim and long-running cult status. In 1995, he returned to this realm of hardcore Hell for *The Devil in Miss Jones 5: The Inferno*. As a direct result of this film, Greg immediately got to direct the music video "The Bit" for the Melvins.

I wrote the screenplay to *DMJ5*, under my nom-de-poon "Selwyn Harris." Aside from the movie's metallic themes, the soundtrack is all guitar-shredding madness. Greg Dark told me that Stan Lee, lead axeman of L.A. punk titans the Dickies, performed all the music, but then he also told me that Slash secretly provided the soundtrack for one of his *New Wave Hookers* sequels. I love Greg, but he smoked a lot of weed. He went on to become the hottest director of MTV videos in the late '90s/early 2000s, first with a series of clips for SoCal ska-core stoners Sublime, and then for the era's pop-tart royalty, including Britney Spears, Christina Aguilera, Mandy Moore, Jessica Simpson, and the Backstreet Boys.

THE DEVIL RIDES OUT

(1968), AKA THE DEVIL'S BRIDE

(DIR. TERENCE FISHER; W/CHRISTOPHER LEE, LEON GREENE, CHARLES GREY, NIKE ARRIGHI)
✶ SATAN ✶ HAMMER HORROR

Christopher Lee stars in Hammer Films' *The Devil Rides Out*, but, surprisingly, not as the title character. He's Duc de Richlieu, an occult expert investigating a satanic cult in 1930s England. Charles Grey (the deadpan Criminologist from *The Rocky Horror Picture Show*) costars as the Crowley-esque cult leader Mocata. After de Richlieu rescues two bewitched inductees from their "Devil's baptisms," Mocata fights back, first with temptations from comely virgin Tanith (Nike Arrighi) and then by invoking demonic apparitions, a skull-faced Angel of Death on horseback, and the goat-horned (and snouted and eared) Satan himself.

The Devil Rides Out is colorful, energetic, and unique. Lee captivates, as always, even in the "hero" role, and Gray is devilish, indeed—seductive and sardonic, be he in a sharp Savile Row suit on his English estate or a garish purple robe at an outdoor blood ritual.

Adapted from a novel by Dennis Wheatley (writer of *To the Devil, a Daughter*), *The Devil Rides Out* was originally proposed by Hammer in 1963, but stalled over censorship fears. The finished movie looks as though it were made then (regardless of its retro setting), rather than in the era of Anton LaVey as a media sensation and hippies groovily experimenting with black magic. *The Devil Rides Out* explicitly ushered the Prince of Darkness and his depraved worshippers onto the big screen, Hammer style, showing us what was only hinted at in *Rosemary's Baby*.

DEVIL'S ANGELS (1967)

(DIR. DANIEL HALLER; W/JOHN CASSAVETES, BEVERLY ADAMS, MIMSY FARMER, BUCK TAYLOR)

✠ MOTORCYCLES

A follow-up to Roger Corman's breakthrough *The Wild Angels* (1966), *Devil's Angels* follows the dustups and beat-downs of biker gang the Skulls after a member accidentally kills a bystander and they lam it out on the highway. The Skulls roll into a little seaside community just in time for the town fair. A local hussy (Mimsy Farmer) stirs up some shit and prompts full-on warfare between the bikers and law enforcement, much to the chagrin of philosophical Skulls leader Cody (John Cassavetes).

Jus Oborn, head sorcerer for Electric Wizard, singles out *Devil's Angels* for high praise in the '60s biker flick canon, especially its music—featuring Mike Curb compositions and songs by Davie Allan and the Arrows. "*Devil's Angels* is so apocalyptic and doom ridden," Oborn told an interviewer. "The song 'Devil's Rumble' is probably the first doom track around."

THE DEVIL'S RAIN (1975)

(DIR. ROBERT FUEST; W/ERNEST BORGNINE, WILLIAM SHATNER, EDDIE ALBERT, IDA LUPINO, JOHN TRAVOLTA)

✠ SATAN ✠ BLACK MASS

A once-in-a-deranged-*Love-Boat*-episode cast of campy greatness converges in a small desert town to succumb to a satanic washout in *The Devil's Rain*. Ernest Borgnine plays Jonathan Corbis, a devil-worshipping high priest in pursuit of a demonic book. He eventually turns into a long-horned goat man in a pentagram-emblazoned robe. William Shatner costars as Mark Preston, a hothead who attempts to defeat Corbis. He fails and becomes a puppet of Lucifer. Ida Lupino is Preston's mom. She, too, gets drafted into the goat-priest's congregation.

Eddie Albert, of TV's *Green Acres*, saves the day as a psychic investigator. He unleashes the devil's storm at a gathering of Corbis's followers. The skies open, a downpour ensues, and the occultists, hilariously, melt like the Wicked Witches of the West before our eyes. Amidst the shaky camerawork and crayon-on-the-radiator visual effects, one face stands out as it yells, "Blasphemer! Blasphemer!" Witness John Travolta in his debut movie role.

Not one moment of *The Devil's Rain* is coherent. Each scene seems disconnected from whatever happened before it, and dull spots deaden the film like raindrops during a hurricane. Nonetheless, *The Devil's Rain* is a crackpot classic. What seemed like an amazing joke when it first opened has remained in the popular consciousness ever since. Church of Satan founder Anton LaVey is credited as *The Devil's Rain*'s "technical advisor." He designed the movie's satanic altar and appears in a helmet alongside Borgnine and Lupino.

The Devil's Rain largely ruined director Robert Fuest. After making Vincent Price's phenomenal *Dr. Phibes* movies and the popular post-apocalypse head-scratcher *The Final Programme* (1973), the British filmmaker cast his lot with Hollywood and this immediately lambasted misstep was the result. Fuest fled to television production in the aftermath. His only other theatrical project was a 1982 soft-core sex flick, *Aphrodite*, about the Greek goddess. Fuest died in 2012.

THE DEVIL'S REJECTS (2005)

(DIR. ROB ZOMBIE; W/SID HAIG, BILL MOSELEY, SHERI MOON ZOMBIE, WILLIAM FORSYTHE)

✠ EVIL CLOWNS ✠ TORTURE

The abominable Firefly brood from *House of 1000 Corpses* (2003) returns in *The Devil's Rejects*. This time, the criminal family comes minus Dr. Satan, and Leslie Easterbrook (*Police Academy*) replaces Karen Black in the role of Mother Firefly. Overall, a much heavier, more pungent, and painful air hangs over the proceedings. *Rejects* is not exactly a sequel to *Corpses*; it's more like a spelunk inside the same universe, delving numerous dark levels downward. Wit and sick comedy abound, but nothing cartoony. Even creep show bozo Captain Spaulding (Sid Haig), grotesque but largely likable at first, reveals his lethally nasty nature here. He also turns out to be the father of Baby Firefly (Sheri Moon Zombie).

The movie opens during a Waco-style siege on the Firefly compound. The family, wanted for forty-seven homicides and tagged by the media as "the Devil's Rejects," blasts their way through law enforcement to the tune of the Allman Brothers' "Midnight Rider." Texas Sheriff John Quincy Wydell (William Forsythe) takes the escape personally. The Firefly clan killed his brother, and this movie's action centers on the lawman's chase and the family's wicked and sadistic side trips as they elude him. Victims pile up fast and bloodily. Firefly leader Otis (Bill Moseley) kidnaps a traveling country-western act, Banjo and Sullivan, and turns their motel room into a roadside torture dungeon. Sexual atrocities, knifings, and naked highway splatter result.

Wydell teams with merciless hitmen the Unholy Two (Danny Trejo and Diamond Dallas Page) and they pursue the Rejects to a whorehouse owned by Captain Spaulding's brother (Ken Foree). The climactic blood-for-all showdown includes a nice callback to House of 1000 Corpses. For an encore, Lynyrd Skynyrd's "Free Bird" plays.

As the crystallization of Rob Zombie's smilingly savage worldview and cruel cool aesthetic, The Devil's Rejects is note-perfect. This represents a major milestone in Heavy Metal Movies, wherein a musician translates, flawlessly, what he did with sound to that most daunting avenue of expression, the motion picture. Coming full circle, Zombie and coproducer Jesse Dayton released an entire album of "Banjo and Sullivan" songs, even though the group never performs in the film.

Emerging as much from the '70s grindhouse affronts (I Spit on Your Grave, The Hills Have Eyes) as from direct-to-DVD extreme horror of the 2000s (Scrapbook, August Underground), Rejects lit up movie screens as a beacon of uncompromised transgression. "This is our world of hurt,"

Zombie proclaims to fellow travelers via The Devil's Rejects. "Let's make it something to see and let's make some fuckin' noise!"

As with House of 1000 Corpses, the spirit of The Texas Chain Saw Massacre (1974) drips, lovingly, all over The Devil's Rejects. Both films' most direct connection to that classic is Bill Moseley as Otis Driftwood. In the heinously underappreciated The Texas Chainsaw Massacre 2, Moseley is brilliant as the steel-plate-headed homicidal hippie Chop Top. He'd earn still more Heavy Metal Movie points a few years hence, portraying Luigi Largo in Repo! The Genetic Opera (2008).

Devil's Rejects' supporting cast is the most remarkable collection of cult movie and TV veterans ever intentionally assembled. Look for Brian Posehn, Danny Trejo, pro wrestler Diamond Dallas Page, Ken Foree (Dawn of the Dead), Michael Berryman (The Hills Have Eyes), E. G. Daily (Dottie from Pee-Wee's Big Adventure and nude in Valley Girl), Tom Towles (Otis from Henry: Portrait of a Serial Killer), and Deborah Van Valkenburgh (of The Warriors, Streets of Fire, and Too Close for Comfort). The sexy naked matron who bounces on Captain Spaulding's big top is '80s adult-film icon Ginger Lynn Allen, showcasing the maturing loveliness that has transformed her into a MILF porn superstar.

The MPAA branded Rejects with an NC-17 seven times before minor adjustments earned an R rating on the eighth go-round. The movie was released on video in its original, unrated form.

The Devils (1971)

(Dir. Ken Russell; w/Oliver Reed, Vanessa Redgrave, Christopher Logue, Michael Gothard)
✶ Witch Hunt ✶ Martyrs ✶ Nunsploitation

In 1969, director Ken Russell established himself as the firebrand of British film with Women in Love. Two years later he cranked up the heat via The Devils, his monumentally incendiary adaptation of Aldous Huxley's fact-based historic novel, The Devils of Loudun, about atrocities committed by the Catholic church in seventeenth-century France. Beefy, wild-eyed Oliver Reed stars as Father Urbain Grandier, a priest who is well liked in the walled city of Loudun, especially by the various women with whom he defies his vow of chastity. Local convent head Sister Jeanne (Vanessa Redgrave) is sexually consumed with thoughts of Grandier, far past the point of madness. Her hysteria rapidly spreads to the nuns in her charge who, pent up by lifetimes of frustration, toss off their frocks and orgy in throes of demonic ecstasy.

By the time big, bad Cardinal Richelieu (Christopher Logue) catches on, word is that Grandier has bewitched Loudun, and the Vatican dispatches psychotic, rock-star witch-hunter Father Pierre Barre (Michael Gothard) to level the city. Grandier has to pay personally. He's shaved bald and subjected to repulsive tortures that culminate with burning at the stake. Loudun is demolished, and the movie ends with Sister Jeanne using one of Grandier's charred bones to masturbate.

Thick with dialogue and visually sumptuous, *The Devils* is a breakneck-paced whirlwind through hell on earth. The setting, the action, and the bleaker-than-pitch-black parting message line up perfectly with heavy metal's rigid assessment of the corruption of organized religion when it runs up against the natural human appetites. True doom is too often delivered by dastardly agents cloaked in guises of the divine.

The Devils has battled censorship for more than forty years. It was initially rated X in both the U.S. and the UK, and edited versions were the best many audiences could ever hope to see. To date, *The Devils* is not readily available on home video in most of the world.

Diary of a Madman

(1963)

(Dir. Reginald Le Borg; w/Vincent Price)
✣ **Demonic Possession**

Vincent Price, on a horror hot streak with Roger Corman's Edgar Allan Poe adaptations *The Pit and the Pendulum* (1961) and *The Raven* (1963), keeps the Technicolor gothic spookery going in *Diary of a Madman*. Price plays a French magistrate and amateur sculptor circa 1900 driven batty by an evil spirit called a "Horla." This Horla intermittently takes possession of our troubled local politician, its presence signaled by a visor-like green light glowing across Price's eyes, driving him to bad behavior up to and including artful murder. *Diary of a Madman* is a notch below Price's truly classic work of this period, but it's a lush production and the star throws himself into it madly.

Playing up his effete side, Vincent is shown early on adoring his pet canary. During a bit of Horla interference, he squishes the bird in his fist, and then ham-tastically goes to pieces when it becomes stickily clear to him what he has done. Maybe Ozzy Osbourne, who already borrowed this movie's title in 1981 for his second classic Randy Rhoads–era album, took this bird-squishing scene to heart.

Disasterpieces (2002)

(Dir. Matthew Amos; w/Slipknot)
✣ **Concert Footage**

Disasterpieces puts Slipknot fans front and center, providing point-of-view access to even the roughest edges of a February 2002 live concert spectacle mounted at London Dockland Arena. Director Matthew Amos fixed twenty-six cameras around the performance space, many on the band members' instruments and bodies. Percussionist Shawn Crahan and editor Paul Richardson then watched every second of footage and assembled a brilliant psycho-spasm crystallization of the action among the masked nine as they destroy the universe onstage.

Two decades earlier, *Disasterpieces* would have played theaters and blown midnight movie audiences' minds, eardrums, and nervous systems worldwide. During the DVD era, the video is a perfect complement for the most visually and sonically adventurous big-ticket harsh-metal shit-disturbers of the 2000s.

Disc 2 of the *Disasterpieces* DVD contains every official Slipknot music video released prior to 2002, including two versions of "Wait and Bleed"—one a live performance, the other a Claymation fantasy.

Dogtown and Z-Boys
(2001)

(DIR. STACY PERALTA; W/SEAN PENN (NARRATOR), JAY ADAMS, TONY ALVA, TONY HAWK, JEFF AMENT)
✻ SKATEBOARDING ✻ SOUNDTRACK (BLACK SABBATH, LED ZEPPELIN, ALICE COOPER, BLUE ÖYSTER CULT, JIMI HENDRIX, THE STOOGES)

Pro skateboarder Stacy Peralta traces the history of his high-speed art form in the documentary *Dogtown and Z-Boys*. Zooming upward from empty Southern California swimming pools in the free-for-all 1970s, the Zephyr skate team—of which Peralta was an exalted member—transformed skateboarding from kid stuff to previously inconceivable aerodynamic acrobatics and a world-class sport. The blazing long-haired burnout rock of the day effectively underscores the action, just as it did in real life. In the years after Zephyr's heyday, hardcore punk and thrash metal would become synonymous with skating, but it's good to see the sport's musical roots on display along with its high-rolling pioneers.

Dogtown and Z-Boys' soundtrack incorporates great hard rock songs, including: "Generation Landslide" by Alice Cooper, "Into the Void" by Black Sabbath, "Godzilla" by Blue Öyster Cult, "Ezy Rider" and "Freedom" by Jimi Hendrix, "Achilles Last Stand" by Led Zeppelin, and "Gimme Danger" by Iggy and the Stooges.

Dominator (2003)

(DIR. TONY LUKE, JR.; W/DANI FILTH, DOUG BRADLEY, SEERA BACKHOUSE, ALEX COX, INGRID PITT)
✻ COMICS ✻ SOUNDTRACK (CRADLE OF FILTH)

The comic strip *Dominator* debuted in 1988 as a feature in *Metal Hammer* magazine. By 1993, *Dominator* existed as a standalone publication, invoking Japanese comics for adults by calling itself the first of the "New Wave of British Manga." *Dominator*'s cult following was large enough to spawn what its creators billed as "England's first-ever all-CGI movie".

Dani Filth of Cradle of Filth voices the title character, a sort of Transformer-looking general in the army of Lord Desecrator, who has recently defeated Lucifer for command of hell.

Ever rebellious, Dominator steals the key to hell, which looks like an electric guitar, and is summoned to earth by three daughters of an exorcist who accidentally play the forbidden "lost chord." Demonic soldiers barrel through the hole torn open between the two realms and everybody fights to Cradle of Filth songs.

Doug Bradley, Pinhead of the *Hellraiser* movies, provides the voices of both Lord Desecrator and the Exorcist. Ingrid Pitt voices Desecrator's ex-girlfriend, Lady Violator. Pitt spoke the role of Countess Elizabeth Bathory on Cradle of Filth's 1998 concept album, *Cruelty and the Beast. Heavy Metal vs. Dominator* (2005) is a totally overlooked, fifteen-minute sequel wherein Dominator meets the evil green rock from *Heavy Metal* (1981).

Don't Go in the House (1980)

(DIR. JOSEPH ELLISON; W/DAN GRIMALDI, ROBERT OSTH, CHARLES BONET, JOHANNA BRUSHAY)
✻ EXTREME HORROR ✻ BANNED VIDEO NASTY

Blasting its way with a literal flamethrower through the extremely crowded post-*Halloween* slasher movie glut of 1980, *Don't Go in the House* has aged horrifically well. Though campy in spots, especially during the discothecque scenes, the film remains harrowing in a more real sense than many of its exploitation brethren. This one really scorches the earth.

Donny Kohler (Dan Grimaldi) grew up suffering at the hands and fiery stovetop of his psychopath mother. She aimed to literally burn the evil out of him. As an adult, Donny works at a factory, where he is paralyzed by the sight of open furnaces. By night, this disturbed man cons women into entering his spooky hilltop home, where he drugs them, strips them, chains them up in a steel-lined burn chamber, and torches them with a flamethrower.

The first kill scene, with Johanna Brushay dangling naked and being scorched alive to skinless goo, is a masterpiece of tension, revulsion, and brilliant special effects. *Don't Go in the House* immediately repelled American critics. Nearly every review featured some variation of a lament on the decline of morality and humanity. Across the pond, the movie figured as one of the key "video nasties" banned in Britain.

House was filmed in various towns along the New Jersey shoreline. Star Dan Grimaldi would achieve Garden State immortality later as Patsy, one of the Tony's key soldiers on *The Sopranos*.

Don't Look Now (1973)
(DIR. NICOLAS ROEG; W/DONALD SUTHERLAND, JULIE CHRISTIE)
✵ WITCHCRAFT

Married British couple John (Donald Sutherland) and Laura (Julie Christie) leave their home for Venice while mourning the death of their five-year-old daughter. The soul-wrenching situation is complicated when an old woman claiming to be a psychic tells them that the girl is attempting to make contact from the afterlife. Soon thereafter, John starts seeing a childlike figure in his daughter's red raincoat running along the Venice canals. Director Nicolas Roeg uses impressionistic visuals both to thrust us into the parents' grief and to subtly introduce the supernatural components that lead up to *Don't Look Now*'s famously heart-stopping climax. Prior to *Don't Look Now*'s release, controversy arose over Sutherland and Christie's sex scene and, to be sure, it's a doozy. Once audiences saw the film, though, the focus became all about the shock ending. No spoilers here: see it and feel your organs attempt to leap up out of your skin.

The Doom Generation
(1995)
(DIR. GREGG ARAKI; W/ROSE McGOWAN, JAMES DUVAL, JOHNATHON SCHAECH, PERRY FARRELL)
✵ APOCALYPSE ✵ SOUNDTRACK (MEAT BEAT MANIFESTO, NINE INCH NAILS)

The Doom Generation is the middle entry in avant-garde filmmaker Gregg Araki's "Teenage Apocalypse Trilogy," sandwiched between *Totally Fucked Up* (1993) and *Nowhere* (1995). Soaked with 1990s scenery, the action follows the cross-country crime spree of three-way lovers Rose McGowan, James Duval, and Johnathon Schaech. Any time they purchase something from a gas station or fast food joint (instead of stealing it), the register totals $6.66. Perry Farrell cameos as a convenience store clerk and drops a Porno for Pyros song ("Dogs Rule the Night") into an industrial-driven soundtrack (Nine Inch Nails, Front 242, Meat Beat Manifesto). Doom marches to a drum machine.

The Doors (1991)
(DIR. OLIVER STONE; W/VAL KILMER, MEG RYAN, KYLE MacLACHLAN, FRANK WHALEY, KEVIN DILLON)
✵ NATIVE AMERICAN MYSTICISM ✵ PAGAN MAGICK

The oral history tome *We Got the Neutron Bomb: The Untold Story of L.A. Punk*, by Marc Spitz and Brendan Mullen, posits that front man Jim Morrison of the Doors was California's founding punk rocker. Maybe, but Mr. Mojo Rising's long hair, leather pants, Death Valley acid trips, invocations of Native American shamanism, declarations of celestial solidarity with Dionysus, the Greek god of wine, and overall ritual madness played a major role in building the swagger of metal frontmen from Glenn Danzig to Henry Rollins to Ian Astbury to Phil Anselmo.

Oliver Stone's Morrison biopic *The Doors* is over-the-top and indulgent, exploding with psychedelia, philosophical bombast, poetry, and rock star excess while stressing the Lizard King's occult interests and black magic sexual exploration with

Pagan high priestess Patricia Kennealy (Kathleen Quinlan). In the lead role, Val Kilmer proves to be in good voice and fills Morrison's rawhide pantaloons just fine. With rabid fan Oliver Stone at the helm, *The Doors* deifies Morrison to the point that when a the head of a Dionysus statue is superimposed on Jimbo's face, it's a moment of relative subtlety.

Down: Diary of a Mad Band— Europe in the Year of VI (2010)

(Dirs. Jim VanBebber, Mike King, Pepper Keenan, Jimmy Bower; w/Phil Anselmo, Pepper Keenan, Kirk Windstein, Rex Brown, Jimmy Bower)

✱ Concert Footage

Down is the occasionally existing, always ass-beating supergroup out of New Orleans made up at the time of filming of Phil Anselmo of Pantera on vocals, Pepper Keenan of Corrosion of Conformity on guitar, Kirk Windstein of Crowbar on guitar, Jimmy Bower of Eyehategod on drums and Rex Brown of Pantera on bass. With former Skid Row guitarist Dave "Snake" Sabo on board as tour manager, *Mad Band* captures these Southern-blasted outlaws embarking on their first European tour in 2006. The film, most of which consists of seventeen songs performed in concert, depicts Down tearing the Continent up and leaving the Old World screaming.

In Norway, Anselmo launches into an onstage rant about how the local black metal rockers run around in the forest, covered in corpse paint, because they're actually "cultivating marijuana." After the show, he apologizes to Fenriz of Darkthrone and Satyr and Frost of Satyricon for saying "some really stupid shit." They're cool with it, or more like they don't seem to notice. Other backstage tour guests include members of Venom and Witchcraft.

Codirector Jim VanBebber is the underground filmmaking legend behind *Deadbeat at Dawn*

(1988) and *The Manson Family* (2003); Anselmo provided music for the latter film, and also performs the voice of Satan. Anselmo also figures prominently in a documentary on VanBebber: *Diary of a Deadbeat* (2012).

Dr. Alien (1989)

(Dir. David DeCoteau; w/Billy Jacoby, Judy Landers, Troy Donahue, Edy Williams)

✱ Sex Mutants

The way-out science-fiction/teen sex comedy hybrid *Dr. Alien* chronicles high school nerd Wesley Littlejohn (Billy Jacoby) transforming into a campus stud after a substitute teacher from outer space, Ms. Xenobia (Judy Landers), injects him with extraterrestrial hormones. Billy becomes immediately irresistible to females, including the school bully's girlfriend and a busty gym instructor (Edy Williams). A boner-like antenna starts popping out of Wesley's head when he gets aroused.

Further personality transformations prompt Billy to become lead singer of the Sex Mutants, a metal band that enjoyably embodies how cheap 1989 movies presented metal bands. The Sex Mutants song "Killer Machine," performed onstage at a rock club in front of a pretty cool skeleton mural backdrop, could feasibly have landed on radio at the time, or at least the Friday night *Metalshop* show on your local FM home of rock 'n' roll.

Supporting the Sex Mutants is a girl group called the Poon Tangs, among whose members are scream queen Linnea Quigley (who plays graveyard stripper Trash in *Return of the Living Dead*) and 1980s porn star Ginger Lynn (see also her star turn in Metallica's "Turn the Page" video and short film). *Dr. Alien* filmmaker David DeCoteau, a semi-legendary schlockmeister, started in gay porn and is credited with well over one hundred directorial efforts, including the Heavy Metal Movie fave *Dreamaniac* (1986).

They will make cemeteries
their cathedrals
and the cities will be
your tombs.

DARIO ARGENTO
presents

DEMONS

"DEMONS"
A Film By **Lamberto Bava**

Music Performed By:
Billy Idol · Motley Crue · Pretty Maids · Rick Springfield
Go West · The Adventures · Accept · Saxon
Produced By DARIO ARGENTO For DACFILM

Released by Ascot Entertainment Group © Copyright 1986 All Rights Reserved

THE ORIGINAL SOUNDTRACK · MUSIC BY JIMMY PAGE
DEATH WISH II

JUDGEMENT IS COMING
DREDD
3D

Clockwise from top left: *brides of Dracula*; Demons
*(1985) rule; El Dia De La Bestia (1995); an excellent metal
character is redeemed in Dredd (2012); W.A.S.P. plays*
Dungeonmaster *(1984).* Center: *Jimmy Page jams* Death
Wish II *(1982)*

Dr. Butcher, M. D. (Medical Deviate)

(1980), aka Zombie Holocaust

(Dir. Marino Girolami; w/Donald O'Brien, Ian McCulloch, Alexandra Delli Colli)

✠ Zombies ✠ Cannibals ✠ Medical Deviant

Nearly the toughest decision faced in the making of this book was whether to list this movie as *Dr. Butcher, M.D. (Medical Deviate)* or as *Zombie Holocaust*. *Zombie Holocaust* is how it was initially billed, outside the U.S, in a brazen attempt to exploit the success of George Romero's *Dawn of the Dead* (1978), Lucio Fulci's *Zombie* (1979), and Ruggero Deodato's *Cannibal Holocaust* (1980). So my head says *Zombie Holocaust*.

Yet my heart belongs to *Dr. Butcher, M.D. (Medical Deviate)*. After an opening involving a New York morgue attendant chowing down on the spoils of his job, the action switches to a tropical locale where flesh-eating natives do battle with non-carnivorous living dead folk. Yet even with that unique premise and its requisite intense mutilation mayhem, *Zombie Holocaust* might not be a singularly standout entry in the Italian-made ultra-disgusto canon—except that it was sliced, diced, slapped together with some new footage involving a gore-mad medico (Donald O'Brien), and promoted and seen in trashpits across America and then embraced on big-box VHS as *Dr. Butcher, M.D. (Medical Deviate)*.

Director Marino Girolami made quick use of leftover sets from Lucio Fulci's *Zombie* to shoot *Dr. Butcher, M.D.* Far from being a secondary cash-in, though, *Dr. Butcher* delivers the grotesque goods, particularly with Donald O'Brien in the title role reinventing the Hippocratic oath as, "First, do ALL harm." This production truly is without peer when it comes to Panzer-strength promotional attacks. Commercials aired for *Dr. Butcher, M.D.*, in saturation numbers on regional TV and FM rock stations. Voice-over god Adolph Caesar intones: "His name is Doctor Butcher, M.D.—Medical Deviate. He's a depraved sadistic rapist, a bloodthirsty homicidal killer, AND he makes house calls!"

Dr. Butcher's trailer, which ran continuously in video machines outside theaters on Manhattan's Forty-Second Street grindhouse row, is a highlights compendium of gore scenes and expands on the commercial's sales pitch with lines such as: "Dr. Butcher loves New York—there are so many attractive patients to operate on!"

Beyond the aforementioned mass-media campaigns, Aquarius Releasing unleashed upon Manhattan a flatbed truck known as the Butchermobile. This sizable, unwieldy vehicle zoomed up and down the city's streets bedecked with flags and banners promoting the film's title. Two guys in blood-spattered mad-scientist costumes, along with two screaming female "victims," rode on the truck's back, waving knives and cleavers and telling passersby where to go see the movie.

Dr. Butcher's Butchermobile stand-ins were no less iconic horror giants than *Gore Gazette* publisher Rick Sullivan and *Psychotronic Encyclopedia of Film* author Michael Weldon. The nubile human medical specimens were their girlfriends. Acting as perfect punctuation to this all-star incident was a line in 1987's *Guide for the Film Fanatic* by Danny Peary: "I nearly got run over by the Butchermobile."

Dracula (1931)

(Dir. Tod Browning; w/Bela Lugosi, Dwight Frye, Helen Chandler, Edward Van Sloan)

✠ Vampires

The most famous film incarnation of the most infamous vampire is an early Heavy Metal Movie masterwork, one of cinema's most agelessly lovable and creepy spine-tinglers. Directed by silent movie horror master Tod Browning, *Dracula* stars Bela Lugosi in the lead role he created on the Broadway stage. The adaptation of Bram Stoker's eponymous 1897 novel is Hollywood's first feature-length supernatural thriller of note.

There are no comic subplots, and Dracula's tone aims to terrify from first frame to last, which represented a gamble for Universal Studios. Fortunately, the public was clamoring for the right scare, and *Dracula* got the entire world screaming. The plot is familiar, so what distinguishes *Dracula* is, indeed, Browning's air of dread, which drifts in like fog that just keeps coming.

What's more, Bela Lugosi paralyzed audiences with fear. The better part of a century later, his screen presence still looms larger than death. He swallows every scene whole with his soul-piercing eyes, diabolical smile, and that slow, studied, menacingly loaded delivery of dialogue ("I never drink . . . wine."). The other deathless performance in Dracula is Dwight Frye as Renfield, the count's insane, insect-devouring assistant.

What we know and adore about the character Dracula almost entirely comes from this milestone movie: his power to turn into a bat; his skills as a seducer who then sinks his fangs into a victim's neck; his fear of the Christian cross; his sleeping by daylight in a coffin; and his vulnerability to a stake through the heart (which is delivered here by tireless vampire slayer Dr. Van Helsing, played by Edward Van Sloan).

Consider how Black Sabbath chose its band name and developed its signature sound, heavy metal music is rudimentally an outgrowth of horror cinema. The 1931 *Dracula* is one of the most crucial cornerstones of fright films. To visit the primordial blood-spring from which metal would eventually leap up among us, just knock on the big wooden door of Castle Dracula right here. No more apt celebration of darkness has ever been spoken than the count's immortal declaration: "Listen to them. Children of the night. What music they make!"

Despite all of Dracula's myriad sequels, spin-offs, and imitations, Lugosi only played the count one more time, in *Abbott and Costello Meet Frankenstein* (1948), which remains Hollywood's greatest horror comedy to date; to paraphrase Quentin Tarantino, the funny parts are really funny and the scary parts are *really* scary.

Dracula 2000 (2000)

(Dir. Patrick Lussier; w/Gerard Butler, Justine Waddell, Christopher Plummer)

✠ Vampirism ✠ Soundtrack (Pantera, Monster Magnet, Slayer, Static-X, System of a Down)

Initially touted as *Wes Craven's Dracula 2000*, this glossy contemporary romp with the Count follows the neo-*Scooby-Doo* teen mystery formula of Craven's *Scream* years, with a twist that is worth the wallow. Here Dracula (Gerard Butler) started his human life as Judas, the betrayer of Jesus Christ. The cherry on top of that concept is a topless scene by willowy blonde Colleen Fitzpatrick, aka teen pop star Vitamin C, who also had a minor global hit song in 2000 called "Graduation." The *Dracula 2000* soundtrack is a dandy sampler of commercial metal's harder end at the end of the century, but alas, no Vitamin C.

Dracula's Daughter (1936)

(Dir. Lambert Hillyer; w/Gloria Holden, Otto Kruger, Marguerite Churchill, Nan Grey)

✠ Goth Chick ✠ Lesbian Vampire

Dracula's Daughter picks up in London moments after the conclusion of 1931's *Dracula* (the one with Bela Lugosi). Gloria Holden, perfectly spooky-hot in the title role, snatches her old man's body from Scotland Yard and torches it, hoping to cure her own vampirism. Nothing doing. Countess Marya Zaleska (as Drac's daughter is properly known) remains blood-crazed, and bewitches her victims with a cursed ring.

Truly cinema's original archetypal goth chick, the countess gets an itch to paint, and then can't help but seducing sexy nude model Lili (Nan Grey). She then hopes to mate with Dr. Garth (Otto Kruger), a psychiatrist to whom she's attracted, by kidnapping his girlfriend Janet (Marguerite Churchill) and hightailing it back to Transylvania. It all ends with a wooden arrow in her heart.

This 1936 movie sizzled under the tagline: "She gives you that WEIRD FEELING!" The lesbian elements are still stunning. At the time, the *New York World Herald* singled out how the countess roamed London "giving the eye to sweet young girls." The nude painting sequence is topped by the Countess slowly leaning in to lay her lips on Janet's, which fans describe as "the longest kiss never filmed." Aristocratic rock madman Screaming Lord Sutch paid homage in his song "Dracula's Daughter."

DRAGONSLAYER (1981)
(DIR. MATTHEW ROBBINS; W/PETER MACNICOL, CAITLIN CLARKE, RALPH RICHARDSON, JOHN HALLAM)
✵ SWORDS & SORCERY ✵ DRAGON

Disney's *Dragonslayer* competed for fantasy blockbuster popularity against *Raiders of the Lost Ark* and *Clash of the Titans,* and ended the hot summer of 1981 with its decapitated noggin on the end of a pike. The mouska-studio should be lauded for making the movie, but they also should have warned away parents somehow. Freaked-out moms had to console tykes who were traumatized by the film's cold, gloomy evocation of Dark Ages blight. Far from the mood of *Fantasia, Dragonslayer*'s spectacularly scary dragon effects pack legitimately shocking horror and gore. If *Dragonslayer* had abandoned all hope of kiddie matinee dollars and fully taken advantage of an R rating, it would rank alongside the same year's *Excalibur* as a full-fledged classic.

To appease a towering dragon named Vermithrax Perjorative, each year King Casiodorus (Peter Eyre) sacrifices a local virgin girl drawn by lottery. The system works fine until the king's daughter, Princess Elspeth (Chloe Salaman), spites her father by rigging the contest so her name comes up to be dragonated. The king calls on teenage sorcerer's apprentice Galen (Peter MacNicol) to slay the dragon. Adventure follows, bolstered by magnificent visual effects from George Lucas's Industrial Light & Magic. Chief among the sights that dwarf modern cinema's best CGI efforts: Vermithrax itself—a physical wonder praised by filmmaker Guillermo Del Toro (*Pan's Labyrinth, Hellboy*) as "one of the most perfect creature de-

signs" in movie history; the Lake of Fire that protects the dragon's underground lair; and a pair of baby dragons that sloppily feast on the princess's leg with red-fanged gross-out glee you'd only expect in Italian zombie/cannibal epics.

After a booming final battle, *Dragonslayer* ends with clear, hard cynicism drenched in metal. The local rabble praise God for killing the dragon, while the king shows up after the fact, drives a sword into its carcass, and declares himself supreme slayer. Galen and his female co-warrior Valerian (Caitlin Clarke) know the truth: no gods, no masters—it was pagan rites, heathen magic, and literal heavy metal that killed the beast.

Ian McDiarmid plays a village priest who decrees Vermithrax to be Satan. The holy man leads his flock against the dragon and is gloriously incinerated, as is the rest of the town, including the church. McDiarmid's next big role was that of the Emperor Palpatine, the ur-baddie of the *Star Wars* saga, in *Return of the Jedi* (1983).

Dragonslayer bands popped up in Chile, Poland, Spain, and the UK. Thrash gods Slayer have also been associated with the name, but guitarist Kerry King has denied the connection. Their moniker could just have easily have been inspired by *The Slayer* (1982) or the Slayer henchmen in *Krull* (1983). George R. R. Martin, creator of *Game of Thrones*, names *Dragonslayer* as the fifth-greatest fantasy film of all time.

DREAM DECEIVERS: THE STORY BEHIND JAMES VANCE VS. JUDAS PRIEST (1992)
(DIR. DAVID VAN TAYLOR; W/ROB HALFORD, K. K. DOWNING, IAN HILL, JAMES VANCE)
✵ BACKWARD MESSAGES ✵ METAL REALITY

This documentary, whose title is paraphrased from a Judas Priest song, intelligently and non-hysterically covers a 1990 lawsuit against the band by a failed suicide survivor. At issue were claims that Priest's "subliminal messages" caused his tragic actions. In 1985, Nevada heshers James Vance, twenty, and Raymond Belknap, eighteen, blew their minds on cheap grass, hooch, and "Better by You, Better Than Me" from Judas Priest's *Stained Class* album. Drunk, high, and armed, they ambled into a church playground to blow their heads off. Belknap ate the full shell and died. Vance missed, blasting off most of his face. Then he turned litigious.

On July 16, 1990, a Nevada court entertained Vance's lawsuit against Judas Priest that posited the band inserted a backward vocal on "Better by You" consisting of the order "Do it!" *Dream Deceivers* introduces us to Vance, whose mangled mug can only invite sympathy. He opens the movie by puffing on a cigarette and emitting smoke through blowholes that should never exist on any human face.

Rather than shirking the rather ludicrous charges, which would have likely been easier than traveling to Sparks, Nevada, Judas Priest appears to face the court. Rob Halford does well during testimony while barely being able to conceal his incredulity at the charges. At one point, he is called on to sing the disparaged song, and the god of metal vocalists wails a cappella in the courtroom.

Ultimately, Halford makes a crucial point. While maintaining that the record contains no hidden messages of any kind, he suggests that even if there was a backward command to "Do it!" those words could be ascribed to anything. Only listeners who were already suicidal would take "Do it!" to mean "Kill yourself." The presiding judge dismissed Vance's lawsuit several weeks into the trial, and the movie ends with all the participants going back to their shattered-to-varying-degrees lives. The message: if you shoot yourself, don't blame heavy metal.

Flabbergasted to the end, Halford points out that if the band were going to plant subliminal messages on their albums, they would compel the audience to "buy more of our records!" Anyone who has ever been to a Judas Priest show knows that no subliminal assistance is needed to hammer that point home.

DREAMANIAC (1986)
(DIR. DAVID DECOTEAU; W/THOMAS BERN, ASHLYN GERE, SYLVIA SUMMERS, CYNTHIA CRASS)
✠ SUCCUBUS ✠ BLACK MAGIC ✠ ZOMBIES

As happens in films directed by David DeCoteau, *Dreamaniac* opens with a strapping young bohunk, Adam (Thomas Bern), , stripping bare-ass naked. He walks down a hall, steps into a bathroom, and is greeted in the shower by a perky-breasted nude female. Girls being icky and all, she claws him bloody. The dude wakes up, and since he's already wearing a sleeveless Def Leppard Union Jack tee in a bed beneath Iron Maiden posters, he rises and gets back to being a "heavy metal musician." Largely, that involves a few guitar strums, some cigarettes, and a black magic ritual to conjure a succubus named Lily (Sylvia Summers). Thinking Lily has to be a dream, Adam goes downstairs to a party being thrown by his mousse-intensive girlfriend Pat ('90s porn star Ashlyn Gere, billed under her real name, Kim McKamy). Lily crashes and feasts on blood, the dead return as zombies, somebody finds a power drill, and then, pow, the crazy dream turned real nightmare is over.

Dreamaniac is essentially some tepid kill scenes and male-emphasizing sex sequences padded out with wacky bits involving '80s stereotypes, including a yuppie who freaks about not being able to check the stock market and a Valley girl who, when asked about heavy metal, chirps "I'm into Lionel Richie!" Adam's bedroom walls are a time capsule of great heavy metal ephemera, which would be fun to freeze-frame on and pick apart if the movie weren't so out of focus. As it is, few of the images are legible, except for Jello Biafra hovering over Adam's pillow.

A coproduction by the affably metal Empire Pictures and the supremely metal Wizard Video, *Dreamaniac* was actually shot on VHS tape. As such, the film, along with (notably) *Blood Cult* (1985) and *Video Violence* (1987), represents an interesting, too-early attempt to legitimize tape as an accepted B-movie medium. Their forerunner, *Boardinghouse* (1982), actually played movie theaters—with its transferred-to-film blurriness billed as "Horrorvision."

Dreamaniac is the breakout of director David DeCoteau after his gay-porn debut *New Wave Hustlers* (1985). DeCoteau made a couple of okay late-era grindhouse efforts, *Creepozoids* (1987) and *Sorority Babes in the Slimeball Bowl-O-Rama* (1988). He then pumped out a staggering number of direct-to-Blockbuster shelf-fillers before hitting upon the gimmick for which he was born: male-focused soft-core teen horror. *The Brotherhood* (2001) is DeCoteau's young dude rip-off of the goth-girl cult fave *The Craft* (1996), with an all-buff high-school boys' swim team indulging in the occult. It has since spawned five sequels, and enabled DeCoteau to launch the similar *1313* series (installment titles of which include *Wicked Stepbrother*, *Actor Slash Model*, and *Boy Crazies*).

DREDD (2012)

(Dir. Pete Travis; w/Karl Urban, Olivia Thirlby, Wood Harris, Lena Headey)

✠ Comic Books ✠ Post-Apocalypse

Overtaking and obliterating Sylvester Stallone's pointless *Judge Dredd* attempt, *Dredd*—or, more specifically, *Dredd 3D*—effectively plugs into the post-doomsday "third-millennium" universe of the late-'70s-born British antihero who, arguably, may rule as the most heavy metal comic book character ever. Karl Urban (who amazed as Dr. McCoy in the 2009 *Star Trek* movie) dons the helmet of the flying-motorcycle-piloting embodiment of ironfisted societal order—and he keeps it on the whole time, never revealing his face, just like in the comic book. That's metal.

Dredd employs the *Training Day* template of having the scariest of all judge-jury-and-executioner officers ordered to take rookie Judge Anderson (Olivia Thirlby), who happens to be psychic, on her first day of patrol over Mega City One. At issue is the emergence of a street drug known as Slo-Mo, controlled by narcotics queenpin Ma-Ma (Lena Headey). It's a good setup for muscular future-hell visuals, and Dredd offers evidence that CGI is finally capable of conveying some cinematic weight or, appropriately, heaviness.

Urban modeled his *Dredd* voice on Clint Eastwood's raspy growl. Dirty Harry after the fall of society served as the conceptual model for the original Judge Dredd comic book character, while his look was inspired by David Carradine's Frankenstein character in *Death Race 2000* (1975). Of course, New York thrashers Anthrax introduced the Judge Dredd character to U.S. pop culture with their 1987 ode "I Am the Law."

DRIVE ANGRY (2011)

(Dir. Patrick Lussier; w/Nicolas Cage, Amber Heard, Billy Burke, William Fichter)

✠ Satan ✠ Human Sacrifice

Nicolas Cage pilots a muscle car in the role of John Milton, an eternally damned career criminal whose raging determination allows him to roar back to this earthly realm from a place where the flames burn but do not consume. He is hell-bent on rescuing his baby granddaughter from Satanic cult leader King (Billy Burke). Milton blazes a trail across the American Southwest, sexing a floozy (Charlotte Ross) and picking up hot waitress Piper (Amber Heard) as a companion. Hot on their heels is a sharp-dressed villain known as the Accountant (William Fichter). He's got to get Milton back to hell, pronto.

As CGI-driven Nicolas Cage supernatural action movies go—Christ, there are so many of them—*Drive Angry* leaves metal fans the least angry. The violence is berserk. The nudity is full frontal. And the devil is in every one of its details. The name of Cage's character, John Milton, is a shout-out to the author of *Paradise Lost*, the 1667 epic poem from which our modern concept of Satan and the kingdom of hell arises. The *Drive Angry* soundtrack showcases some cool classic rock stormers from the ninety-nine-cent vinyl bins: "I Like to Rock" by April Wine, "Laser Love" by T. Rex, and "Raise a Little Hell" by Trooper.

DRIVER 23 (1998)
(DIR. ROLF BELGUM; W/DAN CLEVELAND)
✠ PROG METAL ✠ OBSESSION ✠ CONCERT FOOTAGE

Meet Dan Cleveland. He's a Minneapolis vocalist, bipolar delivery driver, and grandiose rock theoretician who helms the progressive metal ensemble Dark Horse with an obsessive-compulsive intensity so maniacally all-consuming that it is impossible for him to function in life, let alone actually usher Dark Horse anywhere near his own hallucinations of greatness.

Driver 23, the first of two documentaries by the star's childhood friend Rolf Belgum, focuses on Cleveland's singular vision as it crowds out his African-American wife (a professional clown whom we first see while she's applying whiteface makeup) and prompts him to habitually overdose on his psychiatric medication. Dan's inborn conditions and/or his haphazard chemical regimen also inspire bizarre misengineered undertakings. We first sense something is wrong when he constructs an insanely complicated, useless ramp intended to help Dark Horse load equipment faster. As the device tears apart his staircase and he struggles to work around the damage, the rest of his band just lugs its gear up the stairs as usual. He jerry-rigs the world's worst weight bench (a comic highlight). Eventually, abandoned by nearly everyone, Cleveland obsessively covers virtually his entire life with duct tape.

At the center of Cleveland's self-inflicted mental disarray is his music. As his inventions are not really useful, his playing is not quite music. The singing parts, in particular, are far out of sync with humanity. As one Dark Horse player puts it: "Dan cat-howls outside of his range." Musicians, a veritable merry-go-round of characters from the want ads, come and go.

The Atlas Moth picks up several years later, with Cleveland producing Dark Horse's debut album, *Guts Before Glory*, in his newly but expectedly

ramshackle basement studio. Dark Horse is stripped to power trio status, with drummer Jon Mortensen, a professional nature photographer, and bassist Sean Cassidy, who raises enormous moths in his own basement. Mortensen and Cassidy hold their own against Cleveland as worthy documentary subjects. One choice interlude: Cassidy fires off an angry letter to Marvel Comics over an *Incredible Hulk* plot point). Weirdly, they have become extraordinarily good at their hobbies. The never-say-die obsessiveness of their fearless leader has rubbed off in unexpected positive ways, and the band becomes little more than an extended pretext for much-needed friendship.

DROP DEAD ROCK (1995)
(DIR. ADAM DUBIN; W/ADAM ANT, DEBORAH HARRY, IAN MAYNARD, ROBERT OCHIPINTI)
✠ THRASH METAL ✠ SOUNDTRACK (WARRIOR SOUL, THE STONED)

The members of bone-brained Long Island metal band Hindenburg kidnap British punk star Spazz-O (Ian Maynard) at the same time that his manager (Adam Ant) and porn star wife (Chelsey Parks) put out a hit on him. Music mogul Thor Sturmundrang (Deborah Harry) enters the fray, looking to sign Hindenburg fronted by Spazz-O, if they can keep him alive. Tomfoolery in party-store rocker costumes ensues!

This amateurish farce enhances most of its punch lines with cheap cartoon sound effects ("Boing!" "Quack!" "Ding!" "Gulp!"), and weirdly feels about ten years later than its time. Halfway through the Lollapalooza decade, '80s-style glam/thrash hybrids were hardly the shorthand for "garage rock." The top-billed new wave stars were faded. All would be forgiven if the rock rocked or the comedy was funnier. As is, *Drop Dead Rock* is not quite as insulting as the average Troma dreck, but somewhere in that league.

Tom Araya and Jeff Hanneman (Slayer), Rick Allen (Def Leppard), Tommy Victor (Prong), Tom Petersson (Cheap Trick), and Joey Ramone cameo as part of an ersatz MTV ("MVN—Music Video Network") reporting on the abduction of

Spazz-O. Hanneman says, "Spazz-O? I hope they kill the fucker!" to which Araya adds, "Fucker deserves it, man. He was a real jerk!" Rick Allen says, "Before a show he'd shove a banana down his trousers. It wasn't to make him look bigger, it's just that he liked it there."

Spazz-O's hit song "Inseminator" is performed, oddly, by "acid punk" angst-bangers Warrior Soul, under the name "Space Age Playboys" (their best-known album). *Drop Dead Rock* director Adam Dubin made the video for the Beastie Boys' "Fight for Your Right to Party," an achievement especially notable in my mind for sneaking a glimpse of partygoer Kerry King of Slayer into heavy MTV rotation way back in 1986.

Duck! The Carbine High Massacre (1999)

(Dirs. William Hellfire, Joey Smack; w/William Hellfire, Joey Smack)

✶ **School Shooting** ✶ **Concert Footage**

Bad taste blasts the screen like gym-class buckshot in *Duck! The Carbine High Massacre*, a sick-joke reenactment of Colorado's real-life 1999 Columbine High School shooting. The movie was made by fetish-porn outlaws and showcases a live performance by Nashville noise-mongers Today Is the Day, tearing through a pair of ear-pulping numbers at a "youth meeting."

Scary-skinny weirdoes William Hellfire and Joey Smack, who also cowrote and directed, star as metal-pumped teenage outcasts who don black leather trench coats, bust out a cache of weapons, and open fire on their classmates before shooting one another to death. In the aftermath, a cop finds a bomb planted by the killers and, unlike in the actual incident, it goes off.

Aside from Today Is the Day playing "Spotting a Unicorn" and "The Color of Psychic Power," *Duck*'s highlight is an early appearance by Erin Brown as "Bible Girl." Luminous and utterly commanding the screen even in this brief role, Brown proclaims her love for the Lord and gets

shot. Brown, along with Hellfire and the rest of *Duck!*'s cast and crew, emerged from Factory 2000, a hard-kink S&M studio operating out of New Jersey. Shortly after *Duck!*, Erin took on the screen name Misty Mundae and reigned briefly as filmdom's final soft-sex B-movie superstar before free Internet porn annihilated the genre. Hellfire directed a good number of her efforts.

Dune (1984)

(Dir. David Lynch; w/Kyle MacLachlan, Virginia Madsen, Sting, Max von Sydow)

✶ **Science Fiction**

Frank Herbert's universe-spanning 1965 science-fiction novel *Dune* has inspired countless millions of heavy metal fans and thousands of musicians, expanding the concept of headbanging to incorporate the outer realms of mind-blowing. Prog rock, space rock, stoner metal, even founding cosmic gods such as Black Sabbath, Iron Maiden, and (of course) Hawkwind have grains of *Dune*'s sands shot through their DNA. The prospect of converting *Dune* into a single motion picture, though, seemed a madman's errand.

In the early 1980s, movie mogul Dino De Laurentiis thought he'd found the perfect madman: David Lynch, the boundlessly freaky-deaky director of *Eraserhead* (1977) and *The Elephant Man* (1980). Naysayers sneered that not even Lynch could make *Dune* work on film, and their sneers were soon vindicated. Moments of brilliance do flicker fitfully, and the curiosity factor is enough to carry anyone through the beginning of *Dune*'s vast, cold weirdness, but the complete journey is not an easy or enjoyable task.

Unfortunately, Dune's soundtrack was not composed by Rush or Black Sabbath or Voivod, but instead is the work of Toto. The band's guitarist Steve Lukather played all the guitar parts on Michael Jackson's "Beat It" except for Eddie Van Halen's finger-tapping solo, and that was the most metal thing he ever did. By virtue of the cult of the book *Dune* and the cult of Lynch and the sheer, mammoth, über-'80s sprawl of the production, however *Dune* can boast its own semi-substantial cult following.

The most celebrated previous attempt to adapt *Dune* for the screen took place in 1974, when *El Topo* auteur Alejandro Jodorowsky mapped out a ten-hour movie that would star Orson Welles, Mick Jagger, David Carradine, Gloria Swanson, and Hervé Villechaize. Salvador Dalí was to play the emperor while perpetually perched atop a towering toilet. Music would come from Pink Floyd, Magma, and Henry Cow. Jodorowsky labored on the design elements of *Dune* with Moebius and H. R. Giger. After spending two years and two million dollars in preproduction, the backers bailed on Jodorowsky's *Dune*, and what sounds like the heaviest movie of all time imploded into a black hole.

DUNE WARRIORS (1991)
(DIR. CIRIO H. SANTIAGO; W/DAVID CARRADINE, RICK HILL, JILLIAN MCWHIRTER, LUKE ASKEW)
✴ POST-APOCALYPSE ✴ MOTORCYCLES

William (Luke Askew) is post-nuke marauder, a freewheeling sadist who massacres entire villages and makes off with their water. He screws up when he slaughters the family of Michael (David Carradine). Seeking revenge, Michael assembles a team of outlaw skull-crackers, to defend innocents and unseat the wicked William. The results are part *Dune* rip-off and very *Seven Samurai*—but made for about seven bucks.

Besides *Dune* and *The Road Warrior*, *Dune Warrior* also acknowledges *Star Wars*, with hooded dwarves roaming the desert, Jawa style. The motorcycle jousting of *Knightriders* is also purloined. As plagiarized concoctions go, those are some supremely respectable heavy metal source materials. Producer Roger Corman is a legendary recycler. David Carradine's costume and sword were put to previous use in *The Warrior and the Sorceress* (1984) and *Wizards of the Lost Kingdom II* (1989). That wardrobe is almost like a Slayer guitar riff that repeats itself in new heavy jams.

THE DUNGEONMASTER
(1984), AKA RAGEWAR
(DIRS. VARIOUS; W/RICHARD MOLL, JEFFREY BYRON, LESLIE WING, W.A.S.P.)
✴ SWORDS & SORCERY ✴ MONGOL HORDES

No fewer than seven directors labored on Empire Pictures' ambitious, bargain-bin fantasy omnibus *The Dungeonmaster*. Computer dork Paul (Jeffrey Byron) and his fiancée, Gwen (Leslie Wing), only think they've got a bumpy romance until demonic overlord Mestema (Richard Moll, from TV's *Night Court*) zaps them both into his hellacious underworld. Holding Gwen hostage, Mestema challenges Paul to rescue her by surviving waves of tribulations in the video game form.

The opponents include a giant, stop-motion-animated stone statue, a gremlin king, rock-tossing trolls, post-nuke car geeks, and defrosted "historical" villains Genghis Khan and the Wolfman. Plus plenty of zombies. Paul is consistently able to overpower them by tapping a couple of times on his proto-Nintendo power glove. Any one of these elements, along with the imaginative flair with which they're executed (particularly in light of the sub-basement budget), would assure *The Dungeonmaster*'s place in the pantheon of killer headbanging cinema. And then W.A.S.P. shows up and we have a legit instant classic.

In a segment titled "Heavy Metal," Mestema conjures the most unholy racket in all the cosmos, and Paul is zapped into the crowd at a W.A.S.P. concert. The band tears through "Tormentor" while frontman Blackie Lawless pokes, gropes, and whips Gwen, who is chained, in full metal vixen gear, to a stack of amps. Turning their own volume against them with his magic oven mitt, the movie's hero succeeds where Tipper Gore and the PMRC failed: he makes W.A.S.P. disappear. *The Dungeonmaster* is a multilevel must-see for any devotee of Heavy Metal Movies.

Dungeons & Dragons

(2000)

(Dir. Courtney Solomon; w/Jeremy Irons, Thora Birch, Marlon Wayans)

✠ Swords & Sorcery ✠ Dungeons & Dragons

My initial experience of *Dungeons & Dragons,* the decades-late movie adaptation of the game, was catching it video-projected on the big screen at the Fair theater in Queens. The Fair is one of two still-grinding porn theaters in New York City (the other: Brooklyn's Kings Highway Cinema. Tell them Selwyn Harris sent you).

My sum total impression of this big-budget CGI superbomb—in which Marlon Wayans clowns it up and Thora Birch keeps her top on throughout typically cartoony medieval nonsense—was: "Remember that time I tried to play Dungeons & Dragons? And then when I first saw a minute of this movie at the porno theater?"

Dungeons & Dragons devotees: this is your Hollywood bone-toss. You're not getting another one. You don't need this. *Mazes and Monsters* exists.

Dunkelheit: The Tale of Varg Vikernes

(2009)

(Dir. Andrew Garfield; w/Brant Zimny, Cooper Arellano, Justin Corbett, Troy Guiragossian)

✠ Black Metal ✠ Metal History

For decades, the most popular Heavy Metal Movie has been *This Is Spinal Tap,* with different qualifications bringing to mind *Conan the Barbarian, The Road Warrior, Some Kind of Monster,* and so on. More people need to see *Dunkelheit.* For twenty minutes, this seemingly earnest but outrageously campy high school film lauds the worst person ever, Varg Vikernes, while simultaneously making a laughingstock of him and everyone involved in the early days of the Norwegian black metal scene. The result is a naïve piece of junk that is incredibly charming but also infuriating in its dunderheadedness, a wild combination.

The action opens Norway, 1993. Varg Vikernes (Brant Zimny) leads his black metal band Burzum on a blistering rave-up of "Ea, Lord of the Depths" in the semi-icy wilderness. After the jam, Varg, in a fantastically earnest accent, enthuses to his compadres about his Viking berserker ancestors and how his music is all about "unearthly fantasy and magic" in opposition to his country's Christian oppressors. Varg also explains his feelings toward rival group Mayhem: the drummer Hellhammer (Troy Guiragossian) is a good guy, but the lead guitarist is "a real prick" and "a damn wimp and an idiot."

Cut to said prick, Euronymous (Cooper Arellano), with a drawn-on Sharpie mustache and soul patch, calling from jail, which looks, not surprisingly, like a school conference room. The phone wakes up Snorre Ruch (Justin Corbett), Mayhem's other guitarist, and Euronymous asks for a ride home. Mr. Ruch's terrible fake accent, remarkably, is basically Irish as represented in Lucky Charms breakfast cereal commercials.

Euronymous exposes the facts longhand: "It's all about Varg now, not about Mayhem, some band he once played bass for! And the media doesn't care about the music we play! They just care about how evil Varg is for burning down eight churches!" Everything is ludicrous but based on tragic real events that continue to cast an eerie aura over black metal music. Writer-director Andrew Garfield created the film in high school as his senior project before graduating in 2009. The actors are his friends. They're all charming in their bizarre Vaudevillian accents. For much of *Dunkelheit,* Varg wears a Burzum T-shirt and Euronymous wears a Mayhem T-shirt. It's handy.

The unintentional parody here is relentless. When Snorre and Hellhammer jam on "From the Dark Past," Euronymous bursts in and cockily declares: "This band sounds dildos without my guitar playing!" Euronymous also produces an ornate sacrificial knife, alludes to previously offing "that Polish guy," and declares his intent to make "a necklace of Vikernes's bones."

Pressure builds as these the irresistible forces of Euronymous and Varg draw near one another. Meanwhile, "War" by Burzum plays over a montage, setting up the ultimate confrontation. As tension mounts between the two alpha metalheads, Snorre asks in his Irish brogue if he can tag along to their showdown to see Euronymous, because "I've got some riffs I want to show him!"

When Varg buzzes the door at his foe's apartment in the middle of the night, the voice of Euronymous comically blares over the intercom: "Who goes there?" Varg approaches his enemy, and the non-factual black metal battle royale breaks out. Varg stabs Euronymous in the skull, depicted in shadow, followed by a shot of the victim's eyes rolling back into his head like those of a cartoon character.

Afterward, from his jail cell, Varg vaingloriously cries self-defense and the filmmakers seem to back that claim, although nothing in the movie supports that plea at all. Then the credits roll as "Dunkelheit" by Burzum cements the film's adulation of a real creep.

With the possible exception of the West Memphis Three case, Varg murdering Euronymous is the most media-saturated true-crime saga in the annals of heavy metal. Yet for all the hack shockumentaries and flat-footed attempts to craft art films explaining the outbreak of violence in Norway in the early 1990s, no other moving picture comes close to the moxie of *Dunkelheit*. This film, created by teenagers and full of bad decisions, is the best way to experience the faulty thinking and actions of metalheads not much older than themselves.

The Dunwich Horror (1970)

(Dir. Daniel Haller; w/Dean Stockwell, Sandra Dee, Ed Begley, Donna Baccala)

✠ H. P. Lovecraft ✠ Sex Magick

Wicked wizard Wilbur Whateley (Dean Stockwell) aims to unleash the extra-dimensional Old Ones. After stealing a spell book, *The Necronomicon*, Whateley plans to use Miskatonic University lab assistant Nancy (Sandra Dee) in a mating ritual involving a tentacled monster in a closet. Whatever that thing is, it likes to fuck, as brunette coed Elizabeth finds out when she opens a wrong door.

The Dunwich Horror was producer Roger Corman's attempt to tap the mythos of über-metal author H. P. Lovecraft, as the filmmaker had previously done with the work of Edgar Allan Poe throughout the 1960s. This didn't turn out as well, and the world had to wait a quarter-century for good Lovecraft movies including *From Beyond* (1986) and *Dagon* (2001). This movie is laden with groovy visuals, though, and maintains a cult following among stoner rock aficionados, who no doubt have their own creative means of dealing with *Dunwich*'s woozy slow pace.

The Dunwich Horror is now a band in the U.S., and Malhavoc and others have penned "Dunwich Horror" songs. Justin Oborn of doom lords Electric Wizard has hailed *Dunwich* thusly: "An 'electric wizard' is not fuckin Gandalf and all that gay elf-loving shit. *Dunwich Horror* is cool as hell and sums up the whole Electric Wizard ethos... psychedelic black mass horror!"

Famous for the squeaky-clean beach party movie *Gidget* (1959) and best known via the "Look at me" line in the *Grease* song that invokes her name, Sandra Dee long embodied the idea of the well-scrubbed all-American girl. Her participation in a demon-sex drive-in movie is eyebrow-cocking enough, but note that *The Dunwich Horror* also contains the only known incident of Sandra Dee nudity.

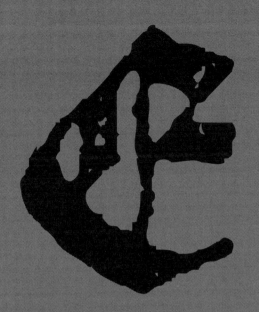

EASY RIDER �֎ EAT THE RICH ✷ ELECTRIC DRAGON 80,000 V ✷ EMANUELLE AND THE LAST CANNIBALS ✷ EMANUELLE IN AMERICA ✷ THE EMPIRE STRIKES BACK ✷ END OF THE CENTURY: THE STORY OF THE RAMONES ✷ ENDGAME ✷ THE ENTITY ✷ ENTRAILS OF A VIRGIN ✷ EQUALIZER 2000 ✷ EQUINOX ✷ ERASERHEAD ✷ ERIK THE VIKING ✷ ESCAPE 2000 ✷ ESCAPE FROM NEW YORK ✷ THE EVIL ✷ THE EVIL DEAD ✷ EVIL DEAD II: DEAD BY DAWN ✷ EVILSPEAK ✷ EXCALIBUR ✷ THE EXORCIST ✷ EXORCIST II: THE HERETIC ✷ EXORCIST III ✷ THE EXTERMINATOR ✷ EXTERMINATORS OF THE YEAR 3000

EASY RIDER (1969)

(DIR. DENNIS HOPPER; W/PETER FONDA, DENNIS HOPPER, JACK NICHOLSON, TONI BASIL)

✷ BIKER MOVIE ✷ TRIP SEQUENCE ✷ SOUNDTRACK (STEPPENWOLF)

I like smoke and lightning, *heavy metal thunder*!" So roars Steppenwolf in "Born to Be Wild," the instant-anthem-of-a-generation that underscores *Easy Rider*'s iconic opening credits sequence. Atop hard-charging motorcycles, hippie biker Billy (Peter Fonda), in his star-spangled helmet, and buckskin-clad burnout Wyatt (Dennis Hopper) roar forth onto an endless open highway, newly loaded from a cocaine deal and with no destination in mind. "Born to Be Wild" provides the most potent motor-power in movie soundtrack history. This brilliant mythmaking moment is the definitive coinage of the term *heavy metal* as far as the inherent promises held for long-haired young searchers.

Overall, *Easy Rider* is more of a moment than an actual movie. The opening is heavy enough to carry to the ending, when *Easy Rider* tunes way, way *down*. The film's famously hopeless conclu-

sion depicts shotgun-cracking rednecks expressing distaste for our biker heroes through the end of two barrels. In the last five minutes, Fonda yells, "We blew it!"; the boys are blown away; and the new wave of American cinema is blasted with a gaping doom metal hole in its heart. After that, the debut of Black Sabbath a few months later was the only thing that made any sense.

EAT THE RICH (1987)

(DIR. PETER RICHARDSON; W/NOSHER POWELL, RONALD ALLEN, NIGEL PLANER, MIRANDA RICHARDSON)

✷ CANNIBALS ✷ SOUNDTRACK (MOTÖRHEAD)

E*at the Rich* is the big-screen debut of the British comedy troupe featured on the TV series *The Comic Strip Presents . . .*, the same core of people responsible for *The Young Ones*. The group was attempting to step up into movies with a debut on par with *Monty Python and the Holy Grail* (1974). Alas, this muddled story about a disgruntled waiter who turns cannibal cook–cum-terrorist proved to be a misfire for nearly everyone except Motörhead. Not only does frontman Lemmy appear in a cameo, *Eat the Rich*'s eponymous theme song became an instant

Motörhead classic. Motörhead contributed six songs to the *Eat the Rich* soundtrack. In addition, the film features "Bess," a solo song by late Motörhead guitarist Würzel. Numerous other UK personalities cameo, including Rik Mayall of *The Young Ones* and the great metal spoof band, Bad News, which also emerged from *The Comic Strip Presents . . .*

Electric Dragon 80,000 V (2001)

(Dir. Sogo Ishii; w/Tadanobu Asano, Masakatsu Funaki, Masatoshi Nagase)

✵ **Science Fiction** ✵ **Electricity**

Dragon Eye Morrison (Tadanobu Asano) is a detective specializing in reptile recovery. Having been struck by lightning as a child, he can channel and conduct electricity. The accident also made him unable to control his furious inner "dragon." To cope, he administers nightly shock treatments to himself and shreds with omnipotence on electric guitar. Now you're playing with *Electric Dragon 80,000 V*.

At the same time, satellite dish repairman Thunderbolt Buddha (Masatoshi Nagase) is obsessed with electric weapons. He uses them to hunt mobsters, vigilante style. When Thunderbolt catches wind of another high-voltage warrior in town, he challenges Dragon Eye to plug in and charge hard for a rooftop battle to determine the ultimate electro-supremacy. Sparks, at great volume, do fly.

Electric Dragon 80,000 V is the weird-wired brain-blossom of Gakuryu Ishii, under the name Sogo Ishii, also known as the director of nuclear punk picture *Burst City* (1982) and leader of Tokyo-based industrial noise marauders MACH-1.67. Not only does the group provide the movie's score, but its propulsive overall aesthetic runs through every frame. Insanely.

Emanuelle and the Last Cannibals (1977), aka Trap Them and Kill Them

(Dir. Joe D'Amato; w/Laura Gemser, Gabriele Tinti, Nieves Navarro, Monica Zanchi)

✵ **Gore** ✵ **Cannibals** ✵ **Banned Video Nasty**

Italian shock lord Joe D'Amato transformed Laura Gemser's benign Black Emanuelle soft-core film series into a scalding cesspool of sadism and death with *Emanuelle in America* (1977). Whereas that transgressive classic dropped our heroine into a snuff film ring, D'Amato immediately upped the carnage by rushing out *Emanuelle and the Last Cannibals*.

Intrepid girl reporter Emanuelle (Gemser) goes undercover in a mental hospital. When a hot female patient bites off the breast of a nurse, Emanuelle deduces that the girl must have been raised by cannibals. Emanuelle then gets the scoop by diddling the bloody-mouthed lass about the clitoris. Our lusty Lois Lane and some pals follow up by heading into the Amazonian jungle to press flesh with real, live flesh-eaters. Graphic, gut-plunging atrocities on par with those of *Cannibal Holocaust* (1977) and *Make Them Die Slowly* (1982) go down, including castration, evisceration, and a horrendously real-looking nipple removal. These jolts get punctuated intermittently by lyrical sex interludes such as a lesbian lagoon dip that's leered at by a cigarette-smoking chimpanzee.

Emanuelle and the Last Cannibals is a hot cauldron of canned Muzak and raw gore—a heady, if not exactly tasteful, stew. In 1984, New York's Forty-Second Street strip of grindhouse movie theaters went Italian bloodbath wild. To cash in on the two-year run of *Make Them Die Slowly* at the Liberty, *Emanuelle and the Last Cannibals* was renamed *Trap Them and Kill Them* and bounced around from one Deuce screen to another for the next eighteen months. I saw it, the first time, at the Empire.

Emanuelle in America (1977)

(Dir. Joe D'Amato; w/Laura Gemser)

✠ Gore ✠ Snuff ✠ Banned Video Nasty

With its innocuous-title, *Emanuelle in America* appeared to be just another entry in the lighthearted Black Emanuelle soft-core sex series that starred Laura Gemser as an erotic world traveler. Yet *Emanuelle in America* represents one of cinema's most severe and inexplicable left turns, the musical equivalent of which would be tuning into a light rock station to hear Journey and Foreigner and then having Anal Cunt and Pig Destroyer blare out between the soccer-mom commercials instead.

For *Emanuelle in America*, our horny heroine becomes an investigative reporter assigned to blow the lid off the international snuff film underground. So what begins as yet another fluffy skin romp becomes, without warning, a brain-lacerating bastion of graphic rape, enslavement, human trafficking, horrifically inventive torture, murder, and actual on-screen bestiality.

In the early '80s, sci-fi splatter visionary David Cronenberg (*The Brood, The Fly*) was appalled by *Emanuelle in America* on cable in a hotel room. He wondered what kind of irredeemable perverts could be entertained by such hideousness. From that experience, Cronenberg conceived *Videodrome* (1983), his masterpiece about a TV station broadcasting snuff porn encoded with a death ray to eliminate anyone who would choose to watch it.

Along with other Joe D'Amato efforts, *Emanuelle in America* has faced censorship the world over, including a run on the UK's list of forbidden "video nasties." The top issue, usually, is a scene of an unnamed actress manually pleasuring a horse. The scene really depicts her hand, and a real horse. She really does what's necessary to get that huge hose flowing, and we really do see it all.

D'Amato also mounts a horribly realistic kinky death orgy, where power brokers and global politicians wreak lethal havoc on screaming slave girls. One victim is forced to drink boiling mercury through some sort of horn; another undergoes a sudden and anesthesia-free double mastectomy. That kind of sickness makes all the difference. So hail to the steel balls alone of *Emanuelle in America*, and the unforgettably heinous staging by sadistic Italian B-movie madman Joe D'Amato.

The Empire Strikes Back (1980)

(Dir. Irvin Kershner; w/Mark Hamill, Carrie Fisher, Harrison Ford, Billy Dee Williams)

✠ Science Fiction ✠ Cryogenics ✠ Amputation

Pretentious saps who want to convince you they're smarter than the type of people who like *Star Wars* movies (meaning, smarter than literally *everyone* else) automatically name *The Empire Strikes Back* as their favorite in the series. That's fine, but then they always tag on, "because it's so dark." Whatever, young Jedi. There are about six hundred sixty-something other movies in this book alone that offer a more accurate conception of "darkness."

Empire is rife with heaviness, though, and studded with great metal moments. Among them are: the ice planet Hoth, which looks a Frank Frazetta pulp novel cover come to freezing life; Han Solo (Harrison Ford) slicing open a Tauntaun to stuff wounded Luke Skywalker (Mark Hamill) into its oily bowels; pint-size green goblin Yoda in his swamp spouting backward philosophy; and bounty hunter Boba Fett freezing Han in carbonite. A current of genuine rage runs through the proceedings, coming to a head when our hero Skywalker has his hand lightsabered off by Darth Vader just before the big reveal: "I am your father!"

The only *Star Wars* character to rival Darth Vader for sheer metal ferocity and hard rock fan reverence is Boba Fett. The mercenary bounty hunter who pursues Han Solo at the behest of Jabba the

Hut dresses like an MX missile with a bullet-shaped helmet covering his entire head. He also fires heat-seeking explosives, carries a huge laser rifle, and never says a word. Boba Fett first appeared as a costumed character in September 1978 at the San Anselmo Country Fair parade, near George Lucas's northern California headquarters. The general public got its first dose of Fett in November 1978, during the trippy, *Heavy-Metal*-magazine-style animated segment of the universally lamented *Star Wars Holiday Special* on CBS. Fun start for a guy who hunts humans and other sentient creatures for a living.

End of the Century: The Story of the Ramones (2003)

(Dirs. Jim Field, Michael Gramaglia; w/the Ramones, Rob Zombie, Kirk Hammett)
✴ Black Leather ✴ Metal History

End of the Century, an excellent documentary on the history of this endlessly influential band, points out that the Ramones started as metal fans. Besides worshipping the Stooges and the MC5, they loved Black Sabbath, with whom they toured, not successfully, in 1978. "Inspired by Sabbath's "Paranoid," front-freak Joey Ramone composed the group's initial songs simply by rearranging the three main chords of Alice Cooper's "I'm Eighteen." For the love of power chords, Van Halen opened for the Ramones well before famously opening for Sabbath!

The Ramones even set out to be metal, aiming to compete in stadiums with Aerosmith and Kiss. The specific nature of their talents dictated another route. But that was also cool. Instead creating something loud and fast called punk rock, the Ramones remained the most relatable punk band to metalheads during the days when the two tribes did not mesh. As punk became hardcore and metal evolved into thrash in the mid-1980s, the notion of "shorter, faster, louder" ruled, and Ramones T-shirts became as com-

mon as Motörhead tees in band photos. In fact, Motörhead recorded the song "Ramones" in tribute, and Metallica recorded six Ramones covers. Sodom's take on "Surfin' Bird" shows their blunt, minimalist debt to the Ramones. Anthrax, L.A. Guns, Powermad, and Soundgarden have followed suit.

End of the Century provides an alternately hilarious and heartbreaking examination of a musical powerhouse forever off the curve, inventing what rock became while never being able to reap any attendant rewards, let alone riches. The film humanizes the iconic Ramones personalities—living sideshow Joey, right-wing taskmaster Johnny, dope fiend Dee Dee, shy original drummer Tommy, and his Brooklyn mook replacement, Marky. So when the interpersonal relationship stuff hits, the impact feels especially gnarly. In the early '80s, Johnny steals Joey's beloved girlfriend and then marries her. Joey and Johnny never speak again. Dee Dee seethes. Johnny gets beaten by a thug within a power chord of death. Joey smiles. Dee Dee continues seething. Everybody falls out with everybody. Twenty years go by. Joey dies of cancer. Dee Dee fatally overdoses. At the Ramones' Rock and Roll Hall of Fame induction in 2002, Johnny says, "God bless George W. Bush," but only Tommy mentions the deceased Joey.

Johnny Ramone repeatedly proves to be the Ted Nugent of punk (that's a compliment). A year after *End of the Century* debuted, Johnny Ramone also died. His loss sadly rendered this film even more valuable. It's a fitting and worthy epitaph for this glue-sniffing, cretin-hopping, brat-beating battalion of genuine originals.

Endgame (1983)

(Dir. Joe D'Amato; w/Al Cliver, Laura Gemser, George Eastman, Dino Conti)
✴ Post-Apocalypse

Predating *The Running Man*, to say nothing of *Battle Royale* and *The Hunger Games*, and setting the action in a post-nuke cosmopolis—the better to rip off both *Rollerball* and *The Road*

Warrior—Endgame stars Al Cliver (*2020: Texas Gladiators*) and Laura Gemser (the mighty Black Emanuelle herself) in a bloody mess helmed by Italian exploitation giant Joe D'Amato (*The Blade Master, Emanuelle in America*).

Endgame is a TV-show-within-a-movie in which metaled-up gladiators battle to the death in urban combat zones. Mutants with the faces of apes and fish, along with a tribe of cowboys, provide additional challenges. Each *Endgame* is broadcast by the Nazi-inspired ruling class in order to keep the surviving rabble at home and pacified. The most popular competitor to date is Ron Shannon (Cliver), and he mucks up the latest adventure by falling for telepathic mutant girl Lillith (Gemser).

Endgame supplies all the wildly goofy costumes and tricked-out vehicles that fans of after-the-bomb action cinema demand, along with no dearth of naked flesh and flowing blood. Though it's not a classic, *Endgame* is like a generic thrash metal band. You put it on the cassette, everything works like it's supposed to, and maybe your head's banging even if you know better. Come on, let's hear it for the cheap stuff!

Joe D'Amato directed at least two hundred films in his lifetime. Inexplicably, he once named *Endgame* as his personal favorite among his dozens of efforts. Sadly, D'Amato died in 1999, so we'll never get a more in-depth explanation—although I'm not entirely convinced he's isn't still churning out movies.

The Entity (1982)
(Dir. Sidney J. Furie; w/Barbara Hershey, Ron Silver, David Labiosa, George Coe)
✴ Demon Rape

The Entity is a largely dismissible haunted house movie rendered entirely unforgettable due to repeated scenes of star Barbara Hershey being stripped nude, fondled, and forced into sex with the invisible monster of the title. Headbangers who rented *The Entity* in a sweaty VHS shack or tuned into one of its many, many cable showings were universally dumbstruck by these attack scenes, which are highlighted by amazing special effects of Hershey's naked breasts being squeezed by unseen hands. In time, parapsychologists think they capture the entity with frozen helium. Alas, when our heroine returns to her house, the front door slams itself shut, and a booming voice intones: "Welcome home, cunt." Only at that point does she move out.

As with many other beloved exploitation movies of a preposterous nature, *The Entity* claims to be "based on a true story." Acheron, Count Raven, Nocturnus, Sacrifice, and Slavestate responded with true metal songs in tribute.

Entrails of a Virgin
(1986), aka Guts of a Virgin
(Dir. Kazuo "Gaira" Komizu; w/Saeko Kizuki, Naomi Hagio, Megumi Kawashima)
✴ Extreme Gore ✴ Demon Rape

Somewhere in Japan, three male photographers and three female fashion models embark on a lovely weekend retreat to the woods. After some posing and snapping, they go off in various configurations to engage in soft-core sex. However, the fornicators are each interrupted by a mud-splattered demon with a monstrous baseball-bat dick. This beast, played by Kazuhiko Goda, bears the official character name "A Murderer." Big Muddy massacres the dudes, then rapes the women. And then he massacres the women, too.

Entrails of a Virgin plays like a series of R-rated pseudo-porn loops that all end the same way. It's fuzzy looking and dull. The sequel, *Entrails of a Beautiful Woman* (1986), offers a gangster spin along with some occult magic.

Nonetheless, *Entrails*'s lurid moniker and exotic lineage made it a sensation on the bootleg VHS-trading circuit of the '80s and '90s, a fertile milieu which for many metalheads was a natural extension of cassette tape trading. By either title—*Entrails of a Virgin* or *Guts of a Virgin*—the film seems like B-grade death metal. In fact, *Guts of a Virgin* was the name of the 1991 Earache Records debut album by Painkiller, a jazz-and-grindcore group consisting of saxophonist John Zorn, bassist Bill Laswell of Material, drummer Mick Harris of Napalm Death, and occasionally Yamatsuka Eye of the Boredoms.

EQUALIZER 2000 (1987)

(DIR. CIRIO H. SANTIAGO; W/RICHARD NORTON, CORINNE WAHL, ROBERT PATRICK, WILLIAM STEIS)
✠ POST-APOCALYPSE

Equalizer 2000 distinguishes itself among the *Road Warrior* rip-off herd due to its setting, Alaska. The Eskimos get really weird after the bomb, and everybody fights everybody. The movie's title refers to a multifaceted super-rifle invented by strongman Slade (Richard Norton). He aims to use the wonder weapon to overthrow the Ownership, a fascist regime oppressing the frozen survivors of nuclear winter. Slade fires that Equalizer 2000 a lot in the movie. Every single scene—save for one goofy romantic interlude between Slade and his lady (Corinne Wahl)—is a go-for-broke action sequence. All these nonstop blowups and shootouts are cheap and silly but, in a way, that makes *Equalizer 2000* all the more metal: use what you've got to rock as hard as you can, all the way to Alaska if necessary.

Incidentally, the number *2000* attached to the end of a film title seems to pack an inherent Heavy Metal Movie wallop. Consider: *Camille 2000* (1969), *Cherry 2000* (1987), *Cinderella 2000* (1977), *Death Race 2000* (1975), *Dracula 2000* (2000), *Escape 2000* (1982), *Godzilla 2000* (1999), *Holocaust 2000* (1977), *Heavy Metal 2000* (2000), and *Lolita 2000* (1998). For exploitation filmmakers, the year 2000 must have represented the turning point when all hell would break loose and heavy metal sensibilities would take over everything. Pretty much right on!

EQUINOX (1970), AKA EQUINOX . . . A JOURNEY INTO THE SUPERNATURAL; THE BEAST

(DIRS. JACK WOODS, MARK THOMAS MCGEE, DENNIS MUREN; W/FRANK BONNER, JACK WOODS)
✠ ASMODEUS ✠ BLACK MAGIC ✠ HELL

The original 1970 poster for *Equinox* defines the title as meaning the "occult barrier between good and evil," and it makes a lot of promises. "SEE four teenagers fight a devil cult! SEE the ring that enslaves and destroys! SEE the symbol that defies the hosts of Hell! SEE the unleashed power of the 1,000-year-old book!"

Atypical of similar exploitation ballyhoo, *Equinox* makes good on and surpasses those boasts with invention, imagination, and youthful energy. As with many a debut metal album, the makers' greatest strength may have lain in not knowing what they were doing—because they therefore had no sense of what they could "not" do.

Two picnicking teenage couples catch the malevolent attention of Asmodeus, the Talmudic king of demons, who has taken the form of—of all things—a forest ranger. During a post-meal exploration of a cave, an old man presents the foursome with an ancient magic book, which proves handy when they're quickly forced to battle monsters sent by Asmodeus to kill them. Fantastic destruction and doom follows.

The joy of *Equinox* is in those creatures—stop-motion-animation and forced-perspective wonders that brandish weight, presence, and charm light-years beyond anything achievable with CGI—and the makeshift action in the youthful cast's solution. You'll marvel at the scaly-faced, blue-skinned caveman in a fur toga who stands about twenty feet tall; the green, ridge-browed, tusk-mouthed ape-colossus; and Asmodeus's true form as a bright red Claymation devil with massive bat wings and pterodactyl foot-claws.

The occult beasts of *Equinox* evoke heavy metal, but the spirit of their creation by first-time moviemakers expanding on an unfinished student film is even more heartfelt and headbanging. One of the movie's male heroes is played by Frank Bonner, who later became lecherous commercial salesman Herb Tarlek on *WKRP in Cincinnati*. Ed Begley Jr. served as assistant cameraman on *Equinox*, his greatest Heavy Metal Movie connection next to serving as drummer John "Stumpy" Pepys in *This Is Spinal Tap*.

☾RASERHEAD (1977)

(DIR. DAVID LYNCH; W/JACK NANCE, CHARLOTTE STEWART, JEANNE BATES, JUDITH ANN ROBERTS)
✣ MUTANTS ✣ DYSTOPIA

Eraserhead, both the classic midnight movie and its famously high-haired central character, is as alienating as anything that's not an industrial doom metal record could be. Weirdmaster General of filmdom David Lynch described his breakthrough creative effort as "a dream of dark and troubling things." Like the grossness of watching "man-made chickens" wriggle and spew goo when you try to cut them for dinner (as characters do in *Eraserhead*), Lynch nails it with that summation.

Buttoned-up oddball Henry Spencer (Jack Nance) has a foot-high hairdo. He works in a nonsensical factory and occupies a hellhole apartment in an industrial building where every molecule seems toxic. He visits the insane family of his girlfriend Mary X (Charlotte Stewart) and learns that he's become a father. The baby, who looks like a fetal cow with no skin, is not exactly human but screams and is definitely unhealthy.

Mary and the baby move into Henry's place and then, believe it or not, things really begin to get strange. As the baby wails inconsolably, Mary leaves. Henry envisions a scarred mutant named the Man in the Planet (Jack Fisk) who pulls loud cranks. He also dreams of his own head falling off and being turned into pencil erasers.

Comfort arrives when the Lady in the Radiator (Laurel Near) rises into the air to perform a dance where she stomps on sperm-like creatures,

arousing Henry's sexuality. After the Beautiful Girl Across the Hall (Judith Ann Roberts) breaks Henry's heart, the baby laughs. In a rage, Henry attacks the baby with scissors and it volcanically mutates into a grotesque murderous giant.

Shot in pulsating black-and-white, *Eraserhead*'s visuals are hypnotic and repulsively beautiful. The film's instantly indelible grotesqueries worked their way into the aesthetics of hard rock steadily and irrevocably as *Eraserhead* endured as a midnight movie experience and gross-out home-video stomach-lining test, bearing notable impact on the imagery employed by industrial metal, prog, and extreme power electronics. *Eraserhead* manifested frequently on black T-shirts worn by guys in metal bands. Rush guitarist Alex Lifeson wore an *Eraserhead* button onstage for years, and the movie's poster looms overhead in the band's "Limelight" music video.

Perhaps even more groundbreaking though, at least musically, is *Eraserhead*'s unprecedented sound work. A continual clatter of clanks, pings, shattering glass, gears grinding, and metal machines malfunctioning, the film's scary aural layers construct a perfectly unnerving universe of alienation and humanity-forsaken pain. The *Eraserhead* soundscape is as fundamental to industrial music of the '80s as krautrock, Throbbing Gristle, Boyd Rice, or living too close to a twenty-four-hour construction site.

In hallucinogenic terms, *Eraserhead* is a bad trip. It's a cosmic bummer with a sick version of a happy ending that seems like a lie of consolation told by an agonized, dying brain. Director Stanley Kubrick screened *Eraserhead* for his cast and crew before making *The Shining*, telling them to aim for the movie's all-encompassing milieu of isolation and no escape. On every level, *Eraserhead* is a work of damned, doomed genius, right there in black-and-white.

Eraserhead himself, star Jack Nance, lived an authentically bleak existence off camera as well. His second marriage was to porn star Kelly Van Dyke (aka Nancee Kelly), who sometimes threatened suicide. In November 1991, Nance attempted

TERRORIFICAMENTE MUERTOS

RENAISSANCE PICTURES Presenta
TERRORIFICAMENTE MUERTOS (EVIL DEAD 2)
Con BRUCE CAMPBELL • SARAH BERRY • DAN HICKS • KASSIE WESLEY • RICHARD DOMEIER
Música de JOSEPH LO DUCA   Efectos Especiales de Maquillaje MARK SHOSTROM   Montador KAYE DAVIS
Director de Fotografía PETER DEMING   Productores Ejecutivos IRVIN SHAPIRO • ALEX DE BENEDETTI
Guion de SAM RAIMI • SCOTT SPIEGEL   Producida por ROBERT TAPERT   Dirigida por SAM RAIMI

TRI FILMS

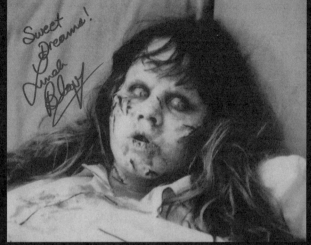

Sweet Dreams!
Linda Blair

Remember the little kid you used to pick on?
Well, he's a big boy now.

Evilspeak

SYLVIO TABET Presents EVILSPEAK
A LEISURE INVESTMENT COMPANY • CAMILL FILM CORPORATION PRODUCTION
Starring CLINT HOWARD • R.G. ARMSTRONG • JOSEPH CORTESE • CLAUDE EARL JONES
HAYWOOD NELSON • DON STARK • CHARLES TYNER • Director of Photography IRV GOODNOFF
Associate Producers GERALD HOFMAN and H. HAL HARRIS • Executive Producer SYLVIO TABET
Screenplay by JOSEPH GAROFALO and ERIC WESTON Based on a Story by JOSEPH GAROFALO
Produced by SYLVIO TABET and ERIC WESTON Directed by ERIC WESTON
A LEISURE INVESTMENT COMPANY Release / Distributed by THE MORENO COMPANY

ROBERT IANNUCCI • ALICIA MORO

EXTERMINATORS OF THE YEAR 3000

ALAN COLLINS • EDUARDO FAJARDO • FRED HARRIS • BERYL CUNNINGHAM • LUCAS FORD
Directed by JULES HARRISON

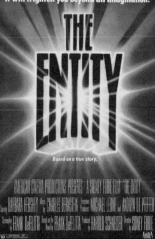

A story so shocking, so threatening,
it will frighten you beyond all imagination.

THE ENTITY

Based on a true story.

AMERICAN CINEMA PRODUCTIONS PRESENTS • A SIDNEY FURIE FILM • THE ENTITY
BARBARA HERSHEY • CHARLES PERSON • MICHAEL LEONE and ANDREW DE PFEFER
Screenplay by FRANK DeFELITTA Based on a Novel by FRANK DeFELITTA • HAROLD SCHNEIDER • Directed by SIDNEY FURIE

SOMEWHERE BETWEEN SCIENCE AND SUPERSTITION, THERE IS
ANOTHER WORLD. THE WORLD OF DARKNESS.

WILLIAM PETER BLATTY'S
THE EXORCIST

Directed by WILLIAM FRIEDKIN

ELLEN BURSTYN • MAX VON SYDOW • LEE J. COBB
KITTY WINN • JACK MacGOWRAN • JASON MILLER
LINDA BLAIR • WILLIAM PETER BLATTY
NOEL MARSHALL • WILLIAM PETER BLATTY

処女のはらわた

激烈・血しぶきエクスタシー!!

Clockwise from top left: Evil
Dead II *(1987); Linda Blair
signs off on* The Exorcist *(1973);*
The Entity *(1982); Entrails of
a Virgin (1986); The Exorcist's
Captain Howdy with little brainy
buddy Pazuzu; Clint Howard
dials up Satan in* Evilspeak
*(1981). Center: Exterminators of
the Year 3000 (1983)*

to cheer up Van Dyke over the phone from the set of *Meatballs 4*, but to no avail. She hanged herself. Van Dyke's body was then discovered by her friend Lisa Loring, the grown-up actress who played little Wednesday on the *Addams Family* TV series. Five years later, Nance got punched in the face outside of a Winchell's Donut House after, as he put it, he "popped off to a couple of beaners." He died the next morning from a sub-dural hematoma, death by literal headbanging.

ERIK the VIKING (1989)

(DIR. TERRY JONES; W/TIM ROBBINS, MICKEY ROONEY, EARTHA KITT, JOHN CLEESE, IMOGEN STUBBS)

✷ **NORSE MYTHOLOGY**

Erik the Viking looks like it should be Monty Python doing for Norse mythology what they did for the legend of King Arthur in *Monty Python and the Holy Grail* (1974). Instead it stars Tim Robbins in the title role, as a Norseman too demure to pillage, let alone (Susan Sarandon forbid!) rape. "You look like you haven't raped anyone in your life," accuses one skeptical would-be victim as Erik stumbles before ravishing her.

Python member emeritus (and *Holy Grail* codirector) Terry Jones helmed this curiously huge, nonsensical production, and he appears as King Arnulf. Fellow Python-ite John Cleese does what he can as Halfdan the Black. Axes and skull helmets abound. *Erik the Viking*'s mythological setup is loaded with references and images the likes of which would later populate the lyrics of Amon Amarth, Enslaved, and other horn-helmeted metal luminaries. The plot involves the goddess Freya, the moon-swallowing wolf Fenrir, Ragnarök, and Valhalla. And then there's Tim Robbins, who essentially counts as both comedy and adventure Götterdämmerung.

Given the genius of *Holy Grail* and, as film historian Danny Peary is quick to point out, how physically intimidating the members of Monty Python are, and taking into account the cruel, gore-drenched satire of their final film, *The Meaning of Life* (1983), a Viking vehicle for Python,

even in a fragmented form, should have rocked. I can only say that *Yellowbeard* (1983) is better, and more metal. But *Yellowbeard* is terrible.

ESCAPE 2000 (1982),
AKA TURKEY SHOOT;
BLOOD CAMP THATCHER

(DIR. BRIAN TRENCHARD-SMITH; W/STEVE RAILSBACK, OLIVIA HUSSEY, MICHAEL CRAIG, LYNDA STONER)

✷ **POST-APOCALYPSE** ✷ **SOUNDTRACK (BRIAN MAY)**

One of the most imaginative and colorfully brutal post-apocalypse action potboilers of the early '80s, *Escape 2000* takes place at an Australian prison camp where inmates can run for their freedom while being hunted by wealthy decadents. Steve Railsback (*Helter Skelter*) stars as the new runner out to turn the tables on his captors. Sexy Olivia Hussey and Lynda Stoner join him in the fight. The villains—headed up by chrome-domed, mustachioed meanie Charles Thatcher (Michael Craig)—drive crazy futuristic vehicles, use crazy futuristic weapons, and die gory, old-fashioned deaths in spectacular, no-organs-barred-from-being-visibly-liquefied fashion.

Escape 2000 is a fermented energy shot of wild exploitation movie greatness from legendary Aussie director Brian Trenchard-Smith (*Stunt Rock*, *BMX Bandits*). He'd revisit a similar scenario with a bit more punky new wave flair in *Dead-End Drive In* (1986). See *Escape 2000* first. Like the musical score by Queen's Brian May, it's a jolt of solid metal. *Turkey Shoot*, the movie's original title, bombed in Australia. Renamed *Escape 2000*, it also flopped in the U.S. Shortly after Margaret Thatcher became prime minister of England, however, the film opened in the UK as *Blood Camp Thatcher*, where it broke box office records.

Of all the warped delights of *Escape 2000*, none is more charming than Alph (Steve Rackman), sidekick of hunter Tito (Michael Petrovitch). Alph is some kind of beast-man/werewolf, but never is his beast-man/werewolf status explained or even acknowledged. Alph's big moment comes when he casually tears off a prisoner's toe and chomps it down as a snack. Such insane little touches make this movie easy to love.

Escape from New York (1981)

(Dir. John Carpenter; w/Kurt Russell, Adrienne Barbeau, Ernest Borgnine, Isaac Hayes, Lee Van Cleef, Donald Pleasence, Harry Dean Stanton)
✠ Post-Apocalypse ✠ Eye Patch

Growing up in the scary, scummy New York City of the '70s frequently felt like being jailed among the criminally insane, right there out in the dirty open air and broad daylight that offered no protection. John Carpenter's *Escape From New York* pushed that reality to a distressingly credible 1997, where Manhattan is an island prison where convicts are dumped with no rules and no regimentation, left to hack out an existence among society's geographical and human ruins.

When crafty inmates shoot down Air Force One and kidnap the U.S. president (Donald Pleasence), security head Hauk (Lee Van Cleef) summons eye-patch-wearing special-forces warrior turned outlaw Snake Plissken (Kurt Russell) to rescue the chief of state in exchange for a full pardon. Snake takes the deal and lands a glider atop the World Trade Center, armed with his own agenda. Snake's journey, then, is ours, too, as the movie interconnects action sequences by exploring New York after its fall. This is the world of *The Warriors* (1979) writ universal. As de-evolution barrels onward, every citizen-scavenger becomes his own multi-costumed, one-criminal street gang.

Snake teams with Cabbie (Ernest Borgnine), Maggie (Adrienne Barbeau), and Brain (Harry Dean Stanton) to infiltrate the stronghold of the Duke of New York (Isaac Hayes), where the president is held captive. The running joke—everyone our hero meets says, "Snake Plissken? I thought you were dead!"—works every time.

So does the whole rest of this scrappy, innovative, genre-launching landmark. With his rock star hair, sleeveless shirt, camo cargo pants, leather coat, and, of course, the eye patch, Snake Plissken looks the part of a heavy metal hero. His stoicism, drive for vengeance, loyalty, and good humor complete the package. Kurt Russell, having come of age in Disney comedies, reinvents his screen persona here, and brilliantly embodies a brand new Heavy Metal Movie archetype.

One of the great charms of *Escape From New York* is how the movie scrapes by on limited resources. Shooting largely in St. Louis using B-movie special effects, Carpenter creates a palpable universe that lets details lapse and makes huge leaps in logic, drawing us into the grime by letting the seams show. Compare it with the big-budget, computer-enhanced—and useless—*Escape From L.A.* (1996). For all the carnage and chaos, my favorite interlude is the scene inside an old movie theater, where gross, grizzled men sing and dance onstage in ball gowns and showgirl costumes.

Coupled with *The Road Warrior*, *Escape From New York* inspired scores of low-budget rip-offs worldwide. No country more passionately embraced Snake Plissken than Italy, though, which promptly cranked out three of *Escape*'s most enjoyable, and most metal, direct descendants: *1990: The Bronx Warriors* (1982) and its sequel, *Escape From the Bronx* (1983), along with *2019: After the Fall of New York* (1983).

The Evil (1978)

(Dir. Gus Trikonis; w/Richard Crenna, Joanna Pettet, Andrew Prine, Victor Buono)
✠ Satan ✠ Haunted House

The Evil is a mostly unremarkable late-'70s haunted house flick centering on a shrink (Richard Crenna) attempting to open a drug rehab in a cursed residence. In the closing moments, though, *The Evil* transforms into a supremely metal, positively lunatic treasure by descending into hell.

Eighty minutes of standard spookery climax with Crenna awakening in an ethereal white room. There, clad in a sharp white suit and filling a white throne the way President Taft filled the White House bathtub, is the devil himself, as blobtastically embodied by obese, biblically bearded character actor and stand-up comic Victor Buono (*The Mad Butcher*, *Beneath the Planet of the Apes*). This payoff comes out of nowhere and it will live forever as one of the screwiest cinematic depictions of Old Scratch anywhere.

The Evil Dead (1981)

(Dir. Sam Raimi; w/Bruce Campbell, Ellen Sandweiss, Richard DeManincor)

✵ Undead ✵ Cabin in the Woods

The woods are alive and horny in *The Evil Dead*. Sam Raimi's electrifying debut showcases cinema's first, best rape committed by a tree, and that's just one of many memorable shocks in this low-budget five-kids-in-a-cabin horror film. Ash (Raimi's boyhood friend Bruce Campbell) and four friends venture into a woodland cabin. There, they crack open an old tome marked *The Book of the Dead* and play a cassette they find of occult incantations. Very soon, all hell—or somewhere a lot like hell—rains down upon them.

One by one, demons wreak havoc on the campers, leading to the aforementioned redefining of a "woody," along with pencil stabbing, axe mutilation, shovel decapitation, face removal by shotgun, possessed "deadites" cackling in bondage, blood flowing into lightbulbs, and ferocious imagination hyperanimatedly unleashed by way of Raimi's swooping, soaring, legitimately breathtaking filmmaking techniques. *The Evil Dead* packs real scares. The same can't be said of its sequels, *Evil Dead 2: Dead by Dawn* (1987) and *Army of Darkness* (1993), thereby making this initial adventure with Ash the most metal, as the Mantas/Death song "Evil Dead" and the L.A. thrash band Evil Dead more than demonstrate.

Stephen King hailed *Evil Dead* as "the most ferociously original horror film of the year," instantly establishing this zero-budget undertaking as a must-see film for fright fans. *Evil Dead* first hit theaters in 1983 without an MPAA rating. For its 1997 video release, it scored a full-blown NC-17. *Evil Dead: The Musical* came near Broadway in 2006, bringing gory blood showers so much like a Gwar show that the theater handed out rain ponchos for ticketholders in the first few rows.

Grindhouse Releasing, which counts Blood Farmers guitarist Dave Szulkin among key staff, successfully rereleased *The Evil Dead* in movie theaters in 2010. Then fans of the original *Evil Dead* and its two sequels reacted unhappily when Raimi announced he'd be producing a 2013 remake—with a female Ash. That rancor turned to rage when its screenwriter was revealed to be *Juno* perpetrator Diablo Cody. The remake came and went, sucking and blowing like the wind.

Evil Dead 2: Dead by Dawn (1987)

(Dir. Sam Raimi; w/Bruce Campbell, Denise Bixler, Sarah Berry, Dan Hicks, Ted Raimi)

✵ Necronomicon ✵ Demonic Possession

Evil Dead 2 hits a reset button on *The Evil Dead* (1981), with locomotive-chinned hero Ash (Bruce Campbell) doing much more of what he did in the first movie. Ash and Linda (Denise Bixler) go to an isolated forest cabin, play a tape of an archaeologist reading aloud from the spell book *Necronomicon Ex-Mortis*, and, look out, here come the demonic forces. Linda's head is removed, but then she gets up and dances around with it in the style of Fred Astaire twirling a top hat. Ash's hand comes off, but then he rigs the stump with a chainsaw. Blood splatters, limbs twist, and the woods quake and moan with malevolent energy.

More victims arrive at the cabin. Each receives a spectacular dispatching and, frequently, zombified resurrection. Of particular note is Ted Raimi, director Sam Raimi's brother, as "Possessed Henrietta." The surprise ending—with Ash being sucked through a time portal and landing in some medieval age when knights fall to their knees before him—was all kinds of a surprise. Campbell established his ongoing off-Hollywood celebrity here, battling evil forces played by Raimi's dive-bombing camera and his own demonically animated hand with unique star power. Employing all that crazy kinetic roller-coaster cinematography and gleefully pushing horror to the furthest possible reaches of slapstick comedy, Sam Raimi is the true breakout talent here. His bravura visuals made *Evil Dead 2* the de rigueur headbanger bong-circle video entertainment of the late '80s. The gruesome laughs when Ash's own scrambling, disembodied hand flips him the bird and scurries off like a rat play to the blackened funny bones inside heavy metal humor.

Raimi's successful Hollywood career is its own testimony. So are the hyperactivity of subsequent violent movies to follow the trails mowed by *Evil Dead 2*. I swear, sometimes I think it's every single one of them. Metal bands that issued songs called "Dead by Dawn" include Deicide, Agony Column, Mortifier, and Mutilation.

EVILSPEAK (1981), AKA COMPUTER MURDERS

(DIR. ERIC WESTON; W/CLINT HOWARD, RICHARD MOLL, R. G. ARMSTRONG, JOE CORTESE, HAYWOOD NELSON)

✠ SATAN ✠ BLACK MASS ✠ SWINE ✠ CHURCH MASSACRE ✠ BANNED VIDEO NASTY

The almighty *Evilspeak* commences in Dark Ages Spain, where a cabal of devil-worshipping monks led by Father Esteban (Richard Moll, "Bull" from TV's *Night Court*) sacrifices a bare-bosomed beauty. Centuries later, bullied military academy cadet Stanley Coopersmith (Clint Howard) unearths the remains of Father Esteban and his devious disciples, along with all their Black Mass paraphernalia. The potential to use these uncovered spells for revenge is compelling to the sniveling Stanley.

At first, *Evilspeak* dwells too long on a colossal array of early-'80s movie notes; everyone gives Stanley the business, from the priests to a gym coach, who actually spanks him. Then the film ramps up to a dizzily dated high-tech high when Father Esteban chooses to return via a program on Stanley's Apple][computer! A red pentagram flashes on the monitor screen, and from there, *Evilspeak* goes literally hog wild through an escalating series of gratifying vengeance kills that include saber beheadings, live human incineration, beating-heart extraction, and flesh-devouring attacks by wild black boars from hell itself, the most delicious of which is visited upon the sexy school secretary as she showers.

At the unhinged heart of all this is Mr. Clint Howard, Ron's adorably troll-like kid brother, whose entire career as an oddball character actor is an exercise in heavy metal tenacity. *Evilspeak* provides Clint with one of his few lead roles, and he feasts upon it like a satanic swine let loose on a soapy nude brunette.

In his authorized biography, Anton LaVey, Black Pope of the Church of Satan, praised *Evilspeak* as being "very satanic." For sure, a nail from a crucifix in the campus chapel pries itself loose and flies like a bullet into a priest's head. The film production itself actually tormented a man of the cloth in real life. Scouts located an abandoned church in South Central L.A., and the crew painted and repaired the church for the film. Meanwhile, a nearby minister dropped by and loudly thanked God that the dilapidated house of worship would be redeemed. Alas, the sprucing up was but a false promise; less than a week later the building was burned beyond recognition to in the filming of *Evilspeak*'s thunderous and blasphemous climax.

EXCALIBUR (1981)

(DIR. JOHN BOORMAN; W/NIGEL TERRY, NICOL WILLIAMSON, HELEN MIRREN, LIAM NEESON)

✠ SWORDS & SORCERY ✠ KING ARTHUR ✠ MAGIC

Surpassed only by *The Lord of the Rings*—and maybe the Bible—the legend of King Arthur has proved to be an endless well of ideas, iconography, and aesthetics for heavy metal. Infinite swords can be pulled from this particular stone! Aside from bands from nearly a dozen countries named for the blade itself, Excalibur, thousands of bands are perched on the tales of Arthur, Guinevere, Lancelot, Merlin, Morgana, Mordred, the Knights of the Round Table, the Holy Grail, and the Lady in the Lake. No need to even mention Rick Wakeman's 1974 opus *The Myths and Legends of King Arthur and the Knights of the Round Table,* an adaptation of which was mounted in Wembley Stadium as *King Arthur on Ice*.

In his definitive cinematic take on the Arthurian legends, director Boorman (*Deliverance, Exorcist II, Zardoz*) throws every one of the components of Camelot on-screen in one long, exhausting rush. At times, *Excalibur* is frenzied, but it also plods. Overall, *Excalibur* is visually awe-inspiring, setting new highs in production design, cinematography, set dressing, and costuming. These are knights in some seriously shining armor. Nicol Williamson is a good, rock-star-like Arthur. Nicol Williamson as Merlin transcends hammy acting to achieve some kind of sublime scenery chewing. Helen Mirren, as incestuous sorceress Morgana, is ever her spellbinding seductress self.

Excalibur's many battle scenes, though confusing, are mighty assemblages of hacked-off limbs, flaming spears piercing armor, and chaotic carnage on horseback. Yet the unpredictable pace and bracingly bold sights also convey a disorienting and trippy air. Percival the Knight's quest for the Holy Grail is peppered several times by a hallucination of the sacred cup floating before him in midair, giant-size, and tipping forward to spill the blood of Christ onto the seeker. Heavy. Merlin trapped in a stalagmite is pure doom. And the "golden boy" mask and full-body armor worn by Mordred (Robert Addie) are just downright disturbing. It's just some freaky shit. If ever a display of medieval mayhem might be enhanced by conjuring up the smoky spirits within a bong named Excalibur, this would be the film for it.

The Exorcist (1973)

(Dir. William Friedkin; w/Linda Blair, Ellen Burstyn, Max von Sydow, Jason Miller)

✠ Satan ✠ Demonic Possession

Satan, of course, is the bad guy in *The Exorcist,* although his demonic minion, Pazuzu, actually takes over the corporeal vessel of young Regan (Linda Blair). Regan is the twelve-year-old daughter of a movie actress (Ellen Burstyn). The girl begins to exhibit disturbing behavior that quickly becomes terrifying and perhaps even supernatural. After a series of grotesque medical procedures prove inconclusive, Father Damien Karras (Jason Miller), a priest who also works as a psychiatrist, calls in veteran demon-fighter Father Merrin (Max von Sydow) to perform a full-strength exorcism.

The result is a philosophical thrill ride, a soul-deep adventure fraught with pain and sadness that invites us to ponder the nature of good and evil. The humanity-rupturing power of *The Exorcist* is twofold. First, obviously, there is its shock value. The possessed Regan urinates on the living room carpet and jams a crucifix into her vagina while yelling, "Let Jesus fuck me!" She spins her head around 360 degrees and famously turbo-vomits pea soup into Father Merrin's unimpressed face. The moment when the words *help me* appear to be scratched from the inside of the child's stomach is especially wrenching.

More subtly—and I believe this is what truly makes *The Exorcist* endure as a classic—is the moving, beautifully acted story of Father Karras doubting his faith and reeling with guilt over putting his mother in a nursing home, smack up to his final, fatal challenge to Pazuzu. It's one thing to hear Regan roar to the priest in a monster tone, "Your mother sucks cocks in hell!" but it's far more upsetting when she speaks in the voice of Karras's Greek immigrant mother, pleading, "Damey? Why you do this to me?"

At the movie's conclusion, the forces of darkness are banished, temporarily, through ultimate sacrifice. Outside the theaters, however, the entire world went devil-happy. An instant box office blockbuster and cultural thunderbolt, *The Exorcist* unleashed Satan into the neighborhood theaters of America and, from there, into casual conversation, news reports, church sermons, special TV episodes, lurid paperbacks, exploitation movie knock-offs, and, most potently, into dark and scary rock music. The Lake of Fire's landlord and all his works thereby turned the 1970s into heavy metal's most diabolically delectable decade—and all by way of a movie made in cooperation with and the full approval of the Catholic Church.

The most chilling screen image is the flash of a proto-corpse-painted figure that appears in Father Karras's nightmare. That's Pazuzu. Necrophagia, among numerous other metal outfits, has incorporated the stark white, red-eyed, rotten-fanged face into its own iconography. Countless metal songs invoke *The Exorcist* lyrically, and many more feature dialogue samples. The best known of these songs is "The Exorcist" by Possessed, which has in turn been covered by Cannibal Corpse, Sadistic Intent, and Cavalera Conspiracy. None match the ice of the hell-shriek Regan emits when Pazuzu leaves her body; in actuality, the sound was taken from a recording of pigs squealing during a mass slaughter, now a mandatory move aped by many of today's slam death metal extremists.

EXORCIST II: THE HERETIC (1977)

(DIR. JOHN BOORMAN; W/LINDA BLAIR, RICHARD BURTON, JAMES EARL JONES, LOUISE FLETCHER)

✣ DEMONIC POSSESSION ✣ LOCUST PLAGUE

Regan MacNeil (Linda Blair), the twelve-year-old girl possessed by the demon Pazuzu in *The Exorcist* (1973), has blossomed into a seemingly healthy, possibly telepathic, positively buxom teen in *Exorcist II: The Heretic*. Pazuzu, alas, is not quite through with her. Father Philip Lamont (Richard Burton) visits Regan and uses a biodynamic feedback device to probe the corners of her mind still spooked by the possession. He sees a boy in Africa named Kokumo who, decades earlier, successfully battled Pazuzu when the demon took the form of swarming locusts. Today, Kokumo is a scientist (played by James Earl Jones) who studies insects. This revelation prompts the deathless declaration from Father Lamont, "Kokumo can help me find Pazuzu."

An interesting plot twist arises concerning Father Merrin (Max von Sydow), the elderly exorcist from the first film. He believes that telepathic healers like Regan and Kokumo are modern saints representing an evolutionary leap forward for humanity. That provocative notion is torpedoed during the climax, when Pazuzu assumes the form of a succubus Regan and Lamont tears its heart out while they're swarmed by locusts. The real Regan then shows up to perform Kokumo's original demon-vanquishing ritual, which, goofily, looks a bit like a tap dance.

Exorcist II is entertaining, but not good. The sequel is one of cinema's most intriguing failures, however, rendered wickedly metal by Ennio Morricone's score. The greatest of all film composers created an incandescent masterwork for *Exorcist II*, topped by the movie's theme song, "Magic and Ecstasy"—a 666-alarm fire of wailing rock guitars, whinnying synthesizers, a ghostly chorus, and tribal electronic beats.

Audience anticipation was so high for *Exorcist II* and viewers' disappointment so immediate and intense that news of hooting and derisive laughter at some screenings was followed by reports of vandalism and riots at others. In a panic, Warner Bros. twice summoned director John Boorman to recut the film—the most expensive production in the studio's history—before it rolled out nationwide. After creating a new master print at great expense for distribution, Boorman personally traveled to theaters where *Exorcist II* was playing and made physical changes to the movie on the spot. Once that version was laughed off the screen as well, Warner Bros. temporarily pulled the movie from the market for Boorman to re-

Mike McPadden

171

reedit. These emergency surgeries didn't help. *Exorcist II* bombed hellaciously.

Exorcist II is an interesting bridge in the career of metal movie starlet Linda Blair. After her instant icon-making turn in *The Exorcist*, Linda proceeded to a series of spectacularly lurid TV films, including *Born Innocent* (1974), *Sarah T: Portrait of a Teenage Alcoholic* (1975), and *Sweet Hostage* (1975). For prepubescent boys, these outings had the aura of actual porno movies.

Unavoidably bosomy by her late teens, Linda followed *E2* with sexy turns in *Roller Boogie* (1979) and *Hell Night* (1981) before dating Rick James at the height of his superfreakness and posing nude in *Oui* magazine. She then embarked on her '80s run of grindhouse greats: *Chained Heat* (1983), *Savage Streets* (1984), *Night Patrol* (1984), *Red Heat* (1985), and *Savage Island* (1985).

ℰxorcist Ⅲ (1990)
(DIR. WILLIAM PETER BLATTY; W/GEORGE C. SCOTT, ED FLANDERS, JASON MILLER, BRAD DOURIF)
✠ DEMONIC POSSESSION

William Peter Blatty, author of the original novel *The Exorcist*, adapted his own follow-up book—1983's *Legion*—for the screen as *Exorcist III*. The action ignores *Exorcist II: The Heretic* (1977) and begins with a police Lieutenant William Kinderman (George C. Scott) investigating a gruesome series of church-related murders, including the crucifixion of a twelve-year-old boy and the beheading of a priest. Further slayings take place at a mental hospital, where one patient is a dead ringer for Father Alex Karras (Jason Miller) ,who, in the first *Exorcist*, challenged the demon Pazuzu to enter his body and release the possessed Regan MacNeil (Linda Blair). The inmate says he's the reincarnation of a criminal called the Gemini Killer, but there's more Pazuzu at play here than at first meets the popped-out eye. Enter the spiritual warriors with the holy water and the iron constitutions when it comes to pea soup power-puked right to the kisser.

Largely a detective thriller with occult over-

tones—and one huge jump-from-your-seat scare—*Exorcist III* attracted a cult following immediately, and comes up often when talking horror with fans of more esoteric heavy metal. *E3* kind of rules in the black noise and power electronics undergrounds. No small element of the *Exorcist III* cult centers around the film's various incarnations. Blatty begged Universal to release the movie simply as *Legion*, in order to bypass the public's memory of *Exorcist II*.

The studio not only wanted ties to the original blockbuster, it ordered Blatty to shoot an entirely different ending, laden with "power of Christ compels you" special effects. As a result, devotees have snatched up and shared elements of the director's original vision, finally bringing forth a fan edit titled *Legion* that appeared online in 2011. The film was screened by costar Brad Dourif at a horror convention and has developed a cult of its own minus all the exorcist trappings.

Blatty directed one other film, the bizarre *The Ninth Configuration*, aka *Twinkle, Twinkle Killer Kane* (1980). Stacy Keach delivers a screen-pulverizing performance and Joe (*Maniac*) Spinell costars, which makes the film mandatory.

ℭhe ℰxterminator (1980)
(DIR. JAMES GLICKENHAUS; W/ROBERT GINTY, SAMANTHA EGGAR, STEVE JAMES)
✠ REVENGE ✠ PSYCHO 'NAM VET ✠ FLAMETHROWER

Chipmunk-cheeked Robert Ginty doesn't naturally look the part of a Vietnam-trained urban killing machine, but he sure plays the part to the hell-hammered hilt in *The Exterminator*. The action begins in Vietnam, as John Eastland (Ginty) and his platoon mates are captured and tortured by Vietcong, building toward as heinously realistic a decapitation as was ever created for a camera prior to al-Qaeda's publicity shorts.

The POWs escape and we jump ahead to the war zone of New York City circa 1980. After a street gang called the Ghetto Ghouls paralyzes Eastland's 'Nam buddy Michael Jefferson (Steve James) with a meat hook to the spine, Eastland transforms into a one-man fusillade of vengeance against criminal scum all over the rotten, worm-infested Big Apple. He defeats the Ghetto Ghouls via flamethrower, machine gun, hungry rats, and sheer hatred. He then moves on to the Mafia, feeding a kingpin into an industrial meat grinder and moving onward from there.

The most fantastically sleazy segment pits the Exterminator—the nickname Eastland earns from all this human vermin removal—against a New Jersey state senator in an underage-boy whorehouse. The naked, blubbery politician is played by character actor David Lipman, recognizable now as a judge on *Law & Order* but at the time familiar as "the Miracle Whip guy" from TV commercials. What the Exterminator reduces him to may fit inside a Miracle Whip jar.

Clad in pitch-black from his from motorcycle helmet to his leather boots and approaching every situation with a policy of "slaughter everyone on the loading dock first, ask questions later," Ginty's Exterminator is a ferociously metal figure: the pent-up loner who became, as the poster puts it, "the man they pushed too far!" Sometimes a man like that will pick up drumsticks or a guitar. Other times, he's the subject of a movie like this grindhouse great. The ad campaign was a killer: "He's not a Taxi Driver . . . and he doesn't have a Death Wish. . . ."

Special-effects legend Stan Winston (*The Terminator*, *Predator*) oversaw *Exterminator*'s brutal and gruesome Vietnam sequence. Those powerful moments took up 20 percent of the movie's total budget, with $25,000 alone spent on the incredible beheading. Money well spent. Writer-director James Glickenhaus went on to a remarkable grindhouse career. He followed *The Exterminator* with the wildly violent espionage film *The Soldier* (1982), the Jackie Chan adventure *The Protector* (1985), and the beyond-berserk buddy crime flick *Shakedown* (1988), which takes place largely in and around the great fleapit theaters of New York's Forty-Second Street, where movies such as this always played. Under the Shapiro-Glickenhaus Entertainment banner, he also

produced *Maniac Cop* (1988) and *Frankenhooker* (1990), before returning to write and direct the grotesque serial-killer thriller *Slaughter of the Innocents* (1993).

As a movie, *The Exterminator* hops off any rails of coherency when the CIA takes an interest in this vigilante, but it kicks keister all the way through, up to and including a really uncomfortable mercy killing at the end. *Exterminator 2* (1984) picks up the lunacy nicely and, for once in cinema history, responds to fan demands in a way that make the movie better. *Exterminator 2* contains nonstop flamethrower maiming, scorching, and annihilation. Thanks, Shapiro-Glickenhaus.

EXTERMINATORS OF THE YEAR 3000 (1983)

(DIR. GIULIANO CARNIMEO; W/ROBERT IANNUCCI, ALICIA MORO, LUCIANO PIGOZZI, FERNANDO BILBAO)
✳ **POST-APOCALYPSE**

Among the *Exterminators of the Year 3000*, the big one dropped long ago, although the "3000" figure is probably just hyperbole. No new civilization has arisen from the rubble. Everything is just desert and fancy motor vehicles. Water is scarce. Crazy Bull (Fernando Bilbao) and his flamboyant biker army control every drop. A band of peaceful survivors need a drink. Hope comes up the road in the form of a warrior named Alien (Robert Ianucci).

Exterminators is not merely one of a million Italian *Road Warrior* rip-offs, but rather the supreme standout among Italian *Road Warrior* rip-offs. Such slavish dedication to aping detail denotes balls of steel. Director Giuliano Carnimeo is a longtime veteran of exploitation moviemaking. Most of his career was spent helming spaghetti westerns, including this unforgettably named trilogy of films all released in 1970: *Light the Fuse . . . Sartana Is Coming*; *I Am Sartana, Trade Your Guns for a Coffin*; and *Have a Good Funeral, My Friend . . . Sartana Will Pay*.

FACES OF DEATH ✠ FADE TO BLACK ✠ FANTASIA ✠ FANTASTIC PLANET ✠ FAST TIMES AT RIDGEMONT HIGH ✠ FASTER, PUSSYCAT! KILL! KILL! ✠ FAUST ✠ FAUST: LOVE OF THE DAMNED ✠ FEAR NO EVIL ✠ FIRE AND ICE ✠ FIRST BLOOD ✠ FIVE DEADLY VENOMS ✠ FIX: THE MINISTRY MOVIE ✠ FLASH GORDON ✠ FLESH AND BLOOD ✠ THE FLY ✠ THE FOG ✠ FOR THOSE ABOUT TO ROCK: MONSTERS IN MOSCOW ✠ FORBIDDEN ZONE ✠ FOXES ✠ FRANKENHOOKER ✠ FRANKENSTEIN (1910) ✠ FRANKENSTEIN (1931) ✠ FREAKS ✠ FREDDY VS. JASON ✠ FREDDY'S DEAD: THE FINAL NIGHTMARE ✠ FRIDAY THE 13TH ✠ FRIDAY THE 13TH PART VI: JASON LIVES ✠ FROM DUSK TILL DAWN ✠ FROM HELL ✠ FROSTBITER: WRATH OF THE WENDIGO ✠ FUBAR ✠ FUBAR II: BALLS TO THE WALL ✠ FULL METAL VILLAGE ✠ THE FUNHOUSE

FACES OF DEATH (1978)

(DIR. ALAN BLACK (JOHN ALAN SCHWARTZ); W/ MICHAEL CARR, SAMUEL BERKOWITZ, MARY ELLEN BRIGHTON, BRAINY THE MONKEY)

✠ SNUFF ✠ SATANIC BLOOD ORGY ✠ MONKEY BRAINS ✠ BANNED VIDEO NASTY

The Internet has become a utility for rubber-neckers with iron guts, displaying around-the-clock hot and cold terrorist beheadings, auto and industrial mishaps, misuse of live animals, and every other conceivable physical transgression committed against sentient organic beings. Before the Internet, though, there was only *Faces of Death*. For the adolescent '80s headbanger coming of age in the era of Iron Maiden's *Piece of Mind* and Grim Reaper's *See You in Hell* on cassette, Twisted Sister and Mötley Crüe all over MTV, and Jason and Freddy slashing up neighborhood theaters, *Faces of Death* on VHS

emerged as the final, crucial badge of honor.

Dr. Francis B. Gröss (Michael Carr), a shaggy-looking coroner, is the clinical narrator delivering choice bons mots on the nature of mortality. A parade of clips narrated by the dour doctor then brings on the Reaper in the form of actual footage of autopsies, accidents, assassinations, animal slaughter, and napalm-inflamed military engagement. Mixed in are hilarious fakeries that include an electric-chair execution that takes several attempts, a cannibal orgy, a guy getting chomped by an alligator, and, most notoriously, decadent diners whacking a monkey with hammers, peeling the skin off its skull, and then chowing down on the brainy goodness therein. All the nonsense is presented as being as genuine as the shots of a plane crash, baby seal clubbing, and news footage of a surfer drowning.

As a movie, *Faces of Death* is deadly ridiculous, sloppily assembled, and maybe even boring. As

Faces of Death, however, it's perfect—the right experience, with the right moniker, arriving at the right time to culturally thrust the armies of the night (horror fans and metalheads) one massive leap further. At first, *Faces of Death* consisted only of stock footage and news films. Japanese investors suggested spiking the punch with dramatized atrocities. Those are, of course, the only parts of the movie that anyone remembers.

Faces of Death ran in grindhouse theatres worldwide for several years before being distributed on tape by Gorgon Video (a Chicago company created expressly to handle this property) and swelling into one of the VHS era's earliest word-of-mouth juggernauts. Initially, *FOD* circulated among devotees of the extreme, but it fairly quickly became a rite of passage for any teenager who had access to a VCR beyond the scope of prying parental eyes. By 1984, the news media had caught on to what was making all those high schoolers shout, "Whoa, GNARLY!" in basement rec rooms. Reports and editorials decrying this fresh, unholy threat to pubescent sensibilities cropped up everywhere. Even Dan Rather promoted the panic on the *CBS Evening News*.

Five sequels followed, along with the compilation *The Worst of Faces of Death* (1987) and *Faces of Death: Fact or Fiction?* (1999), a "documentary" on the phenomenon that is, admirably, just about as bogus as the original enterprise. In the first film, director John Alan Schwartz, credited in the movie as "Alan Black," appears as the leader of the cannibal cult that enjoys an organ-meat orgy. Weirdly, Schwartz emerged from obscurity in 2012 to grant a long, informative interview to the sports blog *Deadspin*. He reveals that the monkey brains were made of cauliflower and that he suspected (as did I) that Steven Spielberg stole that idea from him for *Indiana Jones and the Temple of Doom*. Schwartz also claims that *Faces of Death* has grossed more than $40 million to date, of which he only pocketed fifteen thousand smackers. That's bad monkey business.

FADE TO BLACK (1980)

(DIR. VERNON ZIMMERMAN; W/DENNIS CHRISTOPHER, TIM THOMERSON, GWYNNE GILFORD, MICKEY ROURKE)

✠ '80s Slasher ✠ Dracula

Directly after his star-is-born performance in the surprise hit and 1979 Best Picture Oscar nominee *Breaking Away*, Dennis Christopher followed up with *Fade to Black*. Here, he plays chain-smoking, sad-sack film freak Eric Binford who, after getting jilted by an Australian Marilyn Monroe look-alike (Linda Kerridge), takes to elaborately dressing up like various movie icons and committing murders in keeping with the characters. Eric's MO is effective enough when he plays Dracula at a *Night of the Living Dead* screening and then drinks the blood of a dead hooker, or when his mummy getup scares his mean boss into a heart attack. Where it gets laughable is when Eric takes on the persona of cowboy star Hopalong Cassidy to shoot a bullying coworker (Mickey Rourke—really), as well as when he imitates a series of classic gangster movie protagonists. The fact that *Fade to Black* squanders its own wacko premise and turns out to be as boring as any other generic post-*Halloween* slasher cash-in only makes it weirder. So does Dennis Christopher. He is career-killingly terrible here—to the extent that he wasn't asked to participate in a real movie again until 2012's *Django Unchained*.

Christopher's weird professional path post-*Fade to Black* is cool, though. He became a regular on mainstream TV dramas (from *Moonlighting* to *Law & Order* to *Criminal Minds*) while simultaneously starring in an ongoing succession of metallically madcap B-movies. Among those worth hunting down: *Alien Predator* (1985), *Jake Speed* (1986), and the post-nuke freak show *Circuitry Man* (1991) along with its (lesser, but still metal enough) sequel, *Plughead Rewired: Circuitry Man II* (1994).

Fantasia (1940)

(Dirs. Norm Ferguson, Unknown; w/Leopold Stokowski, Deems Taylor, Mickey Mouse)

✴ Satan ✴ Sorcery ✴ Animation

You don't have to be Yngwie Malmsteen to understand the connection between classical music and heavy metal. You just need ears. Walt Disney's audacious sensory experiment *Fantasia* delivers the auditory delights to accompany unprecedented visual audaciousness. The epic film brings to life a series of classical music pieces with lush, overwhelming animations incorporating abstract imagery and a rich cascade of proto-metal totems, including dinosaurs, fairies, centaurs, dancing mushrooms, black magic run amok, a pissed-off wizard, doomsday, Greek and Roman gods, and Satan himself.

Headbangers can tap into the "head"-y aspects of *Fantasia* at any point, but two segments bang especially metallic. "The Sorcerer's Apprentice" is a driving piece composed by Paul Dukas, based on a poem by metal literary icon Johann Wolfgang von Goethe (author of *Faust*, if you need his cred). Mickey Mouse, as the title character, dons his boss's famous hat and mucks about with magic books in order to get out of doing his chores (as any hesher would). He ignites a bad trip of anthropomorphic brooms and flash-flood conditions.

"Night on Bald Mountain," Fantasia's finale, is one of the most metal sequences in all of cinema. First, there is the music by Modest Mussorgsky, a rolling thunderstorm of doom that builds to absolute apocalyptic perdition. The mountain itself awakes and transforms into a muscular colossus with glowing eyes, pointed ears, long horns, and mighty black wings. Officially, he is Chernabog, a dark god of ancient Slavic religions, but both Disney and *Fantasia* host Deems Taylor referred to the character as "Satan." Either way, he's the devil and he's awesome.

As night falls like black death across the countryside, Chernabog celebrates the pagan occasion of Walpurgis Night by summoning restless souls to rise. Ghosts spring up from graves, witches ride in the sky, skeletons walk, demons maraud, zombies stomp, goblins wail, fire women dance, and animals squeal in the grip of demonic possession. No more transcendent or vivid bacchanal of satanic abandon has ever unspooled on-screen. (Glenn Danzig's band Samhain seems to owe a debt to this sequence, especially for their *November Coming Fire* album artwork.) Chernabog and his minions finally get beaten back to hell by the power of church bells and holy folk singing "Ave Maria." But that's how these things always go.

In 1969, Disney reissued *Fantasia* specifically with drug-tripping rock and roll audiences in mind. Bolstered by a psychedelic poster, *Fantasia* was shown at college campuses and given midnight screenings and generated a Disney memo to theater owners assuring them that the "unwashed, pot-smoking" youth audience who would "offer advice to Mickey Mouse on-screen" was harmless and could essentially be trusted. Interesting to note: *Fantasia* did not turn a profit until that 1969 rerelease.

An important influence on *Fantasia* was heavily metal surrealist Salvador Dali. The master Spanish painter idolized Disney as a visionary artist, as he did Alice Cooper in the '70s. In 1946, Disney and Dali collaborated on an animated short, *Destino*, that was abandoned as Disney faced bankruptcy following World War II. In 2003, Walt's nephew Roy Disney completed the six-minute film.

Fantastic Planet (1973), aka La Planete Sauvage

(Dir. René Laloux; w/Eric Baugin, Jennifer Drake, Jean Topart, Jean Valmont)

✴ Animation ✴ Science Fiction

The psilocybin-soaked forerunner of *Heavy Metal* (1981), *Fantastic Planet* is the heady cartoon saga of Terr (Eric Baugin), a human kept as a pet on another world by giant, blue-skinned Draags. By Draag standards, humans are about the size of mice, and they get treated similarly: as pests or pets. A Draag named Tiwa (Jennifer Drake) grows close to Terr, and he is able to learn how his captors communicate. Armed with this knowledge, Terr escapes to lead the planet's other humans in an uprising.

Fantastic Planet was directed and designed by French painter René Laloux in collaboration with multimedia artist Roland Topor. It is a surreal masterwork, visually heavy, and beautifully communicates timeless themes. The basic message of irrepressible freedom and its creators' fluid, sensual, exploratory sci-fi presentation make *Fantastic Planet* a natural favorite among prog fans in general and Rush nuts in particular.

Fantastic Planet ran as a midnight movie at art theaters and on college campuses throughout the '70s. It was also a popular feature on the USA Network's legendary *Night Flight* omnibus program of way-out rock and roll wonders. As far as impeccable endorsements go, Michel "Away" Langevin, the Voivod drummer responsible for the band's incredible visual style, claims *Fantastic Planet* as his favorite film.

Fast Times at Ridgemont High (1982)

(DIR. AMY HECKERLING; W/SEAN PENN, PHOEBE CATES, JENNIFER JASON LEIGH, JUDGE REINHOLD)

✷ LED ZEPPELIN ✷ VAN HALEN ✷ CHEAP TRICK
✷ SOUNDTRACK (SAMMY HAGAR, BILLY SQUIER)

The pinnacle of teen sex comedies, *Fast Times at Ridgemont High* is a masterpiece of time and place, a high-flying fantasy grounded in the heartache of actual adolescence. You don't have to be fourteen to love *Fast Times*—as long as you were fourteen once. All *Fast Times* is missing is real hard rock on the soundtrack. Instead, the movie gave heavy metal a new icon: ganja-zonked surf dude Spicoli (Sean Penn), the prototype for Beavis and Butt-Head, Bill & Ted, and any number of dudes smoking homegrown weed behind the gym in a Judas Priest *Screaming for Vengeance* painter's cap.

Fast Times opens not at Ridgemont High but at the local mall, where the plot's central characters work and congregate. Stacy (Jennifer Jason Leigh) and Linda (Phoebe Cates) wait tables at Perry's Pizza. Mark "Rat" Ratner (Brian Backer) ushers at the movie theater. His best friend, Mike Damone (Robert Romanus), peddles scalped concert tickets. Mingling at the video arcade are Spicoli and football star Charles Jefferson (Forest Whitaker), each hustling in their own way. Nearby, Stacy's brother Brad (Judge Reinhold) manages All-American Burger.

From there, the interconnected stories converge in high points that have become cultural touchstones. Damone teaches Rat how to romance chicks until both are exposed as the opposite of their put-on personas. Brad daydreams about Linda emerging topless from his backyard swimming pool, then gets busted by her as he masturbates. Stacy's clumsy attempts at sexual liberation lead to an abortion. Dent-headed biology teacher Mr. Vargas (Vincent Schiavelli) reaches into a human cadaver and yanks out the heart, prompting Spicoli to proclaim, "Gnarly!" And, of course, Spicoli and Mr. Hand (Ray Walston) do battle in a series of classroom skirmishes—plus one final showdown in Spicoli's stoner-heaven bedroom—that remain as funny as any comedic face-off in the history of the movies. In the wake of *American Graffiti* (1973), numerous coming-of-age comedies appropriated wishful nostalgia and retro settings (including 1982's mighty *Porky's*), but *Fast Times* makes clear: these kids live now and this is how they do it.

Back to that issue of music, though. *Fast Times* takes place in the Southern California of the early 1980s. By any realistic measure, Stacy and Linda would be listening to new wave on KROQ, while Spicoli would be surfing and skating to Iron Maiden, Def Leppard, and Quiet Riot. Even culturally numb hustler Damone's bedroom wall and button-adorned jacket are plastered with images of Devo, Elvis Costello, and Pat Benatar, while he hustles tickets to Van Halen and Blue Öyster Cult. He launches into a phenomenal sales presentation for Cheap Trick, praising:

"The magnetism of Robin Zander! The charisma of Rick Nielsen!" Why, then, is the *Fast Times* soundtrack dominated by *Rolling Stone* baby-boomer dreck like Jackson Browne, Jimmy Buffett, Graham Nash, and no fewer than four members of the Eagles? Director Amy Heckerling blames studio interference. *Fast Times* producer Irving Azoff was the personal manager of the Eagles—what a shame Rod Smallwood didn't get the script first.

What hot rock did make the cut, though, rocks just fine. Sammy Hagar performs the thunderous "Fast Times at Ridgemont High" and Billy Squier's swinging, horn-driven "Fast Times" perfectly underscores Jefferson's gridiron carnage. What matters, ultimately, is what's on the screen. *Fast Times at Ridgemont High* concludes with the revelation that Spicoli went on to rescue Brooke Shields from drowning and spent the reward money hiring Van Halen to play his birthday party. The television edit of *Fast Times* includes a whopping fourteen extra minutes, including a Spicoli story about Mick Jagger giving him a guitar pick, and Linda assessing whether Mark is "still in his heavy metal phase."

Fast Times at Ridgemont High was adapted for the screen by *Rolling Stone* journalist Cameron Crowe, based on his own nonfiction book of the same title. In 1981, Crowe, who was twenty-four, posed undercover as a student for a year at Clairemont High School in San Diego. While writing for *Rolling Stone* as a teenager, Crowe developed personal friendships with the members of Led Zeppelin. As a result, Zeppelin's presence is all over the *Fast Times* movie, in multiple graffiti images, on the T-shirt of a kid looking to buy BöC tickets, and on Rat's car stereo. The final piece of romantic advice Damone doles out to Rat is, "When it comes down to making it, whenever possible, put on side one of *Led Zeppelin IV*." The movie then cuts immediately to Rat driving Stacy while blaring "Kashmir." Zep fans recognized right off that "Kashmir" is on *Physical Graffiti*, not *IV*. Crowe has explained that they made that choice to point out Rat's charming cluelessness. Led Zeppelin is famously stringent

about not allowing their music to be used in films or on TV. Here, they made an exception for their pal and created a great movie moment.

FASTER, PUSSYCAT! KILL! KILL! (1965)

(DIR. RUSS MEYER; W/TURA SATANA, HAJI, LORI WILLIAMS, SUSAN BERNARD, STUART LANCASTER)
✹ AMAZONS

Shock filmmaker extraordinaire John Waters has called Russ Meyer's *Faster, Pussycat! Kill! Kill!* "the best movie ever made, and possibly better than any movie that ever will be made." Meyer himself described *Faster Pussycat* as his "ode to violence in women." The picture looks and feels like what hard rock circa 1965 sounded like: tough and angular, fast and frantic, voluptuous and hot—and built like a brick brassiere in the miracle of black-and-white.

Miraculous-mammaried drag racing go-go dancers Varla (Tura Satana), Rosie (Haji), and Billie (Lori Williams) mix it up in the desert with wannabe speedster Tommy (Ray Barlow). Varla breaks Tommy's back with her bare hands, and the three dancers kidnap his girlfriend Linda (Susan Bernard). Hitting the road, they come across the Old Man (Stuart Lancaster), a nasty coot rumored to have a fortune hidden in the crappy ranch house he shares with his rape-happy mentally deficient son, the Vegetable (Dennis Busch). The big screen can barely contain these wild women as they wreak gender vengeance and just get their kicks, man.

With *Faster Pussycat*, Meyer blew past his "nudie cutie" beginnings (1959's *The Immoral Mr. Teas*) and sweaty cleavage melodrama phase (1965's *Mudhoney*) into a robust, brazen, crackpot cinema paradise all his own. *Beyond the Valley of the Dolls* (1970) is Meyer's towering-torso masterpiece above all others, but *Faster Pussycat* is his initial full blast forward. L.A. hair metal stars Faster Pussycat not only took their name from the movie, they never failed to champion Russ Meyer whenever possible. Other bands named in tribute to Meyer films include Mudhoney, Vixen, the Black Snakes, and Motorpsycho. White Zombie also sampled *Pussycat* and recreated the look for the "Thunder Kiss '65" video.

FAUST (1926)

(DIR. F. W. MURNAU; W/GÖSTA EKMAN, EMIL JANNINGS, CAMILLA HORN, FRIDA RICHARD)

✠ MEPHISTO ✠ FOUR HORSEMEN OF THE APOCALYPSE

Faust, an educated man who sells his soul to the devil, is a figure of German folklore dating back centuries. His story has inspired countless works, heavy metal and otherwise. The most metallic movie version of this myth is one of the first; German expressionist master F. W. Murnau's cosmically sweeping supernatural follow-up to his *Nosferatu* (1922). The demon Mephisto (Emil Jannings) bets an Archangel (Werner Fuetterer) that he can corrupt the soul of a kindly alchemist named Faust (Gösta Ekman). Through the use of a plague, the temptations of an Italian duchess (Hanna Ralph), and a return to youth, Mephisto gets his man—ensnaring him at least enough for sword fights, a frozen baby, and a voluntary burning at the stake.

The plot is doom-laden enough—it's driven by the devil and culminates in our hero going up in smoke—but Murnau's unmatched artistry creates a visual vocabulary that will echo forever in all aspects of heavy metal. Right off, the Four Horsemen of the Apocalypse charge through the heavens. Soon after, a giant-size Mephisto casts a black shadow over Faust's village simply by spreading his devil wings (the final line of Black Sabbath's "War Pigs" most assuredly comes to mind). Most mesmerizing is Faust flying on Mephisto's cape, soaring through a dragon-filled sky and looking down on the unwitting souls below. Ungodly delights, occult wonders, and eternal damnation as the price of each comprise so much of heavy metal's basic DNA. Murnau's *Faust* is the complete picture of that double helix.

FAUST: LOVE OF THE DAMNED (2000)

(DIR. BRIAN YUZNA; W/JEFFREY COMBS, MARK FROST, ANDREW DIVOFF)

✠ FAUST ✠ MEPHISTOPHELES ✠ SOUNDTRACK (BRUJERIA, CARNIVORE, COAL CHAMBER, CRADLE OF FILTH, DEICIDE, FEAR FACTORY, ILL NIÑO, MACHINE HEAD, OBITUARY, SEPULTURA, SPINESHANK, SOULFLY, TYPE O NEGATIVE)

Veteran horror director Brian Yuzna (*Bride of the Re-Animator, Return of the Living Dad III*) here updates the age-old German folktale to modern-day Spain by way of the loony, blood-soaked comic book of the same name. John Jaspers (Mark Frost), an aspiring artist, sells his soul to the devilish M (Andrew Divoff). Jaspers shortly thereafter dies and returns as a horn-headed superhero with a villainous streak. He aims to thwart M's plans to release a monster called the Homunculus and thereby open the gates separating hell from earth.

A curvaceous curse blows up one woman's breasts and buttocks to Japanese monster movie proportions. *Faust* climaxes with an unexpectedly arousing bondage scene between demonic dominatrix Monica Van Campen and innocent Isabel Brook, who's caged and wearing a see-through chain-mail bikini above the pits of hell. Add in a great underappreciated metal soundtrack, and the film is not quite a lost classic, but definitely a worthwhile wig-flipper. Roadrunner Records really emptied out its catalogue here, with a mind-liquefying round-up of thrash masters, death metal giants, extreme punk, and turn-of-the-century metal, including double doses of both Max Cavalera (via Sepultura and Soulfly) and Peter Steele (via Carnivore and Type O Negative).

Fear No Evil (1981), aka Lucifer

(Dir. Frank LaLoggia; w/Stefan Arngrim, Elizabeth Hoffman, Kathleen Rowe McAllen)

✤ ANTICHRIST ✤ ZOMBIES

The Antichrist goes to high school in *Fear No Evil*. Like a lot of us, he gets bullied about his supposed lack of manliness, and he suffers the violent slings and assholes of gym-class humiliation. Unlike anyone else, though, telepathic Andrew (Stefan Arngrim) avenges the first indignity by forcing female breasts to grow on a jock in the school shower, and the second by willing the phys-ed teacher to murder a classmate in a lethal game of dodgeball. An archangel in elderly woman form (Elizabeth Hoffman) teams with a teen angel (Kathleen Rowe McAllen) to battle Andrew. Their task gets more baroque after Lucifer's son steals off to a castle, drinks the blood of a sacrificial dog, and transforms into a demon with rockabilly sideburns and sheer black lingerie. The concepts of "flaming" and "hellfire" have rarely combusted with such specific heat. Before all the fun's over, Andrew psychically attacks a Catholic theater group performing a passion play and raises a scabby white-faced army of the undead.

That's just a taste of the admirable insanity of *Fear No Evil*. Shame then, that for so elementally metal a topic, *Fear No Evil* went with a punk and new wave soundtrack.

Fire and Ice (1983)

(Dir. Ralph Bakshi; w/Randy Norton, Susan Tyrrell, Stephen Mendel, Maggie Roswell)

✤ SWORDS & SORCERY ✤ FRANK FRAZETTA
✤ ANIMATION

After a box office hit with *American Pop* (1981) and a bungled release of his '50s greaser pastiche *Hey Good Lookin'* (1982), head-trippy animator-for-adults Ralph Bakshi returned with *Fire and Ice* to the fantasy realm of his magic warfare classic *Wizards* (1977) and the ugly but profitable *Lord of the Rings* (1978). This time, Bakshi collaborated with the most heavy metal of all visual artists—Frank Frazetta—and the result is a thoroughly satisfying cartoon sword-and-sorcery adventure that came and went and criminally mostly remains unnoticed.

The plot is a standard fantasy operation. Wicked Queen Juliana (Susan Tyrrell) and her hilariously effete evil son Nekron (Stephen Mendel) attempt to freeze the world from their castle in Icepeak. The good guys of Firekeep get involved when snow-creeps kidnap their remarkably robust Princess Teegra (Maggie Roswell). After escaping, Teegra teams with heroic human Larn (Randy Norton) and mysterious battle-ax badass Darkwolf (Steve Sandor) to set things right— which they do, awesomely.

The look, design, and action of *Fire and Ice* set the film apart, as this is the movie where all those Frank Frazetta album covers come to life and stomp ass in mescaline-friendly rotoscopic splendor! The Frazetta landscapes loom impossibly brutal and sumptuously beautiful, whether alien worlds, medieval kingdoms, arctic tundras, storming seas, or lush sex-jungles. His warriors ripple with Mighty-Joe-Young-meets- Mighty-Thor musculature and his women are explosively ripe, bursting alive in voluptuous perfection.

What Bakshi brings to the bash is his controversial rotoscoping process, where animators trace over live actors performing on film. The practice is as old as cameras—in the 1930s, Disney's *Snow White* and Max Fleischer's *Popeye* series utilized rotoscoping—but Bakshi pushed it to unprecedented levels in the 1970s, often invoking charges of laziness. Hindsight, though, has proven the power of Bakshi's vision. His mixed-media onslaughts anticipated the everything-at-once nature of today's entertainment, and Bakshi movies have aged spectacularly well—*Fire and Ice* high among them. Attention bong-hoovering, D&D-vet skull-thumpers—high time now to turn this film into an institution fit to share a throne with 1981's similar (albeit sexier) *Heavy Metal*!

First Blood (1982)

(Dir. Ted Kotcheff; w/Sylvester Stallone, Richard Crenna, Brian Dennehy, Jack Starrett)

✵ Revenge ✵ Psycho 'Nam Vet ✵ Metal Reality

Taxi Driver is Hollywood's ultimate punk rock Vietnam vet adventure; *First Blood* is the heavy metal equivalent. Low-budget exploitation flicks had been mining the disgruntled Nam returnee motif while the war was still raging (see 1971's *Revenge Is My Destiny*) with a swell after *Taxi Driver* (see 1976's *My Friends Need Killing*) and then in a grindhouse Tet Offensive after the late-'70s prominence of *The Deer Hunter* and *Apocalypse Now* (see 1980's *Cannibal Apocalypse* and *The Exterminator*).

First Blood begins with former special forces P.O.W. John Rambo (Sylvester Stallone) as a shaggy, unshaven, cigarette-smoking loser wandering Washington State in a dirty fatigue jacket (a far cry from the single-handed-slaughterer-of-nations superhero Rambo became in the cartoonish sequels). His grungy appearance riles the local sheriff (Brian Dennehy), who attempts to run Rambo out of town as a drifter. Rambo won't cooperate. Thus begins a battle of wills that escalates to a woodland war game played for real, with Rambo utilizing his Green Beret guerilla combat know-how to battle the authorities.

After thrillingly executed action sequences and with a sense of doom continually ratcheting upward, Rambo's beloved superior officer, Colonel Trautman (Richard Crenna), is brought in to talk the enraged veteran down. Rambo makes a famous speech about the plight of those who fought in Vietnam, particularly upon returning home to get spit on and be sneered at as a "baby killer and all kinds of vile crap." Like *Billy Jack* (1971), the film ends with a cop-fighting hero surrendering and being led off in handcuffs by cops. Unlike in *Billy Jack*, there is no mass of youthful revolutionaries to raise their fists—and, by extension, our spirits—in solidarity. And that was Rambo's point all along.

The triumph of inescapable dread, coupled with the sylvan setting of the Pacific Northwest, is the movie's final metal note. Rambo has been a heavy metal figure all along: his hair is long, his background is roughneck, the Powers That Be come down on him based on how he naturally looks, and they ultimately aim to eliminate him simply for standing tall.

Contrast that with punk icon Travis Bickle in *Taxi Driver*. Bickle lives and wigs out in New York City, he intentionally makes himself a visual object of distress by way of a Mohawk haircut, and he concocts his own mission to violently correct a societal wrong, after which the media hail him as a hero (much the way Manhattan rock critics carbuncled themselves to punk in hope of absorbing some "bad kids" cred).

First Blood and *Taxi Driver* are both great films. One is metal. One is punk. We never got the great "crossover" 'Nam vet opus that would unite both mind-sets and forge a new continuum. We certainly got more wars, though.

Hollywood had been attempting to adapt David Morrell's novel *First Blood* since its 1972 publication. The most intriguing version that almost got made would have been directed by Sam Peckinpah, with Kris Kristofferson as Rambo, Gene Hackman as the sheriff, and Lee Marvin as Colonel Trautman. In *First Blood*'s original ending, Rambo grabs Colonel Trautman's gun and kills himself. Test audiences deemed it "too depressing." Metalheads would have been more understanding.

Five Deadly Venoms (1978), aka Wu Du

(Dir. Chang Cheh; w/Chiang Sheng, Sun Chien, Philip Kwok, Lo Meng, Wei Pai)

✵ Extreme Kung Fu

Multiple generations into home video, to say nothing of YouTube, the existence of kung fu movie theaters is almost entirely forgotten. At least as ubiquitous as hard-core porn tugitoriums, theaters dedicated exclusively to running English-dubbed martial arts movies were common and popular in urban locations all over America throughout the 1970s. Video stores, of course, delivered the fatal blow to "chop socky" grindhouses, but their resolve was first weakened in the early 1980s by Asian karate epics shown via syndicated TV packages such as *Drive-In Movie* in New York and *Kung Fu Theatre* in Los Angeles.

The TV packages also created a new spate of kung fu cult movies, chief among them *Five Deadly Venoms*. Better martial arts films exist than *Five Deadly Venoms*, but none has a superior or more metal opening sequence. A dying master tells his final student that his five previous pupils, each trained in a manner patterned after an animal, have broken bad and are returning to rob the temple. The colorfully masked and costumed Venom Mob soon appears and demonstrates all species of weird martial arts.

Deadly Venom #1, the Centipede, is wiggly and quick, fighting as though he had a hundred limbs. Deadly Venom #2, the Snake, attacks with bent fingers on one hand as fangs, and straight fingers on the other as rattling tail. Deadly Venom #3, the Scorpion, performs crazy backward kicks from everywhere and nowhere at once. Deadly Venom #4, the Lizard, is so fast and so full of vibrating energy that he can walk on walls. Deadly Venom #5, the Toad, is a stout defensive powerhouse who can withstand almost any attack, including blades and poison. After that amazing kickoff, the movie plays out as a largely standard Hong Kong beat-'em-up, but those first fifteen minutes make *Five Deadly Venoms* a genre classic.

Texas-based blackened psych-prog band Shaolin Death Squad performs in traditional Asian makeup and costumes, performing songs inspired by martial arts movies. Their 2010 album *Five Deadly Venoms* is a song-by-song retelling of the film.

Fix: The Ministry Movie (2011)

(Dir. Doug Freel; w/Al Jourgensen, Trent Reznor, Lemmy Kilmister, David Yow)

✤ Ministry ✤ David Yow's Penis

Fix: The Ministry Movie documents the career of Chicago industrial metal juggernaut and chemical acolyte Al Jourgensen. Beginning life as a weak-tea death disco musician and then evolving into the hugest-sounding metal machine of its time, Jourgensen did not invade the mainstream so much as, like he says in the movie, the mainstream came to him. In the immediate wake of grunge on the radio, Ministry's danceable metal sold out Madison Square Garden in 1993 sans advertising. And then suddenly Nine Inch Nails, Marilyn Manson, Korn, and their souped-up sicko ilk were peddling diabolical decadence on MTV and in teenybopper magazines. That aspect of Ministry's existence alone could propel a fascinating documentary. Jourgensen, though, has been at it for decades, always adding new chapters and sinkholes to his own saga.

Nonetheless, *Fix* is pretty much a drag, not so much about Jourgensen the musician as it is about Jourgensen the junkie. Much of his surface appeal has had to do with Al the "drug god," and if that's what draws you to Ministry, consider *Fix* your hard-core porn find of the century. Between long ramblings on the topic of dope sprees past, present, and future, Jourgensen injects himself with intoxicants nonstop on camera. More frustrating is that the assembled metal royalty—including Lemmy, Maynard James Keenan, Buzz Osborne, Jonathan Davis, Jello Biafra, Dave Navarro, and Nivek Ogre—give interviews passing lip service to Al's transformation of music so that they can get to their own (endless) stories about Al getting high and fucking shit up. David Yow of Jesus Lizard at least has the decency to keep taking his clothes off.

FLASH GORDON (1980)

(DIR. MIKE HODGES; W/SAM J. JONES, MAX VON SYDOW, TIMOTHY DALTON, TOPOL, MELODY ANDERSON)
�֍ SPACE ✷ HAWKMEN ✷ SOUNDTRACK (QUEEN)

Suspenseful percussion builds. "FLASH! Ah-AHHH!" erupts a chorus of voices. "Savior of the universe!" *Flash Gordon*'s unmistakable theme song by Queen is the most perfectly superheroic and galactic hard rock for this pop-art madness. Like Queen, this flop blockbuster turned cult touchstone is equal parts self-aware irony and uncontrolled garish excess. Flash's theme goes on to describe him saving every one of us because he's invincible and the king of the impossible. What a man!

In the lead role, Sam J. Jones delivers a triumph of anti-acting. He plays a bleached-blond ex-quarterback of the New York Jets in a skintight T-shirt emblazoned with his own name in a lightning logo. As in the age-old *Flash Gordon* comic strip and the groundbreaking movie serials of the 1930s starring Buster Crabbe, Flash, his lady faire Dale Arden (Melody Anderson), and Dr. Hans Zarkov (Topol) blast off for the planet Mongo, where evil emperor Ming the Merciless (Max von Sydow), resplendent with his chrome-dome and Fu Manchu mustache, aims to explode Earth. Once on Mongo, Ming's daughter Princess Aura (Ornella Muti) rescues Flash from her father. To defeat Ming, Flash teams with Prince Barin (Timothy Dalton) and winged, Viking-like Hawkmen led by the barrel-chested, bearded, boisterously stoner metal Vultan (Brian Blessed).

After the sex film spoof *Flesh Gordon* (1974) and the animated *New Adventures of Flash Gordon* (1979) brought back the goofy original sci-fi franchise, the big-screen *Flash Gordon* was a minor hit on arrival in 1980 and has grown more beloved and enjoyable with age. Winking retro-camp elements such as the comic-panel opening credits and the Robin Hood getups of Prince Barin's men have melded gloriously with the unintentional campiness of the film's gleaming chrome art direction.

Above it all, there is Queen, rocking the coalition of the righteous on to victory. The band's songs and riffs comment on the action, cheer for the good guys, and build up the baddies, and Queen wail and rumble and like a 1970s concept album come to life. Jack Black's comedy duo Tenacious D, known for cherishing Dio and all classic metal, regularly opened shows with an acoustic cover of Queen's *Flash Gordon* theme.

Flash Gordon found new relevance in 2012 when the movie played a key role in Seth MacFarlane's comedy blockbuster *Ted*. Sam J. Jones even donned the "Flash" shirt again to play a parody of what we fans have always wished he went on to be like. When I say "we fans," I mean that at my wedding in 2010, Lady McBeardo approached the marrying altar to the strains of Queen's "Wedding March" from the *Flash Gordon* soundtrack.

FLESH AND BLOOD (1985)

(DIR. PAUL VERHOEVEN; W/RUTGER HAUER, JENNIFER JASON LEIGH, TOM BURLINSON, JACK THOMPSON)
✷ MEDIEVAL MAYHEM ✷ BARBARIANS ✷ PLAGUE

Merciless mercenaries led by power pillager Martin (Rutger Hauer) run rampant over 1501 Europe in *Flesh and Blood*. The screen fills repeatedly with each of the title elements. As the black plague rages around the endless sword combat and general brutality, a statue of St. Martin emerges from the ground. The local priest takes it as a sign from on high that Martin is a divinely anointed leader, thereby granting this slaughter-happy barbarian full backing to mount a raid on a nearby castle, along with rights to the virginity of a previously betrothed princess (Jennifer Jason Leigh).

The first English-language film by Dutch master Paul Verhoeven (*RoboCop*, *Starship Troopers*), *Flesh and Blood* hammers home the mire and misery of medieval living (and, far more often, dying) between battle sequences sufficiently savage enough to elicit winces amidst flying fist-pumps. *Flesh and Blood*'s original title was *God's*

Own Butchers. Also noteworthy, Jennifer Jason Leigh giggles through a fleeting lesbian tussle with Nancy Cartwright, who soon became the voice of Bart Simpson.

The Fly (1986)

(Dir. David Cronenberg; w/Jeff Goldblum, Geena Davis, Leslie Carlson, John Getz)

✠ Science Fiction

In this remake of a 1958 horror classic, scientist Seth Brundle (Jeff Goldblum) builds a teleportation device. The machine works dandily until he unwittingly beams himself into a chamber containing a housefly, thereby mixing his own DNA with that of the insect. The first results are odd hair growths and increased strength. Rapidly, though, Seth seriously mutates, with parts of his body grotesquely dropping off and fresh ones emerging. "Be afraid. Be very afraid," he warns.

Seth refers to himself as a new creature altogether: Brundlefly. His girlfriend, Veronica (Geena Davis), is taken aback, to say the least. Eventually, Brundlefly goes mad, attacking a rival with his sickening fly abilities and setting up a horrific, heartbreaking conclusion. "All romance ends in tragedy," director David Cronenberg once said of *The Fly*, "especially the ones that go on forever."

The Fly, then, buzzes high among heavy metal cinema's great romantic sagas. Love will make you stronger and give you wings, but it's also monstrous, it's heavy, and it'll make you puke to death. A more metal take on love relations is hardly conceivable. The themes of doom, Gothicism, operatic power, and noble nihilism dominate. Watch for Cronenberg's cameo during a nightmare scene. He's the obstetrician who extracts a larval maggot from Geena's vagina.

Revered composer Howard Shore (*Lord of the Rings*), who created the score for *The Fly*, adapted the story into an opera that ran in 2008 at the Théâtre du Châtelet in Paris. Meanwhile, the sticky, dark, mechanical, and greenish milieu of *The Fly* was replicated in countless metal videos.

The Fog (1980)

(Dir. John Carpenter; w/Jamie Lee Curtis, Adrienne Barbeau, Hal Holbrook, John Houseman)

✠ Leper Ghost Pirates

Halloween (1978) astonished moviegoers with an operatic command of terror that wielded big blockbuster impact. Director John Carpenter was quickly labeled "the new Hitchcock" by a world that was obviously desperate for one. Then he just as quickly dashed any such talk by following up *Halloween* with *The Fog*.

The setup is promising: a glowing, supernatural fog besets a Northern California fishing town on the eve of its centennial. Inside the mist are the ghosts of lepers whose ship was sunk to establish the existing community on land that had been reserved for their colony. The spooks are back for one night of carnage to even the score and collect some booty.

Numerous horror aficionados, especially those near the action in the San Francisco Bay Area, love this purposefully slow seaside ghost story, but Carpenter's subsequent two efforts—*Escape From New York* (1981) and *The Thing* (1982)—are far superior. The highlight of the whole film is the sound a ghost's sword makes when it whacks a priest smack in the gullet. Better yet are the best of the many metal songs inspired by the movie, particularly those by Necrophagia and Orange Goblin.

For Those About to Rock: Monsters in Moscow (1992)

(Dir. Wayne Isham; w/AC/DC, Metallica, Pantera)

✠ Concert Footage

Documenting the first major metal show in post-Communist Russia, *For Those About to Rock: Monsters in Moscow* is a straightforward concert chronicle shot in September 1991 as 1.6 million newly liberated metalheads gathered to go nuts at Russia's Tushino airfield. For the movie, the order of bands is reversed so that headliners AC/DC play first, running through four solid classics with brio.

Metallica, just months after the Black Album hit the world like Oppenheimer hit Hiroshima, are in prime form for playing to the huge crowd. The crowd-pleasing anthem "Enter Sandman" has never seemed so totally justified and righteous. After a highly skippable Black Crowes performance, Pantera, ascending to their role as the most important pure metal band of the '90s, slay during their powder-keg set. Local heroes E.S.T. close the movie with a single song. They play stripped-down hard rock reminiscent of AC/DC, bringing everything full circle.

The show at hand took place only a few weeks after the old-guard totalitarian Soviet regime tried a final grab at power and failed. There is no more metal feeling than that of a captive who has broken his chains, and that hard and heavy joy radiates all over the proceedings here. Unfortunately, that joy terrified the overqualified security force on-site, the late-to-freedom Russian army, who reacted to the chaotic outpouring of energy by beating countless metalheads senseless.

FORBIDDEN ZONE (1982)
(DIR. RICHARD ELFMAN; W/HERVÉ VILLECHAIZE, SUSAN TYRRELL, TOSHIRO BOLONEY [MATTHEW BRIGHT], DANNY ELFMAN, JOE SPINELL)
✣ SATAN ✣ JOE SPINELL ✣ ANIMATION

Richard Elfman's eye-popping, mind-whirling, seat-wetting, black-and-white live-action-cartoon musical phantasmagoria *Forbidden Zone* may not be hard-as-steel metal. Yet allow me to point out the presence of perpetually metal Joe Spinell (*Maniac*, *Starcrash*) as a drunken sailor, and Danny Elfman as Satan, who leads the Mystic Knights of the Oingo Boingo through a hallucinatory and hellfire-hot rejiggering of "Minnie the Moocher," one of cinema's most diabolically joyful representations of the Dark One ever.

The rest of *Forbidden Zone* combines lunatic

'40s jazz with late-'70s L.A. new wave, to bring to life such sights as Hervé Villechaize (Tattoo from *Fantasy Island*) as the King of the Sixth Dimension, lording over an underworld of naked slave girls; the wonder nipples of Gisele Lindley, playing a perpetually topless blonde princess; an obscene revamp of the Three Stooges' "Alphabet Song" complete with a blaxploitation gang harmonizing; a giant tap-dancing frog in a tuxedo; fake gorillas; real Hollywood skid-row bums; David Lynch–style animation gone amok; and every racial stereotype ever created—including a dour Swede!

All who watch *Forbidden Zone* leave amazed. Among those most profoundly impacted is director Tim Burton, who pocketed Danny Elfman to compose all of his movie scores and absorbed many, many visual tropes that ultimately came to comprise signature style. Compare *Forbidden Zone*'s Satan scene with the bogeyman-versus-Santa-Claus number in Burton's *The Nightmare Before Christmas* (1993) for very direct evidence of . . . let's call it "borrowing."

FOXES (1980)
(DIR. ADRIAN LYNE; W/JODIE FOSTER, CHERIE CURRIE, SCOTT BAIO, RANDY QUAID, SALLY KELLERMAN, ANGEL)
✣ JAILBAIT ✣ SOUNDTRACK (ANGEL)

Foxes was sold as a wild high school party movie, one of the percolating teen sex geysers that would blow skyward after *Porky's* (1982). In reality, *Foxes* is closer to the naturalistic fatalism of *Over the Edge* (1979) than to the goofy fun of *Fast Times at Ridgemont High* (1982). Absolutely nothing would move these deadpan teen foxes to declare anything "Awesome. Totally awesome."

The sunny San Fernando Valley at Christmastime is just a world of hurt. Latchkey kid Jeanie (Jodie Foster), stoner wreck Annie (Cherie Currie), high-strung Madge (Marilyn Kagan), and wannabe sophisticate Deidre (Kandice Stroh) traverse the dark, dangerous, all-drugs/no-fun land of late-'70s high school. Infinitely upping the scary/scummy quotient is their access to pimp and pusher-laden Hollywood Boulevard.

Relief should come in the guise of an Angel concert, but even that brief escape only sees Jeannie being let down by her absentee road manager dad in a backstage men's room. Farther along, parents supply beer. A mope who today would be on *To Catch a Predator* gets to happily marry his prey. Somebody dies. The acting is uniformly excellent and the script is impressively serious. First-time director Adrian Lyne's stylized take on what might otherwise have been cheap material launched him into an A-list career. Watch for an acne-ravaged Anthony Kiedis in a ruffled tux during the girls' attempt at a fancy dinner party.

Cherie Currie, fresh from ceding her status as lead singer of the Runaways to Joan Jett, is star-is-born dynamic as the doomed doob-and-'lude victim Annie. She deserved a real movie career, but instead followed up with the terrible but cool 3-D monster movie *Parasite* (1982) and the nudie comedy *The Rosebud Beach Hotel* (1984).

As for Angel, Casablanca Records' long-maned, Lycra-pant-wearing (non-Kiss) glam combo does provide quite the time capsule as they perform the movie's theme song—"Twentieth Century Foxes"—onstage. Dig that keytar solo! In fact, Angel proved themselves so screenworthy in *Foxes* that Casablanca Film Works commissioned and actually shot a full concert movie, *Angel at Midnight*, which was likely never completely and definitely never released.

FRANKENHOOKER (1990)

(DIR. FRANK HENENLOTTER; W/PATTY MULLEN, JAMES LORINZ, JOANNE RITCHIE)

✠ MONSTERS ✠ MEDICAL DEVIANT ✠ SEX FANTASY

Frankenhooker is the last gasp of genuine New York exploitation moviemaking from one of the greats in the field, *Basket Case* creator Frank Henenlotter. Sadly, by 1990, the grindhouse theaters that would once have showcased a nasty *Frankenstein* variation about a mad scientist assembling the body parts of murdered prostitutes into a perfect sex partner had mostly either collapsed or been converted into churches.

Frankenhooker, then, had to appeal to a jokey, self-aware art-house audience; in doing so, the movie absorbed the worst elements of what those frauds bought into as "so bad it's good" bullshit. Loaded with winks and nods to its own schlockiness, the comedy is killed with unfunny self-aware mentions of the shoddy plotting and insultingly crappy special effects. All that elevates *Frankenhooker* by the thinnest of plucked pubes is a glorious crackpot lead performance by James Lorinz as monster-maker Jeffrey Franken. *Penthouse* centerfold Patty Mullen, though, is neither sexy nor funny (let alone scary) as Frankenhooker herself. But, alas, the Frankenhooker character is unique (enough) in the annals of horror, and she definitely reflects the grossest aspects of the dying days of mainstream hair metal to warrant a nod here.

After two *Basket Case* sequels, *Frankenhooker* was the third collaboration between director Henenlotter and his co-screenwriter, Robert Martin. To a generation of horror fanatics, "Uncle Bob" Martin is best known as the demigod creator of *Fangoria* magazine. Beginning in 1979 just in time to catch the wave of slasher movie mania, *Fangoria* chronicled every aspect of the fright-film world, illustrated with shockingly gory photographs. Uncle Bob departed *Fangoria* in 1986, just after the post–*Night of the Living Dead* golden age of extreme horror burned out and, ironically, gave way to self-conscious goofball shit such as *Frankenhooker*.

FRANKENSTEIN (1910), AKA THOMAS EDISON'S FRANKENSTEIN

(DIR. J. SEARLE DAWLEY; W/AUGUSTUS PHILLIPS, CHARLES OGLE, MARY FULLER)

✠ HORROR ✠ MEDICAL DEVIANT

The first movie adaptation of Mary Shelley's novel *Frankenstein* came from the Edison Manufacturing Company, produced by the man himself who patched together several existing ideas and invented the movie camera. Edison's attraction to the story of a scientist whose invention achieves a dream, only to have it go horrifically awry, is itself interesting. This sixteen-minute silent exercise features an amazingly crazy-looking take on the monster. He's a tall, spindly, hunchback wrapped in rags, with a big white face, piles of filthy hair, giant feet, and long, serpent-like fingers. No shortage of metal flyers and other artwork has incorporated the Edison Frankenstein monster, possibly without knowing the identity of the creature. The film employs a great gimmick: The shock scenes are tinted orange.

Edison wanted in on the burgeoning movie business, but he knew moral crusaders already had the form in their crosshairs. Establishing a tradition heralded forever after by exploitation film producers and shock-rock promoters, Edison publicized *Frankenstein* with a letter declaring the film's upstanding moral intentions. He wrote: "Edison Co. has carefully tried to eliminate all actual repulsive situations and to concentrate its endeavors upon the mystic and psychological problems that are to be found in this weird tale. Wherever, therefore, the film differs from the original story it is purely with the idea of eliminating what would be repulsive to a moving picture audience." His plan worked like a charm.

☩FRANKENSTEIN (1931)
(DIR. JAMES WHALE; W/BORIS KARLOFF, COLIN CLIVE, DWIGHT FRYE, MAE CLARKE)
✠ FRANKENSTEIN ✠ MEDICAL DEVIANT

It's alive! IT'S ALIVE!" So much of modern horror and a great deal of heavy metal comes from director James Whale's unparalleled adaptation of Mary Shelley's novel *Frankenstein*. Starring Colin Clive as the mad scientist, Dwight Frye as the hunchback assistant, and Boris Karloff, immortally, as the monster, the story is as familiar as anything from Mother Goose or the Bible. In a castle laboratory, Dr. Frankenstein constructs a man out of stolen body parts and, unknowingly, a defective brain. He brings the creature to life with lightning, after which it escapes and ac-

cidentally drowns a little girl. Feeling rage at his creator, the creature attacks the doctor's fiancée. A mob of peasants then chases the monster down and kills him with torches and pitchforks.

Frankenstein is the doctor; the monster doesn't have a proper name. But it's the sympathy, affection, and outright love garnered by Karloff's brilliant, soulful performance that makes the world identify with the creature. We adore the monster. We cherish him. We long to help him. We identify with him. We are him. Horror master David Cronenberg has said that *Frankenstein* cracks open the universal fear of a child being abandoned by a parent and, by extension, humanity being abandoned by God. Heavy metal is the music of latchkey kids and cultural orphans. From Black Sabbath onward, it is the soundtrack of souls condemned never to know heaven. Frankenstein, the monster, is our stand-in. Heavy metal is our battle cry against the torches and pitchforks of a world too scared to understand.

The Frankenstein movie monster does not resemble the creature described in the book. Karloff's look is the invention of makeup genius Jack Pierce. All future depictions of Frankenstein have come from Pierce's design. Karloff's Frankenstein boots weighed thirteen pounds apiece, dwarfing even Gene Simmons's dragon-faced footwear. In the final credits, Universal Studios' globe logo is tilted far to its right. Normally the globe is upright; the shift suggests that *Frankenstein* depicts a world out of balance.

☩FREAKS (1932)
(DIR. TOD BROWNING; W/WALLACE FORD, HARRY EARLES, OLGA BACLANOVA, DAISY AND VIOLET HILTON)
✠ MIDWAY MAYHEM ✠ CENSORSHIP

We accept her, we accept her, one of us, one of us, gooble-gobble, gooble-gobble!" So goes the famous chant among the deformed, disabled, and amazingly talented sideshow performers of director Tod Browning's still shocking, one-of-a-kind horror masterpiece, *Freaks*. The chant is the highlight of a ritual in which these outcasts—

limbless men and women, conjoined twins, dwarfs, giants, hunchbacks, hermaphrodites, human skeletons, microcephaly victims (pinheads), and others—initiate a newcomer into their close-knit, protective circle. This key sequence of *Freaks* has also long resonated as a metaphor for what happens when any downtrodden and displaced untouchable finally finds his or her place among like minds and similar souls in any underground or anti-mainstream subculture.

The Ramones claimed *Freaks* for punk with their 1977 anthem "Pinhead" (although they changed the "gooble-gobble" to "gabba-gabba-hey") but, as with so many elements of those long-haired leather jacket miscreants, the sentiment also extends to heavy metal. The moment of discovery when a new headbanger finds a place in moshpit society—that's what *Freaks* is all about.

As far as the story, *Freaks* deals with a traveling circus wherein a glamorous, standard adult–size trapeze artist named Cleopatra (Olga Baclanova) schemes with her strongman boyfriend Hercules (Henry Victor) to defraud the suddenly wealthy midget Hans (Harry Earles). Cleopatra seduces and pretends to be in love with Hans. After being welcomed into the circle of freaks on their wedding night, she poisons his wine. In short order, the sideshow gang gets wise to her evil deed, and they hunt down Hercules and Cleopatra to mete out freak justice. The strongman is castrated, as evidenced by his off-camera screams reaching successively higher pitches. Cleopatra, in turn, is torn apart and eventually reconstructed with webbed hands into a quacking grotesquerie billed as "the human duck."

No one in 1932 was prepared for *Freaks*. Audiences and critics alike reacted with revulsion. Reports of people fainting and vomiting in droves during the movie's initial screenings seem entirely credible. In the few places *Freaks* did manage to play, the film was routinely censored to ribbons. The film remained outright banned in the UK for more than thirty years. Tod Browning, renowned for brilliant silent film work with Lon Chaney and for directing Bela Lugosi in *Dracula*

just a year earlier, saw his career screech to a halt. For decades, *Freaks* was largely considered "lost," and some segments are actually gone. Hippies and counterculture rebels embraced it in the 1960s, though, and, after decades as a midnight movie, Browning's crowning achievement spawned a cult that continues to thrive.

Heavy metal is freak music by freaks, for freaks. *Freaks*, then, is one of the archetypal—and most beautifully misshapen and misunderstood— Heavy Metal Movies. We accept it as one of ours.

Freddy Vs. Jason (2003)
(Dir. Ronny Yu; w/Robert Englund, Ken Kirzinger, Monica Keena, Jason Ritter, Katharine Isabelle)
✠ Slasher ✠ Supernatural Horror
✠ Soundtrack (Hatebreed, In Flames, Lamb of God, Sepultura, Type O Negative)

Long in the making, this is the big one with the big two. Along with Sabbath vs. Zeppelin, Priest vs. Maiden, or Slayer vs. Metallica, *Freddy vs. Jason* realized the dream of pitting one ultimate bloodletting icon against another in anticipation of spectacular results. That the resulting smackdown between *A Nightmare on Elm Street*'s Freddy Krueger and *Friday the 13th*'s Jason Voorhees works, pretty spectacularly, is even more surprising after nearly fifteen years of false starts and dead ends.

The action in *Freddy vs. Jason* actually begins at the end of the ninth *Friday the 13th* installment, *Jason Goes to Hell*. After the killer receives an explosive, seemingly final shellacking, the camera focuses on his shattered hockey mask discarded in the dirt. All of a sudden, the ground opens, a familiar razor-clawed glove reaches up and pulls the mask back down with it, and the earth reseals itself.

I saw *Jason Goes to Hell* opening night at the packed Harris Theater on Forty-Second Street's grindhouse row. The audience went giddily berserk and could not be contained (relatively speaking) well into the second feature. The remarkably unenlightened sleaze zine *Happyland*

Humans are such easy prey

H. P. LOVECRAFT'S
From Beyond
From the Creators of Re-Animator

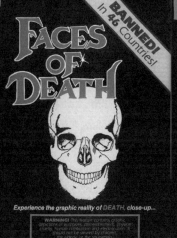

BANNED!
In 46 Countries!

FACES OF DEATH

Experience the graphic reality of DEATH, close-up...

WARNING! This feature contains graphic depictions of autopsies, dismemberment, physical cruelty, human combustion and electrocution. It should not be viewed by children, the elderly or the squeamish.

VHS

a GORGON VIDEO release

ROGER CORMAN PRESENTS
A NEW WORLD PICTURE

FANTASTIC PLANET

DIRECTED BY RENE LALOUX · SCREENPLAY BY ROLAND TOPOR · RENE LALOUX
BASED ON THE NOVEL BY STEVEN WUL · MUSIC BY ALAIN GORAGUER · METROCOLOR · LES FILMS ARMORIAL   PG

FIRE AND ICE

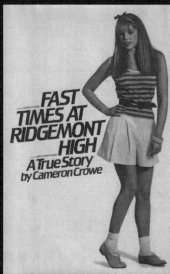

FAST TIMES AT RIDGEMONT HIGH
A True Story
by Cameron Crowe

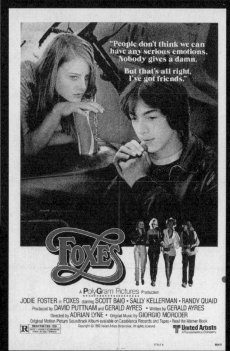

"People don't think we can have any serious emotions. Nobody gives a damn. But that's all right, I've got friends."

FOXES

A PolyGram Pictures Production
JODIE FOSTER in FOXES starring SCOTT BAIO · SALLY KELLERMAN · RANDY QUAID
Produced by DAVID PUTTNAM and GERALD AYRES · Written by GERALD AYRES
Directed by ADRIAN LYNE · Original Music by GIORGIO MORODER
Original Motion Picture Soundtrack Album available on Casablanca Records and Tapes. Read the Warner Book.
Copyright © 1980 United Artists Corporation. All rights reserved.

R RESTRICTED

United Artists
A Transamerica Company

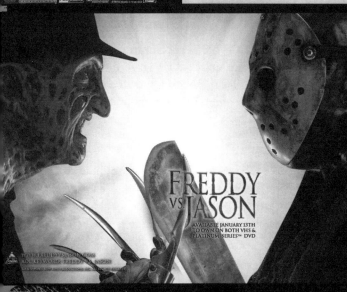

FREDDY VS JASON

AVAILABLE JANUARY 13TH
TO OWN ON BOTH VHS &
PLATINUM SERIES™ DVD

WWW.FREDDYVSJASON.COM
AOL KEYWORD: FREDDY VS JASON

Clockwise from top left: *Lovecraft/ Gordon go* From Beyond *(1986)*; Faces of Death *(1978)*; Fantastic Planet *(1973)*; *fantastic* Foxes *(1980)*; Freddy vs. Jason *(2003)*, *the big one with the big two*; *Frazetta paints* Fire and Ice *(1983)*. Center: Fast Times at Ridgemont High *original paperback* reported on the moment by noting: "No such joyful noise, in terms of volume and endurance, had been made by these people since The Emancipation Proclamation." A young father next to me, explaining the cause for celebration to the toddler on his lap, happily yelled: "Freddy wants someone to play with—IN HELL!" Ten years later, Hollywood granted his wish.

Burnt-up child-killer Freddy, tired of messing only with those already damned for eternity, realizes that he can return among the living by feeding on earthly teenage fears. He's then able to send Jason back up top, where the terror generated by his homicidal rampages can power Freddy's return. Once they're both back up among horny high-schoolers, though, they realize this earthly realm ain't big enough for the both of them. And we get the bloody blowout of our nightmarish dreams.

Hong Kong director Ronny Yu (*The Bride With White Hair*) does for these two monsters of rock what he did for everybody's favorite killer doll in *Bride of Chucky* (1998); he knowingly taps into the strength of each powerhouse to give fans what they want while making the movie faster, wittier, and even gorier than expected. The *Friday* and *Nightmare* series reached their best and most effective possible conclusions here, even as the drag-down battle ends in a cosmic draw. With nowhere else to go, these characters were relegated to the horror of big-budget Hollywood remakes, neither of which was horribly offensive nor, in any real way, memorable.

After decades of neglect, The *Freddy vs. Jason* soundtrack, issued by Roadrunner Records, continued the tradition of highly metal and nü-metal horror soundtracks in the 2000s, this time with contributions from Slipknot, Lamb of God, Type O Negative, Hatebreed, In Flames, Killswitch Engage, and Mike Patton teaming with Sepultura.

FREDDY'S DEAD: THE FINAL NIGHTMARE (1991)
(DIR. RACHEL TALALAY; W/ROBERT ENGLUND, LISA ZANE, YAPHET KOTTO, ALICE COOPER)
✠ SUPERNATURAL HORROR ✠ ALICE COOPER

Freddy Krueger in 3-D!" was the gimmick that propelled *Freddy's Dead: The Final Nightmare* to the biggest-opening box office weekend in the *Nightmare* series. The stupefying shittiness of the movie itself led to lethal word of mouth among horror fans, and in short order this Freddy outing was deservedly dead. The 3-D didn't even represent the best of that ever-shaky technology by 1991 standards. You got cardboard red-and-blue glasses to watch the ten-minute climax, and then you got to take your headache home.

As revealed in *A Nightmare on Elm Street 2*, razor-fingered dream-killer Freddy Krueger is the product of a nun's gang rape, thereby earning the title "the bastard son of a hundred maniacs." The lone nice touch of *Freddy's Dead* comes in casting Alice Cooper as the poor stay-at-home maniac who actually got stuck raising the little bastard.

FRIDAY tHE 13TH (1980)
(DIR. SEAN S. CUNNINGHAM; W/KEVIN BACON, BETSY PALMER, ARI LEHMAN, ADRIENNE KING)
✠ SLASHER ✠ TEEN SEX ✠ HOCKEY MASK

Like many metal subcultures, *Friday the 13th* combined one influence with another influence (cynics might even hurl the word *imitation*) to create something original that, itself, became monstrously influential. For *Friday*, Sean S. Cunningham, producer of Wes Craven's nihilistic milestone *Last House on the Left* (1972), combined the teenage milieu and ominous holiday title of shock blockbuster *Halloween* (1978) with some gross-out gore murder sequences similar to Italian thriller *Twitch of the Death Nerve* (1971), directed by Mario Bava of *Black Sabbath* fame.

The result ruptured popular culture and immediately established the predominant template for the horror explosion of the 1980s. Horny adolescents venture into the woods despite the warnings of a local wack job, whereupon a seemingly supernatural psycho offs them one by one until the lone virgin female turns the tables (or, more accurately, machetes and chainsaws) and escapes, running straight toward a sequel.

In this first *Friday*, Jason Voorhees, the series' homicidal goalie-faced antihero, appears only as a postscript nightmare vision. Even then, he's in the waterlogged form of an undead special-needs kid, awesome but not imposing. Even throughout *Friday the 13th Part 2*, Jason wears overalls and a bag over his head, not donning the hockey mask until *Part 3* in 3-D. Like that of countless other metal icons, Jason's evolution took a few projects to hit its perfect stride. Even Judas Priest began life in Panama hats and satin hippie robes.

Although the summer-camp-massacre theme spawned innumerable metal songs and albums, a smaller slew of bands including December Wolves, Evil Army, Frightmare, and Prowler have written songs called "Friday the 13th." The real-life youngster who played the first Jason, Ari Lehman, has fronted a number of bands, the most prominent of which is named First Jason.

Friday the 13th Part VI: Jason Lives (1986)
(Dir. Tom McLoughlin; w/Thom Mathews, Jennifer Cooke, David Kagen, C. J. Graham)
✠ Slasher ✠ Soundtrack ("Man Behind the Mask" theme by Alice Cooper)

Friday the 13th Part VI opens with a desecrated grave. The headstone reads "Jason Voorhees." An elderly groundskeeper—the sort who, in previous *Fridays*, would have warned the doomed pack of camping teens—sets out to fill the hole. While shoveling dirt, Gramps mumbles about vandalism, turns to the camera and, looking right at you, deadpans: "Some people have a strange idea of entertainment!"

After the wild (and wildly misnamed) *Final Chap-*

ter and the universally loathed (as it doesn't even feature Jason) *A New Beginning*, this sixth *Friday* is a bit of a different beast. A rainstorm scares off the old man and the grown-up version of "Tommy," the kid who killed Jason two movies back (originally played by Corey Feldman), shows up. He jams a long metal pole into the heart of the unearthed corpse, which promptly gets struck by lightning and—BLAMMO!—reanimates the dead killer in a newly unstoppable, electrified form (a nice nod to classic horror tropes).

Jason leaps up, kills Tommy, and throws a knife toward the camera, kicking off a parody of the famous James Bond credits. There can be no mistake: *Jason Lives* is the "funny" *Friday the 13th*. The tone keeps with humor-infused classics that capped the Golden Age of splatter horror—*Fright Night, Re-Animator, Night of the Creeps, The Texas Chainsaw Massacre Part 2*—and it works. A few years hence, wisecracking killers would sink the slasher cycle altogether. But director Tom McLoughlin (*One Dark Night*) keeps *Jason Lives* moving briskly, uses rib-tickling asides only to complement thoroughly effective bloodletting.

Shock-rock god Alice Cooper, a full decade past even his *Hollywood Squares* nadir, hoped *Jason Lives* would do for his career what that lightning rod does for the movie's antihero. "The Man Behind the Mask," Alice's theme song, enjoyed a prominent mention on the movie poster, and the video briefly hit heavy rotation on MTV. The song itself is a curious attempt to update Alice to the mid-'80s synth-pop of A-ha and Nu Shooz while also trying to keep him scary.

From Dusk Till Dawn (1996)
(Dir. Robert Rodriguez; w/George Clooney, Salma Hayek, Harvey Keitel, Quentin Tarantino)
✠ Vampires ✠ Native American Spirituality

The high point of Quentin Tarantino's immediate post–*Pulp Fiction* capers, his coscripted *From Dusk Till Dawn* is a serial murder black comedy morphing into an apocalyptic Mexican vampire massacre at a lawless strip bar with a cast of A-list Hollywood actors (George Clooney, Harvey Keitel, Salma Hayek) commingled with cult exploitation legends (Tom Savini, Fred Williamson, John Saxon). Despite all those promising elements, director Robert Rodriguez presents as big as a mess as you might present yourself following a from-dusk-till-dawn burrito binge.

The first garlic in the wound is the casting. Tribal neck tattoos notwithstanding, Clooney's inherent smugness works against the whole conceit, as opposed to how *Pulp Fiction* turned Bruce Willis's similar traits into a strength. Quentin Tarantino, appearing as Clooney's crime partner, displays screen-crumbling bad acting skills as always. Again, *Pulp Fiction*, in which the material made his wrongness beyond right, proves the exception. *From Dusk Till Dawn* doesn't just feel divided into two halves—it's more like the movie just stops dead and then an hour-long vampire fight begins. A great director might be able to make that work, but not Robert Rodriguez.

A no-holes-barred tequila whorehouse called the Titty Twister showcases the bane of post-PG-13 moviemaking: strippers who don't strip. Salma Hayek, as snake-charming feature dancer Satanico Pandemonium, is supposed to embody ancient demonic Aztec sexuality, yet what kind of limitless evil makes sure to always keep its bikini top on? Although ZZ Top provides *From Dusk Till Dawn*'s theme song, "She's Just Killing Me," the Titty Twister's house band is Tito and Tarantula, the heavy blues stoner rock project of Tito Larriva, former leader of Latino punk legends the Plugz and roots rockers the Cruzados. The Plugz, notably, perform the theme song "Electrify Me" to the Dark Brothers' transgressive porn milestone *New Wave Hookers* (1984).

Two direct-to-video follow-ups came out in 1999: *From Dusk Till Dawn 2: Texas Blood Money*, about a bank heist that goes the way of the Titty Twister, and *From Dusk Till Dawn 3: The Hangman's Daughter*, a prequel set at the turn of the twentieth century revealing the origin of Satanico Pandemonium. (The actual name "Satanico

Pandemonium" alludes to the 1975 Mexican nunsploitation shocker titled *Satánico Pandemonium*, aka *La Sexorcista*.) Each of the sequels is a good modern B-movie.

FROM HELL (2001)
(DIR. ALBERT HUGHES, ALLEN HUGHES; W/JOHNNY DEPP, HEATHER GRAHAM, IAN HOLM, ROBBIE COLTRANE)
✷ JACK THE RIPPER ✷ FREEMASONRY ✷ COMICS

As detailed in Judas Priest's standard "Ripper," in 1888, Jack the Ripper stalks the darkness and fog of London by night, ripping open streetwalking prostitutes with a knife. Scotland Yard inspector Frederick Abberline (Johnny Depp) takes the case: his psychic visions help him, but the task is definitely complicated by his falling in love with endangered hooker Mary Kelly (Heather Graham). Abberline deduces that the crime is linked to the secret society of Freemasons, inviting a heap of high-powered trouble his way.

Surprisingly, *From Hell* is the highest-profile Jack the Ripper movie made to date. The cramped production is based on a popular graphic novel by the heavily metal Alan Moore (*Watchmen*, *V for Vendetta*) but, in an ill-fitting match if ever there was one, directed by Detroit's Hughes Brothers, who previously specialized in African-American drama (*Menace II Society*) and contemporary urban action (*Dead Presidents*). The movie tries but never squirms alive. Watch for a cameo by Anthony Parker as John Merrick, the Elephant Man, a reminder of David Lynch's far more gruesome 1980 visit to Victorian London.

FROSTBITER: WRATH OF THE WENDIGO (1995), AKA WENDIGO; FROSTBITER: LEGEND OF THE WENDIGO

(DIR. TOM CHANEY; W/RON ASHETON, LORI BAKER, DEVLIN BURTON, PATRICK BUTLER)

✴ RON ASHETON ✴ SUPERNATURAL ✴ INDIGENOUS SPIRITUALITY

Ron Asheton—yes, guitarist of the Stooges—stars in this cut-rate horror comedy as a redneck hunter who shotguns a Native American mystic and thereby unleashes *Frostbiter: Wrath of the Wendigo*. Among the Algonquin peoples, a wendigo is an evil animal-human hybrid spirit. Bison B.C., Rhino, Rozz, and Scissorfight have all penned songs in praise of this being. Here, it's an amorphous force that can turn skeletons, a pot of chili, and other inanimate objects into flesh-hungry monsters. A ragtag gaggle of character types hole up in a cabin to fight back, staking their hopes on psychic Sandy (Lori Baker).

Shot in 1988 but not released until 1995, *Frostbiter* is a blatant *Evil Dead* knockoff rescued only by funny and impressive zero-budget special effects; particularly the stop-motion animated chili creatures. Weirdly, throughout the '80s and '90s Ron Asheton put together a below-the-radar acting career in a series of similarly barely existent Z-grade horrors: *The Carrier* (1988), *Hellmaster* (1992), *Frostbiter* (1995), *Mosquito* (1995), and *Legion of the Night* (1995). There is a film festival waiting to happen.

FUBAR (2002); FUBAR II: BALLS TO THE WALL (2010)

(DIR. MICHAEL DOWSE; W/DAVID LAWRENCE, PAUL SPENCE, GORDON SKILLING, ANDREW SPARACINO)

✴ BEER ✴ SOUNDTRACK (AC/DC, IRON MAIDEN, GIRLSCHOOL, THOR, BLACK SABBATH, BLUE CHEER)

Fubar is a comic mockumentary study of Dean (David Lawrence) and Terry (Paul Spence), two deadbeat metalheads from Calgary, Alberta, sporting "hockey hair" and aging ungracefully. Potential drama arises when Terry reveals he's battling testicular cancer. The boys go camping, bond with other Canuck headbangers, drink enough beer to capsize the *Queen Mary* in Lake Ontario, and talk a lot. The word *fuck* is verbalized 274 times.

The characters, which Lawrence and Spence developed in live comedy performances, are funny and believable. Given *Fubar*'s no-budget, digital video format, though, eighty minutes is a long time to spend going nowhere fast, eh?

For the sequel, Terry and Dean rise again in another mockumentary. This time, our hapless metalhead heroes seek work on an oil pipeline. As in the first film, the dialogue is all improvised and the performers are good, but the result doesn't quite add up to a movie. *Fubar II* and its soundtrack album feature Dean's fictional group Night Seeker. Justin Hawkins of the Darkness and Mikey Heppner of Priestess provide guest vocals.

Full Metal Village (2006)

(Dir. Sung Hyung Cho; w/Uwe Trede, Lore Trede, Klaus H. Plähn)

✴ Metal Reality ✴ Concert Footage
✴ Soundtrack (Amon Amarth, Judas Priest, Kreator)

Germany's Wacken Open Air festival, an annual tent-city gathering of hundreds of thousands of metal pilgrims, falls under the deadpan eye of documentarian Sung Hyung Cho. Seventy slow, vaguely mocking minutes chronicle the doings of the local townsfolk of Wacken as they prepare to host seventy thousand incoming headbangers. The climactic festival footage is over too fast. A condescending air hangs distastefully over the entire production. By the end, *Can't Stop the Music* (1980), starring the Village People, is more authentically metal than *Full Metal Village*.

However, leather-and-denim-bedecked travelers descending, enthusiastically but peacefully, upon this tiny German hamlet almost makes the deadly dull, hour-plus warm-up worth the slog. A joyous, slow-motion mosh pit erupts in front of the Wacken Fire Department's brass band as they oompah through traditional German ditties. A number celebrating a pig to be slaughtered for sausage is just great. "Sausage! Sausage!" everybody chants.

Kreator blazes across the main stage in the movie's only actual concert action. Warming up to play "Pleasure to Kill," frontman Mille Petrozza roars to the crowd: "People of Wacken! Are you ready to kill? Are you ready to kill? Are you ready to kill EACH OTHER?" Bangers looking for blazing musical Wacken action will be better served by Sam Dunn's *Metal: A Headbanger's Journey*, but *Full Metal Village* still raises the metal child inside us all.

The Funhouse (1981)

(Dir. Tobe Hooper; w/Elizabeth Berridge, Shawn Carson, Kevin Conway, Wayne Doba)

✴ Carnival Carnage

Texas Chain Saw Massacre director Tobe Hooper's *The Funhouse* is a pretty damn great, pretty woefully unsung variation on the monster-on-the-midway formula in which screaming teens get trapped overnight night in a traveling carnival where a mutant in a Frankenstein mask picks them off. The plot remains mostly that simple, with an aside about the freak-face murdering a hooker/fortune-teller, and his evil carny barker father helping him get rid of the witnesses.

Hooper is a master of atmosphere and obviously loves the circus/sideshow/fairground elements. Every happy clown face, every animatronic mannequin, every corn-dog sign, every stuffed-animal prize, and every Tilt-a-Whirl light becomes a beacon of menace. Impressive, too, is the monster makeup on the killer (Wayne Doba) once his mask comes off. With his oversize albino head, with red eyes treacherously far apart and a mouth full of busted tusk-teeth, he really does look like one of those freak exhibit babies-in-a-bottle all grown up.

The rock-versus-disco war that climaxed most places with Steve Dahl's violent "Disco Demolition" at Chicago's Comiskey Park in 1979 took more than a decade to bite the dust in Brooklyn. In time, it evolved largely into metal versus disco. One of New York City's most popular discos in the '80s was called the Fun House. In 1983, my fellow fourteen-year-old headbanger Michael "Vito" Rovito introduced me to a guy who sported what was the coolest painting I've ever seen on the back of a denim vest: an image of Iron Maiden's Eddie, Godzilla-size, crushing the Fun House with his giant, claw-fingered fist.

.

Galaxy of Terror (1981),
aka Mindwarp:
An Infinity of Terror

(DIR. BRUCE D. CLARK; W/EDWARD ALBERT, SID HAIG,
ERIN MORAN, ROBERT ENGLUND, RAY WALSTON)

✠ SCIENCE FICTION ✠ BEAST SEX ✠ PARANORMAL

Galaxy of Terror is a berserk, mega-violent, oc-cult-infused *Alien* rip-off starring Oliver Wen-dell Douglas from *Green Acres* (Edward Albert), Joanie Cunningham from *Happy Days* (Erin Mo-ran), Freddy Krueger (Robert Englund), Captain Spaulding (Sid Haig), and Mr. Hand from *Fast Times at Ridgemont High* (Ray Walston). Lunatic soft-core auteur Zalman King and buxom blonde Taaffe O'Connell are also onboard for this saga of a spaceship rescue team torn apart by creatures that spring from their own fears.

Galaxy of Terror's beyond-metal poster features a ferociously vivid painting of a distressed vixen clutching a busted ray gun as she's overcome by a giant insect-dragon with a fanged human skull for a head. Ms. O'Connell's louche undoing is highly memorable: she is nakedly raped to death by a twelve-foot-long slug that pukes slime from every pore. Even considering that outrageous

pinnacle, the rest of the deaths are on right on par in terms of sadistic creativity and abundant, propulsive bloodletting. All this madness and graphic hard-line cruelty pouring onto such a storied cast lends *Galaxy of Terror* the strange air of something resembling *Love Boat on the River Styx*.

Though a cheapie produced by B-movie guru Roger Corman, *Galaxy of Terror*'s visual effects, set design, and fantastically realized creatures speak volumes about the young talent assembled to make it all fly right; among them production designer and second unit director James Cam-eron. Taaffe O'Connell's lethally carnal worm en-counter was directed by Roger Corman himself and initially earned *Galaxy of Terror* an X rating.

Alien imitations proved to be a potent Heavy Metal Movie subgenre of the early 1980s. *Galaxy of Terror* beats all, but don't miss *Forbidden World* (1980). The two were frequently paired as a double feature, sometimes adding New York–set Italian space-egg opus *Alien Contamination* (1980). *Inseminoid* (1981) and *Xtro* (1982) expand and toxify *Alien*'s sexual undercurrents into ab-solute insanity. Neither could come more highly recommended.

The Gate (1987)

(Dir. Tibor Takács; w/Stephen Dorff, Christa Denton, Louis Tripp)

✠ Satanic Panic ✠ Backward Masking
✠ Goblins ✠ Fake Metal Band (Sacrafyx)

The most charming of the endlessly charm-filled monumental heavy metal horror films of the 1980s (*Black Roses, Terror on Tour, Trick or Treat*, etc.) is the too-often overlooked *The Gate*, a rollicking homunculi-in-a-haunted-house fantasy by Hungarian filmmaker Tibor Takács. While his parents are away and his teenage sister Al (Christa Denton) takes charge, junior-high rocketry enthusiast Glen (Stephen Dorff) and his dorky headbanger pal Terry (Louis Tripp) unwittingly open a portal to hell in the backyard. Weirdness supernaturally bubbles over. Glen levitates, and beloved family mutt Angus keels over, kaput, out of nowhere.

Fortunately, Terry is the sort of kid who sports Venom and Killer Dwarfs back-patches on his denim vests and sleeps in a room plastered with Iron Maiden posters (as well as one killer Cramps cartoon portrait). He knows where to turn: the backward messages on his heavy metal records. Terry deciphers a sheet of freaky words they found in a nasty egg-thing from the hell-hole by consulting the album *The Dark Book* by black-magic rockers Sacrafyx. Everything should be okay, he reasons, because no corpse of living sacrifice was placed in the pit—that is, until Al's dopey boyfriend buries dead dog Angus in the dumbest place possible.

From there, the gate to hell opens up and *The Gate*, the movie, expands into a wonderfully imaginative, thrillingly realized childhood nightmares of various worst-case scenarios regarding what might happen if you performed that spooky ritual you knew you shouldn't, but you just tossed and turned in bed fighting the urge to jump up and try.

The Gate demonstrates exactly what happens. Warty monster arms shoot out from under the bed, frantically grasping at your ankles. A zombie bursts through a wall, grabs your buddy, and drags him back inside, sealing up the hole as he goes. Your poor, buried ex-dog simply refuses to stay in his final resting place. And armies of foot-tall, claylike hobgoblins run amok—jumping and climbing and biting and, when injured, reassembling into even more of themselves—in preparation for their Big Daddy, a King Kong–size super-goblin with six limbs, four eyes, and at least a million teeth. Then, just when it seems like you've been as spooked as spooked gets, you grow a working eyeball in the middle of your hand and you know the only way to start unmaking this mess is by driving a stiletto smack through that palm-pupil. Ouch. By spinning the Sacrafyx record in reverse, Glen picks up on a Luciferian message regarding the light of love and, in the spirit of explosive NASA genius and Crowley disciple Jack Parsons, our young hero uses a heartfelt missile launch to undo the undoing of the universe currently in progress.

With perfect timing, *The Gate* arrived between Tipper Gore's anti-metal PMRC circus in summer 1985 and Geraldo Rivera's 1988 Halloween special on devil worship, the latter of which offered King Diamond a shot at NBC prime time. The "satanic panic" of this era may never have been as widespread or taken as seriously as metal commentators pro and con will insist it was, but for '80s kids, hard rock demonology loomed everywhere: on T-shirts and blaring from the stereos of their older siblings, keeping congregants wide-eyed and worried during Sunday church sermons, and delivering socko TV news ratings one Ricky Kasso-style fuck-up at a time.

For all its wondrous special effects and effective storytelling, the greatest triumph of *The Gate* may be its subtle, but unmistakable, message regarding scary devil music: after Glen and Terry get mixed up and freaked out en route to adolescence—what with its girls and jocks and other frightening figures–they use heavy metal not only to make sense of the perils befalling them, but to successfully negotiate a way through each torment and trial. That's not a dead-on analogy

...PRAY IT'S NOT TOO LATE.

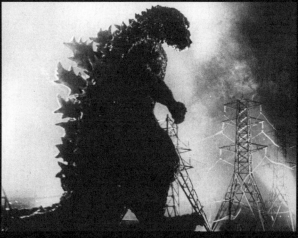

Clockwise from top: Galaxy of Terror (1981)'s sex mutant gore; backwards messages open the The Gate (1987); Gojira stars in Godzilla (1954); Jacob Reynolds soaks in Gummo (1997); Oliver Reed shines in Gor (1987); Get Thrashed (2006)

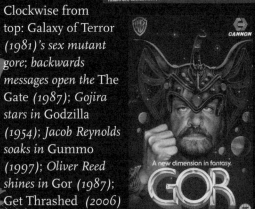

for every high school bone-brain who successfully turned headbanger and triumphed over the monsters in his way. Headbangers aren't looking for a portal to hell, but for an escape from the hell we are already inside.

Get Him to the Greek
(2010)
(Dir. Nicholas Stoller; w/Russell Brand, Jonah Hill, Rose Byrne, Lars Ulrich)
✶ Danish Drummer

Picking up not quite exactly where the barbed 2008 rom-com *Forgetting Sarah Marshall* dumped off, *Get Him to the Greek* chronicles the misadventures of record company shlub Aaron Green (Jonah Hill) attempting to deliver bad-boy rock star Aldous Snow (Russell Brand) to a big concert. Fans of both films featuring Aldous Snow claim numerous boosters. Lars Ulrich, who cameos prominently here, must be among them. Ulrich plays a parody of his public persona. First he wakes up in bed next to Snow's girlfriend (Rose Byrne), which sets up a later scene for Snow to yell at him: "Why don't you go and sue Napster, you little Danish twat?"

Get Thrashed: The Story of Thrash Metal (2006)
(Dir. Rick Ernst; w/Metallica, Slayer, Megadeth, Anthrax, Exodus, Testament, Kreator, Overkill)
✶ Thrash Metal ✶ History ✶ Concert Footage

A labor of love seven years in the making, the feature documentary *Get Thrashed* delivers the Reebok-stomping, hair-twirling, neck-snapping, sped-up-polka-beat goods. Director Rick Ernst, an MTV producer who began as a *Headbangers Ball* intern, fleshes out the beginning, breakthrough, and bust-up of metal's burliest 1980s form with good humor, good storytelling, and participation from many of the era's most important players.

Highlights include reminders of the wall that separated metal and punk until thrash melted it like lava; scene profiles of thrash's primary geographic fronts (San Francisco, Los Angeles, New York, Germany); serious respect paid to Suicidal Tendencies; in-depths explorations of moshing and dress codes; and Dave Mustaine explaining how—by starting in Metallica, creating Megadeth, and teaching Slayer's Kerry King to play rhythm guitar—he, perhaps more than anyone else, invented the thrash riff.

Representatives of every canonical thrash ensemble happily sound off. It's always gratifying, as well, to see vintage performances by fallen metal heroes such as Metallica's Cliff Burton and Exodus frontman Paul Baloff. Pantera singer Phil Anselmo, as ever, entertains and informs, representing thrash's last bastion in the '90s and the myriad forms metal has taken since then. He's the perfect bridge into the film's final section on thrash descendents of the 2000s such as Lamb of God, God Forbid, and Slipknot, whose Corey Taylor is another standout talking head.

Mainstream rock media focuses on how '80s punk and college radio transformed the rock landscape with DIY techniques and guerilla warfare intensity, paying off with grunge's pop triumph at the turn of the decade. Brian Fair of Shadows Fall, though, correctly shines a light on the crucial role thrash performed in creating a new world of musical possibilities, from the tangible—as in pressing records at home and booking your own tours—to the ethereal: a rejection of aesthetic limitations, coupled with all-out insistence on self-determination.

"The legacy of bands like Metallica, Megadeth, Anthrax, Slayer will live on forever," Fair says. "Whether it's in the punk rock scenes, hardcore scenes, or metal scenes, that stuff's there forever. It's imprinted in my DNA at this point."

A nod to Lars Ulrich: the most recognizable member of the most popular heavy metal band of all time routinely participates in and applies his highly marketable presence to numerous low-budget, fan-driven projects like *Get Thrashed*.

Not that his star power is overplayed. In and out of metal circles, much is made of thrash's "Big Four"—Metallica, Slayer, Megadeth, and Anthrax. *Get Thrashed* essentially expands that number to a "Big Five," by rightly giving equal time to Bay Area mayhem masters Exodus.

The Ghost Galleon (1974), aka Horror of the Zombies

(Dir. Amando de Ossorio; w/Jack Taylor, Maria Perschy, Barbara Rey)

✠ Cloaks ✠ Zombies ✠ Knights Templar

The Blind Dead, the zombified remnants of the thirteenth-century Knights Templar, take to the high seas in *The Ghost Galleon*. First the hooded, skeletal spooks lay waste to two supermodels whose boat becomes lost in a fog. When rescuers from the modeling agency and elsewhere come searching, the blood feast continues.

After the first two Blind Dead films—*Tombs of the Blind Dead* (1971) and *Return of the Evil Dead* (1973)—*Ghost Galleon*, despite the cool title, is a major step down in budget, production, and imagination. That the vaunted vessel is a small model is laughably obvious. Cathedral paid tribute with their song "La Noche Del Buque Maldito" (Ghost Ship of the Blind Dead).

Ghost Rider (2007)

(Dir. Mark Steven Johnson; w/Nicolas Cage, Eva Mendes, Wes Bentley, Peter Fonda, Sam Elliott)

✠ Satan ✠ Motorcycles ✠ Faust ✠ Hell

The debate rages as to which Marvel Comics hero is the most metal: Wolverine, Sgt. Fury, the Punisher, or Ghost Rider. It's hard not to favor the circus motorcycle stunt performer who sells his soul to the devil and then rides the earth with a flaming skull for a head, collecting souls of the damned by means of a burning chain he can crack like a whip. Nicolas Cage supplies his standard amped-beyond-amphetamine acting chops to this origin story, where we see how pro rider Johnny Blaze gets conned into working for Old Scratch. Once Johnny goes inferno-faced as Ghost Rider, he's got to contend with Beelzebub's even more evil son Blackheart, who aims to destroy the earth and with it the souls his not-proud papa exists to acquire. As a TV news reporter, Eva Mendes supplies cleavage. As a Civil War–era horseback Ghost Rider, Sam Elliott supplies mustache. Mephistopheles, Satan's dealmaker, is played by cycle movie icon Peter Fonda (*Easy Rider, The Wild Angels, Race With the Devil*), which is a nice touch.

Ghost Rider: Spirit of Vengeance (2012)

(Dirs. Mark Neveldine, Brian Taylor; w/Nicolas Cage, Violante Placido, Ciarán Hinds, Idris Elba)

✠ Satan ✠ Motorcycles ✠ Faust ✠ Hell

For at least a decade, beginning with *Lord of War* (2005), Nicolas Cage has created a strain of insane-to-the-point of incoherent billion-dollar B-movies all his own. The first *Ghost Rider* (2007) fits smack into this singular subgenre. Writer-director team Mark Neveldine and Brian Taylor enjoy a markedly similar run, creating the frantic, physically impossible CGI violence festivals *Crank* (2006), *Crank: High Voltage* (2009), *Gamer* (2009), and *Jonah Hex* (2010). That turgid twain doth meet in *Ghost Rider: Spirit of Vengeance*, with Cage returning as Marvel Comics' flaming-skulled undead biker hero for an irrational, exhausting adventure helmed by Neveldine and Taylor. In 3-D!

This time, Johnny Blaze (Cage) comes out of hiding in Eastern Europe to save a kid (Fergus Riordan) being hunted by the devil (Ciarán Hinds). You will not be surprised when Ghost Rider saves the lad. Neveldine and Taylor's nü-metal sensibilities can pack some eye-poppers. Seemingly every frame is composed, via computer, to look like a selection from the ultimate stoner bedroom poster collection. Their attempt to give *Ghost Rider* visuals a garish high-tech makeover is mostly seeds and stems, man.

To promote *Ghost Rider: Spirit of Vengeance*, Nicolas Cage did a *Saturday Night Live* bit in which he described one of his acting rules as being "every line of dialogue must be either whispered or screamed." When it comes to this film, Cage was whispering and screaming the truth.

GHOUL SCHOOL (1990)
(DIR. TIMOTHY O'RAWE; W/WILLIAM FRIEDMAN, MARY HUNER, JACKIE MARTLING, JOE FRANKLIN)
✤ FAKE METAL BAND

You can't really sink lower than Troma for insultingly pointless gore "comedy," but *Ghoul School* gives it the ol' undead high school swim team try. Metal comes by way of a hair band practicing in the school auditorium for the big dance. Were they taken out of context, you might smirk at just how inefficiently synced the actors' "playing" and the sound supposedly coming out of the instruments is. All told, *Ghoul School* is really bloody, and really, really unfunny. That it delivers the body fluids at least puts it one nose-hair ahead of most horror comedies. The only real reason to investigate *Ghoul School* is for the amusing wedging-in of Joe Franklin (an ancient-school local New York broadcasting legend) and Jackie "The Joke Man" Martling (Howard Stern's head writer and guffaw guy for two decades). Jackie's ex-wife Nancy Sirianni also appears as a metal chick.

GHOULIES II (1988)
(DIR. ALBERT BAND; W/PHIL FONDACARO, DAMON MARTIN, ROYAL DANO, KERRY REMSEN)
✤ W.A.S.P. ✤ EVIL TOILET GOBLINS

From the toilet they came in the original *Ghoulies* (1985), and up from commode pipes again come even more rubber-mugged goblin bobblers in *Ghoulies II*. This time, though, they bring W.A.S.P. along with the theme song "Scream Until You Like It." As *Gremlins* rip-offs go, the *Ghoulies* gang always seemed a rung down from the *Critters* crew, but this second installment is a leap forward from the murky original thanks to

fun puppets, a carnival setting, and super-cool stop-motion animation of ghoulies run amuck on the midway. After their crapper resurrection, the ghoulies reside in a traveling carnival's haunted house attraction called "Satan's Den." By engaging in their slime-slinging mayhem, they make it the most popular ride on the fairgrounds.

On the VHS compilation *W.A.S.P.: Videos . . . In the Raw*, Blackie Lawless talks about working with the ghoulies puppets (and puppeteers) for the "Scream Until You Like It" music video: "We were approached with the idea for a movie [tie-in], for *Ghoulies II*. We looked at the footage and we decided that 'Scream Until You Like It' would be the perfect song. To me, it's one of the better experiences I've had, because the people that ran these creatures made them come to life when we were doing this video, and after it was done, in all honesty, to watch these little guys be put in the box left me with a strange feeling."

GIMME SHELTER (1970)
(DIRS. ALBERT MAYSLES, DAVID MAYSLES, CHARLOTTE ZWERIN; W/THE ROLLING STONES, THE HELLS ANGELS)
✤ MOTORCYCLES ✤ CONCERT FOOTAGE

From their roots in souls-for-sale-at-the-crossroads blues to *Their Satanic Majesties Request* to "Sympathy for the Devil," the Rolling Stones were the first steely-eyed rock act to conquer universal consciousness and ignite the frightening demon fires that begat heavy metal. Maybe more significantly, they played a murderous concert at Altamont Raceway in December 1969 that effectively killed off the summer of love and made a darker new way of looking at things imperative. Enter Black Sabbath, three months later, with a frame of reference that included a healthy respect for the capacity of humans to do evil.

The greatest documentary ever made, *Gimme Shelter* chronicles the Rolling Stones' legendary, lethal free concert at Altamont. Not long after the groovy triumph of Woodstock, the '60s counterculture pushed its luck again and this time unleashed an army of fascist drunks in denim and leather astride iron neck-breaker machines. Just in case you didn't quite comprehend the visuals, the vests spell out their intentions via the moniker Hells Angels. The flower children opened the garden to these swastika-emblazoned marauders and, to be sure, all hell followed with them.

Crowds file into the cold, dusty Altamont race car park and the vibe is instantly fraught with menace. A fat guy on acid strips nude and nobody's cool with it. A couple makes out on a blanket while keeping a rope around the neck of what may be a dog or a goat but definitely is some kind of ominous underworld beast. A white chick collects alms for the Black Panthers, reminding everybody who's not giving her money: "They're just Negroes, you know."

In front of the stage, the Hells Angels—hired as "security" and paid with $500 worth of beer—park their choppers in a line of demarcation. Anybody who touches a bike gets pummeled with hairy fists and sawed-off pool cues. As the crowd swells by thousands upon thousands, the brew-fueled lawgivers keep busy cracking hippie skulls. When Jefferson Airplane's Marty Balin sees the Angels roughing up the crowd, he jumps into the fray and is punched unconscious. Things will not get better.

The Stones take the stage deep in the night, and mayhem grips the masses. Mick Jagger attempts to bring calm with frantic, high-pitched pleas of "Babies, babies, babies!" that are searingly intercut with footage of Angels honcho Sonny Barger looking upon this fey, tarted-up Englishman with genocidal fury. "Sympathy for the Devil" kicks in and the self-anointed minions of the devil rain down figurative death on the peace-and-love dreams of the '60s and literal death on concertgoer Meredith Hunter, a black man who may or may not have pulled a gun, but was definitely guilty of being on a date with a blonde woman.

Right on camera, an Angel drives a fatal blade into Hunter and we see rock and roll's first human sacrifice bleed out before the eyes of the world. The shell-shocked Stones are ushered away in a helicopter that brings to mind the world upside-down fighting in Vietnam, while the desperate, terrified audience members left behind must fend for themselves until they can flee in relative safety at dawn. *Gimme Shelter*'s title song, a chillingly believable cry of fear and confusion, plays over the closing credits as the night's refugees wander off in breaking daylight.

Gimme Shelter is a southward-spiraling nightmare of impossible negative power. The action begins with the Stones coming off a victorious run at Madison Square Garden and, step by step, drags us on a descent through miscalculations and decadent ignorance that ends with a public execution by an armed death squad. In perhaps the least heavy metal of all movie moments, the Grateful Dead arrive and catch wind of the bad storm brewing. "The Angels are beatin' on the musicians?" Jerry Garcia asks. When told yes, Captain Trips just says, "Bummer." Then he gets on a helicopter and hightails it out of there.

GINGER SNAPS (2000)

(DIR. JOHN FAWCETT; W/KATHERINE ISABELLE, EMILY PERKINS, KRIS LEMCHE, MIMI ROGERS)

✠ WEREWOLF ✠ GOTH CHICKS ✠ SOUNDTRACK (FEAR FACTORY, HATEBREED, MACHINE HEAD, SOULFLY)

The deep, sad, and soulful *Ginger Snaps* holds a mirror up to metalhead adolescence and bends it back through the prism of lycanthropy. That Ginger (Katherine Isabelle) is a girl adds an extra dimension to the body horror, given the inherent bloody mutation young ladies contend with in puberty. And that's to say nothing of the emotional nightmares.

On the night of her first period, gothy, late-blooming Ginger, sixteen, is attacked by some kind of hairy beast. She convinces her even odder and more death-fixated sister Brigitte (Emily Perkins) that the assailant was a werewolf. The siblings team with school stoner Sam (Kris Lemche) to find a cure, racing toward a full-moon-on-Halloween conclusion and a final transformation as an allegory of family separation into adulthood: independence is all you ever want when you're a kid, then the scariest thing that could ever happen once you get there.

Karen Walton's script, served by John Fawcett's subtle direction, tells a pointedly female story. The music that Ginger and Brigitte listen to—Fear Factory, Machine Head, and Soulfly—paints an even more specific image of who they are.

Ginger Snaps stirred a bit of a cult buzz upon its release in 2000, but it seemed to get overpowered in terms of promotion and media buzz by the vastly inferior supernatural adolescent-adrift drama from the same time: *Donnie Darko*. Fortunately, *Ginger Snaps* begat two follow-up movies, both released in 2004. *Ginger Snaps Unleashed* is a direct sequel, about sister Emily becoming a werewolf. *Ginger Snaps Back: The Beginning* is a period piece, casting the sisters at a traders' fort in 1815 Canada.

To his undying credit, director Fawcett refused to use CGI, and insisted on only employing prosthetics, makeup, and practical effects for the werewolf scenes.

Global Metal (2008)

(Dirs. Sam Dunn, Scot McFadyen; w/Sam Dunn, Lars Ulrich, Tom Araya, Max Cavalera)

✠ World Metal ✠ Metal Reality

Sam Dunn and Scot McFadyen create a more than worthy follow-up to their instant classic, *Metal: A Headbanger's Journey* (2005). Toronto anthropologist Dunn, who expertly chronicled the rise of European and American heavy metal in his first documentary, takes on the rest of the planet in *Global Metal*. Utilizing the same interview format, Dunn examines what has arisen from metal's boot print in Brazil, Japan, India, China, Indonesia, Israel, and Dubai.

While *A Headbanger's Journey* commenced with the mammoth Wacken Open Air festival in Germany, *Global Metal* kicks off at Brazil's equally huge but more outwardly passionate Rock in Rio gathering. Sepultura's Max Cavalera talks about metal emerging from the fall of the country's military dictatorship in 1985, and we see that metal is as abundant in Brazil as the green of their jungles and the junk of their ladies' trunks.

Next stop is Asia. In Japan, Dunn talks to members of Sigh and highlights the glam-freak visual kei movement and the Megadeth-friendly TV showcase *Death Panda*. The metalheads of Mumbai, India, declare sonic war on their country's traditional culture, in particular the giddy music of Bollywood movies. In China, Kaiser Kuo of rockers Tang Dynasty discusses the rapid ascent of metal in just the past twenty-five years it's been available, and Dunn takes us to a music school full of burgeoning shredders.

Indonesia is the most fascinating stop. In a country emerging from its own totalitarian history with a fearsomely fanatical Muslim population on the rise, metal serves as an underground outlet for personal rage and political action. The metal scene there is explosive, as Lars Ulrich tells us from firsthand experience.

The Middle East provides the movie's closing chapters. First, members of Orphaned Land provide a guide to the metal culture of Israel. Then Dunn goes to Dubai, where he meets musicians from a number of Islamic countries that forbid not only documentarians chronicling heavy metal, but everything else related to heavy metal, period. Dunn ends *Global Metal* by declaring that metal connects with people regardless of their cultural, political, or religious backgrounds. After all, metal is freedom.

God Bless Ozzy Osbourne (2011)

(Dirs. Mike Fleiss, Mike Piscitelli; w/Ozzy Osbourne, Sharon Osbourne, Kelly Osbourne)

✠ Metal History ✠ Prince of Darkness

God Bless Ozzy Osbourne motivated me to look up the word *hagiography*. Watching *God Bless*, from its falsely ironic title to its triumph-of-reality-TV-star climax, I had a hunch that the term was a fit description. Now I know it is. Should we expect anything else when watching a documentary produced by Ozzy's son Jack? Perhaps not, but in terms of surprising or even previously unfamiliar content, *God Bless* is a little godforsaken.

Ozzy grew up in steely shithole Birmingham, UK. He flipped for the Beatles, conquered all knowable worlds in Black Sabbath, drank booze and took drugs in excess, then became a bat-biting solo madman who snorted ants and executed a houseful of cats. He mourned hard over the plane crash demise of guitarist Randy Rhoads, had some big pop hits, consumed more booze and drugs, launched Ozzfest, starred in the last thing anyone watched on MTV, and presently reigns as one of pop culture's most affable rock and roll elders. His wife and two youngest kids got famous, too.

My mother probably knows this much about Ozzy Osbourne, and *God Bless* doesn't provide much more than those basic facts. The Ozzy episode of VH1's *Behind the Music* and the *Classic Albums* installment on Black Sabbath's *Paranoid* are more in-depth, and the singer's many, many interviews in other documentaries could easily be cobbled together paint a more engaging picture of one of metal's most towering gods.

Still, Ozzy never misses a chance to proclaim his devotion to the Beatles, so it's great to see Paul McCartney return the good cheer here. Also, eldest Osbourne daughter Aimee, who shuns public attention and refused to appear on MTV's *The Osbournes*, speaks at length in *God Bless*. She's a dark-eyed, slightly spooky beauty who, in passing, brings to mind the mystery woman on the cover of the first *Black Sabbath* album.

GODZILLA (1954), AKA GOJIRA
(DIR. ISHIRO HONDA; W/AKIRA TAKARADA, MOMOKO KOCHI, RAYMOND BURR)
✻ GIANT MONSTER ✻ RADIATION

Godzilla arose in reaction to early 1950s hydrogen bomb tests in the Pacific by the U.S., UK, and USSR that critically sickened fishermen at sea and stirred heinous memories onshore. The movie, not coincidentally, opens with a scene of Japanese freighters engulfed by flames as the titanic terror announces his presence while the ocean bubbles pure doom. From there, Godzilla rises and takes on Tokyo, and Japan relives the gnarliest agonies of World War II complete with panicked citizenry, martial law, and dialogue regarding bomb shelters and black rain. Scientists ultimately defeat Godzilla by employing yet another previously unthinkable weapon, the Oxygen Destroyer, and we are left to ponder the consequences of this new lethal game changer.

All this deeper meaning enhances what we come to Godzilla for in the first place: a dude in a bumpy lizard costume kicking the crap out of balsa-wood neighborhoods and model airplanes. Purists are best served by the original *Gojira* with Japanese subtitles and about forty extra minutes of footage. Also check out the dubbed Hollywood version, which hilariously stars, via choppy editing, Raymond Burr, referred to almost exclusively as "famous reporter Steve Martin."

In any of his myriad forms, Godzilla rules as one of the biggest, most destructive icons of heavy metal, as championed by in the 1970s by Blue Öyster Cult's "Godzilla" or in the 2000s by French metal monsters Gojira. No longer were Japanese films just art house meditations on feudal history and ancient tradition. *Godzilla* declared that, even when confronting the ultimate horrors of Hiroshima and Nagasaki, the Land of the Rising Sun was on hand to scorch all challengers in the realm of monster mayhem.

THE GOOD, THE BAD, AND THE UGLY (1966)
(DIR. SERGIO LEONE; W/CLINT EASTWOOD, LEE VAN CLEEF, ELI WALLACH)
✻ SPAGHETTI WESTERN ✻ SOUNDTRACK ("THE ECSTASY OF GOLD")

The Italian film genre known as spaghetti western is the European heavy metal of cowboy movies, and *The Good, the Bad, and the Ugly* is the ultimate spaghetti western. As emulated by Motörhead on the cover of *Ace of Spades*, Italian-produced westerns reworked the archetypal American form in the 1960s to include filth, grit, surrealism, suspense, and extreme violence with an intensity bordering on horror. Before this outing, the form's unholy trinity—director Sergio Leone, star Clint Eastwood, and composer Ennio Morricone—had previously conspired to make *A Fistful of Dollars* (1964) and *For a Few Dollars More* (1965).

Sprawling to the point of being cosmic, *The Good, The Bad, and the Ugly* utilizes the American Civil War and westward expansion as a backdrop. The epic plot details an episodic quest to locate buried Confederate gold by the heroic Man With No Name (Clint Eastwood, "The Good"), heartless mercenary killer Angel Eyes (Lee Van Cleef, "The Bad"), and rat-like hustler Tuco (Eli Wallach, "The Ugly"). Bounty hunting scams, shootouts, cannon warfare, a brutal dragging through a desert, more shootouts, internment in a prisoner-of-war camp, numerous daring escapes, and still more shootouts lead up to the definitive "Mexican standoff" as our three players face each other down at simultaneous gunpoint.

The Good, the Bad, and the Ugly is biblically proportioned, caked in blood and dust, and sinking into the soul by way of Morricone's most deservedly celebrated and imitated instrumental theme. The familiar refrain of the tune was meant to mimic the cry of a hyena. The more bombastic "The Ecstasy of Gold" has been Metallica's pre-concert introduction since the early 1980s, and the band has performed the song with the San Francisco Symphony Orchestra.

Quentin Tarantino has declared *The Good, the Bad, and the Ugly* "the best-directed film of all time" and nothing less than "the greatest achievement in the history of cinema." Saddle up and ride hard into the inferno alongside these three horsemen of the spaghetti western apocalypse. Heed Eli Wallach's advice to a failed assassin like a heavy metal commandment: "When you have to shoot—shoot! Don't talk!"

Good to See You Again, Alice Cooper

(1974)

(DIR. JOE GANNON; W/ALICE COOPER, DENNIS DUNAWAY, MICHAEL BRUCE, NEAL SMITH)
⚜ ALICE COOPER

Billed as "The Film That Outgrosses Them All," *Good to See You Again, Alice Cooper* documents Alice's larger-than-lust stage show of the 1973 *Billion Dollar Babies* tour. Intercut between unceasingly stellar tracks like "No More Mr. Nice Guy," "Hello, Hooray," "Billion Dollar Babies," "Raped and Freezin'," "Elected," "Sick Things," "Dead Babies," "I Love the Dead," "School's Out," and "Under My Wheels" are vintage black-and-white Hollywood movie clips and pieces of a narrative Alice movie that got scrapped.

Circa '73, Alice Cooper lorded darkly over rock as the biggest star on earth, and this document makes plain why. Cooper's charisma drips, screams, bleeds, and rocks right off the screen, from an opening performance of "The Lady Is a Tramp" in what appears to be white-tuxedo heaven; through some goofy comedy sketches; to the Roman Colosseum–worthy spectacle of two concerts shot in Dallas and Houston. "Killer" the giant snake hisses and flicks his tongue, and constricts. Whips crack. Money flies. Horrible things happen to mannequins and baby dolls. Alice's crotch bulges. *Good to See You Again, Alice Cooper* proves that the legend of live Alice shows in the band's prime is true.

Originally shot as *Hard Hearted Alice* and focused on a plot with Cooper fleeing a mad movie director and going on trial in Texas as "the rock and roll scourge of America", *Good to See You Again* contains scenes from that abandoned project. Despite delaying the concert segments, they manage to charm in time-capsule terms.

GOR (1987),

AKA JOHN NORMAN'S GOR

(DIR. FRITZ KIERSCH; W/URBANO BARBERINI, REBECCA FERRATTI, JACK PALANCE, OLIVER REED)

✤ SWORDS & SORCERY ✤ CANNON FILMS

Staples of drugstore book racks and many an older brother's skunk-scented bedroom throughout the 1970s, John Norman's prolific output of *Gor* novels featured magnificent fantasy art covers, often by masters such as Boris Vallejo, and they oozed bizarre, kinky, and copious outer-space slave-girl sex. Unlike with Frank Herbert's more highbrow *Dune* series or Edgar Rice Burroughs's *John Carter of Mars* books, no one had been fretting about how to best make a *Gor* movie—except its creator. Norman's lawyers worked tirelessly to get around *Gor* publisher Ballantine Books' disinterest in a film version and, finally, in 1987, the proper loophole was located. Cannon Films' schlock gods Menahem Golan and Yoram Globus snatched the rights, *Children of the Corn* director Fritz Kiersch was hired, and *Gor* hit celluloid hard.

Mild-mannered physics professor Tarl Cabot (Urbano Barberini) is zapped to the planet Gor, the "Counter-Earth." It's a typical post-Conan landscape of barbarian troublemaking lorded over by evil priest Sarm (Oliver Reed, wearing a helmet with metal bat wings). Amusingly fast, Tarl becomes a sword master, kills Sarm's son, picks up slave girl Talena (Rebecca Ferratti), attends a slave-girl wrestling match and a freaky slave-girl orgy, and ultimately defeats Sarm to free all the slave girls. Talena cozies up to the triumphant hero and says, "Now that you have helped us break the bonds of slavery, we owe a service to you."

Tarl cocks an eyebrow and says, "We can discuss that." A sequel, *Outlaw of Gor* (1989) followed.

The first *Gor* novel debuted in 1966, and follow-ups have come out consistently ever since. There were two—*Conspirators of Gor* and *Smugglers of Gor*—in 2012 alone, bringing the running total to thirty-two. "John Norman" is actually the nom de plume of academic and philosopher Dr. John Frederick Lange. He believes that men should dominate all they survey and that women are, by nature, submissive to men. Thus, that's how the ever-abundant sadomasochistic sex works in the *Gor*-niverse. The author's attitudes and the books' content created a feminist backlash in the '80s, with Lange being disinvited from science-fiction conventions and shunned by the mainstream fantasy community ever since.

Even Michael Moorcock, the sci-fi author who collaborated with heavy metal heroes Hawkwind, said that *Gor* books should be kept out of reach of casual browsers, stating, "I'm not for censorship, but I am for strategies which marginalize stuff that works to objectify women and suggests women enjoy being beaten."

Fittingly, then, women (and men) who enjoy being beaten—and/or who enjoy administering the beatings—have become great champions of *Gor* and its creator. *Gor* is the premier sci-fi series in the BDSM community. Numerous websites and organizations have arisen to embrace "Gorean" sexuality, and all the leather, chains, whips, candles, and screaming that entails.

GOREGASM (2007)

(DIR. JASON MATHERNE; W/STEVE WALTZ, RIC KAUFFMAN, DANA KIEFERLE, VALERIE LOMBARD)

✤ SLASHER ✤ GRINDCORE

This sexually berserk slasher movie tells the tale of "the Cockface Killer," who hunts horndogs in and around a porn store crammed with video booths. Not quite a feature film, *Goregasm* exists largely as a piling-up of massively repulsive atrocities set to the appropriate strains of scuzzy doom gods Saint Vitus and Debris Inc., and blackened death grindcore marauders Synapse Defect. Female nudity is copious, attractive, and ob-gyn-level explicit. Shit eating, shredded genitals, and wound fucking abound. *Goregasm* is a laudable mess.

Adding further intrigue to *Goregasm*'s slasher

plot—along with a lot more tits, open vaginas, and visible anus holes—is a lesbian separatist gang called the Clitoral Legion Against Mankind (C.L.A.M.) that kidnaps penis bearers, ass-bangs them with strap-ons, and forces them to serve as anonymous openmouthed glory hole receptacles. It's an original touch! Cameos by Goatwhore's Sammy Duet, Eyehategod/Down's Jimmy Bower, and Saint Vitus' Dave Chandler seal the deal.

Gorgon Video Magazine Vols. 1 & 2

(1989)

(Dirs. Various; w/Michael Berryman, Wes Craven, Stuart Gordon, Penn and Teller, Rick Sullivan)

✠ Gwar ✠ '80s Horror

Gorgon Video arose in the 1980s on its blockbuster rerelease of all-time shockumentary champion *Faces of Death* (1978). The company then built a mini empire on subsequent *FOD* sequels and other fright titles, usually catering to the barf-bag community. In the great metal-horror crossover, Gorgon's green-headed-monster logo was to video what Earache, Megaforce, and Metal Blade were to records. The sickening sight signified: "This is for YOU!"

Just like the record labels, Gorgon tried its bloodied hand at the never-quite-successful video magazine format. *Gorgon Video Magazine Volume 1* explores the vibrant horror culture of the day in a *60 Minutes*–type format, free of the censorship of TV or the MPAA. If *GVM* came off just a mite clunky at the time, however, just a few years later it had aged into a time capsule to be treasured.

Michael Berryman, bald baddie from 1977's *The Hills Have Eyes*, introduces segments on *Hills* director Wes Craven, the wizards of gore at the KNB special effects studio, scream queen Linnea Quigley, Troma Films, and theatrical metal messmakers Gwar. Rick Sullivan, publisher of the groundbreaking DIY horror screed-sheet *Gore Gazette*, reviews movies. The brash, quick-witted Sullivan shows clips and awards "four skulls" to *Bad Taste* (1987), *Vicious* (1988), and *Henry: Portrait of a Serial Killer* (1985), and then hilariously dumps all over the Troma pickup *Cameron's Closet* (1987). Various shock clips and trailers fill out the tape's running time.

Around the same time as *GVM*, Gorgon also produced *Impact Video Magazine*, hosted by Alex Winter (Bill of the *Bill and Ted* movies). Its aim was more generally countercultural, as it showcased underground animation, comedian Bill Hicks, and rap group Public Enemy. *Impact* does boast an interesting metal presence, though, via profiles of Jane's Addiction, the Butthole Surfers, and painter Robert Williams, creator of the original, quickly censored cover image for Guns N' Roses' *Appetite for Destruction*.

Gorgon Video Magazine Volume 1 proved so commercially successful—that is, not at all—that *Gorgon Video Magazine Volume 2* was never released to the public. That's a shame, but ever-resourceful horror mavens seized and duplicate a few screener copies, and the video then made the rounds. *The Hills Have Eyes'* Michael Berryman crops up again between visits with filmmaker Stuart Gordon (on and off the set of *Bride of the Re-Animator*), Linnea Quigley, Penn and Teller (promoting their 1989 flop, *Penn and Teller Get Killed*), special effects creator Screaming Mad George, and, most remarkably, *Zap Comix* artists Robert Crumb and S. Clay Wilson. Rick Sullivan returns as well to rattle off wisenheimer fright flick reviews. Clips and trailers abound.

Many of the participants (Penn Jillette, most loudly) knock the then-thriving big-ticket slasher franchises *Halloween*, *Friday the 13th*, and *A Nightmare on Elm Street*. Every metalhead and horror hound loves those movies now. Once we get a few years past the 2000s, let's see what happens to all those pearl-clutchers who so publicly exhausted themselves fretting over the "torture porn" of *Saw* and *Hostel*.

Gorgoroth: Black Mass Krakow 2004 (2008)

(Dirs. Gorgoroth; w/Gaahl, King Ov Hell, Infernus, Apollyon, Kvitrafn, Goat Pervertor)

✠ Black Metal ✠ Church Scandal

Witness a national scandal and, if you're lucky, lose your soul in the process! *Gorgoroth: Black Mass Krakow 2004* is an hour-long documentation of the Norwegian black metal marauders' celebrated aesthetic assault of February 1, 2004, in which they pulled out all the satanic stops during a filmed performance at a TV station in totalitarian Catholic Poland. Nude women hung on crosses, sheep heads on pikes, eighty liters of animal blood, and wall-to-wall devil worship provided visual enhancement to the band's pummeling, dragon-barf unholy black metal.

Since the performance occurs in a broadcast facility, the concert itself looks and sounds great. The nude chicks and severed barnyard trappings are so much godless gravy splattered all over the top. Following this mass media abomination, Gorgoroth faced charges in Poland of animal cruelty and "religious offense." The band beat the rap by pointing out that they just bought the heads and blood at a butcher shop, and claiming ignorance of any legal stipulations against upsetting pope fans in the land of John Paul II.

Gremlins 2: The New Batch (1990)

(Dir. Joe Dante; w/Zach Galligan, Phoebe Cates, John Glover, Christopher Lee)

✠ Slayer ✠ Christopher Lee

Joe Dante's original *Gremlins* (1984) put teeth and anarchic humor in executive producer Steven Spielberg's otherwise overly sanitary mid-'80s factory output. *Gremlins 2: The New Batch* is Dante's go-for-broke attempt at making the ultimate Looney Tune, a picture overrun by self-aware dragon homunculi hungry for human flesh and family-friendly cuteness.

Gremlins 2 spikes its subversive scorched-Hollywood campaign with a re-creation of Nazi dental torture from *Marathon Man* (1976); two cameos by Daffy Duck at war with his own animators; gremlins breaking into the projection booth at the theater in which you're watching the movie (only to be thwarted by Hulk Hogan); and a hilariously deadpan Christopher Lee, as disease-collecting, giant-pod-toting genetic scientist Dr. Catheter.

Dante and his cabal ultimately ice their sugar-coated poison cake by inviting Slayer to the ruckus. The *Gremlins 2* soundtrack features not just any Slayer, but specifically "Angel of Death" from *Reign in Blood*, the album-opening paean to the Third Reich's most repellent atrocity architect, Dr. Josef Mengele. Slayer's best-known song blares as Mohawk, the biggest and most evil of the gremlins, breaks into Dr. Catheter's lab, downs a beaker of noxious brew, and mutates into a heinous spider-goblin. Using just the song's guitar solo and thereby slipping its lyrical content past der Spielberg is the greatest prank in a movie bursting with them.

Grindcore: 85 Minutes of Brutal Heavy Metal (1991)

(Dir. unknown; w/Digby Pearson, Napalm Death, Morbid Angel, Nocturnus, Paradise Lost, Godflesh, Bolt Thrower, Entombed, Carcass)

✠ Grindcore ✠ Death Metal

Grindcore is a special edition of *Hard N Heavy* video magazine that hit hard and hit deep in 1991. Debate might arise whether every band on the roster rightly falls under the "grindcore" imprimatur. They don't, and "death metal" would likely be a better catchall, but who cares?

What matters is that this is vintage interview and performance footage of extreme hard rock acts during the "lost" period wherein the mainstream media smarmily and excitedly declared heavy metal "dead" and grunge its immediate and only replacement.

These band members and this music expose that lie. And they completely kick ass, as does having *Grindcore: 85 Minutes of Brutal Heavy* as a time capsule and permanent record. Dig of Earache Records talks tape trading and zine publishing. He appears between each band segment. Intercut with "If Truth Be Known" and "Suffer the Children," Napalm Death comes off jokier than anybody would ever expect, declaring that no band is ever going to be faster or more extreme. Showing off his tattoos, drummer Mick Harris wisecracks: "I'm going for a full Japanese body suit. Then I'll be chuffed!"

David Vincent of Morbid Angel discusses Satanism, and the band plays "Immortal Rites." After playing "Dead Emotion," members of Paradise Lost say they feel "sexy and moist." Jennifer of Sonic Relief Promotions says, "Grind can be defined as a death metal with a thoughtful edge." Her partner Grob jokes, "They're just dirty hippies playing very loud music."

Justin Broadrick and Paul Neville of Godflesh look amazed to be outside in Los Angeles on a beautiful night. "Everything we use is intense and extreme," Broadrick says, "because that's the only thing we can relate to, is extremities." As they're being interviewed, a car happens by with "South of Heaven" by Slayer blaring from its speakers. Everybody has an appreciative laugh.

GROTESQUE (2009),
AKA GUROTESUKU
(DIR. KOJI SHIRAISHI; W/TSUGUMI NAGASAWA, HIROAKI KAWATSURE, SHIGEO OSAKO)
✳ JAPANESE HORROR ✳ TORTURE PORN
✳ CENSORSHIP

Just as the pseudo-snuff *Guinea Pig* film series represented Japanese cinema's reaction to and ante upping of '80s slasher movies, *Grotesque* is the Land of the Rising Sun's definitive weighing-in on 2000s torture-porn horror. Do not gorge yourself on sushi prior to viewing.

A mad doctor (Shigeo Osako) kidnaps, rapes, and horrifically abuses Aki (Tsugumi Nagasawa) and Kazuo (Hiroaki Kawatsure). That's all that happens. The devil is in Grotesque's vile creativity and surgically presented details. A final travail, in which the maimed young man must walk across a room while a hook unravels his intestines, plays out like a gurgling slam death metal album cover.

Guinea Pig came into a world where such rank sado-horror was easily mistaken for actual crime footage. A quarter century later, long since Marilyn Manson and Slipknot brought true satanic decadence and death metal's homicidal hate to T-shirt stores at your local mall, *Grotesque* embodies the adjustments necessary to remain heavy.

Suitably, *Grotesque* remains banned in the archetypal heavy metal strongholds of England and Norway. The head of the British Board of Film Classification tore down *Grotesque* with a fervor unappreciated since Tipper Gore took on the Mentors in 1985. "Unlike other recent 'torture'-themed horror works, such as *Saw* and the *Hostel* series," he said, "*Grotesque* features minimal narrative or character development and presents the audience with little more than an unrelenting and escalating scenario of humiliation, brutality and sadism." He's not wrong.

GROWING UP METAL
(2007)
(DIR. BRANDON FARIS; W/CHRISTIAN MCELFRESH, CHRISTINE MCELFRESH, DANNY MCELFRESH)
✳ METAL REALITY

Meet the McElfreshes. Long-haired Nordic dad Danny and hot rocker mom Christine are lead guitarist and frontwoman, respectively, of chugging Cincinnati metal squad Wicked Intent. Their young adult son Christian is the main focus of the seven-minute documentary *Growing*

Up Metal. The short offers an intriguing glimpse into what seems to be a happy family life studded with black T-shirts, late-night practice sessions, and Christian's little brothers and sisters composing original songs such as "Hush, Little Rock Star." Christian talks about being in his mother's womb at a Bon Jovi concert and possibly headbanging. Alert to anyone under forty: Bon Jovi started out as "heavy metal." Ever wanted to see a death metal Chris Farley? Check out Wicked Intent bassist Ryan Hamman.

GUINEA PIG 2: FLOWER OF FLESH AND BLOOD

(1985), AKA SLOW DEATH: THE DISMEMBERMENT

(DIR. HIDESHI HINO; W/HIROSHI TAMURA, KIRARA YUGAO)

✠ EXTREME HORROR ✠ SNUFF ✠ SACRIFICE

Consider the extremes to which Japan has pushed heavy metal, from the druggy guitar heroics of Speed, Glue & Shinki to the hairhopped power of Loudness to the blackened thrash of Sabbat to the stoner rock of Boris to the avant-garde electronic mercilessness of Merzbow to the visual kei insanity of Nightmare, among many, many other variations, tangents, and breaking developments. Now imagine how the Japanese responded to increasingly gruesome and explicit horror in the mid-'80s. The goal, actually, of Japan's landmark *Guinea Pig* film series was to not allow you to just imagine anything: here, at last, was unblinking exposure to the most relentless sadism of which the human psyche could conceive and the most unbearable physical agony that the human body could endure and then some.

The inaugural entry, best known as *Guinea Pig: Devil's Experiment* (1985), is forty-three minutes of up-close unpleasantness as a group of men capture a young woman and subject her to beatings, burnings, fingernail removal, insect infestation, and a horrendously real-looking needle

through the eyeball. She doesn't make it.

Guinea Pig 2: A Flower of Flesh and Blood is a step up cinematically, but a step or two away from the "you-are-there" uneasiness of its predecessor. A loon in a samurai suit (Hiroshi Tamura) chloroforms an innocent nubile (Kirara Yugao), ties her to a mattress, and does what paying customers of films like this one hope he will. The killer sacrifices a chicken over his prey, then steadily removes parts of the live girl's body until it no longer resembles a body, nor is she alive.

Even when I first saw it on a bootleg VHS, *Flower of Flesh and Blood* was followed by *The Making of Guinea Pig*, an hour-long documentary (full 25 percent longer than either of the films themselves) about the fluid-squirting latex effects involved. Seeing actress Kirara Yugao alive and giggling on the set, especially as technicians are wiring her body to gush fluids in ever direction, doesn't come so much as a relief as add to the Japanese weirdness of the *Guinea Pig* enterprise.

Guinea Pig 2 became especially notorious in 1991 when Hollywood star Charlie Sheen—he of the Tiger Blood and all that—somehow got a copy of the movie, believed it was an actual snuff film, and turned it over to the FBI. The feds poked around and let the *Anger Management* actor know that Kirara Yugao remained intact and ambulatory over in Japan.

GUMMO (1997)

(DIR. HARMONY KORINE; W/CHLOE SEVIGNY, JACOB SEWELL, JACOB REYNOLDS, LINDA MANZ)

✠ SATANIC RITUALS ✠ GLUE SNIFFING
✠ SOUNDTRACK (ABSU, BETHLEHEM, BURZUM, BRUJERIA, DARK NOERD, DESTROY ALL MONSTERS, EYEHATEGOD, NIFELHEIM, SLEEP, SPAZZ)

Writer-director Harmony Korine's white-trash-magorical scum-dream *Gummo* spellbinds and sickens in roughly equal amounts, and almost always simultaneously. This is a sustained Heavy Metal Movie masterpiece made by an asshole who, if he were any less of an asshole, could not have created this specific Heavy Metal

Movie, let alone any kind of masterpiece.

Bunny Boy (Jacob Sewell) wears floppy pink ears and wanders about tornado-doomed Xenia, Ohio, engaging in antisocial behavior whose deadpan instances serve as the town's sole outlet for socializing. Teen creeps grope and grind, slutty sisters duct-tape their nipples, Satanic rituals honor the Unholy Father, and kids say the filthiest, most loathsome things—and then do them.

One recurring storyline in *Gummo* concerns Mohawk-adorned, mutant-faced kid Solomon (Jacob Reynolds), who, with an air rifle, hunts stray cats to sell to a Chinese restaurant. Solomon's strongest on-screen moments involve him "working out" under the supervision of his gravel-voiced mom (Linda Manz) using taped-together silverware as dumbbells, and then joyfully consuming a plate of spaghetti while submerged in the black water of a filth-basted bathtub.

Gummo's other eye-punches include a boy pimping his Down's syndrome–afflicted sister; a hesher horde beating a chair into splinters with fantastically hilarious unhinged enthusiasm; skinhead siblings boxing in a kitchen; and Korine making a cameo as a horny sad-sack coming on hard to a disinterested black dwarf. Underscoring these and other float-by visions of casual cruelty is a perfectly selected and arranged soundtrack that functions as a brilliant snapshot of extreme metal circa 1997. The songs of *Gummo* range from the marijuana stomp of Sleep and brute-sludge of Eyehategod to the blackened Norse fury of Burzum and Nifelheim to the industrial death orgy of Electric Hellfire Club.

Harmony Korine is one of the most easy to dislike cinema provocateurs. Do yourself a profound favor and avoid him in the 2008 black metal documentary *Until the Light Takes Us*. Korine struck and masterfully crafted freak-show gold with *Gummo*, though—a feat he could not replicate until *Spring Breakers* (2013). Lightning does strike twice on occasion—ride it when it happens.

Hack Job (2011)

(Dir. James Balsamo; w/James Balsamo, Lynn Lowry, Debbie Rochon, Oderus Urungus)

❋ Satan ❋ Televangelists ❋ Soundtrack
(F.K.Ü, Ghoul, Satan's Host)

Hack Job tempts a lot of fate with its title. A pair of dorks named "Argento" and "Fulci" sell their souls to Satan to make the ultimate fright film. The Dark Lord gives them a screenplay containing three scenarios that we see play out. Nazis fight mummies. An alien crashes a battle of the bands and eats the musicians. A guy is possessed by a spirit commanding him to kill televangelists. The never-amusing Lloyd Kaufman, president of Troma Films, yuks it up as a comical rabbi. His career-long anti-funny streak remains intact. The music is dominated by horror punk and psychobilly from the likes of the Koffin Kats, the Hellbound Hepcats, and Bloodsucking Zombies From Outer Space. For sure, this horror-comedy anthology does not present itself as anything more than what it is. Gwar frontman Oderus Urungus cameos, and '70s drive-in goddess Lynn Lowry and power-lunged scream queen Debbie Rochon fleetingly manage to class everything up.

Hack-O-Lantern (1988),
aka Halloween Night
(Dir. Jag Mundhra; w/Gregory Scott Cummins, Katina Garner, Hy Pyke)

✷ Halloween ✷ Satanic Cult ✷ Antichrist

Hack-O-Lantern relates the thorny tale of teen-age Tommy (Gregory Scott Cummins), a Deep South metalhead with square siblings, a clueless mom (Katina Garner), and a Grandpa (Hy Pyke) that will make your flesh crawl. Gramps not only conducts satanic rituals in the family barn, he incinerates Tommy's dad alive for interrupting the black magic process. The bulk of the local townsfolk rank among devotees of the old man's diabolical cult, and they signal their membership frequently—and rather hilariously—by flashing devil horns as they pass by one another while going about their local dullsville business.

With Halloween approaching, Tommy is yanked away from dreaming up music videos for Seattle hair-glammers D. C. Lacroix to learn that he's the result of an incestuous union between Grandpa and his mom, the unholy fruit of an act they committed to usher in the age of the Antichrist. Guess what that makes Tommy?

Hack-O-Lantern could only exist on VHS, and will forever embody the late-decade, end-of-the-first-generation of semi-homemade fright flicks that '80s headbangers rented and re-rented and perhaps "dubbed" for their private files, getting a little unexpectedly chilled by its amateur attempts at communicating evil. Also add points for Hack-O-Lantern's pipe-organ musical score.

The importance of the female-fronted (so not surprisingly Kim Fowley–affiliated) Medusa Records stars D. C. Lacroix to *Hack-O-Lantern* shouldn't be underplayed. At one point, the movie stops, the band does their thing, and then we're back to the apocalyptic matters at hand. During a moment of frustration, Tommy tunes out his nagging mom by popping in a D. C. Lacroix cassette, closing his eyes, and fantasizing a full-blown MTV clip for his favorite Pacific

Northwest poodle-coif squad and their non-hit "The Devil's Child." In this music video reverie, the protagonist is a dark-skinned Eastern goddess figure whose multiple arms seem to belong to different races, maybe even genders. She shoots lasers from her eyes that blow up each band member; then the destroyer deity jams a trident into Tommy's jugular and his whole head comes off. That's some fantasy!

Director Jag Mundhra was a Bollywood vet who cranked out this and the Adrienne Barbeau slasher flick *Open House* (1987) almost immediately upon hitting Hollywood. Mundhra soon pioneered the "erotic thriller" genre, making R-rated, skin-packed suspense films that actually played theaters before hitting late-night cable TV.

For all of *Hack-O-Lantern*'s hackiness, Hy Pyke is unnerving as Grandpa. Best known as replicant Taffey Lewis in *Blade Runner* (1982), Pyke also played a weird bus driver in *Lemora: A Child's Tale of the Supernatural* (1973) and was Sancho Panza in soft-core musical *The Amorous Adventures of Don Quixote and Sancho Panza* (1976).

Halloween (1978)
(Dir. John Carpenter; w/Jamie Lee Curtis, Donald Pleasence, P. J. Soles, Nancy Loomis, Tony Moran)

✷ Slasher

Writer-director John Carpenter reinvented horror in its entirety with *Halloween*, melding Hitchcock-level suspense with his own fluid visual storytelling. The familiar story opens with a 1963 Halloween night double knifing viewed through the eyes of six-year-old killer Michael Myers (Will Sandin) in a single, bravura, career-making tracking shot. Exactly fifteen years later, the adult Myers (Tony Moran) escapes from a mental hospital and returns to his childhood home, where virginal Laurie (Jamie Lee Curtis) is babysitting. After dispatching Laurie's teen friends in nearby houses, Michael moves in to finish the kill. Dr. Sam Loomis (Donald Pleasence), Michael's medical caretaker, thwarts the final slaughter—temporarily, it turns out.

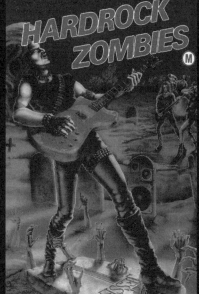

HARDROCK ZOMBIES

They came back from the grave to rock and rave and misbehave!

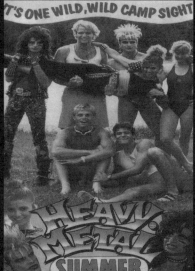

IT'S ONE WILD, WILD CAMP SIGHT

HEAVY METAL SUMMER

Clockwise from top left: *Silver Shamrock's shock stock* in Halloween III *(1982);* Hard Rock Zombies *(1985)* "came back from the grave to rock and rave and misbehave"; *Satan is a Swede in* Häxan *(1922);* The Howling *still (1981);* Heavy Metal Summer *(1988)aka* State Park

This plot would be duplicated endlessly throughout the '80s slasher movies. A handful of imitative classics emerged in this surprise blockbuster's direct wake. So did several dozen enjoyable variations, and countless dud rip-offs. Jamie Lee Curtis starred in some from each category! None of *Halloween*'s spawn could claim John Carpenter's directorial genius. No moment is as simultaneously chilling and cool as when masked Michael Myers pegs a guy to a kitchen wall with a carving knife and then, slowly, inquisitively, tilts his head from side to side, studying his work.

Just as NWOBHM is called "classic metal played with punk attitude," *Halloween* is rooted in the terrifying emotional mastery of Alfred Hitchcock and visual virtuosity of Orson Welles, but revved up with the hammer-pounding intensity of *Night of the Living Dead* (1968) and *The Texas Chain Saw Massacre* (1974). Old meets recent, original element gets added, and an entire form is reborn. Well into the 1990s, *Halloween* ruled as the most profitable independent film ever made.

Carpenter's original title was *The Babysitter Murders*, a killer name for a drive-in movie; but I have to think that had *Halloween* been released under that moniker, it never would have been championed so loudly by audiences, let alone critics. Across the board, *Halloween*'s sequels reek. The lone exception: *Halloween III: Season of the Witch* (1982), which does not involve Michael Myers.

The most harrowing musical moment happens when Laurie and Annie (Nancy Loomis) tool around town in a VW bug toking a joint, while Blue Öyster Cult's "Don't Fear the Reaper" plays pointedly on the car radio.

HALLOWEEN (2007)

(DIR. ROB ZOMBIE; W/MALCOLM MCDOWELL, SCOUT TAYLOR-COMPTON, TYLER MANE, WILLIAM FORSYTHE, SHERI MOON ZOMBIE)

✶ SLASHER ✶ SOUNDTRACK (ALICE COOPER, BLUE ÖYSTER CULT, KISS, THE MISFITS, RUSH)

In what could be termed *Michael Myers: The Biopic*, Rob Zombie's *Halloween* remake supplies insight to the man behind all those murders (and that famous emotionless white spray-painted William Shatner mask). Beginning with Michael Myers' abusive childhood at the fists and taunts of a stripper mom (Sheri Moon Zombie), white-trash stepdad (William Forsythe), and a school bully (Daryl Sabara), Zombie creates pathos for the killer, who goes on his first slaying spree at age ten. We then see psychiatric hospital pediatrician Dr. Sam Loomis (Malcolm McDowell) attempt to emotionally connect with Myers for fifteen years, but the patient remains silent. He communicates only by making and wearing a series of masks. When Michael is an adult (played by Taylor Mane), he escapes and returns home—where all those babysitters are just giggling and goofing around like sitting ducks on Halloween night. *White Zombie*, the 1932 spooker from which the director's former band got its name, plays on a background TV. Loomis, of course, gives chase.

The first part of this *Halloween* is all Zombie's invention; the latter is largely a retelling of John Carpenter's 1978 original. The nurse Michael kills is played by '80s B-movie goddess Sybil Danning (*Chained Heat*, *They're Playing With Fire*). As always, Rob Zombie directs with a clenched fist, and the screen boils with the blood of its creator—as well as that of more than a few victims of Michael Myers.

HALLOWEEN II (2009)

(DIR. ROB ZOMBIE; W/MALCOLM MCDOWELL, SCOUT TAYLOR-COMPTON, TYLER MANE, SHERI MOON ZOMBIE, BRAD DOURIF)

✶ SLASHER ✶ SOUNDTRACK (BAD BRAINS, DIAMOND HEAD, MC5, MOTÖRHEAD, SCREAM, VOID)

With *Halloween II*, Rob Zombie creates a brand-new story to follow his 2007 *Halloween* remake, adding elements of psychedelia, mythology, satirical barbs aimed at celebrity doctor culture, and severe mommy issues. A year after the events of the previous film, Laurie Strode (Scout Taylor-Compton) suffers nightmares about her run-in with Michael Myers (Tyler Mane), while Dr. Loomis works the talk-show circuit shilling his book on the case. Michael, of course, is on the loose, fired up by visions of his mother (Sheri Moon Zombie) astride a snow-colored stallion instructing him to find Laurie and "bring her home"—you know, with a knife. Any and all who stand in his way must be savagely dispatched.

Michael loses his mask and, for the only time in the entire *Halloween* series, walks around fully visible without it. Mother Myers's transformation from white-trash stripper to angel in white, which corresponds with Dr. Loomis morphing from a concerned pediatrician to an exploitative hack, are measures of *Halloween II*'s hallucinatory tone and warped point of view. Zombie's first *Halloween* humanized Michael Myers with a backstory. This sequel makes us a part of his nightmare.

Halloween III: Season of the Witch (1982)

(Dir. Tommy Lee Wallace; w/Tom Atkins, Stacey Nelkin, Dan O'Herlihy, Dick Warlock)

✡ Pagans ✡ Witchcraft ✡ Human Sacrifice ✡ Evil Corporations

Commercials for the Silver Shamrock mask company play an infectious jingle: "Five more days till Hall-o-ween, Hall-o-ween, Hall-o-ween / Sil-ver Sham-rock!" The company is selling three incredibly cool masks—a skull, a witch, and a jack-o-lantern. All seems candy-corn perfect in Silver Shamrock's base town of Santa Mira, California, until dapper assassins, self-immolation, and the murder of the local gag shop owner portend something far more tricky than treat-y.

Halloween III: Season of the Witch exposes a conspiracy in which Silver Shamrock honcho Conal Cochran (Dan O'Herlihy) taps into the bloodletting Samhain ritual of his Irish roots by implanting each mask he sells with a piece of Stonehenge itself. He has actually transported the ancient site to the basement of his factory, somehow erecting impostor rocks back in England. On Halloween night, a special Silver Shamrock commercial will trigger the occult magic contained in the Stonehenge sliver, causing the head of every kid wearing a mask to explode in a mess of spiders and snakes. Tom Atkins, as Dr. Dan Challis, makes a great hero who aims to thwart Silver Shamrock's Samhain shenanigans. Dan O'Herlihy makes an even greater villain. *Halloween III* combines sci-fi, horror, and Celtic witchery to create an unholy holiday favorite that is—like what happens to the tyke in the mask—completely mind-blowing.

The first shock of *Halloween III: Season of the Witch* occurred when ads turned up on TV and fans of the previous two films pieced together that this installment would not feature super-slasher Michael Myers. There was outrage. There was despair. And then everyone went to see the movie anyway, and it was an instant classic that stands head and scary rubber faces above other *Halloween* follow-ups. Series creators John Carpenter and Debra Hill, in fact, only agreed to carry on with *Halloween* movies if each one featured a wholly new, unrelated story. Given *Halloween III*'s initial lackluster box office, the idea was abandoned. This is a shame.

Producer Moustapha Akkad revived the franchise by bringing back Michael Myers for *Halloween 4* (1988) and *Halloween 5* (1989). Those films have their devotees. Director Tommy Lee Wallace went on to make the monstrous Stephen King ABC mini-series *It* (1990).

Hard Ride to Hell (2010)

(Dir. Penelope Buitenhuis; w/Miguel Ferrer, Katharine Isabelle, Laura Mennell, Brent Stait)

✡ Bikers ✡ Human Sacrifice ✡ Torture

This arousing and occult-spiked modern B-take on *The Hills Have Eyes* (1977) dodges the fatal mistake of too many self-aware, post-Tarantino Red Box rentals: cowriter-director Penelope Buitenhuis plays it straight. College-age do-gooders drive an RV through remote Texas and run afoul of Babylon-worshipping cannibal bikers. Jefé (George Clooney's cousin Miguel Ferrer), their one-eyed honcho, is seriously depleting the local nubile young female population in search of an ideal vessel for his heir. He finds her in the corruptible form of Tessa (Laura Mennell). Special forces vet turned cutlery salesman Bob (Brent Stait) arrives, though, to sever the family line.

Ferrer has a clear blast as Jefé, the look and presence of the bikers is a riot, and there's a real sense of danger supplied by the cast and filmmakers. *Hard Ride to Hell* is a horrific hoot. In flashback, Jefé reveals the jerk who cost him his eye: no less a metal icon than sorcerer supreme Aleister Crowley (Mackenzie Gray), through a bloody bit of time-bending black magic.

Hard Rock Nightmare

(1988)

(DIR. DOMINICK BRASCIA; W/GREG JOUJON-ROCHE, ANNIE MIKAN, LISA ELAINA, TROY DONAHUE)
✵ WEREWOLF ✵ FAKE BAND (THE BAD BOYS)

Rock and roll group the Bad Boys venture to a woodland cabin to lay down their latest tracks, but when a werewolf disrupts their jam sessions, it turns into a real . . . *Hard Rock Nightmare!* That's the premise and about all there is to this lost pseudo-slasher flick. The Bad Boys are more bar band than hard rock, let alone heavy metal. Given the timing, I believe the film's title is actually a subdued-to-the-point-of-sleepwalking rip-off of the mighty and magnificent Thor vehicle *Rock-'N'-Roll Nightmare* (1987). I also really love the name of the actor who plays Bad Boy Sammy: Robert D. Peverley.

Hard Rock Zombies

(1985)

(DIR. KRISHNA SHAH; W/E. J. CURSE, SAM MANN, JENNIFER COE, PHIL FONDACARO, JACK BLIESENER)
✵ EVIL DWARVES ✵ NAZIS ✵ ZOMBIES

The Year of Our Dark Lord 1985 serves as dramatic a line in the evolution of heavy metal

as any other. On one cloven hoof, 1985 yielded Slayer's *Hell Awaits*, Celtic Frost's *To Mega Therion*, and Iron Maiden's *Live After Death*, in addition to the Black Sabbath and Led Zep reunions at Live Aid. Then, from atop the bald mountain known as Capitol Hill, senator's wife Tipper Gore organized an uncool-mom anti-metal coven known as the Parents Music Resource Center and pronounced herself Head Harpy in Charge. In the context of 1985, then, *Hard Rock Zombies* not only makes sense but seems inevitable.

A traveling four-piece band identified by a stencil on their van as Holy Moses rocks a bar made out of spare lumber and black spray paint. They look like a party-store version of Manowar and sound like a dentist's office version of Journey. And they kind of break-dance. Post-gig, the group poses backstage with some of the least plaster-cast-inspiring groupies ever assembled, and from there, it's off to the next gig in a bucolic hamlet called Grand Guignol.

Virginal young Cassie (Jennifer Coe) stops the rockers in their tracks and advises them to keep driving, warning, "THEY don't want you there!" She also clearly takes a shine to mullet-skulled lead singer Jessie (E. J. Curse), and good luck taking your eyes off her rabid-caterpillar eyebrows, each of which easily dwarfs the frontman's entire *Magnum P.I.* mustache. The "THEY" she means are Grand Guignol's assemblage of locals who, when read as a list, promise a far greater experience than any film, let alone *Hard Rock Zombies*, would be capable of delivering. Regardless, here goes: two evil dwarves in tuxedoes (one of whom has a literal rubber face), a hitchhiking blonde bombshell who thrill-kills naked, somebody's werewolf grandmother locked in an attic, various mute perverts, and Hitler. Yes, Hitler. THEY are all Nazis, too, even the poor dwarves. And that's only in the joint where the band shacks up!

Elsewhere, the citizenry is represented by a town council comprised of a redneck sheriff, a madcap professor, an ancient Methuselah with a plastic beard, and as motley a gaggle of extras ever ordered to sit in folding chairs and act incensed, all of whom unite to ban rock and roll. Our long-haired heroes, naturally, are gorily dispatched by Grand Guignolians, only to rise from some hilariously shallow graves after Cassie plays a cassette of occult chanting over a semi-Sabbath-sounding bass line. The band members, transformed now into zombie marauders, spend the rest of the movie exacting revenge. And kind of break-dancing.

Again, consider the atmosphere from which *Hard Rock Zombies* emerged. In 1985, to love metal was to be under fire. The year even ended on that tragically literal note when Judas Priest fans James Vance and Ray Belknap punctuated their playground *Stained Class* listening party with a couple of shotgun blasts to their own kissers. Rather than piss and moan, though, *Hard Rock Zombies* demonstrates the metalhead's drive to rock on—live after death indeed—no matter how stupid, ridiculous, and desperate his would-be oppressors may be. And while the movie is to be commended for that moxie and for never teetering over into the insulting self-consciousness of Troma Films, the terms *stupid*, *ridiculous*, and *desperate* will never be out of place in any *Hard Rock Zombies* review. Take that as an endorsement.

Hard Rock Zombies was originally a twenty-minute segment of the goofwad farce *American Drive-In* (1985). Specifically, it was meant to be the movie the crowd watched on the outdoor screen. Investors saw such potential in the tribulations of Holy Moses, though, that they backed this entirely separate movie. Mumbai, India–born director Krishna Shah started on Broadway and wrote for TV before helming *Hard Rock Zombies*. He later produced numerous art flicks and B-movies, including *Sleepaway Camps II* and *III*. Diminutive costar Phil Fondacaro is one of the hardest-working little people in show business. His other signature roles include Torok the Troll in *Troll* (1986), Greaser Greg in *The Garbage Pail Kids Movie* (1987), and Cousin Itt in *Addams Family Reunion* (1988)

HARDBODIES (1984)

(DIR. MARK GRIFFITHS; W/GRANT CRAMER, COURTNEY GAINS, TEAL ROBERTS, DARCY DEMOSS, VIXEN)

✠ Bikinis ✠ Hair Metal

Scotty Palmer (Grant Cramer) rules Muscle Beach, California. What this smooth-talking babe magnet can't do, though, is pay his rent. Stumbling onto the sand come three shlubby, middle-aged disasters hoping to score big-time bikini candy. Enter Scotty as their high-priced pickup guru. Accompanied by his spaz best bud Rag (Courtney Gains), Scotty moves into the clueless trio's sweet seaside pad, runs afoul of his hot but uptight lady love Kristi (Teal Roberts), and plans a monstrous, utterly mind-roasting house party with the all-girl hard rock band Diaper Rash—but, first, he changes the group's name to . . . Hardbodies!

With way more exposed female flesh than is typical even for its boob-and-pube-driven genre, *Hardbodies* stands out proud and hard. The script is also, along with *Screwballs* (1984), noteworthy for its anarchic, any-joke-is-possible approach to comedy. Running amok among various unclothed bathing beauties is a dog trained to snatch bikini tops. Both male leads don drag in separate scenes. A big fat party animal in a "Boogie Till You Puke" shirt blasts 45 Grave's "Party Time" from his boom box (long before the song became the de facto theme of *Return of the Living Dead*). Ultimately, the hero escapes danger on a motorized surfboard and communes with seals.

While rehearsing in a garage, the Hardbodies band performs the highly topical "Computer Madness" ("You pulled the plug!") before the movie cuts to them rocking "Maria" and "Be With Me" at Scotty's surfside swing house. On the beach for the hardbody contest, they play "Mr. Cool." In real life, the Hardbodies rapidly evolved into Vixen and scored a few MTV hits at the mousse-imbued height of hair metal mania, the biggest being "Edge of a Broken Heart." Who knows how huge that might have gotten had they just stuck with the name Hardbodies? The entire beach tableau functions as a reminder of the airhead side of the sleazy L.A. glam scene happening down the Strip.

As with the mighty *Preppies* (1984), *Hardbodies* was made to air on the Playboy Channel, but producers knew they had dynamite on their hands at the height of teen sex comedy craze, and so flung it into theaters. This same year, Courtney Gains made Heavy Metal Movie history as Malachi, the slayer, in *Children of the Corn*. Gains should be worshipped for that role, but it's hard to top his demonstrations here of how to flip someone off in every language known to man.

Hardware (1990)

(Dir. Richard Stanley; w/Dylan McDermott, Stacey Travis, Iggy Pop, Lemmy Kilmister)

✠ Post-Apocalypse ✠ Killer Cameos
✠ Soundtrack (Motörhead, Ministry, Iggy Pop)

South African cinema fantasist Richard Stanley broke through with *Hardware*, a post-nuke sci-fi horror hybrid that mutates a 1950s robot-run-amok premise into an end-of-the-millennium exercise in brutality. In the nuke-ravaged twenty-first century, a returning soldier (Dylan McDermott) buys a disembodied robot head for his sculptor girlfriend (Stacey Travis). Once attached to more metal, the robot becomes sentient and builds a body for itself out of other sculptures; the machine's indestructible, insatiably kill-crazy nature quickly becomes gorily evident.

The plot of *Hardware* is simple. The movie's style and execution elevate it to A-level B-movie glory. Check out Lemmy as a whiskey-swilling, gun-toting water taxi driver. Listen for Iggy Pop as W.A.R.-radio deejay "Angry Bob." Watch for Gwar performing on a TV set, but listen to the music that comes out—it's actually Ministry. From its title to its hyperviolence to its cameos, *Hardware* is iron-knuckles-to-the-skull metal.

Richard Stanley built his reputation making high-impact music videos, including some for Marillion and Fields of Nephilim. He cowrote and began directing the notorious 1996 *Island of Dr. Moreau* remake with Marlon Brando. He was fired four days into shooting, then snuck back on to the set, and remained there, wearing a dog-man costume.

Hated: GG Allin & the Murder Junkies (1994)

(Dir. Todd Phillips; GG Allin, Dee Dee Ramone, Geraldo Rivera)

✠ Metal Reality ✠ Obsession ✠ Poop

Jesus Christ Allin—better known, whether you wanted to or not, as GG Allin—was a dope-addled psychopath who fronted various metallic punk bands and sang love songs about AIDS-infected rapists and serial slayers. He physically pulverized audiences, publicly flaunted what may be the smallest penis ever photographed, and, most notoriously, routinely stopped his shows to defecate and consume his own waste product (and that of others)—and then fling the leftovers.

Such an unprecedented shock factor kept Allin infamous for years. He appeared on Geraldo Rivera's afternoon trash-TV gabfest in 1992. As once noted by GG's beloved Howard Stern—who absolutely refused to allow this menace in his studio—"he had something; there was something there to what he was doing."

GG's combination of literal shit-show and more profound provocation attracted NYU film student Todd Phillips to make the documentary *Hated: GG Allin & the Murder Junkies*. Phillips also lucked into being around for the immediate aftermath of GG's ultimate stunt in June 1993: causing a semi-riot at an outdoor gig in New York City, then overdosing on heroin and dying like a dog in a junkie hellhole.

As a movie, *Hated* is no great shakes. As a gross-out subject nonpareil, GG Allin is pure brown gold. The film presents interviews and performances spiked with lowlife highlights such as GG drinking piss at a party and puking it back up. For years prior to *Hated*, GG plumbed the depths of testing how much stink, abuse, and violation audiences could take. The movie offers more of the same, only better lit. Plus, *Hated* includes footage of GG's hilariously irreverent funeral.

Dee Dee Ramone testifies to GG's talents, and Allin is likewise lauded as a truly irredeemable Iggy Pop by members of confrontational punk-metal genre-fuckers Antiseen, Eyehategod, and the Dwarves. *Hated* served to expand GG's post-humous legend as a violently transgressive hate guru that endures still; GG Allin bobbleheads are now available for sale. His songs have been covered by numerous metal acts, including Faith No More, Queens of the Stone Age, and Watain.

The film launched Todd Phillips en route to Hollywood heavy-hitter status, as he went on to direct *Road Trip* (2000), *Old School* (2003), and all three *Hangover* movies. Phillips, clearly, has always had an eye for kooky characters.

The Haunted World of El Superbeasto

(2009)

(Dir. Rob Zombie; w/Tom Papa, Rosario Dawson, Cassandra Peterson, Paul Giamatti)
✶ **Medical Deviant** ✶ **Nazi Zombies**

Rob Zombie's antic animated lark *The Haunted World of El Superbeasto* took three years to complete, features characters from his live-action films (Sid Haig as Captain Spaulding, Bill Moseley as Otis Driftwood, Paul Giamatti as Dr. Satan), and boasts more cartoon boobs and bloodletting than any single production since 1981's original *Heavy Metal*.

The title character (Tom Papa) is a former Mexican wrestler turned exploitation movie star. He teams with his sexy, eye-patch-adorned sister Suzi X (Sheri Moon Zombie) to thwart the diabolical Dr. Satan from conquering the world by marrying super-stripper Velvet Von Black (Rosario Dawson), who bears a 666 birthmark on her butt. Zombie himself has described *El*

Superbeasto as being "like if SpongeBob and Scooby-Doo were filthy." Among the off-Hollywood icons in the skewed voice cast: Cassandra Peterson (aka Elvira), Ken Foree (*Dawn of the Dead*), Danny Trejo (*Machete*), Laraine Newman (*Saturday Night Live*), and Dee Wallace (*E.T.* and *Cujo*). Tura Satana reprises her role as Varla from *Faster, Pussycat! Kill! Kill!* (1965). Heavy metal comedian Brian Posehn voices Suzi X's robot sidekick, Murray.

Häxan: Witchcraft Through the Ages (1922)

(Dir. Benjamin Christensen; w/Benjamin Christensen, Clara Pontoppidan, Oscar Stribolt)
✶ **Satan** ✶ **Black Mass** ✶ **Nunsploitation**
✶ **Inquisition** ✶ **Scandinavian Darkness**

Six decades before Bathory raised hell on vinyl, Scandinavia satanically scandalized movie screens via *Häxan* ("The Witches"). Writer-director-star Benjamin Christensen's multipart history of black magic, devil worship, and its Christian combatants made a staggering $3 million in 1922. Christensen took inspiration from *Malleus Maleficarum*, a fifteenth-century German witch-hunting handbook, but in no way did he want to merely adapt it for the screen. "I seek to find a way forward to original films," he said.

What an original vision *Häxan* turned out to be. Divided into four parts, the film begins with classical depictions of witches and demons in medieval culture. Part two dramatizes early beliefs of the powers of Satan to corrupt women. Part three depicts a witch trial. The concluding segment takes us to modern times, where what was once believed to be the work of the devil is now recognized as mental illness.

Christensen was a major theatrical and visual artist, and *Häxan* is his thrilling, media-transforming masterwork. With garish resplendence—nuns run wild, fallen women fly on demon wings—the movie evokes the excitement of sin and sorcery, as well as the horror of false accusations and all-too-real inquisitions. Every frame is brilliantly realized. *Häxan*'s highlight is a still-mesmerizing trip to hell itself, a rambunctious inferno of torturers and the tormented, exquisitely rendered with massive sets, wondrous costumes, and extras—some of them, shockingly, nude—gnashing and wailing and flailing as though full-on possessed by Old Scratch for real.

Like the deepest occult heavy metal, *Häxan* is a celebration of things which, historically, have spooked humanity most—the possibility of evil personified as a force beyond our control, and the damnable acts of those who try to control it anyway. Christensen himself appears as *Häxan*'s famous, flat-faced Satan (he always sort of looked like a monkey to me), as well as Jesus Christ during a segment set in heaven.

In 1968, *Häxan* was reissued for American stoner audiences as *Witchcraft Through the Ages*, featuring narration by author William S. Burroughs and a jazz score by Daniel Humair and Jean-Luc Ponty. This version remained on the midnight-movie circuit well into the 1980s.

Heaven Can Help (1989)

(Dir. Tony Zarindast; w/Jinx Dawson, Tony Bova, Dianne Copeland, Diane Hayden)

✠ Satan ✠ Soundtrack (Coven)

The nearly-impossible-to-unearth satanic shocker *Heaven Can Help* stars Jinx Dawson—frontwoman of original occult rockers Coven—as Vyra, a witch who, after dying, cuts a devious deal with the Prince of Darkness. Landing in hell, Vyra asks for another shot up above; in exchange, she'll corrupt an innocent soul, damning her victim to eternal flames. Satan agrees, and he reincarnates the witch as a wicked-hot hard rock singer, not a huge leap for Jinx.

Cosmic conflict flares up when heaven dispatches an angel to battle Vyra. With her natural beauty and vibrant ice-demon charisma, Jinx would elevate *Heaven Can Help* to noteworthy metal status even without her Coven history and goth-queen anointment. The rock scenes, where she fronts a 1989 incarnation of Coven, are endearing. Jinx burns up the screen, though, during the black magic bits and in her final showdown with various agents of the afterlife.

Heaven Can Help was never released to the public, and it may not have even been officially finished. It's so rare it doesn't appear on director Tony Zarindast's IMDB page. It's tough to imagine that the maker of *Cat in the Cage* (1978), *Hardcase and Fist* (1981), and *Werewolf* (1995) would not want the one and only Jinx Dawson witch movie on his résumé.

Heavy Mental: A Rock-n-Roll Bloodbath (2009)

(Dir. Mike C. Hartman; w/Josh Hooper, Bart Allen Burger, Brenna Roth, Monique Dupree)

✠ Splatter ✠ Possessed Guitar

Gore gags, bare boobs, chicks making out, and some surprisingly proficient heavy metal are crammed into this camcorder-shot splatter comedy, made in Detroit and picked up for distribution by Troma Films. Hard rock hopeful Ace Spades (Josh Hooper) acquires a guitar possessed by a legendary heavy metal player, which he uses to wage comically hyperviolent warfare against the bikini-clad (and unclad) female assassins of local crime boss Mrs. Delicious (Brenna Roth). What you expect to go down, come off, and get squashed into bloody piles, all happens right there on-screen. Watch for a juicy cameo by Morbid Melvin (Adam Showers), an obese man-boy character from the local Detroit horror movie TV series *Wolfman Mac's Chiller Drive-In*.

Heavy Metal (1981)

(Dir. Gerald Potterton; w/John Candy, Joe Flaherty, Eugene Levy, Harold Ramis, Richard Romanus, John Vernon)

✠ Swords & Sorcery ✠ Dystopia ✠ Animation

With a theme song by the Eagles' Don Felder and prominent soundtrack selections by

Devo and Stevie Nicks, *Heavy Metal* looks more metal than it sounds, but it feels even more metal than it looks. This animated anthology of pornographically flesh-drenched, skull-crushingly hyperviolent science-fiction mind-blowers is as absolutely metal as movies get. This is the final destination in animation for monster-jugged nympho maidens, human sacrifice, hints of Chthulu, barbarian swordplay, fatal space exploration, robot-bimbo sex, furry alien narcotic use, and a way-out cartoon sequences set to Dio-era Black Sabbath, Blue Öyster Cult, and Grand Funk Railroad. Plus the main character is a sinister talking rock!

After an astronaut dad pilots a 1960 Corvette from his ship to earth, he's vaporized by a green meteorite he brought home for his young daughter. The luminous nugget verbally identifies itself as the sum of all evils and orders the little girl to look into its glow and watch replays of its intergalactic adventures. First up is "Harry Canyon," a comedic, film-noir saga of a New York City cab driver in 2031. He gets double-crossed by a two-bit dame who shows her two very big bits during a sex scene that would push anything but a cartoon into heavy XXX-territory.

Second, and most endearing, is John Candy as a high school nerd who awakens in a universe of '70s van-panel art come to life. He transforms into a naked muscleman named Den, and he immediately rescues a would-be virgin sacrifice. The grateful maiden thanks Den by making it impossible for her to requalify for that particular ritual. He also gets to bang an evil queen and royally waste whole armies of barbarians. *Heavy Metal* then careens into a couple of lesser segments, one involving the trial of an arrogant space station commander, and the other pitting a plane full of World War II air force fighters against zombification. The latter is actually pretty scary; very much the stuff of stoned metal lyricists.

Drugs figure more literally in "So Beautiful, So Dangerous," wherein a spacecraft beams up a mountain-mammaried Jewish American Princess, who promptly sleeps with an onboard robot, wanting to know if he'll get circumcised. Two goofy alien crew members, voiced by Harold Ramis and Eugene Levy, pour out yards upon yards of some kind of space-cocaine and then, after declaring, "Nosedive!" hoover up every flake through their elongated snouts. Listen for the convulsive laughter and watch for hysterical bodies rolling down the aisle to figure out who's on space dust in the theater with you.

The last segment, "Taarna," contains *Heavy Metal*'s signature imagery: the badonka-busted blonde warrior woman brandishing a broadsword atop some sort of pterodactyl who's famously pictured on the movie's poster. Turns out she's really good at fighting, and never more awesomely than during a major blowout underscored by Sabbath's "The Mob Rules." At the conclusion, the evil space rock explodes and the little girl hops on Taarna's space-bird. She grows long blonde hair, sprouts huge boobs, and flies away. Has there ever been a happier ending?

Heavy Metal started in 1977 as a comics-heavy adults-only fantasy magazine of the same name, itself an adaptation of a French publication with the impossibly cool title *Metal Hurlant* (Screaming Metal), which was imported to the U.S. by the heroic folks at *National Lampoon*. The big-screen version of *Heavy Metal* is a Canadian production overseen by *Lampoon*'s movie honchos Ivan Reitman (*Rabid*, *Stripes*, *Ghostbusters*) and Matty Simmons (*Animal House*). That explains why virtually the entire male cast of *SCTV* provides vocal talent. Also listen for John Vernon, Dean Wormer from *Animal House*, as a prosecutor. The future cabbie is voiced by Robert Romanus, who went on to play Damone in *Fast Times at Ridgemont High*.

In March 2008, *South Park* aired a *Heavy Metal* parody titled "Major Boobage." It took eight times as long to complete as an average *South Park* episode, and was the first one to be rated TVMA for "language, sexual situations, and violence." Talk has long burbled of a high-tech, all-star 3-D *Heavy Metal* sequel to be overseen by powerhouse moviemaker David Fincher (*Fight Club*, *The Social Network*). Among the A-list directors who volunteered to supply segments are James Cameron (*Avatar*), Zack Snyder (*300*), Guillermo del Toro (*Hellboy*) and Gore Verbinski (*Pirates of the Caribbean*). Bring it on!

Heavy Metal 2000
(2000), aka Heavy Metal: F.A.K.K.2—The Movie

(Dirs. Michael Coldewey, Michel Lemire; w/Julie Strain, Michael Ironside, Billy Idol, Sonja Ball)
✶ Space Sex ✶ Soundtrack (Apartment 26, Coal Chamber, Machine Head, Monster Magnet, Pantera, Puya, System of a Down)

The long-stalled follow-up to the genre-defining *Heavy Metal* (1981), *Heavy Metal 2000* is an animated showcase for larger-than-lust *Penthouse* Pet and comic book cult queen Julie Strain, who voices and provides the non-exaggerated physical model for the movie's superhumanly curvaceous heroine. *Heavy Metal 2000* doesn't work well as a stand-alone adult-oriented sci-fi cartoon, or as a sequel, or as the basis for a series of new *Heavy Metal* movies. Still, you get a lot of tits, monsters, and ridiculously gory and grotesque death in space, so fire up the bong, ease back, and enjoy.

Once again, a glowing green space rock makes a mess of things. This time, though, there's just one story and it's about how the rock transforms a miner named Tyler (Michael Ironside) into a monomaniacal population-killer. Tyler's rampage rouses the wrath of Julie (Julie Strain), and she pursues him through a universe of multi-boobed strippers, sex robots, lizard people, rock dwarves, and a mysterious guru named Odin (Billy Idol). In a nod to the original, the movie climaxes with Julie prepping for battle by repeating the ritual of Heavy Metal's Taarna, encasing her curvy body in skimpy, skintight leather and arming herself to the teats. *Heavy Metal* is a trip that fans can (and do) easily take two thousand times. *Heavy Metal 2000*, on the contrary, may as well have been titled *Heavy Metal One and Done*.

One glowing difference between the two *Heavy Metal* movies is in the actual metal content of their soundtracks. While the initial installment features Black Sabbath, Blue Öyster Cult, Nazareth, Sammy Hagar, Grand Funk Railroad, and Cheap Trick, it also donated tracks to Stevie Nicks, Donald Fagen of Steely Dan, and "Open Arms" by Journey. *Heavy Metal 2000*'s song selection is actual metal and hard rock, often with an appropriately industrial bent (even on the Insane Clown Posse number).

Heavy Metal auf dem Lande (2006), aka
Heavy Metal in the Country

(Dir. Andreas Geiger; w/Markus Staiger, Oliver Barth, Johannes Braun, Michael Siegl)
✶ Germany ✶ Metal Reality

The documentary *Heavy Metal Auf Dem Lande* studies the juxtaposition between the bucolic Southern Germany town of Donzdorf and the company for which it is most famous: the monstrous heavy metal record label Nuclear Blast. We learn the story of how local lad Markus Staiger founded the imprint in 1987, focusing on hardcore punk at first and then branching out into black metal, power metal, melodic death metal, prog metal, and grindcore. With the help of seemingly everyone in town, Staiger grew Nuclear Blast into the standard bearer of international excellence it is today.

Nuclear Blast is perfectly at home in Donzdorf, employing village housewives to handle mail order (in a funny scene, they deal with bloody skull promos), and hosting listening sessions at the corner pub. At a local outdoor festival, headbangers in full slaying metal gear joyfully mosh to a lederhosen-clad brass band. *Heavy Metal Auf Dem Lande* is a delightful slice of metal-as-normal-life made weird by its soft-spoken interview subjects and the pastoral backdrop of the Swabian mountains. There have to be trolls and witches and goblins up in those hills, right?

Heavy Metal Basement (2006)

(Dir. Jeff Krulik; w/Jim Powell, Jeff Krulik)

✠ Obsession

Jeff Krulik, creator of *Heavy Metal Parking Lot*, spelunks into the memorabilia-crammed Maryland basement of Metal Grind records honcho and *Grinder* zine publisher Jim Powell. The action consists of Krulik asking questions and Powell answering while showing off and talking about his records, cassettes, shirts, posters, laminates, toys, and—you name it, he's got it down there.

It's a zippy forty-nine minutes of treasure exploration guaranteed to amuse and inspire envy. Mr. Powell, to the surprise of no veteran headbanger, also boasts quite the tower of collectible beer cans. *Heavy Metal Basement* appears as a bonus feature on a *Heavy Metal Parking Lot* DVD released in 2007.

Heavy Metal Britannia (2010)

(Dir. Chris Rodley; w/Tony Iommi, Rob Halford, Bruce Dickinson, Lemmy Kilmister, Ian Gillan)

✠ British Metal

Heavy Metal Britannia is a homegrown documentary created by England's BBC Four channel, after similar efforts on Soul Britannia and Synth Britannia (which sort of says much about the priority that BBC Four ascribes to hard rock). The range spans from the 1960s, with proper attention paid to Arthur Brown, to the early '80s and the end of the New Wave of British Heavy Metal.

Much of the narrative in *Heavy Metal Britannia*'s brisk ninety minutes is well covered in other metal docs. Tony Iommi tells the story of losing his finger and creating the false tip from which he birthed the devil's tritone on "Black Sabbath." Rob Halford talks about growing up and breathing in literal heavy metal from nearby factories. Lemmy connects punk and speed (in every sense) to where Motörhead hurled the music. Discussions ensue about metal's connection to classical music and its longtime dearth of female followers and/or practitioners. You get the picture.

Footage of '70s headbangers carting paper and balsa-wood guitars to play along with the music at the legendary Soundhouse metal club, along with rare footage of Budgie, Saxon, Uriah Heep, and other UK powerhouses that go underrepresented in mainstream metal overviews, at least makes *Heavy Metal Britannia* sanguine and seaworthy. Also, the ever-cheery Geezer Butler of Black Sabbath nails the gulf between Carnaby Street pop and his own scary lot: "We came from Aston. There weren't a lot of flowers being handed out."

Heavy Metal in Baghdad (2007)

(Dirs. Suroosh Alvi, Eddy Moretti; w/Firas Al-Lateef, Marwan Reyad, Faisal Talal, Suroosh Alvi)

✠ World Metal

Shot on the literally explosive streets of Iraq in the wake of the 2003 U.S. military invasion, *Heavy Metal in Baghdad* documents the country's only aboveground metal band, Acrassicauda. They play for the devil in a land where the wrong black T-shirt can get you lynched and where simply being near the right mortar target at the wrong time can get you vaporized. A more dramatic demonstration of the rebellious nature of metal could not possibly exist.

Almost stumbling into Iraq by accident after being denied access to Iran, *Vice* magazine correspondents chronicle the tribulations of the members of the band as the country falls apart at their feet. Acrassicauda plays a show, a few dozen brave Iraqi headbangers show up to headbang in resistant solidarity, the power goes out, and the reality of Islamic fundamentalism on one hand and ballistic death from above on the other forces everyone to scatter again. As you'd expect, the drama creates itself. Band members are forced out of their homeland, and ultimately their practice space is blown to ribbons. The parting shot is a square kick in the nuts.

Acrassicauda more than acquits itself musically, playing a number of originals including "The Youth of Iraq," and a number of barnstorming covers, include Metallica's "Fade to Black" and Europe's "The Final Countdown." The latter song prompts the *Vice* narrator to not be able to resist a flash of condescension. Fair enough, since he did actually strap on a flak jacket and go to Iraq, more than once, to make this movie.

A daring documentary on metal in Syria during the conflict there, *Syrian Metal Is War*, is currently in production by fearless local director Monzer Darwish.

Heavy Metal Junior
(2005)
(Dir. Chris Waitt; w/Hatred)
✴ Heavy Metal Kids ✴ Metal Reality

Hatred is a heavy metal band from Scotland. Each member is under thirteen years old. Singer Paul McArthur is eleven, and the total average age is ten. They suck. *Heavy Metal Junior*, director Chris Waitt's twenty-four-minute, deadpan documentary on Hatred, is sufficiently smirking and ironic to have gotten the movie issued in the U.S. by twee-über-alles publishing house McSweeney's. Those a-holes hate heavy metal. Hatred's first original song, performed at a family funfair, is titled "Satan Rocks."

YouTube is bursting with preteen metal talents who warrant serious documentary examination, including Argentinean family act Los Gauchos; Colorado's impressively dark and irresistibly cute elementary-school-age Rammstein acolytes the Children Medieval Band; and England's the Mini Band, who perform an ace cover of Metallica's "Enter Sandman," showcasing eight-year-old Zoe Thomson absolutely shredding on lead guitar.

Heavy Metal Massacre (1989)
(Dirs. David DeFalco, Steven DeFalco, Ron Ottaviano; w/Bobbi Young, David DeFalco, Nick Hasomeris, Michele De Santis, Sami Plotkin)
✴ Soundtrack (Electric Afterburner Band)

Rhode Island reprobate David DeFalco wrote, produced, edited, and codirected *Heavy Metal Massacre* under the nom-de-mousse Bobbi Young. We learn this over the course of a credit sequence that goes on for a full ten minutes. When Bobbi Young finally appears, he is resplendent in yard-high teased peroxide coif, fishnet half-shirts, pink lipstick, clanking necklaces, neon checkerboard boxer shorts, and spandex leggings.

Billed as "The Rock Horror Movie" with "an all-metal explosive sound track," the camcorder-shot *Heavy Metal Massacre* took on brief life as a pass-around tape conducive to group sessions where participants cough smoke and ask, "What the fuck is this shit we're watching?" Mr. Young plays the Killer. He prowls the Dungeon, a metal club, for females to lure back to his kill room. Once there, the girls get topless and the Killer kills them, almost always in slow motion, with each hammer blow or chainsaw chop enhanced by cheap late-'80s home video visual effects and wavy screen wipes. *Heavy Metal Massacre* sputters toward an eighty-minute feature length, and when it ends, it just ends. No resolution of story; it was just time for Bobbi to take the tape out of the machine.

Blazing almost nonstop on the soundtrack are songs by Electric Afterburner Band. Facts about the group are elusive, and one would naturally assume DeFalco was a member except, jarringly, their kind of sludgy semi-hardcore power riffing isn't half horrendous. Fifteen years later, DeFalco reinvented himself as the foaming-mouthed, muscleman creator of the unsanctioned *Last House on the Left* remake, *Chaos* (2005).

THIS IS THE NIGHT OF THE NIGHTMARE...THE DAY OF THE UNDEAD!

A story that goes beyond the boundries of the Supernatural to the half-world of the living dead. Where a woman's soul inhabits a fly's body, where Vengeance is only a voice and where vampires suck only the blood of those they love the dearest.

AMERICAN INTERNATIONAL presents

BORIS KARLOFF STARRING IN

Black Sabbath

...The most gruesome day in the calendar of the Undead!

IN PATHÉCOLOR

ALSO STARRING MARK DAMON · MICHELE MERCIER · DIRECTED BY MARIO BAVA · AN AMERICAN INTERNATIONAL PICTURE

What are you afraid of? It's only rock & roll.

trick or treat

Clockwise from top: *Mario Bava's* Black Sabbath *(1963), the movie that inspired Geezer Butler and started it all;* Taarna *in the decade-defining* Heavy Metal *(1981); Skippy meets Satan in metal exploitation film* Trick or Treat *(1986)*

SOUND YOU CAN SEE IN THE MOVIE YOU CAN FEEL!

CHEAP TRICK

EARTH, WIND, & FIRE

DEBBIE HARRY

LOU REED

IGGY POP

ROCK & RULE

THE BEAUTY...THE BEAST...THE BEAT

LE CAMION DE LA MORT
BATTLETRUCK

An epic drama of adventure and exploration

...taking you half a billion miles from Earth... further from home than any man in history. Destination Jupiter.

MGM PRESENTS A STANLEY KUBRICK PRODUCTION

2001 a space odyssey

CINERAMA Super Panavision and Metrocolor

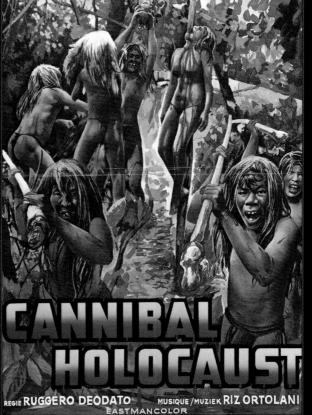

CANNIBAL HOLOCAUST

REGIE RUGGERO DEODATO   MUSIQUE / MUZIEK RIZ ORTOLANI
EASTMANCOLOR

Clockwise from top left: *The war on rock gets animated in* Rock & Rule *(1983); the most metal vehicle of all time is* Battletruck *(1982);* Cannibal Holocaust *(1980) action at its finest; "An epic drama of adventure and exploration,"* 2001: A Space Odyssey *(1968)*

Clockwise from top:
Evil Dead (1981);
The Dunwich Horror
(1970); Inseminoid,
aka Horror Planet
(1981); the aptly-named
Bummer! (1973);
French poster for The
Abominable Dr. Phibes
(1971). Center: *Latin
American lobby card
celebrating* Day of the
Dead (1985)

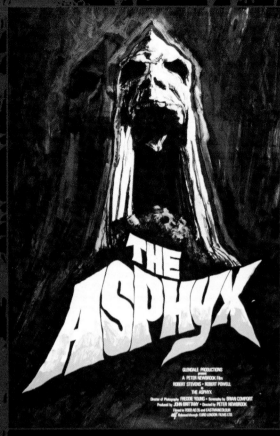

Clockwise from top left: *hand-drawn poster artwork for* The Asphyx *(1973); Joe D'Amato's unbelievably gruesome* Anthropophagus *(1981); Sheri Moon Zombie, Bill Haig, and Blll Moseley in* The Devil's Rejects *(2005); the irrepressible Lips in* Anvil! The Story of Anvil *(2008); heavy metal elements to the hilt in* Land of Doom *(1986)*

A lusty epic of revenge and magic, dungeons and dragons, wizards and witches, damsels and desire, and a warrior caught between.

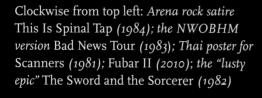

Clockwise from top left: *Arena rock satire* This Is Spinal Tap *(1984); the NWOBHM version* Bad News Tour *(1983); Thai poster for* Scanners *(1981);* Fubar II *(2010); the "lusty epic"* The Sword and the Sorcerer *(1982)*

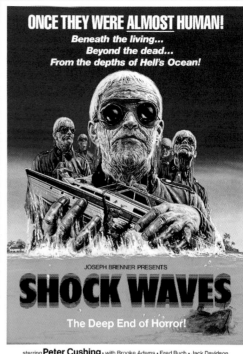

ONCE THEY WERE ALMOST HUMAN!

**Beneath the living...
Beyond the dead...
From the depths of Hell's Ocean!**

JOSEPH BRENNER PRESENTS

SHOCK WAVES

The Deep End of Horror!

starring **Peter Cushing** · with Brooke Adams · Fred Buch · Jack Davidson
Luke Halprin · D.J. Sidney · Don Stout · and **John Carradine**
A Zopix Presentation · screenplay by John Harrison, Ken Wiederhorn
music by Richard Einhorn · produced by Reuben Trane · directed by Ken Wiederhorn
Released by JOSEPH BRENNER ASSOCIATES, INC. · in EASTMANCOLOR

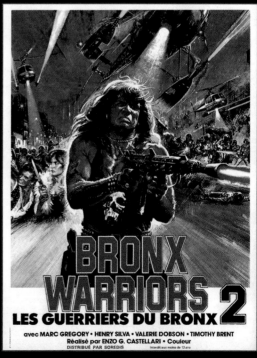

Clockwise from top left: *Saruman inspects an Uruk-hai in* Lord of the Rings *(2001);* Shock Waves *(1977); French poster for* Escape From the Bronx *(1993); politics in* Beneath the Planet of the Apes *(1970); Zappa's* 200 Motels *(1971)*

can you survive

The Texas Chain Saw Massacre

X (LONDON)

...it happened!

THE TEXAS CHAIN SAW MASSACRE
A Film By TOBE HOOPER · Starring MARILYN BURNS and GUNNAR HANSEN as "Leatherface"
Story & Screenplay by KIM HENKEL and TOBE HOOPER
Produced and Directed by TOBE HOOPER · COLOUR

LES MONSTRES
des planètes secrètes

A recent article in a New York newspaper reported that there were large colonies of people living under the city...

The paper was incorrect. What is living under the city is not human.

C.H.U.D. is under the city.

They're not staying down *there*, anymore!

C.H.U.D.
(Cannibalistic. Humanoid. Underground. Dwellers.)

ANDREW BONIME · JOHN HEARD · DANIEL STERN · CHRISTOPHER CURRY · C.H.U.D.

There is one horror that goes beyond the living dead!

AUTOPSY

It'll take you...apart!

black death

Clockwise from top: *"It happened!"* The Texas Chain Saw Massacre (1974); *cannibalistic humanoid underground dwellers;* Black Death (2010); Autopsy (1975) *takes on* NOTLD; *Eddie blazes into battle.* Center: War of the Gargantuas (1966), *hugely popular in France* (1966)

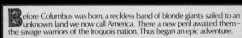

Clockwise from top left: *Werewolves loose in* The Howling *(1981);* Night of the Living Dead *(1968) at its sexiest; lurid Thai poster for* Nightmare on Elm Street 3 *(1987);* Dragonslayer *(1981) soundtrack art; Lee Majors in* The Norseman *(1978)*

Heavy Metal Parking Lot (1986)

(Dirs. John Heyn, Jeff Krulik; Headbangers)
✤ **Metal Reality**

Heavy Metal Parking Lot bangs the pavement outside a 1986 Judas Priest show in the suburbs of Washington, D.C., documenting seventeen minutes of unalloyed joy. The movie is one of life's stand-alone perfect experiences. Documentarians John Heyn and Jeff Krulik, armed with no agenda, wander about and introduce one indelible character after another.

Twenty-year-old air force pledge Dave tilts his Budweiser aside to tongue-kiss his date, Dawn, who happily announces she's thirteen. A shirtless drug legalization advocate says his name is Graham, "You know, like gram of dope!" When asked where he is, Graham responds, "I'm on acid!" Beer-gutted, belly-shirted John, asked to perform air guitar, hands over his mason jar full of screwdrivers, strums a nearby female, and howls "I Get Around" by the Beach Boys.

Zebraman, as the film's fans have dubbed him, is dressed in a sleeveless zebra-print shirt that only enhances his intense opinions. Regarding punk, Zebraman says: "Heavy metal rules. All that punk shit sucks. It doesn't belong in this world. It belongs on fuckin' Mars, man! Circle of Shit and the Dicks!" Of Madonna, he notes: "She's a dick."

A bare-chested, suspender-clad, Star of David pendant–bedecked junior David Lee Roth announces, "Ian Hill, I'm a former bass player, you're an inspiration of mine. Everybody else, you're rocking. Robert Halford, I don't know about you, but everybody else, you're definitely dynamite! Rock! Okay! All right!"

We even meet the fallen who couldn't be there: Timmy, who died in a car accident, and Michael Foster, who's in the hospital.

Sex arises in the form of a mousse-heightened redhead who says, in a crab-cake-thick Maryland accent, that if Rob Halford were there, "I'd jump his booownes!" A blonde proudly shows off knee-burns earned in the course of in-car copulation. One hopped-up honey shouts, "Glenn Tipton, we love you! Glenn Tipton, we LOVE you! We want to FUCK your brains out!" while her friend gyrates in agreement.

Cascading throughout are shots of the young, the drunk, the stoned and the younger, the drunker, and the more stoned, along with a befuddled Jamaican security guard and, maybe my favorite, two drunks happily petting police horses.

Every single second of Heavy Metal Parking Lot counts as a highlight, and each viewing is as fresh and hilarious and exhilarating and transcendent as the first. For years, the movie was an underground milestone, one of the most-passed-around and heavily bootlegged VHS tapes of all time. Perhaps because of its longtime outlaw status, Heavy Metal Parking Lot became a phenomenon. It penetrated the mainstream via music video parodies by the Backstreet Boys and pop-punk weasels Less Than Jake and American Hi-Fi. In 2009, Lady Gaga paid homage with a series of Pop Culture Parking Lot videos, documenting the crowds outside her concerts.

For the twentieth anniversary in 2006, filmmakers Heyn and Krulik settled music rights issues with Judas Priest and issued a deluxe DVD version. They also returned to the Capital Centre and made Neil Diamond Parking Lot, which is itself a wonder to behold.

Heavy Metal Picnic (2010)

(Dir. Jeff Krulik; w/Tito Cantero, Rudy Childs, Billy Gordon, Ken Guilette)
✤ **Concert Footage**

Jeff Krulik and John Heyn, creators of Heavy Metal Parking Lot (1986), turn their documentarian gaze on Maryland's 1985 Full Moon Jamboree in Heavy Metal Picnic. The jamboree was a three-day, anything-goes gathering of metalheads at "The Farm," a word-of-mouth party plateau for heshers and longhairs in a remote pocket of the town of Potomac. Metal hustler Billy Gordon organized the event, providing for bands to play on a dangerously makeshift stage, with doom lords Pentagram and Asylum headlining.

Rudy Childs patrolled the proceedings, interviewing his fellow headbangers using a Panasonic camcorder and CBS News microphone pilfered from the 1984 Reagan inauguration. *Heavy Metal Picnic* consists of Childs's original footage coupled with new material shot by Krulik and Heyn that reunites the original good-time knuckleheads we see running wild twenty-five years earlier. The reunited friends revisit the Farm, long since scrubbed of teenage dirtbags, and a great uprising of metal nostalgia is resurrected and forever preserved on film.

Heavy Metal Summer

(1988), aka State Park

(Dirs. Kerry Feltham, Rafal Zielinski; w/Isabelle Mejias, Jennifer Inch, Peter Virgile, Louis Tucci)
✠ Concert Footage

Arriving too late to the party in the great '80s teen sex comedy cycle, the Canadian tax write-off production *Heavy Metal Summer* pits campers at Weewankah Park against evil industrialist Mr. Rancewell (Walter Massey), who wants to pollute their bucolic retreat with toxic waste. For a movie sold as a raunchy hot-weather romp that opens with a guy in a bear suit addressing the camera, *Heavy Metal Summer* turns out disappointingly tepid. A half-decade before this romantic, female-focused trifle, genius codirector Rafal Zielinski gifted the teen sex comedy genre with its most insane high point, *Screwballs* (1983).

Heavy Metal Summer earns its title (which was changed to *State Park* for U.S. release) by way of Johnny Rocket (Peter Virgile) and Louis (Louis Tucci), a pair of Mötley Crüe–modeled hair-bangers, the former of whom falls for snobby Marsha (Isabelle Mejias), a prude who repeatedly expresses disgust for anything having to do

with heavy metal. Louis, with Tommy Lee stripes under his eyes, does manage to fitfully amuse en route to *Summer*'s climactic rock show, which surprisingly features non-Canadian metal god Ted Nugent joining in on the live jam, but he doesn't even try to whack the guy in the bear suit. Walter Massey, who plays dastardly Mr. Rancewell, also costars with Jon Mikl Thor in *Zombie Nightmare* (1986).

Heavy: The Story of Metal (2006)

(Dir. Michael John Warren; w/Everybody)
✠ Metal History ✠ Concert Footage

Heavy: The Story of Metal is a mammoth, four-hour, four-part overview of our favorite music genre, bursting with great historical archive footage, killer live performances, and a varied cast of talking heads that ranges from Tony Iommi and Dee Snider to Ian Christe and Richard Christy.

"Part One: Welcome to Our Nightmare" revels in the emergence of the original gods, from proto-pioneers such as Blue Cheer and the MC5 to unholy inventors Sabbath, Led Zep, and Deep Purple to their first generation of progeny—AC/DC, Kiss, Blue Öyster Cult, Aerosmith, Ted Nugent, Thin Lizzy, etc.

"Part Two: British Steel" focuses on the rise of the New Wave of British Heavy Metal (Iron Maiden, Judas Priest, Def Leppard), with a nod to the party-hearty rocking emerging in California courtesy of Van Halen.

"Part Three: Looks That Kill" delves into the high-haired, hyper-glam pop metal of Mötley Crüe, Poison, and their ilk, with nods toward the landmark Heavy Metal Movies *This Is Spinal Tap* (1984) and *The Decline of Western Civilization Part II* (1988). Also, we meet Washington's anti-metal censorship organization, the Parents Music Resource Center.

"Part Four: Seek and Destroy" parallels the ascent of thrash with the short-lived world conquest of Guns N' Roses and explores Marilyn

Manson, Ozzfest, nü metal, and the misguided link to the 1999 Columbine school shooting.

No one is capable of making a single perfect heavy metal history documentary. *Heavy: The Story of Metal* does rank high, however, up in the category of "as good as it gets." Throughout the second half of the 2000s, *Heavy: The Story of Metal* functioned essentially as the VH1 Classic channel's default programming, twenty-four hours a headbanging day.

HELL COMES to FROGTOWN (1987)

(DIRS. DONALD G. JACKSON, R. J. KIZER; W/"ROWDY" RODDY PIPER, SANDAHL BERGMAN, WILLIAM SMITH)

✠ POST-APOCALYPSE ✠ FROGMEN

Hell Comes to Frogtown is one of Heavy Metal Cinema's all-time great movie titles. The plot promises something that, in more competent hands, would have been a genuinely thrilling cult classic. As it is, incompetence reigns here.

"Rowdy" Roddy Piper plays Sam Hell, a fertile, sperm-shooting World War III hero who wanders America after the big one has fallen. Almost everyone else is sterile. Hell gets wrongly accused of rape by the female-run government and he is forced to take a deal that will send him to rescue a gaggle of fertile women who have been kidnapped by the "greeners." Once he saves the ladies, he has to knock them all up.

The aforementioned greeners, it must be noted, are full-size humanoid beings with the heads and hands of frogs. They live in Frogtown, so Hell literally goes to Frogtown. The movie is fun but not great, and though totally metal, it should be heavier! Codirector Donald G. Jackson is the creator of the loco-in-the-coco post-nuke roller-skating nuns movie *Roller Blade* (1986), along with its multiple sequels. Robert Z'Dar took over the role of Sam Hell in *Frogtown II* (1992). He was replaced by Scott Shaw for the second sequel, *Toad Warrior* (1996).

HELL HOUSE (2001)

(DIR. GEORGE RATLIFF; W/JIM HENNESSY, BILL HUMPHREY, JANE KING)

✠ SATAN ✠ BLACK MASS ✠ ETERNAL DAMNATION

Every year since 1990, the Pentecostal Trinity Church of Cedar Creek, Texas, has mounted its Hell House, a sins-on-parade-themed spook show aimed at scaring the hell out of all those who pass through its doors. *Hell House*, the movie, documents the creation of the 2000 edition. We meet the earnest participants, including the adults who mount the unexpectedly elaborate production, and the teenagers who audition and debate whether the rape or suicide roles are more fun to play.

The documentary climaxes with a walk through the "Hell House" in action. Visitors move from one room to the next as the high school thespians act out various sins and their gory wages. We see AIDS death; a plasma-gushing crotch, resulting from an "abortion pill" gone wrong; an essential re-creation of Pearl Jam's "Jeremy" lyrics (the character, who shoots himself at school, is even named Jeremy); and flashes of a Black Mass with a Star of David painted on the floor—accidentally, no doubt—in place of a pentagram. Masked demons and a cardboard-winged angel act as intercessors on behalf of their Lower and Higher Powers.

Interestingly, where any version of a Hell House in the past would have singled out heavy metal music, in 2000, it focuses instead on electronic music and the rave scene, culminating with a date-rape-drug tragedy.

The big tragedy, of course, is eternal. Hell House ends in hell. A black-clad skinhead painted up like the Crow stands in for the Father of Lies and explicitly tortures the wicked whose works we have witnessed. Visitors can then step into a prayer room before leaving, or go directly hit the nacho truck.

As a documentary, *Hell House* is fuzzy and unstructured, and it is riddled with dull spots, particularly in the middle. To director George Ratliff's credit, his movie is no agenda-fueled hammer job like *Jesus Camp* (2006), where the filmmakers' sole motivation is hatred for the movie's own subjects. Instead, *Hell House* brings us into the lives of sympathetic people, particularly the single dad whose youngest son has cerebral palsy, as they search for relief from the world's woes and aim to forge a connection with their fellow pilgrims through the arenas of music, art, and theater. Just like metalheads.

In fact, despite surface opposition, the church members even use the identical tropes as headbangers: blood, screaming, face paint, scary masks, crushing riffs, the whole works. References to occult practices abound, even if the movie skimps a bit on the details, and their hell looks cool.

Outside the Hell House, though, a gaggle of dissenters socks it to one of the church elders. Particularly enraged is a youth in a Fear Factory tee and backward Slipknot ball cap. "Who are you to say what's right and wrong?" he seethes before flipping the bird. His cooler-headed girlfriend, wearing a Slipknot bowling shirt, suggests expanding the Pentecostal view on homosexuality. Weirdly, then, one of their pals says, "If it wasn't for the Catholic Church, you Protestants wouldn't even have your Bible!" Take that!

Hell Night (1981)

(Dir. Tom DeSimone; w/Linda Blair, Vincent Van Patten, Peter Barton)

✠ Slasher ✠ Linda Blair

Hell Night hit the 1980s slasher cycle early and hard, depicting an unprepared crew of fraternity and sorority pledges challenged to spend the night in a creaky mansion where a gruesome mass slaughter took place years earlier. Their campus cohorts, of course, will try to spook them out of the place with Halloween record sound effects and skeletons rigged to pop out of closets, but the real frights get supplied by the mutant victim who didn't quite get murdered enough, and who now knows how to slice, twist, skewer, and otherwise bloodily expel mewling teenage meddlers in high style. The rubber-faced, Hulk-strong monster is plenty metal, but what really makes *Hell Night* a hot, heavy hoot is Linda Blair as the lead screamer. *Hell Night* launched Linda on an exploitation hot streak as great as anybody else's in the last days of drive-in movies.

Director Tom DeSimone made his bones under the name Lancer Brooks, helming vintage gay porn (including 1970's remarkably bluntly titled *How to Make a Homo Movie*). DeSimone would go on to make the even more metal *Reform School Girls* (1986), which features a lot of nudity from the Plasmatics' Wendy O. Williams.

Hell's Bells: The Dangers of Rock-n- Roll (1989)

(Dir. Eric Holmberg; w/Eric Holmberg)

✠ Censorship ✠ Satanic Panic

Coming in a bit after the '80s satanic panic had crested, *Hell's Bells: The Dangers of Rock-n-Roll* is a five-part documentary clocking in at no less than three hours, and hurling the usual evangelical Christian charges against the devil's music. Aside from its Herculean running time, mullet-headed writer-director-producer Eric Holmberg's labor of love stands out due to comedy bits and clever editing touches. Killer soundtrack, too.

Hell's Bells opens with a parody of the classic *Freedom Rock* album TV commercial. Two old hippies sit on a park bench and frown when a homeboy sashays by blaring rap from a boom box. "Man, whatever happened to good music?" one burnout says. "I'm talkin' AC/DC, 'Highway to Hell'!" Both space-cases fall all over each other singing and grooving.

An announcer intones via voice-over: "Missing those great heavy metal songs that set the world's feet a-stomping? . . . Alice Cooper, 'Go to Hell'; Kiss, 'Hotter Than Hell"; Cramps, 'Aloha From Hell'; Grim Reaper, 'See You in Hell'; CJSS,

'Citizen of Hell'; Rigor Mortis, 'Condemned to Hell'; Twisted Sister, 'Burn in Hell'; Cheap Trick, 'Gonna Raise Hell'; Mercyful Fate, 'Princess of Hell'; Raven, 'Hell Patrol' . . ."

Hell's Bells 2: The Power and Spirit of Popular Music is a 2004 follow-up that incorporates grunge and Marilyn Manson. Holmberg's mullet is gone, and so is the nonstop goofwad comedy approach, but high anti-metal entertainment is to be had (particularly if you, too, are high).

HELLRAISER (1987)

(Dir. Clive Barker; w/Andrew Robinson, Clare Higgins, Sean Chapman, Ashley Laurence, Doug Bradley)

✠ Hell ✠ BDSM

"I have seen the future of horror," declared Stephen King at the peak of his mid-'80s influence, "and his name is Clive Barker." King's quote haunted British author Barker as his words became celluloid in the form of the botched *Underworld*, aka *Transmutations* (1985), and the minor cult item *Rawhead Rex* (1986). Knowing the future of horror must involve film, Barker directed his next adaptation himself. The result was *Hellraiser* (1987), an instant classic that sent fright genre lunging forward and warped the parameters of popular culture. Though far from flawless, *Hellraiser* reverberates as proof that "good" can often be the enemy of "great."

Married couple Larry (Andrew Robinson) and Julia (Clare Higgins) move into a home sort of haunted by Larry's not-exactly-dead, not-exactly-human brother Frank (Sean Chapman). Skinless, limbless Frank fell prey to the pleasures and pains of a sorcerer's puzzle box. By twisting the sides, he disappeared into a flaming nightmare world of sadomasochistic atrocities run by kinky, glowing-skinned, bodily-modified freak-creatures called the Cenobites. Chief among these deviant demons is Pinhead (Doug Bradley), so named for the dozens upon dozens of nails artfully hammered into his face and skull. Julia falls for Frank, who needs to feed on human flesh and blood to corporeally escape the dimension of Cenobites. Julia provides for him by bringing home horny dudes to be slaughtered. The Cenobites, who are loath to let Frank go, also turn their attention to Julia's nubile daughter Kirsty (Ashley Laurence), turning her escape from their otherworldly pull into *Hellraiser*'s famously clumsy climax. As he's being torn to literal bits by hooks and chains, Frank screams out, "Jesus wept!" Those two words comprise the shortest book in the Bible, John 11:35.

Barker's filmmaking inexperience and many points where the movie turns ludicrous don't detract from the experience. The monsters are what matters. *Hellraiser* is a hellacious triumph of imagination and conceptual architecture. It boasts inventive makeup effects and creature design, and it marks the debut of one of horror's enduring antiheroes in the form of Bradley's chilling, diabolically charismatic Pinhead.

In metal terms, *Hellraiser* is the aesthetic bridge between the dank, avant-garde noise-polluters of the '80s such as Foetus and Nurse With Wound, and the rampaging '90s alt-metal of the high Lollapalooza era à la Ministry, White Zombie, and beyond. After the film, Hellraiser bands appeared in Denmark, France, Indonesia, Russia, and the U.S. Dozens of bands penned "Hellraiser" tracks in the years following, although in Lemmy Kilmister and Ozzy Osbourne's case the inspiration was mercenary. The film producers recognized the link between heavy metal and horror and hired them to write a song for a sequel soundtrack.

Industrial band Coil composed and performed *Hellraiser*'s original soundtrack. Barker chose Coil after calling them the only group whose records he had to take off because they made his bowels churn. Unfortunately, studio interference led to a soundtrack by a nameless "house band." Coil released their score as the album *The Unreleased Themes of Hellraiser*.

Piercing, tattoos, scarification, BDSM, and occult realms that can be experienced only in the shadowland between pain and pleasure all existed

世界中で大ブーム！サイバーパンク・ショック超大作！

ヘル・レイザー
HELLRAISER

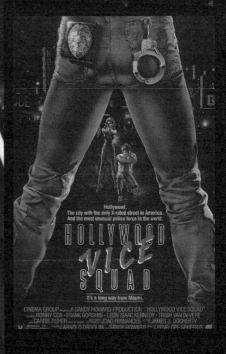

Clock wise from top left: *Zebraman rocks the mic in* Heavy Metal
Parking Lot *(1986); Japanese montage poster for* Hellraiser *(1987);*
Hollywood Vice Squad *(1986) poster rips off* Ms. 45; Halloween *(1978)*
reissue promo—"Everyone is entitled to one good scare"

long before *Hellraiser*. Nonetheless, this '80s splatter horror film put it all together for mass consciousness. In true metal fashion, *Hellraiser* allowed the culture to catch up with burbling underground notions and then press forward. Then came RE/Search's *Modern Primitives* book, the Jim Rose Circus Sideshow, and the fact that both your mom and your kid sister now have tattoos.

Hellraiser III: Hell on Earth (1992)

(Dir. Anthony Hickox; w/Doug Bradley, Terry Farrell, Paula Marshall, Kevin Bernhardt)

✠ Hell ✠ Soundtrack (Motörhead, Armored Saint, Tin Machine, Chainsaw Kittens, House of Lords)

Hellraiser III: Hell on Earth was the last movie in the kinky horror franchise to get a wide theatrical release and the first to get a real tie-in soundtrack album, which is, appropriately, heavily metal. Pinhead turns artful in *Hellraiser III*—literally—after he gets trapped in a carving called the Pillar of Souls that is purchased by decadent nightclub owner J. P. Monroe (Kevin Bernhardt). Pesky TV reporter Joey Summerskill (Terry Farrell) investigates the pillar and ultimately unearths the demon-releasing puzzle box from the first two *Hellraiser* movies. Soon enough, Cenobites are running wild. The ghost of World War I RAF captain Elliot Spencer (the pre-hammer-faced human incarnation of Pinhead), comes to the rescue. Armored Saint appear as themselves when TV newswoman Joey goes to a rock club.

After a decent sequel in *Hellbound: Hellraiser II* (1988) and a four-year wait, *Hellraiser III* felt like a general sputtering-out, despite decent moments such as a climax involving Cenobites tearing up city streets and Pinhead making a mockery of the Christian mass. From here, the series devolved into the barely released anthology *Hellraiser: Bloodline* (1996), which was abandoned by multiple directors, and a fitful series of straight-to-video follow-ups, the most recent of which, *Hellraiser: Revelations* (2011), moved the franchise to Mexico. An announced big-screen remake of the original, to be directed by series creator Clive Barker, has not materialized.

"Hellraiser," the movie's theme song, is performed by Motörhead and written by Lemmy, Ozzy Osbourne, and Zakk Wylde. Ozzy initially included his version of the song on the 1991 *No More Tears* album.

The Hellstrom Chronicle (1971)

(Dirs. Walon Green, Ed Spiegel; w/Lawrence Pressman)

✠ Apocalypse ✠ Insect Overlords ✠ Beasts Gone Berserk

"The earth was created not with the gentle caress of love, but with the brutal violence of rape," warns *Hellstrom*'s first line. Orgasmic lava gushes with terrifying sound effects ensue. Written by David Seltzer, author of *The Omen*, and burrowing its way into minor phenomenon status, *The Hellstrom Chronicle* is a shining, squirming example of that woefully underappreciated 1970s staple, the nature exploitation documentary. And it won an Academy Award! All for a bunch of bugs.

The movie itself is narrated by the fictitious Dr. Hellstrom (Lawrence Pressman). He assures us that the matter-of-fact violence and heartless efficiency of the insect kingdom guarantees that creepy-crawlers are in the process of conquering and eliminating humanity. The "good" doctor's proclamations join groundbreaking microscopic photography of ants, spiders, roaches, wasps, and their ilk in savage action. The breathtaking natural photography is why *The Hellstrom Chronicle* scored the 1971 Best Documentary Oscar. The hysterical narration, doomsday paranoia, liberal use of vintage monster movie clips, and an ad campaign promoting the film as a sci-fi/horror-fright fest are what make it a Heavy Metal Movie. All hail our new insect overlords!

HELTER SKELTER (1976)

(DIR. TOM GRIES; W/STEVE RAILSBACK, GEORGE
DiCENZO, NANCY WOLFE, MARILYN BURNS)
✠ MANSON FAMILY

Helter Skelter, the CBS TV movie adapted from the true crime book by L.A. DA Vincent Bugliosi, terrified America over two nights in 1976, thanks largely to a career-unmaking brilliant performance by Steve Railsback as Charles Manson. The movie focuses on the legal case against Manson following the notorious 1969 Tate-LaBianca murders. Even though Manson was not present during the crimes, Bugliosi tries to pin murder conspiracy charges on the long-haired, demon-eyed, babble-prone embodiment of the Establishment's fear of hippies. Manson Family members, particularly blood-drinking forced-abortion provider Susan Atkins (Nancy Wolfe), lighten Bugliosi's prosecutorial burden through crazed testimony and a devotion to Charlie that evokes demonic possession.

Helter Skelter is an excellent '70s TV movie by any standard, and a must for Heavy Metal Cinema fans due to its subject matter and Steve Railsback's creepy fucking nightmare eyes. Haunted by how much he resembled the mad killer and his inescapably unnerving stares, Railsback never shook Charlie's specter. Among subsequent career highlights: *The Stunt Man* (1980), a damned odd action-movie meditation on reality versus cinema; *Deadly Games* (1982), a big-box VHS slasher favorite; *Escape 2000*, aka *Turkey Shoot* (1982), one of the great Australian post-apocalypse skull-crushers; and *Ed Gein* (2000), in which he played the eponymous real-life cannibal killer and producers made the most of his Manson connection. Hilariously, filmmaker Martin Scorsese turned down an offer to play the Manson role in *Helter Skelter*.

HENDRIX (2000)

(DIR. LEON ICHASO; W/WOOD HARRIS, BILLY ZANE,
DORIAN HAREWOOD, VIVICA A. FOX)
✠ METAL HISTORY

This unremarkable Showtime biopic casts Wood Harris as the magic-fingered fret-shaman and generically runs through the events of his life and death in cut-rate "this happened, that happened, he OD'd, the end" style. Stock footage montages connect the dull dots ("Look! It's Beatlemania! Now it's Woodstock! Now he's dead!"). Harris went on to better work as Avon Barksdale on HBO's *The Wire*.

Hendrix includes the notorious episode where Jimi was repeatedly booed off the stage while opening for the Monkees on tour in 1967. VH1's Monkees biopic *Daydream Believers* actually does the storied mismatch more justice, pointing out that Hendrix opened at the Monkees' behest. They were awestruck fans who, as Monkees songwriter Tommy Boyce put it, "just wanted to watch Hendrix every night."

HENRY: PORTRAIT OF A SERIAL KILLER (1986)

(DIR. JOHN McNAUGHTON; W/MICHAEL ROOKER, TOM
TOWLES, TRACY ARNOLD)
✠ SERIAL KILLERS

Henry: Portrait of a Serial Killer is a horror movie for audiences that hate horror movies until they've been instructed by Some Respectable Authority to love one in particular; the most recent example being 2008's *Let the Right One In*. Loosely inspired by real-life murderer Henry Lee Lucas, *Henry* dispassionately follows the title character (Michael Rooker) arriving in Chicago to stay with his dunderheaded prison pal Otis (Tom Towles) and Otis's sister Becky (Tracy Arnold). While in town, Henry slays human prey at will and teaches Otis his various tricks for eluding the law. Tracy, meanwhile, goes and messes up their good thing by falling in love with Henry.

Made in 1986, *Henry* was rescued from obscurity as a midnight feature at Chicago's Music Box Theater in 1989. Siskel and Ebert dropped by and raved about it on TV, setting a phenomenon in motion. From there, *Henry* rolled out to the country's art houses and, city by city, horror dorks and mainstream critics alike foamed in rapturous unison about this being a new high point in the low art of fright films.

The truth: *Henry* was never more than an okay B-movie distinguished by some A-plus acting. Michael Rooker announces his talent in the title role and that's about it. The sequences that unnerved and haunted reviewers, like the videotaped family massacre, always come off hokey, whereas the more self-consciously "hokey" bits, like clumsily killing a guy with a TV set, at least play like honest moviemaking. Despite Rooker's command of the screen, there are "actor-y" parts where Henry, Otis, and Becky sit around talking all, you know, "white trash."

So what? Countless heavy metal fans love *Henry: Portrait of a Serial Killer*. Fantômas and other bands have penned songs about Henry Lee Lucas and specifically this movie. Stripped of the fake acclaim bestowed by anti-horror interlopers, it's okay. *Henry* initially garnered an X rating from the MPAA for its "tone," meaning that no edits to actual violence or visual content could be made to get the movie rated R. It was eventually released unrated. A numbnuts cash-in sequel, *Henry: Portrait of a Serial Killer Part II* (1996), played for a nanosecond in theaters before landing on home video. None of the stars or makers of the original were involved.

HERCULES (1958)
(DIR. PIETRO FRANCISCI; W/STEVE REEVES, SYLVA KOSCINA, FABRIZIO MIONI, IVO GARRANI)
✦ SWORDS AND SANDALS ✦ GREEK MYTHOLOGY

American bodybuilder Steve Reeves became the highest-paid movie star in Europe by portraying the Greek god of strength in the Italian-made *Hercules* (1958) and its sequel, *Hercules*

Unchained (1959). He later became the subject of the Thor song "Hail Steve Reeves." Although creaky by today's standards, *Hercules* packed theaters all over the planet with its straightforward saga of the title hero teaming with Jason (Fabrizio Mioni) and the Argonauts to recover the stolen Golden Fleece. While severely lacking in special effects, *Hercules* makes up for that with the monolithic screen presence of Reeves.

Considerably more beefy and gym-sculpted than even the most macho of prior movie stars, Reeves is the obvious prototype for Arnold Schwarzenegger, along with all the other physical powerhouse action movie marauders presently populating our blockbusters. Reeves got the iron pumping, injecting sweat-wrought heavy metal into fantasy filmmaking. *Hercules* ignited a craze for "peplum movies" throughout the 1960s. Also known as "sword and sandal" films, these adventures took place mostly in ancient Rome (sometimes Greece) and often involved mythology and magic. Usually, these movies were aimed at kids, and were cranked out in Europe on the severe cheap. The peplum genre is inherently proto-metal in the garage phase, larger-than-life on a shoestring.

HERCULES (1983)
(DIR. LUIGI COZZI; W/LOU FERRIGNO, SYBIL DANNING, BRAD HARRIS, INGRID ANDERSON)
✦ GREEK MYTHOLOGY

Rushed into production to capitalize on *Conan the Barbarian* (1982), *Hercules* casts Der Arnold's *Pumping Iron* nemesis, Lou Ferrigno (*The Incredible Hulk*), as Greek mythology's half-man/half-god/all-muscle tower of power. After the infant demigod strangles serpents in his cradle, Hulk-turned-Herc Lou is a riot, complete with a dubbed voice. He comes of age by wrestling a bear, defeating it, and tossing the animal into space. The special effects live up to your hopes. Luigi Cozzi's watchful eye seems to have wandered a little following his prior triumphs *Starcrash* (1979) and *Alien Contamination* (1980).

Hercules battles evil witch Ariadne (Sybil Danning) and evil wizard King Minos (Brad Harris), and rescues innocent Cassiopea (Ingrid Anderson) from virgin sacrifice on the not-yet-sunken isle of Atlantis. Then he visits Zeus on the moon and we're done. Interestingly, this PG-rated *Hercules* aimed for the Saturday afternoon kiddie matinee crowds. Alas, that tradition had become ancient Greek history by 1983. *Hercules* caught on subsequently with bad movie geeks and ganja-giddy headbangers in front of VCRs, prone to spraying bong- water out of their noses. A 1985 sequel, *The Adventures of Hercules*, proved similarly friendly to hallucinogen-enhanced home video viewings.

Surprisingly, heavy metal seems to have largely passed over Hercules as a direct lyrical and conceptual inspiration. The Mightiest Man on Earth has flourished for thousands of years in story, poetry, paintings, sculpture, opera, animation, movies, TV, and, during the late 1970s, even a giant-size pinball machine, which featured a standard billiards cue ball and bumpers the size of tire irons. Then came heavy metal, and the muscleman is still waiting for a proper earsplitting tribute.

Hercules in New York (1969), aka Hercules Goes Bananas

(Dir. Arthur Allan Seidelman; w/Arnold Schwarzenegger, Arnold Stang, Deborah Loomis)

✣ Greek Mythology

Arnold Stang meets "Arnold Strong" in *Hercules in New York*. That's how Arnold Schwarzenegger was billed in his first film appearance, a kid-friendly comedy of Olympian stupidity. The bespectacled, bow-tied, Brooklyn-accented Stang was beloved for years for playing prototypical nerd types on radio and TV. Here, Stang costars as sidewalk pretzel salesman "Pretzie," who befriends Hercules (Der Arnold, of course) after the demigod ditches Olympus for Manhattan.

"Laff riot" aptly describes this archetypal old-school turkey, a lovably inept botch job studded with maybe a thousand dull moments (as these things usually are) and porn-flick production values.

Arnold wrestles a bear in Central Park. To call his opponent a "bear" is an act of supreme charity toward whoever designed what's passed off here as a bear costume. The movie climaxes with Herc taking the reins of a horse-drawn chariot and charging through Times Square. Along with my bodybuilding cousin Martin Snow, I was lucky enough to catch on the big screen during its quick *Conan*-cash-in 1982 rerelease. Yes, I'm bragging.

Hercules in the Haunted World (1961)

(Dirs. Mario Bava, Franco Prosperi; w/Reg Park, Christopher Lee)

✣ Hades ✣ Greek Mythology ✣ Vampire Zombies

"Superhuman Strength Versus Supernatural Evil!" promised the ads, and this movie backs them up in high style, due largely to codirector Mario Bava's visual panache and Christopher Lee as a literal underworld boss. Muscleman Reg Park took over demigod duties from original Hercules movie series star Steve Reeves. In his second go-round, after 1961's *Hercules and the Captive Women*, he's solid granite.

In order to cure his girlfriend Princess Deianira (Leonora Ruffo) of amnesia, Hercules descends into Hades to acquire the Stone of Forgetfulness. Among the surreal, expertly staged adventures that ensue are encounters with living stone creatures, psychedelic lava, and vampire zombies. Lee magnificently chews up the beautifully lit scenery in full-blown diabolical mode; albeit, stupidly, with somebody else's voice dubbed over his famous baritone. *Hercules in the Haunted World* serves as the bridge for Italian horror maestro Mario Bava between his amazing international breakthrough *Black Sunday* (1960) and the heavy-metal-spawning *Black Sabbath* (1963). He would go from there to make a number of symphonic masterpieces of movie terror.

HESHER (2010)

(DIR. SPENCER SUSSER; W/JOSEPH GORDON-LEVITT, DEVIN BROCHU, NATALIE PORTMAN, RAINN WILSON)

✠ SOUNDTRACK (METALLICA)

Writer-director Spencer Susser says he conceived the title character of *Hesher* as a "heavy metal Mary Poppins," a conceit that reeks of indie-flick co-opting of lower-class "cool." T.J. (Devin Brochu) is a kid around ten years old whose mother has recently died. Into T.J.'s troubled world storms Hesher (Gordon-Levitt). He's a violent, foul-mouthed, chain-smoking dirtbag who never wears a shirt (so as to show off his incredibly fake middle-finger tramp stamp). Hesher also drives a shitty black van, and he simply moves into T.J.'s house

From the get-go, Hesher's an asshole. He bursts in on T.J. at school, draws dicks on stuff, burns property, trashes a stranger's swimming pool, and fucks Nicole (Natalie Portman), the supermarket cashier on whom the kid has a crush. Of course, in this universe, all of Hesher's repulsive destruction is precisely what T.J.'s shattered, uptight American family needs to cut loose and fully realize what it is to be alive.

No actual "hesher" could have been involved in the making of this film. Be assured, this is the product of creators pretending to honor the "wisdom" and "nobility" of people they'd call the cops on if they got within a Prius-fume of their local NPR meet-up. Forget Mary Poppins: Hesher is the heavy metal equivalent of that loathsome cinema archetype, "the Magical Negro."

Joseph Gordon-Levitt says he based *Hesher* on deceased Metallica bassist Cliff Burton, leading to famously movie-shy Metallica enriching the soundtrack with numerous songs from their first four albums. "I was actually moved, because I grew up headbanging to Metallica," said Gordon-Levitt. Sure you did, Jojo.

HIGHLANDER (1986)

(DIR. RUSSELL MULCAHY; W/CHRISTOPHER LAMBERT, SEAN CONNERY, CLANCY BROWN, BEATIE EDNEY)

✠ SWORDS & SORCERY ✠ SCOTTISH MYTHOLOGY
✠ SOUNDTRACK (QUEEN)

Highlander tanked on arrival in theaters in 1986. But this heavy metal vision, so perfectly attuned to its audience, was destined to rise again and live forever—much like the immortals of *Highlander*'s mythology. The action gets rolling in a 1986 Manhattan parking complex, where swordsman Connor MacLeod (Christopher Lambert) beheads a rival, creates a power surge, and is busted by the NYPD. In custody, he flashes back to how he got there: In 1518 Scotland, MacLeod easily shakes off what should be a mortal wound in battle. This spooks the villagers, and they ban him to the Scottish highlands. The exiled MacLeod meets a colorful Spaniard, Juan Sanchez Villa-Lobos Ramirez (Sean Connery), who explains that they are both immortals whose only weakness is decapitation. Ramirez trains MacLeod in sword fighting, because immortals are constantly attempting to de-noggin one another, as it results in a transfer of power known as "The Quickening."

After coexisting not exactly peacefully, the world's immortals gather in New York City for a battle royal because, as they each say, "There can only be one!" Though the film makes little sense, *Highlander* still rocks, albeit it largely as nostalgia. Lambert is a strong hero, and Connery's long cameo is one of his most enchanting screen turns, which is saying something. Superpowered swordsmen slice each other relentlessly from the neck up, set to a great score by Michael Kamen bolstered by seven original Queen songs, each of which deserved to be a hit.

Although *Highlander* is not a great movie, it is immortal. For one thing, it looms large as one of history's most retroactively successful box office bombs. After performing well in non-U.S. theaters, the movie became a home video blockbuster and frequently rerun favorite on cable TV. This second life generated three big-screen sequels, two direct-to-video sequels, two live-action TV series, an animated TV series, numerous novels and comics, and multimedia games.

Apart from the cosplay enthusiasts and live-action role-play adaptations it spawned, the most directly metallic real-world offshoot of *Highlander* is the "wall of death" ritual that occurred with regularity during Lamb of God concerts in the early 2000s. Whenever Virginia's reigning groove goliaths played the song "Black Label," the mosh pit would split in two halves as if preparing for a lethal game of red rover, with crowd members eyeballing one another as the pulsating rhythm simmered. When the breakdown hammer fell, both groups charged forward into an explosive collision, emulating the classic full-body combat first cinematically realized in *Highlander* and then later in *Braveheart* (1995).

Highlander II: The Quickening is much more massively scaled and big-budget, yet few films so huge are so utterly baffling and insane.

Highway to Hell (1991)

(Dir. Ate de Jong; w/Chad Lowe, Kristy Swanson, Patrick Bergin, C. J. Graham, Richard Farnsworth)

✠ Satan ✠ Lita Ford ✠ Cerberus ✠ Flaming Boobs

Charlie (Chad Lowe) and Rachel (Kristy Swanson) drive through a desert to get married in Las Vegas. Along the way, crater-faced demon Sgt. Bedlam, aka Hellcop (C. J. Graham), kidnaps the bride-to-be and drags her down to the fiery hereafter. Charlie, to win her back, must travel the *Highway to Hell*. A curiosity that only gets more inexplicable with time, *Highway to Hell* is a wacky comedy about Satan and damnation that largely misses its marks but is still dotted with enough laudably amusing weirdness and gags to recommend it to Heavy Metal Movie fans.

Funniest among *HTH*'s laugh nuggets is an all-star table in Hades where Hitler (Gilbert Gottfried), Attila the Hun (Ben Stiller), and Cleopatra (Amy Stiller) bicker and kibbitz as though they're at an early-bird dinner in the Catskills. Patrick Bergin plays a "satanic mechanic" named Beezle, who, as you might guess, reveals his last name to be "Bub." There's also the three-headed guard dog, Cerberus; a guy who pisses toxic waste; a zombie diner; a strip club of the damned, where boobs burst into flames; and a roadside construction crew (of the Good Intentions Paving Company) that seems to consist of multiple Andy Warhols. And Lita Ford cameos as a hitchhiker. *Highway to Hell* is a headbanging knee-slapper.

The History of Iron Maiden, Part 1: The Early Days (2004)

(Dir. Matthew Amos)

✠ Metal History ✠ NWOBHM ✠ Eddie

The History of Iron Maiden, Part 1: The Early Years delivers the studded leather goods. Utilizing a family-tree flowchart, *History* introduces every version of the revered British metal band from their formation as metallic hair-raisers through the group's 1983 conquest of U.S. stadiums with *Piece of Mind*.

Almost every band member recounts his experiences. All are upbeat and insightful. Rare video footage abounds, much of it from the New Wave of British Heavy Metal's endlessly fascinating era. Early singer Dennis Wilcock practices sword swallowing and pukes enough stage blood to knock out an audience member. The band's first attempt at a mascot is a giant Kabuki-style mask that bleeds from the eyes and breathes red smoke. Cover artist Derek Riggs reveals the inspiration for zombie mascot Eddie to be a photo of a human noggin on a Vietnamese tank. Former frontman Paul Di'Anno—resplendent in earrings, sculpted goatee, silver NFL jersey, and a baseball cap that reads fuck—salutes his successor, Bruce Dickinson, as Iron Maiden's greatest vocalist. Then comes the first ten-foot-tall Eddie to wander out on stage. Maiden heaven.

The History of Iron Maiden, Part 2 (2008)

(Dir. Matthew Amos)

✵ Metal History ✵ NWOBHM ✵ Eddie

Picking up in 1984 where *The History of Iron Maiden, Part 1* dropped us off, *Part 2* maintains the format of that milestone and continues the saga through the albums *Powerslave* and *Live After Death,* along with ensuing tours. Bassist and Maiden mastermind Steve Harris coolly runs the show. Vocalist Bruce Dickinson is cheekily good-humored as always. And mascot Eddie the Head transforms into a King Kong–size mummy who emerges from behind the drum kit and repeatedly almost gives skin-pounder Nicko McBrain a concussion.

Part 2 also demonstrates the group's video evolution, both in promo clips and long-form concert tapes, and touches on the tour exhaustion that would repeatedly almost decimate the band going forward. For all their hellfire aesthetics and damnation energy, Iron Maiden has endured in no small part due to how funny its members are and how amused they become by their circumstances. *Part 2* details Maiden producer and martial arts enthusiast Martin Birch challenging swordsman Bruce Dickinson to a winner-slays-all karate-vs.-fencing showdown. Dickinson also reveals how he purchased his ridiculous feather "hawk's head" stage mask from a Hollywood S&M shop.

We get the full scoop behind the legendary band fight B-side, "Mission From 'Arry". The track consists of Harris and McBrain arguing with obscene flair not heard since the Troggs tapes that inspired *This Is Spinal Tap*. Dickinson secretly recorded the verbal melee, even riling his bandmates up again after they'd calmed down. The audio attack ends, uproariously, with Harris spewing, "Some cunt's recording this!" We need to be grateful that when it comes to Iron Maiden, somebody was always recording something.

The History of Iron Maiden Part 2 debuted as a bonus item on the 2008 DVD version of the band's landmark 1985 concert video, *Live After Death*. Also included is *'Ello Texas*, a fifteen-minute short in which the lads visit the Alamo. Check out Bruce in a sombrero and giant novelty sunglasses.

The History of Iron Maiden, Part 3 (2013)

(Dir. Andy Matthews)

✵ Metal History ✵ NWOBHM ✵ Eddie
✵ Killer Cameo (Tom Jones)

Unlike the first two installments that chronicled the long meteoric ascent of one of metal's most cherished bands, *The History of Iron Maiden Part 3* begins with a crash. After the monumental *Powerslave* tour, Maiden's members are shattered by exhaustion. Alas, Maiden being Maiden, their planned six-month respite gets cut to four months and work commences on 1986's *Somewhere in Time*.

Part 3 takes us from the recording of that classic up to the end of Maiden's *Seventh Son of a Seventh Son* tour in 1988, blending new interviews with vintage footage. The documentary divulges eye-opening and often gut-busting episodes from the group's ongoing journey. Here, we learn how Welsh pop powerhouse Tom Jones crashed Maiden's New York hotel room with champagne and listened to early tapes of *Somewhere in Time* with them until dawn. The tour designers go nuts with new inflatable technology to the point that members can play in the palms of mascot Eddie's mammoth hands. When Maiden finally makes it to Japan, Dickinson takes a bit of mystery out of one of rock's most storied arenas. "You're thinking, 'Oh, Budokan!'" he says, "Well, 'budokan' actually means 'karate hall.' You get there and it's just a gym!"

The Hobbit (1966)

(Dir. Gene Deitch; w/Herb Lass)

✠ J. R. R. Tolkien

Hollywood's first official crack at J. R. R. Tolkien's fundamentally metal universe of Middle Earth, *The Hobbit* is cartoon director Gene Deitch's twelve-minute semi-animated folly. The illustrative but barely moving frames consist of warm and colorful paintings reminiscent of Deitch's work for Terrytoons studios, where he created Sidney the elephant. The largely altered story, now involving a princess love interest, comes to life with lighting effects and minimal movement of cutout images. A Mr. Peabody–esque narrator talks over canned music. The end result is puzzling, and decades later remains a curiosity perfectly suited for computer viewing. Producer William L. Snyder rushed *The Hobbit* into production as the clock ran down on his licensing contract with the Tolkien estate. The finished cartoon took less than a month to make, and was screened exactly one time in a Manhattan theater—on the same day that Snyder's contract was up.

The Hobbit (1977)

(Dirs. Jules Bass, Arthur Rankin Jr.; w/Orson Bean, John Huston, Richard Boone, Brother Theodore)

✠ J. R. R. Tolkien ✠ Dragon

Rankin-Bass Studios is best known for its classic stop-motion animated TV Christmas specials (*Rudolph the Red-Nosed Reindeer; The Year Without a Santa Claus*) and one howlingly great Halloween big-screen release (1967's *Mad Monster Party*). In 1977, Rankin-Bass abandoned holidays to adapt J. R. R. Tolkien's *The Hobbit* as an ABC-TV movie. The result is seventy-seven brisk minutes of beguiling storytelling with a perfect voice cast that's ideal for introducing kids to the progressively more heavy metal wonders of Tolkien's Middle Earth stories.

Bilbo Baggins (Orson Bean) is a fat and happy Hobbit whose simple existence is upended by a visit from wizard Gandalf the Grey (John Huston) and a gaggle of dwarves. The dwarves whisk Bilbo off on an adventure to reclaim their treasure from the dragon Smaug (Richard Boone). Among the oddities they encounter along the way is the slithering Gollum (Brother Theodore).

The Hobbit is reasonably exciting throughout and ends on a warm note of self-discovery. A child's road to heavy metal often begins with being terrified by a song or an album cover into wanting to know more; Tolkien—and his interpreters in this version of *The Hobbit*—offers a gentler path. Treat a kid you know to it. *The Hobbit* also adapts Tolkien's original lyrics from the book into a series of original songs.

The Hobbit: An Unexpected Journey (2012)

(Dir. Peter Jackson; w/Martin Freeman, Ian McKellen, Richard Armitage, Andy Serkis, Christopher Lee)

✠ J. R. R. Tolkien ✠ Dragon

After shepherding the *Lord of the Rings* trilogy to its victorious cinematic realization, director Peter Jackson returned to the first book in J. R. R. Tolkien's realm of Middle Earth—and then he split that into three movies, too. *The Hobbit: An Unexpected Journey* introduces the little fellow of the title, Bilbo Baggins (Martin Freeman), who, at the urging of his wizard friend Gandalf (Ian McKellen), accompanies thirteen noisy, blustery dwarves on a quest to recover a magic ring from the dragon Smaug. Jackson and company work the same magic here that they did in *LOTR*, barreling full-bore at the forefront of technology to translate Tolkien's beloved headbanger story to the screen. *The Hobbit: An Unexpected Journey* employed a revolutionary high-frame-rate 3-D filming process that looked like nothing audiences had seen before. Early reports of seasickness and panic attacks only hyped the technique further. Mexico's contemporary horror master Guillermo del Toro (*Hellboy, Pan's Labyrinth*) cowrote *The Hobbit*'s screenplay. *The Hobbit: The Decimation of Smaug* followed admirably in 2013.

Hollywood Vice Squad (1986)

(Dir. Penelope Spheeris; w/Ronny Cox, Frank Gorshin, Leon Isaac Kennedy, Carrie Fisher)

✡ Sunset Strip

Penelope Spheeris, just before she permanently (and perfectly) crystallized '80s L.A. hair metal in *The Decline of Western Civilization Part II* (1988), pocketed one more exploitation-movie paycheck in the form of *Hollywood Vice Squad*. Most likely inspired by Roger Corman's concurrent, fantastically sleazy *Angel* movies ("High school honor student by day, Hollywood hooker by night!") and borrowing the plot of Paul Schrader's peerless *Hardcore* (1979), *HVS* dips back, title-wise, to the grimy greatness of Gary Sherman's *Vice Squad* (1982).

Given that likably lowbrow lineage and an unlikely B-movie dream cast (Ronny Cox, aka the dead guitar player from *Deliverance*! Frank Gorshin, aka the Riddler from *Batman*! Leon Isaac Kennedy, aka Too Sweet from *Penitentiary*! Princess Freakin' Leia as a hooker!), it's a borderline tragedy that *Hollywood Vice Squad* ended up such a forgettable whimper. Spheeris, evidently, had bigger and harder-rocking things on her mind.

Filmed at the crest of poodle-head glam flashiness, the numerous establishing shots are heavily studded with mousse-imbued metal maniacs making their way from one rock club to the next record store to the next back alley blow-job/regurgitation station in colorful numbers.

The Holy Mountain (1973)

(Dir. Alejandro Jodorowsky; w/Horacio Salinas, Zamira Saunders, Ana De Sade, Chucho-Chucho)

✡ Heavy Psych

Alejandro Jodorowsky invented the midnight movie with *El Topo* (1971); then he came back with the even more ambitious *The Holy Mountain*. The Thief (Horacio Salinas) resembles Jesus Christ and embarks on a quest for enlightenment that begins in earnest after he defecates into a box and an alchemist (Alejandro Jodorowsky) turns the feces to gold, stating: "You are excrement. You can turn yourself into gold." En route to the holy mountain where this will take place, the Thief is accompanied by seven archetypal professionals who embody the counterculture's major bum trips circa '73. They include a weapons manufacturer, a political financier, a cosmetics manufacturer, and a maker of toy guns. Each symbolic human undergoes hallucinatory death and rebirth as they ascend the holy mountain. The Thief ends up partnered with a prostitute (Ana De Sade) and a chimpanzee (Chucho-Chucho), living the ultimate dream of many a stoner metal devotee. The alchemist finally puts a stop to the action. He breaks the fourth wall, points out that all this is just a movie, and orders the audience out of the theater to take on "real life."

The Holy Mountain is a visual masterwork and as fitting an accompaniment for psychedelic derring-do today as it was four decades ago. Much as vintage acid rock lyrics may sound dated and naïve today, but the grooves and riffs still transport the listener to a higher plane, so it is with the specifics of *Holy Mountain*. Enjoy the hippie nonsense as nostalgia, allow the heavy poetry and brutal beauty of the filmmaking to take you to the mountaintop. The 1992 stoner metal masterpiece *Sleep's Holy Mountain* by Sleep does not synch up with *The Holy Mountain* the way Pink Floyd's *Dark Side of the Moon* so famously does with *The Wizard of Oz*, but try it anyway.

Horror Hospital (1973),
aka Computer Killers
(Dir. Antony Balch; w/Michael Gough, Robin Askwith, Vanessa Shaw)
✠ British Horror ✠ Zombie Bikers

Horror Hospital opens with a live performance by British doom band Mystic. The group dazzles a stoned rock club audience with an ode to black magic while a glammed-up transvestite lies in a trance at the foot of the fog-shrouded stage. Jason (Robin Askwith) spoils the spell by getting mad over how Mystic ripped off the song from him. He takes off on a package tour sold to London's groovy upstarts billed as "Hairy Holidays." The tour is a front, naturally, to get young bodies into the laboratory of the diabolical Dr. Storm (Michael Gough), who lobotomizes hippies and makes them his undead slaves. Storm's henchmen include his dwarf assistant Frederick (Skip Martin) and a battalion of zombified bikers. His Rolls-Royce is equipped with pop-up blades to decapitate any potential escapees. Horror Hospital ably infuses wacko fright elements with cheeky British humor for a thoroughly satisfying and quintessentially early-'70s hard rock romp.

Horror of Dracula
(1958), aka Dracula
(Dir. Terence Fisher; w/Christopher Lee, Peter Cushing, Melissa Stribling, Valerie Gaunt)
✠ Dracula ✠ Hammer Films

Christopher Lee is the ultimate Heavy Metal Movie vampire. Peter Cushing is his ultimate foil. Hammer Films is the ultimate heavy metal studio. Horror of Dracula is almost where it all began. Actually, the previous year's Curse of Frankenstein—with Lee as the monster, and Cushing as the mad scientist—commenced Hammer's reign as horror's premier production house. That worldwide blockbuster hit established Hammer's signature look and tone, and exposed audiences to unprecedented levels of redder-than-red blood on-screen. Horror of Dracula followed suit, with director Terence Fisher concocting new black magic by casting Lee in the cape and fitting his mouth with fangs. The screen's greatest Dracula—no disrespect to pioneering icon Bela Lugosi—was born, undead and amped up to spook forever. Cushing makes a singularly great Dr. Van Helsing, the tireless vampire hunter.

Horror of Dracula retells the familiar story of the bloodsucking count, but it does so with Hammer's one-of-a-kind style. Hyperreal sets and costumes, studied suspense, flare-ups of terror, a rich gothic atmosphere, lush colors, and blood—that thick, flowing, dripping, fang-coating, crimson-beyond-compare blood—all add up to a wellspring of bubbling plasma of enduring inspiration. Hammer Films emerged as an institution, bringing so many elements to metal, starting with those rain sounds and church bells that open Black Sabbath's debut album.

As with Curse of Frankenstein before it and the music of heavy metal to come, Horror of Dracula riled censors and other guardians of public decency. The British censor board complained Hammer Films: "The curse of this thing is the Technicolor blood: why need vampires be messier eaters than everyone else?"

Horror of Dracula did spectacular business worldwide, prompting Universal Studios to grant Hammer Films full rights to remake all their classic monster movies. Hammer immediately followed up with The Mummy (1959), again directed by Terence Fisher, starring Cushing as an archaeologist and Lee as the resurrected Egyptian high priest Kharis.

Lee played Dracula in seven films. Each is a Heavy Metal Movie essential: Horror of Dracula (1958), Dracula: Price of Darkness (1966), Dracula Has Risen From The Grave (1968), Taste the Blood of Dracula (1970), The Scars of Dracula (1970), Dracula A.D. 1972 (1972), and The Satanic Rites of Dracula (1973). Decades later, he performed on albums by Manowar and Italy's Rhapsody of Fire, and even released a heavy metal album of his own at the ripe young age of ninety-one.

Horror of the Hungry Humongous Hungan

(1991)

(Dir. Randall Dininni; w/ Joseph E. Miller, Brenda Moyer, David A. Yoakam)

✢ Voodoo ✢ Hair Metal ✢ Zombies

Originating as *The Hungan* and then pukey-cute renamed by Troma Films for VHS release, this film presents a flesh-hungry Frankenstein-style patchwork creature reanimated by a voodoo priestess. He has a mask for a face, claws for hands, and a flannel-heavy lumberjack wardrobe. Inadvertently due to that last touch, *Hungan* embodies the changing state of hard rock when the movie was filmed.

The monster dresses pure grunge, but the on-screen musical talent at a house party is California hair metal ensemble Cry Wolf. The party's dancing revelers—including a fully costumed Pee-Wee Herman impersonator—really dig Cry Wolf's glammy Sunset Strip sound, so much so that they block our view of the band throughout two (long) numbers, "Can't Get Enough of You" and "It's Getting Better." That level of anti-competence renders *Hungan* a must for fans of movies that are terrible.

Horror Planet (1981),

aka Inseminoid

(Dir. Norman J. Warren; w/Jennifer Ashley, Robin Clarke, Stephanie Beacham, Judy Geeson)

✢ Science Fiction ✢ Space Horror ✢ Alien Rape

Shot under the delectably lurid title *Inseminoid*, *Horror Planet* manages to inventively rip off *Alien* (1979) by having the space monster slaughter a spaceship crew by possessing the body of luscious blonde astronaut Sandy (Judy Geeson). Of course, the evil space fiend rapes and impregnates her first.

Horror Planet traffics in heavy metal imagery on a low budget that suits it well. A movie's got to know its limitations. Given its similar focus on forced sex between intergalactic species, *Horror Planet* is often doubled up in the public's mind with the same year's even better *Galaxy of Terror*.

Horsemen (2009), aka

Horsemen of the Apocalypse

(Dir. Jonas Åkerlund; w/Dennis Quaid, Ziyi Zhang, Lou Taylor Pucci, Patrick Fugit)

✢ Apocalypse ✢ Soundtrack (The Sword)

Dennis Quaid stars in *Horsemen* as Aidan Breslin, a weary detective mourning the recent death of his wife. A platter of human teeth and the flaying-by-hooks of a pregnant woman send Breslin on the trail of a killer paying homicidal homage to the Bible's Four Horsemen of the Apocalypse: Pestilence, War, Famine, and Death. More bloody, contraption-oriented slayings follow, and the final mystery unravels around several youths who are working out not even particularly severe parental issues.

Horsemen is horseshitty, for sure, but bears the distinction of being directed by Jonas Åkerlund, the original drummer for Swedish black metal pioneers Bathory. In 2011, *Horsemen*'s Book of Revelations serial murder and forced-body-modification motifs turned up in equally lukewarm form on the much-lambasted season six of the TV series *Dexter*.

Hostel (2005)

(Dir. Eli Roth; w/Jay Hernandez, Derek Richardson, Eythor Gudjonsson, Jennifer Lim)

✢ Torture

Saw bloodied Halloween 2004 as the harbinger of a new, ugly age in Hollywood horror. After a 2005 warm-up at festivals, *Hostel* solidified that advent as the first major U.S. studio release of 2006, prompting fright-film-loving *New York* magazine critic David Edelstein to crystallize the genre development, for better or worse, as "torture porn." He also suggested "gorno."

The "torture porn" tag posited that *Hostel* and *Saw* use sadistic violence to sexually arouse the audience and then dismemberment, death, or both to deliver viewers to climax. Though hardly a new selling point in exploitation films, the context was unprecedented, as Edelstein acknowledged: "Explicit scenes of torture and mutilation were once confined to the old Forty-Second Street, the Deuce, in gutbucket Italian cannibal pictures like *Make Them Die Slowly*, whereas now they have terrific production values and a place of honor in your local multiplex."

Heavy metal had long been plumbing these toxic depths by the time *Saw* and *Hostel* came to be. What makes the torture-porn-movie phenomenon significant here is how it intertwined with metal from altogether new angles. Movies had always led the culture previously. From its Black Sabbath birthing point, metal followed the lead of film, first echoing gothic spook flicks and the elegant blood-red terror of Hammer Films. As horror edged into the increasingly explicit slasher cycle and chunk-blower zombie adventures, heavy music responded with progressively more savage sounds and lyrics, ultimately spawning death metal. And then came grindcore and power electronics, and metal surpassed motion pictures in terms of mining the most unconscionably evil extremes in the human psyche and vividly representing the violation of the last conceivable taboos. *Saw* and, more substantially, *Hostel* are where the movies played catch-up.

Two ugly American frat bros (Jay Hernandez and Derek Richardson) and their Icelandic pal (Eythor Gudjonsson) backpack across Europe, acting thoroughly despicably. Blindingly gorgeous Eastern European sirens persuade to them head for Bratislava, where constant war and hardship have depleted the male population, meaning that "there is *so* much pussy" and it is desperate. Upon arriving, our trio of nonheroes goes to what they're told is a youth hostel, but is in fact an abandoned factory that has been converted into a human slaughterhouse. The slaughtering doesn't happen quickly. Or cleanly. Or for nothing.

Before we can piece together what, exactly, is going on inside the hostel, a Japanese businessman wanders out of it, dazed and seeming postorgasmic. "You can spend all your money in there," he warns. The customer is played by Japan's premier horror cinema visionary, Takashi Miike (*Audition, Visitor Q, Ichi the Killer*). He makes a fantastic creep.

The shock twist of *Hostel* offers a live wire of dread in 2005 that no movie had achieved for ages. The killing house is a resort for superwealthy sickos set up by post-Soviet gangsters. Young people are dispatched to the facility by seductive, good-looking scouts, and then the highest bidder is allowed to do absolutely anything he or she desires to the purchased victim. The individual atrocities displayed thereafter are suitably awful and cinematically impressive, but the movie's more subtle shadings hammer home the living nightmare: a gang of criminal children roaming the streets, the failed doctor's monologue as he preps for forced fatal surgery, and the lack of sympathy elicited early on by the three assholes, for whom we must then root.

The true horror of *Hostel* is, in fact, its truth: the entire thing is just so soul-sickeningly believable. It's a fucked-up world in which we live and die. Extreme metal and torture-porn horror keep us sane. But what escalating extremes are necessary, then, to truly go *insane*?

HOSTEL: PART II (2007)

(DIR. ELI ROTH; W/LAURA GERMAN, BIJOU PHILLIPS, HEATHER MATARAZZO, MONIKA MALACOVA)

✠ TORTURE PORN ✠ COUNTESS BATHORY
✠ CANNIBALS

Hostel: Part II returns to the human slaughterhouse. Among members of the sick secret circle who pay to torture and murder unwitting victims there, a bidding war ensues over the coming arrival of a trio possessing the most highly prized characteristics: they're healthy, white, attractive, college-age young women from America. Laura German, Bijou Phillips, and

Heather Matarazzo play the Americans. Predictably heinous fates await them. Bijou dies grossly. Heather's demise is the central set piece of the film and perhaps the most explicitly heavy metal horror moment of cinema in the 2000s.

The former "Wienerdog" of *Welcome to the Dollhouse* (1996) is all grown up and quite attractive. She awakens naked, hung upside down above an elaborate bathtub. An elegant European woman (Monika Malacova), obviously of noble breeding and vaguely vampiric, enters in a velvet cape, strips bare, and lies in the tub. The reclining woman then reaches up to Heather with a scythe and slashes her twitching body repeatedly, orgasmically bathing in the blood that rains down. The noblewoman's name, in order to dispel any doubts as to the reference, is Mrs. Bathory.

Laura German turns the tables on her captor at *Hostel: Part II*'s climax. Writer-director Eli Roth really swings to knock it out of the park with the single most grotesque dismemberment ever depicted in a Hollywood film, but it falls a bit short. While no film of *Hostel: Part II*'s caliber has ever graphically and unflinchingly displayed the amputation of a penis and its accompanying testicles that are then tossed to hungry dogs as this one does, the showboat element diminishes the blow. Like Yngwie Malmsteen and other technical masters of metal guitar heroism: all the notes and speed and precision are there, but what's missing is the soul.

Eli Roth is a different kind of horror master. He's the real deal and his original *Hostel* is fraught with soul. *Part II* veers off a bit too far into wanky solo territory. Regardless, in the twenty-first century, nobody shreds better. The character named "the Italian Cannibal" is played by Ruggero Deodato, director of *Cannibal Holocaust* (1980). Roth charmed French beauty and exploitation movie goddess Edwige Fenech out of retirement to cameo as an art professor.

Hot Moves (1984)

(Dir. Jim Sotos; w/Michael Zorek, Jill Schoelen, Adam Silbar, Jeff Fishman, Monique Gabrielle)

✴ Athletic Rock

Hot Moves begins with a static shot the front door of a high school. It's the last day of class. As the credits zoom on- and offscreen, we hear an off-camera teacher ask, "So what do you hope to accomplish in the next three months, Barry?"

"Well, Mrs. Harrison," the student answers, "my friends and I have decided to do something to really enhance our personal growth and self-awareness this summer—we're gonna get LAID!" Cut immediately to a montage of hot fun in the SoCal swelter season set to the driving sounds of New Wave of British Heavy Metal high-flyers Raven pounding out the title track.

Hot Moves is a brash, very funny, never-a-dim-moment entry in the '80s teen sex comedy movie canon. The plot follows four teenage dorks who pledge to pop their cherries before school starts again in September. One of them is played by Michael Zorek, who was Bubba "the Ultimate Party Animal" Beauregard in 1983's *Private School*. From that righteous kickoff, Raven rocks the freewheeling boobs-and-barf spirit into motion and the movie rolls on from there. *Hot Moves* all the way.

Hot Moves's opening segment keeps with Raven's aesthetic. The band proudly described itself as "athletic rock" and even performed in sports gear. As they wail through hot moves, we see a parade of hard-bodied revelers surfing, running, skating, pumping iron, flinging Frisbees, breakdancing, BMX biking, and jet-skiing. One rad dude even juggles bowling balls.

House of 1000 Corpses (2003)

(Dir. Rob Zombie; w/Sid Haig, Bill Moseley, Sheri Moon Zombie, Karen Black, Erin Daniels)

✠ Medical Deviants ✠ Scary Clown ✠ Torture

Rob Zombie transitioned from shock rock superstar to overlord of his own movie subgenre with *House of 1000 Corpses*. Zombie's music videos (esp. "More Human Than Human") pointed toward where his filmmaking would go, combining classic Universal horror of the 1930s and '40s with 1950s fright comics, sci-fi, and pinup imagery as fed through brazen grindhouse barbarism of the '70s and hallucinatory, future-looking, cutting-edge tech of the here and now.

House of 1000 Corpses opens with a time-honored horror premise: a quartet of young adults (Erin Daniels, Chris Hardwick, Rainn Wilson, and Jennifer Jostyn) embark on a road trip, make a scary detour into the roadside Museum of Monsters and Madmen overseen by creepy clown Captain Spaulding (Sid Haig), and then pick up Baby Firefly (Sheri Moon Zombie), a very troublesome hitchhiker. This mistake leads the travelers into the ghoulish torture hovel of the title, home of the hideous Firefly family. In addition to Baby, there's Mother Firefly (Karen Black), adopted son Otis T. Driftwood (Bill Moseley), Grampa Hugo (Dennis Fimple), and giant mutant offspring Tiny (Matthew McGrory). Dr. Satan lives, and practices some unspeakable form of decidedly non-healing medicine, in the basement. Underscoring all the atrocious action is Dr. Wolfenstein hosting an all-night monster movie on TVs strewn about each room.

From this setup, *House of 1000 Corpses* reels off an imaginative, amphetamine-furious cavalcade of candy-colored evil, merry mutilation, and trippy gross-outs, jolted to ever increasing degrees of intensity by sideways soirees into genuinely chilling doom. Zombie's simultaneously berserk and powerfully controlled vision in *House* was a one-of-a-kind experience until he returned with *The Devil's Rejects* (2005) and his *Halloween* revamps. As it stands now, *House of 1000 Corpses* is the table of contents for Rob Zombie's directorial canon—a growing terror trove to which he is always adding new and unexpected ingredients. Being the first, though, *House* jumps and pulsates and crackles with a vicious, feral zest.

Sid Haig's Captain Spaulding became an instant horror icon. Zombie did for Haig here what Quentin Tarantino did for John Travolta in *Pulp Fiction* (1994), resurrecting him for an entirely new generation. Haig lit up lots of the most remarkable cult and grindhouse films ever made, including *Spider Baby* (1964), *THX 1138* (1970), and *Galaxy of Terror* (1981). He costarred with Pam Grier in *The Big Doll House* (1971), *The Big Bird Cage* (1972), *Black Mama, White Mama* (1973), *Coffy* (1973), and *Foxy Brown* (1974).

From *Easy Rider* (1969) onward, Karen Black ruled as one of gritty '70s Hollywood's most esteemed and prolific actresses—and, in her choice of roles, one of the weirdest. When not appearing in acclaimed films such as *Five Easy Pieces* (1970) and *Nashville* (1975), Karen starred in eccentric curiosities such as *The Pyx*, aka *The Hooker Cult Murders* (1973), *Airport 1975* (1974), *Burnt Offerings* (1976), and Alfred Hitchcock's final effort, *Family Plot* (1976). Karen Black forever earned her horror-queen bones in the TV movie *Trilogy of Terror* (1975). The third segment of this anthology proved to be an instant classic, with Karen battling a foot-high "Zuni fetish doll" come to spear-throwing, fang-gnashing homicidal life inside her apartment.

One segment elevates *House of 1000 Corpses* to a higher plane of witty and sadistic fun. Following a montage of cops discovering Firefly family abominations set to the tune of "I Remember You" by Slim Whitman, Otis places a pistol barrel against the forehead of a deputy (Walton Goggins of *The Shield* and *Justified*). He then forces the cop to his knees. The soundtrack goes silent and the camera slowly climbs skyward, building unbearable suspense as we wait to see if Otis will squeeze the trigger. In these masterful, merciless twenty-five seconds, Rob Zombie establishes himself not just as a legitimate filmmaker, but as a premier pathfinder who determines where horror will venture across the next decade.

The House of the Devil (2009)

(Dir. Ti West; w/Jocelin Donahue, Tom Noonan, Mary Woronov, Greta Gerwig)

✠ Satan ✠ Devil Worship ✠ Satanic Panic

"During the 1980s, 70% of Americans believed in the existence of abusive Satanic Cults," reads a pre-title card at the start of *The House of the Devil.* "Another 30% rationalized the lack of evidence due to government cover-ups. . . ."

Amidst the era of that amusingly questionable statistic, Long Island college student Samantha (Jocelin Donahue) takes a babysitting gig on the night of a full lunar eclipse. She gets a lift to a spooky house in the woods from her pal Megan (Greta Gerwig), meets the supremely unnerving Mr. and Mrs. Ulman (Tom Noonan and Mary Woronov), and learns that the job is not exactly as advertised. Thereafter, all hell breaks loose.

First, though, Samantha snoops around the house, dancing to "One Thing Leads to Another" by the Fixx on her Walkman, and continuously tries to call Megan. Donahue's screen presence and writer-director Ti West's adept control create a slow burn that adds infinite impact to what happens when the unholy fireworks do finally go off. See the payoff yourself and shriek.

House of the Devil's costumes, set design, and art direction create a movie that, were you to happen to catch it on TV, really might make you wonder if it wasn't from the early 1980s. More than the feathered hair and the loud rotary phone, the effectiveness of this trope is due to tone, pacing, and typically unnoticed technical aspects such as lighting and editing. Those features alone would announce Ti West as a dynamic talent; the movie's climactic satanic rapture indicated a new master of horror had arrived.

In keeping with the retro authenticity, MPI issued *House of the Devil* as a special-edition VHS tape, complete in an oversize box reminiscent of '80s horror video labels Wizard, Vestron, Monterey, Lightning, and Video Gems.

House of Psychotic Women (1974), aka Blue Eyes of the Broken Doll; House of Doom

(Dir. Carlos Aured; w/Paul Naschy)

✠ Giallo

Throughout the first half of the 1980s, *House of Psychotic Women* seemed to materialize from nowhere as a VHS tape in every video store on the planet. Nobody had ever heard of the movie before seeing the garish and salacious box cover in horror rental sections, and nobody has spoken much about it since.

House is a Spanish-made film starring the country's primary horror superstar, Paul Naschy, as Gilles. He's a drifter who goes to work in a house owned by three mentally untrustworthy sisters. Shortly after Gilles' arrival, a murderer wearing black gloves (the signature image of the Italian giallo thriller) takes to slaughtering blue-eyed female locals and plucking out their peepers. It's all very European and semi-gothic and amped up with nudity and by the end it makes no sense, but still . . . it's *House of Psychotic Women.*

In 2012, the great film journalist and former Alamo Drafthouse movie curator Kier-La Janisse published her book *House of Psychotic Women,* a masterful memoir in which she recounts her life as reflected in horror films about decidedly disturbed females.

The House with Laughing Windows

(1976)

(Dir. Pupi Avati; w/Lino Capolicchio, Francesca Marciano, Pietro Brambilla)

✠ Giallo ✠ Christian Martyr ✠ Evil Priest

Art restorer Stefano (Lino Capolicchio) travels to an Italian village to fix up the local church's St. Sebastian fresco. The painting was created by the mentally unhinged town creep, Legnani, who specialized in portraits of people near death—the more painful, the better. Legnani long ago disappeared with his two equally insane sisters, and they are all presumed dead, but the more Stefano learns about him, the more gruesome things start happening, including a series of murders.

The House With Laughing Windows is a haunting giallo devoid of many of the genre's staples (no gloved killer, little sexual torture) and builds to a memorably shocking payoff. As an otherworldly group, Roman Catholic martyrs rank among the most metal entities outside of the realms of Satan. St. Sebastian, the subject of all the tumult in Laughing Windows, is particularly metal. Tied nude to a stake and shot through with dozens of arrows, he appears as a statue in the prayer closet in Carrie (1976) and has been adopted by gay Catholics as their unofficial heavenly patron.

How to Train Your Dragon (2010)

(Dirs. Dean DeBlois, Chris Sanders; w/Jay Baruchel, Gerard Butler, America Ferrera)

✠ Vikings ✠ Dragons ✠ Animation

File this film in the children's section of the Heavy Metal Movies library in the sky. Dragon spins the saga of a young Viking warrior who chooses to spare a fire-breathing monster. The two natural opponents learn to understand one another and team up to fight reptilian prejudice amongst the Norsemen. How to Train Your Drag-on is a beautifully animated Viking adventure that surpasses any surface political correctness to interest young minds in Norse mythology. There are some even mildly scary battles between trained dragons and evil ones, so it's not a total wuss-out. Nobody ever said a kid's gateway to heavy metal couldn't be cute.

Howard the Duck (1986)

(Dir. Willard Huyck; w/Lea Thompson, Tim Robbins, Ed Gale)

✠ Space Mutants ✠ Comics ✠ Fake Band (Cherry Bomb)

Emerging in 1973 from a cosmic swamp as a background character in Marvel's archetypically stoner rock comic Man-Thing, Howard the Duck brought absurdism, philosophy, and deadpan dada humor to the funny papers. He smoked cigars and wore a jacket and tie (but, in classic tradition, no pants). The neurotic duck also romanced female "hairless apes" (as he called humans) and engaged in such timely pursuits as hanging out with samurai-costumed John Belushi. At one point, the duck investigated a movie called Waste, modeled after real-life 1976 grindhouse shocker Snuff.

Alas, Howard the Duck, the movie, didn't fly onto screens until 1986, the summer of Top Gun. So this character who once weaved together the crass flippancy of Frank Zappa with the metaphysical explorations of Rush and the sci-fi guile and earthy humor of Hawkwind was forced to fit the slick, stupid tenor of the times. Even with Poison, Cinderella, and Bon Jovi around, no real hard rock band was featherweight enough to match what executive producer George Lucas needed. The movie had to invent one. The band Cherry Bomb is the multi-ethnic, all-female glam metal group with whom Howard becomes involved after beaming to Cleveland from his home planet of Duckworld. They have got electric drum pads, a keytar, Joan Collins shoulder-pads, and everything else there was to hate about 1986. While performing the theme song, at least they have a duck guitarist.

Crimp-maned Cherry Bomb frontwoman Beverly Switzler (Lea Thompson) falls for the web-footed extraterrestrial, and they somehow get mixed up with the Dark Overlord of the Universe, resulting in a shit-show of pointless Industrial Light & Magic special effects. The least special of these is Howard himself. Lucasfilm must have known their duck was a turkey, because they chose to promote the movie by building mystery around Howard's appearance. He is six different tiny actors—including Ed Gale, aka Chucky from the *Child's Play* movies—in a terrible bird costume, with Disney-fied "cute" facial features and a satin baseball jacket. Critics cried "fowl," audiences flew the coop, and one of the all-time great cartoon beasts had his goose cooked by Hollywood.

THE HOWLING (1981)

(DIR. JOE DANTE; W/DEE WALLACE, PATRICK MACNEE, DENNIS DUGAN, BELINDA BALASKI)

✣ WEREWOLVES

Joe Dante's hairy, scary werewolfapalooza *The Howling* stars Dee Wallace as a newscaster stalked by a serial killer who turns out to be a willfully shape-shifting lycanthrope. Working from a witty screenplay by heady indie filmmaker John Sayles, Dante applies to *The Howling* the same barbed, semi-satiric sensibility that made his *Piranha* (1978) a drive-in classic and *Gremlins* (1984) a world-conquering smash. The transformation effects—bubbling skin, cartoon silhouettes, and torsos elongating into what Dante once deemed "Smokey the Bear" monsters—looked great at the time, and, in the aftermath of CGI, they look even better now.

The Howling packs a ferocious (and furry!) surprise payoff that matches where heavy metal was heading when the movie was released: the being we thought we knew was about to violently morph into a whole new kind of wolfman.

The year 1981 proved to be the watershed moment for heavy metal werewolf movies. *The Howling* tore up theaters in springtime and then, come late summer, *An American Werewolf in London* opened on August 21. Joe Dante cut his

teeth editing trailers for legendary exploitation producer Roger Corman. He also profoundly loved Corman's films and others like them. As a result, *The Howling* is packed with appearances by classic horror, B-movie, and cult figures, including John Carradine, Slim Pickens, Dick Miller, and Kenneth Tobey. *Famous Monsters of Filmland* publisher Forrest J. Ackerman is shown brandishing his own magazine in an occult bookstore. Corman himself makes a cameo too. He's waiting for a phone booth.

Like 1981's never-ending torrent of Judas Priest clones, *The Howling* begat a series of increasingly unrelated sequels. Each, in its own way, qualifies as heavy metal. The first couple are best. *Howling II: Your Sister Is a Werewolf* (1985) is a crazy romp fortified by Christopher Lee and a shot of Sybil Danning ripping her top off that gets shown over and over again during the closing credits. *Howling III: The Marsupials* (1987) goes daffy and Down Under for an admirably insane Australian spin on lycanthropy that includes werewolf ballet dancers—with pouches.

THE HUMAN CENTIPEDE (FIRST SEQUENCE) (2010)

(DIR. TOM SIX; W/DIETER LASER, ASHLEY C. WILLIAMS, ASHLYNN YENNIE, AKIHIRO KITAMURA)

✣ MEDICAL DEVIANT

The much ballyhooed *Human Centipede* is what false metal looked like in 2010. Like a lame scenester band cobbling together breakdowns via cut-and-paste software, crazed German scientist (Dieter Laser) attaches two women and a man to one another, lips to anus. The victims then wobble around as a new single being, the Human Centipede. The guy in front (Akirhiro Kitamura) gets to eat food, which he then defecates into the mouth of the chick in the middle (Ashley C. Williams) who, in turn, dumps the twice-shit mix into the oral cavity of the unfortunate lady bringing up the rear (Ashlynn Yennie). Not much else goes down in *The Human Centipede*.

Despite the screamingly repeatable premise

that infiltrated water cooler talk, the movie itself is not gory, graphic, or disturbing—save for a single, hilarious moment of the old Kraut braying, "Feed her! FEED her!" The entire film is a punch line in search of a premise; a six-legged exercise in faux-outrageousness, utterly safe for consumption. Writer-director Tom Six is to be applauded for realizing that people would want "more blood and shit in the sequel." *The Human Centipede II (Full Sequence)*, which chronicles the construction of a ten-person creature, does broker heavily in body fluids. Again, though, the movie itself is a just dumb and ineffective, and pretentiously presented in black-and-white.

Humanoids From the Deep (1980), AKA Monster;

Beneath The Darkness

(Dir. Barbara Peeters; w/Doug McClure, Ann Turkel, Vic Morrow, Lynn Schiller)
✵ **Monster Rape** ✵ **Banned Video Nasty**

"They're not human. But they hunt human women. Not for killing. For mating."

Humanoids From the Deep may be the last completely kick-ass effort from B-movie legend Roger Corman, and by any standards it is also one of the most metal sexploitation horrors to ever bubble up among 1980s headbanger VCR gatherings. The title creatures are green prehistoric fish-men roughly of the *Creature From the Black Lagoon* school, although one has razor arms and one might be a kind of midget. One such humanoid attacks a beachfront tent during the opening scene, raping the topless nubile inside and killing her ventriloquist boyfriend. Only the dummy makes it out intact.

Several more times, walking sea monsters carnally violate a screaming nude woman and slay the dude with her, until local townsfolk put aside their differences to defeat the scaly menace. First they have to learn to be nice to Native Americans. The action builds to a flesh-and-blood-soaked humanoid invasion of a carnival that turns into

an orgy of sex, violence, and sexual violence.

Humanoids is not entirely played straight (one of the heroines wears her sash from the "Miss Salmon" pageant and, as noted, the movie opens with ventriloquist copulation), but it's unflinching and intense and, in the annals of rubber-suit abominations, a pure, shimmering, and glorious beast.

Director Barbara Peeters asked for her name to be removed from the film after producer Roger Corman hired someone else to shoot and insert additional nudity and gore. Peeters's name is still on *Humanoids*, but she publicly distanced herself from Corman, and went to work in television. The movie's name was tarnished in 1996 by a limp remake as part of Showtime's largely counterproductive series, *Roger Corman Presents . . . .*

Hype! (1996)

(Dir. Doug Pray; w/Bruce Pavitt, Jonathan Poneman, Soundgarden, Melvins)
✵ **Distortion** ✵ **Metal Reality** ✵ **Concert Footage**

Hype!, the preeminent grunge documentary, admirably tilts toward the music's metal side. For AM radio pop addicts of the '70s, who dove into teenage punk in the first half of the '80s, then grew some hair following *Master of Puppets* in 1986 and *Locust Abortion Technician* in 1987, grunge was the greatest of all possible worlds: "the Beatles plus Black Sabbath plus Black Flag."

At *Hype!*'s core is the rise and then super-rise of Seattle's Sub Pop Records, the original home of Green River, which spun off into Mudhoney (yay!) and Pearl Jam (nay!); the label also brought the world Soundgarden and Tad, and set Nirvana on the road to "Smells Like Teen Spirit." *Hype!* fills viewers in on the heavier side of the Seattle sound, mainly via incendiary live performances from a time when all of these bands were raw and wild.

By the time *Hype!* debuted at the Sundance Film Festival, in 1996, though, grunge seemed like something already a generation older. The moment when the counterculture crashed the culture had already happened. The film combines shell-shocked "What the hell is happening?" breathlessness with a hungover "What the hell happened?" haziness to grungy effect.

Hysteria: The Def Leppard Story (2001)

(Dir. Robert Mandel; w/Orlando Seale, Karl Geary, Tat Whalley, Anthony Michael Hall)
✻ NWOBHM ✻ Concert Footage

The New Wave of British Heavy Metal's reigning pop crossover act gets the VH1 biopic treatment and, as with other installments on Meat Loaf and the Monkees, it's breezy despite tragic pitfalls, well played, and damned entertaining. *Hysteria* fetishizes the car wreck that cost drummer Rick Allen his left arm, opening with a foreshadowing game of roadway chicken, flashing back to Leppard's '70s beginnings, and then building to the crescendo of the appendage-decimating crash. But that's just giving the audience what it wants.

Similarly handled in cheapie TV movie style is guitarist Steve Clark's alcoholism, which ultimately proved fatal in 1991. Since this is a band-okayed VH1 cash-in, any attempt as "tastefulness" would actually ruin the campy fun. Snippets of Leppard hits float across the soundtrack. You get what VH1 was willing to pay for. The inevitable montage set to "Hello America" does prove inevitable. And Anthony Michael Hall is a howl as Leppard super-producer Mutt Lange.

I

I COME IN PEACE ✡ I DRINK YOUR BLOOD ✡ I KNOW WHO KILLED ME ✡ I LOVE YOU, MAN ✡ I SPIT ON YOUR GRAVE ✡ ICHI THE KILLER ✡ ILSA, SHE WOLF OF THE SS ✡ I'M NOW: THE STORY OF MUDHONEY ✡ IMMORAL TALES ✡ INCIDENT AT CHANNEL Q ✡ THE INCUBUS ✡ INFERNO ✡ INSIDE ✡ INTERCESSOR: ANOTHER ROCK 'N' ROLL NIGHTMARE ✡ INTREPIDOS PUNKS ✡ INVASION OF THE BLOOD FARMERS ✡ INVASION U.S.A. ✡ INVOCATION OF MY DEMON BROTHER ✡ IRON EAGLE ✡ IRON MAIDEN AND THE NEW WAVE OF BRITISH HEAVY METAL ✡ IRON MAIDEN: FLIGHT 666 ✡ IRON MAIDEN: 12 WASTED YEARS ✡ IRON MAIDEN: BEHIND THE BEAST ✡ IRON MAIDEN: BEHIND THE IRON CURTAIN ✡ IRON MAIDEN: DEATH ON THE ROAD ✡ IRON MAN ✡ ISI/DISI: AMOR A LO BESTIA ✡ IT'S SLEAZY

I Come in Peace (1990), AKA Dark Angel

(Dir. Craig R. Baxley; w/Dolph Lundgren, Betsy Brantley, Brian Benben, Matthias Hues)

✡ Science Fiction ✡ Horror ✡ Alien Drugs

I come in peace," says extraterrestrial drug trafficker Talec (Matthias Hues), prior to slaying many victims with a deadly flying CD. Houston vice cop Jack Caine (Dolph Lundgren) responds, finally dispatching the space pusher, "You go—IN PIECES!"

I Come in Peace is the best of Dolph Lundgren's highly metal and enjoyable late-'80s/early-'90s grindhouse action run. Output like this kept his name on drive-in double bills and in the fun part of the video store alongside contemporaries Steven Seagal and Jean-Claude Van Damme. Fast-paced and fantastically violent, *Peace* starts as a straightforward hard-boiled cop thriller, then adds in somebody killing people with vibrating discs that defy gravity. The explanation is almost worthy of David Cronenberg: Talec pumps his targets full of heroin, then siphons their overdosing endorphins to peddle to junkies back on his home planet. Ultimately, our hero teams with an alien cop named Azeck (Jay Bilas) who's been chasing this menace all over the galaxy.

Dolph starred as He-Man in the 1987 *Masters of the Universe* movie; to me, though, the gnarly, Hong Kong–esque version of *The Punisher* (1989) in which he starred remains the most metal Marvel Comics film adaptation ever. Also recommended as metallically Dolph-rific: *Red Scorpion* (1989), *Showdown in Little Tokyo* (1991), and *Universal Soldier* (1992).

Similar to Dolph's streaking comet of a career as a B-movie draw is that of *I Come in Peace* director Craig R. Baxley. The veteran stuntman first helmed the cult Carl Weathers blowout *Action Jackson* (1988), then went on to the incredible Brian Bosworth biker stomp *Stone Cold* (1991), in which, I shit you not, the Mississippi Supreme Court is assassinated on-screen with machine guns.

I Drink Your Blood (1970)

(Dir. David E. Durston; w/Bhaskar Roy Chowdury, Lynn Lowry, Jadine Wong, Rhonda Fultz)

✠ Satan ✠ Black Mass ✠ Manson Family

Let it be known, sons and daughters, that Satan was an acid head. Drink from his cup; pledge yourselves. And together, we'll all freak out!"

So speaketh long-haired hippie cult leader Horace Bones (Bhaskar Roy Chowdury) in his LSD benediction that opens up *I Drink Your Blood*, the greatest of all Manson Family exploitation movie cash-ins and an angry, rampant outbreak of hallucinogenic heavy horror that will fry even the soberest and most un-metal of minds. Bones and his seven dosed disciples descend on a small town and rough up some residents. For revenge, a local kid injects meat pies with blood from a rabid dog and feeds them to the scraggly interlopers. In short order, the satanists transform into blood-parched, drug-amped, foaming-at-the-mouth zombies who attack the townsfolk. One groovy chick even offers herself up for gangbang purposes to a group of construction workers. That's how *I Drink Your Blood* proves that there's one sure way to bring hippies and hard hats together: rabies.

Everyone and everything goes nuts. Limbs and heads get hacked off. Blood flies. A pitchfork pierces flesh. And it all ends with a police-mounted massacre of the rabid ones, and my single favorite closing line in all of cinema: "Death from hydrophobia is agony." *I Drink Your Blood*, from beginning to end, is Heavy Metal Movie ecstasy. Raise your devil horns—because that's what the cult members all do in the opening seconds of this 1970 classic.

Exploitation maven Jerry Gross, distributor of I *Drink Your Blood*, purchased the rights to a black-and-white 1964 voodoo snooze called *Zombies*, which he retitled *I Eat Your Skin*. Gross paired the two as a double feature that ran in grindhouses and drive-ins throughout the '70s. Upon seeing a newspaper ad for *I Drink Your Blood/I Eat Your Skin* during its 1977 rerelease, I was inspired to cut it out, and thus began my childhood hobby of making scrapbooks of crazy movie stuff, which eventually led to me writing this book.

I Know Who Killed Me (2007)

(Dir. Chris Sivertson; w/Lindsay Lohan, Julia Ormond, Neal McDonough, Michael Adler)

✠ Torture ✠ Soundtrack (Dead Meadow, Melvins, the Sword)

Lindsay Lohan stars as a stripper (who doesn't strip) in *I Know Who Killed Me*, a box office bomb and Razzie Award–type alleged "bad" movie that, of course, is infinitely more bizarre and interesting and worthwhile than the piddle-whiz our cultural tastemakers insist is good. Movies, quite often, are like heavy metal in that way.

I Know Who Killed Me delves into metal country with hallucinatory sequences of abduction, punishment, and possibly amputation, plus a tricky double-identity motif that boils over from psychological fright to lava-lamp-lit body horror. Lilo is at her most naturally beautiful and charismatic. Her most intense real-life downward spiral to date remained just around the corner at this point. *I Know Who Killed Me*'s soundtrack leans heavy on stoner metal. I take it as a message to Lindsay: switch to weed, sweetheart.

I Love You, Man (2009)

(Dir. John Hamburg; w/Paul Rudd, Jason Segel, Rashida Jones, Lou Ferrigno, Rush)

✠ Rush ✠ Lou Ferrigno

Paul Rudd is the uptight groom-to-be. Jason Segel is the lovably unkempt perpetual adolescent. *I Love You, Man* is the "bromantic" comedy in which this odd couple comes together. On paper, that plot's a groaner, but *I Love You, Man* is elevated by a state-of-contemporary-comedy cast having a blast, a funny subplot involving Lou

Ferrigno's mansion, and that the bonding point of snob and slob is none other than progressive metal gods Rush.

After jamming to "Tom Sawyer" in Segel's man cave, the dudes attend a Rush concert accompanied by Rudd's stick-in-the-mud fiancée (Rashida Jones), and the scene wittily captures the agony being stuck at a metal show with the wrong chick. Rudd and Segel wail and flail and sing along with "Limelight" while Jones stands with her arms folded, rolling her eyes, and bitching about getting bumped. We've all been there.

I Love You, Man concludes with the heroes performing "Limelight" at Rudd's wedding, and they pull the bride onstage to join them. Rocking well is the best revenge.

Director John Hamburg is a lifelong Rush devotee who chased his famously shy idols with humble persistence. Hamburg told the website *Coming Soon*: "Once Rush got that I wasn't poking fun at them, that I'm genuinely a fan and the main characters of the movie are fans…that's when they came onboard."

Rush so enjoyed appearing in *I Love You, Man* that their 2010–11 Time Machine tour included a video featuring Rudd and Segel backstage as their characters from the movie.

I Spit on Your Grave
(1978), aka Day of the Woman
(Dir. Meir Zarchi; w/Camille Keaton, Eron Tabor, Richard Pace, Anthony Nichols)
✠ Rape and Revenge ✠ Banned Video Nasty

The "Stairway to Sexual Assault Heaven" of rape and revenge grindhouse potboilers, *I Spit on Your Grave* boasts one of the best-known exploitation movie titles—and yielded one of the most vividly remembered Heavy Metal Movie viewing experiences. New York City novelist Jennifer Hills (Camille Keaton, a distant relative of Buster) travels to a riverfront Connecticut cottage to complete a book. After she has an uncomfortable encounter with some local men, they

beat, rape, and humiliate her for two horrifically sustained segments that equal 25 percent of the total film time.

Close to death but also fully alive, Jennifer builds her strength back up and exacts gruesome vengeance on her assailants. She slowly hangs the mentally deficient Matthew (Richard Pace), and then seduces macho Johnny (Eron Tabor) with a hot bath. Upon stroking him just to the point of orgasm, Jennifer slips a knife into the water and slices off his genitals. Gentlemen: if you've ever wanted a movie to make you feel as though you're going to faint, fast-forward right to that bathtub scene.

Finally, Jennifer dispatches Andy (Gunter Kleemann) with an axe and speeds a boat out to Stanley (Anthony Nichols), who is flailing in the river. Stanley begs for mercy, but Jennifer backs the motor right into his gut, repeating the words he used while raping her: "Suck it, bitch!"

From a metal perspective, the scenes showing Jennifer's phoenix-like resurrection cascade like an acoustic folk metal interlude (very woodland-like), and then those showing her wreaking vengeance upon the creeps are power metal mixed with more horror-focused elements of the New Wave of British Heavy Metal.

I Spit ran for years on grindhouse and drive-in bills, and did shockingly huge business in the early days of home video. It is inextricably linked to heavy metal and extreme culture of the early '80s, when time and technology united a new generation of the dark-hearted curious to converge over music and movies that spoke especially to them.

Filmed as *Day of the Woman*, the movie bombed under that title. Renamed *I Spit on Your Grave* for a 1981 rerelease, it packed theaters and sent moral guardians into ticket-selling tizzies. Gene Siskel and Roger Ebert dedicated an entire thirty-minute episode of their PBS series *Sneak Previews* to decrying *I Spit on Your Grave*.

"This woman has just cut, chopped, broken, and burned five men beyond recognition," the

DOLPH LUNDGREN

DARK ANGEL

SKYROCK

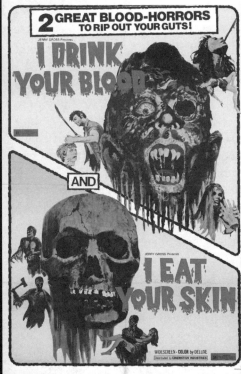

2 GREAT BLOOD-HORRORS
TO RIP OUT YOUR GUTS!

JERRY GROSS Presents

I DRINK YOUR BLOOD

AND

JERRY GROSS Presents

I EAT YOUR SKIN

WIDESCREEN · COLOR by DELUXE
Distributed by CINEMATION INDUSTRIES

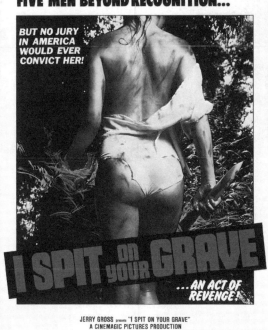

THIS WOMAN HAS JUST
**CUT, CHOPPED, BROKEN, and BURNED
FIVE MEN BEYOND RECOGNITION...**

BUT NO JURY
IN AMERICA
WOULD EVER
CONVICT HER!

I SPIT ON YOUR GRAVE

...AN ACT OF
REVENGE!

JERRY GROSS presents "I SPIT ON YOUR GRAVE"
A CINEMAGIC PICTURES PRODUCTION
A MEIR ZARCHI FILM

starring CAMILLE KEATON · ERON TABOR · RICHARD PACE · ANTHONY NICHOLS

DISTRIBUTED BY THE JERRY GROSS ORGANIZATION   Color By METROCOLOR ®

R RESTRICTED

Clockwise from top left: Dark Angel, *aka* I Come in
Peace *(1990); a legendary double bill;* Iron Maiden:
Flight 666 *(2009) and* Iron Maiden: The Early Days
*(2004); he is Iron Man (2008); "No jury in
America would ever convict her!"*

movie's famous tagline, is erroneous. Jennifer only kills five men, and no one gets burned (not in the literal sense, anyway; I suppose getting your dick cut off is a real "burn," though).

I Spit on Your Grave generated a worthless 2010 remake of the same name—and that stupidity shat out its own 2013 sequel. As usual, the imitations and knockoffs are more interesting. My favorite of these is *I Spit on Your Corpse, I Piss on Your Grave* (2001), from Wicked Pixel studios, starring Emily Haack of the harrowing *Scrapbook* (2000). Emily's fearless performance includes making hard-core full-penetration love to a broomstick and forcing her assailant's face into a pile of horribly real-looking human shit.

After making *I Spit on Your Grave*, Camille Keaton and director Meir Zarchi were briefly married. Imagine that honeymoon!

Ichi the Killer (2001)
(Dir. Takashi Miike; w/Nao Omori, Shin'ya Tsukamoto, Tadanobu Asano, Alien Sun)
✳ Extreme Japanese Gore ✳ Censorship

Filmmaker Takashi Miike is a creative leviathan who mastered the hardest-edged material in Japan's ultraviolent cinema and then pushed upward and onward into avant-garde experimentation and brain-smashing breakthroughs. Miike rose through direct-to-DVD "V-Cinema" movies (Japan's equivalent of Red Box rentals and Syfy original films). His breakthrough came via his one-of-a-kind sickening romantic torture story *Audition* (1999), and the insanely violent yakuza saga *Dead or Alive* (1999). *Ichi the Killer* is Miike's signature film, though, and a psychotic tsunami of heavy metal perversity and gore splashing in the highest of Japanese styles.

Homicide broker Ichi (Nao Omori) is a meek sexual degenerate who only becomes truly aroused when witnessing or, better yet, perpetrating acts of ludicrous physical violation. A mystery figure uses Ichi to knock off yakuza gangsters one at a time, by associating each with a traumatic incident in the killer's past (childhood bullying, rape, more rape, etc). The manipulator outfits Ichi in a leather superhero-style getup equipped with easy-flip razor-sharp blades. Clad in this archetypically metal outfit, he wastes humanity in mind-boggling manners and numbers.

There is something cartoonish about the general overkill of *Ichi*, but not to the point that the movie, while witty, ever becomes a joke. It's like watching a virtuoso guitarist teeter from shredding into ridiculousness—you'll smile, you might laugh, but only because you and he both know, at heart, that it's serious. In the tradition of Heavy Metal Movie greats of the grindhouse era such as *Mark of the Devil* (1970), *Ichi the Killer* patrons received barf bags when the movie played film festivals in Stockholm and Toronto.

Ilsa: She Wolf of the SS (1974)
(Dir. Don Edmonds; w/Dyanne Thorne, Gregory Knoph, Uschi Digard, George "Buck" Flower)
✳ Nazi "Camp" ✳ Banned Video Nasty

Heavy metal and the Third Reich are two unsavory flavors that oftentimes make brilliant bad taste together. Now, to be sure, I am not referring to National Socialist Black Metal and/or the punk-influenced stuff that whips up skinheads at white-power rallies. Such examples, I believe, betray the purpose of metal, which is to wage sonic and aesthetic warfare against obedient groupthink, authoritarian collectivism, and general faith in the assholes in charge.

Metal's freedom-fighting arsenal, however, should lob—and always has lobbed—taboo ideas and images against all enemies. And in polite society, no more verboten wellspring of iconography exists than that of Adolf Hitler and his merry Mengele (along with the rest of those devious *dummkopfs*). So from Lemmy Kilmister's Axis uniform collection to "Angel of Death" by Slayer to the iron spiky logo of MTV's *Headbangers Ball* to Marilyn Manson's fixation on swastikas, metal has long exploited Teutonic totalitarianism to achieve its own goals.

Exploitation movies operate the same way. The grindhouse-gashouse twain started to meet with *Love Camp 7* (1969), then detoured through the art house via *The Night Porter* (1974), before ascending to the "Stairway to Himmler" of Nazisploitation cinema: *Ilsa, She Wolf of the SS*. Aryan Amazon Dyanne Thorne embodies the titular figure like a Panzer assault in and out of jackboots. Ilsa runs a prison camp where no limits exist when it comes to use and abuse of the human inmates. The women are sex slaves; when used up, they become subjects for inhuman scientific experiments. A different male services Ilsa each night—only to be castrated and executed immediately upon ejaculation. An American GI infiltrates both the compound and Ilsa herself, turning the movie from a connect-the-atrocities series of sicko set pieces into a pulp story out of a vintage men's adventure magazine.

The acting in *Ilsa* is very strong. Director Don Edmonds keeps everything moving in tight, exciting fashion. Like *Bloodsucking Freaks* (1976), *Ilsa, She Wolf of the SS* is a cultural transgression. One scene in the movie crystallizes *Ilsa*'s metallic Bavarian brutality: a bound, naked teenage girl is placed standing atop a block of ice as the centerpiece of a long Nazi banquet table. Around her neck is a wire noose. As the *schweinhund* officers drink and dine, they barely notice the ice melting and the girl gradually choking to death.

Alp-endowed German milkmaid Uschi Digard and bombastically robust natural redhead Sharon Kelly die horrendously in *She Wolf*, but then they both appear good-as-nude in the follow-up, *Ilsa, Harem Keeper of the Oil Sheiks* (1976). Of the sequels, *Oil Sheiks* is a worthily repugnant follow-up, diminished simply by its dearth of Nazis. *Ilsa, the Tigress of Siberia* (1977) is amusing but, aside from a chainsaw arm-wrestling scene (with dudes, to boot), it's a weak comedown from the first two. *Ilsa, the Wicked Warden* (1977), directed by Jess Franco, began life as *Wanda the Wicked Warden*, and then was retitled to count as a franchise film. Thorne runs a South American women's prison. It's disgustingly fantastic.

Rob Zombie's *Werewolf Women of the SS* trailer in *Grindhouse* (2007) is his tribute to Nazisploitation in general, and *Ilsa* in particular. Metal tributes have come with "Ilsa" songs by At War and Impaled Nazarene spin-off Diabolos Rising, along with Pungent Stench's hilarious and foul Iraq War reworking "Lynndie, She-Wolf of Abu-Ghraib." Today, in actual life, Dyanne Thorne works as the minister of a wedding chapel in Las Vegas. As for the real-life Ilse Koch, "the Bitch of Buchenwald," she was the first noteworthy Nazi war criminal to face a U.S. military trial. Despite announcing that she was eight months pregnant, presumably by an American guard, the court showed no sympathy or patience for her at all.

I'M NOW: THE STORY OF MUDHONEY (2012)

(DIR. RYAN SHORT; W/MUDHONEY, KIM THAYIL, STONE GOSSARD, JEFF AMENT, TAD DOYLE)

✠ DISTORTION ✠ PROTO-METAL ✠ FLANNEL

Mudhoney circa 1988 is like Metallica circa 1982. For just as Metallica boomed forth a new era of hard rock with *Kill 'Em All* by injecting their metal with punk, Mudhoney heralded the definitive sound of the upcoming decade by power-fortifying their punk with metal. "Touch Me I'm Sick," Mudhoney's signature anthem, ruptured the world like the Stooges with Tony Iommi playing lead. They built the Seattle sound in a mucky garage, a pack of combustive youths who grew up naturally absorbing every connection between the Dicks and Kiss, the Sex Pistols and Cheap Trick, T.S.O.L. and Ted Nugent, and the Melvins and Celtic Frost.

Before Mudhoney, there was Green River, an inadvertent proto-grunge supergroup featuring Mark Arm on vocals, Stone Gossard on guitar, and Jeff Ament on bass. A split led to Gossard and Ament forming Pearl Jam after a stop in Mother Love Bone, while Arm teamed with axe master Steve Turner and ex-Melvins bassist Matt Lukin to create Mudhoney. No matter what else was brewing up in the Pacific Northwest, "Touch

Me I'm Sick" was the handmaiden that delivered into the popular consciousness the likes of Soundgarden, Tad, Screaming Trees, L7, Nirvana, and all your flannel-flying favorites.

I'm On: The Story of Mudhoney does a top-notch job of chronicling that origin story, but then the movie seems to pull its punches at the moment when Nirvana—essentially perceived as Mudhoney's kid-brother band early on—not only surpassed the relatively elder statesmen, but conquered the entire universe in 1991 (side by side with, fittingly, the post–Black Album Metallica).

More than two decades have passed since that dawn period, and *I'm On* provides a great look at the history of '90s rock that had no choice but to soldier on in the shadow of Nirvana. Killer concert footage, funny interviews, and the constant presence of Sub Pop records (Mudhoney's famous launch pad) turn the movie into a natural and valuable follow-up to the grunge-just-after-ground-zero documentary *Hype!* (1996).

Immoral Tales (1974)
(Dir. Walerian Borowczyk; w/Paloma Picasso, Charlotte Alexandra, Florence Bellamy)
✠ Countess Bathory ✠ Lucrezia Borgia

Immoral Tales is a four-part erotic anthology by Polish surrealist Walerian Borowczyk. The opening salvo is a seaside "my first blow job" chronicle livened up by the teen characters being cousins. Next up is a bit of sacrilege with luscious French dish Charlotte Alexandra thinking of Christ and consuming vegetables not with her mouth. The third immoral tale reckons with heavy metal. Paloma Picasso (yes, Pablo's daughter) stars as Countess Elizabeth Bathory, the inspiration for Sweden's black metal pioneers and countless other heavy metal marauders.

Featuring no dialogue, the film weaves a spell of complete arousal as Borowczyk sumptuously photographs dozens upon dozens of naked nubiles in Bathory's lair while they wait for their opportunity to bed the notorious noblewoman. Unknown to the girls is that the countess's

sapphic indulgence teeters over into sanguine madness: after sex, she slaughters her concubines and bathes in their blood. When the red stuff flows—in volumes that would make *The Shining*'s Overlook Hotel elevators jealous—the camera shoots it as lovingly as all the fresh flesh and dewy adolescent awakening that, moments earlier, had been so bewitching. Of the screen's many representations of Countess Bathory, *Immoral Tales'* twenty-four-minute interlude remains the sexiest, the most evocative, and by far the most drenched in blood.

Immoral Tales' fourth quarter is a clunker, but depicts another decadently depraved European aristocrat, incest-happy pope-fucker Lucrezia Borgia (Florence Bellamy).

A fifth chapter of *Immoral Tales* was developed into its own movie. 1975's *La Bête* (*The Beast*), also directed by Borowczyk, documents a fevered affair between a betrothed virgin (Finnish sex symbol Sirpa Lane) and a huge, hairy, black Sasquatch creature that blasts semen all over her naked body from his ebony-hued elephant-trunk dick. I told you Borowczyk was a surrealist.

Incident at Channel Q (1986)
(Dir. Storm Thorgerson; w/Al Corley, Joe Janus, David Dreisin, Lisa Lees)
✠ Censorship ✠ Music Videos ✠ Soundtrack
(Lita Ford, Iron Maiden, Kiss, Motörhead)

In a feat of money saving that must have made notorious B-movie cheapskate moguls Roger Corman and Lloyd Kaufman bow like Wayne and Garth before Alice Cooper, *Incident at Channel Q* incorporates eleven music videos into just enough plot to achieve a feature-length running time. These are not original music sequences created for the film; they are preexisting promo clips made and paid for by record companies that had already been through the MTV rotation mill. Instant movie!

Channel Q is a rock video network that broadcasts from a quiet suburban hamlet. All goes kablooey upon the arrival of a new motorcycle-jacketed, chain-jangling VJ (Al Corley). He's had enough of Channel Q's bland programming, so he locks himself in the studio and storms the airwaves with totally radical programming, mostly consisting of videos that were a couple of years old by the time the movie came out. Outside, the locals go as ballistic as the budget allows. They wield "Stop Video Filth" picket signs and give fake interviews to fake TV news teams. Thus "metalheads" square off against "straights," interrupted on occasion by the revolutionary likes of "Twilight Zone" by Golden Earring and "In and Out of Love" by Bon Jovi.

As a metal exploitation curiosity and a relic of its moment, *Incident at Channel Q* would be invaluable even if it didn't contain the clip for Deep Purple's comeback anal sex anthem, "Knockin' on Your Back Door." Among the other *Radio 1990* fodder in this film are "Aces High" by Iron Maiden, "All Hell's Breakin' Loose" by Kiss, "The Body Electric" by Rush, "Gotta Let Go" by Lita Ford, "Iron Fist" by Motörhead, and "Rock You Like a Hurricane" by Scorpions.

The movie is officially rated R, and a legitimate soundtrack album was released, but no newspaper ads or other evidence of a theatrical run exists. Still, I must try to believe paying customers entered a public auditorium and were shown old music videos on a big screen, which would have been an exploitation triumph.

THE INCUBUS (1982)

(DIR. JOHN HOUGH; W/JOHN CASSAVETES, KERRIE KEANE, DUNCAN MCINTOSH, JOHN IRELAND)

✠ DEMON RAPE ✠ WITCHCRAFT

During a savage wave of rape-murders in a small New England town, local pathologist Dr. John Cordell (John Cassavetes) repeatedly has to clean "red sperm" out of female corpses. Meanwhile, his daughter's troubled boyfriend Tim (Duncan McIntosh) suffers visions of hooded torturers laying into bound women. Are the two connected? Has an actor ever had a grosser way with the word *ruptured* than Cassavetes?

When Tim worries about whether he might be responsible for the crimes, he ducks into a theater where, lo and behold, New Wave of British Heavy Metal dynamos Samson are rocking onstage. Everybody's good headbanging time is harshed when yet another woman is banged to death in the bathroom. As the title suggests, the culprit is actually the incubus, a shape-shifting evil force looking to impregnate witches.

An occult spin on the slasher film cycle, *The Incubus* never quite pushes its repugnant concept to effective cathartic horror or cheap cheeseball thrills. Mostly, between fitfully impressive brutality, it's just downbeat and deadening, albeit original. Extra points for Samson's appearance, though it is actually culled from the unfinished film *Samson: Biceps of Steel*, by Julien Temple.

The Incubus introduced the word *incubus* to the heavy metal lexicon, leading to a baby boom of over a hundred songs with that title and nearly a dozen bands taking the moniker.

Incubus director John Hough is also a Hammer horror vet (1971's *Twins of Evil*), who also made *The Legend of Hell House* (1973) and brought post-*Fantasia* metal to Disney movies in the form of *Escape to Witch Mountain* (1975) and *Return From Witch Mountain* (1978).

INFERNO (1980)

(DIR. DARIO ARGENTO; W/IRENE MIRACLE, LEIGH MCCLOSKEY, ELEONORA GIORGI, DARIA NICOLODI)

✠ '80S ITALIAN HORROR ✠ DARIO ARGENTO

The most incomprehensible of Italian terror master Dario Argento's classics—and that, for sure, is saying something—*Inferno* is a lot of loose pieces that add up to a heavy metal symphony of crazy horror. The plot centers on an ancient book titled *The Three Mothers*, about three evil sisters who lord over humanity with darkness, sorrow, and tears. Anywhere the book goes, convulsive murder follows.

Inferno drips with gothic witchery and fiery eroticism, all lit up with vivid colors and visual shocks. Argento's mentor, Mario Bava (*Black Sabbath*), created some of Inferno's most striking visual effects and took over shooting in spots when the director became ill with hepatitis. Bava, sadly, died just before *Inferno* was released.

INSIDE (2007),
AKA À L'INTÉRIEUR
(DIRS. ALEXANDRE BUSTILLO, JULIEN MAURY; W/ BEATRICE DALLE, ALYSSON PARADIS)
✠ HORROR ✠ FRANCE

The French shocker *Inside* is the closest any movie has ever come to actually making me toss my baguettes. The film begins as an affecting drama about hugely pregnant Sarah (Alysson Paradis), alone on Christmas Eve and mourning her husband, who died in a car crash four months earlier. A character known only as the Woman (Beatrice Dalle) appears on Sarah's doorstep. She is clad head to toe in black, with bright white skin, plump red lips, and straight, inky-dark hair, resembling a witch from a Dario Argento movie. She turns out to be much worse than that. The Woman attacks Sarah and attempts to cut the baby from her belly. That assault is ongoing for the remainder of the movie.

Sarah's mother, local policemen, even a pet cat get in the way of the Woman and—well, they don't stay in the way. For over an hour, *Inside* is a cat-and-mouse chase between two almost superhuman females—one who seems programmed to obtain a baby at any cost, the other biologically wired to protect the same baby. I was shaky through almost all of this *Inside*'s running time. Right before something unthinkable involving scissors happens, I felt intense physical nausea. Bear in mind, please, that I am no wilting flower. My life has been spent in endless pursuit of heinous and horrific cinematic images.

Inside grinds nerves and bludgeons emotions while building to an awesome volcanic climax.

The film is one of two crown jewels among an unexpected explosion of extreme horror coming from France in the 2000s. *Martyrs* (2008) is the other. That pair of merciless masterworks—along with fellow horror contenders such as *In My Skin* (2004), *High Tension* (2005), *Frontier(s)* (2007), and *The Hunt* (2010) plus the art film outrages of Gaspar Noe and Catherine Breillat—mirror France's ascendant nihilistic metal output of the same decade by way of Deathspell Omega, Antaeus, Aosoth, Arkhon Infaustus, Artefact, Dagoba, Gojira, and Year of No Light.

INTERCESSOR: ANOTHER ROCK 'N' ROLL NIGHTMARE (2005)
(DIRS. BENN MCGUIRE, JACOB WINDATT; W/JON MIKL THOR, CHRIS ALLEN, RACHEL BERNHARDT)
✠ THOR

This spiritual sequel to *Rock 'n' Roll Nightmare* (1987) relights the star of mighty metal man Jon Mikl Thor in the title role. He is a specific superhero type who wields a hammer of the gods. When demons Mephisto (Craig Bowlsby) and Zompira (Dave Collette) attempt to besmirch the "last two innocent souls on Earth," the Intercessor steps in on their behalf. While no official soundtrack album has been released, you can pick up the movie's theme song, "Intercessor," on the 2002 Thor album, *Triumph*. The album also contains "Fubar Is a Super Rocker" from *Fubar: The Movie* (2002), and "Hail Steve Reeves," a tribute to the original *Hercules* star.

INTREPIDOS PUNKS (1983)
(DIR. FRANCISCO GUERRERO; W/ROSITA BOUCHOT, MARTHA ELENA CERVANTES, EL FANTASMA)
✠ MOTORCYCLES ✠ NUNSPLOITATION ✠ MEXICAN GANGS ✠ SATANIC ORGY

The berserk Mexican biker movie revamp *Intrepidos Punks* is a loud, frantic, and batshit loco piece of cinematic warfare. Far from the fashionista punk rockers of CBGB, these are violent hairy brutes living in caves, whose purple Mohawks are basically afros held in place by colorful spray paint. My kind of guys!

The first sight is a quartet of nuns entering a bank and tossing off their habits to reveal that they are machine gun-wielding, high-heeled female members of the Intrepidos Punks gang, led by leather-bikini-clad Beast (Princess Lea). They're there to rob the joint. The punkettes need money to free their locked-up male partners from jail, including gang honcho Tarzan (El Fantasma, a big-shot *luchador* wrestler in Mexico). The wildly made-up women then kidnap the wives of prison officials. This results in a suburban rape orgy set to the jams of acid rock house band Three Souls in My Mind, who set up band practice in the living room and pound away at the movie's theme song ("*Sex y drogas y violencia*!") while the abuse of the cop wives continues. This vivid tableau climaxes with Beast chopping off a victim's hand to mail to the correctional facility as a threat.

After the hand-in-the-mail ploy pans out, the newly reunited Intrepidos Punks tear through town and retreat to the desert on dune buggies, motorcycles, muscle cars, tricked-out trikes, and other wacky vehicles, including one of those half-motorcycle/half–VW Bug numbers with a giant Yes band logo painted on the back. Along the way, they speed about firing off guns, howling, and setting people on fire. Then the real party begins. The punks get wasted and throw themselves lustily into a black magic orgy in their satanic lair, complete with post-orgasm crying jags. Big boobs abound and bounce freely.

A pair of scuzzy, hairy-lipped, pussy-hound cops half-assedly pursues the punks, setting up a fittingly colorful firefight finale. Nothing indicates that *Intrepidos Punks* takes place in a post-apocalyptic world, except the punks themselves—e.g., the way they look, the garish death machines they drive, the fact that they seem to operate out of a cave, etc. Still, this movie should be properly categorized as a *Road Warrior* cash-in.

The public record lists *Punks*' production year as 1980, but, really, there's just no way this film so pointedly influenced *Road Warrior* and not vice versa. Other sources date *Punks* being made in 1983, which makes sense, except that the non-punk sequences look and feel like 1973. The music played by Three Souls in My Mind throughout the movie is not even remotely "punk," but is bluesy garage-psych that would have grooved perfectly on the soundtrack of any '60s biker movie. *Intrepidos Punks,* for that and countless other reasons, really does clamp down on the concept of "timeless. The sequel, *La Venganza De Los Punks* (1987), is noticeably nastier.

INVASION OF THE BLOOD FARMERS (1972)

(DIR. ED ADLUM; W/NORMAN KELLEY, TANNA HUNTER, BRUCE DETRICK, CYNTHIA FLEMING)

✡ DRUIDS ✡ HUMAN SACRIFICE

Invasion of the Blood Farmers begins with a history lesson all about the ongoing practices and religious rituals of blood-eating druids from outer space. Most importantly, we learn that these druids live among us now—even in northern Westchester County, New York! The blood farmers in question are good-ole-boy types led by Creeton (Paul Craig Jennings), who love to guzzle Miller High Life, hang dogs, and grab female victims in the shower. They just want to revive their blonde queen (Cynthia Fleming), who lies comatose in a glass coffin. Dr. Roy Anderson (Norman Kelley) does high-minded battle against the fiends.

Looking and feeling like Andy Milligan's cracked horror cheapies, but not as turn-you-to-cement boring, *Blood Farmers* is hilariously confusing and actually quite watchable. The story has great a metal premise and pleasingly inept execution. Cringe along and love it. Director Ed Adlum previously made a sexploitation flick with a killer proto-metal title: *Blonde on a Bum Trip* (1968). He followed *Blood Farmers* with the Yeti-run-amok movie *Shriek of the Mutilated* (1976).

Edlum shot *Blood Farmers* over three weekends for $24,000. He claims the movie never earned back that investment. He also says most of the actors were paid in six-packs of beer; Miller, no doubt—the cans are all over the place on-screen.

In spite of fantastically lurid VHS-box artwork (a raging Blood Farmer is about to harvest a busty blonde screamer with a pitchfork), *Invasion of the Blood Farmers* slipped under many metal radars by virtue of being rated PG. At the time *Blood Farmers* was released, renting a PG horror movie would have been the equivalent buying the clean version of a heavy metal album. The great horror-drenched doom metal band Blood Farmers can probably take credit for reviving the film's reputation in recent years.

Invasion U.S.A. (1985)

(Dir. Joseph Zito; w/Chuck Norris, Richard Lynch, Melissa Prophet)

✠ Chuck Norris ✠ Massive Destruction

Seeing the stakes raised by *Red Dawn* (1984) and upping the ante insanely (albeit on a much lower budget), *Invasion U.S.A.* is a Cannon Films creation in which Chuck Norris, as ex-CIA agent Matt Hunter, goes up against a full-scale Soviet infiltration of southern Florida. As happens in such films, the real battle comes down to Hunter against Russian operative Mikhail Rostov (Richard Lynch), and global conflict gets settled by way of a climactic mano a mano whack-down.

Invasion U.S.A. is an ass-beating riot, and two sequences hold up as high headbanging entertainment today: Norris piloting his pickup truck against enemy bullets through a mall crowded with holiday shoppers, and Lynch's rampage in which he plunges a woman's head down onto the metal straw through which she's snorting cocaine and turns her nostrils into blood hoses, after which he shoves his gun down a guy's pants and fires directly into the jerk's dick.

Invasion U.S.A. joins S.O.D.'s breakthrough hardcore-metal crossover milestone, *Speak English or Die*, and arcade games like *Contra*

in a unique category of comically over-the-top violently patriotic mid-1980s entertainment. God bless *that* America.

Invocation of My Demon Brother (1969)

(Dir. Kenneth Anger; w/Kenneth Anger, Anton LaVey, Bobby Beausoleil, Rolling Stones)

✠ Occult ✠ Anton LaVey ✠ Manson Family

Avant-garde filmmaker and trippy Crowleyan occultist Kenneth Anger made use of his late-'60s friendship with mystically curious rock superstar Mick Jagger to concoct *Invocation of My Demon Brother*. The eleven-minute whirlwind of nonsensical images, seductively assembled, consists of scraps of Anger's long-in-gestation *Lucifer Rising*, which was not completed until 1972. As a Moog synthesizer score by Jagger plays away, *Invocation* hurls sights including Rolling Stones concert snippets, a bong made from a real human skull, Church of Satan leader Anton LaVey performing a devilish funeral for a cat, and a black cherub holding a sign that reads: "ZAP—YOU'RE PREGNANT—THAT'S WITCHCRAFT."

The same year that *Invocation* came out, Bobby Beausoleil, who plays Lucifer, was arrested while driving the car of a man he had stabbed to death days earlier. Beausoleil was a member of the Manson Family, and this "political piggy" murder launched their infamous Helter Skelter killing spree. Bobby remained close to Kenneth Anger for years, and even composed and performed the score for *Lucifer Rising* from behind bars.

Iron Eagle (1986)

(Dir. Sidney J. Furie; w/Louis Gossett, Jr., Jason Gedrick, Tim Thomerson, Caroline Lagerfelt)

✠ Military Action ✠ Soundtrack (Dio, Helix, King Kobra, Queen, Twisted Sister)

Iron Eagle beat *Top Gun* to the box office by nearly six months in 1986, yet it wasn't exactly a hit. Perhaps this Reagan-age adventure just primed the populace for USA #1 aerial bravura and Tom Cruise to swooped in to reap the benefits. The movie's misfire is a minor shame because *Iron Eagle* moves faster than *Top Gun*. Plus the movie features a score by Dio, Helix, and King Kobra. And as for official theme songs, Queen ("One Vision") beats Kenny Loggins ("Danger Zone").

Jason Gedrick expected to be a behemoth movie star after *Iron Eagle*, and that's how he plays the lead, a cocky novice flyer charged with rescuing his shot-down air force officer father (Tim Thomerson). Master pilot Colonel Charles "Chappy" Sinclair (Louis Gossett Jr.) is his tutor. Together, they make a lot of oily Arab bad guys go boom.

The silliness of *Iron Eagle* seems to contradict its serious military film pedigree. Gossett was still riding high from an Oscar-winning performance in *An Officer and a Gentleman* (1982). Director Sidney J. Furie had previously made the Vietnam drama *The Boys in Company C* (1978), which enormously influenced Stanley Kubrick's *Full Metal Jacket* (1987). By the mid-'80s, they were each ready to ride the dum-dum *Iron Eagle* express for the next decade. Three sequels followed: *Iron Eagle II* (1988), *Aces: Iron Eagle III* (1992), and *Iron Eagle on the Attack* (1995). Lou Gossett appears as Chappy in each film.

Dio's *Iron Eagle* contribution "Hide in the Rainbow" was released in 1986 on the UK-only release *The Dio EP*. The EP also includes "Hungry for Heaven," a rather surprising "Baba O'Reilly" sound-alike that graced the Madonna-laden soundtrack for the great Matthew Modine high school wrestling movie *Vision Quest* (1985).

IRON MAIDEN AND THE NEW WAVE OF BRITISH HEAVY METAL (2008)

(DIR. ROB JOHNSTONE; W/PAUL DI'ANNO, NEIL KAY, BRIAN TATLER, BARRY "THUNDERSTICK" GRAHAM)
✸ NWOBHM ✸ METAL HISTORY

Amidst the unexpected groundswell of stylized talking-head heavy metal history documentaries such as the movies of Sam Dunn and the TV production *Heavy: The Story of Metal* came the unauthorized but eminently entertaining English production *Iron Maiden and the New Wave of British Heavy Metal*. The usual suspects appear (Geoff Barton, Malcolm Dome, Joel McIver, Garry Bushell), but IMATNWOBHM stands out by showcasing talks with pioneering metal club owner Neil Kay and under-interviewed musicians along the lines of Paul Di'Anno and Dennis Stratton (Iron Maiden), Brian Tatler (Diamond Head), Barry "Thunderstick" Graham (Samson), and Robb Weir (Tygers of Pan Tang), as well as all four members of Girlschool.

IRON MAIDEN: FLIGHT 666 (2009)

(DIRS. SAM DUNN, SCOT MCFADYEN; W/IRON MAIDEN, RONNIE JAMES DIO, VINNY APPICE)
✸ CONCERT FOOTAGE

Directors Sam Dunn and Scot McFadyen also helmed *Metal: A Headbanger's Journey* (2005), *Global Metal* (2008), and *Rush: Beyond the Lighted Stage* (2010). Iron Maiden hits the air, literally, in a private Boeing 757 piloted by frontman Bruce Dickinson. The occasion is the first leg of the band's early 2008 Somewhere Back in Time tour, the largest of their career, with stops in India, Australia, Japan, the U.S., Canada, Mexico, and South America.

The members of Maiden prove not just to be survivors (this is the rare metal documentary devoid of tragedy), but great company. Dickinson, in particular, keeps up his engaging British chatter, familiar to anyone who's seen them live, and remains in constant motion. Just like the plane—which is named, in honor of Maiden's famous undead mascot, "Ed Force One."

Lively interviews and expertly shot concert footage are bolstered by visits with Maiden fans all over the globe. One of them is Reverend Marcus Motolo, a Brazilian priest who earned the nickname "Father Iron Maiden," in part, because he sports "162 Iron Maiden tattoos" and counting. Father Iron Maiden's countryman Bruno Ismael Zalanduskas catches a drumstick tossed by Nicko McBrain. Bruno erupts into tears and can't stop crying for thirty-eight tremendously moving seconds, as genuine an exhibit of human emotion captured anywhere in documentary cinema.

Flight 666 played theaters for a "one-off screening" worldwide on April 9, 2009. The movie is a love letter to its audience from one of the true monoliths of beloved evil music. "It's about integrity," Dickinson says. "We did it our way."

Iron Maiden: 12 Wasted Years (1987)

(Dir. Julian Caidan; Steve Harris, Neal Kay, Charles Webster, Paul Di'Anno)

✠ **Metal History** ✠ **NWOBHM** ✠ **Eddie**

The deadpan and profoundly British documentary *Iron Maiden: 12 Wasted Years* offers a selective history of the band from their mid-1970s formation on to their World Slavery tour and the recording of *Somewhere in Time* in 1986. This early summary is by no means exhaustive, but the overall tone captures the essence of the group. Highlights include stunning rare footage of shirtless Paul Di'Anno rip-roaring through "Charlotte the Harlot" in 1980. Steve Harris provides a tour of the Ruskin Arms pub, where the cult of Maiden first amassed. EMI exec Charles Webster explains his professional dedication to the band whilst sitting on a park bench next to two befuddled old ladies.

Roadies, managers, and other behind-the-scenes figures sound off, including Neal Kay, DJ at the Bandwagon, the New Wave of British Heavy Metal's hottest room. Several offhand references are made to paper and cardboard guitars wielded by early Maiden fans, but we don't actually see them. Check out the twenty-minute black-and-white Music Box documentary included as a bonus on *Iron Maiden: The Early Years* to witness that crucial moment in time.

12 Wasted Years appears as a bonus feature on the 2013 DVD reissue of the concert video *Maiden England '88*. Each complements the other screamingly well.

Iron Maiden: Behind the Beast (2012)

(Dir. Andy Matthews; Bruce Dickinson, Janick Gers, Steve Harris)

✠ **Metal Reality** ✠ **Concert Footage**

The astonishing Iron Maiden documentary *Flight 666* (2009) is a tough act to follow. This later film, *Iron Maiden: Behind the Beast*, attempts a different angle. The band loads up onto its famous Boeing 747, Ed Force One, for a 2011 world tour. Now the focus is on the behemoth technical undertakings involved in making every aspect of the Maiden organization fly.

Sorry to lower the altitude here, but *Behind the Beast* is lackluster. Roadies, electricians, flight attendants, art directors, stage managers, business managers, Eddie managers; any or all of these essential support staff could be essential viewing with Iron Maiden as a backdrop. Alas, *Behind the Beast* comes off like all the stuff you didn't know you were glad was left out of *Flight 666*.

This feature is included as a bonus on the 2012 concert DVD *En Vivo!*, shot in Santiago, Chile. Stick with the musical aspects of that package.

Iron Maiden: Behind the Iron Curtain (1984)

(Dir. Kenny Feuerman; Iron Maiden)

✠ **Metal History** ✠ **NWOBHM** ✠ **World Metal**

Iron Maiden: Behind the Iron Curtain runs just a half hour, but the production was a home video landmark, portraying the group at a new height of its own power in the dangerously unknown territory of Communist Poland. For these iron curtain metalheads, Iron Maiden rolling into town ignited the equivalent of Beatlemania. The band arrives at the airport to find a legion of fans sitting on the actual building. One kid tells vocalist Bruce Dickinson that he longs to play heavy metal on a synthesizer. Another kid charms concert tickets for himself and two comrades out of a cameraman with a passionate speech about how much Iron Maiden means to him. The state police are shockingly accommodating, because, as Steve Harris puts it, "They're all fans!"

The Poles may have bought black-market bootlegs of the albums, but the ticket sales were real. Maiden performs: "2 Minutes to Midnight," "Hallowed Be Thy Name," and "Run to the Hills." Also, after searching the streets unsuccessfully for an open pub, the band crashes an actual wedding and jams Deep Purple's "Smoke on the Water" for the delighted partygoers.

Iron Maiden's 2008 *Live After Death* DVD contains a fifty-eight-minute version of *Behind the Iron Curtain* with extra performance footage.

Iron Maiden: Death on the Road (2005)

(Dir. Matthew Amos; w/Bruce Dickinson, Janick Gers, Steve Harris)

✵ **Iron Maiden's Let It Be**

Iron Maiden: Death on the Road is a multimedia release built around a 2003 Maiden performance in Dortmund, Germany. In addition to video of the concert itself, the DVD includes a seventy-minute documentary on the recording of Iron Maiden's thirteenth album, *Dance of Death*, with producer Kevin Shirley.

The DVD special-feature material is pretty standard, made noteworthy for including the first officially issued footage of the group actually laying down tracks in a studio. We see the members playing in black-and-white, broken up by full-color talking-head interviews. Technical minutiae are hashed out. Licks are rehearsed and played several times before being rehearsed and played several more times. Maiden completists will be in behind-the-scenes heaven; all others will likely be best served by sticking with the concert disc.

Iron Man (2008)

(Dir. Jon Favreau; w/Robert Downey Jr., Gwyneth Paltrow, Jeff Bridges, Terrence Howard)

✵ **Iron Man** ✵ **Soundtrack (Black Sabbath, AC/DC, Suicidal Tendencies)**

Marvel Comics' only openly alcoholic superhero provided the perfect rehab vehicle for Hollywood's most ludicrously alcoholic bad-boy-bouncing-back. As billionaire playboy turned mechanized crime-fighter Tony Stark, Robert Downey Jr. is perfectly matched with a witty script and deft direction by Jon Favreau. *Iron Man* is the zestiest, most enjoyable, and lightest of all the modern comic book blockbusters.

Stark's first attempt at building an Iron Man suit, while he's held hostage in a cave in Afghanistan, results in a retro-metal masterpiece; gray, huge, and vintage sci-fi robotic. If early 1970s proto-metal (Sir Lord Baltimore, Dust, Budgie) could be a mechanical monster, this is exactly what it would look like. The movie ends with one of modern cinema's great parting shots. At a press conference, Tony Stark leans into a microphone and cockily announces, "I am Iron Man!" The screen cuts, immediately, to the Black Sabbath anthem pounding over the end credits.

Isi/Disi: Amor a lo Bestia (2004)

(Dir. Chema de la Peña; w/Santiago Segura, Florentino Fernández, Jaydy Michel)

✵ **Spanish Metalheads** ✵ **Soundtrack (AC/DC covers, Sin City Six)**

Isi (Santiago Segura) and Disi (Florentino Fernández) are thirtysomething metalhead brothers and best buds in Spain who get into slapstick mishaps on par with their equivalents in Los Estados Unidos, Wayne and Garth and/or Beavis and Butt-Head. Given the looser limitations on comedy in earthy European productions, the movie's two big gags involve one woman getting sperm-hosed in the face and another undergoing unexpected sodomy.

The jokes are dumb and reveal no new or credible knowledge of headbanger customs or lifestyle, but those aforementioned punch lines are quite *el metallico*. "Isi Disi" is the Spanglish pronunciation of AC/DC. The movie's heroes are huge AC/DC fans, and several cover songs appear on the soundtrack.

It's Sleazy (2001)

(Dir. Dave Brockie; w/Gwar)

✡ Massive Destruction ✡ Dismemberment

It's Sleazy ends the ten-year cycle of Gwar concept videos commenced by the Grammy-nominated *Phallus in Wonderland* (1992). The alien heavy metal marauders appear as guests on the *Jerry Springer*–like TV talk show of their preposterously pompadour-adorned manager, Sleazy P. Martini. The topic: "Gwar Ruined My Life." Parody commercials, explosions of gore, sexual mayhem, and rip-roaring, fluid-spewing performances by theatrical metal's all-time champs fill out the bill. When "Marilyn Manson" (not actually him) disdainfully tells Gwar to "go back to art school," the band graphically tears off his skin. *It's Sleazy* is the final Gwar video to feature veteran members Danielle Stampe (Slymenstra Hymen) and Hunter Jackson (Techno Destructo).

Jackass: The Movie

(2002)

(Dir. Jeff Tremaine; w/Johnny Knoxville, Steve-O, Bam Margera, Ryan Dunn)

✠ Youth Revolt ✠ Soundtrack (Slayer, Misfits)

Jackass: The Movie does exactly what Jackass the MTV show did, only bigger, louder, and more naked. Johnny Knoxville leads his fear-free merry miscreants through Three Stooges–style slapstick sans special effects, basically embodying the cartoonish violence of Beavis and Butt-Head made apparently indestructible flesh. By extension, the Jackass gang lives out, and nearly dies over, the dumbest, most hilariously self-destructive impulses cooked up by every testosterone-drunk gaggle of young male metalheads out to challenge the boundaries of mortality. Henry Rollins and Andrew WK make cameos.

Two sequels followed. Each one is crucial viewing; taken together, the Jackass films comprise one of Heavy Metal Movies' most titanically idiotic and indispensible trilogies. Jackass Number Two (2006) ups the gross-out ante, and adds Turbonegro, Wolfmother, and more Slayer to its soundtrack. Jackass 3D (2010) features a proper intro by Beavis and Butt-Head.

Jason and the Argonauts (1963)

(Dir. Don Chaffey; w/Todd Armstrong, Nancy Kovack, Gary Raymond, Honor Blackman)

✠ Greek Mythology ✠ Sword-Fighting Skeletons

The Greek myth turned Technicolor legend Jason and the Argonauts is stop-motion animator Ray Harryhausen's towering masterpiece. His vividly implanted sights later shaped heavy metal album covers, songwriting, fashion, and daydreams. Various humans portray the gods and mortals in the story of heroic Jason and his Argonauts' quest to find the golden fleece, but the real stars are the supremely metal objects and monsters, all imbued with movement, presence, and vitality by Harryhausen and model builders and animators. Jason and the Argonauts is a classic metal wonderland, a direct connection to eternal mysteries and ancient revelations.

Four visual segments in particular reign monumentally. In one, bat-winged harpies attack a blind soothsayer in a sustained assault of terror; in another, the sea god Triton (son of Poseidon) rises from the waves to part narrow mountains so that Jason's ship, the Argo, may pass through them. Talos, a ten-story bronze statue, comes to life and stomps Argonauts all over a beach. Most spectacularly metal of all, after Jason slays the seven-headed, dragon-like Hydra, a thief sows the beast's teeth in the ground, and from each tooth a skeleton warrior rises to do battle. The Argonauts go steel-to-steel and flesh-to-bone against these relentless enemies in a spectacular spray of visual effects. *Army of Darkness* (1993) is essentially an entire homage to this sequence.

JAWBREAKER (1999)

(DIR. DARREN STEIN; W/ROSE MCGOWAN, REBECCA GAYHEART, JULIE BENZ, MARILYN MANSON)
✠ HIGH SCHOOL HELL

*J*awbreaker attempts to update the classic pitch-black teen satire *Heathers* (1999) for the post-Lollapalooza, pre–*Mean Girls* set, and the result is thoroughly loathsome—albeit not in the "deliciously evil" way that writer-director Darren Stein would have it. Rose McGowan and pals Rebecca Gayheart and Julie Benz accidentally choke a classmate at Reagan High to death with the titular candy, and then attempt to cover it up.

Somehow this leads to a makeover comedy "subverted" by Rose sodomizing a high school jock with a Popsicle (off-camera) and Marilyn Manson as a jailbait-chasing bar skeeze. At the time, Rose, described here as "Satan in heels," was the real-life Mrs. Manson. Beyond the forced presence of Mr. Antichrist, *Jawbreaker* only gets about as metal as an ironic use of the Scorpions' "Rock You Like a Hurricane."

THE JERKY BOYS: THE MOVIE (1994)

(DIR. JAMES MELKONIAN; W/JOHN G. BRENNAN, KAMAL AHMED, ALAN ARKIN, OZZY OSBOURNE, HELMET)
✠ PRANK PHONE CALLS

*J*ust as metal titans from Bathory to Metallica arose on the power of fans exchanging endlessly copied cassettes, the original batch of prank phone call recordings by the Jerky Boys

were passed around, en masse, from one class clown and office cutup to another throughout the early '90s, creating a semi-secret society bonded by passwords like "sizzle-chest," "needle-nips," and "Look, *jerky*, I don't need to talk to *you!*"

After Howard Stern repeatedly aired the tapes, the Boys scored an Atlantic Records contract in 1993, sold eight million CDs, went to number one on the *Billboard* charts, and became the stars of the only Disney-financed multimillion-dollar motion picture based on a couple of mooks from Queens harassing clueless clods via telephone. *The Jerky Boys: The Movie* is a genuinely funny Mafia farce that plays to the strengths of stars John G. Brennan and Kamal Ahmed, casting with big-time actors who know how to make mobsters hilarious (Alan Arkin, William Hickey, and Vinny "Big Pussy" Pastore among them).

Ozzy Osbourne cameos as the manager of Helmet. New York's most dressed-down alt-metal foursome were coming off a weird moment as the first underground act to cash in on the post-Nirvana major label gold rush (and then hardly delivering *Nevermind* numbers with the resulting Interscope album, *Betty*).

Helmet must have either been good sports or under professional pressure (somehow I can't imagine frontman Page Hamilton busting up over "Tarbosh the Egyptian Magician"). Either way, they make the most of their rock club moment with a searing take on Black Sabbath's "Symptom of the Universe."

JESUS CHRIST SUPERSTAR (1973)

(DIR. NORMAN JEWISON; W/TED NEELEY, CARL ANDERSON, YVONNE ELLIMAN, JOSH MOSTEL)
✠ TORTURE ✠ CRUCIFIXION

*J*esus Christ and the devil's music, heavy metal, are not entirely strange bedfellows, beginning in the 1960s with hippie psych groups such as Agape, Jesus People, and the Resurrection Band, then on through Stryper's glam and Trouble's doom in the '80s, all the way to religious nü-metal courtesy of System of a Down and Christian metalcore in the 2000s. Then there is the fact that in the hands of innumerable anti-Christian bands, Christ on the cross is proven metal fodder. *Jesus Christ Superstar*—from its initial 1970 concept album to its 1971 Broadway triumph to Norman Jewison's psilocybin-scented 1973 movie version—just might be that cosmic cross section's heaviest incarnation.

First off, Judas is the hero, the protagonist, and the most sympathetic character. *Superstar* opens with the Apostle who would peddle his spiritual guru for thirty pieces of silver wailing through "Heaven on Their Minds," a scathing, bad-trip masterpiece detailing Judas's doubts as to all this "Son of God" hoo-hah. And things spiral down from there. The last days of Christ on Earth come to us from the point of view of his traitor. It's all pain, doubt, weeping women, rage at the establishment, mindless followers out for their own self-interests, Jesus sweating blood as he ponders his own beating, humiliation, and execution. The film then ends with the crucifixion and not, tellingly, anybody's resurrection.

The music may only occasionally flirt with metal—the Pharisees' number "This Jesus Must Die," as you'd imagine, comes closest—but does contain elements of acid rock, heavy psych, prog, retro-burlesque, even krautrock tape loops and soundscapes. Equally a product of its time is how Jewison and his art directors chose to mount the movie. Like some distant relatives of the Manson Family, a troupe of actors pulls up to a series of minimalist sets in a stony desert. They goof around, try on costumes, and then get to acting out the story. All the dialogue is sung, and the action takes place on self-consciously unfinished constructions among the rocks.

Unfortunately, Jesus himself (Ted Neeley) lacks the superstar qualities that would make the movie as vital as the original record. It's cosmically frustrating to ponder what the film might have been had a deal been struck with any of the A-list names initially attached to star, including

John Lennon and Mick Jagger. On the 1970 *Jesus Christ Superstar* concept album, Deep Purple vocalist Ian Gillan sings the part of Jesus. Jewison wanted Ian to star in the movie. Gillan asked for a sizable salary, and also insisted that the other members of Purple be paid, as filming would disrupt their tour plans. Among the supporting cast, Paul Thomas, who plays Peter, went on to work for decades as a porn performer and then director.

In the end, the movie is a worthy, interesting take on composer Andrew Lloyd Webber and lyricist Tim Rice's Heaviest Story Ever Sung. The flogging of Christ, depicted here in real time via thirty-nine long, bloody lashes, is gruesome. The film also packs a divine wallop on the eve of the Crucifixion, when Neeley-as-Christ sings the epic number "Gethsemane." He belts pure rage to God over the fate awaiting him and wonders if he should just walk away and let the world be damned. At the crescendo—an explosion of soul-wrenching horns—Jewison intercuts a close-up montage of medieval passion paintings. One by one, the blood-red colors and images of agony hammer home the physical horror of Christ's sacrifice to devastating cinematic effect.

JIMI HENDRIX (1973),
AKA A FILM ABOUT JIMI HENDRIX
(DIRS. JOE BOYD, JOHN HEAD, GARY WEIS; W/JIMI HENDRIX, MICK JAGGER, LITTLE RICHARD)
✵ CONCERT FOOTAGE

The biographical documentary *Jimi Hendrix*, which hit theaters just three years after the guitar god's death, combines performance footage that's since become familiar (from Woodstock, the Isle of Wight, and the *Jimi Plays Berkeley* movie) with talking-head interviews involving classic rock royalty still in their prime. Mick Jagger is particularly engaging when he candidly admits he doesn't know if Jimi's demise has any deeper meaning. As a film, *Jimi Hendrix* is nothing revolutionary. As a straightforward time capsule regarding a musical revolution—

Clockwise from top left: Jason and the Argonauts *(1963) make Greek mythology even more metal;* Jimi Hendrix *(1973) lives (on film);* John Carter *(2012) flees Martian mutant maneaters; Caiaphas and company conspire to crucify* Jesus Christ Superstar *(1973)*

ary, it's a gem. *Jimi Hendrix* does afford us a rare filmed treat: the master working his magic acoustically. Jimi's transcendent performance of "Gettin' My Heart Back Together" on a twelve-string is mesmerizing. Little Richard talks about firing Hendrix as his guitar player for being too flamboyant. Watching Little Richard run through his anecdotes at his high-haired, bug-eyed, squealing maddest, the mind reels at what that could have possibly meant. Also included for your mind-spinning amusement: Jimi, appearing chemically modified while tripping out *The Dick Cavett Show*.

Jimi Plays Berkeley (1971)

(Dir. Peter Pilafian; w/Jimi Hendrix, Mitch Mitchell, Billy Cox)

✡ Concert Footage ✡ Youth Gone Wild

The title describes what you get in *Jimi Plays Berkeley*. After a few minutes of "sign of the times" footage of hippies up to what they were up to in 1970 (which includes picketing a theater showing *Woodstock*), we get a full Jimi Hendrix performance shot at the Berkeley Community Theater on May 30, 1970. Intercut with scenes of more unrest among the unwashed (including a full-blown campus riot) are shots of Hendrix, with Billy Cox on bass and Mitch Mitchell on drums, thundering through "Purple Haze," "The Star Spangled Banner," "Little Wing," "Voodoo Child," "Machine Gun," "I Don't Live Today," "Hey Baby," "Lover Man," and what would stand as the most mind-frying cinematic take on "Johnny B. Goode" until the Sex Pistols gave it a shot in *The Great Rock 'n' Roll Swindle* (1980). In campus theaters and art house venues, this documentary was as much a staple of late-night film programming of the 1970s and '80s as *Harold and Maude* (1971), *Phantom of the Paradise* (1974), *The Song Remains the Same* (1977), and even *The Rocky Horror Picture Show* (1975).

Jodorowsky's Dune (2013)

(Dir. Frank Pavich; w/Alejandro Jodorowsky, H. R. Giger, Nicholas Winding Refn)

✡ Science Fiction ✡ Alternate Reality

This instant must-see documentary is the closest we can get to laying our eyes on what might be the heaviest and most metallic movie never made: master surrealist Alejandro Jodorowsky's big screen interpretation of Frank Herbert's line-in-the-cosmic-sand 1965 sci-fi novel, *Dune*. The glorious insight provided here by director Frank Pavich is that *Dune* may well be the most influential movie never made.

The list of talent Jodorowsky had assembled in 1974 remains skull-popping. *Dune* was to star Mick Jagger, Marlon Brando, David Carradine, Gloria Swanson, and—as an emperor atop a giant toilet throne—Salvador Dali. Production design and special effects were underway by future *Return of the Living Dead* creator Dan O'Bannon, French comic book genius Moebius, and Switzerland's supreme metal visual artist, H. R. Giger, who designed both the title creature of *Alien* and painted the cover image of Celtic Frost's *To Mega Therion*. Soundtrack music was planned from Pink Floyd, Magma, and Peter Gabriel. And again, all this would be filtered through the cracked genius director of *El Topo* and *The Holy Mountain*. The Jodorowsky take on *Dune* embodied 1970s Hollywood at its most madly imaginative and inventively ambitious. We all know now that David Lynch made *Dune* in 1984—here's the same story with an alternate beginning.

Joe Dirt (2001)

(Dir. Dennie Gordon; w/David Spade, Brittany Daniel, Jaime Pressly, Kid Rock)

✡ Def Leppard Bashing ✡ Soundtrack (Argent, Thin Lizzy, April Wine)

Joe Dirt is David Spade's intentionally illiterate love letter to mullet-coifed, denim-vested, blonde-mustached specimens of lower-income

Caucasian manhood most prevalent circa 1974–84. The picture comes courtesy of Adam Sandler's forever metal-friendly Happy Madison production studio. Spade stars as the title character, a janitor who sets forth on an adventure wherein he encounters white-trash wonder women (Brittany Daniel and Jaime Pressly, each at her height of hotness); a mobster named Clem (Christopher Walken); and a bully in need of comedic comeuppance (Kid Rock).

Joe Dirt is overall too lightweight, and lacks the courage of its Southern scumbag–lampooning convictions, but Kid Rock calls it correct when he hollers after a retreating Spade: "Def Leppard sucks!" And I do always laugh when the dog's balls are frozen to the front porch.

John Carter (2012)

(Dir. Andrew Stanton; w/Taylor Kitsch, Lynn Collins, Willem Dafoe, Samantha Morton)
✠ Science Fiction ✠ Swords & Sorcery

Pulp author Edgar Rice Burroughs is most famous for inventing Tarzan, but his second-best-known creation is even more metal than the Lord of the Apes: John Carter of Mars. Introduced in the 1917 novel *A Princess of Mars*, Carter was a Confederate captain in the Civil War who, during the gold rush, was spiritually projected to Mars, or "Barsoom," as the planet is known to natives. There, Carter becomes a warlord, romances Princess Dejah Thoris, and has centuries of adventures battling space aliens and mythical beasts since, due to the atmosphere of Mars, he can leap huge distances and perform mighty feats of strength. Also, he can't die.

John Carter was immediately popular and proved hugely influential on subsequent characters such as Superman and Flash Gordon. The imagery surrounding John Carter of Mars largely set the template for heavy metal fantasy art. Everything from sexy space-girl novel covers to airbrushed scenarios on Chevy van panels to the entirety of *Heavy Metal* magazine (and the movie) emerge from this wellspring. Marvel's *John Carter, War-*

lord of Mars and *Conan the Barbarian* ruled as the most metal comic books of the 1970s.

Throughout the 1930s, Warner Brothers animator Bob Clampett repeatedly tried to make a full-length animated *John Carter of Mars* feature, but it wasn't until the twenty-first century that another animator, Pixar director Andrew Stanton, finally made a properly epic *John Carter* movie for Disney. *John Carter* falls short—they didn't even properly call it *John Carter OF MARS*, for Barsoom's sake—but not for lack of attempting to melt our faces and rock our skulls. Carter (Taylor Kitsch) does his best swinging a sword and taking on CGI landscapes and opponents that obviously aren't there (especially in 3-D). He romances Princess Dejah (Lynn Collins) and fights a walking city, and it all looks like a very loud video game that someone else is playing. In the end, *John Carter* lost more than $200 million for Disney and resulted in the exile of Rich Ross, the studio boss in charge at the time, to Mouska-Siberia. That's some kind of metal accomplishment. An orchestral cover of Led Zeppelin's "Kashmir" appeared in the *John Carter* trailer, recorded by the female string quartet Bond.

Direct-to-DVD "mockbuster" studio the Asylum rushed out their own *Princess of Mars* with Antonio Sabato Jr. as John Carter and Traci Lords as Dejah. *Princess of Mars* looks like PC-desktop moviemaking crap, but Sabato ain't half-terrible leading this sub-Syfy-channel nonsense. Lords, still luminously luscious in her forties, makes a fantastically sexy heroine. And *Princess* had the last laugh, beating the trouble-plagued big-screen version to market by three years.

Johnny Got His Gun (1971)

(Dir. Dalton Trumbo; w/Timothy Bottoms, Kathy Fields, Jason Robards, Donald Sutherland)
✠ "One" ✠ War Is Hell

Directed by Dalton Trumbo from his classic 1939 antiwar novel, the film version of *Johnny Got His Gun* first found a sympathetic audience at the height of America's Vietnam conflict, and then an unwitting one nearly two decades later when clips from the movie appeared in the popular MTV video for Metallica's musical adaptation of the story, "One."

The title makes reference to a U.S. armed forces recruiting slogan: "Johnny, get your gun!" Here, the "Johnny" is young Joe Bonham (Timothy Bottoms), a World War I infantryman who gets his arms, legs, eyes, nose, and mouth blown off by an artillery shell. Kept alive in a hospital, he's fully conscious but unable to see or communicate, a prisoner of his own broken body. Attempting to deal with his fate, Joe alternately thinks back to his old life and dreams of being put on display in a traveling road show to reveal the actual human cost of war. In time, Joe is able to "speak" to his doctors and a sympathetic nurse by banging his head on his pillow in Morse code. He tells them of his road-show plan. If they can't make that happen, Joe says, they should kill him. The army, of course, honors neither of this hardest-fallen soldier's requests.

Short of the tale of Christ on the cross, *Johnny Got His Gun* may well be Western culture's Heaviest Story Ever Told. Christ himself appears (in the form of Donald Sutherland) intermittently throughout the film, offering Joe no solutions and no answers.

"One," Metallica's breakthrough single from its 1988 . . . *And Justice for All* album, retells the concept of *Johnny Got His Gun* as seven minutes and twenty-four seconds of unprecedented machine-gun storytelling. Metallica had previously avoided making videos. After . . . *And Justice* went double platinum without MTV, the band felt it had made its point. For their first-ever music video, Metallica simply bought the rights to *Johnny Got His Gun*. The video intercuts black-and-white footage of the band performing "One" with snippets from the movie, creating the most powerful peace polemic to ever dominate MTV's Viewer Request Top 10.

Dalton Trumbo, creator of the book and film, died in 1976 and could not have imagined that

Johnny's message would live on in teen hearts via gnarly heavy metal thrash-beasts. He was a die-hard leftist, but no pacifist. Once Hitler invaded Russia, Trumbo pulled *Johnny* from publication. Now he wanted American boys to go save the Soviet Union and communism from the Nazis. As for Metallica, they certainly changed their position on music videos in the years ahead.

JONAH HEX (2010)

(DIR. JIMMY HAYWARD; W/JOSH BROLIN, MEGAN FOX, JOHN MALKOVICH, MICHAEL FASSBENDER)

✶ OCCULT COWBOYS ✶ NATIVE AMERICAN MYSTICISM

Introduced by DC Comics in 1972 as the star of the Weird Western Tales line, Jonah Hex is a repulsively disfigured, alcoholic, son-of-a-whore ex-Confederate soldier turned relentless Old West bounty hunter. So many good stories start that way. Here Josh Brolin, a powerful presence under repellent CGI face-rot, holds the distractingly busy screen well as Hex. He contends with John Malkovich as General Turnbull, his hospital-torching former commanding officer who tried to crucify Jonah and watched the fiery murder of Mrs. Hex and Junior Hex.

Years after their personal Civil War battles, Hex is imbued by Native Americans with the power to talk to the deceased, and Turnbull gets hold of a proto-atomic super-cannon aimed at the U.S. Capitol building. Only Jonah Hex can stop the mad general, unless his affections for saloon gal Lilah (Megan Fox) interfere. Fortunately, he has the Native Americans and plenty of dead friends on his side.

Over-the-top action filmmaking duo Mark Neveldine and Brian Taylor (*Crank, Crank: High Voltage, Ghost Rider: Spirit of Vengeance*) scripted *Jonah Hex*—with a vengeance! The visuals are nicely trippy on occasion and the music is impressively composed and performed in large part by progressive metal powerhouse Mastodon. Describing their score to *Ain't It Cool News*, Mastodon's Brent Hinds explained: "Some of it was heavy, some of it was very moody. A lot of it was spacey: Melvins B-sides, Pink Floyd–like, surreal outer space, like Neil Young's *Dead Man*. Swirling, nausea music." Hinds also cameos in the movie as a soldier onboard a railroad train.

In comic book form, Jonah Hex eventually left the American West of the 1870s and was transported to the post-apocalyptic twenty-first century. The eighteen-issue 1985 series titled *Hex* chronicles Jonah's new life as a Mad Max–type antihero.

Judge Dredd (1995)

(Dir. Danny Cannon; w/Sylvester Stallone, Diane Lane, Armand Assante, Rob Schneider)

✠ Judge Dredd ✠ Post-Apocalypse
✠ Soundtrack (White Zombie)

Hollywood's first crack at England's most metal comic book antihero clanked on arrival. Sylvester Stallone is miscast in the lead of *Judge Dredd*, piloting his flying motorcycle over "third-millennium" New York City, going mano a mano with a crappy CGI super-robot, enduring comic relief from Rob Schneider, and barking the judge's signature line with chuckle-inducing ineffectiveness through his signature sideways-mouth affect: "I AM DA LAHW!" Nothing works in *Judge Dredd*, including the music. The character's late-1970s sci-fi comic birth and the high-tech, apocalyptic violence in which he engages demand the sounds of heavy metal, particularly Anthrax, whose 1987 Dredd paean "I Am the Law" is responsible for 99 percent of the character's popularity in North America. With the exception of "Supercharger Heaven" by White Zombie, the *Judge Dredd* album traffics in limp weenies such as the Cure, The The, and Cocteau Twins. Suffice to say that until the sleeper *Dredd* (2012), this character remained most justly served by the thinly veiled tribute *RoboCop* (1987).

Judgment Night (1993)

(Dir. Stephen Hopkins; w/Emilio Estevez, Cuba Gooding Jr., Denis Leary, Stephen Dorff)

✠ Urban Warfare ✠ Soundtrack (Biohazard, Faith No More, Helmet, Living Colour, Mudhoney, Slayer)

The last gasp of grindhouse theaters begat some kick-ass medium-budget action movies in the early 1990s. Most noteworthy are the career streaks of Steven Seagal and Jean-Claude Van Damme. Most overtly heavy metal, due to its gimmick soundtrack, is *Judgment Night*. Yuppies Frank (Emilio Estevez) and Mike (Cuba Gooding Jr.) and a couple of pampered pals get lost in the Chicago ghetto, where they suffer a collective dark night of the soul, as well as numerous ass beatings at the hands of multiracial drug thugs employed by street crime kingpin Fallon (Denis Leary).

As an urban-guerilla-warfare cheap-thrill machine, *Judgment Night* works fine. As a cross-genre music marketing stunt to take advantage of the new "alternative rock" radio format that was conquering American teens en masse, the soundtrack is legendary. *Judgment Night* the music CD paired rap stars with hard rock and metal acts to create new songs and sounds. Team-ups included Slayer and Ice-T; Faith No More and Boo-Yaa T.R.I.B.E.; Living Colour and Run-DMC; Mudhoney and Sir Mix-a-Lot; and Biohazard and Onyx. The mixture of machismo seemed like a cool idea in pop music, until Limp Bizkit formed the following year and made *Judgment Night* rock into a bad thing. Limp Bizkit's DJ Lethal appears with House of Pain here on their track with Helmet, earning the ultimate nü-metal pedigree.

THE KEEP (1983)

(DIR. MICHAEL MANN; W/IAN MCKELLEN, GABRIEL BYRNE, SCOTT GLENN, ALBERTA WATSON)

✴ DEMON ✴ NAZI HORROR

The Keep, directed by Michael Mann after *Thief* (1981) but before *Miami Vice*, chronicles Nazis fighting a newly liberated demon in a Transylvanian castle-prison to a soundtrack by Tangerine Dream. In the best way, that sounds like a trippy sprawl into high-gloss Hades, and for its first half, *The Keep* makes good. Mann's cinematography of Romanian landscapes and their ancient, stony villages is breathtaking, and the SS death squads led by young Gabriel Byrne are more terrifying than the amorphous beast they unleash. Then an uncharacteristically hammy Ian McKellen devours all scenery within reach as a Jewish demonology scholar and inexplicably glowing-eyed wanderer Scott Glenn engages in interminable, early-'80s-perfume-commercial-style sex with Alberta Collins. What a relief when a rubber-suit smoke-machine monster finally appears. Originally presented in 70 mm and amped-up Dolby surround sound, *The Keep* is nonetheless a worthy notch in the Heavy Metal Cinema canon. Like spandex pants on men, somebody thought it looked good at the time.

KILL OR BE KILLED (1976)

(DIR. IVAN HALL; W/NORMAN COOMBES, RAYMOND HO-TONG, JAMES RYAN)

✴ KARATE ✴ NAZIS ✴ DWARF HENCHMAN

Longhaired rock and roll karate ace Steve Chase (James Ryan) stumbles upon a plot to settle old World War II scores by means of a martial arts battle royale. Baron von Rudloff (Norman Coombes) is a ex-Nazi general who still smarts over Japan out-karate-chopping Germany at the 1936 Berlin Olympics. So, many years later, the Baron invites Japanese fighting legend Miyagi (Raymond Ho-Tong) to oversee a rematch in a remote castle. Steve Chase is the guy to beat, and both sides are ready to beat the snot out of him.

Action segments do the trick. When Rudloff's dwarf henchman Chico (Daniel Duplessis) suffers the indignity of karate guys playing keep-away with his favorite hand puppet, the diminutive powerhouse flips out and opens a plus-size can of ass-kick all over his tormentors.

Filmed in South Africa in 1976, *Kill or Be Killed* didn't see proper release until 1980. When the movie proved hugely popular in the U.S., schlock studio Film Ventures rushed out a sequel, *Kill and Kill Again* (1981). The second movie features "bullet time" special effects nearly two decades before *The Matrix* but, alas, no dwarf henchmen.

KILLADELPHIA (2005)

(DIR. DOUG SPANGENBERG; W/RANDY BLYTHE, MARK MORTON, WILLIE ADLER, JOHN CAMPBELL, CHRIS ADLER)

✠ CONCERT FOOTAGE ✠ MUSIC VIDEOS

Killadelphia assembles a couple of December 2004 Lamb of God shows at Philly's Trocadero into a face-frying concert film. The group blows the roof off the joint, then invites us to peer behind the scenes into all the action a hotheaded band of marauders can muster. Firing on all cylinders, operating at a high level, they occasional struggle just to keep it together. The band follows in the footsteps of Metallica and Pantera as far as mastery of home video is concerned. Uniquely, the *Killadelphia* DVD is constructed to let viewers to watch the show and the offstage material either as separate entities, or edited together into a positively pulverizing, three-hour-long big-picture documentary.

The musical elements are top-tier: the band opens with "Laid to Rest" and tears through fifteen more numbers. Sound and visuals rock completely. The documentary scenes include the band skydiving, and, alternately, arguing and having a blast on the road. The blistering segment for which *Killadelphia* is best known is a vicious bare-knuckled brawl between singer Randy Blythe and guitarist Mark Morton; the rest of the group can't break it up until the vocalist is bleeding and heaving on the pavement. Lamb of God followed *Killadelphia* with the similarly excellent, even more epic DVD *Walk With Me in Hell* (2008).

KILLDOZER (1974)

(DIR. JERRY LONDON; W/CLINT WALKER, NEVILLE BRAND, ROBERT URICH)

✠ BULLDOZER ✠ MUTANTS ✠ METEORS

"Everyone knows a machine can't kill," teases the tagline to *Killdozer*, one of the 1970s' most warmly remembered attempts at TV movie horror, "except the machine!" The homicidal bucket of bolts in question is the most metal of heavy equipment vehicles, a bulldozer, and the killing starts soon after a mighty morphin' meteorite crashes near the device on an island oil-drilling site. Once the alien-possessed bulldozer becomes sentient, it rampages all around this tropical landscape, hunting down roughneck crewmembers to kill by dozing. Slowly. And stupidly.

Though the movie lasts just seventy minutes, *Killdozer* is lethally lethargic. Still, the film, adapted from a 1944 story by sci-fi titan Theodore Sturgeon, did inspire a fantastically dorky Marvel comics spin-off. In 1983, Wisconsin noise punks Killdozer honored the movie by taking its name and plowing through metal-adjacent towers of raucous sound alongside fellow Midwest boundary annihilators such as Big Black and Jesus Lizard.

KILLER PARTY (1986)

(DIR. WILLIAM FRUET; MARTIN HEWITT, RALPH SEYMOUR, PAUL BARTEL)

✠ SLASHER ✠ SOUNDTRACK (WHITE SISTER)

Killer Party announces on its poster that it's "*dead*-icated to the class of '86." I graduated high school in 1986, so I've always appreciated that touch, along with the pleasures of karate-kicking, spandex-sporting, comb-over-mulleted Pasadena AOR combo White Sister blasting through their anti-hit "April (You're No Fool)" during *Killer Party*'s opening credits. The entire rest of the movie is a dim trudge about a nondescript slasher carving his way through an April Fool's Day costume bash at a sorority house.

"April (You're No Fool)" typifies the mousse-damaged hair metal only heard on movie soundtracks in the '80s. *Killer Party* honors this peculiar genre by lifting the curtain. "Here you go, folks," the film seems to say. "This is White Sister. They actually play this crap. Look at them go! We knew you were wondering." Also please note White Sister's guitar strings—there are none.

Aside from two legit albums (one on the Heavy Metal Records label), White Sister's other significant cultural contributions are both hor-

Clockwise from top: *Ace Frehley
battles his robot clone in* Kiss Meets
the Phantom of the Park *(1978);*
King Kong *(1933) reigns, airplanes fall
like rain; Marvel's krazily kollectible*
Killdozer *(1974) komic;* Kill or Be
Killed *(1976)*

ror soundtrack cuts: "Save Me Tonight" from the classic *Fright Night* (1985) and "Dancin' on Midnight" from the not-classic *Halloween 5: The Revenge of Michael Myers* (1989). The group never topped their *Killer Party* appearance, and neither did anyone else involved in this movie.

KING KONG (1933)
(DIRS. MERIAN C. COOPER, ERNEST B. SCHOEDSACK; W/FAY WRAY, BRUCE CABOT, ROBERT ARMSTRONG)
✴ URBAN MAYHEM ✴ ANIMAL REVENGE

King Kong is a loud, hairy ape who feels misunderstood metalhead pain. Dragged from Skull Island, preoccupied with a hot blonde, and forced into "civilized" society to perform for disdainful squares, Kong beats his chest, roars, busts loose, squashes his opposition, grabs the girl, and ascends to the highest peak within freak-out distance. The big guy ultimately goes down hard, but he goes down swinging—bashing to bits the very best the bastards had to launch against him. When it comes to building and then unleashing the rage of the forty-foot-tall gorilla within *King Kong*—both the beast and his beauty of a movie—no more metal mission of a film has ever been so inspiringly accomplished.

King Kong spawned numerous sequels, remakes, and rip-offs. Producer Dino De Laurentiis's big-budget 1976 *King Kong* boasts some terrific, nutty '70s cinema excesses. Peter Jackson's 2005 CGI remake is unfortunately a bust. Of the knockoffs, Korea's crackpot *A*P*E* (1976) rocks in its original 3-D (especially when the giant gorilla flips the bird). *Mighty Peking Man*, aka *Goliathon* (1977), stands out for flaxen jungle beauty Evelyne Kraft giving a leopard a boner.

KISS LOVES YOU (2004)
(DIR. JIM HENEGHAN; W/SEBASTIAN BACH, BILL BAKER, DEE SNIDER, DICK MANITOBA, JERRY ONLY)
✴ METAL REALITY

Kiss Loves You follows the ups and downs of hard-core Kiss Army followers over a ten-year period. Starting in 1994, Kiss is floundering as

close as they've ever come to the edge of obscurity. Fan enthusiasm shifts from the unmasked group itself to cover bands that employ the makeup and pyrotechnics of Kiss's '70s heyday. Finally getting the hint in 1996, Gene Simmons and Paul Stanley race up ahead of the pack, reuniting with original members Ace Frehley and Peter Criss to embark on their own tour with face paint, dragon boots, blood spitting, and smoking guitar solos.

Kiss Loves You studies the impact of Kiss's resurgence on a cross section of devotees, in particular the tribute acts Strutter and Hotter Than Hell, along with a four-piece Brooklyn clan calling itself "The Kiss Family," whose members include a four-year-old Paul Stanley lookalike and what might be the world's fattest uncle in Gene Simmons drag. The most compelling subject is Ace Frehley disciple Bill Baker, who has devoted his life to emulating his idol and acquiring every possible fiber of Ace ephemera. The fate of him and his cover combo Fractured Mirror may well make you shed a single, dramatic tear in the manner of Gene at the end of the "World Without Heroes" video.

The opening montage of Kiss fans' vintage home movies and memorabilia collections sets a perfect tone of nostalgia and camaraderie that makes the unexpected results of Kiss slapping the makeup back on all the more moving. Interjected throughout is commentary by rock familiars, including Sebastian Bach, Dee Snider, Jerry Only, and the Dictators' Dick Manitoba.

KISS MEETS THE PHANTOM OF THE PARK (1978)
(DIR. GORDON HESSLER; W/GENE SIMMONS, PAUL STANLEY, ACE FREHLEY, PETER CRISS)
✴ KISS ✴ ROBOT KISS ✴ CARNIVAL CHAOS

To hear the members of Kiss tell it, cartoon mega-studio Hanna-Barbera (*Flintstones*, *Scooby-Doo*, *The Banana Splits*) sold them on the idea of starring in a TV movie that would be *"A Hard Day's Night* meets *Star Wars."* In some ways, the schlocky, dorky, cynically of-its-moment final product, *Kiss Meets the Phantom of the Park*, rises above its formula and emerges as a zeitgeist-plasticizing, rock-as-kid-stuff anti-spectacular best enjoyed if you were nine years old and staying up late to catch it on a school night, three days before Halloween in 1978.

The opening moments explode with the band members, King Kong size, stomping all over the Magic Mountain amusement park rides they dwarf while roaring through "Rock and Roll All Nite." They hop into flying bumper cars—Gene and Paul in one, Ace and Peter in the other, of course—and soar up and over and around the hills and loops of lit-up roller coasters. Somehow, from there, *Kiss Meets the Phantom of the Park* only gets more wicked-tough-awesome-cool. Gene breathes fire and speaks in lion roars. Paul's starry eye shoots lasers that he can use to walk through space. Peter sings "Beth." Ace inexplicably turns into an African-American gentleman wearing the trademark "Spaceman" makeup for one scene, a switcheroo made after a mortified Ace fled the set, forcing his stunt double to don the face paint. All the superhero crap fourth-grade kids made their Kiss dolls do was really happening!

The phantom is actually a mad scientist (Anthony Zerbe) who builds look-alike Kiss robots who are so evil that instead of singing "Hot! Hot! Hotter than hell!" they sing "Rip! Rip! Rip and destroy!" Fortunately, the flesh-and-blood Kiss taps into the supernatural powers of their talisman amulets—i.e., a bunch of stupid shapes on necklaces—to defeat their malevolent mechanical twins. They also play "Shout It Out Loud" a bunch of times.

For a generation of future headbangers, Kiss was a gateway band, and *Kiss Meets the Phantom of the Park* is the welcoming, candy-coated reception area of a heavy metal wonderland. In a move of semi-admirable gall that predates Kiss condoms and Kiss coffins, the band found they

could charge admission to their TV movie to paying audiences in Europe. The film slipped into murky ownership status in the '80s, and semi-legal video companies flooded drugstore bargain bins with VHS copies. The film was remastered as *Kiss in Attack of the Phantoms*, another attempt to cash in on *Star Wars*, for inclusion in the 2007 *Kissology* box set.

KNIGHTRIDERS (1981)
(DIR. GEORGE A. ROMERO; W/ED HARRIS, TOM SAVINI, GARY LAHTI, PATRICIA TALLMAN, BROTHER BLUE)
✣ MOTORCYCLES ✣ KNIGHTS IN ARMOR

Perhaps at a Renaissance Faire somewhere during the late 1970s, after a few tankards of mead, a full troupe of medieval knights jousting on motorcycles might not seem bewildering. As a movie premise, though, this is helmet-scratching weirdness for the ages. King Billy (Ed Harris) leads *Knightriders*' automotive roundtable, struggling to keep his traveling act together. Tom Savini forgoes his usual horror-makeup duties to costar as the Black Knight who's tempted to "sell out." *Knightriders* is, in fact, akin to other eccentric coming-of-middle-age professional films of its day, particularly Clint Eastwood's 1980 *Bronco Billy*, about a Wild West show on the ropes, and has larger implications about status and society. But the specifics of *Knightriders* are so uniquely metal: knights on bikes directed by zombie guru George Romero. Watch for a cameo by Stephen King and his wife Tabitha as loutish fairgoers. King dropped by the set while preparing to collaborate with Romero on *Creepshow* (1982).

KROKUS: As Long as WE Live (2004)
(DIR. RETO CADUFF; W/CHRIS VON ROHR, FERNANDO VON ARB, FREDDY STEADY, MARC STORACE, MARK KOHLER)
✣ METAL HISTORY ✣ SWITZERLAND.

Krokus: As Long as We Live is a high-spirited documentary made to coincide with the

Clockwise from top left:
Nice axe! But Kevin Sorbo's
Kull *(1997) is a clunker;*
the cracked sci-fi epic Krull
(1983), in which Colwyn
faces the Slayers; George A
Romero's Knightriders *(1981)*
is cool; but not the rubber-suit
monster of The Keep *(1983)*

Heavy Metal Movies

thirtieth anniversary of Switzerland's all-time biggest-selling heavy metal rock band. With so much film and literature dedicated only to the darkest and most extreme Swiss heavy metal (Celtic Frost, Coroner, Hellhammer), the party-hearty mainstream hard rock of Krokus comes as a refreshing icy blast. The overall lightness of tone and sex-drugs-and-leather-pants bliss are still blitzed at points by real tragedy.

A few years after forming in a haze in 1974, Krokus caught an AC/DC show. According to bassist and original vocalist Chris Von Rohr, the Swiss band took a new direction, following the Australian juggernauts straight down the highway to hell. Von Rohr even assesses the 1982 Krokus release *Once Vice at a Time* as "the album AC/DC never made," and he's absolutely right.

Krokus: As Long as We Live conveys the band's journey through riotous vintage video and new talking-head interviews. The trip is a damned fun ride up until the final exits. With the arrival of multi-octave wailer Marc Storace, a Maltese immigrant to Switzerland, the band hit big on MTV in America. Money poured in, vices piled up, and bodies were carried out. Founding guitarist Tommy Kiefer's heroin addiction got him fired in 1986. Shortly thereafter, Kiefer discovered he was HIV positive and took his own life. The documentary conveys the depth of his loss, and hammers home how that nonstop '80s hair metal party packed a motherfucker of a hangover.

Krokus: As Long as We Live more or less follows the classic *VH1: Behind the Music* narrative, right up to reunion performances among the survivors. Much like the keg-bash metal of Krokus itself, that's more than good enough.

KRULL (1983)

(DIR. PETER YATES; W/KEN MARSHALL, LYSETTE ANTHONY, FREDDIE JONES, LIAM NEESON)

✳ SWORDS & SORCERY ✳ OUTER SPACE ✳ SLAYERS

The signature totem from the sci-fi fantasy cheese-and-light show *Krull* is the Glaive: an asterisk-shaped, five-knifed retractable throwing weapon that returns to its wielder like a boomerang. Prince Colwyn (Ken Marshall), he of the meticulously blown-out hairdo, unearths the Glaive from a rocky cave and uses it to battle his ideally metal-monikered enemies: a gargantuan reptile known as the Beast, along with an army of Slayers, who terrorize the galaxy together in a monster-faced mountain spacecraft known as the Black Fortress. Backing Prince Colwyn are Ergo the Magician (David Battley), Rell the Cyclops (Bernard Bresslaw), and a cabal of convicts who will each be freed if they join the fight.

Astoundingly, Krull only gets more metal from there. Our female object of rescue is Lyssa (Lysette Anthony), an enchantress imprisoned in the lair of the Crystal Spider. That bugger is nothing compared to the Fire Mares that enable the good guys' escape: Clydesdales that run so fast, flames shoot from their hooves until they actually take flight through the sky.

Krull just rocks. It's King Arthur, *Star Wars*, Tolkien, and *Clash of the Titans* consumed by old-school nerds and power-puked back out via the technology of *Megaforce* and ColecoVision. The entire movie looks like the cover of Judas Priest's *Screaming for Vengeance* come to life. Unlike most of your cassettes from that era, it still plays fantastically well. And in the halls of Heavy Metal Movie gadgetry, the Glaive hangs somewhere between Conan's sword and Bill and Ted's time-traveling phone booth. Hail the Glaive!

Krull generated an epic arcade game designed by Gottlieb, an Atari 2600 video game, a Parker Brothers board game, and one of the most brain-damaged promo gimmicks in history: a mass wedding at Columbia Studios uniting a dozen couples. Each had written essays explaining why their "fantasy come true" would be to have a *Krull* wedding in Hollywood. The spawn of these marriages must have some stories to tell!

Kull the Conqueror
(1997)

(Dir. John Nicolella; w/Kevin Sorbo, Tia Carrere, Thomas Ian Griffith, Harvey Fierstein)

✠ Swords & Sorcery ✠ Robert E. Howard

Kull opens by explaining how sorceress queen Akivasha once ruled humanity with an army of demons, until the god Valka kicked her ass and established the kingdom of Valusia. Centuries later, Kull (Kevin Sorbo) has a nice life there. When we first meet Kull, he's trying to join an elite warrior force, only to be pulled into a bloodbath in a throne room where he ends up getting crowned king. And it's not an easy time to be the king. General Taligaro (Thomas Ian Griffith) aims to overthrow the human regime by resurrecting the wicked Akivasha. Since she is Tia Carrere, she has no problem bamboozling Kull, marrying him, and forcing him from the throne. The rest of the movie is a series of silly struggles for Kull to regain the title that came to him almost by accident early in the movie.

Kull began its interesting life in 1987 as *Conan the Conqueror*, slated to be the third entry in the Conan series. After Arnold Schwarzenegger stumbled with *Red Sonja* (1985) and *Raw Deal* (1986), though, producer Dino De Laurentiis dropped his contract. Ironically, the original *Conan the Barbarian* (1982) employed many elements of Robert E. Howard's Kull stories, including arch-nemesis Thulsa Doom, whereas *Kull the Conqueror* is based mostly on Howard's Conan writings. In 1994, Kevin Sorbo took on the lead role in several *Hercules* TV movies, leading to the briefly popular weekly series *Hercules: The Legendary Journeys* (1995–97). The show was lightweight and campy, and Sorbo played the titular god as such. He infects the Kull character with the same lack of believability, which explains why Hercules was so totally surpassed by its own spin-off, *Xena: Warrior Princess*. Lucy Lawless, for sure, would have been better here as the star.

Kurt & Courtney (1998)

(Dir. Nick Broomfield; w/Courtney Love, Kurt Cobain, El Duce)

✠ El Duce ✠ Nirvana ✠ Soundtrack (Earth)

British journalist Nick Broomfield comes off unequal parts admirable and awful in his documentaries, with *Kurt & Courtney* providing a prime example. Although its fun to watch Broomfield set up Courtney Love here and lay her to waste, *Kurt & Courtney* ultimately seems slapdash. The central mystery of how directly involved in the death of Nirvana singer Kurt Cobain was his wife is only pushed irretrievably into the cutout bin of wild ideas.

As a spiritual stand-in for the deceased Cobain, we meet his best friend, Dylan Carlson, he of the muscle cars and, at this point, profound, facial-sore-raising drug addiction. Although central here as the angel of death who handed Cobain his fatal shotgun, Carlson is also the single most heavy injection of metal into the whole Seattle Sub Pop rock scene. Leading his band Earth, as Black Sabbath was also once called, Carlson slowed the centrifugal pull of the planet's spin with experimental, evil drone metal. His rock-bottom interview here about his friend's final days is chilling.

And then comes El Duce! The bloated, bedraggled Eldon Hoke—leader of "rape rock" provocateurs the Mentors—takes a superstar turn where even the PMRC invoking his "anal vapor" lyrics and guest spots on *Hot Seat With Wally George* had failed. His stumbling, staggering on-camera claim that Courtney Love offered him $50,000 to kill Kurt Cobain makes this repugnantly lovable lunatic a sick kind of reality star. Then, within a week of talking to Broomfield, a passing train turned El Duce into trackside pizza. Bend up and smell the conspiracy theories.

L

LABYRINTH ★ LADIES AND GENTLEMEN, THE FABULOUS STAINS ★ LADYHAWKE ★ THE LAIR OF THE WHITE WORM ★ LAND OF DOOM ★ LAND OF THE MINOTAUR ★ LASERBLAST ★ THE LAST ACTION HERO ★ LAST DAYS HERE ★ THE LAST EXORCISM ★ THE LAST HORROR FILM ★ LAST HOUSE ON DEAD END STREET ★ THE LAST HOUSE ON THE LEFT ★ THE LAST SLUMBER PARTY ★ THE LAST TEMPTATION OF CHRIST ★ THE LAST UNICORN ★ LEATHERFACE: THE TEXAS CHAINSAW MASSACRE III ★ LED ZEPPELIN: CELEBRATION DAY ★ LED ZEPPELIN: THE FIRST CUTS ★ LED ZEPPELIN PLAYED HERE ★ LEGALIZE MURDER ★ LEGEND ★ THE LEGEND OF BLOOD CASTLE ★ THE LEGEND OF BOGGY CREEK ★ THE LEGEND OF THE 7 GOLDEN VAMPIRES ★ LEMMY ★ LESS THAN ZERO ★ LET SLEEPING CORPSES LIE ★ A LETTER FROM DEATH ROW ★ LIFEFORCE ★ LIKE FATHER LIKE SON ★ LISA AND THE DEVIL ★ LISZTOMANIA ★ LITTLE COREY GOREY ★ LITTLE NICKY ★ THE LIVING DEAD GIRL ★ THE LOBO PARAMILITARY CHRISTMAS SPECIAL ★ LONE WOLF ★ THE LONELINESS OF THE LONG-DISTANCE RUNNER ★ THE LORD OF THE RINGS (1978) ★ THE LORD OF THE RINGS: THE FELLOWSHIP OF THE RING ★ THE LORD OF THE RINGS: THE TWO TOWERS ★ THE LORD OF THE RINGS: THE RETURN OF THE KING ★ THE LORDS OF SALEM ★ LOST HIGHWAY ★ LOVEDOLLS SUPERSTAR ★ LUCIFER RISING

LABYRINTH (1986)

(DIR. JIM HENSON; W/DAVID BOWIE, JENNIFER CONNELLY, TOBY FROUD)

★ FANTASY ★ GOBLINS ★ FAIRIES ★ EVIL MUPPETS

Hot off of Dario Argento's *Phenomena*, teenage Jennifer Connelly is Sarah, a high school girl who wishes goblins would carry away her baby brother Toby (Toby Froud, actual son of production designer Brian Froud). The goblins oblige her. Enter an owl that transforms into Jareth, King of Goblins (played by infinitely mutating rock god David Bowie). Jareth informs Sarah that she can have the kid back if she can work her way through his labyrinth homeland in thirteen hours. Into the mystical maze our girl goes, where it's all dwarves and knights and knaves and freaky beasties and goblins galore.

Muppet maven Jim Henson directed and designed *Labyrinth*'s thousands of fantastic creatures. *Star Wars*' supreme being, George Lucas, produced the film, and Monty Python's Terry Jones wrote it. For some, *Labyrinth*'s massive, elaborate, obviously labor-intensive coming-together of talents yielded a story of dark wonder, a beloved treasure of fantasy filmmaking. For others, *Labyrinth*'s tally of incredible ingredients adds up to a screen full of stuffed animals and a big shrug. Other people's dreams can be so boring.

Ladies and Gentlemen, the Fabulous Stains (1982), aka All Washed Up

(Dir. Lou Adler; w/Diane Lane, Fee Waybill, Paul Simonon, Laura Dern)

✠ Concert Footage ✠ Fake Band (the Metal Corpses)

At once candy-colored and gritty, dreamy and pissed-off, the proto-riot-grrrl opus *Ladies and Gentlemen, The Fabulous Stains* is saturated in new wave luminosity and—seeing as how it costars the bassist from the Clash and literally half the Sex Pistols—it pulsates with genuine punk musculature. The movie's metal comes, spectacularly and unexpectedly, by way of the Tubes, specifically Fee Waybill, real-life lunatic frontman of the theatrical San Francisco shock rockers. Waybill plays the face-painted, fright-wigged, leather-clad Lou Corpse, singer for fading '70s arena rockers the Metal Corpses on whose tour the all-teenage-girl Stains tag along. The Metal Corpses' logo is rendered in Iron Maiden's famous angular lettering.

Tragedy strikes early when the Corpses drummer overdoses in his dressing room, and the metal vets bow out, leaving the punky supporting acts to headline the rest of the way. Even without Lou Corpse, the story of the Stains finding their own aggressive footing is an invigorating charge to all metal hopefuls. Diane Lane delivers a star-making performance as singer Corinne "Third Degree" Burns, who creates a cult of pubescent worshippers who mimic her skunk-stripe hair, torn fishnets, and see-through blouses. The film pulls the rock out from under itself, though, with a sour-note conclusion that, rather shockingly, negates the messages of mainstream resistance and corporate refusal that it touted all along.

Ladies and Gentlemen, the Fabulous Stains never received a proper theatrical release, but found a fast and vocal cult following on cable TV (particularly thanks to USA Network's landmark *Night Flight* series). In 1985, *Stains* earned a brief art-house run in some big cities before slipping back into an enduring life as a tape-traded fan favorite. Along with Allan Moyle's decidedly more rough-hewn *Times Square* (1980), *Fabulous Stains* provided a wellspring of ideas and a specific blueprint for what, in the early 1990s, would blossom into the DIY riot grrrl movement, an incubator for a massive unshaven metal takeover of the Pacific Northwest in the 2000s.

Ladyhawke (1985)

(Dir. Richard Donner; w/Michelle Pfeiffer, Rutger Hauer, Matthew Broderick, John Wood)

✠ Swords & Sorcery

Ladyhawke mildly skewers the post-*Conan* sword-and-sorcery craze and tames its action-fantasy heroics for a family audience. As such, it's agreeable afternoon matinee entertainment—certainly not heavy, and just mildly metal. In a magic-riddled medieval milieu, Matthew Broderick plays Mouse, an escaped thief on the run. A knight (Rutger Hauer) and the knight's majestic, mysterious hawk are happy to assist him. The bird, it turns out, is a shape-shifting woman named Isabeau (Michelle Pfeiffer), who been cursed to transform each night. Together, they fight to overturn evil noblemen and free the Ladyhawke from her spell.

Ladyhawke's anthemic musical score combines Gregorian chants with electric guitars, full-kit drums, and synthesizers. It was composed by Andrew Powell and produced by his frequent collaborator, prog-rock god Alan Parsons. While scouting Italian locations for *Ladyhawke*, director Richard Donner listened to Alan Parsons Project albums (on which Powell performed) and said he ultimately couldn't envision the movie apart from that type of musical accompaniment. Italian prog metal act Shaggoth later recorded its own metal interpretation, "Ladyhawke."

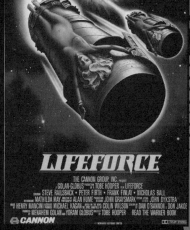

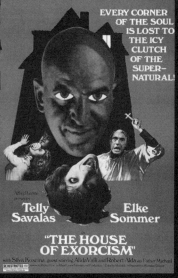

Clockwise from top left: *Pentagram doc* Last Days Here *(2011)*; Lair of
the White Worm *(1988)*; *alternate and way sexy* Lifeforce *(1985) poster*;
Laserblast *(1978) is a blast for sure*; Land of the Minotaur *(1976)*; *Telly
Savalas as Satan in* Lisa and the Devil *(1974), aka* The House of Exorcism

THE LAIR OF THE WHITE WORM (1988)

(DIR. KEN RUSSELL; W/AMANDA DONOHOE, HUGH GRANT, CATHERINE OXENBERG, SAMMI DAVIS)

✠ LESBIAN VAMPIRE ✠ DEMONS

The last great film by the great, great Ken Russell (*The Devils, Tommy, Altered States*) adapts the final novel written by *Dracula* creator Bram Stoker. *The Lair of the White Worm* is a rapturous Russell romp, replete with outrageously obvious phallic symbols in every frame, gothic Scottish occultism gone wild, and Amanda Donohoe unhinged and unclothed as Lady Sylvia Marsh—a mysterious noblewoman who reveals herself to be an undying demon priestess who heads a cult dedicated to the serpent god Dionin. The film's visuals cut deep into the metal psyche, from the lush countryside to the medieval castles to the climactic rampage of Lady Sylvia sprouting fangs and frantically aiming her wooden strap-on dildo in the direction of a sacrificial virgin's snake pit.

Ken Russell made *Lair of the White Worm* as part of a multi-picture deal that required one horror movie. He scored a home-video hit with *Gothic* (1986), a stylized account of how young Mary Shelley came to write *Frankenstein* in 1818. He decided to push the boundaries of period spookiness to its maddest ends with *White Worm*. The stony domain of *White Worm*'s snake god is actually the incredibly heavy natural cavern called Thor's Cave in Staffordshire, UK. Netherlands-based melodic death metal group God Dethroned released their album *The Lair of the White Worm* in 2004, with cover artwork depicting Lady Sylvia in almost entirely serpentine form.

LAND OF DOOM (1986)

(DIR. PETE MARIS; W/DEBORAH RENNARD, GARRICK DOWHEN, DANIEL RADELL, FRANK GARRET)

✠ POST-APOCALYPSE ✠ RAPE AND REVENGE

Harmony (Deborah Rennard) is the "Mad Maxine"–style heroine of the post-nuke waste-'em-up *Land of Doom*. While on the run from the usual punked-up raiders who raped and pillaged her desert village—emphasis definitely on the former activity—she ducks into a cave and meets wounded warrior Anderson (Garrick Dowhen). Man-hating Harmony decides she trusts Anderson enough to team with him to combat the armies of leather daddies on tricked-out motorcycles who serve local mayhem-lord Slater (Daniel Radell).

In 1986, Rennard was halfway through her decade-long stint on the nighttime soap *Dallas*, on which she played Sly Lovegren, the sly secretary of evil oil magnate J. R. Ewing (Larry Hagman, R.I.P.). *Land of Doom* seems an odd choice for Rennard's shot at screen stardom, but she acquits herself handsomely enough. *Land of Doom* had one of the coolest and most heavy-looking VHS boxes in the video stores of its day—so cool it surpassed the film itself. The main image on the cover is that of a mutant muscleman wearing a half-face leather mask, brandishing a razor-fingered combat glove that contains its own built-in crossbow. A biker marauds on the lower left while, over the main figure's shoulder, a woman clearly meant to suggest Brigitte Nielsen in *Red Sonja* shoots out a smoldering look. Nothing in the movie is as cool as any of that, but it's far from the first time an exploitative ad campaign or cockeyed power metal album cover has dwarfed the product it was promoting.

LAND OF THE MINOTAUR (1976), AKA THE DEVIL'S MEN

(DIR. KOSTAS KARAGIANNIS; W/PETER CUSHING, DONALD PLEASENCE, LUAN PETERS)

✠ SATAN ✠ GREEK MYTHS

With the head of a bull, the body or a Spartan warrior, and a demeanor that implies he's permanently on the prowl for a mosh pit, the minotaur is one of ancient mythology's most heavily metal rump-stompers. *Land of the Minotaur* involves robed satanists in a Greek cave who pray to a talking statue of the titular beast, an imposing creature that blows smoke out its nostrils. British horror giant Peter Cushing stars as a devil-worshipping baron, with the similarly credentialed Donald Pleasence as a Jesus-worshipping priest. Brian Eno composed the spooky electronic score.

"The Devil's Men," *Land of the Minotaur*'s theme song, is a '70s action-movie funk-metal rave-up sung by "Paul Williams"—not the ubiquitous mid-'70s Paul Williams of *Phantom of the Paradise* fame; this Paul Williams is actually a British blues singer from the band Juicy Lucy.

LASERBLAST (1978)

(DIR. MICHAEL RAE; W/KIM MILFORD, CHERYL "RAINBEAUX" SMITH, EDDIE DEEZEN)

✳ ALIENS ✳ HORROR

Billy was a kid who got pushed around," states *Laserblast*'s tagline. "Then he found the power!" That sounds like a premise repeated hundreds of times in early MTV heavy metal music videos during the 1980s, but in the case of Billy (Kim Milford), the power is an arm cannon that shoots death rays. The gun is left lying around in the desert during the movie's opening scene by a green-faced man who is disintegrated by completely awesome stop-motion animated aliens that look like upright turtles without shells. After frying the gun guy, they zoom away on a spaceship. Once Billy gets his mitts on the weapon, he uses it to blow up the car of a couple of bullies who were attempting to rape his girlfriend Kathy (Cheryl "Rainbeaux" Smith).

Up on their spaceship, the aliens catch sight of this and head back to earth. Billy, in the meantime, turns green, sprouts fangs, and tears off on a laser-cannon rampage until he, too, is ultimately vaporized by the space turtles. *Laserblast* is nothing short of that: a blast. The movie is an exciting, almost homemade-looking cheapie that quakes with late-'70s Southern California hard rock Chevy-van charm, mixed with '50s alien puppet terror. In one of the most metal moments in cinema (as well as one of the most admirably

subversive), Billy aims his laser cannon at a *Star Wars* billboard and blasts that fucker to bits.

For its successful March 1978 theatrical run, *Laserblast* was presented as half of a double feature with the Christopher Lee thriller *End of the World* (1977). The TV commercial for the duo was hilarious and seriously effective. An announcer hyped the film as all sorts of amazing images appeared on-screen: the spaceship, the aliens, Billy blasting stuff with death rays, the luminous Rainbeaux. The montage suddenly froze on a static shot of planet Earth in space. The announcer intoned solemnly: "Also showing: END . . . of the WORLD!" And the Earth blows up.

In 1974, *Laserblast* lead Kim Milford played singing muscleman Rocky Horror in the original Los Angeles stage production of *The Rocky Horror Show*. Tragically, most people who know of *Laserblast* do so because it was featured on the loathsome, un-fucking-funny TV series *Mystery Science Theater 3000*. *Laserblast* has also been twice remade in spirit. That's a nice way of saying it has been ripped off, first by the obscure *Deadly Weapon* (1989), then a decade later by the even more obscure *Alien Arsenal* (1999).

THE LAST ACTION HERO (1993)

(DIR. JOHN McTIERNAN; W/ARNOLD SCHWARZENEGGER, AUSTIN O'BRIEN, F. MURRAY ABRAHAM, TOM NOONAN)

✳ DEATH ✳ SLASHER ✳ SOUNDTRACK (AC/DC, ANTHRAX, MEGADETH, QUEENSRŸCHE)

Meta meets metal in *The Last Action Hero*, as Arnold Schwarzenegger plays himself *and* a movie character based on his film persona *and* that film persona itself. The three Arnolds costar in an action movie that contains another action movie and a "real life" story that comments on the nature of action movies. In the midst of this, Tom Noonan (the Tooth Fairy from *Manhunter*) also portrays himself *and* a cinematic axe murderer called the Ripper, who battles Arnold. In the meantime, the cosmic rupture separating real life from the movie universe unleashes the character of Death from Ingmar Bergman's *The Seventh Seal* (here played by Sir Ian McKellen) to saunter through Times Square, re-created in its super-seedy grindhouse glory of the '70s and '80s. And all of this is set to a wailing heavy metal soundtrack.

The Last Action Hero is not lacking for ideas. The makers did lack the courage to totally challenge the summer blockbuster audience, though, and lots of inherent headiness is boiled down into soft-brained mush. Critics launched an anti-Arnold backlash and soon the greatest action hero was handed his first box office bomb. Arnold came back big the following summer with *True Lies* (1994), but the misfire of *The Last Action Hero* is one of the worst missed opportunities in mythically ambitious pop filmmaking.

In concept-metal terms, the idea began as *2112* or *Operation: Mindcrime* but the final product ended up akin to *Tales from the Elder*. And that's enough to make us Arnold fanatics shed a single, dramatic tear just like Gene Simmons in the "World Without Heroes" video. "Big Gun" by AC/DC was the first single from *The Last Action Hero*'s remarkably metallic soundtrack. The tie-in video showcases Arnold playing guitar onstage with the band, wearing full Angus Young schoolboy regalia.

Last Days Here (2011)

(Dirs. Don Argott, Demien Fenton; w/Bobby Liebling, Sean "Pellet" Pelletier, Phil Anselmo)
✵ Pentagram ✵ Addiction ✵ Concert Footage

Described often, and accurately, as a "street-level Black Sabbath," Pentagram is one of the hard rock's greatest and most tragically unrealized juggernauts, and an a ongoing focus of obsession for doom metal fanatics. At the heart of the Pentagram fascination is founder and lone constant member Bobby Liebling, an asteroid-eyed war wizard. Liebling looks like a starved Salvador Dalí in Bobby Sherman outfits, and he rocks a stage like Mick Jagger stuck with a cattle prod. The documentary *Last Days Here* is Bobby

Liebling's story. He built the Pentagram cult through decades of false starts and underground-traded recordings, beginning in 1971 and achieving success, finally, in the mid-2000s. A ferocious 1974 tear-through of "Forever My Queen" encapsulates the mightiness of Liebling and his fellow players, as well as what rock has missed out on owing to the singer's inability to ever successfully get it together.

For any rock band to survive for that long on little recognition is remarkable enough; that an insane, omnivorous narcotic enthusiast on the scale of Liebling is still breathing, let alone shaking his hip-huggers in performance, should be biologically impossible. *Last Days Here* begins with the offstage Liebling, a fiftysomething man-child-*cum*-cadaver who festers among filth heaps between crack hits and drug runs in his parents' suburban Maryland basement. Observes dad Don, a Department of Defense advisor for multiple U.S. presidents: "They call us enablers." Yes, based on evidence presented here, we do! Footage of Liebling, arms completely bandaged, crawling on his knees for crack rocks, is upsetting beyond any "human picture of death," and manages to be horrifying without turning exploitative. The climb ahead is massive.

Pentagram worshipper and longtime Relapse Records go-to guy Sean "Pellet" Pelletier befriends Liebling and, as a manager, aims to get the band up and active again. Everybody's got their work cut out for them. Challenged repeatedly by psychotic delusions (the "parasite infestation" segments come close to warranting a barf bag) and a self-destructive hardwiring that, back in the '70s, led him to blow an audition for Kiss wherein Gene Simmons and Paul Stanley *came out to his own home*, Liebling is a never less than a nightmare—except when he performs. Slowly, steadily, we see Liebling transform from barely living remains to the witchy wild man of his stage persona. Backstage at a Down show, Bobby humbly accepts praise from a long line of metal musicians, culminating with Phil Anselmo working a deal for a new Pentagram album on his label and declaring, "It would be an honor!"

Creeping back from the sub-basement, Bobby dyes his hair, grows his mustache, breaks out shiny paisley shirts purchased in 1967—and then he meets a girl. That, of course, totally fucks shit up. The climax of *Last Days Here* focuses on Bobby battling inner torment over his relationship with Hallie, a radiantly attractive Pentagram devotee half his age. He struggles to mount a comeback concert in New York, and gets there. Just before the credits roll, we see that Bobby and Hallie went on to get married and that a Bobby Liebling Jr. rocks among us now—a happy ending that is ostensibly unimaginable.

As a devoted fan, I wished the movie contained more Pentagram—more of the band's music (a common shortcoming of rock documentaries), and more details regarding the forty-plus-year evolution of this freakishly unique outfit. For example, *Last Days Here*'s entire storyline builds to the Manhattan comeback show, but on the big night we can't hear the damn band! The phenomenon of Hallie is also perplexing. This young beauty pops up seemingly from nowhere to romance the mummified, drug-blooded phantom reptile Bobby Liebling. This topic warrants a little more on-camera exploration.

To date, Bobby remains on top of the world, recording new music, touring the world for the first time, and enjoying family life. Everybody won, especially the filmmakers, who arrived years earlier on a scene featuring very little light. Let the rallying cry for a sequel begin!

The Last Exorcism (2010)

(Dir. Daniel Stamm; w/Patrick Fabian, Ashley Bell, Iris Bahr, Louis Herthum)

✡ Satan ✡ Exorcism ✡ Small-Town Devil Cult

The Last Exorcism imagines the classic 1972 documentary *Marjoe*, about a child preacher turned faithless mercenary out for one last haul of Christian cash, as a found-footage horror film. Patrick Fabian stars as Cotton Marcus, a retiring exorcist who invites a film crew to record his final performance. Upon reaching poor "possessed" teenager Nell Sweetzer (Ashley Bell), Marcus discovers his phony special effects are clearly no match for whatever demonic force actually seems to be in play. The unforeseeable shock ending comes from the groovy depraved universe of early-'70s occult TV movies, putting a perfectly metal cap on one of the heaviest horror movie experiences of the film's decade.

Last Exorcism screenwriters Huck Botko and Andrew Gurland made their way to Hollywood by way of savage underground movies traded informally during the last days of VHS and since preserved via the dark corners of the Internet. Botko made a series of "dessert-umentaries" such as *Graham Cracker Cream Pie* (1999) in which he does unconscionable things to baked goods and then serves them to his family. And in this case "unconscionable" includes having tubercular homeless men hock mucus and male porn stars ejaculate into the pie mix before baking.

Along with *The Hangover*'s Todd Phillips, Gurland codirected the *HBO America Undercover* installment "Frat House," an ode to homoerotic violence and vomit that was deemed impossible to air. Together, Botko and Gurland created the fake documentary shorts *Gramaglia* (2000) and *Broken Condom* (2004), along with the very good feature-length male-humiliation comedies *Mail Order Wife* (2004) and *The Virginity Hit* (2010). Ludicrously, *The Last Exorcism Part II* emerged in 2013, and was viewed by an audience of zero.

The Last Horror Film (1982), aka The Fanatic

(Dir. David Winters; w/Joe Spinell, Caroline Munro, Judd Hamilton, Mary Spinell)

✡ '80s Slasher ✡ Joe Spinell

Joe Spinell and Caroline Munro, stars of the splatter classic *Maniac* (1980), reunite for *The Last Horror Film*. A strange, disjointed, oftentimes laughable movie on its own terms, *The Last Horror Film* is absolutely essential viewing for headbangers intrigued by *Maniac* and its fat, greasy, endlessly fascinating star. Spinell stars as Vinny Durand, a *Fangoria*-reading New York City taxi driver obsessed with actress Jana Bates (Munro), the "queen of horror films." Hoping to get Jana to star in his own movie, Vinny follows her to the Cannes Film Festival, where she's promoting her latest opus, *Scream*. After Jana's handlers keep Vinny at a distance, they start to turn up dead. *The Last Horror Film* tracks Vinny's descent into all-out Jana-obsessed madness, complete with an unforgettable scene of a shirtless Spinell erotically caressing his own bosom in ecstasy as Jana's images are projected onto his scarred, blobby torso. The action climaxes in a spooky graveyard and then pays off with a jaw-dropping surprise that must be seen for a shock, and then rewound over and over again for the sheer freaky joy of it. The final punch line of *The Last Horror Film* will answer every question you ever had about Joe Spinell.

Director David Winters previously made Alice Cooper's 1975 TV special *Welcome to My Nightmare*; he went on to helm the 1986 skateboard movie *Thrashin'*. Winters and Spinell shot *The Last Horror Film* at the Cannes Film Festival guerilla style, without any kind of legal permits. The incidental fun here is checking out the movies being shown and sold that year: one marquee displays the blood-red title *Make Them Die Slowly* (aka *Cannibal Ferox*).

Last House on Dead End Street (1977)

(Dir. Roger Watkins [as Victor Janos]; w/Roger Watkins, Ken Fisher, Kathy Curtain)

✯ Snuff

One of extreme cinema's dankest underground oddities, *Last House on Dead End Street* plays like an unmarked, beat-to-shit, fished-from-the-gutter crust-grind cassette demo that may or may not have been inefficiently recorded over loops of power electronics. Greasy, ape-like, pissed-at-society lowlife Terry Hawkins (played by writer-director Roger Watkins) is sprung from jail after doing a year on drug charges. At first, he wonders where his next paycheck will come from. A buddy suggests slaughterhouse work—illustrated here by actual, PETA-propaganda-worthy footage of animals being killed—but Terry dreams bigger. He wants to go into showbiz—specifically, the snuff-film division.

Tout de suite, Terry sets up shop in a warehouse with a Manson Family–like cabal of assistants, including deliciously hairy nude hippie chicks. They commence 8mm-immortalizing their heinously creative, gut-rupturing gory dispatches of assorted victims. The plot suggests straightforward horror, but nothing about this *Last House* is straight or forward. Looking beyond the forced power drills to the head, and the live, wriggling surgical procedures, the movie's most indelible passages are all about budget and resource limitations forcing improvised weirdness. The gang don huge Greek theater masks to torment victims while the soundtrack cuts to numerous voices half-moaning, half-chanting "Terry is the answer. . . . Terry is the answer." The effect is chilling. Later, Terry grabs a taxidermied deer leg, pushes it through his open pants zipper, and forces a restrained man to fellate the hoof. Try shaking that sight out of your head.

Shot on the empty, dead-of-winter SUNY Oneonta campus in 1972 as *The Cuckoo Clocks of Hell* (in a version that ran three full hours!), the movie looks and sounds not just cheap and amateurish, but grimy and wrong. Technical shortcomings only add to a rank air of freakish believability. Nothing in the film looks like an actual snuff killing, yet the scum-bucket studio that later released the movie to theaters in 1979 certainly encouraged rumors that the killings were real. More than anything, the feral, disgusting people on-screen come off as legit. Viewers are forced to ponder whether art alone can teeter over into something criminal.

Film promos included terrifically misleading newspaper ads and FM rock-radio spots, both of which stole *Last House on the Left*'s "It's only a movie!" tagline in an attempt, beyond just the

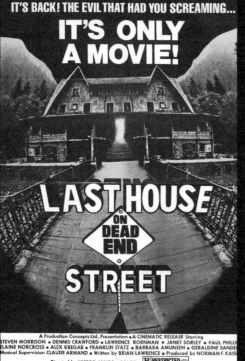

IT'S BACK! THE EVIL THAT HAD YOU SCREAMING...

IT'S ONLY A MOVIE!

LAST HOUSE ON DEAD END STREET

A Production Concepts Ltd., Presentation ● A CINEMATIC RELEASE Starring
STEVEN MORRISON ● DENNIS CRAWFORD ● LAWRENCE BORNMAN ● JANET SORLEY ● PAUL PHILLI
ELAINE NORCROSS ● ALEX KREGAR ● FRANKLIN STATZ ● BARBARA AMUNSEN ● GERALDINE SANDE
Musical Supervision CLAUDE ARMAND ● Written by BRIAN LAWRENCE ● Produced by NORMAN F. KAIS
Directed by VICTOR JANOS ● COLOR   R RESTRICTED

LAST HOUSE ON THE LEFT · IS FOREVER!

THE NATION'S #1 CULT MOVIE NEVER DIES!

CAN A MOVIE GO TOO FAR?

CHECK THESE GROSSES:
APRIL 11-TO-17

5 D.I. MINNEAPOLIS RUN
ALL D.I.'s HOLDING 2nd WEEK
($2100 TOTAL ADVERTISING)

MARI, SEVENTEEN, IS DYING. EVEN FOR HER THE WORST IS YET TO COME!

TO AVOID FAINTING KEEP REPEATING, IT'S ONLY A MOVIE ...ONLY A MOVIE ...ONLY A MOVIE ...ONLY A MOVIE ...ONLY A MOVIE ONLY A MOVIE

THEATRE	GROSS
LUCKY TWIN D.I.	8,103
COON RAPIDS D.I.	6,004
FLYING CLOUD D.I.	5,123
CORALL D.I.	7,288
ROSE D.I.	10,102
TOTAL:	$36,620

ALSO CHECK THIS
UNPRECEDENTED 5 WEEK
WINTER ENGAGEMENT:
REDWOOD D.I.-SALT LAKE CITY

2/7-13	3,439
2/14-20	3,818
2/21-27	2,000
2/28-3/6	2,355
3/7-13	2,395
TOTAL:	$14,007

LAST HOUSE ON THE LEFT

WARNING! NOT RECOMMENDED FOR PERSONS OVER 30!

NOW AVAILABLE WITH A COMPLETELY NEW CAMPAIGN!

NEW PRINTS — NEW PRESS BOOK
NEW RADIO — T.V. — AND — THEATRICAL TRAILER
— CONTACT YOUR LOCAL —
A.I.P. EXCHANGE FOR DATES
IN NEW ENGLAND · JUD PARKER FILMS · BOSTON, MASS. · 617-542-0744

VOTRE SYSTÈME NERVEUX SERA ICI-ALLEMENT MIS
A RUDE ÉPREUVE, AUSSI, CONSEILLONS-NOUS AUX
PERSONNES IMPRESSIONNABLES OF S'ABSTENIR...

LE MASSACRE DES MORTS VIVANTS

The Legend of Boggy Creek
A TRUE STORY

A HOWCO INTERNATIONAL PICTURES RELEASE
A PIERCE-LEDWELL PRODUCTION   G

The Most Controversial Horror Film Ever Is Finally Here.

The Saw is Law

The terror begins the second it starts.

LEATHERFACE
THE TEXAS CHAINSAW MASSACRE III

NEW LINE CINEMA PRESENTS LEATHERFACE: THE TEXAS CHAINSAW MASSACRE III
WITH Annette Benson DIRECTOR OF PHOTOGRAPHY Mick Strawn PRODUCTION DESIGN James L. Carter

Clockwise from top left: Last House on Dead End Street *(1977) is back from somewhere;*
Last House on the Left *(1972) kills...at the box office;* Leatherface *(1990)'s saw is the law; tall tale*
The Legend of Boggy Creek *(1972); Let Sleeping Corpses Lie (1974) in furious original French*

title, to confuse patrons into thinking this was either Wes Craven's 1972 classic or some sort of follow-up. That level of chutzpah is practically worthy of Nikki Sixx. Fake quotes from nonexistent movie critics are an exploitation-movie staple. In addition to having "CULT CLASSIC" stamped on it, the *Last House on Dead End Street* poster boasts a legendary example: "'Worst film . . . Kids love it.'—Atlanta Film Festival."

Last House on Dead End Street languished for at least seven years before unspooling on a commercial movie theater screen. In 1979, the film got a decent release in New York City grindhouses and nearby drive-ins. Creator Roger Watkins says he only knew the movie was out when a passerby stopped him on a New York sidewalk and said, "You look like the guy throwing animal guts around in that movie playing on Forty-Second Street!" Watkins was responsible for quite a few movies that lit up theater marquees at New York's infamous "Deuce" entertainment center. Under various pseudonyms, including "Richard Mahler," Watkins directed a number of highly regarded "Golden Age" porn films, including *Her Name Was Lisa* (1980), *The Pink Ladies* (1981), *Midnight Heat* (1983), and *Corruption* (1984). As you might guess, Watkins's porn movies typically deal with pitch-black themes, including drug overdoses, suicide, and murder for hire.

In the early 2000s, Watkins went on the Internet and was astonished to find that *Last House on Dead End Street* had developed a worldwide cult following. In fact, no one had even ever been sure who exactly had directed this movie until Watkins came forward online. From there, fan interest and interaction prompted him to get involved in the horror community and oversee the making of an incredible *Last House on Dead End Street* DVD in 2005. He passed away soon after. The special-edition DVD features a video for "They Dwell Beneath" by horror-driven death-metal mavens Necrophagia, featuring scenes from *Last House on Dead End Street*. The intensity of the song, matched with scenes from the film, is terrifying.

The Last House on the Left (1972)

(Dir. Wes Craven; w/David Hess, Sandra Peabody [as Sandra Cassell], Jeramie Rain, Fred Lincoln)

✠ Rape and Revenge ✠ Banned Video Nasty

Night of the Living Dead (1968) did for horror cinema what Black Sabbath's self-titled 1970 debut did for rock and roll. Twin apocalypses descended, forever rendering what had existed before quaint and domesticated, while simultaneously dictating that whatever might follow would have to continually surpass all previous transgressions in darkness, dread, and terror. After Sabbath, rock festered for nearly a decade before reaching the accelerated evil of Iron Maiden, Angel Witch, and the New Wave of British Heavy Metal and from there death metal, black metal, and the rest of modern-day terror. Movies reached a new boiling point within just a few ungroovy years of the first zombie invasion, thanks to *Last House on the Left*.

Written and directed by Wes Craven (and produced by future *Friday the 13th* helmer Sean S. Cunningham), *Last House on the Left* is a sick and repulsive punishment that has neither mellowed nor lightened with age. Unlike the classic metal albums of 1972—giants including *Vol. 4* by Black Sabbath, *Machine Head* by Deep Purple, *School's Out* by Alice Cooper, and Blue Öyster Cult's eponymous bow—*Last House on the Left* possesses no element that may be construed by any non-diseased mind as "fun." The arch hardness begins when suburban girl Mari (Sandra Cassell) celebrates her seventeenth birthday by going with her friend Phyllis (Lucy Grantham) to see the band Bloodlust play in New York City. The teens attempt to buy pot from sniveling junkie Junior (Marc Sheffler), but he leads them to the lair of his criminal father Krug (David Hess) and his scumbag cohorts Sadie (Jeramie Rain) and Weasel (Fred Lincoln). The doom sets in. And then keeps on settling.

The gang kidnaps Mari and Phyllis and drives

them to the woods. Krug forces the girls to wet their pants and have sex with one another. One by one, each thug rapes them. When Mari manages to run away, Weasel stabs Phyllis repeatedly and Sadie unreels the girl's intestines from her wounds. Krug catches Mari, carves his name in her chest, and, as she tearfully prays, shoots her to death. So much for act 1. Audiences that could endure (or contain themselves over) *Last House*'s opening level of unprecedented brutality then watched Krug and company unwittingly take shelter at the home of Mari's parents. After Mom and Dad catch on as to what happened and that their guests are the creeps responsible, they mount a vengeance campaign—slashing Sadie's throat, biting off Weasel's penis, and chainsawing Krug to ribbons. Interestingly, Junior's demise—Krug furiously talks him into eating a bullet—may be the most lacerating of all.

Last House on the Left hit big at the box office with its unforgettable ad campaign: "To avoid fainting, keep repeating, 'It's only a movie. . . . It's only a movie. . . .'" Unlike almost every other exploitation film, *Last House* surpassed its marketing, savaging viewers and sending them gasping for fresh air. The impact is all the more impressive by how much of *Last House on the Left* is a goddamned mess. Unlike *Night of the Living Dead* or the subsequent *The Texas Chain Saw Massacre* (1974), *Last House* is not a masterwork of controlled filmmaking, but a shaky amateurish effort that veers deliriously (and even stupidly) off tone and off point repeatedly. The film was originally intended to be hard-core pornography, with all the performers agreeing to perform penetrative sex, which says a lot about the visible production values and ethereal sense of abandon.

Last House is built on that crucial foundation of rough edges. The absence of polish, and the air of guerilla warfare combine to wallop one's senses with brickbats (and knives and teeth and chainsaws) of horribly credible cruelty. The heinous sense of realism changed our reality and changed moviemaking. And as its slick, big-budget 2009 Hollywood remake makes clear, improving on imperfect perfection is impossible.

Last House's signature "To avoid fainting . . ." ad campaign had actually been employed by two previous films, each of them suitably metal in nature: goremeister Herschell Gordon Lewis's *Color Me Blood Red* (1964) and William Castle's gothic Joan Crawford shocker *Strait-Jacket* (1965). Many, many flicks helped themselves to the gimmick after *Last House*.

David Hess is disgusting as Krug. The New York native had a remarkable songwriting career before deciding to explore an interest in acting. Hess composed hits for Sal Mineo, Elvis Presley, Andy Williams, and Pat Boone, and in 1970 cowrote the Grammy-winning "electric rock opera" *The Naked Carmen*, later mounted as a stage show in Berlin. Hess also wrote and performed the music for *Last House*, including the hopeless theme song, "The Road Leads to Nowhere."

Last House on the Left is based on Ingmar Bergman's 1960 art-house classic *Jungfrukällan*, aka *The Virgin Spring*, itself an adaptation of a medieval Swedish ballad. In his indispensible *Wes Craven's Last House on the Left* (FAB Press, 2001), an exhaustive-beyond-imagination book on this film, David Szulkin presents profound interviews with all principal persons, providing endless insights into the movie. He ends the volume with a translation of the original poem "Töre's Daughters in Vänge."

As gleefully revealed by Daniel Ekeroth in his exploitation powerhouse *Swedish Sensationsfilms* (2011), although Bergman hated all the trashy rape-revenge knockoffs his film inspired, *Jungfrukällan* won awards at Cannes and the Golden Globes, and remains the only Bergman film to win Best Foreign Language Film at the Oscars. *Last House on the Left* did not follow suit.

The official Hollywood remake, *Last House on the Left* (2009), isn't terrible when taken at glossy teen-idol face value. Garret Dillahunt, as Krug, does interesting things with the character. As Sadie, singing comedian Riki Lindhome conveys feral sexual menace, and she honors a great exploitation movie tradition by dying with her boobs out. Infinitely more fascinating than the big-studio take, and arguably more horrific than the 1972 original, is the unofficial *Last House* remake, *Chaos* (2005). That fucker leaves a mark.

The Last Slumber Party (1988)

(Dir. Stephen Tyler; w/Jan Jensen, Nancy Meyer)
✠ Slasher ✠ Soundtrack (Fyrstryke)

School's out for the summer, and a jubilant sleepover is on for ready-made teenage slasher targets Tracy (Nancy Meyer), Chris (Jan Jensen), and Linda (Joann Whitley). You will not be surprised when an escaped mental patient crashes the bash, scalpel-first. *The Last Slumber Party* is simultaneously mind-numbing and liquefying, a gorily ramshackle exercise in anti-horror made on a budget that may not have stretched into the double digits. The terribleness is truly something "special."

Pumping heavy metal into *Last Slumber Party*'s ketchup-scented bloodbath is the job of Tulsa, OK, cock rockers Fyrstryke. The band and its 1986 album, *Just a Nightmare*, worked up enough of a Midwest following beyond *Last Slumber Party* that they were invited to reunite to play the glam-tilted 2010 Rocklahoma festival along with Tesla, Krank, Cinderella, and other poodle noodlers.

The Last Temptation of Christ (1988)

(Dir. Martin Scorsese; w/Willem Dafoe, Barbara Hershey, Harvey Keitel, David Bowie)
✠ Satan ✠ Sacrilege ✠ Censorship

As blasphemy goes, this film may not have the immediately pulse-pounding effect of naming an extreme metal band Headless Christ or Rotting Christ or Raping Christ or Sarcoma in Christ but it is one hell of a Hollywood insult. Director Martin Scorsese's *The Last Temptation of Christ* opens with Jesus of Nazareth confessing to some cenobite-intense sadomasochistic

expressions of self-loathing while manufacturing crosses for the extermination of Jewish rabble-rousers. Played by Willem Dafoe exactly like his messianic counterfeiter character from *To Live and Die in L.A.* (1985), Jesus does all kinds of wacky shit including, but not limited to, conversing with a snake, a lion, a pillar of flame, and Satan in the form of a twelve-year-old girl (Juliette Caton). John the Baptist offers Jesus a choice similar to a situation in *Shogun Assassin* (1980), where Lone Wolf asks his toddler Daigoro to choose between a sword and a ball to decide his fate. The kid picks the sword. Jesus has to choose between an axe and a beating human heart. The son of God picks the beating heart.

Hanging on the cross at the end of the film (I hope that's not a spoiler for you), Jesus imagines what life would be like had he just given in and nailed tattooed prostitute Mary Magdalene (Barbara Hershey, showcasing the not-quite-finest facelift surgery available in ancient Judea). When, after writhing in pain, Jesus yells, "It is accomplished!" I think he means the fact that you can see his holy penis.

On cue, Jesus people worldwide rose up to belly-ache about *Last Temptation* belittling their beliefs. One extremist French front borrowed an approach typically associated with another Middle East–based religion of peace, and firebombed a theater in Paris showing the movie. Fourteen patrons suffered severe burns and the theater took three years to rebuild.

Last Temptation of Christ came hot on the unholy heels of *Hail Mary* (1985), a modern retelling of the birth of Christ by French provocateur Jean-Luc Godard. Despite the protestors out front at the time, I promptly fell asleep about ten minutes into the movie. The type of people who spend their weekends outside in the freezing cold, picketing movie theaters, were way more on the money the first time I braved the their hysterical catcalls to see the maniacally metal killer Santa Claus masterpiece *Silent Night, Deadly Night* (1984).

THE LAST UNICORN (1982)

(DIRS. JULES BASS, ARTHUR RANKIN JR.; W/MIA FARROW, JEFF BRIDGES, ANGELA LANSBURY, ALAN ARKIN, BROTHER THEODORE)

✳ UNICORN ✳ WITCH

Animation studio Rankin-Bass followed up TV movie versions of *The Hobbit* (1977) and *The Return of the King* (1980) by adapting the Peter S. Beagle fantasy book *The Last Unicorn*. Mia Farrow voices the title character. She's a lonely beast on a journey. She is caged by a witch for a circus, then escapes and frees the other animals, transforms into a human girl, falls in love, and rescues her unicorn pals from the mad Red Bull.

The Last Unicorn did okay during its initial run and then seemed to fade away. Kids loved it just because it was a cartoon, but grew up to appreciate the great voice work and the story's meaningful take on uniqueness and freedom. A thrilling sequence depicting hundreds of unicorns charging up from the sea to crumble a castle into dust ranks alongside the "Mob Rules" raiders sequence of *Heavy Metal* (1981) as most metallic cartoon scene ever. *The Last Unicorn*'s songs, though, written by Jimmy Webb ("MacArthur Park") and performed by the group America ("A Horse With No Name") may well actually be the diametric opposite of heavy metal.

LEATHERFACE: THE TEXAS CHAINSAW MASSACRE III (1990)

(DIR. JEFF BURR; W/KATE HODGE, WILLIAM BUTLER, KEN FOREE, VIGGO MORTENSEN, R. A. MIHAILOFF)

✳ CHAINSAWS ✳ SOUNDTRACK (LAAZ ROCKET, DEATH ANGEL, SACRED REICH, HURRICANE, MX MACHINE, OBSESSION, WASTED YOUTH, WRATH)

By your humble reviewer's estimation, *The Texas Chain Saw Massacre* (1974) is the greatest horror film ever made, and *The Texas Chainsaw Massacre Part 2* (1986) is the greatest horror comedy. Given that lineage, and the promise of a thrash soundtrack, not to mention a starring role for *Dawn of the Dead*'s Ken Foree, *Leatherface: The Texas Chainsaw Massacre III* is a letdown that sucks a rusty Black & Decker. The plot is close enough to the original to call it a total Hollywood remake (except that audiences didn't tolerate such travesties yet). A young couple (Kate Hodge and William Butler) takes the wrong road in Texas and runs afoul of a boring new incarnation of Leatherface (R. A. Mihailoff) and his cannibal Sawyer clan. One of the miscreants is "Tex," played by future *Lord of the Rings* king Viggo Mortensen. He doesn't help things here. Much was made of the MPAA repeatedly branding *Leatherface* with an X rating, and thereby forcing edits to secure an R. The end result is an inane mess. Bootleg variations of the film later surfaced, but none of the extra footage helped.

Directors who almost made *Leatherface* include *Chainsaw* series creator Tobe Hooper, future *Lord of the Rings* mastermind Peter Jackson, and splatter makeup genius Tom Savini. Instead, the job went to Jeff Burr, director of the pretty good Vincent Price horror anthology *The Offspring* (1987) and the worthless *Stepfather II* (1987). The novelty in 1990 of hearing Death Angel, Sacred Reich, and Laaz Rocket blaring through movie theater speakers was fun, though. Unsung Bay Area thrashers Laaz Rocket scored a *Headbanger's Ball* moment with their video for the theme song, "Leatherface." The clip features the band performing among desert rocks while scenes from the movie run in the sky behind them.

LED ZEPPELIN: CELEBRATION DAY (2012)

(DIR. DICK CARRUTHERS; W/ROBERT PLANT, JIMMY PAGE, JOHN PAUL JONES, JASON BONHAM)

✳ CONCERT FOOTAGE

A document of Led Zeppelin's much-vaunted 2007 reunion performance, *Celebration Day* takes its name from track three of *Led Zeppelin III*. The occasion that raised these rockers from retirement: a charity gala for Atlantic Records founder and Zep music biz guru Ahmet Ertegun. *Twenty million* hopefuls applied for 18,000 available seats London's O2 Arena. For the first time since drummer John Bonham went belly-up in 1980, Led Zeppelin's three surviving members headlined a full-length performance.

Led Zep had limped through an outing at the Atlantic Records fortieth anniversary show in 1988, but this time they aimed to get it right. They committed to six weeks of intense, lockdown rehearsal. Come showtime, these rock gods were nothing less than godlike. Kicking off with "Good Times, Bad Times," the set, played with Jason Bonham (John's son) on drums, is a greatest-hits canon erupting with newfound life and creating a palpably mystical communion between the performers and the audience that truly conveys the sense of the movie's title.

Director Dick Carruthers (*Heavy Metal: Louder Than Life*) conveys the anxiety of these veterans that gets surpassed only by their excitement—and their final, electrifying execution—over one more (one last?) opportunity to ascend, as only they can, that certain stairway to somewhere.

Because of the band's exacting technical specifications, *Celebration Day* took five years to complete. It premiered in October 2012 at New York's Museum of Modern Art with Robert Plant, Jimmy Page, John Paul Jones, and Jason Bonham in attendance. The film garnered such praise and the event elicited such warmth that calls for a Zeppelin reunion tour became inevitable. "I think it's disappointing for people when the answer is no," Page said, shooting the notion down. "That's what it is now."

Led Zeppelin Played Here (2014)

(Dir. Jeff Krulik; w/Jimmy Page, Dave Grohl, Barry Richards, Mario Medious, Richard Cole)

✡ Metal Reality ✡ Metal Mythology

Maryland documentarian Jeff Krulik has created a unique Heavy Metal Movie genre wherein he chronicles suburban and working-class hard rock fandom as a folk-art exercise in alternate reality. Most famously, Krulik codirected (with John Heyn) the 1986 landmark *Heavy Metal Parking Lot*, a spectacular fifteen-minute film of fans outside a D.C.-area Judas Priest blowout. Krulik's lesser-known *Heavy Metal Picnic* (2010) is a loving look back at the amateur 1985 Full Moon Jamboree rock festival along the Potomac River, headlined by Pentagram.

Led Zeppelin Played Here is the latest chapter in Krulik's Old Line State metal history. He tracks down a rumor that on January 20, 1969—the night of Richard Nixon's inaugaration—no less a rock monolith than Led Zeppelin mounted a concert on the basketball court of the dinky Wheaton Youth Center in suburban Maryland. Estimates of the crowd range from fifty to two hundred, but most accounts agree that the hall was largely empty and that the band earned $200—supposedly the lowest fee Zep ever accepted.

Nicely nailed by a *Washington Post* reviewer as "a rock and roll *Rashomon*," *LZPH* gathers testimonies from those who claim to have been present for the gig—including legendary show promoter Barry Richards—as well as from skeptics like local music columnist Mike Oberman. Flashy Atlantic Records promo hustler Mario Medious can't remember the gig, but bearded Warner Brothers PR man Eddie Kalika swears he was there. He claims the event was slapped together quickly with no advertising. Highly believable either way are Richards' and Kalicka's accounts of Zeppelin's brute manager Peter Grant threatening violence unless he received gas money.

But did it really happen? This mystery ("the Loch Ness Monster of Maryland rock and roll") makes for an intriguing tale, especially as fans display their memories and ephemera from other Youth Center shows by Dr. John, Rod Stewart, Rare Earth, Spirit and, remarkably, the Stooges (much is made of Iggy Pop making his trademark peanut butter mess). We also see a personal photo of Alice Cooper performing atop a table in a nearby community college cafeteria.

Led Zeppelin Played Here climaxes outside a 2012 Kennedy Center gala. Krulik quizzes Jimmy Page himself about the '69 show. The guitarist doesn't remember either way, but he offers that some D.C. pals were in the room when he conceived the concept for the band. As with Krulik's previous projects, the real pleasure of *Led Zeppelin Played Here* is getting inside the metal heads of some likeable mid-Atlantic maniacs.

LED ZEPPELIN: THE FIRST CUTS (1990)

(DIR. JOE MASSOT; W/ROBERT PLANT, JIMMY PAGE, JOHN BONHAM, JOHN PAUL JONES)

✠ CONCERT FOOTAGE

Led Zeppelin: The First Cuts consists of footage excised from *The Song Remains the Same* (1976) played over performances of "Dazed and Confused," "Moby Dick," "The Song Remains the Same," and "Whole Lotta Love." Zep manager Peter Grant once deemed *Song* "the most expensive home movie ever made." *The Last Cuts* seems like some cheap leftovers by Joe Massot, original director of *Song*, who was fired mid-production. Massot's previous credit of note was the psychedelic wig-flipper *Wonderwall* (1968), which featured a weird soundtrack by George Harrison that was released as the first solo Beatles album. If you couldn't get enough of Robert Plant's Viking fantasy in *Song*, enjoy five more minutes of it here, costarring his wife Maureen.

LEGALIZE MURDER (2007)

(DIR. NICK WARDEN; W/NICK WARDEN, PHILLIP ADAMS, JOSEPH SALERNO, AMY QUANT)

✠ BLACK METAL

Welsh writer-director Nick Warden stars in the mock documentary *Legalize Murder* as Dominick Dalrymple, a pretend journalist profiling black metal maniacs Jack and Vic Norsemen (Phillip Adams and Joseph Salerno, respectively). The fundamental gag of *Legalize Murder* is that these goofs perform everything from the most mundane chores to black magic rituals to Satan in full corpse paint and at top demonic intensity. The actors are funny and Warden is clearly familiar with the church arsons and peculiar black metal violence upon which he goofs.

LEGEND (1985)

(DIR. RIDLEY SCOTT; W/TOM CRUISE, MIA SARA, TIM CURRY, BILLY BARTY)

✠ FANTASY ✠ LORD OF DARKNESS ✠ FAIRIES, GOBLINS, DEMONS, ALL THAT

Ridley Scott's slickly stylized *Legend* is a by-the-numbers fantasy adventure elevated by the director's visual flourish and eye-popping character design. Jack O' the Green (Tom Cruise) lives in an enchanted forest where everything is peachy until the Lord of Darkness (Tim Curry) chops off the one remaining unicorn's horn. Blight falls upon the wooded land, and Darkness kidnaps Princess Lili (Mia Sara). Jack teams with elves, fairies, dwarves, and such to set things right. Pretty to look at and largely uninteresting, *Legend* works best as a vehicle for floating on deep bong hits. Curry's Lord of Darkness, it must be stated might be the most visually arresting representation of Satan in cinema. Designed by Rob Bottin (*The Howling, The Thing*), Darkness's skin is fire-engine red, his face is an elongated contusion of harsh angles, and he sports mammoth, bull-like black horns that extend three feet up above his pointed ears. In other words, he's even more terrifying than Tom Cruise.

THE LEGEND OF BLOOD CASTLE (1973), AKA FEMALE BUTCHER; CEREMONIA SANGRIENTA

(DIR. JORGE GRAU; W/LUCIA BOSÉ, EWA AULIN, ESPARTACO SANTONI, ANA FARRA)

✠ COUNTESS BATHORY ✠ BATS

Countess Elizabeth Bathory (Lucia Bosé) needs blood, particularly young, female virgin blood. She needs enough to fill a bathtub, in fact, as she believes it to be the elixir that will rejuvenate her aging body. The story of this Hungarian noblewoman is kept alive through heavy metal, both abstractly and specifically via the band Bathory and Cradle of Filth's *Cruelty and the Beast* album. The countess has also been the subject of numerous films detailing her many exploits, and *The Legend of Blood Castle*, after a slow build, stands as one of the more compelling (if sadly infrequently fleshy and bloody) treatments. Director Jorge Grau followed up *Blood Castle* with the also metal *Let Sleeping Corpses Lie* (1974).

THE LEGEND OF BOGGY CREEK (1972)

(DIR. CHARLES B. PIERCE; W/WILLIAM STUMPP, VERN STIERMAN, JUDY BALTOM, CHARLES B. PIERCE JR.)

✠ BIGFOOT ✠ '70S DRIVE-IN ✠ MASS HYSTERIA

Leaving the largest footprint in the Bigfoot movie subgenre, this mock documentary chases an eight-foot-tall, hairy Arkansas man-beast called the "Fouke Monster" (after nearby town Fouke, no foukin' kidding.) Director Charles B. Pierce combines interviews with down-home folk with reenactments of their beastly encounters. After taking some fire from a group of hunters, the Fouke Monster messes up some stuff and eats a couple of dogs off-camera. He also, hilariously, scares a cat to death, on camera. Jaunty banjo tunes drive home the Deep South setting, as does the unexpectedly creepy gothic atmosphere of the swamp. Beyond the inherent heavy metal fortitude of Bigfoot, *The Legend of Boggy Creek* is so close to not being a real movie that it becomes more real than most movies you'll ever see. The cheapness works in the same way that zero-fidelity black metal can sometimes conjure an overwhelmingly creepy atmosphere.

Charles B. Pierce was a Texarkana advertising salesman who realized his dream of making a movie by borrowing $100,000 and calling on local talent to create *The Legend of Boggy Creek*. The ramshackle production, staffed largely by high school students, played the drive-in circuit

for a decade and earned in excess of $20 million. Pierce later directed the scary retro-slasher *The Town That Dreaded Sundown* (1976) and the metallic Lee Majors vehicle *The Norseman* (1978). Three sequels followed: *Return to Boggy Creek* (1977), starring Dawn Wells of *Gilligan's Island* and young Dana Plato of *Diff'rent Strokes*; *The Barbaric Beast of Boggy Creek Part II*, aka *Boggy Creek II: The Legend Continues* (1985), which is, yes, the third film in the series; and the straight-to-DVD *Boggy Creek: The Legend Is True* (2011).

Cold Mourning wrote the song "Boggy Creek." Kansas City death metal band Troglodyte paid homage with their 2011 album, *Welcome to Boggy Creek*. In addition to startling cover art of Bigfoot detaching an unfortunate's face, songs include "Symphonies of Sasquatch," "Mummified Yeti Hand," "Bring Me the Head of Big Foot," and "Skunk Ape Rape: The Rapture."

THE LEGEND OF THE 7 GOLDEN VAMPIRES (1974), AKA THE 7 BROTHERS MEET DRACULA

(DIRS. ROY WARD BAKER, CHANG CHEH; W/PETER CUSHING, JOHN FORBES-ROBERTSON, DAVID CHIANG)

✠ VAMPIRES ✠ KUNG FU ✠ HAMMER FILMS

England's Hammer Films may be the most metal of all horror movie studios. Hong Kong's Shaw Brothers is inarguably the most metal of all kung fu movie studios. These two powerhouses combine gothic British Dracula and '70s kung fu mayhem and combust in *The Legend of the 7 Golden Vampires* to create an alloy of bloodsucking, bone-snapping, hell-raising grindhouse greatness. In 1904, the venerable Professor Van Helsing (played by the even more venerable Peter Cushing) travels to China to lecture on a legend about seven "golden vampires" terrorizing a village. The great Dracula-hunting Van Helsing, of course, knows this is no mere legend. When one of the seven bloodsuckers is slaughtered, Count Dracula (John Forbes-

Robertson) also hightails it to China, where he disguises himself as a warlord to support the remaining six, and to battle his nemesis Van Helsing again. The professor rallies martial arts experts to do combat with the vampires. The ensuing action sequences play out as they do in the best Shaw Brothers productions—they're funny, painful, mesmerizing, ridiculous, shocking, and thoroughly exciting all at the same time. *Golden Vampires* is the fifth and final performance of Peter Cushing in the role of Van Helsing.

LEMMY (2010)

(Dirs. Greg Olliver, Wes Orshocki; w/Lemmy Kilmister, Slash, Ozzy Osbourne, Metallica)

✠ METAL HISTORY ✠ CONCERT FOOTAGE ✠ GOD

In this documentary, you hear over and over (and over and over) again: "Lemmy is an icon!" and "Lemmy is a badass motherfucker!" and "Lemmy *is* rock and roll!" and "Lemmy is God!" For once, the reason you hear all this hyperbole is because it's true. To establish all such proclamations as legit, *Lemmy*, the movie, only needs to focus on Lemmy, the iconic badass motherfucker rock and roll god who founded Motörhead and rewrote heavy metal in his own punk-biker-cowboy-pirate image.

Wisely, first-time documentarians Greg Olliver and Wes Orshocki choose that route. Lemmy drinks whiskey, smokes cigarettes, fires a German tank, and plays trivia games at the Rainbow and slot machines in Vegas. With pleasure, we simply witness and listen to him crack wise and witty in that famous dragon-gargle. Backing up the facts are high-profile testimonies from usual suspects Ozzy, Alice, and Slash; rare treats from members of Hawkwind and The Damned; and surprise contributions from New Order bassist Peter Hook and Pulp oddity Jarvis Cocker. There's also fun studio footage of Lemmy jamming with Dave Grohl on Chuck Berry's "Run, Run Rudolph," and an invigorating performance of "Damage Case" wherein Lemmy joins Metallica onstage. Motörhead blows the screen out, too.

Music, booze, bad behavior and all, we see the real Lemmy and we know for sure that this larger-than-lust embodiment of metal mayhem is everything we say he is. Surprises arise in the form of Lemmy pal Billy Bob Thornton being his freaky self, Hawkwind's four-decades-hence nude dancer Stacia looking luminous while wielding a cigarette ash as impossibly sizable as her legendary chest, and a powerful moving moment between Lemmy and his son. As the camera explores the innumerable trinkets, trophies, treasures, and trash of Lemmy's overflowing Sunset Strip apartment, he's asked: "Of all these things, what do you treasure most?" Automatically, Lemmy responds, "My son!" and then gives his progeny, long-haired rocker Paul Inder, a pat as we see them seated side by side.

LESS THAN ZERO (1987)

(DIR. MAREK KANIEVSKA; W/ANDREW MCCARTHY, ROBERT DOWNEY JR., JAMI GERTZ, JAMES SPADER)

✠ SOUNDTRACK (SLAYER, DANZIG, AEROSMITH)

Less Than Zero adapts Brett Easton Ellis's mondo shocko roman à clef detailing Caligula-scoped decadence among the teenage offspring of Beverly Hills and big money Hollywood. Clay (Andrew McCarthy) returns to sunny SoCal from college in New England. He's been gone one semester. Four months. In that time, his high school girlfriend Blair (Jami Gertz) has developed a cocaine addiction, and his old pal Julian (Robert Downey Jr.) is so far gone he's almost sucking schlong for heroin at drug pusher hot tub parties. Julian dies. Clay talks Blair into plucking the spoon from her honker and heading east with him. Everything is L.A.'s fault. The end.

Decadence notwithstanding, *Less Than Zero* deserves mention for bringing Slayer to the big screen via the landmark Def Jam soundtrack assembled and produced by Rick Rubin. The big hit single was the Bangles' surprisingly hard-edged revamp of Simon and Garfunkel's "Hazy Shade of Winter." The record also features Aerosmith doing "Rockin' Pneumonia and the Boogie Woogie Flu"; Glenn Danzig's first two post–Misfits/Samhain solo recordings, which predate his Danzig debut on Def Jam the next year; Slayer slaying "Inna Gadda da Vida" by Iron Butterfly; and Poison chewing on "Rock and Roll All Nite" by Kiss. In addition, Public Enemy also gives Anthrax a shout-out in "Bring the Noise." Though they do not appear on the soundtrack, Red Hot Chili Peppers perform on-screen at length in their original form with late guitarist Hillel Slovak. This crucial line-up wore sweat-socks on their johnsons, inspired Faith No More, and was responsible for a late-1980s funk metal craze that saw even hard-core thrashers Exodus recording covers of funk songs.

As usual, the book *Less Than Zero* was better than the movie, and a litany of censor-slaughtering interludes were discarded on the way to the screen. Bret Easton Ellis, after the 1987 premiere, called the movie "pretty, boring, and pretty boring." That represents the only recorded incident, ever, of that author employing understatement.

Let Sleeping Corpses Lie (1974), aka The Living Dead at Manchester Morgue

(Dir. Jorge Grau; w/Christine Galbó, Ray Lovelock, Arthur Kennedy, Aldo Massasso)

✵ '70s Horror ✵ Zombies ✵ Manson Family

Observers often note how the 1960s didn't seem to die until the end of 1973. *Sleeping Corpses* proves that the dreams of the decade died hard and, as the plot progresses, unhappily enough to wake the dead. George (Ray Lovelock), an occult book specialist, heads out for a countryside vacation. He catches a ride with sexy hippie chick Edna (Christine Galbo). En route, a deranged, red-eyed man who looks like a plague victim attacks them. The pair takes refuge in a small town, only to be accused by a local police inspector (Arthur Kennedy) who suspects that George and Edna are Manson-style counterculture murderers responsible for a rash of recent grotesque slayings. The deaths are, of course, the work of zombies, who are rising rapidly due to

chemical pesticides from nearby farms infecting burial grounds. This plot point ratchets up the suspense considerably, as the couple must now flee both the undead and the law.

An Italian/Spanish coproduction set in England, *Let Sleeping Corpses Lie* brings much of the continent's best horror elements to a masterfully rendered feast of doom metal bleakness and earthquake-riffed fear. The movie's no-longer-sleeping corpses shamble about breathing heavily and making gross rattling noises. These sounds are also used to unnerving effect in the eerie score by director Jorge Grau. At one point, zombies tear big, heavy tombstones out of the ground and throw them at cops.

The inspector's rants against the heroes are brilliantly typical of what headbangers hear their whole long-haired, denim-vest-clad lives. In the best outburst, the authority figure rails: "You're all the same, with your long hair and your faggot clothes, drugs, sex, every sort of filth. And you hate the police, don't you?" (The reply to that: "You make it easy!")

Sleeping Corpses' masterfully evoked dread is exemplified by an early segment showing George piloting his motorcycle to the country. The scenery is all bleak and decaying, consisting of pollution, dead animals, and gray-faced passersby too numb to even notice a sexy female streaker as she attempts to inject some naked life into the living shambles of the pastoral English countryside. *Let Sleeping Corpses Lie* is almost equally as well known by its most common British name, *The Living Dead at Manchester Morgue*.

Electric Wizard shaman Jus Osborn rates *Sleeping Corpses* "a grade-A classic! Every frame is saturated with doom and gloom; bleak mountains and deserted graveyards, and [I like] the whole subtext of the cops thinking it's the sick hippy Satanists and not the living dead."

A Letter From Death Row (1998)

(Dirs. Bret Michaels, Marvin Baker; w/Bret Michaels, Martin Sheen, Charlie Sheen)

✡ Prison ✡ Poison

During a lull between imitating David Lee Roth's hair weave in the 1980s and starring in countless VH1 reality shows in the 2000s, Poison frontman Bret Michaels wrote, codirected, and starred in *A Letter From Death Row* as Michael Raine, a prisoner awaiting the electric chair after being convicted of murdering his girlfriend. A concerned woman from the governor's office (Lorelei Shellist) interviews him, and questions arise as to Raine's guilt or innocence. Martin Sheen shows up briefly. Charlie Sheen shows up even more briefly. You might not want to miss the shots of Michaels performing karate moves alone in his cell. Somebody is fried at the end, but the movie keeps you guessing as to whether or not it's Raine. Try not to guess too hard. Michaels also wrote and performed *Death Row*'s musical score.

Lifeforce (1985)

(Dir. Tobe Hooper; w/Mathilda May, Steve Railsback, Patrick Stewart, Peter Firth)

✡ Sci-Fi Horror ✡ Space Vampires

Halley's Comet, which in real life was due to fly by Earth in 1986, brings with it a space ship full of humanoid alien human-eaters in 1985's *Lifeforce*, and they make a terrible mess of London. The space killers land, escape from sleep pods on their ship, and casually walk the streets of Old Blighty, draining the vital essence—the "life force"—from countless victims. (Christopher Jagger, who plays "First Vampire," is Mick Jagger's younger brother.) What seems like hundreds of scientists, policemen, and scientists run amok, shouting and panicking, as they attempt but fail to address the problem at hand. After two stamina-pulverizing hours, the movie just pulls the plug and says, "Go home."

Unlike the finished movie, the *Lifeforce* ad campaigns were sensational. Commercials opened with an extreme close-up of a female eye from the side, looking downward. The eye blinks, the camera pulls back, and it's revealed to be looking south toward Earth. This image also made for a strong poster. Better still were *Lifeforce*'s Japanese posters: airbrushed van art–style spacescapes with the nude Space Girl strapped, asleep, to a rocket hurtling through the heavens.

Director Tobe Hooper, light years past his *Texas Chain Saw Massacre* triumph, botched virtually every element of what should have been the greatest science-fiction/horror hybrid since *Alien* (1979). Hooper aced one flawless aspect of *Lifeforce*: he cast French stunner Mathilda May as "Space Girl"—and got her to leave her clothes off. Suspended in her pod, May is so mesmerizingly beautiful it's actually shocking. And she is so entirely exposed, it's as though she somehow creates some whole new category of nudity.

This is savvy filmmaking, as Mathilda's role is to wake up, break free, approach strangers, strike them dumb with her bare gorgeousness, and then suck the juice from their very existences. That she remains completely naked in full view the entire time can be viewed as something of a gimmick during this long goddamned movie, but it's of a piece with the actress's fearlessness and star power. Given its Britishness, hoary sci-fi storyline, and curvaceous naked space siren, *Lifeforce* brings to mind Stacia, the bombastically busty nude dancer with intergalactic rock patrol Hawkwind. For years, I referred to *Lifeforce* as *Stacia: The Motion Picture.*

Like Father Like Son (1987)

(Dir. Rod Daniel; w/Kirk Cameron, Dudley Moore)

✡ Concert Footage ✡ Soundtrack (Aerosmith, Mötley Crüe)

Possibly the lightest-weight of all Heavy Metal Movies, *Like Father Like Son* essentially gives a sex change to the 1976 Jodie Foster Disney classic (remade in 2003 with Lindsay Lohan) *Freaky Friday*, wherein a parent and child change places. Dudley Moore plays the father, a pent-up surgeon. Kirk Cameron plays the son, a totally rad high school dude who's big into the AOR clones turned hair band Autograph. When drinking a magic potion causes them to switch bodies, junior heads off to work at the hospital and classical-music-loving dad lands in the rowdy audience at a no-holds-barred Autograph concert.

Autograph scored heavy MTV rotation in 1985 with "Turn Up the Radio," now an egregious signifier of the high hair-metal era. Neither Autograph song in *Like Father Like Son*—"She Never Looked That Good for Me" and "Dance All Night"—was a hit. This soundtrack also features Aerosmith, Mötley Crüe, and the Ramones. The film became an international blockbuster, enabling the green-lighting of a spate of 1988 adult-and-child body-switch movies. Among them: *18 Again*, *Big*, *Dream a Little Dream*, and *Vice Versa*—which showcases Malice in concert.

LISA AND THE DEVIL (1974), AKA HOUSE OF EXORCISM

(DIR. MARIO BAVA; W/TELLY SAVALAS, ELKE SOMMER, ALIDA VALLI, ALESSIO ORANO)

✵ SATAN ✵ EXORCISM ✵ '70S ITALIAN HORROR

Elke Sommer is Lisa, a tourist visiting Toledo, Spain. Telly Savalas is Leonardo, a local who's a dead ringer for the painted image of devil in a medieval fresco that caught Lisa's eye. Eventually, Lisa's escalating fear spins her out into a colorful frenzy of surrealism—the type always masterfully handled by director Mario Bava. The original Italian version of the movie ends there. In America, a heavily edited version featuring new scenes of sex and violence played at the bottom of drive-in and grindhouse triple feature bills under the title *House of Exorcism* to cash in on *Exorcist* mania. In Woody Allen's *Annie Hall* (1977), a montage meant to convey the vapidity of Los Angeles includes a shot of a theater marquee where *House of Exorcism* is playing along

with *Messiah of Evil* (1974). Extra footage or not, Telly Savalas as the devil is just fundamentally heavy. "Who loves Satan, baby?"

LISZTOMANIA (1975)

(DIR. KEN RUSSELL; W/ROGER DALTREY)

✵ CLASSICAL SHRED ✵ SOUNDTRACK (RICK WAKEMAN)

Ken Russell, British cinema's most incendiary surrealist showboat, does for nineteenth-century classical composer Franz Liszt in *Lisztomania* what he did for that deaf, dumb, and blind kid who played a mean pinball in *Tommy* (1975). That kid himself is back; the Who frontman Roger Daltrey, who played Tommy, takes on the role of Liszt. Russell's film posits that Liszt was, in fact, the great rock star of his time and that the term "Lisztomania" really was coined in 1844 to describe the rabid fan reaction to his music. His popularity and effect upon audiences rivaled that of Elvis, the Beatles, and those who followed him a century hence. From that grounding in actuality, however, *Lisztomania* departs maniacally into its own universe of meta-musical madness.

Years before Yngwie Malmsteen, *Lisztomania* reeks rampantly of neoclassical metal via its bizarre visual flourishes. Yes keyboardist Rick Wakeman's synth-driven score melds Liszt's lyricism with lustiness of mid-'70s hard rock. At some point, rival composer Richard Wagner (Paul Nicholas) evolves into a hybrid of Dracula, Frankenstein, and Hitler, and mows down mass victims with a hybrid machine gun and electric guitar. Furthermore, Ringo Starr plays the pope, while wearing cowboy boots.

LITTLE COREY GOREY (1993)

(DIR. BILL MORRONI; W/TODD FORTUNE, BRENDA POPE, GREG SACHS EDENIA SCUDDER)

✵ TEEN REVENGE ✵ FAKE METAL BAND (CREATURE)

Put-upon teen Corey Gorey (Todd Fortune) suffers endless harangues and humiliations from his repulsively fat, Coors-guzzling mom (Edenia Scudder) and coke-peddling asshole-jock brother Biff (Greg Sachs). For non-homicidal entertainment, Corey turns on and rocks out to face-painted, Kiss-like theatrical metal rockers Creature, whose music video "Wicked Witch" and songs like "Evil Kiss" are constantly blaring from the TV and other electronic orifices.

After Corey sacrifices eighteen dollars for Ozzy Osbourne tickets, Biff steals them and date-rapes the snotty object of Corey's affection, Jackie. The pent-up violence comes to a boil as Corey ties up his mom, then goes on a full-on slaughter spree, flattening the female letter carrier with the family car. The metal-tinged horror comedy *Little Corey Gorey* was principally shot in 1988, completed in 1993, reduced in two separate butchered DVD forms, and finally made available for free in its uncut silly, savage splendor at its own website in 2012. After never making a dime, the director is making one last stab for glory, and he deserves some for this minor chintz-metal gem.

LITTLE NICKY (2000)

(DIR. STEVEN BRILL; W/ADAM SANDLER, HARVEY KEITEL, PATRICIA ARQUETTE, OZZY OSBOURNE)

✠ Satan ✠ Ozzy Osbourne ✠ Soundtrack (AC/DC, Deftones, Ozzy Osbourne, Scorpions)

Adam Sandler's opening one-two punch as a movie star—the surreal slapstick masterworks *Billy Madison* (1995) and *Happy Gilmore* (1996)—could not have been more of a knee-slapping knockout. *The Wedding Singer* (1998) and *The Waterboy* (1998), both blockbusters, don't reside in the same sphere, but are funny and made Sandler an enjoyable regular multiplex option. *Little Nicky* promised the big-budget wish fulfillment of the suddenly hugest comedy star in the world unleashing his baby-talking lunacy on Satan and heavy metal. The damnation of this situation is that *Little Nicky* sucks cocks in hell. The movie is misshapen and mirthless to the point that Sandler seems to have sold his soul for those first four successes, and is now rendering payment due in the form of a disaster where every joke bombs and every metal moment is false.

Sandler plays the title role, the son of Satan (Harvey Keitel). The character reprises the repulsive, slurring rock critic he did on quick *Saturday Night Live* "Weekend Update" segments. Here, this mongoloid-mouthed mess must carry the movie. Nicky ditches the elaborately comic hell for New York, where he falls in love with a geeky Valerie (Patricia Arquette) and gets a talking bulldog, voiced by Robert Smigel. Also "up north" is Nicky's evil brother Adrian (Rhys Ifans), who finds minions in a pair of devil-happy metalheads (Jonathan Loughran and Peter Dante). The brothers duke it out, Nicky visits heaven, and Ozzy Osbourne saves the day by biting off Adrian's head.

Marilyn Manson agreed to do a cameo but bowed out. When *Little Nicky* stiffed at the box office, it left behind an embarrassing pile of ephemera: dolls, models, T-shirts, an elaborate video game, and lots more. Someone, somewhere must have collected all these hellacious gewgaws, right?

THE LIVING DEAD GIRL (1982)

(DIR. JEAN ROLLIN; W/FRANCOISE BLANCHARD, MARINA PIERRO, CARINA BARONE)

✠ Zombies ✠ Lesbian Vampire ✠ Toxic Waste

French splatter-eroticist Jean Rollin is at his best in *The Living Dead Girl*, bringing lyrical allure to a toxic-waste-spawned, flesh-eating zombie flick. Blonde Catherine (Francoise Blanchard) is the corpse in question. She leaps up from her coffin, famished for blood, after industrial chemical dumpers make the mistake of trying a little grave robbing on the side. They never leave the tomb of their dirty deed; one's eyes and the other one's entire face quickly end up in Catherine's entrails.

Freaked out and zombified, but still quite sexily human, Catherine reconnects with dark-haired Helene (Marina Pierro), her bosom childhood buddy and "blood sister." Helene bathes Catherine in a scene emblematic of director Rollin's eye for arousal. From there, Helene grows obsessed with nurturing her friend back to normalcy, but to do so she must keep Catherine fed with victims lured to their chateau.

Living Dead Girl's kill scenes pack a gnarly wallop, with each attack leading to grotesque close-ups of Catherine puncturing and tearing her meal's flesh, then sucking and chewing on all the mess that spills out. Less in-your-face (so to speak) but equally captivating is the film's evocation of damaged female friendship turned mad obsession, the kind of frantic line-blurring that riot grrrls screamed songs about and goth-chick cutters indulge in during sanguine sleepovers.

Sophisticated cinephile metal chicks, whether they lean most heavily goth or industrial or folk metal or whatever, often profess a soft spot for Rollin's work. Even Rollin's titles evoke a gender-intensive connection: e.g., *Rape of the Vampire* (1968); *The Iron Rose*, aka *The Vertical Smile* (1973); *Once Upon a Virgin*, aka *Lips of Blood* (1975); *The Grapes of Death* (1978); and *Femme Dangereuse* (1989). Britain's satanic-sex-heavy Redemption Films has done an ace job of preserving and presenting *Living Dead Girl* and other Rollin films on DVD and digital formats. Rob Zombie tipped his tattered top hat with the radio hit "Living Dead Girl."

THE LOBO PARAMILITARY CHRISTMAS SPECIAL (2002)

(DIR. SCOTT LEBERECHT; W/ANDREW BRYNIARSKI, TOM GIBIS, MICHAEL V. ALLEN)
✠ COMIC BOOKS ✠ SOUNDTRACK (MACHINE HEAD, PRIMER 55, ROB ZOMBIE)

Among the reigning giants of comic books, Marvel is more metal than D.C. With *Lobo*, D.C. attempted to even up the heavy score. The Aquaman and Wonder Woman company's answer to rivals such as Ghost Rider, Wolverine, and the Punisher could not be more explicitly metal. He has red eyes and long black hair, he wears leather and chains, and the skin on Lobo's face is naturally patterned like corpse paint.

This booze-gulping, cigar-puffing, hyper-muscular space alien also runs solely on combustive hate and gets off so intensely on slaying that he murdered the entire population of his home planet.

The Lobo Paramilitary Christmas Special is a short made by American Film Institute student Scott Leberecht in which a whoremongering, fluffy-dicked Easter Bunny hires this most villainous of super-antiheroes to assassinate Santa Claus. The results are as violent and obscene as expected, and the film is extremely well made, with dead-on performances and Hollywood-caliber special effects. Three songs feature prominently in the fourteen-minute film: "Davidian" by Machine Head, "Living Dead Girl" by Rob Zombie, and "Tricycle" by Primer 55.

LONE WOLF (1988)

(DIR. JOHN CALLAS; W/DYAN BROWN, KEVIN HART)
✠ WEREWOLVES ✠ SOUNDTRACK (TYXE)

The year 1981 unleashed both *The Howling* and *An American Werewolf in London*. However, unlike the vampire and zombie takeovers to come, metal-charged cinematic lycanthropy never engulfed the mainstream. As a result, hairy howler movies since tend to be a terrifically odd lot. *Lone Wolf* enjoyably exemplifies late-'80s lupine fright flicks: low-budget horror made for the VHS market. In this case, *Lone Wolf*'s full-moon-averse protagonist, Joel Jessup (Kevin Hart), happens to front a heavy metal band that specializes in playing high school dances.

The plot is straightforward: mysterious wild dog attacks terrorize a Colorado college town. Poor Joel knows he's the canine in question. *Lone Wolf* rises above its corn syrup bloodbaths and animatronic rubber puppet effects. Such devices looked silly at the time but, after so much CGI exhaustion, they provide a bracing blast of breath of fresh awesomeness. The tall, long-clawed, pulsating-faced werewolf gorily crashing a high school Halloween party especially rocks.

The songs by Joel's band are also surprisingly rocking. They lip-synch to a series of hard-and-heavy numbers by a group called Tyxe. Based on some kick-ass power ballads and party stompers in *Lone Wolf,* Tyxe deserved a career scoring home video horror. The band makes good on titles such as "Rock You All Night," "Let It Rock," and "Raised on Rock & Roll."

The Loneliness of the Long-Distance Runner (1962)

(Dir. Tony Richardson; w/Tom Courtenay)

✡ Youth Gone Wild

A decade and a half prior to punk and the New Wave of British Heavy Metal, *The Loneliness of the Long-Distance Runner* embodied the first rumblings of an English youth rebellion in bloom, initially as a short story by Allan Sillitoe and most indelibly in the stark, black-and-white film adaptation by director Tony Richardson. The tale of a juvenile delinquent, Colin Smith (Tom Courtenay), who runs endless miles to mentally escape the confines of reform school also gets a memorable Iron Maiden treatment in the song "The Loneliness of the Long-Distance Runner" on the band's 1986 *Somewhere in Time* album.

The straightforward, second-person narrative details the hero's endless drive to just keep hurling forward away from the forces of oppression, while refusing to allow his hard-won freedom to be co-opted by any contest that would just reinforce the deadening conformist system. Maiden's alternately sweeping and elegiac take is a great tribute to the powerfully moving 1962 film. Less so is Agoraphobic Nosebleed's 2009 grindcore spin on the material, "The Loneliness of the Long-Distance Drug Runner."

The Lord of the Rings (1978)

(Dir. Ralph Bakshi; w/Christopher Guard, William Squire, Michael Sholes, John Hurt)

✡ J. R. R. Tolkien ✡ Animation

Hollywood's first attempt at translating J. R. R. Tolkien's seminal heavy metal saga to the big screen seemed to have landed in the right hands: adventurous animation visionary Ralph Bakshi. The previous year, Bakshi delivered the Tolkienesque beguiler *Wizards* (with a lot of unacknowledged co-optation of the work of cartoonist Vaughn Bode), so having him transition to more wizards—along with hobbits, elves, dwarves, orcs, etc.—seemed natural. Unfortunately, the post–*Star Wars* and everybody-seems-to-be-on-cocaine era of late '70s Hollywood pushed out a rushed production further hindered by Bakshi's decision to create most of the movie by rotoscoping—that is, filming live actors performing the action and then tracing it onto animation cells. Used judiciously, as in 1930s Popeye cartoons and Bakshi productions *American Pop* (1980) and *Fire and Ice* (1982), rotoscoping looks cool. In *Lord of the Rings,* it looks like Gollum puke.

Straight up, this nonsensical, stamina-obliterating, Technicolor headache is one of metal cinema's supreme misfires. Bakshi deserves some form of horns raised for braving an attempt. But just toss his *Rings* into Helm's Deep and move on to Peter Jackson's properly crafted (and also largely animated) epic versions. Bakshi wanted Led Zeppelin to score his movie, and that, for sure, would have been a game changer. Notorious music mogul Saul Zaentz, producer of *Lord of the Rings,* refused the request because he would not be able to release a Zep soundtrack on his Fantasy Records label. The band had already cribbed lyrics from the pages of the books, however, and could have made an interesting rock and roll hobbit mosh pit out of things.

In 1965, the Beatles fought to acquire the movie rights. Stanley Kubrick was to direct. Cast was to be Paul McCartney starring as Frodo, Ringo Starr as Sam, George Harrison as Gandalf, and John Lennon as Gollum. Kubrick ultimately declared the books impossible to film, given the special-effects technology of the time.

However, Peter Jackson credits Ralph Bakshi's animated *Lord of the Rings* with inspiring him to read the books and, ultimately, make the his version of the movies twenty years later. For that we are eternally grateful.

The Lord of the Rings: The Fellowship of the Ring (2001)

(Dir. Peter Jackson; w/Elijah Wood, Ian McKellen, Sean Astin, Viggo Mortensen, Christopher Lee)

✠ J. R. R. Tolkien

After decades of false starts, misfires, and other Hollywood slip-ups through the Cracks of Doom, the one right filmmaker at the one exact right time, culturally and technologically, arose to translate J. R. R. Tolkien's biblically heavy metal *Lord of the Rings* trilogy into a trio of worthy movie classics. Writer-director Peter Jackson's *The Lord of the Rings: The Fellowship of the Ring* honors an unspoken covenant between the metalheads who worship the books and the threat of movie adaptations: if you're even going to try, do not fuck it up. Jackson and his armies of assembled talent do not fuck it up. No movie theaters anywhere were torched by metal throngs.

In fact, the first movie of the trilogy arrived to universal acclaim. Jackson's background in perverse puppets (1989's *Meet the Feebles*) and comically surreal splatter horror (1992's *Dead Alive*) prepared him nobly for *Lord of the Rings*' fantastical creatures and vast scope. Jackson drives the complicated story with grace, fluidity, and speed.

All the characters that inspired legions of metal songs, concept albums, and band names are here, stunningly enacting their pursuit of the One Ring: hobbits Frodo Baggins (Elijah Wood) and Samwise Gamgee (Sean Astin), good wizard Gandalf (Ian McKellen), evil wizard Saruman (Christopher Lee), rightful king Aragorn (Viggo Mortensen), elf lord Elrond (Hugo Weaving), elf archer Legolas (Orlando Bloom), elf beauties Arwen (Liv Tyler) and Galadriel (Cate Blanchett), bearded dwarf Gimli (John Rhys-Davies) and, most awe-inspiringly, slimy, raspy, grotesque but still kind of lovable One Ring junkie Gollum (Andy Serkis). There is no dearth of orcs, either.

Hammer horror veteran Sir Christopher Lee had been a hard-core devotee of Tolkien's books since the 1950s. He was reportedly the only cast member who actually met Tolkien during his lifetime, and he claimed to read *The Lord of the Rings* once every year. As the fallen wizard Saruman the Black, he held down the film's considerable darkness with obsidian-like intensity.

All three *Lord of the Rings* films contain magnificent music by Howard Shore. He based the scores on the work of supreme proto-metal classical composer Richard Wagner, and thus the music rings with the Wagnerian majesty of metal acts including Manowar, Emperor, Warlord, Nightwish, and Rhapsody of Fire.

The extended-edition DVD of *The Fellowship of the Ring* runs twice as long. The sequels follow suit in extra-long fashion. No one's complaining.

The Lord of the Rings: The Two Towers (2002)

(Dir. Peter Jackson; w/Elijah Wood, Ian McKellen, Sean Astin, Viggo Mortensen, Christopher Lee)

✠ Tolkien ✠ Swords & Sorcery ✠ Undead

The Lord of the Rings: The Two Towers continues the tale begun with *The Fellowship of the Ring*, even more vividly realizing the most beloved heavy metal aspects of J. R. R. Tolkien's Middle Earth saga. Heroic hobbits Frodo (Sean Astin) and Sam (Sean Astin) pick up Gollum (a magnificently cracked Andy Serkis) en route to Mordor to destroy the One Ring. Gandalf (Ian McKellen) returns from death. Wandering hobbits Merry and Pippin (Billy Boyd) enlist Treebeard and his tribe of sylvan giants, the Ents, to their cause. All the story elements culminate in the hyper-metal Battle of Helm's Deep, a massive cinematic spectacle to behold. Director Peter Jackson cameos during the prolonged fight, tossing a spear.

As a middle chapter in heavy metal's most influential epic yarn, *The Two Towers* stands mighty tall on its own. In addition to showcasing the eco-metal and pagan metal deities made wooden flesh the Ents, the Two Towers introduces metal archetypes the Nazgûl, witch knight "dark riders" in service to Sauron, *Lord of the Rings'* embodiment of evil, who takes form primarily as a giant, sometimes flaming disembodied eye, as sung about by Led Zep in "Ramble On."

The Lord of the Rings: The Return of the King (2003)

(Dir. Peter Jackson; w/Elijah Wood, Ian McKellen, Sean Astin, Vigo Mortensen, Andy Serkis, Christopher Lee)

✣ Tolkien ✣ Swords & Sorcery ✣ Undead

Peter Jackson's suitably monumental three-part movie realization of J. R. R. Tolkien's *The Lord of the Rings* concludes with a whole lot of bangs, followed by a sizable round of hobbit whimpers. *The Return of the King* details the many battles to place Aragorn (Viggo Mortensen) on his rightful throne and, primarily, the journey of Frodo (Elijah Wood), Sam (Sean Astin), and Gollum (Andy Serkis) to destroy the One Ring. The story incorporates some of Middle Earth's most inspired beings, such as the giant, hobbit-eating spider Shebon; the ghostly King of the Dead leading his ghostly Army of the Dead; and the Witch-King

of Angmar, who doubles as Lord of the Nazgûl, a dark rider whose evil-intensive titles should be self-explanatory. More metal still are settings such as Mordor, the residence of the unspeakably destructive evil eyeball Sauron, and Amon Amarth, aka Mount Doom, which contains the singularly heavy-sounding Crack of Doom.

With a lot of loose ends to tie up, *Return of the King* does succumb to what seem like about a dozen endings too many, many featuring weeping hobbits. Regardless, Peter Jackson and his legions of cast and crew adapt literature's most epic heavy metal saga into the ultimate heavy metal blockbuster movie trilogy. Headbangers beguiled by the books may well cry along with those hobbits, but out of sheer appreciation and joyful respect. The entire *Lord of the Rings* film series is, as Gollum hisses, PRECIOUS!

The Lords of Salem (2013)

(Dir. Rob Zombie; w/Sheri Moon Zombie, Meg Foster, Bruce Davison, Judy Geeson)

✣ Satan ✣ Witchcraft ✣ Black Metal
✣ Backward Masking ✣ Soundtrack (John 5)

The seminal 1980 text *The Golden Turkey Awards* by Harry and Michael Medved contains an interview with Phil Tucker, director of the cult classic 1953 stink bomb *Robot Monster*. After discussing this infamous 3-D sci-fi gutbuster starring a guy in a gorilla suit with a diving helmet, Tucker laments a movie he made that was completely lost, called *Space Jockey*. "My other films are *okay*," Tucker says, "but that *Space Jockey*—that's a *real* piece of shit."

Rob Zombie's *Space Jockey* is *The Lords of Salem*, a film about Salem witches being resurrected in modern day by means of a subliminal messages on a rock album. What sounds like the ultimate Heavy Metal Movie turns out to be, well, a real piece of shit. Rob's wife Sheri Moon Zombie stars as Heidi LaRoc Hawthorne, one-third of the biggest radio team in the Boston area. The show seems to run in the middle of the night, presenting a numbing combination of extreme metal, '80s oldies, and rapid-fire morning-zoo sound effects. A vinyl LP by a band identified only as the Lords materializes from nowhere at the radio station. Its cacophonous drone hypnotizes Sheri and all the women tuned in to her, and a coven that was burned alive during the Salem with trials soon returns to earth.

Into this framework are scattered a contemporary sorceress cabal led by Heidi's landlady (Judy Geeson), flashbacks to old Salem (with a nude sixty-five-year-old Meg Foster), a lumpy dwarf monster that looks like the red M&M from the candy ads, and fitful appearances by Count Gorgan, frothing frontman for black metal marauders Leviathan the Fleeing Serpent. *Lords of Salem* is numbingly dull when it's not jarringly inept, especially the dialogue, and the black metal bits prove to be especially galling. Through his blank-brained misunderstanding and mishandling of black metal, Rob Zombie finally becomes the square 1960s dad trying on love beads and flashing a peace sign while chirping, "Groovy!" For Rob, though, it's corpse paint, a sword, and insincere calls to the hailing of Satan.

The Lords of Salem deserves to burn, but is not cool enough to do so in Hell. Count Gorgan and his group are the black metal equivalent of the punks on the celebrated 1982 "Next Stop, Nowhere" episode of NBC's *Quincy, M.E.* (note that the Mohawk-adorned band was named Mayhem!). At least real fans can watch *Quincy* and also the stupendous 2009 "Mayhem on a Cross" episode of the Fox mystery series *Bones* and laugh at what square TV execs guess so clumsily what's eating kids today. The gap between media boardroom and high school hopheads was never greater or more hilarious. Zombie's misfire just comes off as smug and insulting. Even the atrocious fake-1950s music of *The Lords of Flatbush* kicks the plastic bullet belts clean off the faux black metal of *The Lords of Salem*.

The modern witches include Dee Wallace Stone (*The Howling, Cujo*) and Patricia Quinn (Magenta from *The Rocky Horror Picture Show*). Ken Foree

of *Dawn of the Dead* plays one of the disc jockeys. Horror icons and Zombie regulars Sid Haig and Michael Berryman cameo as old-timey executioners. Petrifying and dull as the final cut of *Lords of Salem* is, the mind calcifies to consider the epic-length original version that contained a movie-within-a-movie called *Frankenstein vs. the Witchfinder*. The excised material stars cult figures Udo Kier, Camille Keaton, Clint Howard, and Richard Lynch. Watch for it as a Blu-ray special feature, but not at my house.

Lost Highway (1997)
(Dir. David Lynch; w/Patricia Arquette, Bill Pullman, Balthazar Getty, Robert Blake)
Soundtrack (Trent Reznor, Nine Inch Nails, Marilyn Manson, Rammstein, Smashing Pumpkins)

SoCal surrealist David Lynch whips up a white-line-fever dream involving Bill Pullman and Balthazar Getty as shifting souls of a single character, Robert Blake donning a chalk face and blowing minds, and lots of Patricia Arquette's big, naked breasts. Cameos include Henry Rollins playing a guard, and Marilyn Manson and Jeordie White (known then as Twiggy Ramirez) creeping it up as snuff-porn ghouls. The appearances make effective use of the rockers' public persona, even if they break the dream effect of the movie: "Hee hee! It's Henry Rollins!"

Nine Inch Nails' Trent Reznor assembled the *Lost Highway* soundtrack, which includes original instrumental score pieces written and performed by Reznor, as well as NIN's "The Perfect Drug." As a result, *Lost Highway* is not only the sole David Lynch film to produce a hit soundtrack, it also spun off a bona fide pop chart smash. Lynch himself selected two Rammstein songs: "Rammstein" and "Heirate Mich." The official music video for the former is a direct tie-in to *Lost Highway*, containing film clips.

Lovedolls Superstar (1986)

(Dir. David Markey; w/Jennifer Schwartz, Kim Pilkington, Janet Housden, Jeff McDonald, Steve McDonald, Jello Biafra)

✠ Concert Footage ✠ Cult ✠ Manson Family

All the principal players of *Desperate Teenage Lovedolls* (1984) return for this equally outrageous pop-trash sequel, wherein the surviving members of an all-girl supergroup reunite to conquer rock stardom and the entire universe. While still pulsating with bubblegum joy, *Lovedolls Superstar* ups the punk factor over the original's metallic tint, as Redd Kross morph into hardcore hardheads Anarchy 6. (Hunt down their ultra-rare tie-in LP *Hardcore Lives!* however possible.) The Dead Kennedys' Jello Biafra guest stars as the president of the United States.

Metal plays into *Superstar* irregularly but awesomely. Drummer Patch (Janet Housden) moves to the desert, changes her last name to Christ, and founds a Manson/Jim Jones–esque cult of teenage throwaways who worship her. Steve McDonald plays Rainbow Tremaine, twin brother of *Desperate Teenage Lovedolls*' sleaze-pimp rock impresario Johnny Tremaine. Unlike his late sibling, however, Rainbow has been enlightened by his time with "Jean and Billy Jack at the Freedom School." Also, a possessed Gene Simmons doll orders the onstage assassination of Bruce Springsteen, and his wish is fulfilled to the max.

Lucifer Rising (1972)

(Dir. Kenneth Anger; w/Kenneth Anger, Bobby Beausoleil, Marianne Faithfull, Jimmy Page)

✠ Lucifer ✠ Occult Ritual ✠ Manson Family

Fever-brained infidel Kenneth Anger is the most dynamically influential underground filmmaker of the twentieth century, and the highest-profile continual practitioner of occult magic since the demise of grand magus Aleister Crowley. Anger, active since the late 1940s and still alive and hurling hexes from his shoebox apartment on New York's Eighth Avenue, largely invented modern editing and image-based storytelling techniques. Check his acclaimed, continually studied breakthrough *Scorpio Rising* (1963), a film about rock and roll bikers at Coney Island, to see how Hollywood and everyone else absorbed Anger's fluid camerawork and use of pop artifacts. With *Lucifer Rising*, he sought to incorporate rock and roll mysticism into his bitchy brew of avant-garde visuals, homoerotica, and Crowleyan Thelemic spirituality.

Six years in the making, *Lucifer Rising* is typical of Anger's other work, if a little more explicitly psychedelic. Beautiful lights and colors swirl with vibrant energy while seductively evil sights float about. Anger befriended Led Zeppelin guitarist and fellow Crowley devotee Jimmy Page during the anything-goes days of the late '60s. *Lucifer Rising* was to be their collaboration, with Page appearing in the film and providing its score. After a falling out (as is inevitable with Anger), the director discarded Page's music and instead asked for a new soundtrack from *Lucifer Rising*'s lead actor: aspiring musician and dangerous Manson Family member Bobby Beausoleil.

The twenty-eight-minute *Lucifer Rising* spent six years in production. In the interim, Beausoleil was sent to prison for the murder of Gary Hinman, and he actually composed the film score behind bars. Jimmy Page can be seen, uncredited, in the finished movie (he's staring at a portrait of Crowley). That's more than *Death Wish 2* and *3* can say, although they feature Page scores. In 2012, Page released the movie music on an album titled *Lucifer Rising and Other Soundtracks*. His official statement: "The collection has been exhumed."

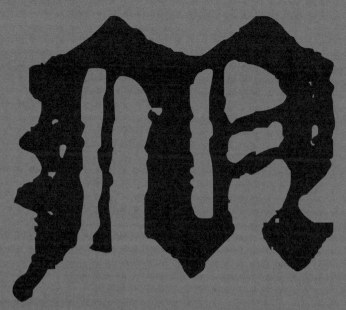

THE MAD BUTCHER ✳ MAD FOXES ✳ MAD MAX ✳ MAD MAX BEYOND THUNDERDOME ✳ MADMAN ✳ MAIDEN HEAVEN ✳ A MAN CALLED HORSE ✳ MANHUNTER ✳ MANIAC ✳ THE MANITOU ✳ MANOWAR: HELL ON EARTH, PARTS 1‚Äì5 ✳ MANSON ✳ THE MANSON FAMILY ✳ MARIMBAS FROM HELL ✳ MARJOE ✳ MARK OF THE DEVIL ✳ MARTIN ✳ MARTYRS ✳ THE MASQUE OF THE RED DEATH ✳ MASSACRE IN DINOSAUR VALLEY ✳ MASTERS OF THE UNIVERSE ✳ THE MATRIX ✳ MAUSOLEUM ✳ MAXIMUM OVERDRIVE ✳ MAY ✳ MAZES AND MONSTERS ✳ MEGAFORCE ✳ MEN BEHIND THE SUN ✳ THE MENTORS: A PIECE OF SINEMA ✳ METAL: A HEADBANGER'S JOURNEY ✳ METAL MESSIAH ✳ METAL MESSIAH: BORN AGAIN SAGE ✳ METAL RETARDATION ✳ METAL SKIN ✳ METALHEADS: THE GOOD, THE BAD & THE EVIL ✳ METALLICA: SOME KIND OF MONSTER ✳ METALLICA: THROUGH THE NEVER ✳ METALLIMANIA ✳ METALOCALYPSE: THE DOOMSTAR REQUIEM ✳ METALSTORM: THE DESTRUCTION OF JARED-SYN ✳ MISSING IN ACTION ✳ MONKS: THE TRANSATLANTIC FEEDBACK ✳ MONSTER DOG ✳ MONTEREY POP ✳ MONTY PYTHON AND THE HOLY GRAIL ✳ MORBID ANGEL: TALES OF THE SICK‚ÄîA CLOSER LOOK ✳ MOTEL HELL ✳ MOTHER OF TEARS ✳ MR. BRICKS: A HEAVY METAL MUSICAL ✳ MUNSTER, GO HOME! ✳ MURDERS IN THE RUE MORGUE ✳ MUSICAL MUTINY ✳ THE MUTILATOR ✳ MY AMITYVILLE HORROR ✳ MY BLOODY VALENTINE ✳ MY SWEET SATAN

THE MAD BUTCHER

(1971)
(DIR. GUIDO ZURLI; W/VICTOR BUONO, KARIN FIELD)
✳ TEUTONIC CANNIBALS

Rotund stand-up comic and character actor Victor Buono is best known for donning a 5XL pharaoh getup as King Tut on the 1960s *Batman* TV series. He also scored a supremely weird Heavy Metal Movie moment by making a surprise cameo as a surrealistic Satan at the end of 1978's *The Evil.*

Buono's metal cinema credentials additionally boast *The Mad Butcher*, a cruddy horror comedy shot on blatant studio sets in which he plays Otto, a Viennese meat merchant whose signature sausage bears a secret ingredient that's exactly what you would expect from a horror comedy called *The Mad Butcher.* While light on blood, *Butcher* does boast a sleazy Euro sex comedy's worth of topless Austrian frauleins.

Clockwise from top left: A Man Called Horse *(1970) soundtrack LP;* The Manitou *(1978) VHS box;* Mausoleum *(1983), the movie, not the Belgian record label; Alice Cooper meets (and meats)* Monster Dog *(1984);* Madman *(1982) is from Marz;* Megaforce *(1982), the movie, not the New Jersey record label;* Sacrifice!, *aka* The Man From Deep River *(1972);* Manson *(1973) the documentary*

Following a ubiquitous rental run during the early days of VHS, *Mad Butcher* earned metal immortality after German thrashmeisters Destruction released their 1987 *Mad Butcher* EP, featuring the bona fide thrash metal classic title track. The exquisitely rendered cover painting depicts an obese cleaver wielder who looks a lot like *Plan 9 From Outer Space* hulk Tor Johnson, and stuck around as band mascot. Mad butchah!

MAD FOXES (1981), AKA LOS VIOLADORES

(DIR. PAUL GRAU, AKA PAUL GRAY; W/ROBERT O'NEAL, SILVIA GODO, ANNE ROCCA)

✠ NAZI BIKERS ✠ RAPE REVENGE

"Easy Rocker" by Krokus is the theme song of *Mad Foxes*—ironic, considering the lack of "easy rocking" during this brain-smashing trash-bash. Stingray-driving Hal (Robert O'Neal) and his indeterminate-aged girlfriend annoy a motorcycle gang by running one of their members off the road. He dies in flames, which prompts the bikers to beat the puke out of Hal and rape the virginity out of his girlfriend (then laugh at their bloody fingers). Hal retaliates by leading some karate school pals to the funeral of the dead biker, where hand-to-gland hell breaks loose. One martial artist chops off the gang leader's penis and force-feeds it to him. Then the bikers mow down the karate dudes with gunfire.

Incredibly, from there the warfare escalates between Hal and the Hitler-worshipping hog riders (when they walk outside, their swastika armbands become inexplicably devoid of swastikas). The bikers massacre Hal's parents, blasting his wheelchair-bound mother at point-blank range with a shotgun. They celebrate this victory by violating, disemboweling, and/or orgying with anyone and everyone they encounter. Hal takes them down one at a time with guns, grenades, and lots and lots of gusto. A coproduction of Spain and Switzerland (homeland of Krokus), *Mad Foxes* is the maddest seventy-seven minutes of uneasy rocking imaginable.

MAD MAX (1979)

(DIR. GEORGE MILLER; W/MEL GIBSON, JOANNE SAMUEL, HUGH KEAYS-BYRNE, STEVE BISLEY)

✠ POST-APOCALYPSE ✠ BIKERS

After the superpowers up north nuke one another, life Down Under inches ever more rapidly toward full-on collapse. Motorcycle gangs arise as agents of chaos. To combat them, a new breed of high-octane highway cops form the Main Force Patrol. The most skilled and effective patrolman is erstwhile family man Max (Mel Gibson). A chase ends with Max killing gang leader the Nightrider (Vincent Gil), prompting the latter's minions to run riot. They commit mass rape, incinerate Max's partner Goose (Steve Bisley), and ultimately run down and murder Max's wife, Jessie (Joanne Samuel), and baby son.

From there, Max earns his nickname. Mad Max hunts down the bikers one by one and dispatches them in spectacular fashion, saving particular rage for Toecutter (Hugh Keays-Byrne), whom he splatters face-first into a speeding truck, and Johnny (Tim Burns), whom he turns into an ankle-cutter by chaining his leg to a time-bomb and handing him a hacksaw.

Mad Max qualifies as a biker movie, a rogue cop story, revenge exploitation, and post-apocalypse sci-fi. Mel Gibson seizes the screen with unprecedented hate, but what truly grips us is the hurt emanating from his shattered heart. No other actor can pull that off better, and he did it here first. The film opened a fresh frontier in Australian cinema, and offers motor vehicle fetishists their wettest dream. Director George Miller shoots the cars and motorcycles as though they are objects of worship. The stunts surpass all previous crash-'em-ups both in their impossible-to-believe execution and in Miller's brilliant means of making sure we see—and feel—every iota of impact.

A blockbuster in its homeland and a sleeper hit worldwide, *Mad Max* changed movies. This hero is a pent-up powder keg clad in leather and armed with tons of steel hurled heavily at deadly velocity. Mad Max became an instant metal icon, of the same ultra-butch breed as *Killing Machine*–era Rob Halford, circa 1978. The German heavy metal band Mad Max soon emerged, as did a slew of "Mad Max" metal songs. Max's muscle-bound, mustachioed, chrome-domed boss is Captain Fred McPhee (Roger Ward). That he calls himself "Fifi" is a nice bit of metal irony akin to that displayed by the mighty bands that took on the monikers Budgie and Pink Fairies. Max's last name, spoken regularly here but rarely elsewhere in the film series, is the amazingly metal-sounding "Rockatansky."

Mad Max Beyond Thunderdome (1985)

(Dirs. George Miller, George Ogilvie; w/Mel Gibson, Tina Turner, Bruce Spence)

✷ Post-Apocalypse ✷ Battles

Two men enter! One man leaves!" With its barbarian death dealers, mutant underworld, gladiatorial combat as public splatter spectacle, and a tribe of warrior children mistaking our antihero for their messiah, *Mad Max Beyond Thunderdome* is the most overtly '80s heavy metal film in the series. Though the least satisfying of the series, *Mad Max Beyond Thunderdome* cannot help but rock under the black heels of Mad Max (Mel Gibson) plus the awesome vision of the structure, that Aunty Entity (Tina Turner) calls, "the THUNNN-DAH DOME!"

Life hasn't picked up for Max since his prior adventure in *The Road Warrior* (1982). He stumbles into rough-and-tumble Bartertown, a makeshift community fueled by pig feces and lorded over by the ruthless Aunty Entity. Master (Angelo Rossitto) is the dwarf who runs the pig-shit plant, protected by the hulking, muscular Blaster (Paul Larsson). When the former climbs atop the shoulders of the latter, they operate as a single entity: Master/Blaster. Legal issues and mass entertainment in Bartertown are handled the same way: by casting the disputing parties into the Thunderdome, where they bounce from wall to wall on bungee cords, grabbing weapons to wield against one another. Naturally, Max is forced to battle Master/Blaster. After being banished from Bartertown, Max is rescued by a group of kids who believe he is the embodiment of a prophesied messiah. He, in turn, goes on to deliver them from the encroaching horrors of Bartertown and, as a savior, lives up to their expectations.

Beyond Thunderdome flirts with the greatness of its predecessors but never achieves the perfect exploitation poetry of *Mad Max* (1979) or the brilliant art-punk ferocity of *The Road Warrior*. The PG-13 rating is certainly a hindrance. When the movie does deliver, though—mostly during the fight scenes—*Mad Max Beyond Thunderdome* is like prog rock with crust punk trappings, not as uncommon a combo as you might think during the '80s, as the mass-media industries struggled to contain and agglomerate the underground musical happenings of the era.

Nearly as metal as the Thunderdome is Aunty Entity's judgment wheel. "Break a deal, face the wheel" is the only local law that really matters, and when the time comes to prosecute, Aunty spins a metal disc marked with a series of outcomes. The fates include: Amputation, Forfeit Goods, Gulag, Hard Labor, Life Imprisonment, Death, Spin Again, Aunty's Choice, and, the best, Complete Acquittal, which means being tortured to death.

Madman (1982)

(Dir. Joe Giannone; w/Paul Ehlers, Tony Fish, Carl Fredericks, Gaylen Ross, Jan Claire)

✷ '80s Slasher ✷ Madman Marz

Madman introduces us to "Madman Marz," a creatively homicidal antihero, by way of an oft-told campfire legend. Marz, it's said, offed his family with an axe in their woodland home, only to subsequently survive getting axed in the face himself and then escape a hangman's noose. Since then, he's continued to haunt the forest, and he shows up if you speak his name above a whisper. Somebody does. Without being as iconic as the *Friday the 13th* and *Nightmare on Elm Street* movies, *Madman* may be the most archetypal '80s slasher film. The picture is set at a summer camp, and involves awakening a monstrous and indestructible camper killer by stating his name out loud. Furthermore, teenage sex proves to be the quickest route to stylized slaughter. As played by Paul Ehlers, the long-haired, mountain-bearded Madman Marz makes for an outstandingly memorable villain. On *Madman*'s DVD commentary track, Ehlers says he ran from the set to a hospital for the birth of his daughter in the full Madman Marz getup; what a terrifyingly metal way for a kid to come into the world. Marz's name is definitely spoken above a whisper in the songs written about him by Mortician and Savage Thrust, so beware.

Maiden Heaven (2010)
(DIRS. RONAN DOYLE, AARON NOONAN; W/RONAN DOYLE, AARON NOONAN, JANICK GEARS, IRON MAIDEN)
✤ Iron Maiden ✤ Concert Footage

The documentary *Maiden Heaven* opens in 2010 with Iron Maiden announcing their "Final Frontier World Tour." Irish Maiden fanatics Ronan Doyle and Aaron Noonan immediately hit the road to catch every show of the tour's European leg. As the poster points out, *Maiden Heaven* spans "7,000 kilometres, 7 countries, 10 days," and these upbeat headbanging lads make it a pleasurable jaunt, if not a particularly fascinating stand-alone movie. While not exactly at the same level as the epic *Iron Maiden: Flight 666* (2009), *Maiden Heaven* does make an interesting travel companion.

A Man Called Horse (1970)
(DIR. ELLIOT SILVERSTEIN; W/RICHARD HARRIS, JUDITH ANDERSON, MANU TUPOU, IRON EYES CODY)
✤ Native American Spirituality ✤ Torture

A *Man Called Horse* is the legend of a British nobleman called John Morgan (Richard Harris) who is captured by a Sioux tribe in the American West. He is beaten, humiliated, dragged over rocks for miles, and treated like the animal that the Sioux name him: Horse. In time, Horse's resilience earns him respect from his captors, and he comes to understand them. After Horse scalps two enemy Shoshone scouts, he asks to undergo a full-blown Sioux warrior initiation ritual. Then comes the stuff that made *A Man Called Horse* a sensation in 1970: proto-torture-porn, modern-primitive, BDSM gnarliness that climaxes with Horse suspended in the air by hooks through his nipples.

Richard Harris plays Horse with perfect intensity. His way-out wig-outs six years later in *Orca*, while a whale of good time to watch, come off almost as a parody of the serious determination on display here. As a result, *A Man Called Horse* is rendered very metal as its sympathies stand boldly with the "savages." The film shocked the shit out of audiences with images later utilized by bands from Rammstein on down. Although the movie is largely forgotten today, the marker it placed for "torture porn" films like *Saw* or *Hostel* in the 2000s is clearly laid out on the poster tagline: "A man called 'Horse' becomes an Indian warrior in the most electrifying ritual ever seen!"

Horse had an even more immediate influence on Italian exploitation cinema. *Sacrifice!* (1972), directed by Umberto Lenzi, is largely a *Horse* remake set in modern times in the Amazonian rainforest. From that came the formula for Italy's barf bag cannibal cycle, e.g., *Emanuelle and the Last Cannibals* (1977), *Mountain of the Cannibal God* (1977), *Cannibal Holocaust* (1980). Lenzi himself rode that progressively grosser train from there through *Eaten Alive* (1980) to his masterpiece, *Cannibal Ferox* aka, *Make Them Die Slowly* (1982).

Note that the old squaw character (Judith Anderson) is named "Buffalo Cow Head." Two sequels followed, each a more conventional western than the original: *Return of a Man Called Horse* (1976) and *Triumphs of a Man Called Horse* (1983). Meanwhile, the song "A Man Called Horse" by

Finnish doomsters Lord Vicar eloquently retells the film's story through ten-plus minutes of grandiose heaviness.

MANHUNTER (1986)

(DIR. MICHAEL MANN; W/WILLIAM PETERSON, BRIAN COX, TOM NOONAN, KIM GREIST)

✣ CANNIBALS ✣ SLASHER

Hot from masterminding *Miami Vice* on TV, Michael Mann returned to the big screen with *Manhunter*, bringing his fluorescently stylized and icy flair to an adaptation of the Thomas Harris novel *Red Dragon*, wherein the world was introduced to Dr. Hannibal Lecter. Lecter, of course, became one of the all-time great horror icons by way of Anthony Hopkins's portrayal in *The Silence of the Lambs* (1991). In *Manhunter*, British thespian Brian Cox plays the cannibalistic medico in considerably more low-key fashion. Hannibal is a background character here, consulting with FBI agent Will Graham (William Peterson) in pursuit of a serial slayer of suburban families known as "The Tooth Fairy" (a great, terrifying Tom Noonan). Iron Butterfly's epic 1968 proto-metal anthem "In-a-Gadda-da-Vida" underscores Graham's final pursuit of the Tooth Fairy, amping up the madness of their confrontation to sheer tripping-balls levels. True-life murderer Dennis Wayne Wallace, who became obsessed with and ultimately killed a woman with whom he'd had hardly any contact, inspired Mann's use of "In-a-Gadda-da-Vida": Wallace believed the Iron Butterfly anthem was "their song."

As masterful and culturally dominant as *Silence of the Lambs* is, *Manhunter* actually achieved a deeper and longer-reaching influence. The film bombed upon release and never achieved more than a cult following, but it established the direct template for *Lambs* and all of television's modern crime procedurals. Not for nothing was William Peterson cast as the lead in *CSI: Crime Scene Investigation*, guiding that program to become literally the world's most popular TV show. Peterson first rocked the obsessive, self-narrating, connection-making case-cracker role in *Manhunter*, and

if you revisit the film now, you'll see that he still rocks it best—right along with Iron Butterfly.

Manhunter was originally named *Red Dragon*, after its source novel, but marketing tests showed that audiences were convinced it was a karate movie under that moniker. (Producer Dino De Laurentiis was still smarting over the box office disaster of the previous summer's *Year of the Dragon*). Of course, after *Silence of the Lambs* hit, all bets were off, and NBC re-aired *Manhunter* in 1991 as *Red Dragon: The Curse of Hannibal Lecter*. The novel was again adapted under its original name in 2002 for a film with Anthony Hopkins and Edward Norton. That movie sucks.

MANIAC (1980)

(DIR. WILLIAM LUSTIG; W/JOE SPINELL, CAROLINE MUNRO, ABIGAIL CLAYTON)

✣ SLASHER

Frank Zito never got to discover heavy metal. He is the character played by Joe Spinell in *Maniac*, the heaviest, most metallic, and flat-out greatest slasher film ever made. Zito is a fat, pockmarked, greasy, lonely loser in his middle forties. He is a survivor of wretched child abuse at the hands of his prostitute mother, and his sole coping mechanism involves stalking, slaying, and scalping young women around New York City. Frank also hangs his victims' hair on mannequins scattered about his Brooklyn basement apartment. *Maniac* introduces us to Zito through a series of these variously horrific attack scenes, beginning with a knife slaughter on a beach, and reaching its most vomit-eliciting crescendo with a point-blank shotgun blast to the head of a young lothario.

Unexpectedly, between murders, Zito attempts to romance British fashion photographer Anna D'Antoni (Bond girl Caroline Munro). After noticing her snapping photos, he pretends to be a potential client by donning oversize eyeglasses and a gaudy suit, imitating Robert De Niro ("You talkin' to me?"), and offering to take Anna out for clams casino (at a place actually called the Clam

Casino). She's charmed. Zito, of course, can't keep it together forever, and his relationship with Anna ends in a graveyard, where she clocks him with a shovel and sets off a series of hallucinations that lead to his questionable demise. Zito's mannequins may or may not come to life and tear the flesh from his obese body. This type of toxic imagery shouldn't be easy to watch, but *Maniac* mesmerizes from first frame to last. The film brings out the best from ace exploitation director William Lustig (*Vigilante, Maniac Cop*) and splatter-effects guru Tom Savini (who also plays the guy whose head is blown into a geyser of hamburger). Composer Jay Chattaway's squelchy analog synth score ranks high among fright cinema's most potent.

Lead actor Joe Spinell wrote *Maniac*'s screenplay. The larger-than-life-and/or-death New York character actor was previously most recognizable as a Corleone soldier in the first two *Godfather* movies and Stallone's loan shark boss in the original *Rocky* (1976). He had to create a character big enough for his presence and personality, and Frank Zito was certainly it.

Setting the stage for the metal-censoring '80s of Tipper Gore and the PMRC, *Maniac* met with protests, angry editorials, public outrage, and some outright bans. Even in Times Square, hardly a beacon of decency, the group Women Against Pornography staged demonstrations outside a theater showing the film. As any exploitation movie huckster will tell you, "pickets sell tickets." *Maniac* became a worldwide box-office smash, spawning a die-hard cult that continues unabated.

Taking a cue from *Dawn of the Dead, Maniac* opened in theaters unrated, bearing on its advertisements the self-imposed warning: "There is no explicit sex in this picture. However, there are scenes of violence which may be considered horrifying. No one under 17 admitted." Also like *Dawn, Maniac* drenched late-night TV with terrifying commercials. The ads flashed images of the movie's attack scenes set to synthesizer blasts brought to a jarring halt by an announcer sneering, "Maniac! It'll *tear* the *life* out of you!"

Amazingly, this most savage of slasher abominations did directly inspire a number one pop hit. "Maniac" by Michael Sembello from the *Flashdance* soundtrack—yes, that song—is a tribute to this film. As he explains to Lustig in a special feature on the *Maniac* Blu-ray, Sembello and his cowriter were haphazardly creating the song's central riff on a keyboard and jokingly started singing about the movie. Their original chorus included the line "he'll kill your cat and nail him to the door." By the time the song ended up in *Flashdance*, those words were changed to "and she's dancing like she's never danced before."

Watching *Maniac*, I sometimes wonder what Frank Zito might have been like had he just happened upon *Sabbath Bloody Sabbath* or Iron Maiden's *Killers* at a crucial crossroads in his life. Zito is a type of outcast to whom heavy metal inherently appeals, and whom it often saves. Maybe had Frank once wandered over to legendary metal club L'Amour: Rock Capitol of Brooklyn, his creepiness might have subsided. He might have moshed a little bit, found some friends, and made things work with all kinds of French photographers instead of slaughtering hookers and nurses.

Elijah Wood reprised the Joe Spinell role (in theory only) in a 2012 remake.

The Manitou (1978)

(Dir. William Girdler; w/Tony Curtis, Susan Strasberg, Michael Ansara, Stella Stevens)
✳ Native American Spirituality

The Manitou is a '70s fever trip of paleface Native American sympathy, a "birth horror" picture in the vein of *It's Alive* (1974) and *Demon Seed* (1977), offering a variation on the Zuni fetish doll from *Trilogy of Terror* (1975), via ESP, and featuring some ass-kicking optical visual effects. Tony Curtis stars as Harry, a phony psychic whose ex-girlfriend, Karen (Susan Strasberg), has what she believes is a tumor growing on her neck. That's not a tumor, though, but Misquamacas—a Native American spirit being called a Manitou. In this case, the Manitou is the spirit of a four-hundred-year-old tribal warrior returning to exact revenge on whitey.

Odd deaths occur, Tony attends a séance, and Misquamacas whelps himself, magnificently, from Karen's neck-womb. You have not lived until you see goo-slimed dwarf actor Felix Silla in an old American Indian mask do his dirty magic as the Manitou. Help comes from Native American spiritualist John Singing Rock (Michael Ansara), who battles the spirit during an indoor blizzard. Meanwhile, Karen channels the power of all the computers in a hospital to float in space and shoot lasers at Misquamacas. Importantly, her top falls off and her boobs come out as she does this.

The Manitou is a vision quest wherein you simply will not (and maybe even should not) believe your eyes. Invitations to the 1978 premiere of *The Manitou* in South Africa were printed on barf bags. *The Manitou* is the last film of remarkable Kentucky auteur William Girdler. He died shortly afterward in a helicopter crash. In just six years, Girdler directed nine movies, many of which live on as cult classics. Particularly worth seeing are *Three on a Meathook* (1973), *Abby* (1974), *Sheba, Baby* (1975), *Grizzly* (1976), and *Day of the Animals* (1977). Bands named Manitou popped up in wake of this film in Finland, Netherlands, Norway, and Poland, and Venom's "Manitou" is arguably the final song of the band's golden era.

Manowar: Hell on Earth, Parts 1-5

(2001–2010)

(Dir. Neil Johnson; w/Joey DeMaio, Eric Adams, Karl Logan, Scott Columbus, Donnie Hamzik)

✠ Concert Footage ✠ World Metal ✠ Blood ✠ Fire ✠ Steel ✠ Fantasy ✠ Metal Reality

In the eyes of founding bassist Joey DeMaio, vocalist Eric Adams, shredder Karl Logan, and skin-pounder Scott Columbus, Manowar is life, and life is an ongoing, endlessly energized attack against false metal, via epic leather singalongs played at soul-shattering volume with galaxy-rattling joy. The band's exhaustive, days-long home video series *Hell on Earth* is a crushing overload of pure metal power, built on examples of exaggerated excess that make run-of-the-mill heavy metal bombast seem demure.

Nearly forty years into muscle-bound Manowar's masterful musical conquest of all they survey, the band's ongoing documentary series lays bare one universal truth: chicks show their boobs to Manowar. *Manowar: Hell on Earth, Part 1* (2001) kicks off the cycle with a skinternational bevy of eye-poppers doffing their tops for the rippling-bicep brotherhood. Invigorated by the recent addition of guitarist Logan, to say nothing of the perpetual onslaught of flashed flesh, Manowar trots the globe on a fourteen-country tour with stops in Europe (with outstanding live performances in Belgium, Germany, and Italy); Cleveland (for a particularly over-the-top New Year's Eve bacchanal); and, for the first time, South America. As you'd guess, in a continent where even the most casual headbanger comes off as a 666th-level "Manowarrior," the crowds rapturously respond as though true gods have materialized into leather-clad, riff-pounding reality right before their ecstatic eyes. Other adventures see the boys filming a music video for "Return of the Warlord," jamming with an orchestra on "Courage," taking in a Spanish bullfight, and revving all engines at a Midwinter Motorcycle Madness festival. The head-scratcher is how these guys can roam the planet like the second coming of Led Zeppelin while maintaining next to no profile at home in America. Like everything else they do, Manowar takes "big in Japan" status to the biggest, loudest, and furthest level.

Manowar: Hell on Earth II—Fire and Blood (2002) is more purely music-oriented than the previous year's *Hell on Earth, Part 1*, focusing largely on live performances during the band's Hell on Stage tour in 1998. Disc one spotlights the leather-strapped demigods gigging throughout Europe, highlighted by powerful performances of "Guyana (Cult of the Damned)" in Belgium and "Dark Avenger," complete with Orson Welles narration, in Portugal. Disc two, "Blood in Brazil" showcases the band triumphing over thirty thousand frantically dedicated fans at a 1998 Monsters of Rock show in Sao Paulo. Manowar mania completely reigns throughout the thirteen-song set. The bonus features are more or less pedestrian, but remember, this is Manowar. Their version of "mundane" is any other band's version of dragon-fire barbarian Armageddon.

Manowar: Hell on Earth III (2003) hammers home five hours and twenty minutes more of Manowar. Of course, any *true* metalhead is living, breathing, fighting, fucking, and bleeding pure, uncut Manowar during every single second of existence; certainly that's what bassist Joey DeMaio tells you repeatedly. Believers will be inspired and non-converts will come to their Mano-senses. The first disc follows the band from Brazil through Western Europe and Scandinavia on into Estonia and Russia. The boys pound booze, let babes rub all over them, and stomp false metal to smithereens with every riff and every riotous post-gig debauch. On disc two, Manowar storms Germany's Ringfest 2002 for a nine-song decimation of any other band who dared take the stage. Again, DeMaio will assure you that's correct. The concert is followed by eight music videos, including some live clips and short "making-of" segments and a couple of quick documentaries: one on the state of Manowar circa 2003, the other on Ringfest. Whew!

Power metal. Viking metal. Epic metal. Metal metal. Manowar. All these iconic concepts merge in the audio-video bombardment of *Manowar: Hell on Earth IV* (2005) to the point that it becomes pointless to ponder how any other form of music—let alone metal—can possibly compete in sensory-overwhelming awesomeness. Disc one features mind-bending action from Manowar's 2002 Warriors of the World tour, capturing footage from no fewer than thirty-five different cities. Disc two contains behind-the-scenes documentaries and, fascinatingly, a solid hour of Manowar appearances on European TV shows.

Again, abroad Joey DeMaio and Eric Adams are treated like Pete Townshend and Roger Daltrey, while the band's last significant U.S. TV appearance seems to be a Nickelodeon slot in 1984.

No one could ever accuse the Kings of Metal of skimping one scintilla of a saber slice when it comes to overpowering all expectations. *Manowar: Hell on Earth V* (2010) boasts that, unlike the four previous rapid-fire installments, this production was "five years in the making." In fact, it shows. This fifth video package ups the band's firepower in terms of high-tech video work, glossy presentation, and overall aesthetics—not to mention helicopter shots.

Fret not, *Hell on Earth V* still includes gloriously excessive concert clips from Europe and Moscow, intermingled with party-hearty post-show torrents of beer, booze, boob-flashing groupies, and extended declarations of Manowar's true metal magnificence. As usual, the double-disc package also boasts music videos, behind-the-scenes documentaries, and the expected bounty of too-much-is-never-enough stuff.

Hell on Earth V goes further by delving into *The Asgard Saga*, a multimedia collaboration between the band and German fantasy author Wolfgang Holbein about Thor and Odin roaming earth among the Vikings. Snowy swordfights and thunderous hammer slams abound in the short *Asgard Saga* film, scored by Manowar and screened for the first time at the band's own 2009 Magic Circle Festival along the Rhine River. The movie is intended to be just one aspect of a deluge of dimensions including websites, video games, social media, and other outlets detailed in a bombastically entertaining "making of" feature. Perhaps all that will be included in *Hell on Earth, Part DCLXVI*.

MANSON (1973), AKA
MANSON AND SQUEAKY FROMME
(DIRS. ROBERT HENDRICKSON, LAURENCE MERRICK; W/CHARLES MANSON, VINCENT BUGLIOSI, LYNETTE "SQUEAKY" FROMME, GEORGE SPAHN)
✣ MANSON FAMILY

Taking cues that only he could detect from the Beatles' near-metal "Helter Skelter," counterculture villain Charles Manson embodied acid rock's ultimate bum trip. The devil-eyed, unwashed Manson was a guitar-strumming, songwriting, Dumpster-diving LSD freak who ranted in his desert lair about being the Antichrist. He summoned a long-haired youth army to conquer the planet, and attempted to sire a dynasty to inherit the spoils. When Charlie ordered his creepy-crawlers to attack—well, you don't have to be Roman Polanski to know how that went down.

The documentary *Manson* focuses on this Ohio River hoodlum turned global bogeyman and his followers, the Manson Family, through the prism of their conviction for the legendarily gruesome Tate-LaBianca murders in 1969. A rock-solid introduction to the man and his various associated manias, the documentary features copious news footage of the group's sensational mass-murder trial. Newly filmed interviews include one with prosecutor Vincent Bugliosi, who went on to write his own conspiracy-laden account, *Helter Skelter*. *Manson* also catches up with George Spahn, the old blind dude who owned the movie-set ranch where the Manson Family lived; and several nonconvicted Family members.

As scarily exhilarating as it is watch Manson launch into one of his cyclonic baby-talk hyper-babbles, the breakout star of the documentary is poison pixie Manson girl Lynette "Squeaky" Fromme. Holding a rifle with fevered erotic devotion, she coos: "You have to make love with it. You have to know it [moans]. You have to know every part of it. And to know you know it is to know it, so that you could pick it up, at any sec-

ond, and SHOOT!" In 1975, Squeaky fought for a face-to-face meeting with Led Zeppelin's Jimmy Page. While Zep was playing a concert in Los Angeles, she repeatedly told the group's management that she had to warn Page about a vision of doom she had regarding "bad energy" heading his way. She never got to see him. Later in 1975, Squeaky attempted to assassinate President Gerald Ford. In an unintended homage to Ford's famous clumsiness, Squeaky's pistol misfired.

Along with Altamont, Black Sabbath, and Alice Cooper, the hippie Manson pissed homicidal hate all over the flower-power movement. Among the metal Manson-isms: "These children that come at you with knives, they are your children. You taught them. I didn't teach them. I just tried to help them stand up."

A wannabe rock star who didn't even need a hit song to garner a flock of groupies willing to kill and die for him, Charles Manson looms as one of popular culture's most entrancing antiheroes. Slipknot samples the movie *Manson* in the song "742617000027," and Guns N' Roses, White Zombie, Marilyn Manson, and Redd Kross have covered Charles Manson songs. Many others, including Infected, Negative Theory, Superjoint Ritual, Postmortem, Disgust, Righteous Pigs, and Church of Misery, have penned Manson-inspired anthems.

The film earned an Academy Award nomination for Best Documentary Feature, but lost to another Heavy Metal Movie classic, *Marjoe* (1972). After Squeaky Fromme's attempted offing of President Ford, producers immediately rushed the documentary back into theaters under the title *Manson and Squeaky Fromme*. A judge temporarily blocked the movie from distribution out of fear that it would prevent Squeaky from receiving a fair trial.

Around the same time, *National Lampoon's Animal House* (1978) began conceptual life as *Charlie Manson Goes to High School*. Writers Harold Ramis, Chris Miller, and Doug Kenney envisioned a fantastical origin for Manson as a clean-cut teen who would develop into the Charlie we know before graduation and turn cheerleaders into his acid-fried followers. The poster was to have depicted a well-scrubbed adolescent with Charlie's famously diabolical eyes under a parody of *American Graffiti*'s tagline ("Where were you in '62?") that read: "Where was HE in '63?" Financiers balked at the notion of characters below the age of eighteen, and thus the plot evolved into the beloved college comedy.

The Manson Family
(2003)
(Dir. Jim VanBebber; w/Marcelo Games, Marc Pitman, Leslie Orr, Jim VanBebber, Phil Anselmo)
✣ Manson Family ✣ Soundtrack (Charles Manson, Necrophagia, Superjoint Ritual)

More than a decade in the making (writer-director Jim VanBebber literally sold his blood to keep the production going), *The Manson Family* finally arrived in 2003. What DIY director VanBebber promised for so long, *The Manson Family* delivered like a carving fork to the belly. The movie opens and closes with a wraparound story set in the early 2000s about modern primitive–type dopers who worship Charles Manson and the hippie followers who terrorized Los Angeles with mass murders in 1969. The the film takes us back to those heady, harrowing days; unwashed, acid-blasted, and lethally groovy.

At a ranch in the California desert as the 1960s waned, career criminal and wannabe rock star Manson (Marcelo Games) assembles a "Family" made up of counter-culture castoffs. He lures these longhairs with drugs, orgies, the promise of perilous thrills, and charismatic suggestions that he may be both the Messiah and Satan incarnate. Then he talks one hell of a game about starting a race war, after which the Manson Family will rule the entire planet. VanBebber, who also costars as homicidal henchman Bobby Beausoleil, conjures a seedy, hellish, but powerfully seductive milieu. Manson's ludicrous notions, as a result, become convincing and even logical. Compounding this feat is that the one actor who

comes up short (no pun intended) is Games in the lead role. What should be an unconquerable hole in the center doesn't detract from the film's impact, due as much to an otherwise fully committed cast and VanBebber's wild hybrid of storytelling techniques.

The script opens a gusher of gore, explicit sex, a dog sacrifice, occult outrages, and sufficient visual savagery so that when the famous murder of the pregnant Sharon Tate occurs, it's that relief when VanBebber, respectfully, declines to exploit the sight of the fatal Caesarian section forced upon her. *The Manson Family* does not go easy on us in any way, though. But VanBebber handles the material seriously, and he realizes his intentions effectively. (Unlike Manson himself!)

Bolstering *The Manson Family's* visual whiplash is an aural nightmare of an electronic score by Download, a splinter group of industrial death gurus Skinny Puppy, along with tracks by Manson himself, Necrophagia, and numerous contributions by the various projects of ex-Pantera frontman Phil Anselmo—who also supplies the film's voice of Satan. VanBebber has since directed music videos for Skinny Puppy, as well as for soundtrack contributors Necrophagia.

Marimbas from Hell
(2010)
(Dir. Julio Hernández Cordón; w/Don Alfonso, Blacko, Chiquilin)
✣ Concert Footage ✣ World Metal

Don Alfonso is a down and nearly done marimba player in Guatemala. Blacko drums for blackened death combo Metal Warriors, and is an ex-satanist turned born again Christian who keeps kosher. Don's glue-huffing nephew Chiquilin brings these two oddballs together, and the three of them become the band Marimbas From Hell. Writer-director Julio Hernández Cordón's deadpan semi-documentary about three outcasts who find purpose in crafting a wholly new form of heavy metal is a lopsided love letter to the uniting and transformative power of hard rock. *Marimbas From Hell*, which opened L.A.'s first Heavy Metal Film Festival in 2011, suggests the world needs to see and hear more from the Guatemalan underground.

MARJOE (1972)

(DIRS. SARAH KERNOCHAN, HOWARD SMITH; W/MARJOE GORTNER)

✣ TELEVANGELISTS

The 1972 Academy Award winner for Best Documentary Feature (beating out the equally metal *Manson*), *Marjoe* chronicles grown-up child preacher Marjoe Gortner as he confronts becoming, as the *New York Times* put it, "evangelism's answer to Mick Jagger." Newsreel footage shows precocious little Marjoe, at age four, preaching the gospel and performing marriage ceremonies in the Eisenhower-era Bible Belt. Come the early '70s, Marjoe is a tall, handsome, lanky hippie topped with a fiery red rock-star mane. He mesmerizes congregants with his top-of-the-lungs tent-revival razzle-dazzle. Then he steps offstage, embraces his foxy black girlfriend, and lets us in on the fact that it's all a scam.

Marjoe lost the faith and he invited filmmakers to record his farewell tour before departing west for a secular Hollywood career (much like metal comedy icon Sam Kinison, who came to show business after making a living preaching on the tent-revival circuit). The resulting movie is a potent, pungent time capsule that fuels criticism of religion as a moneymaking proposition. Yet if Marjoe and those like him inspire audiences to be happier and live better lives, is he really ripping them off? On the other hand, if he pushes them toward more bitterness and hateful isolation, is he really responsible? In the '80s, professional evangelism, particularly on television, preoccupied countless heavy metal lyrics. *Marjoe* is a first-rate nonfiction film and a great look at from where all that anger initially blossomed.

Marjoe Gortner's post-preaching filmography is a heavy metal B-movie marvel. Among the highlights: *Pray for the Wildcats* (1974), a bizarre TV movie about bikers played by William Shatner, Andy Griffith, and Robert Reed; *Earthquake* (1974), in Sensurround; *Bobby Jo and the Outlaw* (1976), costarring Lynda "Wonder Woman" Carter, who bares what bobbled beneath her eagle-wing breastplate; *Food of the Gods* (1976), about rats and chickens grown to the size of hippos and giraffes; *Starcrash* (1978), a *Star Wars* rip-off with Joe Spinell as an ersatz Darth Vader; and *Mausoleum* (1983), where busty Bobbie Bresee's boobs turn into hungry monster faces and bite chunks out of anyone who hugs her. Marjoe also directly inspired the great found-footage horror film *The Last Exorcism* (2010).

MARK OF THE DEVIL (1970)

(DIR. MICHAEL ARMSTRONG; W/UDO KIER, HERBERT LOM, OLIVERA VUCO, REGGIE NALDER, GABY FUCHS)

✣ WITCH HUNT ✣ TORTURE

The Michael Reeves–Vincent Price masterwork *Witchfinder General* (1968) was a blockbuster only in Germany. *Mark of the Devil* represents a direct cash-in on that success, and far exceeded the grosses in every sense of its role model. The exploitation mavens at Hallmark Releasing made horror-hype history in marketing this German import for its 1972 U.S. release. "Positively the most horrifying movie ever made!" screamed the ads, which also claimed the movie was "Rated V for Violence." Most spectacularly, patrons were issued branded barf bags with every ticket. The *Mark of the Devil* campaign packed drive-ins and grindhouses for years, and influenced much ensuing '70s ballyhoo.

Mark of the Devil takes place in 1770s Germany and chronicles witchfinder Count Christian von Meruh (Udo Kier), He undergoes a crisis of faith while witnessing the brutality visited upon screaming nubiles in the name of Christ by wicked Lord Cumberland. During the opening credits, an unholy Thug of God named Albino (Reggie Nadler) attacks a group of nuns, raping and killing all but three. That trio, having

I WARNED YOU NOT TO GO OUT TO NIGHT

MANIAC

"Maniac" Starring **Joe Spinell · Caroline Munro**
Associate Producer **John Packard** · Special Make-Up Effects by **Tom Savini** · Music by **Jay Chattaway** · Screenplay by **C.A. Rosenberg** and **Joe Spinell** · Executive Producers **Joe Spinell** and **Judd Hamilton**
Produced by **Andrew Garroni** and **William Lustig** · Directed by **William Lustig**
A Magnum Motion Picture · Copyright © 1982 Movies Productions
Color by TVC · **DOLBY STEREO** · Distributed by **ANALYSIS FILM CORPORATION** A NEW FILM DISTRIBUTION COMPANY

PERDIDOS EN LA VALLE DE LOS DINOSAUROS
"STRANDED IN DINOSAUR VALLEY"

con: **MICHAEL SOPKIN · SUZANNE CARVALL** - producido: **CHARLES LEMICK** "DORAL FILM N·Y"
dir: **MICHEL E. LEMICK**

THE MAD BUTCHER

MEAT IS MEAT BUT THIS SAUSAGE WAS SPECIAL

VICTOR BUONO

Clockwise from top left: Maniac *bulges in legendary loin-busting outrage;* Manowar *raises* Hell on Earth; *Frank Langella makes like* Skeletor *in* Masters of the Universe; The Mad Butcher; Massacre in Dinosaur Valley *is a lie—no dinosaurs!*

survived, is then accused of witchcraft. The lashings, thumbscrews, butt-spikings, and burnings play out in graphic glory. Nobody gets it more gruesomely than blonde Gaby Fuchs, who is stretched on a rack and then has her tongue forcibly removed (an image promoted on posters and barf bags). The production is hateful and colorfully repugnant, setting a visual template for the many heavy metal ensembles who wielded this cross for shock value (and anti-Christian righteousness). Cathedral relied on footage from the film for its "Hopkins (Witchfinder General)" music video, and Pagan Rites named an album *Mark of the Devil*, while Autopsy Torment, Kult ov Azazel, Mystic Circle, Lurking Corpses, and many others wrote songs inspired by this film.

Martin (1976), aka
Martin the Blood Lover;
Martin the Vampire
(Dir. George Romero; w/John Amplas)
✣ George Romero ✣ Vampires

John Amplas stars as Martin, a disturbed youth whom we first see drugging a woman on a train, slitting her wrists, and siphoning blood from the wound. He's been dispatched to Braddock, Pennsylvania, to live with his old-world granduncle Tateh Cuda (Lincoln Maazel). Martin fantasizes (in black and white) about being a vampire. Tateh Cuda believes his nephew is the real deal, and attempts to keep him in check with crosses and garlic, but Martin assures him that being a vampire doesn't involve any "magic." Lonesome Martin becomes a popular regular known as "the Count" on a local late-night radio show, calling in to chat before sneaking off to Pittsburgh to escalate his vampire attacks. Tateh Cudah, in turn, moves on from rosary beads and holy water to a hammer and stake. The movie is ambiguous about whether Martin actually bears a supernatural curse, or whether he and his granduncle are just tragically bonkers.

Martin is a vampire film and a George Romero movie like no other. Minus fangs and a cape, this vampire represents a new, ultra-real kind of terror. The director names *Martin* as one of his own favorite films. The movie is a sad, eerie excursion into dead-end teenage isolation. *Martin*, both the movie and the character alike, detail what can happen when an adolescent succumbs to real darkness and horror. In Europe, *Martin* played under the title *Wampyr*, and featured a new score by Romero's frequently used prog squad, Goblin.

Martyrs (2007)
(Dir. Pascal Laugier; w/Morjana Alaoui, Mylene Jampanoï, Catherine Bégin, Robert Toupin)
✣ Martyrs ✣ Human Sacrifice

Just as Italy defined extreme horror filmmaking in the 1980s, France pushed all fright movie limits throughout the 2000s. *Martyrs* may be the country's *coup de gross*. Relentlessly unpleasant but lingeringly thought-provoking, *Martyrs* is a profound meditation on metaphysical violence and the nature of human sacrifice. Such an ambitious melding of high-art concepts and grindhouse histrionics has rarely hurt so much.

Battered young Lucie (Mylène Jampanoï) escapes from horrific captivity. She is hospitalized, then raised in an institution, where she befriends fellow abuse victim Anna (Morjana Alaoui). Fifteen years later, with Anna's help, Lucie executes what seems to be a charming suburban family, claiming that the parents were her captors. Following the murders, Lucie remains tormented by a scarred, monstrous creature (Isabelle Chasse).

After Lucie nearly tears herself to literal pieces, Anna discovers a torture chamber beneath the dead family's home. There she discovers Emilie Miskdjian as La Suppliciée, "The Torture Victim." She wears a chastity belt and has a metal mask nailed into her scalp. Lucie and the other victim are shot to death, and we meet Mademoiselle (Catherine Bégin). The older woman runs a cult that seeks to learn what lies beyond death by physically punishing an individual's body until the mind achieves the ecstatic state of grace experienced by Joan of Arc and other martyrs.

Mademoiselle notes that the best subjects for this work are young women, which does not bode well for Anna. Not at all.

Upon first viewing, I loathed *Martyrs*, as it seemed empty and cold and calculated to shock. But the film stuck with me. France's previous cookie-toss champion, the Beatrice Dalle pregnancy freak-out *Inside* (2007), rattled me right away, almost becoming the first film to actually make me throw up. *Martyrs* is a different experience on each of its many levels.

If *Inside* feels like what happens when a hell-bent human monster chases you, *Martyrs* conveys what it must feel like after you've been caught. The explicit lack of sexuality in *Martyrs'* abominations is an obvious anomaly in the realm of teen-damsels-in-all-kinds-of-distress cinema.

Martyrs is not simply exploitation, but high-art meditation in exploitation garb, loaded with subtext and allusions, reaching back through the centuries to the original horror stories that first kept conscious humans sane. The concepts in which *Martyrs* traffics are really the great mysteries of existence, as summed up by the cult's singular ambition and, impressively, by the viewer's ordeal of making it to the last scene.

The Gallic horror explosion of the 2000s was paralleled by a concurrent ascent of extreme metal bands from France, many of which matched the films in topics and tonality by commingling the sublime and the sadistic. Among the standouts: Antaeus, Aosoth, Deathspell Omega, Arkhon Infaustus, Benighted, Dagoba, Gojira, Gorod, Scarve, and Year of No Light.

The Masque of the Red Death (1964)

(Dir. Roger Corman; w/Vincent Price, Hazel Court, Jane Asher, Patrick Magee)

✶ Satan ✶ Plague ✶ Edgar Allan Poe

Roger Corman, the world's best-known hyperproductive B-movie producer, also directed his fair share of drive-in program fillers early on

and, in doing so, occasionally knocked out a masterpiece. One is *Little Shop of Horrors* (1960). Another is *The Wild Angels* (1966). Between them is the greatest of all, Corman's take on Edgar Allan Poe's *The Masque of the Red Death*, starring Vincent Price as Prospero, a Satan-worshipping prince in twelfth-century Italy.

Upon learning that a plague called the Red Death is ravaging his countryside, Prospero kidnaps Francesca (Jane Asher), a young peasant woman, and invites local nobility to stay in his castle until the disease runs its course. Eeriness and intrigue abound, including a hallucinatory occult ceremony wherein Francesca becomes a bride of Satan. The diabolically decadent Prospero hosts a grand costume ball. After the dwarf Hop-Toad (Skip Martin) incinerates his gorilla-suited enemy to the guests' amusement, a mysterious figure in red appears. Prospero believes that to be the devil himself, on hand to show his approval. In fact, the visitor is the Red Death. Doom runs scarlet.

Masque of the Red Death is Corman's symphonic, philosophical homage not just to Poe, but to art films as well, specifically those made by Ingmar Bergman (*Seventh Seal* is a clear influence) and Luis Buñuel (father of this movie's colors, claustrophobia, and psychedelic nightmares). The flawlessly crafted film is hypnotic and lands a final crushing blow, which there is no hope of dodging. *Masque of the Red Death* is beauty and beguilement at its darkest and most macabre.

Heavy metal and Edgar Allan Poe meet in required high school English classes, and become bonded for life. This particular story has spawned "Masque of the Red Death" songs by Abstract Agony, Axemaster, Crimson Glory, Hades, Malhavoc, Manilla Road, Outcast, Overlorde, and Stormwitch, to name a few.

The Masque of the Red Death is the second-to-last in Corman's series of Poe adaptations, most of which feature Vincent Price, including *House of Usher* (1960), *The Pit and the Pendulum* (1961), *The Premature Burial* (1962), *Tales of Terror* (1962), *The Raven* (1963), *The Haunted Palace* (1963), and *The Tomb of Ligeia* (1964).

Massacre in Dinosaur Valley (1985), aka Stranded in Dinosaur Valley

(Dir. Michele Massimo Tarantini; w/Michael Sopkiw, Suzane Cavalho, Marta Anderson)

✠ Cannibals ✠ Slaves ✠ '80s Italian Horror

Massacre in Dinosaur Valley does not boast the bite of earlier, better-known, more fantastically disgusting entries in the 1980s chunk-blower Italian cannibal exploitation cycle, but the movie remains well worth a wallop. A team of American archaeologists crash-lands in the Amazon jungle. They immediately encounter piranhas, leeches, booby-traps, quicksand, and cannibals who obviously favor their human female meat properly raped before cooking. Even that surprisingly rare exploitation movie/grindcore transgression, forced lesbian gang-sex, is rendered. Once the survivors escape, they fall into the clutches of white slavers. Out of a literal frying pan and into a figurative fire.

Once Michael Sopkiw (who previously starred as Mad Max stand-in Parsifal in the post-apocalyptic fave *2019: After the Fall of New York*) brings some cheeseball Indiana Jones spark to the proceedings, this almost becomes an adventure movie. Female leads Suzane Carvalho and Susan Hahn look spectacular naked, which makes the bulk of *Massacre in Dinosaur Valley* itself look rather nakedly spectacular. Only consider yourself warned: THERE ARE NO FUCKING DINOSAURS!

Masters of the Universe (1987)

(Dir. Gary Goddard; w/Dolph Lundgren, Frank Langella, Meg Foster, Courteney Cox)

✠ Swords & Sorcery ✠ Cannon Films

Heavy metal's greatest Saturday morning spin-off, the 1983–85 toy-promoting TV cartoon series *He-Man and the Masters of the Universe*, plugged elementary school kids directly into the prevailing ass-kicking force of all things metal. This was older siblings' scary album covers brought to animated life and made good, clean things. Muscular but mild-mannered Prince Adam, when pressed, would raise a broadsword skyward like a member of Manowar and invoke transformative occult forces with the cry "By the power of Grayskull!" He then shape-shifted into He-Man, who looked exactly like Prince Adam, except he wore severely butch, body-revealing S&M gear that might have made metal queen Lee Aaron blush. He-Man's enemy is the satanic-seeming, skull-headed Skeletor, and their universe is populated with figures co-opted (to varying degrees of shamelessness) from pulp fantasy novels, Frank Frazetta paintings, and other mainstays of weed-whacked '70s heavy metal motifs, including the aforementioned Castle Grayskull, a place that looks exactly like it sounds.

When it came time for this kiddie cartoon to do battle on the big screen, Cannon Films scooped up *He-Man*. The studio had executed some of the decade's most brutally metal action flicks (Bronson and Norris, 'nuff said). Alas, Cannon had no clue as to how to approach a movie for children. As a result, the *Masters of the Universe* movie is only the best Cannon could do for really, really cheap.

Hot off *Rocky IV* and not yet an early-'90s B-movie action draw, Dolph Lundgren seemed a perfect choice for He-Man, but he wasn't. Master thespian Frank Langella may well have also been a great Skeletor, but he wears an overwhelming skull mask and you kind of can't hear him. Meg Foster, with the creepiest eyes in Hollywood outside of *Helter Skelter*'s Steve Railsback, looks the part as wicked sorceress Evil-Lyn. Young Courteney Cox is the human lead. She'd clearly rather be dancing terribly with Bruce Springsteen. She-Ra, Princess of Power is spared any such indignity by not even being included. It's up to Billy Barty as slapstick dwarf Gwildor (subbing for the cartoon's floating, Jawa-esque sidekick Orko) to carry the adventure once they all get beamed to 1987 Earth. Billy does what he can. However crappy the *Masters of the Universe* movie turned out, it's still the *Masters of the Universe* movie, and was mandatory viewing for tens of millions of future metal maniacs.

Masters of the Universe began life in 1982 in the cauldron of Heavy Metal Movies, when the Mattel toy corporation signed a deal to manufacture dolls based on Arnold Schwarzenegger's 1982 *Conan the Barbarian* movie. Faced with the impossibility of peddling such a sex-and-violence-tainted line to kids, Mattel came up with a remarkably Conan-like character it promoted via Wonder Bread who was named "Won-Dar." That guy evolved, rather quickly and under the duress of a lawsuit, into He-Man.

The Matrix (1999)

(Dirs. the Wachowski Brothers; w/Keanu Reeves, Laurence Fishburne, Carrie-Anne Moss)

✠ Post-Apocalypse ✠ Man vs. Machine ✠ Soundtrack (Deftones, Marilyn Manson, Monster Magnet, Rage Against the Machine)

The ultra-modern *2001* arrived two years early when the Wachowskis cracked open the cosmic egg in multiplexes the world over with theological sci-fi action blowout supreme *The Matrix*. Computer hacker Neo (Keanu Reeves) goes down an existential rabbit hole when Morpheus (Laurence Fishburne) rescues him from relentless Agent Smith (Hugo Weaving). Neo awakens to the fact that humanity is asleep, sharing a mutual dream—the Matrix—supplied by intelligent machines and mistaken for actual life. Clad in black leather and equipped to bend physical reality to their will, the rebels rage against the Matrix machines to a machine-gun metal soundtrack and with unprecedented visual wizardry. The bullet-slowed-in-time effect was heart stopping, and came to define life in 1999.

The blank-faced cyber warriors and their slick, green-hued data battlefield influenced heavy metal as much as axe-swinging barbarians had done in the 1980s. Everyone from Fear Factory to Static X to Samael to Ulver plugged into a metal matrix of dystopian science fiction, cyberpunk, graphic novels, and anime that echoed this film's ethos: question what's presented to you, destroy what's wrong about it, and forge your own reality. As Morpheus tells Neo: "I'm trying to free your mind. But I can only show you the door. You're the one that has to walk through it."

Sadly, the *Matrix*-metal crossover temporarily soured after the April 1999 Columbine High School massacre. The teenage shooters were outspoken fans of many of the bands on the film's soundtrack (particularly Rammstein). Clad in black leather, they deemed themselves "the Trench Coat Mafia." Images from the shooting, with the killers whipping shotguns out from under their long garments, automatically brought to mind similar scenes in *The Matrix*.

Sequels followed, and sucked. *The Matrix: Reloaded* (2003) is lame metal. *The Matrix: Revolutions* (2003) is false metal.

Mausoleum (1983)

(Dir. Michael Dugan; w/Bobbie Bresee, Marjoe Gortner, LaWanda Page, Norman Burton)

✠ '80s Horror ✠ Satanic Possession

Busty blonde scream queen Bobbie Bresee stars in *Mausoleum* as Susan Farrell, a well-heeled housewife who is possessed by Satan. After she steps into her mother's aboveground internment facility, Susan's eyes glow green, she telekinetically tosses objects and people through the air, and she occasionally transforms into sexy beast-creature with monster faces on her breasts that chomp anyone who hugs her. Oliver (Marjoe Gortner), Sue's husband who's smarting after getting bitten by her tit-teeth, conspires with her psychiatrist (Norman Burton) to release the woman from her torment by placing a crown of thorns on her head. This leads to a climactic round of human ring-toss in a cemetery.

Mausoleum is off-the-rails insane and, as a blast from the big-box-VHS-rental days of the past, a heavy metal viewing party you must experience. Just be careful about who you hug afterward.

Bobbie Bresee earned a Saturn Award nomination for Best Actress from the Academy of Science Fiction, Fantasy, and Horror Films. She lost to Louise Fletcher in *Brainstorm* (1983). What a robbery! LaWanda Page, Aunt Esther from TV's *Sanford and Son*, plays an Old Hollywood–style housemaid. Upon witnessing supernatural doings, she says: "Great googly moogly! Enough grievin', I'm leavin'!" Then she slugs from a hidden bottle of hooch, and hightails it away from all those crazy white folk.

Maximum Overdrive (1986)

(Dir. Stephen King; w/Emilio Estevez, Pat Hingle, Laura Harrington, Yeardley Smith)

✠ Stephen King ✠ Soundtrack (AC/DC)

After a decade of having his books turned into movies by other filmmakers (from Brian De Palma's *Carrie* in 1976 up to Lewis Teague's 1985 *Cat's Eye* anthology), monstrously prolific horror maven King plopped into his own director's chair and adapted the short story "Trucks" into *Maximum Overdrive*. The plot is a simple *Twilight Zone*–style scenario: a passing comet brings earth's electrical machinery to life. Unfortunately, everything from can openers to Coke machines to steamrollers is homicidally pissed.

After giving us overview of the mechanical mayhem decimating the suburbs, the focus shifts to a hardscrabble mix of humanity at the Dixie Boy truck stop in North Carolina. These survivors are pinned inside the diner by a convoy of kill-crazy eighteen-wheelers. Our sort-of heroes take up primitive arms against anything technical. The resulting body splatters are spectacular. Emilio Estevez, channeling a southern-fried spin on Otto from *Repo Man* (1984), makes for a winning simpleton of a hero. The great character actor Pat Hingle has a ball in his redneck role as Bubba Hendershoot. Yeardley Smith is a riot, as she was in *The Legend of Billy Jean* (1985). All the while, AC/DC wails on the soundtrack.

Overdrive's opening montage of the comet's effects achieves a great nervous balance of wit and doom. We follow a little kid peddling his bike from one sudden accident to another, to cars intentionally crashing themselves, to a soda machine that launches cans at Little Leaguers, and to supermarket time-savers turning fresh produce into deadly projectiles. King himself cameos at an ATM, shouting, "Honeybun, this machine just called me an asshole!" The pacing and editing fall rhythmically right on target to "Chase the Ace," an ultra-rare AC/DC instrumental (the 1976 B-side "Bonny" had been the only previous one). For a first-time director, this segment is amazingly assured. Critics dumped on *Maximum Overdrive* upon first impact and even King kind of disowned the movie, likening himself to a worthy heir to Ed Wood. *Maximum Overdrive* is not great, but still deserves to be championed for more than just its director's brand-name recognition.

Hard rock fanatic King knew all along he wanted AC/DC to do the soundtrack, and he was delighted when the band agreed. King similarly reached out to the Ramones to provide a theme song for *Pet Sematary* (1989). In addition, King's pen name "Richard Bachman" is a tribute to Bachman Turner Overdrive, and when the rock radio station near his Maine headquarters announced it would change formats, the author drove over and bought it with cash to make sure it would keep pumping out heavy tunes. The *Maximum Overdrive* soundtrack, which is actually titled *Who Made Who*, was an instant classic. In large part an AC/DC greatest hits package, it also included the aforementioned "Chase the Ace" and another track sans vocal, "The D.T."

May (2002)

(Dir. Lucky McKee; w/Angela Bettis, Anna Faris, Jeremy Sisto, James Duval)

✠ Goth Chicks ✠ Dario Argento

If *Carrie* (1976) is the power-metal movie meditation on coming-of-age female isolation turned outward into creative homicidal fury, *May* is the riot-grrrl-influenced lo-fi goth-metal version. Each packs its own wallop. Angela Bettis is May, an oddball veterinary assistant in her early twenties whose childhood eye troubles have kept her at a distance her entire life. May sews her own clothes, and her one constant companion is an eerie doll she keeps in a glass coffin, even into young adulthood. Conflict arises when May takes up a sexual come-on from party girl Polly (Anna Faris) and falls hard for mechanic Adam (Jeremy Sisto), who turns her on to the films of Italian fright master Dario Argento. After each entanglement hurts May further, Adam will regret sharing that education.

First-time director Lucky McKee builds a funny, brisk structure for *May*'s deeply sad and heartfelt story. Angela Bettis, all herky-jerky and heartbreaking, creates an instant horror icon. *Carrie* speaks to anyone who remembers harrowing teen moments. *May*, more pointedly, resonates with damaged, desperate outcasts, of any gender, who have longed only for someone with whom they can share what they feel when experiencing gore movie highs and heavy metal revelations. *May* grabbed public attention when Roger Ebert gave it a four-star review. It played nine theaters largely as a pre-DVD pit stop, but Ebert taking up the movie's mantle did for *May* what his rave had done two decades earlier for *Henry: Portrait of a Serial Killer* (1985).

Angela Bettis immediately followed *May* by starring as Carrie White in the TV miniseries remake of *Carrie* (2002). Bettis and Lucky McKee have gone on to a fruitful professional relationship. She starred in his Showtime's *Masters of Horror* episode "Sick Girl" (2006), and he acted in her directorial debut, *Roman* (2006), a gender-inverted take on a story similar to *May*.

Mazes and Monsters

(1982)

(Dir. Steven Hilliard Stern; w/Tom Hanks, Wendy Crewson, Chris Makepeace, Murray Hamilton)
✠ Dungeons & Dragons ✠ Satanic Panic

Campus pals Robbie (Tom Hanks), Wendy (Kate Finch), Jay Jay (Chris Makepeace), and

Daniel (David Wallace) idly while away the semester like all the coolest Ivy League students do: by exhaustively engaging in the fantasy role-playing game Mazes and Monsters. Poor Robbie was already booted out of Tufts for playing too much M&M, but he quickly falls in with new players at New York City's (fake) Grant University (which looks a lot like Columbia). Soon enough, Robbie is dropping classes, donning cloaks, and hunting a beast named Gorvil in a steam tunnel.

Ultimately, Robbie believes he can cast a spell if he jumps from the top of "the Two Towers"—the World Trade Center. After a dramatic talk-down—with the gang in full M&M garb—Robbie gets permanently lost in the world of the game. He thinks his parents' house is an inn, where he pays for his keep with a magical coin that keeps reappearing at his bedside when he wakes up each morning.

As inept, overzealous, unintentionally gut-busting "cautionary" TV movies go, *Mazes and Monsters* ranks right up there with the mightiest. As with the heavy metal scare movie *Black Roses*, *Mazes and Monsters* accepts that every scary thing you've heard about the subject is absolutely true. The acting, particularly by Makepeace ("Wudy da Wabbit da Winna" from 1979's *Meatballs*) is across-the-board atrocious. The rest of the cast, especially seasoned professionals like Murray Hamilton as a cop, are impressively less than professional. Hanks, of course, came off as a movie star from the first episode of his sitcom *Bosom Buddies* (or his quick appearance in the 1980 fright flick *He Knows You're Alone*). His presence, like his Afro, is undeniable. Hanks overpowers everything else on-screen simply by playing his zany role straight, except during his great flip-out scene, where he screams into a pay phone: "There's BLOOD on my KNIFE!"

In terms of campiness, *Mazes and Monsters* hilariously fleshed out the TV gap between the 1982 episode of *CHiPs* where Donny Most played Ozzy-KISS hybrid "Moloch" and Geraldo Rivera's legendary 1988 Halloween brouhaha *Exposing Satan's Underground*. The 1980s was the decade of the Moral Majority battling bad influences on airwaves, Tipper Gore fighting Mentors songs in Senate hearings, and Women Against Pornography picketing slasher movies. Terror over what the suddenly popular, immersive, demon-laden *Dungeons and Dragons* might be doing to America's youth was real, even if nobody involved in making this film seems to have any conviction about that message. Don't enter expecting Dio, either; the music is a downpour of not-ready-for-radio soft rock ballads. Your gonads will wither.

Five minutes in, Chris Makepeace inexplicably wears a spiked Kaiser helmet while bitching out his mom. Throughout the rest of the movie, he wears wacky headgear including WWI pilot goggles. Makepeace deserved the attention: he was to have starred in the never-completed Kiss movie, *The Elder*, spun off their 1981 concept album, *Music From The Elder*.

Mazes and Monsters' eponymous source novel by romance writer Rona Jaffe took inspiration from the urban legend known as "the Steam Tunnel Incident." In 1979, sixteen-year-old prodigy James Dallas Egbert III disappeared into utility passages under Michigan State University to kill himself with pills. Egbert survived and went into hiding, prompting the news media to pick up a rumor that, as a result of his dedication to Dungeons & Dragons, he was down below chasing trolls. Really, he was just depressed, and he fatally ate buckshot a year later.

Director Steven Hilliard Stern previously helmed the 1981 Disney Faust spoof *The Devil and Max Devlin* (with Bill Cosby as Satan), and later directed an episode of *The Crow: Stairway to Heaven*.

MEGAFORCE (1982)
(DIR. HAL NEEDHAM; W/BARRY BOSTWICK, PERSIS KHAMBATTA, MICHAEL BECK, EDWARD MULHARE)
✲ TIME TRAVEL ✲ MOTORCYCLES

New Jersey's Megaforce Records, the heavy megalith built in 1983 by Metallica's *Kill 'Em All* (and early albums by Mercyful Fate, Manowar, Raven, Exciter, Anthrax, Overkill, and

Testament), took its name from *Megaforce*, a futuristic sci-fi adventure romp that bombed in theaters but lives today as a cult curiosity. The film is hilariously hokey and charmingly cheap, while also being thoroughly imaginative and mostly exciting.

In the movie, the Megaforce organization's motto is "Deeds, not words," and the team is described as "a phantom army of super elite fighting men whose weapons are the most powerful science can devise." (Again, much like Metallica circa '82.) The Megaforce fleet includes motorcycles equipped with handlebar rocket-launchers and dune buggies that fire lasers. These come in handy during the endless desert battles against dudes with tanks. The Megaforce uniforms are skintight silver bodysuits with proto-*Flashdance* headbands stretched around mega-forcefully blow-dried hair. What plot exists serves just to showcase the cutting-edge (albeit medium-budget) early-'80s visuals, and the overall feeling throughout is that this is a kids' movie, ready made for toy lines and cartoon spinoffs.

Twentieth Century Fox produced *Megaforce* in conjunction with legendary Hong Kong martial arts studio Golden Harvest, and promoted the movie with an ad campaign in comic books. Kids could send in one dollar and join the Megaforce, and be able to prove that status with official membership cards, patches, and reflective bike decals—courtesy of team leader "Ace Hunter."

Ace Hunter is portrayed by Barry Bostwick, relatively butched up after being Brad in *The Rocky Horror Picture Show* (1975). He leads a cast studded with cult stars that includes Persis Khambatta, aka the bald chick in *Star Trek: The Motion Picture* (1979); Michael Beck, who played Swan in *The Warriors* (1979); Edward Mulhare, the spooky sea captain on TV sitcom *The Ghost and Mrs. Muir*; and rectangle-faced Henry Silva (*Alligator*, *Chained Heat*), in his usual role as the villain. Beyond its off-Hollywood acting lineup, *Megaforce* is the work of Hal Needham, former stuntman turned auteur of the first two *Smokey and the Bandit* movies and both *Cannonball Run* installments. His death in 2013 at the ripe old age of eighty-two is the best argument yet for the annihilation of speed limits.

Men Behind the Sun (1988)

(Dir. Mou Tun-fei; w/Hsu Gou, Tie Long Jin, Zhaohua Mei, Gang Wang)

✠ World War II Atrocities ✠ Real Autopsy ✠ Animal Sacrifice

Almost as volcanically offensive as the mock documentary *Farewell, Uncle Tom* (1971), by evil Italian *Mondo Cane* (1962) shockumentary creators Gualtiero Jacopetti and Franco Prosperi, is *Men Behind the Sun*. Writer-director Mou Tun-fei claims his film is based on true events. Set in China during World War II, the film focuses on Japanese-run science center Unit 731, a site where prisoners were subjected to unconscionably atrocious biochemical weapons experiments. A plot regarding soldiers of a youth corps serves as a through line, but the movie really showcases dreadfully realistic atrocities in scenes with uncomfortably convincing special effects. Professional performances just compound the awfulness of what we're witnessing.

The most blatantly disgusting of these episodes involves a man in a depressurizing chamber who shits out his intestines. The most heartbreaking depicts a young mother whose crying baby gets casually tossed and buried in the snow. She is then subjected to subzero temperatures and warm water until her flesh can be easily peeled off down to the bone. There are many, many other impossible-to-erase sights; some violate universal taboos and, had the movie been made in the age of the Internet, likely would have resulted in director Mou having to go into hiding. One scene shows a live, screaming cat being devoured by thousands of starving rats. Later on, the rats are burned alive before our eyes. Director Mou claims he used a prop cat covered with red-dyed honey that the rats licked off. But the no-doubt-about-it incineration of the live rats after the fact casts doubt on his claims.

Another guts-melting moment is an actual autopsy of a boy who looks to have been about ten years old. The Japanese murdered the mute child for his organs. For the sequence in which the body parts are harvested, Mou convinced parents who recently lost their school-age son to allow the crew to film his post-mortem medical examination. The parents thought that the finished movie would shed light on the horrors perpetrated upon China during the war. Separate from the autopsy, numerous dismembered body parts are all actual human remains. War is hell, and *Men Behind the Sun* is one war movie that hurts like hell to watch.

The Mentors: A Piece of Sinema (1992)

(Dir. Various; El Duce, Sickie Wifebeater, Dr. Heathen Scum, Wally George)

✠ Rape Rock ✠ Censorship

Along with W.A.S.P., the Mentors owe much of their infamy to Tipper Gore. Even more than the former's buzz-saw codpiece "F*ck Like a Beast" album cover image, Tipper invoked the lyrics of the latter to flip the wigs of her Washington, D.C., coven, the Parents Music Resource Center (PMRC). Voice of sanity Frank Zappa, arguing on behalf of free speech, noted with amusement that the U.S. Congressional record would forever contain transcriptions of Mentors lyrics about using someone's face as toilet paper.

Fronted by bloat-bellied behemoth Eldon Hoke, aka El Duce, the Mentors dealt in "rape rock," spewing hilariously catchy calculated-to-offend anthems in a pre–Sam Kinison/Andrew Dice Clay world. They wore executioner hoods, they were in terrible shape, they signed to Metal Blade Records just as the label was starting to take note of punk bands, and they were awesome.

The Mentors: A Piece of Sinema compiles a few of the group's sloppy, scatological video efforts and tabloid-talk-show appearances. The first film, *Get Up and Die* (1983), offers an instrumental version of the band's song of the same name to accompany El Duce narrating a parade of images depicting naked hate-sex, zany violence, and documentary-style drug adventuring. *The Mentors Fuck Movie* (1987) is even less coherent but more fun. The best I can make of it is that it's a preview for a movie that doesn't exist, showcasing more of the sort of stuff contained in *Get Up and Die*, intercut with footage of El Duce prowling Hollywood streets, attempting to convince women to star in a porno film. Fortunately, El Duce was a barker at Hollywood sub-grindhouse porno pit the Ivar Theatre, and he knew plenty of women "professionally" who were happy to oblige. These two early Mentors videos reputedly were made as fluff trailers to get Ivar patrons in the mood for the main features.

We also get a visit by El Duce to *Hot Seat*, the early-'80s L.A. talk show hosted by hyper-right-wing crankcase Wally George—angry white forerunner of Morton Downey Jr., and Bill O'Reilly. Finally, *A Piece of Sinema* closes with proper music videos for two of the Mentors' most potent anthems: "Four F Club" and "Golden Showers."

An equally strong whiff of dirty rock nostalgia, and just as puzzling to newcomers, *The Mentors: El Vita Duce*, is a 2007 DVD reworking of the 1990 home video *The Wretched World of the Mentors*, also a collection of videos and interviews. Jump right in, but pull your executioner hood down tight over your nose.

METAL: A HEADBANGER'S JOURNEY (2005)

(DIRS. SAM DUNN, SCOT MCFADYEN, JESSICA JOY WISE; W/SAM DUNN, ALICE COOPER, TONY IOMMI, RONNIE JAMES DIO, LEMMY KILMISTER, DEE SNIDER)
✠ METAL HISTORY ✠ CONCERT FOOTAGE

Filmmaker Sam Dunn travels the earth to talk to metal icons, including the crème-de-la-crunch from all four decades of metal, with the usual documentary suspects (Alice Cooper, Lemmy Kilmister, Dee Snider); less typically chatty icons (Tony Iommi, Geddy Lee); and surprising representatives of many metal subgenres, including death metal (Cannibal Corpse), black metal (Emperor, Enslaved), and modern American extreme rock (Slipknot, Lamb of God).

The spectacularly ambitious *Metal: A Headbanger's Journey* attempts to encapsulate and analyze all that Black Sabbath hath wrought over the previous thirty-five years. Dunn introduces himself as a career anthropologist who aims to turn his skills on his favorite form of music. He's a terrific on-screen host and the movie ably conveys the relentless effort he put into making interviews happen and, once they were secured, making them worthwhile.

The standout innovation of *Metal: A Headbanger's Journey* is Dunn's division of metal into a series of subgenres, which we see laid out in the style of a family tree. Between segments, the tree is animated to emphasize the next form to be examined (e.g.—hard rock, punk, death metal, Swedish death metal, grunge, etc.) with Dunn providing a quick, informative lesson via voice-over. For those in search of one go-to overview documentary, *Metal: A Headbanger's Journey* ably rises to the occasion, horns first.

Dunn walks through the concert grounds of Germany's massive Wacken Open Air festival, a mini-metropolis of thousands upon thousands of tents housing many more thousands upon thousands of metal fans, gathered outside peacefully to slam and groove to the devil's music.

When Norwegian fans complained about the movie's examination of the notorious church burnings and other violence committed by their black-metal countrymen, Dunn returned and interviewed those who contacted him, along with a well-spoken Christian priest. The resulting featurette is included on the *Metal: A Headbanger's Journey* DVD and is an outstanding documentary in itself, culminating with Dunn standing beside gigantic sculptures of Viking swords that stupefy with their awesomeness.

In summing up the metal attitude, Tom Morello of Rage Against the Machine, flips the bird, and quotes his own band's biggest Top 40 hit: "Fuck you, I won't do what you tell me!" As a Mao-espousing millionaire in a baseball cap marked "Commie," Morello, of course, endorses a totalitarian police state "for the greater good," but let's give the doofus his due here. His on-camera declaration is completely accurate.

Metal Messiah (1978)
(DIR. TIBOR TAKACS; W/JEAN PAUL YOUNG, DAVID HENSEN, LIANE HOGAN, RICHARD WARD ALLEN)
✠ SHOCK ROCK ✠ CRUCIFIXION ✠ ALIENS

One of the damnedest motion picture miscarriages an audience has ever braved, *Metal Messiah* is a freak fume vaguely emanating from Canada's brink-of-new-wave underground. Richard Ward Allen wanders about as Raymond Chandler, the mystery writer, narrating in Raymond Chandler fashion. The Messiah (Richard Hensen) reveals himself as a metal-covered (meaning silver-painted) space alien. Some noisy cabaret action ensues, a macho army guy in a rubber mask appears, and a scary spaceman undergoes surgery; then comes the "rock show."

The Messiah fronts a stunningly kick-ass '70s doom combo (à la Pentagram) that boasts aggressively kinky theatrics in their live show (à la the Tubes). Gyrating lingerie girls collapse in a pleasantly nude lesbian grope orgy onstage. After naysayers sing their charges against the alien, the whole endeavor climaxes, as these things must, with the Messiah nailed to cross.

The first half of *Metal Messiah* is too disjointed and amateurish for the rest to work, which is a shame for the musical performance and fantasy sequences buried in the back end. The actors and other on-screen performers share music credit with a band called Moses. Even if they never saw the film, Judas Priest and the Great Kat liked the title enough to write songs with that name. Director Tibor Takacs later directed the great heavy metal teen terror classic *The Gate* (1987).

Metal Messiah: Born Again Sage (2010)
(DIR. NICK WELLS; W/PHANTOM HILLBILLY, TODD ROBINSON, CANDI MENCHESTER, MILO ARR)
✠ FAUST MYTH ✠ SATAN ✠ SOUNDTRACK (APOCRYPHA, BLACK CHRIST, PANZERGOD)

In late-1980s Oregon, Sage Negadeth (Phantom Hillbilly) attends "a high school where nobody ever graduates" and seeks to assemble the greatest metal band ever forged in hellfire. He teams with a Rastafarian rhythm section to create Nigger Christ, which inevitably is softened to Black Christ. After years as a typical dead-end hesher, Sage sells his soul to the devil, goes to hell and back, converts to Christianity, and plans a Sunday school metal musical adaptation of the Bible's Book of Revelations.

Metal Messiah is digital-video labor of obvious love, ably carried by leading man Phantom Hillbilly. Coming off as a wiry combination of Ernest P. Worrell and Otto from *The Simpsons*, he's a likable, laugh-getting hero. The writing is good, and the other actors do well, too. Even the fake porno titles that crop up warrant a chuckle ("Blow-meo and Screw-liet"). The movie also provides cool incidental looks at Portland's contemporary metal scene, with corpse-painted black metal purveyors Panzergod blitzkrieging through several performances and even acting a little. Plus, Portland wouldn't be the same without some topless, tattooed rock and roll chicks.

Sage and his friends concoct a language substituting band names for various words. The more impressively complex this slang becomes, the faster they spew it out. The movie's cheapo vision of hell ain't half-terrible, either. The burning crucifixion victims are cool, and Sage's head engulfed in flames actually looks pretty good. Bonus slack awarded for excellent employment of vintage checkerboard '80s painter's caps with drop-down flaps.

METAL RETARDATION
(2009)
(DIR. BILL ZEBUB; W/KING DIAMOND, TYPE O NEGATIVE, DARKTHRONE, MY DYING BRIDE, CANDLEMASS, NEVERMORE, VENOM, GWAR, S.O.D., ENSLAVED)
✠ METAL HISTORY

Bill Zebub's charmingly insane magazine *The Grimoire of Exalted Deeds* printed interviews with various heavy metal figures, from stadium-stuffers to subbasement dwellers, typified by the publisher's bizarre questions spoken in broken Middle English. *Metal Retardation* allows us to watch Zebub in action, and his Q&A subjects are a majorly impressive lot. Some of them are amused, some are confused, and some are annoyed. The process is funny throughout, occasionally hilarious, and at times even amazing.

Despite the title, *Metal Retardation* provides such a backdoor, fun-house-mirror view of the musicians being profiled that it will actually raise your hard rock IQ; all apologies to Mr. Zebub, as that could not possibly have been his intention.

The standout recurring bit sees Zebub incessantly hounding Cannibal Corpse frontman George "Corpsegrinder" Fisher to sing, "Mary Had a Little Lamb." When Fisher finally agrees, he bungles the words and Zebub immediately tells him that previous Cannibal Corpse vocalist Chris Barnes would have gotten it right.

METAL SKIN (1994)
(DIR. GEOFFREY WRIGHT; W/ADEN YOUNG, TARA MORICE, BEN MENDELSOHN, NADINE GARNER)
✠ CHURCH DESECRATION ✠ ANIMAL SACRIFICE

In downbeat suburban Australia, car fanatic buddies Psycho Joe (Aden Young) and Dazey (Ben Mendelsohn) work in a supermarket, where they fall in with Savina (Nadine Garner), a lovely young satanist. She gets her kicks in the form of blasphemous church vandalism, live animal offerings to the Dark Lord, and illegal street races. A final car chase provides a heart-pounding

throwback to Aussie automotive mayhem cinema (*The Road Warrior, Dead End Drive-In*). Everything ultimately spins out of control and Satan doesn't save a single soul.

Geoffrey Wright also directing the down-under potboiler *Romper Stomper* (1992), starring Russell Crowe as a white-power skinhead.

METALHEADS: THE GOOD, THE BAD & THE EVIL (2008)
(DIR. BILL ZEBUB; W/BILL ZEBUB, EMILY THOMAS, TOM GOODWIN, CARL WILLIAMSON)
✠ METAL MAYHEM

Long after multimedia metal gadfly Bill Zebub ceased publication of his uniquely demented zine *The Grimoire of Exalted Deeds*, he made copious heavy-music documentaries. Even more threatening to world sanity were his narrative films such as this one. Zebub stars here as Bill, a layabout hesher too lazy to even bang his head. Emily Thomas plays Elaine, his foxy metal babe who just wants him to get a job. Bill's buds are typical stoner dorks, except for Evil Metalhead (Carl Williamson), who encourages our hero to "rampage." That does not, as you might guess, lead him to employment.

Neanderthal slapstick, dirty jokes, and naked chicks dancing to doomy guitar tracks add up to an experience somewhere between a headache, a belly laugh, and a simultaneous fart and belch with some puke in it. Yes, that is praise.

As moviemaking technology becomes simpler, cheaper, and lighter to carry around, Bill Zebub only becomes more prolific. A sampling of the eleven features the Zebub empire has produced since *Metalheads* include *The Worst Horror Movie Ever Made: The Remake* (2008), *Metal Retardation* (2009), *Forgive Me for Raping You* (2010), *Zombiechrist* (2010), *Jesus the Total Douchebag* (2010), and *Antfarm Dickhole* (2011).

Metallica: Some Kind of Monster (2004)

(Dirs. Joe Berlinger, Bruce Sinofsky; w/James Hetfield, Lars Ulrich, Kirk Hammett, Robert Trujillo, Dave Mustaine, Bob Rock)

✠ Metal Reality ✠ Rehab ✠ Danish Drummer

"Never will you more want to slap two grown men in the face!" So declared one typically frustrated Metallica fan upon witnessing *Some Kind of Monster*, the acclaimed documentary chronicling the world's all-time biggest hard rock band making their all-time most despised album. The smack-happy critic was referring to James Hetfield and Lars Ulrich, Metallica's singer and drummer, respectively. By the time *Some Kind of Monster* came out, even if that gruesome two-some's most steadfast apologists could look past them cutting their hair, headlining Lollapalooza, and pissing in Napster's free-music-for-every-body punch bowl, this self-financed film paints them as unprecedented prima donnas. You'll want your *Master of Puppets* T-shirt money back.

First we see their dismissive treatment of departing bassist Jason Newsted. Then Hetfield claims his sobriety requires him to spend no more than twenty consecutive minutes in the studio lest he explode into spontaneous drunkenness. Then Lars Ulrich grotesquely sweats the prospect that his art collection might not command the eight-figure sum at auction for which he's hoping. (Don't worry, he gets even more dough!).

Throughout the embarrassment of embarrassments, producer Bob Rock looms like a sad-sack Barney Rubble; the dildo visionary who infused Metallica with that something special he brings to other clients such as Veruca Salt.

Everybody hates each other, except maybe lead axeman Kirk Hammett, who escapes by surfing. In order to complete their album, Metallica brings in "performance enhancement coach" Phil Towle, a Cosby-sweatered boob who once revoked his own therapist license before a regula-tory board could do it for him. Towle proves to be one of the great comically incompetent villains not only in the realm of documentaries, but maybe in all of cinema. When the band ultimately sends Towle packing—as he begs to stay—a corner is turned. We start rooting for these billionaire crybabies to make great music again.

The fact that the end result was the universally disdained *St. Anger* doesn't even matter. By the occurrence of the movie's climactic prison video shoot and stadium show finale, the members of Metallica have allowed us unfettered access to themselves at their least sympathetic and most despicable. And it works. *Some Kind of Monster* is some kind of triumph all the way through.

Monster's most moving moment may be the reunion of Lars Ulrich and original Metallica guitarist Dave Mustaine. After decades of silence, the two speak candidly about Mustaine's being fired for drinking and how, even while fronting Megadeth, he has always felt hurt by existing in their shadow. Mustaine later said he didn't want the footage used, but he'd already signed a release. For a while he pouted that this was Metallica's "last betrayal" of him but, in 2010, he played several "Big Four of Thrash Metal" shows with his ex-mates.

The movie's other most emotionally gripping moment occurs when Lars visits his father, Torben Ulrich, a Danish tennis legend and accomplished jazz player. Looking like his name sounds, the wizard-bearded Torben casually denigrates his son's work, listening to a new track and simply stating: "Delete that." To witness the way Lars (and Metallica's management) crumples is to say, "Growing up with that, maybe I'd be a douche about a lot of things, too."

Robert Trujillo, from Ozzy Osbourne's band, wins the bassist slot vacated by Jason Newsted. Almost immediately, Newsted began a brief stint as bassist for Ozzy Osbourne. An even trade? Not when you consider that Trujillo soon appeared in cartoon form with the rest of Metallica on *The Simpsons* in 2006. Newsted ended up in a reality TV show band with Tommy Lee.

Metallica: Through the Never (2013)

(Dir. Nimród Antal; w/Dane DeHaan, Metallica)

✠ Concert Footage ✠ Apocalypse ✠ In 3-D!

A multidimensional triumph, *Metallica: Through the Never* is an unexpected firestorm of metal might and rock cinema grandeur. Epic stadium-concert footage is rapturously brought to life to create a skull-shattering end-of-the-world midnight movie. In 3-D! IMAX 3-D!

Though this praise sounds preposterous, seeing and hearing and ducking tons of urban mayhem debris flying off the screen is believing. The band performs fourteen songs on a multitiered, endlessly morphing, mechanical marvel of a stage built atop the entire hockey rink at Rogers Arena in Vancouver. The concert aspects alone make *Metallica: Through the Never* an instant milestone.

Better still is the movie's plot-driven through line. Towheaded Metallica crew grunt Trip (Dane DeHaan) is dispatched from the big show to collect a leather satchel. The bag is located in a broken-down truck that sits on a street somewhere. Mission accepted, Trip heads out to find society collapsed; the city is raining fire and blood down around him. Bandana-masked rebels attack faceless totalitarian riot police in combustive street combat. Glass shatters. Heads splatter. Bodies explode. Chaos reigns.

The Rider (Kyle Thomson)—a combination of Lord Humongous from *The Road Warrior* and Frank Frazetta's "Death Dealer" painting—thunders through the melee atop a black steed. He lassoes resistance fighters, hanging them from lampposts to kick, squirm, and die. Trip navigates this savage, surreal landscape.

The show, meantime, spectacularly goes on. *Through the Never* either punctuates Metallica's elder-statesman status gracefully or sets up their next chapter on a note of victory. Because if not Metallica to forge ahead with these expensive large-scale metal visions, who else?

Metallimania (1997)

(Dir. Marc Paschke; w/Metallica, Slayer, Anthrax, Rob Halford, Madonna)

✠ Metal Reality

Remember Alcoholica? *Metallimania* consists of the ripping thrash metal turned mainstream heavy metal band's sweaty home movies. The self-proclaimed "most unreasonable rock and roll documentary ever produced," *Metallimania* captures the final moments before Metallica started second-guessing themselves. Cobbled together from thousands of hours of camcorder goofiness from Metallica's 1994–96 tour, the film stars the shirtless, beer-snotted, mullet-headed hesher nation that worshipped Metallica, engaging in buzzed buffoonery in honor of a band they recognized as four of their drooling, belching, booger-flicking, fight-picking own.

Wolverine-whiskered Eric Braverman hosts. A metal DJ and band manager who contributed articles mocking Metallica to the band's fan magazine and was loved for it, Braverman ultimately served as best man at bassist Jason Newsted's wedding. At one point he bellies up to a luminous blonde at a bar and throws some anti-charm in her direction; it's Madonna. He is obnoxiously up to the task of interviewing fans as they spit, cry, and sometimes collapse. They explode in anger and in joy, and often in a state that can't be determined. Racial epithets abound. Punches are thrown, and they never connect. Rob Halford, Tom Araya, and Josh Homme seem so atypically lighthearted during their appearances that watching them yuk it up starts to feel heavy. All the while, the band members yell, laugh, drink, curse, tell jokes, and have a great time looking stupid. *Metallimania* is some kind of whole other beast, an excellent hair of the dog to quell any nausea brought on by the later Metallica doc *Some Kind of Monster*.

It's High Noon at the End of the Universe.

METALSTORM
THE DESTRUCTION OF JARED SYN
3D

By sword
By pick
By axe
Bye bye

THE MUTILATOR

America's Funniest Family
in their FIRST FULL-LENGTH FEATURE
in TECHNICOLOR

Munster, Go Home

Herman races the world's fastest cars with his DRAG-U-LA special!

FRED GWYNNE · YVONNE DeCARLO
AL LEWIS · BUTCH PATRICK and DEBBIE WATSON
also starring TERRY-THOMAS · HERMIONE GINGOLD
screenplay by GEORGE TIBBLES, JOE CONNELLY and BOB MOSHER

Clockwise from top:
Mel Gibson as Mad Max;
Metalstorm: The Destruction
of Jared-Syn; *nuts of the round
table in* Monty Python and
the Holy Grail; Munster, Go
Home *theatrical poster; Buddy
Cooper's debut and swan song,*
The Mutilator

Metalocalypse: The Doomstar Requiem— a Klok Opera (2013)

(Dir. Mark Brooks; w/Brendon Small, Malcolm McDowell, Jack Black, "Corpsegrinder" Fisher)

✠ Rock Opera ✠ Animation

The all-singing, all-shredding, all-slaying *Metalocalypse: The Doomstar Requiem—A Klok Opera* debuted Halloween 2013 on the Adult Swim cable channel. C'mon, can you imagine trying to fit that title on a movie theater marquee? Adult Swim is also the home battle station/slaughterhouse of the mind-frying *Metalocalypse* animated series from which this epic is spawned.

Picking up where season four of the show left off, *Doomstar* makes good on the threat of being *A Klok Opera* as every word of dialogue is sung and performed in the melodic death metal style of Dethklok, the cartoon band at the heart of the series. There are occasional hops between metallic subgenres and moments of orchestral sweep, but growling and grinding is the overwhelming system of dialogue delivery.

Dethklok rhythm guitarist Toki Wartooth and producer Abigail Remeltindrinc are held captive by the Revengencers, an unholy alliance between fired Dethklok axe-slinger Magnus Hammersmith and the Masked Metal Assassin (voiced by George "Corpsegrinder" Fisher of Cannibal Corpse). At first, the band attempts to soldier on without Toki, employing a malfunctioning hologram for a live concert, but they ultimately recognize that they must rescue their brother. High, bloody, occult-infused adventure erupts before our eyes and against our eardrums.

The Doomstar Requiem successfully blows out the microscopically metal layers of the mega-multitiered Dethklok universe into a grand, mad, forty-seven-minute opus that soars further and lunges deeper than if the producers had merely strung three typical quarter-hour episodes. *Doomstar* was originally intended to represent the end of *Metalocalypse*, but the opera's punch line—involving classically Rudolf Schenker–mustached bass monster William Murderface—indicated that the show will go on, most brutally.

Metalstorm: The Destruction of Jared-Syn (1983)

(Dir. Charles Band; w/Jeffrey Byron, Tim Thomerson, Kelly Preston, Richard Moll)

✠ Post-Apocalypse ✠ Swords & Sorcery ✠ 3-D

Bringing up the rear of the early-'80s 3-D movie outburst, *Metalstorm: The Destruction of Jared-Syn* is typical of writer-director's Charles Band's more likable efforts (such as 1984's *The Dungeonmaster*). Band mashes up the reigning B-movie ingredients of the day into a possibly post-nuke adventure that sends space cowboy Dogen (Jeffrey Byron) and renegade Finder Rhodes (Tim Thomerson) to rescue distressed damsel Dhyana (Kelly Preston) from malevolent mutant Jared-Syn (Michael Preston) and his cyborg son Baal (R. David Smith). In 3-D! With the help of a Cyclops tribe led by Hurok (Richard Moll) and sky-bikes created to directly cash in on the same summer's obscure release *Return of the Jedi*, our heroes score the magic mask necessary to secure the destruction of Jared-Syn, thereby making the movie's subtitle a spoiler.

Like many Charles Band efforts of the '80s, *Metalstorm* has aged well and is forever associated with the flashier and more obvious *objets d'metal musique* of its moment, namely Quiet Riot videos and Grim Reaper's *See You in Hell* cassette. The concept of a Metal Storm was powerful enough to spawn bands with that name in Germany and the U.S., plus songs called "Metalstorm" by Iron Angel, Rigor Mortis, and Slayer.

Moreover, the entire 3-D revival of 1981 through 1983 ripples with metal. Indeed, essential British metal mag *Kerrang!* offered 3-D glasses with 3-D Hanoi Rocks and Kiss posters in two issues. Among the cinematic delights are *Comin' at Ya!*

(1981), a loony spaghetti western starring Tony Anthony; *Friday the 13th Part III* (1982), wherein Jason dons the hockey mask for the first time; *Parasite* (1982), Charles Band's first 3-D effort, featuring the Runaways' Cherie Currie and the final nude appearance by my all-time favorite actress, Cheryl "Rainbeaux" Smith; *Revenge of the Shogun Women* (1982), martial arts mayhem with hot nuns; *Rottweiler* (1982), Southern drive-in auteur Earl Owensby's attack-dog epic; *Jaws 3-D* (1983), in which Dennis Quaid's girlfriend attempts to show off psychotic great white sharks at Sea World; and *Amityville 3-D* (1983)—the flop that basically killed the moment.

Missing in Action (1984)

(Dir. Joseph Zito; w/Chuck Norris, M. Emmet Walsh, David Tress, Lenore Kasdorf, James Hong)

✠ Vietnam War ✠ Cannon Films

Missing in Action catapults Chuck Norris from karate-flick cult hero to almost-mainstream stardom. The film was still too nasty and rough-hewn to make Chuck a leading man ready for prime time, but that's just another way of saying it was too metal! Chuck stars as veteran Colonel James Braddock, who returns to Ho Chi Minh City ten years after escaping a Vietcong prison. He's looking for left-behind P.O.W.s, and, when he finds them, he frees them. M. Emmet Walsh charms as Braddock's booze-, gun-, and girl-running pal, and James Hong is nicely serpentine as the villain General Trau. The whole thing rocks.

Aside from the poster image of Chuck firing a cannon under the tagline "The war isn't over until the last man comes home!" *MIA*'s signature image depicts in every degree of heavy metal our hero slow-motion leaping up out of a river to royally machine-gun a trio of bad guys to bits. *Missing in Action* was filmed immediately after *Missing in Action 2: The Beginning* (1985). Cannon Film honchos Menahem Golem and Yoram Globus decided that the sequel was the better of the two movies and therefore released it first. The previously shot movie was then held for a year and opened as a "prequel."

Monks: The Transatlantic Feedback (2006)

(Dirs. Lucia Palacios, Dietmar Post; w/Gary Burger, Larry Clark, Dave Day, Roger Johnston, Eddie Shaw)

✠ Metal History ✠ Sacrilege ✠ Cold War

Five men with monk-ring haircuts take the stage in black vestments. Nooses hang around their necks. The drummer pounds tribal bombast. Fuzz-bomb guitars rage with feedback. The singer vomits out madness regarding atomic warheads, James Bond, King Kong, and Vietnam. And the crowd dances to the racket. Outside, totalitarian tanks a short drive away hang the nuclear sword of Damocles over humanity's head. It's 1965 Hamburg—and these are the Monks.

Monks: The Transatlantic Feedback documents the inadvertent revolution mounted by five American GIs stationed in West Germany who formed a rock and roll band. Barely twenty years after World War II, they tapped into the dark energy that eventually manifested in full as heavy metal. The movie lays out the story. After a routine British Invasion–era start-up on an army base, the five-piece group took a serious turn following the JFK assassination. Local avant-garde art provocateurs Walther Niemann and Karl H. Remy caught a performance, and the ensuing collaboration resulted in the group naming itself the Monks. The members shaved their heads bald in the middle, donned black capes, and boiled their music down to minimalist affronts that packed the power of a Panzer tank. Their 1966 album *Black Monk Time* connected with all the right fans and lives on as an opening volley in the evolution of mean and heavy hard rock.

The Monks lobbed joyful danger everywhere they played, and were the all-around "anti-Beatles" (An archetypal song sentiment: "I hate you, baby . . . but call me!"). The band collapsed under its own weirdness quickly. They were tempted to tour Vietnam rock clubs during the war, then reconsidered when a rock band was blown up onstage there. All five original members—Gary Burger (vocals), Eddie Shaw (bass), Larry Clark (organ), Dave Day (electric banjo), and Roger Johnston (drums)—share their stories on camera. Vintage photos and performance clips, especially of the Monks playing German TV dance shows, prove mesmerizing. The band enthralls and amazes during a 1999 reunion show at New York's Cavestomp Festival, bringing *The Transatlantic Feedback* to a happy climax. Afterward, the members part ways again. Some are thrilled to have been Monks, some are lukewarm, but each player is grateful for having had the chance to create (what their high-art cohorts correctly nailed as) "the music of the future."

MONSTER DOG (1984)

(DIR. CLAUDIO FRAGASSO; W/ALICE COOPER, VICTORIA VERA, CARLOS SANTURIO, PEPA SARSA)
✠ WEREWOLF

Monster Dog stars Alice Cooper at a weird point in his career; namely, the point when he was available to star in *Monster Dog*. Alice plays rock star Vincent Raven. In the music video for "Identity Crisis" that opens the movie, Alice-as-Vincent appears as James Bond, Billy the Kid, Sherlock Holmes, and Jack the Ripper. Though Alice provides the vocal track to the song, anytime he speaks in this movie, veteran voice actor Ted Rusoff dubs his lines. That odd touch makes this whole endlessly padded, shot-in-Spain mess all the more aberrant and memorable.

After the video, Vincent trucks the crew and his girlfriend Sandra (Victoria Vera) back to his childhood home, which happens to look like Castle Dracula. Nobody is terribly surprised when nearby wild dogs take to chewing on the townsfolk. The canine attacks present immediate complications for Vincent, as his father was a werewolf who was lynched by locals. Naturally, when junior returns—"Identity Crisis" rock star or not—word spreads that he's up to some old-dog lycanthropic tricks.

The Monster Dog of the title shows up, looking like a beef-jerky sock puppet. Some real dogs accompany him, and they attack with gore galore. All the while, European B-flick actors pretend to fight off the cheap toy that's supposed to be biting them. Alice performs one more number ("See Me in the Mirror"), and he finally does wolf out via a really cool, bubbling-skin transformation involving an animatronic mannequin head.

Monster Dog is overall monstrously dull, but any Alice Cooper werewolf movie is essential. Director Claudio Fragasso also helmed *Troll II*. If he only made that and *Monster Dog*, he would already be a legend. Fortunately, he also made *Hell of the Living Dead* (1980), *Rats: Night of Terror* (1984), and maybe even *Zombi 3* (1988).

Ted Russof, who supplies Vincent Raven's speaking voice, is a voice-over legend. His other Heavy Metal Movie credits include *Beyond the Darkness* (1979), *Nightmare City* (1980), *Absurd* (1981), *Piranha II: The Spawning* (1981), and *The Last Temptation of Christ* (1988). Way less heavily, *Monster Dog*'s two non-Alice soundtrack songs are performed by the Alan Parsons Project.

MONTEREY POP (1968)

(DIR. D. A. PENNEBAKER; W/THE JIMI HENDRIX EXPERIENCE, THE WHO, JEFFERSON AIRPLANE)
✠ BURNING GUITAR ✠ CONCERT FOOTAGE

Monterey Pop, the movie, documents the Monterey Pop Festival, a three-day rock concert mounted by promoter Lou Adler and John Phillips of the Mamas and the Papas. Even with its beautifully natural Northern California setting and the presence of light-leaning acts such as the Byrds and Simon and Garfunkel, Monterey Pop turns out to lead the front-line battle charge for hard and heavy acid rock. Of paramount importance is the Jimi Hendrix Experience, a group that transforms rock with a literally scorching performance. In addition, the Who roar out a proto-metal take of "My Generation"; the Animals storm through the Stones' "Paint It Black"; plus-size biker boogie behemoths Canned Heat do the blues number "Rollin' and Tumblin'"; and Jefferson Airplane psychedelizes an entire generation with "High Flying Bird" and "Today."

The bright inspirational moment for heavy metal comes when Jimi Hendrix burns rock to the ground with an apocalyptic deconstruction of the Troggs' "Wild Thing." The song culminates with him lighting his guitar ablaze, smashing it on the stage, and throwing the neck to the crowd. He tramples flower power and announces dark and thunderous sights and sounds, filled with seemingly frivolously destructive gestures that ignite new worlds of rock, riots, and revolution.

Monterey Pop director D. A. Pennebaker previously made the earth-shaking Bob Dylan documentary *Don't Look Back* (1967), and went on to make the rock docs *Alice Cooper* (1970) and *Ziggy Stardust and the Spiders From Mars* (1973).

Monty Python and the Holy Grail (1975)

(Dir. Terry Gilliam, Terry Jones; w/Graham Chapman, John Cleese, Terry Gilliam, Eric Idle, Terry Jones, Michael Palin)

✠ **Swords & Sorcery** ✠ **Black Plague**

The Monty Python troupe delivers an uproariously metallized take on the legend of King Arthur and his pursuit of Christ's cup. Directed by Terry Jones and Terry Gilliam, *Holy Grail* pioneered the thoroughly metal splatter comedy genre with an unrivaled wit. That it's rated PG is one of those "only in the '70s" moments.

This convincing Arthurian epic's most metal interludes invoke the most violent laughter. Black plague bodies pile up while corpse collectors push wheelbarrows through the streets, shouting, "Bring out your dead!" The Black Knight is slowly dismembered, with each wound gushing a faucet of blood until, finally, he is just a stump in black metal insisting he can still fight. Sir Lancelot single-handedly massacres most of an entire village's wedding celebration in order to "rescue" Galahad from a throng of virgin handmaidens

who only want to be spanked and provide oral sex to him at Castle Anthrax. Then comes the Rabbit of Caerbannog, chomping off heads. By executing these gags so seriously, *Monty Python and the Holy Grail* is heavy metal made hilarious—as great heavy metal often willingly is.

Monty Python's follow-up movies are each also steeped in metal motifs and concepts. *The Life of Brian* (1979) parodies life under Roman rule during the time of Christ. Due to its religious satire, the movie faced censorship worldwide, prompting the tagline: "So funny it was banned in Norway!" The final original Python project, The *Meaning of Life* (1983), is a full-on graphic assault against religion and society by means of blood, guts, and projectile vomit. Metalheads noticed. Countless songs sample "bring out yer dead," and "Follow the Blind" by Blind Guardian samples *Holy Grail*'s Latin funeral prayer.

Morbid Angel: Tales of the Sick— A Closer Look (2009)

(Dir. Juan Gonzalez; w/David Vincent, Trey Azagthoth, Richard Brunelle, Pete Sandoval)

✠ **Death Metal** ✠ **Metal History**

Morbid Angel: Tales of the Sick—A Closer Look revisits the recording of the Tampa death metal originators' 1991 milestone *Blessed Are the Sick*. David Vincent speaks from a red bedroom lit by gothic candles. Wraparound sunglasses protect him from the glare. Producer Tom Morris delves deep into his process. General Morbid Angel go-to employee Dieter "Monster" Szczypinski shares his memories, as does guitar-tech-turned-attorney Eric Partlow. Ultimately, no amount of explanation can satisfactorily explain what Morbid Angel did, but it's nice just to wallow in the immediate aftermath. Nile members Karl Sanders, Dallas Toler-Wade, and George Kollias speak at length of love for *Blessed Are the Sick*. So how about a concept split EP where Nile's Egyptian gods battle Morbid Angel's Sumerian gods?

Motel Hell (1980)

(Dir. Kevin Connor; w/Rory Calhoun, Paul Linke, Nancy Parsons, Wolfman Jack)

✠ Splatter ✠ Cannibals

It takes all kinds of critters to make Farmer Vincent's fritters!" That's the slogan of independent organic butcher Vincent Smith, played by veteran cowboy actor Rory Calhoun, and his sister Ida (Nancy Parsons, aka Miss Beulah Balbricker from the *Porky's* movies). The agrarian siblings also run the Motel Hello, the sign for which, because of shot neon in the *O*, reads as *Motel Hell*. The "all kinds of critters," of course, is really just one kind: human critters. Farmer Vincent booby-traps the motel, captures its visitors, and then "plants" the victims in his garden up to their necks, where they are fattened en route to slaughter and fritter conversion.

Motel Hell is a great, sick joke that doesn't skimp on scares or gore in its pursuit of guffaws. Legendary rock radio DJ Wolfman Jack is a howl, indeed, in his role as Reverend Billy. *Motel Hell*'s signature moment—that of Farmer Vincent wearing an actual decapitated hog's head over his own during a duel with extra-long chainsaws—is one of the most perfectly metallic images in all of cinema. Just remember: "Meat's meat, and a man's gotta eat!"

Mother of Tears (2007)

(Dir. Dario Argento; w/Asia Argento, Daria Nicolodi, Moran Atias, Udo Kier)

✠ Witchcraft ✠ Apocalypse

Dario Argento identifies *Mother of Tears* as the final chapter in his "Three Mothers" trilogy, preceded by *Suspiria* (1977) and *Inferno* (1980). Maybe it is, or maybe that's just how he got the movie made and secured a decent worldwide release for it. *Mother of Tears* is, in fact, a cheap ladling of crappy CGI gore atop the ludicrously silicone-pumped bare boobs of Moran Atias, who sucks all life right out of the screen in the centerpiece role as Mater Lacrimarum.

Asia Argento, nude for dad as usual (thanks), plays somebody. You won't know and you won't care. She's investigating odd doings plaguing Rome, such as mass suicides and a mom tossing an obvious doll we're supposed to believe is a baby off a bridge (the "thunk" effect of the doll hitting its head en route to the water, admittedly, gave me a chuckle). Everything comes crashing down right before the final credits, when Asia, presumably as a stand-in for Papa, emerges into a post-apocalyptic landscape and laughs hysterically right at each of us sitting in the audience.

Only two sequences semi-redeem *Mother of Tears* from the all-time feces heap. The first is a tracking shot of a gaggle of chic European witches sashaying through an airport. They cackle, they bully, and they trample any and all they come across, creating an uncomfortably funny moment. The second is a nasty gore sequence where a woman's head is mashed by a train door repeatedly slamming shut. Two cool riffs do not a symphonic metal concept album make.

Mr. Bricks: A Heavy Metal Musical (2012)

(Dir. Travis Campbell; w/Tim Dax, Nicola Fiore, Vito Trigo, Sharmeen Azmudeh)

✠ Metal on Broadway ✠ Soundtrack ("Outlaw" by Motörhead)

Describing his youth in the '80s and '90s, Travis Campbell—director of *Mr. Bricks: A Heavy Metal Murder Musical*—told *Decibel* magazine: "There was nothing like getting a pizza, watching a VHS of the newest *Texas Chainsaw*, *Friday the 13th*, or *Nightmare on Elm Street* sequel and then later turning on *Headbangers Ball*! What a Saturday night!" That description nails all righteous heavy metal cinema hard on its banging head, and sums up the personal touch Travis brings to *Mr. Bricks*. As promised, this is a full-blown heavy metal murder musical. Some characters burst into song, others engage in gory slaughter. Quite a few do both.

Mr. Eugene Bricks (Tim Dax) begins the movie

as a muscle-bound, body-modified berserker with tattoos covering 90 percent of his face, and a bullet wedged 100 percent inside his brain. He kidnaps hot female cop Scarlet Moretti (Nicola Fire) and embarks on a hell-bent-for-homicide mission to win her heart. Between and during explosions of violence, Bricks sings directly into the camera in hyper-aggro, hardcore-influenced style that's reminiscent of Biohazard's Evan Seinfeld. (New York hardcore veteran Tony Enz of the band Reason Enough supplies his singing voice.)

The music, composed and performed by Campbell, largely veers toward metalcore. The songs are well executed (pun, as usual, intended), as are the movie's concussive beat-downs, action outbursts, and horror components. One caveat: CGI gore. Campbell and his fully committed cast get a full horns-up, while *Mr. Bricks*'s distributor, Troma Films, warrants half a metal hand salute for picking up an original work outside the normal realm of their insultingly self-mocking nonsense—and not the usual half horn one throws toward Troma, either.

  Leading lady Nicola Fiore has become a DVD horror scream queen. *Mr. Bricks* makes use of her natural energy (she previously played bass in a hardcore band), and serves as the culmination of her sexily aggressive rise to B-movie stardom through *Terror at Blood Fart Lake* (2009), *Bloodbath in the House of Knives* (2010), *She Wolf Rising* (2011), *Slaughter Daughter* (2012), and the eyebrow-raising *Ms. Cannibal Holocaust* (2012).

Munster, Go Home! (1966)

(Dir. Earl Bellamy; w/Fred Gwynne, Yvonne DeCarlo, Al Lewis, Butch Patrick)

✠ Monsters ✠ Cars

The *Addams Family* may have been classier, headier, and more subtly demonic, but from its surf-guitar theme song to the episode where Eddie turns into a trumpet-blowing beatnik complete with goatee, to Herman recording a hit version of "Dry Bones"—*The Munsters* always had

one size-36 grave-digging boot firmly planted in the realm of rock and roll. *Munster, Go Home* is a full-color big-screen spin off released the summer after the series was canceled (and it played on a double bill with the Don Knotts romp *The Ghost and Mr. Chicken*. Those were the times!).

Herman (Fred Gwynne), Lily (Yvonne De Carlo), Grandpa (Al Lewis), Eddie (Butch Patrick), and Marilyn (Debbie Watson) travel to England. Herman, to everyone's surprise, has been named Lord Munster of Munster Hall. Their adventure climaxes with a car race wherein Herman pilots a coffin converted by Grandpa into the "Drag-u-la" speed machine. Watch for horror icon John Carradine (David, Keith, and Robert's father) as Cruikshank, the scheming British butler.

Rob Zombie is not just a fanatic of *The Munsters* TV show, he's a particular fan of *Munster, Go Home!* Zombie scored a huge hit in 1998 with the song "Dragula," and footage from Herman's car race appears in his directorial movie debut, *House of 1000 Corpses* (2003)

Murders in the Rue Morgue (1932)

(Dir. Robert Florey; w/Bela Lugosi, Sidney Fox, Leon Ames, Arlene Francis, Charles Gemora)

✠ Slasher ✠ Edgar Allan Poe

Bela Lugosi followed up his star turn in *Dracula* (1931) by portraying mad scientist Dr. Mirakle in the Edgar Allan Poe adaptation *Murders in the Rue Morgue*. Mirakle tours nineteenth-century Paris with a sideshow, exhibiting his intelligent ape Erik (Charles Gemora, in a suit that makes him look like a cross between a gorilla and an orangutan). By night, the devious doctor kidnaps women and injects them with simian blood. Both Mirakle and Erik fixate on beautiful Camille (Sidney Fox). The beast eventually strangles his master in a jealous rage, and then is shot trying to flee into the night with his female prey.

Rue Morgue is a creaky relic to be sure, but its misty Paris setting and atmospheric direction by Robert Florey, along with the incomparable Lugosi, come together to create a palpably creepy experience. There's even a moment involving Erik that made me jump. That's no mean feat for any movie, let alone one this ancient that costars a guy in a monkey costume.

Iron Maiden's 1981 tour de force "Murders in the Rue Morgue" presents a fascinating alternative telling of the tale on *Killers*, itself a kind of grindhouse multiplex of seedy horror stories. Vocalist Paul Di'Anno sings as one of the foreign witnesses to the original crimes. He points out that he "can't speak French," and so he decides to run. The rest of the song recounts his horror at the sight of the dead bodies, and his terror over being blamed for the killings.

Murders in the Rue Morgue was remade in 1971 with Jason Robards and as a 1986 TV movie with George C. Scott. Stick with the Lugosi version.

Musical Mutiny (1970)

(Dir. Barry Mahon; w/Brad F. Grinter, Iron Butterfly, the Fantasy, the New Society Band)

✠ Iron Butterfly

Florida schlock-movie impresario Barry Mahon trafficked in all manner of drive-in fodder and discount matinee programming, with a particular knack for oddball nudie flicks (*Fanny Hill Meets Dr. Erotico*(1969)) and, toward the late-1960s end of his run, amazingly cheap kiddie piddle (*Santa and the Three Bears* (1970)). Many of those later gems were shot in and around a Florida amusement park called Pirate's World.

For *Musical Mutiny*, Mahon aimed his cameras at teenagers—the demographic between his typical audiences (those being for either *The Wonderful Land of Oz* or *PPS: Prostitutes Protective Society*). Who better to lead the youth movement of 1970 than an eighteenth-century swashbuckler who emerges from the sea spouting hippie jive, declaring that the time has come for a "musical mutiny!"?

Rebellion comes in the form of a concert film featuring psychedelic opening acts the Fantasy and the New Society Band. Then we get a full set from the headliners, proto-metal freak-gods Iron Butterfly. This includes a nine-minute, lip-synched take on "In-a-Gadda-da-Vida."

Mahon's lone visual concession to the swinging times is a psychotic employment of a zoom lens to swoop in and out as the performers jam. This Dramamine-begging footage is jarringly punctuated by shots of clean-cut Florida families just sort of taking it all in while waiting in line for cotton candy or the Ferris wheel. Laugh now, but remember: "In-a-Gadda-da-Vida" really can have all kinds of wild effects on people.

The Mutilator (1985), aka Fall Break

(Dir. Buddy Cooper; w/Matt Mitler, Bill Hitchcock, Ruth Martinez, Morey Lampley)

✠ Slasher

By sword. By pick. By axe. Bye bye." That was *The Mutilator*'s all-time great advertising tagline, appearing on posters and in TV commercials. The movie itself never flirts with being as clever, but was still a standout, late-cycle '80s slasher. As a kid, Ed Junior (Matt Mitler) accidentally shoots his mom to death, sending Ed Senior (Jack Chatham) into a psychotic tailspin. Years later, college-age Ed Jr. hears from his estranged pop, who offers an invite to come visit him at his beach house. Ed piles some pals into his jalopy and off they go—straight into surfside slaughter at the hands (and swords and picks and axes, etc.) of the deranged dad.

The kills in *The Mutilator* impress with the ingenuity and intense levels of gore. A wall lined with human heads as trophies even manages to spook a little. Otherwise, this is standard heavy-breathing POV stalk-and-slaughter moviemaking. What elevates *The Mutilator* to metal status, then, is its bluntness. Writer-director Buddy Cooper made the film under the clumsy title *Fall Break*, but distributors widely changed the name to the straight-up brutal *The Mutilator*. Beyond mere marketing, the name matches the movie's straightforward carnage. Released the same year as the death-metal-defining *Seven Churches* by Possessed, and the same year that Belo Horizonte, Brazil's mighty Mutilator was formed, *The Mutilator* heralded a new upfront face value to come in rip-your-face-off entertainment.

The Mutilator's ads prominently announced that the movie was "written, produced, and directed by BUDDY COOPER" as though his name were a selling point. Despite *The Mutilator*'s success and lingering reputation, BUDDY COOPER never wrote, produced, or directed another movie.

My Amityville Horror (2013)

(Dir. Eric Walter; w/Daniel Lutz, Laura DiDio, Lorraine Warren)
✶ Haunted House

*M*y Amityville Horror introduces us right away to bald, chain-smoking, agony-eyed Daniel Lutz, one of the kids who spent a month in the notorious Long Island home that spawned a cottage industry of books, movies, T-shirts, and other horror ephemera during the 1970s. Lutz is thirty-seven now, and shattered. Part tearfully, part defiantly, he recounts his demonic possession, the swarms of flies that overtook him, Jodie the pig peering in an upper floor window with "red laser eyes" and "teeth like a wolf," and all the other details on the record since the 1977 publication of *The Amityville Horror*.

This UPS deliveryman (and heavy metal guitarist) emotes with horrible credibility about abuse he claims to have suffered at the hands of his stepfather, George Lutz, the ex-marine who became a media sensation once he sold the story of his haunted house. The filmmakers just let Daniel Lutz talk, which is smart. He's a magnetic figure who looks like a combination of metal-loving comedian Jim Norton and Michael Chiklis as Vic Mackey from *The Shield*. Better still, sequences are punctuated with footage of Lutz wailing and shredding on guitar in his garage.

My Amityville Horror errs by not providing us with more. Lutz's siblings do not participate. The opinions of various demonologists and parapsychologists are presented at face value. Daniel talks about running away as a young teen and living in the desert—with no details of any depth as to what those years were like, nor how he came to father and support two children, let alone how he came by his guitar skills. The short movie quickly racks up a series of missed opportunities.

A visit to parapsychologist Lorraine Warren is weirder and way scarier than anything in any other *Amityville* movie. Her overstuffed home contains several huge, colorful show chickens kept, seemingly cruelly, in individual indoor cages. Every so often, one of the fowls emits a bloodcurdling scream. It's freaky enough when Lorraine has Daniel kiss a relic she claims came from the true cross upon which Christ died; it's one hell of a freaky jolt to have the action interrupted by raging cries of rooster anguish.

My Bloody Valentine (1981)

(Dir. George Mihalka; w/Peter Cowper, Paul Kelman, Lori Haller, Neil Affleck, Cynthia Dale)
✶ Slasher

*O*n Valentine's Day 1960, in a mining town called Valentine Bluffs, a group of miners died in an accident caused by the crew bosses quitting early to attend a Valentine dance. You could understand the reticence of sole survivor Harry Warden (Peter Cowper) to be at peace around February 14 after that, but he takes his agitation to the extreme, cutting out the hearts out of those negligent foremen and leaving the organs as a warning to the town to never ever celebrate Valentine's Day again.

Twenty years pass. The local youth figure that it's time to safely break out the cupid decorations and "Be Mine!" cards again but, this being a slasher movie, Harry—in full miner gear with a scary gas mask and a sharpened pickaxe—returns to pump the punch bowl full of plasma.

My Bloody Valentine stood out among the early-'80s slasher glut for its memorable title, the inherent fright factor of its villain, the original use of coal mines and underground tunnels for suspense sequences, and the genuinely grotesque sight of freshly torn-out human hearts delivered to unsuspecting recipients in candy boxes. If there's one horror movie weapon to rival the chainsaw for heavy metal might, it's the pickaxe. The MPAA instantly branded *My Bloody Valentine* with an X rating, demanding cuts to every kill sequence. The fully restored film remained out of circulation until 2009, when an uncut Blu-ray release was tied in to the remake, *My Bloody Valentine 3D*.

Early-'90s Irish rock band My Bloody Valentine is typically considered Britpop or shoegaze (like a lot of black metal these days), but their droning riffs, monstrous distortion, and intensely loud swirling walls of noise have always placed them in the alternative metal camp in my mind. In 1992, MBV's ominous buzzing overkill made me check my ears for blood and left made me nauseated and gasping for air. Many metal bands have covered My Bloody Valentine material, including Airs, Earthenwomb, Nadja, and the Provenance.

My Sweet Satan (1994)

(Dir. Jim VanBebber; w/Jim VanBebber, Terek Puckett, Alydra Kelly)

✡ Ritual Homicide ✡ Acid King

Mad metal moviemaker Jim VanBebber (*Deadbeat at Dawn*) celebrated the tenth anniversary of Long Island's teenage "Acid King" Ricky Kasso committing satanic ritual murder by making a movie about it. VanBebber stars as the killer, here named Ricky Kasslin. *My Sweet Satan* is a nineteen-minute descent into suburban burnout hell that opens with Kasslin hanging himself in a jail cell. In flashback, we see what led to the moment: Ricky's a drug-dropping high-school metal fan who commits his soul to the devil, gets burned on a dope deal by another teen, and responds by stomping the deadbeat's skull to mush. After he's arrested, he rigs up a noose and goes to meet his dark master.

VanBebber's screen presence is terrifying and his direction is self-assured. The gore effects during the murder, and the way the camera forcibly presents what happens to that head, are stomach-voiding. Well done. The title *My Sweet Satan* is a reference to what many claim can be heard when playing Led Zeppelin's "Stairway to Heaven" backward.

Napalm Death: The Scum Story (2012)

(Dir. Pete Bridgewater; w/Napalm Death)

✠ Grindcore ✠ Metal History ✠ Birmingham

Suitably bare-bones and direct, the forty-eight-minute documentary *Napalm Death: The Scum Story* is actually longer by a third than the album it commemorates. Drummer Mick Harris engagingly talks about the hows and whys of *Scum* rising, and he leads an entertaining tour of the locations where the eruption of his former band went down. These hot spots include the still-active Rich Bitch recording studios and the shuttered shambles of the Mermaid, a legendary punk club where Napalm Death gigged with Amebix, Chaos UK, and other genre-warping grind and punk legends.

Harris is lively and likable, and other valuable input comes from Earache Records founder Digby Pearson and Turner Prize–nominated visual artist Mark Titchner. Always chipper music journalist Malcolm Dome discusses how the personnel changes that took place in Napalm Death between the band's recording *Scum*'s side A and side B reflect the record's chronological evolution from punk to metal. Dome hails Mick Harris—the only member to play on both sides of the record—for bringing the record to scum-tastic fruition.

Among the interesting revelations: original bassist Nik "Napalm" Bullen chose Rich Bitch because female-fronted crossover pioneers Sacrilege U.K. had recorded there. We also learn that Napalm Death only rehearsed each song on side B exactly one time before entering the studio. Best of all, Harris divulges his youthful penchant for leading other group members in kicking at least one door off its hinges at every gig. The band always paid for the damages, but stopped after a show at Covington University. "We kicked too many doors down, and the security guy was waiting for us behind the last door!" There is a metaphor there, just waiting to be kicked open.

Natural Born Killers (1994)

(Dir. Oliver Stone; w/Woody Harrelson, Juliette Lewis, Robert Downey Jr., Rodney Dangerfield)

✠ Serial Killers ✠ Soundtrack (Jane's Addiction, Nine Inch Nails, L7)

In the pre-Internet early-'90s era of xeroxed zines and self-released records, serial killers inundated heavy metal and punk consciousness the way cat videos pollute our Facebook feeds now. Hollywood latched on to this ugly bubble, and allowed Oliver Stone, a sometimes visionary filmmaker, to gratify his every optical and visceral whim in *Natural Born Killers*. The end result is indulgent to the max.

Woody Harrelson and Juliette Lewis star as married murderers Mickey and Mallory Knox. They represent corporate entertainment's notion of "white trash." *Natural Born Killers* traces their homicidal road trip across the physical and cultural United States, wherein every crime they commit raises their media profile. Stone shoots from cockeyed angles, backwards, and with weird filters. He tells his disjointed story with amphetamine editing, animation, old movie clips, TV parodies, contemporary news reports ("Look! O. J.!"), psychedelic videos, and what I think was literally every trick in his book.

Village Voice critic J. Hoberman rightly described *Killers* as "the most avant-garde Hollywood production since Dennis Hopper's *The Last Movie*." Avant-garde, alas, doesn't always mean good. Given the big-budget violence fetish and beyond-MTV visuals, a cult quickly sprang up around the film, particularly among young hard rock fans. The movie's cred was boosted by several incidents of copycat crimes wherein perpetrators explicitly referred to this film as their inspiration. Murder is always dumb; murder in tribute to a movie where the director's eye-popping panache is squandered because the hammy performances and ham-fisted "messages" are in themselves dumb is somewhere beneath despicable.

Trent Reznor says he watched *Natural Born Killers* more than fifty times to "get in the mood" for assembling the movie's soundtrack. While studded with an occasional okay number, the song choices, like the film itself, largely embody a mainstream tastemaker's limp idea of "edgy." Just consider the inclusion of "Rock N Roll Nigger" by Patti Smith and the fact that the hit single was a cover of "Sweet Jane" by the Cowboy Junkies. Soy milk packs more peril.

At one point, Juliette Lewis wastes a diner full of rednecks while braying along to "Shitlist" by L7. The Jane's Addiction track "Sex Is Violent (Ted, Just Admit It)" features scary vocals by operatic performance art witch Diamanda Galás. Her 1982 debut LP *The Litanies of Satan* influenced numerous heavy metal boundary blasters, and the same year that *Natural Born Killers* came out, Galás teamed with Led Zeppelin's John Paul Jones for the great bluesy *The Sporting Life*.

The everything-and-the-strobe-lit-kitchen-sink approach nails the early-1990s zeitgeist. A deleted scene included on the DVD showcases twin professional bodybuilders as "the Hun Brothers" thanking Mickey and Mallory for chopping their limbs off. The Pauls are better known to viewers as "the Barbarian Brothers," stars of a series of likable schlock projects, including *The Barbarians* (1987), *Think Big* (1989), and *Double Trouble* (1992). Quentin Tarantino penned the original screenplay for *Natural Born Killers*. Stone and several collaborators reworked the material almost completely, prompting Tarantino to distance himself from the finished film.

Near Dark (1987)

(Dir. Kathryn Bigelow; w/Lance Henriksen, Bill Paxton, Jenny Wright, Adrian Pasdar)

✠ Vampires ✠ Western Noir

Near Dark crept into theaters for Halloween 1987, following the pop-metal summer fun of *The Lost Boys* and in direct competition with John Carpenter's demonic math-metal prog horror, *Prince of Darkness*. The season was a great one for upending the wooden-stake tentpoles of various fright genres. In *Near Dark*, Oklahoma farm boy Caleb (Adrian Pasdar) falls for fetching young beauty Mae (Jenny Wright), a member of a hardscrabble, nomadic hillbilly family that travels by camper. It turns out they're vampires. Before long, Caleb is one, too.

Mae and Caleb share perfectly heavy thoughts about the curse of immortality. Mae says, "Listen hard. Do you hear it?"

"Hear what?" Johnny says.

"The night," she replies. "It's deafening."

Caleb's quest to free himself and then Mae of undeadness provides *Near Dark* with its heart, but the movie's soul centers on super-stylized ultraviolence and director Kathryn Bigelow's alternately atmospheric and explosive dustup tributes to the Gatling-gun-western revisionism of Sam Peckinpah (*The Wild Bunch*). Towering performances come from Lance Henriksen as the whiskey-boiled gang leader, Bill Paxton as a particularly sadistic bloodsucker, and Joshua John Miller as a grotesque vampire child-man.

Near Dark builds to a sensationally brutal climax with Mae betraying her vampire brethren while sunlight scorches the skin from her bones, and then it peters out with a silly B-movie postscript. The entire package is beautifully filmed, a haunting back-roads vampire romance infused with blood from throats slit by cowboy-boot spurs and the searing lead kisses of gun slaughter that carries on into infinite darkness.

Joshua John Miller, who plays a Homer, a centuries-old pervert trapped in the pudgy confines of a twelve-year-old miscreant, is also Keanu Reeves's creepy kid brother who disposes of his sister's doll at the beginning of *River's Edge* (1987). *Near Dark*'s music score is by German synthesizer giants Tangerine Dream, creators of killer soundtracks (*Thief*, *Miracle Mile*, *Sorcerer*), and this is one of their best. While not overtly metal in sound, Tangerine Dream has wielded huge influence on metal musicians worldwide, notably Mayhem from Norway, whose instru-

mental "Silvester Anfang" was given to them by early Tangerine Dream member Conrad Schnitzler. Agathodaimon, Eliminator, and Holy Moses have all written "Near Dark" songs, as well.

NECRONOMICON: BOOK OF THE DEAD (1993)

(DIRS. CHRISTOPHE GANS, SHUSUKE KANEKO, BRIAN YUZNA; W/JEFFREY COMBS, RICHARD LYNCH)
✠ H. P. LOVECRAFT ✠ ANTHOLOGY

The careers of extreme '80s splatter classic leading men Bruce Campbell (*The Evil Dead*) and Jeffrey Combs (*Re-Animator*) interestingly parallel those of '70s action superstars Clint Eastwood and Charles Bronson, respectively. Campbell, largely in cahoots with his blockbuster director pal Sam Raimi, graduated from B-flicks to prominent mainstream movie and TV roles (even a 2007 Old Spice commercial) much the way Eastwood went from vigilante cop potboilers to winning multiple Best Picture Oscars. Combs, on the other (chainsawed) hand, has remained one of the hardest-working thespians in low-budget horror and exploitation, much as Bronson dedicated his final decades to brain-smashingly brutal exploitation pictures.

Each route has merits, and each star has imbued metal virtuosity into every effort, but extra hails are due here to Jeffrey Combs, an intense nerd hero like no other who has consistently returned to the realm that launched him: the cosmically thunderous occult literature of über-metal author H. P. Lovecraft. After making his bones as Lovecraft's mad scientist Herbert West in two *Re-Animator* movies and starring in *From Beyond*, Combs takes on the role of the writer himself in the three-part anthology *Necronomicon: Book of the Dead*. Combs plays H. P. Lovecraft in wraparound segments between each of three minithrillers inspired by the dark visionary's work.

Unfortunately, *Necronomicon*'s individual episodes are duds. "The Drowned" wastes the great Richard Lynch (*Bad Dreams*) as a spooky sea captain, and manages to dull even a cameo by the mighty tentacled anti-god Cthulhu. "Cold Air" depicts a cracked doctor (David Warner) who has defeated death, just so long as he keeps his body temperature ice-cold. Finally, "Whispers" follows a pregnant cop (Signy Coleman) who gets tossed in a pit with brain-eating creatures called Migos.

Despite the great cast, beasts included, the interstitial bits are the only highlights, as Combs as Lovecraft pores over a well-worn copy of the book after which the film is named. By the end, the *Necronomicon* is revealed not to belong on the nonfiction shelf, and Lovecraft proves himself lethally skilled as an acrobatic slayer of demons, mutant monks, and other bogus-looking rubber monstrosities he dispatches by way of a sword hidden inside his walking stick. The semi-mind-blowing aspect of all this is that under heavy-duty makeup Combs almost becomes a dead ringer for Bruce Campbell!

NEKROMANTIK (1988)
(DIR. JÖRG BUTTGEREIT; W/DAKTARI LORENZ, BEATRICE MANOWSKI, HARALD LUNDT)
✠ NECROPHILIA ✠ SACRIFICE ✠ CENSORSHIP

Rob (Daktari Lorenz) cleans up crime scenes for a living, and pockets pieces of dead bodies for his own joy. When he scores an entire rotting corpse, Rob elatedly brings it home to Betty (Beatrice M.) and the two of them fuck the maggoty, festering, nonliving shit out of it. In time, Betty comes to prefer the decomposing stiff to her husband, until Rob finally comes home to a note that reads: "Left for good, took the corpse." This cadaverous cuckoldry sends Rob on a suicidal tear wherein he murders a cat and bathes in its guts, strangles a hooker and has sex with the body, and finally stabs himself repeatedly while ejaculating over images of a rabbit being slaughtered.

Nekromantik figured grandly and grotesquely in the second wave of headbanger-beloved videos often watched as a group challenge to determine how much a viewer could stomach. This arty German import followed *Faces of Death* and *Cannibal Holocaust* and other great vomit-inducing VHS faves of the '80s, and was often viewed alongside traded VHS tape comps including footage of Pennsylvania politico R. Budd Dwyer blowing his brains out and Chuck Berry using a pretty blonde as a Port-a-San. That's not to belittle *Nekromantik* as a mere puke-party centerpiece. Like much heavy metal music, it can empty your bowels and raise your consciousness. It's also seriously, seriously German.

Aside from all the mondo disgusto visuals, *Nekromantik*'s most unforgettable component is its driving, upbeat, contextually hilarious musical love theme, "Ménage a Trois." This elegant, propulsive piano piece is pounded out over and over and over again, creating repeated juxtapositions between the lovely song and the repugnantly unlovely sights. You'll never expunge that riff from your head, no matter how hard you barf.

Nekromantik was promptly banned in Australia, Finland, Iceland, Malaysia, New Zealand, and Norway. Just as immediately, "Nekromantik" songs were composed by Haemorrhage, Harmony, and Sabbat. A band called Bowel Fetus covered the "Theme From Nekromantik." *Nekromantik 2* (1991) feeds the fever with more of the same, disgustingly.

NEON MANIACS (1986), AKA EVIL DEAD WARRIORS
(DIR. JOSEPH MANGINE; W/CLYDE HANES, LEILANI SARELLE, DONNA LOCKE, VICTOR BRANDT)
✠ URBAN WARFARE ✠ MUTANTS

Unique and nutty from end to end, *Neon Maniacs* failed to nab even a cult following during its initial theatrical release, its second life on cable and home video, and even when Anchor Bay issued a special-edition DVD. This unsung little gem of screwy-skulled '80s action-horror centers on highly stylized mutants that live—and kill—in the immediate vicinity of San Francisco's Golden Gate Bridge. Serving as foils to these night-raiding freakazoids are a group of teens, the most notable of who is macabre-minded Paula (Donna Locke). She goes to college out in Frisco, but originally hails from the highly metal hometown of Amityville, New York. The youthful targets don't matter, though. As they should be, the Neon Maniacs themselves are the stars here.

Neon Maniacs makes a great complement to any of Charles Band's across-the-board terrific *Puppet Master* movies, as the Maniacs are basically human-size equivalents of Puppet Master Toulon's foot-high marauders. They are wonders of paint and wigs and latex and practical prosthetics and physical mechanics and fantastically rendered costumes and intricate pre-CGI design. To a Maniac, they are metal in appearance; their names indicate precisely how much metal that means: Ape, Archer, Axe, Decapitator, Hangman, Mohawk, Punk Biker, Samurai, Scavenger, Slasher, and Soldier. There are even more Maniacs than just those headliners, but what else could you possibly need?

Never Say Die (2004)
(Dirs. David Gray, Katie McQuerrey; w/Joe Donnelly, Danny Toto, Tom Capobianco)
✣ Metal Reality ✣ New Jersey

Never Say Die chronicles the dawn of the second decade of New Jersey's hardest-banging, heaviest Black Sabbath cover band, Sabbra Cadabra. Garden State metal fans to the marrow, the members of Sabbra Cadabra—vocalist Joe Donnelly, guitarist Danny Toto, bassist Scott Destefanis, and drummer Tom Capobianco—don groovy vintage garb and speak onstage in the British dialects of their idols, performing ritual invocations of unabashed nostalgia in bars and clubs throughout the New York tristate area. "If there's anybody here tonight doesn't want to par-tee," admonishes Donnelly-as-Ozzy from the stage, "go home, listen to Green Day."

Typical rock group drama arises (boredom, burnout, rivalry, excessive intoxication), made entertaining by the peculiar reality of men who imitate preexisting icons. In the early 2000s, everyone but Donnelly formed a Zeppelin tribute act, Black Dog, which frequently opens for Sabbra Cadabra. "The rest of the guys in this band

love Led Zeppelin," Donnelly says. "I can't stand them. I can't stand Robert Plant goin' 'baby baby baby' two hundred fuckin' times. That's just annoying." In response he forms Ozzmosis, an Ozzy solo cover band that generates no end of tension between him and his Sabbra cohorts.

We see footage of the group's first practice in 1993, Donnelly's massive and intricate collection of Micronauts toys, and a tour of Puerto Rico that forever alters the group. A decade after the film debuted, Sabbra Cadabra is still out there doing what they do. Filmmakers David Gray and Katie McQuerrey were assistant editors (he on *Blair Witch 2*, she on *No Country for Old Men*) who made *Never Say Die* as a labor of love. Sabbra Cadabra played their wedding.

Never Too Young to Die (1986)
(Dir. Gil Bettman; w/John Stamos, Vanity, Gene Simmons, George Lazenby, Robert Englund)
✣ Gene Simmons

John Stamos, between TV gigs on *General Hospital* and *Full House*, took a curious stab at big-screen stardom in the hyper-'80s espionage adventure *Never Too Young to Die*. He failed, but the movie is an abominable heavy metal triumph. Lance Stargrove (Stamos) is the gymnast son of a CIA agent (George Lazenby, the only one-and-done James Bond) who teams with super-spy Danja Deering (Vanity) to thwart megalomaniacal hermaphrodite Velvet Von Ragnar from poisoning L.A.'s water supply. Gene Simmons plays the he-she supervillain. And how! Kiss actually postponed part of the *Animalize* tour so Gene could be Velvet Von Ragnar. Simmons's resplendent costume for the character had been worn previously by Lynda Carter; she donned the duds for a 1980 TV special where she sang Kiss's disco stomper, "I Was Made for Loving You."

For some reason, *Never Too Young to Die* does not boast a robust and vocal cult following. The tagline alone should be actively keeping this mess in midnight screenings: "Vanity: The New Breed

Wer glaubt, den besten Thriller zu kennen, hat diesen Schocker nicht gesehen!

MANIACS DIE HORRORBANDE

Clockwise from top: Napalm Death: The Scum Story; *the western vampire noir* Near Dark; *Robert Mitchum spells it out in* Night of the Hunter; *Hell comes to Londontown in* Night of the Demon (1957) *(beating the movie reviewed here by decades);* Neon Maniacs *looks even more maniacal in German*

of Temptress! Stamos: The New Breed of Hero!" Lump that up with the God of Thunder in full drag queen regalia, Robert Englund (well known as Freddy Krueger) as an evil computer cowboy, and a bosom-unbinding homage to *Beyond the Valley of the Dolls*, and it's never too late to get the word out about *Never Too Young to Die*.

New York Ripper (1982)

(Dir. Lucio Fulci; w/Jack Hedley, Almanta Keller, Howard Ross, Andrea Occhipinti)

✙ Slasher ✙ Giallo ✙ Banned Video Nasty

Emanating from the Rotten Apple during its last orgasmic outburst of open-market public carnality, Lucio Fulci's *New York Ripper* tracks a prostitute-patronizing NYPD detective (Jack Hedley) in pursuit of a mad slasher who quacks like a duck when murdering hookers, live-sex peep-show performers, and anything else with a vagina into which he can sink a straight razor or a broken bottle. You did read that right, by the way. The killer quacks like a duck. That off-the-wall affect adds big-time to *Ripper*'s disconcerting spelunk into savage violence and venereal shock, as does dreamily shot footage of decadent, early-'80s Times Square overflowing with porn theaters, massage parlors, and hellholes of even lower (and so much greater) repute.

New York Ripper pulsates with the vibrant blood-red metallic horror of its day. Even for Lucio Fulci (*Zombie*), the film is sleazy, sexual, fast moving, and prone to ricochet into insane detours. The wide views of New York City are stunning. Walking down a hospital corridor, a coroner pauses to lift up a sheet and briefly survey a young female cadaver unrelated to the storyline. "Another," he sighs, a one-second lament for the charnel house New York has become. A disgusting sort-of rape in a Puerto Rican pinball parlor uptown also reveals the kinky turn-ons of the Manhattan elite. These brutal shocks, alongside *Maniac* and *The Amityville Horror*, are the birthing spasms in the background of the outer-borough and bridge-and-tunnel heavy metal explosion of the 1980s.

Night of the Hunter (1955)

(Dir. Charles Laughton; w/Robert Mitchum, Shelley Winters, Lillian Gish)

✙ Evil Preacher ✙ Noir

Robert Mitchum creates a heavy metal archetype in the expressionistic *Night of the Hunter*. The great sloe-eyed Hollywood tough guy plays Reverend Harry Powell, a sweet-talking Southern Man of God with a hell's worth of hate in his psycho-killer heart. He wears black parson's hat and a western bow tie, and he brandishes the words *LOVE* and *HATE* tattooed across his fists. All this charming preacher wants to do is murder a pair of innocent children who know where a stolen ten grand is hidden.

A lyrical horror noir with brilliant evocations of childhood terror, *Night of the Hunter* is the only film directed by Charles Laughton, a legendary actor best known for playing creeps such as Quasimodo in the legendary *The Hunchback of Notre Dame* (1939). Critics and audiences freaked out and fled *Hunter* upon its initial release, but the film's artful, bewitching power turned it into a classic now long revered as a masterwork.

Night of the Hunter has served a wellspring of visions for filmmakers including David Lynch and Rob Zombie (not to mention Spike Lee). The number of metalheads with knuckle tattoos today is incalculable. In addition, *Poltergeist II*'s diabolical Reverend Henry Kane (Julian Beck)—as seen on the cover of Anthrax's *Among the Living*—is really just a supernatural extension of Mitchum's all-too-horribly down-to-earth clergy monster.

Nightbreed (1990)

(Dir. Clive Barker; w/Craig Sheffer, David Cronenberg, Anne Bobby, Charles Haid)

✙ Mutants

Hellraiser gets all the attention, but I've always been partial to horror author Clive Barker's second movie effort as a director, *Nightbreed*. It's an adaptation of Barker's highly metal-titled novel *Cabal*, about an outcast society of mutants and monsters living in a city underneath a graveyard called Midian to hide away from humanity. Both Midian and its freakazoid inhabitants are marvels of glorious pre-CGI special visual effects. Not surprisingly, *Midian* and *Nightbreed* have both been adopted as heavy metal band names.

Craig Sheffer stars as Boone, a disturbed youth spooked by visions of Midian. David Cronenberg (yes, the director of *Scanners* and *The Fly*) plays Dr. Decker, his psychiatrist, who is, in fact, a masked serial killer of entire families. He aims to pin the murders on Boone. The escalating mind games between patient and doctor, along with Boone's girlfriend (Anne Bobby) making her way inside Midian, set in motion a war between a nearby redneck militia, led by police chief Eigerman (Charles Haid, in a great, near-parody spin on Renko, his *Hill Street Blues* character), and the previously peaceful superhuman creatures who come barreling up from beneath the tombstones. The battle climaxes with Midian's generals dropping their horned, hairy, living equivalents of the nuclear option by way of roaring, "RELEASE THE BERSERKERS!" As was required of fright films of its era, *Nightbreed*'s conclusion sets up at least a sequel, if not an entire movie series, only in this case a sequel would have been welcome, with Boone transforming into mutant leader Cabal and Decker taking on the air of an Antichrist.

Barker has blamed *Nightbreed*'s falling through the cracks on the studio's marketing it as typical slasher junk. The movie's meaningless poster depicts a close-up of a scared girl's eyes under the words "Lori thought she knew everything about her boyfriend. Lori was wrong!" *Nightbreed* did garner a devoted following, and rightly so. The story of Midian and its secret misfit underworld is a potent metaphor and rallying cry for metalheads, punks, goths, and other like-minded denizens of more-than-just-musical subcultures. When the dominant population doesn't want you, just leave. Fuck 'em. Just . . . secede. Go find your own tribe, your own nightbreed. And when the time comes: RELEASE THE BERSERKERS!

Night of the Demon
(1980)
(Dir. James C. Wasson; w/Michael Cutt, Joy Allen, Bob Collins, Jody Lazurus)
✷ Bigfoot ✷ Black Magic ✷ Virgin Sacrifice
✷ Banned Video Nasty

Bigfoot is cryptozoology's most heavy metal creature, and this is Bigfoot cinema's most heavy metal movie. *Night of the Demon* delivers Bigfoot big-time, plus plenty of backwoods black magic, virgin sacrifice, a mutant Bigfoot baby being burned alive, college-student slaughter, and all kinds of Bigfoot sex crimes. The intensity of violence and gore spraying on-camera is mind-boggling, made much more so by all this insanity being stomped down upon us deadly straight.

No moment in *Night of the Demon* is more serious than when Bigfoot tears the penis off a biker who mistakenly pees on Bigfoot's big feet. Bigfoot also attacks two twenty-five-year-old women who are supposed to be Girl Scouts—at least, their T-shirts read "GIRL SCOUTS." The victims whip out knives to slay the beast, but Bigfoot repeatedly bashes them together like a pair of orchestral cymbals, causing the Girl Scouts to accidentally stab one another over and over while an upbeat flute wails on the soundtrack.

In our plane of reality, Bigfoot may or may not exist. No matter how many times I watch *Night of the Demon*, I'm not entirely convinced this movie actually exists, either. But is right here beside me. I better check it one (million) more time(s).

Night of the Demons
(1988), aka Halloween Party
(Dir. Kevin S. Tenney; w/Amelia Kinkade, Linnea Quigley, Cathy Podewell, Hal Havins)
✷ Séance ✷ Demonic Possession

Angela (Amelia Kinkade) and Suzanne (Linnea Quigley) throw an All Hallows' Eve bash at the spooky old funeral parlor Hull House. All the teen flick archetypes are invited: sweethearts

Frannie (Jill Terashita) and Max (Philip Tanzini); preppy Jay (Lance Fenton); right-on black bro Roger (Alvin Alexis); mousy Helen (Allison Baron); outcast Stooge (Hal Havins); and virginal Judy (Cathy Podewell), who will likely survive.

The revelers attempt a séance, and their *Halloween Party* turns into a *Night of the Demons*. Specifically, what the partygoers unleash is green smoke emitted by a bug-monster from a broken mirror. One by one, the kids become possessed, wig out, and then chase and sometimes slaughter whoever hasn't smoked up yet. Nudity, gore, and a high-flying sense of good, gruesome fun render *Night of the Demons* an above-average '80s schlock-fest; an entirely unexpected, jaw-dropping special effects piece in which Linnea Quigley inserts a lipstick through her nipple and into her breast makes it a one-of-a-kind wonder that inspired two sequels and a 2009 remake.

Released in Detroit in September 1988, and rolled out cross-country that fall, *Night of the Demons* shocked the movie industry by breaking box-office records wherever it opened. Theater audiences turned out for the movie's simple concept, effective TV campaigns, and a cool poster in which a fang-faced gorgon girl beckoned you to join her celebration. The tagline read: "Angela is having a party, Jason and Freddy are too scared to come . . . But You'll have a hell of a time."

Night of the Demons 2 (1994)

(Dir. Brian Trenchard-Smith; w/Amelia Kincade, Merle Kennedy Darin Heames, Jennifer Rhodes)

✠ Demons ✠ Nuns

The unspoken metal undercurrent of the original *Night of the Demons* (1988)—hair, fashions, overall tacky late-'80s vibe—is more tangible in *Night of the Demons 2* (1994). Defiantly, at the peak of the alt-rock Lollapalooza era, the soundtrack is dominated by death metal devils Morbid Angel. Mouse (Merle Kennedy), the shy and bullied kid sister of the evil-friendly party thrower Angela (Amelia Kincade), is tricked by a trio of proto–Mean Girls into attending a Halloween bash at the haunted Hull House. The cruel setup goes bloodily bonkers once Angela returns in a full-blown flesh-eating fury. Only Catholic school disciplinarian Sister Gloria (Jennifer Rhodes) can rescue the girls by revealing her previously secret succubus-battling skills.

Night of the Demons 2, directed by Australian B-movie veteran Brian Trenchard-Smith (*Stunt Rock*, *Escape 2000*), is a good deal lighter in tone than its predecessor, and features a possessed lipstick and a combat-ready nun. Angela emerges at a Catholic high school Halloween dance, sexily resplendent in a slit-all-over goth getup. She hops up on a table and hurls herself into an erotic dance interpretation of "Rapture" by Morbid Angel. The teens at her feet fall into her rapture—who wouldn't?

Night of the Living Dead (1968)

(Dir. George Romero; w/Duane Jones, Judith O'Dea, Karl Hardman, Marilyn Eastman)

✠ Zombies

George Romero's *Night of the Living Dead* is to horror cinema what Black Sabbath's self-titled 1970 debut album is to heavy metal: a decisive end point for all that had come before it and the starting line for a new era that is darker, deeper, and more multidimensional than any before it. When the proper array of forces converged to make the film and the band possible, the outcome in both cases was really fucking scary.

Maybe that green woman on the cover of *Black Sabbath* was one of the living dead? The link between *Black Sabbath* and *Night of the Living Dead* is so profound that the album can serve as an aural counterpoint to the movie—not really a soundtrack, per se, but a song-by-song parallel to the apocalyptic saga on-screen.

Start with "Black Sabbath": *Night of the Living Dead* opens with corny-looking siblings Barbara (Judith O'Dea) and Johnny (Russell Streiner).

Tall, goony Johnny taunts his sister with a ghoul moan, "They're coming for you, Barbara." Unfortunately, he's right. Zombie #1 (Bill Hinzman) shuffles up, cracks Johnny's head against a tombstone, and attempts to eat Barbara. She flees to a farm and flips out at the sight of a half-devoured cadaver. Ponder that alongside the song "Black Sabbath," with its cataclysmic tritone sounding an avalanche of unhappy possible outcomes, and lyrical references to supernatural figures of damnation spreading panic.

Next consider "The Wizard": As Barbara freezes at the sight of more zombies, Ben (Duane Jones) heroically appears, kicks some undead ass, and whisks her into the farmhouse, where other frightened people have hunkered down. Sabbath sings in "The Wizard" of a mystic figure whose charms and abilities uplift and empower all he encounters. Ben fills that role. He takes charge of fortifying the dwelling against zombie attacks, while confidently providing all those gathered with purpose and determination. When Barbara freaks out, he casts a spell on her the most direct way possible: knocking her unconscious so the rest of them can get some work done.

Moving along to "Behind the Wall of Sleep": While Barbara is comatose, the extent of the zombie dilemma becomes clear by way of news broadcasts and marauding ghouls trying to get at the band of survivors. One zombie takes a bite out of little girl Karen (Kyra Schon). Her parents, Harry (Karl Hardman) and Helen (Marilyn Eastman), stash her away in the basement, hoping to protect her from further injury. Words about a "sleeping wall of remorse" turning one's body to a corpse, coupled with "Behind the Wall of Sleep"'s charging groove provide a perfect comment on the ensuing grimness.

As far as "N.I.B." is concerned: After hearing about military-run rescue stations on TV, teenage couple Tom (Keith Wayne) and Judy (Judith Riley) aim to make a break for it. They don't get far. A fuel pump explodes and the zombies munch on barbecued adolescent, an act depicted in gory detail. The empty promises of Lucifer as detailed in "N.I.B." mirror the false hope for salvation and protection spewed by the state. Those who fall for offers made by the Father of Lies end up tormented by demons and consumed in hellfire. Tom and Judy fall prey to reanimated incisors and go up in a blaze of petroleum.

If your version of the first Sabbath album includes "Evil Woman," note that Armageddon invades the safe house by way of female appetite gone amok. Little Karen rises from death, famished for flesh, and she gnaws on the physical remains of her father. "Wickedness lies in your moistened lips," sings Ozzy on "Evil Woman."

Next up, "Sleeping Village": *Night of the Living Dead*'s climax is an onslaught of unthinkable carnage visited upon what, just a day earlier, was a pastoral country setting. Sabbath's lyrics in "Sleeping Village" are ironic, given the gothic storm of the music. Try playing it simultaneously with the wild action of the zombies carrying off Barbara and Ben shotgun-blasting the resurrected Helen and Harry.

And then comes the closing cataclysm of "Warning": *Night of the Living Dead*'s ending stands with the final moments *Planet of the Apes* (1968) and *The Wicker Man* (1973) as doom metal's definitive celluloid incarnation, plus it came first. Having made it through the titular dusk-to-dawn gauntlet, Ben waves to a law enforcement posse outside the farmhouse, shouting to let them know he's alive. Mistaking our hero for a zombie, they blow his head off. A jarring, surreal series of still photographs then shows Ben being tossed in a heap of other dead bodies and lit on fire. Given that imagery, and that message, there is nothing at all ironic about the title, or the message, of the song that ends the album Black Sabbath by Black Sabbath: "Warning."

Doom is doom is doom. Is doomed.

Again like Sabbath, *Night of the Living Dead* reset the parameters and possibilities of movies, igniting a revolution in newly extreme horror that carried on through *Last House on the Left* (1972), *The Exorcist* (1973), *The Texas Chainsaw Massacre*

(1974), *Halloween* (1978), its own sequel *Dawn of the Dead* (1979), and *Friday the 13th* (1980) along with the subsequent slasher cycle of the next half decade, culminating with *Re-Animator* (1985), *Return of the Living Dead* (1985), and *The Texas Chainsaw Massacre 2* (1986).

Classic heavy metal begins with Sabbath's debut and concludes sixteen years later with Slayer's *Reign in Blood*. Everything after sounds like part of a later generation. Timewise, Black Sabbath and *NOTLD* ran the same course, influencing everything in their paths, and both are still alive in the DNA of all metal and fright films.

Night of the Seagulls

(1975)

(Dir. Amando de Ossorio; w/Victor Petit, María Kosty, Susana Estrada)

✠ Zombies ✠ H. P. Lovecraft

The final film in the Blind Dead saga, *Night of the Seagulls* opens in the thirteenth century, as Knights Templar kill a young man and drag his girlfriend off to be sacrificed to their monstrous, fishlike deity. Flashing forward to 1975, Dr. Henry Stein (Victor Petit) and his wife Joan (María Kosty) move to a Spanish fishing village. Soon enough, they discover that for seven nights, every seven years, the now-zombified Knights Templar have risen from the dead to claim blood offerings from the townsfolk. That black magical week is just about to kick off. The locals intend to toss virginal Lucy (Sandra Mozarowsky) to the ghouls. The doctor aims to intervene.

As an improvement over 1974's *The Ghost Galleon*, *Night of the Seagulls* returns the Blind Dead—awesomely spooky skeletal figures in robes and hoods—to the Iberian seaside, where they reside in a Gothic castle, swing their swords, and ride bone-chilling blind horses along the beach—a rock-solid note on which to end the series.

Night of the Seagulls borrows heavily from the work of H. P. Lovecraft, in particular his stories "Dagon" and "Shadow Over Innsmouth," which

focus on sacrifices to a sea god. The seagull aspect—the locals believe the many gulls contain the souls of sacrificed maidens—is also reminiscent of the whippoorwills in Lovecraft's "The Dunwich Horror" who cry at night when spirits leave their bodies. Ever cognizant of all things relating to Dunwich and the blind dead, Cathedral stepped forward with their own rumbling blind-dead hymn "Night of the Seagulls."

The Night Stalker

(1972)

(Dir. John Llewellyn Moxey; w/Darren McGavin, Carol Lynley, Barry Atwater, Simon Oakland)

✠ Vampire

Gritty newspaperman Carl Kolchak (Darren McGavin) pursues a blood-draining serial killer along the Las Vegas strip. Kolchak's hunch is that the murderer is a vampire. Not only is he right, the vampire turns out to be ancient Romanian nobleman Janos Skorzeny (Barry Atwater), and it's up to Kolchak to take him out old-school.

McGavin's funny, unexpectedly courageous Kolchak, who always looks rumpled inside his fresh seersucker suits, is one of TV's great cult characters. *The Night Stalker* spawned a Seattle-set sequel, *The Night Strangler* (1974), wherein Kolchak battles an evil alchemist, and finally a short-lived, but severely beloved series, *Kolchak: The Night Stalker*. On the show, Kolchak operated in Chicago and took on zombies, witches, werewolves, and a headless motorcycle rider, among other variations on spook faves. He even had to squeeze out of a contract with Satan.

X-Files creator Chris Carter always credits *The Night Stalker* as one of his chief inspirations. In *Danse Macabre*, Stephen King lauds the TV series but questions Kolchak's journalistic skills. He points out that since Kolchak is battling a new supernatural monster every week, shouldn't he figure out that some kind of larger phenomenon is going on? Right there is the difference between *The Night Stalker* and *The X-Files*.

In popular consciousness, the term *night stalker* shifted in 1985 from describing Carl Kolchak to describing true-death serial slayer Richard Ramirez, who was given the nickname in the press. Ramirez was a harder-than-hard-core AC/DC fan who left a band-logo baseball cap at a crime scene and was especially taken with the song "Night Prowler." The media got the name of the song wrong, and the "Night Stalker" was born. Wolf, Anthem, Blitzkrieg, Hades, Cloven Hoof, Enthroned, Guillotine, and Skelator stepped forward with songs by that name.

₦IGHTMARE (1981), AKA ₦IGHTMARES IN A ĐAMAGED ฿RAIN; ฿LOOD ₷PLASH; ₷CHIZO
(DIR. ROMANO SCAVOLINI; W/BAIRD STAFFORD)
✴ SPLATTER ✴ BANNED VIDEO NASTY

Nightmare opens with mental patient George Tatum (Baird Stafford) being sprung from a nut hut and beating a fast path to a Times Square peep show. The vintage Forty-Second Street footage is simply dazzling and golden, popping with cheap sex and sleaze. While watching a fetching female performer attempt to do her thing in a whack shack, George succumbs to a seizure that has him foaming at the mouth. The violent episode is just the latest in his series of troubles—and everyone else's. Young George, we graphically see, caught his dad strapped to a bed while a dominatrix slapped him bloody. Unable to process the situation in any healthy manner, the young boy axed the two of them into tomato puree. As an adult, even the slightest sexual tension brings flashbacks to his secret boyhood hatchet tantrum, prompting George to kill and kill again. Officially a missing person, he slashes his way down to Daytona Beach, graphically killing all women and children in his path. The unsettling implication throughout is that George has been programmed to kill by the CIA for some sort of dirty trick. A greasy, cigar-smoking trench-coat type pushes heavily for George's capture.

Nightmare erupted into New York City theaters

the week before *Halloween* in 1981, raining blood and lashing out at audiences like a natural follow-up to Joe Spinell's landmark slasher outrage *Maniac* (1980). This loony, disjointed, English-as-an-alien-language slaughter-fest was an immediate mini-blockbuster. *Nightmare* topped local NYC box-office charts the weekend it opened and then played all the way into the summer of '82 before bouncing around the lower halves of grindhouse double features. From there, *Nightmare* lived on as big-box VHS rite-of-puke-passage for a spell before slipping into obscurity among all but the most die-hard psycho-killer movie devotees—many of whom are also heavy metal headbangers.

Maybe New York crowds liked the chaotic storytelling, or the over-the-top lurid performances. While Michael Myers in *Halloween* and later Jason Voorhees in the *Friday the 13th* sequels hid their homicidal impulses under impassive masks, lead actor Baird Stafford here appears to lose his mind completely in every third frame of film, with eyes bugging, and teeth clenched in a death grimace. Death metal supergroup the Ravenous, featuring members of Nuclear Assault, Autopsy, and Necrophagia, took note of this terrifying quality in the song "Nightmares in a Damaged Brain."

British censors quickly and prominently banned *Nightmare* as a "video nasty." They were alerted to the movie by two promotional gimmicks: a giveaway barf bag and a contest to guess the weight of a brain in a jar. Filmmakers who wish for the free publicity brought by a good censorship charge, take warning! Distributor World of Video 2000 went bankrupt after producer David Grant was jailed for a year in the U.K. for sneakily showing the film in theaters without making tiny cuts demanded by censors. Licensors in other countries were less foolish, and cut this film to varying running times. Today's fully restored editions are Frankensteins of film qualities, as seconds were salvaged from all generations and types of print.

Nightmare's poster and newspaper ads blatantly

Clockwise from top left: Night of the Living Dead, *Italian-style; the Blind Dead ride on a* German *Night of the Seagulls* one-sheet; *Max Schreck as* Nosferatu (1922), *still the creep's creep*

touted Tom Savini as "Special Effects Director." While Savini did provide some consultation to the filmmakers, he threatened to sue over so nervy a misrepresentation. By the time the distributor had to make the change though, the impression had already been made on the public that *Nightmare* was a pure Savini effort. Even mentioning the connection here contributes to poor Savini's headache!

A Nightmare on Elm Street (1984)

(Dir. Wes Craven; w/Robert Englund, Heather Langenkamp, John Saxon, Johnny Depp)

✷ Slasher ✷ Bogeyman

First with *Last House on the Left* (1972) and again with *The Hills Have Eyes* (1977), horror maven Wes Craven sporadically redefined the genre he had entered as a filmmaker only reluctantly. Craven never shook up the box office more apocalyptically, though, than when he unleashed razor-fingered bogeyman Freddy Krueger into humanity's collective *unconsciousness. Nightmare on Elm Street* arrived unheralded at the crest of the 1980s slasher movie cycle, when simple indestructible slicey-dicey masked maniacs populated grindhouse theaters and VHS machines. These killers and their flicks packed their own pleasures but became increasingly predictable. *Nightmare*, and its all-fears-to-all-victims antihero Freddy, was something terrifyingly original.

The *Elm Street* plot has transcended cinema to become a real part of American folklore. A series of bizarre, seemingly impossible splatter murders befalls teens in the vicinity of Elm Street. Each had been complaining of recurring nightmares involving a burnt-faced, knife-gloved slayer in a brown fedora and ratty striped sweater. Nancy (Heather Langenkamp), daughter of the local police chief (John Saxon), interacts with the phantom figure, named Freddy Krueger (Robert Englund), and learns that he was a child molester who escaped prison on a technicality, only to be burned alive by neighborhood parents.

A decade later, he returns to the kids' dreams to exact revenge. Nancy figures out a means of pulling Freddy into the waking world, and there they do battle in a setting where, as in a nightmare, anything is possible.

The shock of *Nightmare* came from its ferociously imaginative visuals (Nancy's phone turning into a tongue and slurping her mouth, Johnny Depp being eaten by his bed and vomited back up as a geyser of blood), a horribly logical storyline, and Craven's command of suspense.

Celebrated by the S.O.D. song "Freddy Krueger" months after the film's release, *Elm Street* tapped into classic fright films and fear archetypes. The movie also barreled ahead into uncharted territory via innovative special effects and a basic premise in which anything the mind could conceive could (and would) be played out before our eyes—as long as it was heavy and horrifying.

Freddy went on to become a homicidal stand-up comic promoting a cottage industry of collectibles in the *Elm Street* sequels; but the same could be said for the thrash metal that initially came to popularity alongside the *Elm Street* movies. For the original *Nightmare*'s ninety-one minutes, horror-loving metal fans got the teenage agony of Metallica, the supernatural ravages of Slayer, Megadeth's hatred of authority, and Anthrax's love of scary movies in one perfect cinematic firestorm—lorded over by an escapee of hell clawing his way into the minds of youth by way of solid metal appendages.

Nightmare is scariest when it goes most classically surreal. This is especially true during the first dream sequence when, out of the fog in a back alley, a bleating goat runs right toward us. Freddy then introduces himself by elongating his arms like the main character out of a *Plasticman* panel guest-illustrated by Salvador Dalí. (The goat would return in *Freddy vs. Jason* (2003).)

Alfred Hitchcock once explained that suspense is not surprising an audience, it's letting them know exactly what's coming and then forcing them to wait. Wes Craven understood that. At the moment when Nancy yanks Freddy out from her dream, she springs awake, and then it's a just a matter of time before Krueger pops up and dives for her. Anticipating that moment made me so tense that when Freddy finally appeared, I leapt up from my seat in Brooklyn's now-gone Kingsway Theater and crashed back down, twisting my ankle. Normally I'd have had to be caught in a mosh at L'Amour to get properly mangled by entertainment like that.

A Nightmare on Elm Street 3: Dream Warriors (1987)

(Dir. Chuck Russell; w/Robert Englund, Heather Langenkamp, Patricia Arquette, Craig Wasson)

✠ Slasher ✠ Bogeyman ✠ Soundtrack (Dokken, Bruce Dickinson)

After the misstep of 1985's *A Nightmare on Elm Street 2: Freddy's Revenge* (hilariously gay locker-room towel-snapping murder notwithstanding), key players from the first film returned to glory with *A Nightmare on Elm Street 3: Freddy's Revenge.* And they were also rockin' with Dokken, courtesy of the tightly melodic hair band's title song, "Dream Warriors." (Dokken's other great metal movie milestone is being the opening act for Judas Priest in *Heavy Metal Parking Lot.*)

Original Freddy killer Nancy (Heather Langenkamp) teams with Dr. Neil Gordon (Craig Wasson) to counsel teens in a mental health facility who are suffering Krueger dreams. The nightmares on-screen are triumphs of horrific imagination and brilliant practical-effects execution. They include Freddy yanking veins and tendons from a victim's limbs and making him dance like a marionette; the infamous razor gloves turning into syringes to deliver multiple hot shots to a reformed heroin addict; and a tour de force that begins with Dick Cavett turning into Freddy and attacking Zsa Zsa Gabor, ending with a Kruegerized TV set growing arms, grabbing Patricia Arquette, and "welcoming her to prime time" as a he slams her head through the screen. John Saxon returns as Nancy's sheriff father, battling Freddy's stop-motion-animated skeleton with a shovel in an auto graveyard.

We also learn Freddy's supremely metal origin from his mother, Amanda Krueger (Nan Martin), now a spooky nun—and maybe be a ghost. Years earlier (who knows how many), young Amanda was locked in a holding facility with scores of criminally insane degenerates. They gang-raped her for days on end, and nine months later, she birthed young Frederick—"the bastard son of a hundred maniacs."

Nightmare on Elm Street 3 climaxes with the surviving teens figuring out how to enter Freddy's non-waking world in order to "kick that motherfucker's ass all over dreamland." Freddy goes down hard but of course he gets the last wink, which is immediately followed by Dokken's "Dream Warriors" underscoring the closing credits. Nearly a decade into its existence, Dokken had proven to be a reliable mainstream metal presence, but a bona fide pop hit eluded them. "Dream Warriors" fixed that, largely by way of a music video in crazy rotation on MTV in which the band members defended Patricia Arquette from the various machinations of Freddy Krueger. At the end of the Dokken video, Freddy wakes up from slumber and shakes his head as though we've just been watching his nightmare. "Who *were* those guys?" he moans, holding his burned head. Ho, ho. Beavis and Butt-Head would eventually make great, sarcastic fun of that parting shot for all of us.

Dream Warriors is one of the great fright sequels, one of the most inventive films of any genre in the '80s, and a visceral embodiment of the spirit shared by heavy metal and horror movies. What a scream. One of the key factors in *Dream Warriors* is that Freddy Krueger is still scary. The movie is fun, and our antihero is given to wisecracks, but he's not yet the full-time supernatural serial killer turned Borscht Belt comedian he would become in *Elm Street 4.* Freddy remained in that jokester vein up until the hugely weird

Wes Craven's New Nightmare (1994).

A Nightmare on Elm Street 4: The Dream Master (1988) ditched metal for rap, turning over its hoped-for hit-single slot to the Fat Boys' "Are You Ready for Freddy?" Alas, the single sunk. Overall, the Dream Master soundtrack is a Top 40 hodgepodge featuring Billy Idol, Blondie, Sinead O'Connor, and the like. Vinnie Vincent and Love/Hate represent the metal front.

A Nightmare on Elm Street 5: The Dream Child (1989), the sole box-office disappointment in the series' lucrative run, divided its soundtrack entirely between metal and rap, with a track by busty Britpop tart Samantha Fox splitting the difference. Metallically, there's "Savage" by W.A.S.P., "Can't Take the Hurt" by Mammoth, "Heaven in the Back Seat" by Romeo's Daughter, and "Bring Your Daughter to the Slaughter" by Iron Maiden's Bruce Dickinson.

Iggy Pop assumed theme song duties for Freddy's Dead: The Final Nightmare (1991) via "Why Was I Born? (Freddy's Dead)." That soundtrack also includes the stalwart "In-A-Gadda-Da-Vida" by Iron Butterfly, and three songs by then–Metal Blade recording artists the Goo Goo Dolls.

NIGHTSTALKER (2002)
(DIR. CHRIS FISHER; W/BRET ROBERTS, ROSELYN SANCHEZ, JOSEPH MCKELHEER, DANNY TREJO)
✶ SERIAL KILLERS

Nightstalker plays loose with the facts regarding the mid-'80s serial murderer Richard Ramirez, and spins them off at the epileptic speed of a herky-jerky Marilyn Manson music video. Bret Roberts stars, both as Ramirez (although he's only called "Nightstalker"), and as the bald, white-painted demon that makes the screen rattle and apparently forces all those terrible crimes to get committed. Whereas the real Ramirez left an AC/DC baseball cap at a crime scene and professed affection for the band's spooky song "Night Prowler," Nightstalker features death metal by Crematorium and Defiled.

When it comes to famous serial killers, Richard

Ramirez, aka "the Night Stalker," is as metal as those creeps get. Survivors testified that Ramirez invoked Satan during his atrocities, and he drew pentagrams on some of his victims (at least once in lipstick). While on trial, Ramirez affirmed his religious affiliation by carving a pentagram in his own palm and occasionally shouting, "Hail Satan!" Metal bands in Germany and Greece repaid the tribute by naming themselves Nightstalker. The Ramirez phenomenon has also been examined in song by Cloven Hoof, Macabre, Phantasm, and, most thoughtfully, Hades.

THE NINTH GATE (1999)
(DIR. ROMAN POLANSKI; W/JOHNNY DEPP, FRANK LANGELLA, LENA OLIN, EMMANUELLE SEIGNER)
✶ SATAN ✶ OCCULT BOOKS ✶ BLACK MASS

Director Roman Polanksi returned to the occult realm of his 1968 masterpiece Rosemary's Baby for The Ninth Gate. Johnny Depp plays Dean Corso, a rare-book dealer who picks up an old tome reportedly written by Satan himself in the year 1666. When the volume's engravings are read properly, they will raise the author up from his fiery kingdom to visit you. Corso pursues the mystery of the book from New York to Spain to literally the final fence of the title, which separates Earth from the flaming pit of eternal suffering, a place made of stupid CGI flames. You know the term "boring as hell"? The Ninth Gate really makes you understand it.

Turns out that Depp and Polanski met at the Cannes Film Festival. Depp was promoting his loony, ultra-rare directorial debut The Brave (1997), in which he costars with Marlon Brando. It's about a Native American father who, to improve his family's financial lot, sells himself as on-camera talent to a maker of snuff films (Brando). Iggy Pop provides the soundtrack. Norway's blackened doom band Faustcoven summoned a brief tribute with the song "Ninth Gate."

No Code of Conduct (1998)

(Dir. Bret Michaels; w/Bret Michaels, Charlie Sheen, Martin Sheen)

✠ Metal Reality

Bret Michaels, lead headband of Poison and auteur/star of *A Letter From Death Row* (1998), returns—along with slumming *Death Row* paycheck-cashers Charlie and Martin Sheen. Unlike the Sheens' brief cameos in their first film with Michaels, Charlie stars here as a scandal-tarnished cop and Martin plays his no-nonsense lawman dad. Bret Michaels plays an undercover narc whose drug bust goes violently wrong (beneath late-'90s strobe lights) and sets in motion a standard direct-to-video police drama that lacks even subpar action sequences.

Criminally underused is Mark Dascascos as Charlie's partner. But do look out for a sleazeball named "Pappy." He's played by Joe Estevez, Martin's brother, Charlie and Emilio's uncle, and a modern B-movie stalwart. Joe might be the most metal of the whole lot. Charlie Sheen is credited with cowriting the script. You'll believe it.

Bret Michaels may not have panned out as much of a filmmaker, but have you tasted his "Bret's Blend Tea Trop-a-Rocka" iced tea that Snapple spun off from *Celebrity Apprentice*? It's delish. You'll open up and say . . . mmm!

The Norseman (1978)

(Dir. Charles B. Pierce; w/Lee Majors, Cornel Wilde, Mel Ferrer, Jack Elam, Susie Coehlo)

✠ Vikings ✠ Native Americans

The Lee Majors vehicle (and "Charles B. Pierce/Fawcett-Majors Production") *The Norseman* bears essentially the same plot as acclaimed filmmaker Nicolas Winding Refn's weighty, existential *Valhalla Rising* (2009): turn-of-the-first-millennium Vikings row their dragon boat to North America and run afoul of the native tribes. While I would never declare *The Norsemen* "better" than *Valhalla Rising*, the former stars the Six Million Dollar Man with a perfect bionic mustache alongside NFL legend Deacon Jones in a horned helmet. Together, they fight (slightly) extra-tan surfer dudes made up like Halloween party Indians. Metal has more than one mood. Choose your Norsemen accordingly.

Lee Majors' big screen follow-up to *The Norseman* cast him as the world's greatest construction worker who comes out of truck-driving retirement to assemble a "Magnificent Seven"–style team of bricklayers and pipe fitters. The 1979 film's title is quintessentially metal: *Steel*.

Nosferatu (1922), aka Nosferatu: A Symphony of Horror

(Dir. F. W. Murnau; w/Max Schreck, Gustav von Wangenheim, Greta Schroder, Alexander Granach)

✠ Vampire

The great F. W. Murnau's (*Satanas, Sehnsucht, Faust, Tabu*) German expressionist horror masterpiece *Nosferatu* is actually an unauthorized adaptation of Bram Stoker's blockbuster 1897 novel, *Dracula*. That's right—just as *Snakes on a Train* (2006) and *Transmorphers* (2007) hit DVD before *Snakes on a Plane* (2006) and *Transformers* (2007) opened in theaters, *Nosferatu* was the result of its studio failing to secure the rights to *Dracula* and then just making the movie anyway and calling it something different. Granted, the leap from Count Dracula to Count Orlok and from the term *vampire* to *nosferatu* represents a small creative step, but it's the same story, same castle, same coffin, and same creep factor. As much as *Nosferatu* helped itself to *Dracula*'s specifics, the movie introduced the notion that sunlight kills vampires. That idea quickly became part of the folklore.

Murnau's visionary direction and the the terrifying lead performance by Max Schreck as the chrome-domed, bug-eyed, devil-eared, fang-faced, claw-fingered Orlok conjure a the most hideously metal vision of bloodsucking nobility. *Nosferatu* has endured as an icon on album art, flyers, stickers, and T-shirts. Nearly one hundred metal songs have been titled "Nosferatu," by bands including Jag Panzer, Hellwitch, Solace, English Dogs, God Forbid, Coroner, Helstar, and a lot more. *Nosferatu* haunts metal's bloody gothic doom aesthetic, a fact made especially powerful when you realize that many who continue to employ Schreck's soul-starved visage don't even know from where it originated. They just know he's the fuckin' heaviest.

Nosferatu: The First Vampire (1998) makes the most of this film's expired copyright and shrewd soundtrack marketing by "remastering" the movie and adding a fully licensed suite of previously released songs by Type O Negative.

The film *Shadow of the Vampire* (2000) fictionalizes the making of *Nosferatu* and proposes that the power of Schreck's performance stems from him being an actual undead bloodsucker. It's a fun movie with John Malkovich as F. W. Murnau and Willem Dafoe as Schreck, directed by E. Elias Merhige (*Begotten*).

ᚿosferatu the ᚢampyre (1979)

(Dir. Werner Herzog; w/Klaus Kinski, Isabelle Adjani, Bruno Ganz, Roland Topor)
✠ Vampires

Germany's premier contemporary filmmaker, Werner Herzog, casts the country's all-time most intense (not to mention insane) screen icon, Klaus Kinski, as the lead in *Nosferatu the Vampyre*, a highly stylized reimagining of the 1922 silent masterpiece that put Teutonic expressionism on the map. F. W. Murnau's original *Nosferatu* implanted an undead bloodsucking count from Transylvania into our collective nightmares. Herzog's version pays tribute to the first movie and takes into account what the most famous vampire had become in the decades since.

Kinski, as Count Dracula, re-creates the famous

bald, pointy-eared, razor-toothed, claw-fingered character invented, indelibly, by Max Schreck. But he's Klaus Kinski, so this vampire is all his own. Kinski proves himself a demented deity of Heavy Metal Movies. Werner Herzog worked with him repeatedly, often literally risking his life to do so. Do not miss Herzog's posthumous documentary on their storied, masterwork-producing friendship, *My Best Fiend* (1999).

Nosferatu the Vampyre's renowned electronic score by krautrock band Popol Vuh pulsates with the same tightly bolted musical tension that runs through German metal bands from Scorpions to Sodom to Kreator to Helloween to Rammstein. Meanwhile, the fog, the fancy dress, and the almost painful nudity bring to mind early Iron Maiden, in the era of their first two albums, when they were strictly a horror metal band and, just like this film, in a league of their own.

ᚿova ᚱex: ᚨin't ᚬasy ᚤeing ᚿheesy (2011)

(Dir. Dean Robinson; w/J. P. Cervoni, Kevin Tetz, Kenny Wilkerson, Mark Wolfson)
✠ Glam Metal

For a hot, hair-hopped minute in the 1980s, Nova Rex was the biggest glam metal band in Indianapolis. All these years later, *Nova Rex: Ain't Easy Being Cheesy* assembles home videos and new interviews with the group members into a passably professional documentary that recounts the exploits of guys who maybe could have been metal contenders—if they had ever gotten around to contending. Director Dean Robinson published the hard rock magazine *HiJinx* from 1989 to 1994. Nova Rex bassist Kenny Wilkerson is a Florida tanning salon kingpin these days. That's got to be like drawing a "Get Out of Glam Metal Free" card.

THE OBSESSED: THE CHURCH WITHIN (1994)

(DIR. BRIDGET T. ROY; W/SCOTT "WINO" WEINRICH, GUY PINHAS, GREG ROGERS)

✤ DOOM METAL ✤ WASHINGTON, D.C.

The half-hour promotional VHS production *The Obsessed: The Church Within* was created during the band's brief stint with Columbia Records. The aim was to bring the music world up to speed on the band, with testimony from members of Fugazi, L7, the Melvins, Gumball, Pantera, Cathedral, C.O.C., White Zombie, and Henry Rollins. Tesco Vee of the Meatmen, Tom Lyle of Government Issue, and a slew of other surprisingly non-metal voices chime in on the band's legend.

Henry Rollins (Black Flag/Rollins Band) and Ian MacKaye (Minor Threat/Fugazi) dominate the film's narrative, recounting funny, scary stories of how the Obsessed won over the chrome-domed D.C. hardcore scene at a time when long-haired metal was viewed as the ultimate enemy. They wax rapturously about how, as teenagers, they were terrified, awestruck, and charmed by

Obsessed frontman and guitar monster Scott "Wino" Weinrich. Colorful contributions also arrive from Melvins drummer Dale Crover, Phil Anselmo during his Pantera days, and L7 bassist Jennifer Finch, who reveals that drummer Greg Rogers taught her how to say "Your eyelashes look like the hairs on my butt" in Spanish.

Truly to be treasured is a glimpse of Wino's pre-Obsessed band Warhorse playing at a Maryland high school in 1978. As expected, the band is mammoth and righteous. Afterward, a teen jock huffs, "I'd rather go grocery shopping with my mother than watch that concert. You gotta be a big freak to watch that concert!" A long-haired stoner counters, "It was jammin', you know. It's our type of music, not old fogey music, not disco. It's just the right kind of music." Right on!

THE OLD DARK HOUSE (1932)

(DIR. JAMES WHALE; W/BORIS KARLOFF, MELVYN DOUGLAS, CHARLES LAUGHTON, EVA MOORE)

✤ HAUNTED HOUSE

Director James Whale and actor Boris Karloff followed up their terror landmark *Franken-*

Clockwise from top left: *Charlton Heston is legend in* The Omega Man; *Harvey Spencer Stephens as little devil Damien in* The Omen *(1976); Richard Harris raises a harpoon in vain against* Orca

stein (1931) with *The Old Dark House*, a horror comedy that became tremendously influential. The movie still works because the scary parts are really scary, and the funny parts are really funny, and examples litter the horror landscape with warnings about how easy it is to bungle those two essential ingredients.

In the midst of a late-night downpour in rural Wales, five travelers led by army veteran Roger (Melvyn Douglas) seek shelter in the aged, unlit structure. The ghoulish, speechless butler Morgan (Karloff) greets them, and they learn that the estate belongs to the Femm family. The Femms, whom they meet one by one, are a bunch of spine-tingling, bone-chilling, rib-tickling creeps.

Virtually all movies about innocents accidentally trapped in a spooky mansion filled with malevolent eccentrics are spun directly from the template of *The Old Dark House*. Perhaps the most famous such descendent, *The Rocky Horror Picture Show* (1975), sticks close enough to the specifics to essentially count as a parody. *The Old Dark House* is one of Phil Anselmo's top ten horror films, and also the subject of the song "Old Dark House" by Raven Bitch.

THE OMEGA MAN (1971)
(DIR. BORIS SAGAL; W/CHARLTON HESTON, ANTHONY ZERBE, ROSALIND CASH, LINCOLN KILPATRICK)
✣ POST-APOCALYPSE ✣ MUTANTS ✣ LAST MAN ALIVE

Smack between *Planet of the Apes* (1968) and *Soylent Green* (1973), *The Omega Man* is the middle chapter in Charlton Heston's heavy metal sci-fi trilogy supreme. Chuck plays Colonel Robert Neville, an L.A. scientist who survived the biological warfare that apparently wiped out the rest of earth's human population. As a plague hit, Neville injected himself with an experimental serum and it worked. Now, in 1977, he hunkers down in a fortified bunker. For kicks, he tries on leisure suits in empty Hollywood stores and watches the *Woodstock* movie repeatedly in an empty theater. The crowd scenes, depicting hundreds of thousands of fresh faces frolicking

at the famous concert in lovely Bethel, New York, connect him to humanity and bring him to tears.

What survivors do exist are albino mutants who have formed a cult called the Family, centered on charismatic leader Matthias (Anthony Zerbe). The Family hates any remnants of how life used to be, and so all they want to do is burn Colonel Neville at the stake on the pitcher's mound in Dodger Stadium. Foxy black chick Lisa (Rosalind Cash) rescues Neville from the Family and takes him to a hidden band of humans who are infected with the plague but have not yet mutated. Neville's challenge is to re-create the healing serum from his own blood in order to cure his new friends and, possibly, transform the Family members back into healthy people. The Family is happy as is, and a final battle storms up.

Everything carries on in dizzy metal spirit, with superior execution. The ending will test of your last strand of sanity. Neville looks up at a balcony and finally gets Matthias in the crosshairs of his machine gun. His weapon jams, though, and Matthias wings a spear at Neville, which pierces the colonel smack in the right-side rib cage. He falls back into a fountain, mortally wounded. With his last breath, Neville hands a human cohort a flask of his blood serum, from which medicine can be made to heal any other survivors. Having saved humanity with the gift of his blood, Neville collapses with his arms outstretched and dies in a full cruciform position. *The Omega Man* goes, in that moment, from one of the great doom metal movies to the single greatest Christian metal movie of all eternity.

The Omega Man is based on the 1954 novel *I Am Legend*. The first movie adaptation of the book is *The Last Man on Earth* (1964) with Vincent Price, which is creepy and great. The most recent version was *I Am Legend* (2007) with Will Smith. Famously right-wing Charlton Heston was an outspoken advocate of civil rights in the 1960s. He marched in demonstrations with Martin Luther King and believed that racial equality was perfectly in keeping with his other conservative values. His interracial sex scene with Rosalind

Cash in *The Omega Man* ruffled the expected feathers, but certainly not Chuck's. In his monumental 1995 autobiography *In the Arena*, though, Heston states that it even gave Cash herself some whim-whams, due to her having grown up watching him in iconic movies such as 1956's *The Ten Commandments*. Heston writes that Cash told him: "It's a spooky feeling to screw Moses."

THE OMEN (1976)

(DIR. RICHARD DONNER; W/GREGORY PECK, LEE REMICK, DAVID WARNER, HARVEY SPENCER STEPHENS)

✠ ANTICHRIST

The cultural Satan-mania ignited by *The Exorcist* begat not only a cottage industry of cheap exploitation rip-offs, but also *The Omen*, a big-budget prestige production that proved to be 20th Century Fox's top blockbuster prior to the subsequent summer's *Star Wars* (1977). Whereas *The Exorcist* is a serious-minded exercise in doom aesthetics and philosophy, *The Omen* is hotheaded power metal bordering on camp. Each film executes its own heavy milieu perfectly.

In the weeks leading up *The Omen*'s release, the saturation TV and radio ad campaign was inescapable. "Good morning," the commercials intoned. "You are now one day closer to the end of the world." Waking up to that was really scary.

Hollywood legend Gregory Peck stars as Ambassador Robert Thorn, the USA's man in London. His wife, Katherine (Lee Remick), gives birth to a son, the baby dies immediately, and a priest convinces Thorn to take home a newborn whose destitute mother died in childbirth. Nobody tells Katherine. They name the changeling Damien. All's kosher with Damien (Harvey Spencer Stephens) until his fifth birthday. His grand backyard party gets pooped when the boy's noose-adorned nanny (Holly Palance, daughter of Hollywood ass-kicker Jack Palance) emerges on a ledge above the festivities and announces: "Look at me, Damien! It's ALL for you!" She then leaps forward, hangs herself, and crashes through a window. The replacement nanny, Mrs. Baylock

(Billie Whitelaw), is even weirder, a diabolically dour old crone constantly accompanied by a monstrous Rottweiler.

As similarly odd occurrences mount, a priest (Patrick Troughton) and a photographer (David Warner) piece together that Damien is the son of Satan as predicted in the Bible's Book of Revelations. He is the Antichrist who will bring with him Armageddon and the end of our world. The elder Thorn initially scoffs his best Gregory Peck scoff, but once normal boyhood mischief turns freaky (Damien scares zoo baboons) and perilous (he shatters his mother's back with his tricycle), the ambassador gets on board.

The quest to kill Damien with the seven daggers of Megiddo brings with it several more iconic horror high points: the grave-robbing discovery that Damien's birth mother was a jackal; a sheet of glass sliding slowly off the back of a truck and decapitating the photographer; the discovery of a 666 birthmark on Damien's scalp, and the final shot of Damien, triumphant, turning to the camera; looking right at us, and smiling. That little literal son of a bitch (and son of Satan) rules.

Blue-eyed, chubby-cheeked Harvey Spencer Stephens, as Damien, says few words, but delivers one of the most enduring performances in horror. He is a cherubic tyke, and also a menace. Stephens auditioned for the part when he was four. To see if he could convincingly pull off the role's rough stuff, director Richard Donner said, "Can you beat me up?" The boy launched himself into the task, making sure to deliver a haymaker to Donner's testicles. He got the part.

Jerry Goldsmith's score is a masterwork of neoclassical foreboding and terror. The movie's theme song, "Ave Satana" ("Hail Satan"), is pure metal mayhem, and features Latin chanting that translates roughly as "We drink the blood, we eat the flesh, raise the body of Satan." Goldsmith conducted a performance of the piece at the 1977 Academy Awards, complete with smoke, chains, and demonic female dancers. He rightly went home that night with an Oscar. Countless metal bands, albums, and songs named after Damien,

Damien Thorn, and *The Omen* draw directly from this score.

The Omen is one of Hollywood's supposedly "cursed" movies. Numerous lightning mishaps plagued the cast and crew, and the animal handler went on to be eaten by lions. Eeriest of all was an August 1976 car accident involving special effects artist John Richardson. His female passenger was decapitated in much the same way that David Warner gets beheaded in the movie—an effect Richardson created. It happened on Friday the 13th.

Despite all-grown-up Harvey Spencer Stephens making a cameo as a tabloid journalist, there is no need to see the useless 2006 remake of *The Omen*. Void of all charm, the movie was made solely to cash in on the highly marketable release date June 6, 2006—6/6/6, get it?

⍟MEN ⅢⅠ: ⍦HE ⍦INAL ⍊ONFLICT (1981)

(DIR. GRAHAM BAKER; W/SAM NEILL, DON GORDON, ROSSANO BRAZZI)

✠ ANTICHRIST ✠ BLACK MASS

Omen III: The Final Conflict opens with a bravura montage of dialogue-free storytelling that traces the route of the daggers of Megiddo—the weapons necessary to kill the Antichrist—from a construction dig in Chicago where a worker pawns them to a monastery in Italy where a monk prays over them. Alas, then people start talking, and *Omen III* pretty much goes to hell—but not in the way you hope.

Now thirty-two, Antichrist-in-waiting Damien Thorn (Sam Neill) is a billionaire businessman who is appointed U.S. ambassador to Great Britain (his earthly stepfather's old gig). Fully embracing his satanic origins and apocalyptic mission, Damien performs Black Mass rituals in his lair and organizes a cabal of mesmerized disciples. A second Star of Bethlehem tips off Damien that a new Christ child is on the way, prompting him to take aggressive action. The

Italian monks with the knives of Megiddo, meanwhile, chase Damien around trying to shank him when he's not looking. *Omen III*'s sole saving grace is its hilarious anticlimax. Damien strolls through a cathedral courtyard, calling out Jesus for a fight. "I'm here, Nazarene," he bellows. "Where are you? It's time! Show yourself!"

The Son of God casts a shadow. The Son of Satan is taken aback just long enough for his girlfriend to become a literal backstabber by Megiddo-knifing him in the heart from behind. We get a quick, reassuring look at the giant, glowing Jesus, and then some Bible quotes flash on the screen. End of apocalypse. Until the TV movie *Omen IV: The Awakening* (1991).

⍟NE ⍙AN ⍙ETAL, ⍢ARTS 1 AND 2 (2012)

(DIR. J. R. ROBINSON; W/J. R. ROBINSON, JEF WHITEHEAD, RUSSELL MENZIES, SCOTT CONNOR)

✠ BLACK METAL

The three-part *Vice* production *One Man Metal* documents three men its narrator describes as black metal's "true loners—artists who play all their own instruments and don't just scream about isolation and misanthropy, they live it." *Part One* and *Part Two*, running fifteen minutes apiece, paint gripping portraits of three one-man black metal band subjects: Leviathan, Striborg, and Xasthur. The stark cinematography, appropriately, bludgeons in black-and-white.

First up is burly, bearded Oakland tattoo artist Jef Whitehead, who records as Leviathan. Whitehead came up through the skateboard world and has performed under the name Wrest in numerous bands. Leviathan is the result, he says, of always being in bands he just wished would play harder and sound more punishing.

Striborg, aka Russell Menzies, aka Sin Nonna, is next. Living and recording on a farm in Tasmania, Menzies takes *Vice* correspondent J. R. Robinson on a hike through a nearby, majestically lush woodland. Striborg, he says, is just the medium to convey what exists there: "My guitar would be the mists, the frost, the snow; drums would be the heart of the land, the trees and the rocks and certain things like that; the vocals are like the voice of the forest. Atmosphere is important, nothing else matters."

Finally, we meet Scott Connor, the L.A.-area recluse who records as Xasthur. Revealing his face on camera for the first time and emotionally on guard, Connor is bald and pasty and comes off as tragically depressed. One observation Connor makes is haunting: "I don't recall ever making claims I can't back up in my lyrics, like 'I'm going to kill myself.' I don't do that. Instead, I just say, 'Hey, you know, here's a few reasons for you listening to this—you might want to look into dying and killing yourself.'" Then again, after checking out Xasthur's one-room world in *One Man Metal*, you probably feel okay about soldiering on for another day.

Director and on-screen interviewer J. R. Robinson is himself a one-man sonic assault artist. Based in Chicago, he records and performs as Wrekmeister Harmonies, creating aural whirlwinds of blackly metallic soundscapes.

One Man Metal Part 3 was delayed by Jef Whitehead facing a thirty-four count indictment for sexually assaulting his girlfriend in 2011, which the *Chicago Sun-Times* reported thusly: "A tattoo artist raped his girlfriend using tattoo tools above a near West Side tattoo parlor, authorities allege." In 2012, Whitehead was ultimately convicted only of a single count of aggravated domestic battery and received two years probation.

ORCA (1977), AKA ORCA: THE KILLER WHALE

(DIR. MICHAEL ANDERSON; W/RICHARD HARRIS, CHARLOTTE RAMPLING, BO DEREK, WILL SAMPSON)

✠ ANIMAL UPRISING ✠ NATIVE AMERICANS

Tinseltown titan Dino De Laurentiis, pumped from the triumph of his crackpot 1976 *King Kong* remake, cast his money nets toward the oceanic box-office records of *Jaws* (1975). The result: *Orca*, a fabulously ludicrous rip-off that, for sheer foot-stomping, beer-through-the-nose-squirting laughs and raucous metal insanity, simply devours its source of inspiration. At issue immediately is that killer whales, despite their name, are never scary, but rather are *always* adorable. Witness the hilarious opening segment, as this movie's killer-whale protagonist ("Orca") frolics and makes undersea love to his lady whale in tune to Ennio Morricone's lilting score.

Sexy scientist Dr. Rachel Belford (Charlotte Rampling) attempts to circumvent this crippling cuteness by lecturing on the killer whale's rows of teeth and claiming that the ancient Romans called the beasts "the bringer[s] of death." No, they did not. They saw them and went, "Awwww," just like the rest of us. Much more threatening is crusty old salt Captain Nolan (acting and drinking legend Richard Harris), who aims to capture a killer whale and peddle it to an aquarium. First, Nolan and his crew (Robert Carradine, Keenan Wynn, and Bo Derek) battle a great white shark, and get saved by Orca! Then the ungrateful humans set their sights on Orca himself.

Nolan helpfully nicks Orca in the fin with a harpoon, so we'll always know exactly which whale is on-screen, but the business end of the weapon ends up in the extremely pregnant Mrs. Orca. Rather than give birth in captivity, she throws herself into the boat's propeller. The screen goes red and the soundtrack squeals a lot. Trying to save the momma whale, Harris hoists her up on deck by the tail and—you will not believe you are seeing what you are seeing—Mrs. Orca erupts into spontaneous whale abortion, expelling her disturbingly humanoid fetus onto the boat. In a panic, Harris power-hoses the miscarriage over the side. In the heat of the melee, we see two close-ups on Orca's eye. First, he sheds a tear. Then the image of Harris appears on Orca's cornea, and the whale blinks, as though taking a picture, committing this scurvy-looking case of late-stage alcoholism to memory. Revenge is inevitable. And amazing. And hilarious.

Orca spends the rest of the movie sinking boats, knocking shit down, annihilating the local fish supply, blowing up the little seaside down where his wife and kid got killed, and thereby pressuring Nolan to come out and give chase. The final pursuit seems to lead to the actual North Pole. Keenan Wynn doesn't make it. Carradine doesn't make it. Bo Derek's leg doesn't even make it—as Orca wreaks some havoc on Nolan's waterfront property, Bo breaks her shin bone. Later, on the boat, Orca finishes the job by jumping up and chomping off Bo's cast-encased limb, then swimming away with the bleeding stump like he stole a french fry. After some passion amidst the icebergs, Nolan and Orca have it out.

The highest-profiled of the highly metal 1970s eco-horror cycle, *Orca* is also the most solidly entertaining of its vengeful-wildlife brethren. Among the others: *Night of the Lepus* (1972), *Food of the Gods* (1976), *Day of the Animals* (1977), and *Kingdom of the Spiders* (1977). Will Sampson, riding out his popularity as Chief from *One Flew Over the Cuckoo's Nest* (1975), appears in Orca as Umilak, a Native American local with many mystical revelations to share about homicidal sea life. Also in 1977, Sampson costarred as Crazy Horse alongside Charles Bronson as Wild Bill Hickok in *The White Buffalo*. Horns up.

In terms of plot, *Orca* is really a variation on *Moby-Dick*, using *Jaws* as a moneymaking template. In promoting the film, Richard Harris resented any comparisons between *Orca* and *Jaws*, throwing colorful tantrums before reporters. Mr. Harris was known to imbibe daily about the amount of fluid that remains constantly on-screen in *Orca*—only he wasn't chugging water.

Herman Melville's cosmically proportioned novel *Moby-Dick* is one of the great wellsprings of heavy metal inspiration, most explicitly in the form of the 2004 concept album *Leviathan* by Mastodon. Many attempts have been made to film the epic tale of a mad Captain Ahab piloting his ship to ruin in lethally reckless pursuit of the white whale who ate his leg, The 1956 Technicolor adaptation directed by John Huston (*The Maltese Falcon*) and written by Ray Bradbury (*Fahrenheit 451*) does the best job.

Outlaw of Gor (1989), aka Outlaw; Gor II

(Dir. John "Bud" Carlos; w/Urbano Barberini, Rebecca Ferratti, Russel Savadier, Jack Palance)

✠ Swords & Sorcery ✠ Cannon Films

The second adaptation of John Norman's sadomasochistic sci-fi series of *Gor* space-sex novels, *Outlaw of Gor* hurls physics professor Tarl Cabot (Urbano Barberini) and his lovelorn pal Watney (Russel Savadier) back to Gor—a PG-13 world of rocks, wizards, and limitless access to sexy submissive slave girls. *Outlaw of Gor* is cheaply funny, but forgettable enough except for the interloping of that enemy of all things worthwhile in cinema: *Mystery Science Theater 3000*. *MST3K* featured *Outlaw of Gor* under the title *Outlaw*. My raging hatred toward that nonsense knows no depth. Having three jerk-offs make fun of wild, inventive, endlessly entertaining movies that didn't adhere to their idea of "proper" standards is the equivalent of having *Rolling Stone* critics or Pitchfork bloggers go through your record collection and fake-laugh loudly at every mention of Satan or dragons or violent mass nuclear Armageddon. Fuck that; fuck them.

Over the Edge (1979)

(Dir. Jonathan Kaplan; w/Matt Dillon, Vincent Spano, Pamela Ludwig, Michael Kramer)

✠ Youth Gone Wild ✠ Metal Reality
✠ Soundtrack (Van Halen, Ramones, Hendrix)

"A kid who tells on another kid is a dead kid." Inspired by a 1973 incident in a planned community outside of San Francisco, *Over the Edge* was actually filmed in Greeley, Colorado, less than an hour's drive from where the Columbine High School massacre would take place in 1999.

New Granada is a "planned community" in a Colorado with everything its residents could want—except for anything at all that appeals to its massive teenage population. As a result, the kids go berserk with boredom and frustration, feeling like rodents locked in a maze that is itself trapped inside a prefabricated prison. In fact, the original title of director Jonathan Kaplan's downbeat (yet inspiring) youth-in-revolt masterpiece was *Mouse Packs*, named for a magazine article about an actual teen crime spree that screenwriter Tim Hunter thought would make a good jumping-off point for what he deemed "an exploitation movie." Although created with a drive-in market in mind, *Over the Edge* transcends such classification, having endured now as a rite of passage for three generations and counting who see themselves in drunk, stoned, mad-as-hell dead-end young hotheads coming of rage in a middle-class paradise.

Left to their own devices, New Granada's youth gravitate toward destruction. The movie opens with Richie (Matt Dillon) and Claude (Vincent Spano) shooting a BB gun at a cop car belonging to vicious Officer Doberman (Carl Northup), then getting busted for carrying a knife. When plans for a drive-in theater and a bowling alley are soon revealed to have fallen by the wayside, tension rises from simmering to bubbling. A ramshackle youth center is all the kids have, and the authorities want to close that, as it basically functions as a hub for drug dealing and plotting petty crimes. The kids are left, then, to sneak booze, get high, break stuff, and physically attack one another to hard rock blaring from boom boxes. The only real fun they have comes from utterly vandalizing unsold tract homes. The incidents escalate until Richie points a gun at Doberman and Doberman points his back and fires.

An emergency PTA meeting is called at the local high school. Once the town's parents, teachers, policemen, and lowlife business leaders are inside, the kids lock the doors shut with bicycle chains and rage with abandon in the parking lot—smashing cars, burning tires, destroying anything they can tear down, and threatening to torch the entire adult population. Few movie scenes have ever been as simultaneously uplifting and terrifying.

As with another movie about teen freaks battling the man, *Billy Jack* (1971), *Over the Edge* works through its tragedies to conclude on a note of hope. The "ringleaders" of the New Granada rebellion get carted off to a juvenile detention facility called the Hill, but as their bus leaves town, the kids they left behind line up to wave and cheer and show their support. The heavy metal '80s lie just ahead.

Having readied the film for release directly in the wake of gang violence at theaters showing *The Warriors* (1979), Orion Pictures panicked about *Over the Edge* generating copycat incidents. Orion's solution was to dump the movie on a handful of screens and sell it as horror—complete with ads showing the eyes of the young cast whited out to zombielike effect. Then, for two years, *Over the Edge* sat on a shelf. In 1981, it was shown at a festival of "lost" films at the Public Theater in New York, earning a rave review in the *New York Times* and finding new life via HBO and home video. As with the heavy metal music of its day, the exact kids who needed to see *Over the Edge*, and who loved it, made sure to keep it alive and keep passing it along.

With its metal feel and metal themes (and even its near-metal soundtrack), *Over the Edge* works as an '80s youth-gone-vile bookend with the even harder-hearted *River's Edge*, directed by this film's cowriter Tim Hunter. Based just on those two titles, Hunter concocted a perfectly hurtful and heartfelt antidote to the overprivileged suburban teen world of the John Hughes movies (*Sixteen Candles*, *The Breakfast Club*, *Pretty in Pink*).

Over the Edge is fourteen-year-old Matt Dillon's first film. He was discovered at an upper-middle-class high school in Westchester County, New York, where a talent scout asked what his parents did for a living. Dillon shot back, "My father's a fuckin' stockbroker, and my mom, she don't do shit." He got the part, and turned it into not-quite-instant stardom.

Ozzy Osbourne: Don't Blame Me (1991)

(Dir. Jeb Brien; w/Ozzy Osbourne, Alice Cooper, Lemmy Kilmister, Black Sabbath, Mötley Crüe)

✠ Metal History ✠ Concert Footage

The slick video documentary *Ozzy Osbourne: Don't Blame Me* traces metal's foremost madman from birth to his No More Tears tour, then being touted as his last. The package includes twenty-four songs; cool insight into Black Sabbath forming as heavy blues hippies Earth; the legal dirt on a the case in which "Suicide Solution" was blamed for a young man killing himself; and a genuinely moving segment on the 1981 death of Ozzy's daredevil guitarist Randy Rhoads, during which Lemmy reminisces about the fun he had consistently beating his late friend Rhoads at the video game Asteroids.

Caveat banger: The DVD edition of *Don't Blame Me* runs shorter than the original VHS, with various edits made throughout. Shell out for the tape on eBay.

Ozzy Osbourne: The Prince of F*?$!@# Darkness (2002)

(Dirs. Various; w/Ozzy Osbourne, Tony Iommi, Geezer Butler, Bill Ward, Rob Halford)

✠ Metal History

Rushed out by questionable DVD purveyors Brentwood Video to cash in on MTV's *The Osbournes*, the quickie *Ozzy Osbourne: The Prince Of F*?$!@# Darkness* assembles interviews, performances, and other odds and sods into an artless biography. No new insights will be gleaned, but there's some cool and unusual material such as Black Sabbath being awarded a place on Hollywood's Rock Wall of Fame. Even for the prince, it's not all f*?$!@# darkness. This quasi-legal video is worth hunting down for the inclusion of a super-rare making-of promo, created in 1986

to be played in video stores to promote heavy metal horror classic *Trick or Treat*, wherein Ozzy plays a rock-hating televangelist. It's a pure f*?$!@# treat.

PAGAN METAL: A DOCUMENTARY (2009)

(DIR. BILL ZEBUB; W/PRIMORDIAL, ENSIFERUM, FINNTROLL, KORPIKLAANI, TURISAS, TYR)
✶ PAGAN METAL ✶ CONCERT FOOTAGE

One-head banging machine Bill Zebub turns his slapdash but entertaining filmmaking techniques toward the alternately airy-faerie and swordy-slashy realms of Europe's burgeoning pagan metal underground. The title *Pagan Metal: A Documentary* is slightly misleading—no in-depth exploration is offered for this occult-folk/hard-rock hybrid. Still, the interviews and performance footage are inherently valuable raw materials. And *raw* describes the operative approach in this rough-hewn enchanted forest.

Of particular interest are the rivalries and clannishness that emerge from various interviews.

The Finnish groups insist pagan metal is a Finn phenomenon. The Swedes and Irish and everybody else have different ideas. Nationalism and anti-immigrant emotion bubble under a fair deal of the chatter—sometimes amusingly, sometimes uncomfortably, especially for the band members themselves. The common spiritual thread among these seekers seems to be spirits themselves, as in booze! Tales of Finland's ancient drinking culture alone make *Pagan Metal* worth a mighty flagon of *glögg*.

PAGANINI HORROR (1989)

(DIR. LUIGI COZZI; W/DONALD PLEASENCE)
✶ PAGANINI ✶ '80s ITALIAN SPLATTER HORROR

Italian violinist Niccolo Paganini was to nineteenth-century classical music what Eddie Van Halen was to late-1970s guitar rock: an unprecedented phenom whose technical virtuosity and wild innovation redefined the powers of his instrument. The fiery fiddler was also the original Black Sabbath, as fevered performances and uncanny techniques earned him the nicknames "Devil's Son" and "Witch's Brat." Stupefied audiences stumbled off, convinced such skills could only arise from a pact with Satan.

On top of his flamboyant approach to violin, Paganini boozed, smoked, snorted snuff, and banged scores of groupies, truly cementing his reputation as Europe's first rock star. He eventually crashed and burned in Paris after opening the Casino Paganini, which went bust. Upon dying in 1840, he was denied a sanctioned burial by the Catholic Church, which was still skittish about his demonic talents. All this lore is natural grist for a rip-roaring heavy metal splatter movie, particularly from Paganini's home country during its decade of gore-geyser dominance.

In *Paganini Horror*, an all-girl rock group aches for a hit, so they buy mysterious sheet music from the extremely drunk Mr. Pickett (Donald Pleasence—Method acting, I'd wager) and hire a horror flick director (Pietro Genuardi) to shoot their music video in a spooky mansion owned by a sinister landlady (Daria Nicolodi). "'No one else has ever done anything like this before,' one of the rock babes declares, "except for Michael Jackson and 'Thriller,' and his fantastic video clip!"

The new tune tops even "Thriller" by awakening the homicidal ghost of Niccolo Paganini, who then hunts them down and dispatches them to various blood-spraying degrees by way of his razor-sharp violin bow. Unfortunately, writer-director Luigi Cozzi (*Contamination*, and both Lou Ferrigno *Hercules* movies) is all fumble-fingers, producing a succession of sour notes squawked out, boringly, on broken strings. Paganini himself deserves a horror movie that's better than this one—or at least truly bad.

The same year as *Paganini Horror*, titanic terror thespian Klaus Kinski wrote, directed, and starred in his own biopic of the composer, *Kinski Paganini*—his final film before dying in 1991.

PAM AND TOMMY LEE: STOLEN HONEYMOON

(1998)

(DIR. TOMMY LEE; W/PAMELA ANDERSON, TOMMY LEE)

✷ SEX AND OUTRAGE

Hot on the heels of heavy metal tape trading, *Pam and Tommy Lee: Stolen Honeymoon* began life as what seemed like several million shitty bootleg VHS tapes passed from perverts to collectors to the curious. *Baywatch*'s buoyantly buxotic blonde and her Mötley Crüe drummer husband claimed the cassette had been swiped from them. The couple made questionable efforts to sue someone, but they eventually decided that it you can't beat 'em, at least reap some cash from all of 'em beating off.

Thus the bootleg Pam Anderson and Tommy Lee sex tape became the officially licensed *Pam and Tommy Lee: Stolen Honeymoon*, racking up six hundred thousand copies sold to become the best-selling adult video in history (until *Night in Paris* arrived in 2003). Shot on a boat and in Pam's trailer on the set of the movie *Barb Wire* (1996), the players' various genital exhibitions deserve praise, and generated many Tommy Lee "drumstick" jokes. The eroticism is offset by airhead dialogue. If you can maintain tumescent intractability amidst squeals of "I love you, lover!" you're a closer man to Tommy Lee than I.

Pam also costars with Poison frontman Bret Michaels in a sex tape from several years earlier. Michaels legally blocked any kind of official tape, but Google away if you're so inclined. Pam talks dirty into Bret's mic stand and can now be viewed being unskinny bopped by him on more seedy websites than a rose has thorns.

PANTERA: 3 VULGAR VIDEOS FROM HELL (1999)

(DIR. VARIOUS; W/PHIL ANSELMO, DIMEBAG DARRELL, VINNIE PAUL, REX BROWN)

✠ METAL REALITY ✠ CONCERT FOOTAGE

Built to kill and discharged in 1999, *3 Vulgar Videos* combines a trio of the Texas band's popular long-form home videos into two devastating DVDs of ferociously funny and frightening metal intensity. Disc one combines *Cowboys From Hell: The Videos* (1991) and *Vulgar Video* (1993). Disc two presents *3 Watch It Go* (1997) plus three songs from the 1991 Monsters in Moscow Festival. Simply Pantera was great at filling the audio-visual void left when MTV canceled *Headbangers Ball* in 1995.

Commingled among the nearly four hours of Pantera action are live performances, music videos, and an epic parade of cameos by hard rock royalty. Watch out for (among many others) Ace Frehley, Gene Simmons, Kerry King, Jeff Hanneman, Scott Ian, Marilyn Manson, Layne Staley, Jerry Cantrell, Tommy Lee, Trent Reznor, Billy Corgan, and Yngwie Malmsteen. Yet these *Vulgar Videos* are never more alarming than when the band members are just kicking back, doing their version of "relaxing," or pursuing some kind of vicious, hair-raising laugh.

The nonmusical elements of *3 Vulgar Videos* include close-range fireworks aimed at one another, nudity-laden visits to strip clubs owned by drummer Vinnie Paul, a rapturously uncomfortable encounter with religious zealots who attempt to pray for the band, and intoxicant consumption on a level that may be perilous simply to watch. Nobody did metal with the power of Pantera in the '90s, and their party videos became cherished guests of honor at headbanger gatherings. *3 Vulgar Videos From Hell* is the hulking, maybe hazardous, historical touchstone that welcomes all comers to the demented inner workings of the last heavy metal band minted to arena rock status.

PARADISE LOST: THE CHILD MURDERS AT ROBIN HOOD HILLS (1996)
PARADISE LOST 2: REVELATIONS (2000)
PARADISE LOST 3: PURGATORY (2011)

(DIRS. JOE BERLINGER, BRUCE SINOFSKY; W/JASON BALDWIN, DAMIEN ECHOLS, JESSIE MISSKELLEY)

✠ SATANIC PANIC ✠ METAL ON TRIAL
✠ SOUNDTRACK (METALLICA)

Originally airing on HBO, *Paradise Lost: The Child Murders at Robin Hood Hills* powerfully illuminated the questionable circumstances surrounding the 1994 convictions of three teenage Arkansas headbangers accused of a heinous triple murder. Jason Baldwin (age sixteen), Damien Echols (age seventeen), and Jessie Misskelley (age eighteen)—soon known as "the West Memphis Three"—faced imprisonment and execution for the 1993 murder and sexual mutilation of three eight-year-old boys, Chris Byers, Michael Moore, and Steve Branch. The teens' predilection for black clothing and heavy metal music sparked talk among local zealots that the killings were performed as a satanic ritual. Prosecutors ran with the human sacrifice theory and won a death penalty against Echols and lengthy convictions for Baldwin and Misskelley. Documentary makers Berlinger and Sinofsky initially thought they were documenting a ritual killing, but in the course of filming they leaned toward believing that the legal deck had been stacked against the defendants. Based on intimate access to prosecutors, the defense team, and the victims' families, the film makes compelling arguments for innocence, without totally dispelling doubts.

The story took years to catch on, but ultimately

the documentary provoked a vast outraged reaction and generated a continual current of real-life worldwide support for the West Memphis Three. Among those first moved by their plight were the members of Metallica. *Paradise Lost* is the first film in which the group allowed its music to appear, and naturally songs like "Nothing Else Matters" were cleared for free. Metallica went on to donate songs to *Paradise Lost 2: Revelations* (2000) and *Paradise Lost 3: Purgatory* (2011). In 2003, Berlinger and Sinofsky repaid the relationship by creating the bizarre landmark documentary *Metallica: Some Kind of Monster.*

Over the course of two follow-up films, more incredible events unfold, including the turnaround of John Michael Byers, stepfather of one of the murdered boys. He is portrayed here as a wild-eyed gunslinger blasting pumpkins apart as proxies for the heads of the three accused teenagers. After being unfairly pinpointed as a likely alternative suspect in the follow-up film, he eventually supports the West Memphis Three.

Paradise Lost 2: Revelations is the dire middle chapter of the tragic documentary series. The convicted teenagers are now young men, and the film details the rise of a newfangled Internet support community around the inmates during their appeals. Much is made of mismatched bite marks appearing on the victims. The court seems uninterested in considering the evidence, leading to monumental frustration and desperation on the part of the West Memphis Three and their families and supporters.

What look to be the absolutely criminal misdeeds of the Arkansas legal system in motion are infuriating and heartbreaking. As the defendants take their appeal to higher legal authorities, they find themselves time and time again facing the same judges and prosecutors, as those men made careers and won elections on the backs of the case they railroaded through the system.

Fortunately, this film, and its 1996 predecessor, *Paradise Lost: The Child Murders at Robin Hood Hills*, galvanized the public to demand justice. The rise of online networking enabled a

previously unprecedented virtual community of moral, financial, and legal support for the West Memphis Three defendants. The webmasters of WM3.org are specifically profiled here, and stand out as earnest and educated coastal interlopers, the opposite of the disenfranchised trailer park families who backed their sons in the first movie. This movie plainly wants to point a finger at the theatrically angry John Mark Byers. He does himself no favors by ranting and staging a mock cremation of the convicts. After we learn that he's had multiple entanglements with the law and that he once forced a child to use a knife in a fight; it's clear directors Berlinger and Sinofsky want to see him fully investigated. Yet once again, *Paradise Lost 2* ends with the West Memphis Three locked up and doomed to execution, where they stayed for another decade.

In 2011, science caught up with consensus: the West Memphis Three did not kill those children. After eighteen years in prison, DNA evidence excluded the possibility that Jason Baldwin, Damien Echols, and Jessie Misskelley killed three little boys in 1993, and they walked out of jail free men, no longer teenagers.

John Mark Byers, whose threats and obnoxiousness made him the ostensible "villain" of the first two *Paradise Lost* movies, apologizes to the West Memphis Three and campaigns for their release. However, another victim's father, relatively mildmannered Terry Hobbs, starts to appear guilty in light of physical evidence and conflicting alibis.

When *Paradise Lost 3* concludes with Baldwin, Echols, and Misskelley cutting a deal and emerging from prison, the moment is simultaneously exhilarating and heartbreaking. The deal they sign in exchange for freedom essentially precludes them from suing the state of Arkansas; they are not legally innocent, only free. The battle now shifts to clearing their names, proving that the state of Arkansas wrongly caged the West Memphis Three and held them for nearly two decades to save face.

After three films and nearly two decades, the *Paradise Lost* trilogy survives as a testament to the

EMBASSY Home Entertainment

PROM NIGHT

LESLIE NIELSEN · JAMIE LEE CURTIS
Dirigida por PAUL LYNCH

DONALD PLEASENCE EM

PAGANINI HORROR

QUELA MÚSICA NÃO PODIA SER TOCADA.

Direção LEWIS COATES

yellow

ACADEMY AWARD NOMINEE

THE 18-YEAR FIGHT TO PROVE THE INNOCENCE OF THE WEST MEMPHIS THREE

PARADISE LOST 3:
PURGATORY

A FILM BY JOE BERLINGER AND BRUCE SINOFSKY

Die endgültige erotische Erfahrung

nach dem erotischen Comic-Klassiker

Gwendoline

JENNIFER HAS A FEW MILLION CLOSE FRIENDS.
SHE'S GOING TO NEED THEM ALL.

From Dario Argento the master of terror...

Creepers
IT WILL MAKE YOUR SKIN CRAWL

Clockwise from top left:
splashy Prom Night *Spanish VHS;* Paganini Horror; *Jennifer Garner in most metal Argento offering* Creepers, *aka* Phenomena; *nuns want no fun in* Persepolis; *Paradise Lost 3 has a "happy" ending;* Center: *kinky German poster for* The Perils of Gwendoline in the Land of the Yik-Yak

Clockwise from top left: Phantasm *has balls;* Phantom of the Paradise *has it all;* Psychomania *rides from the grave;* Planet of the Apes *really is "unusual and important".*

power of metal and movies, particularly when combined in a cause of righteousness. These men were robbed of their youth and livelihoods for wearing black clothes, possessing Megadeth and Metallica cassettes, and checking out books about witchcraft from the local public library. Without the documentaries, they would likely not be alive. As far as Heavy Metal Movies go, this trilogy is a lifesaver.

PARASITE (1982)

(DIR. CHARLES BAND; W/ROBERT GLAUDINI, DEMI MOORE, LUCA BERCOVICI)

✠ POST-APOCALYPSE ✠ SCIENCE FICTION ✠ 3-D!

The parasite of *Parasite* is a lab creation of Dr. Paul Dean (Robert Glaudini). Slimy and slug-like, with ferocious fangs, this organism bores into human intestines before exploding forth *Alien* style to find a new host. There might be lots of them. Poor Dr. Dean was forced to concoct the monsters by the Merchants, the totalitarian class that rules the post-atomic-incident future-world of America 1992. Dr. Dean sneaks out one of the parasites in his gut, hoping to destroy the thing before the Merchants can fully weaponize it. He teams with plucky young Patricia Welles (Demi Moore—in her second film), and together they drive an ambulance across the wasteland while a hired gun in a DeLorean gives chase. Adding to the challenge is a gang of not-quite-typical after-the-apocalypse thugs, led by tough girl Dana, who's played by Runaways singer Cherie Currie. Many, many times during *Parasite*, the parasite itself falls right into our viewing faces—in 3-D!

Ads for *Parasite* promoted it as "the first futuristic monster movie in 3-D"—a ridiculous claim, as the original 3-D craze of the 1950s had futuristic monsters popping off movie screens everywhere—but it was a likably silly way to distance itself from summer 1982's other R-rated 3-D hair-raiser: *Friday the 13th Part 3*. Director Charles Band returned to the medium of three dimensions the following summer with the even more overtly metal *Metalstorm: The Destruction of Jared-Syn* (1983).

Parasite contains one of the last roles by '70s drive-in movie goddess Cheryl "Rainbeaux" Smith. Playing "Captive Girl," she looks hard, sad, and ragged, with a poodle-metal hairdo and no shirt, and she dies early on. My favorite actress made only two more movies after *Parasite*. She was the stand-in for Veronica Lake in the Steve Martin vintage movie cutup comedy *Dead Men Don't Wear Plaid* (1982), and then she had a small role in the Texas-set art-house romance *Independence Day* (1983). From there, Rainbeaux dimmed into an existence of addiction and jail time, culminating in her tragic passing twenty long years after we last saw her as "Captive Girl."

THE PASSION OF tHE CHRIST (2003)

(DIR. MEL GIBSON; WITH JIM CAVIEZEL, MONICA BELLUCCI, ROSALINDA CELENTANO)

✠ CRUCIFIXION ✠ TORTURE ✠ SATAN

Beating (and whipping and nailing and spitting on) the "torture porn" horrors of *Saw* and *Hostel* by more than a year, *The Passion of the Christ* is hyper-charismatic Catholic Mel Gibson's visceral conjuring of biblical ultra-violence and fever-brained faith, filtered through his own personal furies and arterial-spray hard-gore visual effects. The results are miraculously disgusting.

Gibson has been a heavy metal hero from *Mad Max* onward. Naturally, he delivers might and the madness, pain and devastation, and hypnotic otherworldliness. Just for a mind fuck, all the dialogue is spoken, gasped, and choked in the dead language Aramaic. Like it or not, you know the story, as told in two other towering Heavy Metal Movies for Jesus—*Jesus Christ Superstar* (1973) and *The Last Temptation of Christ* (1988). Interestingly, here and in *Last Temptation*, Satan is a woman (you know us Catholics).

Churchy folk packed theaters, some Jewish groups claimed anti-Semitism, and Gibson followed up by making *Apocalypto* (2006), a decapitation-happy explosion of pre-Columbian slaughter and sacrifice among the Mayans.

Pee-wee's Big Adventure (1985)

(Dir. Tim Burton; w/Pee-wee Herman, Elizabeth Daly, Mark Holton, Twisted Sister)

✠ Motorcycles

The red-bow-tied fun-house universe of *Pee-wee's Big Adventure*, a masterpiece by any sane standard, hardly seems the stuff of heavy metal. But Pee-wee Herman's intense nerdiness is so radical that he might as well be covered in leather and spikes. He is definitely a man-child set apart from his peers, living by his own rules, with a soft spot for the burnout older brothers of the world, as evidenced by the appearance of bikers and Twisted Sister in his breakthrough star vehicle. After a nationwide odyssey to recover his stolen bicycle, the *Big Adventure* climaxes with Pee-wee pedaling madly through Warner Brothers' studio lot, crashing across one archetypal Hollywood scene being filmed after another. Since this is 1985, that roster includes Twisted Sister shooting a video for the song "Burn in Hell." Surrounded by requisite video vixens, Dee Snider and his fellow Long Island longhairs preen and play atop a slow-rolling Cadillac convertible. Pee-wee caroms past with a speedboat, Santa's sleigh, and Godzilla in pursuit. The Sisters abandon the Caddy just before impact, and a great heavy metal pileup goes down.

Like every other moment in *Pee-wee's Big Adventure*, Twisted Sister's "Burn in Hell" moment is a gift from comedy heaven. Besides, Pee-wee won our hearts already in Cheech and Chong movies. He also gave young Rob Zombie his first big-league art job as a production assistant on the over-the-top set of the *Pee-wee's Playhouse* TV show. So when the authorities cracked down on Pee-wee (and the media piled on) for pulling his pee-wee in a Florida dirty movie theater, we were all rooting for him and still are.

Perdita Durango (1997), aka Dance with the Devil

(Dir. Alex de la Iglesia; w/Rosie Perez, Javier Bardem, James Gandolfini, Screamin' Jay Hawkins)

✠ Witchcraft ✠ Santeria

A decade before his star turn as a dead-eyed killing machine in *No Country for Old Men* (2007), Javier Bardem is pure terror in *Perdita Durango*, slaying souls wholesale along the same Texas-Mexico border. Instead of Old Men's tight-lipped mercenary with a '70s bubblegum pop star haircut, Bardem here plays Romeo Dolorosa, a jaguar who takes the form of a human witch doctor with long hair, tattoos, and an inner inferno that would fit right in at a Sepultura soccer-stadium show. Perdita (Rosie Perez) is Dolorosa's female companion. Together, they kidnap teenage couple Duane (Harley Cross) and Estelle (Aimee Graham). Individually, they rape them. Dolorosa's ultimate intention is to kill the girl in a sacrificial Santeria ritual overseen by voodoo priest Adolfo (Screamin' Jay Hawkins). In hot pursuit is a mealymouthed DEA agent (James Gandolfini) who is repeatedly mowed down by high-speed vehicles.

Hot off his Spanish-language Antichrist fright-comedy *The Day of the Beast*, director Álex de la Iglesia used *Perdita Durango* to barrel into the post-Tarantino half of the indie-film '90s. Unfortunately, this sick, brutal, and witty fever rush got lost in the quirky crime movie onslaught of its day. *Perdita Durango* reeks of blood and tears and cocaine and it burns like sun-cracked evil and it gleams like a (frequently used) machete.

R&B madman Screamin' Jay Hawkins often goes underappreciated as a pioneer of heavy metal. Back in the 1950s, he took the stage in a coffin, wore animal skins and long capes, and waved a skull-topped walking stick over mesmerized crowds while howling about black magic. Hawkins's time-honored persona makes him a natural fit in *Perdita Durango*.

The Perils of Gwendoline in the Land of the Yik-Yak

(1984), aka Gwendoline

(Dir. Just Jaeckin; w/Tawny Kitaen, Brent Huff, Zabou Breitman, Bernadette Lafont)

✤ S&M ✤ Amazons

The same year that her torn clothes and ripped body made Ratt's *Out of the Cellar* a smash pop-metal success, Tawny Kitaen kinked things up to headbanger levels in the sci-fi S&M exploitation adventure *The Perils of Gwendoline in the Land of the Yik-Yak*. Tawny stars as voluptuous Gwendoline, who ventures into an exotic jungle to pursue a rare butterfly that eluded her scientist father. Along for the hunt are sexy French maid Beth (Zabou Breitman) and burly mercenary Willard (Brent Huff). The trio contends with cannibals and is captured by the Yik-Yak, a tribe of barely clad female warriors who worship a wicked lesbian queen (Bernadette Lafont). The fetish-mad matriarch's plan is to keep Gwendoline and Beth naked and chained up until they submit to the whips of her will. She aims to force Willard to mate with her ovulating gladiator champion before executing him.

The queen, of course, doesn't get her way, but en route to a literally volcanic climax, *Gwendoline* provides soft-core sex cinema with many of its most metallically unique sights and sensualities. Beyond Tawny and her luscious female costars up front, *Gwendoline* displays a controlled-but-combustive sexuality that's equal parts *Heavy Metal* magazine and actual heavy metal equipment, plus the film is infused with post-apocalyptic-seeming aesthetics (i.e., steel pony costumes on bare-assed girl soldiers, endless chrome mirrors turning every hallway into a kaleidoscope of exposed female flesh, and so on, all of it sumptuously staged and photographed).

Several years later, Tawny Kitaen would reinvent herself in a plethora of Whitesnake hits as MTV's definitive heavy metal video vixen. *The Perils of Gwendoline* reveals Tawny as a different sort of metal minx—one who really leaves a mark where you can feel it. Black leather, metal studs, whips, chains, handcuffs, ropes, racks, dungeons of the decadent—all these were tropes of sadomasochistic sex, of course, before they were adopted by heavy metal.

No deviant visionary did more to spread the BDSM gospel than John Willie, the writer, artist, and publisher of the groundbreaking underground kink journal *Bizarre*, which ran from 1946 to 1959. Among *Bizarre*'s bondage spreads, high-heel homages, and giddy humiliation stories was a comic strip titled "Sweet, Sweet Gwendoline," which limned the ongoing story of a curvaceous heroine who repeatedly falls prey to dominatrix types. Pioneering erotic filmmaker Just Jaeckin (*Emmanuelle*, *The Story of O*) based *The Perils of Gwendoline* on Willie's wild creation.

Persepolis (2007)

(Dirs. Marjane Satrapi, Vincent Paronnaud; w/ Chiara Mastroianni, Catherine Deneuve)

✤ Youth Revolt ✤ Animation ✤ World Metal

Persepolis is an emotionally moving, black-and-white animated film based on an autobiographical graphic novel by Marjane Satrapi. The film's stylized images and deft vocal casting detail Satrapi's life as a young girl coming of age in 1970s Iran under totalitarian Muslim rule. Among Marjane's modes of rebellion is her discovery via the black market of the music of Iron Maiden. She also gets into Tool and Whitesnake, along with punk rock. Iggy Pop supplies the voice of revolutionary Uncle Anoush.

Phallus in Wonderland (1992)

(Dirs. Judas Bullhorn, Distortion Wells)

✤ Concert Footage ✤ Censorship

Gwar's *Phallus in Wonderland* translates the Godzilla proportions of the band's famous foam-rubber-and-fluid-dispensing stage show into something close enough to an actual movie. The monster costumes, the breast and penis fixations, the mutilations, the beheadings, and the testicle pulverizing are all on display here, with a little bit of plot to boot.

Phallus rattles off the origins of Gwar quickly enough: they're space warriors who crash-landed in Antarctica and recently thawed to become a planet-wasting heavy metal collective. Once unleashed on the public, frontman Oderus Urungus (Dave Brockie) has his sentient monster-schlong—the Cuttlefish of Cthulu—removed so it can face obscenity charges. Gwar fights back with every method of mayhem and weapon of tight-ass destruction conceivable.

Leading the assault on Gwar is Edna P. Granbo (Hunter Jackson), a Tipper Gore stand-in, and her rock-censoring Morality Squad, a cabal of mutant superheros. Gwar's bombastic slaughtering of these enemies incorporates the shock tactics of their stage performances and occasionally treats us to more in-depth details. The kills are calculated to gratify headbangers. For example, the Morality Squad's Father Bohab, a child molester of the cloth, gets his comeuppance by being sodomized with a crucifix and spanked with a Bible. A subplot details Gwar hawking a children's cereal fortified with crack cocaine.

Shot as a companion piece to the band's 1992 album *America Must Be Destroyed*, *Phallus in Wonderland* nabbed a Grammy nomination for Best Long Form Video but lost to Annie Lennox. *Phallus* also launched an impressive series of direct-to-video Gwar movies, including *Skulhedface* (1994), *The Return of Techno Destructo* (1996), *Rendezvous With RagNaRock* (1997), *A Surprising Burst of Chocolaty Fudge* (1998), *Dawn of the Day of the Night of the Penguins* (1998), *It's Sleazy* (2001), and *Blood Bath and Beyond* (2007). Distinct from Gwar's straight concert videos, each home video runs about an hour and somehow extends the boundaries of the Gwarniverse.

PHANTASM (1979)

(DIR. DON COSCARELLI; W/ANGUS SCRIMM, REGGIE BANNISTER, MICHAEL BALDWIN, BILL THORNBURY)

✠ HORROR ✠ SUPERNATURAL

"If you've ever listened to a bright, imaginative eight-year-old child make up a ghost story," wrote the normally stodgy *New York Times* film critic Vincent Canby, "you'll have some idea of what it's like to watch *Phantasm*."

Phantasm, the breakout effort of writer-director Don Coscarelli, remains one of the most loopy and original joys in horror cinema. Young Mike (Michael Baldwin) happens upon spooky doings at the Morningside Mortuary. First he catches the grimmest of all undertakers, the Tall Man (Angus Scrimm) easily lifting a loaded casket by himself. Poking around inside the funeral parlor, Mike sees a silver sphere that flies through the air, sprouts a little metal drill, and gorily bores a hole in an unsuspecting victim's forehead (who then wets his pants, postmortem). Mike teams with older brother Jody (Bill Thornbury) and long-haired, guitar-shredding ice cream man Reggie (Reggie Bannister) to pry open the secrets of Morningside during a trip to a dark side that includes vicious versions of *Star Wars*' Jawas that act as guardians of a portal to an alien planet.

Phantasm is a cyclone ride through sci-fi and horror fan Coscarelli's fevered headspace and one of the most inventive adventures you'll see in any genre. The movie's metallic tone and clean timbre are heavy metal to the amputated finger-bone, and its signature images have been employed and expanded upon by countless metal artists. Phantasm was the name of the L.A. thrash metal supergroup featuring Ron McGovney (ex-Metallica) and Katon W. DePena (Hirax). Possessed, Acid Reign, Marduk, Rigor Mortis, and many others have penned songs inspired by the film. Swedish death metal gods Entombed incorporated the eerie, otherworldly score into their landmark song "Left Hand Path."

One of Don Coscarelli's cornerstone influences

was Frank Herbert's sci-fi opus *Dune*. He pays tribute by naming a bar in the movie Dune. Never to be forgotten, *Phantasm* boasts one of the all-time best horror movie taglines: "If this one doesn't scare you, you're already dead!" Four sequels followed over the subsequent 35 years.

Phantom of the Opera

(1925)

(Dir. Rupert Julian; w/Lon Chaney, Mary Philbin, Norman Kerry, Arthur Edmund Carewe)

✸ Faust ✸ Horror

The ghoul of *The Phantom of the Opera*, as portrayed by Lon Chaney in a history-making performance, is a shadowy masked figure who skulks around the catwalks and catacombs of the Paris Opera House. Though musically gifted, he is a monster who cannot find love due to his horrible visage, which may or may not reflect inner evil. No wonder metal bands from Iron Maiden to Nightwish have latched onto this story!

Via letter, the Phantom insists to opera management that singer Carlotta (Mary Philbin) be promoted from understudy to lead performer in *Faust*. When it doesn't happen, he saws a chandelier off of the ceiling during the crowded opening night and kidnaps Carlotta, carrying her away on a gondola through the Paris sewers into his fantastically creepy lair. There, Christine tears off the Phantom's mask and reveals his monstrously disfigured face in one of cinema's earliest shock scenes that made audiences members faint, vomit, and/or flee from theaters in terror.

Phantom of the Opera horrified and delighted audiences worldwide for years, setting in motion Universal Studio's classic monster movies of the 1930s and '40s. The film's gothic setting, imbued with the power of opera, and its exploration of unrequited love between an ugly dude and a hot chick singer—along, of course, with Chaney's über-creepy Phantom kisser, which became an instant and permanent Halloween fixture—add up to an early high note in heavy metal cinema.

Chaney was known as the Man of a Thousand Faces because he designed and executed his own makeup. To create the Phantom, he pulled the tip of his nose upward with wire, painted his eye sockets and nostrils black, covered his actual eyeballs with egg membranes, glued his ears back against his head, and wore a full mouthpiece with stumpy false teeth.

The Phantom of the Opera has been made into a number of subsequent films of lesser but fitfully worthwhile heavy metal fortitude. Claude Rains (*The Invisible Man*) brought sound and color to the 1943 *Phantom*. Inspector Clouseau's erstwhile police chief nemesis Herbert Lom stars in the 1962 Hammer Films version. Robert Englund ditches Freddy Krueger's hat for the famous mask in the 1989 *Phantom of the Opera* that costars *The Stepfather*'s Jill Schoelen, and is a pretty good B-movie of its era.

Dario Argento applied his own *pazzo* touches, such as having the Phantom being raised from infancy on by sewer rats, to his 1998 take, which is otherwise only notable for his directing daughter Asia Argento nude—once again. The big, splashy 2004 *Phantom of the Opera* is a lavish adaptation of the ongoing stage musical by Andrew Lloyd Webber (*Jesus Christ Superstar*) with Gerard Butler (*300*) and Emmy Rossum (the hot daughter from TV's *Shameless*).

Phantom of the Paradise (1974)

(Dir. Brian De Palma; w/Paul Williams, William Finley, Jessica Harper)

✸ Faust ✸ Music Business Horror

Phantom of the Paradise is a one-of-a-kind, only-in-the-'70s, rib-tickling, head-banging, rip-roaring, rock and roll musical Armageddon that combines *Phantom of the Opera*, glam, *Faust*, silent films, Edgar Allan Poe, doo-wop, *Frankenstein*, psychedelia, *The Picture of Dorian Gray*, and the singular madness of writer-director Brian De Palma at the apex of his split-screen, multimedia, tear-cinema-down-to-rebuild-it powers.

Scrawny composer Winslow Leach (William Finley) naively pitches his rock opera/cantata based on the legend of Faust to Swan (Paul Williams), the ruthless impresario of Death Records. Swan promptly steals Winslow's music to debut it at the opening of his new rock showplace, the Paradise. To silence Winslow, Swan has the musician beaten, sent to Sing Sing and, eventually, mutilated by a record press—which melts his face and silences his voice—and left for dead. Winslow, of course, is alive and hell-bent on revenge. Donning a leather suit, black cape, and silver bird mask, he reinvents himself as the Phantom, committed to wreaking havoc however possible on Swan's Paradise. Humanizing Winslow's hate is Phoenix (Jessica Harper), a singer with whom he falls in love. Pushing our antihero further into rage, however, is Beef (Gerrit Graham), a sissified he-man glam rocker (à la Gary Glitter) and the makeup-donning horror-metal combo the Undead (a la Kiss). Swan casts them both in the production of Faust.

Finally frightened enough by the Phantom to be willing to negotiate, Swan signs a contract in blood, allowing Phoenix to sing the cantata at the Paradise. Alas, the double-crossings do not end. Neither does the fun in this way-out, beyond-OTT celebration of rock and pop, horror and comedy, art and trash.

Brian De Palma was inspired to create *Phantom* when he saw Paul Williams regally exiting an elevator. The five-foot-two actor and composer wore a cape, smoked a cigar, and had a girl on each arm. "He was a rock and roll Napoleon," De Palma says. Williams was a major star throughout the '70s. In addition to writing hits for the Monkees, the Carpenters, Three Dog Night, and others, he costarred as an orangutan in *Battle for the Planet of the Apes* (1973), as Little Enos Burdette in *Smokey and the Bandit* (1977), and on seemingly every TV show of the decade. His other film scores include *Bugsy Malone* (1976), *The Muppet Movie* (1979), and *Ishtar* (1987).

Williams's songs for *Phantom* are works of wonder. They range from '50s greaser ballads to '60s surf group harmonies to the incredible, one-two punch of the Undead and Beef—where the movie turns explicitly heavy metal. The Undead, in their black-and-white face paint that echoes Arthur Brown, Alice Cooper, and Kiss (and portends King Diamond and countless Norwegian church-burners), introduce Beef with "Somebody Super Like You," a driving run-up punctuated by hisses and hideous screams. Then Beef emerges, Frankenstein-like, belting out the rousing anthem "Life at Last"—only to be topped by the Phantom zapping him with a metal lightning bolt.

Originally, the movie was written as *Phantom of the Fillmore*, in homage to Bill Graham's rock palaces in New York and San Francisco.

Swan's record label was initially to be called Swan Song. Led Zeppelin's Swan Song imprint precluded that, necessitating the birth of Death Records. Nonetheless, the original Swan Song logo appears on several items, including a tape recorder and Beef's towel.

Jessica Harper, as Phoenix, is a runner-up for the all-time Cult Movie Queen tiara. Demure and deep-voiced, the Chicago native also starred in the making-of-a-silent-porn-film comedy *Inserts* (1974), the 1981 *Rocky Horror* semi-sequel *Shock Treatment* (as Janet), and the Steve Martin musical *Pennies From Heaven* (1981). Harper's most metal role is the lead in Dario Argento's Goblin-scored splatter masterwork, *Suspiria* (1977).

PHENOMENA (1985), AKA CREEPERS

(DIR. DARIO ARGENTO; W/JENNIFER CONNELLY, DONALD PLEASENCE, DARIA NICOLODI, DALILA DI LAZZARO)

✡ ITALIAN HORROR ✡ SOUNDTRACK (GOBLIN, IRON MAIDEN, MOTÖRHEAD)

Dario Argento's proper follow-up to his masterpiece *Suspiria* (1977) opens with a similarly jaw-dropping jolt of operatically executed teen girl slaughter. Vera (Fiore Argento, the director's eldest daughter) wanders into a house in the woods where someone, or something, breaks free of chains upon her arrival. An unseen assailant attacks Vera with scissors and chases her up against a window overlooking a rushing stream. The girl falls backward, the window shatters, and she is decapitated by a sheet of glass—in slow motion. Vera's severed head tumbles into the water below and floats away quickly on the cascading current. *Buongiorno!*

Jennifer (Jennifer Connelly, at age fourteen) is an American student newly arrived at Vera's Swiss boarding school. Her telepathic connection to insects turns on resident entomologist John McGregor (Donald Pleasence), who is confined to a wheelchair and has a chimpanzee assistant named Inga. More murders and intrigue follow, with Jennifer eventually crawling through a pool of oozing maggots and larvae to discover a monster-faced mutant-child, from whom she barely escapes with her head, thanks to her Aquaman-equivalent connection to bugs. Noggins continue to roll, until the surprise straight-razor ending, a sequence that has always driven me ape with joy.

Phenomena belongs in the upper stratosphere of the Argento canon. The director makes his usual cameos—providing the hands that commit all the on-camera atrocities—and his nightmare logic here does not engender terror so much as it does giddiness. Italian prog-rock maestros Goblin, as always, powerfully complement the action and inner workings of the characters with their keyboard-driven whirlwinds of sound. *Phenomena*'s unique tone may be even more perfectly matched, though, by the two metal songs that appear prominently: "Flash of the Blade" by Iron Maiden and "Locomotive" by Motörhead. Of all Argento's films, *Phenomena* is the most head-banging, and I'm not just talking about all those heads rolling down the Alps on-screen.

Phenomena opened in the U.S. as *Creepers*, promoted with ads that stressed the movie's metal content. The poster touted the contributions by Iron Maiden and Motörhead, as did commercials on FM rock stations. Argento calls *Phenomena* his most personal film. I long hoped that meant

he could commune with grasshoppers or that he had an ape that would kill for him, but the director has since revealed that events detailed in the heart-crumbling story that Jennifer tells about her mother abandoning the family on Christmas Day actually happened to him as a boy.

Pieces (1982)
(Dir. Juan Piquer Simón; w/Christopher George, Lynda Day George, Edmund Purdom, Ian Sera)

✤ Slasher

No horror experience is quite on par with a movie whose ads proclaimed, "It's exactly what you think it is!" and, "You don't have to go to Texas for a chainsaw massacre!"

Pieces' plot sounds like standard horror stuff, commencing in a boy's bedroom, where a spindly tyke is assembling a jigsaw puzzle containing an image of a naked lady. Mom busts in and gives junior grief, and he axes her into pieces. Some years later, a masked figure is power-tooling coeds to death at a university. He then makes off with bodies in bloody hunks. Teaming up to nab the mystery mangler are cigar-chomping cop Lieutenant Bracken (Christopher George), undercover tennis pro Mary (Lynda Day George), and Jimmy-Olsen-like college dork Kendall (Ian Sera). Top suspects include the ghoulish Dean (Edmund Purdom) and a Bluto-like groundskeeper (Paul L. Smith, who actually played Bluto in Robert Altman's 1979 *Popeye*). Piece after piece gorily piles up until the post-climax payoff that, truly, no rational being can possibly anticipate.

If you're not aware of *Pieces*' parting shot, I beseech you not to learn about it before watching the movie. Just see *Pieces* and let the ending happen to you. You will hobble away in pieces.

Pieces includes water-bed murder, and a close-up of a frightened woman's crotch as she wets her pants in terror. The final moment still swamps them both. Bruce Lee imitator Bruce Le (that is the correct spelling) makes a sidesplitting cameo. Producer Dick Randall imported him from his kung fu movie productions in Rome.

Grindhouse Releasing's essential *Pieces* DVD features multiple documentaries and footage of a Hollywood screening of the movie hosted by *Hostel* director Eli Roth, an outspoken fan.

Pink Floyd: The Wall (1982)

(Dir. Alan Parker; w/Bob Geldof, Bob Hoskins, Eleanor David, Jenny Wright)

✶ Animation ✶ Concert Footage ✶ Bricks

The relationship between psych-prog deities Pink Floyd and heavy metal is more than just mingling bong smoke. Emerging from the same space rock scene that launched Hawkwind, and beguiling young prog metallers like Voivod, Floyd bent hard rock through a prism—very much like their *Dark Side of the Moon* cover—to create a place in the pantheon parallel to Led Zeppelin, Deep Purple, and, during some "Hole in the Sky" moments, Black Sabbath. For their 1979 Götterdämmerung of a double album *The Wall*, Pink Floyd employed producer Bob Ezrin (Alice Cooper, Kiss, Hanoi Rocks), and created their most metallic music to date.

Particularly heavy is *The Wall*'s opening number "In the Flesh?" and its climactic, question-mark-free reprise. Bassist and overall mastermind Roger Waters says he composed the song's soaring, swooping, bombastic riff to be a parody of overwhelming arena rock that would simultaneously work as a straight-up power anthem on its own. Filmmaker Alan Parker adhered to that same principle in adapting the album into the midnight movie milestone *Pink Floyd: The Wall*.

Bob Geldof, real-life singer of the Boomtown Rats, stars as Pink. *The Wall* begins with Pink's father being atomized in World War II. We then watch young Pink (Kevin McKeon) smothering under the ministrations of an overbearing mother and suffering the sadism of British schoolmasters. The action jumps from there to Pink's adult life as a stadium-filling rock star. Offstage, he's a cuckolded husband and a hotel-trashing, groupie-thrashing, drug-addicted head case.

The Wall turns really weird and deep when Pink's charisma and influence spawn a fascist movement symbolized by crossed hammers. He serves as rock and roll führer. Each event further isolates Pink from humanity, as bricks fill in the wall. The final act is a hallucinatory trial, which results in the wall getting blown to bits and a conclusion that provides no clues as to the future. The plot is told through songs from the album (which anyone with even the most casual relationship to FM radio knows by heart), Parker's monumentally surreal visuals that bring to mind—and even surpass—Ken Russell and Alejandro Jodorowsky, and gorgeously grotesque animations featuring images by Gerald Scarfe.

"Another Brick in the Wall Part 2"—aka "We Don't Need No Education"—is Floyd's best-known song and it provides the movie's best-known visuals. After Pink's humiliation by a wicked teacher, faceless schoolchildren march and get fed by a conveyor belt into a mammoth meat grinder. They are churned out as blobby strings of nothingness until the song's apex, when the kids still on line tear off their masks and riot, joyfully destroying their books and desks, ganging up to enact physical revenge on their abusive teachers, and burning the school to the ground in an orgy of liberation.

Floyd's only number-one pop hit provides the ideal soundtrack, upping the ante of Alice Cooper's "School's Out" and the Ramones' "Rock 'n' Roll High School" by erasing any humor from the situation. This time when school's out forever, it really means for-fucking-ever.

Everything works. *Pink Floyd: The Wall* is perhaps the greatest narrative rock film and definitely the best movie version of a rock opera. Much about it is overtly metal, but the despair, the desperation, the damnation, and the unpredictable redemption that comes from rock and roll is what makes *The Wall* as heavy as cinema can get.

Planet of the Apes
(1968)
(Dir. Franklin J. Schaffner; w/Charlton Heston, Roddy McDowall, Kim Hunter, Maurice Evans)
✠ Apes ✠ Apocalypse

The heavy metal parts of *Planet of the Apes* include every single scintilla of *Planet of the Apes*: Charlton Heston. Humans as subservient simians. Simians as superior to humans. The horseback net hunts. Mute hottie Nova. Married chimp scientists Cornelius and Zira. Human-hating orangutan Dr. Zaius. Gorilla soldiers. Leather costumes. Stone houses. The Forbidden Zone. The dissonant soundtrack. "Take your stinking paws off me, you damn, dirty ape!" The list goes on, and each element adds another degree of metallic poetry, impact, and annihilation.

Heston, as human astronaut George Taylor, wins freedom from the apes. Joined on a black steed by Nova, he charges off along the coastline into the Forbidden Zone.

"What do you think he'll find out there, Doctor?" Zira asks.

"His destiny!" Zaius tells her.

Sure enough, Taylor rides for a spell and then stops the horse. Spotting a massive, twisted metal structure, he dismounts and collapses to the sand in agony, wailing: "Oh, my God, I'm back! I'm home! All the time it was—you finally really did it! YOU MANIACS! You blew it up! DAMN you! Damn you all TO HELL!" Before him, reaching toward the sky, are the rusted, half-buried remains of the Statue of Liberty.

Planet of the Apes spawned four direct movie sequels, a 1974 prime-time TV series, a 1975 Saturday morning cartoon, a 2001 big-screen "reimagining," and a 2011 reboot film. Even that Tim Burton reboot is worth its weight in metal. Equally part of heavy metal's fiber are all the toys, lunch boxes, games, and other ephemera that flooded the kiddie market throughout the 1970s.

Doom band Blood Farmers pay specific hom-age to the CBS show with their song "General Urko." San Francisco traditionalists Slough Feg have recorded an album called *Ape Uprising*. And Candlemass, Devin Townsend Project, and the Kovenant all have "Planet of the Apes" songs.

Pledge Night (1990),
aka Hazing in Hell
(Dir. Paul Ziller; w/Todd Eastland, Shannon McMahon, Arthur Lundquist, Joey Belladonna)
✠ Slasher

Had *Pledge Night* been made five or even ten years earlier, the film might rank with other delightfully cheeseball slasher movies of the post–*Friday the 13th* blood tsunami. But then again, ten years earlier, *Pledge Night* might well have not secured Anthrax singer Joey Belladonna to put in such an oozingly strong appearance.

Belladonna plays Young Sid, a fraternity hopeful who, on the occasion mentioned in the movie's title, gets boiled alive in a vat of acid. His skin bubbles, his fluids spray, and he hits notes above and beyond anything ever called for even in Anthrax's most ambitious vocal crescendos. What Sid does not do, though, is die. Well, not exactly. He returns years later as Acid Sid (Will Kempe), to kill new pledges and make mayhem. Acid Sid is sort of a hippie incarnation of Freddie Krueger, splattering teens and cracking wise.

As a showcase for an Anthrax member movie cameo, *Pledge Night* seems to make more sense than *Calendar Girls* (2003). That genteel British comedy even goes the extra distance by featuring guitarist Scott Ian, bassist Frank Bello, and erstwhile vocalist John Bush.

Poltergeist (1982)
(Dir. Tobe Hooper; w/Craig T. Nelson, JoBeth Williams, Heather O'Rourke, Zelda Rubinstein)
✠ Haunted House ✠ The Beast

In summer 1982, when they opened just a week apart, *Poltergeist* served as the ferocious flip side to the tear-jerking love ballad of *E.T. the Extra-*

Terrestrial, centering on a suburban California family's home infested by terrifying spooks. Five-year-old Carol Ann (Heather O'Rourke) communicates with the spirits and gets sucked into their realm through the TV. A group of paranormal experts, led by colorful dwarf Tangina (Zelda Rubinstein), battles the demons and their unholy leader the Beast. Mom (JoBeth Williams) dons a white jumpsuit to descend into hell to get the girl back. All seems well until the house erupts with ghouls, maggot storms, animated trees, unearthed corpses, and a massive, pulsating vaginal portal to some great void. Meanwhile across the multiplex, E.T. was mumbling, eating product-placement candy, and phoning home.

Each of these mega-ultra-blockbusters arose from the creative force of Steven Spielberg. *Poltergeist*, directed by Tobe Hooper and produced by a hands-on Spielberg, presented the first real evidence of a visceral, vicious streak that the famously warm-and-fuzzy filmmaker would greatly indulge two summers later via *Gremlins* and the heart-removal, monkey-brain-eating highlights of *Indiana Jones and the Temple of Doom*. Alas, after that, Spielberg's Heavy Metal Movie cred would peter out quickly in a saccharine pop piss-pool of so many *Goonies* and *Hooks* and *Harry and the Hendersons*. At least we will always have that one guy in *Poltergeist* tearing off his face in bloody, gelatinous chunks that pile up in a bathroom sink.

Texas Chainsaw Massacre maker Tobe Hooper is credited as the director. From the get-go, though, nearly everyone involved, from composer to editor, insisted that Spielberg did the real heavy lifting, while Hooper perhaps nodded off in a corner. For all its dated '80s cutesy touches, though, *Poltergeist* was really fucking scary, much more like Texas maverick Hooper than Hollywood golden boy Spielberg. Hooper only made one last good movie—the great *Texas Chainsaw Massacre 2* (1986)—among a succession of shriveling abortions that ultimately reduced him to making Syfy-channel originals. Spielberg does seem to be the film's actual director, and only the vagaries of Directors Guild of America rules prevent that truth from being acknowledged.

Little person Zelda Rubinstein previously voiced "Atrocia Frankenstone" on NBC's Saturday morning *Flintstones* revival in 1980, the series where Fred and Barney become cops partnered with the Schmoo. *Poltergeist* made her a star, and Rubinstein went on to a long career, landing great roles in cult films such as the interesting eyeball horror *Anguish* (1987) and the camp favorite *Teen Witch* (1989). Poltergeist bands have also been summoned from at least Greece, Portugal, Serbia, and Switzerland.

Poltergeist II: The Other Side (1986)

(Dir. Brian Gibson; w/Craig T. Nelson, JoBeth Williams, Zelda Rubinstein, Julian Beck)

✡ Ghosts ✡ Native American Spirituality

Poltergeist II: The Other Side is an unremarkable film speckled with laughably shitty bits including a floating chainsaw; a teen boy's dental braces endlessly unspooling from his mouth and enveloping him in a giant ball of aluminum string; and the entire family flailing aimlessly in some otherworldly void. These scenes were shot when *Poltergeist II* was planned as a 3-D release, and the result is on par with the most hilarious "everything into the camera" bits performed by horror hosts Dr. Tongue (John Candy) and Bruno (Eugene Levy) on *SCTV*.

Director Brian Gibson previously made *Kilroy Was Here* (1983), a fifteen-minute dystopian sci-fi short that introduced the touring Styx stage show for the album of the same name. Styx's anti-PMRC spectacle included, yes indeed, "Mr. Roboto."

Finding themselves spooked again, the Freeling family employs dwarf psychic Tangina (Zelda Rubinstein), who helped them in the first movie. This time she recruits Native American shaman Taylor (Will Sampson, Chief from *One Flew Over the Cuckoo's Nest*). Together they battle the only element of *Poltergeist II* that makes any impact: creepy Julian Beck as Reverend Henry Kane, a demon who assumes the form of a preacher in an Amish hat who has hellfire behind his eyes and one of cinema's most withering evil grins. The reverend is terrifying. Beck's unforgettable performance was then made indelible in the annals of heavy metal by the Reverend Kane waving, front and center, on the cover of the classic 1987 Anthrax album, *Among the Living.*

By the time the movie came out, Julian Beck was no longer among the living himself. He died of stomach cancer after shooting his role. Beck's passing would later be invoked as evidence of a "Poltergeist curse," alongside the untimely demises of costars Dominique Dunn (strangled at twenty-two by her boyfriend) and Heather O'Rourke (dead of septic shock at age twelve).

Poltergeist III (1988), a horrible thing about a high-rise full of haunted mirrors, recast actor Nathan Davis as Reverend Kane. The movie deserved to be cursed just for that.

POP ROCKS (2004)

(DIR. RON LAGOMARSINO; W/GARY COLE, SHERILYN FENN, DAVID JENSEN, DOUGLAS M. GRIFFIN)

✠ HAIR METAL ✠ FAKE BAND (ROCK TOXIN)

A made-for-TV family comedy about a staid bank exec dad getting pulled back into his (squeaky clean) hair metal past, *Pop Rocks* crackles thanks to Gary Cole as the square who has to embrace anew his old flair. Cole plays Jerry Harden, aka "The Dagger," frontman for shock squad Rock Toxin, who stormed the charts and the heavy metal world two decades earlier in Kiss-like face paint and costumes. Cole as Dagger is right on par with other makeup-faced made-for-TV shock rockers, including the all-time champs Donny Most as Moloch on *CHiPs* and Sonny Bono as Deacon Dark on *The Love Boat.*

When Rock Toxin guitarist Izzy (David Jensen) shows up at the long-since-reformed Dagger's office with an offer for big reunion dough, the straitlaced dad considers his teen daughter's college tuition and agrees to don the fright wig and strap on the platform boots for another go-round—as long as he can keep it secret. Cole is always hilarious, which he's proven as Mike Brady in the '90s *Brady Bunch* movies and as Bill Lumbergh in *Office Space.* As it stands, *Pop Rocks* is a funny movie for little kids just grasping the existence of something called heavy metal.

PORNO HOLOCAUST (1981)

(DIR. JOE D'AMATO; W/GEORGE EASTMAN, DIRCE FURNANI, ANNJ GOREN, MARK SHANNON)

✠ ITALIAN HORROR ✠ MUTANTS ✠ LETHAL SPERM

Porno Holocaust is so death metal a name, that if the title didn't first exist as an Italian gross-out, full-penetration, rape-monster movie, Pungent Stench would have invented it. Scientists travel to a Greek island where nuclear testing took place, ostensibly for reasons other than to have sex with each another, but that's all that happens. Halfway through this boring private outrage, a nuke-mutated beast-man arrives to dole out carnal assaults on the women. His victims subsequently die from vaginal poisoning due to intake of "radioactive sperm." The movie delivers "porno" terribly, and "holocaust" not at all. Still, horns-up to whoever put those two words together while brainstorming a crotch-grabbing name to slap on a grindhouse marquee.

PREDATOR (1987)

(DIR. JOHN MCTIERNAN; W/ARNOLD SCHWARZENEGGER, CARL WEATHERS, JESSE VENTURA, KEVIN PETER HALL)

✠ ALIENS

Major Alan "Dutch" Shaefer (Arnold Schwarzenegger) leads his crack special-ops squadron into the Central American jungle to rescue a kidnapped U.S. government official. Once there, they lay righteous waste to an enemy camp and discover skinned human bodies that suggest something more foul is in play than meets the eye (or the thermal heat-sensor vision goggles). Something is watching Dutch and his soldiers: an eight-foot-tall, armor-bodied, tusk-faced space alien with a mouth full of fangs and really cool dreadlocks. He drops by earth to hunt humans, and he enjoys the challenge posed by Dutch and his commandos.

One by one, the Predator gruesomely picks off the fighting men, who include Carl Weathers (Apollo Creed from the *Rocky* movies), Sonny Landham (Billy Lone Bear from *48 Hours*), and Jesse "The Body" Ventura (from pro wrestling and, later, the Minnesota governor's office). Ventura's showstopping weapon is a rotating-barreled machine gun usually found on the side of a helicopter. Arnold ultimately throws down *mano-a-monstero* with Predator, royally kicking the space beast's keister and informing him, "You are one ugly motherfucker!"

Predator is about as perfect a heavy metal movie experience possible without any heavy metal songs. The movie was described as "Rambo meets Alien," but the actual genesis of the film's concept came from a joke about how the only opponent movie boxer Rocky Balboa had yet to square off against was E.T. the Extra-Terrestrial. Something must have rubbed off on the stars. Schwarzenegger was elected governor of California in 2003. Jesse Ventura was elected governor of Minnesota in 1998. Sonny Landham ran for governor of Kentucky in 2003, but lost. Now Carl Weathers should take on an entire state.

PRINCE OF DARKNESS (1987)

(DIR. JOHN CARPENTER; W/DONALD PLEASENCE, JAMESON PARKER, LISA BLOUNT, VICTOR WONG)

✠ SATAN

A lice Cooper stares right at you. No matter what else happens in John Carpenter's *Prince of Darkness* (and plenty does), that's what you'll walk away with. Alice doesn't speak a word of dialogue. He doesn't need to. Using just that glare and a scowl, he spooks profoundly, portraying a skid-row bum possessed by a seven-million-year-old living and sentient liquid that's been hidden in a protective casing underneath an L.A. church long past its expiration date.

As the green goop percolates, a team of scientists determine that this stuff is the essence of Satan himself. Even more alarming is that the slime is

serving to unleash Satan's father—the Anti-God! The curious designation of Satan as the "Prince" of Darkness, as opposed to the "King," never occurred to me before this movie. Leave it to '80s VHS horror to fill me in on theology.

Carpenter's movie is studded with brain blasts of physics *and* metaphysics, but what sticks is the claustrophobic setting and sense of apocalyptic dread as, one by one, the scientists fall under the lethal spell of the devil fluid. That horror is embodied by Alice Cooper, as he stares right at you.

Alice Cooper landed in *Prince of Darkness* as a lark when his friend John Carpenter invited him to the set. For a scene in which the camera pans across an army of homeless people standing motionless and glowering, they decided to put Alice in a vagrant costume and throw him in there—just a neat secret cameo. Alice, however, exuded such screen presence that he got instantly upgraded to leader of the silent hobo infantry, and one of the most iconic images of '80s horror—and Heavy Metal Movies—was born.

PRIVATE PARTS (1997)

(DIR. BETTY THOMAS; W/HOWARD STERN, ROBIN QUIVERS, PAUL GIAMATTI, FRED NORRIS)

✠ METAL REALITY ✠ KILLER CAMEOS

R adio superstar Howard Stern's biopic *Private Parts*, adapted from his 1993 book, traces his rise from Long Island misfit schlub to reigning comedy terror of the airwaves. Stern and his team play themselves. Paul Giamatti became a star as their nemesis program director, the flamingly sensitive prude Pig Vomit. Visually, Howard's on-screen evolution through the early 1980s involves his adopting poodle-metal hair, leather pants, and a skull T-shirt. The movie culminates with an outdoor fan rally where AC/DC rocks with "You Shook Me All Night Long."

In real time, Stern caught a metal vibe upon moving to FM radio in late 1985, well after the action in *Private Parts*. Once there, Howard made frequent guests of Dee Snider of Twisted Sister and Leslie West of Mountain, as well as mondo-metal comedian Sam Kinison. All were considered too crude, too gauche for mass consumption, yet all became popular favorites and reaped massive rewards for sticking to their outré guns.

An early scene in *Private Parts* depicts Stern wandering backstage at "The Music Awards" while wearing his open-butt Fartman costume. Ted Nugent and Dee Snider look him over. Ozzy Osbourne does too, declaring, "What an asshole!" In reality, Stern was lowered from the rafters at the 1992 MTV Video Music Awards, and his presence visibly annoyed Metallica as they accepted a video award for "Enter Sandman."

Prom Night (1980)

(Dir. Paul Lynch; w/Jamie Lee Curtis, Leslie Nielsen, Casey Stevens, Michael Tough)
✷ Slasher

As *Prom Night* opened in the summer of 1980, the post-*Halloween* slasher onslaught went into turbo mode. *Friday the 13th* had been running for months to packed theaters, sending crowds out wired and wide-eyed. Even with genre queen Jamie Lee Curtis top-billed, *Prom Night* just seemed silly (not like really serious shit such as *The Prowler* and *Madman*).

Prom Night's airheadedness, however, proved to be its strength. A group of preteen kids play a game that accidentally gets one of them killed. Six years later, the participants are high school seniors preparing for the big prom; only some psycho starts picking them off before the final dance. But which psycho is it? The none-too-taxing mystery plot and none-too-terrifying or gory murders made *Prom Night* goes-down-easy repeat viewing in drive-ins and beat-the-heat air-conditioned theaters all the way until school started again, eventually proving to be one of the most profitable films of the year. The soft touch allowed a fast path to a Sunday night prime-time airing on NBC, green pastures for boffo ratings.

Given that huge exposure, *Prom Night* set in place many slasher movie rules that endured at least until the movie *Scream* made fun of them.

For example: the killer wears a ski mask and whispers detailed threats to his victims via telephone before striking. In a metal context, *Prom Night* is to slasher films what the processed AOR and glam records of the same era were to heavy metal; a soft-headed battering ram that plowed open a large enough hole to allow through endless variations of real-deal rough stuff. Bow down before *Prom Night*'s bloody boogie.

Prom Night's costumes, dance moves, and even the theme of the big dance—"Disco Madness!"—are all anti-metal to the point of denim and leather disintegration. Leslie Nielsen plays the high school principal, also the father of Jamie Lee's character and the kid who dies early on and sets the film's events in motion. That same summer, Leslie received a permanent comedy makeover in *Airplane!*

Promised Land of Heavy Metal (2008)

(Dir. Kimmo Kuusniemi; President Tarja Halonen)
✷ Finland ✷ World Metal

Sarcofagus guitarist, filmmaker, and proud son of Finland Kimmo Kuusniemi opens his documentary by demonstrating the sonic parallels between Finnish folk music and the hardest of heavy rock. "Finland is the only country in the world where heavy metal is mainstream," Kimmo states, "and I want to find out why."

Promised Land mushes us to Finland, where heavy metal seems to fill the air. The movie visits multiple local metal meccas including the Heavy Corner karaoke bar and the massively packed Music Hunter record store. Helsinki's streets are repeatedly depicted as teeming with leather-clad neo-Vikings in full rock regalia. After paying respect to such '80s Finn metal pioneers as Iron Cross, Riff Raff, and Tarot (bizarrely, not Hanoi Rocks), the movie leaps ahead to the vast array of metallic Finnish sounds by Children of Bodom, Impaled Nazarene, Stratovarius, and heavy metal cello ensemble Apocalyptica.

At the center of Finnish metal mania is Lordi, monster metal marauders who won the 2006 Eurovision songwriting contest with the anthem "Hard Rock Hallelujah." Finland's president Tarja Halonen presents the band with a key to the capital and hosts a swarming outdoor festival. When asked if she minds that she'll be forever associated with honoring Lordi, President Halonen shoots back, "Do I mind? I love it!"

Diving deeper into unique Finnish metal culture, the film reveals that "Hard Rock Hallelujah" was inspired by the Temppeliaukio Church, a dome-shaped Lutheran house of worship carved into a giant rock, where long-haired priests minister to youth with heavy metal masses. Kuusniemi talks to those priests and their congregants, along with psychiatrists, journalists, a theologian, and many other musicians. He never finds a single answer for why his nation has to be so heavy, but for this *Promised Land*, the quest is its own reward.

PSYCHO (1960)

(DIR. ALFRED HITCHCOCK; W/ANTHONY PERKINS, JANET LEIGH, MARTIN BALSAM)

✠ SLASHER

While *Night of the Living Dead* is a more direct black-and-white harbinger of the advent of heavy metal, *Psycho* forced horror films forward in a radical manner worthy of the highest hails. There was scary, and then there was *Psycho*, and afterward *scary* meant something new entirely. Shot on the cheap by the most famous movie director in the history of movies, *Psycho* chronicles the unpleasantness that befalls thieving, sexually active bank teller Marion Crane (Janet Leigh) when she stops for a night at the Bates Motel.

Marion meets lanky, awkward mama's boy Norman Bates (Anthony Perkins), the motel's proprietor, whose hobby is stuffing and mounting dead animals. She joins him for a pleasant enough dinner, and then retires to take cinema's single most celebrated shower. She's interrupted by Mrs. Bates, who hacks her to death with a kitchen knife in an unprecedented onslaught of up-close bloodletting. Marion's boyfriend (John Gavin) and sister (Vera Miles) send private investigator Milton Arbogast (Martin Balsam) out to the motel to see what's up. Arbogast, too, runs into the pointy end of Mrs. Bates's bad manners.

Psycho's shock ending has transcended popular culture lore to simply become part of human consciousness. Mrs. Bates is a rotting corpse in the basement. Norman conducts conversations with himself in her voice and, when warranted, dresses up in his dead mother's clothes and commits murder. Watching the movie is fun and thrilling now, but talk to someone who saw *Psycho* in 1960. They will speak of how it contained loads more suggested sexuality and graphic violence than any movie that had ever been seen, and they will tell you that the *Psycho* damn near killed them with sheer terror. Heavy Metal Movies date back to Thomas Edison's *Frankenstein* (1910), but that was the primitive proto-metal era. The merciless intensity and technical power of modern heavy metal fright films begins with *Psycho*. Bands named Psycho popped up in Canada, Mexico, Singapore, and Boston, and the name Bates Motel has been assumed by heavy metal bands in Canada and the U.K. and is the title of a song by Meliah Rage.

If ever a film did *not* demand a sequel, it was *Psycho*, and yet, we've had a bunch of them. Bates be praised—some have been okay. *Psycho II* (1983) is an unexpectedly sensible extension of the story, and *Psycho III* (1986), directed by Tony Perkins himself, is an interesting meditation on the entire phenomenon. The NBC pilot movie *Bates Motel* (1987) and the made-for-cable *Psycho IV: The Beginning* (1990) are both unbearable. In 1998, director Gus Van Sant made a shot-for-shot remake of *Psycho* for no one, and it was forgotten. A much more interesting venture, the movie *Hitchcock* (2012), stars Anthony Hopkins as the big man, and dramatizes the making of *Psycho*. Somehow, A&E's TV series *Bates Motel*, launched in 2013, turned out great.

PSYCHOMANIA (1973),
AKA THE DEATH WHEELERS; DEATH WHEELERS ARE . . . PSYCHO MANIACS
(DIR. DON SHARP; W/NICKY HENSON, MARY LARKIN, GEORGE SANDERS, ANN MICHELLE)
✵ SATAN ✵ ZOMBIES ✵ MOTORCYCLES

Teenage biker baddie and second-generation British devil worshipper Tom Latham (Nicky Henson) leads his biker gang the Living Dead with an unquenchable drive for chaos. He dreams of pulling off the ultimate antiauthoritarian coup: returning from the dead as an indestructible instrument of motorized mayhem. After a pact with Satan, a suicide, and an incredible scene of Tom roaring forth from his grave atop a motorcycle, Living Dead members Hatchet, Gash, and Chopped Meat follow their leader in dying up to their name. Tom's mom (Beryl Reid) is delighted when Junior returns from Hades. She is a classic British movie satanist, and inhabits an old dark house with a dour butler.

Funky, freaky, and affably of its acid-splattered time—as well as extremely British—*Psychomania* is also suitably violent and spooky. The debates regarding slow zombies versus running zombies may rage forever; *Psychomania*'s zombies ride choppers and hogs, and it makes for one hell of a high, heavy run. Electric Wizard, Insaniac, and the Misfits have all tapped the movie's mojo, one way or another. A review in *The Times of London* declared that *Psychomania* was only suitable to be screened at an "S.S. reunion party." Curvaceous costar Ann Michelle went on to vamp it up in *House of Whipcord* (1974) and shower with her twin sister Vicki Michelle in *Virgin Witch* (1972).

Motörhead's 1984 "Killed by Death" video pays homage to *Psychomania* with Lemmy driving a motorcycle out from his grave. So does the 1994 zombie classic *Dellamorte Dellamore*, aka *Cemetery Man*. In "Celluloid Heroes," the Kinks sing of how even if you covered him with garbage, esteemed English thespian George Sanders "would still have class." Appearing in *Psychomania* may have been just too trashy. Shortly after shooting his scenes, Sanders killed himself. We await his return to earth as a satanic biker.

THE PUNISHER (1989)
(DIR. MARK GOLDBLATT; W/DOLPH LUNDGREN, LOUIS GOSSETT JR., JEROEN KRABBE, KIM MIYORI)
✵ COMIC BOOKS ✵ REVENGE

Comic book fans can slap-fight it out about whether the title of Most Metal Marvel Superhero should go to Wolverine, Ghost Rider, or the Punisher. I'll declare forthrightly here, though, that 1989 *Punisher* is the most metal Marvel superhero film ever made. Too bad that this taut, tough, rollicking B-movie slipped through the cracks prior to the character's joyless Hollywood blockbuster spins in the 2000s.

Director Mark Goldblatt combines high-energy '50 pulp fiction with '70s revenge film plus the "anything goes and everybody gets killed" zeitgeist of Hong Kong's action cinema revolution. Total number of deaths on-screen: ninety-one. Dolph Lundgren is perfect in the lead, a haunted ex-cop kneeling nude in his sewer lair and praying out loud between bouts of massacring New York mobsters and Japanese yakuza bruisers. The fights are thrilling and, most importantly, executed by living stuntmen on physical movie sets, as was the practice in the pre-CGI world.

Nerds complain that Lundgren doesn't don the Punisher's signature skull-logo T-shirt. Is that like King Diamond performing without face paint? Maybe, but he is always King Diamond.

The Punisher's opening and closing monologues, cowritten by Lundgren, ripple with torment: "Come on, God, answer me. For years I'm asking, why? Why are the innocent dead and the guilty alive? Where is justice? Where is punishment? Or have you already answered? Have you already said to the world: Here is justice, here is punishment, here, in me!" Biohazard was impressed enough to sample the dialogue.

The Punisher (2004)

(Dir. Jonathan Hensleigh; w/Thomas Jane, John Travolta, Laura Harring, Roy Scheider)

✡ Comic Books ✡ Revenge ✡ Soundtrack (Damageplan, Hatebreed, Amy Lee)

Thomas Jane puts on the skull-logo shirt and long leather coat as Frank Castle, Marvel Comics' miserable vigilante antihero also known as the Punisher. Jane, a likable star attempting to go dark, holds his own against shaky-cam action, video game gunfire, and lots of other motherfuckers in a convulsively typical 2000s adrenaline overload action blockbuster. John Travolta does bad-guy duties, playing a mob boss who murders Castle's family. His henchmen, by the CGI dozen, get "punished."

For all the generic dullness of this *Punisher* (as opposed to the great, cheapie 1989 version) it's nice to see a splashy, hyperviolent movie shot on location in Tampa, Florida. The sweltering wellspring of Deicide, Morbid Angel, Obituary, and Assück does well as the backdrop for nonstop human slaughter and shouted profanity.

The Punisher's soundtrack CD offers a pretty comprehensive a sampling of mid-2000s commercial metal. Hatebreed represents the most extreme end and a Queens of the Stone Age B-side is tossed in as a curveball. Seether's power ballad "Broken," featuring Amy Lee from Evanescence, was a way bigger hit than the movie.

Punishment Park (1971)

(Dir. Peter Watkins; w/Patrick Boland, Kent Foreman, Carmen Argenziano)

✡ War on Metal ✡ Censorship

The dynamic of authority figures pounding iron fists in response to rock-driven youth culture is at least as old as Elvis's humping hips getting kiboshed by CBS censors on *The Ed Sullivan Show*. Prior to that, teenagers were either children locked away in school or mini-adults slaving in salt pits. Rock and roll brought teenage culture to the fore, and with it teen rebellion. Of all musical tribes pushed into confrontation with the Man, heavy metal has engaged in the most colorful struggle, providing regularly reoccurring satanic panics from imagined backward messages to the misaligned via schoolyard shooters.

Legitimately chilling, of course, was Tipper Gore's 1985 attempt to institute governmental regulation of the music industry—in particular, records by Ozzy and W.A.S.P. (along with "She Bop" by Cyndi Lauper)—via the Parents Music Resource Center (PMRC). The end result of the senatorial PMRC hearings was that Dee Snider triumphantly recast himself as a fang-faced freedom fighter and the Mentors (bless them) sold a few dozen more albums.

A solid fifteen years earlier, British visionary Peter Watkins's *Punishment Park* imagines an America where the likes of the PMRC took over completely. Confronted with hippies gone haywire, the Powers That Be perfect a final solution for rooting out, rounding up, and confining longhairs and rabble-rousers to a desert camp—"Punishment Park" to be precise. If the prisoners can endure the elements and outrun the armed officers in lethal pursuit of them, they'll go free. And if not—well, at least their deaths will count as a lesson learned. Network television cameras broadcast this cruel new version of justice.

Punishment Park plays out as a mock documentary about a group of young radicals and rock and roll naysayers as the long jackboots of the law give chase and stomp them, sending a warning message to anyone else with out-of-line thoughts. Watkins fires his own distress signal as to how the state and its corporate sponsors will eventually silence their critics, and he uncannily nails post-*Survivor* reality TV. Nostradamus is a recurring heavy metal figure of reverence. With Peter Watkins, however, we can be absolutely sure that at least some of his predictions came true.

Prior to *Punishment Park*, Peter Watkins made *Privilege* (1967), a rock and roll fable about the rise of a British pop star who can and will sell anything and everything, right up to the outermost extremes of "God" and "country."

Q: THE WINGED SERPENT (1982)

(DIR. LARRY COHEN; W/MICHAEL MORIARTY, DAVID CARRADINE, RICHARD ROUNDTREE, CANDY CLARK)

✦ INDIGENOUS SPIRITUALITY ✦ URBAN WARFARE

A New York City–based blood cult resurrects Aztec god Quetzalcoatl in the form of a "winged serpent"—a white dragon that nests atop the Chrysler Building and flies around picking off various Manhattanites. David Carradine (*Kung Fu*) and Richard Roundtree (*Shaft*) bring grindhouse heat as cops in pursuit of the monster; Michael Moriarty, in a mostly improvised role, is a piano-playing small-time crook with the scoop on the beaked behemoth's home base.

Q's most metal aspect is the creature itself, a stop-motion-animated puppet that never shies away from the camera, a marvel of practical special effects that will captivate monster movie fans forever, as fitting a representation of an Aztec god as the movies have ever given us.

Director Larry Cohen (*It's Alive, God Told Me To*) is a B-movie genius given to guerilla filmmaking approaches. He shot much of *Q* illegally in New York, and created a near panic when, without telling any authorities, he put Carradine and other actors atop the Chrysler Building during a weekday morning rush hour. They were firing machine guns at a helicopter that was standing in for Quetzalcoatl.

Mormons believe Quetzalcoatl was actually Jesus Christ and that, before ascending into Heaven, he visited Native Americans. And that's just *one* supremely metal aspect of Mormonism.

QUATERMASS AND THE PIT (1967), AKA FIVE MILLION YEARS to EARTH

(DIR. ROY WARD BAKER; W/ANDREW KEIR, JAMES DONALD, BARBARA SHELLEY, JULIAN GLOVER)

✦ SATAN ✦ ALIEN INVASION

London workers dig up what they think is a leftover World War II missile. The projectile turns out to be a rocket from Mars, containing alien corpses that look more than a bit like Satan. Dr. Quatermass (Andrew Keir), stops work on plans to colonize the moon in order to investigate. The rocket soon exudes an evil psychic grip on those who get too close. Soon, London is inflamed with riots. When a giant spectral Martian looms over the city, Dr. Q remembers how to beat the devil, and he saves earth. Cheerio!

Hammer Films' *Quatermass and the Pit* is better known in the U.S. as *Five Million Years to Earth*. The title is a reference to science within the film that perhaps humanity evolved from these devilish creatures all those millennia ago, and also an acknowledgment on the part of the producers that the popular British sci-fi character Dr. Quatermass never caught on stateside.

Clockwise from top left: Q: The
Winged Serpent *as painted by Boris
Vallejo;* Queen of the Damned;
Five Million Years to Earth, *aka*
Quatermass and the Pit; *stone-age*
Quest for Fire *VHS box*

Despite its intriguing premise, the movie is stodgy and silly, particularly when a machine that can record and play back someone's thought patterns on a movie screen is just wheeled out as though it were no more exotic than a Mr. Coffee. Still, the concept of humanity evolving from satanic Martians is a head-banging winner.

Dr. Quatermass is the hero upon which the Hammer Films foundation was laid. The studio's successful Dr. Q movies in the '50s enabled the launch of the Christopher Lee–Peter Cushing horror films that later made Hammer the definitive Heavy Metal Movie production house.

Queen of the Damned (2002)

(Dir. Michael Rymer; w/Stuart Townsend, Aaliyah, Marguerite Moreau, Lena Olin)

✠ Vampires ✠ Sunset Strip

Aristocratic bloodsucker Lestat (Stuart Townsend), the creation of novelist Anne Rice previously portrayed by Tom Cruise in *Interview With the Vampire* (1994), is awakened from a century-long coffin slumber in Los Angeles by the sounds of a gothy nü-metal band. Lestat likes what he hears! In short order, he takes over as the combo's singer. Trouble brews when the Sunset Strip's top-hat-and-bat-wings scene, power-boosted by an actual undead fop, attracts other vampires—in particular Akasha (R&B singer Aaliyah), the unholy mother of all vampires. Akasha wants Lestat as her king, and she'll happily annihilate every mortal being on earth to make it happen. Unfortunately, Lestat is perfectly happy showing off his hot licks and removing Hot Topic garb from his backstage groupies, so he ends up the unlikely champion of humanity.

After the big-budget *Interview With the Vampire*, *Queen of the Damned* comes off as a two-bit rush job, produced to beat a deadline before the studio lost its rights to the story. Aaliyah is certainly easy on the eyes, but she's pure vapor in terms of screen presence. The fact that she died in an airplane crash months before the movie came out

adds a layer of bummer to what would otherwise be a light diversion on late-night HBO.

Queen's soundtrack potently freezes on circular aluminum nü-metal's big hard-rock cultural moment. Lestat's music was made by Korn frontman Jonathan Davis (who cameos as a ticket scalper). Due to contractual restrictions, Davis's vocals could not be used on the soundtrack, so he rounded up a cabal of singers including Marilyn Manson, Wayne Static, David Draiman, Chester Bennington of Linkin Park, and Jay Gordon of Orgy. Talk about queens of the damned.

Quest for Fire (1982)

(Dir. Jean-Jacques Annaud; w/Ron Perlman, Rae Dawn Chong, Everett McGill, Nicholas Kadi)

✠ Saber-Toothed Tigers ✠ Cannibalism

Based on J. H. Rosny's 1911 novel, *Quest for Fire* takes place eighty thousand years in the past. The film chronicles the journey of three Neanderthals (Ron Perlman, Everett McGill, Nicholas Kadi) to find fire for their tribe after their sole source of flame burns out. Along the way, they encounter cannibals (covered in what looks like corpse paint), saber-toothed tigers, wooly mammoths, quicksand, and advanced Cro-Magnons. They learn about weaponry, fine art, sex outside of rape, and, crucially, how to make fire.

Unlike camp-fests on the order of *One Million Years B.C.* (1966), spoofs such as *Caveman* (1981), or more recent CGI junk like *10,000 B.C.* (2008), *Quest for Fire* applies painstaking realism to depict prehistoric life. Told through prehuman language, sheer visual bravura, and brilliant performances, *Quest for Fire* is a powerful adventure and moving hero's journey quite unlike anything else in the movies—heavy metal or otherwise.

Novelist Anthony Burgess, author of *A Clockwork Orange*, famous for its unique future lingo, Nadsat, created the film's caveman language. Iron Maiden's 1983 song "Quest for Fire" from *Piece of Mind* effectively re-creates the movie's scenario (adding a goofy opening line involving dinosaurs walking the earth).

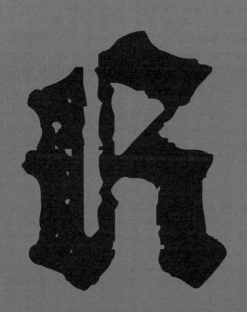

R

RACE WITH THE DEVIL ✠ RAMPAGE ✠ RATS: NIGHT OF TERROR ✠ RAZORBACK ✠ RE-ANIMATOR ✠ RED SONJA ✠ REFORM SCHOOL GIRLS ✠ REJUVENATOR, THE ✠ RENDEZVOUS WITH RAGNAROK ✠ REPO: THE GENETIC OPERA ✠ RETURN OF THE EVIL DEAD ✠ RETURN OF THE JEDI ✠ THE RETURN OF THE KING ✠ RETURN OF THE LIVING DEAD ✠ RETURN OF THE LIVING DEAD 3 ✠ RETURN TO OZ ✠ RICKY 6 ✠ RIOT ON SUNSET STRIP ✠ THE RIPPER ✠ RISE OF THE PLANET OF THE APES ✠ RIVER'S EDGE ✠ THE ROAD WARRIOR ✠ ROADIE (1980) ✠ ROADIE (2011) ✠ ROBOCOP ✠ ROCK & RULE ✠ ROCK 'EM DEAD ✠ ROCK: IT'S YOUR DECISION ✠ ROCK 'N' ROLL NIGHTMARE ✠ ROCK OF AGES ✠ ROCK STAR ✠ ROCK'N WITH SATAN ✠ THE ROCKER ✠ ROCKTOBER BLOOD ✠ ROCKULA ✠ THE ROCKY HORROR PICTURE SHOW ✠ RODRIGO D: NO FUTURO ✠ ROLE MODELS ✠ ROLLER BLADE ✠ ROSEMARY'S BABY ✠ R.O.T.O.R. ✠ ROTTING CORPSE: CIRCUS OF FOOLS ✠ RUIDO DAS MINAS ✠ RUNAWAY ✠ THE RUNAWAYS ✠ THE RUNNING MAN ✠ RUSH: BEYOND THE LIGHTED STAGE

Race With the Devil

(1975)

(Dir. Jack Starrett; w/Peter Fonda, Warren Oates, Loretta Swit, Lara Parker)

✠ Satan ✠ Black Mass ✠ Human Sacrifice

Hollywood hard-men Peter Fonda and Warren Oates costar as regular California Joes piloting a Winnebago RV toward a Colorado vacation. They have dirt bikes, skis, and their wives in tow, and nothing but blue skies ahead. Come nightfall, though, these gents accidentally witness an outdoor satanic ritual that culminates in a human sacrifice. When they are spotted, the devil worshippers give chase, and the heroes have to, as the title says, *Race With the Devil*.

Director Jack Starrett earned his colors with hard-driving biker movies (*Run, Angel, Run!*; *The Losers*) and booty-stomping blaxploitation (*Slaughter, Cleopatra Jones*), and he proves equally deft here with a hybrid of small-town occult horror and engine-gunning cat-and-mouse highway pursuit. Whenever the movie seems to be settling into *Race* mode (the nerve-wracking navigation of a flaming Winnebago through twisty mountain byways), out leaps a fresh injection of *Devil*, like the cultists' use of rattlesnakes. The overall storm brewed by *Race With the Devil* makes it an unsung drive-in metal movie classic, and a hell of a good time. Only Starrett knows if the title derives from the hard-hitting 1968 proto-metal jam by Gun titled "Race With the Devil," which was later covered by Judas Priest, Girlschool, and Church of Misery.

Rampage (2009)

(Dir. Uwe Boll; w/Brendan Fletcher, Shaun Sipos, Michael Paré, Matt Frewer, Lynda Boyd)

✠ Killing Spree

After suffering as one of Internet's universal punching bags, director Uwe Boll struck back through a trio of boundary-free fury exercises: the kitchen-sink sicko comedy *Postal* (2007), the plain old sicko serial-killer movie *Seed* (2007), and *Rampage*, his rapid-fire poison-pen letter to the *Grand Theft Columbine* generation.

Borrowing the setup but ditching the mitigating attempts at liberal Hollywood "gray-shading" of Michael Douglas movie *Falling Down* (1993), *Rampage* introduces us to Brendan Fletcher as torn-up teenager Bill. As life's escalating irritants gnaw his core, a botched coffee order finally sends Bill to his stash of automatic weapons, high-powered explosives, and Kevlar body armor. Bill, as you might guess, then cavalierly marches about Main Street blasting in every direction.

Alas, these walk-and-shoot orgies get pretty damn depressing pretty damn quick, but the movie's final political diatribe is ham-fisted and lunkheaded enough to be likable. *Rampage* represents Uwe Boll at his most thoughtful and, even more shocking, cinematically competent. A five-minute restricted audience "red band" trailer for *Rampage* supplies a highlight loop of the movie's carnage set to the thunderous nü-metal of the song "Die, Motherfucker" by the band Dope. Subtlety-seekers need not investigate.

Rats: Night of Terror (1984), aka Rats; Blood Kill

(Dir. Bruno Mattei; w/Ottaviano Dell'Acqua, Geretta Geretta, Massimo Vanni, Richard Cross)

✠ Post-Apocalypse ✠ Mutants ✠ Rat Zombies

In the year 225 a.b.—"After the Bomb"—humanity's survivors are split between those in underground cities and the hardscrabble surface dwellers known as the New Primitives. As this is an Italian *Road Warrior* knock-off, you can be quite sure that any such new primitivism does not suffer from a lack of tricked-out motorcycles and deathmobiles. *Rats: Night of Terror* does put an interesting spin on the post-nuke template, though. The villains are not just some rival band of punky bikers and muscle thugs, but the actual title creatures; mutated rodents with razor-sharp fangs and an insatiable hunger for human flesh. And there are *lots* of them going tooth and tiny nail against the *Mad Max* types here in the urban wreckage of Armageddon.

Rats, in fact, comes to resemble a zombie film with fuzzy, squeaking little fuckers in place of reanimated corpses. The movie's cheapness keeps it from being scary but also makes it hilariously memorable. The rats themselves were, in fact, guinea pigs painted black. The poor things get repeatedly tossed at our heroes and, in a moment meant to suggest a horrifying swarm of these creatures, dozens of them are dumped onto a conveyor belt and sent forward into the action. A credit at the end of *Rats* ought to read: "All animals were harmed in the making of this motion picture."

Razorback (1984)

(Dir. Russell Mulcahy; w/Gregory Harrison, Arkie Whiteley, Bill Kerr, Judy Morris)

✠ Man Against Nature ✠ Giant Killer Pig

The star of crazy Aussie oinksploitation ripper *Razorback* is a dump-truck-size wild boar that terrorizes the Outback after developing a taste for human hog slop. This beast remains cinema's nearest dead ringer for Motörhead's snaggle-toothed War Pig logo. American Gregory Harrison (Dr. Gonzo Gates of TV's *Trapper John, M.D.*) turns Great White Hunter after the Great Bristle-Backed Beast devours his animal-activist wife. She had traveled Down Under to expose dog food companies illegally harvesting kangaroo meat. Her shrimp ends up on the barbie.

Razorback, the movie and the monster alike, looks great. Director Russell Mulcahy (who went on make two *Highlander* films) renders a unique, neon-hued, Dalí-esque universe shot with high-end mid-'80s music-video aesthetics. The snarling, hard-charging pig is a whirlwind of tusks, teeth, flaring nostrils, and glaring eyes. He surrealistically spellbinds while bulldozing through entire houses, and deserves his own heavy metal concept album.

RE-ANIMATOR (1985)

(DIR. STUART GORDON; W/JEFFREY COMBS, BARBARA CRAMPTON, DAVID GALE)

✠ EXTREME GORE ✠ H. P. LOVECRAFT

Science-fiction and dark fantasy author H. P. Lovecraft (1890–1937) is one of the supreme priests of heavy metal culture and aesthetics. The visionary and peculiar Rhode Island native has come to be most revered among headbangers for his creation of intricate worlds filled with demonic overkill and kinky sex, populated by freak-out creatures such as the tentacle-faced hate-deity Cthulu (see also Metallica's "Call of Ktulu") and the horny Dagon fish-men.

Though Lovecraft horror has been a part of metal since Black Sabbath first asked "What is this that stands before me?" the initial VHS-era glimpses of the author's visions came via *Re-Animator*, filmmaker Stuart Gordon's uproarious, over-the-top adaptation of the short story, "Herbert West—Reanimator." Like the breakneck thrash metal movement that coincided with its rise, *Re-Animator* is exhilarating and repulsive, brutal and goofy, inspiring and insane. (The movie is in league with a half-dozen "Re-Animator" bands worldwide, and a slew of songs by Rigor Mortis, Vulture, and Disemboweled Corpse.)

In the film, Herbert West (Jeffrey Combs) is a nerdy but crazily charismatic medical student at Miskatonic University (a frequent Lovecraft locale). He concocts a chemical that can restore life to the dead, but they come back psychotic, super-strong, and driven to kill. Herbert is okay with those side effects. His on-campus enemy, Professor Hill (David Gale), is not. Their conflict results in a lot more than just academic broadsides getting pumped up, blown out, and chewed to bits. Their laboratory setting offers countless cadavers ripe for experimentation.

One unforeseen scientific breakthrough befalls the dean's gorgeous daughter, Megan (Barbara Crampton). After Professor Hill gets decapitated, West reanimates both the dead man's head and body. This leads to a scene where Hill's walking corpse straps Megan nude to a table and, holding his own head in his hands, lowers it tongue-first between her legs and goes lick wild—cinema's ultimate outrageous example of "giving head." The image also seems to have inspired the orally affectionate zombies on the cover of Cannibal Corpse's *Tomb of the Mutilated*.

The perfect period at the end of the Golden Age of Extreme Horror that began in 1968 with *Night of the Living Dead, Re-Animator* was a crucial extra-musical component of mid-'80s metal. The shocks and gory sights poured like liquid petroleum on the kindling of underground death metal, oozing into the underground and helping to ignite the extreme metal conflagration with humor and flair, and real horror. Following *Re-Animator*, Stuart Gordon became cinema's premier interpreter of H. P. Lovecraft, devoting his life to crafting an unspeakable torrent of Heavy Metal Movie essentials: *From Beyond* (1986), *Castle Freak* (1995), and *Dagon* (2001). Heavy metal has responded with Reanimator bands hailing from Canada, Russia, Slovakia, the UK, Ukraine, and the United States, plus dozens of "Reanimator" songs featuring the grossest musical visions known to humanity.

RED SONJA (1985)

(DIR. RICHARD FLEISCHER; W/BRIGITTE NIELSEN, ARNOLD SCHWARZENEGGER, SANDAHL BERGMAN)

✠ SWORDS & SORCERY ✠ AMAZONS

Six foot one, sexily muscular, and enunciating in a northern European accent at least as impenetrable as the utterances of her costar Arnold Schwarzenegger, Brigitte Nielsen emerged from the land of Lars Ulrich to swing a broadsword toward superstardom in *Red Sonja*. Despite the stink-bomb movie, she connected. Nielsen stars as Sonja, a redhead born into the Hyborian Age. After wicked lesbian Queen Gedren razes her village, she dedicates her life to learning sword combat and exacting vengeance. Yes, the setup is identical to that of *Conan the Barbarian*. In case anyone missed that, the queen also is played by a *Conan* costar, Sandahl Bergman. Red Sonja actually debuted as a Marvel comics character in 1973, based on a similar character ("Red Sonya") created by *Conan* author Robert E. Howard.

En route to Gedren's castle, Sonja acquires a magic talisman that provides her with superhuman fighting skills, and she hooks up with Lord Kalidor (Schwarzenegger). Their adventures are typical, spiced up by Gedren coming on hot and heavy to Sonja, and by the appearance of a stupidly likable amphibious monster called the "Icthyan Killing Machine."

Despite the right cast and director, (Richard Fleischer made 1984's okay *Conan the Destroyer*), *Red Sonja* is duller and less inventive than even many of the cheapest sword-and-sorcery stinkers of its day. When it comes to these movies, badness is acceptable, but boring is not.

In his 2012 memoir, *Total Recall: My Unbelievably True Life Story*, Arnold Schwarzenegger confirmed Nielsen's prior claim that the bruise-some twosome engaged in an affair while shooting *Red Sonja*. Schwarzenegger considers *Red Sonja* the worst film he ever made, and jokes that uses it to discipline his children: "I tell them, if they get on my bad side, they'll be forced to watch *Red Sonja* ten times in a row. Consequently, none of my kids has ever given me much trouble."

Even though the film tanked, Nielsen became a pop-culture fixture upon the release of *Red Sonja*. She took up offscreen with Sylvester Stallone, and costarred with him as a scheming Soviet boxing promoter in the most metal of all pugilism films, *Rocky IV* (1985).

REFORM SCHOOL GIRLS

(1986)

(DIR. TOM DESIMONE; W/WENDY O. WILLIAMS, SYBIL DANNING, LINDA CAROL, PAT AST)

✠ WOMEN IN PRISON

Reform School Girls tore up grindhouses after a hot spate of women-in-prison flicks throughout the early '80s, the greatest of which is the Linda-Blair-vs.-Sybil-Danning smackdown of the über-bitches, *Chained Heat* (1983). There, Sybil played the wicked queen bee of an evil jailhouse girl gang. *Reform School Girls* flips the nips. As a warden of the titular reform school, Sybil bumps up hard and heavy against problem student Charlie Chambliss, portrayed at full snarl by Plasmatics front-dervish Wendy O. Williams.

Nudity is copious (strip searches, group showers, fire-hose discipline, etc.), as is comically over-the-top(less) cruelty, such as a deliciously sick scene of Wendy branding a gang symbol with a hot wire hanger on the supple seat of a squirming new fish (Sherri Stoner). *Reform School Girls* is a spoof but delivers the necessary ingredients for a properly metal babes-behind-bars exploitation diversion. W.O.W. is a wonder throughout, shooting hate bullets from her eyes, real bullets from assorted weapons, and closing the proceedings by glowering at the camera and roaring, "See you in Hell!"

Wendy O.'s only other screen credit of note is an appearance in the hard-core porn comedy *Candy Goes to Hollywood* (1979). She appears on a TV parody called *The Dong Show*, performing the feat that financed her early Plasmatics days when she worked the live sex shows on Forty-Second Street: shooting Ping-Pong balls out of her vagina.

THE REJUVENATOR (1988),
AKA REJUVENATRIX

(DIR. BRIAN THOMAS JONES; W/VIVIAN LANKO, JOHN
MACKAY, VIVIAN DUBLIN, GODDESS AMBROSIA)
✠ '80s HORROR ✠ MEDICAL DEVIANT

Aging glamour-puss Ruth Warren (Vivian Dublin) would just about kill to be young again. Enter mildly mad scientist Gregory Ashton (John MacKay), and she gets multiple chances to do just that. Upon ingesting Dr. Ashton's unsteady youth serum, Ruth transforms into her former self (played by sprightly Vivian Lanko), but just for a few hours at a time. After that, she morphs into a series of splatter-tastic variations on late-'80s latex horror makeup monstrosities—sprouting fangs, oozing slime, and hungry for humans.

Adding octaves and Aqua Net to the glop and gore on display is a cameo appearance by all-female Long Island quartet Poison Dollys, doing what they do loudly onstage in a rock club.

Rejuvenator's grotesque visual effects are the warped handiwork of Ed French, a New York B-movie mainstay who also made eye-pop candy for *Nightmare* (1981), *Amityville II* (1982), *Sleepaway Camp* (1983), and *C.H.U.D.* (1984) before going big time with *Terminator 2* (1991).

RENDEZVOUS WITH RAGNAROK (1997)

(DIRS. DAVE BROCKIE, DON DRAKULICH, HUNTER
JACKSON; W/GWAR)
✠ EVIL PUPPETS ✠ GORE ✠ CONCERT FOOTAGE

Theatrical metal monstrosities Gwar return with more costumes, more puppets, more gore galore, mutilation merriment, and another mini-movie expansion of their Gwarniverse. As the destructive comet Ragnarok hurls toward Earth, aliens steal a sperm sample from Gwar frontman Oderus Urungus and use it to impregnate side-woman Slymenstra Hymen. The mutant baby heralds the arrival of evil Cardinal Syn, a robot who feeds on infants who contain high levels of "jizmoglobin" (one of Gwar's favorite bodily fluids to spray all over an audience).

Rendezvous With Ragnarok offers blood, feces, genital pulverization, heavy metal, and Gwar, as expected. The video for "Saddam a Go-Go," featured on *Beavis and Butt-Head*, is also included. This humble Gwar video impressively predates *A Serbian Film* (2010) in crossing a final boundary of shock concepts, albeit comically. Apologizing to Slymenstra after committing this ultimate transgression, Oderus says: "I'm sorry I raped our baby, but here, I bought you this nice purse."

REPO: THE GENETIC OPERA (2008)

(DIR. DARREN LYNN BOUSMAN; W/ALEXA VEGA,
ANTHONY HEAD, BILL MOSELEY, OGRE, PARIS HILTON)
✠ POST-APOCALYPSE ✠ EXTREME GORE

Repo! The Genetic Opera offers the agonized, ugly, and unloved adolescents of the twenty-first century the same pleasures bestowed upon previous generations by its combined influences: theatrical rock, nü metal, British punk, industrial music, goth, splatter horror, and sick jokes. Thus, *Repo* automatically gets an A for intention, with all other grades coming in on a generously sliding scale.

Set in a murky Dystopia in the year 2057, *Repo* chronicles lowlifes and big shots in a world where elective surgery is humanity's primary rush. GeneCo, the corporation that supplies the body parts, occasionally has to yank their products back for nonpayment. Semi-grown-up *Spy Kids* kid Alexa Vega stars as a teenage recluse who may or may not be stricken with a rare malady. Her father (Anthony Head) cares for her by day. By night, he dons leather and power tools and acts as a Repo Man, re-harvesting unpaid-for human organs while they're still in use.

Out among the gutter dregs, a grave robber (Terrance Zdunich) plies his trade to pilfer a body fluid sought after by surgery addicts. At the opera

JUDGE, JURY,
AND EXECUTIONER.

R.O.T.O.R.

PETER FONDA · WARREN OATES
ARE BURNING THEIR BRIDGES AND A LOT OF RUBBER
ON THE DEADLIEST STRETCH OF ROAD IN THE COUNTRY!

RACE
WITH THE
DEVIL

LORETTA SWIT · LARA PARKER

RATS

¡Entre locuras y giras, el rock y el amor se imponen!

LOS LOCOS CAMINOS
DEL ROCK

A 300 ans,
il a décidé de monter
son groupe de rock !

ROCKULA

CANNON

SPECIAL EDITION

Rock 'n' Roll
Nightmare

WHEN THE BAND STARTS TO ROCK...
HEADS START, TO ROLL!

Billy's back from the dead...
with a message from Hell!

Rocktober
Blood

Clockwise from top left: R.O.T.O.R. *rips off the coolest images;* Race With the Devil; Rats: The
Night of Terror; *Meat Loaf meets Alice Cooper in Roadie; ideal double feature:* Rock 'N' Roll
Rocktober Blood *and* Rock 'N Roll Nightmare; *Spanish* Rockula

house, Blind Mag (Sarah Brightman) projects stuff from her mechanical eyes (a cool effect) and belts out high notes for audience members whose faces are too tight to express any emotional reactions. Paul Sorvino shows off his classically trained pipes as the head of GeneCo. His unworthy heirs are played by Bill Moseley (Chop Top from *Texas Chainsaw Massacre 2*), Ogre from Skinny Puppy, and Paris Hilton.

Even with that plot and that cast, *Repo* contains not one scintilla of irony, self-awareness, or even the slightest outside perspective. From the high-tech industrial metal underpinnings of the music to the shockingly explicit innards-ripping, *Repo*'s airs of misery, isolation, and self-loathing radiate out in operatic proportions. As such, *Repo* echoes heavy metal's utter respect for a grievously angst-afflicted adolescent audience of all ages.

In 2010, I saw *Repo* at a sold-out midnight screening in Chicago's Music Box Theatre, where *Rocky Horror* still plays. The teenage crowd in which I sat booed a trailer for *Twilight*, then went orgasmic for *Repo*'s opening credits and stayed that way until the final fadeout. They greeted each musical number with wild shrieks, sang along with every word, and rapturously applauded each conclusion. At no juncture was the atmosphere less than thick-as-brick with glee— over gore-sopped pain and suffering expressed in song. As stated, *Repo*'s music is Internet-age sing-along metal that's not really for me, but it perfectly serves the film's devotees.

RETURN OF THE
EVIL DEAD (1973), AKA
ATTACK OF THE BLIND DEAD;
RETURN OF THE BLIND DEAD
(DIR. AMANDO DE OSSORIO; W/TONY KENDALL, FERNANDO SANCHO, ESPERANZA ROY, JOSÉ CANALEJAS)
✣ ZOMBIES ✣ KNIGHTS TEMPLAR

Not to be confused with Sam Raimi's *Evil Dead* series (or 1985's *Return of the Living Dead*), *Re-*

turn of the Evil Dead is the first sequel to *Tombs of the Blind Dead* (1971), a classic Spanish spooker about the zombified resurrection of the Knights Templar. *Return* opens with a flashback to thirteenth-century Bouzano, Portugal, where peasants overpower the Knights for practicing black magic, poking their eyes out with torches before finally burning them to death. In 1973 Bouzano, the town preps for an anniversary bacchanal in celebration of the Knights' blinding and execution. Village idiot Murdo (José Canalejas) kills a woman as a blood sacrifice to the Knights and, sure enough, it works. The Blind Dead—hooded, robe-wearing skeletons who brandish swords and ride blind horses—rise to slaughter and feast on the festival's revelers. In terms of action and real scares, *Return of the Evil Dead* is quite a leap forward from *Tombs of the Blind Dead* and remains a popular favorite in the series.

RETURN OF THE JEDI (1983)
(DIR. RICHARD MARQUAND; W/MARK HAMILL, CARRIE FISHER, HARRISON FORD, BILLY DEE WILLIAMS)
✣ SCIENCE FICTION ✣ EVIL EMPIRE

The original *Star Wars* saga ends not with a bang but with a pagan bacchanal around woodland bonfires. That would be fine and metal, indeed, if the pagans were anybody other the utterly non-metal Ewoks. Alas, Ewoks is what you get in *Return of the Jedi*, along with a bunch of so-so adventuring done better in the first two *Star Wars* movies, apart from a pretty wicked chase through a forest on flying motorcycles.

Jedi's metal strength is all front-loaded. Jabba the Hut, a fantastically obese gangster worm, stuffs his face as his minions attend constantly to his other pleasure portals in a den of otherworldly decadence. Princess Leia (Carrie Fisher) is chained to Jabba's girth in a metal bikini. Just outside Jabba's hot, sandy libertine lair is the deathtrap into which he feeds his enemies: a giant, pulsating, toothed space-vagina.

Consider the power fantasies of any teenage metalhead as thunder riffs blare in his bedroom, pizza cheese slides into his maw, a jizz sock lies stiff on the floor alongside the latest porno delivery system, and visions of lame-asses at school eat shit in the warzone just beneath his unwashed long hair. Jabba the Hut embodies all that in rotund mollusk form, with the intergalactic racketeering funds to pull it off right. Badass motherfucker.

Return of the Jedi originally bore the decidedly more metal title *Revenge of the Jedi*. Posters and other tie-in products were made until Star Wars creator George Lucas decreed that "Jedi are not vengeful." The mind reels over what *Jedi* might have been had the directing duties been taken by George Lucas's initial choice: *Eraserhead* and *Wild at Heart* madman David Lynch.

The Return of the King (1980)

(DIRS. JULES BASS, ARTHUR RANKIN JR.; W/ORSON BEAN)

✠ J. R. R. TOLKIEN

Television animation studio Rankin-Bass followed up their well-received version of *The Hobbit* (1977) with an adaptation of the final book in author J. R. R. Tolkien's *Lord of the Rings* trilogy, *The Return of the King*. *Return* aired as an ABC TV special and stands as an unofficial follow-up to Ralph Bakshi's big-screen botch of *The Lord of the Rings* (1978). Like *The Hobbit*, it's aimed at children.

Orson Bean does double vocal duties as both Frodo and Bilbo Baggins, backed by fellow *Hobbit* returnees John Huston as Gandalf and Brother Theodore as Gollum. The perfect voice cast continues with Roddy McDowall as Sam, Theodore Bikel as Aragorn, and William Conrad as Lord Dethenor. If the more foot-hair-raising elements of Frodo and Samwise Gamgee's journey to Mount Doom seem watered down here, remember that these cartoons provide a welcoming gateway for kids to discover the heavy metal wonders that lay ahead in the realm of Tolkien's Middle Earth.

Brother Theodore, so great here as the voice of Gollum/Smeagol, was a cult figure whose sinister persona and tumultuous life story is rife with heavy metal elements. Born Theodore Gottlieb in 1906 Germany, he survived the Nazi death camp Dachau; moved to Switzerland, where he was deported for "chess hustling"; and then high-tailed it to the U.S. with the help of family friend Albert Einstein. In the '50s beat era, Theodore became a pitch-black comic monologist who scored numerous TV appearances before fading into obscurity. He came back big in the early '80s, though, via unforgettably unhinged appearances on *Late Night With David Letterman*, and a weekly one-man stage show in New York.

Theodore's other movie roles exude fitting, metallic-tinged weirdness. Among them are Nazi Captain Carl Clitoris (a non-sex role) in the hard-core porn *Jaws* parody *Gums* (1976); a bit as himself in the German disco vampire comedy *Nocturna* (1979); the voice of a carnival barker in *The Last Unicorn* (1982); and serial-slaying next-door neighbor Uncle Reuben Klopek in *The 'Burbs* (1989).

Return of the Living Dead (1985)

(DIR. DAN O'BANNON; W/LINNEA QUIGLEY, JAMES KAREN, CLU GULAGER, DON CALFA)

✠ ZOMBIES ✠ NUCLEAR HOLOCAUST

Return of the Living Dead is the mid-'80s punk-metal crossover in celluloid form. The opening was perfectly timed in August 1985, smack in the middle of *Speak English or Die* by Stormtroopers of Death, *Dealing With It* by Dirty Rotten Imbeciles, *Animosity* by C.O.C., and *In My Head*, the long-haired final album by Black Flag, one and all milestones that annihilated the wall between heavy metal and punk. Amidst that wellspring, *Return of the Living Dead* arrived, and suddenly everyone could relate to each other!

Return opens in a Louisville morgue, where incompetent workers release a toxic gas that reanimates corpses and makes them hungry for brains. Bad enough that these goofs are in a bunker full of dead bodies; even worse, there happens to be a cemetery right next door. The initial victims to reap the wrath of the rising zombies are a gaggle of leather-clad, safety-pinned, Mohawk-adorned rockers boozing and canoodling among the graves. Sexy punkette Trash (Linnea Quigley) strips completely nude atop a tombstone, while the escaped gas arouses a sudden eruption of ghouls up out of the ground.

At first, the rules set by previous zombie films apply: the dead lurch forward, arms outstretched and teeth gnashing, chomping anyone they can catch and thereby making more of themselves. But soon enough the zombies run, talk, and, upon devouring a couple of EMT workers, grab an ambulance radio and order: "Send more paramedics!" Even disembodied appendages spring to kill-crazy life, along with surgically halved canines known as laboratory "split dogs" that simply can't be destroyed. A captured zombie, strapped to a medical table, moans and flails as she explains that eating brains provide momentary comfort because "it hurts to be dead!"

The authorities' final solution is to rain Armageddon onto the infected area. *Return of the Living Dead* remains, to date, the only major film to end with the nuclear destruction of Louisville. But wait, there's more, and the suspiciously metal "Partytime" by former pallid death rockers .45 Grave explodes on the soundtrack, as vocalist Dinah Cancer wails: "Do you wanna par-tay!" The film ends on an ultimate note of doom, then sneaks in a sick-joke punch line promising warped fun to come.

The antic madness and killer performances of *Return of the Living Dead* are unrivaled among the canon of zombie film greats. Along with *Fright Night* and *Re-Animator*, each released within weeks of one another, this remains one of the last great examples of the movie genre that seems most difficult to pull off: the horror comedy. *Return of the Living Dead* marks the directorial debut of writer Dan O'Bannon, a former collaborator with John Carpenter, and also a

coscreenwriter of *Alien* (1979). Originally *Return* was slated by to made by *Texas Chainsaw Massacre* helmer Tobe Hooper—in 3-D!

Return is scary and funny; it's also disgusting—yet inspiring. The appeal was metal and punk together in the great crossover movie of its day. No small coincidence, either, that this was the multiplex precursor to the major-label debuts by Big Four thrash metal bands Metallica, Slayer, Anthrax, and Megadeth, all heavily punk-influenced and looking to party under the mushroom cloud of this specific time in popular ghoul culture. The world was ready.

Return of the Living Dead 3 (1993)
(Dir. Brian Yuzna; w/Melinda Clarke, Kent McCord, Sarah Douglas, James T. Callahan)
✵ Zombies ✵ Goth Chick ✵ Body Modification

Bearing only vague thematic connections to its crackpot predecessors, mainly about the army creating zombies with sloppy use of toxic gas, *Night of the Living Dead 3* is a romantic fright film laden with heavy gore and played entirely straight. The scares and the romance work, which makes *ROTLD3* even more of a rarity than a non-despicable horror-comedy!

Young Curt Reynolds (J. Trevor Edmond) finds out that his military dad is secretly in the zombie production division. We're treated to numerous instances of graphic zombie abuse, some of which really deliver the gross-out goods. After Curt's mall-punk girlfriend Julie (Melinda Clarke) gets killed in an accident, he sneaks her body into Pop's lab and doses her with undead fumes. What results is the scene that turned *ROTLD3* from a castoff sequel into a cult favorite all its own. Julie transforms—slowly, painfully, and in up-close agonizing detail—into the sexiest flesh-eating goth chick in movie history.

Set in the mid-1990s, Julie's metamorphosis is highly Lollapalooza and alt-metal-influenced. She pierces her skin (naked nipples included) with broken glass shards; inserts scraps of metal all over her body; sexily scarifies her extremities; and emerges in torn fishnets and leather with all her hotness fully exposed.

Giving proper kudos to the creature design, the real credit goes to Melinda Clarke for pulling this off. Had *ROTLD3* been stuck with a lesser glamour ghoul, it would simply have sunk and sucked. As it stands, *ROTLD3*'s Julie's is one of heavy metal cinema's most headbanging femmes fatale—and I mean way, way fatale. Ten years after *ROTLD3*, Melinda Clarke reinvented herself as a primetime MILF as the party-hearty mother of Mischa Barton's doomed bisexual teen drunk character on the Fox TV drama *The O.C.*

RETURN TO OZ (1985)
(DIR. WALTER MURCH; W/FAIRUZA BALK, NICOL WILLIAMSON, JEAN MARSH, EMMA RIDLEY)
✠ POST-APOCALYPSE ✠ WITCHCRAFT

Eleven-year-old Fairuza Balk fills the ruby slippers as miserable little Dorothy in the ill-conceived, inappropriate, and monumentally metal *Return to Oz*, Disney's whacko sequel that scarred a generation left alone with the home video. Six months after the Oz adventure we all know about, Auntie Em ships Dorothy to a draconian mental hospital, where the child is subjected to shock therapy. Dorothy escapes with her pet chicken Billina, surfs a river back to Oz, and finds the place in ruins. The Yellow Brick Road is destroyed. The Emerald City, robbed of its emeralds, is a pit of despair. The Scarecrow and the Tin Man have been turned to stone. The munchkins—don't even ask. The only good news is that the chicken obtains the power of speech.

A wobbly robot named Tik-Tok explains that how the evil Nome King (Nicol Williamson, Merlin of *Excalibur*) caused this mess. Jack Pumpkinhead, whose body is made of tree branches with a head just like it sounds, joins them. They soar off on the Gump, a flying sofa with the head of a talking moose. All-out terror arises when Dorothy visits Mombi, a witch with a gallery full of interchange-able heads. The disembodied noggins moan, roll their eyes, and gnash their teeth from inside glass jars lined up next to each other on shelves. Mombi selects one and wears it atop her neck.

Princess Ozma (Emma Ridley), who looks like she does on the cover of the Melvins' *Ozma* album, eventually saves the day and sends Dorothy back to Kansas. The good news, once our little heroine gets back, is that she'll never have to go to the nut hut again, because it got struck by lightning and burned down. Better still, the a-hole doctor in charge died in the fire, and his sadistic nurse got carted off to prison in a chicken coop.

Tornados of trippy shit and black-brained doom never let up. The original *Wizard of Oz* took us over the rainbow. *Return to Oz* is a rainbow in the dark. Upon its summer 1985 release, critics immediately, and accurately, flipped out over *Return to Oz*'s bleakness and horror. Audiences stayed away, and the movie lost Disney nearly $30 million. Oddball movie fans discovered the film quickly, though, and created a cult that has snowballed through the ensuing decades.

RICKY 6 (2000),
AKA DAY YOU LOVE SATAN
(DIR. PETER FILARDI; W/VINCENT KARTHEISER, CHAD CHRIST, SABINE SINGH, KEVIN GAGE)
✠ SATAN ✠ LSD ✠ SOUNDTRACK (IRON MAIDEN, VAN HALEN, DIO, KROKUS, DISEMBOWELMENT)

The low-budget, Canadian-made *Ricky 6* bor-rows its name and essential story elements from Long Island's notorious 1984 case of Satan-worshipping teenage "Acid King" mur-derer Ricky Kasso. As with the actual crime story, Ricky (Vincent Kartheiser) is a high-school untouchable in 1983 who attains what he thinks is power through LSD and ritual appeals to the Prince of Darkness. Numerous optical effects do well to convey the already schizophrenic Ricky's slide into psychedelic-onset homicidal rage. At one point, Jesus Christ chases Ricky through a supermarket during an acid trip. When the

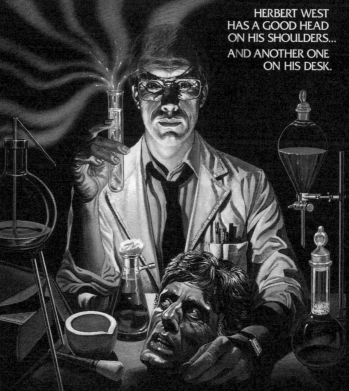

HERBERT WEST
HAS A GOOD HEAD
ON HIS SHOULDERS...
AND ANOTHER ONE
ON HIS DESK.

H.P. Lovecraft's classic tale of horror

RE-ANIMATOR
...It will scare you to pieces.

THE SAGA CONTINUES.

STAR WARS
REVENGE OF THE JEDI

Coming May 25, 1983 to your galaxy.

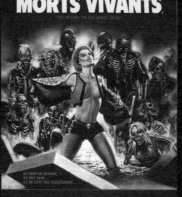

UN FILM DE DAN O'BANNON

LE RETOUR DES
MORTS VIVANTS

Clockwise from top left:
Red Sonja *foreign release;*
Re-Animator *alternate poster;*
Return of the Living Dead
delights in French; Revenge-
ful early Return of the Jedi
poster; Reform School Girls
camp it up

campfire slaughter eventually comes, we feel the pain of both perpetrator and victim.

Ricky 6 utilizes a period soundtrack well, particularly after the murder. Then the "Black Beast" that Ricky hoped to summon appears in his mind, to the strains of "Your Prophetic Throne of Ivory" by Australia's doom-death comminglers Disembowelment, to devastating effect.

Riot on Sunset Strip (1967)

(Dir. Arthur Dreifuss; w/Aldo Ray, Mimsy Farmer, Laurie Mock, Hortense Petra)
✠ Sunset Strip ✠ Concert Footage

Twenty rock-solid years before *The Decline of Western Civilization Part II*'s poodle-heads invaded the same sidewalks, L.A.'s stretch of Sunset Boulevard running from Havenhurst drive in Hollywood to Sierra Drive in Beverly Hills had already been ground zero for troublesome longhairs. *Riot on Sunset Strip* is a colorful, campy exploitation docudrama filmed within six weeks of a real-life December 1966 youth uprising. At issue was a teen curfew enforced on the area's burgeoning music scene.

Mimsy Farmer (*Four Flies on Grey Velvet, Hot Rods to Hell*) takes on Alice duties as she trips down the Strip's rabbit hole of rock clubs, hippies, bikers, pot parties, LSD, square business owners, police brutality, and even the groove-bummer known as gang rape. The *Sunset Strip* can't always be a riot.

Heavy metal is right on the horizon by way of some killer garage-psych performances. The Standells blast out the punkish title song and the hauntingly downbeat "Get Away From Here"— the group's greatest media appearance next to their 1964 guest-star spot on TV's *The Munsters*. The Enemies flip wigs with the fuzz-soul rave-up "Jolene" (not the Dolly Parton song).

Most unmistakably proto-metallic, however, are the two numbers by the Chocolate Watch Band, "Sittin' There Standing" and "Don't Need Your

Loving." The band wails rapturously, as though itching to soon hear Jimi Hendrix. Highly Morrison/Jagger–infected frontman Danny Aguilar exudes a slithering charisma that conjures up its own Lizard King–size devilish sympathy.

The Ripper (1985)

(Dir. Christopher Lewis; w/Tom Savini, Tom Schreier, Mona Van Pernis, Wade Tower)
✠ Slasher

Horror cinema's go-to gore effects guru (following his work with George Romero and on the *Friday the 13th* series and other plasma-sopped '80s chunk-blowers), Tom Savini finally got to splatter his victims in front of the camera in *The Ripper*. That is what is noteworthy about this shot-on-video tale of a haunted ring that turns its victims into Jack the Ripper on a campus laden with slashable coeds: Savini plays Jack the Ripper

The Ripper was writer-director Christopher Lewis's immediate follow-up to the definably metal *Blood Cult* (1985), which was accurately promoted as "the first movie made for the home video market" and made a heap of blood money.

Rise of the Planet of the Apes (2011)

(Dir. Rupert Wyatt; w/James Franco, Andy Serkis, Freida Pinto, John Lithgow)
✠ Animal Revenge

Atoning for Tim Burton's hugely despised 2001 *Planet of the Apes* remake, the hugely beloved *Rise of the Planet of the Apes* tells the origin story of the monkey planet through the prison conversion of highly intelligent chimpanzee Caesar (played, via motion capture, by Andy Serkis). Caesar grows up in the home of scientist Will Rodman (James Franco), where he grows proficient in sign language. After Caesar intimidates the neighbors, authorities place him in a cruel sanctuary for primates. There, aided by gorilla Buck and orangutan Maurice, Caesar organizes the animals into an army. Escaping from the sanctuary, Caesar steals canisters of a new intelligence-raising drug in gas form. Upon returning, he sets off the gas, and leads the apes on a spectacular invasion of San Francisco, en route to setting up what will be their new home in the Redwood forest.

Rise of the Planet of the Apes is symphonic in its build-up and thunderous in its resolution. The human actors are terrific, but the mostly CGI apes finally justify that most frustrating movie effects technology. Oppressed beings triumphing up over captors and abusers is the essence of heavy metal. *Rise of the Planet of the Apes* makes such heaviness sing. And swing from the trees!

Rise also pays clever homage to the cherished original *Planet of the Apes* films. The female chimp Cornelia is named after Roddy Mc-Dowall's Cornelius, and Maurice is a tribute to Maurice Evans, who played orangutan Dr. Zaius. The character Caesar (sort of) first appeared in *Conquest of the Planet of the Apes* (1972), and was also played by Roddy McDowall. He was the son of Cornelius and Zira (Kim Hunter), born in contemporary America in *Escape From the Planet of the Apes* (1971). After a plague kills all of earth's cats and dogs, apes are enslaved to work for humans. When Milo displays superior intellect, he's given an encyclopedia and asked to select what he should be called. He chooses Caesar. "A king's name!" his keeper marvels. Caesar goes on to lead the full-scale ape revolution.

RIVER'S EDGE (1986)
(DIR. TIM HUNTER; W/KEANU REEVES, IONE SKYE, CRISPIN GLOVER, DENNIS HOPPER)
✠ GRIM REALITY ✠ SOUNDTRACK (SLAYER, HALLOWS EVE, FATES WARNING)

River's Edge is what lower-class high school heavy metal fandom looked and felt like around the time *Reign in Blood* debuted. While Hollywood was asking mid-'80s teens to accept Judd "Nostrils" Nelson in *The Breakfast Club* as the closest thing to the metalheads gathered everywhere around them, genuinely indepen-

dent filmmaker Tim Hunter gifted us with *River's Edge*. Having already written *Over the Edge* (1979), Hunter proved the anti–John Hughes, and this is his *666 Candles*.

Down by the river embankment, teen hulk Samson "John" Tollet (Daniel Roebuck) strangles and dumps the body of his nude girlfriend Jamie (Danyi Deats). He then shows her remains, individually and in groups, to his posse of alcoholic, stoner, denim-and-leather-ensconced high school classmates, and they do nothing. Pangs of conscience nip at Matt (Keanu Reeves) and Clarissa (Ione Skye), but Clarissa's boyfriend, manic speed freak Layne (Crispin Glover), nips any proper impulses in the bud. All Layne wants to do is protect John, so he holes his friends up with veteran head-case Feck (Dennis Hopper), who long ago murdered his own girlfriend, and who now can only relate to a blow-up sex doll named Ellie. Nobody ends up happy.

River's Edge depicts a stone-cold world where your mom accuses you of dipping into her weed stash (and adds, "You were all mistakes anyway!); your twelve-year-old brother is a sadistic drunken drug addict who can and will shoot you once he gets a gun; and the only semblance of adulthood is an ex-hippie teacher self-importantly lamenting whatever the hell happened between his generation and yours ("We stopped a war, man!"). In such an existence, leaving your dead, naked friend in the woods and protecting her killer makes sense. In 1986, the only sound that made that life endurable was Slayer, and for once a soundtrack supervisor bludgeons the nail on the head with four early Slayer songs.

Keanu Reeves and Crispin Glover set the templates for their respective careers in *River's Edge*, transforming themselves into Heavy Metal Movie archetypes. Reeves took the dazed, dumbfounded essence of *Fast Times at Ridgemont High*'s Jeff Spicoli to terribly believable dark places, only to sweeten the part up again in the *Bill and Ted* movies. Glover represents pure explosive eccentricity, a full-bodied, spastically involuntary channel for the thunder and lightning behind his empathetic-then-scary-then-vacant eyes. These character types went on to serve both actors well through the years, and viewers, too.

Screenwriter Neal Jimenez based *River's Edge* on an actual 1981 case in Milpitas, California, of a sixteen-year-old raping and strangling his fourteen-year-old girlfriend, and then showing off her corpse to thirteen of his friends. No one reported the crime for two days.

The Road Warrior
(1982), AKA Mad Max 2
(Dir. George Miller; w/Mel Gibson, Bruce Spence, Emil Minty, Kjell Nilsson, Vernon Wells)
✷ Post-Apocalypse

With its neon-hued Mohawk haircuts, improvised trash-heap fashions, and pop-art visual evidence of "no future" everywhere, *The Road Warrior* adds a wild early-NWOBHM punk sheen to a leather-hide, heavy-machinery heart, and the blazingly metallic tale of the power of a lone hero against the encroaching forces of damnation. Writer-director George Miller and star Mel Gibson return from *Mad Max* (1979), a surprise drive-in and grindhouse hit that took on a second life as an art-house attraction and midnight movie. As in *Mad Max*, Gibson stars in the title role as an Australian highway cop whose violent, hyperspeed patrols represented society's last grab at maintaining some semblance of order after an unnamed global catastrophe had already ruptured all that had been "normal."

By the time of *The Road Warrior*, society has clearly lost that struggle. The landscape is entirely lawless "post-apocalypse." Gasoline is humanity's most precious commodity. Embittered by the murder of his family in the first movie, but too noble to simply go savage, Max drives the desert blacktops accompanied by an Australian cattle dog. They share cans of slimy pet food. After fending off a band of marauders led by Wez (Vernon Wells) and teaming with madcap helicopter pilot Gyro Captain (Bruce Spence), Max heads to a compound populated by

survivors with a working oil refinery.

The people of the compound are just and peaceful. They reveal that Wez is part of the outlaw brigades of sadistic madman Lord Humungus (Kjell Nilsson). After several skirmishes with the forces of Humungus, Max deigns to help the compound members, and their precious fuel, escape to safety. He'll also, happily, get to waste countless members of Team Humungus in the process.

The Road Warrior's climactic highway battle is the most epic chase scene in the history of the movies. With air support from Gyro Captain, and frontline bravery by the boomerang-tossing Feral Kid (Emil Minty), the hockey-armored Warrior Woman (Virginia Hey), and numerous other ragtag combatants, Max pilots an armored tanker truck against the enemy's tricked-out death machines, hell-bent for glory in the ashes of Armageddon. Spectacularly, they get there.

For all its unique style and surprising inventiveness, *Mad Max* was, at its core, simply a killer B-movie. *The Road Warrior* is a quantum leap forward—a Hollywood-scale blockbuster, as broad and blazing as its outback setting, and as game-changing as any adventure film to bedazzle worldwide audiences before or since. When we leave Max at the end, a redeemer alone on the road that he is doomed to travel, we know that this cannot be the end of his story; not even at the end of the world.

Max's beaten-up, black, supercharged V-8 pursuit special is the embodiment of heavy gearhead metal. A full year before Jason Voorhees of the *Friday the 13th* movies donned his hockey mask, the mighty Lord Humungus put his to terrifying use here. He assembles his hordes outside the compound, torturing two of the mini-society's inhabitants that his minions captured. A goggle-wearing goof (reminiscent of '70s funnyman Arte Johnson) introduces Humungus as "the Ayatollah of Rock-n-Rollah!" The chain-wielding, muscle-bound villain then launches into a booming speech that demands immediate surrender or utter annihilation.

Like the spirit of squatter punk made skunky eight-year-old-boy flesh, the Feral Kid interrupts Humungus. Emerging from one of his rat tunnels, the Kid whips his boomerang skyward and kills Wez's pretty-boy cycle bitch. When Wez then launches the weapon back, it ends up slicing off Arte Johnson's fingers. The Feral Kid whoops in triumph and backflips back down inside his tunnel. No gods, no masters!

In *Not Quite Hollywood*, the great 2008 documentary on Australian exploitation movies, Quentin Tarantino points out: "NOBODY shoots cars like the Aussies." That's true, as is the fact that nobody ever had cars—or trucks or motorcycles o the Gyro Captain's bizarre mini-helicopter—as great to shoot as the tricked-out, chopped-up, remodeled, superpowered vehicles rampaging in *The Road Warrior*.

In 2004, *Mad Max* fans created a highway driving event called *Roadwar USA* that evolved, by 2009, into the full-blown Wasteland Weekend, re-creating the world of the Mad Max movies with custom cars, costumes, campsites, stunts, fireworks, and all manner of recreational mayhem in service of a "four-day post-apocalyptic party". I don't know if anybody made it out alive, and I prefer to leave it that way.

ROADIE (1980)

(DIR. ALAN RUDOLPH; W/MEAT LOAF, ALICE COOPER, KAKI HUNTER, BLONDIE, DON CORNELIUS)

✠ CONCERT FOOTAGE ✠ SOUNDTRACK (ALICE COOPER, CHEAP TRICK, STYX, PAT BENATAR)

Meat Loaf stars in *Roadie* as good old boy Travis W. Redfish, a Texas truck driver and electronic-gizmo whiz who hitches his wagon to the Alice Cooper–struck eyes of teenage groupie Lola Bouilliabase (Kaki Hunter, future leading lady of the *Porky's* movies). Together, Travis and Lola travel cross-country to press the flesh with Cooper, and along the way they meet all manner of music greats, including down-home legends Roy Orbison, Hank Williams Jr., and Asleep at the Wheel, as well as new-wavers Blondie, who

really show a knack for slapstick. Travis uses his genius with gadgets and his all-around Texas tornado of a personality to earn the title of Greatest Roadie of All Time, while Lola sort of gets her boa-constrictor-strewn man in the end. Alice's big reveal to Lola that he's a soft-spoken fellow by day who just pretends to be a blood-drinking maniac by night comes off honest and unrehearsed. The moment is the sort of thing an actual roadie might overhear and keep to himself. The movie does well by sharing it with us.

Alas, *Roadie* never quite gels into anything more than scrambled evidence of Hollywood's turn-of-the-'80s cocaine problem—the repeated cuts away from musical performances become enraging. Today, the movie is tough to take, even as nostalgia. As a fan with "M-E-A-T" and "L-O-A-F" tattooed on his knuckles, I mourn for the movie-star-making turn that *Roadie* might have been!

ROADIE (2011)

(DIR. MICHAEL CUESTA; W/RON ELDARD, JILL HENNESSY, BOBBY CANNAVALE, LOIS SMITH)

✠ BLUE ÖYSTER CULT ✠ SOUNDTRACK (BÖC, RAMONES)

Except for one element, *Roadie* is an altogether typical low-budget, New York indie flick featuring Queens streets, stilted "local color" dialogue, and actors familiar from semi-gritty productions of this ilk (including every variation of TV's *Law & Order*). The one element that separates *Roadie* from its wee-hour cable and last-choice Redbox rental brethren, though, is that the damn thing is all about Blue Öyster Cult!

Ron Eldard stars as Jimmy, a fortysomething equipment-carrier for BÖC who returns home to his dotty mom (Lois Smith) after the band leaves on tour without him. Patrolling his neighborhood, Jimmy runs into high school bully Randy (Bobby Cannavale, a creep who could be the romantic lead in a she-male porn) and childhood crush Nikki (Jill Hennessy, always terrible when she tries to play working class). The two old friends are married now and they are assholes.

Jimmy's an a-hole, too. And so is Jimmy's mom. And, sort of, so is the entire movie; but then there's the goddamned Blue Öyster Cult angle and *Roadie* consistently, remarkably reloads and just keeps getting that essential ingredient exactly right. In one truly weird scene, the three main characters get coked up in a motel room. Talk turns to BÖC as "thinking man's metal," with an intricate, accurate description of Buck Dharma's writing philosophy and playing techniques. Randy interrupts to let it be known he'll play cuckold while Jimmy bulls Nikki. That doesn't happen, nor do we get to hear much more about Blue Öyster Cult.

Special kudos have to go to director Ron Cuesta (who coscripted *Roadie* with his brother Gerald) for recognizing and reviving late-'70s/early-'80s hard-rock should-have-beens the Good Rats, former band of longtime Kiss guitarist Bruce Kulick. Long Island local heroes who opened for Aerosmith, Kiss, Rush, Ozzy, and other titans of arena rock while awaiting a breakthrough hit that never happened, the Good Rats get a lot of love in *Roadie*, both via dialogue and soundtrack play.

ROBOCOP (1987)

(Dir. Paul Verhoeven; w/Peter Weller, Nancy Allen, Michael Ironside, Dan O'Herlihy)

✠ Near-Apocalypse Detroit ✠ Tough Justice ✠ Corporate Scum

Given its lineage of General Motors, Ted Nugent, the Stooges, and the MC5, along with Kiss serenading it as the preeminent "Rock City" and urban strife that has led to its "Mad Max times," to quote Moe from *The Simpsons*, Detroit has long ruled as one of headbanger history's most metal metropolises. Who better, then, to keep the peace through superior firepower in such a literally headbanging milieu than a man who is mostly made of actual metal? That's the premise of director Paul Verhoeven's savage, brilliant, near-future satire *RoboCop*, a masterpiece by any standard and a high point in the pantheon of Heavy Metal Movie milestones.

Our hero, Murphy (Peter Weller), is a regular "New Detroit" beat cop who is blasted to purée by street baddies. Barely alive, he is rebuilt by heartless corporate moneymen as a cyborg tool of law enforcement: RoboCop. While raining bullets and terror down on New Detroit's criminal class, RoboCop struggles to reconnect to his human past, to break free from the hypercapitalist overlords who dictate his existence, and to blow away the scum who messed him up in the first place. By the end, all of his and our wishes come face-meltingly, gut-blastingly, skull-smashingly true, thousands of rounds of ammo at a time.

With its exquisite film-craft, pulp sci-fi ancestry, artful splatter, and a spirit that is at once fascistic and freedom-minded, *RoboCop* is pure metal and pure brain-stomping joy. Peppering the mayhem are mock TV broadcasts that send up media manipulation, complete with eye-popping prescience in the form of a proto-reality-TV game show, *I'd Buy That for a Dollar!*

RoboCop was the big-ticket Hollywood breakthrough for mad Dutch filmmaker Verhoeven. He had previously scored worldwide art-house hits and helmed the metallic 1985 cult favorite *Flesh + Blood*. He went on to bring still more perverse humor and action mastery to his subsequent Heavy Metal Movie triumphs *Total Recall* (1990) and *Starship Troopers* (1997).

The Verhoeven-less *RoboCop 2* (1990), scripted by comic book visionary Frank Miller, savagely upped the dark-hearted carnage, perhaps to the point of no return. *RoboCop 3* (1993) aimed for a PG-13 family market, as did two short-lived TV series, one of which was an afternoon cartoon. A PG-13, CGI remake stunk up multiplexes in 2014—hopefully a violent robot cop will appear in real life to gun down everyone involved.

Rock & Rule (1983)

(Dir. Clive A. Smith; w/Paul LeMat, Susan Roman)

✠ Animation ✠ Post-Apocalypse ✠ Demonology ✠ Soundtrack (Cheap Trick, Iggy Pop)

Rock & Rule begins with narration informing us that nuclear war has come and gone "a long time ago" (1983, to be exact). The sole survivors are "street animals"—dogs, cats, and rats—that have evolved into humanlike races. One surviving trait is the desire to rock, along with a greedy drive from on high to exploit any such rockers.

Rat-faced music mogul Mok seeks one perfect voice to unleash an inter-dimensional demon that looks like fire puke. From there, Mok will be permanently empowered to "rock and rule." Struggling songstress Angel has the voice. Mok bedazzles her and whisks her away from homey Ohmtown to Nuke York City to commence the demonic summoning. Angel's good-guy bandmates Omar, Dizzy, and Stretch give chase.

Canadian cartoon studio Nelvana produced *Rock & Rule* with signature fluid animation and oddball vibes familiar to '70s kids from the TV specials *A Cosmic Christmas, The Devil and Daniel Mouse*, and, most awesomely, the cartoon segment of the 1978 *Star Wars Holiday Special* that introduced Boba Fett. While too mild to rank alongside *Heavy Metal* (1981), *Rock & Rule* is still a trippy, feature-length cartoon about a cokehead rock rat seducing a virginal blonde to conjure forth the forces of hell.

Despite its on-screen drug consumption, occult rituals, sexy cat-chicks and everything else that makes rock rule, MGM had no idea how to market *Rock & Rule*. The movie, as a result, never played theaters in the U.S. and no soundtrack album was ever issued. Fans sought out *Rock & Rule* on video (and USA Network *Night Flight* airings), traded tapes, and kept the movie alive. I even saw a bootlegged 16mm print at SUNY Purchase in 1986. In 2005, Unearthed Films put out a two-disc special edition loaded with extras.

Rock 'Em Dead (2007)

(Dir. George Streicher; w/Chris Grubner)

✠ Faust ✠ Satan ✠ Soundtrack (Sacred Relic)

High school power metal bassist Nick "Rockin'" Martin (Chris Grubner) longs like hell to *Rock 'Em Dead*. Unfortunately, after corpse-painted chief songwriter Leroy (Remington Roberts) quits his group in a huff, Nick is stuck with composer duties. Salvation seemingly arrives in the form of sartorial music producer/impresario/scary golfer Lucius DeMion (Stephen Yost).

Lucius offers Nick a bargain: surrender the soaring pipes of vocalist Joe (Chris Lundy), and our young struggler will attain instant metal god might. Nick takes the deal; then he breaks it. A modest-budget version of all hell breaks loose.

Clocking in at under a half hour and populated by teenage non-actors, *Rock 'Em Dead* is as entertaining as the garage-slop anthem for which Nick gambles (and loses) a zombie bloodbath and eternal damnation. Writer-director George Streicher operates with his own distinctive voice. Since *Rock 'Em Dead*, he's made more than a dozen short features, most horror-based, and all bustling with palpable passion. Maybe someday George will have to pay an eternal price, but for now it is fun to watch his movies.

Rock: It's Your Decision (1982)

(Dir. John Taylor; w/Ty Taylor, Laura Branscum)

✠ Satanic Panic ✠ Censorship

Surly high schooler Jeff Sims (Ty Taylor) gets into it with his (oddly pointy-knockered) mom over "that noise" he listens to in this fifty-three-minute film made for churches and Christian schools that bills itself as "a stirring portrayal of teenage conflicts over music." Those hoping for some genuinely wild-eyed, fire-and-brimstone hysteria about the caterwauling of Satan may feel cheated. There's anti-rock preaching aplenty, but it's just so goddamned limp.

Jeff's buttoned-up youth pastor gently lectures the troubled youth on the importance of listening only to music that wouldn't "embarrass God." Metal gets its usual holy grilling, but what distinguishes *R:IYD*, and makes it a fun watch, is how lumps AC/DC and Kiss together with Barry Manilow and the Captain and Tennille. The session concludes with Jeff delivering a ten-minute sermon about his liberation from rock, centered on the lyrics of "One of These Nights" by the Eagles. If you're searching for the daughter of the devil, like rock in general, it's your decision.

After visiting a record shop, Jeff flips out: "The average age of a person buying a Kiss album is twelve. I even saw a little kid buying the Rolling Stones' 'Start Me Up'!" Jeff yells right into his mom's party-hat boobs: "You with your nose in those soap operas all day! They're nothing but sex with commercials!" AC/DC really fires up Jeff's brimstone as he runs through their song titles: "'Rock 'n' Roll Damnation,' 'Let There Be Rock,' 'Highway to Hell,' and—this is the best— 'Hell . . . Ain't . . . a . . . Bad . . . Place . . . to Be'!"

None shall for escape Jeff's wrath, as proven when he decries the Captain and Tennille and Rod Stewart. His outrage knows no bounds: "Even Barry Manilow wrote in one of his hits, 'Come into my arms and let me know the wonder of all of you,' and he's supposed to be mild!" God forbid this nervous Nelly ever gets hold of a Prostitute Disfigurement MP3, sheesh!

Rock 'n' Roll Nightmare (1987), aka The Edge of Hell

(Dir. John Fasano; w/Jon Mikl Thor, Jillian Peri)
✸ Jon Mikl Thor ✸ Satan ✸ Puppetry

Canuck muscle-monster Jon Mikl Thor stormed through the 1970s fronting a hard rock act known for his showstopping ability to bend actual steel bars with his teeth. The most enduring monument to Jon Mikl Thor's might, however, remains *Rock-'N Roll Nightmare*, a charmingly cheapo heavy metal horror film in which our hero and his new combo, The Tritons, attempt to lay tracks at a recording studio out in the woods, only to be hassled by demons portrayed, not convincingly, by hand-puppets.

Nightmare's climax seems to be somebody's supremely personal dream come true. Thor transforms into a sort of leather-and-spike-clad Super-Thor. With his hair teased-up like a mid-'80s explosion at the mousse factory, our he-man hero battles a mannequin riding atop some kind of wobbly dolly device that's billed as Satan. They throw Play-Doh octopi at one another. Thor wins, but adds: "We'll meet again, Old Scratch!"

Rock 'n' Roll Nightmare deftly balances awareness of its own cut-rate ridiculousness with an unvarnished desire to entertain and, above all, to rock. This feature ripples with stupid success on every headbanging count. For Heavy Metal Movie fans, 1987 really was the Nightmare Year of Our Thor. In addition to *Rock 'n' Roll Nightmare*, he also starred in the nearly-as-nuclear-kooky *Zombie Nightmare*, costarring Adam West (*Batman*).

Intercessor: Another Rock 'n' Roll Nightmare (2005) is a semi-sequel that casts Thor as an interdimensional warrior for righteousness who battles minions of Mephisto. Had it existed prior to the CGI era, *Intercessor* might have been great.

Rock of Ages (2012)

(Dir. Adam Shankman; w/Tom Cruise, Julianne Hough, Russell Brand, Alec Baldwin)
✸ Sunset Strip ✸ Censorship

Rock of Ages is sexless, joyless, and antiseptic, to the point of being a hate crime against sex, joy, and all things gloriously septic about heavy metal. It's 1987 on L.A.'s Sunset Strip, just months before the action in Penelope Spheeris's *The Decline of Western Civilization Part II*. Only it's not. Embarrassingly, we are tested by a loathsomely lazy nostalgia reenactment peppered with cameos by Sebastian Bach, Nuno Bettencourt, and Kevin Cronin. "The Bourbon Room," the movie's stand-in for the Rainbow and Whisky a

Go Go, is a multi-floored rock haunt owned by Dennis Dupree (Alec Baldwin) and managed by Lonny (Russell Brand). Outside, an ersatz PMRC group pickets "heavy metal," led by political wife Patricia Whitmore (a ghastly wax-museum version of Catherine Zeta-Jones).

Into this bogus bouillabaisse of party-store "rocker" wigs stumble star-crossed hopefuls Sherrie Christian (a contrived Julienne Hough) and Drew Boley (Diego Boneta). Tom Cruise is interesting for half a moment, stretching the "Hey, that's Tom Cruise!" stunt from *Tropic Thunder* (2008) into a tattoo-nippled turn as a David Lee Roth/Axl Rose/Jim Morrison/Michael Jackson hybrid named Stacee Jaxx.

The music is mostly obvious '80s pop metal, long pulverized by omnipresent, brainwash-level overexposure into meaninglessness and finally into anger: "Here I Go Again" by Whitesnake; "I Wanna Rock" by Twisted Sister; "Just Like Paradise" by David Lee Roth; "Paradise City" by Guns N' Roses; and "Rock You Like a Hurricane" by Scorpions. Keep in mind that these are rendered as show tunes by the cast. A few old hits by Van Halen, Poison, Quiet Riot, and Warrant round out the soundtrack. The movie mocks New Kids on the Block, though it definitely stems from the same music factory tradition.

Despite the movie's faux outrage over Zeta-Jones's pseudo–Tipper Gore, we all know how in real life the Alec Baldwins of the world fawned over Mrs. Gore and her metal-stomping PMRC censor coven in 2000 once her husband, Al, became their team's presidential candidate. Metalheads still haven't forgotten the PMRC. Hollywood wants to congratulate itself by dressing up in exaggerated heavy metal costumes and reducing what is truly liberating and inspiring and upwardly propulsive about hard rock to "Harden My Heart" by Quarterflash.

"It lies," says Father Merrin in *The Exorcist* regarding the power tactics of evil, "and it lies by mixing truth with lies." Heed those words. In short, *Rock of Ages* sucks cocks in hell.

ROCK STAR (2001)

(DIR. STEPHEN HEREK; W/MARK WAHLBERG, JENNIFER ANISTON, DOMINIC WEST, TIMOTHY OLYPHANT)

✠ FAKE METAL BAND (STEEL DRAGON)

Inspired by the real-life story of Judas Priest during the 1990s (and originally titled after the Priest song "Metal Gods"), Mark "Marky Mark" Wahlberg and the director of *Bill and Ted's Excellent Adventure* take on the true-life excellent adventure of Ripper Owens, a cover band lead singer who ultimately spent some time fronting his favorite band for real. Wahlberg portrays Chris "Izzy" Cole, long-haired Pittsburgh devotee of British metallers Steel Dragon. By day, he's a ponytailed Xerox technician. Living after midnight, Izzy transforms into screamer for a tribute band, Blood Pollution, perfectly mimicking Steel Dragon singer Bobby Beers (Jason Flemyng). Twin guitar leads notwithstanding, Steel Dragon sounds a lot more hair metal than Judas Priest, but we are stuck with Hollywood perceptions of heavy metal in cases like this. (In reality, Miljenko Matijevic, of Connecticut poodle-noodlers Steelheart, provides Wahlberg's vocals).

Steel Dragon's singer, like real Priest vocalist Rob Halford, steps up to the microphone offstage, as well. He splits from the group at the height of their stadium-packing success, in whiny exasperation over his bandmates' homophobic razzing. Thanks to a rock-chick-submitted performance video, Steel Dragon recruits our hometown hero. From there, we get a typical too much, too soon, too insulting cautionary tale. Izzy parties harder than he's supposed to (to the thunderous beats of INXS and Frankie Goes to Hollywood), going so far as to swallow a funny pill and kiss, like, three whole girls in one night. He pays insufficient attention to his devoted beloved, even though she's (hubba! hubba!) Jennifer Aniston.

Other clichés abound. The end is purely a Hollywood dullard's idea of redemption, as Izzy ditches the Dragons to don clean flannel and chirp out an acoustic Verve Pipe tune at a Seattle coffee house. The message: heavy metal forces you to make gay jokes, drive gas guzzlers, and objectify naked groupies, so don't do it, kids! Be nice and conscientious, like Pearl Jam! Atop many metal-qua-metal mistakes, *Rock Star* displays a dismissive, even contemptuous attitude toward the specific music world in which it traffics.

Though *Rock Star* seems to be a heavy metal movie made by people who are only familiar with heavy metal from other movies, metal fans tend to like it. The Steel Dragon lineup boasts an impressive lineage of hard rock heavy hitters, including Black Label Society guitar whiz Zakk Wylde, Dokken bassist Jeff Pilson, and drummer Jason Bonham, the Son of Bonzo himself. Similarly, the B-level tribute schlub band Blood Pollution features Black Label Society's Nick Catanese on guitar and Slaughter drummer Blas Elias.

Rock Star might have hewn more closely to the story of Ripper Owens joining Judas Priest, but producers claim natural creative impulses moved the plot in a different direction. Never one to ripple any currents, Owens has said that the true story probably wouldn't pony up big box office. On VH1 Classic, though, the real Priest singer, Rob Halford, definitively proclaiming about *Rock Star*: "I think it sucks!" So mote it be.

Rock'n with Satan (2002)

(Dirs. Adam Starr, Justin Karoway-Waterhouse, Jared Starr; w/same three jokers)

✠ Satan ✠ Fake Band (White Scorpion)

The too-early-for-YouTube cheapie *Rock'n With Satan* somehow required three directors, each of whom also stars. High school 1980s glam metal fans Ricky Steele (Justin Karoway-Waterhouse) and Billy Love (Adam Starr) are the only visible members of metal squadron White Scorpion. An ancient tome filled with sheet music summons ominous hustler Radical Z (Jared Starr). Rock and roll dreams come true, a teacher is electrocuted, a monster face appears, and the boys defeat evil. The filmmakers/thespians have stated that they paid the movie's crew in gas money. "Gaseous" sounds about right.

The Rocker (2008)

(Dir. Peter Cattaneo; w/Rainn Wilson, Christina Applegate, Emma Stone, Jason Sudeikis)

✠ Hair Metal

Rainn Wilson fleshily embodies the title role in *The Rocker*. He is Robert "Fish" Fishman, drummer for '80s glam-metal wonders Vesuvius. In 1988, the band opts to open for Whitesnake on the condition that they fire Fish, he vows to start a new act that will eclipse Vesuvius. Twenty years of loserdom ensue, until Fish teams with his nephew's garage combo A.D.D. Thanks to unwittingly starring in a YouTube video titled "Naked Drummer" that goes viral, Fish is able to realize his dream—with a lot of spandex, slapstick, and hard-thrown finger-horns in along the way. In the tradition of many authentic '80s glamsters, Rainn Wilson is a man possessed of a, let us say, non-Olympic-athlete physique, who is nonetheless eager and quick to display as much of his bare flesh as possible. The rest of the movie is less funny than that.

Rocktober Blood (1984)

(Dirs. Ferd and Beverly Sebastian; w/Tray Loren, Donna Scoggins, Nigel Benjamin, Cana Cockrell)

✠ Slasher ✠ Soundtrack (Sorcery)

Rocktober Blood rocks ridiculously, right away. Billy Eye (Tray Loren), frontman of the band for whom the movie is named, wails operatically in a recording studio before heading out for a date at four thirty in the morning. "What can I say?" chuckles Billy, who resembles a younger but no less bloated version of Kenny Powers from *Eastbound and Down*, "She wants my body!"

Backing vocalist Lynn (Donna Scoggins) resents ex-lover Billy's caddish ways, particularly when she's now supposed to sing the song he composed for her, "Rainbow Eyes." Frustrated, she calls it quits for the night and heads for a naked, pre-dawn dip in the studio's convenient Jacuzzi. Such tan lines they simply do not make anymore. In the meantime, Billy returns and goes batty. He kills two studio workers, tells Lynn "I'm going to show you what a rock and roll whore is all about" as he slices her shoulder. Cut to black, then a title card, "Two Years Later."

While some goof in a rubber monster mask break-dances on stage surrounded by twenty or so real-life headbangers in Japanese battle-flag T-shirts, a hotshot reporter (David Mables) from rock channel "MVTV" brings us up to speed. Billy Eye "massacred twenty-five rock and rollers" two years earlier and was executed. Lynn has assumed lead vocals for the band, now named Head Mistress. She's ready to announce their upcoming 1984 tour. Shortly thereafter, somehow, Billy appears backstage. Not happy.

Lynn continually encounters the undead and bloodthirsty Billy en route to Head Mistress's kickoff performance. No matter how hard she does aerobics with her hot friends, or how naked she gets for yet another bath, nothing can stop Billy's harassment of Lynn, typified by an obscene phone call wherein he pants, "I want your hot, steaming pussy blood all over my face!"

Head Mistress manager Chris (Nigel Benjamin) and buxom blonde Honey (Cana Cockrell) accompany Lynn to dig up Billy's grave to prove he's dead. Sure enough, when they crack open the coffin, the worm-covered skull inside is wearing a tight red headband in the fashion of Faster Pussycat's Taime Downe. No mistaking Billy!

So who shows up at Head Mistress's big show and forcibly assumes the vocals? First he belts out the hit "Killer on the Loose" through a demon mask and creates all manner of carnage before showing his face. It *is* Billy! Only it's not! And it's not just because he's wearing cheap stage makeup that would embarrass Lou Corpse from *Ladies and Gentlemen . . . the Fabulous Stains* (1984). The madman is actually Billy's evil twin brother, John—he is the real killer and the real composer of all those great songs! As these loopy revelations sink into our skulls, he erupts into a new signature anthem, "I'm Baaack!"

See *Rocktober Blood* once and, for sure, you'll

never forget him. But if you're the type who could watch *Rocktober Blood* just once, what are you doing reading this book?

Nigel Benjamin, who plays manager Chris, briefly fronted Mott the Hoople after Ian Hunter went solo. He provides the vocals when we see Billy singing. Lynn's voice comes courtesy of Susie Major from the band Face Down. As with their legendary movie showcase *Stunt Rock* (1978), the songs by Sorcery not only kick ass, they crystallize the state of popular hard rock at the moment of their delivery. Flush with Sorcery's own theatrical music mega-flair, *Rocktober Blood*'s numbers surpass the post-Van Halen, pre-Poison mid-'80s pop metal moment of Quiet Riot, Ratt, and Mötley Crüe's *Theatre of Pain*.

Sorcery, the band that took metal stage histrionics to undreamt-of new lunacies, kicks out the jams during Head Mistress's climactic live spectacular. Opening with a near cover of Eddie Van Halen's "Eruption," the show involves screaming blondes writhing in chains around the band. One by one, Billy/John slaughters the ladies while performing, tossing bloody organ meats to the crowd and, in the final case, the unlucky victim's still twitching, openmouthed head.

The final on-screen credit is particularly metal: "A SPECIAL THANKS TO ALL OUR FRIENDS WHO APPEARED IN THE ROCK AND ROLL PARTY SCENE." We thank them also.

Rockula (1990)

(Dir. Luca Bercovici; w/Dean Cameron, Toni Basil, Thomas Dolby, Susan Tyrrell, Bo Diddley)

✻ Vampires ✻ Curses ✻ Pirates ✻ Sunset Strip

Here's what Rachel McPadden has to say:

Underdog deadbeat Ralph (Dean Cameron) is just another lazy twentysomething nonpracticing vampire living with his smothering, smoldering, gothic boogie-woogie bugle babe mom, played by avant-weirdo choreographer Toni Basil of "Hey Mickey". Ralph is doomed to repeat a centuries-old curse in a twenty-two year cycle: meet dream girl Mona (Tawny Fere), and then watch helplessly two weeks later on Halloween as she's murdered via hambone by a pirate with a rhinestone peg leg. This time, Ralph and his fatal gal are plopped right in the middle of the fading Sunset Strip hair metal days. Mona is a sexy huge-haired hard sort-of rock singer who performs half-dressed in a cage at Club Hell.

Ever a sucker for that chick and that curse, Ralph starts his own band with a local bartender (Susan Tyrrell, Queen Doris of *Forbidden Zone*) and some tavern cronies, including Bo Diddley. Bo Diddley is in the actual band Rockula. Mayor of the Sunset Strip, KROQ's Rodney Bingenheimer, who legendarily brought Gene Simmons to see Van Halen open for the Boyz at the Starwood in 1976, makes a cameo as himself in the backstage gauntlet of admirers following Rockula's Club Hell debut.

Ralph hits the streets desperately seeking Mona; a flyer-covered wall features a bill for Saint Vitus's filming party with heavy psych dudes Electric Peace at Club 88, a former strip club turned punk and metal palace. Another poster promotes Sunset Strip hair metal rockers Shel Shoc. A third just claims, "I'm Pregnant With Satan's Baby!" At one point, Ralph morphs into a grotesquely adorable farty anthropomorphic bat troll portrayed by "World's Shortest Actress" Tamara De Treaux, who not only helped bring that E.T. costume to life, but breathed evil into elf-from-Hell Greedigut in "Ghoulies."

Eventually, Rockula blows minds at Club Hell; Ralph gets the girl, loses the girl, and performs some weird hallucination mind-meld that transfers a hit rock ballad duet and strange skid row (the community, not the group) video idea to Mona to propel her to instant stardom. In the end, Ralph musters the cold marble balls to fight for his fine piece of rocker-chick ass.

"Rapula" also happens, because there is virtually no genre loyalty from anyone in this movie.

Thomas Dolby, uncredited keyboard sweetener of early Def Leppard albums, appears as Stanley "Stan the Man" Wilson, sadistic used-car sales-

man of the afterlife. He owns Stanley's Deathpark, "where we take the death out of dying," and wants to start a record label called Morgue Records, Death Music, or R.I.P. One of his inventions is a coin-operated tombstone that vends flowers. Metalheads would buy anything sold from a tombstone quarter-machine.

The Rocky Horror Picture Show (1975)
(Dir. Jim Sharman; w/Tim Curry, Susan Sarandon, Barry Bostwick, Richard O'Brien, Meat Loaf)
✠ '70s Glam ✠ Denim and Leather
✠ Cannibalism

As a teenage ritual, as a leather-and-longhair public dress-up opportunity, and as a "corrupting" (read: liberating) influence on wayward youth by means of sex, monsters, and rock and roll, *The Rocky Horror Picture Show* is a strange bedfellow of heavy metal. Toss in the direct, all-encompassing influence of Dr. Frank N. Furter (Tim Curry) on every aesthetic aspect of '80s hair metal, Meat Loaf as a half-brained psychobilly motorcycle thug, and the invocation of a "satanic mechanic," and *Rocky* grows more metallic still.

Most of all, there is the essential plot: pent-up virgins Brad (Barry Bostwick) and Janet (Susan Sarandon) stumble across a castle full of hedonists steeped in devilish music, sodomy, weed, God-mocking experimentation, group rituals, no-limits sexuality, and rejection of any and all societal norms in the pursuit of the highest goal: "Don't dream it, be it." Coming out the other side, Brad and Janet face the world as new creations—leading with their crotches, ferociously experienced, and ready to rock all comers. Viewed in that black light, *Rocky Horror* is the story of heavy metal fandom.

During the 1999 *Rocky Horror Show* Broadway revival, Skid Row's Sebastian Bach played Riff Raff, the butler. In 2009, *Time Warp: A Metal Tribute to The Rocky Horror Picture Show* was announced. Set to perform on the record were "current and former members "of (among others)

Alice Cooper, Black Sabbath, Kiss, Megadeth, Mountain, L.A. Guns, Warrant, Macabre, and My Life With the Thrill Kill Kult." I know I'm not alone in still waiting for that record.

Rodrigo D: No Futuro (1990)

(Dir. Victor Gaviria; w/Ramiro Meneses, Carlos Mario Restrepo, Vilma Diaz)

✠ Metal Reality ✠ Colombia ✠ Soundtrack (Amén, Agressor, Blasfemia, Ekiron, Mierda, Necromantic, Profanacion)

Sometimes, post-apocalyptic bleakness doesn't require nuclear bombs. Consider the Medellín, Colombia, slums of *Rodrigo D: No Futuro*. In what was literally the most dangerous city on earth in 1990, youth culture amounts to committing violent crimes against anyone, everyone, and one another. The kids are also constantly getting "disappeared" by the local police, who are brutally corrupt to the soles of their jackboots.

Rodrigo, the teenage loner of the film's title, fits in nowhere. Played with real intensity by Ramiro Meneses, he taps out endless rhythms with a pair of drumsticks, and forever searches the pits and pockets of the planet's murder capital for a full drum kit in hope that he can put together a punk group. Punks and *metaleros*, in fact, represent the only vitality, humanity, and interconnectedness among the kids in Medellín. Through such music, Rodrigo dares to dream of perhaps departing somehow for a better tomorrow. Alas, the movie isn't subtitled *No Futuro* just to sell more Sex Pistols T-shirts to the Latin market.

Rodrigo D's soundtrack thunders with metal from several South American outfits. In an unforgettable scene in a cinder-block hellhole turned practice space, we meet curly-maned, headbanging twin sisters Piedad Castro and Vicky Castro (one of whom wears a Sodom T-shirt). They blast out a desperate metal song as short and savage as the precarious lives all around them.

Role Models (2008)

(Dir. David Wain; w/Paul Rudd, Seann William Scott, Christopher Mintz-Plasse)

✠ Kiss ✠ Medieval LARPing

Danny (Paul Rudd) and Wheeler (Seann William Scott) are two directionless, thirtysomething schlubs who peddle the energy drink Minotaur to schoolkids by way of "stay off drugs" assemblies. After a traffic scuffle, they're sentenced to community service; they take gigs as Big Brother–type mentors to wayward kids. Danny lands with Augie (Christopher Mintz-Plasse), a teen dork into metal-adjacent, sword-and-sorcery-heavy Live Action Role Play (LARP).

Role Models is very funny, teaming *American Pie*'s Stifler and *Superbad*'s McLovin for a series of raunchy slapstick adventures. The soundtrack is dominated by Kiss, and the exciting LARP climax involves our heroes donning Gene-Paul-Ace-and-Peter war paint and heading into battle with fungo bat swords among cardboard castles. Rudd closes the movie with a serenade of "Beth," accompanied by medieval minstrels on lute.

Roller Blade (1986)

(Dir. Donald G. Jackson; w/Suzanne Solari, Jeff Hutchinson, Barbara Peckinpaugh)

✠ Post-Apocalypse ✠ Nunsploitation

In no way affiliated with any form of inline skating, the heroines of the hair spray–heightened post-nuke circus *Roller Blade* travel on wheeled skates of the old-school variety in this magnificently batshit bonkers production. The self-propelled females are nuns belonging to a sect known as the Bod Sisters. They patrol a seaside boardwalk and knife-fight with evildoers straight from the extras casting session of the next Twisted Sister music video. Most importantly, they enjoy a lot of topless hot tub time.

The Bod Sisters' uniform—when they do manage to wear any—is fantastically metal: a blue robe worn over black tights with a hefty black leather belt around the waist. On top, each Bod

Clockwise from top left: *Mark Wahlberg plays* Rockstar; *Keanu Reeves dons denim for* River's Edge; *Lord Humungus gets set to release berserker Wez in* The Road Warrior; *Colombian kid hell in* Rodrigo D: No Futuro

Sister wears a red, pointed executioner hood emblazoned with a black Maltese cross. When one Bod Sister is wounded, the others load her into the Jacuzzi and pray to a deity who appears in the form of a flashing smiley face that takes over the screen.

Overseeing the Bod Sisters is Mother Speed (Katina Garner). Though confined to a wheelchair, she also wears roller skates. The villain is Saticoy, a man in a leather mask who bickers with the blue-faced puppet on his right hand. Helping the Bods in their struggle is skate punk Marshall Goodman (Jeff Hutchinson, who also appears as the Wrong Ryder, Samurai Devil, and as members of the Spikers and Three Wise Guys gangs).

Roller Blade is pure antic energy, off-the-wall insanity, and cheese-metal supremacy. It spawned four lesser sequels, but I still wish they'd make more. Writer-director Donald G. Jackson performed the same duties on each of the follow-ups: *Roller Blade Warriors: Taken by Force* (1989), *The Roller Blade Seven* (1991), *Legend of the Roller Blade Seven* (1992), and *Return of the Roller Blade Seven* (1992). Jackson's best-known non–*Roller Blade* effort is the highly metal "Rowdy" Roddy Piper vehicle *Hell Comes to Frogtown* (1988).

Rosemary's Baby (1968)

(Dir. Roman Polanski; w/Mia Farrow, John Cassavetes, Ruth Gordon, Sidney Blackmer)

✠ Satan ✠ Black Mass

Two towering classics emerged in 1968 that influenced the imminent arrival of heavy metal. The first was low-budget, feral, and graphic, gut-shocker *Night of the Living Dead*. The other is the high-profile, elegant, gothic, and slow-building soul-chiller *Rosemary's Baby*. In hindsight, both seem intertwined by predestination with the music that was bubbling up through the tar of creation, soon to be birthed by Black Sabbath in 1970. While *Night* erupted from the underground to redefine terror, *Rosemary* shrouded public consciousness from on high. Based on Ira Levin's best-selling novel, the movie involves a witch's brew of collaborators including Hollywood pros, master thespians, an avant-garde director, and a spooky-movie huckster producer.

Mia Farrow stars as Rosemary, wife of New York theater actor Guy Woodhouse (John Cassavetes). They move into an opulent but faded apartment building, the Dakota on Central Park West, and become friendly with eccentric elderly neighbors Minnie (Ruth Gordon) and Roman (Sidney Blackmer). Eerie doings loom, leading up to Rosemary passing out during dinner. She has a nightmare about being raped by a figure intensely reminiscent of Satan.

Unnerving suspense increases until New Year's Eve, when revelers gather around Rosemary to ring what they call "the Year One." With difficulty, Rosemary delivers a son, Adrian. Looking in on his cradle after the fact, she shrieks the famous lines: "What have you done to him? What have you done to his eyes, you maniacs!" Adrian, she is finally informed, "has his father's eyes."

Rosemary's Baby is a creepshow extraordinaire. that combines formal filmmaking with dynamic new storytelling techniques. The eyes have it, *Rosemary's Baby* points out. Heavy metal, duly inspired, further drove home that the ears are windows to the soul all their own. Doomstone, Fantomas, and Psychonaut are a few of the bands to have recorded songs based on the movie, or sampled snippets of dialogue.

Director Roman Polanksi suffered the real-life horror of having his pregnant wife Sharon Tate murdered by the "Helter Skelter"-obsessed Manson Family in their infamous 1969 massacre. Murmurs of a *Rosemary's Baby* "curse" were inevitable. Really, if any such nonsense ever flirted with plausibility, it would be that one. The chills continued in 1980 when real-life Dakota resident John Lennon was gunned down on the sidewalk just steps outside in the building.

Rosemary's Baby was produced by famed horror movie hype man William Castle, who peddled his productions with fun, creative, and charming gimmicks. Among the affable, stogie-puffing

Castle's cooler ballyhoo techniques were wiring theater seats to buzz audience members during *The Tingler* (1959), and the miracle of "Emergo" for *House on Haunted Hill* (1959), wherein an actual skeleton would fly down on a wire from up above the screen and sail out above the audience's heads when a skeleton appeared in the movie. For *Rosemary's Baby*, Castle let the power of the film act as its own gimmick.

Anton LaVey, founder (in 1966) of the Church of Satan, claimed he served as "technical advisor" for the devil worship aspects of *Rosemary's Baby*. LaVey often indulged the sins of pride and bearing false witness simultaneously, so that boast is likely not true, although no one connected to the movie has ever actually denied it. Definitely false is the myth that LaVey portrayed the Devil who impregnates Rosemary. That role of honor belongs to character actor Clay Tanner, who later appeared in the Satan-themed heavy metal drive-in hit *Race With the Devil* (1975)

R.O.T.O.R. (1988)

(Dir. Cullen Blaine; w/Richard Gesswein, Carroll Brandon, Jayne Smith, Margaret Trigg)

✠ Science Fiction ✠ Horror

Robotic Officer of the Tactical Operations Research/Reserve Unit," yes indeed, that's what *R.O.T.O.R.* stands for. And what *R.O.T.O.R.*, the movie, does is rip off and mash up *RoboCop* and *The Terminator*—in Texas!—by chronicling an experimental police android that escapes from the lab before it's finished. A proper rampage of slaughter and destruction results.

R.O.T.O.R. is not good, but the concept resonates. The incredible painting on the movie's VHS cover burns the eyes with like the classic *Mad Max* poster. But this artwork is far more entertaining than the bucket-of-bolts movie inside.

R.O.T.O.R.'s rival for the most unwatchable *RoboCop* cash-in of the '80s is *Robo Vampire* (1988), a Hong Kong production that incorporates Chinese black magic and endlessly uninspired martial arts sequences.

Rotting Corpse: Circus of Fools (2006)

(Dir. Steve Larsen; w/Walter Trachsler, Jim "Moe" Mulqueen, John Perez, Lennon Lopez)

✠ Thrash Metal ✠ Texas ✠ Metal History

Arising from the blood and sweat of members of Pantera's early road crew, the down and dirty Rotting Corpse first detonated its explosive Texas thrash in 1985. As articulated by ultra-amiable guitarist and head corpse Walter Trachsler: "This shit was for rejects. This was music for people who didn't fit in." Rotting Corpse so totally ran with its against-the-grain ethos that the band never came to terms with any record label that came knocking. They thrived as a word-of-mouth sensation among tape traders, creating a succession of frantically traded demos in the back half of the '80s. (The tapes sounded good; they were recorded by Pantera's Vinnie Paul in exchange for payment of a motorboat, which promptly sank.)

Circus of Fools viscerally chronicles the organic ripped-jeans ascent of thrash metal by way of priceless vintage home videos, interviews with many players in the revolving Rotting Corpse lineup, and testimony from Jason McMaster (Watchtower, Dangerous Toys), metal DJ Wes Weaver, and Texas Metal Underground records honcho Scott Fulwiler. As the videocassette rolls, frontman Moe Mulqueen loses his shoe to a mob and refuses to sing until he gets it back. Trachsler constantly abuses his cherished cheetah-print stage guitar, given to him by Pantera, and must repeatedly rebuild the axe so his mentors don't kill him. Trachsler was also Dimebag Darrell's first guitar tech, and you have to believe that all his Exodus-inspired passion on display was crucial to Pantera giving up hair spray in favor of tough-guy groove metal in the 1990s.

The documentary also goes on to trace the fits and starts of Rotting Corpse into the twenty-first century, with a wealth of material culled from the group's 2005 reunion tour of Texas.

Ruido das Minas (2011)

(Dir. Filipe Sartoreto; w/Paulo Xisto Pinto Jr., Claudio David, Bozó, M. Joker)

✠ Metal History ✠ World Metal

Ruido das Minas: A Origem do Heavy Metal em Belo Horizonte, in English, means "Noise Mines: The Origin of Heavy Metal in Belo Horizonte." Director Filipe Sartoreto is a former miner, and here he has made an insightful and indispensible documentary on the up-from-the-underground heavy metal explosion in Brazil's mining country. Sartoreto and his interview subjects are so unique and engaging, in fact, that I watched *Ruido Das Minas* in its original Portuguese and didn't feel like I missed a thing.

In the beginning, Brazil hosted a familiar fan-fueled metal scene involving zines (*Mongol Banger*), record stores (the Modern Sound and Woodstock), and tape trading. The outside world loomed incredibly large, notably the incredibly fertile inspiration of Iron Maiden at Rock in Rio, Twisted Sister on MTV and, surprisingly or not, Queen in general. Among the homegrown bands in Belo Horizonte Overdose emerges to prominence first, followed and superseded by Sepultura. Sarcofago, Sextrash, Mutilator, and others follow. From there, *Ruido das Minas* progresses through the decades, displaying how metal's grip on the nation has never let up, and tracing the influence of Brazilian metal worldwide.

The metal mines in this film are loaded with gold. Seeing 1985 camcorder live footage of a teenage Sepultura in face paint is weird. Overdose happily harmonizing on a wholesome TV dance show around that time is even weirder. Standouts among the on-camera interviews include Paulo Jr. of Sepultura in a lunch joint; Holocausto's Anderson and Valerio in camouflage face masks; Gerald Incubus and M. Joker of Sarcofago haunting a graveyard; and Overdose's Claudio David and Bozó laughing and joking and having a blast. What a world.

Runaway (1984)

(Dir. Michael Crichton; w/Tom Selleck, Gene Simmons, Cynthia Rhodes, Kirstie Alley)

✠ Science Fiction

Aside from *Kiss Meets the Phantom of the Park* (1978), the science-fiction thriller *Runaway* marks the acting debut of demon/bassist/God of Thunder Gene Simmons. As you'd expect, he's the bad guy. Tom Selleck is the hero, Sgt. Jack Ramsay, a Chicago cop in a future where robots are commonplace. Every so often, one of mechanical buggers goes berserk. Ramsay's job is to catch and laser-gun down any such "runaways."

Gene brings the high-tech conflict as evil computer genius Charlie Luther. He develops a chip to be implanted into robots specifically to turn them against their masters. You can imagine where this leads—trouble!

Runaway bombed in theaters, but you only get to see Gene Simmons kick off his acting career once. Simmons says that his audition consisted of writer-director Michael Crichton asking the rock star to convey the desire to commit murder using only his eyes. Gene stared wordlessly at Crichton for a full minute and got the part.

The Runaways (2010)

(Dir. Floria Sigismondi; w/Dakota Fanning, Kristen Stewart, Scout Taylor-Compton)

✠ Metal History ✠ Drama

Produced by Joan Jett and based on Cherie Currie's memoir, *The Runaways* is brisk and glossy and, to employ a double entendre worthy of the band's publicity machine, it goes down easy. The stunt casting of *Twilight* virgin Kristen Stewart as Runaways guitarist Jett and actual underage nymph Dakota Fanning as vocalist Currie is in keeping with the band's ethos, as well. Too soon, though, the jailbait juggernaut screeches to a well-scrubbed halt.

Connecting the glammy bubblegum of Sweet and Kiss to the burgeoning punk movement (and, ultimately, whelping the hair-metal '80s), the Runaways were teenage girls assembled by megalomaniacal music biz maven Kim Fowley to conquer all comers with monster riffs and roller-skating *Lolita* carnality.

Michael Shannon, so great as the conflicted Christian G-man on HBO's *Boardwalk Empire*, approximates Fowley's Frankenstein leer, but he never quite swings the necessary Svengali swagger. The real-life Fowley, a Top 40 producer turned rock impresario, is terrifying, fascinating, and funny. As overseer of the Runaways, he embodied a Hollywood sleaze moment smack between Charles Manson convincing hippie chicks to off the pigs for him and Roman Polanski slipping Quaaludes into root beer in order to slip himself into a thirteen-year-old.

The Runaways acknowledges such rancid venality, but from a disinfected distance. An unfortunate side effect is that that approach dilutes the upside of soaring out of the gutter: the giddy danger, the exhilarating abandon, the ecstatic oblivion—all the stuff runaways run away for.

Guitar goddess Lita Ford, by far the most metal member of the original Runaways line-up, had nothing to do with the film. She claims that Jett's manager offered her a thousand dollars total for the right to her life story and she told him to go close his eyes forever. Unlike the establishment-respected Jett and the Hollywood-bound Currie, Lita plunged ahead from the group into the disreputable Sunset Strip metal of the next decade. We can only wonder how she might have scorched the movie to make it more real, more rock and roll, more like the actual Runaways.

The Running Man (1987)

(Dir. Paul Michael Glaser; w/Arnold Schwarzenegger, Richard Dawson, Jesse Ventura)

✠ Post-Apocalypse ✠ Killer Cameos

The Running Man is the name of totalitarian-state America's most-watched reality TV hit in 2017. The show provides condemned criminals a shot at freedom if they can outwit, outplay, and outlast an onslaught of floridly costumed, lethally gimmicked "stalkers" whose sole goal is to slaughter the contestants on air.

Arnold Schwarzenegger is Ben Richards, a military pilot incorrectly blamed for a massacre. *Running Man* host Damon Killian convinces Richards to give the show a try, and that's when the fun starts. The boozy, schmoozy, chain-smoking (off camera) Killian is played by real-life *Family Feud* emcee Richard Dawson in one of the most smashing and unexpected villain turns in the history of the movies. He's hilarious, scary, and never less than 100 percent credible.

Dawson as Killian is especially mammoth in a movie exploding with some of the most colorful bad guys ever thrown at the ultimate larger-than-'80s-special-effects action hero. Among the "stalkers" dispatched to disembowel our hero are Buzzsaw (Gus Rethwisch), a motorcycle ace equipped with multiple chainsaws; Subzero (Professor Tanaka), a hockey player who wields a razor-sharp sticks and exploding pucks; Fireball (Jim Brown), who flies with a jetpack and fights with a flamethrower; Dynamo, an obese, opera-singing expert in electricity; and Captain Freedom (Jesse Ventura), the champion *Running Man* stalker with the highest number of kills.

If this sounds like a mash-up of pro wrestling, He-Man, *Rollerball*, B-movie science fiction, grindhouse violence, and kids playing with all their different action figures at once, it is. All those elements are intoxicatingly metal, which makes *The Running Man* one power-packed cocktail of a wild '80s metal alloy.

The Running Man was adapted from a novel by Stephen King, written under his pseudonym, Richard Bachman. Director Paul Michael Glaser is better know as the darker half of '70s TV super-cops *Starsky and Hutch*. George P. Cosmatos, who directed *Rambo: First Blood Part II* (1985), had *The Running Man* gig in the bag until he insisted on setting the entire movie inside a shopping mall. Producers balked. Mick Fleetwood of Fleetwood Mac and Dweezil Zappa both play resistance fighters in the movie.

Rush: Beyond the Lighted Stage (2010)

(Dirs. Sam Dunn, Scot McFadyen; w/Geddy Lee, Alex Lifeson, Neil Peart, Jack Black)

✴ Metal History ✴ Canada

Dynamic documentarian duo Sam Dunn and Scot McFadyen (*Metal: A Headbanger's Journey, Iron Maiden: Flight 666*) roll the bones on prog metal's most towering power trio in *Rush: Beyond the Lighted Stage* and everyone wins. With boisterous energy and deep, obvious love, the movie presents a point-by-point history of Rush packed with fascinating, often surprisingly funny insights that even lifelong devotees would not have previously been able to access.

Like a Bizarro World anti-version of James Hetfield and Lars Ulrich in *Metallica: Some Kind of Monster*, frontman Geddy Lee and guitarist Alex Lifeson, best friends since childhood, are the two most immediately and severely likable figures in rock doc history. One outstandingly warm and amusing moment with the pair occurs when Lee and Lifeson, who have worked literally side by side for decades, sit in a local eatery booth and demonstrate how everyone recognizes the singer in public and no one recognizes the guitar player. Famously standoffish drummer Neil Peart opens up as well, satisfactorily explaining his reticence to press the flesh in the manner of his fellow bandmates. Peart says he was the world's biggest fan of the Who growing up, but he never wanted to go pound on their hotel room doors—the music they gave him was enough. It's really quite a killer point.

Every conceivable aspect of Canada's hardest rocking export gets the in-depth treatment: the ongoing hatred from rock critics; the proper pronunciation of "Peart" as "peert"; former tour mates Kiss good-naturedly goofing on them for going to bed early (and alone); Peart blowing the other dudes' minds with Ayn Rand books; "Take Off to the Great White North"; the New Wave influence that pushed them over the top in the '80s; even the rapping, joint-smoking skull in the "Roll the Bones" video (which Peart, adding to his masterful mightiness, credibly defends).

Like many classic rock warhorses, Rush ceased to have mass-market pop hits after FM radio shut the door on new material in the late '80s. *Rush: Beyond the Lighted Stage* is especially valuable, then, for non-hard-core fans who have felt out of touch since the 1987 "Time Stands Still" video with Aimee Mann flying around the screen. The documentary proves that the threesome has been every bit as expansive and influential in its second two decades as on its high-profile way up; check out the surprise blockbuster success of their 2012 concept album, *Clockwork Angels*.

The narrative flow of *Rush: Beyond the Lighted Stage* is bridged together by an honor roll of hard rock's heaviest humbly, and in minute detail, laying bare their devotion to Rush with unguarded enthusiasm that, repeatedly, becomes emotionally moving. In alphabetical order, the roster includes: Sebastian Bach, Jack Black, Mick Box (Uriah Heep), Danny Carey (Tool), Jimmy Chamberlin (Smashing Pumpkins), Les Claypool (Primus), Tim Commerford (Rage Against the Machine), Billy Corgan (Smashing Pumpkins), Kirk Hammett, Taylor Hawkins (Foo Fighters), Vinnie Paul, Mike Portnoy (Dream Theater), Trent Reznor, Gene Simmons, and Zakk Wylde.

S

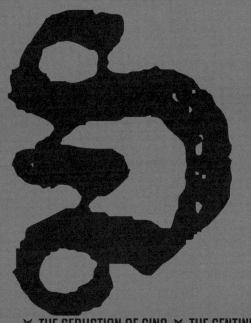

SACRED SIN ✶ SALEM'S LOT ✶ SALO: 120 DAYS OF SODOM ✶ SAM KINISON: WHY DID WE LAUGH? ✶ SANTA SANGRE ✶ SATAN RIDES THE MEDIA ✶ SATAN'S BABY DOLL ✶ SATAN'S CHEERLEADERS ✶ SATAN'S MISTRESS ✶ THE SATANIC RITES OF DRACULA ✶ SATANICO PANDEMONIUM ✶ SATANIS: THE DEVIL'S MASS ✶ SAVAGE STREETS ✶ SAW ✶ SAW II ✶ SAW III ✶ SAW IV ✶ SAW 3D ✶ SAWBLADE ✶ SAXON: HEAVY METAL THUNDER ✶ SCALPS ✶ SCANNERS ✶ SCHOOL OF ROCK ✶ SCREAM BLOODY MURDER ✶ SCREAM DREAM ✶ SCREAMERS ✶ SEASON OF THE WITCH ✶ THE SEDUCTION OF GINA ✶ THE SENTINEL ✶ SEPULTURA: UNDER SIEGE ✶ A SERBIAN FILM ✶ THE SEVENTH SEAL ✶ SEVERED WAYS: THE NORSE DISCOVERY OF AMERICA ✶ SGT. PEPPER'S LONELY HEARTS CLUB BAND ✶ SHE ✶ THE SHINING ✶ SHOCK 'EM DEAD ✶ SHOCK WAVES ✶ SHOCKER ✶ SHOOT 'EM UP ✶ THE SIGN OF THE CROSS ✶ SILENT NIGHT, DEADLY NIGHT ✶ SIMON, KING OF THE WITCHES ✶ THE SISTERHOOD ✶ SKULHEDFACE ✶ SKULLDUGGERY ✶ SLAUGHTERHOUSE ROCK ✶ THE SLAYER ✶ SLAYER: LIVE INTRUSION ✶ SLAYER MAILBOX ✶ SLEEPAWAY CAMP ✶ SLOW SOUTHERN STEEL ✶ SLUMBER PARTY MASSACRE ✶ SNUFF ✶ SODOM AND GOMORRAH: THE LAST SEVEN DAYS ✶ SODOM: LORDS OF DEPRAVITY, PART I ✶ SODOM: LORDS OF DEPRAVITY, PART II ✶ SOLDIERS UNDER COMMAND ✶ THE SONG REMAINS THE SAME ✶ SONS OF STEEL ✶ SORCERESS ✶ THE SORROWS OF SATAN ✶ SOYLENT GREEN ✶ THE SPIRAL STAIRCASE ✶ SPUN ✶ STAIRWAY TO HEAVEN ✶ STAR TREK II: THE WRATH OF KHAN ✶ STAR WARS ✶ STAR WARS: REVENGE OF THE SITH ✶ STARCRASH ✶ THE STONED AGE ✶ THE STORY OF ROCK 'N' ROLL COMICS ✶ STRANGE DAYS ✶ STRANGELAND ✶ STREET TRASH ✶ STRYKER ✶ STUNT ROCK ✶ SUPER DUPER ALICE COOPER ✶ SUCH HAWKS SUCH HOUNDS ✶ SUCK ✶ SUNSET STRIP ✶ SUSPIRIA ✶ SWAMP THING ✶ THE SWORD AND THE SORCERER ✶ SWORD OF THE BARBARIANS

Sacred Sin (2006)

(Dir. Michael Ninn; w/A. J. Bailey, Brooke Banner, Dee, Heather Vuur, Jassie, Monica Mayhem, Nevaeh, Jean Val Jean)

✶ Soundtrack (Eddie Van Halen)

Aiming for perfume commercial aesthetics, video pornographer Michael Ninn pioneered CGI work in smut and created a high-end niche so distinct that the subgenre bears his name. His *Sacred Sin* is the complicated story of a mother rejecting God after the death of her son, intertwined with the tale of a cop losing his family. Their existential grief leads to a lot of artificially shot fornication involving latex masks, arm-length gloves, and cigarette holders. Just as it would in real life.

Ninn's pal Eddie Van Halen composed and performs two instrumental pieces on the *Sacred Sin* soundtrack, "Rise" and "Catherine," as well as several interstitial piano interludes. The *Sacred Sin* DVD contains three original Eddie Van Halen music videos. These songs represent the bulk of new material released during the 2000s decade by the once-prolific guitarist. Unfortunately, in an X-rated world of Fleshbot, Kink Studios, Joanna Angel, Madison Young, Courtney Trouble, and even Black Sabbath devotee Sasha Grey, the digitally scrubbed faux-profundity of Michael Ninn is just false fucking metal!

Salem's Lot (1979)

(Dir. Tobe Hooper; w/David Soul, James Mason, Lance Kerwin, Bonnie Bedelia)

✠ **Vampires** ✠ **Stephen King**

Stephen King's excellent 1975 novel *Salem's Lot* provides the source material for director Tobe Hooper's three-hour TV miniseries, the scariest thing ever made for the tube. Novelist Ben Mears (David Soul) returns to the titular town, where he grew up, to write about the spooky old Marsten House, which always had a reputation for being haunted. When Mears notices bizarre changes in the residents' behavior, he starts to connect it to the dashing but off-putting Richard Straker (James Mason), who has purchased the Marsten property. Sure enough, Marsten is the personal assistant of an ancient vampire. The locals are falling prey to the bloodsucker, prompting Mears to do battle with wooden stakes and holy water alongside young horror movie buff Mark (Lance Kerwin) and the local doctor (Ed Flanders).

Salem's Lot is spooky, tense, and, in a few spots, jolting enough to make you jump. For years, *Salem's Lot* ran on TV as a Halloween perennial, and a return visit is always welcome. The original version of *Salem's Lot* runs three hours and was aired over several nights on CBS. A two-hour version, *Salem's Lot: The Movie*, played theaters in Europe and was an early hit on home video.

When the vampire is finally revealed, he resembles bald, pointy-eared, long-fanged Max Schreck in *Nosferatu* (1922). By coincidence, Werner Herzog's remake with Klaus Kinski, *Nosferatu the Vampyre*, was also released in 1979. Deadly Blessing, Katharsys, and Israeli band Salem later stepped up with "Salem's Lot" songs.

Salo: 120 Days of Sodom (1975)

(Dir. Pier Paolo Pasolini; w/Paolo Bonacelli, Giorgio Cataldi, Umberto Paolo Quintvale, Aldo Valletti, Elsa De Giorgi)

✠ **Marquis De Sade** ✠ **World War II** ✠ **Black Mass**

Salo: *120 Days of Sodom* updates a 1785 novel by the Marquis De Sade so the story takes place in Mussolini's fascist Italy during World War II. The Duke (Paolo Bonacelli), the Bishop (Giorgio Cataldi), the Magistrate (Umberto Paolo Quintvale), and the President (Aldo Valletti) commit to a ritual exploration of the outer limits of pleasure. This cabal, in cahoots with four female prostitutes, kidnaps eighteen physically beautiful teenagers, nine of each gender. The teens are sequestered, nude, in a remote castle.

A cavalcade of atrocities ensues, as the men subject their prisoners to every imaginable sexual abuse, torture, humiliation, and misery, including a lush banquet where every course consists of human shit. We're also privy to a Black Mass wedding and a final massacre of the teens via scalping, scalding, and eye and tongue removal. This sounds like a gross-out parade on the order of *Bloodsucking Freaks* (1976) or *A Serbian Film* (2010), and it is—somewhat. *Salo* is also a revered masterwork by Italian art world giant Pier Paolo Pasolini, held in esteem and defended from censorship by highbrow cinema provocateurs on the order of Martin Scorsese, Michael Haneke, and Catherine Breillat.

Beyond overlapping braininess with barf-bag material, Pier Paolo Pasolini is one of twentieth century Europe's most engaging thinkers. He wrote, painted, made films, and also enjoyed rough gay sex in the company of male street prostitutes. Pasolini died in 1975 after being run over repeatedly with his own car. Giuseppe Pelosi, a seventeen-year-old street hustler, confessed to the crime.

An often-heard rumor about *Salo* is that Pelosi was one of the teen actors in the film, and that he became so unhinged by what Pasolini had put him through on set that he exploded in a fit of vehicular homicide. However much one wants to believe that, it's simply not reality.

Sam Kinison: Why Did We Laugh? (1998)

(Dir. Larry Carroll; w/Sam Kinison, Rodney Dangerfield, Richard Pryor, Jay Leno)

✠ Raw Comedy ✠ Soundtrack ("Wild Thing")

Like Aleister Crowley, rotund hedonist and ex-evangelical preacher Sam Kinison was nicknamed "The Beast," and his stand-up comedy career was elementally intertwined with heavy metal. Kinison first caught the public's ear with a performance on a 1984 HBO special that was a literal scream. Squat, pent-up, and long-haired, Kinison exploded into an obscene tirade about curing world hunger ("Don't send those people food! Send them U-Hauls! They're in the DESERT!") and a scary star was born, wailing. Regular slots on *Saturday Night Live* followed, along with albums and more specials, weeklong sit-ins with Howard Stern, and a full-on mutual embrace from the hard rock community.

With an appetite for drugs and alcohol in volumes revealed by his stage voice, Kinison never seemed destined for a long run among mortals. He burned numerous Hollywood bridges and, in 1992, died in a car crash outside Las Vegas. The documentary *Sam Kinison: Why Did We Laugh?* intersperses copious Kinison performance footage with shots of other comedians telling stories about the insanity of knowing Sam and how his metal-inflamed fervor forever reshaped the crossroads where humor meets hellfire.

In 1988, Kinison took up romantically with Jessica Hahn, a church secretary turned *Playboy* model who took down televangelist Jim Bakker with a sex scandal. *Why Did We Laugh?* covers the making of a music video for Kinison's 1988 metal cover of the Troggs' "Wild Thing" in which Hahn handled scantily-clad-vixen duties. Singing along in the video are Steven Tyler, Joe Perry, Slash, Steven Adler, Steve Vai, Billy Idol, Jon Bon Jovi, Richie Sambora, and Dweezil Zappa. Sam delivers a blistering guitar solo. Axl Rose later joked to Howard Stern that while shooting the clip Slash used Hahn "as a spittoon." Haw, haw, haw, Axl!

Santa Sangre (1989), aka Holy Blood

(Dir. Alejandro Jodorowsky; w/Alex Jodorowsky, Blanca Guerra, Guy Stockwell, Thelma Tixou)

✠ Evil Circus ✠ Slasher

The last masterpiece by Alejandro Jodorowsky (*El Topo*, *The Holy Mountain*) stars his son Alex as Fenix, a mental patient putting his memories together through a series of horrific and hallucinatory visions. Fenix grew up performing magic in a Mexican circus family. As a young man, he does a sexy knife-throwing act with the Tattooed Woman (Thelma Tixou). Fenix's mother, Concha (Blanca Guerra), becomes the fanatical head of the Church of the Holy Blood ("Santa Sangre"), which ultimately prompts his father, Orgo (Guy Stockwell), to cut off her arms. Years later, Fenix teams with his mother, acting as her "arms" to enact a spree of violent revenge.

A bare-bones plot description of *Santa Sangre*, while weird, does not convey the sensory overload. The parade of nightmares includes a baby elephant spraying endless blood from its trunk, a hell-hot feast for headbangers on a trip for the next visual high. Coscreenwriter Claudio Argento is the older brother of Italian splatter maestro Dario Argento. A band named Santa Sangre once rocked in Chile, and Soulgrind recorded an album by that name.

Satan Rides the Media (1998)

(Dir. Torstein Grude; w/Varg Vikernes, Oystein Aarseth, Svein Erik Krogvold)

✠ Norwegian Black Metal

Made in Norway by Norwegians, the documentary *Satan Rides the Media* provides an unusually close angle on the country's notorious early-1990s black metal arson and murder outbursts. The film's position is that sensationalist newspaper and TV coverage actually created the atmosphere in which corpse-painted delinquents felt compelled to one-up one another, resulting in more dozens of churches reduced to ashes and an occasional prematurely filled grave.

Director Torstein Grude makes a convincing case as he connects bombastic media reports about "satanic" transgressions to copycat crimes all over Europe. There is more than one way, it becomes apparent, to commit arson. For what it's worth, in 2004, Varg Vikernes wrote a typically distracted and off-topic review of *Satan Rides the Media*, but he did laud filmmaker Grude as "indeed far more knowledgeable and trustworthy than everybody else that has tried to unveil the secrets of this milieu."

Satan's Baby Doll (1982), aka La Bimba di Satana; A Girl for Satan

(Dir. Mario Bianchi; w/Jacqueline Dupre, Mariangela Giordano, Marina Hedman)

✠ Satan ✠ Italian Horror ✠ Nunsploitation

A funeral in a haunted gothic castle sets the stage. Soon enough, teenage Miria (Jacqueline Dupre) is possessed by the spirit of her recently deceased, hyper-promiscuous mother. With mom working her mind and *Mons Venus* alike, Miria beds all comers and murders most of them, including a sexy nun named Solo (Mariangela Giordano). Satan is invoked throughout but does not make an explicit appearance.

A remake of the colorfully titled *Malabimba: The Malicious Whore* (1972), *Satan's Baby Doll* is fine Italian sleaze with a blackened heavy metal soul, all spiced up meatball-like in its extended version with hard-core sex scenes. For all its occult intercourse and Bride of Christ homosexuality, the truly metal selling point of *Satan's Baby Doll* is its poster: a modified version of the Boris Vallejo painting *Demon Lover* that depicts a winged, reptile-skinned monster-man in unholy embrace with a nude woman who we see from behind. The demon in the original artwork is green-tinged, but for the poster he's re-colored hellfire red. In some versions, a wisp of smoke hides a portion of the female figure's lush butt crack.

Heavy metal album covers by the Peru-born Vallejo include *The Ultimate Sin* by Ozzy Osbourne, *Take No Prisoners* by Molly Hatchet, *Penetrator* by Ted Nugent, and *No Place for Disgrace* by Flotsam and Jetsam. Other mega-metal movie posters bearing his art are *Barbarella* (1968), *The White Buffalo* (1977), *Knightriders* (1981), *Q: The Winged Serpent* (1982), *Deathstalker* (1983), *Barbarian Queen* (1985), and *Warrior Queen* (1987).

Satan's Cheerleaders (1977)

(Dir. Greydon Clark; w/John Ireland, Yvonne De Carlo, John Carradine, Kerry Sherman)

✠ Satan ✠ Black Mass

"When these girls raise hell," goads the tagline of *Satan's Cheerleaders*, "there's the devil to pay!" Gross high school janitor Billy (Jack Kruschen) scouts virgins for the local devil-worshipping sheriff (John Ireland) and his evil high priestess wife (Yvonne De Carlo—Lily Munster herself). They kidnap the local gridiron booster squad in hopes that at least one will qualify for a maiden sacrifice. Nothing goes as planned.

Satan's Cheerleaders (pretty much) makes good on its phenomenal title and potent premise; a mix of standard pom-pom drive-in cheapie tropes

Clockwise from top left: The Sisterhood *slays;* The Sword of the Barbarians *seems to be an axe;* Satan's Baby Doll *with censored seat meat;* Street Trash *on Arrow Blu-ray;* Saxon: Heavy Metal Thunder; Satanico Pandemonium *aka* La Sexorcista (pranks, locker room nudity, a touch football game on the beach) that morphs into satanic small-town conspiracy, imperiled nubiles on the run, and a fantastically '70s surprise ending. The girls overpower an entire town full of Lucifer lovers, but sometime after their adventure, pretty Patty (Kerry Sherman) brandishes a pentagram on the football field and telepathically heals the quarterback's injured ankle with the power of Old Scratch. Satan wins! Rah-rah-rah!

The occult scenes are creepily effective, especially when red-lit Lily Munster commands, "Answer my prayers, Satan! Kill! Mutilate!" One theatrical ad campaign tried to pass *Satan's Cheerleaders* off as a spoof, with posters declaring it "Funnier than *The Omen*, scarier than *Silent Movie*!" but *Satan's Cheerleaders* actually plays it straight.

Inspired by the film, an Austin, Texas, coven of tattooed vixens in 1995 formed a provocative pep squad called "Satan's Cheerleaders." These horn-raising evil-spirit boosters performed onstage with numerous local metal acts, ultimately leading to live gigs with Mötley Crüe and the Misfits.

Satan's Mistress (1982), aka Demon Rage; Fury of the Succubus; Dark Eyes

(Dir. James Polakof; w/Lana Wood, John Carradine, Britt Ekland, Kabir Bedi)
✶ Satan ✶ Demon Sex ✶ Demonic Possession

Diabolically voluptuous housewife Lisa (Lana Wood) lazes about her beachfront home, bored and pent-up, until a mysterious gentleman deemed only the Spirit (Kabir Bedi) raises hell with her between the sheets. Given that the movie is called *Satan's Mistress*, the Spirit is clearly more horns-on-the-head than mere horn-dog. Lisa surrenders to naked carnal abandon, the Spirit attempts to possess his mistress's daughter, and highly billed horror veteran John Carradine babbles while wearing priest garb for about four minutes.

Satan's Mistress was an early VHS hit, sending countless burgeoning headbangers home from the horror section of the video store with the promise of substituting raw flesh for the usual blood and guts. Quite devilishly, it delivered. Lana Wood is the younger sister of actress Natalie Wood. She first made a splash as Bond babe "Plenty O'Toole" in *Diamonds Are Forever* (1971). Lana also got all the boobs in the family.

As with 1982's other occult-intercourse thriller, *The Entity*, *Satan's Mistress* claims to be based on true incidents. Make no mistake, though the story is fake, Lana Wood's breasts are very, very real.

The Satanic Rites of Dracula (1973), aka Count Dracula and His Vampire Bride

(Dir. Alan Gibson; w/Christopher Lee, Peter Cushing)
✶ Satan ✶ Dracula ✶ Hammer Films

The final Hammer Films production to date to features Christopher Lee as the Count, the 1973-set *The Satanic Rites of Dracula* gets an extra metal nod for that extraordinarily evocative title alone. Plus it features Peter Cushing as Professor Van Helsing, a descendent of the original Drac-hunter, Doctor Van Helsing.

Satanic Rites boasts a great premise: Dracula wants to kill himself by ending the entire human race, and so he seduces world leaders through occult magic. Unfortunately, the movie feels exhausted. Put a stake in it. The film's supremely metal *Satanic Rites* moniker spooked distributors in the United States, who changed it to the meaningless *Count Dracula and His Vampire Bride*. The film later played on American television all the time under the original title, and inspired songs by Gore Obsessed and Tjolgtar.

Lee portrayed Dracula once more, in the non-Hammer *Dracula and Son* (1976), a French-made spoof cashing in on *Young Frankenstein* (1974).

Satanico Pandemonium

(1975), AKA La Sexorcista

(DIR. GILBERTO MARTINEZ SOLARES; W/CECILIA PEZET, ENRIQUE ROCHA, CLEMENCIA COLIN)

✠ SATAN ✠ NUNSPLOITATION

Cecilia Pezet stars as tempted, tormented Sister Maria in this arty Mexican nunsploitation nugget. Sister Maria wanders an idyllic countryside reminiscent of Eden. She picks flowers and cuddles a lamb until Enrique Rocha shows up naked as Lucifer. He offers her an apple, Maria takes it, and her world goes to hell.

Gore, anti-religious fervor, and rampaging nude nuns run amok at the climax. During one sexy interlude, Maria gets it on with another clergywoman who transforms into Lucifer and literally puts the devil inside our confused Bride of Christ. You might sweat a little more than holy water over that. Salma Hayek's character in *From Dusk Till Dawn* is named Satanico Pandemonium in homage to this film, and the bands Eviscerated and Pandemia have also penned songs with that name.

Satanis: The Devil's Mass (1970)

(DIR. RAY LAURENT; W/ANTON LAVEY, DIANE LAVEY, ZEENA LAVEY)

✠ SATAN ✠ BLACK MASS ✠ CHURCH OF SATAN

In the "Year of the Dark Lord 1966", chrome-domed provocateur Anton LaVey founded the Church of Satan in San Francisco and published his best-selling manifesto of self-will draped in sinister bunting, *The Satanic Bible*. For countless metalheads, LaVey's black book with the white pentagram on the cover proved to be as indispensible a tool for bonding, enlightenment, and, yes, troublemaking as anything in their record collection. Pointy-eyebrowed, goateed, and given to wearing capes, LaVey was a carny showman and lion tamer in his previous occupations, and that hustler spirit shines through the spooky tropes

in the documentary *Satanis: The Devil's Mass*.

LaVey makes a captivating interview subject, amusing and even a little bit scary as he pitches his combination of Ayn Rand selfishness, Aleister Crowley ritualism, and haunted-house gimmickry. Shot in the highly saturnalian summer of '69, the film has LaVey, "Black Pope" of the Church of Satan, leading us around the antireligion's "Black House" headquarters in San Francisco. He plays his *Phantom of the Opera*–like organ and leads a number of minions through an array of kinky satanic ceremonies, including a full-blown Black Mass using a naked woman as the altar. Various church members opine on satanic philosophy, often while nude. We learn that LaVey's neighbors think he's a hell of a guy. We also meet Mrs. LaVey, a blonde witch named Dianne, and the couple's young daughter, Zeena.

Satanis was made and peddled as a cheap, hokey exploitation flick, and that's just part of what's so devilishly charming about it. One of *Satanis*'s topless, post-orgy revelers looks like a diner waitress named Blanche. Through a cigarette croak, she babbles about how her new Satan-won sexual freedom enabled her to encourage her teenage son to cure his acne by masturbating. It's funny, skeevy, and uncomfortably arousing all at once.

The Black Mass has been a touchstone of heavy metal since Coven's landmark 1969 LP *Witchcraft Destroys Minds and Reaps Souls*. Inside the album's gatefold was a photo of the band engaged in devil worship, with a dark priest about to plunge a sacrificial dagger into naked lead singer Jinx Dawson. On the record itself, side two is comprised entirely of an audio recording of a Black Mass ritual.

Young Zeena LaVey grew up to marry Nicholas Schreck, founder of the experimental "death rock" outfit Radio Werewolf. Throughout the late-'80s "satanic panic," the couple appeared on numerous TV talk shows to do battle with worked-up Christians and pro-censorship hotheads.

A wacky handful of celebrities have openly associated with the Church of Satan, including Jayne

Mansfield and Sammy Davis Jr. Anton LaVey ordained Marilyn Manson as a "reverend" in the Church of Satan in 1993.

SAVAGE STREETS (1984)

(DIR. DANNY STEINMANN; W/LINDA BLAIR, JOHN VERNON, LINNEA QUIGLEY)

✴ RAPE AND REVENGE

The metal-scented grindhouse great *Savage Streets* injects '70s *Death Wish*–style vigilantism into a '50s-era *Blackboard Jungle* juvenile delinquent plot. The combo combusts in a blood-red, big-haired rage of '80s exploitation mayhem. Linda Blair stars as Brenda, leader of the all-girl high school posse the Satins, and older sister of deaf waif Heather (an insanely young-looking, pre-breast-implant Linnea Quigley). Brenda's main source of conflict is the Scars, the leather-jacketed bad-boy cabal on campus, although she also tangles with a throng of female classmates during a naked catfight in the gym shower.

Brenda's run-ins with the Scars escalate from vandalism and vehicle theft to the gang rape of Heather. One of the Satins is tossed off a bridge. Our heroine transforms from mere badass to an angel of deadly vengeance clad in a cat suit, and armed with a crossbow and a plethora of homemade booby-traps. One by one, the Scars go down and Brenda takes them there—in pieces.

Savage Streets boasts an obvious punker (Scott Mayer as Red, a bad guy), and oozes '80s metal from the first frame to the last. The movie was created as a star vehicle for ex-Runaways singer Cherie Currie. She shot at least a day's worth of footage and departed for reasons unknown. Both hot off the women-in-prison classic *Chained Heat* (1983), Blair and human frown John Vernon battle one another anew in *Savage Streets*. In *Heat*, Blair and Vernon played inmate and warden; here they extend their range as high school student and principal. Vernon has no patience for these teenage turf wars. He barks out a series of brilliant one-liners, the apex of which is "Go fuck an iceberg!"

The multi-boobed rumble in the shower is pure hard rock party time. Plug in, crank up, and ride the naked lightning. Later in *Savage Streets*, a gratuitous Linda Blair bathtub scene comes on like a guitar instrumental. The movie stops so we can ogle her enormous chest while she puffs a smoke and plots mass homicide in clear water. Like Eddie Van Halen's "Eruption," Linda demonstrates unique skill here. No matter how much anybody else practices or tries to duplicate the effect, this moment is hers and hers alone.

Finally, the pile-on violation of Linnea Quigley is just ugly and scary, making a connection, however ephemeral, to real evil. Petite and playing deaf, prepubescent-looking Quigley is vulnerability incarnate. The gang sets upon her brutally and drags her into the boys' bathroom, where they strip her nude, draw all over her tiny torso, and take turns raping her, eventually fracturing her skull. Since her character is "mute," Quigley attempts to scream over and over, but no sound comes out. The effect is horrifying and genuinely blood-curdling. It's not just metal then. That's when *Savage Streets* gets heavy.

SAW (2004)

(DIR. JAMES WAN; W/CARY ELWES, DANNY GLOVER, MONICA POTTER, SHAWNEE SMITH, TOBIN BELL)

✴ TORTURE ✴ SOUNDTRACK (FEAR FACTORY, FRONTLINE ASSEMBLY)

Saw buzzed fast and gorily into the popular consciousness with a gruesome ad campaign, a grossly fertile premise, a worthily surprising surprise ending, and a fixation on brutality that audiences did not expect from Hollywood. *New York* magazine critic (and horror-loving mensch) David Edelstein didn't concoct the term *torture porn* until *Hostel* came along in early 2005, but *Saw* hit that cannily defined jugular first.

Two men awaken in a horrible bathroom, each chained by the ankle to a pipe. A corpse lies in a pool of blood between them. They find two hacksaws, which fail to work on their chains. The men realize that the saws are meant for their feet. Such is the handiwork of a killer named Jigsaw (Tobin Bell). A game of puzzles and snares ensues, told largely through flashbacks, about how Jigsaw captures those to whom he wants to impart a lesson on valuing their lives, and how he subjects them to nightmarish mechanical murder machines that they can escape if they make absolutely perfect choices.

Danny Glover plays a detective hunting Jigsaw. Dragged down by his terrible acting, this first entry ranks weakest among the seven-film *Saw* series. Cary Elwes, as first victim and the movie's sort of hero, is bad enough to be curiously effective. Bell makes a good impression as Jigsaw, and Shawnee Smith is great as a junkie survivor of a steel-jawed-bear-trap head-attachment challenge. Former Nine Inch Nails keyboardist Charlie Clouser contributes the musical score.

Saw's corporeal rupturing and even the sadism weren't new, but director James Wan's presentation was: gnat's eye close-ups of unthinkable suffering edited with epileptic energy, burrowing into viewers' brains in earsplitting tune to the movie's industrial metal soundtrack. What slasher films were to the '80s (metal), torture porn would be to the 2000s (extreme metal). *Saw* got the incendiary pain-giving device rolling.

The movie created its own horror icon, not with Jigsaw himself, but with a tricycle-riding puppet nicknamed "Billy." The white-faced, spiral-cheeked, red-eyed toy has a movable jaw like a ventriloquist dummy, and speaks for Jigsaw when the killer sets up one of his traps. The Billy puppet is an homage to the knife-swinging doll in Dario Argento's *Deep Red* (1975). He rocks.

SAW II (2005)

(DIR. DARREN LYNN BOUSMAN; W/TOBIN BELL, SHAWNEE SMITH, DONNIE WAHLBERG, DINA MEYER)

✠ TORTURE ✠ EVIL PUPPETS ✠ SOUNDTRACK (BUCKETHEAD, BLOOD SIMPLE, MARILYN MANSON, MUDVAYNE, PUSCIFER, QUEENS OF THE STONE AGE)

A sizable improvement over the first installment, *Saw II* taps the inherent strengths of the *Saw* concept and creates a formula for future sequels. Righteous madman Jigsaw (Tobin Bell) sends victims through a "fun house" of tortures. If they survive, they will become enlightened in new ways to the value of life. The soundtrack again combines original music by Charlie Clouser with a mixed bag of contemporary hard rock.

Don "Donnie Don" Wahlberg and Dina Meyer play cops who discover Jigsaw, weak and grotesquely sick from cancer, monitoring the progress of eight such test subjects on video screens. We learn a bit of Jigsaw's backstory (he survived a suicide attempt), and we watch amazingly creative torture devices in fantastically repugnant action. Shawnee Smith returns from the first *Saw* as a junkie who once got away from the killer's head-trap known as "the jaw-splitter." Here, she is forced to jump into a pit filled with dirty hypodermic needles, as wince-inducing a scene as any through which you will ever squint, grunt, and clench your teeth.

As police drive Jigsaw to his lair, they ask him to point out where it is. "It's the last house on the left," he says. Nice touch.

SAW III (2006)

(DIR. DARREN LYNN BOUSMAN; W/TOBIN BELL, SHAWNEE SMITH, ANGUS MACFADYEN)

✠ TORTURE ✠ EVIL PUPPETS ✠ SOUNDTRACK (ALL THAT REMAINS, AVENGED SEVENFOLD, BULLET FOR MY VALENTINE, DETHKLOK, HELMET, DISTURBED, LAMB OF GOD, MASTODON, MINISTRY, SLAYER)

Saw III hacks off the best of what came before it and forces new, frightening, and ever heavier pieces together into something fresh and ferocious. This is not just the best entry in the *Saw* franchise or the best of the 2000s "torture porn" cycle; it's one of the decade's best horror films, period. *Saw III* is a bona fide shocker that churns one's bowels while also managing to stimulate activity north of one's neck, powered by screaming musical accompaniment that sounds like somebody left the Sirius XM Liquid Metal channel circa 2006 playing forever.

Jigsaw (Tobin Bell), assisted by hot hench-junkie Amanda (Shawnee Smith), turns his lesson-teaching torture machinery on Jeff (Angus Macfadyen), a father who cannot let go of his anger and hatred of life in the aftermath of his young son being hit by a car and killed. In the meantime, an unhappy physician (Bahar Soomehk) is forced to keep the cancer-stricken Jigsaw alive in his lair, which is laden with stolen medical equipment. The doctor is forced into a collar containing five shotgun shells hooked up to Jigsaw's heart monitor. If he dies, the shells detonate into her face and brain. We learn more about Jigsaw's previous life, as well as the power of devotion that Amanda feels for him.

As the stories play out, breathtakingly inventive torture devices defile the screen. A naked woman is hung up in a subzero meat freezer and repeatedly hosed with ice water. A drowning pool slowly and noisily fills with pork-sludge as whole hogs fall into a one-of-a-kind pig-liquefying contraption. *Saw III*'s twist ending is not as surprising as what goes down in the first movie, but it's dramatically more satisfying, just like everything else in the movie.

The atrocities we witness not only supersede the mechanical horrors of prior installments, they actually invite thought and discussion. My colleague Aaron Lee pondered Jigsaw as a metaphor for the United States and his test subjects as Iraq. I went back even further and pondered the God of the Old Testament challenging Abraham to sacrifice his own son. If that seems like a serious comparison for a second sequel to a gross-out Halloween box-office attraction, it is!

Taking a red page from Kiss's Marvel Comic where the band members' blood was mixed in with the red ink, *Saw III* sold posters to benefit the Red Cross that contained blood in their coloring from Jigsaw himself, Tobin Bell. Former Nine Inch Nails keyboardist Charlie Clouser, who scored the first two *Saw* films, returned for this one as well. The official *Saw III* soundtrack album is essentially a time capsule of its day's left-of-mainstream hard rock, a sort of *Now That's*

What I Call Popular Extreme Metal compilation. The inclusion of Dethklok, the cartoon band with its own television series and movie, represents some kind of super-groovy rift in cosmic reality.

Saw IV (2007)
(Dir. Darren Lynn Bousman; w/Tobin Bell, Shawnee Smith, Donnie Wahlberg, Dina Meyer)
✦ Torture ✦ Evil Puppets ✦ Soundtrack (Avenged Sevenfold, Drowning Pool, Every Time I Die, From Autumn to Ashes, Fueled by Fire, the Human Abstract, Ministry, Nitzer Ebb, the Red Chord, Sixx:A.M.)

Saw IV is a step down from *Saw III*, but is still bloody good. From beyond the grave, or wherever his body ended up, Jigsaw (Tobin Bell) continues to run his malevolent torture contraptions via tapes he left behind (including one in his own stomach), assisted by someone wearing a wickedly cool hooded pig mask. In addition to vicious mechanical traps, we are treated to a lot more of Jigsaw's backstory, even watching him interact years earlier with his pregnant wife, Jill (Betsy Russell). Seeing über-creep Tobin Bell try to play pre-jiggy Jigsaw as a young(ish), hopeful dad-to-be in a red hoodie is a treat.

Saw IV's opening gambit is engagingly gnarly: a man with his eyes sewn shut and a man with his mouth sewn shut are chained to a winch inside a mausoleum. There's only one key, and they have no way of communicating. Things end gloppily.

The soundtracks for the *Saw* movies grew aggressively more metal. *Saw IV* veers off on a specifically more industrial-metal track; pioneers Nitzer Ebb do *Saw IV*'s theme song, "Payroll."

After helming the previous two installments, director Darren Lynn Bousman departed the series after *Saw IV*. He went on to make *Repo: The Genetic Opera* (2008) and a really great remake-in-name-only, *Mother's Day* (2010).

Saw 3D (2010),
aka Saw: The Final Chapter
(Dir. Kevin Greutert; w/Tobin Bell, Shawnee Smith, Betsy Russell, Chester Bennington)
✳ Torture ✳ Evil Puppets ✳ Soundtrack (Dir En Grey, Krokus, Lordi, Nitzer Ebb) ✳ 3-D

Saw V (2008) stunk on ice. *Saw VI* (2009) was a thaw in the proper direction but was slaughtered at the box office by the surprise blockbuster *Paranormal Activity* (2009). The level heads behind the *Saw* franchise saw the writing on the receipts and powered down their Jigsaw juggernaut with *Saw 3D*. The plot reaches back to the first *Saw* and a "greatest hits" parade of mechanized mutilators is rolled out and revitalized, along with a plethora of new gross-out gadgets. In 3-D.

Nü-metal was the early 2000s music genre despised by seemingly everyone, yet capable of peddling millions of CDs and packing stadiums. Among nü-metal's most loathed—and best-selling—was rap-rock combo Linkin Park. In *Saw 3D*, Linkin frontman Chester Bennington plays a white-power skinhead. Jigsaw's assistant superglues Nazi Chester to a car seat, then launches him forward so that all his skin is torn from his body. That would be awesome even if it happened to someone besides a Linkin Park guy.

As with prior *Saw* releases, the soundtrack leaned almost entirely metal. One interesting touch is the presence of Japanese cult acts, including experimental metal artists Dir En Grey, electronica weirdos Boom Boom Satellites, and punkers Wagdug Futuristic Unity.

Sawblade (2010),
aka The Buzzsaw Murders
(Dir. Dennis Devine; w/Reggie Bannister, Mark Alan, Brittany Madelynn Daniels, Jed Rowen)
✳ Fake Band (Sawblade)

Sawblade is about a heavy metal band—conveniently named Sawblade—that plans to spend twenty-four hours locked in an old slaughterhouse, where they'll create a new "hard-core" music video. Unbeknownst to the ambitious headbangers, a homicidal maniac named Elliot Benson (Jed Rowen) was murdered, mutilated, and buried on the site. That doesn't mean he's exactly dead, though. Elliot rapidly rises to hack and slash through the group and its groupies with—what else?—a series of saw blades!

Director Dennis Devine, who keeps busy cranking out direct-to-DVD wonders like this, also made chick-metal horror flick *Dead Girls* (1990).

Saxon: Heavy Metal Thunder (2012)
(Dirs. Sven Offen, Hans Christian Vetchen, Various; w/Lemmy Kilmister, Lars Ulrich)
✳ NWOBHM ✳ Danish Drummer

British bruisers Saxon crystallized the New Wave of British Heavy Metal with their anthem "Denim and Leather," and then tried and nearly succeeded in conquering America during the 1980s. Created exclusively for Saxon's fan club and narrated by Toby Jepson (of Brit rockers Little Angels), this three-hour documentary on the Barnsley bombers serviceably recounts Saxon's mid-1970s birth as pub band Son of a Bitch. By 1980, they had become a NWOBHM force on par with Iron Maiden and Diamond Head. Interesting turns come in the mid-'80s when this quintessentially English ensemble goes after Hollywood hair metal money. And an inevitable dip into near-decimation brings a tale of evolution and survival that continues onward.

Nearly every available member of the group appears on camera. Drummer Pete Gill, he of the satin jogging shorts, who also served a brief tenure in Motörhead, is notably missing. Superstar guitarist Graham Oliver and founding bassist Steve Dawson are here; their breaks from the group were public and bitter, ultimately resulting in their 1999 attempt to wrangle the name Saxon back from the existing organization. The documentary doesn't shy from such rough patches, allowing all involved to speak their piece without pummeling us with legal details.

Talking-head endorsements come from Metallica's Lars Ulrich, Doro Pesch of Warlock, and both Lemmy Kilmister and Fast Eddie Clarke from Motörhead. Also included in the DVD are three hours of Saxon rarities, archival footage, and performance videos, including a 1981 German TV appearance that pours out of the speakers like a Panzer tank. Denim and leather may have brought us all together, and *Saxon: Heavy Metal Thunder* will always keep us that way.

Ᏸcalps (1983)

(Dir. Fred Olen Ray; w/Jo-Ann Robinson, Richard Hench, Roger Maycock)
✠ **Slasher** ✠ **Native Spirituality** ✠ **Revenge**

Clueless archaeology students mess with an ancient Indian burial ground and unleash the vengeful spirit of cosmically ticked-off warrior Black Claw. He wants their scalps. Hence, we get the title of this splatter oddity, *Scalps*. As with the Viking-gone-Voorhees curiosity *Berserker* (1987), *Scalps* gets props for injecting a heavy metal obsession into the already super-metallic slasher movie cycle: Native American motifs, particularly vengeance for past paleface atrocities.

The gore is pretty great. Black Claw is terrifically freaky looking. Kirk Alyn (who starred as Superman in 1940s movie serials) plays the victims' college professor. *Famous Monsters of Filmland* publisher Forrest J. Ackerman cameos. There's also a chintz-cool demon with a mechanical lion's head, and the musical score is pure '80s horror-flick synthesizer fun. At the end a sequel—*Scalps II: The Return of D.J.*—is promised. The rule of thumb is that such overenthusiastic sequel announcements almost never materialize.

Ᏸcanners (1981)

(Dir. David Cronenberg; w/Jennifer O'Neill, Stephen Lack, Patrick McGoohan)
✠ **Gore** ✠ **Mind Control**

In *Scanners*, heads bang for *real*. David Cronenberg's ingenious sci-fi/horror/espionage opus is a one-of-a-kind thriller that became an instant classic due to its early scene of a guy's head exploding from within. Matched up before an audience against a hostile telekinetic "scanner" (Michael Ironside), a human male subject (Louis Del Grande) sweats, rocks, convulses, grits his teeth, quakes his limbs, and then, *blammo*! From the neck up, he's raining red paint and raw hamburger.

The larger plot of *Scanners* is a sprawling story of a weapons corporation trying to control and utilize people who possess the ability to read minds and, literally, blow them. Cronenberg masterfully executes suspense and raises heavy questions about what constitutes the proper use of our individual talents and abilities in a context of freedom. And when it's gore time, scan yourself up a raincoat.

Special effects technicians created *Scanners'* exploding head by loading a latex model full of wet dog food and fresh rabbit livers, then blasting it from behind with a 12-gauge shotgun—a real heavy metal volcano, at last.

Ᏸchool of Ꭱock (2003)

(Dir. Richard Linklater; w/Jack Black, Joan Cusack, Mike White, Sarah Silverman)
✠ **Rock Redemption** ✠ **Soundtrack (AC/DC, Cream, Metallica, Ramones, the Stooges)**

Jack Black, who earned his metal wings with Dio-worshiping duo Tenacious D, cleans up his mouth but keeps the music down and dirty in *School of Rock*, a musical *Bad News Bears* with face-melting guitar solos and its heart—and hard-thrown horns—in the right place. Black plays Dewey Finn, a thirtysomething boy-man still attempting to live out his rock and roll delusions. We first see him hurling his shirtless butterball body off a rock club stage in an attempt to crowd-surf that lands him face-first on the floor. That's indicative of how well his dream is going.

When the rent comes due, Dewey impersonates his roommate Ned (screenwriter Mike White) and takes a substitute-teaching job at a fancy school. When the ten-year-old students display musical expertise, he immerses them in a hard and heavy rock education, and organizes the young prodigies to enter a battle of the bands—where he'll be the frontman and collect the cash prize. Dewey's grifter scheme, of course, gives way to affection and respect for his prepubescent bandmates. When the kids' moment to shine arrives, playing their original song "School of Rock," Dewey steps aside. But he joins them for a rousing encore of AC/DC's "It's a Long Way to the Top (If You Wanna Rock 'n' Roll)."

Black made himself a superstar with this raucous performance, becoming a twenty-first century John Belushi who, unlike Belushi, allows his warm side to dispel the demons that drive his antic madness. His rapport with the kids, who are also uniformly awesome, is funny and feels real. He wants rock to do for them what it did for him—and he finds a way to make it happen.

Musically, *School of Rock* gets the facts straight and presents them passionately. Dewey maps out an amazing interconnected history of rock on a blackboard, which kicks off a montage set to the Ramones' "Bonzo Goes to Bitburg." Images of the musicians being taught to the kids float by, dominated by hard rock greats including Jimi Hendrix, the Who, Pink Floyd, Black Sabbath, AC/DC, Rush, and Yes.

Led Zeppelin notoriously refuses to allow their music in movies made by anyone other than their friend Cameron Crowe. To secure "Immigrant Song," then, director Richard Linklater shot a video of Black and the kids onstage, leading a crowd in a chant, pleading to "the gods of rock" to allow them to use the track. Zeppelin were charmed and, as a result, one of *School of Rock*'s great moments is Black invoking the

"hammer of the gods" to his young pupils as "Immigrant Song" wails. The begging video is included on the *School of Rock* DVD.

This is clearly the work of people deeply inspired by headbanging, slam-dancing, finger-tapping, blast-beating, and overall rocking out. The movie embodies the liberating moment when, as a kid, loud and heavy music ceases to be noisy and scary and starts to sound like freedom and joy. Then the louder, heavier, noisier, and scarier the music gets, the more freeing and joyful it becomes from there on out.

Scream Bloody Murder (1973),

aka The Captive Female

(Dir. Marc B. Ray; w/Fred Holbert, Leigh Mitchell, Robert Knox, Angus Scrimm)
✶ Gore ✶ Blasphemy

Scream Bloody Murder billed itself as "the first motion picture to be called GORE-NOGRAPHY!" That's such a thoroughly metal concept, I'd raise my hook hand in salute if I were like Matthew (Fred Holbert), the movie's amputee antihero. Farm boy Matt inexplicably murders his father with a tractor and loses his left mitt. He is shipped to the nut hut for a few years, comes home to find his mother remarried, and launches into a slaughter spree that culminates with his kidnapping redheaded country hooker Vera (Leigh Mitchell) and keeping her on a leash.

Cheap and crazy, *Scream Bloody Murder* delivers on sights both sanguine and sick. The deaths look painful and Matthew's sudden psychedelic visions of cackling witches are pretty scary, building to a berserk, incest-dipped climax in a church where you just know nobody asked for permission to shoot "GORE-NOGRAPHY!"

Patrons of *Scream Bloody Murder* received a free blindfold at the box office. The poster also warned: "Because of the explicit violence in this film, theater-goers must have a sound mind and a strong stomach." Watch for an early appearance by Angus Scrimm, under the name Rory Guy, playing Dr. Epstein. Scrimm would become a horror icon as the Tall Man in *Phantasm* (1979).

This film is in league with "Scream Bloody Murder" songs by Blood Farmers, Exciter, and Realm, and "Gorenography" by the keen-eyed Impaled. Likewise, a record with a strong claim on being the first death metal album ever, Death's *Scream Bloody Gore*, seems to be in cahoots.

SCREAM DREAM (1989)
(DIR. DONALD FARMER; W/CAROL CARR, MELISSA MOORE, NIKKI RIGGINS)
✠ DEVIL WORSHIP ✠ EVIL PUPPETS

Rocking in at sixty-nine salacious minutes, the shot-on-video *Scream Dream* centers on a Tennessee-accented hard rock combo called Rikk-O-Shay, fronted by "queen of heavy metal" Michelle Shock (Carol Carr). The group's followers, we're told, are such "hard-core heavy metal fans" that they "think Van Halen is elevator music!"

The movie begins with a topless blonde being chainsawed vagina-first. Don't worry one little bit, she's only playacting in Rikk-O-Shay's new music video, "Scream Dream." No wonder this band is selling out every stop on their tour and firebombing the pop charts. Alas, when Rikk-O-Shay's manager suspects that Michelle is actually a satanic witch, he fires her for attracting too much public interest and media attention. Isn't that always the way?

Michelle, of course, is so much more than just some leathered-up spell caster. Backstage, she orally services a male groupie (who swiped his girlfriend's car payment to make the show), and then orally extracts his penis. Afterward, Michelle performs an occult ritual. When she is interrupted by poodle-head backup singer Derrick, the two duke it out. Derrick ends up making fatal knife-music all over Michelle's body.

Shirt-averse B-movie boob star Melissa Moore joins Rikk-O-Shay as replacement singer Jamie Summers and ably leads them through a musi-

cal opus titled "Ball Buster." Upon discovering Michelle's throat-slit corpse, Jamie does what comes naturally; she sucks blood from the neck wound. An inevitable demonic possession transforms Jamie into a horn-headed, fang-faced, pointy-eared, bare-bosomed sex monster. A rubber demon hand puppet also commences to run wild over the surviving members of the Rikk-O-Shay organization, biting Derrick on his dick.

Sandwiched between his *Cannibal Hookers* (1987) and *Vampire Cop* (1989), *Scream Dream* is rural auteur Donald Farmer's great contribution to outhouse-budget videotape metal horror. Farmer has since kept busy, with *Shark Exorcist* due in 2014. Melissa Moore added the middle name "Anne" and has appeared in thirty-one movies to date; in the bulk of them she appears nude (*Sorority House Massacre II*, *Bikini Drive-In*). Minus Michelle Shock, Rikk-O-Shay was reportedly a real metal band that gigged in bars and VFW halls around Tennessee. *Scream Dream* remains the group's most high-profile project, and it's unlikely anybody could really top what they accomplished here.

SCREAMERS (2006)
(DIR. CARLA GARAPEDIAN; W/SYSTEM OF A DOWN, BARONESS COX)
✠ CONCERT FOOTAGE

Heavy-hitting international journalist Carla Garapedian follows System of a Down in *Screamers* as the band tours the world in 2005. Along the route, SOAD super-charges audiences with soaring, diving, thunderously powerful mutations on prog metal, and then educates those freshly blasted-open minds regarding the horrors of mass murder. The members of System of a Down fight with particular passion to honor and memorialize the victims of the Turkish-led Armenian Genocide of 1915. Those slayings killed many of the band's actual ancestors, as has been lyrically explored in numerous SOAD songs.

Screamers is an odd, enlightening hybrid of a rock tour documentary and a political protest

Is it a Nightmare?
or is it...
The Slayer

R

Clockwise from top left: The Slayer; Severed Ways: *Cecil "Beastly" DeMille's* Sign of the Cross *(1932)*; Shocker *(1989)*; *Death as looming adversary in Ingmar Bergman's* The Seventh Seal

SEVERED WAYS
THE NORSE DISCOVERY OF AMERICA

film, intermingling System of a Down performances with horrifying atrocity footage, testimony from survivors, and interviews with scholars and activists. With SOAD performing live, the movie can't help but rock. What's especially moving is witnessing how the band's youthful audience has been enlightened on the topic of state-mounted slaughter because of the music, and how the kids connect their own personal struggles with larger matters that connect us all to the human race. Neither System of a Down nor this remarkable film ever comes off pedantic or preachy. Instead, *Screamers* demonstrates the power of metal to actually move the world.

Hrant Dink stands out in *Screamers* as the funny and courageous publisher of a Turkish-Armenian newspaper in Turkey. For criticizing his home nation over its ongoing denial of the Armenian Genocide, Dink endured three prosecutions for "denigrating Turkishness." Shortly following the 2007 premiere of *Screamers* in Turkey, a Turkish nationalist shot Dink to death and shouted, "I killed the infidel!" The gunman was seventeen years old, the perfect age for System of a Down, and it's hard not to imagine that exposure to the band's message might have radically changed his poisoned outlook.

Season of the Witch (2011)

(Dir. Dominic Sena; w/Nicolas Cage, Ron Perlman, Claire Foy, Christopher Lee)

✠ Witchcraft ✠ Inquisition ✠ Crusades ✠ Plague

On the heels of interesting detours via *The Bad Lieutenant: Port of Call New Orleans* (2009) and *Kick-Ass* (2010), Nicolas Cage returned in *Season of the Witch* to out-special-effect all the PG-13 CGI bombast that typically surrounds him in what seems to be several dozen instant-bomb comic book releases every year. Battle-hardened Catholic Crusaders Behmen (Cage) and Felson (Ron Perlman) are charged by mostly dead Cardinal D'Ambroise (Christopher Lee, in rotting-flesh face makeup) to transport the Girl (Claire Foy) to a Hungarian monastery. She's a witch, see; only those monks can destroy her and thereby end the bubonic plague that's decimating Europe. The plot sounds great, and might have been if the movie had been made forty years earlier with adults in mind. Alas, *Season of the Witch* looks like a kids' video game as viewed by a fully seizing epileptic.

This picture is not to be confused with George Romero's *Hungry Wives* (1972), rereleased in 1985 as *Season of the Witch*; nor with *Halloween III: Season of the Witch* (1982).

Although metal bands, notably the Jon Oliva–fronted Savatage side project Doctor Butcher, have written many songs by this name, the classic "Season of the Witch" is the spooky 1966 hit by folk star Donovan. Hard and heavy covers have been performed by Vanilla Fudge, Suck, and even Robert Plant. Acid-rock tabla player Sam Gopal recorded a version in 1969 featuring his band's guitarist Lemmy Kilmister on vocals.

The Seduction of Gina (1984)

(Dir. Jerrold Freedman; w/Valerie Bertinelli, Michael Brandon, Ed Lauter)

✠ Soundtrack (Eddie Van Halen)

Valerie Bertinelli stars as Gina in this crisis-of-the-week TV movie concerning gambling addiction. Gina visits the glamorous casinos of Lake Tahoe (where, twenty years later, Sammy Hagar opened a Cabo Wabo tequila bar franchise), and oh boy, is she ever seduced. Of note are three synthesizer compositions by the star's then husband, Mr. Edward Van Halen, one of which contains a guitar solo. His involvement here delayed work on Van Halen's *1984* album, at least in the eyes of singer David Lee Roth, contributing to tensions that culminated in Roth leaving the band. At least the world got one more terrible TV movie out of it.

The Sentinel (1977)

(Dir. Michael Winner; w/Cristina Raines, Chris Sarandon, Ava Gardner)

✴ Satan ✴ Hell

The Sentinel takes place in 1970s Brooklyn, and is scarily Catholic and chock full of freaks just like my real-life childhood. In this film, a Brooklyn Heights brownstone is earth's gateway to hell. Ancient, blind Father O'Halloran (John Carradine) sits alone on the top floor of the house, making sure demons don't burst through onto Joralemon Street. As the old clergyman nears death, it's time for a new Sentinel, and suicidal fashion model Alison Parker (Cristina Raines) is unwittingly the ideal candidate.

Hell does break loose eventually, but The Sentinel is mostly a misfire that squanders a cast of glorious Hollywood veterans including Carradine, Ava Gardner, Burgess Meredith, Eli Wallach, Sylvia Miles, José Ferrer, Arthur Kennedy, and Jerry Orbach (plus whippersnappers Christopher Walken, Jeff Goldblum, and Beverly D'Angelo).

Director Michael Winner also made the first three Death Wish movies. Instead of being Rosemary's Baby for the 1970s, or even Love Boat on the River Styx, The Sentinel is mostly like a collection of blown solos and out-of-tune notes. The movie courted controversy by featuring disfigured people and circus sideshow workers as demons from hell. Their big scene remains disconcerting. Is a guy really frighteningly evil just because he has messed-up legs?

Sepultura: Under Siege (1991)

(Dir: Steve Payne; w/Max Cavalera, Andreas Kisser, Paulo Jr., Igor Cavalera)

✴ World Metal ✴ Concert Footage

Opening with ominous B-roll footage of riot police on the ground back in their native Brazil, Sepultura charges the stage in Barcelona and the crowd immediately explodes to life in Sepultura: Under Siege. An hour-long acid bath with São Paulo's most ferocious death thrashers ensues. The band burns through mostly the brand-new Arise album, with a nuclear parting shot by way of a cover of Motörhead's "Orgasmatron."

The band is reaching its prime, and thrilled to be embraced halfway across the world by a rabid Spanish-speaking audience. Short interviews allow band members to explain the desperate poverty, corruption, religious oppression, and inevitable uprisings of their homeland. Frontman Max Cavalera ruminates on moshing and stage diving as alternatives to actual violence. Brother Igor Cavalera recalls a 1990 São Paolo show that became a deadly riot.

Sepultura returned to the VHS concert documentary arena with Third World Chaos (1995), which follows a similar format, but features guest talking-head appearances from Pantera, Evan Seinfeld of Biohazard, and Jello Biafra of the Dead Kennedys. The 2002 release Sepultura: Chaos DVD compiles both films, along with the 1996 video EP We Are What We Are.

A Serbian Film (2010)

(Dir. Srdjan Spasojevic; w/Srdjan Todorovic, Sergej Trifunovic, Jelena Gavrilovic)

✴ Torture ✴ Rape Without Revenge

If all the most heinous, hateful, toxic and repellent porno-grind and sick death metal lyrics or artwork were assembled in one foul stack, you could absorb the shock for days and still be sure to see worse here. A Serbian Film is the ultimate brutal blast, and I'm going to spoil it for you. But not really, because no amount of spoilers could possibly soften the blow.

A Serbian Film is an arty exploration of an ex-porn star's descent into a snuff-film underworld—and is the first commercially made and openly exhibited motion picture to depict, in unflinching detail, a screaming baby plucked fresh from the womb and graphically raped to death before our eyes. "Newborn porn!" is what the movie's diabolical filmmaker character calls it.

To be sure, the victim we actually see on camera is a rubber doll and the penis that does her in (along with the many, many other lethally wielded erections on display) clearly looks to have been bought by the gross from a not particularly high-end adult bookstore. Nonetheless: this is it. *A Serbian Film* represents one definite finality of extreme cinema, showing us the absolute worst thing that can possibly be conceived by any human mind. Now what?

This quagmire is what makes *A Serbian Film* so grind. With intentionally and inventively repulsive sonic assaults and lyrical celebrations of cannibalism, necrophilia, and pederasty (many times all at once), grindcore pushes heavy metal as far as possible in terms of musical offense. Bulldozing through the art form's most remote limits with a buzz-saw codpiece, however, grindcore quickly becomes a final Big Dead Empty of its own nihilism, pedaling fast with no traction.

A Serbian Film, in cinematic terms, is exactly that sort of buzzkill. The baby rape occurs relatively early in the action. Once you see that, the feeling is: Okay, that happened and it's in my brain now, but the world's still turning—is it even necessary for this to continue with still more child abuse, sodomy that climaxes with machete decapitation, a corpse orgy, and forced homosexual skull-buggery?

Technically well made (albeit prone to pseudo-Slipknot music video aesthetics) and admirable in its gall, *A Serbian Film* is certainly worth subjecting yourself to at least once. But maybe the hopped-up heavy breathing connects a bit too directly to the desperate "transgressive" nerd movement of the 1990s, when high school wedgie victims grew up to masturbate over serial killer fanzines and tried to out-"sick" each other by collecting murder-scene tchotchkes. Talk about being fucked at birth in suburban America.

All that stated, the arch pretentiousness of the title *A Serbian Film* is absolutely charming. Above all, maybe *A Serbian Film* works best as a wondrous antidote to show to anyone who claimed to be impressed by *Human Centipede*.

The Seventh Seal

(1957)

(Dir. Ingmar Bergman; w/Max von Sydow, Bengt Ekerot, Bibi Andersson, Gunnar Björnstrand)

✠ Death ✠ Witch Hunt ✠ Plague

Swedish master director Ingmar Bergman forged the apex of cinematic heaviness with *The Seventh Seal*, creating a meditation on life, death, and the nature of God and humanity (possibly God *versus* humanity). The movie's indelible images and apocalyptic mind-set forever altered filmmaking and culture altogether, even creating an elemental visual vocabulary and a passageway for cosmic despair that will be utilized forever by heavy metal.

Max von Sydow stars as Antonius Block, a world-weary Danish knight returning home from the Crusades. His country is under siege by the bubonic plague. Death (Bengt Ekerot) appears as a pale-faced reaper, complete with a hooded black robe and a scythe. He tells Block his time on earth is up, but the knight challenges the reaper to a game of chess. The prize is his life.

The people around Block cannot see Death, and they believe the knight is playing alone. The plague, in the meantime, upends their existence, and we see the turmoil of the day, including an accused witch (Maud Hansson) who is condemned to be burned at the stake. In the meantime, amidst universal suffering, God remains silent. *The Seventh Seal* concludes with Block imploring the heavens, "Have mercy on us, for we are small and frightened and ignorant," followed by a vision of the knight and his people being led into the horizon by Death.

The reaper commands his followers to sing and join hands, creating a *danse macabre*—as chilling an image as has ever been realized. Nobody beats Death. And God keeps his almighty mouth shut.

A legion of bands have penned songs titled "Seventh Seal," including Van Halen, Double Diamond, Funeral Rites, Lefay, and Vulcano. *Bill* and *Ted's Bogus Journey* (1991) directly parodies the movie. Instead of chess, the movie's metalhead heroes challenge Death to bouts of Battleship, Clue, electronic football, and Twister. Party on, dudes.

Severed Ways: The Norse Discovery of America (2009)

(Dir. Tony Stone; w/Tony Stone, Fiore Tedesco, Gaby Hoffman, David Perry, Noelle Bailey)
✵ Vikings ✵ Church-burning ✵ Soundtrack (Judas Priest, Morbid Angel, Burzum)

Orn (Tony Stone) and Volnard (Fiore Tedesco), Norsemen accompanying Leif Eriksson to Vinland, are left behind and must contend with North America's harshest elements: grueling winter, hostile "Skraeling" (native peoples), and Irish missionaries. Mostly devoid of dialogue, this shot-in-the-wild film features on-camera human defecation, chicken decapitation, a monk giving Volnard a homoerotic pedicure, and a native woman doping and date-raping Orn.

The comings and goings of our forest-bound heroes play out anachronistically to a soundtrack of metal (Judas Priest, Morbid Angel) and prog (Brian Eno, Popul Vuh), along with Burzum at its most atmospheric. Writer-director-star Tony Stone shot *Severed Ways* mostly in rural Vermont with (really) shaky handheld video cameras, using only natural light. The result may well be the damnedest thing to secure a legitimate theatrical release in the first decade of the twenty-first century.

For most of the duration, someone falling over a log constitutes a minor action sequence, so a full-blown church burning is beyond the height of excitement. After Orn and Volnard stumble across a couple of Irish monks in the woods, the Norsemen torch the missionaries' makeshift cabin of worship. In a film that indulges in countless pagan metal fantasies, this is clearly a great, pithy call-out to Norway's church burnings of the 1990s. Stone underscores the arson with music by Burzum, aka Varg Vikernes, the most infamous real-life villain of Norwegian black metal, imprisoned for church arson and the murder of a friend.

In true old-school black-metal demo fashion, Tony Stone made his opus with cheap equipment on the fly, starting it as a college project and finishing it over several years in fits and starts dictated by available time and money. The film as an entity is just supremely weird. What began as a freaky home movie in essence was treated like a bona fide film, showing in real movie theaters, being reviewed by prominent critics. As this horn-helmeted head-scratcher hypnotically shakes and stumbles and hisses along, somewhere in time it becomes a real movie.

Sgt. Pepper's Lonely Hearts Club Band (1978)

(Dir. Michael Schultz; w/the Bee Gees, Peter Frampton, George Burns, Alice Cooper)
✵ Concert Footage

A legendary megaton stink-bazooka presenting nonstop evidence of how cocaine completely basted every brain cell in late-'70s Hollywood, Peter Frampton and the Bee Gees' *Sgt. Pepper's Lonely Hearts Club Band* does idiotically manage to entertain throughout. For the duration of Aerosmith's performance of "Come Together" as FVB, the Future Villain Band, this fast-food sugar overdose of a movie even manages to rock. (Kiss turned down the villian band role to instead film *Kiss Meets the Phantom of the Park*.)

Alice Cooper, with a rare mustache, is less rocking in the role of Father Sun, a big projected face amidst a psychedelic disco jizz-spill light show. He sings "Because" from *Abbey Road* in the sneering, high-register voice he uses as backup on "Billion Dollar Babies" and comes off sounding like Johnny Carson's "Art Fern" character.

The film's polyester-and-Formica syntheticscape

piles up like a car crash for "Our Guests at Heartland," an uproariously pathetic attempt to recreate the original *Sgt. Pepper* album cover with a grotesque singing chorus of willy-nilly rock, pop, and soul curiosities. Hard rock is represented by Johnny Winter, Rick Derringer, Jack Bruce of Cream, and Jim "Dandy" Mangrum of Black Oak Arkansas. Also available to show up on an Astroturf movie set were Sha Na Na, Carol Channing, Leif Garrett, and Cousin Brucie.

She (1982)

(Dir. Avi Nesher; w/Sandahl Bergman, David Goss, Quin Kessler)

✠ Post-Apocalypse ✠ Soundtrack (Bastard, Motörhead) ✠ Swords & Sorcery

The same year she costarred in *Conan the Barbarian* (1982), Sandahl Bergman took top billing in *She,* a post-nuke variation on an adventure story adapted from the 1886 fantasy novel *She* by H. Rider Haggard. The tale was first filmed by Thomas Edison's production company in 1909, and has been remade numerous times since then. This version involves Mrs. Conan, mutant mummies, a giant in a tutu, motorcycle sword fights, and a musical score by Rick Wakeman of Yes, and is therefore the best in life.

Twenty-three years after a civilization-ending event known as "The Cancellation," our eponymous heroine She accompanies a pair of warrior brothers to free their kidnapped sister from the typical band of baddies in cheapo '80s apocalypse movies; one wears a football helmet, one seems to be a bloodsucking gay clown, and a bunch of them are werewolves in togas. Mohawk hairstyles abound.

She is all dopily enjoyable Nerf-metal fun, helping itself to *Star Wars*' garbage-compactor scene and tossing in a Frankenstein robot for good measure. Motörhead's *She* contributions, interestingly, are all instrumentals.

The Shining (1980)

(Dir. Stanley Kubrick; w/Jack Nicholson, Shelley Duvall, Scatman Crothers)

✠ Haunted House ✠ Stephen King

The Shining is one of cinema's most towering horror accomplishments, and one of heavy metal's most fundamental extra-musical touchstones. The Overlook Hotel, the otherworldly centerpiece of the action in *The Shining,* is remote and grand and certainly haunted, with a madly detailed topiary labyrinth. As we come upon this setting in the dead of winter, as snowstorms further envelop the Overlook in ethereal foreboding and dread, the Torrance family arrives. Novelist dad Jack (Jack Nicholson), housewife mom Wendy (Shelley Duvall), and psychic tot Danny (whose telepathic gift is called "the shining") are there to act as the Overlook's off-season caretakers. During their stay, the Hotel proves to be malignantly alive with ghosts, curses, and a lugubrious, excessive version of death.

The Shining's slow-motion avalanche of terror is flecked by visual high points that have become cultural icons: little Danny channeling "Redrum"; murdered twin girls asking Danny to play; and old crone bathing in room 237; the phantom bartender, alone at the elegant bar; the bear blowing the butler; and certainly the endless typed-out reams of "All work and no play makes Jack a dull boy." Finally, Jack's rabid freak-out while he chases Wendy and Danny with an axe is the stuff of nightmares. "Heeeeeere's Johnny!" *The Shining*'s most famous line, was improvised on the spot by Jack Nicholson.

The simmering unease, the battle of one man against Some Great Evil Beyond, and whirlwinds of chaos are all in director Stanley Kubrick's vise-like control. So are the coldness, the hardness, the isolation, the mammoth sense of space, and, inevitably, the inward violence surging outward. Multilevel gothic flourishes abound, too, given the elegance of the ghosts (and their perversions), along with death-metal hatchet-murder flare-ups and that ultimate gore-grind wet night-mare when the hotel's elevators barf out oceans of blood.

As a horror movie, *The Shining* may well be flawless. As a Heavy Metal Movie, is the absolute picture of perfection—framed and mounted for eternity, just like the party portrait that comprises the film's chilling final shot. Even barren of warlords, motorcycles, sword slayers, chainsaws, nuns, and demons, *The Shining* is wedged into the shivering soul of heavy metal; the name has been taken up by bands in the Netherlands, Norway, and Sweden, and songs called "the Shining" have been offered by Black Sabbath and many others. Redrum is also a popular band name and song title.

During shooting, Kubrick screened three definitive Heavy Metal Movie Classics for the cast and crew to establish the mood he was seeking: *Rosemary's Baby* (1968), *The Exorcist* (1973), and *Eraserhead* (1977). Stephen King, who wrote the original novel upon which *The Shining* is based, has long stated that he never liked what Stanley Kubrick did to his story. Mr. King has always been the best friend heavy metal has ever had in the publishing world, but he is just wrong not to completely love this movie.

SHOCK 'EM DEAD (1991)

(DIR. MARK FREED; W/TRACI LORDS, STEPHEN QUADROS, TROY DONAHUE, ALDO RAY)

✠ SATAN ✠ HAIR METAL ✠ SUNSET STRIP
✠ VOODOO ✠ FAKE BAND (SPASTIQUE COLON)

Released the year that rock critics would remind you was when grunge broke, *Shock 'Em Dead* is a amusing last gasp of high-'80s Sunset Strip hair metal, going out with an appropriately schlocktastic bang tango.

Hollywood glam squad Spastique Colon needs a lead guitarist. Enter Martin (Stephen Quadros), a by-the-numbers '80s movie nerd who quits his job at Pizza Playland to try out for the gig. Front-man Johnny Crack (Markus Grupa) lambastes Martin's playing and sends him, humiliated, into

the path of a face-painted witch named Voodoo Woman (Tyger Sodipe), who operates out of one of Los Angeles's numerous trailer parks.

Martin asks to be transformed into the "greatest rocker in the world." Voodoo Woman slaps a whamma jamma on him and, after a brief sojourn wherein he becomes a werewolf and meets the actual heavy metal Satan, our hero awakes as Angel Martin—the "greatest rock star in the world" (apparently a world with a tremendously liberal notion of greatness).

Angel shreds on the axe, has naturally pumped-up dollar store "rocker wig" hair, and he cohabitates in a sweet pad with a number of often topless concubines. After he usurps Johnny Crack as both lead guitarist and lead singer in Spastique Colon, the eye of his crotch focuses hard on the band's manager, Lindsay (Traci Lords).

The downside, revealed by his in-house female companions who cut similar blood bargains, is that after Martin sacrificed his soul for rocking rewards, he must kill and kill and kill to stay alive. Practical effects mutations, splatter murders, satanic optical effects, and an onslaught of naked gazongas (although none belonging to Traci) all pile up on the way to *Shock 'Em Dead*'s literally headbanging payoff.

Hair metal had its day, and then died of dumbness. *Shock 'Em Dead* will live on into eternity, too dumb to perish.

Angel Martin's lightning-fingered guitar wizardry is supplied by world-renowned shredder Michael Angelo Batio of Nitro. Director Mark Freed has assured fans that he used no special effects in presenting Batio's playing.

Shock 'Em Dead is the final film of veteran character actor Aldo Ray, who plays pizza-making hothead Tony. Ray starred in numerous tough-guy movie classics of the 1950s. A few decades later, he specialized in cheapies such as this one, with a few weird gems among them; e.g., *Don't Go Near the Park* (1979), *Biohazard* (1985), and *Evils of the Night* (1985). Dear old Aldo's nuttiest showcase ever, though, was his non-sex-villain role in the big-screen hard-core porn western *Sweet Savage* (1979). He even won best actor at the X-Rated Critics' Organization Awards.

My favorite Spastique Colon song title is "Hairy Cherry." Who dares me to make a Traci Lords joke here?

𝕾hock 𝖂aves (1977), AKA 𝕬lmost 𝕳uman; 𝕯eath 𝕮orps
(DIR. KEN WIEDERHORN; W/PETER CUSHING, BROOKE ADAMS, JOHN CARRADINE, FRED BUCH)
✠ NAZI ZOMBIES ✠ PETER CUSHING

Ken Wiederhorn's *Shock Waves* is a still-impressive tale of an elite group of unstoppable, not-quite-living SS supermen known as the Death Corps who have been waiting since World War II to kill again. The opportunity arises when vacationers shipwreck on an island occupied by a fugitive Nazi officer (Peter Cushing). He's been storing the blonde, goggle-wearing Death Corps zombies on the bottom of the ocean. In short order, the monsters emerge from beneath the waves for a series of uniquely chilling attacks.

Shock Waves' paranormal Nazi element, particularly under the command of Hammer horror great Cushing, is supremely metal. The zombies here are a powerful and intimidating force, somehow no less formidable by way of being killable if someone pulls off their goggles. Underground hit *Shock Waves* remains the Nazi zombie Heavy Metal Movie to beat (I guess by pulling off its goggles). Classic heavy metal bands Bow Wow, Killer, and Leather all heard the call and created headbanging material in response.

𝕾hocker (1989)
(DIR. WES CRAVEN; W/MITCH PILEGGI, MICHAEL MURPHY, PETER BERG)
✠ SATAN ✠ SLASHER ✠ SOUNDTRACK (BONFIRE, DANGEROUS TOYS, MEGADETH)

Horace Pinker (Mitch Pileggi) is a TV repairman who serial-kills on the side. Lt. Don Parker (Michael Murphy) is the detective whose family Pinker murders when the law gets too close. Jonathan Parker (Peter Berg) is the cop's adopted son who connects to Pinker through his dreams. Wes Craven is the director in search of a proper follow-up to *A Nightmare on Elm Street* (1984). *Shocker* is the movie. And it is no *Nightmare on Elm Street*.

Pinker gets caught and fries in the electric chair, but finds a new lease on ending lives when he makes a pact with the devil to return to earth as "pure electricity" able to possess human bodies. Jonathan is faced, then, with forcing Pinker out of the realm of pure energy and into the "real world" so he can finally be stopped.

Horace Pinker, as played by Pileggi, shows potential as a horror antihero on par with the razor-fingered villain from whom he was essentially cloned. Overall, the movie embodies Wes Craven at his worst, displaying the bloat and pompousness of his college professor background intertwined with the drive to cash in that led him to producing a big-bucks remake of *Last House on the Left*. Every so often, somehow, Craven pumps out a masterpiece. That's the real shocker.

The executed serial killer brought back to life by the same methods used to execute him became quite a thing in late-'80s horror. In addition to *Shocker*, *The Horror Show* (1989) attempted to forge a new Krueger out of Max Jenke (Brion James), and there was also *The Chair* (1988), *Prison* (1988), and *The First Power* (1990). Years later, "shocker" would come to describe a potent variation on metal's finger-horns—with the thumb and ring finger joined as the rest of the digits are pointedly extended to indicate "two in the pink, one in the stink."

𝕾hoot 'em 𝖀p (2007)
(DIR. MICHAEL DAVIS; W/CLIVE OWEN, PAUL GIAMATTI)
✠ SOUNDTRACK (MOTÖRHEAD, MÖTLEY CRÜE)

True to the title, *Shoot 'Em Up* aims and misses at being be the shoot-'em-up movie to end all shoot-'em-up movies. This swing for the ultraviolent fences comes on like an avalanche of firearms and firepower and exploding squibs and post-*Matrix* "bullet time" visuals and "Fuck you, motherfucker!" dialogue. Essentially, the highlights add up to the experience of watching a video game being played by someone else.

The double-barreled battles here involve death machines Clive Owen and Paul Giamatti warring over baby Oliver, an infant who can only be soothed by the sound of heavy metal music. His mother lived near a metal club, and thus little Oliver remembers hard rock vibrations from the womb. He grows happy upon hearing AC/DC, Motörhead, and Mötley Crüe. Even with more than 150 visible on-screen kills, a guy getting a carrot punched through the back of his throat, and Monica Bellucci as a lactating hooker, this baby is still the heaviest part of the film. Hail, little guy!

The Sign of the Cross (1932)

(Dir. Cecil B. DeMille; w/Fredric March, Claudette Colbert, Charles Laughton)

✠ Ancient Rome ✠ Sacrifice ✠ Bestiality

Pioneering cinema giant Cecil B. DeMille adapted the Bible three times. Each is an epic of appropriate proportions, juiced with sufficient sex and violence to render everything scripturally accurate and also heavily, heavily metal. DeMille did the Old Testament in *The Ten Commandments* (1923), and the New Testament in *King of Kings* (1927). In *The Sign of the Cross,* he re-creates the plight of the early Christians as only he (or the actual Emperor Nero) could: with lavish spectacles of perverse decadence, unnatural sex, and gruesome executions staged in the Roman Colosseum for the lust-crazed beguilement of the masses.

Effeminate, slug-lipped, roly-poly Charles Laughton (*The Hunchback of Notre Dame*) makes a perfectly slimy Nero. After burning down Rome, he blames the inferno on the burgeoning Christian cult. Centurions then round up any suspected Jesus worshippers and haul them to the Colosseum for spectacularly entertaining dispatch. In between martyr-makings, Claudette Colbert unsubtly flashes both boobs in a buoyant milk bath; Joyzelle Joyner performs the positively pornographic "Dance of the Naked Moon" to seduce a teenage girl; and orgies abound featuring a cast of thousands in various stages of toga removal.

Still, it's *Sign*'s cavalcade of Christian-killing grotesqueries that no fan of horror and/or heavy metal should miss. Elephants trample and splatter Christians in the arena, then carry off their broken bodies with their tusks; burlesque legend Sally Rand gets tied to a log and set upon by live crocodiles who chew her ample and supple flesh; and gladiators battle with nets and tridents to one gory death after another. Most ape-shit insane of all, a nude maiden is bound to a post, whereupon a gorilla circles her and ponders what to do with unmistakable intent. Once the beast lunges for her, the movie cuts to observers in the stands, where the men all look delighted as the women hide their eyes in horror. Interspecies rape? *Sign of the Cross* has it! For all its horrific and depraved innovations, the *Penthouse* magazine production of *Caligula* (1979) was not without precedent. From Hollywood! In *1932*!

The Sign of the Cross proved to be a huge hit, so naturally, someone stepped in to do something about it. The Catholic-led National Legion of Decency emerged in 1933 directly from some church officials' outrage over *The Sign of the Cross*. The League endured, dictating to papists what films they could and could not see under pain of eternal hellfire, until 1966. Hollywood similarly instituted the fun-killing Hays Code in 1933, which led to *The Sign of the Cross* only being shown in highly censored form until it was fully restored in the 1990s. The film buffs in Iron Maiden paid tribute with their song "Sign of the Cross" in 1995.

Silent Night, Deadly Night (1984)

(Dir. Charles Sellier; w/Robert Brian Wilson, Linnea Quigley)

✵ Slasher ✵ Scary Nuns ✵ Censorship

The king of all Killer Kris Kringle flicks, *Silent Night, Deadly Night* would be a rip-roaringly robust slasher blast even without its ho-ho-horror gimmick—and oh how it delivers its insane, angry gifts! In 1971, yuletide unpleasantness befalls young Billy Chapman by the sackful, culminating with a drunk in a Santa Claus costume shooting Billy's father and raping the boy's mother to death. This leads Billy to a miserable upbringing in an orphanage at the hands of sadistic nuns. When he's sprung at age eighteen, Billy (Robert Brian Wilson) gets a job at Ira's Toy Store. Just in time for the holidays.

Billy is seized by nightmares of a demonic Father Christmas—and normal sexual feelings drive him into spasms of guilt. When the store manager insists that Billy don the Santa suit, the merry massacre is on. Various fornicators (including scream queen Linnea Quigley) experience Santa's lethal outreach. In the movie's *coup de gross*, one reveler is beheaded while riding a sled, and we see his disembodied noggin tumbling down a snowy hill after the rest of him speeds by.

Silent Night, Deadly Night is one of two movies I actually crossed a picket line to attend. I saw it at Brooklyn's Kingsway multiplex, happily invoking a chorus of "Shame! Shame!" from a gaggle of annoyed mothers waving signs outside the box office. *Silent Night, Deadly Night* realizes the notion of an evil Santa bringing death house to house with the power of eight decapitated reindeer. This slasher goes for the jugular, and from first slaying to last, it jingle-bell rocks.

The sequels to *Silent Night, Deadly Night* are admirably nutzoid. *Silent Night, Deadly Night Part 2* (1987) consists of nearly 50 percent recycled footage from the first movie. *Silent Night, Deadly Night 3: Better Watch Out!* (1989) introduces a

psychic teen to the saga; the movie was directed by Monte Hellman, whose *Two Lane Blacktop* (1971) once made him the great avant-garde hope of Hollywood. *Silent Night, Deadly Night 4: Initiation* (1990), was directed by Brian Yuzna (*Bride of Re-Animator*) and focuses on Christmas witches. *Silent Night, Deadly Night 5: The Toy Maker* (1991) features Mickey Rooney as the title figure, Joe Petto, who has an oddball son named Pino. You can pretty much take it from there.

The two other psycho-Santa movies from the 1980s fall just below *Silent Night, Deadly Night* in terms of inclusion in the Heavy Metal Movies canon, but each is still great on its own. *Christmas Evil* (1980) explores themes similar to those of *Silent Night, Deadly Night* but packs a walloping Santa Claus surprise at the end. With good reason, John Waters counts it among his favorite films. The extremely British *Don't Open Till Christmas* (1984), a mystery with barbaric gore effects, flips the script and has the mad mangler offing innocents who are dressed as Santa Claus.

Simon, King of the Witches (1971)

(Dir. Bruce Kessler; w/Andrew Prine, Brenda Scott, George Paulsin, Ultra Violet)

Simon's tagline says it all: "The Black Mass . . . The Spells . . . The Incantations . . . The Curses . . . The Ceremonial Sex . . ." Andrew Prine (*Barn of the Naked Dead*) opens *Simon, King of the Witches* by directly addressing the camera. "My name is Simon," he says. "I live in a storm drain. Some people call me a warlock. But I really am one of the few true magicians." A streetlight mystically illuminates overhead. Then Simon is busted for vagrancy. Such knowing pinpricks run throughout *Simon*, compounding the dated charm of this psychedelic occult overdose. Robert Phippeny, Simon's screenwriter, claimed to be a practicing warlock.

Simon's visual highlights are a trip, particularly a loopy goat-worshiping ceremony conduced by Andy Warhol cohort Ultra Violet and a trippytrailed light stint through a looking glass ripped off from the end of *2001*. Try playing the movie with the sound down and the sound turned up on any given album by Electric Wizard, Witchcraft, or Jex Thoth. The risk of your soul will be worth the high.

The Sisterhood (1988)

(Dir. Cirio H. Santiago; w/Rebecca Holden, Chuck Wagner, Lynn-Holly Johnson, Barbara Hooper)

✠ Post-Apocalypse ✠ Witchcraft ✠ Amazons

Coming late in the *Road Warrior* rip-off game, *The Sisterhood* puts a likable spin on the expected heavy metal trappings, tricked-out motor vehicles, and intersex swordplay.

After the big one drops, men rule over women with an iron dick. Female survivors are slaves—sexual, domestic, and otherwise. The exception is a band of vagina-bearing outlaws rumored to be witches. Their name? *The Sisterhood*. Two sisters, Alee (Rebecca Holden) and Vera (Barbara Hooper), do possess extraordinary powers. Together they recruit teenage Marya (Lynn-Holly Johnson), who shares a psychic bond with her pet crow. Bearded baddie Mikal (Chuck Wagner) kidnaps Marya, takes her through the Forbidden Zone and into Calcara, "the city of ultimate pleasure." The Sisterhood gives chase, unearths working weaponry, and brings down the two-boobed boom.

In 1983, Chuck Wagner also starred in the ABC-TV sci-fi misfire *Automan*. He played the *Tron*-like computer-generated superhero of the title.

Skulhedface (1994)

(Dir. Melanie Mandl; w/Gwar, Jello Biafra, Sebastian Bach)

✠ Puppetry ✠ Jizmoglobin

Gwar amplifies the ambitions displayed in their Grammy-nominated *Phallus in Wonderland* (1992). The production is bigger and more polished, and equally bent on reworking the band's famously grotesque stage show as a proper movie. This time, stranded space warriors Gwar feed humans to a giant maggot in Antarctica, hoping the beast will sprout wings so they can fly it away to their home planet.

In Hollywood, meanwhile, entertainment mogul Boss Glom (Jello Biafra) aims to sign Gwar to GlomCo and water their music down for mass consumption. Gwar respond by graphically slaughtering everyone at GlomCo. Boss Glom rips away his skin mask to reveal he is Skulhedface, an alien supervillain out to sap Gwar of their "jizmoglobin." Skid Row's Sebastian Bach cameos as himself. You get the picture. Gwar's amazing costumes and puppets all come in to play, as does the band's visceral fixation on chopped-off appendages that spew geysers of rancid body fluid. *Skulhedface* also introduces peripheral Gwar character Flopsy, a dwarf with female genitals for a face.

Skullduggery (1983), aka Warlock; Blood Puzzle

(Dir. Ota Richter; w/David Calderisi, Wendy Crewson, Thom Haverstock)

✠ Satan ✠ D&D ✠ Satanic Panic

It started as a game . . . until DEATH started playing!" Upping the satanic-panic ante of the 1982 TV movie *Mazes and Monsters* by actually involving Satan himself, *Skullduggery* is a low-budget Canadian horror cash-in on Dungeons & Dragons hysteria. Adam (David Calderisi) is a Trotterville Community College student involved in a D&D-like game that takes place at a costume shop. He's also been cursed by the devil. All these factors converge when Adam dons a knight outfit, envisions coeds as witches and succubi to be slaughtered, and gorily has at them.

Wendy Crewson, who costars, was also the female lead in *Mazes and Monsters*, a year earlier. What kind of bizarre typecasting was she going for? This movie is not to be confused with 1970 Burt Reynolds sci-fi flick *Skullduggery*, centering on the discovery of a race of monkey-men called the Tropi, which is fairly metal in itself.

Slaughterhouse Rock (1988)

(Dir. Dimitri Logothetis; w/Toni Basil, Nicholas Celozzi, Donna Denton, Tom Reilly)

✠ Occult Studies ✠ Native American Mythology ✠ Fake Band (Bodybag)

Slaughterhouse Rock casts Toni Basil, famous for her 1982 one-hit wonder "Hey Mickey," as the ghost of Sammi Mitchell, murdered frontwoman of the heavy metal group Bodybag. Sammi the spook hangs around Alcatraz until college student Alex (Nicholas Celozzi) shows up along with his occult studies professor (Donna Denton) and some pals. Alex has been stricken with some pretty well visualized nightmares regarding the famous island prison, and he's now there to confront his fears. The plan goes kablooey when one of the gang is possessed by a flesh-famished demon.

A new wave oddity studded with metal, *Slaughterhouse Rock* boasts impressive horror effects, nude knockers courtesy of *Playboy* poser Hope Marie Carlton, multiple Devo songs, and a general likability. Sammi Mitchell and Bodybag are described as pushing metal to shockingly macabre extremes, including decorating their set with "real human cadavers!" Just imagine.

The Slayer (1982), aka Nightmare Island

(Dir. J. S. Cardone; w/Sarah Kendall, Frederick Flynn, Carol Kottenbrook, Carl Kraines)

✠ '80s Slasher ✠ Banned Video Nasty

In need of a vacation, artist Kay (Sarah Kendall) jets off to a remote fishing island with her husband, brother, and sister-in-law. Upon arriving, she has a series of garish, grotesque dreams about her loved ones being murdered by a man on fire she calls "the Slayer." The situation goes from bad to horror movie when Kay's nightmares gorily come true.

The Slayer is a slasher movie that's fallen through the cracks and not without reason, but given its sacred provenance, hitting trash-pit theaters and VHS racks just as Araya, Hanneman, King, and Lombardo were donning satanic makeup in SoCal—its place in heavy metal is solid. In the mid-'80s, *The Slayer* was packaged on a rare double-feature VHS tape with the homicidal-Native-American slasher movie *Scalps* (1983). Used copies of that gem are running about $250 these days.

Slayer: Live Intrusion (1995)

(Dir. Phil Tuckett; w/Tom Araya, Jeff Hanneman, Kerry King, Paul Bostaph)

✠ Concert Footage ✠ Arm Carving

Slayer: Live Intrusion captures the band barnstorming Arizona during the 1995 *Divine Intervention* tour. The fifteen-song set opens with "Raining Blood" and wraps up with "Chemical Warfare," and is a great document of the band's time with drummer Paul Bostaph. He replaced original Slayer member Dave Lombardo first in 1992, and again in 2013. One major highlight is a spine-snapping cover of Venom's "Witching Hour" with the help of mayhem-makers Chris Kontos and Robb Flynn of Machine Head.

The live melée was directed by Phil Tuckett and his team of battle-hardened veterans from NFL Films, who hyped *Live Intrusion* by reporting that the full-contact violence of Slayer's mosh pits far exceeded anything the crew had encountered during years on the gridiron. Also, this Slayer movie kicks off (as pictured on the *Divine Intervention* disc itself) with a fanatic actually carving "SLAYER" into his arm in bloody real time.

Slayer Mailbox (2010)

(Dir. Andrew Shearer; w/Rachael Deacon)

✠ Metal Reality

Out on some sunny suburban road, "Slayer 185" is emblazoned in silver on the side of a mailbox. A heavily tattooed, robustly curvaceous death siren approaches. She's mesmerized. She removes the mailbox and takes it to a zoo, or wherever this place is that houses an owl, two alligators, a turtle, and a sleeping bear behind barbed wire. Something special is in bloom. The lady and mailbox share one milk shake with two straws. The mailbox pops open to give her flowers. Strawberries and champagne follow. Candles are lit, a black dress comes off, a mailbox flag rises; and the ending is a surprise.

Slayer Mailbox, written by and starring Pittsburgh provocateur Rachael Deacon, is five minutes long and it's a masterwork of economic storytelling for maximum effect—much like *Reign in Blood*. Ms. Deacon swears on Kerry King's gut-length goatee that it's a re-creation of a true story, although only she and the mailbox would really know for sure.

ⳫLEEPAWAY ⳭAMP (1983)

(DIR. ROBERT HILTZIK; W/FELISSA ROSE, MIKE KELLEN, JONATHAN TIERSTEN, CHRISTOPHER COLLET)

✠ SLASHER ✠ SURPRISE!

You only get to see *Sleepaway Camp* for the first time once. If you haven't yet, stop reading and see it. Then come back. *Sleepaway Camp* irrevocably bonds everyone who experiences it to everyone else who has ever experienced it. Take it in once and you're a lifelong member. Like the aftermath of hearing Voivod or Napalm Death or Immortal for the first time, Camp Arawak is a place you can never fully leave.

The insanity of *Sleepaway Camp* flares up in frame one, as severely Long Island–accented tots Peter and Angela endure a tragic boating accident with their two gay dads. The next scene jumps ahead a few years. Angela (Felissa Rose)—the sole survivor of the water crash—is about twelve and nearly catatonic. She and her cousin Ricky (Jonathan Tiersten) are departing for a summer at Camp Arawak, sent off by her indescribably off-the-fucking-wall Aunt Martha (Desiree Gould, in the single most bizarrely campy performance in cinema history).

Camp Arawak seems like a lovely facility, turned into a hellhole by the inexplicably angry, universally sewer-mouthed campers. These kids are awful, and they all hate each other. The best exchange takes place at a miserably unpleasant softball game where an opponent snarls, "Eat shit and die, Ricky!" to which Ricky responds, "Eat shit and live!" These are the children of wise-ass New York, and you know they would have been bringing M.O.D. and Carnivore cassettes to camp within a few years.

Anyone who crosses the infuriatingly silent, bug-eyed Angela the wrong way ends up kaput in a series of graphic murders delivered with shockingly effective visual panache. The obese, child-molesting cook Artie (Owen Hughes) is scalded into screaming hideousness. A drowning victim washes ashore and a snake eerily slides out of his mouth. A nasty jock taking "a wicked dump" gets a beehive to his naked crotch. Villainous tough girl Judy (Karen Fields) is held down and raped to death with a hot curling iron.

The movie's level of rage and violence is stupefying—but not nearly so much as its rippling homoerotic moments, which burst repeatedly to the surface. Consider the onslaught: an elaborate naked ass-crack-to-the-face prank in the boys cabin; a hilariously gratuitous all-male skinny-dipping butt parade (censored on all but the original VHS); the ball-hugging short-shorts sported by muscle-counselor Ronnie (Paul DeAngelo); Angela's visualized freak-out with her nude dads cuddling in a spinning bed; and, of course, *Sleepaway Camp*'s ultimate dangling denouement.

Sleepaway Camp is one of a handful of films—*2001*, *Showgirls*, and *Forbidden Zone* come to mind—that strike repeatedly with the same soul-shaking, brain-blasting, consciousness-shattering impact. This champion crackpot artwork would be metal even without the crazily overwrought power ballad "Angela's Theme" running under the closing credits.

Two sequels followed in rapid succession, minus the original writer and director: *Sleepaway Camp II: Unhappy Campers* (1988) and *Sleepaway Camp*

III: Teenage Wasteland (1989). Pamela Springsteen—kid sister of the Boss and the vocally irritated cheerleader in *Fast Times at Ridgemont High*—portrays a post-op female Angela in both. The sequels have cults of their own, and are pretty fun, but would fare better as stand-alone slasher flicks not tied to the original masterpiece.

Sleepaway Camp creator Robert Hiltzik returned with a worthy, sexually deranged follow-up of his own in 2008, *Return to Sleepaway Camp*.

$SLOW $SOUTHERN $TEEL (2011)

(DIRS. DAVID LIPKE, CHRIS TERRY; W/"DIXIE" DAVE COLLINS, PHIL ANSELMO, HANK III, EYEHATEGOD)

✶ SOUTHERN METAL

The overbearing focus on New York in various punk rock histories has long annoyed me. I never blinked at perhaps the similar amount of excess attention paid, American metal-wise, to the Sunset Strip and the Bay Area until I saw *Slow Southern Steel*. This swamp-hot brain-boiler of a documentary forcibly wrapped my head in a Confederate flag and punched my peeper-sockets with skull-ringed fists until I could see straight.

Narrated by "Dixie" Dave Collins of Buzzov✶en and Weedeater, *Slow Southern Steel* is a blistering journey through the post-grunge metal scene of the land below the Mason-Dixon Line. As its name indicates, *Slow Southern Steel* focuses heavily on sludge metal, largely in the form of bands such as Eyehategod, whose Mike Williams proves to be a colorful Q&A subject.

Black Flag and the Melvins are invoked repeatedly as life-changing agents of infinite hard rock possibilities. The monster-riff mud stomping of both bands ripples in the music here, swirling in among country radio, church choirs, rap, and non-aural elements such as sweet tea, fried food, and spooky backwoods playgrounds. (Not to mention whiskey, weed, and what have you.)

Directors Chris Terry (of the band Rwake) and David Lipke shot interviews with more than forty bands in clubs, bars, basements, back alleys, practice spaces, and all manner of locations that evoke the physical and aesthetic realm of southern metal. The photography, editing, and pacing of these first-time filmmakers is on par with the best professionally made "rock docs" without ever slipping into slickness. New Orleans demon Phil Anselmo looms large in the later part of the film, which focuses on metal survivors of Hurricane Katrina. Hank III, grandson of country-western god Hank Williams and son of southern rock hellraiser Hank Williams Jr., would also be a standout regardless of his family history.

Admirably, no one shies away from discussing Confederate flag imagery. Norfolk, VA's, Beaten Back to Pure takes the most confrontational stand. Their message echoes a metal take on Southern hospitality, repeated countless different ways: the musicians don't need outsiders, they don't care about outsiders, but they will rock the fuckin' shit out of any and all comers.

$LUMBER $PARTY $MASSACRE (1982)

(DIR. AMY HOLDEN JONES; W/MICHAEL VILLELLA, MICHELLE MICHAELS, ROBIN STILLE, DEBRA DELISO)

✶ SLASHER

Amidst the great glut of 1982 slasher films, *Slumber Party Massacre* made its mark immediately by boasting the greatest possible title for such an enterprise. The picture then delivered with a no-frills delivery of sexy slaughter, flecked with some humor, to become a sticky staple of metalhead horror movie marathons of its day. Sexy Trish (Michelle Michaels) takes advantage of her parents being away to host the other members of her high school girls' basketball team for a sleepover. They smoke weed, giggle, and gab about boys until a serial murderer with an expertise in power-drilling crashes the affair (as detailed in songs titled "Slumber Party Massacre" by Frightmare and Lustmord).

Slumber Party Massacre was made from a script (titled *Don't Open the Door*) by highly regarded lesbian feminist author Rita Mae Brown. She intended it as a parody of slasher films, but director Amy Holden Jones wisely shot a straightforward dead-teenager opus. It works both ways (which must make Ms. Brown extra proud). Despite the movie itself being made by women, *Slumber Party Massacre* drew heat for its "misogynistic" poster image. The one-sheet depicts lingerie-clad nubiles cowering beneath the spread legs of a male assailant, thrusting a long power drill in their direction straight from his crotch. The furor recalled the upset over the scalp-with-boner painting on the poster for *Maniac* (1980).

$NUFF (1976)

(DIRS. MICHAEL FINDLAY, HORACIO FREDRIKSSON, SIMON NUCHTERN; W/MIRTHA MASSA, ALDO MAYO)

✵ SNUFF ✵ MANSON FAMILY ✵ MOTORCYCLES

In the "anything goes" 1970s, *Snuff* aimed to go too far. As *Deep Throat* popularized hard-core pornography, Black Sabbath promulgated satanic rock, and every network sitcom actress was ordered to the set sans bra, public consciousness reeled at where society's new permissiveness might finally arrive. Thus arose the legend of "snuff films"—movies in which a living human is murdered on camera for the gratification of perverts at subsequent underground screenings.

Married New York exploitation movie mavens Michael and Roberta Findlay, always quick to go where the stink was, smelled a hot gimmick in snuff films. They had already cashed in on Manson Family hoopla by making the hippie-cult biker flick *The Slaughter* (1971), which was now just lying around. So the Findlays tacked some nonsense onto the end of *The Slaughter* and mounted a brilliant ad campaign that got tongues wagging as to how this, finally, was the outrage that broke that final taboo.

Using the studio and equipment of X-rated director Carter Stevens (*Teenage Twins*, *Punk Rock*), the Findlays shot a "snuff" scenario in which an actress is held down on a bedroom movie set. The multiple indignities she suffers include

having her finger clipped off with pliers and her hand removed by buzz saw before a final disemboweling. Red paint oozes everywhere, out from her plastic wounds. The screen goes white, and a voice announces, "Shit! We ran out of film!"

Next came the real artistry, the hype. "The movie they said could never be shown!" blared *Snuff*'s ads. "The film that could only be made in South America, where life is CHEAP!" Word of mouth exploded. Moral guardians howled. Thrill-seekers packed grindhouses and drive-ins. The Findlays counted the cash.

New York district attorney Robert Morgenthau launched an investigation into the film. At a press conference afterward, he announced that the kill scene was "nothing more than trick photography, as is evident to anyone who sees the movie." In truth, the brouhaha surrounding *Snuff* is all there is. The Manson/biker stuff is a snooze, despite the leader being named "Satan," and the money shot at the end is not just bogus, it's laughably, charmingly so. As a cultural phenomenon, though, *Snuff* obliterated obstacles that might have stood in the way of other emerging artistic transgressions. Never look down upon the origins of your extremes.

In 2003, video company Blue Underground issued *Snuff* on DVD. Blue Underground is renowned for its deluxe, extras-loaded packages, but in keeping with the movie's "illegal" reputation, *Snuff* came in a box resembling brown paper wrapping. You put the DVD in, and the movie just starts—no warnings, no credits, nothing. When the movie's over, it just starts again.

In 1976, I was an eight-year-old who cut movie ads out of the newspaper for scrapbooks. Horror and kid stuff were my favorites (I didn't dare clip the pornos; I only studied those like catechism); but I was seriously shaken up by the promos for *Snuff*. Lying awake in a freak-out state over the idea of a movie that showed people getting killed—and, worse, that other people would want to see it—I talked to Pops McBeardo about it.

A few days later, Pops took me to meet a detective friend of his who had actually worked the *Snuff* case. The policeman assured me that the girl from the movie was fine, and that he'd even talked to her. Both Pops and the detective lamented in their Brooklyn accents that the world was full of "sick bastahds," but you just have to avoid them. I rested easier for a while. Then I grew up to write this book.

Sodom and Gomorrah: The Last Seven Days (1975)

(Dirs. Artie Mitchell, Jim Mitchell; w/Sean Brancato, Joan Devlon, Gina Fornelli)

✠ Sodom and Gomorrah ✠ Porn Chic

Hippie-era San Francisco decadents raised by a pro gambler father, the enterprising brothers Artie and Jim Mitchell first mastered the loonier-than-lust naked-dance hall business, then eased into adults-only cinema and created the X-rated milestone *Behind the Green Door* (1972). That blue-movie blockbuster was speckled with surreal horror elements and included a highly metal scene of lesbian nuns administering a group tongue-bath. Star Marilyn Chambers was a pretty model who had previously posed holding a baby for the wholesome image adorning every box of Ivory Snow detergent.

After sullying America's 99-and-44/100% pure dream girl in *Green Door* (and again the following year in *The Resurrection of Eve*), the Mitchell brothers aimed to spray their dirty money all over the Good Book. *Sodom and Gomorrah: The Last Seven Days* re-creates the Old Testament's famous twin cities of polymorphous perversion and salacious sin—the most metal locales in all of scripture, championed in songs by Sodom, Therion, Entombed, Venom, and so many more—as mega-budget, cocaine-ripped pornographic madness involving sex all over the desert, sex in trees, sex in the street, sex with animals, sex with vegetables, one guy performing oral sex on himself, and all of it executed by a hairy, attractive cast done up in *Ben Hur* garb.

The mad King of Sodom (Sean Brancato) goes Caligula for a bit, covering a dude's dick with honey and stuffing it down an anthill, and ordering some kind of giant wineskin rape of a fornicating woman. After observing all the deranged decadence from on high, Yahweh—a chimpanzee in a flying saucer who drawls with the voice of a John Wayne imitator—deigns to "castrate the pre-verts." After initiating the practice of circumcision, Yahweh sees no hope for redemption and he thereby declares the citizens of Sodom and Gomorrah "a bunch of liberal assholes." His biblical destruction rains down forthwith.

Sodom: Lords of Depravity, Part 1 (2006)

(Dir. Tom "Angelripper" Such; w/Tom "Angelripper" Such, Chris "Witchhunter" Dudek, Frank "Blackfire" Gosdzik, Josef "Peppi" "Grave Violator" Dominic, Atomic Steif)

✠ Thrash Metal ✠ Metal History ✠ Concert Footage

Before forging a heavy metal attack squadron that raged against common notions of God and Christianity in no uncertain terms, human Rottweiler Tom "Angelripper" Such of Germany needed to look no further than the Bible. In 1982, Such named his three-piece soul-wrecking machine after earth's most unholy location as described by the so-called holy book: Sodom. The fact that Sodom, and the common language offshoot "sodomy," is most often associated with homosexual anal intercourse didn't stop Angelripper and his Almighty-hating band from charging forward as a key force in the creation of Teutonic thrash.

History of Depravity is a three-hour documentary included in the massive DVD package *Sodom: Lords of Depravity Part 1*. The ambitious film traces the band from the members' origins as the sons of miners, inspired by Venom and their

"1000 Days in Sodom" to fight a war against Euro techno-wimps such as Nena and Falco. Most extraordinary, this only covers the story through 1995, the key early period during which Sodom rules along with Destruction and Kreator as the kings of German thrash metal. Every living member of Sodom appears here, along with friends, collaborators, producers, fans, groupies, bartenders, members of other bands, and an amazing array of participants in the history of this groundbreaking über-group.

The size alone of *History of Depravity* should be saluted, but even more praiseworthy is the band's unvarnished self-portrait. Particularly uncomfortable is the segment regarding the firing of beloved drummer Chris "Witchhunter" Dudek. Angelripper calls it "the hardest decision in the career of Sodom" and the documentary truly makes you feel it.

For anyone afraid of subtitles, take note: *History of Depravity* is in German. Watch and read along, or just watch. The power of Sodom transcends such trifles as mere language. Also included is a second DVD, collecting live performance clips edited together to create a single live playlist that spans the band's first thirteen years.

Sodom: Lords of Depravity, Part II
(2010)
(DIR. TOM "ANGELRIPPER" SUCH; W/SODOM)
�֢ Thrash Metal ✻ Metal History ✻ Concert Footage

The first disc of the double-DVD release *Sodom: Lords of Depravity Part II* contains an exhaustive four-hour follow-up to 2006's three-hour documentary *History of Depravity Part I*. Once again, the filmmaking is remarkably in-depth and, as a result, *Part II* works best for hard-core Sodom fanatics.

Whereas the first installment enthralls even the most casual admirer with its tale of a new band on the rise, pounding out a whole new form of

heavy metal between 1982 and 1995, the next dozen years revolve around Angelripper and his revolving Sodom cohorts as established heroes. Angelripper's country metal side project Desperado gets a fair amount of attention. A second DVD presents Sodom's huge twenty-fifth anniversary show at Wacken Open Air in 2007.

Soldiers Under Command (2003)
(DIRS. JAMES L. REID, MATT LUEM, GREG FIERING; W/ MICHAEL SWEET, ROBERT SWEET, OZ FOX, TIM GAINES)
✻ Christians ✻ Concert Footage ✻ Metal Gatherings

Open your Bible now to Isaiah 53:5: "But he was wounded for our transgressions, he was bruised for our iniquities: the chastisement of our peace was upon him; and with his stripes we are healed." Seizing on scripture nobody else had ever noticed, Stryper, a credibly rocking quartet of *Circus* magazine pinups from Orange Country, California, became the only multiplatinum glam metal ensemble of the MTV '80s whose lyrics and lifestyle were overtly Christian. After throwing thousands of disposable Bibles into audiences and selling a reported seven million records, Stryper broke up in 1992, victims of (as any viewer of hair metal *VH1 Behind the Music* episodes can recite by rote) "the Seattle scene."

Striking a tone best described as "semisweet," the short documentary *Soldiers Under Command* drops in on the band's one-off reunion in 2003, which takes place at the Second Annual Stryper Expo at a Christian college somewhere outside L.A. (Yeah, it's kind of weird that it's the *second* one). Fans of all shapes line up and radiate gratitude toward the band's sonic salvation. A smiling pair of beefy longhairs who must be identical twins are especially charming as they recall their first Stryper show at Magic Mountain "in 1984 . . . or '85." All four original band members talk warmly about the band's history, with drummer Robert Sweet being the most vocal about them holy rolling on the road again. (He's the most vocal about a lot of things.) Janice Sweet, identified as "Stryper Mom and Manager," oversees the official stall selling thrown Bibles and other pricey merch. Swedish Christian metal outfit Laudamus clanks through a number, as does Christian hip-hop group Priesthood. Christian skateboarders do their thing alongside the music stage.

Soldiers Under Command concludes with Stryper taking the stage and blasting out "Sing Along Song" with sufficient chops and stage mastery to beg the question, Why *don't* they get back together? In real life, that's exactly what happened, and Stryper have remained active ever since—praise something or other!

The Song Remains the Same (1976)

(Dirs. Peter Clifton, Joe Massot; w/Robert Plant, Jimmy Page, John Bonham, John Paul Jones)

✠ Concert Footage

Led Zeppelin rocks Madison Square Garden, and you are there! Robert Plant sword-fights and searches for the Holy Grail, and you are there! Jimmy Page climbs a mountain in search of enlightenment, and you are there! John Paul Jones rides the midnight streets of Victorian London with masked horsemen, and you are there! John Bonham hangs out at home, plays snooker, and then goes driving. You are still there!

The Song Remains the Same chronicles Led Zep's mighty three-night stand at the Garden in 1973, showcasing the band in full flight and top power. Interspersed throughout are fantasy sequences and odd offstage moments. A blotto-wasted fan runs afoul of security, only to get his buzz harshed behind a locked door. At one point, the group learns its cash haul has been heisted from a hotel strongbox. Nobody was ever caught.

In the pre-MTV, pre-VCR world, *The Song Remains the Same* supplied the only opportunity for fans to experience a Zep show outside the fact. With nothing but album covers to go by, people barely knew when the band looked like. As a result, in 1977 alone, the movie grossed $10 million at the box office—impressive even for a mainstream Hollywood production, let alone a tripped-out, two-hour-and-seventeen-minute hard rock fantasia, replete with violin bows and Bonzo's complete "Moby Dick" drum solo. The verbal virtuosity of Zep's manager Peter Grant is also on grand display, as the legendary strongman unloads eighteen variations of the terms *fuck* and *cunt* on a promoter inside of three furiously hard-boiled minutes.

At one point, the camera approaches Jimmy Page as he jams on a hurdy-gurdy along the bonny banks of Loch Ness. He faces away, and when he finally spins to face us, Page's eyes glow demonic red. Hail Satan's favorite guitar player!

The Song Remains the Same has remained in constant circulation as a midnight movie, a home-video rite of teenage passage, and the ideal visual and sonic companion piece for the recreational employment of upright tabletop water pipes. May that always remain the same.

Sons of Steel (1988)

(Dir. Gary L. Keady; w/Rob Hartley, Roz Wason, Jeff Duff, Dagmar Bláhová)

✠ Post-Apocalypse ✠ Black Alice

Sons of Steel is a late entry in Australia's Ozploitation cycle (which gave us, most notably, the *Mad Max* movies) and a cult item from the land of AC/DC, Mortal Sin, and Wolfmother. This hard rock musical involves post-doomsday barbarians who resurrect '80s heavy metal frontman Black Alice (Rob Hartley) to travel back in time so he can prevent the nuclear apocalypse. The film's broad, vulgar comedy is often funny, and Black Alice makes a good lunatic hero, be he wailing to a savage beauty in a rawhide bikini or rescuing the Sydney Opera House from imminent detonation.

Black Alice looks like Maynard James Keenan of Tool did in the early '90s. But Black Alice did the semi-shaved-head longhair thing in the late '80s. Similarly uncanny is the appearance of a pair of dreadlocked, albino twins, a decade and a half before those weirdoes in the Matrix sequels.

Sorceress (1982)

(Dir. Jack Hill; w/Leigh Harris, Lynette Harris, Martin LaSalle, Bruno Rey)

✠ Swords & Sorcery

Fabulously crappy van art come to life in the form of Playboy twins, sorcerers, sword fighting, a Viking, a goat boy with a hard-on, a battle-ready tribe of apemen, zombies, and a bat-winged lion. Buxom blonde twins Leigh Harris and Lynette Harris star, collectively, as the titular figure (za-zing!) in the Roger Corman produced super-quickie *Sorceress*. The Harrises come by their stunning curves naturally. The same cannot be said for their acting talent. No matter: their stiffness (and, subsequently, that of the viewers) only add to the buoyant fun.

After being rescued from sacrifice and raised by a warrior, our heroines —who are psychically linked under the guise of "The Two Who Are One"—venture out into their medieval world dressed as "men" (wearing fur hats and baggy cloaks). They join forces with Krona (Martin LaSalle); a hunky barbarian type, Erlick (Bob Nelson); Valdar the Viking (Bruno Rey), Pando the boner-popping satyr (David Milbern); and a bunch of guys in gorilla suits. Together, they battle the twins' evil sorcerer father. When he finally sets zombies loose on them, they respond by conjuring their god Vitahl—a giant, flying lion in full cut-rate stop-motion-animation glory.

Sorceress also reveals, in its travails, that if one twin experiences arousal and/or orgasm, the other one does too. So in the movie's final shot, Erlick wraps his arms around the sisters, clearly heading for *twincest* Valhalla and smirks, "You see—the two ARE one!" Valdar the Viking gets a big, hearty laugh out of that.

Sorceress is the final film directed by '60s and '70s grindhouse legend Jack Hill and the first written by '80s stalwart Jim Wynorski. Among the cult masterpieces previously helmed by Jack

Hill are *Spider Baby* (1968), *The Big Doll House* (1971), *Coffy* (1973), *Foxy Brown* (1974), and *Switchblade Sisters* (1975). Jim Wynorski followed *Sorceress* by scripting the most insane '80s teen sex comedy, *Screwballs* (1984), and then directing around a hundred films. Highlights include *Chopping Mall* (1986), *Deathstalker II* (1985), *Big Bad Mama II* (1987), *Scream Queen Hot Tub Party* (1991), and dozens of direct-to-video wonders.

The Sorrows of Satan (1926)

(Dir. D. W. Griffith; w/Adolphe Menjou, Ricardo Cortez, Carol Dempster)

✠ Satan ✠ Faust

Poor, pitiful writer Geoffrey Tempest (Ricardo Cortez) does what all poor, pitiful writers do: he curses God. This time, he gets lucky and summons Satan, who appears in the guise of dapper chap Prince Lucio (Adolphe Menjou). A deal is cut, Tempest becomes rich, and then bad things happen—until our tortured soul triumphantly rejects the false promises of the Prince of Darkness. An otherwise standard Faustian saga is rendered significant in *The Sorrows of Satan* by D. W. Griffith's typical mastering-this-as-I-make-it-up direction, Menjou's portrayal of Old Scratch as a top-hatted dandy, and scenes of fleshly decadence leading to otherworldly redemption—all in dreamy, silent black-and-white.

The Sorrows of Satan opens with St. Michael the Archangel and his army of winged warriors tossing Lucifer out of heaven. During his brilliantly lit and powerfully evocative way down, Lucifer transforms into the black-horned, goat-legged devil we know. A fallen angel—and a star—is born. An immediate worldwide hit and silent-film classic, *The Sorrows of Satan* is based on an 1895 novel of the same name by Marie Corelli. The book is regarded as one of the world's first best-sellers. There has always been lucre, filthy and otherwise, in the Lucifer business.

SOYLENT GREEN (1973)

(DIR. RICHARD FLEISCHER; W/CHARLTON HESTON, EDWARD G. ROBINSON, LEIGH TAYLOR-YOUNG)

✴ POST-APOCALYPSE ✴ CANNIBALISM

"Soylent Green is people!" That may be a spoiler, but it is also the only thing anybody remembers about *Soylent Green*. On its arrival in weary and disillusioned 1973, this film was a blockbuster, bursting with metal themes such as humanity's self-directed damnation and a high-tech spin on cannibalism, along with suitably grand but downbeat prog rock visuals driving home the misery of not yet being dead, processed, peddled, and eaten.

In the grim New York City of 2022, reckless overpopulation and environmental ruin have depleted food sources to the point that most nutrition is sold to the masses by the Soylent Corporation. The most in-demand product is Soylent Green, a new concoction said to come from "high-energy plankton" but—well, you already know what that means. Charlton Heston, riding high on his heftily metal apocalyptic sci-fi star run after *Planet of the Apes* (1969) and *The Omega Man* (1971), plays the police detective who blows the lid off Soylent Corporation's cannibalistic repurposing project. Edward G. Robinson, in his final role, dies on-screen magnificently.

One question from the possibly even more disillusioned and bleak world forty years later: if you were eking out survival in a doomed, poisonous, lethally crowded urban hell where there was nothing to eat, would you *care* that Soylent Green is people? I would chow down happily and hope that Soylent Green was people I didn't even really like in the first place. Yum! Pair with supple servings of metal by the bands Soilent Green from Louisiana, and Soylent Green from both Germany and Spain.

THE SPIRAL STAIRCASE (1945)

(DIR. ROBERT SIODMAK; W/DOROTHY MCGUIRE, ELSA LANCHESTER, GEORGE BRENT, ETHEL BARRYMORE)

✴ HAUNTED HOUSE

One of Phil Anselmo's top ten horror favorites, this moody, lushly shot serial-murder movie centers on mute Helen (Dorothy McGuire) as a killer is targeting "women with afflictions." Suspense builds to one particularly dark and stormy night, when the staircase in question and the spooky mansion containing it are lit by lightning and shaken by thunder. For serious horror fans whose interests extend beyond extreme gore, *The Spiral Staircase* is masterpiece of atmosphere and brilliant black-and-white cinematography.

Elsa Lanchester, who plays a sly maid, is most famous for her high-haired performance in the title role of *Bride of Frankenstein* (1935).

SPUN (2002)

(DIR. JONAS ÅKERLUND; W/JASON SCHWARTZMAN, BRITTANY MURPHY, JOHN LEGUIZAMO, MENA SUVARI)

✴ DRUGS

Spun is a nihilistic indie-flick dervish whirling in and out of various lives interlocked by the manufacture, marketing, and/or consumption of methamphetamine. Ex-Bathory drummer Jonas Åkerlund directs with speed-freak franticness (appropriately) as various hipster-circa-2002 thespians pretend to be down-and-out druggies.

The strobe-light-paced production of *Spun* is given to self-conscious sick jokes (naked stripper Chloe Hunter remains tied to a bed for days) and obscene soliloquies (Mickey Rourke's meth cook waxes rhapsodic about "the pussy" in America's character), and is peppered with "cool" cameos ("Look! That lesbian is Debbie Harry!") straight out of post-Tarantino screenwriting classes. If you can also tolerate Jason Schwartzman and John Leguizamo under any circumstances—let alone here, respectively, as a cute junkie and a motormouthed pusher—then *Spun* might be right up your art-school-pussies-talkin'-tough alley.

On the other hand, Rob Halford cameos as a porn shop owner. He wears a leather vest and a T-shirt emblazoned with "PIG," and he thumbs through a whack-mag titled *Bathhouse B/J.* That's worth at least one pipe hit.

Stairway to Heaven

(1946)

(Dirs. Michael Powell, Emeric Pressburger; w/ David Niven, Kim Hunter, Robert Coote)
✴ Metal History

Given Zep's notorious habit of helping themselves to existing musical compositions, it's not unimaginable to deduce that they copped the title of their anthem-of-anthems from this well-regarded celestial WWII romance.

Royal Air Force pilot Peter Carter (David Niven) is slated to die when his bomber crashes. As he parachutes out, though, heaven can't find him "in all that fog." Landing safely Carter falls in love with an American woman, so when the afterlife comes calling, he has to plead his case to stay before a heavenly court. In *Stairway to Heaven*, the actual stairway to heaven is an escalator!

Star Trek II: The Wrath of Khan (1982)

(Dir. Nicholas Meyer; w/William Shatner, Leonard Nimoy, Ricardo Montalban, Kirstie Alley)
✴ Science Fiction ✴ Torture ✴ Armageddon

Spinning off of the 1967 TV episode "Space Seed," *Star Trek II: The Wrath of Khan* pits the starship *Enterprise* against Ricardo Montalban as the villain Khan Noonien Singh. Genetically altered for beyond-human strength and intellect, Khan is a former dictator turned space prisoner. He reels in Federation do-gooders Commander Chekov (Walter Koenig) and Captain Terrell (Paul Winfield) with a false distress signal, only to implant hideous brain-eating eel-things inside their ears.

Captain Kirk (William Shatner), Mister Spock (Leonard Nimoy), and the regulars set their phasers to "Rescue." Scrimmages with Khan all over the galaxy result in the ignition of a doomsday device that is only undone when Spock sacrifices his own life. When the expiring Vulcan croaks his farewell "live long and prosper," no catastrophic sacrifice has ever been so pointedly moving—or so pointed-eared.

Star Trek: The Motion Picture (1979) was a monstrously bloated, mammoth-budgeted mega-bore. In order to make a sequel, Paramount cut financing from $46 million to $11 million, and removed nitpicky *Trek* creator Gene Roddenberry from nuts-and-bolts decision making. Numerous stadium-filling metal bands give lip service to their desire to go back to the garage to reconnect to their raw roots. Here it actually happened, and paid off in the lean, mean *Wrath of Khan*.

Star Trek's motif of space exploration and consciousness expanding is inherently prog rock. Khan, above all other *Trek* characters, turned the series metal. Montalban, a great "Latin lover" in movies of the 1940s and '50s, had reinvented himself as white-suited host-of-mystery Mr. Roarke on the ABC series *Fantasy Island*, only to "go evil" here as Khan—bare-chested, bodybuilder-armed, and resplendent beneath a proto-David-Coverdale poof-wig.

Chekov and Paul Winfield getting brain-eating mollusks in their ears is the second most metal moment in the *Star Trek* canon. The most metal moment all of *Star Trek*, period, is when Kirk erupts with such fervor he can be heard throughout the entire universe: "Khaaaaaaaaan!!!"

Star Wars (1977)

(Dir. George Lucas; w/Mark Hamill, Carrie Fisher, Harrison Ford, James Earl Jones)

✴ Science Fiction ✴ Darth Vader

Since the release of *Star Wars* on May 25, 1977, no aspect of human existence has gone untouched by the movie, especially not heavy metal. But which came first—the effect of *Star Wars* on heavy metal, or heavy metal's effect on *Star Wars*? Consider, below, how each can be seen as interlocked with one another.

The opening crawl is symphonic metal. The Death Star is drone metal. The Jawas are doom metal. The Tusken Raiders are crust punk. The land speeder is '70s van rock. The Max Rebo Band is groove metal. Han Solo is thrash. Han Solo shooting Greedo first is death metal. Chewbacca is stoner rock. Obi-Wan Kenobi is prog metal. The Force is Pagan metal. C-3PO is mathcore. R2-D2 is Nintendo-core. The Empire is black metal, with more than a few particular nods to NSBM. Grand Moff Tarkin is New Wave of British Heavy Metal. The giant eel in the garbage compactor is sludge metal. Luke and Leia's incestuous kiss is that weird corner of metal occupied by Anal Cunt, the Melvins, the Mentors, and the Butthole Surfers. The aerial dogfight between the X-wings and the TIE fighters is power metal. The big ceremony at the end where everybody gets a medal is Viking metal.

And Darth Vader, of course, is all aspects of all forms of heavy metal in every possible permutation. Only perpetually heavier. And perpetually more metal, as proven by the awesome Polish death metal band Vader.

Star Wars. That's all. It's *Star Wars*.

Star Wars: Revenge of the Sith (2005)

(Dir. George Lucas; w/Hayden Christensen, Natalie Portman, Ewan McGregor, Jimmy Smits)

✴ Evil ✴ Science Fiction ✴ Christopher Lee

The last of the *Star Wars* prequels, *Revenge of the Sith* is the worst of the bunch, which is pretty damn shitty. Nonetheless, Darth Vader is who he is among heavy metal icons and this dumb, broken-video-game idea of a movie is his official coming-out story.

While studying to join the benevolent Jedi knights, Anakin Skywalker (Hayden Christensen, the worst) escalates in a series of tantrums until he quits and joins evil rival group the Sith. There's a disappointing visit to the Wookiee planet (longed for since the 1978 *Star Wars Holiday Special*), and Luke Skywalker and Princess Leia are born at the end.

Succumbing to Grown Men of the Internet who demand that the nursery school artifacts to which they cling should be "dark," *Sith* showcases not-yet-Vaderized Anakin slaughtering children (or, as Yoda nauseatingly calls them, "younglings") and light-saber-fighting Obi-Wan Kenobi (Ewan McGregor) on a stupid planet made of CGI lava. As a result, *Revenge of the Sith* is the only *Star Wars* movie to be rated PG-13. Christopher Lee plays Sith honcho Count Dooku, aka Darth Tyranus. Hang on to every precious second of his brief screen time. And please keep in mind that the Austrian band Sith and the Noothgrush song "Sith" both predate all this silliness.

STARCRASH (1978),
AKA FEMALE SPACE INVADERS
(DIR. LUIGI COZZI; W/MARJOE GORTNER, CAROLINE MUNRO, DAVID HASSELHOFF, JOE SPINELL)
✠ SCIENCE FICTION ✠ ITALIAN EXPLOITATION

Eyepoppingly colorful and brain-blastingly metal, *Starcrash* is an Italian *Star Wars* rip-off, the cheapness of which has only added to its charm. The movie boasts a once-in-a-career-low-point assemblage of highly entertaining marginal movie superstars. Ex-Bond babe Caroline Munro (*The Spy Who Loved Me*) stars as space smuggler Stella Star. Kid-preacher turned drive-in flick great Marjoe Gortner (*Marjoe, Food of the Gods*) plays Akton, Stella's sidekick. The Emperor (Christopher Plummer, Captain Von Trapp from *The Sound of Music*) hires this duo to reclaim his kidnapped son Simon (David Hasselhoff!) from the clutches of evil Count Zarth Arn (Joe Spinell, *Maniac*'s maniac).

Unlike most of the *Star Wars* movies, *Starcrash* is always amusing and compelling, punched up with amazing moments. Unlike every *Star Wars* movie, only *Starcrash* showcases a crimson-caped slasher star like Joe Spinell chewing the galaxy clear out of scenery while sporting semi-Princess-Leia hair curls. Spinell and Caroline Munro reunited for the metal splatter masterwork *Maniac* (1980) and again in *The Last Horror Film* (1982), Spinell's insane meditation on the success and meaning of *Maniac*. Director Luigi Cozzi went on to make Lou Ferrigno's two '80s *Hercules* movies.

THE STONED AGE (1994)
(DIR. JAMES MELKONIAN; W/MICHAEL KOPELOW, BRADFORD TATUM, RENEE GRIFFIN, CLIFTON GONZALEZ)
✠ HESHERS ✠ SOUNDTRACK (BLACK SABBATH, BLUE ÖYSTER CULT, FOCUS, MONTROSE, TED NUGENT)

Unfortunately overshadowed by *Dazed and Confused* (1993), *The Stoned Age* is a dirtier, dorkier, and, at times, funnier take on '70s hard rock nostalgia. The looks are right, the tunes are cranking, and the chicks are naked. Keep on truckin', man!

Sometime deep into the "Stairway to Heaven" decade, hard-up longhairs Joe (Michael Kopelow), a zitty redhead, and Hubbs (Bradford Tatum), who seems mildly violent, putter around Torrance, California, in a VW station wagon, "the Blue Torpedo." Of particular note is that Joe has apparently not been the same since attending a Blue Öyster Cult show where he was shot by a laser coming out of a giant eyeball.

These dudes aim for beer, weed, women, and wild times—in whatever order—and pick up oily Tack (Clifton Gonzalez Gonzalez), who says he knows where there's a babe-packed party. Nothing goes as planned, but they do meet insane-o hot blonde Lanie (Renee Griffin) and down-to-earth hippie chick (China Kanter) en route to a gut-buster climax in which a pissed-off dad beats the snot out of an entire party of teenagers. Joe also learns the secret of the BÖC laser eye.

While *Dazed and Confused* is an acknowledged coming-of-age classic, *The Stoned Age* is scrappier and nastier, best embodied by acne-ravaged Joe bellyaching about how he only wants *"fine* chicks, man"; an honest appraisal of the ups and, by far, more downs of growing up metal.

A post-credits scene shows Joe and Hubbs after a BÖC show. Leaving a convenience store, two hairy dudes hustle them to buy five-buck concert shirts. Joe and Hubbs refuse, calling the merchandise bootleg. The bogus shirt pushers are played by Eric Bloom and Buck Dharma—vocalist and lead guitarist, respectively, of Blue Öyster Cult.

Tack describes tall, full-bodied, flaxen-maned party girl Lanie as "looking like that chick on the *Virgin Killers* album." Now Renee Griffin, who plays Lanie, in no way resembles the naked pre-pubescent girl on Scorpions' most controversial cover, but it's a hilarious in-joke to metalheads and/or scary perverts in the audience. At one point, Griffin wears a *Tyranny and Mutation* T-shirt. Better still: she takes it off.

The Story of Rock 'n' Roll Comics (2005)

(Dir. Ilko Davidof; w/Todd Loren, Alice Cooper, Mojo Nixon, Cynthia Plaster Caster)

✷ Comic Books

"Unauthorized and Proud of It" proclaimed the company tagline of Todd Loren's Revolutionary Comics, a semi-outlaw publishing house best known for the line Rock 'n' Roll Comics. The series began with Guns N' Roses and remained rooted in metal. Between 1989 and 1994, Revolutionary's black-and-white comic books chronicled the lives and legends of music stars, by means of not always precise research and almost always terrible artwork. They were schlocky, ballsy, sometimes even grotesque, and lovable.

Axl Rose constantly threatened to sue Revolutionary. Bon Jovi and Skid Row made similar grumbles. Only New Kids on the Block actually followed through, and the result was a semi-landmark First Amendment decision indicating that comic books did not need to be authorized if they operated as news reportage or parody and avoided trademarked logos. Previously, Revolutionary specialized in sloppily copied logo co-optation.

The only force that could stop Loren, in fact, was a knife, plunged into him multiple times during what police think was a gay sex pickup gone wrong in 1992. The Story of Rock 'n' Roll Comics chronicles Loren's saga by way of archival video, interviews (notably with Alice Cooper, Cynthia Plaster Caster, and Mojo Nixon), and ingenious animation of comic-book panels. This is a compelling documentary that manages to entertain and amuse despite its sad subject manner.

Underground cartoonist Dennis Worden, whose Stickboy series was published by Revolutionary, reads an editorial he wrote right after Loren's murder. "His comics were schlock (except for mine, of course), but his audaciousness amused me. Schlockmeister General, I salute you! And to everybody else: FUCK YOU!!!"

A tape plays of Gene Simmons calling the Revolutionary Comics office. Shock of shocks, he praises the company and gives their Kiss comics an across-the-board "A-plus." Rather than put them out of business, he wanted to, and did, join in the production and sale of the company's later Kiss material.

Cynthia Plaster Caster corrects one comics panel, pointing out that her quick-drying material did stick to Jimi Hendrix's pubic hair but that he did not cry out in pain when she pulled it off.

Alice Cooper points out that Rock 'n' Roll Comics would be hard-pressed to exist today, because how could you turn Dave Matthews into a comic book hero?

Wild Eye Video's DVD release of The Story of Rock 'n' Roll Comics is a first-class package, loaded with extras. How charmingly unlike the products to which the movie pays tribute!

Strange Days (1995)

(Dir. Kathryn Bigelow; w/Ralph Fiennes, Juliette Lewis, Angela Bassett, Tom Sizemore)

✷ Snuff ✷ Soundtrack (Prong, Skunk Anansie, Testament)

Copping its name from a Doors album (the title cut is covered by Prong here), Strange Days takes place on the verge of 1999 teetering over into the new, technology-driven millennium. Not even Hollywood's most perceptive prognosticators predicted the Internet to develop as it did, so Strange Days brokers in a mortifyingly dated '90s trope: virtual reality. Grifting a bit from William Gibson's classic cyberpunk novel Neuromancer, Strange Days tracks Ralph Fiennes as a broker of black-market point-of-view videos. Watched with the proper headpiece, you experience exactly what the person shooting the tape did, whether sex, violence, or even death. That last thrill engenders an explosion of virtual-reality snuff films. Director Kathryn Bigelow shoots big and the script, cowritten by James Cameron, aims for giant ideas, but it's a muddle.

Mainstream metal grew too amorphous in the

rave/techno/Lollapalooza '90s. *Strange Days*, trading as it does in metal topics and looking like an X-ray of Perry Farrell's mind as he gets sodomized with candy by the clown from Prodigy, reflects that. The state of mid-'90s hard rock is reflected in the aggressively groovy soundtrack. For the "Strange Days" cover, Prong is joined on keyboards by the Doors' Ray Manzarek.

STRANGELAND (1998)

(DIR. JOHN PIEPLOW; W/DEE SNIDER, LINDA CARDELLINI, KEVIN GAGE, ELIZABETH PEÑA, AMY SMART, ROBERT ENGLUND)

✣ BONDAGE ✣ BODY MODIFICATION
✣ SOUNDTRACK (DEE SNIDER, TWISTED SISTER, ANTHRAX, COAL CHAMBER, CRISIS, MEGADETH, MARILYN MANSON)

Twisted Sister's Dee Snider wrote and stars in *Strangeland*, a noble and fitfully effective attempt to translate his lifelong love of extreme horror into a state-of-the-sickness outrage. Alas, Snider did not turn out to be Rob Zombie, but *Strangeland* proved to be a likable addition to the Heavy Metal Movie canon. A gaggle of teens messing with Internet chat rooms are seduced, one by one, into the lethal BDSM torture dungeon of heavily pierced and tattooed sex sadist Captain Howdy (Snider).

When Genevieve (Linda Cardellini), the daughter of a hard-nosed cop (Kevin Gage), succumbs to the Captain, the full force of the law brings the sicko to justice—only to have him walk a few years later by reason of insanity. *Strangeland*, from there, chronicles Captain Howdy raining modern-primitive revenge on his persecutors, the most redneck of whom is a vigilante played, in a nicely ironic touch, by Robert Englund (aka *Nightmare on Elm Street*'s Freddy Krueger).

Strangeland predated the post-*Saw* "torture porn" horror cycle by most of a decade. Other than that, the movie is solidly of its moment. It's dated, to be sure, but what a time capsule. Captain Howdy, named for the demon Linda Blair contacts via Ouija board in *The Exorcist*, looks like what the most way-out metalheads were going for as Marilyn Manson bridged the gap between the Lollapalooza '90s and Ozzfest 2000.

When Captain Howdy is sprung from jail and transforms, via psychotropic medication, into mild-mannered Carleton Hendricks, angry neighbors gather outside his house. One holds a picket sign bearing the words of Snider's best-known song: "We're Not Gonna Take It!"

After years of pooh-poohing claims of offended audience members storming out of movie theaters, I finally witnessed it firsthand at a 1997 test screening of *Strangeland* in midtown Manhattan. When one of Captain Howdy's nubile victims screams with her mouth sewn shut, the flesh on her lower face tears apart and her lips gorily slide off. From the back of the screening room, a gussied-up blonde in high heels announced, "That's it!" and clacked her way toward the exit. Just before she left, she sarcastically sneered, "GREAT movie, guys!"

STREET TRASH (1987)

(DIR. J. MICHAEL MURO, AKA JIM MURO; W/MIKE LACKEY, BILL CHEPIL, VIC NOTO)

✣ BROOKLYN ✣ TOXIC BOOZE ✣ GORE

A scuzzball liquor-store owner discovers a mysterious case of bottles of a Day-Glo booze called Tenafly Viper, and he decides to peddle the stuff to derelicts that hang out in a nearby junkyard. The fluid causes drinkers to melt from the inside out, reducing one vagrant after another to blood, guts, and bubbling ooze. This splatter orgy is something of an extreme horror milestone, beloved by many heavy metal cultists, but I call *Street Trash* false metal. It just might flip your party-store rock-star wig the way you like it, but, for me, a loathsome lack of nerve to play anything straight is slopped all over *Street Trash*.

Mitigating factors that elevate *Street Trash* include a hilarious performance by James Lorinz (who similarly almost saved 1990's *Frankenhooker*) and mesmerizingly fluid camera work from director J. Michael Muro. In fact, *Street Trash* was Muro's ticket to become the number-one Steadicam operator in Hollywood for decades after. Obscurities he's shot include *Titanic, Terminator 2, The Fast and the Furious,* and the *X-Men* movies.

STRYKER (1983)

(Dir. Cirio H. Santiago; w/Steve Sandor, Andrea Savio, Mike Lane, William Ostrander)

✠ Post-Apocalypse ✠ Amazon Tribe

Shot in a Philippines rock quarry by that island nation's legendary B-movie cranker-outer Cirio H. Santiago, *Stryker* pits a lone-wolf hero (Steve Sandor) against the expected mutant criminal packs in a post-nuke world where clean water is the object of every survivor's homicidal desire. *Stryker* begins, as it should, strikingly. Apocalyptic hottie Delha (Andrea Savio) speeds her amped-up motor-trike down a sun-scorched highway with a pack of leather-clad hell-raisers piloting a muscle car in hot pursuit. Delha is rescued by Stryker and his pal/rival Bandit (William Ostrander), whereupon she reveals that hook-handed baddie Kardis (Mike Lane, delightfully diabolical) lords over a castle under which is a top-secret oasis that's bubbling with fresh H_2O. This means, of course, low-budget car-wrecking, explosions-in-the-desert war.

Spicing up the normal-to-above-average action sequences are a tribe of warrior women in football shoulder pads (a funny detail to rip off from *The Road Warrior*) and pint-size desert dwellers as clearly meant to conjure thoughts of *Star Wars*' Jawas, as were the "Road Eyes" in the Neil Young concert epic *Rust Never Sleeps* (1979). *Stryker* is solidly metal, a prime example of boob-baring, bloodletting, after-the-bomb sci-fi the likes of which countless headbangers grooved to between bong hits and adjusting the tracking on their VCRs.

The Heavy Metal Movie onslaught directed by Filipino madman Cirio H. Santiago deserves a flooding river of praise. Among the gems this maniacally prolific filmmaker has given us as director, producer, or both are *Women in Cages* (1971), *The Big Doll House* (1971), *The Big Bird Cage* (1972), *The Hot Box* (1972), *TNT Jackson* (1974), *The Muthers* (1976), *Vampire Hookers* (1978), *Firecracker* (1981), *Caged Fury* (1983), *Wheels of Fire* (1985), *Silk* (1986), and *Caged Fury II: Stripped of Freedom* (1994).

STUNT ROCK (1980), AKA CRASH; SORCERY

(Dir. Brian Trenchard-Smith; w/Grant Page, Monique van de Ven, Margaret Gerard, Sorcery)

✠ Stunts ✠ Rock

Stunt Rock's tagline—"*Death Wish* at 120 Decibels!"—might not accurately reflect the content of the movie, but the bravado is right on, as is the blaring volume at which you should watch this lovably oddball combustion of daredevil derring-do and fantastically theatrical late-'70s heavy metal.

Real-life stunt man Grant Page travels from his native Australia to Hollywood for a TV gig. He hooks up with his cousin, Curtis Hyde, a master magician who portrays the Prince of Darkness in sensory-walloping, Kiss-like live performances by L.A. metal coven Sorcery. (The producers originally approached arena-rock supergroup Foreigner to star in *Stunt Rock*. When they passed, Van Halen got the call. When Van Halen opted out, it came down to Sorcery, for whom Van Halen had opened several years prior.)

Part phony documentary about Page, part legit rockumentary about Sorcery, and studded with wild action (including numerous, out-of-nowhere clips from other movies, including *Danger Freaks, Mad Dog Morgan,* and *Gone in 60 Seconds*), *Stunt Rock* is amazing, exhausting, and insane. While the heavy but ultra-catchy Sorcery vamps in concert, Hyde stages battles with Merlin (Paul Haynes) in a war of massive illusions that incorporate elaborate props, costumes, scenery, and, of course, stunts. Page, naturally, is quite taken with the sights and sounds of Sorcery. In short order, both a journalist investigating "career obsession" (Margaret Gerard) and Dutch

TV star Monique van de Ven (as herself) become equally taken with the rugged risk-taker from Down Under, particularly as he demonstrates his death-defying skills willy-nilly in between Sorcery shows. For no particular reason, Sorcery's masked drummer punctuates the weirdness with odd interjections spoken in a synthesized high-pitched warble.

Australian director Brian Trenchard-Smith told the journal *Cinema Papers* that the *Stunt Rock* concept struck him in the shower: "Something clicked in my commercial mind which said, 'Famous Australian stuntman meets famous rock group. They interrelate; much stunt and much rock takes place. Kids will tear up the seats.'" Trenchard-Smith is one of the giants of Ozploitation cinema, having also helmed *Turkey Shoot* (1982) and *Dead-End Drive-In* (1986). As Quentin Tarantino exclaims on *Stunt Rock*'s DVD cover: "If you don't like Brian Trenchard-Smith . . . get the fuck out of here!"

Super Duper Alice Cooper (2014)

(Dir. Sam Dunn, Scot McFadyen, Reginald Harkema; w/Alice Cooper, Shep Gordon, Bob Ezrin, Dennis Dunaway)

⚔ **Metal Reality** ⚔ **Musical** ⚔ **Wolfman Jack**

Billed as the first "doc opera," *Super Duper Alice Cooper* rousingly filets and displays Alice Cooper's early life and first two decades of one-of-a-kind hard rock/high camp/heavy metal superstardom. Maestro metal documentarians Sam Dunn and Scot McFadyen (*Iron Maiden: Flight 666*, *Rush: Beyond the Lighted Stage*) are joined by filmmaker Reginald Harkema (*Manson: My Name Is Evil*). Their film, which largely surpasses Alice's own concert films and acting stints, weaves incredible vintage performance and interview clips with animation of ultrarare photos. By presenting current-day memories and testimonials only via voice-over—as opposed to intercutting talking head Q&As—the movie allows the mythical, mystical visual elements of

the Alice Cooper saga to dazzle and overwhelm unabated.

Alice narrates his development from square son-of-a-preacherman childhood to high school rock and roller to transvestite shock platoon leader to biggest rock monster on earth to alcoholic outcast to cocaine gargoyle to his clean and sober, live MTV concert on Halloween night, 1986. Along the way, *Super Duper* chronicles his involvement with music icons such as Frank Zappa (who produced the first Alice album because he thought of the group as "male GTOs," his in-house all-girl party platoon); manager Shep Gordon (suggested by a member of the Chambers Brothers to handle the band's business strictly because he was Jewish); producer Bob Ezrin (who went on to record Kiss's *Destroyer* and Pink Floyd's *The Wall*); and the indestructible original Alice Cooper group members Glen Buxton, Dennis Dunaway, and drummer Neal "The Platinum God" Smith. In addition, Alice cavorts with unlikely showbiz admirers on the royal order of Groucho Marx, George Burns, Jack Benny, and Frank Sinatra (who called him "Coop"). Alice also creates several mind-melting collaborations with master surrealist Salvador Dalí.

Iggy Pop recounts the night in 1970 when the Alice Cooper Group returned to Detroit from a failed Hollywood adventure and successfully conquered a concert after the Stooges and the MC5 had played. Elton John tells of attending an Alice blowout at the Hollywood Bowl where the grand finale was a helicopter bombing the audience with women's panties. John Lydon espouses Alice's profound influence on the Sex Pistols; he testifies that he will always follow whatever Cooper does "except golf!" And Twisted Sister's Dee Snider sums up his generation profoundly: "Alice Cooper raised us! He raised a bunch of sick motherfucking little children of the '70s who became sick motherfucking '80s rock stars. We came from this man's loins. He ejaculated and glam metal was born."

Such Hawks Such Hounds (2008)

(Dirs. Jessica Hundley, John Srebalus; w/Scott "Wino" Weinrich, Matt Pike, Scott Reeder)

✠ Stoner Rock ✠ Doom ✠ Metal History
✠ Concert Footage

*S*uch Hawks, Such Hounds: Scenes From the American Hard Rock Underground asks three questions of its on-camera participants: First, what is heavy? Second, what is doom? And third, what is stoner rock? This engaging documentary plows into the early hard rock strains that originated with Blue Cheer and Black Sabbath, flowered in megaton vinyl slabs throughout the '70s (climaxing with Motörhead), detoured deep into punk, crossed paths with thrash, emerged for a spell as grunge (climaxing with the Melvins), and has since mutated into a fuzzed-out, buzzed-up, psychedelic convergence of desert dreamscapes, Sasquatch physicality, and blissed-out pagan abandon.

The movie rightly focuses early and heavily on Pentagram, and Scott "Wino" Weinrich's one-two doom punch of the Obsessed and St. Vitus. Stay-at-home dad Wino takes us on a tour of his pepper garden. The interview with ex-Pentagram drummer Geof O'Keefe provides more insight to his legendary band than the entirety of *Last Days Here* (2011), a documentary on the personal struggles of frontman Bobby Liebling.

Later, a long segment covers the epic saga of Sleep's *Jerusalem/Dopesmoker* album. Along the way, numerous genre giants share their thoughts, including members of Kyuss, Acid King, Nebula, Mudhoney, Thrones, Bardo Pond, and Atomic Bitchwax. Medulla-oblongata-obliterating live music performances punctuate each segment as well. Toward the end, we meet numerous visual artists (Arik Roper, Seldon Hunt, Stephen O'Malley, Stacie Willoughby) essential in creating stoner rock's graphic aesthetic.

Sound of the Beast author Ian Christe speaks authoritatively on the effect of ultra-powerful Marshall, Laney, and Orange amplifiers. "A large part of early hard rock music," Christe says, "is just trying to make sense of what you do with all this distortion and all this volume."

In conclusion, ex–Skin Yard guitarist turned Nirvana producer and heavy sound guru Jack Endino says: "To me, stoner rock is just grunge, and grunge was just '70s rock—continued."

Suck (2009)

(Dir. Rob Stefaniuk; w/Rob Stefaniuk, Jessica Paré, Malcolm McDowell, Alice Cooper, Iggy Pop, Henry Rollins, Moby, Alex Lifeson, Dimitri Coats)

✠ Vampires

*T*itling your movie *Suck* points to either obliviousness, a sneaky lowering of expectations, or pure balls. Canadian comedian Rob Stefaniuk wrote and directed this amiable rock and roll vampire musical, and stars as the leader of a sad-sack Canuck rock combo, the Winners. Sexy bassist Jennifer (Jessica Paré) succumbs to Tim-Burton-ish vampire kingpin Queeny (Burning Brides vocalist/Off! guitarist Dimitri Coats) and, subsequently, a trail of drained corpses follows the Winners' tour hearse. Malcolm McDowell, as Eddie Van Helsing (get it?) pursues them. That's all that happens, but it's funny.

Suck surpasses its limitations of genre and budget with clever rock-nerd Easter eggs, out-of-nowhere stop-motion animation, and witty cameos. Look for the staged re-creations of classic album covers. Watch for Henry Rollins as a wacky morning DJ, Alex Lifeson guarding the U.S. border against Canadians, and, most amusing of all, techno-vegan Moby as Beef, a hyper-carnivorous, leather-clad metal frontman. Alice Cooper is nice as an undead barkeep, and Iggy Pop excels as a life-draining record producer. Though slight, *Suck* rocks—even Moby shows his hardcore roots.

SUNSET STRIP (2013)

(DIR. HANS FJELLSTAD; W/OZZY OSBOURNE, LEMMY KILMISTER, SLASH, JOHNNY DEPP)

✠ SUNSET STRIP ✠ HAIR METAL

An up-close look at Los Angeles's three-and-a-half-mile-long nightlife district, *Sunset Strip* serves up talking-head sit-downs with the usual suspects (Lemmy, Slash, Perry Farrell, Lou Adler); testimony from some big-name actors (Johnny Depp, Mickey Rourke, Keanu Reeves); and plenty of skeezy evidence of Hollywood at its most skin-crawling. Director Hans Fjellstad previously made the synthesizer documentary *Moog* (2004) and worked as an editor on Adult Swim's mighty *Metalocalypse*.

As immortalized in *The Decline of Western Civilization Part II* (1988), heavy metal pulsates through the history of the Strip from the heaviness of the Doors onward. The metal years in this film are represented by Ozzy Osbourne, Dave Navarro, Stephen Pearcy of Ratt, Taime Downe of Faster Pussycat, *Headbangers Ball* host Riki Rachtman, and poodle-head Sha Na Na descendents Steel Panther (no offense to Sha Na Na). In addition, the Sex Pistols' Steve Jones amusingly reminds us how he moussed his mane in the late '80s to get in on Doheny Avenue back-alley blow jobs.

In addition to *Decline II*, better films regarding the Sunset Strip include the hippie exploitation fave *Riot on Sunset* (1967) with Stonesy garage combo the Chocolate Watch Band tearing it up; *Mayor of the Sunset Strip* (2003), a moving documentary about KROQ DJ Rodney Bingenheimer (look out for David Lee Roth's unbelievable fur boots!); and the quasi-legal *Los Angeles Plays Itself* (2003), a mesmerizing three-hour compendium of existing movie scenes edited together to lay the City of Angels bare.

SUSPIRIA (1977)

(DIR. DARIO ARGENTO; W/JESSICA HARPER, STEFANIA CASINI, FLAVIO BUCCI, JOAN BENNETT)

✠ WITCHCRAFT ✠ BLACK MASS ✠ ZOMBIES ✠ SOUNDTRACK (GOBLIN)

Italian splatter maestro Dario Argento is one of horror's most supremely heavy metal filmmakers. *Suspiria* is his supreme visual achievement. Italian prog-rock demons Goblin rank high among cinema's most metal soundtrack composers and performers. *Suspiria* is their all-time greatest musical score. As such, *Suspiria* may be the most operatically horrific of all Heavy Metal Movies, Italian or otherwise.

American ballet student Suzy (Jessica Harper) arrives in Germany to study at a mysterious dance academy. On her way inside, she is throttled by a girl fleeing in terror. The girl runs off, only to be murdered with a knife, a noose, and stained glass. Her exposed heart is bludgeoned until her lifeless body dangles and leaks fluids to Goblin's jarring, crackly music blasts. *Suspiria* thereby immediately establishes a new cinematic high in luscious shock and inventive sadism, and that death is only the beginning.

Once inside the school, where the twisting hallways are lined with cornea-scorching red velvet, Suzy falls prey to blood-spraying fits and feverish hallucinations. The most chilling of these incidents involve her hearing the word *witch* whispered, slowly and repeatedly, as more students die in rapturously ugly fashion. After thousands upon thousands, maybe even millions, of maggots rain from the ceiling onto shrieking ballerinas, Suzy realizes the school's matriarchs are witches. She exposes them as they perform a satanic ritual in the presence of their undead figurehead. The academy building itself then comes to evil life (and explosive death) while Suzy flees amidst an onslaught of brain-blasting visuals and earsplitting aural overwhelm that can only exist in this mercilessly realized universe of visceral madness.

Nothing is the same after *Suspiria* ends. Especially you. You stumble away from *Suspiria* rattled, questioning your own mental state, and unable to piece together what you've just been through. Every time. Argento's surreal, color-soaked brutalism—in perfect synch with Goblin's gorgeously cacophonous, constantly blaring score—lacerates and leaves scars that are both indelible and inspirational. Much as learning to shred on guitar involves developing finger calluses, repeat exposure to *Suspiria* (and, yes, you must see it more than once) builds up useful hard parts on the surface of your soul, all the better to access the searing truth within—and then to get it out.

Suspiria is utterly, discombobulatingly incoherent, a state which only adds to its power. *Village Voice* critic J. Hoberman rightly called it "a film that only makes sense to the eye."

Argento fashioned *Suspiria*'s famous color scheme after Walt Disney's *Snow White and the Seven Dwarfs* (1937). He cast Jessica Harper in the lead based on his love of her performance in *Phantom of the Paradise* (1974).

As scary as *Suspiria* is, the film's late-night TV ad campaign during summer 1977 stopped my heart with sheer terror. The notorious *Suspiria* commercial commences with a shot of a woman from behind. She's brushing her long, lovely black hair while a singsong female voice intones: "Roses are red, violets are blue. . . ." She then puts a flower in up behind her ear and says, "The iris is a flower. . . ." And then this seemingly nice lady spins to face the camera and HER HEAD IS A SKULL and she shrieks, "AND THAT WILL MEAN THE END OF YOUUUU!!!" A grotesque spelling-out of the title fades in. Each letter looks like a veined, pulsating organ, and an evil whisper hisses: "Susss-SPEEE-reee-ahhhhh!"

This abject horror has summoned Suspiria bands in France, Germany, the UK, Norway, and the U.S. Miranda Sex Garden and others named albums *Suspiria*. Many Suspiria songs also exist, notably "Thrones of Suspiria" by Thornspawn and "A Witness to Suspiria" by great Virginia horror mavens Deceased.

Swamp Thing (1982)

(Dir. Wes Craven; w/Ray Wise, Adrienne Barbeau, Louis Jourdan, Dick Durock)

✠ Mutant ✠ Medical Deviant ✠ Comic Books

The eponymous freak/hero of *Swamp Thing* first emerged in 1971, the star of a standalone story in the DC Comics horror title *The House of Secrets*. Readers fell fast and hard for the mega-muscled, seven-foot-tall, part-man, part-vegetation, all-sludge creature of high intelligence, dark emotions, and acute sensitivity. Swamp Thing was quickly spun off into his own comic book, and, a decade later, into the cult movie written and directed by scare maven Wes Craven. This longtime favorite among headbangers delivers a warm, witty take on the saga with cool rubber-suit fights and stoner-rock atmosphere galore.

Ray Wise plays Dr. Alec Holland, a chemist who is battling world hunger by developing serums for aggressive vegetation ("Imagine a tomato that can grow in the desert!"). As happens in tales like this one, Holland is dosed with his own concoctions. Swamp Thing results. French thespian Louis Jourdan camps it up as Dr. Anton Arcane, an evil rival scientist who downs the go-green juice and discovers that it only makes you more of what you are; just as Holland transformed into the noble Swamp Thing, Arcane becomes a hulking woodland jerk. The two beasts literally sling mud at one another during the ripsnorting climax. Leading lady Adrienne Barbeau adds to the rockin' good times by taking a topless dip among the lily pads that is rather eye-popping for a PG-rated production. Those were the times!

With the film championed by Gene Siskel and Roger Ebert as a "buried treasure," and the comic book substantially overhauled in a legendary run written by Alan Moore (*Watchmen*), *Swamp Thing*'s following grew sufficiently during the 1980s to beget a sequel, *Return of Swamp Thing*. Unlike the original, the 1989 edition is smarmy and self-aware, trading the first movie's psychedelic doom soul for the crappy mall-rock attitude of the MTV hair metal of the moment. Case in point(less): female lead Heather Locklear, married at the time to Mötley Crüe's Tommy Lee, contributes nothing to even remotely threaten *Return*'s PG-13 rating.

The Sword and the Sorcerer (1982)

(Dir. Albert Pyun; w/Lee Horsley, Richard Lynch, Simon MacCorkindale, Richard Moll)

✯ Swords & Sorcery (natch)

Lee Horsley stars as Talon, a cheeky, fur-wrapped hero who slays like *Conan* and japes like *Magnum, P.I.* (Fittingly, Horsley followed up *S&S* with three seasons on ABC's *Magnum* knock-off, *Matt Houston*). In a unique stroke, Talon's sword boasts three blades, two of which he can launch like rockets. Real-life burn victim Richard Lynch stars as real-life British military ruler Oliver Cromwell, England's most metal dictator ever. Here, probably unlike in real life, Cromwell conquers all comers by using a black witch and conjuring Richard Moll (*Night Court*) as giant slime-beast Xusia; pronounced *Shoo-sha*, just like the sexpot South American kiddie-show hostess.

Simon MacCorkindale (NBC's future *Manimal*) plays Prince Mikah, rightful heir to the throne usurped by Cromwell. Kathleen Beller ("Kirby" from *Dynasty* and off-screen wife of Thomas Dolby) is his sister, Princess Alana. When Talon crash-lands into a naked concubine chamber, the princess is in the midst of a nude lesbian butt massage. Talon likes what he sees. You will too.

S&S boasts some terrific special effects, too, including a wall of goop-slopped faces of the damned moaning into eternity and Xusia ripping his human skin off to reveal his nuclear gelatin visage. Throughout its entire running time, *The Sword and the Sorcerer* is fast-paced, exciting, and funny while never degenerating into parody.

A title card at the end promises that Talon will be back in *Tales of an Ancient Empire*—"coming soon," a promise that is almost never true. Director Albert Pyun did coax Lee Horsley out of semi-retirement to pick up the tri-saber one more time, but not for twenty-eight years. A finished sequel is rumored to exist, *Tales of an Ancient Empire* (2010), but remains somewhere in Pyun's closet. *Tales* reportedly closes with the promise of third Talon saga, *Red Moon*.

On May 14, 1982, Hollywood blockbuster *Conan the Barbarian* tore into theaters and ignited a global super-storm of B-movie rip-offs and cash-ins. At the end of its initial eight-week run, *Conan* had grossed $38,513,085. Rushed into theaters early by greedy producers on April 25, 1982, penny-ante grindhouse attraction *The Sword and the Sorcerer* commenced a city-by-city cross-country rollout over those same eight weeks, becoming the first and the fastest of the Conan clones to hit the market. By year's end, the film had taken in $39,103,425. Yes, *The Sword and the Sorcerer* beat *Conan the Barbarian* at the box office. *Conan*, of course, lives on as a pop culture staple, video perennial, and source of revenue streams ranging from T-shirts to dolls for grown men. By 2007, Conan had earned Universal Studios in excess of $300 million, and it's still making bank. *The Sword and the Sorcerer*, on the other hand, is a minor cult item that lives on chiefly among steel-knuckled admirers.

As with records regarding muscle-savages, occult adventures, and medieval mayhem—Heavy Metal Movies and heavy metal music each soar highest when their parent genres use both their homegrown and megalithic dragon-wings to take full flight. The only requirement is awesomeness: *Conan* is a great Hollywood blockbuster, and *The Sword and the Sorcerer* is a great drive-in bash-'em-up. Both are muscularly metallic to the center of their molten souls.

Sword of the Barbarians (1982), aka Barbarian Master; Sangraal, The Sword of Fire

(Dir. Michele Massimo Tarantini; w/Pietro Torrisi, Yvonne Fraschetti, Xiomara Rodriguez)

✵ Swords & Sorcery ✵ Goddess of Fire
✵ Apemen ✵ Cannon Films

Sword of the Barbarians features plenty of swords, but its focus is mostly on one very large barbarian. Sangraal (Pietro Torrisi) is a prince sent into exile as a baby. He returns to his homeland as a muscle magazine cover–type adult who's resplendent in the art of blade combat. The conquering hero runs afoul of Rani, the Goddess of Fire (Xiomara Rodriguez), and spends much time trying to resurrect his dead wife. As happens with surprising frequency in '80s Italian exploitation movies, a tribe of apemen eventually figures importantly in the action.

Sword of the Barbarians is slow-witted Conan rip-off from the country that made the most and many of the best of them. For the completist in pursuit of every movie that seems like a Manowar album cover come rumbling to life, this one ought to do.

Sangraal's father is King Ator, a tie-in to Italy's then-contemporary worldwide sword-and-sorcery hit, Ator the Invincible (1982). Sangraal is the name of the Holy Grail that's so famously sought after in the legends of King Arthur.

Star Pietro Torrisi's previous roles include Accardo's Thug in Flatfoot in Hong Kong (1975), Burglar in Violent City (1975), Hitman in Convoy Buddies (1976), Tattooed Gypsy in Salon Kitty (1976), Rapist in Werewolf Woman (1976), Orso's Henchman #2 in Uppercut (1978), and Orso, a Thug, in Popeye (1980).

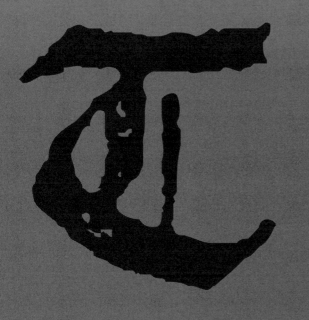

TAPEHEADS ✡ TAXI DRIVER ✡ TEACHERS ✡ TEENAGE TWINS ✡ TEN TO MIDNIGHT ✡ TENACIOUS D IN THE PICK OF DESTINY ✡ TENEBRAE ✡ TENSION: 25 YEARS UNDERGROUND ✡ THE TERMINATOR ✡ TERMINATOR 2: JUDGMENT DAY ✡ TERROR ON TOUR ✡ TERRORVISION ✡ TETSUO: THE IRON MAN ✡ THE TEXAS CHAIN SAW MASSACRE (1974) ✡ THE TEXAS CHAINSAW MASSACRE (2003) ✡ THE TEXAS CHAINSAW MASSACRE 2 ✡ THEATRE OF BLOOD ✡ THEY LIVE ✡ A THIEF IN THE NIGHT ✡ THE THING ✡ THE THIRST ✡ THIS IS SPINAL TAP ✡ THOR ✡ THOR: THE ROCK OPERA ✡ THRASH ALTENESSEN: EIN FILM AUS DEM RUHRGEBIET ✡ THRASHIN' ✡ THRILLER: A CRUEL PICTURE ✡ THE THRONE OF FIRE ✡ THUNDER AND MUD ✡ TO THE DEVIL A DAUGHTER ✡ TOMBS OF THE BLIND DEAD ✡ TOMMY ✡ EL TOPO ✡ THE TOXIC AVENGER ✡ TRACES OF DEATH III ✡ TRAUMA ✡ THE TRIAL OF BILLY JACK ✡ TRICK OR TREAT ✡ TRILOGY OF TERROR ✡ TROLL ✡ TROLL 2 ✡ TROLLHUNTER ✡ TROMEO AND JULIET ✡ TRUE NORWEGIAN BLACK METAL ✡ TRUTH ABOUT ROCK ✡ TUFF TURF ✡ TURBULENCE 3: HEAVY METAL ✡ TURN THE PAGE ✡ THE TWILIGHT SAGA: ECLIPSE ✡ TWITCH OF THE DEATH NERVE

TAPEHEADS (1988)

(DIR. BILL FISHMAN; W/JOHN CUSACK, TIM ROBBINS, TED NUGENT)

✡ MUSIC VIDEOS ✡ FAKE BAND (BLENDER CHILDREN)

Created by some of the team behind 1984's *Repo Man* for a cult following that never quite materialized, *Tapeheads* chronicles the misadventures of a video production studio opened by wheeler-dealer Ivan (John Cusack) and creative type Josh (Tim Robbins). Hollywood's notion, at the time, was that "music videos" would sort of take the form of what the Internet turned out to be (the '80s were on cocaine, kids). Thus,

Tapeheads is an exploration of just how wild and wacked-out the medium could get.

Our proto-slacker heroes churn out new wave promo clips, rap commercials for Roscoe's Chicken N' Waffles, and other unsalable products that manage to deliver no dearth of odd celebrity cameos, some of which are heavy metal in nature.

Stiv Bators' goth supergroup Lords of the New Church plays a parody metal band called the Blender Children who star in a graveyard-set music video. Occasional Lords collaborator Michael Monroe of Hanoi Rocks does not join them. Ted Nugent (or someone just like him) also swings by, and Jello Biafra plays an FBI agent.

TAXI DRIVER (1976)

(DIR. MARTIN SCORSESE; W/ROBERT DE NIRO, JODIE FOSTER, CYBILL SHEPHERD, HARVEY KEITEL)

✠ URBAN WARFARE ✠ PSYCHO 'NAM VET

Taxi Driver is a punk movie masterpiece. From its setting in mid-'70s New-York-City-as-Hell-on-Earth to its antihero, Travis Bickle, giving himself his famous Mohawk to its skanky, arty, sewer-pipe apocalypse energy, *Taxi Driver* gushes punk rock. However, the movie's sheer violent trauma and Robert De Niro's creation of Travis Bickle as cinema's ultimate psycho Vietnam vet also bleed heavy metal.

Two *Taxi Driver* characters stand out as total metal. One is Peter Boyle as the world-weary cabbie who imparts knowledge and has thus earned the affectionate nickname "Wizard." The other is Harvey Keitel as Sport, the pimp of Jodie Foster's twelve-year-old-hooker character, Iris. Sport has long black hair, fistfuls of rings, and one long, painted fingernail that's most likely for scooping cocaine but which also seems like some kind of black-magic bedevilment tool, particularly potent for luring virgins in to be sacrificed. Sport is *Taxi Driver*'s evil wizard.

The movie's dialogue has been sampled many times, notably in a cover of Kiss's "God of Thunder" by White Zombie. Martin Scorsese has said that if he could, he would go back and film *Taxi Driver* again . . . in 3-D!

TEACHERS (1984)

(DIR. ARTHUR HILLER; W/NICK NOLTE, JOBETH WILLIAMS, RALPH MACCHIO, CRISPIN GLOVER)

✠ SCHOOL SHOOTINGS ✠ SOUNDTRACK (.38 SPECIAL, FREDDIE MERCURY, NIGHT RANGER, ZZ TOP)

Teachers must have initially been intended as a high-minded, bare-knuckled satire of education on the order of *Network* or *. . . And Justice For All,* but it seems to have only gotten made to reap Clearasil cash from the teen-sex-comedy craze of the '80s. Either genre could have resulted in a sufficiently heavy metal end result, but the muddled *Teachers* works neither as insightful commentary nor as nakedly outrageous puberty rave-up.

Teachers, instead, scores what metal grades it can by virtue of a mainstream hard rock soundtrack and a subplot in which Crispin Glover, fittingly, goes proto-Columbine by keeping a gun in his locker. Also, JoBeth Williams, the mom from *Poltergeist*, ends the movie by stripping nude and running down a crowded high school hallway.

Blue Öyster Cult composed and performed three original songs for the *Teachers* soundtrack that were not used: "Double Talk," "I'm a Rebel," and "Summa Cum Laude." "I'm a Rebel" was later reworked into the song "Shadow Warrior," but all three tracks remained unreleased until 2012, when they were included on BÖC's fortieth-anniversary box set.

TEENAGE TWINS (1976)

(DIR. CARTER STEVENS; W/BROOKE YOUNG, TAYLOR YOUNG, TIA VON DAVIS, ERIC EDWARDS, LEO LOVEMORE)

✠ SATAN ✠ NECRONOMICON ✠ SATANIC INCEST

You'd think a porn film built around on-camera incest between real-life identical twin sisters would be odd enough. *Teenage Twins*, alas, goes beyond the thrill of breaking all existing sex statutes, known and unknown, and centers its plot on satanic rituals and the H. P. Lovecraft–created occult tome, the Necronomicon. Horny-go-lucky Hope (Brooke Young) and relatively straitlaced Prudence (Taylor Young) share a psychosexual bond. When one gets aroused, the other feels it. Relief comes when they engage in full-on lesbian sex. Seeing as how Prudence has never been penetrated by a man, her witchcraft-obsessed father arranges for her to be the centerpiece of a gang bang involving all the family members, atop a pentagram.

Shot in three days at director Carter Stevens's house, for the price of the masking tape used to make the five-pointed star, *Teenage Twins* has endured because of its taboo gimmick. The

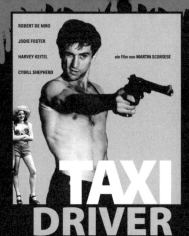

ROBERT DE NIRO
JODIE FOSTER
HARVEY KEITEL
CYBILL SHEPHERD

ein Film von MARTIN SCORSESE

TAXI DRIVER

TOP GOVERNMENT SECRET UNCOVERED!

THE TROLL HUNTER

YOU'LL BELIEVE IT WHEN YOU SEE IT

CONSUME

You see them on the street. You watch them on TV.
You might even vote for one this fall.
You think they're people just like you.
You're wrong. Dead wrong.

JOHN CARPENTER'S

THEY LIVE

A Thief in the Night
...and there will be no place to hide.

MARK IV PICTURES Presents A THIEF IN THE NIGHT
Starring PATTY DUNNING
JIM GRANT Executive Producer RUSSELL S. DOUGHTEN JR.
Screenplay Produced and Directed by DONALD W. THOMPSON

ACTION

HOT.
RECKLESS.
TOTALLY INSANE.

THRASHIN'

FRIES ENTERTAINMENT PRESENTS
AN ALAN SACKS PRODUCTION
OF A DAVID WINTERS FILM "THRASHIN'"
STARRING JOSH BROLIN ROBERT RUSLER
and introducing PAMELA GIDLEY as Chrissy CHUCK McCANN
Executive Producers CHARLES FRIES MIKE ROSENFELD
Written by PAUL BROWN and ALAN SACKS
Produced by ALAN SACKS
Directed by DAVID WINTERS

Clockwise from top left: Taxi Driver; *Norway needs*
The Troll Hunter; *some Clowns in* Terror on Tour; *law
enforcement exposed in* They Live; *thrashed* Thrashin'
VHS; A Thief in the Night; They Live *poster*

Mike McPadden

devil-worship stuff is a worthy bonus. Though the movie lacks the black-metal soundtrack of *Phallusifier: The Immoral Code* (2007), *Teenage Twins* does boast action that even the grooviest of religions would deem "ungodly." Doubling the ante of Linda Blair's crucifix in *The Exorcist* (1973), the twins masturbate with a Bible.

Prolific porn filmmaker Carter Stevens additionally helmed the X-rated *Punk Rock* (1977) and numerous titles for notorious bondage studio Avon Films, where satanism and black magic frequently figured into the plots. The Taylor twins made one other film, *Double Your Pleasure* (1978), also directed by Stevens. They not only have sex with each other again, they get it on with a pair of identical twin brothers (not the Nelson twins—they were still growing out their hair—and not the Björler twins from At the Gates; they were only five years old.)

Ten to Midnight (1983), aka 10 to Midnight

(Dir. J. Lee Thompson; w/Charles Bronson, Gene Davis, Andrew Stevens, Lisa Eilbacher, Ola Ray)

✠ Slasher ✠ Charles Bronson ✠ Cannon Films

Roger Ebert's zero-star review of Charles Bronson's fabulously repugnant *Ten to Midnight* calls the movie a "scummy little sewer," a "cesspool," and a "garbage disposal." Ebert is correct in those assessments, and you should consider them high praise. Warren Stacy (Gene Davis) is a kink-driven Los Angeles serial killer who strips nude to do his dirty work and then gets off on knifing his victims' bodies. Prepare early to see Davis naked, a lot. Bronson, as a frazzled L.A. cop on Stacy's trail, eventually plants evidence on the killer in order to bust him. When Stacy beats the rap, though, he focuses his homicidal lust on Bronson's daughter (Lisa Eilbacher)—and then *Ten to Midnight* becomes *really* gnarly.

For all its myriad excesses and devoted followers, *Ten to Midnight* remains alive in the popular consciousness of even casual '80s cable viewers due to two scenes. The first is when Bronson is interrogating Stacy and whips out a bizarre motorized suction-dildo sex toy that he swiped from the murderer's bathroom. "Ever see one of these, Warren?" Bronson seethes. "What's it used for? What's the matter—CAT got yer tongue? It's for JACKIN' OFF—isn't it?"

The second occurs during the movie's final moments, when Stacy stands in the middle of a street—stripped bare, as usual—and babbles madly as Chuck approaches. "You can't punish me! I'm sick!" Stacy shouts. "You can't punish me for being sick! You can just lock me up. But I'll be back. And you'll hear from me again! You and the whole fucking world!" Bronson, stone-faced, just says, "No, we won't." Then he shoots Warren Stacy right in his naked head. *Ten to Midnight*'s searing nastiness makes it every bit as metal as the *Death Wish* sequels that Bronson made at the same time, the latter films' Jimmy Page soundtracks notwithstanding.

Tenacious D in the Pick of Destiny (2006)

(Dir. Liam Lynch; w/Jack Black, Kyle Gass, Ronnie James Dio, Meat Loaf, Dave Grohl)

✠ Satan ✠ Dio ✠ Sasquatch

Tenacious D in The Pick of Destiny opens with an amazing mini–rock opera in which young Jack Black (Troy Gentile) suffers in Kickapoo, Missouri, under the wailing put-downs of his father (Meat Loaf) until his Ronnie James Dio poster springs to life and instructs him to go to Hollywood and form the greatest rock band of all time. From that perfect setup, it seems clear that Tenacious D has created the modern *Up in Smoke* (1978), in which the great marijuana-motivated rock and roll comedy duo of its day flawlessly translates its short-attention-span joys to the medium of film. Better still, *The Pick of Destiny* updates Cheech and Chong's hippie hijinks with the comedic hellfire of heavy metal.

Jack Black and Kyle Gass form Tenacious D, naming the band for birthmarks on their fat asses. Together, they uncover the deepest secret in rock: that the greatest guitar gods, from Tony Iommi to Jimmy Page to Angus Young to Randy Rhoads and beyond, have all played with one pick that was created by a dark wizard to battle Satan. Black and Gass embark on a cross-country trek to steal the Pick of Destiny, as it's known, and thereby absorb its "supranatural" powers ("supra," it is explained, is one level above "super"). Along the way, Black frolics with Sasquatch (John C. Reilly) and Gass parties with sorority girls. After the pair swipes the Pick of Destiny, Satan (Dave Grohl) appears. Tenacious D challenges him to a "rock-off" which concludes with Tenacious D turning Satan's horn into "the Bong of Destiny."

The Pick of Destiny seemed destined for Heavy Metal Movie immortality, particularly for fans of Tenacious D's music and HBO series. The ingredients for greatness are all there, but something went wrong. Maybe too many rollers spoiled the spliff? Maybe they just needed Brian Posehn. For whatever reason, the overall result is dim and dull. On the air with Howard Stern in 2006, Jack Black predicted that *Pick of Destiny*'s opening weekend gross would be in the range of $25 to $30 million. It actually brought in just $3 million and ended with a final tally of $8.2 million. Hilariously, the title track of Tenacious D's far more successful 2011 album opens with the observation "When *The Pick of Destiny* was released, it was a bomb" and then goes on to declare how the duo has risen from those ashes.

Tenebrae (1982), aka Unsane
(Dir. Dario Argento; w/Anthony Franciosa, Giuliano Gemma, John Saxon, Daria Nicolodi)
✠ Italian Horror ✠ Soundtrack (Goblin)

Tenebrae is horror maestro Dario Argento's return to giallo murder mysteries. Holding a special place in the hearts of the filmmaker's devotees, the film radiates a crazily heavy metal intensity throughout. Anthony Franciosa stars as an American thriller novelist in Italy who learns that a copycat straight-razor slasher is piling up bodies in the same fashion described in his latest

book. Nutzoid erotic flashbacks, one of which involves gorgeous transsexual Eva Robin's, and a cinematically bravura depiction of a lesbian couple's murder imbue *Tenebrae* with an overtly sexual atmosphere. As usual for Argento, the plot details don't make a heap of sense or matter much; the real star attraction is the fluid directorial style and surrealistically explicit violence.

"Tenebrae" is also the name of a Christian religious service held on the three mornings directly preceding Easter Sunday. Bands from Canada, Finland, Poland, Portugal, and the U.S. have adopted the name, and Helvis, Mortician, Order From Chaos, and Satan have all written songs by that name.

Tension: 25 Years Underground (2011)
(Dir. Rudy Childs; w/Tom Gattis, Billy Giddings, Michael Francis, Petio Petev)
✠ Metal History

Tension: 25 Years Underground documents the short, tense life of a long-running Maryland metal squad whose troubles began when things started finally getting good for them. Formed in 1978 as Deuce, the band boasted future Megadeth guitarist Marty Friedman as a member in the early years. After Capitol Records signed them in 1984, during an actual recording session in L.A. another band named Deuce issued them an order to change their name. Given the disastrous equipment Capitol provided (Pat Benatar and Bob Seger were hogging the good stuff in adjoining studios), the moniker Tension fit, and it stuck. Not too much else did, however, and that's really the story told by *Tension: 25 Years Underground*.

The band issued the cult classic album *Breaking Point* in 1986 and the well-regarded *Epitome* in 1987, and called it quits in 1988. During that brief period Tension experience a lot, as the metal scene saw the apex of thrash, PMRC censorship, MTV pop metal, and the furious emergence of heavy metal as truly global music.

25 *Years Underground* brings it all to light. One Tension booster prominently wears an Anvil T-shirt. Here's hoping some of that sympathic documentary mojo rubs off; the film did catch top prizes at two regional film festivals in 2012.

The Terminator (1984)

(Dir. James Cameron; w/Arnold Schwarzenegger, Linda Hamilton, Michael Biehn, Paul Winfield)

✠ Automaton ✠ Time Travel

The killing machine at the mechanical heart of *The Terminator* is a living object of flesh, fluid, and single-minded "kill 'em all" determination layered around a skeleton made of heavy metal. So is everything about writer-director James Cameron's apocalyptic template changer. Cameron borrowed from the French post-nuke time-travel curiosity *La Jetée* (1962) and works by esteemed writer Harlan Ellison. Then he blasted a quantum leap forward in science-fiction and action movies, teaching the world, at last, how to say "Schwarzenegger."

The Terminator's now archetypal plot concerns single woman Sarah Connor (Linda Hamilton) being pursued by the Terminator (Arnold, of course), a human-looking robot sent by machines from the future to kill her. The purpose is to prevent the future birth of her son John Connor, who will grow up to lead a revolution. Following the Terminator to the past is Kyle Reese (Michael Biehn), a soldier sent to protect Sarah Connor. The story's brain-bending time-space origami, coupled with cosmic contemplations of fate and technology, instantly elevated *The Terminator* above its B-movie roots. So did Cameron's A-plus mounting of suspense, chaos, and carnage. The movie's heart, though, lies in Arnold's lovably heartless creation.

Arnold became "Der Arnold," mightiest heavy metal movie star of all time, as a result of *The Terminator*. After previously playing Hercules and Conan (and beating out O. J. Simpson for this role), Arnold falls almost silent here in his first turn as a villain. He's really scary, but the muscleman's affable, heavy-accented ball-buster persona bleeds through the cold-blooded-executioner facade. That's what made instant catchphrases—such as "I'll be back!"—out of his scanty dialogue,

Arnold became a heavy metal godfather, inspiring a dozen or more Terminator bands worldwide, plus wiseacre brutalizers including Stormtroopers of Death and the San Diego thrash metal side project Austrian Death Machine, a Schwarzenegger tribute band featuring a bad Arnold imitator on lead vocals.

The Terminator was the right machine in the right movie at the right moment, forever altering the future. *Terminator 2: Judgment Day* (1991) is equally metal, but different. *Terminator 3: Rise of the Machines* (2003) surprised everyone by being pretty good, from its bare-butted cyborg Valkyrie villain (Kristanna Loken) to its end-of-the-world parting twist. The most metal thing about the PG-13-rated *Terminator: Salvation* (2009) is the audio that leaked online of star Christian Bale rabidly chewing the fuck out of the cinematographer who made noise on the movie set and messed up his scene.

Terminator 2: Judgment Day (1991)

(Dir. James Cameron; w/Arnold Schwarzenegger, Linda Hamilton, Edward Furlong, Robert Patrick)

✠ Apocalypse ✠ Urban Warfare ✠ Time Travel

He said he'd be back, and, for sure, Arnold Schwarzenegger returns as yet another killing machine in *Terminator 2: Judgment Day*. This time he's sent to kill a third killing machine. Writer-director James Cameron also reintroduces Sarah Connor (Linda Hamilton, who looks like Arnie showed her how to do pull-ups), along with John Connor—the future revolutionary at the center of all these time-tripping assassination efforts—played by future tabloid-copy supplier Edward Furlong.

In terms of technology, scope, and ambition,

T2 dwarfs its B-movie-rooted predecessor and blasted way, way ahead at the box office. The liquid metal Terminator, embodied with feline ferocity by Robert Patrick, remains a wonder of visual effects innovation. The judgment day of the title—a nuclear attack on Los Angeles—stands as the last, best on-screen Armageddon before cheap CGI made such explosive annihilation ho-hum.

These leaps "forward" moved the *Terminator* series away from its original heavy metal heart and toward the cold, corporate-rock destiny of its desperate twenty-first-century sequels, *Terminator 3: Rise of the Machines* (2003) and *Terminator: Salvation* (2009). In fact, the cheapie Italian rip-off *Terminator II* (1990), a non-follow-up in stolen name only (that actually imitates Cameron's other blockbuster sequel project, *Aliens*) feels more metal to me than *T2* proper. When it comes to L.A. bands, the first movie is like early Slayer, but the amorphous flowing *T2* is more like Fear Factory; great band sometimes, but nobody said they were 100 percent metal.

Just ahead of the *Use Your Illusion* albums, Guns N' Roses scored a big summer hit and achieved total MTV saturation with *T2*'s theme song, "You Could Be Mine." The music video intercut movie clips with new footage of Arnold as the Terminator stalking the band at a concert. His computer eyes evaluate W. Axl Rose and determining the singer's status as "waste of ammo."

TERROR ON TOUR (1980), AKA DEMON ROCK

(DIR. DON EDMONDS; W/RICK STYLES, CHIP GREENMAN, RICH PEMBERTON, LISA RODRIGUEZ)

✣ SLASHER ✣ FAKE BAND (THE CLOWNS)

Heavy metal horror cinema of the 1980s is a genre unto itself, and some wailing pioneer had to be the first in each field. For '80s heavy metal horror flicks, that particular wailer is *Terror on Tour*. Shot in 1980 and lingering in remote grindhouse oblivion until hitting home video two years later, *Terror on Tour* opened the backstage

exit through which everything from *Trick or Treat* (1986) and *Black Roses* (1988) all the way up to *Lords of Salem* (2013) would rush in.

The tour of *Terror* at hand belongs to theatrical shock rockers the Clowns. Their dark-tinged, party-hearty goof metal sounds like a cheapo commingling of Alice Cooper and Kiss and is matched by gruesome visual tropes and violently histrionic stage shows. Each Clown wears a costume consisting of an Afro wig with colored stripes, a black leotard, a black cape, and a white, half-faced mask worn over black-and-white clownish face paint. The Clowns rock, and performances are studded with gore-gushing simulations of the band decapitating and mutilating their orgasmically screaming groupies. After each gig comes a party described by the Clowns manager as "loose women, drugs, booze—you know the scene!"

The good-time tent comes crashing down on to clownland when real female acolytes of the band turn up slashed, bashed, and dumped in rock club toilet stalls at each tour stop. Although the musicians seem to have alibis, the mad stabber dresses like a Clown, prompting the cops to cut a deal with lanky bad girl Jane (Lisa Rodriguez) to go undercover as a sex-mad fan. The movie may contain the greatest metal wish-fulfillment dialogue line ever, when one ripe Clowns groupie coos, "That cocaine made me really horny!"

Shot over a short week by the director of *Ilsa, She Wolf of the SS* (1975) and *Ilsa, Harem Keeper of the Oil Sheiks* (1976), *Terror on Tour* is a three-ring riot and a historic relic, enthralling for every one of its ninety minutes. By hitting celluloid first, *Terror on Tour* actually bridges the valley between the post-*Halloween* slasher glut in movie theaters and the sporadic bursts to come of more purposefully metal-minded horror films made with a focus on a home-video afterlife. As such, *Terror on Tour* is a sincerely stupid and lovable Rosetta Stone of B-movies and rock music alike that captures an otherwise under-chronicled "in between" moment just past FM rock dominance and before the advent of MTV.

One cultural trend earlier, the Clowns might have been taken seriously. One trend later, they might have been too instantly mockable to exist. *Terror on Tour* arrived at the only possible moment. Bone-brained or not, proper heavy metal horror cinema came along with it. Hail to the Clowns, happily energetic hard rockers portrayed by an actual band from Rockford, Illinois, called the Names (not be confused with the Belgian post-punk combo of the same moniker).

Terrorvision (1986)

(Dir. Ted Nicolaou; w/Diane Franklin, Gerrit Graham, Mary Woronov, Jon Gries)

✠ Science Fiction ✠ TV Casualties

The candy-colored gross-out horror comedy *TerrorVision* seemed to emerge from a cool retro pocket of the '80s where the nerve of punk and the kitsch of new wave successfully commingled with the might and scope of heavy metal, creating a new rise of funny, disgusting, mean-spirited extreme entertainment. Not much really came of that dream except *TerrorVision*, but I love it.

In outer space, an extraterrestrial sanitation worker converts a slimy, car-size reptilian monster into an electronic signal and beams it to the farthest reaches of the galaxy, somewhere within the range of planet Earth. Down in Southern California, doltish dad Stanley Putterman (Gerrit Graham) installs a massive TV satellite dish in his backyard and then hits the suburban swinging circuit with sexy MILF Raquel Putterman (Mary Woronov). Meanwhile, teen daughter Suzy (Diane Franklin) preps for a date with her properly denim-and-leather-encased, W.A.S.P.-T-shirt-wearing headbanger boyfriend O.D. (Jon Gries).

Between their primping and kinking, the satellite sucks the googly-eyed, Jabba-the-Hut-like monstrosity from the sky and dumps it into their indoor pool. Then it squishes the heads, one by one, of those who stumble within tentacle-reach. Ten-year-old army nut Sherman Putterman (Chad Allen) and survivalist Grandpa (Bert Remsen) battle the creature, in cahoots with mega-busty TV horror hostess Medusa (Jennifer Richards). A final encounter with the alien garbageman is disgusting, laugh-out-loud funny, and, because it involves the planetary-proportioned cleavage of Medusa, uncomfortably sexy.

TerrorVision delivers on all fronts, and earns heavy respect. Headbanger O.D. tries to negotiate with the head-squishing space blob by pointing out how metal the creature is. He's not wrong, and the ploy almost works. Jon Gries previously gobbled up the screen as punk-rock Pac Man champ King Vidiot in *Joysticks* (1983). The older crowd are no posers, either; Gerrit Graham delivers a great metal movie musical number as Beef in *Phantom of the Paradise* (1974).

Tetsuo: The Iron Man (1989)

(Dir. Shin'ya Tsukamoto; w/Shin'ya Tsukamoto, Tomorowo Taguchi, Kei Fujiwara)

✠ Extreme Gore ✠ Apocalypse ✠ Japan

Tetsuo: The Iron Man was tagged as "cyberpunk" upon arrival, but this 16mm, sixty-seven-minute explosion of insane Japanese violence, Cronenberg-style body horror, and *Eraserhead*-esque industrial doom ranks among the most literally "heavy metal" films ever welded. The Metal Fetishist (played by writer-director Shin'ya Tsukamoto) slashes open his leg and stuffs a steal rod in the gash. Afterward, a businessman (Tomorowo Taguchi) plows his car into the Metal Fetishist, who appears to die. The driver and his girlfriend (Kei Fujiwara) hide the body.

The businessman begins to transform into a being made of scrap metal. He is chased by a woman who is also mutating into metal, clearly at the otherworldly behest of the Metal Fetishist. At dinner, the businessman sees that his penis has become a massive steel power drill. He gorily drives his mechanized phallus into his girlfriend and finally becomes the all-metal Iron Man. This insanity climaxes with the Iron Man and the Metal Fetishist fusing their bodies into a two-headed metal monster. They storm the streets of

Japan, aiming to turn the entire world into metal and bring about an apocalypse by rust.

Tetsuo is maniacally entertaining, and heavy metal down to its steel essence. Two sequels followed, each as metallic, but neither as dizzyingly heavy: *Tetsuo II: Body Hammer* (1992) and *Tetsuo: The Bullet Man* (2009).

𝔗𝔥𝔢 𝔗𝔢𝔵𝔞𝔰 ℭ𝔥𝔞𝔦𝔫 𝔖𝔞𝔴 𝔐𝔞𝔰𝔰𝔞𝔠𝔯𝔢 (1974)

(DIR. TOBE HOOPER; W/GUNNAR HANSEN, MARILYN BURNS, EDWIN NEAL, JIM SIEDOW)

✠ **SLASHER** ✠ **GORE** ✠ **CANNIBALISM** ✠ **CHAINSAWS**

Only two films in my experience tap into "prehuman" intensities of fear. The first is *Night of the Living Dead* (1968) and the other is the original *The Texas Chain Saw Massacre*. Both were directorial debuts, made on the fly by amateurs, and both exploded across global consciousness like nuke-backed napalm. Viewer by viewer, *Night* and *Massacre* leveled previous conceptions of the ability of art to terrify an audience. These milestones ran nonstop for more than a decade each in neighborhood theaters, drive-ins and art houses and at midnight screenings before reaching untold new numbers on home video. All who witnessed them sustained unprecedented psychological and emotional damage.

Night and *Massacre* expelled crowds back out into the living world cathartically cleansed and inwardly shattered. Having survived, viewers were newly equipped to confront the real horrors of life, large and small, with imaginations savagely torn open. In comparative terms, one often hears about the line-in-the-sand experiences of a metal fan discovering heavy music: "I heard [Sabbath/Priest/Slayer/Pantera/Carcass] and that was it. I changed and I could never go back." *Night* melds '50s EC horror comics with gothic graveyard spookery and apocalyptic dread, punctuated by a surreal coda. *The Texas Chain Saw Massacre*, however, incorporates those all those elements, but it also anticipates and lays out multiple forms of psychotic blood-splattered carnage.

Five teens pilot a van through the desert roads of the Lone Star State. They're college-age, long-haired, bell-bottomed stoner types, hugely typical of the time, with the exception of fat, nasty, wheelchair-bound Franklin (Paul A. Partain). Already, the metal spirit is evident in the rock and roll youth atmosphere and the violation of a taboo: we hate the handicapped guy. As you'd expect, the kids pull over for a hitchhiker (Edwin Neal). Their new passenger's grimy appearance and spastic vocal mannerisms evoke Charles Manson. First it's uncomfortable, and then it's appalling. The Hitchhiker produces a straight razor, slashes his own hand, and then turns the blade on Franklin. The kids kick him out onto the blacktop. Then the freak-out starts.

Texas isn't just weird. It's also scary. And it will kill you in horrible, creative ways. Scary Texas metal bands like deadhorse and Agony Column proved this, as did Butthole Surfers and broken-brained local casualty Roky Erickson.

The longhairs stop at a gas station, where the Old Man (Jim Siedow) in charge says he's waiting for a fuel delivery to fill his pumps. The kids decide to stay. Some look for a swimming hole. Kirk (William Vail) and Pam (Teri McMinn) approach a farmhouse to use a phone. They step inside and knock on a giant steel door, which slams open. There's Leatherface. This behemoth slob in a bloody butcher smock and a mask made of human skin slams in Kirk's skull instantly with a sledgehammer. The young jock collapses and spasms uncontrollably. Pam stares in dead-eyed horror. Leatherface pounds Kirk's head repeatedly until the shaking stops. He then drags the body into the other room, glares at Pam, and slams the massive door shut. Silence follows.

Viewers are right there with Pam—frozen, choked, and reeling with fear. The introduction of Leatherface immediately establishes the type of antihero that would become *the* crucial figure in horror and heavy metal. His appearance recalls Alice Cooper explaining that he was tired of hearing about "rock and roll heroes" and thus created himself as the first "rock and roll villain."

Leatherface is the embodiment of all things frightening and repulsive, as well as everything that's appealing about what's frightening and repulsive. In large part, that's about power. He looks like a monster, and, noticeably, he's decked out in skins. Rock and roll villains—from Gene Simmons to GG Allin to Marilyn Manson to corpse-painted hordes the world over—have been following his lead ever since.

Attempting to flee, Pam sees that the farmhouse is inundated with thousands upon thousands of human bones, and skin, too, and meat. Most remains are piled in nauseating heaps, but some are fashioned into grotesque furniture, like a homicidal caveman's take on an H. R. Giger (*Alien*) design. A live chicken clucks maniacally in a cramped, suspended cage. Like Sally, the bird is trapped. We are too. The sight of the *Chain Saw* living room is as disturbing as movies get. There is terrible logic to the arrangement of bones and splattered organs. The sheer volume reveals that countless humans have been slaughtered here, and that it's been going on for years and years and years and years.

Pam turns to run from the house, but Leatherface grabs her and carries her off, wailing and flailing, to his kill room. Horribly, he impales Pam alive on a meat hook. Here, we witness the birth of an entire new level of horror—a quickening and increasing of the heaviness, as Pam squeals and reels on that hook. *Chainsaw* then chronicles the pursuit and extermination of the young travelers. The film is gritty, merciless, and shot almost documentary style, with bare-bones barbarism. Eventually, only Sally (Marilyn Burns) survives. There is a dreadful moment when she reaches the Old Man at the gas station for help, feels a glimmer of relief, and then realizes that he, too, is part of the cannibal clan.

Back at the house, *Chain Saw* climaxes with the motherfucker of all death metal milieus. The Hitchhiker, the Old Man, and Leatherface—who's now dressed as the mom of the bunch—tie Sally to a chair at their family table to serve her dinner. Director Hooper achieves a Hitch-

cock-level triumph of suspense he cuts from the tormentors to the ghastly menu items to searing close-ups of Sally's frantic darting eyeballs as she takes in the horror. Enter Grandpa (John Dugan). This cadaverous, barely breathing ancient will kill their dinner guest. Sally's head is held over a bucket as Grandpa hits her with a hammer—but his blow is too soft, and he drops the tool. And so, over and over again, Grandpa slams Sally's head and drops the hammer. She screams and bleeds and the assembled psychos laugh and cheer, and Grandpa gives it another go. And then another. The movie theater has never heard so much screaming, as this process is excruciatingly hard to watch. With some distance, this scene is the height of *Chain Saw*'s black comedy. Grandpa forces the death metal ingredients to their brutal limit—and then he keeps going.

Sally manages to break free and jumps through an upstairs glass window. A final dance of doom ensues. Leatherface and the Hitchhiker pursue their prey onto a highway. An eighteen-wheeler trucker flattens the Hitchhiker spectacularly. Leatherface slices his own leg in the melee, and Sally manages to hop in the back of passing pickup. She laughs like a lunatic, her mind snapped, as Leatherface swings his chainsaw by the roadside, dancing and squealing while the sun rises behind him.

Jarringly, it's over. After the dawn, there is only more darkness. Deeper and bleaker. Hurling ever downward into forever. If a more heavy metal experience is to exist in the annals of horror films, you, reader, are going to have to make it. Look for inspiration to "Texas Chainsaw Massacre" and "Leatherface" songs by Blood, Last House on the Left, Burnt Offering, Lääz Rockit, Legion of Death, Revenge, Skitzo, and other miscreants.

The Texas Chainsaw Massacre (2003)

(Dir. Marcus Nispel; w/Jessica Biel, Jonathan Tucker, Erica Leerhsen, R. Lee Ermey)

✠ Gore ✠ Chainsaws ✠ Soundtrack (Pantera, Hatebreed, Lamb of God, Morbid Angel, Meshuggah, Fear Factory, Mushroomhead)

With the 2003 *Texas Chainsaw Massacre,* dodgy super-producer Michael Bay presents an un-wanted, unnecessary remake of the greatest horror film of all time, stuffed with gorgeous Generation Y hardbodies, directed by TV com-mercial and music video slickster Marcus Nispel, and pumped up with a too-calculated metal soundtrack.

Five teens in a van pick up the wrong hitchhiker and steer straight into flesh-masked power-tool enthusiast Leatherface (Andrew Bryniarski) and his family—who don't even seem to be cannibals here. Jessica Biel models a wet tank top effec-tively during her endless loops of running and screaming. *Full Metal Jacket*'s R. Lee Ermey, as Leatherface's cranky elder, yells a lot, too.

This soulless, scare-less *Chainsaw* mock-up made big Halloween-season bucks and so loosed the execrable avalanche of big-ticket Hollywood horror remakes throughout the 2000s. Direc-tor Nispel alone helmed the miserable reboots *Friday the 13th* (2009) and *Conan the Barbarian* (2011). For a while, he was busy ruining *The Fly.* The *Texas Chainsaw Massacre* soundtrack album does pack a death punch, assembling a definitive snapshot of mainstream-leaning extreme hard rock circa 2003.

The Texas Chainsaw Massacre Part 2 (1986)

(Dir. Tobe Hooper; w/Dennis Hopper, Bill Moseley, Caroline Williams, Jim Siedow, Bill Johnson)

✠ Cannibalism ✠ Chainsaws ✠ Cannon Films

"After a decade of silence," announced ads for *The Texas Chainsaw Massacre Part 2,* "the buzz is back!" The quiet after the first *Massacre* was broken by the sweet prospect of a sequel helmed by original director Tobe Hooper, scripted by Lone Star intellectual L. M. Kit Carson (who'd written 1984's acclaimed *Paris, Texas*) and pro-duced by Cannon Films, the most metal movie studio of the '80s. On top of that, *Part 2* starred wild card Dennis Hopper. Still, the finished movie surpassed all expectations.

Texas Chainsaw Massacre Part 2 is a self-aware riot, a profound meditation on the global phe-nomenon of the first film, a visceral send-up of horror filmdom's psychosexual dysfunctions, a joyful paean to the often lethal weirdness of Texas, a literally gut-busting black comedy, and, most importantly, a rip-roaring horror epic that feels as though it will split right through the screen and slice the entirety of the world into giddy ribbons.

Jim Siedow, the gas station attendant of the origi-nal, film returns now as the Cook, proprietor of a chili truck called the Last Round-Up. Replac-ing the Hitchhiker is Bill Moseley as napalm-brained, homicidal hippie-with-a-head-of-steel Chop Top. Leatherface is on hand, here played with pantomime grace by Bill Johnson. Grandpa (Ken Evert) is back, too. We are also treated to visions of "Grandma." She is gross.

Chainsaw Part 2's plot revolves around the Sawyer cannibal clan attacking a radio station, kidnapping foxy DJ Stretch (Caroline Williams), and defending their underground lair against an attack from Hopper as hell-bent-for-revenge Texas lawman Lefty Enright. From its yuppie-decapitating opening to its transmigration-of-power-tool-madness finale, *Chainsaw Part 2* is as invigorating, boundless, and inspiring as the thrash metal explosion happening during the year of this film's release.

Texas Chainsaw Massacre Part 2 made good on the craziest hopes of the original's devotees in the way that thrash fulfilled many specific desires of hard rock fans. With thrash, it was: "I wish there was heavy metal that incorporated punk, and that sometimes sang about being a teenage loser, and other times sang about Nazi war criminals and still other times sang about Satan and decapitations and stuff. And sometimes it should be funny and sometimes it should be depressing."

With *Chainsaw Part 2*, it was: "Let's see what the cannibal family's lair would look like under a huge old Civil War–themed amusement park, and let's get to hear from somebody whose face has been sliced off to be worn as a mask and, holy fuck, let's see Dennis Hooper battle Leatherface in a massive chainsaw duel to the death!"

The film also delves into chainsaw sex. At the radio station, Stretch aims to escape Leatherface's killer tool by using her feminine wiles. Straddling an ice chest and spreading her shapely legs, she seduces the killer into faux-fucking her by gently rocking his chainsaw blade back and forth. When it touches the ice, the saw smokes and Leatherface squeals orgasmically. He then runs off in terror—not knowing how to handle this new feeling. Those given to interpretations of sexual repressions and explosiveness in horror, let alone phallic symbolism, are encouraged to have a thousand field days with this.

Under contract with Cannon to deliver *Chainsaw Part 2* for an August 1986 release, Hooper rushed the movie through its final edits up until virtually the last possible minutes. When the Tom Savini gore effects prompted an X rating from the MPAA, *Chainsaw Part 2* hit theaters unrated, bearing the highly metal warning statement: "Due to the nature of this film, no one under 17 will be admitted."

Chainsaw's frantic production is legendary and, frankly, that's how Tobe Hooper should have kept making movies. The pressure obviously did him (and the film) good. Hooper stupefied the world with the original *Chainsaw* in 1974, made the excellent gothic alligator horror *Eaten Alive* (1977), and triumphed on TV in 1979 with the *Salem's Lot* miniseries, and his monster-on-the-midway romp *The Funhouse* (1981) is a hoot. *Poltergeist* (1982) should have been Hooper's once-and-forever leg up to top-ticket Hollywood productions, but Steven Spielberg always implied that he took over directing duties. One is immediately inclined to say fuck Spielberg, but consider how Tobe Hooper fared in the aftermath. *Lifeforce* (1985) is wretched. *Invaders from Mars* (1986) doesn't even rate. Then there's *Chainsaw Part 2*—as incandescent and masterfully made as the first one. Afterward: nothing.

Tobe Hooper never made a movie that got a legitimate theatrical release again (a 2:30 a.m. screening I caught at Mann's Chinese Theatre in Hollywood of 1995's *The Mangler* doesn't count). He's specialized in direct-to-video schlock, the nadir of which, so far, has been a 2004 remake-in-name-only of *The Toolbox Murders*. Somebody give this guy a killer script and not enough time or money to make it, please.

THEATRE OF BLOOD (1973),
AKA MUCH ADO ABOUT MURDER
(DIR. DOUGLAS HICKOX; W/VINCENT PRICE, DIANA RIGG, ROBERT MORLEY, MILO O'SHEA)
✣ **BRITISH HORROR** ✣ **VINCENT PRICE**
✣ **SHAKESPEARE**

The intersection of heavy metal and Shakespeare is nearly as pronounced and undeniable as the core DNA strands shared by metal and classical music. Lust. Murder. Power. Vengeance. Black magic. And cascading seas of blood. Shakespeare, like metal, delivers all that on the grandest and most thunderous of scales and he uses words the way metal uses music: to communicate all of life's sound and fury that rouses the soul and rocks the corpus to the greatest heights of inspiration. One such result is the hair-raising, gut-busting, pitch-black horror comedy *Theatre of Blood*.

Vincent Price, newly revitalized by the triumphs of his *Dr. Phibes* movies in the previous years, stars as Edward Lionheart—a flamboyant British ham who believes he is the most divinely talented thespian to ever light up the London stage. Lionheart is lonesome in this opinion. Through his long, loony career, England's theater critics have savaged the actor time and again. Finally, bolstered by the Bard, Lionheart executes his vengeance.

After faking his own death, Lionheart murders the poison-penned reviewers who have hurt him most—each one dies a grotesque death in the manner of those limned in the works of Shakespeare. We see public butchering (*Julius Caesar*), false accusations of adultery igniting homicidal jealousy (*Othello*), spearing and horse-dragging (*Troilus and Cressida*), a sixteen-ounce heart pulled out (*The Merchant of Venice*'s "pound of flesh"), drowning in wine (*Richard III*), electrocution by hair curlers (mimicking Joan of Arc's fiery demise from *Henry VI*), sword fighting on a trampoline (a take on *Romeo and Juliet*), and, most awesome of all, poodles baked in a pie and force-fed to a fat queen who calls them his "babies" (a spin on the child-eating climax of *Titus Andronicus*).

Price has the time of his life doling out these deaths. He gets to explode into Shakespeare passages repeatedly and then pull off one bizarre, heinous, action-packed assassination after another. *Theatre of Blood* gets a standing ovation, a banging head, and every possible horn up. All is well that ends dead.

Goth metal fave Diana Rigg of *The Avengers* plays Lionheart's henchwoman daughter. She eventually exits the stage like Cordelia in *King Lear*.

They Live (1988)

(Dir. John Carpenter; w/"Rowdy" Roddy Piper, Keith David, Meg Foster, George "Buck" Flower)

✡ Science Fiction ✡ Mind Control ✡ Dystopia

John Carpenter's dystopian pulp masterpiece *They Live* infuses '50s horror comic-book and sci-fi movie motifs with the self-aware violence of its own era and age-old issues regarding authority, society, and what it means—along with what it takes—to truly be free. That sounds like heavy metal's own mission statement, because it is, give or take some medieval dragons and the eternal hellfire of Satan and such.

Pro wrestler Roddy Piper began what should have been a prolific movie career as Nada, a drifter who happens upon a pair of sunglasses that, when worn, display the world as it actually is. Earth, he sees, has been conquered by hostile, skull-faced space aliens who control humanity through subliminal commands sent via mass media. Broadcasts, billboards and endless advertisements secretly hammer home messages such as "CONSUME," "OBEY," "WATCH TV," and "DON'T THINK." Nada puts together what's going on and, after engaging in cinema's all-time most insanely awesome fistfight, convinces his friend Frank (Keith David) to try on the sunglasses. Together, they then fight frantically to liberate their species from enslavement.

Like the best of Carpenter's work (*Halloween*, *Escape From New York*), *They Live* uses its small budget to its advantage in communicating big ideas as huge entertainment. The movie ripples with vitality and good humor (the R-rated parting shot is truly a nut-/gut-buster for the ages), and is truly a rallying cry and visceral prod to wake up, stand up, and raise hell. YOU live!

"I'm here to chew bubble gum and kick ass," Nada announces in *They Live*'s most celebrated line, "and I'm all out of bubble gum!" The back-alley beat-down between Nada and Frank goes on for five and a half uninterrupted minutes. Amazingly, it gets better as it goes along. John

Carpenter says that the fight took three weeks to stage and rehearse. The effort was worth it.

As noted, Roddy Piper should have rallied on from *They Live* to a legendary action movie career. He had a good run as a wrestler and low-profile actor, but his only other feature film of note is *Hell Comes to Frogtown* (1988). *Frogtown*—about a post-apocalyptic world overrun with frog-headed mutants—had the promise of an instant classic, but it turned out just so-so. Regardless, I still hope "Hot Rod" gets a role in one of Sylvester Stallone's sequels to *The Expendables*.

Carpenter himself is outspokenly left wing, politically. To his endless credit, he left any such specifics out of *They Live*. The movie's attitude is anti-consumerism on its surface, and antiauthoritarian to its core of its soul. As a result, the iconography of *They Live* is regularly employed by graphics-makers on every point in the political spectrum. You are just a likely to see the movie's monster politician in front of an "OBEY" sign at an Occupy Wall Street rally as you are on the website of a hard-right radio talk show host. *They Live* unifies anyone who aims to shatter the shackles of those in charge and forge his or her own destiny, by any ass-kicking means necessary.

A Thief in the Night
(1973)
(DIR. DONALD W. THOMPSON; W/PATTY DUNNING, MIKE NIDAY, COLLEEN NIDAY, RUSSELL S. DOUGHTEN JR.)
✴ ANTICHRIST ✴ APOCALYPSE

A *Thief in the Night*, titled after the biblical description of Jesus Christ's sneaky return to Earth, is the first in a series of low-budget but highly imaginative films about the Rapture. Beginning with a song and an apocalypse,

Thief details the end times predicted by the Book of Revelations as experienced by groovy blonde chick Patty Jo Myers (Patty Dunning). She's stuck in Iowa after awakening to find her devout family vanished into heaven. Bum deal. Faced with the imminent arrival of the four horsemen, Patty

recognizes the one-world government UNITE (United Nations Imperium of Total Emergency) to be the Antichrist. She does whatever she can to avoid being branded with UNITE's legally mandated stamp—the mark of the beast.

Shot for $60,000 using Midwestern locals as totally believable extras, *Thief* is loaded with a '70s wah-wah guitar and funky keyboard music score, and plenty of recognizable contemporary characters fighting a surprisingly credible take on the Antichrist as a totalitarian regime. While this isn't exactly a good movie, the action is steady and rich with factors that appealed to long-haired rock fans (especially those predisposed to anything Satan-related), including horror movie suspense; a cobra attack; a helicopter; a sinful carnival; gonzo facial hair; the spooky title song "I Wish We'd All Been Ready"; and, of course, the end of the world.

Terrifying a captive, and unfortunately not totally stoned, audience, *Thief* played for decades in U.S. drive-ins, church basements, Sunday schools, and religious TV stations. Contemporary end-times entertainment purveyors such as the creators of the *Left Behind* series cite *A Thief in the Night*— a true triumph of self-financed indie filmmaking—as the bedrock from which the entire industry arose. Rational estimates place the number of Christians who have viewed writer-director Donald W. Thompson's movie at 300 million. Three sequels followed, each dragging more than the last: *A Distant Thunder* (1978), *Image of the Beast* (1980), and the post-nuclear *The Prodigal Planet* (1983). Producer Russell S. Doughten appears in each film as long-haired, fire-eyed, Bible-doubting survivalist Rev. Matthew Turner. Did any Christian kids sit through the later films and ever actually see a devil?

The Thing (1982)

(Dir. John Carpenter; w/Kurt Russell, Keith David, T. K. Carter, Wilford Brimley)
✵ Horror ✵ Space Invasion

Ostensibly a remake of Howard Hawks's *The Thing From Another World* (1951), John Carpenter's first major studio effort adheres more faithfully to the original source material, the novella *Who Goes There?* by John W. Campbell. At the bottom of the world, an Alaskan malamute dog flees pursuit by a helicopter, from which an apparently insane Norwegian scientist is frantically firing a rifle at the animal. Members of an American research team rush out of their Antarctic station to see the commotion. The copter crashes, a shootout ensues, which the Norwegians lose, and the dog is welcomed into the camp. That was the Americans' big mistake.

The Thing of the movie's title is a shape-shifting, ethereal being from another planet that moves from one organic host to another with spectacularly gory and painful results. This entity arrives in the dog, and then moves among the humans at the facility, one by one, mutating with each transition into a new horror never previously witnessed in your worst deranged nightmare. In its most searing visual incarnation, the Thing bursts out of Norris (Charles Hallahan), turns the dead man's decapitated head upside down, sprouts disgusting spider/crab legs, and scurries forward. Palmer speaks for all us: "You gotta be fucking kidding me!"

Kurt Russell plays scientist R. J. MacReady. Along with team member Childs (Keith David) he maintains the nearest thing to a grip on sanity as the Thing literally tears through friends and colleagues. Russell and David are powerful, but *The Thing*'s true star is special effects genius Rob Bottin, whose team built and designed the film's indelibly horrific visions (except the unforgettable monster the dog becomes, which was created by FX giant Stan Winston). The final moments of *The Thing*, in which MacReady and Childs crack a bottle of scotch and accept their inescapable, icy demise at the actual lowest spot on Earth, would be a great time to surrender to a monumental slab of funeral doom. The fatal frost of the South Pole sets in and the Thing dies with our heroes. But the chill lasts forever.

Released two weeks after *E.T. the Extra-Terrestrial* in 1982, *The Thing* bombed at the box office, making more room for Steven Spielberg's decidedly upbeat take on alien-earthling relations. On video, cable TV, and even laser disc, *The Thing* rapidly found a ferociously devoted audience attracted to the movie's isolated setting, hopeless outlook, and obscenely creative expression of inner rage turned outward aggression.

As for Hollywood's 2011 "prequel" to *The Thing*, the effects are all CGI and the Kurt Russell part is played by young and lovely starlet Mary Elizabeth Winstead. Read into that what you will.

The Thirst (2006),
aka Twilight Thirst
(Dir. Jeremy Kasten; w/Matt Keeslar, Clare Kramer, Jeremy Sisto, Adam Baldwin)
✵ Vampires

Desperately lovelorn vampires of the twenty-first century are dominated by the celibate teens of *Twilight*; check out this movie's hilariously crass mock-mockbuster alternate title. A decade earlier, though, art-house theaters were overrun with arch, pretentious vampire movies clamoring to stake your brain with sentimental goth notions of similarities between bloodsuckers and dope-shooters. Michael Almereyda's *Nadja* (1994), Abel Ferrara's *The Addiction* (1995), Larry Fessenden's *Habit* (1995)—each was more precious and awful than the next.

The Thirst, however, improves on that premise by simply stealing vampire motifs from *Near Dark* (1987) and junkie freak flare-ups from *Requiem for a Dream* (2000). Then the movie dumbs all the fuck down, bloodies everything in sight, and casts Mr. Medium Budget Horror of the 2000s, Jeremy Sisto, as kinky undead kingpin Darius, who's tormenting two recovering narcotics fiends (Matt Keeslar and Clare Kramer), turned Nosferatu-like.

Tossing an extra treat to the *exact* crowd that would likely snag *The Thirst* from a Redbox or download it for wee-hours perusal, Otep Shamaya of nü-metal noisemakers Otep cameos as a dominatrix vampire at a flame-decorated industrial rock club. On Otep's MySpace page, Shamaya wrote of *The Thirst*: "Beware, danger-ously lame B-movie ahead."

Tнιs Ιs Spinal Tap

(1984)

(DIR. ROB REINER; W/CHRISTOPHER GUEST, MICHAEL McKEAN, HARRY SHEARER, ROB REINER)

✴ METAL HISTORY ✴ CONCERT FOOTAGE

The question is not whether or not *This Is Spinal Tap* is the greatest of all Heavy Metal Movies; the question is whether or not it's the greatest of all movies, period. And it's a heavy question. As a comedy, *Spinal Tap* is superb; as a send-up of heavy metal specifically, and rock and roll more generally, it is without peer. *Spinal Tap* is also a dead-on spoof of documentary film-making, from its creaky "vintage" TV clips to its deadpan on-camera interviews. Not one note is off in *This Is Spinal Tap*—especially not the ones they screw up on purpose.

Grinningly sincere filmmaker Marty DiBergi (Rob Reiner) introduces *This Is Spinal Tap* as his documentary tribute to a band he first caught as hippies playing Greenwich Village in the '60s. They had already, by then, morphed from Mersey Beat mop-tops to paisley-gilded love children crooning, "Listen to the Flower People." In due time, Spinal Tap struck metal, and that's the band we meet as the movie begins, long-haired leather-warriors hitting the road to promote their latest opus, *Smell the Glove*.

The cataclysmic tour that ensues is a collection of all-time classic movie scenes, each more bril-liantly hilarious than the last: the album *Shark*

Sandwich reviewed as "Shit Sandwich"; guitarist Nigel Tufnel (Christopher Guest) showing off his amplifiers that "go to eleven"; the plans revealed for a Jack the Ripper musical titled *Saucy Jack*; bassist Derek Smalls (Harry Shearer) getting trapped onstage in his plastic pod; the twenty-inch Stonehenge; the exploding drummers; the comeback in Japan; and on and on.

Punctuating each set piece are pitch-perfect performances from Reiner and the band mem-bers—who also composed and performed the breathtakingly accurate, eminently rocking songs ("Big Bottom," "Sex Farm," "Tonight I'm Gonna Rock You Tonight"); as well as National Lampoon editor Tony Hendra as manager Ian Faith, Paul Shaffer as music biz schmoozer Artie Fufkin, Fran Drescher as nasally offended publicist Bobbi Flekman, and Billy Crystal as a mime.

Beyond pop stardom and moviemaking, though, *This Is Spinal Tap*, a self-described "rockumen-tary," is really the story of every rock and roll band, from stadium superstars to mom's-base-ment trash-can bangers. This has been explicitly confirmed, time and again, by countless big-name musicians (Axl Rose, Pete Townsend, Tom Petty, and U2 just top the list), but the film's soul-deep truth of the perils of creating electri-fied music are instantly recognizable to anyone who has ever attempted to play in a group.

There is David St. Hubbins (Michael McKean) befouling the brotherhood with his meddle-some lady love (June Chadwick); the horrifically awkward failure to harmonize at the grave of Elvis Presley, when it counts; the infighting, the lost gigs, the gang-ups, the storm-offs; and the instant "all is forgiven" rapture of even just one single thing going right. *This Is Spinal Tap* flawlessly crystallizes these inevitable collapses, spinouts, and rebounds to the point of making the movie painfully funny on a much deeper, more literal level. In every respect, *This Is Spinal Tap* goes to eleven.

For all of *Spinal Tap*'s incandescent moments, the definitive jewel is Nigel Tufnel—equal parts confident and dim-witted—showing off his super-stacked equipment. Glowingly, Nigel points out to Marty DiBergi how, whereas "most blokes only go to ten", his amps are all numbered to eleven for when he needs that "extra push over the cliff."

When DiBergi says, "Why not just make ten louder and make ten be the top?" Nigel can only blankly respond, "These go to eleven!" Ladies and gentlemen, there it is: the most Heavy Metal Movie moment in the history of Heavy Metal Movies. Less is less, and more is more.

Spinal Tap fans campaigned for November 11, 2011—aka 11/11/11—to be celebrated as "Nigel Tufnel Day." Aside from the drive's massive Facebook popularity and local observations on radio stations and at rock clubs, Spinal Tap themselves—Michael McKean, Christopher Guest, and Harry Shearer—screened the movie at the Brooklyn Academy of Music and took audience questions in character. In 2002, the Library of Congress declared *This Is Spinal Tap* "culturally, historically, or aesthetically significant." It was selected for permanent preservation in the United States National Film Registry.

Spinal Tap was initially created for a 1979 television pilot called *The TV Show*. Hosted by Rob Reiner, the premise was a *Kentucky Fried Movie*–style collection of sketches, linked by some dude flipping channels on the tube. At one point, he comes across a parody of *The Midnight Special*, where Reiner, as Wolfman Jack, howlingly introduces Spinal Tap. The fully formed metal gods power through the song "Rock and Roll Creation."

David St. Hubbins and Nigel Tufnel's climactic clash where the expletives *fuck* and *fucking* rain down like volcanic ash is a direct homage to the widely circulated gem "The Troggs Tapes." During twelve minutes taped at a rehearsal, the Troggs—the '60s garage rockers who gave us the proto-metal "Wild Thing"—explode into fireballs of hatred and obscenity so toxic its hard to believe the actual tape didn't combust ("Oh, we'll put some fairy dust over it! I'll piss on the tape!").

B-movie scream queens Linnea Quigley and Brinke Stevens put in quick appearances as Spinal Tap groupies. W.A.S.P. frontmaniac Blackie Lawless appears in a mock commercial for *Heavy Metal Memories*, a Spinal Tap greatest-hits collection that was used in 1984 to promote the movie. It's a parody of TV ads for records that features Blackie romancing a metal chick as an announcer rattles off his spiel and dozens of Spinal Tap song titles scroll by on-screen.

THOR (2011)
(DIR. KENNETH BRANAGH; W/CHRIS HEMSWORTH, NATALIE PORTMAN, STELLAN SKARSGÅRD)
✠ NORSE MYTHOLOGY ✠ COMIC BOOKS

The power metal portions of *Thor* are good, but *Thor* being a big-studio summer tentpole comic-book adaptation—in the anti-miracle of modern 3-D, no less—the dial tilts too often to power ballad, and stays there. Still, there is much to happily flip one's winged helmet over here. As long as Thor remains in supernatural realms, particularly the Norse deities' homeland Asgard, the movie is an engaging realization of the tale of the Viking god who has arguably wielded the most influence on heavy music, from the garage rock of Thor's Hammer in the '60s to the giggly stoners of Valient Thorr today.

Early on in Asgard, Thor (Chris Hemsworth) assembles a superpowered Mod Squad (amusingly described later on by a cop on Earth as, "Xena, Jackie Chan, and Robin Hood") to stomp frost giants in the land of Jotunheim, and the ensuing blowout is spectacular to the point of godliness. Our hero whips up a whirlwind of ice shrapnel and plows down an onslaught of Snow-Misers-Gone-Wild by hurling his hammer toward them and letting go; the "clank-clank-clank" sound as they crash into each other and smash to bits is a blast. (If that goat-headed bruiser on the cover of Bathory's *Under the Sign of the Black Mark* could see this fight in zillion-dollar 3-D, he would jump to life and join the fray.) Unfortunately, Thor wasn't supposed to pick that battle, so Odin banishes him to Earth, stripped of god powers. Even more unfortunately, the movie goes there with him and sticks around, for a long, long while.

Thor lands in New Mexico but, really, he gets stuck in a Natalie Portman movie. By the time Loki (Tom Hiddleston), the Father of Hell, attempts to assassinate Thor with no more than a fire-breathing robot, it's too late to care and everybody's eyes are in revolt from the 3-D glasses. Salvation arrives in the form one final, highly satisfying tail-stomping in Asgard and a trippy, cosmos-trotting end credits sequence that suddenly makes the 3-D seem worth it. A 2013 sequel followed, and will not be the last.

THOR: THE ROCK OPERA (2010)

(DIR. JON MIKL THOR; W/JON MIKL THOR, LESLIE EASTERBROOK, DAN ROEBUCK, MARK MULCAHY)
✵ NORSE MYTHOLOGY ✵ SOUNDTRACK (THOR)

For four decades, Jon Mikl Thor has created muscleman hard rock, along with classic heavy metal horror movies—*Zombie Nightmare* (1986) and *Rock 'n' Roll Nightmare* (1987). *Thor: The Rock Opera* is not a rock opera at all, but rather a hodgepodge of film clips, music videos, live performances, and barbarian babes going wild. The package supplies more Jon Mikl Thor than you can bend a steel bar in your teeth at, and that alone is satisfyingly operatic.

Costar Leslie Easterbrook is best known as mega-busty ball-smashing Sergeant Callahan in the *Police Academy* movies. She has since begun working for director Rob Zombie, stepping in for Karen Black as Mother Firefly in *The Devil's Rejects* (2005), and playing a hospital guard in *Halloween* (2007).

THRASH ALTENESSEN: EIN FILM AUS DEM RUHRGEBIET (1989)

(DIR. THOMAS SCHADT; W/ROB FIORETTI, MILLE PETROZZA, RAPHA, STONEY, PEPPY)
✵ GERMAN THRASH METAL

Thrash Altenessen: Ein Film Aus Dem Ruhrgebiet is a drop-in on a depressed and deprived German village that, during the course of the movie, is in the process of launching thrash kings Kreator. Altenessen is the band's hometown, a suburb of Essen; the movie's secondary title means "A Film of the Ruhr Area." Ruhr's musical fertility is the backseat focus of documentarian Thomas Schadt. His focus is sociological, capturing the natives of a coal-mining town long after the mines were shut down.

The members of Kreator and their pals from the neighborhood talk and joke and come off as a dead-end gaggle of dirty longhairs on the dole who simply sit around, drink up, and rock out (save for one shattered sad sack who says he "broke" his liver). *Thrash Altenessen* often veers in the direction of becoming *Das Gummo*. We also meet the town elders, who are mostly disenfranchised, unemployable ex-miners. Some organize against a proposed highway that would disrupt their living spaces. Others guzzle booze on public steps and toss the bottles atop ancient litter mountains. Horrible sirens wail through the streets constantly, and everything's crumbling to shit.

One local standout is the father of bassist Rob Fioretti, who makes it plain he regrets leaving his native Italy. Another is a fifteen-year-old flamenco guitar player who impresses a crowd gathered for a thrash show.

Schadt jolts the film to life every so often by inserting a live performance by Kreator. It's clear they're getting out of Ruhr (the movie ends with Kreator on tour). The left behind just remain where they are—getting wasted, staying wasted, being wastes. The gang's names, as intoned by Schadt's deadpan, sound like those of the Bavarian Bowery Boys: Stoney, Peppy, Psycho, Lerche, Schenz, Packo, and Rapha.

Among the songs Kreator performs are "Love Us or Hate Us," "Flag of Hate," "Extreme Aggression," and "Toxic Trace," along with an open jam or two.

Thrashin' (1986),
aka Skate Gang

(Dir. David Winters; w/Josh Brolin, Robert Rusler, Pamela Gidley)

✠ Skateboarding

Skateboarding, professional and otherwise, has been associated with hard rock from its wheels-down get-go. The '70s era, on display in documentaries such as *Dog Town and Z-Boys* (2001), was about taking over empty swimming pools to the sounds of Hendrix, Nugent, and Kiss. Early-'80s skating is typically associated with punk and hardcore. By the second half of the decade, this high-speed opportunity to bang your head all kinds of ways figured strongly as a component of thrash metal, as long-haired ragers Metallica, Anthrax, and the Accüsed found their way into *Thrasher* magazine and onto skate ramps everywhere.

The Romeo-and-Juliet-themed skateboard exploitation movie *Thrashin'* gets its title right, but blows the soundtrack with pop floss by the Bangles and Animotion. Fear and Circle Jerks bring the SoCal hardcore, Red Hot Chili Peppers appear in a club playing "Black Eyed Blonde," Screamin' Sirens offer cowpunk, and somebody in an office somewhere slipped in some AOR hard stuff from White Sister and Rebel Faction. The bass-popping title song is performed by Meat Loaf, though, so no actual thrash features!

Regardless, *Thrashin'* kick-flips into the Heavy Metal Movie canon by virtue of being the go-to movie for young skaters in 1986, replete with cameos from pro skate heroes Tony Hawk, Lance

Mountain, and Christian Hosoi; plus enough stunt footage to create a cult time capsule. Josh Brolin stars as L.A. skate rat Corey, who falls for Chrissy (Pamela Gidley). It turns out she's sister of Hook (Robert Rusler), the leader of a thuggish Venice Beach skate gang and Corey's competition for an upcoming tournament. You know, from there, how these things go.

Thriller: A Cruel Picture (1973), aka They Call Her One Eye; Hooker's Revenge

(Dir. Bo Arne Vibenius; w/Christina Lindberg, Heinz Hopf, Despina Tomazani, Solveig Andersson)

✠ Swedish Sensationsfilm ✠ Rape and Revenge

Poor Frigga. At the beginning of *Thriller: A Cruel Picture*, a monstrous childhood rape renders this young Swedish beauty mute.

When she becomes a teenager, played by June 1970 *Penthouse* Pet Christina Lindberg, Frigga hitches a ride to speech therapy class from a stranger named Tony (Heinz Hopf). Unfortunately, Tony kidnaps Frigga, rapes her, beats her, and gets her addicted to heroin so that he can pimp her out as a sex slave. Things, from there, only go downhill.

We see Frigga earning her shots of dope by means of hardcore porn "inserts"—i.e., genital penetration footage incongruously injected into the film but featuring other actors from other films. These are not loving encounters, and their appearance in *Thriller* during early days of Netflix must have caught somebody by unhappy surprise. Frigga does get to enjoy some hot sex with a lesbian (Despina Tomazani), but after she scratches the face of a male john, Tony shoves a knife into her eye and half-blinds her. She then finds out that her parents, who never stopped searching for her, have died.

At last, Frigga has had e-frigga'n-nuff. She dons an eye patch, kicks the junk cold turkey, takes karate lessons, and gets her hot mitts on a shotgun. You can imagine what happens next. Only, really, you can't. That's why you've got to see *Thriller* for yourself. As opposed to the normal fever blood boiling in rape and revenge films such as *I Spit on Your Grave* (1977) and *Ms. 45* (1981), *Thriller* is cold and remote. But it's also mesmerizing and inspiring. Much like Sweden. Everything about *Thriller* is definitively of the land that has also given us Ingmar Bergman, Bathory, Greta Garbo, and Amon Amarth. Bo Arne Vibenius's slow, studied direction summons hallucinatory hyperviolence flowing from the unique screen command of the breathtaking Ms. Lindberg. Like the harshest black and death metal onslaughts to emanate from the same ice and snow a few years later, *Thriller*, for sure, is cruel, but it's a cruelly beautiful picture, too.

Quentin Tarantino paid homage to Christina Lindberg and *Thriller* in his *Kill Bill* movies by having Daryl Hannah sport an eye patch. "Of all the revenge movies I've ever seen, that is definitely the roughest," the director said of *Thriller* to *Movie Treasures*. "There's never been anything as tough as that movie."

The indispensible *Swedish Sensationsfilms: A Clandestine History of Sex, Thrillers, and Kicker Cinema* by Daniel Ekeroth (Bazillion Points, 2011) lays bare the brain-blasting story behind *Thriller*. The movie's cold-blooded producers took out massive life insurance policies on Christina Lindberg, as they wouldn't spring for blanks and had her firing live ammo during the shotgun scenes. The book also boasts a charming introduction by Lindberg, still as seductive as ever.

The Throne of Fire

(1983)

(Dir. Franco Prosperi; w/Sabrina Siani, Pietro Torrisi, Harrison Muller, Benny Cardoso)

✠ Swords & Sorcery ✠ Witchcraft ✠ Ghost Knight

The Throne of Fire is crammed with as much cool-seeming cheapie Italian *Conan* knock-off crap as possible. Belial, "the devil's messenger," forces sex on a witch and she gives birth to merciless barbarian Morak (Harrison Muller). At the same moment, heroic Siegfried (Pietro Torrisi) comes into the world, destined to challenge Morak for the titular throne, which was forged by no less incendiary a craftsman than the great god Odin. Also up for grabs is the shapely and combat-ready Princess Valkari (Sabrina Siani). Only the man she marries will remove her teeny suede bikini and sit on the throne without it bursting into flames.

In the course of the resulting struggle, Siegfried is tossed into the Well of Madness, a network of subterranean caverns that provides *Throne of Fire* with its lone noteworthy visual sequence, in which a series of belligerent hallucinations attack our hero. These include a panther, a giant snake, floating heads that jabber at him, and a ghost knight in a suit of armor. Despite such potent-sounding details, *Throne of Fire* remains obscure in the early-'80s sword-and-sorcery canon because it's largely a confusing snooze. Nonetheless, the concept of a throne of fire was appealing enough to spark songs by Altar, Damnations Hammer, Ravenclaw, and Impending Doom.

Director Franco Prosperi previously codirected *Hercules in the Haunted World* (1961) with Mario Bava. *Throne*'s Well of Madness scenes momentarily recall that surreal muscle-head classic. Deliciously bottom-heavy beauty Sabrina Siani, who's just nineteen in *Throne of Fire*, went on to Heavy Metal Movie immortality as the perpetually topless, gold-masked villainess Ocron in Lucio Fulci's mighty *Conquest* (1983). Siani costars with *Throne*'s Pietro Torrisi in two other broadsword adventures: *The Invincible Barbarian* (1982) and *Sword of the Barbarians* (1982).

Thunder and Mud (1990)

(Dir. Penelope Spheeris; w/Jessica Hahn, Tawn Mastrey, Tiffany Million, Wally Ann Wharton)

✠ Mud Wrestling ✠ Soundtrack (Nuclear Assault, Tuff, Grave Danger, Young Gunns)

Not-quite-hot on the platform heels of her history-making documentary *The Decline of Western Civilization Part II: The Metal Years* (1988), director Penelope Spheeris got down (conceptually) and dirty (literally) with *Thunder and Mud*. What began as a pay-per-view cable special then briefly occupied VHS rental-store space, soon slipped into oblivion, and now occupies a warm place in the cockles of hearts of a certain sort of headbanger of a certain sort of vintage.

The concept: five bikini-clad mud wrestlers meet four height-of-hair-metal Sunset Strip glam groups—and Nuclear Assault. Each girl reps a band in the mud pit, and the winning combo plays a number before the next bout. Comedy bits and pseudo-metal '80s bombshell Jessica Hahn help spice things up, or at least they try. In an *Onion* profile years later, Spheeris proclaimed *Thunder and Mud* "a flaming piece of crap."

This nonsense is probably best enjoyed in brief tastes via online video sites. Nuclear Assault shines as the only real metal band. In a gleamingly idiotic bit they goofily perform a mass massage on a barely swimsuit-adorned model. Since few of us will ever string all the clips together and sit through this entire feature, it's okay to spoil the ending. All-female band She-Rok wins *Thunder and Mud*. They are actually quite capable as musicians. Bass player Mary Kay was a co-founder of Detroit's legendary proto-punkers the Dogs. Singer Emi Canyn became one of Mötley Crüe's nun-costumed backup singers, the Nasty Habits and, in due time, Mrs. Mick Mars.

Jessica Hahn remains an über-'80s timepiece, setting the template for reality-TV-type trash queens for decades to come. She's also profoundly intertwined with the pop-culture side of metal in the '80s. Long Island church secretary Hahn had sex with married televangelist Jim Bakker, and the ensuing 1987 scandal destroyed his empire. Hahn posed for *Playboy*, became a featured Howard Stern regular, and romanced screaming metal funnyman Sam Kinison.

To the Devil a Daughter (1976)

(Dir. Peter Sykes; w/Nastassja Kinski, Christopher Lee, Richard Widmark)

✠ Satan ✠ Virgin Sacrifice ✠ Hammer Horror

Warning! This Motion Picture Contains the Most Shocking Scenes This Side of Hell!" screeches the poster, a taste of classic exploitation ballyhoo. The non-horned title character of *To the Devil a Daughter* is teenage nun Catherine (Nastassja Kinski). Her mother died in an incident involving a long, scary knife and baptism by blood immediately after Catherine's birth, and the girl has since been sequestered in a convent run by heretical Catholic priest Father Michael Rayner (Christopher Lee). You can imagine where this particular padre is sending our girl for her eighteenth birthday. Occult writer John Verney (Richard Widmark) shows up on behalf of her earthly pop (Denholm Elliott) to whisk this young Sister Anti-Christian away from her sulfurous coming-out party, which involves no small amount of uncovered virginal flesh.

Somehow, despite this premise, that cast, and one of the all-time killer titles, *To the Devil a Daughter* misses the fun and frights inherent in its massive black promise. Adapted from a novel by Dennis Wheatley, *To the Devil a Daughter* was the final horror movie production of England's legendary Hammer Film Studios (prior to the 2007 revival). Hammer initially approached Ken Russell (*The Devils*) and then Mike Lodge (*Get Carter*) to make *Daughter*. Director Peter Sykes previously helmed Hammer's gothic incest spooker *Demons of the Mind* (1972).

Yet although the movie is talky and overcomplicated, Nastassja Kinski kicked off one of the all-time great taboo-busting careers in the movies here. And all in the name of Satan. The not-even-barely legal Kinski was born in 1961. *Daughter* was released in 1976. For all *Daughter*'s dullness and disappointments, there is something inherently metal and classically satanic, about a fifteen-year-old exposing her nubile nakedness atop a pentagram. As was the case with Scorpions' scandalous *Virgin Killer* album cover, keep in mind that many teenage headbangers saw this sight for the first time while still young enough to consider a fifteen-year-old an older woman.

TOMBS OF THE BLIND DEAD (1971), AKA NIGHT OF BLIND TERROR; REVENGE FROM PLANET APE

(DIR. AMANDO DE OSSORIO; W/CÉSAR BURNER, MARIA ELENA ARPÓN, LONE FLEMING)

✠ ZOMBIES ✠ KNIGHTS TEMPLAR

Virginia (Elena Arpón) and Roger (César Burner), a young couple traveling through Spain, run into Virginia's old pal Betty (Lone Fleming) on a train. After the ladies reminisce about their schoolgirl lesbianism, Roger gets plenty aroused, but Virginia seeks to further spice things up by leaping off the moving train. Just by coincidence, she lands in an abandoned village on "the night of blind terror." Once a year, zombified forms of the Knights Templar rise in the village in search of blood. The Knights were a thirteenth- century secret society that sought immortality through black magic. They were summarily blinded and executed by the Catholic Church. As we see, they didn't stay dead forever.

The Blind Dead themselves are hooded, robed skeletons who brandish swords and ride horseback along the Spanish coastline. Their spooky steeds are also blind. The Knights Templar became a hot topic in the 2000s courtesy of Dan Brown's ungodly popular novel *The Da Vinci Code*. Stick with the *Blind Dead* movies, including *Return of the Evil Dead* (1973), *The Ghost Galleon* (1974), and *Night of the Seagulls* (1975).

Some shoddy U.S. distributors of *Tombs of the Blind Dead* attempted to cash in on the mania for *Planet of the Apes* by retitling it *Revenge From Planet Ape*! Slapped-together prologue narration recasts the Knights Templar as super-intelligent apes defeated and blinded by humans after a battle three thousand years ago. The ape leader vows to return in the future for revenge. You can watch this jaw-dropping intro on Blue Underground's *Tombs of the Blind Dead* DVD.

TOMMY (1975)

(DIR. KEN RUSSELL; W/ROGER DALTREY, ANN-MARGRET, OLIVER REED, ELTON JOHN, TINA TURNER)

✠ ROCK OPERA ✠ PINBALL ✠ SOUNDTRACK (THE WHO)

Cinematic madman Ken Russell declared his movie adaptation of the Who album *Tommy* to be "the greatest work of art the twentieth century has yet produced." For a while there in the second half of the '70s, many a long-haired, midnight-movie-attending Chevy van pilot was inclined to totally far-fuckin'-out agree. Who vocalist Roger Daltrey stars as the well-known "deaf, dumb, and blind kid" who amasses a rapturous cult of devotees by being a pinball wizard. *Tommy*'s hesher fan base and monolithic stadium-rock foundation qualify it as metal, and Russell's still-shocking visuals up the heaviness magnificently.

On the fun side are Elton John's eight-foot-high Doc Martens and Keith Moon as Uncle Ernie "fiddlin' about, fiddlin' about, fiddlin' about." Eric Clapton's Marilyn Monroe–worshipping faith healer is too low-key, but not without totemic merit. The queasy eroticism of Ann-Margret (Oscar nominated as Tommy's mother) climaxing in a great King-Kong-proportioned money shot of baked beans is unexpectedly sexy.

The "bum trip" aspect of *Tommy* is where the metal truly clangs. Tina Turner's narcotic-pumping Acid Queen is a searing harpy. Even more scabrous is Paul Nicholas as creative sadist Cousin Kevin, who subjects Tommy to water torture, hot irons, and a nail-studded toilet seat. Make what you will of Who honcho Pete Townshend and the music he composed for *Tommy*, but credit Townshend with Heavy Metal Movie points in perpetuity for trusting Russell to convert what might have become merely a relic of its time into a continually vibrant rock and roll carpet bombing of the senses.

The sidebar saga of youthful Tommy fanatic Sally Simpson (Victoria Russell) culminates with her marrying a rock star from California (Gary Rich), a guitar-slinging Frankenstein monster in a cowboy outfit. That freak is metal as fuck.

El Topo (1970)

(Dir. Alejandro Jodorowsky; w/Alejandro Jodorowsky, Brontis Jodorowsky, Mara Lorenzio)

✠ Western ✠ Gore

El Topo infuses the already peyote-fumed air of classic spaghetti westerns (e.g., *The Good, the Bad, and the Ugly*) with uncut acid as though every grain of sand on screen is a fully dosed tab. Writer-director-producer Alejandro Jodorowsky stars as a pilgrim making all kinds of hallucinatory progress. He's a black-clad gunfighter who rides the Mexican desert accompanied by his naked seven-year-old son. After ditching Junior with a cabal of monks, El Topo charges into the heat with slave girl Mara (Mara Lorenzio) to battle four master gunfighters, each symbolizing a different major world philosophy or religion. One is actually a legless man riding on the back of an armless man, predating the setup of Master/Blaster in *Mad Max Beyond Thunderdome*.

Mara comes across a mysterious woman (Paula Romo) and shoots El Topo to commence her new life as a lesbian. Years later, El Topo comes out of a coma inside a cave where he's worshipped as a god by dwarves, cripples, amputees, and other people with deformities. They're trapped in this underground lair until El Topo manages to free them. Running out to freedom, the prisoners are gunned down by cultists led by El Topo's now-adult son (Robert John). El Topo lights himself on fire, and the movie ends with Junior riding off with his dead father's girlfriend.

Far fuckin' out, right? You have no idea, until you actually experience *El Topo*. Aside from spaghetti westerns, Jodorowsky's visuals and the specifics of El Topo's quest for enlightenment stem from comic books, kung fu cinema, occult ephemera, science fiction, dwarf mythology, and sexploitation. If heavy metal had existed prior to *El Topo*, it for sure would be in that mix, too.

Although other films had certainly screened at midnight prior to *El Topo*, it was its long, exclusive, seven-night-a-week 12 a.m. run at the Elgin Theater in New York that established the midnight-movie market. *El Topo* so flipped John Lennon's spectacles that he convinced Beatles attorney Allen Klein to buy the rights and market the film at midnight screenings worldwide.

Jodorowsky has announced numerous sequels to *El Topo*, none of which has yet emerged. In 2002, he proclaimed that Marilyn Manson, an outspoken champion of the original, would star. Jodorowsky and Manson also announced a collaboration on another film, *Holy Wood*, that never came to be. It still sounds cool.

The Toxic Avenger (1984)

(Dirs. Lloyd Kaufman, Michael Herz; w/Mitch Cohen, Mark Torgl, Andree Maranda)

✠ Mutants ✠ Metal Reality

The best-known by-product of New York's schlock-processing plant Troma Films, *The Toxic Avenger* bridges the studio's early standout transgressions (*Bloodsucking Freaks, Mother's Day*) and the cynical, cutesy-poo rubber vomit jokes with which it later became synonymous. All these years and all those terrible Troma movies later, *The Toxic Avenger* remains grossly likable and worthily metal.

As with the *Crazy* magazine Teen Hulk series from a year or two earlier, the central Incredible Hulk horror-parody concept is great. Here a weakling janitor in radioactive toilet-town Tromaville, New Jersey, is transformed by glowing ooze into a hyperviolent, mop-wielding super-monster. The movie's over-the-top attitude results in a number of bona fide shocks: not only does a kid gets his head splattered by a car in an up-close shot, one of the female perpetrators later masturbates to Polaroids of the carnage. *Toxic Avenger* features so many fantastically atrocious moments: nerdy Melvin foaming and bubbling as he transforms into Toxie; Cigar Face showing off how he got his nickname, by smashing a lit stogie into a cop's kisser; the shotgun execution of a blind girl's guide dog; death by milk shake maker; the effect of gravity on a gym rat's head under the weights of a bench-press machine; and the entertainingly obese mayor of Tromaville ceaselessly stuffing his fat mug.

Toxic Avenger falters when the lack of budget inspires not creativity and innovation but cheap dodges and a general tilt toward slipshod amateurism. Those shortcomings are forgiven, given how the movie does deliver, launching a new genre of literally headbanging exploitation hybrids. The movie caught on like uranium burns and spawned a sea of descendants, first in decades of Troma crap, and more recently in higher-profile faux-grindhouse fabrications such as *Hobo With a Shotgun* (2011).

The MPAA branded *Toxic Avenger* with an X for violence before it opened in theaters unrated. As such, it is the only X-rated film to generate a kids' TV cartoon. *Toxic Crusaders* ran on Fox for thirteen episodes. *The Toxic Avenger Part II* (1989) and *The Toxic Avenger Part III: The Last Temptation of Toxie* (1989), filmed as one feature and then split into two, are utter dung. *Citizen Toxie: Toxic Avenger IV* (2000) represents a mild, semi-hardened improvement over utter dung.

The original movie is a metal touchstone, appealing for both its repulsiveness and its black-humored take on environmentalism. Exodus penned its thrash-dance hit "The Toxic Waltz" in the movie's aftermath. In 1992, Metallica's James Hetfield suffered third-degree burns onstage, and he since describes his bubbling, smoking skin as looking like the metamorphosis scene from *The Toxic Avenger*. "Toxic Avenger" tribute songs have also appeared from Devastated, Gore Obsessed, Lethal Death, and others.

Traces of Death III

(1995)
(DIR. BRAIN DAMAGE; W/BRAIN DAMAGE)
✢ Medical Deviant ✢ Snuff ✢ Soundtrack
(Deceased, Dismember, Merzbow, Repulsion)

Traces of Death III introduces us, straight off, to a gentleman in a Relapse Records T-shirt. Ceremonial red candles stand alight on displays around him. "I am BRAIN . . . DAMAGE . . . producer of the first two shockumentary series, *Traces of Death* . . . Welcome to *Traces of Death III*! I have pieced together for you the most brutal and vile acts of inhumane atrocities ever compiled on film. You will see horrifying scenes of the aftermath of terrorist suicide bombers! And watch the gut-wrenching torture inflicted by the El Salvador death squad. And much more!"

Not missing a double-bass beat, Brain Damage gets to the meat of his message—using mondo gross-out footage as a marketing tool for death metal bands! "*Traces of Death III* also brings to you some of the HOTTEST talent in the metal industry! Bands like Ma-SHOO-gah, Core, Deceased, Hypocrisy, Dead World, Mortician, and Gorefest, to name a few. My blackened soul is proud to announce the release of the *Traces of Death III* soundtrack! At the end of this ghastly spectacle of gore, I will tell YOU how to get it! As much as your brain may fight, KEEP your eyes and ears open and let the carnage continue!"

Traces of Death is the brain-damaged child of Damon Fox of L.A. power metal battalion Stormtrooper. Fox hosts the first two volumes. *Traces of Death IV* emerged in 1996; *Traces of Death V* in 2000. Since then, we've seen nary a trace.

TRAUMA (1993)

(DIR. DARIO ARGENTO; W/ASIA ARGENTO, CHRISTOPHER RYDELL, PIPER LAURIE, FREDERIC FORREST)

✶ GIALLO

The Dario Argento giallo *Trauma* assembles the Italian horror visionary's expected stylized hyperviolence in a typically over-the-top murder mystery, but it scores a distinguished Heavy Metal Movie nod for the introduction of its leading lady. Eighteen-year-old Asia Argento, the director's daughter, stars in *Trauma*, where she immediately grabbed the horror world by the short hairs and dug her claws in deep.

Asia is all goth beauty and smoldering erotic menace. She went on to be a crackpot cinema icon, both as an actress and a director who never sees a taboo she won't lunge herself at to shatter and splatter in a feral commitment absolute freedom. If you've ever wanted to see a busty teenage girl get naked in an arousing milieu and captured on film by her father, *Trauma* provides the finest of all such opportunities to date.

THE TRIAL OF BILLY JACK (1974)

(DIR. FRANK LAUGHLIN; W/TOM LAUGHLIN, DELORES TAYLOR, VICTOR IZAY, TERESA LAUGHLIN)

✶ PSYCHO 'NAM VET ✶ SCHOOL MASSACRE

The Trial of Billy Jack opens with a My Lai–style massacre of native villagers in Vietnam, and ends with a Kent State–style massacre of hippie kids at the totally groovy Freedom School in New Mexico. Those two big countercultural dots need some heavy-duty connective tissue to add up to a movie, and this three-hour sequel to the 1971 drive-in masterpiece *Billy Jack* is just the unfettered ego trip to do it. The film is a firestorm of heavy metal ideas, imagery, and impact.

Billy Jack, our half-Indian, ex–Green Beret, ass-kicking pacifist hero aids the Freedom School's muckraking journalism department, which has a "Nader-like" daily newspaper, a TV station, and a helicopter. Then he sits in on a heated American Indian tribal council, where step-and-fetch-it locals who suck up to white people are derided as "Uncle Tom-myhawks." Finally, before the National Guard guns down everybody's good time, Billy Jack goes on a hilariously ham-fisted vision quest, a sequence to end all other psychedelic awakenings. The hallucinogenic high point of this vision quest occurs as Billy Jack slaps Jesus Christ in the face.

Every exchange of dialogue in this picture is an inflamed call to revolution, every beat-down is an exercise in forced enlightenment, and every point is made with the subtlety of Billy Jack's bare foot delivered via roundhouse-thrust smack into one's frontal lobe. If that level of blaring, combative, sustained overkill isn't metal, then don't even bother telling me what is—I'll be too busy teaching a kid with no hands to play the guitar, then protecting him with my own body from National Guard bullets after he runs into the line of fire to save his pet bunny rabbit.

TRICK OR TREAT (1986)

(DIR. CHARLES MARTIN SMITH; W/MARC PRICE, ELISE RICHARDS, GENE SIMMONS, OZZY OSBOURNE)

✶ BACKWARD MASKING ✶ TELEVANGELISTS
✶ SATANIC PANIC ✶ SOUNDTRACK (FASTWAY)

Headbangers of a certain vintage will feel nostalgic attachment for *Trick or Treat*, a gambit by mega-mogul Dino De Laurentiis to cash in simultaneously on mid-'80s heavy metal mania and teen horror hysteria. *Trick or Treat* makes for some downright homely viewing years later, but does pack enough treats to not feel totally like a trick. I mean, Gene Simmons appears as an ersatz Wolfman Jack metal DJ, and Ozzy Osbourne portrays the world's worst televangelist!

Our protagonist is a likable, put-upon dork Eddie Weinbauer (Marc Price, aka Skippy Henderson from TV sitcom *Family Ties*). He lives and breathes hard rock and is shaken by the death of his heavy metal hero, Sammi Curr (Tony Fields). Hard rock disc jockey Nuke (Gene Simmons) consoles Eddie by giving him a one-of-a-kind

Clockwise from top left: *classic posters for*
TerrorVision *and* The Texas Chain Saw
Massacre; Tombs of the Blind Dead *in Thai;*
Zuni fetish doll superstar in Trilogy of Terror;
original pre-sensation Toxic Avenger *poster*

Sammi Curr acetate. When Eddie plays the record backward at home, hidden messages from Sammi steadily imbue him with powers to conquer the school bully (Doug Savant) and seduce the honey in gym class (Elise Richards). One near-violent incident follows another. Most frustrating is the bad guy almost getting his eyeball power-drilled by possessed machines in shop class—only to have Eddie turn off the power.

At the Halloween dance, Sammi Curr materializes from beyond the grave, takes over frontman duties for the onstage metal band, and proceeds to kill kids all over the school gym. His weapon of choice is cartoony lightning bolts fired from his guitar; a flash of light, a sound effect, a cheap explosion, and then smoky nothingness! With all due respect to Sammi Curr's metal might, even the 1982 Scott Baio/Willie Aames slapstick telekinesis farce *Zapped!* is scarier.

The surprisinglyl bloodless movie earns its R rating with a sexy scene in which Elise Richards listens to Sammi Curr and falls into an ecstatic trance. Animated green smog emerges from her headphones, representing heavy metal lust. The smoke cascades down her writhing body, takes on the form of a hand, and pops open her bra. Just as it's working on her pants button, she awakes and it turns into a big rubbery shrieking monster, then disappears. A whole movie of that would have been great.

But still, *Trick or Treat* is *our* movie, made specifically for headbangers and horror hounds alike. I will defend it to my last moshing breath. Many years later, it almost seems like a prescient before-the-fact Columbine allegory. An outcast teen obsessed with heavy metal evens the score against those who humiliate and oppress him, driven by Sammi Curr's declaration, "Rock's chosen warriors will rule the apocalypse!"

Speaking of the bitter end, note that Marc Price goes bottomless about two minutes in. At least it's intended as comedy, as he's being humiliated in the school gym. That's more than can be said Ron "Arnold Horschack" Palillo's bare-ass action in *Hellgate* (1990)—there, the *Welcome Back, Kotter* veteran is attempting to be "sensual."

Trick or Treat was conceived with the intention of having Blackie Lawless of W.A.S.P. play Sammi Curr. Judging by the band's appearance in *The Dungeonmaster* (1984), it's a pity that never happened. Hard rock fogies Fastway, featuring ex-members of Motörhead and Humble Pie, were already waning when tapped to provide the theme song. W.A.S.P. would have made infinitely more sense. When Blackie didn't pan out and Gene Simmons also passed (agreeing only to his radio DJ cameo), the role went to *Solid Gold* dancer Tony Fields. Prolific TV actress Elaine Joyce plays Eddie's mom. She has an amusing and arousing aerobics moment. Aerobics and heavy metal really did go together in the '80s.

Fitting as 1986 was the year of punk-metal crossover, Eddie wears a T-shirt emblazoned with the logo of the Dead Kennedys record label, Alternative Tentacles. The hero's on-screen collection contains records by Megadeth, Exciter, Impaler, and Savatage; his room is hung with posters of Anthrax, Judas Priest, Kiss, Mötley Crüe, Raven, Twisted Sister, and Ozzy Osbourne; and there's a Lizzy Borden sticker for good measure.

Ozzy Osbourne's cameo as a preacher condemning heavy metal on television exists simply so viewers could say, "Look! That's Ozzy Osbourne as a preacher condemning heavy metal on television!" and that really is reason enough. He pops up again after the final credits.

Trilogy of Terror (1975)

(Dir. Dan Curtis; w/Karen Black, He Who Kills)

✠ Supernatural ✠ Native American Mysticism

The ABC Movie of the Week *Trilogy of Terror* contains three stories, but the reason anyone remembers *Trilogy of Terror* is for one story, the concluding segment, "Amelia," which pits hyper-'70s superstarlet Karen Black against a foot-high Zuni "fetish doll" carved to resemble a ferocious warrior, complete with razor-like fangs and a sharp spear. The doll is said to house the actual spirit of a hunter deity named "He Who Kills," but as long as the gold chain around the thing's neck stays intact, it won't come to life and go slay-crazy all over Karen Black. The chain remains intact for about thirty seconds.

The remainder of the story consists of He Who Kills pursuing Karen Black all over her high-rise apartment. And the twelve-inch-tall, fully ambulatory creature is truly a wonder to behold: he screams, he babbles, he runs, he stalks, he lunges, and he leaps through the air. He steals a carving knife and stabs Karen in the ankles mercilessly. Karen tries to drown her tiny tormentor in a bathtub, and she momentarily traps him in a suitcase, but the little fucker keeps breaking loose until she tosses him into the oven and he goes up in smoke. Not peacefully. Not quietly.

He Who Kills is aboriginal heavy metal in miniature—a wailing embodiment of native rage come to supernatural homicidal life. Fireball Ministry cared enough to write a song about him. The famously off-the-wall *Trilogy of Terror* remained so potent that a sequel was made twenty years after the original. He Who Kills returns in *Trilogy of Terror II* (1996), again starring in the final segment. This time he torments Lysette Anthony.

TROLL (1986)

(DIR. JOHN CARL BUECHLER; W/MICHAEL MORIARTY, SHELLEY HACK, JULIA-LOUIS DREYFUS, SONNY BONO)

✠ TROLLS ✠ FAIRIES ✠ GOBLINS ✠ NYMPHS

The charms of *Troll* have multiplied through the years, independent of its better-known 1990 sequel-in-name-only *Troll 2*. First is the semi-mind-blowing fact that Michael Moriarty and Noah Hathaway play a father and son named "Harry Potter" (Senior and Junior, respectively). Then consider the casting: Gary Sandy (Andy Travis on TV's *WKRP in Cincinnati*) plays a Rambo wannabe, future *Seinfeld* star Julia Louis-Dreyfus becomes an ivy-clad woodland nymph after her apartment transforms into an enchanted forest, and Sonny Bono sprays oily erotic charm as a San Francisco swinger who is turned into a giant pickle. Those are all side effects of the main story, about an evil troll and a kindly witch taking their centuries-old battle to an apartment complex that is soon overrun with fairies, goblins, and other charming rubber puppets.

At one point, for no particular reason, Michael Moriarty slams the brakes on the action in *Troll* to announce he's going to put on and enjoy his favorite record: "Summertime Blues" by Blue Cheer. Moriarty's full-on possessed lip sync and flailing pantomime of the acid rock rave-up is one of the most metal moments in movie history. The only cinematic use of iconic proto-metal that comes close is the final pursuit in *Manhunter* set to "In-A-Gadda-Da-Vida" by Iron Butterfly.

TROLL 2 (1990)

(DIR. CLAUDIO FRAGASSO; W/MICHAEL STEPHENSON, GEORGE HARDY, MARGO PREY, CONNIE MCFARLAND)

✠ GOBLINS ✠ NO TROLLS ✠ CANNIBALISM

Okay, here we go. Connected only in name to the sleeper fantasy hit *Troll* (1986), *Troll 2* is an off-the-rails excursion into cheapie horror that blossomed into one of cinema's great cult sensations. Shortly after dad Michael Waits (George Hardy) plans a family vacation in the rural town of Nilbog, young son Joshua (Michael Stephenson) is visited by his grandfather's ghost (Robert Ormsby). Gramps warns that Nilbog—spell it backward—is a hotbed of vegetarian goblins who turn humans into plants to be eaten.

Technical foul-ups, goblin costumes consisting of goofball masks worn over ponchos, people eating green slime and then becoming green slime, and a double-decker bologna sandwich wielded as a weapon are just the tip of *Troll 2*'s pleasures. The unique costumes came courtesy of sexploitation star Laura Gemser, best known as the Thai-born lead in the Black Emanuelle film series.

Troll 2's sleepover-friendly PG-13 rating and relentless presence on HBO during the '90s beguiled a generation with its incompetent Italian-made madness. Fans celebrate *Troll 2* today with midnight screenings, parties, fan sites, and an actual convention. *Troll 2* was briefly the absolute lowest-rated film on the IMDB, a distinction celebrated in the documentary *Best Worst Movie* (2010), made by the actor who plays Joshua here.

Troll 2 director Claudio Fragasso also made the notorious Alice Cooper vehicle *Monster Dog* (1984). *Troll 2*'s reputation as the world's worst film has never amused Fragasso; he claims he did better than anyone else could have, given his limited resources. Filled with frustration, Fragasso crashed a cast reunion and had to be removed, screaming all the way out that the participants were "dogs" and "liars." We still love him.

TROLLHUNTER (2010)

(DIR. ANDRÉ OVREDAL; W/OTTO JESPERSEN, GLENN ERLUND TOSTERUD, TOMAS ALF LARSEN)

✠ TROLLS ✠ NORWAY

From Norway—where else?—comes the best and most deadpan variation on *The Blair Witch Project*. Here, film students take to the woods to track down something spooky, thought to be an unusual series of bear attacks. Things get interesting with the arrival of an oddball hunter, unknown to local licensed bear killers.

Of course, bears are not biting cars in half and kicking over hillsides. The culprits are giant trolls, taller than the trees, some with three heads. The bearded weirdo is a troll hunter, commissioned by the government to wipe out any monsters that escape from approved troll territories—and also to keep the public in the dark that such creatures exist. The thing is, the troll hunter is sick of the job, so he invites the young camera crew to accompany him on this final mission.

In the title role, Otto Jespersen creates one of horror cinema's most brilliantly hilarious characters. Exhausted, stone-faced, and never less than 100 percent believable, he goes about the business of coating himself in troll stink, messily dispatching the beasts, and then slavishly filling out the xeroxed government forms required for each kill. The troll mythology is similarly realized with utter credibility, as evidenced in the hunter's confession that, "back in the '70s" he committed a massacre on an entire society of these "dumb animals." That wound weighs on him heavily.

Trollhunter is suspenseful, frightening, funny, and deadpan Norwegian to the extreme. If the country had produced strain of black metal whose main aim was to jolt you out of your seat but charm a smile onto your face, it would feel like this movie. The trolls themselves are movie monsters you have longed to see, created using actors and puppets with presence and weight. Through the use of forced perspective (like the goblins from *The Gate*), they absolutely appear to be running and roaring and gnashing their terrifying teeth. These are the type of stunningly believable creations Hollywood has banished since embracing CGI. We need them back!

TROMEO AND JULIET (1996)

(DIR. LLOYD KAUFMAN; W/JANE JENSEN, WILL KEENAN, LEMMY KILMISTER, DEBBIE ROCHON)

✠ GORE ✠ SHAKESPEARE ✠ SOUNDTRACK (MOTÖRHEAD, BRUJERIA, UNSANE)

Shakespeare's tale of star-crossed lovers is updated to 1996 and given the Troma Films treatment in *Tromeo and Juliet*. Motörhead leader Lemmy Kilmister appears on-screen to narrate. Tromeo (Will Keenan) is a tattoo artist. Juliet (Jane Jensen) is a rich girl sequestered by her domineering family, and cared for sexually by her sexy nurse (B-movie goddess Debbie Rochon). The basic Shakespeare plot plays out with gore, nudity, sick sex, rubber monsters, and a funny punch line involving incest-mutant kids.

Starting with the inclusion of Lemmy (who knocks it out of the park), *Tromeo* makes a shocking amount of right decisions for a Troma movie. Screenwriter James Gunn had the sound sense to hightail it to Hollywood, where he penned the 2004 *Dawn of the Dead* remake and directed *Slither* (2006) and *Super* (2010). Around the time of *Tromeo*'s release, lead actress Jane Jensen released an electronic dance-metal album titled *Comic Book Whore*.

True Norwegian Black Metal (2007)

(Dirs. Ivar Berglin, Peter Beste; w/Gaahl, Peter Beste, Ivar Berglin, King ov Hell)

✸ Soundtrack (Gorgoroth, Trelldom)

Produced by *Vice* magazine and hosted by *Vice* Scandinavia correspondent Ivar Berglin, thirty-two minute documentary *True Norwegian Black Metal* is misleadingly titled. The central figure is Gaahl, face-painted practitioner of torture and lead vocalist of Gorgoroth. After getting a quick run-through of the genre, complete with Venom, Bathory, Mayhem, and church burnings, we meet Gorgoroth. Along with footage from the "Black Mass" performance in hyper-Catholic Poland, where the stage was lined with decapitated sheep heads and nude, crucified actors, bassist King describes the band's agenda: "Everything we do is to promote the message of Satan."

Next the crew visits Gaahl's snowy wilderness family home, where he talks about individualism and shows his paintings. He seems cool for a dude sent to prison for tying some guy down for six hours while squeezing his balls and collecting his blood in a cup. The long black leather coat Gaahl wears to go mountain hiking is the tits. The movie ends when Gaahl feels annoyed by a question as to whether he feels lonely. He sits silently for nearly three minutes. The effect goes from weird to uncomfortable to scary.

The soundtrack features various Gaahl projects beyond Gorgoroth that include Trelldom and Warduna. It atmospheric power blends excellently with visuals of untamed Norwegian landscapes in wintertime. Along with the documentary, *Vice* issued a companion book, *True Norwegian Black Metal*. This sizable coffee table art object showcased great photography of contemporary black metal bands by Peter Beste, along with a slew of sample artwork and writing by the crew behind the essential history of Norway's extreme scene, *Metalion: The Slayer Mag Diaries*.

Truth About Rock (1983)

(Dirs. Dan Peters, Steve Peters; w/Dan Peters, Steve Peters)

✸ Censorship ✸ Satanic Panic

Take the next few minutes," a representative of Truth About Rock Ministries advises, "to hear about rotten songs such as Alice Cooper's song about necrophilia, which is making love to a dead body. Hear how Aerosmith likes girls who are bleeding; Ted Nugent on masochism, which is pleasure in sex through pain; and those clean-cut Australians AC/DC, who encourage oral sex. Hear of Kiss's fornicating with teenage girls, and Wendy O. Williams' enjoyment of public nudity!"

That's the "truth" about heavy metal in the intro to *Truth About Rock*, a breathlessly delirious deconstruction of the whole of hard grooves as experienced via the eyes, hairdos, and slick drawls of evangelical siblings Dan and Steve Peters. They ask us, in unison, to their own amusement: "What the DEVIL is wrong with rock music?"

When not making dent-headed quasi-documentary screeds, the brothers travel Jesus Country, coordinating youth-group record bonfires. We see numerous video clips of perfectly good metal and totally non-metal records being melted, while the brothers gleefully keep the tally: "more than five million dollars' worth of rock burned!"

Spewing their hilarious hatred at a speed-metal pace, the Peters boys hold up album covers, identify occult influences, quote *Rolling Stone* interviews, invoke scripture, boast about their LP infernos, and occasionally allow a commercial interjection advising where to send your money if you want the Peters boys to come incinerate your own blasphemous vinyl. Could be fun?

Tuff Turf (1985)

(Dir. Fritz Kiersch; w/James Spader, Kim Richards, Robert Downey Jr., Paul Mones)
✠ Knife Fights

With its "neon palm tree" look, surprise musical numbers, and a soundtrack weirdly dominated by retro soulsters like Southside Johnny and Jack Mack and the Heart Attack, calling *Tuff Turf* "metal" seems like a stretch until you see it. The experience of being a torn-up youth in the 1980s pours off the screen. The floor-to-ceiling temple to Mötley Crüe above Kim's makeup mirror reaches out to the headbangers in the audience. The movie lets us know it gets us. Pounding at the center of its *Tuff* heart is metal.

Singing, dancing, and knife-fighting its way to cult status amidst a hyper-'80s teenage wasteland, *Tuff Turf* is situated right between Hollywood underdog stories such as *Footloose* (1984) and *The Karate Kid* (1984) and rougher-hewn campus revenge potboilers like *Young Warriors* (1983) and *3:15: The Moment of Truth* (1986). James Spader is the new kid, Paul Mones is the psycho juvenile delinquent, and Kim Richards (grown up from Disney's *Witch Mountain* movies) is the crimp-coiffed maiden fair over whom they do battle. Robert Downey Jr. is the good guy's Hawaiian-shirted sidekick.

Also throw a horn to the totally tubular appearance of new wave nihilists the Jim Carroll Band, performing at a teen warehouse dance as "the Crypt." Robert Downey Jr. sits in on drums, whipping through "It's Too Late (If You're in Love With Sharon Tate)." Jim Carroll has also collaborated with and written lyrics for Blue Öyster Cult. His landmark Lower East Side heroin memoir, *The Basketball Diaries*, even inspired the title of the ultimate book on Norwegian black metal, *Metalion: The Slayer Mag Diaries*.

Turbulence 3: Heavy Metal (2001)

(Dir. Jorge Montesi; w/John Mann, Gabrielle Anwar, Craig Sheffer, Rutger Hauer)
✠ Doomsday Cult ✠ Psycho 'Nam Vet ✠ Fake Metal Star (Slade Craven)

Slade Craven (John Mann) is a black-maned, makeup-encased Marilyn Manson stand-in. He plans to perform a concert onboard a wide-body airplane that, via the miracle of live Internet streaming, will be watched by "ten million people." Simon Flanders (also John Mann) is Craven's exact double. He's the leader of an apocalyptic cult called Guardians of the Gateway that believes a sacrifice will unleash hell on Earth by way of Stull, Kansas—again, a place so unholy that "even the pope" refused to fly over it.

Flanders ties up and hides the real Craven after takeoff. He then assumes the rocker's identity to create havoc at thirty thousand feet. The rugged pilot (Rutger Hauer), who says Craven's music reminds him of 'Nam, may be a hiding secret, as well. With help from a hacker on the ground, Craven breaks his restraints and transforms into a hilariously inappropriate action hero, launching *Turbulence 3: Heavy Metal* upward into ridiculously enjoyable B-movie altitudes.

A knowing slyness appears, as though the film itself appreciates its own audacity. The movie doesn't skimp on suspense or violence, though. The same attributes can be applied to much of the type of rock that Slade Craven represents (including, to be sure, Manson and Cradle of Filth), making *Turbulence 3: Heavy Metal* a perfectly engaging discount package of prefabricated evil.

In 1997, the first *Turbulence* played movie theaters and featured Ray Liotta as a psycho who kills everyone onboard an airline flight. The straight-to-video *Turbulence 2: Fear of Flying* (1999) stars Craig Sheffer as an airplane engineer stuck on a hijacked jet. Weirdly, Sheffer returns here as an entirely different character, a computer hacker teamed with the FBI.

Turn the Page (1999)

(Dir. Jonas Åkerlund; w/Ginger Lynn Allen)
✠ Metal Reality ✠ Soundtrack (Metallica)

Ex-Bathory drummer Jonas Åkerlund directs the music video for Metallica's 1998 single "Turn the Page," a cover of the 1970s Bob Seger ode to how much it sucks to be a rock star. Porn legend Ginger Lynn Allen stars as a transitory sex worker, slinging her goods one motel room, one strip club, and one pickup trick at a time. Along for the ride is her daughter (Anders Templeman), who looks about eight years old and just stoically endures.

This fifteen-minute film short fills in the far bleaker explicit details of the music video's downbeat narrative, using much of the same footage accompanied by the daughter's narration, and intercut with footage of Allen answering questions we don't hear with uncomfortable earnestness. The interview segments prove compelling, as Allen is obviously speaking about her own real life as the "It Girl" of mid-'80s porn who left the business only to return later as a single mom to cash in on the MILF fetish. She's very good here.

As they ride in a surprisingly sensible Volvo station wagon (a nod to the director's homeland?), the daughter says: "We listen to the car radio a lot. Mom likes hip-hop, and I like country-western songs." They compromise by tuning into "Unforgiven II" by Metallica. Ginger ends the movie being roughed up royally by a john to Metallica's "Fixxxer." *Turn the Page* won the Bronze Medal at the Flagstaff Film Festival 1999.

The Twilight Saga: Eclipse (2010)

(Dir. David Slade; w/Kristen Stewart, Robert Pattinson, Taylor Lautner, Dakota Fanning)
✠ Vampires ✠ Werewolves ✠ Native Mysticism

I swear to Christopher Lee, Lon Chaney Jr., and the Manitou that I had no previous interest in *Twilight*. But this lushly photographed adrenaline candy action movie about warring teen vampires and Native American werewolves teaming up to go fang-and-claw against rogue bloodsuckers in the Pacific Northwest won me over just enough.

Aside from the great song "Friends" by Band of Skulls on the *New Moon* soundtrack, I promise that I won't go to bat for any other *Twilight* movie. If you can overcome your own understandable prejudice, try to think about the myriad goofball mainstream entry points that initially propelled you to heavy metal; you might enjoy *Eclipse*.

Bauhaus vocalist and king goth Peter Murphy makes a cameo here as "The Cold One," one of the original vampires. "I'm sure 'Bela Lugosi's Dead' helped inspire the naming of Bella," Murphy said, invoking the song Bauhaus performs in 1983's *The Hunger*. "I'm not a *Twilight* geek, but if I had to choose between Bela Lugosi and Bella Swan, I would choose Bella Swan."

Twitch of the Death Nerve (1971), aka A Bay of Blood; Blood Bath; Carnage; Last House on the Left—Pt. II

(Dir. Mario Bava; w/Claudine Auger, Luigi Pistilli)
✠ Italian Horror ✠ Slasher

Mario Bava's *Twitch of the Death Nerve* set the template for '80s slasher movies nearly a decade early (just as the perfect Slayer riffs found on Flower Travellin' Band's 1971 record *Satori* were a psychic premonition of thrash metal). Four teenagers venture into a woodland cabin on a bay, where they are stalked by an unseen assailant. One girl immediately skinny-dips and gets a hooked blade in her throat. A dude in the house takes the same blade to the face. The two remaining teens fuck in an upstairs bedroom until a killer thrusts a spear through both their bodies at once. Each of these murders is re-created, to varying degrees of exactness, in the first two *Friday the 13th* films, and it would be hard to tally the imitators who took over from there.

Twitch deviates from post-*Halloween* hack-'em-ups via a complicated husband-and-wife real-estate-scam plot. This realtor chicanery bloodily racks up its own body count, and the movie ends with the crooked spouses' own children happily shotgunning them to death. The total death count is thirteen. Make of that what you will (and what every exploitation movie maker in the U.S. eventually did).

Hallmark Releasing Corporation, which had successfully sold *Mark of the Devil* (1970) as "the First Film Rated V for Violence," retitled *Twitch* as *Carnage* and peddled it in America as "the Second Film Rated V for Violence." Twitch of the Death Nerve is also a band from England, and the title of songs by bands including Blue Holocaust, Dead Child, Serpent Eclipse, and Subm

The Ultimate Revenge: Combat Tour Live (1985)

(Dir. Tony DeMartino; w/Slayer, Exodus, Venom)
✖ Thrash Metal ✖ Concert Footage

The prime-era thrash metal video documentary *The Ultimate Revenge: Combat Tour Live '85* opens with the image of a *Saturday Night Fever* poster going up in flames. Across the smoldering image, a superimposed dateline reads: "April 3, 1985, Studio 54, NYC." On the soundtrack, the unmistakable rallying cry of Exodus frontman Paul Baloff: "I wanna know how many of you people go out in the streets looking to kick someone's fuckin' ass. Maybe a couple of posers, you know, head on down to the local disco and hang out and waste a couple of people. . . . If you like metal, I wanna hear you fuckin' screeeam! Yeah! Yeeaah!! YEEEAAAHHH!!!"

Cut to a fired-up throng of denim-and-leather-encased teenage headbangers, all male, of various races, gathered around a police barricade outside, yes indeed, Manhattan's notorious disco palace, Studio 54. The long-haired kids throw horns, flip birds, and hail Satan, and they definitely all make sure to "fuckin' scream!" In the course of its first 120 seconds, *Ultimate Revenge Combat Tour* feverishly conveys what it was to be young, off the chain, and engulfed by thrash on the streets of New York City smack in the middle of the most metal of decades.

Inside Studio 54, Exodus blaze into "Piranha." Slayer follow with a blitzkrieg-quick "Die by the Sword," and then Venom take it to the heart of fog machine hell itself with a preexisting video promo clip for "Witching Hour." Three titanic forces, three different approaches, three prongs of metal might at various peaks of their upward onslaught.

Down "in the bowels of Studio 54," Venom's Cronos and Abaddon slug Jack Daniel's and liken the group's collective impact to that of "a brick." The interviewer jokes, "So there's no truth to the rumor you're going to sacrifice Madonna onstage tonight?" Cronos shoots back, "I would fuck her onstage!" Members of Slayer, about 666 sheets to the wind, remind us that "disco is dead" and pledge allegiance to Agnostic Front, Verbal Abuse, D.R.I., Black Flag, Bach, Beethoven, and Tchaikovsky. Then they perform "Antichrist," "Hell Awaits," and "Chemical Warfare." Cronos further expounds on the punk-metal crossover.

The original VHS release of *Ultimate Revenge Combat Tour Live '85* ends with a post-credits promo featuring a barked-out voice-over by "Major Mayhem" touting the latest releases by the three featured acts ("Ride with these guys and the devil is your copilot!"), followed by an accounting of Combat Records' "Special Forces" roster, which includes Talas, TKO, and Tokyo Blade. ("These boys specialize in administering violence, with taste!") "Combat Ranger" status is accorded to Megadeth, Abattoir, Savatage. ("If there's a dirty job to be done, you send in the rangers—and pray to God that you live!") Next, the "Combat Army" marches with Mercyful Fate, Oz, the Rods, and Trouble. ("Get your combat boots stompin'!") Finally, there's the "Combat Ultra Assassin Squad": Impaler. ("So hideous, even I don't get too near them!")

A follow-up, *Ultimate Revenge 2* (1992), showcases metal heading into a phase of genre-diversification. This October 1988 show, taped at Philadelphia's Trocadero, features Raven, Dark Angel, Death, Faith or Fear, and Forbidden. The bloom of the original's charming naïveté is, inevitably, gone; so, too, are any interview segments. Sometimes metal can be *too* stripped down, you know.

Under a Serpent Sun: The Story of At the Gates (2010)

(DIR. ANDERS BJÖRLER; W/ANDERS BJÖRLER, JONAS BJÖRLER, TOMAS LINDBERG, ADRIAN ERLANDSSON, MARTIN LARSSON, ALF SVENSSON)
✠ METAL HISTORY ✠ SWEDISH DEATH METAL

Under a Serpent Sun: The Story of At the Gates documents the evolutions and revolutions of the Swedish death metal deities quite literally from an insider's point-of-view; the director is guitarist Anders Björler. Multiple years in the making, *Under a Serpent Sun* is unsurprisingly meticulous its details and rich with photos, videos, and original interviews. What will make you kiss the burning sky, however, is how talented Björler proves to be as a filmmaker.

At the Gates emerged from the band Grotesque in 1990 and cocreated the limitlessly influential Gothenburg sound, a ruthlessly melodic variation of death metal. The band released five classic albums in six years and split up. Extreme metal felt every moment of the band's absence. The group reunited for shows in 2008, where

fans embraced them with fervor befitting long-lost heroes emerging as if they had never gone away . Over the course of a fast two hours and eight minutes, Björler recounts every high and low point with utterly fluid verbal and visual storytelling. As wicked as he is on guitar, Anders Björler is equally precise and targeted.

Under a Serpent Sun is the first disc in the triple-DVD 2010 release *At the Gates: The Flames of the End*. Disc two contains the band's instant-legend reunion show at Wacken Open Air 2008. Disc three collects twenty-six live performances from throughout the band's history. Anders Björler deemed *The Flames of the End*, "a fine last document," but a new 2014 album revived the ghost. Make more movies, Björler!

Under Surveillance

(2006), AKA Dark Chamber

(DIR. DAVE CAMPFIELD; W/ERIC CONLEY, FELISSA ROSE, MARK LOVE, DESIREE GOULD)
✠ RICKY KASSO

Twenty-plus years after he gouged out a drug buddy's eyes while insisting "Say you love Satan!" Long Island's "Acid King" killer Ricky Kasso was continuing to inspire fright flicks.

Under Surveillance tells the story of college-age Justin (Eric Conley), who moves into his father's apartment complex. When a female tenant is murdered in what seems to be a satanic ritual, Justin and his pals spy on the other residents. The amateur sleuths eventually turn up evidence of a diabolical cabal called the Black Circle. One character is named "Rick." Need to know more?

Shot for under twenty-five thousand dollars near the actual Kasso crime scene, *Under Surveillance* forgoes the normal horror sensationalism for more mannered suspense. The film reunites two key cast members of the horror classic *Sleepaway Camp* for small roles: Felissa Rose, who played Angela, and Desiree Gould, who was Aunt Martha. They are less memorable here.

Until the Light Takes Us (2008)

(DIRS. AARON AITES, AUDREY EWELL; W/VARG VIKERNES, FENRIZ, HELLHAMMER, ABBATH, FAUST)

✠ NORWEGIAN BLACK METAL

Everybody hates *Until the Light Takes Us*, and everybody is right for once. You probably already hate this movie, and you know exactly why. Still, *Until the Light Takes Us* is the highest-profile North American documentary to date on the infamous Norwegian black metal church burnings and lethal violence of the '90s. The film centers, as attention to this topic too often does, on Varg Vikernes, the former Count Grishnakh, who knifed to death fellow corpse-paint aficionado Øystein "Euronymous" Aarseth. Varg speaks at length from his dorm-like prison setup. He's loquacious, seductive, and convincing as he talks about Christianity forcibly usurping Norse spirituality and capitalist globalism poisoning the purity of nature's true order. He knows what topics to tap when wanting to jerk around big-city American media types who just want to think someone has been gosh-darned misunderstood.

Filmmakers Aaron Aites and Audrey Ewell have already been criticised for not pressing Varg to further elaborate on his racial anger and neo-Nazi ideology. They seem too busy being impressed with how Norway really aims to rehabilitate its murderers, unlike their mean old homeland. A missing piece that glares gallingly in this fact-based chronicle of black metal music makers is the mystifying lack of actual black metal music. The sound of black metal is repeatedly described; the coldness, the hardness, the darkness, and the open-sky sense of space. So many words about black metal are here, but so few actual songs.

Then, infuriatingly, Harmony Korine literally tap-dances into the picture. After more than an hour of prostrating attempts to get black metal taken seriously, the instantly despicable indie auteur squeals that he only listens to black metal because it's the most "evil music in the world." This is played over footage of Korine at some New York City art function, launching into shuck-and-jive gyrations that, in one of his "shock" videos, he would likely perform in blackface (and blackface, for sure, is not corpse paint).

Until someone makes a less hipster-ninny documentary on the topic, *Until the Light Takes Us* is the most complete presentation out there. Fenriz provides a quote on camera that, as usual, makes absolute comic but dead serious sense: "Part of me wishes this whole thing hadn't become a trend, but, you know, people like to dress up."

Up in Smoke (1978)

(DIR. LOU ADLER; W/CHEECH MARIN, TOMMY CHONG, STACY KEACH, TOM SKERRIT)

✠ DRUGS ✠ SOUNDTRACK (ALICE BOWIE BAND)

Cheech and Chong bring uproarious stoner antics from seed-and-stem-flecked record albums to the baked screen in their debut film. They pull off one of comedy's most perfect translations between media, a masterpiece of THC-soaked slapstick absurdity, and a warmhearted, red-eyed celluloid testament to the connection between heavy metal and the sweet leaf.

Up in Smoke's climactic "Rock Fight" was shot at the legendary Roxy on L.A.'s Sunset Strip. The audience is packed with many of the same punks who appear in Penelope Spheeris's documentary *The Decline and Fall of Western Civilization* (1979), rejects who made quick bucks for looking weird at early-morning movie shoots.

As the Alice Bowie Band, Cheech and Chong win the Rock Fight by performing the song "Earache My Eye." The pulverizing central riff powers a knockout metal hit that's been covered by Soundgarden, Korn (with and without Metallica), Rollins Band, Raging Slab, the Hookers, Scatterbrain, Cuff, and countless others. In concert, Rush has ended "The Big Money" with an homage to the opening thunderbolts of "Earache."

Reports of a new Cheech and Chong movie in 2014 single-handedly boosted marijuana consumption in 23 states.

VALHALLA (1986)

(DIRS. PETER MADSEN, JEFFREY J. VARAB; W/DICK KAYSO, PREBEN KRISTENSEN, LAURA BRO)
✖ COMIC BOOKS ✖ NORSE MYTHOLOGY

Based on a popular comic book and set in ancient Denmark, the animated *Valhalla* begins when Norse deities Thor and Loki drop by the woodland cottage of brother and sister Tjalfe and Røskva and offer to take them across the rainbow bridge to Asgard, home of the gods. Turns out it's a raw deal, as the kids immediately are put to work shining hammers and polishing thunderbolts. Fellow underage laborer Quark recruits Tjalfe and Røskva in a children's crusade against the higher-ups, leading to an epic skirmish of Danish kids versus gods and giants. Who wins? Well, you don't see any gods or giants around here, do you?

Valhalla was Denmark's first major effort at animated filmmaking. At $3.8 million, it was also the nation's most expensive production of 1986. In *Valhalla*'s German-language version, Thor is voiced, fluently, by Christopher Lee.

VALHALLA RISING (2009)

(DIR. NICOLAS WINDING REFN; W/MADS MIKKELSEN, MAARTEN STEVENSON, ALEXANDER MORTON)
✖ VIKINGS ✖ NATIVE AMERICANS ✖ TORTURE

Get ready to bang your head very slowly. One Eye (Mads Mikkelsen), a Viking captive named for the most logical of reasons, starts out tied to pole in the middle of a cold, muddy field in a.d. 1000. His bare torso reveals a lifetime of scarring horrors, some of which we see inflicted in graphic enough detail to rival *Martyrs* and *The Passion of the Christ*. In time, One Eye gorily slays his captors and heads for the hills, allowing a ten-year-old Aryan slave boy (Maarten Stevenson) to tag along. They encounter a squadron of freshly zealous Christian Norseman, hop on a longboat with them, and become lost in fog for what seems like an eternity.

Amidst the infinite cloudiness, One Eye and Blonde Kid's fellow travelers become spooked, and nastiness ensues. At long last, the boat lands in America. The Norsemen guess the natives ashore are either Arabs (the crew intended to hit the Holy Land) or demons. They soon discover that, whoever these tan-skinned locals are, they know a thing or two about greeting questionable visitors with arrows and clubs. At the end, One Eye makes a final, grand gesture.

Valhalla Rising is a little bit of masterpiece: beautifully mounted, expertly paced to cast a spell, and more or less unforgettable—if you can stay awake. While its title conjures the music of Enslaved or Amon Amarth at its most anthemic, *Valhalla Rising* is more akin to Sunn O)))'s day-long ambient drone-dirge beat-downs—paralyzingly slow, but uniquely rewarding. If you don't stick with it, nobody will blame you. Grand Magus did and wrote a song in tribute to the film.

Director Nicolas Winding Refn says he conceived *Valhalla Rising* as "an acid trip" and credits Mario Bava's *Planet of the Vampires* and Jodorowsky's *El Topo* as cinematic inspirations. He modeled One Eye's single prosthetic eye on the fake peeper worn by Kirk Douglas in *The Vikings* (1958). This film's original script had One Eye single-handedly defeating an entire army of Native Americans, then boarding a spaceship and blasting off to the stars. How could Refn not have gone with that?

Vampyros Lesbos (1971)

(Dir. Jesus Franco; w/Soledad Miranda, Ewa Strömberg, Dennis Price, Jesus Franco)
✠ Lesbians ✠ Vampires

Spooky beauty Soledad Miranda stars as Countess Nadine Oskudar, a centuries-old sapphic succubus who seduces new blood on her private island off the coast of Turkey. The countess sets her sights, fangs, and other sexily unshaven parts on Ewa Strömberg, playing a German traveler. They lock holes for an unholy affair to last through eternity.

Vampyros Lesbos is the artistic zenith of Jesus "Jess" Franco, Spain's maniacal moviemaking machine behind some of the most—and least—remarkable European horror and exploitation films from the 1960s to the 1980s. Lovely Miranda served as Franco's most inspiring artistic muse. The dedication the director put into her signature vehicle shows in the unsettling atmospheres, sumptuous art direction, and omnipresent sexuality that forces you to embrace the word erotic without embarrassment, even when speaking about it out loud. That's no mean feat, but *Vampyros Lesbos* is no mere lesbian vampire flick.

At age sixteen, Soledad Miranda became an international cinema sensation as a fresh-faced, singing and dancing ingénue in a variety of features released over the first half of the 1960s. She reinvented herself between 1969 and 1970, embarking on a remarkable run of films with Jess Franco that includes *The Devil Came From Akasava*, *Eugénie de Sade*, *Juliette*, *Nightmares*

Come at Night, *She Killed in Ecstasy*, and, of course, *Vampyros Lesbos*. While transforming into the premier mysterious goth goddess of the movies, she died tragically in a car accident just before *Vampyros Lesbos* opened. Her beauty, talent, and one-of-a-kind screen presence, thanks largely to this film, remain immortal.

La Venganza de los Punks (1987)

(Dir. Damian Acosta Esparza; w/Juan Valentin, El Fantasma, Olga Rios, Laura Tovar)
✠ Satan ✠ Black Mass ✠ Satanic Orgy
✠ Revenge

Mexico's delightfully maniacal *Intrepidos Punks* (1983) infused a classic 1960s biker-movie plot with a sprinkle of '70s backwoods devil worship and a smoking shitload of early-'80s post–*Road Warrior* color, costumes, high-octane death machines, and wildly attired mayhem vendors. The sequel maintains all those previous ingredients but lunges the mix deep, hard, and viciously into rogue cop revenge, slasher movie splatter, and explicit satanic sex. Marco (Juan Valentin), the cop who imprisoned *Intrepidos Punks* leader Tarzan (El Fantasma), opens the movie with a large family celebration of his daughter's fifteenth birthday. Just as she's about to blow out her candles, the punks barge in and massacre everyone in sight, pausing only to rape the females, including the quinceañera girl.

Tarzan leaves Marco alive, however, to suffer over the horror he brought down upon his loved ones. And suffer Marco does, but not a fraction as heinously as the Punks do once the unhinged lawman transforms himself into a merciless agent of torture and slaughter. Before their day of reckoning, the punks celebrate their evil deeds with a full-on Black Mass before a glowing-eyed statue of Satan. Tarzan leads the gathering in a full-face, rainbow-hued dunce cap and a red cape. He sacrifices some kind of animal—a goat, a dog, or maybe el chupacabra—and his minions carnally commune in the beast's blood.

Alas, their Dark Lord forsakes them once Marco comes poking around their desert cave headquarters. One by one, the killer cop pulverizes the punks (male and female alike) through brutal and elaborate executions that include acid dumping, decapitation, head-spiking, fatal whipping, flamethrower incineration, a snake pit, and asshole impalement. *Venganza* is ugly and sweet.

Whereas *Intrepidos Punks'* music was bluesy garage psych, with a few crucial years of the 1980s passing between films, *Venganza's* score heads hard into heavy metal. Neither film boasts an actual "punk" soundtrack. Tarzan's pre-orgy, Spanish-language rallying cry translates as "Long live death! Long live cocaine! Long live weed! Long live alcohol!" Two years later, like the spawn of some kind of post-disaster baby boom, the band Brujeria was born in Los Angeles.

ᴠERLIERER (1987)

(DIR. BERND SCHADEWALD; W/MARIO IRREK, RALF RICHTER, VIOLENT FORCE)

✷ COLD WAR ✷ METAL GANGS ✷ SOUNDTRACK (DIE TOTEN HOSEN, VIOLENT FORCE)

Verlierer proves that punky new-wave heavy metal urban warfare gangs of the 1980s were not restricted to Cannon Films' Charles Bronson wrecking machines or Italian post-nuke potboilers. *Nein!* The colorfully attired mayhem makers in *Verlierer* live (and die and kill and maim) in Essen, Germany's Ruhrgebiet region, during the downtime between its being the drab industrial hub of Germania and being reincarnated as a gentrified hotspot. These violent, hateful kids— the *verlierers*, or "losers"—emerge like unwanted pests from within the cultural cracks.

Wherever the streets are mean, the cops are creeps, and parents, as ever, just don't understand, heavy metal unites the youth just as surely teenage arrogance and dead-end ignorance will divide them into warring factions. On one side of town strut the Getto Sharks, a ragtag hodgepodge of scruffy ruffians under the command of oily-pompadoured meanie Richy (Ralf Richter).

They would be considered the metal kids in a mainstream American movie of the time. Across the tracks are the more truly metal Rats, a swarm of hoodlums clad in proper black leather jackets and denim battle vests.

Drama arises when Richy's kid brother Mücke (Mario Irrek) wants to join the Sharks (at one point, he even yells, "*Ich bein ein* Shark!"). Richy can't help but want to drop-kick the young fool in any direction away from such a dumb-shit prospect. Between intramural showdowns and throwdowns, each gang harasses and violates the local residents to varying degrees. Quite a tear through a mall ensues as "Eighties" by Killing Joke plays. The lead-up to the big rumble, a battle with pipes, chains, and switchblades, is actually set to the "Baseball Furies Chase" theme from *The Warriors!*

This Heavy Metal Movie careens into precious metal relic territory via a concert sequence where Teutonic thrash battalion Violent Force elicits fresh-flung mosh sweat while ripping through the song "Dead City" at hardcore speed. The enthusiastic performance depicted in loving detail is probably unique in cinema in capturing deathly thrash metal moments before erupting into full-force death metal.

Watch for a secondary gang member played by Campino of Die Toten Hosen, and for an appearance by Mille Petrozza of Kreator. Like the soundtrack of *Heavy Metal* (1981), for some reason the *Verlierer* soundtrack also includes a Stevie Nicks number.

ᴠICE ꙅQUAD (1982)

(DIR. GARY SHERMAN; W/WINGS HAUSER, SEASON HUBLEY, GARY SWANSON, FRED BERRY)

✷ SUNSET STRIP ✷ SOUNDTRACK ("NEON SLIME")

Director Gary Sherman's scabrous potboiler *Vice Squad* is the cinematic embodiment of scary scumbag Los Angeles that got so searingly summed up in sonic form five years later by Guns N' Roses on "Welcome to the Jungle." Taking place over one berserk, exhausting, dusk-

Clockwise from top: *Brazilians Sepultura reaching out to Spain in* Under Siege; Videodrome *quad poster; tasteful original French treatment for* A Virgin Among the Living Dead; Virgin Witch *Spanish poster avoids the hype title* Lesbian Twins

to-dawn stretch, *Vice Squad* tracks the capture, escape, and pursuit of psycho pimp Ramrod (Wings Hauser). The action thereby snakes us through hustler strolls, players' bars, kinky trick scenes, back-alley black markets, and frantic police roundups in Hollywood.

Season Hubley, hot off playing a porn actress in *Hardcore* (1979), essentially re-creates and deepens that role as Princess, the streetwalker at the heart of Ramrod's rage. Gary Swanson as the lead detective is rock solid, and Maurice Emanuel as his cornrow-adorned partner is funky cool personified. Watch for a breakout turn by Nina Blackwood, MTV's original blonde VJ vixen. She sets the savagery in motion powerfully as Ginger, a junkie hooker who attempts to flee Ramrod only to fall prey to his evil charm, and then to his even more evil expertise with a wire hanger. Also Fred Berry—Rerun from *What's Happening!!*—is a riot as "Sugar Pimp." Ramrod claims Sugar and his types have no balls, and then enforces that opinion with his hard-squeezing bare hands.

From frame one, though, *Vice Squad* is Wings Hauser's movie. Familiar to soap opera fans for playing an all-around swell fella on *The Young and the Restless,* Hauser rampages all over every scene—including the ones he's not in—like a Brahma bull on anally injected bath salts. Ramrod may be the most frightening villain in the annals of grindhouse action films and, to be sure, *Vice Squad* ranks high, hard, and hellacious among the genre's greatest kicks to the cranium.

Vice Squad exploded in January 1982, drawing long lines to neighborhood theaters and tawdry trash-pit showplaces alike. It ultimately grossed more than $80 million world wide on an initial investment of $2 million and change. The film's success ignited a familiar chorus among the usual bellyachers, braying "What have we come to?!" The *New York Times* ran a four-page moan about the new level of brutality at the movies. *Newsweek*'s similar *Vice Squad* review appeared under the headline "State of the 'R'."

In lieu of "Welcome to the Jungle," *Vice Squad* offers its own grinding, grimy theme song, the sleaze-bucket blues howl "Neon Slime." Not quite metal, "Neon Slime" is a wicked, hard-rock gut-plunger, with Hauser puking out words about specific street atrocities over a wrenching heavy-blues guitar lead. Director Sherman says that he worked on the concept along with lyricist Simon Stokes and composer Joe Renzetti. They called Hauser, who had his own rock band on the side, to come over and bark it out on the spot. The rest is opening-and-closing-theme history. No metal band that I'm aware of has yet recorded a cover of "Neon Slime." Do it!

VICIOUS LIPS (1986), AKA PLEASURE PLANET

(DIR. ALBERT PYUN; W/DRU-ANNE PERRY, GINA CALABRESE, LINDA KERRIDGE, SHAYNE FARRIS)

✡ HAIR METAL ✡ SCIENCE FICTION

Vicious Lips is named for its heroines: an energetically rocking female foursome who look and sound almost uncannily like the midpoint between Poison and the Bangles. If the Vicious Lips can get themselves off earth, they will perform a gig at the Radioactive Dream, the hottest rock club in the galaxy. Their mission involves getting onboard a spaceship with a none too securely caged monster (Christian Andrews), but then crash-landing on a planet where they meet two sexily bare-assed blonde desert dwellers (Jacki Easton Toelle and Tanya Papanicolas).

The Radioactive Dream club strongly resembles the titular gathering hole in the post-nuke porn masterpiece *Café Flesh* (1982). Manager Maxine Mortogo (Mary Anne Graves) brings to mind both Anne Carlisle in *Liquid Sky* (1982) and Lois Ayers in the Dark Brothers' *The Devil in Miss Jones 3* and *4* (1985/86). All of *Vicious Lips* looks similarly hyper–new wave, albeit five years too late to the geometric makeup airbrush tutorial.

Hair metal to the rescue! With the closing number, "Lunar Madness," the movie goes out on a fine galloping beat worthy of *Headbangers Ball.* Vicious Lips' music is performed by Sue Saad, ex-frontwoman of L.A. new wave squad Sue Saad and the Next. The group also contributed songs to *Roadie* (1980), *Looker* (1981), and Albert Pyun's previous effort, *Radioactive Dreams* (1985)—saluted here via the name of the rock club.

VIDEODROME (1983)

(Dir. David Cronenberg; w/James Woods, Deborah Harry, Sonja Smits, Jack Creley)

✠ Horror ✠ Censorship ✠ Snuff

By 1983, sci-fi/horror mindblower David Cronenberg (*Scanners*) could see Big Brother–esque censorship cabals such as the heavy metal–hating PMRC on the immediate horizon, and he responded in Cronenberg fashion. In the film of the same name, Videodrome is the moniker of a shadowy television service that plays sick and sadistic snuff porn. The content catches the eye of small-time TV station owner Max Renn (James Woods), always on the prowl for a newly sensational attraction. Renn investigates the source of Videodrome and uncovers a global conspiracy of mind control through televised body manipulation; anyone who watches Videodrome is stricken with a cancer ray contained in the broadcast itself.

The organization behind Videodrome explains its motivation simply: anyone who would watch anything like Videodrome deserves to be punished and exterminated. En route to its apocalyptic climax, Cronenberg's vision bends and warps the parameters of reality. Renn experiences grotesque hallucinations that viscerally surpass all previous limits of "body horror." The wild images are anchored throughout by Woods's command performance.

Videodrome is Cronenberg's masterwork, a heady, heavy trip that specifically reaches out to anyone who patrol the outskirts of "acceptable" behaviors and entertainments. "Stay free" is the movie's fundamentally metal message, "and chase that freedom to whatever weird extremes it requires." In the age of the Internet, social media, and instant communication, things will only ever get weirder. And faster. and more dangerous Long live the (forever mutating) new flesh.

Cronenberg's inspiration for *Videodrome* was the notorious 1977 Heavy Metal Movie shocker *Emanuelle in America*, directed by Joe D'Amato and starring Laura Gemser; the film represented the soft-core Black Emanuelle series' freakish leap into nihilism, torture, pseudo-snuff, and hard-core bestiality. Lonely in a hotel one late night, Cronenberg turned on the TV, caught *Emanuelle in America* and wondered what kind of creep would watch this stuff. And then he realized he was still watching. He wondered, from there, about those in power who would act further on his initial feelings of repulsion and moral superiority. *Videodrome* resulted.

VIOLENT SHIT (1989)

(Dir. Andreas Schnaas; w/Andreas Schnaas, Karl Inger, Gabi Bäzner, Wolfgang Hinz)

✠ Extreme Gore ✠ Christ Killing ✠ Cannibalism

Defining "fucked up" in a heavy metal context as only Germans can (see also Lucifer's Friend, Living Death, and Rammstein), *Violent Shit* is a just-the-splats story of mom-cleaving kid Karl who grows up to be notorious murder junkie known as the Butcher (played by writer-director Andreas Schnaas). The Butcher breaks out of jails, slaughters all he comes across, and occasionally pauses to cannibalize a victim. With each kill, his skin further rots off his bones.

When the Butcher encounters a vision of Christ in a forest, he hacks the Messiah open, then slays a few more people outside a church before his own body gives out. The final moments consist of the Butcher tearing his flesh open and peeling it apart, revealing a blood-covered baby inside. As noted: Germany. There's no place else like it. No scheiße. A Violent Shit band appeared in Colombia, and various sordid underground acts including Funeral Rape, Funeral Moon, and Putrid Scum scribbled together songs by the name.

Violent Shit debuted as Germany's first direct-to-video movie in 1989. Three sequels followed:

Violent Shit II: Mother Hold My Hand (1992); Violent Shit III: Infantry of Doom, aka Zombie Doom (1999); and Karl the Butcher vs. Axe (2010).

The Schnaas-made Nikos the Impaler (2003) is not an official sequel, but occasionally turns up as Violent Shit 4: Nikos. Of all the Schnaas movies, Nikos is the best, dealing with an ancient Romanian barbarian resurrected at a snooty New York gallery opening. He massacres the fuck out of every art-douche within sword-slashing distance until he is sent back from whence he came by way of a ceremony involving a vampire woman and Hitler.

A Virgin Among the Living Dead (1973),
AKA Christine, Princess of Eroticism; Zombie 4
(DIR. JESS FRANCO; W/CHRISTINA VON BLANC, BRITT NICHOLS, LINDA HASTREITER, ANNE LIBERT)
✠ Lesbians ✠ Vampires ✠ Haunted House

The virgin among the living dead in A Virgin Among the Living Dead is nubile young Christine (Christina von Blanc), who is haunted by dreams of a giant black phallus and lives forever afraid of the Queen of Darkness (Anne Libert). The living dead may be Christine's ghostly relatives who haunt the spooky castle that she's visiting, or they may be the zombies who turn up, seemingly spliced in from another movie (those creatures would, in fact, actually later get spliced into 1981's Zombie Lake). However you decipher it, A Virgin Among the Living Dead is metal enough to watch. But don't bang your head too hard trying to make sense of it.

Hyper-prolific Spanish director Jess (aka Jesús) Franco does his typical zoom-lens-happy spin on steamy, seamy erotic horror, save for a dream sequence lensed by French wine-zombie director Jean Rollin (Les Raisins de la Mort). Once you know the backstory, A Virgin Among the Living Dead becomes oddly poignant. Following the success of his Vampyros Lesbos (1971), Franco

signed a multipicture deal to create more cinematic showcases for the star of that film—and his creative muse—Soledad Miranda. Tragically, Miranda was killed in a car accident, and A Virgin Among the Living Dead is the first film Franco made in her absence.

Virgin Witch (1972),
AKA Lesbian Twins
(DIR. RAY AUSTIN; W/ANN MICHELLE, VICKI MICHELLE, PATRICIA HAINES, PETER CUSHING)
✠ Lesbian Witch

Twin sisters Ann Michelle and Vicki Michelle star as Christine and Betty, respectively, in Virgin Witch. They're models out to hit it big in swinging London. Christine catches the eye of fashion agent Sybil Waite (Patricia Haines), who is in fact a witch on the prowl for a virgin to induct into her coven.

After Christine eagerly volunteers to be deflowered during an occult ceremony, Sybil eyeballs Betty next. Whatever tension exists is pricked by copious nudity and lots of ritual dancing in praise of Satan. Sexy witchcraft is heavy.

Virgin Witch played in some regions under the title Lesbian Twins. Despite the Michelle siblings being in the buff for a chunk of the movie's running time, Ann and Vicki do not make good on lurid implications of that alternate moniker. Four years later, American sisters Brooke Young and Taylor Young went on to violate any and all screen taboos regarding "twincest" in the hardcore porn curiosity Teenage Twins. Weirder still is that Teenage Twins is loaded with the sort of black magic ceremonies and aesthetics that go on in Virgin Witch—pushing them to the extreme point where a Bible is used as a masturbation aid. You've never done that—have you?

THE VISITOR (1979), AKA STRIDULUM

(DIR. GIULIO PARADISI (AS MICHAEL J. PARADISE); W/ JOHN HUSTON, MEL FERRER, SAM PECKINPAH)

✠ ANTICHRIST ✠ SATAN ✠ SCI-FI/HORROR

A prog-metal mind-melt conjured by an off-the-cocaine-rails cabal of sci-fi-mad late-'70s Hollywood and Italian exploitation movie mavens, *The Visitor* is, like the concept of "rock opera," a thing that should not be. Yet the movie rocks and it's operatic and here we are, heads banging. Telekinetic eight-year-old Katy Collins (Paige Connor) is imbued with the cosmos-cracking power of "Sateen," placing her precariously in a universe-wide tug-of-existential-war between Jerzy Colsowicz (John Huston), God's man from a planetoid full of bald kids, and a universal bad guy whose name sounds a lot like, well, "Sateen." The fact that crusty, hunched-over, Methuselah-like Jerzy travels from the stars and comes into Katy's life by way of a babysitting service is charmingly indicative of how tenuously *The Visitor* connects to our human experience of sanity.

Lance Henriksen resembles a hero as Katy's surrogate stepdad; Joanne Nail is overwhelmed by the sheer weirdness around her as her mother; and the rest of the cast is padded with such golden-age movie stars as Glenn Ford, Shelley Winters, and Mel Ferrer. Aside from the mighty John Huston (director of *The Maltese Falcon*), legendary hard-boiled filmmaker Sam Peckinpah (*Bring Me the Head of Alfredo Garcia*) turns up (and turns his back repeatedly to the camera) as an abortion provider. Best of all is international action superstar Franco Nero portraying—you did *not* guess it—Jesus Christ.

The Visitor is strangely paced and presents utter lunacy as a simple series of given facts, each of which works. The film's popping and pulsing optical visual effects ooze and float off the screen like black-light posters and pulp fantasy illustrations come to cannabis-facilitated life. Acid rock and stoner metal devotees will be hard pressed to find so simultaneously raging and laid-back a cinematic experience as this.

Producer and screenwriter Ovidio G. Assonitis arrived at *The Visitor* after cocreating the *Exorcist* rip-off *Beyond the Door* (1974) and the *Jaws* rip-off *Tentacles* (1977). He maintained his highly metal lowbrow movie run in the decades ahead, producing, among other nutty knockouts, *Piranha II: The Spawning* (1981), *The Curse* (1987), *Iron Warrior* (1987), *Beyond the Door III* (1980), *Sonny Boy* (1989), *Lambada* (1991), and two of the five *American Ninja* adventures.

VIY (1967), AKA SPIRIT OF EVIL

(DIRS. KONSTANTIN YERSHOV, GEORGI KROPACHYOV; W/ LEONID KURAVLEV, NATALYA VARLEY)

✠ WITCHCRAFT ✠ SOVIETS

Adapted from a spooky story by Nikolai Gogol (and based on Ukranian folklore), *Viy* is the story of young seminarian Khoma (Leonid Kuravlyov), who, in order to become a priest, must survive a three-day prayer watch over the corpse of Pannochka (Natalya), a sexy witch who is not going to the afterlife quietly. To keep the undead sorceress trapped where she is, Khoma draws an imprisoning circle in holy chalk around her resting place. Pannochka spectacularly battles back by unleashing ghosts, zombies, demons, and other stunning residents of hell, each of whom does his or her damnedest to break down God's barrier.

Viy boasts visually luscious special effects, taut pacing, and the scary air of a terrifically absorbing fairy tale. The witch rides her coffin like a broom, mutants and monsters spill forth from walls, and then a giant hand suddenly soars up from the floor. Of special interest is that *Viy* was the first horror film sanctioned and produced by the Soviet government. Even under a totalitarian regime, the public's love of occult lore and visceral sensations needed to be slaked—a fact the Soviets acknowledged again with the 1989 Moscow Music Peace Festival that featured Scorpions, Mötley Crüe, Skid Row, Cinderella, and a fresh-from-rehab Ozzy Osbourne. Bon Jovi was there, too—was that anti-U.S. propaganda?

A big-budget 2014 remake, *Viy 3-D*, broke Russian box office records, and the *Viy* story surfaces in Russian metal.

VOLIMINAL: INSIDE THE NINE (2006)

(DIR. SHAWN "CLOWN" CRAHAN; W/SLIPKNOT)
✵ METAL HISTORY ✵ CONCERT FOOTAGE

Slipknot percussionist Shawn "Clown" Crahan spews forth a crazed, impressively impressionistic portrait of Iowa's dirtiest three-quarters-of-a-dozen as the band toxically crop-dusts the planet in support of its 2005 album, *Vol. 3. (The Subliminal Verses)*. *Voliminal: Inside the Nine* splatters a whole lot of Slipknot over two DVDs. The first contains Crahan's nonlinear documentary, which consists of randomly ordered, rapid-fire footage shot with handheld cameras. We see chaotic snatches of performances, practices, backstage booze challenges and road tripping.

As a film, Crahan's vision keeps with Slipknot's mission to demolish expectations and bust apart genres. At times the experience is even stomach-turning, with lots of epileptic editing, and lots and lots of roadies puking. Disc two takes a more straightforward approach, showcasing interviews, full songs taken from concerts across the globe, and music videos.

Disc one features a Slipknot jam session with the band members out of their famous masks and uniforms. Their faces are digitally blurred, but this is still as unguarded an interlude as we've ever gotten from these impeccable masterminds of mayhem. Frontman Corey Taylor explains it all: "Being in Slipknot is a lot like having cysts removed from your body. It's got to be done, and at the end of the day, it feels really, really good."

WAR OF THE GARGANTUAS ✤ FRANKENSTEIN'S MONSTERS: SANDA VS. GAIRA ✤ WARLORDS OF THE 21ST CENTURY ✤ WARRIOR OF THE LOST WORLD ✤ THE WARRIORS ✤ WARRIORS OF THE APOCALYPSE ✤ WARRIORS OF THE WASTELAND ✤ WAYNE'S WORLD ✤ WAYNE'S WORLD 2 ✤ WE SOLD OUR SOULS FOR ROCK N' ROLL ✤ WENDIGO ✤ THE WEREWOLF VS. THE VAMPIRE WOMAN ✤ WEREWOLF SHADOW ✤ WEREWOLVES ON WHEELS ✤ WEST OF MEMPHIS ✤ WHEELS OF FIRE ✤ WHERE EVIL DWELLS ✤ WHITE BUFFALO ✤ WHITE SLAVE ✤ WHITE ZOMBIE ✤ WICKED LAKE ✤ THE WICKER MAN ✤ THE WILD ANGELS ✤ WILD AT HEART ✤ THE WILD LIFE ✤ WINGS OF THE CROW ✤ WITCHBOARD ✤ WITCHCRAFT '70 ✤ WITCHERY ✤ LA CASA 4, WITCHCRAFT ✤ WITCHFINDER GENERAL ✤ WITHOUT WARNING ✤ WIZARDS ✤ WOODSTOCK ✤ WORKING CLASS ROCK STAR ✤ WORLD GONE WILD ✤ THE WORLD'S GREATEST SINNER ✤ THE WRESTLER

WAR OF THE GARGANTUAS (1966), AKA FRANKENSTEIN'S MONSTERS: SANDA VS. GAIRA

(DIR. ISHIRO HONDA; W/RUSS TAMBLYN, KUMI MIZUNO, KENJI SAHARA)

✤ MONSTERS

Because the supremely weird *Frankenstein Conquers the World* (1965) apparently wasn't weird enough—and that mind-melter features an eighty-foot-tall Frankenstein wrestling dinosaurs—Toho Studios doubled the freakadelic man-in-suit fun in its even more spectacular sequel, *War of the Gargantuas*. The battling gargantuas at hand are giant beast brothers—one brown, one green—cultivated from the cells of the original Frankenstein after he was done conquering the world. They are King Kong–size and gorilla-like, but with faces resembling '50s-era caveman novelty masks carved out of stone.

The brown one, named Sanda, was raised by caring scientists (Russ Tamblyn and Kumi Mizno) and resides peacefully in the Japanese Alps. The green meanie, named Gaira, grew up underwater, clearly pissed off. He voraciously hankers for human meat. Gaira's eating tour begins with smashing ships and then laying waste to Tokyo International Airport, scooping up travelers to devour with every pummel. Once Sanda notices the carnage, the monster-size conflict of the title is on, with the gargantuan brothers whaling the tar out of one another.

War of the Gargantuas is an avalanche of fun, especially as a way-out side trip within Toho's *Godzilla*-dominated universe. The creatures are extremely lovable (do not miss baby Sanda at home with his foster parents) and the action is fantastic. The cover art of the 2013 Phil Anselmo/Warbeast split EP *War of the Gargantuas* is a tribute to the movie. Anselmo is depicted as the tender Sanda, while Warbeast (and ex-Rigor Mortis) frontman Bruce Corbitt is pictured as temperamental Gaira.

WARLORD: . . . AND THE CANNONS OF DESTRUCTION HAVE BEGUN (1984)

(DIR. UNKNOWN; W/MARK ZONDER, WILLIAM J. TSAMIS, DAMIEN KING II)

✤ METAL VIDEOS ✤ CONCERT FOOTAGE

On their ambitious home video, relatively unknown but determined early-'80s L.A. power metal band Warlord prove that they possessed the songs, the instrumental chops, and the stage presence to break out of the Metal Blade stable and rise through the ranks. Before they had even recorded a full album, they borrowed Slayer's fog machine to shoot this fantastically weird, forty-minute underground classic.

All Warlord lacked was a sensible plan under all those heaps of hair. Aiming straight for top, they rented out a large theater and filmed a full-scale concert, without an audience—and never having played live. Promoting the band's albums by direct-marketing the video to metal fans made some sense. Bypassing the drudgery of touring was just crazy enough to work—but it did not.

The . . . *And the Cannons* VHS tape captures the most professional-sounding and self-assured amateur band you will ever see. After a prelude featuring a burning logo and some important-sounding narration, the band erupts into "Lucifer's Hammer." This masterfully executed classic stood out on the *Metal Massacre II* compilation. Six songs follow, showcasing Warlord's epic grandeur and deep love of European metal. Between numbers, band members stiffly recite statements of purpose about Warlord's techniques, declaring the band's greatness. You will get an earful of their "minds-first philosophy," and learn how they have been influenced by the early works of Bach and the Scorpions.

Unfortunately for Warlord, classic heavy metal fell out of favor, and those ever-present smoke machines got a lot more use with Slayer. Warlord went through a slew of singers, but this video, intended as a launching pad, became the band's early shining moment. All that changed in the 2000s, when Joacim Cans from Swedish neo-traditionalists Hammerfall took over the vocals of a revitalized Warlord. Lucifer's Hammer smashes again mightily for this four-man strike force.

WARLORDS OF THE 21ST CENTURY (1982), AKA BATTLETRUCK

(DIR. HARLEY COKELISS; W/MICHAEL BECK, ANNIE McENROE, JAMES WAINWRIGHT, JOHN RATZENBERGER)

✤ POST-APOCALYPSE ✤ CARS

New Zealand's rocking contribution to the *Road Warrior* rip-off boom of the early '80s, *Warlords of the 21st Century* delivers the most singularly metal vehicle in any of these movies: the massive, black, iron-and-steel super-tank known as the Battletruck. That thing's piloted by bad guys, headed up by evil Colonel Straker (James Wainright). The good guys are led by Hunter (Michael Beck, aka Swan from *The Warriors*), who rides a tricked-out dirt bike. Everybody fights and the vehicular mayhem rocks. The Aussies may have perfected futuristic-car-crash cinema, but the kiwis do themselves proud.

Nineteen eighty-two was the year of Michael Beck behind the handlebars of some spectacularly goofy/goofily spectacular motorcycle variations. In addition to *Warlords of the 21st Century*, Beck also starred as Dallas in *Megaforce*.

WARRIOR OF THE LOST WORLD (1983), AKA MAD RIDER

(DIR. DAVID WORTH; W/ROBERT GINTY, PERSIS KHAMBATTA, DONALD PLEASENCE, FRED WILLIAMSON)

✤ POST-APOCALYPSE ✤ MEGAWEAPON

Robert Ginty, while awaiting flamethrower upgrades between *The Exterminator* (1980) and *Exterminator 2* (1984), stars in *Warrior of the Lost World*. He plays the Rider, a seeker of higher consciousness who rides a talking motorcycle equipped with a brain, called Einstein. On the other side of some kind of a crack in the cosmos, Enlightened Elders select the Rider to lead rebels called the Outsiders against Omega, a post-nuke totalitarian state controlled by the evil Prossor (Donald Pleasence).

The Rider, teamed with Enlightened Elder made sexy woman Nastassia (Persis Khambatta), defeats mutants known as the Marginals (who look like your assembly-line *Road Warrior* rip-off punks, ninjas, and amazons) and then destroys Omega's flashiest defense vehicle, a lethally tricked-out truck deemed the Megaweapon. *Warrior of the Lost World* is enjoyable Italian trash-fun with sufficiently headbanging metal aesthetic.

Just a year prior to *Warrior of the Lost World*, Persis Khambatta (best known as the bald chick in the first *Star Trek* movie) starred as Major Zara in the high-octane/heavy machinery metal movie favorite *Megaforce*. She returned to post-apocalypse sci-fi in *She Wolves of the Wasteland* (1988), where she plays head villainess Cobalt, who aims to aims to conquer a scorched Earth where only female warriors and one man survive.

The same year as *Warrior of the Lost World*, Fred Williamson took a more prominent role in another glowing spaghetti-nuke nugget, *Warriors of the Wasteland*.

THE WARRIORS (1979)

(DIR. WALTER HILL; W/MICHAEL BECK, JAMES REMAR, DEBORAH VAN VALKENBURGH, DAVID PATRICK KELLY)

✠ URBAN WARFARE ✠ DENIM AND LEATHER

The Warriors, Walter Hill's surreal fantasia of teenage gang violence in a stylized New York hellscape, is the single touchstone film that unites each of the city's three biggest hard rock subcultures: metal, punk, and hip-hop. Based on a 1965 novel that was, in turn, inspired by the ancient Greek adventure text *Anabasis*, *The Warriors* chronicles the Coney Island–based gang of the movie's title across their dark night on the run back home after wrongly being accused of assassinating messianic outcast organizer Cyrus (Roger Hill) up in the Bronx.

"Can you COUNT, suckers?" Cyrus preaches to a crowd of thousands of garishly attired gangs gathered in a public park to hear his message. "I say the future is ours . . . if you can COUNT."

Adding up numbers of "hard-core members" in the five boroughs, Cyrus intones: "That's sixty thousand soldiers. Now there ain't but twenty thousand police in the whole town. Can you dig it? CAN you DIG it? CAN YOU DIG IT!?!" The throngs erupt in geysers of rapture. Anyone who ever felt embraced by heavy metal (or punk or hip-hop) will feel a joyful chill of recognition.

Cyrus gets wasted, and the Warriors get a bum rap courtesy of the slimily insane Luther (David Patrick Kelly) of the Rogues—who actually committed the murder. So begins an saga through subway tunnels and unknown neighborhoods that has since become a parade of iconic cinema encounters: the two-bit Orphans; the all-girl Lizzies; Ajax (James Remar) vs. the decoy cop (Mercedes Ruehl); the roller-skating squad simply known as the Punks; the intel gathering by the Turnbull ACs; the attack of the Baseball Furies; and Luther's finger-clinking "War-eee-uhzz . . . come out to play-aayyyy!" that sets up the final showdown on the sands of Coney Island.

In this rock and roll rebel rampage, the single most metal gang in the movie, the Baseball Furies, also provides one of the most metal moments in all of movie history. Bedecked in pinstriped uniforms and multicolored corpse-paint, these mute freaks charge forward to a terrifying synthesizer score, running through Central Park like automatons at midnight, swinging their Louisville Sluggers with cataclysmic force. Various real-life bands in numerous genres have adopted the look and even the name of the Baseball Furies, but there is no mistaking that the original lineup bleeds pure New York–style black metal.

The Warriors' initial ad campaign was a thing of

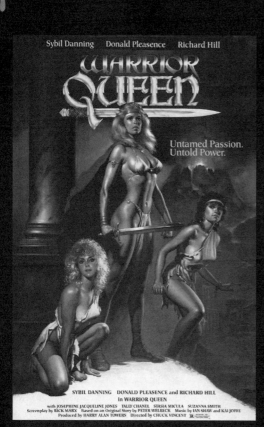

Sybil Danning   Donald Pleasence   Richard Hill

WARRIOR QUEEN

Untamed Passion.
Untold Power.

SYBIL DANNING, DONALD PLEASENCE and RICHARD HILL
in WARRIOR QUEEN
with JOSEPHINE JACQUELINE JONES · TALLY CHANEL · STASIA MICULA · SUZANNA SMITH
Screenplay by RICK MARX · Based on an Original Story by PETER WELBECK · Music by IAN SHAW and KAI JOFFE
Produced by HARRY ALAN TOWERS · Directed by CHUCK VINCENT

Warriors of the Apocalypse

ROBERT GINTY   PERSIS KHAMBATTA
DONALD PLEASENCE

mit FRED WILLIAMSON
HARRISON MULLER

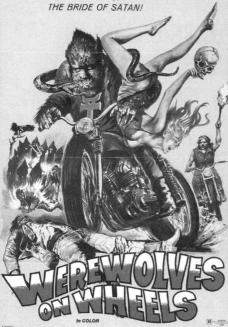

THIS GANG THOUGHT IT WAS TOUGH...

'til it found a new type of hell...
THE BRIDE OF SATAN!

WEREWOLVES ON WHEELS

In COLOR

STEPHEN OLIVER · SEVERN DARDEN

THE LAST WARRIOR

Der Kämpfer einer verlorenen Welt

TIVOLI   DAVID WORTH

Clockwise from top left: Warrior Queen *rendered by
Boris Vallejo;* Warriors of the Apocalypse; Warriors of
the Wasteland *aka* The Last Warrior; Werewolves on
Wheels *found a new type of hell*

terror for anyone living in the savage cesspool of late-'70s New York. Saturation TV commercials and subway posters boasted fake statistics about the presence of gang members (the same ones spouted by Cyrus) while showing images of armies upon armies of tarted-up street thugs overtaking civilization. Violence happened almost immediately at theaters showing the film, cutting short its initial run. As a result, I believe the cult of *The Warriors* sprang up two years later, after ABC showed it as their Friday Night Movie. Safe at home, millions of viewers saw this unique, thrilling adventure that was aired largely uncut. The broadcast created word of mouth that spilled over into rental popularity once home video hit, leading to a perennial presence on cable. By the '90s, *The Warriors* had hit the midnight-movie circuit, where it has since remained.

For such a megalithic cultural touchstone, *The Warriors* spawned only a few direct rip-offs. Many of the Italian post-apocalypse flicks copped their piece of the action —*1990: The Bronx Warriors* is the most obvious example—as did Mexico's *Intrepidos Punks* films. My favorite cash-in may be the motorcycle/frat house/rape-and-revenge/vigilante hybrid *Young Warriors* (1983) with James Van Patten, Ernest Borgnine, and Richard Roundtree. Grand Theft Auto makers Rockstar Games remade *The Warriors* as a hugely popular console video game in 2005.

I am loath to instruct someone to stay away from a movie. However, Walter Hill's director's cut of *The Warriors* is the exception. It contains Internet-drawn comic book panels superimposed on the action, and voice-over narration that actually aborts the original film as you watch it.

Warriors of the Apocalypse (1985)

(Dir. Bobby A. Suarez; w/Michael James, Deborah Moore, Ken Metcalfe, Charlotte Cain)

✴ Post-Apocalypse ✴ Amazon Warriors ✴ Laser Eyes

Shot in the Philippines and set in the jungle "150 years after World War III," *Warriors of the Apocalypse* tracks a ragtag band of hard-scrapping survivors who sport a leather-and-studs that makes Rob Halford look subtle. Our heroes wander the green wasteland in pursuit of the Mountain of Life. Along the way, they skirmish with a tribe of headhunters and a platoon of psychic Pygmies before enjoying some much needed R & R among a tribe of Amazons. When needed, as in the final big battle, the Amazon queen can shoot lasers out of her eyes. And she does.

Warriors of the Apocalypse is odd enough to warrant acknowledgment and may stand as the one artistic enterprise to even begin to tap the heavy metal potential of pygmies. Director Bobby A. Suarez also helmed the Filipino grindhouse action favorites *Cleopatra Wong* (1978) and *The One-Armed Executioner* (1983).

Warriors of the Wasteland (1983), aka The New Barbarians

(Dir. Enzo G. Castellari; w/Fred Williamson, Giancarlo Prete, George Eastman, Anna Kanakis)

✴ Post-Apocalypse ✴ Mutants ✴ Motorcycles
✴ Soundtrack (Claudio Simonetti, Goblin)

A direct rip-off of *The Road Warrior* (1981), enjoyably stocked with kookily comic-book-modified motor vehicles on par with *Megaforce* (1982), *Warriors of the Wasteland* is pretty kick-ass post-nuke schlock from the country that churned such gems out best: the country of Bulldozer, Ufomammut, Children of Technology, and the pope. The Mad Max figure here is Scorpion (Giancarlo Prete). He teams with power-mustached archer Nadir (Fred Williamson) and a ten-year-old car ace called Young Mechanic (Giovanni Frezza) to defend a ragtag squadron of survivors against the Templars, a motorcycle cult led by the One (George Eastman).

Warriors stands out among other after-the-bomb adventures for the surprising punishment that the One bestows upon Scorpion. About two-thirds through, the bad guy captures the good guy and then badly buggers him up his good guy bowels. Yeah, he rapes him. As a result, my friend Vito and I spent most of high school referring to this film as "Warriors Below the Waistband." George Eastman, who plays the One, stars as the lead cannibal Nikos Karamanlis in the barf-bag classic *Anthropophagus*, aka *The Grim Reaper* (1980), along with its deservedly lesser-known sequel, *Anthropophagus 2000* (1999).

Fred Williamson, who masterfully fires off exploding arrows and doesn't get ass-raped as Nadir, is one of the giants of blaxploitation cinema. The pro-football veteran and martial arts master debuted as an actor in *M*A*S*H* (1970), then became a grindhouse superstar as the lead in *Hammer* (1972), and two highly only-in-the-'70s titles, *The Legend of Nigger Charley* (1972) and *The Soul of Nigger Charley* (1973).

Aside from its obvious metal genre influences, *Warriors of the Wasteland* also pays tribute (advertent or otherwise) to spaghetti westerns, especially when Scorpion dons a Clint Eastwood–esque Mexican poncho to conceal a cache of weapons.

WAYNE'S WORLD (1992)

(Dir. Penelope Spheeris; w/Mike Myers, Dana Carvey, Tia Carrere, Rob Lowe, Alice Cooper)

✠ Metal Reality ✠ Soundtrack (Black Sabbath, Alice Cooper, Bullet Boys [covering Montrose], Cinderella, Kix, Ugly Kid Joe)

From his parents' basement in Aurora, Illinois, Wayne Campbell (Mike Myers) broadcasts his public access cable TV show, *Wayne's World*, joined by his bespectacled, dorky best friend, Garth Algar (Dana Carvey)—who is permanently clad in an Aerosmith T-shirt. *Wayne's World* consists of two roughly teenage goofs busting each other up with boob and boner jokes, secretly making fun of local authority figures, and wailing on air instruments. The program proves so popular that a reptilian TV executive (Rob Lowe) aims to take it nationwide—but his real intent is to steal away the totally "babelicious" rock-star-in-the-making Cassandra (Tia Carrere) from Wayne.

The plot of *Wayne's World*, the movie, provides a serviceable structure for translating the source *Saturday Night Live* sketch to the big screen. What transpires is a collection of absurdist interludes—sketches themselves, really—through which we can cheer on the knuckleheaded heroes. Pop culture's premier teen headbangers prior to Beavis and Butt-Head, Wayne and Garth personify and communicate the side of metal that gets lost amidst all the more media-friendly satanism and high school suicide. These guys are youthful, slightly odd, more than slightly immature, but eminently likable bozos in pursuit of the next big laugh, their first big love, and a simple, rocking good time. Metal, with its specific energy and all-things-are-possible ardor, bonds them and buoys them.

Just after the opening credits, Wayne hops into Garth's AMC Pacer (with flames painted on the side) and pops a cassette into the tape deck, cocking an eyebrow and announcing, "I think we'll go with a little 'Bohemian Rhapsody,' gentlemen!" Wayne, Garth, and their two long-haired hesher friends in the backseat sing along as they cruise scenic Aurora. They pull over to pick up their "partied out" pal Phil, wearing a Deep Purple tee, who's desperately trying not to "hurl." Once inside, Phil sings along, leading up to Brian May's monstrous guitar solo. At that point, the whole car erupts into totally excellent spontaneous headbanging.

Wayne's World was an international blockbuster, and the movie's popularity sent "Bohemian Rhapsody" back up pop charts all over the globe.

In the U.S., the song hit number two; when first released in 1976, it had peaked at number nine. Alice Cooper's cameo constitutes his best movie appearance, topping even his disco bellboy number in 1977's *Sextette*. Wayne and Garth meet their idol backstage after a Milwaukee concert (where we see him perform "Feed My Frankenstein"), and he casually launches into a hilariously detailed history of the city.

When the magnitude of the moment truly hits them, Wayne and Garth fall to their knees, and bow worshipfully before Alice, chanting, "We're not worthy! We're not worthy!"

For her big TV debut as a rock and roll frontwoman, Cassandra blasts out a cover of "Ballroom Blitz," the 1973 bubblegum-metal masterpiece by British glamsters Sweet that became a sort of perennial standard in metal after being covered by Krokus, Nuclear Assault, and the Motörhead-themed black leather Midwestern thrashers Iron Fist.

Wayne's World 2 (1993)
(Dir. Stephen Surjik; w/Mike Myers, Dana Carvey, Tia Carrere, Kim Basinger)
✠ Metal Reality ✠ Native American Mysticism ✠ Soundtrack ("Frankenstein" by Edgar Winter, "Louie Louie" by Robert Plant)

Aurora, Illinois's cuddliest basement-broadcasting headbangers return. This time, Wayne and Garth have visions of Jim Morrison and a mostly naked American Indian, prompting them to plan a massive outdoor rock festival called "Waynestock." Aerosmith headlines, and romps through "Shut Up and Dance." This sequel came around a little too quickly in the wake of the 1992 blockbuster and was not helped by the advent of Beavis and Butt-Head stealing Wayne and Garth's heavy metal thunder as the world's best-loved couch-bound rock goofs. The film bombed at the box office and is difficult to find even in the abundant digital streaming era. Still, mark *Wayne's World 2* down as funny and underappreciated.

We Sold Our Souls for Rock N' Roll (2001)
(Dir. Penelope Spheeris; w/Black Sabbath, Slayer, Rob Zombie, Slipknot, System of a Down, Primus, Deftones, Fear Factory, Buckethead)
✠ Metal History ✠ Concert Footage ✠ Ozzfest

Penelope Spheeris, supreme chronicler of hard rock from the gutter up through her *Decline of Western Civilization* movies, expands her scope to football stadiums and the waves of headbanging humanity that flood them in *We Sold Our Souls for Rock N' Roll*, a deft and droll documentary about Ozzfest 1999.

Ozzfest comes across strongly as a traveling carnival (plenty carnal and debatably evil), replete with classic freak shows ("See the Giant Rat!"), shit food ($6 corn dogs), and turn-of-the-century decadence. Spheeris is never more deadpan than when interviewing boob-flashing girls going wild. Perils abound in the mosh pit. Dehydration, alcohol poisoning, and overdoses keep the freak-out tents occupied.

Three years before *The Osbournes* hit MTV, Ozzy is lucid here, even when reading lyrics off movie screen–size teleprompters and quaffing various health-tonic potions between songs. His wife, Sharon, features heavily, too. Each artist interviewed is clearly grateful for the opportunity to hitch his heaviness to this mammoth juggernaut, offering an unusual perspective from men who make raging rackets for a living.

Penelope Spheeris is an unrivaled rock documentarian. Consider the Maysles Brothers and the power of their masterwork. *Gimme Shelter*, which plants you in the immediacy of action. Spheeris observes up close, but she's cannily detached, so that she tells a story with her edits, her song cues, her every cinematic choice. *We Sold Our Souls for Rock N' Roll* is right on par with Spheeris' *Decline* films, a lost classic overshadowed by the marketing avalanche of Ozzfest.

Slipknot visits the Lincoln Memorial in full costume. A visiting eighth-grade class is quite smitten with them. Slayer lets loose about groupies early on, then visits Alcatraz. Rob Zombie hollers, "Fuck Woodstock!" For some reason, Black Sabbath teams up against drummer Bill Ward. In documentaries, this split appears good-natured; a long, hilarious segment here describes how Tony Iommi has repeatedly set Ward on fire through the years. "And he's still got all the scars all over him!" the doubled-over guitarist says through laughter.

Pastor Stan Craig debates Sharon Osbourne on a radio show and suggests she is ignorant of the true practices of the homosexual. "Do you know about rimming?" he asks. "Do you know about golden rain? Do you know about running gerbils up you through a tube in your rear end and all that stuff?" She insists she does not. Seizing the upper hand in his perverse game, Pastor Craig unloads the true depth of his wisdom: "I want you to remember this: Black Sabbath are practicing cannibals." I love this movie.

WENDIGO (2001)

(DIR. LARRY FESSENDEN; W/PATRICIA CLARKSON, JAKE WEBER, ERIK PER SULLIVAN)

✷ WENDIGO ✷ NATIVE AMERICAN SPIRITUALITY

As extolled in songs by Bison B.C., Scissorfight, and others, a wendigo is a malevolent animal spirit in Native American folklore, particularly among the Algonquin tribes. The creature is often depicted with the head of a deer and can possess humans and make them hungry for flesh. In some versions of the tale, a person can become a wendigo after practicing cannibalism. Writer-director Larry Fessenden's *Wendigo* is an arty, low-key curiosity that injects the title legend into the life of a Manhattan family that heads out to a home in the wilderness to escape big-city stress. George (Jake Weber), his wife Kim (Patricia Clarkson), and their ten-year-old son Miles (Erik Per Sullivan) learn about the wendigo from a local Native American shopkeeper who gives the kid a figurine of the monster. From there, misfortune befalls the transplants, building up to

a hallucinatory appearance by the wendigo itself, and the promise of further trouble to follow.

One of the great outrages of all cinema discussions is the notion that in horror films, what you don't see is truly scary. Fortunately, *Wendigo* defies that claim, revealing the titular beast as a ten-foot-tall freak-thing with a fantastically rubbery twelve-point buck head. The monster appears only briefly, but big credit to Fessenden and company for putting a man in a costume and showing him off.

The *Wendigo* DVD features extensive interview footage with Fessenden. He's rather affably pretentious (saying he considers *Wendigo* one of his "naïve films") despite sporting missing teeth, hobo clothes, and long, thin hair that looks like it would break under the weight of shampoo. Fessenden is likable, despite previously making *Habit* (1997), the last in a dreadful series of '90s New York hipster art-horrors that romanticized vampires by likening them to Lower East Side junkies. Others of this rancid ilk include Michael Almereyda's *Nadja* (1994) and Abel Ferrara's *The Addiction* (1995).

THE WEREWOLF VS. THE VAMPIRE WOMAN

(1971), AKA WEREWOLF SHADOW; LA NOCHE DEL WALPURGIS

(DIR. LEON KLIMOVSKY; W/PAUL NASCHY, GABY FUCHS, PATTY SHEPARD, BARBARA CAPELL)

✷ WEREWOLVES ✷ VAMPIRES

The *Werewolf vs. the Vampire Woman* is writer-star Paul Naschy's fourth film as the lycanthropic Waldemar Daninsky, singled out here as the best representation of the series. It also boasts one of cinema's all-time most metal taglines: "See it with someone you hate!"

Waldemar begins this outing as a corpse undergoing an autopsy. When the attending doctors remove two silver bullets from Daninsky's heart, he leaps back to life in wolfman form, eats the physicians, and heads to his castle. Meanwhile, sexy college students Elvira (Gaby Fuchs) and Genevieve (Barbara Capell) get their kicks roaming the Spanish countryside, looking for the tomb of medieval vampire Countess Wandessa. The girls meet Daninsky, who leads them to the grave, and Elvira accidentally resurrects the bloodsucking noblewoman. Voila, we have the vampire woman to go versus the werewolf.

With beautiful colors, lush photography, and an array of European stunners among the female-heavy cast, *Werewolf vs. Vampire Woman* is a dreamy, bloody scream. It's like early power metal with presciently pretty folk passages. You will do more than just howl at it.

Paul Naschy is the stage name of Spanish multi-talent Jacinto Alvarez. In addition to portraying the werewolf Waldemar Daninsky in no fewer than twelve films between 1968 and 2004 (as well as wolfmen in three non-Daninsky movies), Naschy has played Dracula, Frankenstein, the Mummy, and the Hunchback in various entries among his more than one hundred film credits. Early on, Naschy earned the nickname "the Lon Chaney of Spain." In 2001, King Juan Carlos I awarded Spain's Gold Medal of Merit in the Fine Arts to Naschy for his burly body of hair-sprouting work. His uncanny resemblance to John Belushi only makes his movies more fun.

WEREWOLVES ON WHEELS (1971)

(DIR. MICHEL LEVESQUE; W/STEVE OLIVER, DONNA ANDERS, GENE SHANE, BILLY GRAY)

✠ WEREWOLVES ✠ MOTORCYCLES ✠ SATAN ✠ BLACK MASS ✠ ANIMAL SACRIFICE

Outlaw motorcycle organization the Devil's Advocates happen upon a desert monastery where the monks are in the midst of a satanic worship ritual. The unholy men black-magically kidnap biker mama Helen (Donna Anders), prompting the Advocates to stomp the monks into robe-covered piles of slop. Back out on the road, though, that the sect will have its revenge becomes evident when Helen transforms into a howling, fur-sprouting she-beast. In time, she bites another biker and, at last, there we have them: Werewolves on Wheels.

The werewolf makeup is awesomely old-school: glued-on prosthetics and hair with black dog noses. The image of Helen levitating above flames in a beat-up wedding gown is also memorably trippy and eerie. Director Michel Levesque was a former protégé of B-movie mogul Roger Corman who served as art director on the Russ Meyer mam-sterpieces *Supervixens* (1975), *Up!* (1976), and *Beneath the Valley of the Ultra-Vixens* (1979). Other metallically notable Levesque titles are *Bobbie Jo and the Outlaw* (1976), *Ilsa, Harem Keeper of the Oil Sheiks* (1976), *The Incredible Melting Man* (1977), and *Foxes* (1980).

In 2011, specialty label Boomkat issued the *Werewolves on Wheels* soundtrack, full of strange, electronic-laced music by Don Gere, a country music devotee with a psych rock stoner streak.

WEST OF MEMPHIS (2012)

(DIR. AMY BERG; W/JASON BALDWIN, DAMIEN ECHOLS, JESSIE MISSKELLEY)

✠ SATANIC PANIC ✠ METAL REALITY ✠ SOUNDTRACK (MARILYN MANSON, HENRY ROLLINS)

After eighteen years in jail and three history-making *Paradise Lost* films, the documentary *West of Memphis* sums up, with the perfect clarity of hindsight, the notorious bastardization of justice suffered by the wrongly convicted murder suspects known as the West Memphis Three. In 1994, the Arkansas legal system convicted heavy metal teens Jason Baldwin, Damien Echols, and Jessie Misskelley of the grotesque murder and sexual mutilation of three eight-year-old boys. A judge sentenced Damien Echols to death.

Spurring the case was talk among local evangelical Christians that the black-clad, Metallica-listening suspects committed the crime as a satanic ritual. Over the ensuing decades, the court ignored evidence, blocked appeals, and defied the increasingly loud public call for at least a new investigation. Eventually, proper DNA testing crumbled the convictions of the West Memphis Three. In 2011, the men, in their midthirties, were released from prison. Joe Berlinger and Bruce Sinofsky's literally life-saving *Paradise Lost* docs reveal the ins and outs of the story as it happens, while Amy Berg's overarching view here explores the more elusive hows and whys of this tragedy. Damien Echols, who coproduced the movie, emerges as a deeply intelligent thinker and creative personality, as well as a profoundly well-spoken survivor of cosmic wrongness. Getting to know him better in this fashion is painful, but a pleasure.

In allowing them to leave prison, the State of Arkansas offered the three men a deal under the terms of which they cannot sue for restitution. The state is not held liable for wrongdoing and can leave the case closed. With the release of Echols, Baldwin, and Misskelley, however, the focus of public outrage shifted to clearing the men's names outright and finding the true killer. The *Paradise Lost* films sprang three innocents from cages. Here's hoping that *West of Memphis* can further force their cause up the road toward legitimate justice.

Wheels of Fire (1985), aka Desert Warrior

(Dir. Cirio H. Santiago; w/Gary Watkins, Laura Banks, Lynda Wiesmeier, Joe Mari Avellana)

✠ Post-Apocalypse ✠ Cannibals

The character Mad Trace may be one of the most blatant rip-offs of that other post-nuke lone wolf, road warrior hero who, the same year as *Wheels of Fire*, was stepping into the Thunderdome. "If you thought Max was mad," proclaims this movie's poster, "meet Trace!" Played in top scowling Mel Gibson fashion by Gary Watkins, Trace wears head-to-toe black leather, pilots a jet-black muscle car, and kicks the asses of radioactive mutants and punked-up marauders all over the desert highways he patrols.

Trace meets up with his atomic-warhead-breasted sister Arlie (*Playboy* Playmate Lynda Wiesmeier), whom he must in short order rescue from warlord Scourge (Joe Mari Avellana). To pull off this mission, Trace teams with warrior woman Stinger (Laura Banks). En route to Scourge's lair, they torch baddies with the Tracemobile's built-in flamethrower. Peril befalls our heroes as they are briefly captured by pint-size creatures that dwell underground (like the Morlock race in H. G. Wells's *The Time Machine*). Arlie is soon saved, but not before she does a few more scenes with her shirt off.

Wheels of Fire was directed in the Philippines by that country's B-movie madman Cirio H. Santiago, on the heels of his superior *Stryker* (1983), and after-the-bomb action flicks *Future Hunters* (1986) and *Equalizer 2000* (1987). Luminous, naturally super-curvaceous Lynda Wiesmeier ushered the 1980s through puberty one rewind-and-pause on the VCR at a time. The knockout D.C. native also appears nude in *Joysticks* (1983), *Private School* (1983), *Preppies* (1984), *R.S.V.P.* (1984), *Malibu Express* (1985), and *Evil Town* (1987). Judas Priest and Manowar later coughed up "Wheels of Fire" songs, although that may well have been dumb luck in combining two of metal's most active ingredients.

Where Evil Dwells (1985)

(Dirs. David Wojnarowicz, Tommy Turner; w/ Rockets Redglare, Joe Coleman, Nancy Coleman, Lung Leg, Baby Gregor)

✠ Acid King ✠ Soundtrack (AC/DC, Jim Thirlwell, Wiseblood)

The twenty-eight-minute, black-and-white cornea-scorcher *Where Evil Dwells* is the most discombobulating creative offshoot of the drug-fueled 1984 mutilation and murder committed by teenage metalhead (and "Acid King") Ricky Kasso. Hailing from the punk- and industrial-inspired "Cinema of Transgression" scene in New York that produced outlaw filmmakers Richard

Kern and Nick Zedd, *Where Evil Dwells* is a well-done hallucinogenic foray into art-school nihilism cast in the shadow of headbanger bloodshed.

A ventriloquist's dummy comes to life and babbles about Ricky Kasso, then stabs a guy whose eyeballs melt out of his face. Lower East Side heroin hepcats play "hesher" and lower a dummy off an overpass onto a suburban road while "Hells Bells" by AC/DC blares. A guy in a toga stuffs his face. Performance artist Joe Coleman sets off firecrackers in his fancy 1890s suit. Somebody wears a hockey mask and Freddy Krueger claws. Many images appear that could be from an orgy, but the film becomes too blurry. Then the dummy starts babbling again. More eyeballs. A hunchback saunters alongside roller-coaster tracks. A biker chick whips mannequin legs while Leatherface, shirtless, dances like a spaz. Goat-headed Satan appears. The credits roll out of a skull mask on a sheet of paper that gets lit ablaze. The End.

Alongside AC/DC (do you think they collected royalties on this?), *Evil*'s soundtrack pulsates with perfectly suited crushing industrial ugliness from Jim Thirlwell (aka Foetus) and Wiseblood, Thirlwell's collaboration with Swans percussionist (and Celtic Frost producer) Roli Mosimann.

WHITE BUFFALO (1977)

(DIR. J. LEE THOMPSON; W/CHARLES BRONSON, WILL SAMPSON, SLIM PICKENS, JOHN CARRADINE)

✠ MOBY DICK ✠ NATIVE AMERICAN MYTHOLOGY

Smelling green in the water after *Jaws* (1975), Hollywood mega-mogul Dino De Laurentiis rapidly rolled out his own trifecta of giant-animals-run-amok blockbusters. First was De Laurentiis's largely lambasted 1976 *King Kong* remake, an outrageously of-the-moment misfire with Jessica Lange asking the giant gorilla about his zodiac sign. Then came *Orca* (1977), with master British scenery chewer Richard Harris looking admirably drunk, yelling a lot while pursuing the most killer of whales.

Finally, Dino gave us *White Buffalo*. The most overtly metal film of the bunch is sadly also the most boring; no mean feat considering with Charles Bronson as Wild Bill Hickok teamed with Chief from *One Flew Over the Cuckoo's Nest* as Crazy Horse. *White Buffalo*'s title character—a furry albino Moby-Dick stand-in who haunts Hickok's dreams then barrels through a wall to kill him—resembles a minivan laden with heaps of yarn and a giant face from a Mardi Gras float. It shoots dry-ice steam out its nose-holes.

"You won't believe your eyes!" proclaimed the movie's posters, and it was true: Your eyes have never been laid upon anything so hilariously bogus. *White Buffalo* is all buffalo chips.

WHITE SLAVE (1985), AKA AMAZONIA: THE CATHERINE MILES STORY; CANNIBAL HOLOCAUST II

(DIR. MARIO GARIAZZO (AS ROY GARRETT); W/ELVIRE AUDRAY, WILL GONZALES, ANDREA COPPOLA)

✠ ITALIAN HORROR ✠ CANNIBALS ✠ RAPE AND REVENGE ✠ ANIMAL UPRISING

"This film is a faithful reconstruction of a true story," we're told in the opening moments of the documentary-style sleaze bonanza *White Slave*. "The places and events shown are the same as those where, ten years ago, Catherine Miles experienced her incredible adventure." Take that with a grain of blonde pubes among the bloodthirsty savages.

The Catherine Miles in question (Elvire Audray) is a lithe, flaxen beauty boating down the Amazon for her eighteenth birthday. Headhunters crash the celebration and decapitate Mom and Pop Miles. They tie the unconscious teen to a stake like hunted game and carry her back to their village—flanked by her parents' bobbling, disembodied noggins. The image leaps to life like a cross between South American thrash and the proto-metal painted covers of vintage men's magazines. Through a lot of naked, gory tribulations, the natives induct Catherine into the

Clockwise from top: Witchfinder
General, *aka* The Conqueror Worm
UK quad; World Gone Wild *goes VHS*;
Necron 99 aka Peace in Wizards;
burning Wicker Man (1973) *promo*

naked, gory ways of their tribe. She makes do, and even falls in love with local bohunk Umukai (Will Gonzales), but payback secretly propels our heroine all the while.

White Slave climaxes with Catherine returning to European society, where she discovers her uncle and his wife actually set her parents up for jungle slaughter. She then rains down upon the guilty parties some fully "gone native," bare-breasted, bow-and-arrow (and axe and spear) revenge. For all its lurid pleasures, *White Slave* is a relatively minor entry in the Italian barf-bag cinema cycle of the 1980s, but it was noxious enough to have been passed off *Cannibal Holocaust II* in some areas of the world.

White Slave is the creation of screenwriter Franco Prosperi, who also wrote the surrealistically metal *Hercules in the Haunted World* (1961), as well as another cannibal opus, *The Green Inferno* (1988). Like *White Slave*, *Green Inferno* was also renamed *Cannibal Holocaust II* in regions where distributors thought they could get away with it.

White Zombie (1932)
(DIR. VICTOR HALPERIN; W/BELA LUGOSI, MADGE BELLAMY, JOSEPH CAWTHORN, ROBERT FRAZER)
✠ ZOMBIES ✠ VOODOO

Moan, pop your eyes wide, outstretch your arms, and stumble in drooling respect to *White Zombie*, the first feature-length zombie film, as well as the origin of the surname of the twenty-first century's most overtly heavy metal filmmaker.

Newlywed Madeline (Madge Bellamy) honeymoons in that romantic hotspot Haiti, catching the eye of local voodoo master Murder Legendre (Bela Lugosi, who sports repulsive triangular patches of facial hair, a style that Mick Mars later admired enough to adopt as his own). Sugar plantation kingpin Charles Beaumont (Robert Frazer) is sweet on Madeline, so he cuts a deal with Murder Legendre to turn her into a zombie. Black magic never quite works out smoothly, though, and Beaumont runs afoul of Legendre

and his awesome army of the undead.

White Zombie seems like it would have come across as ancient and creaky in 1932. Moribund pacing, amateur acting, and chintzy special effects only increase its otherworldly appeal and make the movie itself come across more enjoyably zombie-like. Some movies belong undead.

Rob Zombie named his game-changing metal band White Zombie after the movie he once called "a great film that not a lot of people know about."

Wicked Lake (2008)
(DIR. ZACH PASSERO; W/CARLEE BAKER, ERYN JOSLYN, EVE MAURO, ROBIN SYDNEY)
✠ CANNIBALS ✠ WITCHCRAFT ✠ SOUNDTRACK
(MINISTRY, PRONG, REVOLTING COCKS)

Wicked Lake will warm the cockles of your Skinemax-nostalgic hard parts, and then slake your bloodlust. The first half of the movie glossily chronicles a foursome of supple female skinny-dippers (Carlee Baker, Eryn Joslyn, Eve Mauro, Robin Sydney) who make out with one another naked; they make too-tempting targets of themselves to rednecks lining the banks of a perfectly nice rural lake. After a half hour of slow-motion lesbian group sex, the bad guys bully our all-natural girls (one old grandpa demands a blow job), but, come midnight, the curvaceous quartet transforms into a coven of cannibal witches.

Al Jourgensen of Ministry scored *Wicked Lake*, loaded the soundtrack with Ministry songs and a guest track by Prong, and also cameos as a dorky art student in the movie's first scene. Other cameos include Angela Bettis (*May*) as a small-town floozy and Tim Thomerson (*Trancers*, *Dollman*) as a coke-snorting cop. Go fucking figure.

The Wicker Man (1973)

(Dir. Robin Hardy; w/Edward Woodward, Christopher Lee, Britt Ekland, Ingrid Pitt)

✶ Paganism ✶ Human Sacrifice

In spirit and execution, *The Wicker Man* is a profoundly pure doom experience akin to the primeval song "Black Sabbath" by Black Sabbath. UK documentarian Mark Gatiss has dubbed this lyrical, mesmerizing, ultimately scarring and nightmare-inducing antihero's journey "British folk horror," along with 1968's *Witchfinder General* and 1971's *Blood on Satan's Claw*.

At the beginning of this endlessly provocative and engaging classic, police Sergeant Howie (Edward Woodward) flies to Summerisle, a pastoral island off the Scottish coast, to look into the disappearance of fourteen-year-old Rowan Morrison. Howie, a dogmatic Christian, is appalled to find the hedonistic residents indulging all manner of desires, and practicing pagan worship of pre-Jesus Celtic gods. Sex permeates the atmosphere, particularly unnerving the middle-aged detective, an unmarried virgin.

Lord Summerisle (Christopher Lee) invites Howie to investigate the island and its inhabitants as they prepare for their upcoming May Day fertility festival. Faced with naked teen maidens practicing maypole routines, couples unabashedly copulating in public, children being taught to honor the phallus in nature, dirty sing-alongs at the pub, and hot blonde Willow (Britt Ekland) stripping nude while crooning a tune a next door, Howie grows increasingly frustrated. His aggravation, compounded by his inability to turn up information on Rowan, pushes him toward madness.

Howie eventually deduces that the missing girl he seeks is being held captive to be sacrificed. When the May Day parade starts, islanders in stunning animal masks prance through the streets and make funny sacrifices to their gods. Meanwhile, Howie disguises himself and searches the empty homes. He finds Rowan tied to a post and cuts her free. She immediately flees through a cave.

Frantically, Howie gives chase. He emerges in the sunlight, shocked, as the girl Rowan embraces Lord Summerisle and the other celebrants. They surround Howie as Summerisle explains how they lured the detective to the island specifically because he is a devout Christian and a policeman and, most importantly, because their gods demand a virgin. As such, Howie will make a perfect sacrifice.

On the beach, Howie is locked inside the "Wicker Man," a forty-foot-tall wooden effigy of a man alongside goats, ducks, chickens, and other animals. The pagans light the statue ablaze and we watch it go up, a sacrifice to the gods. As the flames rise, Howie shouts biblical verse, the animals scream, the islanders revel in their handiwork, and the camera draws back slowly. The Wicker Man burns and burns, its head collapsing into its flaming torso. Behind the inferno, a setting sun casts the sky blood red.

Cinfantastique has declared *The Wicker Man* to be "the *Citizen Kane* of horror movies," but the picture was not an immediate success. Cuts of various lengths were tested throughout the world. A shortened version played as the B feature in England with *Don't Look Now* (1973). In the states, *The Wicker Man* was test-marketed at drive-ins in 1975.

Later, when the film ran the risk of becoming a lost horror treasure in a sea of slasher movies, Christopher Lee personally asked critics to seek and review it, even offering to pay for their tickets! Lee is revered for his portrayal of supernatural villains ranging from Dracula in the Hammer Studios horror epics to Sarumon in the *Lord of the Rings* movies and Count Dooku in *Star Wars*. He is just as charming and chilling as Lord Summerisle, a mortal man capable of inhuman cruelty to serve his supernatural beliefs.

The world has since come around to the film in a big way. *The Wicker Man* was cited by the creators of the famous Burning Man festival as their original inspiration. Never a band to allow a British film classic to go unrecognized in song, Iron Maiden released its "Wicker Man" single in 2000, marking the return of singer Bruce Dickinson, who had been on sabbatical from the band during the 1990s.

Ingrid Pitt, who plays Summerisle's librarian, is the first lady of Hammer horror, starring in *The Vampire Lovers* (1970) and *The House That Dripped Blood* (1971). *Countess Dracula* (1971), with Pitt in the lead, is one of the best cinematic takes on the über-metal legend of Countess Elizabeth Bathory. She revisited the part on Cradle of Filth's 1998 Bathory concept album, *Cruelty and the Beast*, providing narration on several tracks in the voice of the wicked noblewoman.

Pay no attention to the 2006 Nicolas Cage remake. Okay, the YouTube clip with Cage freaking out over "BEES!" is hilarious. But that's it.

The Wild Angels (1966)
(Dir. Roger Corman; w/Peter Fonda, Nancy Sinatra, Bruce Dern, Diane Ladd)
✠ Motorcycles

A biker named Heavenly Blues (Peter Fonda) leads a hell-raising motorcycle gang in *The Wild Angels*. Mike, aka Monkey, is his old lady (Nancy Sinatra, beyond convincing as a leather broad). Loser (Bruce Dern) is the Angels' number two, and quite the loose cannon. Loser's old lady is the eloquently named Gaysh (Diane Ladd). The Angels' existence consists of various indulgences of group violence and sexual assaulted punctuated by beer, weed, and acid parties. Life is bad, filthy fun until Loser bites it and his funeral turns into the Angels' last stand.

A *Life* magazine cover story on the Hells Angels motorcycle club inspired drive-in movie guru Roger Corman to make *The Wild Angels*. In classic Corman style, he made the movie fast, but not quite as cheaply as usual. The kinetic energy and upgraded production values electrify the film, and *The Wild Angels* became a nasty little blockbuster than spawned the entire outlaw-

biker-cinema genre. Medically perilous boozing, joint passing, LSD consumption, near-nude women, rape as normal sexual relations, and the swastika as de rigueur interior design: that's what the Wild Angels' wild fun is made of.

The *Wild Angels* soundtrack is a landmark leap forward for hard rock, consisting of rumbling psychedelic punch-ups and beat-downs by fuzz guitar pioneers Davie Allan and the Arrows. Songs such as "Blues' Theme" and "The Last Ride" represent a muscular coarsening of surf rock and electric blues to sonically incorporate the darkening underbelly of hippie culture.

Heavenly Blues's rousing battle speech ranks high among heavy metal's most inspirational messages, sampled famously by Mudhoney and elsewhere: "We wanna be free! We wanna be free to do what we wanna do. We wanna be free to ride our machines without being hassled by the Man! . . . And we wanna get loaded!"

Wild at Heart (1990)
(Dir. David Lynch; w/Nicolas Cage, Laura Dern, Willem Dafoe, Crispin Glover)
✠ Thrash Metal

T ripmeister David Lynch hits the road with Elvis-obsessed Sailor (Nicolas Cage) and lanky sexpot Lula (Laura Dern) for a dark comic American underworld odyssey highlighted by the director's signature freak show pit stops, wiggy visuals, and outbursts of barbaric violence.

Wild at Heart opens outside a formal banquet in Cape Fear, North Carolina. On the staircase going in, Bob Ray Lemon (Gregg Dandridge) threatens Sailor with a switchblade. In a flash, Sailor overtakes Bob Ray as Powermad's "Slaughterhouse" thunders suddenly on the soundtrack. Sailor then literally and explicitly beats Bob Ray's brains out in time to the music.

After Sailor gets sprung from jail, he takes Lula to a Powermad show. As they thrash on the dance floor to "Slaughterhouse," a punk tries to muscle in on Lula. The band stops as Sailor knocks the guy out. Vocalist Joel DuBay tosses

Sailor the microphone, and the band backs him perfectly as he croons a romantic rendition of Elvis's "Love Me" to Lula. It *is* wild!

The Wild Life (1984)

(Dir. Art Linson; w/Chris Penn, Eric Stoltz, Lea Thompson, Ilan-Mitchell Smith, Lee Ving)

✠ Metal Reality ✠ Psycho 'Nam Vet
✠ Soundtrack (Eddie Van Halen, Steppenwolf, Hanover Fist)

Writer Cameron Crowe followed up his screenplay for *Fast Times at Ridgemont High* (1982) by penning *The Wild Life* as a sequel in spirit to that Amy Heckerling–directed classic. Chris Penn, Spicoli's real-life brother, even appears as ganja-zonked party animal Drake. Although his catchphrase—"It's casual!"—never caught on, this party-boy Penn is funny, too.

The plot uses the first apartment of high school graduate Bill (Eric Stoltz) as a centerpiece for the intersecting lives of various suburban L.A. youths. Donut City waitress Anita (Lea Thompson) dates a married cop (Hart Bochner), who turns mildly scary. Teen metalhead Jim (Ilan Mitchell-Smith) hangs out with always scary junkie 'Nam survivor Charlie (Randy Quaid). The dudes take in Russ Meyer mammazon Kitten Natividad doing her famous bathtub routine at a strip club (I saw it at Show World in 1988). Everything ends with a rager at Bill's place.

As Jim, wormy Ilan-Mitchell Smith makes for an uncomfortably recognizable mid-'80s metal type. He's slimy, angry, pretentious, utterly self-serious, and given to solitary nunchaku practice to the sound of "In the Metal of the Night" by Hanover Fist. You can practically smell the crappy dirtweed coming off his soiled denim. His balloon-squeak voice and ant-like physique complete the picture. Today, Jim would probably be an especially tiresome rock critic. The cable guy who guzzles brews with Drake is played by Fear front-nut Lee Ving, a formidable screen presence as always.

The Wild Life achieved instant metal significance for featuring an instrumental big-screen movie score by Eddie Van Halen. Produced during Van Halen's segue from frontman David Lee Roth to Sammy Hagar, and possibly even helping to precipitate that rupture, *The Wild Life*'s screen music is a pedestrian studio composite of funk groove, finger-popping bass, and patented Eddie guitar acrobatics. Still, in the era when Herbie Hancock's "Rockit," Harold Faltermeyer's "Axel F," and Jan Hammer's "Miami Vice Theme" were storming the pop charts, Eddie Van Halen's decidedly single-ready "Donut City" deserved to be a hit. Elements of Eddie's tracks here were later incorporated into the Van Halen songs "Right Now" and "A.F.U. (Naturally Wired)."

Alas, "Donut City" didn't even make it to the CD version of the *Wild Life* soundtrack, and rights issues made the film itself difficult to find after its initial VHS release.

Wings of the Crow (2000)

(Dir. Jack Williams; w/Jamie Taylor, James Gammon, Danielle Williams, Rachela Williams)

✠ Supernatural ✠ Soundtrack (Black Sabbath, Rammstein, Rob Zombie, White Zombie)

Wings of the Crow is a fan-made, feature-length remake of *The Crow* (1994) that flips the story's gender roles. Series hero Eric Draven becomes Erica Drake (Jamie Taylor), who gets murdered and resurrected a year later, on Devil's Night, to hunt down the evildoers responsible. Obviously made with real passion and a real lack of money, *Wings of the Crow* is a popular pass-around video among *Crow* cultists. The production ably employs heavy metal songs throughout its run time, including "Children of the Grave" by Black Sabbath, "Alter Mann" by Rammstein, "Return of the Phantom Stranger" by Rob Zombie, and "Black Sunshine" by White Zombie.

WITCHBOARD (1986)

(DIR. KEVIN S. TENNEY; W/TAWNY KITAEN, TODD ALLEN, STEPHEN NICHOLS, KATHLEEN WILHOITE)

✠ OUIJA BOARD ✠ DEMONS ✠ VIDEO VIXENS

Barring the original contact made by Captain Howdy in *The Exorcist* (1973), *Witchboard* is the premiere cinematic showcase for Hasbro Inc.'s most indisputably metal of playthings, the Ouija board. This surprise horror hit also provided a dark bridge for temptress Tawny Kitaen to cross between her hard-R comedy antics in 1984's *Bachelor Party* and her reinvention in the decade's second half as MTV's defining metal video vixen via various Whitesnake smashes.

Kitaen stars as Linda Brewster, a unwitting Ouija board amateur who uses the device to contact the spirit of "David," whom she believes is an innocent boy who died at age ten. In fact, though, Linda's otherworldly contact is the demon Malfeitor. Disguised as David, Malfeitor takes possession of Linda and causes typical upsets along the lines of knives throwing themselves across a kitchen and a series of murders occurring that implicate Linda's fiancé Jim (Todd Allen) as the culprit. Most importantly, Malfeitor attacks Linda in the shower, you know, when she's naked!

Except for its remarkable success, *Witchboard* is thoroughly unremarkable. Time has not revealed whatever made this dull thriller so appealing, leading lady aside, of course. Tawny is as Tawny does. For *Witchboard*, that's more than enough. After fleeting topless teases in *The Perils of Gwendoline* (1984), Tawny goes full-frontal nude in *Witchboard*, thoroughly exposing that exquisite anatomy shadowed by torn clothes on the cover of Ratt's *Out of the Cellar* album.

Writer-director Kevin S. Tenney followed up by creating the even more metal horror sleeper, *Night of the Demons* (1988).

Two sequels followed: *Witchboard 2: The Devil's Doorway* (1993) and *Witchboard III: The Possession* (1995). Far more prolific was the *Witchboard* rip-off *Witchcraft* (1988). Over twenty years and twelve sequels, the *Witchcraft* series curiously dipped into and out of soft-core porn, until the spell was finally broken with *Witchcraft 13: Blood of the Chosen* (2008).

WITCHCRAFT '70 (1970), AKA ANGELI BIANCHI . . . ANGELI NERI

(DIRS. LUIGI SCATTINI, LEE FROST; W/ANTON LAVEY, DIANE LAVEY, EDMUND PURDOM)

✠ WITCHCRAFT ✠ BLACK MASS ✠ SATAN ✠ WICCA

Focusing on the occult intrigue raised by the late-1960s counterculture and loading the on-screen rituals with nude female bodies, *Witchcraft '70* is a globe-trotting, Italian-made documentary that was further sexed up with extra naked footage for American grindhouse audiences by exploitation maven Lee Frost (*Love Camp 7*). Various segments depict Wiccan practices, Aleister Crowley rituals, a Macumba exorcism, and a fake hippie cult in Devil's Canyon. The latter is intended to conjure associations with the Manson Family, and to show off flower power chicks sans peasant blouses.

Anton LaVey, founder of the Church of Satan, invites us on a tour of his San Francisco headquarters and runs through a Black Mass "destruction rite." Mrs. LaVey's boobs and pubes serve as the altar. Animal sacrifice is prevalent, including a voodoo practice in which a bare nubile is basted in the blood of a freshly decapitated boar.

Witchcraft '70 is a spookily psychedelic time capsule that will prove of most use to occult completists or very specific fetishists only. A disrobed high priestess challenges the Christian God: "If there be any power left in heaven, let it transfix my breast!" Some kind of Finnish devil ritual requires a pig's head painted pitch-black. If no metal band has copped that idea for a stage prop yet, there is no power left in hell.

WITCHERY (1988),
AKA LA CASA 4; WITCHCRAFT
(DIR. FABRIZIO LAURENTI; W/LINDA BLAIR, DAVID
HASSELHOFF, CATHERINE HICKLAND, HILDEGARD KNEF)
✠ WITCHCRAFT ✠ DEMON RAPE ✠ CRUCIFIXION

David Hasselhoff is the hero of *Witchery*. That's right. The Hoff plays Gary, who, together with his virginal girlfriend Linda (Catherine Hickland), travels to a haunted hotel on off the coast of Massachusetts to research the occult. A storm traps Gary, Linda, and six others—including Linda Blair as an expectant mother—on the island. The tempest turns out to be the crafty work of a local black magic woman who will do everything in her considerable power to make sure no one there gets out alive.

Once *Witchery*'s cauldron really gets bubbling, pretty deep into the proceedings, the film explodes into a catalogue of cruel mayhem that includes a demon forcing intercourse on poor preggo Linda, an elderly woman's mouth being sewn shut, gardening tools penetrating a human throat, gore-spraying voodoo knife-play, and crucifixion on a burning cross—upside down! Only the Hoff can stop the madness!

Witchery may or may not be an official sequel to the Italian spooker *Ghosthouse*, aka *La Casa 4* (1988), which is, in turn, an unofficial, unauthorized follow-up to Sam Raimi's *Evil Dead 2* (1987). Like the movie itself, keeping all this stuff straight can be a challenge.

WITCHFINDER GENERAL
(1968), AKA THE CONQUEROR WORM
(DIR. MICHAEL REEVES; W/VINCENT PRICE, IAN OGILVY,
ROBERT RUSSELL, PATRICK WYMARK, HILARY DWYER)
✠ WITCH HUNT

Michael Reeves's *Witchfinder General* combines horror, adventure, lurid sexuality, and artful visuals in the story of real-life historical figure Matthew Hopkins—England's answer to Spain's Torquemada. Hopkins proclaimed himself Britain's "Witchfinder General" during the English Civil War of the mid-1600s, and waged a moral war with hangings, burnings, and torture in the name of God—all, of course, for a profit.

Witchfinder General is nothing less than spellbinding. Vincent Price devours the screen as Hopkins. With his cape and pilgrim hat and utterly humorless demeanor, Hopkins travels from village to village with his lackey John Stearne (Robert Russell), to round up and extract duress-driven "confessions" by means of extreme agony. The local clergymen then pay handsomely for having their congregations so cleansed. The scam runs afoul when Hopkins sticks needles in the back of an uncooperative priest (Rupert Davies)—to find the "Devil's Mark," naturally—while Stearne rapes the clergyman's nubile niece Sara (Hilary Dwyer). This invokes a vow of vengeance from Richard Marshall (Ian Ogilvy), the girl's fiancé and just-returned war hero.

Action and intrigue ensue, along with shocking proto–"torture porn" elements and a dire mind-snapping payoff after the good guys "win." The movie's final shot mirrors its opening: a woman screams in abject horror over the inescapable dread of her damnation. Wail to England.

Witchfinder General met immediate censorship and condemnation in England, while going unnoticed in the States. It was a blockbuster in Germany, however, spawning a mini-trend of followers including *Mark of the Devil* (1970), *The Bloody Judge* (1970), and *Witches Are Violated and Tortured to Death*, aka *Mark of the Devil Part II* (1973). Vincent Price later correctly named Matthew Hopkins in *Witchfinder General* as the best performance of his storied career. Director Michael Reeves actually wanted Donald Pleasence to star, but deferred to producers banking on Price's international box office power. Because of Price's popular series of Edgar Allan Poe films, *Witchfinder General* was retitled *The Conqueror Worm*, after a Poe poem, for its U.S. release.

Several influential critics championed the film. The iconography, power plays, and occult trappings of the film became heavy metal archetypes, particularly in Britain, inspiring the bands Witchfinder General and Conqueror Worm, plus a rash of songs over the decades by Saxon, Cathedral, Electric Wizard, Pale Divine, Warhammer, and many more.

Like too many other young heroes, brilliantly talented filmmaker Michael Reeves died of a barbiturate overdose at age twenty-five—shortly before *Witchfinder General* even made it to theaters.

WITHOUT WARNING (1980)

(DIR. GREYDON CLARK; W/JACK PALANCE, MARTIN LANDAU, DAVID CARUSO, TARAH NUTTER)

✠ SCIENCE FICTION ✠ PROTO-PREDATOR

An eight-foot-tall, bulb-skulled space alien lands in a lovely wooded area and hunts humans by throwing fanged, starfish-like parasites at them. Once the creatures latch on, they drain their targets of blood and the predator collects another cool trophy. Among the victims are a Cub Scout leader (Larry Storch of TV's *F Troop*) and a gaggle of camping teens that includes young David Caruso. Vintage combat veterans played by Hollywood legends Martin Landau, Jack Palance, Cameron Mitchell, Ralph Meeker, and Neville Brand fight this menace.

Without Warning is a throwback to '50s space invader thrillers amped up on the sudden shocks of early-'80s slasher-movie madness, with extraterrestrials throwing pancakes that drain human bodily fluids. Kevin Peter Hall plays the alien. In 1987, he'd play another hunter from a distant planet opposite Arnold Schwarzenegger in *Predator* (the same year he starred as a Sasquatch in *Harry and the Hendersons*).

Director Greydon Clark is a grindhouse great, having also made *Satan's Cheerleaders* (1977), *Angels Brigade* (1979), *Wacko* (1982), *Joysticks* (1983), and *Skinheads: The Second Coming of Hate* (1989). As Necrophagia frontman Killjoy DeSade has declared about *Without Warning*: "The alien is creepy and the flying vagina–type creatures with teeth ruuuuule!!!"

WIZARDS (1977)

(DIR. RALPH BAKSHI; W/SUSAN TYRRELL, BOB HOLT, STEVE GRAVERS, JESSE WELLS, RICHARD ROMANUS)

✠ SWORDS & SORCERY ✠ ANIMATION

Master animator Ralph Bakshi's fantasia, set two million years past the nuclear annihilation of humanity, *Wizards* is a multimedia wonder of fantasy filmmaking and a 1970s meditation on sorcery versus science, and transcendence versus technology. As the tagline reads, the film is "an epic fantasy of peace and magic."

In the enchanted land of Montagar, kindly wizard Avatar (Bob Holt) battles his evil brother Blackwolf (Steve Graver) for the crown vacated by the passing of their mother, a fairy queen. After a quick showdown, Blackwolf retreats to the harsh realm of Scortch, where he raises a fascist army of angry mutants by projecting Nazi propaganda films in the sky. His goal is to conquer Montagar. Avatar captures and reprograms Peace, one of Blackwolf's Terminator-like robots (as seen on *Wizards*' famous poster). Along with elf spy Weehawk (Richard Romanus) and sexy fairy Elinore (Jesse Wells), he sets out to stop his brother.

Wizards then becomes a *Lord of the Rings*–like heroic journey infused with brilliantly airbrushed Chevy van art and powered by really primo bong steam. Bakshi creates a sumptuous mythical universe as vivid and palpably realized as the urban scumscapes of his *Fritz the Cat* (1972), *Heavy Traffic* (1973), and *Coonskin* (1975). He throws all manner of art styles and visual storytelling approaches on-screen, combining lush oil paintings with Saturday-morning-cartoon action, trippy frame manipulation, and shadow impressionism with nightmarishly rotoscoped footage of Hitler, Panzer tanks, and the Luftwaffe in full blitzkrieg mode. Busty fairy Elinore's tiny shirt showcases nipple-bumps on par with the finest pinball machines of *Wizards*' day.

Ever the smart-ass Jewish kid from Brooklyn, Avatar is a wisecracking, cigar-chomping stand-in for Bakshi. The story's climactic face-off features a punch line that would go on to be "borrowed" in 1981 when Indiana Jones is confronted by a swordsman in *Raiders of the Lost Ark*. Bakshi's street sense adds a perfect wink to the heady mysticism and cosmic tumult with which *Wizards* so mesmerizingly surrounds us.

This feature was originally titled *War Wizards*, but Bakshi's friend George Lucas asked if the name could be changed so as not to lead to confusion with his own concurrent 20th Century Fox release, *Star Wars*. *Wizards* debuted to good reviews and gangbusters business on February 9, 1977. As was the practice at the time, Fox kept the film in circulation and built word of mouth for months, planning a major rollout to more theaters during the warm-weather months. Then *Star Wars* opened on May 25. With all previous box office records going the way of the Death Star, Fox had to devote all their attention to manufacturing more prints of *Star Wars* to fill screens outside of which crowds were literally beating down doors. *Wizards* fell by the wayside.

Mark Hamill, Luke Skywalker himself, voices Sean, leader of the fairies.

WOODSTOCK (1970)

(DIR. MICHAEL WADLEIGH; W/PEACE AND LOVE, MAN)
✵ CONCERT FOOTAGE ✵ SOUNDTRACK (JIMI HENDRIX, SANTANA, TEN YEARS AFTER)

Woodstock, the documentary, does a highly commendable job of conveying Woodstock, three days of peace and music in Sullivan County, New York, in 1969 that shook the world of mainstream rock journalism forever. Using split screens and witty editing choices, *Woodstock* puts you in the mud, the mayhem, and the merriment, conjuring a hugeness of scale, a sense of history, and a general good vibe.

The band performances are exceedingly well filmed, and the power of the people is never louder than when Country Joe gets a half-million humans to yell, "F-U-C-K!" across hundreds of acres of Max Yasgur's farm in Bethel, New York, (the last-minute site of the festival after town

leaders in not-close Woodstock, New York, got cold feet.) The movie is admirably metallic in several spots: as Alvin Lee of Ten Years After shreds his guitar to laser splinters on "I'm Going Home"; Santana summons "Soul Sacrifice"; and Jimi Hendrix wakes up a sea of hippies with his epochal destruction and reinvention of "The Star Spangled Banner," the greatest electric guitar performance until Eddie Van Halen unleashed "Eruption" nearly a decade later.

WORKING CLASS ROCK STAR (2008)

(DIR. JUSTIN McCONNELL; W/RANDY BLYTHE, DAVE BROCKIE, JESSICA DESJARDINS, SHANE IVY)
✵ METAL REALITY ✵ CONCERT FOOTAGE

Working Class Rock Star documents the day-to-day pummeling of life on the road for a trio of up-and-coming metal acts: 3 Mile Scream, Bloodshoteye, and Tub Ring. Shot on the fly, the movie creates effective "you are there" misery during the traveling and deal-making segments, punctuated by invigorating "ah! This is why they are there!" performance numbers. Of the intertwined narratives, the most intriguing story belongs to Bloodshoteye vocalist Jessica DesJardins. She and bandmate Shane Ivy are parents of a little girl, and their struggle to balance child rearing with death metal planet conquering warrants a longer documentary on its own.

Members of 40 Below Summer, Arch Enemy, Bleeding Through, Byzantine, Dog Fashion Disco, Finntroll, the Haunted, Himsa, Mahogany Rush, Strapping Young Lad, and Unearth also feature. Lamb of God's Randy Blythe is especially frank in telling young bands to welcome the suffering of shit gigs, no money, and bum trips. Dave Brockie—otherwise known, in costume, as Oderus Urungus of Gwar—points out that he still maintains a day job.

Veteran guitar wizard Frank Marino of Mahogany Rush fumes like a smoking sage as he lays out the devolution of rock from "concerts" to "shows" to MTV to drunken crowds preferring "drinking man's music" to "thinking man's music." Ultimately, he concludes, "people go into the business now knowing that they're going to get screwed. And they go in anyway."

World Gone Wild (1988)

(Dir. Lee H. Katzin; w/Bruce Dern, Michael Paré, Catherine Mary Stewart, Adam Ant)

✠ Post-Apocalypse ✠ Manson Family

As a late-to-the-Thunderdome *Mad Max* rip-off with sprinklings of satire and smudges of self-awareness, *World Gone Wild* comes as a pleasant surprise. The movie is witty and exciting and boasts the last great movie star performance by the perennially half-crazed Bruce Dern.

In 2087, seventy-five years after nuclear war, Ethan (Bruce Dern) is the grizzled hippie leader of a junkyard commune settled on a precious source of clean water. Three books survived the blast: *Iacocca* by former Chrysler chairman Lee Iacocca ("I understand he was a great president," one of the locals says), *Emily Post's Etiquette*, and *The Wit and Wisdom of Charles Manson*.

That last volume inspires eager reader Derek (Adam Ant) to create a machine-gun cult of Manson-mesmerized followers dressed in white altar-boy cassocks. Ethan casually kills one with a hubcap to the throat, and then summons his mercenary son George (Michael Paré) to assemble a crack team to defend the commune. Many of Derek's zealots, for our gory edification, are hungry cannibals. Details like that, plus a grenade ignited in somebody's mouth, make *World Gone Wild* a work deserving of metallic respect.

The anthemic closing theme, "A World Gone Wild," is performed Michael Des Barres with Steve Jones of the Sex Pistols on guitar.

The World's Greatest Sinner (1962)

(Dir. Timothy Carey; w/Timothy Carey)

✠ The Devil ✠ Soundtrack (Frank Zappa)

Towering, crazy-eyed character actor extraordinaire Timothy Carrey wrote, produced, directed, and stars in *The World's Greatest Sinner*, a black-and-white bazooka blast to the brain. Carey plays insurance salesman Clarence Hilliard. After a revelatory conversation with the devil in the guise of a snake, Hilliard quits his job, changes his name to God, becomes a guitar-slinging rock star, and runs for president.

Listening as the devil preaches the essence of satanic philosophy—"There's only one God, and that's Man!"—God Hilliard rouses his minions with a philosophy promising to make every man and woman into "superhuman beings." He beds female admirers ranging in age from fourteen to eighty. Ultimately, he challenges the real God to a winner-take-all showdown. God wins.

Carey is on fire from frame one, and the inferno only builds. God Hilliard is a heavy metal figure to the hilt, from his self-deification to his escaped-lunatic explosions on guitar. A frequent collaborator with Stanley Kubrick and Marlon Brando, the hulking, hawk-nosed, brute-mannered Brooklyn native made *The World's Greatest Sinner* with his own money and never gave it a proper release. He died from a stroke in 1994.

The Wrestler (2008)

(Dir. Darren Aronofsky; w/Mickey Rourke, Marisa Tomei, Evan Rachel Wood)

✷ Wrestling ✷ Soundtrack (Accept, Cinderella, Quiet Riot, Ratt, Scorpions)

Mickey Rourke returned to big-ticket Hollywood after taking on *The Wrestler* as Randy "the Ram" Robinson, a washed-up, busted-out ex-pro grappler barely hanging on somewhere between nostalgia and death. Rourke is remarkable as the Ram, be he shooting steroids, engaging in two-bit New Jersey school auditorium bouts, attempting to connect to his estranged daughter (Evan Rachel Wood), or halfway romancing Cassidy (Marisa Tomei), a stripper who, in her forties, has also passed her career expiration date.

Like an ill-advised '80s metal reunion concert, *The Wrestler* is not fun. But beyond watching the broken and bedraggled subjects attempt to party like it's 1985, we can really feel the heart and soul that goes into not giving up on old dreams—as well as the tragic lack of brains and faith that makes it impossible to let those passions evolve into something new.

With his flowing golden fleece and signature "Ram Jam" finishing move, Randy Robinson (a horrendously flawed man) is a flawless embodiment of where "the squared circle" flares up into metal magnificence. The Ram bonds with Cassidy over Guns N' Roses when "Sweet Child O' Mine" comes on in a New Jersey bar. They mutually declare adoration for '80s hair rock. "Then that Cobain pussy had to come and ruin it all," Randy laments. "Like there's something wrong with just wanting to have a good time," Cassidy adds. "Fuckin' '90s sucked," they both agree.

Possibly because he agrees with him about the 1990s, Axl Rose granted "Sweet Child O' Mine" for free to the soundtrack due to his friendship with Mickey Rourke.

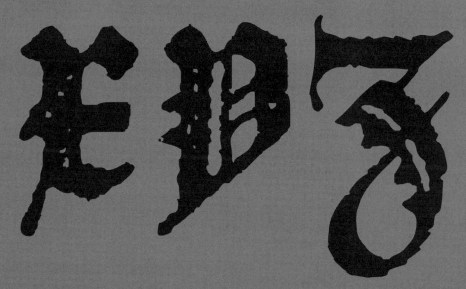

X-MEN ORIGINS: WOLVERINE ✠ XTRO ✠ A YEAR AND A HALF IN THE LIFE OF METALLICA ✠ YOR, THE HUNTER FROM THE FUTURE ✠ YOU'RE GONNA MISS ME ✠ YOUR HIGHNESS ✠ ZAO: THE LESSER LIGHTS OF HEAVEN ✠ ZARDOZ ✠ ZEN OF SCREAMING: VOCAL INSTRUCTION FOR A NEW BREED ✠ ZOMBIE ✠ ZOMBI 2 ✠ ZOMBIE NIGHTMARE ✠ ZOMBIELAND ✠

X-MEN ORIGINS: WOLVERINE (2009)

(DIR. GAVIN HOOD; W/HUGH JACKMAN, LIEV SCHREIBER)
✠ COMIC BOOKS

After *X-Men* (2000), *X-Men 2* (2003), and *X-Men: The Last Stand* (2006), the Marvel Comics mutant crew's most metal member—the one with retractable razor claws and an impressive cigar habit—takes the spotlight. We first meet young Wolvie (Hugh Jackman) in the Canadian Territories in 1840, alongside his brother, who grows up to be Sabretooth (Liev Schreiber). First, though, the bros become Americans, and then fight in every U.S. military conflict from the Civil War (where they pick up Glenn Danzig–esque facial hair grooming that carries them through the next century) to Vietnam. Then they turn into X-Men. Then they fight each other and a bunch of other guys, all in the miracle of shaky-cam and CGI. Comparing Wolverine's solo project here

and the 1978 Kiss solo albums, the movie comes nowhere near the dizzying heights near *Ace Frehley* but is not as lowly as *Peter Criss*, either. Fork over your allowance money accordingly.

Director Darren Aronofsky bizarrely decided to follow up his widely celebrated ballet murder movie *Black Swan* (2010) with a samurai-themed Wolverine return bearing the hilariously arty title *The Wolverine*. He eventually bowed out of that bad idea, but director James Mangold swooped in, and a deservedly underseen sequel by that name limped forth in 2013.

XTRO (1983)

(DIR. HARRY BROMLEY DAVENPORT; W/BERNICE STEGERS, PHILIP SAYER, SIMON NASH, MARYAM D'ABO)
✠ SCIENCE FICTION ✠ HORROR ✠ ALIEN SEX
✠ BANNED VIDEO NASTY

Xtro is a heavy metal supernova of grindhouse sleaze and peculiarly English sexuality that plays like Hawkwind anticipating death metal at

the cosmic nexus of Venom, Sabbat, and Aker-
cocke. While playing outside with his son Tony
(Simon Nash), unassuming dad Sam Phillips
(Philip Sayer) is abducted by a bright light. Cut
to three years later. The light flashes again and
leaves in its wake a slimy, quadruped, half-hu-
man/half-who-knows-what-the-fuck-that-thing-is
monstrosity called Xtro (Tim Dry).

Xtro promptly murders a passing motorist and
rapes a nearby young woman, impregnating her.
She goes through the entire pregnancy process
immediately, and, with grotesque pain, gives
birth to a fully-grown adult man. In fact, the
newborn is the missing father from earlier, Sam
Phillips! Young Tony, in the meantime, suffers
from wild nightmares and awakes soaked in
someone else's blood. Dad returns, even though
Mom has taken up with another dude, and then
the insanity really starts.

Sam is busted eating the eggs of Tony's pet
snake. The father then applies his mouth to the
boy's neck and pumps him full of some sort of
alien fluid. Tony gains superpowers that include
turning a toy soldier and a clown doll into six-
foot killing machines. Even weirder stuff involving eggs follows.

Xtro's ad campaign made use of 1982 cinema's
diametric-opposite space alien adventure with
the tagline "Not all *E*xtra *T*errestrials are friendly!" Hallucinatory, cringingly uncomfortable,
and absolutely fearless in pursuit of its own mad
vision, *Xtro* stood out as bizarre at the time of its
release, and feels even more unique with every
passing year. Let us be glad it beamed down at
all for our perpetual puzzlement and perverse
pleasure.

The handmade fright-movie zine *Gore Gazette*,
sought out by horror hounds and metalheads in
the '80s, was forever changed by the arrival of
Xtro. Publisher Rick Sullivan was as an accountant for Exxon. He used a Xerox machine at work
to produce his profane, hilarious biweekly tip
sheet of the latest mind-rippers to blow through
Times Square shit-pit theaters. To illustrate his
Xtro review, he picked a shot of the alien forc-

ing his space seed on an unwilling recipient. Of
course, that was the image that Sullivan accidentally left on Exxon's copier machine. He was
swiftly encouraged to take his accounting talents
elsewhere.

A Year and a Half in the Life of Metallica

(1992)

(Dir. Adam Dubin; w/Metallica, Bob Rock, Slash)
✠ **Metal Reality** ✠ **Concert Footage**

Metallica by Metallica, aka the Black Album, is
one of the rock's great lines of demarcation.
The record stormed the pop charts of 1991 and
launched Metallica on its way to quickly becoming the biggest hard rock act of all time. The
thrashtastic foursome could never simply return
to the hairy thrash pits from which they arose.
Attempting to expand Metallica's message and
marketplace, the band teamed with producer Bob
Rock, who had mined platinum for fluff-metal
nemeses Mötley Crüe and Bon Jovi. The result is
"Enter Sandman," "Sad But True," and "Nothing
Else Matters." After that, nothing else did matter.

The first ninety minutes of *A Year and a Half
in the Life of Metallica* documents the process
of making "The Black Album" without commentary. Director Adam Dubin previously made
the Beastie Boys' "Fight for Your Right to Party"
video, featuring a cameo by Slayer's Kerry King,
who performs the guitar solo, slipping Satan and
spikes into MTV heavy rotation in the year of
Reign in Blood. Upon its release in 1992, *A Year
and a Half in the Life of Metallica* was a cool gesture toward openness by a band that recognized
the power of its relationships with fans. Now that
every band seems to produce YouTube videos to
document the studio recording of every guitar
solo, it's hard to recall how different Metallica
was by documenting its inner sanctum.

Part two runs two and a half hours, and captures Metallica working the road hard, from
backwoods arenas to major events including the

Freddie Mercury Tribute at London's Wembley Stadium. All four hours of Metallica overload stand as a fascinating time capsule that shows, not so much unflinchingly as unwittingly, musicians struggling to make music in the middle of massive commercial success. The band dynamics become complicated, especially as the members are surrounded by more and more staff, managers, and hangers-on. Needless to say, unerring determination has a strong presence in this production.

The key scene: Metallica frontman James Hetfield and Guns N' Roses guitarist Slash sit at a table drinking before a 1992 tribute to Freddy Mercury. When Slash drunkenly knocks over a beer, Hetfield yells at him, "Don't push it toward me, DICK!" Aside from being hilarious, the moment catches Metallica in the process of supplanting their self-destructing tour mates GNR atop Rock Mountain. Cautionary figures Spinal Tap also appear, chiding Metallica for swiping their all-black *Smell the Glove* "cover artwork" for the Black Album.

Yor, the Hunter From the Future (1983)

(DIR. ANTONIO MARGHERITI; W/REB BROWN, CORINNE CLÉRY, JOHN STEINER, CAROLE ANDRÉ)

✠ ITALIAN EXPLOITATION ✠ POST-APOCALYPSE
✠ SWORDS & SORCERY ✠ DINOSAURS

Yor (Reb Brown) is a perfectly coifed caveman who rescues cavewoman Ka-Laa (Corinne Cléry) first from a dinosaur head (we don't see the body) and then from a tribe of apemen. He is resourceful; he kills a human-size bat and uses its carcass to hang-glide in and save the day. Yor and Ka-Laa's further adventures lead to a desert ruled by a goddess. In her realm, sand mummies, blue cavemen, and android armies protect the nuclear stockpiles of the evil Overlord (John Steiner). The Overlord also has spaceships.

Yor, the Hunter From the Future is an early VHS schlock favorite that was filmed in Turkey and consists of patched-together elements from an Italian sci-fi TV series. The movie is as loony as it sounds, and a lively reminder of its time. The song "Yor's World" by Guido and Maurizio De Angelis is a gut-bustingly inept knockoff of Queen's *Flash Gordon* theme. Whereas in *Flash Gordon*, the refrain "FLASH!" would pop up during the action, scenes in *Yor* are punched up with a falsetto chorus erupting: "He's the MAAAAAAN!"

Director Antonio Margheriti is an Italian exploitation flick *capo*. He also made *Killer Fish* (1979), *Cannibal Apocalypse* (1980), *The Last Hunter* (1980), *Jungle Warriors* (1985), and more than fifty other grindhouse greats. Reb Brown starred as the titular Marvel Comics hero in two laudably crappy TV movies in 1979: *Captain America* and *Captain America II: Death Too Soon*.

You're Gonna Miss Me (2005)

(DIR. KEVEN MCALESTER; W/ROKY ERICKSON, BILLY GIBBONS, GIBBY HAYNES, BYRON COLEY)

✠ TEXAS ✠ ACID ROCK

Amidst a flood in the 2000s of terrific documentaries on outsider music icons that included *MC5: A True Testimonial* (2002), *Mayor of the Sunset Strip* (2003), and *The Devil and Daniel Johnston* (2005), came *You're Gonna Miss Me*, a cinematic portrait of heavy-psych pioneer turned tragic head case Roky Erickson. Unfortunately, this 2005 entry is one fat sour note in a succession of otherwise fine films.

After effectively inventing psychedelic rock with the 13th Floor Elevators ("You're Gonna Miss Me"), singer-songwriter Roky Erickson was busted in 1969 for carrying a single joint. Facing ten years jail time, he pled insanity, and was shipped to the notorious Rusk State Hospital, a mental facility for the criminally insane. There, Erickson was subjected to involuntary electroconvulsive shock treatments and who knows what else. In 1972, he emerged, irrevocably shattered.

After several years of playing with a band he

When Tony grows up, he's going to be just like Daddy!

XTRO

Some extra-terrestrials aren't friendly.

Starring BERNICE STEGERS · PHILIP SAYER · SIMON NASH · MARYAM D'ABO · DANNY BRAININ · Special effects by NEEFX · Special Effects Makeup by ROBIN GRANTHAM
Director of Photography JOHN METCALFE · Associate Producer JAMES CRAWFORD · Written by ROBERT SMITH and IAIN CASSIE · Executive Producer ROBERT SHAYE
Music Composed by HARRY BROMLEY DAVENPORT · Special Synthesizer Effects Created by SHELTON LEIGH PALMER

P.M. PRODUCTIONS
UN FILM DE ANTHONY M. DAWSON

REB BROWN
CORINNE CLERY

YOR LE CHASSEUR DU FUTUR

ALAN COLLINS, JOHN STEINER · and CAROLE ANDRE

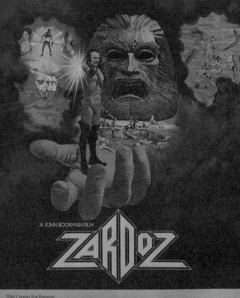

BEYOND 1984, BEYOND 2001, BEYOND LOVE, BEYOND DEATH.

A JOHN BOORMAN FILM

ZARDOZ

20th Century Fox Presents
SEAN CONNERY in ZARDOZ · Written, Produced and Directed by JOHN BOORMAN
Also-starring CHARLOTTE RAMPLING · SARA KESTELMAN And JOHN ALDERTON
PRINTS BY DE LUXE® PANAVISION®

WE ARE GOING TO EAT YOU!

ZOMBIE

...THE DEAD ARE AMONG US!

Clockwise from top left: Xtro *goofs on E.T.;* Yor, the Hunter From the Future *en français;* Zombie *is going to eat you;* Zardoz *is going to blow your mind*

Mike McPadden

541

dubbed Bleib Alien, Erickson recorded again in 1979. He created a new body of music even more powerful than his '60s work, with songs consumed by horror and science-fiction themes that Roky clearly perceived to be reality. He played with intensity to match the horror in his head. Then Roky stepped into a DMV and announced that a Martian had taken control of his body.

As *You're Gonna Miss Me* begins, Roky is in even worse shape than that, sitting in ramshackle hovel with all manner of electronic equipment blaring at once. He has matted hair and life-threatening dental abscesses. He clings proudly to a certificate that "officially" declares him a space alien. Meanwhile, Roky's batty mom drives him even battier than she is. Roky's brother tries to help, but Roky doesn't necessarily want help. Soon, ninety-one inexpertly assembled, miserably depressing minutes have passed.

Roky Erickson still performs. Though he looks spooked, his singing, playing, and stage presence remain cosmic dynamite. His shows are joyous occasions. An exploration of that aspect of Roky Erickson's current life, without ignoring the bleak parts of his existence, would have balanced *You're Gonna Miss Me* tremendously.

Alas, that's not the movie that got made, but he deserves a better, less pitying chronicle of his wonderful and horrible life.

Your Highness (2011)

(DIR. DAVID GORDON GREEN; W/DANNY MCBRIDE, JAMES FRANCO, NATALIE PORTMAN, ZOOEY DESCHANEL)
✤ SWORDS & SORCERY

The hard-toking team of director David Gordon Green and actors Danny McBride and James Franco reunited after their stoner smash *Pineapple Express* (2008) to blow smoke on the heavily metal sword-and-sorcery genre with. McBride plays pot-puffing ne'er-do-nuthin' Prince Thadeous. Franco is his dashing swordsman brother Prince Fabious. They romance Natalie Portman and Zooey Deschanel, respectively, while battling evil wizard Leezar (Justin Theroux).

Despite its pedigree and an admirable aim to comically spelunk lower than lowbrow, *Your Highness* is a bust—and that's never good regarding things reefer-related. The power driving the heroes' quest is "the Fuckening," an immediate laugh-getting spoof of *Highlander II*'s "the Quickening"—except it gets repeated so often that *Highlander II* seems funnier. Worth a mention, though, is how McBride cuts a Minotaur's penis off with a unicorn horn, then wears the dismembered man-bull manhood around his neck (possibly a first in the proud history of cinema).

Zao: The Lesser Lights of Heaven (2005)

(DIR. RYAN DOWNEY; W/DANIEL WEYANDT, SCOTT MELLINGER, RUSS COGDELL, JESSE SMITH)
✤ CHRISTIAN METAL

Zao is a sometimes Christian, sometimes not quite as Christian, metalcore God Squad from western Pennsylvania. Since 1993, they've issued an impressive succession of recordings and embarked on an even more impressive array of tours, building a reputation as live powerhouse that combines sonic elements of Carcass and Neurosis with their own rapturous religious fervor and eagerness to warp genres. Members have come and gone, in sizable numbers typical of even non-Christian metalcore bands.

That's the broad overview. The details, and I do mean all of them, can be discovered and analyzed, one by one, in the meticulously intricate documentary *Zao: The Lesser Lights of Heaven*. Directed by manager Ryan Downey, it's three and a half hours of Zao-ism. For fans: pure *Heaven*. For non-fans: think in terms of *Lesser Lights*. Lest two-hundred-plus minutes of—is it okay to say the "evolution" of Zao?—leave you longing, *The Lesser Lights of Heaven* DVD also comes with hours of live performance footage, including three full-length concerts. Wowee Zao-ee.

ZARDOZ (1974)

(DIR. JOHN BOORMAN; W/SEAN CONNERY, CHARLOTTE RAMPLING, SARA KESTELMAN, JOHN ALDERTON)

✴ POST-APOCALYPSE

Beyond 1984 . . . Beyond 2001 . . . Beyond Love . . . Beyond Death . . ." The ad campaign for writer-director John Boorman's limitlessly ambitious sci-fi opus *Zardoz* made that promise, and the movie absolutely delivers those cosmic goods. In the year 2293, a gigantic, flying stone head resembling a ferocious Greek theater mask floats down from the sky to a green countryside where horseback hunters in red bandoliers drop to their knees in worship. "I am Zardoz!" the head booms across the landscape. "The gun is good. The penis is evil. The penis shoots seeds, and makes new life to poison the Earth with a plague of men, as once it was, but the gun shoots death, and purifies the Earth of the filth of brutals. Go forth . . . and kill!" Then this magnificent Tiki-Stonehenge-on-steroids-in-space Zardoz head spits forth an immense bounty of rifles and ammunition, which the revelers scramble to collect while ecstatically praising Zardoz.

At this moment, nobody would fault anyone else for thinking Zardoz may well be the greatest film ever made. You may even continue to believe that as Zed (Sean Connery) awakes from a pile of grain inside the airborne head's mouth, encounters a clownish pilot of some sort (Niall Buggy), and shoots him. Zed lands inside the Vortex, a highly early-'70s notion of a commune where the uniformly youthful, groovily beautiful, pastel-robed inhabitants look like the audience from *The Rolling Stones Rock and Roll Circus* (1968) and actually act more stoned.

Freckly scientist May (Sara Kestelman) intends to study Zed, while hotheaded Consuela (Charlotte Rampling) insists they kill "it." Some jerk named Friend (John Alderton) uses Zed for slave labor. Everybody wants to know what happened to Arthur Frayn, which is the name of the man Zed shot. A lot of what can only be called "hooey" ensues. A lot. The comely flower people

of the Vortex are immortals. Zed, it turns out, is a mutant superman "bred and led" by Arthur Frayn to bring about the gift of death. This revelation comes amidst ceaseless psychedelic visuals that start out breathtaking and quickly become numbing. Frayn also tips off the origin of the name "Zardoz"—blowing Zed's mind with a library copy of *The Wizard of Oz*.

The final, gory showdown between the Brutals, the killers Zed left behind, and the death-famished Immortals (imagine the climax of 1970's *Gimme Shelter* expanded heavily) does not satisfy. Like all that has preceded it, the scene drags on nonsensically and for too long. A coda, in which we watch an allegorical time-lapse progression of Zed's and Consuela's reinvention as a new Adam and Eve, respectively, actually manages to be charming and goes by quickly.

Despite the demerits, this is *Zardoz*, a grand example of Hollywood at its most daring and most intelligent, when a director like Boorman could be rewarded for box office success (the 1972 blockbuster *Deliverance*) with carte blanche to chase after the sweeping ideals, lofty artistry, and idea-seeking audiences of Stanley Kubrick. *Zardoz* shows us marvels, and at no point is it ever less than commendable. Plus, topless hippie chicks are all over the place.

Boorman made *Zardoz* after his *Lord of the Rings* project fell apart. He used many of the visual effects he developed for *Lord of the Rings* years later in *Excalibur* (1981). *Zardoz* was filmed next to Boorman's house in Ireland. Many of the extras are Travellers, Irish gypsies. Charles Staffell, overseer of *Zardoz*'s monumental visual effects, also brought us the groundbreaking sights of *2001: A Space Odyssey* (1968), *Barbarella* (1968), *Superman* (1978), *Dune* (1984), and *Aliens* (1986).

The Zen of Screaming: Vocal Instruction for a New Breed (2007)

(Dir: Denise Korycki; w/Melissa Cross, Randy Blythe, Andrew W.K.)

✶ Metal Reality ✶ Cookie Monster Vocals

Petite redhead powerhouse Melissa Cross serves as the vocal guru for the most monstrous throats in contemporary heavy metal and extreme hardcore. *Zen of Screaming* is a partially a documentary on her work, but it's mainly an instructional video that demonstrates how she elevates the most guttural growlers to new levels of universe-shattering intensity.

Lamb of God's Randy Blythe and renowned party guy Andrew W.K. are particularly animated on-camera advocates here for the Cross technique, and Cross herself shines in the how-to segments. She makes seemingly impossible feats of decibel derring-do happen. You will not believe the electrocuted Godzilla wails that emerge from this groovy, grounded, meditative earth mama, and the DVD will involuntarily lead you to moan, huff, grunt, and howl along with her. Also watch for cameos by members of All That Remains, God Forbid, Every Time I Die, Shadows Fall, and Madball.

The Zen of Screaming 2 (2007) offers an advanced course with still more interviews. Long may Melissa Cross protect and empower vocal cords while severely damaging eardrums!

Zombie (1979), aka Zombi 2

(Dir. Lucio Fulci; w/Tisa Farrow, Ian McCulloch, Richard Johnson, Auretta Gay)

✶ Zombies ✶ Italy ✶ Banned Video Nasty

A zombie fights a live shark and wins. A splinter pierces a woman's eyeball s-l-o-w-w-w-l-y in unflinching, up-close detail. Undead ghouls chow down en masse and chew with their rotten mouths open. Over and over again, *Zombie* makes good on its notorious tagline, "WE ARE GOING TO EAT YOU!"

As was typical for Italian horror outrages of its era, *Zombie* opens in Manhattan. A run-in with a resurrected bruiser aboard a yacht in New York Harbor sends the boat's owner, Ann Bowles (Tisa Farrow), and investigative journalist Peter West (Ian McCulloch) to the Caribbean island of Matool. That place is teeming with flesh-famished ghouls, and we see them in all kinds of literally stomach-rupturing action.

Lucio Fulci's cult-classic living-dead extravaganza ranks second only to George Romero's *Dawn of the Dead* (1978) in the pantheon of all-time great gross-out undead epics. Partly that's because *Zombie* was sold in much of the world, illegitimately, as a sequel to *Dawn*. *Zombie* is a riot. The movie will make you laugh in spots from astonished incredulity, and its violence is fitful, unpredictable, and overwhelming. The logic in the heat of director Lucio Fulci's realm cannot be deciphered, leaving viewers battle-hardened and disconcerted but invigorated.

The perfect picture for Forty-Second Street grindhouses, where entering was often a savage ordeal itself, *Zombie* foments an experience much like real-life events of creative mayhem and great danger. It's a heavy metal mosh pit punched up with cannibal carnivorousness let loose. The poster image of a filth-caked cadaverous head with vermin gnawing one eye socket and its broken teeth twisting up into a seeming half grin is one of the most ubiquitous and always effective heavy metal icons, right next to the classic

Frankenstein, and Regan from *The Exorcist* in full possessed mode.

Finally, about that zombie-vs.-shark madness: the concept arose after producer Ugo Tucci ran into Mexican schlockmeister René Cardona, who had made the insane "erotic" *Jaws* rip-off *Tintorera: Killer Shark* (1977). Giannetto De Rossi directed the scene in a saltwater tank. Though the shark is obviously real, viewers have to wonder if it is a thousand years old or somehow missing teeth. In fact, the shark had gorged on horsemeat and was tranquilized before filming. The animal's trainer plays the zombie. The resulting underwater pas de deux makes Baryshnikov look like Jerry Lewis—glorious!

Zombie Nightmare (1986)
(Dir. Jack Bravman; w/Jon Mikl Thor, Adam West, Tia Carrere)
✷ Zombies ✷ Soundtrack (Thor, Fist, Girlschool, Motörhead, Pantera, Virgin Steele)

Jon Mikl Thor, the stunt-rocking frontbeast of his hard rock squadron Thor, transitions to gutter-budget heavy metal horror flick icon-on-the-rise in *Zombie Nightmare*. The film is not as perfect as his next effort, *Rock 'n' Roll Nightmare* (1987), but there Thor essentially plays himself. Here he plays as a muscle-bound undead teenage baseball hero who hunts down a sex-and-violence-crazed street gang (whose members include young Tia Carrere) and battles corrupt authority figures, including camp icon Adam West, TV's 1960s Batman. The punch-up action is further pumped by a keister-stomping array of metal songs by established shredders and up-and-comers, including party metal–era 1980s Pantera. Despite the title, nobody has a nightmare about any zombies (nor do any zombies have nightmares).

Zombieland (2009)
(Dir. Ruben Fleischer; w/Woody Harrelson, Jesse Eisenberg, Emma Stone, Abigail Breslin)
✷ Zombies ✷ Midway Mayhem ✷ Soundtrack (Blue Öyster Cult, Metallica, Van Halen)

To my unhappy eyes, the twee zombie-mania of the Internet age—which lumps the undead in with exhausting pass-alongs like bacon rainbows, unicorn drawings, and all those goddamned kitten videos—is for non-horror fans wanting a simulation of the horror experience without feeling anything resembling real *horror*. So pretenders aim to satiate their bloodlust by witnessing gore-exploding massacres of non-living, non-thinking, non-feeling post-humans who must be stopped lest they hurt innocents. However much fun it is to blurt "AWESOME!" over endless ghoul decapitations by shotguns and shovels, such actions carry no consequence. In fact, they're good and wholesome, qualities diametrically opposed to any conception of true horror; and, by extension, true metal.

An ambulatory corpse evokes none of the emotional attachments we feel toward a teenage coed taking a shower, or a couple on their way home, or any other kind of victim worthy of some compassion. Silly attempts to like those made by *Land of the Dead*, *Fido*, and other zombie-sympathizer efforts only hammer that point home. Zombies are pests and they can't help but hurt us. So they have to go. That may result in some mess, but there's no harm, no foul. They're really just video-game targets. And they're funny. Worst of all, they have now become cute. Therein lies a major corruption in contemporary horror cinema. Where zombies are concerned, dilettantes and day-trippers run the show. In musical terms, this is akin to the days when Bon Jovi, Godsmack, and Pearl Jam could be misconstrued as heavy metal bands, but with the whole world backing up that massive mistake.

Zombieland is the most offensively egregious example of this modern malfeasance: a fun-for-the-whole-family romp with a nerdy teen (Jesse

Eisenberg) teaming with a cute chick (Emma Stone) and her plucky kid sis (Abigail Breslin) under the tutelage of a lovably cantankerous ne'er-do-well (Woody Harrelson) to dispatch CGI monsters in clunky live-action cartoon fashion. So infantilized is *Zombieland* that its celebrated cameo by Bill Murray centers on him dressing up in his *Ghostbusters* costume and singing the popular children's theme song from that popular children's film. Moreover, the movie climaxes at an amusement park, where the Ferris wheel and Tilt-a-Whirl are just two more meaningless target-shooting opportunities. Lest the video-game milieu come off as too subtle, the action stops periodically for graphics explaining "The Rules" to pop up on-screen, a technique VH1 borrowed from the Internet for six months in the MySpace era.

The metal content of the *Zombieland* soundtrack only provides more evidence of the movie's prefabricated unit-moving mentality. Sure, there's Blue Öyster Cult, Metallica, and Van Halen but they're represented by "Don't Fear the Reaper," "For Whom the Bell Tolls," and "Everybody Wants Some," inescapable rock radio retreads meant to ease Dad into feeling comfortable between non-hits by faux-edgy *Rolling Stone* critics' poll toppers such as Band of Horses and the Black Keys (for the kids). Mom and everybody else get to chuckle at campy numbers like "Puppy Love" by Paul Anka and "Feels So Good" by Chuck Mangione.

The message of *Zombieland* is its milieu: "The undead apocalypse is so wacky! And cheeky! And, above all, CUTE! How can you not LOVE it!?!"

Puke. Puke! PUKE!!! How did this happen, people? How did a hard-R-rated splatter depiction of post-apocalyptic kill-or-be-cannibalized nightmare get de-gonadified into something just that precious?

What kind of world have we made for our Heavy Metal Movies? And what kind of tampon-scented hell-world has this new version of Heavy Metal Movies, in turn, made for us?

As Per Yngve "Dead" Ohlin of Norway's Mayhem righteously declared shortly before eating a shotgun shell: "Black metal is something that should be feared by normal people!"

Well, turns out "normal" people love *Zombieland*, a feel-good picture that castrated the canary in our shared cultural coal mine, a bellwether of the sugarcoated shock shit that was to come, suffocating us in diabetic coma singularity. In *Zombieland*, and in countless other examples ever since, the key components of Heavy Metal Movies—blood, guts, horror, sex, chaos, and killer riffs—are neutered and made safe and edgeless and sticky-sweet. The ultimate real-life horror is the loss of true horror, as the key ingredients of Heavy Metal Movies are used for the opposite ends of a real Heavy Metal Movie.

The end of horror has arrived not with a big nuke or an uprising of brain-famished corpses or an incoming charge of sword-and-sodomy-happy barbarians, but with a steady, mounting, ultimately inescapable softening and sleepwalk-inducing onslaught of never-ending YouTube black metal parody clips and "Which Goonie Are You?" quizzes and perpetually repackaged takes on other people's gelded kindergarten nostalgia wherein fucking adult men punctuate their written communications with smiley faces. Throw some zombies and teenage vampires and indie-rock-okayed "metal" into the mix, and it's all the same sugar water, the deadly concoction in which we all might drown.

So *Zombieland* serves as one conclusion of the original age of Heavy Metal Movies, riding its own internal laugh track to beat us down and erect a safe-as-cereal-milk grave marker. Feel free to piss on the site. And then, while shaking out those last drops, consider that *Zombieland* will not be the whimpering end of Heavy Metal Movies; it doesn't have to end this way.

Pick your own peeve and pummel it properly, whether "political correctness," social media scolds, corporate interference, a society that coddles couch-bound wussies with video games and shock porn. Looking back ten years in Heavy

Metal Movie terms, I aim both barrels at odious self-aware leeches like Troma and *Mystery Science Theater 3000*, both of whom wrapped the adventure and desperation of B-movies in diaper layers of irony and shtick. We end up mollified and meek, never risking anything publicly until the hopeless outcasts among us either become heavy metal earth-shakers or lose their minds and take an AK-47 into a school hallway.

The greatest creations, of course, often arise from a void or a cultural ruin. Consider heavy metal itself, commencing with Black Sabbath's bleak 1970 debut and leading to Slayer circa 1986, releasing *Reign in Blood* and thrashing themselves Satanically senseless while surrounded by nothing but hair metal bands. Heavy Metal Movies started with feral silent-era shockers like *Thomas Edison's Frankenstein* and *Haxan: Witchcraft Through the Ages*, and nearly a hundred years later have come too far to retire toothlessly with mega-budget theme park gerbil-droppings like *Zombieland* and blockbuster boy-man superhero bilge.

Forget the promise of a better tomorrow—the chance to make this fucking second right now better is more monstrously potent than ever. Virtually every one of us is walking around with a movie studio in his pocket. We can all shoot, edit, score, and distribute our own movies with push-button ease. So just as every year continues to bring forth amazing, unpredictable, and even unimaginably great new heavy metal bands, records, and live performances (have you heard the insanity coming out of Iceland now? Or Singapore?), the power for Heavy Metal Movies to keep pace is finally in our grasp.

Now that your tortured cranium is front-loaded with a thousand different ways to bang that screen that does not bang, put this book down. Dream up your perfect Heavy Metal Movie, then grab that nightmare or fantasy and scream it out through the closest nearby camera. Make that motion picture happen. Make that metal vision real. Push it out of yourself and into the world. Give me something ferocious and killer and kick-

ass and utterly, maniacally metal-to-the-marrow, and I'll see you back here when it comes time to unleash *Heavy Metal Movies II*.

Lights . . . camera . . . TAKE ACTION, YOU HEADBANGING MOTHERFUCKERS!!!

Appendix Ayyyyyye:
The 66.6 Most Metal Moments in Movie History

Here are the cinematic equivalents of hard rock's 100 best riffs, most shredding solos, peak held screams, and the most naked groupies. Fast-forward accordingly, these are the good parts!

1. **This Is Spinal Tap (1984)**
   Nigel Tufnel cranks up his custom amp. "This one goes to eleven!"

2. **The Decline of Western Civilization Part II: The Metal Years (1988)**
   Chris Holmes, paralyzed drunk and floating in a backyard pool with his poor mom standing nearby, empties the remainder of a vodka bottle over his head.

3. **The Wicker Man (1973)**
   Edward Woodward feels the heat as the sacrificial meat within the titular structure that pagans set ablaze.

4. **Heavy Metal Parking Lot (1986)**
   Zebraman unleashed: "Heavy metal rules. All that punk shit sucks. It doesn't belong in this world, it belongs on fuckin' Mars, man! What the hell is punk shit? And Madonna can go to hell as far as I'm concerned. She's a dick!"

5. **Heavy Metal (1981)**
   Laser dragons invade to "Mob Rules" by Black Sabbath.

6. **Rock 'N' Roll Nightmare (1987)**
   Jon Mikl Thor battles foam-rubber cycloptic octopi tossed at him by Satan.

7. **The Song Remains the Same (1977)**
   Jimmy Page violin-bows his guitar.

8. **Iron Maiden: Flight 666 (2008)**
   Brazilian fan Bruno Ismael Zalanduskas catches a drumstick from Nicko McBrain, and weeps for 38 profound seconds.

9. **Conan the Barbarian (1982)**
   Conan on what is best in life: "To crush your enemies, to see them driven before you, and to hear the lamentation of the women."

10. **Wayne's World (1992)**
    Wayne and Garth fall to their knees before Alice Cooper. "We're not worthy!"

11. The Thing (1982)

Upside-down disembodied head sprouts giant spider legs, charges forward. "You've gotta be fucking kidding!"

12. Apocalypse Now (1979)

Helicopters attack to Wagner's "Ride of the Valkyries."

13. Ace Ventura: Pet Detective (1994)

Cannibal Corpse makes its comedy debut.

14. The Exorcist (1973)

Pazuzu-possessed Linda Blair pukes pea soup into the maws of God's men.

15. Metallica: Some Kind of Monster (2003)

Torben Ulrich assesses the first recordings in years by his son's band: "Delete that!"

16. Severed Ways (2007)

Behold: history's first black metal church burning, circa 1007 A.D.

17. Mazes and Monsters (1982)

RPG-cracked Tom Hanks flips out in a phone booth: "There's blood on my knife!"

18. Prince of Darkness (1987)

Alice Cooper stares into the camera, casually shoves a bicycle through someone's chest.

19. Zombie (1979)

Zombie vs. shark. Underwater.

20. Kiss Meets the Phantom of the Park (1978)

Kiss, using full talismanic superpowers, dukes it out with Evil Robotic Kiss.

21. 2001: A Space Odyssey (1968)

Every appearance of the monolith.

22. Anvil: The Story of Anvil (2008)

Taking a mid-morning stage in Japan as the opening act of a three-day festival and fearing the worst, Anvil's cheering sea of joyful fans blows the band away.

23. Planet of the Apes (1968)

Charlton Heston meets the Statue of Liberty. "You finally did it! You maniacs! You blew it up! Damn you! Damn you all to HELL!"

24. Phantom of the Paradise (1974)

The Undead sing "Somebody Super Like You," bringing Beef back to "Life at Last!"

25. The Texas Chain Saw Massacre (1974)

Leatherface introduces himself by delivering a sledgehammer to an unsuspecting skull, resulting in a spasming body at his gut-caked boots. Then he drags away the victim, slamming the steel door behind him, HARD!

26. Jerky Boys (1995)

Helmet performs, managed by Ozzy Osbourne.

27. The Omen (1976)

The little antichrist's nanny hangs herself at a little kid birthday party. "It's all for you, Damien! ALL FOR YOU!"

28. Private Parts (1997)

AC/DC plays the Howard Stern rally on 42nd Street.

29. Star Wars (1977)

Enter Darth Vader, through a cloud of smoke, to John Williams' pure black-hearted doom processional theme.

30. The Dungeonmaster (1984)
W.A.S.P. tears it up on "Tormentor."

31. Black Roses (1988)
A speaker-spawned demon eats Big Pussy.

32. Witchfinder General (1968)
Vincent Price, as Matthew Hopkins, shows his ways of making witches talk.

33. The Stoned Age (1994)
E. Bloom and Buck Dharma peddle bootleg BÖC shirts in a parking lot.

34. Trick or Treat (1986)
Sammi Curr electrifies his audience.

35. Up in Smoke (1978)
Alice Bowie wins the battle of the bands with "Earache My Eye."

36. Black and Blue (1980)
Ronnie James Dio leads Madison Square Garden in a group wail during Black Sabbath's "Heaven and Hell."

37. The Shining (1980)
Axe-mad Jack Nicholson chops through a wooden door, sticks his face in the hole, and unleashes cinema's scariest smile. "Heeeeere's Johnny!"

38. Cremaster 2 (1999)
Slayer's Dave Lombardo drums, while bee-covered Morbid Angel frontman Steve Tucker makes a phone call.

39. A Serbian Film (2010)
Now we've all been subjected to "newborn porn."

40. Bill and Ted's Excellent Adventure (1989)
Wyld Stallyns back up history's greatest heroes in their high school auditorium.

41. Lord of the Rings: The Two Towers (2002)
The Battle of Helm's Deep.

42. Maniac (1980)
Joe Spinell shotguns Tom Savini's head none-too-cleanly off his shoulders.

43. Back to the Future (1985)
Marty McFly fries his dad's mind with a Van Halen cassette.

44. Caligula (1979)
Rome's most metal emperor amuses himself with a mass-decapitation machine.

45. Fantasia (1940)
"Night on Bald Mountain." Nobody does demons like Disney.

46. The Road Warrior (1982)
Lord Humungus—"the warrior of the wasteland, the ayatollah of rock-n-rolla"—addresses Mad Max and the members of the peaceful compound. Feral Kid crashes the moment, boomerang-first."

47. Hardbodies (1983)
Vixen rocks the beach house.

48. Immoral Tales (1974)
Countess Bathory in an all-girl bloodbath.

49. Pee-Wee's Big Adventure (1985)
Our star interrupts Twisted Sister shooting a music video for "Burn in Hell"

50. Burial Ground: The Nights of Terror (1981)
Bewigged midget Peter Bart comes on hard to his mom, bites off her boobs.

51. Gummo (1997)

Riled-up, ready-to-brawl locals mercilessly take on an innocent wooden chair; all they leave behind are splinters.

52. August Underground's Mordum (2003)

Killjoy of Necrophagia shows off his dead body collection.

53. Faces of Death (1978)

Live monkey brains, served fresh.

54. The Gate (1987)

Backward-masked messages on a metal record unleash evil, amazingly cool little homunculi emerge in a young head-banger's backyard.

55. Jesus Christ Superstar (1973)

J.C. sweats blood while contemplating his crucifixion to a montage of exquisitely gnarly medieval passion paintings.

56. The Warriors (1979)

Here come the Baseball Furies!

57. Aqua Teen Hunger Force Colon Movie Film for Theaters (2007)

An innocent "Let's All Go to the Lobby" cartoon erupts into an savage animated etiquette lesson by Mastodon, "Cut You With a Linoleum Knife."

58. Rosemary's Baby (1967)

Mother and child moment. "What have you done to his eyes?"

59. Troll (1986)

Michael Moriarity dances alone to Blue Cheer.

60. Un Chien Andalou (1929)

Salvador Dali and Luis Buñuel drag a straight razor across a human eyeball.

61. Zardoz (1974)

A giant, flying stone head spits out weapons and lays down the law: "The gun is good. The penis is evil. The penis shoots seeds and makes new life to poison the earth with a plague of men, but the gun shoots death and purifies the Earth of the filth of brutals. Go forth, and kill!"

62. Musical Mutiny (1970)

Iron Butterfly plays the Pirate's World amusement park, and even the squares dig the show.

63. The Devil's Rain (1975)

Ernest Borgnine transforms from desert sheriff to goat-headed satanic priest.

64. Foxes (1980)

The girls head to an Angel concert and have fits for Punky's whips.

65. Halloween III: Season of the Witch (1982)

Nobody ever forgets the Silver Shamrock commercials, sung to the tune of "London Bridge": "Happy-happy Halloween/Halloween/Halloween... Sil-ver Sham-rock!"

66. Beware of Mr. Baker (2012)

Ginger Baker whacks his walking stick smack into the director's nose, breaking it (the director's nose, not Ginger's stick).

66.6 Fast Times at Ridgemont High (1982)

Spicoli saves Brooke Shields from drowning and blows the reward money on hiring Van Halen to play his party (only "point six" because we don't get to see the party!)

APPENDIX BLEED: THE UNFIT FIFTEEN, METAL MOMENTS IN NON-METAL MOVIES

Not all that glitters is pure metal. Even the weakest of the towering Heavy Metal Movies in this book still sings with sheer power. But sometimes completely non-metal movies shift into heavy mode for a few blinding seconds. Following are some metal thunderbolts as they ripped through a sea of weakness.

A.I.: ARTIFICIAL INTELLIGENCE (2001)
Stanley Kubrick struggled for decades to adapt a film based on author Brian Aldiss's 1969 short story "Super-Toys Last All Summer Long." Steven Spielberg took over after Kubrick passed away, and softened things up wherever possible—except for a scene involving a "flesh fair," where old robots are disintegrated on stage while dirtbag humans drink, belch, and cheer. Music onscreen comes from Al Jourgensen of Ministry, out of work since no Lollapalooza was happening in 2001, leading an industrial metal ensemble a lot like Ministry.

BETTER OFF DEAD (1985)
Lightning strikes a meat patty, and a fully stacked cheeseburger with the voice of David Lee Roth leaps to life and belts out "Everybody Wants Some." The Claymation marvel dances with a girl burger; croons to a party of French fries who sway with their knees soaking in a pool of liquid cheese; and shreds the song on a mini version of Eddie Van Halen's signature striped guitar.

BLACK SHEEP (1996)
In this slapstick political comedy directed by Penelope Spheeris (*Wayne's World*, *The Decline of Western Civilization*), Mudhoney plays "Poisoned Water Poisons the Mind" at a Rock the Vote benefit. They also clown around a bit with star Chris Farley before and after the performance.

CALENDAR GIRLS (2003)
Calendar Girls is a feel-good movie about the potentially feel-yourself-good true story of a gaggle of British grandmothers who posed nude for a charity calendar. The only real nakedness on display here comes from Helen Mirren, decades after she romped royally for *Caligula* (1979). En route to *The Tonight Show*, the booty-baring biddies carouse by a Hollywood hotel pool with Scott Ian and Frank Bello of Anthrax. Ian admitted his goatee was standing on end: "I was pretty excited to be in a scene with Helen Mirren."

CAN'T STOP THE MUSIC (1980)

Early on in this garish, man-crazy disco fantasia starring the Village People, W.A.S.P. king bee Blackie Lawless appears in a talent agent's office. He wears full hair-dye-to-boot-sole black, bounces up and down like a subhuman, and tries to chew his way through a telephone cord. He still comes off infinitely better than his bandmate Chris Holmes does in *The Decline of Western Civilization Part II* (1988)!

DARK SHADOWS (2012)

Aside from the general monster mosh of beasts lurking in the corners, metal is represented here by Alice Cooper playing himself. After being hired by head bloodsucker Barnabas Collins (Johnny Depp) to perform at the Collinwood Ball, Alice tears through "No More Mr. Nice Guy," then dons a straitjacket for "Ballad of Dwight Fry."

DIARY OF A MAD HOUSEWIFE (1970)

The upper-middle class Manhattan neuroses that engulfed much of 1970s pop culture received a major early boost from *Diary of a Mad Housewife*. So, to more miniscule degree, did the movie career of Alice Cooper. Alice and his boys provide entertainment at a chic loft shindig, grooving through a killer cover of "Ride with Me" by Steppenwolf that turns into a great jam on their own "Lay Down and Die Goodbye."

EMPIRE RECORDS (1995)

In this teen ensemble romantic comedy about clean-cut simple-minded record store workers, Gwar makes an in-store appearance. Little wonder all record stores went out of business!

FOOTLOOSE (1984)

Though not part of the smash hit official soundtrack album until a 1998 reissue, Quiet Riot's "Metal Health" appears in the movie as the key introduction to Kevin Bacon's character as he peels into the school parking lot in his VW Beetle. The song was a Top 40 single the previous year. Rebel cred established, *Footloose* promptly forgets about metal, though metal, much more than dancing was banned during the 1980s.

GREEN HORNET (2011)

Here's a superhero nobody remembers, reborn in the unworthy body of a comic actor (Seth Rogan) that nobody ever wanted to see play a superhero—in 3-D! Sweetening the green mess is Anvil, riding high enough from their 2008 *Anvil! The Story of Anvil* comeback to nab a meagerly explosive scene as the rock band in a rock club—glimpsed on a TV—during this $120 million Hollywood spectacular. They do look good in 3-D, too.

HIDEAWAY (1995)

Hideaway is a pre-*Clueless* Alicia Silverstone vehicle with Jeff Goldblum as a back-from-the-dead dad. He is a chronic cutter who, when self-injuring, can see through the eyes of an occult murderer. Industrial metal titans Godflesh pound out the agonized anthem "Nihil" at a metal club in this Dean R. Koontz adaptation. The middle-of-the-road, consumer-friendly take on inevitable evil is very much of its moment, riding the spirit of tribal tattoos, nose piercings, and serial killers that cracked the mainstream in the mid-1990s.

HOT TUB TIME MACHINE (2010)

In 2010, a trio of fortysomething schlubs revisit the ski resort where they legendarily partied back when Poison headlined "Winterfest '86". The Sunset Strip's most glittering sons are depicted as being superstars, although the band didn't actually catch on until "Talk Dirty to Me" hit MTV in February 1987. Like Poison care one lick about the truth as long as they look good!

JOHNNY BE GOOD (1988)

The curious mission of *Johnny Be Good* is to reconfigure Anthony Michael Hall—the dweeb from *Sixteen Candles* (1984), *The Breakfast Club* (1985), and *Weird Science* (1985)—as a brawny, charismatic quarterback/captain of a top-ranked high-school football team. The curious musical mission of Judas Priest is to venture far off base to cover the immortal Chuck Berry hit title song, then make an awkward video featuring tons of stage-diving because that's what all the young bands were doing in 1988. Fumble!

THE NOMI SONG (2004)

Klaus Nomi was an art-gassed, glam-rocking space case from Germany who touched down in New York just in time for new wave. After performing with David Bowie on *Saturday Night Live* in 1979, Nomi attempted to open for Twisted Sister at a small New Jersey metal club. The Garden State hesher throngs took one whiff of this fey, frail alien in a giant triangular bellboy costume and let him have it. Klaus's bandmates say the Twisted Sister audience terrified their front-freak into nearly irrevocable catatonia. Jay Jay French of Twisted Sister speaks candidly and sympathetically about what happened when Nomi opened for the band. He convincingly talks about how he still feels terrible about the abuse the crowd heaped on Klaus, and his vivid recollection will put you right there for the humiliation.

VICE VERSA (1988)

Riding a weirdly inexplicable wave of late-'80s adult-and-child body-swap movies (*18 Again*, *Big*, *Dream a Little Dream*, *Like Father like Son*) came *Vice Versa*, starring Judge Reinhold and Fred Savage. The band Malice, L.A.'s answer to Judas Priest, performs the movie's theme song, and they blast almost the entirety of their song "Crazy in the Night" onstage at a rock club. After Reinhold becomes ten-year-old Savage on the inside, he takes his classical-music-fan date ('80s teen movie dream girl Corinne Bohrer) into the pit while Malice performs. "These guys are RADICAL!" the man-boy screams before jumping up on stage. His date smiles. She's in love. Who wouldn't be?

The Dudley Moore/Kirk Cameron vehicle *Like Father like Son* boasts on on-camera performance by Autograph, and a soundtrack featuring Aerosmith and Mötley Crüe.

Appendix Must See: TV Casualties, Notable Headbanging on the Small Screen

THE MUNSTERS (1965)
"Will Success Spoil Herman Munster?"

With his mammoth Frankenstein form stuffed into a motorcycle jacket, and a leather cap on his square scalp, Herman Munster jams on an electric guitar. While go-go girls shimmy, he rhymes "groovy junk" with "ever-lovin' punk."

GIDGET (1966) "Gidget's Career"

Beach babe Gidget (Sally Field) ditches her bikinis for corpse-white face paint and a black gothic go-go dress to front a "spooky" pop ensemble, Gidget and the Gories.

THE DICK CAVETT SHOW (1969) Jimi Hendrix

After missing a scheduled appearance the day after Woodstock (can you blame him?), Jimi Hendrix sits in a few weeks later with erudite funnyman Dick Cavett, and cosmic chatter ensues through a whirlwind of hallucinogens.

STAR TREK (1969) "The Way to Eden"

Prog-rock space hippies hijack the starship Enterprise. They mock square Captain Kirk as a "Herbert" and bust out instruments to groove through a series of heavy cosmic jams. At the end, bad acid does them in.

MIDSUMMER ROCK (1970)
The Stooges/Mountain/Grand Funk Railroad

Airing in primetime on ABC, this 90-minute documentary of Cincinnati's 1970 Midsummer Rock Festival is headlined by Grand Funk Railroad and Mountain, but it freakily electrifies a generation of tube-gazing future headbangers when Iggy Pop crowd-surfs and coats himself with peanut butter during a furious Stooges set and Alice Cooper climaxes his performance by taking a pineapple upside down cake smack in the kisser.

IN CONCERT (1972) Alice Cooper

ABC's late-night live music series debuts with Alice Cooper rousing the boob tube rabble with "I'm Eighteen."

THE PAUL LYNDE HALLOWEEN SPECIAL (1976)

The flamboyant funnyman's tricks and treats include the Wicked Witch from *The Wizard of Oz*, Witchiepoo from *H. R. Pufnstuf*, and a black-magical guest shot from Kiss, who jack viewers' lanterns with "Detroit Rock City", "Beth", and "King of the Nighttime World".

LOVE BOAT (1979) "Sounds of Silence"

In full black-white-and-red face-paint that weirdly resembles the stage face of King Diamond, Sonny Bono boards the Pacific Princess as "the demented, the dangerous, the disgusting" Deacon Dark. After an intro from *Laugh-In*'s Arte Johnson, the Deacon charges the ship's lounge in a Zorro hat and cosmic red jumpsuit. He offends the passengers and crew (except Isaac, the bartender, who digs the scene) with a rave-up of "Smash It!" (chorus: "smash it!/bash it!/hit it with a hammer and trash it!"). His band looks a lot like the Clowns from 1980's *Terror on Tour*.

CHIPS (1982) "Rock Devil Rock"

For this Halloween night broadcast, California Highway Patrol hunks Ponch (Erik Estrada) and Jon (Larry Wilcox) contend with Donny Most as Moloch, a face-painted, longhaired, devil-costumed combination of Alice Cooper, Ozzy Osbourne, and, given his penchant for pranks, Most's signature Ralph Malph character from *Happy Days*. Moloch drives a hot-rodded hearse, breathes fire on stage (leading Jon to quip, "I wonder if he does barbecues!"), and rocks a crowd with his hit, "Devil Take Me." Watch also for a cameo from Cassandra Peterson as Elvira, boobing it up at an apple-bobbing party.

US FESTIVAL '83 (1983) "Heavy Metal Day"

Cable television and heavy metal really grew up together. Burgeoning premium cable channel Showtime ushers in the metal '80s with this 90-minute special highlighting outdoor sets at the US Festival 83 before 375,000 sunburnt fans by Quiet Riot (whose *Metal Health* would reach #1 that fall), Ozzy Osbourne, Scorpions, Triumph, Judas Priest, and Van Halen, who earned a million dollars for their drunken late-night bravura performance. Mötley Crüe, who also performed at midday in full black leather, were filmed but do not appear here.

LIVEWIRE (1983) Manowar

To promote the album *Into Glory Ride*, Manowar storms Nickelodeon's original talk and variety show, thundering through "Gloves of Metal" at full volume and in full leather-fur-and-steel barbarian gear to a stupefied audience of preteen kids and their deafened parents. When a mom asks afterward if that was one of the band's more mellow numbers, Manowar mastermind Joey Demaio smiles, "Yeah, that's our love song."

HEAVY METAL MANIA (1985)

MTV's original monthly metal special features host Dee Snider of Twisted Sister. The show presents music videos punctuated by Dee's funny between-song banter, and it develops a warhorse format that will evolve over two years into the weekly *Headbangers Ball*.

IT'S YOUR MOVE (1985) "The Dregs of Humanity"

The short-lived, savagely funny cult sitcom *It's Your Move* stars Jason Bateman as a high school scam artist. His greatest con is rigging up a quintet of robed and hooded skeletons like marionettes and getting his chubby sidekick to work them through a full-blown metal concert in the school gym.

DONAHUE (1986) "New York Hardcore"

This episode shows off punk's buzz-cutted frontline with bruisers from Agnostic Front, Cro-Mags, and Murphy's Law sounding off to a lot of suburban aunts. Representing the city's punk-metal crossover are all four members of Nuclear Assault.

HEADBANGER'S BALL (1987–1995)

MTV takes over Saturday nights with a multi-hour broadcast of metal videos, in-studio interviews, and on-the-road adventures. After awkward hosting bungles by VJs Kevin Seal and Adam Curry and a series of guest emcees, Hollywood rock club impresario Riki Rachtman makes the show his own and pilots it to eight years of zeitgeist-defining, hotter-than-hell metal heaven. *Headbanger's Ball* indoctrinates at least one entire generation into a lifetime devotion to donning leather and denim in perpetual pursuit of metal glory.

GERALDO RIVERA (1988) "Devil Worship: Exposing Satan's Underground"

Not to be outdone by ABC *20/20*'s Venom-laden 1985 exposé of teen metalhead Satanism, NBC offers up two hours of primetime just prior to Halloween for Geraldo Rivera's hysterical high point of pure '80s Satanic Panic. Mixing heavy metal imagery and performance snippets with professional occultists such as Anton LaVey, the special also features a Q&A with Charles Manson, gruesome accounts of real serial murder, and "eyewitness" testimonies of black masses, live sacrifice, and ritual child abuse. Icing the metal cake are appearances by Ozzy Osbourne, who denies he is a Satanist, and King Diamond, who is happy to say that he is one.

DONAHUE (1990) "Indecency & Obscenity"

In light of hip-hop group 2 Live Crew's Florida obscenity trial, hard rockers Wendy O. Williams (Plasmatics), Mike Muir (Suicidal Tendencies), and Jello Biafra (Dead Kennedys) sit on Phil's panel, but a pro-censorship minister who blurts out a rap quote on live TV: "Put the motherfucker in your mouth and suck it till it comes!"

MARRIED... WITH CHILDREN (1992)
"My Dinner With Anthrax"

TV's sexiest teen metal vixen Kelly Bundy (Christina Applegate) and her dud kid brother Bud (David Faustino) win a visit from Anthrax, the most inherently comedic of thrash metal's Big Four. The band shows up ready to party, plays "In My World," trashes the Bundy house, and then joins guest star Edd "Kookie" Burns for a quick doo-wop rendition of his 1959 novelty hit "Kookie, Kookie, Lend Me Your Comb."

THE DREW CAREY SHOW (1998)
"In Ramada Da Vida"

When Drew and his pals form a band, Megadeth's Dave Mustaine shows up to audition for lead guitar. As the guitar hero is shredding away, Drew's sidekicks tell him not to be so nervous and to "slow down." Dave says, "It's supposed to sound that way!" Drew hollers, "Next!"

THE OSBOURNES (2002–2005)

MTV transforms metal's bat-biting Prince of Darkness into a zonked-out reality TV sitcom dad with this momentary cultural phenomenon that also makes enduring stars of wife Sharon Osbourne, and kids Jack and Kelly.

BONES (2009) "Mayhem on a Cross"

The campy days of TV punk episodes returns with this ludicrous dramatization involving "Norwegian death metal" band Spew. In Norway, cops shut down a black metal warehouse concert due to a human skeleton hung on a cross. The stolen bone-rack is what remains of an American bass player named Mayhem who performed with the death metal band Spew. Dr. Brennan (Emily Deschanel) and FBI Agent Booth (David Boreanaz) learn about the various subgenres of extreme metal and explore a musical underground where "concerts are set up at secret locations and only insiders are invited." One such locale is a slaughterhouse infected with mad cow disease, where the authority figures bump up against characters named Pinworm, Grinder, and Murderbreath. Hilarity ensues.

METAL HURLANT CHRONICLES (2012)

Metal Hurlant (which literally means *Screaming Metal*) is the French adult science-fiction and fantasy magazine that was introduced in America in 1977 as *Heavy Metal*. The English-language Franco-Belgian TV series *Metal Hurlant Chronicles* is a steamy sci-fi anthology based on the mind-and-lap-expanding comics of the original publication. And so the cycle continues...

Acknowledgements: Hard, Heavy, and Otherwise

Here's who I thank, and how:

For all that matters most—and then even more: Rachel McPadden. My salamander. My monkey woman. You make me glad, every minute, that I'm a monkey man, too. Rachel relentlessly searched for and discovered countless movies, watched hundreds upon hundreds of them with me, hunted down facts, dug up images, provided honest critiques, travelled to distant locations, physically patched together multiple incarnations of the ludicrously huge manuscript, made me a completely *sick* battle vest and, with every scintilla of everything she's got, supported and promoted and co-shepherded this entire undertaking with grace and wit and unending creativity. I love you, Rachel, and there'd be no me without you, let along a decent reference text that illuminates the connection between Blue Öyster Cult and the *Demonic Toys* film series.

For everything louder than everything else: Ian Christe. Mr. Bazillion Points. Permanent horns up. Thank you for guidance, patience, tirelessness, and hearty humor as you jackhammered and sculpted literally millions of wilding words into a tome of eminent readability and a mammoth object of brute beauty. I'm a longtime fan, now a grateful friend. For the rest of everything: *Tack, tack så mycket*! This I wail while hoisting a horn full of Zingo in honor of Bazillion Points sergeant-at-arms Magnus Henriksson.

For our confederacy of foolishness: Scott R. Miller, I say, "Thank R. You." He helped round up all the book's images and then processed every single one all by his lonesome. Check out his shockingly talented state-of-the-doom artwork: facebook.com/ScottRMillerIllustrationDesign.

For supplies: Quimby's Books is where the inspiration to write *Heavy Metal Movies* struck me and Liz Mason was there, doing what she does best—making Quimby's the heart of our community and Chicago's jewel of lunatic/visionary reading, writing, drawing, and publishing. Go to: Quimbys.com. Katie Rife of Everything Is Terrible converted countless VHS tapes and graced me with a free VCR. Katie is everything (is terrible). Go to EverythingIsTerrible.com. Derrick Ogrodny of Poster Perversion cracked open an entire exotic world of electrifying cinematic promo images. Go to: PosterPerversion.com. Brian Chankin of Odd Obsession Video in Chicago was enormously generous in supplying visuals. Go to OddObsession.com. Shocking Videos kingpin Mark Johnston sent me stacks of freakishly rare DVDs.

Thanks for talking: Alice Cooper and Richard Christy. Additional thanks go to Katherine Turman, the multitalented producer of the *Nights With Alice Cooper* radio show and co-author with Jon Wiederhorn of the landmark *Louder Than Hell*.

For sharing his molten metal genius: David Szulkin, aka Dave Depraved, Blood Farmers' guitar magus and author of the greatest book ever written about a single film, *Wes Craven's Last House on the Left*. Write more books, Dave!

For counsel and commiseration: Jim "Mr. Skin" McBride, Brian Collins, Aaron Lee, Peter Landau, Mike "Springo" Spring, Mike Edison, Joe McGinty, John Fasano, Elle Quintana, Kathy "Metalcakes" Bejma, Tara Slayermag, Zack Carlson, Robin Bougie, John Walter Szpunar, Kier-La Janisse, Joseph A. Ziemba and Dan Budnik (Bleeding Skull rules!), Jimmy Failla, Rob Hauschild, Keara Shipe, Vera Napolean, Velcro "Andy Slater" Lewis, Tressa Slater, Christopher Sienko, Amy Hobby, Michael Lee Nirenberg, Sean Sakamoto, Christine Colby, Maryann Bayer and Kevbayer of Bayerclan Radio, Kimberly Austin of Rock Book Talk, Derek Mullens of Metamorph Tattoo Studios, Dante's Pizza, Kuma's Corner, Owen Daniel Ullrich Uss, and, from the coagulated bottom of my fat bastard heart, Michael "Vito" Rovito. Also, for other reasons, Madonna Boots, wherever she may blonde.

For and with unconditional love: Molly Mullaney (#1), Leo Mullaney (Koo-Koo Man), Jean McPadden, Katie McPadden Mullaney, John McPadden, Andy Mullanney, and my entire family back in, as my (actual) godson Johnny "Gunks" Giusti puts it, "Mick and Guinea Central." Brian McPadden (Pops McBeardo) stormed Green Beret Valhalla in 2012. My heart is always on the frontline with him.

For teaching me how to write, not die, and then live: Allan MacDonell

For initial ignition: Danny Peary, Harry and Michael Medved, Rick Sullivan, Michael Weldon, Bill Landis, Jimmy McDonough, Adam Parfrey, Gerard Cosloy, Joe Carducci, Josh Alan Friedman, all other Bazillion Points authors, and ever-lovin' Peter Bagge. *Heavy Metal Movies* is happiest on your bookshelf alongside titles by any and all of these giants.

Four-three arrivederci,

McBeardo

ABOUT THE AUTHOR

Photo by Chris Roo

Brooklyn-born Mike "McBeardo" McPadden is the head writer of the online phenomenon Mr. Skin. In addition to years of freelance journalism (*Esquire, Black Book, New York Press*), and more than a decade as a *Hustler* editor and correspondent, Mr. McPadden has also done time as a B-movie screenwriter. He lives in Chicago with his wife, xoJane.com editor Rachel McPadden.

BAZILLION POINTS

Earth's heaviest publisher of authoritative books on music and film is the hard-working home of *Swedish Death Metal, Murder in the Front Row, Only Death Is Real, Metalion, Dirty Deeds, Hellbent for Cooking, Mellodrama: The Mellotron Story, Swedish Sensationsfilms*, and many more. Visit us, build your own temple of incredible knowledge, and become the envy of all worlds:

WWW.BAZILLIONPOINTS.COM